D0435176

Canon City Public Library
Canon City, Colorado

LaVyrle Spencer

Three Complete Novels

THREE COMPLETE NOVELS

LaVyrle Spencer

BYGONES

NOVEMBER OF THE HEART

FAMILY BLESSINGS

G. P. Putnam's Sons

New York

Canon City Public Library

Canon City, Colorado

G. P. Putnam's Sons
Publishers Since 1838
200 Madison Avenue
New York, NY 10016

Bygones copyright © 1992 by LaVyrle Spencer
November of the Heart copyright © 1993 by LaVyrle Spencer
Family Blessings copyright © 1993 by LaVyrle Spencer

All rights reserved. This book, or parts thereof,
may not be reproduced in any form without permission.
Published simultaneously in Canada

Library of Congress Cataloging-in-Publication Data

Spencer, LaVyrle.
[Selections.   1996]
Three complete novels / LaVyrle Spencer.
p.   cm.
Contents: Bygones—November of the heart—Family blessings.
ISBN 0-399-14181-2
1. Love stories, American.   I. Title.
PS3569.P4535A6   1996   96-6235 CIP
813'.54—dc20

Printed in the United States of America

1 3 5 7 9 10 8 6 4 2

BOOK DESIGN BY AMANDA DEWEY

Contents

BYGONES

Chapter 1

———⌇⌇———

The apartment building resembled thousands of others in the suburban Minneapolis/St. Paul area, a long brick rectangle with three floors, a set of steps on each end and rows of bruised doors lining stuffy, windowless halls. It was the kind of dwelling where young people started out with cast-off furniture and bargain-basement draperies, where toddlers rode their tricycles down the halls and could be heard through the floors when they cried. Now, at 6 p.m. on a cold January night, the smell of cooking meat and vegetables sifted under the doors, mingled with the murmur of televisions tuned to the evening news.

A tall woman walked down the hall. She looked out of place, dressed in a classic winter-white reefer coat bearing the unmistakable cut of a name designer, her accessories—leather gloves, handbag, shoes and scarf—of deep raspberry red. Her clothing was expensive, from the fifty-dollar silk scarf looped casually over her hair to the two-inch high heels combining three textures of leather. She walked with an air of hurried sophistication.

Pulling the scarf from her head, Bess Curran knocked at the door of number 206.

Lisa flung it open and exclaimed, "Oh, Mom, hi. Come on in. I knew I could depend on you to be right on time! Listen, everything's all ready but I forgot the sour cream for the stroganoff, so I have to make a quick run to the store. You don't mind keeping your eye on the meat, do you?" She dove into a closet and came up with a hip-length jean jacket, which she threw on over her dress.

"Stroganoff? For just the two of us? And a dress? What's the occasion?"

Lisa headed back to the door, digging her keys from her purse. "Just give it a stir, okay?" She opened the door halfway and stopped to call, "Oh! And light the candles and put a tape on, will you? That old Eagles one is there that you always liked."

The door slammed and left Bess in a backwash of puzzlement. Stroganoff? Candles? Music? And Lisa in a dress and pumps? Unbuttoning her coat, Bess wandered into the kitchen. Beyond the galley-style work area that divided it from the living room, a table was set for four. She studied it curiously—blue place mats and napkins cinched into white napkin rings; the leftover pieces of her and Michael's first set of dishes, which she'd given Lisa when she left home; four of her own cast-off stem glasses; and two blue candles in holders she'd never seen before, apparently bought specially for the occasion on Lisa's limited budget. What in the world was going on here?

She went to the stove to stir the stroganoff, which smelled so heavenly she couldn't resist sampling it. Delicious—her own recipe, laced with consommé and onions. As she replaced the cover on the pan, she realized she was famished: she'd done three home consultations today plus two hours in the store before it opened, grabbing a hamburger on the run. She promised herself, as she did every January, to limit the home consultations to two a day.

Returning to the front closet, she hung up her coat and straightened a pile of shoes so she could close the bifold door. She found matches and lit the candles on the dinner table and two others in clear, stubby pots on the living-room coffee table. Beside these a plate from her old dinnerware held a cheeseball waiting to be gouged and spread on Ritz crackers.

The match burned low.

She flinched and flapped it out, then stood staring at the cheeseball. What the devil? She glanced around the room and realized the place was clean for a change. Her old brass-and-glass tables had been freshly dusted and the cushions plumped on the hand-me-down family sofa. The tapes were stacked neatly, and the junk on the bookshelves had been neatened. The jet-black Kawaii piano Lisa's father had given her for high-school graduation hadn't a speck of dust on it. Instead, the key cover was neatly closed, and on top of the piano a picture of Lisa's current boyfriend, Mark, shared the space with a struggling philodendron plant and five Stephen King books in a pair of brass bookends Lisa had received from her Grandma Stella for Christmas.

The piano was the only valuable thing in the room. When Michael had given it to Lisa, Bess had accused him of foolish indulgence. It made no sense at all— a girl without a college education or a decent car or furniture owning a five-thousand-dollar piano that would have to be moved professionally—to the tune of about a hundred dollars per move—how many times before she was finally settled down permanently?

Lisa had said, "But, Mom, it's something I'll always keep, and that's what a graduation present should be."

Bess had argued, "Who'll pay when you have to have it moved?"

"I will."

"On a clerk-typist's salary?"

"I'm waitressing, too."

"You should be going on to school, Lisa."

"Dad says there's plenty of time for that."

"Well, your dad could be wrong, you know! If you don't go on to school right away, chances are you never will."

"You did," Lisa had argued.

"Yes, I did but it was damned hard, and look what it cost me. Your father should have more sense than to give you advice like that."

"Mother, just once I wish the two of you would stop haggling and at least pretend to get along, for us kids' sake. We're so sick of this cold war!"

"Well, it's a stupid gift." Bess had gone away grumbling. "Five thousand dollars for a piano that could finance a whole year of college."

The piano had remained a sore spot. Whenever Bess came to Lisa's apartment unannounced, the piano held a film of dust on its gleaming jet finish and seemed to be used merely as the depository for books, scarves, hair bows and all the other flotsam of Lisa's busy two-job life. It was all Bess could do to keep from sniping, "See, I told you!"

Tonight, however, the piano had been dusted and on the music rack was the sheet music for Michael's favorite song, "The Homecoming." In years past, whenever Lisa sat down to play, Michael would say, "Play that one I like," and Lisa would oblige with the beautiful old television-movie theme song.

Bess turned away from the memory of those happier times and put on the *Eagles Greatest Hits* tape. While it played she used Lisa's bathroom, noting that it, too, had been cleaned for the occasion. Washing her hands, she saw that the fixtures were shining, the towels fluffy and freshly laundered. On the corner of the vanity was the apothecary jar of potpourri she'd given Lisa for Christmas.

Bess hung up the towel and glanced in the mirror at her disheveled streaky-blonde hair, gave it a pluck or two: after the day she'd put in she looked undone. She'd been in and out of the wind, the shop, her car, and hadn't taken time since morning to pause for cosmetic repairs. Her forehead looked oily, her lipstick was gone and her brown eyes looked stark with the eyeshadow and mascara worn away. There were lap creases across the skirt of her winter-white wool crepe suit, and a small grease spot stood out prominently on the jabot of her raspberry-colored blouse. She frowned at the spot, wet a corner of a washcloth and made it worse. She cursed softly, then found a lifter-comb in Lisa's vanity drawer. Just as she raised her arms to use it, a knock sounded at the opposite end of the apartment.

She stuck her head around the corner and called down the hall, "Lisa, is that you?"

The knock came again, louder, and she hurried to answer it, leaving the bathroom light on behind her.

"Lisa, did you forget your—?" She pulled the door open and the words died in her throat. A tall man stood in the hall, trim, black-haired, hazel-eyed, dressed in a gray woolen storm coat, holding a brown paper sack containing two wine bottles.

"Oh, Michael . . . it's you."

Her mouth got tight.

Her carriage became stiff.

He gave her a stare, his eyebrows curled in displeasure. "Bess . . . what are you doing here?"

"I was invited for supper. What are you doing here?"

"I was invited, too."

Their face-off continued while she curbed the desire to slam the door in his face.

"Lisa called me last night and said, Dinner at six-fifteen, Dad."

She had called Bess the night before and said, "Dinner at six, Mom." Bess released the doorknob and spun away, muttering, "Cute, Lisa."

Michael followed her inside and shut the door. He set his bottles on the kitchen cupboard and took off his coat while Bess hustled back to the bathroom to put herself as far from him as possible. In the glare of the vanity light she backcombed four chunks of hair hard enough to push them back into her skull root-first. She arranged them with a few chunks and stabs of the wire hair lifter, slashed some of Lisa's grotesque scarlet lipstick on her mouth (the only tube she could find, considering she'd left her purse at the other end of the apartment), glared at the results and at the dark blob on her jabot. Damn it. And damn him for catching me when I look this way. She raised her brown eyes to the mirror and found them flat with fury. And damn me for squandering so much as a second caring what he thinks. After what he did to me, I don't have to pander to that asshole.

She slammed the vanity drawer, rammed her fingers into her forelock and ground it into a satisfying mess.

"What are you doing back there, hiding?" he called irritably.

It had been six years since the divorce, and she still wanted to arrange his penis with a hot curling iron every time she saw him!

"Let's get one thing clear," she bellowed down the hall. "I didn't know a damned thing about this!"

"Let's get two things clear! Neither did I! Where the hell is she anyway?"

Bess whacked the light switch off and marched toward the living room with her head high and her hair looking like a serving of chow mein noodles.

"She went to the store for sour cream, which I'm cheerfully going to stuff up her nostrils when she gets back here."

Michael was standing by the kitchen table, studying it, with his hands in his trouser pockets. He was dressed in a gray business suit, white shirt and blue paisley tie.

"What's all this?" he threw over his shoulder as she passed behind him.

"Your guess is as good as mine."

"Is Randy coming?" Randy was their nineteen-year-old son.

"Not that I know of."

"You don't know who the fourth one is for?"

"No, I don't."

"Or what the occasion is?"

"Obviously, a blind date for her mother and father. Our daughter has a bizarre sense of humor, doesn't she?" Bess opened the refrigerator door, looking for wine. Inside were four individual salads, prettily arranged on plates, a bottle of Perrier water, and sitting on the top shelf in a red-and-white carton, a pint of sour cream. "My, my, if it isn't sour cream." She picked it up and held it on one hand at shoulder level the way Marilyn Monroe would have held a mink. "And four very fancy salads."

He came to have a look, peering over the open refrigerator door.

"What are you looking for, something to drink?"

The smell of his shaving lotion, which in years past had seemed endearingly familiar, now turned her stomach. "I feel as if I need something." She slammed the door.

"I brought some wine," he told her.

"Well, break it out, Michael. We apparently have a long evening ahead."

She took two glasses from the table while he opened the bottle.

"So . . . where's Darla tonight?" She held the glasses while he poured the pale red rosé.

Over the gurgling liquid he answered, "Darla and I are no longer together. She's filed for divorce."

Bess got as rattled as an eighteen wheeler going over a cattle guard. Her head shot up while Michael went on filling the second glass.

She hadn't spent sixteen years with this man not to feel a mindless shaft of elation at the news that he was free again. Or that he had failed again.

Michael set the bottle on the cupboard, took a glass for himself and met Bess's eyes directly. It was a queer, distilled moment in which they both saw their entire history in a pure, refined state, so clear they could see through it, way back to the beginning—the splendid and the sordid, the regards and the regrets that had brought them to this point where they stood in their daughter's kitchen holding drinks that went untasted.

"Well, say it," Michael prodded.

"Good, it serves you both right."

He released a mirthless laugh and shook his head at the floor. "I knew that's what you were thinking. You're one very bitter woman, Bess, you know that?"

"And you're one very contemptible man. What did you do, step out on her, too?"

He walked out of the room replying, "I'm not going to get into it with you, Bess, because I can see all it'll lead to is a rehash of our old recriminations."

"Good." She followed him. "I don't want a rehash, either. So until our daughter gets back we'll pretend we're two polite strangers who just happened to meet here."

They carried their drinks into the living room and dropped to opposite ends of the davenport—the only seating in the room. The Eagles were singing "Take It Easy," which they'd listened to together a thousand times before. The candles were burning on the glass-top table they'd once chosen for their own living room. The davenport they sat on was one upon which they'd occasionally made love and cooed endearments to each other when they were both young and stupid enough to believe marriage lasts forever. They sat upon it now like a pair of church elders, in their respective corners, resenting one another and the intrusion of these memories.

"Looks like you gave Lisa the whole living room after I left," Michael remarked.

"That's right. Down to the pictures and the lamps. I didn't want any bad memories left behind."

"Of course, you had your new *business,* so it was no trouble buying replacements."

"Nope. No trouble at all," she replied smugly. "And of course, I get everything at a discount."

"So how's the business going?"

"Gangbusters! You know how it is after Christmas—everybody looking at those bare walls after they've pulled down all the holiday paraphernalia, and wanting new wallpaper and furniture to chase away the winter doldrums. I swear I could do half a dozen home consultations a day if there were three of me."

He studied her askance, remaining silent. Obviously she was happy with the way things had worked out. She was a certified interior designer now, with a store of her own and a newly redecorated house.

The Eagles switched to "Witchy Woman."

"So how's yours?" she inquired, tossing him an arch glance.

"It's making me rich."

"Don't expect congratulations. I always said it would."

"From you, Bess, I don't expect anything anymore."

"Oh, *that's* funny!" She cocked one wrist and delicately touched her chest. *"You* don't expect anything from *me* anymore." Her tone turned accusing as she dropped the cutesy pose. "When was the last time you saw Randy?"

"Randy doesn't give a damn about seeing me."

"That's not what I asked. When was the last time you made an effort to see him? He's still your son, Michael."

"If Randy wants to see me, he'll give me a call."

"Randy wouldn't give you a call if you were giving away tickets for a Rolling Stones concert and you know it. But that doesn't excuse you for ignoring him. He needs you whether he knows it or not, so it's up to you to keep trying."

"Is he still working in that warehouse?"

"When he bothers."

"Still smoking pot?"

"I think so but he's careful not to do it in the house. I told him if I ever smell it in there again I'll throw him out."

"Maybe you should. Maybe that would straighten him up."

"And then again maybe it wouldn't. He's my son, and I love him, and I'm trying my best to make him see the light but if I give up on him, what hope will he have? He certainly never gets any guidance from his father."

"What do you want me to do, Bess?" Michael spread his arms wide, the glass in one hand. "I've offered him the money to go to college or trade school if he wants but he doesn't want anything to do with school. So what in the hell do you expect me to do? Take him in with me? A pothead who goes to work when he feels like it?"

Bess glared at him. "I expect you to call him, take him out to dinner, take him hunting with you, rebuild a relationship with him, make him realize he still has a father who loves him and cares about what happens to him. But it's easier to slough him off on me, isn't it, Michael? Just like it was when the kids were little and you ran off with your guns and your fishing rods and your . . . your mistress! Well, I can't seem to find the answers for him anymore. Our son is a mess, Michael, and I'm very much afraid of what's going to become of him but I can't straighten him out alone."

Their eyes met and held, each of them aware that their divorce had been the blow from which Randy had never recovered. Until age thirteen he had been a happy kid, a good student, a willing helper around the house, a carefree teenager who brought his friends in to eat them out of house and home, watch football games and roughhouse on the living-room floor. From the day they'd told him they were getting a divorce, he had changed. He had become withdrawn, uncommunicative and increasingly lackadaisical about responsibilities, both in school and at home. He stopped bringing his friends home and eventually found new ones who wore weird hairdos and army jackets and one earring, and dragged their boot heels when they walked. He lay on his bed listening to rap music through his headphones, began smelling like burned garbage and coming home at two in the morning with his pupils dilated. He resented school counseling, ran away from home when Bess tried to ground him and graduated from high school by his cuticles, with the lowest grade-point average allowable.

No, their marriage was certainly not their only failure.

"For your information," Michael said, "I have called him. He called me a son of a bitch and hung up." Michael tipped forward, propping his elbows on his knees, drawing gyroscopic patterns in the air with the bottom of his glass. "I know he's messed up, Bess, and we did it to him, didn't we?" Still hunched forward, he looked over his shoulder at her. On the stereo the song changed to "Lyin' Eyes."

"Not we. You. He's never gotten over you leaving your family for another woman."

"That's right, blame it all on me, just like you always did. What about you leaving your family to go to college?"

"You still begrudge me that, don't you, Michael? And you still can't believe I actually became an interior designer and made a success of it."

Michael slammed down his glass, leapt to his feet and pointed a finger at her from the far side of the coffee table. "You got custody of the kids because you wanted it, but afterwards you were so damned busy at that store of yours that you weren't around to be their parent!"

"How would you know? You weren't around, either!"

"Because you wouldn't let me in the goddamn house! *My* house! The house I paid for and furnished and painted and loved just as much as you did!" He jabbed a finger for emphasis. "Don't tell me I wasn't around when you're the one who re-fused to speak to me, thereby setting an example for our son to follow. I was willing to be sensible, for the kids' sake, but no, you wanted to *show* me, didn't you? You were going to take those kids and brainwash them and make them believe *I* was the only one in the wrong where our marriage was concerned; and don't lie to me and say different, because I've talked to Lisa and she's told me some of the shit you've told her."

"Like what?"

"Like, our marriage broke up because I had an affair with Darla."

"Well, didn't it?"

He threw up his hands and rolled his eyes to the ceiling. "God, Bess, take off your blinders. Things had soured between us before I even met Darla and you know it."

"If things soured between us it was because—"

The apartment door opened. Bess clapped her mouth shut while she and Michael exchanged a glare of compressed volatility. Her cheeks were bright with anger. His lips were set in a grim line. She rose, donning a veneer of propriety, while he closed a button on his suit jacket and retrieved his glass from the coffee table. As he straightened, Lisa rounded the corner into the living room. Behind her came the young man whose picture stood on the piano.

Had Pablo Picasso painted the scene, he might have entitled it *Still Life with Four Adults and Anger.* The words of the abandoned argument still reverberated in the air.

Finally Lisa moved. "Hello, Mother. Hello, Dad."

She hugged her father first, while he easily closed his arms around her and kissed her cheek. She was nearly his height, dark-haired and pretty, with lovely brown eyes, an attractive combination of the best features of both her parents. She went next to hug Bess, saying, "Missed hugging you the first time around, Mom, glad you could come." Retreating from her mother's arms, she said, "You both remember Mark Padgett, don't you?"

"Mr. and Mrs. Curran," Mark said, shaking hands with each of them. He had a shiny all-American face and naturally curly brown hair, crew-cut on top and trailing in thinned tendrils over his collar. He sported the brawn of a bodybuilder and a hand to match. When he shook their hands, they felt it.

"Mark's going to have supper with us. I hope you stirred the stroganoff, Mom." Lisa headed jauntily for the kitchen, where she went to the sink, turned on the hot water and began filling a saucepan. Right behind her came Bess, snagging Lisa's elbow and forcing her to do an about-face.

"Just what in the world do you think you're doing!" she demanded in a pinched whisper, covered by the sound of the running water and "Desperado" from the other side of the wall.

"Boiling noodles for the stroganoff." Lisa swung the kettle to the stove and switched on a blue flame, with Bess dogging her shoulder.

"Don't be obtuse with me, Lisa. I'm so damned angry I could fling that stroganoff down the disposal and you right along with it." She pointed a finger. "There's a pint of sour cream in that refrigerator and you know it! You set us up!"

Lisa pushed her mother's arm as if it were a turnstile and moved beyond it to open the refrigerator door. "I certainly did. How'd it go?" she asked blithely, removing the carton of sour cream and curling its cover off.

"Lisa Curran, I could dump that sour cream on your head!"

"I really don't care, Mother. *Some*body had to make you come to your senses."

"Your father and I are not a couple of twenty-year-olds you can fix up on a blind date!"

"No, you're not!" Lisa slammed down the carton of sour cream and faced her mother, nose-to-nose, whispering angrily. "You're forty years old but you're acting like a child! For six years you've refused to be in the same room with Dad, refused to treat him civilly, even for your children's sake. Well, I'm putting an end to that if I have to humiliate you to do it. Tonight is important to me and all I'm asking you to do is *grow up, Mother!*"

Bess stared at her daughter, feeling her cheeks flare, stunned into silence. From the countertop Lisa snagged a bag of egg noodles and stuffed them into Bess's hands. "Would you please add these to the water while I finish the stroganoff, then let's go into the living room and join the men as if we all know the meaning of gracious manners."

When they entered the living room it was clear the two men, seated on the sofa, had been doing their best at redeeming a sticky situation in which the tension was as obvious as the cheeseball meant to mitigate it. Lisa picked up the plate from the coffee table.

"Daddy? Mark? Cheeseball anyone?"

Bess stationed a kitchen chair clear across the room, where the living-room carpet met the vinyl kitchen floor, and sat down, full of indignation and the niggling bite of shame at being reprimanded by her own daughter. Mark and Michael each spread a cracker with cheese and ate it. Lisa carried the plate to her mother and stopped beside Bess's rigidly crossed knees.

"Mother?" she said sweetly.

"No, thank you," Bess snapped.

"I see you two have found something to drink," Lisa noted cheerfully. "Mark, would you like something?"

Mark said, "No, I'll wait."

"Mother, do you need a refill?"

Bess flicked a hand in reply.

Lisa took the only free seat, between the two men.

"Well . . ." she said brightly, clasping her crossed knees with twined hands and swinging her foot. She glanced between Michael and Bess. "I haven't seen either one of you since Christmas. What's new?"

They somehow managed to weather the next fifteen minutes. Bess, struggling to lose the ten extra pounds she consistently carried, refused the Ritz crackers with cheese but allowed herself to be socially manipulated by her daughter while trying to avoid Michael's hazel eyes. Once he managed to pin her with them while sinking his even, white teeth into a Ritz. You might at least *try,* he seemed to be admonishing, for Lisa's sake. She glanced away, wishing he'd bite into a rock and break off his damnable perfect incisors at the gums!

They sat down to eat at 7:15 in the chairs Lisa indicated, her mother and dad opposite each other so they could scarcely avoid exchanging glances across the candlelit table and their familiar old blue-and-white dishes.

Setting out the last of the four salad dishes, Lisa requested, "Will you open the Perrier, Mark, while I get the hot foods? Mom, Dad, would you prefer Perrier or wine?"

"Wine," they answered simultaneously.

The older couple sat obediently while the younger one got the bottled water, lime slices, wine, bread basket, noodles, stroganoff and a vegetable casserole, working together until everything was in place. Finally Lisa took her chair while Mark made the rounds, pouring.

When the glasses were filled and Mark, too, was seated, Lisa picked up her glass of Perrier and said, "Happy new year, everyone. And here's to a happier decade ahead."

The glasses touched in every combination but one. After a conspicuous pause, Michael and Bess made a final *tingg* with the rims of their old household stemware, a gift from some friend or family member many years ago. He nodded silently while she dropped her gaze and damned herself for disheveling her hair in an angry fit an hour ago, and for dropping ketchup on her jabot at noon, and for not stopping at home and putting on fresh makeup. She still hated him but that hate stemmed from a fiery pride, bruised at the moment. He had left her for someone ten years younger and ten pounds underweight, who undoubtedly never appeared at social functions with her hair on end, her forehead shiny and lunch on her jabot.

Lisa began passing the serving bowls and the room became filled with the sounds of spoons rapping on glass.

"Mmm . . . stroganoff," Michael noted, pleased, while he loaded his plate.

"Yup," Lisa replied. "Mom's recipe. And your favorite corn pudding, too." She passed him a casserole dish. "I learned to make it just like Mom. Be careful, it's hot." He set the dish beside his plate and took an immense helping. "I figured since you're living alone again you'd appreciate a good home-cooked meal. Mom, pass me the pepper, would you?"

Complying, Bess met Michael's eyes across the table, both of them grossly uncomfortable with Lisa's transparent machinations. It was the first point upon which they'd agreed since this unfortunate encounter began.

Michael tasted his food and said, "You've turned into a good little cook, honey."

"She sure has," put in Mark. "You'd be surprised how many girls today can't even boil water. When I found out she could cook I told my mother, I think I've found the girl of my dreams."

Three people at the table laughed. Bess, discomfited, hid behind a sip of rosé, recalling that one of the things Michael had criticized after she'd returned to college had been her neglecting the chores she'd always done. Cooking was one of them. She had argued, What about you, why can't you take over some of the household chores? But Michael had stubbornly refused to learn. It was one of many small wedges that had insidiously opened a chasm between them.

"How about you, Mark," Bess asked. "Do you cook?"

Lisa answered. "Does he ever! His specialty is steak soup. He takes a big old slab of sirloin and cubes it up and browns it and adds all these big hunks of potatoes and carrots, and what else do you put in it, honey?"

Bess shot a glance at her daugher. *Honey?*

"Garlic, and pearl barley to thicken it."

"Steak soup?" Bess repeated, turning her regard to Mark.

"Mm-hmm," Mark replied. "It's an old family favorite."

Bess stared at the young man who was shaped like Mount Rushmore. His neck was so thick his collar button wouldn't close. His hairdo was moussed on top and girlish on the bottom. And he thickened his steak soup with pearl barley?

Lisa grinned proudly at Mark. "He irons, too."

"Irons?" Michael repeated.

"My mother made me learn when I graduated from high school. She works, and she said she had no intention of doing my laundry till I was twenty-five. I like my sleeves and jeans with nice creases in them, so . . ." Mark raised his hands—his fork in one, a roll in the other—and let them drop. "I'm actually going to make some woman a pretty good housewife." He and Lisa exchanged a smile bearing some ulterior satisfaction, and Bess caught Michael adding it up before he swept his uncertain glance back to her.

Lisa said, "We might as well tell them, Mark." The two exchanged another smile before Lisa wiped her mouth, replaced her napkin on her lap and picked up her glass of sparkling water. "Mom, Dad . . ." With her eyes fixed radiantly on the young man across the table, Lisa announced, "We've invited you here tonight to tell you that Mark and I are going to get married."

In almost comical unison, Bess and Michael set down their forks. They gaped at their daughter. They gaped at each other.

Mark had stopped eating.

The tape player had stopped playing.

From an adjacent apartment the grumble of a TV could be heard through the wall.

"Well," Lisa said, "say something."

Michael and Bess remained speechless. Finally Michael cleared his throat, wiped his mouth on his napkin and said, "Well . . . my goodness."

"Daddy," Lisa chided. "Is that *all* you have to say?"

Michael forced an uncertain smile. "You caught me a little by surprise here, Lisa."

"Aren't you even going to congratulate us?"

"Well . . . yes . . . sure, of course, congratulations, both of you."

"Mother?" Lisa's eyes settled on Bess.

Bess emerged from her stupor. "Married?" she repeated disbelievingly. "But Lisa . . ." *We hardly know this young man. You've only known him for a year, or is it that long? We had no idea you were this serious about him.*

"Smile, Mother, and repeat after me, Congratulations, Lisa and Mark."

"Oh, dear . . ." Bess's gaze fluttered to her ex-husband, back to her daughter.

"Bess," Michael admonished quietly.

"Oh, I'm sorry. Of course, congratulations, Lisa . . . and Mark, but . . . but when did all this happen?"

"This weekend. We're really sold on each other, and we're tired of living apart, so we decided to commit."

"When is the big event?" Michael inquired.

"Soon," Lisa answered. "Very soon. Six weeks, as a matter of fact."

"Six weeks!" Bess yelped.

"I know that doesn't give us much time, but we've got it all figured out."

"What kind of wedding can you plan in six weeks? You can't even find a church in six weeks."

"We can if we're married on a Friday night."

"A Friday night . . . oh, Lisa."

"Now listen, both of you. Mark and I love each other and we want to get married but we want to do it the right way. We both want to have a real church wedding with all the trimmings, so here's what we've arranged. We can be married at St. Mary's on March second, and have the reception at the Riverwood Club. I've already checked and the club's not booked. Mark's aunt is a caterer and she's agreed to do the food. One of the guys I work with plays in a band that'll give us a pretty decent price. We're only going to have one attendant each—by the way, Randy has agreed to be one of them, and he even said he'll cut his hair. With only one attendant there'll be no trouble matching bridesmaids' dresses—Mark's sister can buy one anywhere; and as for the tuxes, we'll rent them. Flowers are no problem. We'll use silk ones and keep them modest. The cake we'll order from Wuollet's on Grand Avenue, and I'm pretty sure we can still find a photographer—having it on a Friday night, we're finding out, makes last-minute arrangements pretty easy. Well?"

Beleaguered, Bess felt her lips hanging open but seemed unable to close them. "What about your dress?"

A meaningful look passed between Lisa and Mark, this one without a smile.

"That's where I'll need your cooperation. I want to wear yours, Mom."

Bess looked dumbfounded. "Mine . . . but . . ."

"I'm pretty sure it'll fit."

"Oh, Lisa." Bess let her face show clear dismay.

"Oh, Lisa, what?"

Michael spoke. "What your mother is trying to say is that she isn't sure it's appropriate under the circumstances, isn't that right, Bess?"

"Because you're divorced?" Lisa looked from one parent to the other.

Michael gestured with his hands: that's how it is.

"I see nothing inappropriate about it at all. You were married once. You loved each other and you had me, and you're still my parents. Why shouldn't I wear the dress?"

"I leave that entirely to your mother." Michael glanced at Bess, who was still laboring under the shock of the news, sitting with her ringless left hand to her lips, her brown eyes very troubled.

"Mother, please. We can do this without your cooperation but we'd rather have it. From both of you." Lisa included Michael in her earnest plea. "And as long as

I'm laying out our plans, I may as well tell you the rest. I want to walk down the aisle between you. I want my mom and my dad both there, one on either side of me, without all this animosity you've had for the past six years. I want to have you in the dressing room, Mom, when I'm getting ready; and afterwards, at my reception, I want to dance with you, Dad. But without tension, without . . . well, you know what I mean. It's the only wedding present I want from either one of you."

The room fell into an uneasy silence. Bess and Michael found it impossible to meet each other's eyes.

Finally Bess spoke. "Where will you live?"

"Mark's apartment is nicer than mine, so we'll live over there."

And the piano will need to be moved again. It took great control for Bess to refrain from voicing the thought. "I don't even know where he lives."

Mark said, "In Maplewood, near the hospital."

She studied Mark. He had a pleasant enough face but he looked terribly young. "I must apologize, Mark, I've been so taken off guard here. The truth is, I feel as though I barely know you. You do some kind of factory work, I think."

"Yes, I'm a machinist. But I've been with the same company for three years, and I make good money, and I have good benefits. Lisa and I won't have any problems that way."

"And you met Lisa—?"

"At a pool hall, actually. We were introduced by mutual friends."

At a pool hall. A machinist. A bodybuilder with a neck like a bridge abutment.

"Isn't this awfully sudden? You and Lisa have known each other—what?—less than a year. I mean, couldn't you wait, say a half a year or so and give yourselves time to get to know one another better, and to plan a wedding properly, and us a chance to meet your family?"

Mark's eyes sought Lisa's. His cheeks colored. His forearms rested on the table edge, so muscular they appeared unable to comfortably touch his sides.

"I'm afraid not, Mrs. Curran." Quietly, without challenge, he said, "You see, Lisa and I are going to have a baby."

An invisible mushroom cloud seemed to form over the table.

Michael covered his mouth with a hand and frowned. Bess drew a breath, held her mouth open and slowly closed it, staring at Mark, then at Lisa. Lisa sat quietly, relaxed.

"We're actually quite happy about it," Mark added, "and we hoped you'd be, too."

Bess dropped her forehead onto one hand, the opposite arm propped across her stomach. Her only daughter pregnant and planning a hasty wedding, and she should be happy?

"You're sure about it?" Michael was asking.

"I've already seen a doctor. I'm six weeks along. Actually I thought maybe you'd guess, because I'm drinking the Perrier instead of wine."

Bess lifted her head and encountered Michael, somber, his food forgotten. He met her dismayed eyes, straightened his shoulders and said, "Well . . ." clearing his throat. Obviously, he was at as great a loss as she.

Mark rose and went to stand behind Lisa's chair with his hands on her shoulders. "I think I should say something here, Mr. and Mrs. Curran. I love your daughter very much, and she loves me. We want to get married. We've both got jobs and a decent place to live. This baby could have a lot worse starts than that."

Bess came out of her stupor. "In this day and age, Lisa—"

Michael interrupted. "Bess, come on, not now."

"What do you mean, not now! We live in an enlightened age and—"

"I said, *not now,* Bess! The kids are doing the honorable thing, telling us their plans, asking for our support. I think we should give it to them."

She bit back her retort about birth control and sat simmering while Michael went on, remarkably cool-headed.

"You're sure this is what you want to do, Lisa?" he asked.

"Very sure. Mark and I had talked about getting married even before I got pregnant, and we had agreed that we'd both like to have a family when we were young, and that we wouldn't do like so many yuppies do, and both of us work until we got so independent that *things* began mattering more than having children. So none of this was nearly as much of a shock to us as it is to you. We're happy, Dad, honest we are, and I do love Mark very much."

Lisa sounded wholly convincing.

Michael looked up at Mark, still standing behind Lisa with his hands on her collar. "Have you told your parents yet?"

"Yes, last night."

Michael felt a shaft of disappointment at being last to learn but what could he expect when Mark's family was, apparently, still an intact, happy unit? "What did they say?"

"Well, they were a little surprised at first, naturally, but they know Lisa a lot better than you know me, so they got over it and we had a little celebration."

Lisa leaned forward and covered her mother's hand on the tabletop. "Mark has wonderful parents, Mom. They're anxious to meet you and Dad, and I promised them we'd introduce you all soon. Right away Mark's mother suggested a dinner party at their house. She said if you two are agreeable, I could set a date."

This isn't how it's supposed to be, Bess thought, battling tears, Michael and I practically strangers to our future son-in-law and total strangers to his family. Whatever happened to girls marrying the boy next door? Or the little brat who pulled her pigtails in the third grade? Or the one who did wheelies on his BMX bike in our driveway to impress her in junior high? Those lucky, simpler times were bygone with the era of transient executives and upward mobility, of rising divorce rates and single-parent homes.

Everyone was waiting for Bess to respond to the news but she wasn't ready yet, emotionally. She felt like breaking down and bawling, and had to swallow hard before she could speak at all.

"Your dad and I need to talk about a few things first. Would you give us a day or two to do that?"

"Sure." Lisa withdrew her hand and sat back.

"Would that be okay with you, Michael?" Bess asked him.

"Of course."

Bess deposited her napkin on the table and pushed her chair back. "Then I'll call you, or Dad will."

"Fine. But you aren't leaving yet, are you? I've got dessert."

"It's late. I've got to be at the store early tomorrow. I really should be going."

"But it's not even eight yet."

"I know, but . . ." Bess rose, dusting crumbs from her skirt, anxious to excape and examine her true feelings, to crumple and get angry if she so desired.

"Dad, will you stay and have dessert? I got a French silk pie from Baker's Square."

"I think I'll pass, too, honey. Maybe I can stop by tomorrow night and have some with you."

Michael rose, followed by Lisa, and they all stood awkwardly a moment, politely pretending this was not a scenario in which parents were running, distraught, from the announcement that their daughter was knocked up and planning a shotgun wedding, pretending this was merely a polite, everyday leave-taking.

"Well, I'll get your coats, then," Lisa said with a quavery smile.

"I will, sweetheart," Mark offered, and went to do so. In the crowded entry he politely held Bess's coat, then handed Michael's to him. There was another clumsy moment after Michael slipped his coat on, when the two men confronted each other, wondering what to say or do next. Michael offered his hand and Mark gripped it.

"We'll talk soon," Michael said.

"Thank you, sir."

Even more awkwardly, the young man faced Bess. "Good night, Mrs. Curran," Mark offered.

"Good night, Mark."

Unsure of himself, he hovered, and finally Bess raised her cheek to touch his gingerly. In the cramped space before the entry door Michael gave Lisa a hug, leaving only the mother and daughter to exchange some gesture of good night. Bess found herself unable, so Lisa made the move. Once Bess felt her daughter's arms around her, however, she clung, feeling her emotions billow, her tears come close to exposing themselves. Her precious firstborn, her Lisa, who had learned to drink from a straw before she was one, who had carried a black doll named Gertrude all over the neighborhood until she was five, and, dressed in feet pajamas, had clambered into bed between her mommy and daddy on Saturday mornings when she got old enough to climb out of her crib unaided.

Lisa, whom she and Michael had wanted so badly.

Lisa, the product of those optimistic times.

Lisa, who now carried their grandchild.

Bess clutched Lisa and whispered throatily, "I love you, Lee-lee," the pet name Michael had given her long ago, in a golden time when they'd all believed they'd live happily ever after.

"I love you, too, Mom."

"I just need a little time, please, darling."

"I know."

Michael stood waiting with the door open, touched by Bess's use of the familiar baby name.

Bess drew back, squeezing Lisa's arm. "Get lots of rest. I'll call you."

She passed Michael and headed down the hall, clasping her clutch purse under one arm, pulling on her gloves, her raspberry high heels clicking on the tiled floor. He closed the apartment door and followed, buttoning his coat, turning up its collar, watching her speed along with an air of efficiency, as if she were late for a business appointment.

At the far end of the hall she descended two stairs before her bravado dissolved. Abruptly she stopped, gripped the rail with one hand and listed over it, the other hand to her mouth, her back to him, crying.

He stopped on the step above her with his hands in his coat pockets, watching her shoulders shake. He felt melancholy himself, and witnessing her display of emotions amplified his own. Though she tried to stifle them, tiny mewling sounds escaped her throat. Reluctantly, he touched her shoulder blade. "Aw, Bess . . ."

Her words were muffled behind a gloved hand. "I'm sorry, Michael, I know I should be taking this better . . . but it's such a disappointment."

"Of course it is. For me, too." He returned his hand to his coat pocket.

She sniffed, snapped her purse open and found a tissue inside. Still with her back turned, mopping her face, she said, "I'm appalled at myself for breaking down in front of you this way."

"Oh, hell, Bess, I've seen you cry before."

She blew her nose. "When we were married, yes, but this is different."

With the tissue tucked away and her purse again beneath an arm she turned to face him, touching her lower eyelids with the fingertips of her expensive raspberry leather gloves. "Oh, God," she said, and emptied her lungs in a big gust. She drooped back with her hips against the black metal handrail and fixed her tired stare on the opposite railing.

For a while neither of them spoke, only stood in the murky hallway, helpless to stop their daughter's future from taking a downhill dive. Finally Bess said, "I can't pretend this is anything but terrible, our only daughter and a shotgun wedding."

"I know."

"Do you feel like you've failed again?" She looked up at him with red-rimmed eyes, shiny at the corners with a new batch of tears.

He drew a deep, tired breath and took stock of their surroundings. "I don't think I want to discuss it in the hallway of this apartment building. You want to go to a restaurant, have a cup of coffee or something?"

"Now?"

"Unless you really have to hurry home."

"No, that was just an excuse to escape. My first appointment isn't until ten in the morning."

"All right, then, how about The Ground Round on White Bear Avenue?"

"The Ground Round would be fine."

They turned and continued down the stairs, lagging now, slowed by distress. He opened the plate-glass door for her, experiencing a fleeting sense of déjà vu.

How many times in the course of a courtship and marriage had he opened the door for her? There were times during their breakup when he'd angrily walked out before her and let the door close in her face. Tonight, faced with an emotional upheaval, it felt reassuring to perform the small courtesy again.

Outside, their breath hung milky in the cold air, and the snow, compressing beneath their feet, gave off a hard-candy crunch like chewing resounding within one's ear. At the foot of the sidewalk, where it gave onto the parking lot, she paused and half-turned as he caught up with her.

"I'll see you there," she said.

"I'll follow you."

Heading in opposite directions toward their cars, they started the long, rocky journey back toward amity.

Chapter 2

They met in the lobby of the restaurant and followed a glossy-haired, effeminate young man who said, "Right this way." Michael felt the same déjà vu as earlier, trailing Bess as he'd done countless times before, watching the sway of her coat, the movement of her arms as she took off her gloves, inhaling the faint drift of her perfume, the same rosy scent she'd worn for years.

The perfume was the only familiar thing about her. Everything else was new—the professionally streaked blonde hair nearly touching her shoulder, the expensive clothes, the self-assurance, the brittleness. These had all been acquired since their divorce.

They sat at a table beside a window, their faces tinted by an overhead fixture with a bowl-shaped orange globe and the pinkish glow of the phosphorescent lamps reflecting off the snow outside. The supper crowd had gone, and a hockey game was in progress on a TV above the bar somewhere around a corner. It murmured a background descant to the piped-in orchestra music falling from the ceiling.

Michael removed his coat and folded it over an empty chair while Bess left hers over her shoulders.

A teenage waitress with a frizzy hairdo came and asked if they'd like menus.

"No, thank you. Just coffee," Michael answered.

"Two?"

Michael deferred to Bess with a glance. "Yes, two," she answered, with a quick glance at the girl.

When they were alone again, Bess fixed her gaze on Michael's hands, wrapped palm-over-palm above a paper place mat. He had square, shapely hands, with neatly trimmed nails and long fingers. Bess had always loved his hands. They were, she'd said many times, the kind of hands you'd welcome on your dentist. Even in the dead of winter his skin never entirely paled. His wrists held a whisk of dark hair that trailed low and made his white cuffs appear whiter. There was an undeniable appeal about the sight of a man's clean hands foiled by white shirt cuffs and the darker edge of a suit sleeve. Oftentimes after the divorce, at odd, unexpected moments—in a restaurant, or a department store—Bess would find herself staring at the hands of some stranger and remembering Michael's. Then reality would return, and she would damn herself for becoming vulnerable to memory and loneliness.

In a restaurant, six years after their divorce, she drew her gaze from Michael's hands and lifted it to his face, daunted by the admission that she still found him handsome. He had perfect eyebrows above attractive hazel eyes, full lips and a head of gorgeous black hair. For the first time she noticed a few skeins of gray above his ears, discernible only under the direct light.

"Well . . ." she began, "this has been a night of surprises."

He chuckled quietly in reply.

"This is the last place I expected to end up when I told Lisa I'd come for supper," Bess told him.

"Me too."

"I don't think you're as shocked by all this as I am, though."

"I was shocked when you opened that door, I can tell you that."

"I wouldn't have been there if I'd known what Lisa had up her sleeve."

"Neither would I."

Silence for a moment, then, "Listen, Michael, I'm sorry about all that . . . well, Lisa's obvious attempt to revive something between us—our old dishes and the stroganoff and the corn pudding and the candlelight. She should have known better."

"It was damned uncomfortable, wasn't it?"

"Yes, it was. It still is."

"I know."

Their coffee came: something neutral to focus on instead of each other. When the waitress went away Bess asked, "Did you hear what Lisa said to me when we were alone in the kitchen?"

"No. What?"

"The gist of her message was, Grow up, Mother, you've been acting like a child for six years. I had no idea she was so angry about our antagonism, did you?"

"Only in retrospect, when she'd talk about Mark's family and how close and loving they are."

"She's talked to you about that?"

His eyes answered above his cup while he took a sip of coffee.

"When?" Bess demanded.

"I don't know—a couple different times."

"She never told me she talked to you so often."

"You put up barriers, Bess, that's why. You're putting up a new one right now. You should see the expression on your face."

"Well, it hurts to know she's talked to you about these things, and that Mark's family knows her better than we know Mark."

"Sure it hurts, but why wouldn't the two of them gravitate toward the family that stayed together? It's only natural."

"So what do you think of Mark?"

"I don't know him very well. I think I've only talked to him a couple of times before tonight."

"That's my point. How could this have happened when they've been dating such a short time that we've scarcely met the boy?"

"First of all, he's not a boy. You have to admit, he certainly faced the situation like a man. I was impressed with him tonight."

"You were?"

"Well, hell, he was there beside her, facing us head on instead of leaving her to break the news by herself. Doesn't that impress you?"

"I guess so."

"And by the sound of it, he comes from a good family."

Bess had decided something on the way to the restaurant. "I don't want to meet them."

"Aw, come on, Bess, that's silly—why not?"

"I didn't say I *won't* meet them. I will, if I have to, but I don't *want* to."

"Why?"

"Because it's hard to be with happy families. It makes our own failure that much harder to bear. They have what we wanted to have and thought we'd have. Only we don't, and after six years I still haven't gotten over the feeling of failure."

He considered awhile, then admitted, "Yeah, I know what you mean. And now for me, it's twice."

She sipped her coffee, curious and hesitant while meeting his eyes across the table.

"I can't believe I'm asking this, but what happened?"

"Between Darla and me?"

She nodded.

He stared at his cup, toying with its handle. "What happened was that it was the wrong combination from the beginning. We were each unhappy in the marriage we had, and we thought . . . well, hell . . . you know. We married each other on the rebound. We were lonely and, like you said, feeling like failures, and it seemed important to get another relationship going and to succeed at it, to sweeten the bitterness, I guess. What it really turned out to be was five years of coming to terms with the fact that we really never loved each other."

After some time Bess said, "That's what I'm afraid is going to happen to Lisa."

His steady hazel eyes held her brown ones while each of them pondered their daughter's future, longing for it to be happier than their own. From the bar around the corner came the whine of a blender.

When it stopped Michael said, "But the choice isn't ours to make for her."

"Maybe not the choice but isn't it our responsibility to make her consider all the ramifications?"

"Which are?"

"They're so young."

"They're older than we were when we got married, and they both seem to know what they want."

"That's what they told us but what else would you expect them to say, under the circumstances?"

He considered awhile then remarked thoughtfully, "I don't know, Bess, they seemed pretty sure of themselves. Mark made some points that had a lot of merit. If they had already talked about when they wanted to have babies, they were a jump ahead of about ninety percent of the couples who get married. And, frankly, I don't see anything wrong with their thinking. Like Mark said, they have good jobs, a home, the baby would have two willing parents—that's a pretty solid start for a kid. You have your kids when you're young, you have more patience, health, zest— and then when they're gone from home you're still young enough to enjoy your freedom."

"So you don't think we should try to talk them out of it?"

"No, I don't. What would the other options be? Abortion, adoption, or Lisa raising a baby alone. When the two of them love each other and want to get married? Wouldn't make much sense at all."

Bess sighed and crossed her forearms on the table. "I guess I'm just reacting like a mother, wanting a guarantee that her daughter will be happy."

His eyes told her what he thought about hoping for guarantees.

After a moment she said, "Just answer me this—when we got married, didn't you think it would be for life?"

"Of course, but you can't advise your child not to marry because you're afraid she'll make the same mistakes you did. That's not realistic. What you have to do is be truthful with her, but first of all you have to be truthful with yourself. If you— I guess I should be saying *we*—can admit what we did wrong and caution them to avoid the same pitfalls, maybe *that's* how we can redeem ourselves."

While Bess was pondering the point the waitress came and refilled their cups. When she went away, Bess took a sip of her steaming coffee and asked, "So, what do you think about the rest? About us walking down the aisle with her and her wearing my old wedding dress and everything?"

They sat silently awhile, their glances occasionally touching, then dropping as they thought about putting on a show of harmony before a couple hundred guests, some, undoubtedly, who'd been guests at their own wedding. The idea revolted them both.

"What do you think, Bess?"

Bess drew a deep breath and sighed. "It wasn't pleasant, getting chewed out by my own daughter. She said some things that really made me angry. I thought, How dare you preach to me, you young whelp!"

"And now?" Michael prodded.

"Well, we're talking, aren't we?"

The question gave them pause to consider the six years of silence and how it had affected their children.

"Do you think you could go through with it?"

"I don't know. . . ." Bess looked out the window at the cars in the parking lot, imagining herself walking down an aisle with Michael . . . again. Seeing her wedding gown in use . . . again. Sitting beside him at a wedding banquet . . . again. More quietly, she repeated, "I don't know."

"I guess I don't see that we have any other choice."

"So you want me to give her the go-ahead for this dinner at the Padgetts'?"

"I think we can fake our way through it, for her sake."

"All right, but first I want to talk to her, Michael, please allow me that. Just to make sure she isn't marrying him under duress, and to assure her that if she makes some other choice you and I will be supportive. May I do that first?"

"Of course. I think you should."

"And the dress, what should I say about the dress?"

This issue touched closer to home than all the others.

"What harm would it do if she wore it?"

"Oh, Michael—" Her eyes skittered away, suddenly self-conscious.

"You think just because you wore it and the marriage didn't last, the thing is jinxed? Or that somebody in the crowd might recognize it and think it's bad judgment? Be sensible, Bess. Who in that entire church besides you and me and possibly your mother would even know? I say let her wear it. It'll save me five hundred dollars."

"You always were putty in her hands."

"Yup. And I kind of enjoyed it."

"Need I mention that the piano will have to be moved again?"

"I'm aware of that."

"On their limited budget, it'll be a drain."

"I'll pay for it. I told her when I bought it I'd foot the bill for the piano-moving for the life of the instrument, or the life of me, whichever ended first."

"You told her that?" Bess sounded surprised.

"I told her not to tell you. You had such a bug up your ass about the piano anyway."

Bess almost laughed. They eyed each other, repressing grins.

"All right, let's back up, boy, to that remark you made about saving five hundred dollars. I take it from that that you're going to offer to pay for the wedding."

"I thought it was damned noble of the two of them not to ask for any help, but what kind of Scrooge would let his kid lay out money like that when he's earning a hundred thousand a year?"

Bess raised her eyebrows. "Oooo . . . you dropped that in there very neatly, just to make sure I'd know, huh? Well, it just so happens I'm doing quite well myself. Not a hundred grand a year but enough that I insist on paying half of everything."

"Okay, it's a deal." Michael extended his open hand above their coffee cups.

She shook it and they felt the shock of familiarity: the fit hadn't changed. Their expressions grew guilt-tinged and immediately they broke the contact.

"Well," Michael said, expanding his chest and touching his stomach. "I've had enough coffee to keep me awake until three."

"Me too."

"You ready to go then?" She nodded and they hitched their chairs back from the table. While they were donning their coats, he inquired, "How's your mother?"

"Indefatigable as always. Makes me breathless just listening to her."

He smiled and said, "Say hi to the old doll for me, will you? I've missed her."

"I'll do that. But if this wedding comes off, you'll undoubtedly be able to say hello to her yourself."

"And your sister, Joan. She still in Colorado?"

"Yes. Still married to that jerk and refusing to consider divorce because she's Catholic."

"Do you ever see her?"

"Not very often. We just don't have anything in common anymore. By the way, Michael . . ." She paused, her coat on. For the first time her eyes softened as she looked at him. "I was very sorry about your mother."

"And I was sorry about your dad."

They had each lost a parent since the divorce but she still had one left. He now had none.

"I appreciated your coming to the funeral. She always liked you," Michael told Bess. She had attended and had taken the children, of course, but had not spoken to Michael. Likewise, he had attended her father's funeral, but they had remained stubbornly aloof from one another, exchanging only the most perfunctory condolences. They had each liked the other's parents. It had been one of the connections hardest to sever.

"It was damned hard when Mother died," Michael admitted. "I kept wishing I had some brothers and sisters, but . . . aw, hell, what good are wishes? I'm forty-three years old. You'd think I'd have gotten used to it by now."

His whole life he'd hated being an only child and had talked about it often with her. She, too, had missed having a sister she was close to. There was a seven years' age difference between herself and Joan, which left them little in the way of childhood nostalgia regarding play, or friends, or even school. In her memory, Joan seemed more like a third parent than a sister. When she'd married and moved to Denver it had made little difference in Bess's life, and though they occasionally exchanged letters, these were merely duty missives.

It felt odd to both Bess and Michael, standing in the doorway of a restaurant, commiserating with each other about their loneliness and their loss of loved ones. They'd handled bitterness well, knew exactly how to handle it, but this empathy was an imposition. It made them eager to part.

"Well," Bess said. "It's late. I'd better be going."

She left the restaurant ahead of him and at the door felt the brief touch of his hand in the center of her back.

Memories.

In the parking lot at the point of parting, he said, "Chances are we aren't going to get through this whole wedding without having to contact each other. I've moved. . . ." He handed her a business card. "Here's my new address and phone number. If I'm not there, leave a message on the recorder, or call the office."

"All right." She put the card in her coat pocket.

They paused, groping for parting words while this present good-bye melded into a montage of a hundred others from their courting years—New Year's Eves, dances and parties, all followed by long passionate sessions on her doorstep. The flashback lasted only seconds before Michael spoke.

"You'll call Lisa, then?"

"Yes."

"Maybe I'll call her, too, just to let her know we're in agreement."

"All right . . . well, good night."

" 'Night, Bess."

Again came that momentary void, with neither of them moving, then they turned and went to their separate cars.

Bess started her engine and waited while it warmed. He had taught her that long ago: in Minnesota a car lasts longer if you let it warm in winter. That was in their struggling days, when they'd kept cars for five or six years. Now she could afford a new one every two years. Presently she drove a Buick Park Avenue. She waited to see what kind of car he was driving—her curiosity some odd possessive holdover she could not control. She heard the muffled growl of his engine as he passed behind her, and caught a glimpse of a silver roofline in the rearview mirror, turning only as he eased into a pool of illumination from a tall pole light to identify a Cadillac Seville. So it was true—he was doing well. She sat awhile attempting to sort out her feelings about that. Six years ago she would gladly have stuck pins in a voodoo doll of Michael Curran. Tonight, however, she felt an inexplicable touch of pride that once, long ago, she'd chosen a winner, and that now, faced with an impromptu wedding, there would be no need to stint their daughter.

Remembering Michael's card, she snapped on the overhead light and fished it from her pocket.

5011 Lake Avenue, White Bear Lake.

He'd moved to White Bear Lake? Back within ten miles of her? Why, when he'd lived clear over in a western suburb of Minneapolis for the past five years? Too close for comfort, she decided, stuffing the card back into her coat pocket and putting her car in gear.

Twenty minutes later she pulled into the horseshoe-shaped driveway of the house she and Michael had shared in Stillwater, Minnesota. It was a two-story Georgian on Third Avenue, high above the St. Croix River, a beautifully balanced home with a center door and bow windows on either side. The entry was guarded by four fluted round columns supporting a semicircular railed roof. From behind the sturdy railing a great fanlight overlooked the front yard from the second story. The place had a look of permanence, of security, the kind of house pictured in children's readers, Bess had told Michael when they'd found it, the kind of house where only a happy family would live.

They had fallen in love with it on sight; then they'd gone inside and had seen the magnificent view, clear across the St. Croix River to Wisconsin, beyond, and the lot itself, cresting the bluff, with its great, grand maple tree dead center out back, and the sparkling river lying below. They had seen the place and had gasped in mutual delight.

Nothing that had happened since had changed Bess's opinion of the house. She still loved it; enough to be making payments on Michael's legal half of it since Randy had turned eighteen.

She pulled into the double attached garage, lowered the automatic door and entered the service door to the kitchen. She'd redone the room since her business had flourished, had installed matte white Formica cabinets with butcher-block tops, a new vinyl floor in shades of seafoam blue and plush, cream-colored carpeting in the attached family room. The new furniture was a blend of smoky blues and apricots, inspired by the view of the river and the spectacular sunrises that unfolded beyond the tall east windows of the house.

Bess bypassed the U-shaped kitchen and dropped her coat onto a sofa facing the wall of glass. She switched on a shoulder-high floor lamp with a thick, twisted ceramic base and a cymbal-shaped shade and went to the window to draw up the blinds. The window treatments were lavish above, simple below: great billowing valances in a busy blue-and-apricot floral, paired with pleated horizontal blinds of pale apricot. The pattern of the curtains was repeated in two deep, chubby chairs; a coordinating splash of waves appeared on the long sofa with its baker's dozen of loose cushions.

Bess drew up the blinds and stood looking out the window at the winter view—the smooth yard, swathed in snow, sloping down to the sheer bluff covered by scrub brush; the granddaddy maple standing sentinel at the yard's edge; the great pale path of the wide river and, on the Wisconsin side, a half mile away, dots of window light glimmering here and there on the dark, high, wooded bank.

She thought of Michael . . . of Lisa . . . of Michael again . . . and of their unborn grandchild. The word had not been mentioned but it had been there in that restaurant between them as surely as their cups of steaming coffee.

My God, we're going to have a grandchild.

The thought thundered through her, brought her hand to her mouth and a lump to her throat. It was difficult to hate a man with whom you were sharing this milestone.

The lights across the river became starbursts and she realized there were tears in her eyes. Grandparenthood had been something that happened to others. It was symbolized by television commercials with sixty-five-year-old gray-haired couples with round, rosy cheeks baking cookies with youngsters; calling their grandchildren long distance; opening their doors at Christmastime and welcoming two generations with open arms.

This child would have none of that. He would have a handsome young grandfather, recently divorced, living in White Bear Lake, and a businesswoman of a grandma too busy for cookie-making, living in Stillwater.

Many times since her divorce Bess had felt regret for the loss of tradition and an unbroken family line but never so powerfully as tonight, when facing the advent of the next generation. She herself had known grandparents, Molly and Ed LeClair, her mother's folks, who'd died when she was in high school. Recalling them brought a wistful expression to her face, for they'd lived right here in Stillwater through her younger years, in a house on North Hill to which she'd ridden her bike whenever she wanted, to raid Grandma Molly's cookie jar or her strawberry patch, or to watch Grandpa Ed paint his birdhouses in his little workshop out back. He'd known the tricks of attracting bluebirds—a house with a slanted roof, no perch and a removable bottom, he'd taught her—and always in the summer their backyard had bluebirds flitting above Grandma Molly's gardens and the open meadow beyond.

Times had changed. Lisa's child would have to visit his grandma in her interior design shop, and his grandfather only after he got old enough to drive a car.

Moreover, the bluebirds had disappeared from Stillwater.

Bess sighed and turned away from the window. She removed her suit and left it on the sofa. Dressed in her blouse, slip and nylons, she built a fire in the family-room fireplace and sat on the floor before it, staring, disconsolate. She wondered what Michael thought about becoming a grandfather, and where Randy was, and what kind of husband Mark Padgett would make, and if Lisa truly loved him, and how she herself was going to survive this charade Lisa was asking of her. Already, after only one night with Michael, she was bluer than she'd been in months.

The telephone rang and Bess glanced at her watch. It was going on eleven. She picked up the receiver from a glass-top table between the two tub chairs.

"Hello?"

"Hi. Just checking in."

"Oh, hi, Keith." Lifting her face to the ceiling, she scooped her hair back from one temple.

"You got home late."

"Just a few minutes ago."

"So, how was the dinner with Lisa?"

Bess flopped onto one of the chairs with her head caught on the rounded back. "Not so good, I'm afraid."

"Why not?"

"Lisa invited me over for more than just dinner."

"What else?"

"Oh, Keith, I've been sitting here getting a little weepy."

"What is it?"

"Lisa is pregnant."

At the other end of the line Keith released a swoosh of breath.

"She wants to get married in six weeks."

"To the baby's father?"

"Yes, Mark Padgett."

"I remember you mentioning him."

"Mentioning him, that's all. Lord, she's known him less than a year."

"And what about him? Does he want to marry her, too?"

"He says he does. They want a full wedding with all the trimmings."

"Then I don't understand—what's the problem?"

That was one of the troubles with Keith. He often failed to understand her problems. She had been seeing him for three years, yet in all that time he'd never seemed sympathetic at the moments she needed him to. Particularly when it came to her children, he had an intolerant side that often irritated her. He had no children of his own, and sometimes that fact created a gulf between them that Bess wasn't sure could ever be bridged.

"The problem is that I'm her mother. I want her to marry for love, not for expediency."

"Doesn't she love him?"

"She says she does but how—"

"Does he love her?"

"Yes, but—"

"Then what are you so upset about?"

"It's not that cut-and-dried, Keith!"

"What? Are you upset about becoming a grandmother? That's a lot of bunk. I've never been able to understand people getting all freaked out about these things—reaching thirty, or forty, or becoming a grandparent. It's all pretty ridiculous to me. What really matters is keeping busy and healthy and feeling young inside."

"That's not what I'm upset about!"

"Well, what then?"

Reclining in the chair, with her chin on her chest, Bess picked up the soiled jabot and toyed with it.

"Michael was there."

Silence . . . then, "Michael?"

"Lisa set us up, she invited us both, then made an excuse to leave the apartment so we'd be forced to confront each other."

"And?"

"And it was hellish."

Silence again before Keith said, decidedly, "Bess, I want to come over."

"I don't think you should. It's nearly eleven."

"Bess, I don't like this."

"My seeing Michael? For heaven's sake, I haven't spoken a civil word to the man in six years."

"Maybe not, but it only took one night to upset you. I want to come over."

"Keith, please . . . it'll take you half an hour to get here, and I should go into the shop early in the morning to do some bookwork. Believe me, I'm not upset."

"You said you were crying."

"Not about Michael. About Lisa."

From his silence she anticipated his reaction. "You're pushing me away again, Bess. Why do you do that?"

"Please, Keith, not tonight. I'm tired and I expect Randy will be home soon."

"I wasn't asking to stay overnight." Though Bess and Keith were intimate, she had made it understood early in their relationship that as long as Randy lived with her, overnights at her house were out. Randy had been hurt enough by his dad's peccadillo. Though her son might very well guess she was having an affair with Keith, she was never going to verify it.

"Keith, could we just say good night now? I really have had a rough day."

Keith's silence was rife with exasperation before he released a sound resembling escaping steam. "Oh, all right," he said, "I won't *bother* you tonight. What I called for was to see if you wanted to go to dinner on Saturday night." His invitation was issued in an acid tone.

"Are you sure you still want me to?"

"Bess, I swear to God, sometimes I don't know why I keep hanging onto you."

Bess became contrite. "I'm sorry, Keith. Yes, of course, I'd love to go to dinner Saturday night. What time?"

"Seven."

"Shall I drive in?" Keith lived in St. Paul, thirty miles away. His favorite restaurants were over in that direction.

"Come to my place. I'll drive from here."

"All right, I'll see you then. And Keith?"

"What?"

"I really am sorry. I mean it."

Across the wire she could sense him expelling a breath and drooping his shoulders. "I know."

After Bess hung up she sat in her chair a long time, curled forward, elbows to knees, her toes overlapped, staring at the fire. What was she doing with Keith? Merely using him to slake her loneliness? He had walked into her store one day three years ago, when she'd been three years without a man, three years trying occasional dates that turned into sexual embarrassments, three years insisting that all men belonged at the bottom of the ocean. Then in walked Keith, a little on the plain side in the looks department, a little on the thin side in the hair department, but one of the best sales reps she'd ever encountered. Known in the trade as a rag man, he'd wheeled in a big 40×20-inch sample case and announced he was from Robert Allen Fabrics and that she had decorated the home of his best friends, Sylvia and Reed Gohrman; he liked the looks of her store; needed a Mother's Day gift for his mother; and if she would look through his samples while he perused her merchandise, they might each find something they liked. If not, he'd be gone and would never darken her door again.

Bess had burst out laughing. So had Keith. He'd bought a forty-dollar vase trimmed with glass roses, and when she was wrapping it she said, "Your mother will be pleased."

He replied, "My mother is never pleased with anything. She'll probably come in here and exchange it for those three frogs that are holding that glass ball."

"You don't like my frogs?"

He glanced at the three ugly brass frogs, covered with green patina, their forefeet raised above their heads, supporting what looked like a large, clear glass marble. He raised one eyebrow and quirked his mouth. "Now, that's a loaded question when you haven't told me what you think of my samples yet."

She had looked, and liked, and been assured by Keith that his company maintained careful quality control of its products, would not keep her on ice for three months then ship flawed fabric, provided *free* samples rather than the "book plan" (which required storeowners to sign a year's contract and agree to pay for all samples), offered delayed billing and followed up every order with a computerized acknowledgment and shipping date.

She was impressed, and Keith went away knowing so.

He'd called a week later and asked if she would like to go to Dudley Riggs's Brave New Workshop with him and his friends Sylvia and Reed Gohrman. She liked his style—live comedy for a first date, which she needed at the time, and mutual acquaintances as reassurance that she wouldn't have another wrestling match on her hands at the end of the evening.

He had been impeccably polite—no groping, no sexual innuendos, not even a good night kiss until their second date. They had seen each other for six months before their relationship became intimate. Immediately afterward, he'd asked her to marry him. For two and a half years she'd been saying no. For two and a half years he'd been growing more frustrated by her refusals. She had tried to explain that she wasn't willing to take that risk again, that running her business had become her primary source of fulfillment, that she still had her troubles with Randy and didn't want to impose them on a husband. The truth was, she simply didn't love him enough.

He was nice (an elementary word but true, when describing Keith) but when he walked into her shop she only smiled, never glowed. When he kissed her she only warmed, never heated. When they made love she wanted the light off, not on. And when it was over, she always wanted to go home to her own bed, alone.

And of course there was that thing about her children. He'd been married once, briefly, during his twenties but being childless he had remained marginally jealous of Lisa and Randy and slightly selfish in his approach to many conflicts. If Bess had to say no to him because of a previous commitment with Lisa, he became piqued. He held that her stand on his sleeping at her house was ridiculous, given that Randy was nineteen years old and no dummy.

Another thing—he coveted her house.

He had come into it the first time and stood before the sliding glass doors, looked out over the river valley and breathed, "Wow . . . I could put my recliner right here and never move."

First off, she hated recliners. Secondly, she felt a trickle of irritation at the very suggestion of him moving into *her* house. For the briefest moment she'd even had a flash of defense on Michael's behalf. After all, it was Michael who'd paid for the house and helped her furnish it. How dare this upstart stand there musing about usurping the spot that had always been Michael's favorite?

There were many facets of Keith that displeased her. So the question remained, why did she continue to see him?

The answer was plain: he had become a habit, and without him life would have been infinitely more lonely.

She sighed and went to the fireplace, screaked open the metal screen and turned the logs, watching sparks rise like inverted fireworks. She sat before it, with her arms crossed on her upraised knees. *Oh, Lisa, don't worsen the mistake you've already made. It's no fun watching a fire alone, wishing things had turned out differently.*

Her face grew hot, and the nylon slip covering her thighs seemed to catch the heat and draw it to her skin. She dropped her forehead onto her arms but remained where she was. The house was so silent and bleak. It had never been as satisfying after Michael left. It was home, and she would never give it up. But it was lonely.

Outside, most of the lights across the river had disappeared. She rose and wandered into the dining room—an extension of the family room—running her fingers over the backs of the unused chairs as she passed them, and on through an archway into the formal living room, which stretched across the entire east end of the house, from the river view at the rear to the street view at the front. At the rear corner, where two immense windows met, a grand piano stood in the shadows— black, gleaming, silent since Lisa had grown up and moved away. On it was a gallery of framed family pictures. On Thursdays the cleaning lady moved the pictures and dusted the piano. At Christmastime a huge arrangement of red balls and greenery ousted the five framed portraits. After New Year's the gallery came back and stayed until the following Christmas. It was the only thing the piano was used for anymore.

Bess sat down on the sleek ebony piano bench and slid across it in her nylon slip. She switched on the music lamp. Its rays shone down upon an empty music rest and a closed key cover. She touched the brass pedals, cold and smooth beneath her nylon-bound toes. She folded her hands and rested them between her thighs and wondered why she herself had given up playing. After Michael left she'd shunned the instrument just as she'd shunned him. Because he had liked piano music so much? How childish. Granted, her life had been busy, but there were moments such as these when the sound of the piano would have been comforting, when the feel of the keys would have soothed.

She rose and opened the bench, leafed through the sheet music until she found what she was looking for.

The cover of the bench clacked loudly as it closed. By contrast, the key cover made a soft, velvet thump as it opened. The music rustled, and her raspberry silk sleeves appeared in the thin band of light illuminating the keys.

The first notes shimmered through the shadowy room, harp-like and haunting as she found the familiar combinations and struck them.

"The Homecoming." Lisa's song. Her father's song. Why Bess had chosen it, she neither dissected nor cared. The compulsion had struck and she'd responded, rusty as she was on this instrument. As she played, the tentativeness left her fingers, the tension left her shoulders and soon she began to feel what a runner feels when he hits his stride, the immense sense of well-being at baring one's teeth to the wind and utilizing some capability that has lain dormant too long.

She was unaware of Randy's presence until she ended the song and he spoke out of the shadows.

"Sounding good, Mom."

"Oh!" She gasped and lifted an inch off the piano bench. "Randy, you scared the devil out of me! How long have you been there?"

He smiled, one shoulder propped against the dining-room doorway. "Not long." He sauntered into the room and sat down on the bench beside her, dressed in jeans and a brown leather jacket that looked as though a fleet of Sherman tanks had driven over it. His hair was black, like his father's, and dressed with something sheeny, spiked straight up and finger-long on top, slicked back over the ears and trailing in natural curls below his collar in back. Randy was an eye-catcher—her clerk at the store said he reminded her of a young Robert Urich—with a lopsided, dimpled grin; a way of letting his head dip forward when he approached a woman; a tiny gold loop in his left ear; perfect teeth and brown eyes with glistening black lashes that were longer than some men could grow their beards. He had adopted the rough-cut look of the unshaved young pop singer George Michael, and an un-hurried manner.

Sitting beside his mother he played a low-register F, holding the key down until the note diminished into silence. Dropping the hand to his lap, he turned his head infinitesimally—all his motions were understated—and unleashed his lazy quarter-smile.

"Been a long time since you played."

"Mm-hmm."

"Why'd you stop?"

"Why'd you stop talking to your dad?"

"Why did you?"

"I was angry."

"So was I."

Bess paused. "I saw him tonight."

Randy looked away but allowed the grin to remain.

"How is the prick?"

"Randy, you're speaking of your father, and I won't allow that kind of gutter language."

"I've heard you call him worse."

"When?"

Randy worked his head and shoulders in irritation. "Mom, get off it. You hate his guts as much as I do and you haven't made any secret of it. So what's all this about? All of a sudden you're buttering up to him?"

"I'm not buttering up to him. I saw him, that's all. At Lisa's."

"Oh yeah, that's right. . . ." Randy dropped his chin and scratched his head. "I guess she told you, huh?"

"Yes, she did."

He looked at his mother. "So, you bummed out or what?"

"Yeah, I guess you could say that."

"I was, too, at first but now I've had a day to think about it and I think she'll be okay. Hell, she wants the kid and Mark's okay, you know? I mean, he really loves her, I think."

"How do you know so much?"

"I spend time over there." Randy ran his thumbnail into the vertical crack be-tween two piano keys. "She cooks me dinner and we watch videos together, stuff like that. Mark's usually there."

Another surprise. "I didn't know that . . . that you spend time over there."

Randy gave up his preoccupation with the keys and returned his hand to his lap. "Lisa and I get along all right. She helps me get my head on straight."

"She said you've agreed to stand up for them."

Randy shrugged and let his eyes rove indolently his mother's way.

"And to cut your hair."

He made a chucking sound, sucking his cheek against his teeth. "There you go. You're gonna like that, huh, Ma?" His grin was back.

"The hair doesn't bother me as much as the beard."

He rubbed it. It was coarse and black and undoubtedly a turn-on for many nineteen-year-old girls. "Yeah, well, it's probably gonna go, too."

"You got some girl who's going to miss it?" she teased, reaching as if to pinch his cheek.

He reared back and brandished both hands, karate-fashion. "Don't touch the nap, woman!"

They poised as if on the brink of combat, then laughed together and hugged, with her smooth cheek against his prickly one, and the smell of his distressed leather jacket engulfing her. No matter the worries he caused her, moments like this were her recompense. Ah, there was something wonderful about an adult son. His occasional hugs made up for the loss of his father, and his presence in the house gave her someone to listen for, someone else moving about, a reason to keep the refrigerator stocked. It probably was time she booted him out of the nest but she hated losing him, no matter how seldom they exchanged banter such as this. When he left there would be only her in this big house alone, and it would be decision time.

He released her and she smiled affectionately. "You're an incorrigible flirt."

He covered his heart with both hands. "Mother, you wound me."

She let his high jinks pass and said, "About the wedding . . ."

He waited.

"Lisa asked your father and I to walk her down the aisle."

"Yeah, I know."

"And it looks as though there's going to be a dinner at Mark's parents' home to introduce the two families." When Randy made no reply, she asked, "Can you handle that?"

"Lisa and I have already got that covered."

Bess's lips formed a silent *oh*. These children of hers had a relationship that seemed to have left her several years behind.

Randy went on. "Don't worry, I won't embarrass the family." After a brief assessment of his mother's eyes, he asked, "Will you?"

"No. Your father and I had a talk after we left Lisa's. We both agreed to honor her wishes. The olive branch has been passed."

"Well then . . ." Randy raised his palms and let them slap his thighs. "I guess everybody's happy." He began to rise but Bess caught his arm.

"There's one more thing."

He waited, settling back into his customary nonchalance.

"I just thought you should know. Your father and Darla are getting a divorce."

"Yeah, Lisa told me. Big deal . . . old love 'em and leave 'em Curran." He gave a disgusted laugh and added, "I really don't give a shit, Mom."

"All right. I've told you." Bess flipped her hands in the air as if excusing him. "End of parental duty."

He rose from the bench and stood in the shadows nearby. "You better look out, Mom, the next thing you know he'll be knockin' on your door again. That's how guys like him work. . . . They gotta have a woman and by the sound of it he's fresh out of one. He made a fool of you once, and I sure as hell hope you don't let him do it again."

"Randy Curran, what kind of an airhead do you take me for?"

Randy swung away and headed for the dining-room archway. Halfway through it he used it to brake himself and turned back to her.

"Well, you were sitting there playing that song he always liked."

"It happens to be one I always liked, too!"

Leveling his gaze on her, he patted out a bongo rap on either side of the door-frame. "Yeah, sure, Mom," he remarked dryly, then gave himself a two-handed push-off and left.

Chapter 3

The St. Croix River valley lay under a cloak of winter haze the following day as Bess left home for her shop. It was a frigid, windless morning. To the south rose an inert white plume from the tall brick smokestack of the Northern States power plant, the immaculate cloud building in a thick, motionless bundle that hovered against a pewter sky. To the north, rime formed a jeweled frosting upon the lacy tie braces of the ancient black steel lift bridge that linked Stillwater with Houlton, Wisconsin, across the water.

Rivertown, Stillwater was called. It snuggled in a bowl of wooded hills, rivers, ravines and limestone bluffs that pressed it close against the placid waters of the river from which the town took its name. It had been a mecca for lumberjacks of the 1800s, who'd worked in the pineries to the north and spent their earnings in the town's fifty watering holes and six bordellos that had long since disappeared. Gone, too, were the great white pines that had once supported the town, yet Stillwater prized its heritage of former sawmills, loggers' rooming houses and Victorian mansions built by the wealthy lumber barons whose names still dotted the pages of the local telephone directory.

It appeared, at first glance, a city of rooftops—steeples, mansards, peaks and turrets of the whimsical structures built in another day—all of them dropping toward the small downtown that rimmed the west bank of the river.

Bess viewed it as she drove down Third Street hill past the old courthouse. A right on Olive and she was at Main: a half-mile strip of commerce stretching from the limestone caves of the old Joseph Wolf Brewery at the south to the limestone walls of the Staples Mill at the north. Main Street's buildings were of another century, ornate, red-brick, with arched second-story windows above, old-fashioned street lamps out front and narrow alleys out back. Steep cobbled sidewalks led down the side streets on their way to the riverfront one block beyond. In summer tourists walked its strand, enjoyed its rose gardens, sat in the shade of the town gazebo at Lowell Park or on the green lawns in the sun while licking ice-cream cones and watching the pleasure crafts nose through the blue water of the St. Croix.

They boarded the stern-wheeler *Andiamo* for scenic rides and sat on the decks of the riverside restaurants sipping tall pastel drinks, eating sandwiches and squinting at the rippling water from the shade of chic terrycloth visors, musing how great it would be to live here.

That was summer.

This was winter.

Now, in droll January, the roses were gone. The pleasure crafts were dry-docked in the valley's five marinas. The *Andiamo* lay ice-bound at her slip. The popcorn wagon on Main Street was battened down and covered with a dome of snow. The ice sculptures in front of the Grand Garage had lost their fine edges and dwindled into crystal memories of the sailboats and angels they had been during the busy Christmas season.

Bess had her usual English muffin and coffee at the St. Croix Club restaurant beside the cheerful gas fire, took another coffee along in a Styrofoam cup and headed for her shop.

It was on Chestnut Street, two doors off Main, an ancient building with two blue window boxes, a blue door and a sign that said BLUE IRIS, HOMESCAPES, with a likeness of the flower underscoring the words.

Inside it was gloomy but smelled of the potpourri and scented candles she sold. The building was ninety-three years old, scarcely wider than a hospital corridor but deep. The front door faced north, creating a cool, shady aspect in summer. This morning, however, cold drafts filtered in.

The walls of the store were papered in shantung-textured cream to match the painted woodwork, and beneath the cove molding ran a border strip of blue irises the same shade as the carpeting. Blue irises also appeared on the signature art that hung behind the desk on the stair wall, and on the paper bags in which customers' purchases were wrapped.

Grandma Molly had grown blue irises in her yard on North Hill. Even as a child Bess had dreamed of owning her own business and way back then had known what it would be called.

Bess picked her way through the maze of lamps, art prints, easels, brass picture frames, small furniture and dried botanicals to the small checkout counter set midway down the left wall against an ancient, steep stairway that climbed to the tiniest loft imaginable. It was pressed close against the ceiling—so close the top of Bess's hair brushed the embossed tin overhead. In the town's heyday some accountant had spent his days up there, penning numbers in ledgers and taking care of cash receipts. It often occurred to Bess that the man must have been either a midget or a hunchback.

She checked at the cash register and found several messages left by Heather the day before, taking them and her coffee up the creaky steps. Upstairs it was so crowded she was forced to balance on one foot while leaning over the clutter of swatch and wallpaper books to switch on a floor lamp, then the fluorescent one on her desk. As an office, the loft was inadequate by anyone's standards, yet every time she considered giving up the store to get a bigger one, it was the loft that kept her here. Maybe it was mornings like this, when her cramped, high work space collected the rising heat and reflected the light off the cream-painted ceiling, and kept the aroma of her coffee drifting close about her head. Or maybe it was the view of the front window and door over her railing. Or maybe it was simply that the loft had character and history, and both appealed to Bess. The thought of a modern office in a sterile cubicle slightly repulsed her.

It was Bess's habit to come early. The hours between 7 and 10 A.M., when the phones were quiet and no customers around, were the most productive of her day. Once 10 A.M. hit and the front door was unlocked, power paperwork was out.

She uncapped her coffee, read Heather's messages, did paperwork, filing, made phone calls and got some design work done before Heather arrived at 9:30 and called upstairs, " 'Morning, Bess!"

" 'Morning, Heather! How are you?"

"Cold." Bess heard the basement door open and close as Heather hung up her coat. "How was your supper at Lisa's?"

Bess paused with the page of a furniture catalog half-turned. Heather knew enough about her history with Michael that Bess wasn't going to open that can of worms yet.

"Fine," she answered. "She's turning out to be a very decent cook."

Heather's head appeared beyond the railing and her footsteps made the loft stairs creak. She stopped near the top of the stairs—a forty-five-year-old woman with strawberry blonde broom-cut hair glazed into fashionable disarray, stylish tortoiseshell glasses and sculptured garnet fingernails bearing tiny rhinestone nail ornaments that flashed as her hand rested on the railing. She had wide cheekbones, a pretty mouth and dressed with insouciant flair, creating a positive first impression when customers walked into the store.

Bess employed three part-time clerks but Heather was her favorite as well as her most valued.

"You have a ten o'clock appointment, you know."

"Yes, I know." Bess checked her watch and began gathering her materials for the house call.

"And a twelve-thirty and a three."

"I know, I know."

"Orders for today?"

Bess handed Heather various notes, gave her instructions about ordering wallpaper and checking on incoming freight, and left the store confident that things would run smoothly while she was gone.

It was a hectic day, as most were. Three house calls left her little time for lunch. She grabbed a tuna-salad sandwich at a sub shop between house calls and ate it in the car. She drove from Stillwater to Hudson, Wisconsin, to North St. Paul and got back to the Blue Iris just as Heather was locking up for the night.

"You had nine calls," Heather said.

"Nine!"

"Four of them were important."

Bess flopped onto a wicker settee, exhausted.

"Tell me."

"Hirschfields, Sybil Archer, Warner Wallpaper and Lisa."

"What did Sybil Archer want?"

"Her wallpaper."

Bess groaned. Sybil Archer was the wife of a 3M executive who believed Bess had a wallpaper press in her back room and could produce the stuff at the snap of a finger.

"What did Lisa want?"

"She didn't say. Just said you should call her back."

"Thanks, Heather."

"Well, I'm off to the bank before it closes."

"How'd we do today?"

"Terrible. A grand total of eight customers."

Bess made a face. The bulk of her business came from her design work; she kept the store chiefly as a consideration for her design customers. "Did any of them buy anything?"

"A Cobblestone Way calendar, a few greeting cards and a couple of tea towels."

"Hmph. Thank God for summer in a tourist town, huh?"

"Well, I'll see you tomorrow, okay?"

"Thanks, Heather, and good night."

When Heather was gone, Bess pushed herself up, left her coat on the settee and headed for the loft. As usual, she hadn't spent nearly as much time as she had hoped on designing. It took an average of ten hours to design most jobs, and she'd barely put in three today.

Upstairs, she kicked off her high heels and scraped back her hair as she dropped to her desk chair, opened a turkey-and-sprout sandwich she'd picked up at Cub supermarket and popped the top on her Diet Pepsi.

Slowing down for the first time since morning, she realized how tired she was. She took a bite of her sandwich and stared at a stack of replacement pages that had been waiting well over two weeks to be inserted in one of the furniture catalogs.

While she was still staring the phone rang.

"Good evening, Blue Iris."

"Mrs. Curran?"

"Yes?"

"This is Hildy Padgett . . . Mark's mother?" A friendly voice, neither cultured nor crude.

"Oh, yes, hello, Mrs. Padgett. It's so nice to hear from you."

"I understand that Mark and Lisa had supper with you last night and broke the news."

"Yes, they did."

"Well, it seems those two are getting set to make us some kind of shirttail relatives or something."

Bess set down her sandwich. "Yes, it certainly does."

"I want you to know right up front that Jake and I couldn't be happier. We think the sun rises and sets in your daughter. From the first time Mark brought her home we said to each other, Now there's the kind of girl we'd like for a daughter-in-law. When they told us they were getting married we were just delighted."

"Why, thank you. I know Lisa feels the same way about both of you."

"Of course, we were a little surprised about the baby coming but both Jake and I sat down and had a long talk with Mark, just to make sure that he was doing what he wanted to do, and we came away assured that he had every intention of marrying Lisa anyway, and that they both wanted the baby and are quite excited about it."

"Yes, they told us the same thing."

"Well we think it's just wonderful. Both of those kids really seem to have their heads on straight."

Once again Bess felt a twinge of regret, perhaps even jealousy, because she knew Mark and Lisa as a couple so much less intimately than this woman seemed to.

"I have to be honest with you, Mrs. Padgett, I haven't met Mark many times but last night at supper he certainly seemed straightforward and sincere when he told us this marriage is what he wants, what they both want."

"Well, we've given them our blessings and now the two of them want very much for all of us to meet, so I suggested a dinner party here at our house and I was hoping we could get together on Saturday night."

"Saturday night . . ." Her date with Keith; but how could she put one ordinary date before this? "That sounds fine."

"Say seven o'clock?"

"Fine. May I bring something?"

"Lisa's brother, is all. All of our kids will be here, too—we've got five of them—so you'll get a chance to meet them all."

"It's very kind of you to go to all this trouble."

"Kind?" Hildy Padgett laughed. "I'm so excited I've been getting up nights and making lists!"

Bess smiled. The woman sounded so likable and breezy.

"Besides," Hildy went on, "Lisa volunteered to come over and help me. She's going to make the dessert, so all you have to do is be here at seven and we'll get those kids off to a proper start."

When she'd hung up, Bess sat motionless in her swivel chair, melancholy in spite of the plans she'd just made. Outside, dusk had fallen, and in the window downstairs the brass lamps were lit, throwing fern-shadow through a plant that hung above the display. In the loft only the desk lamp shone, spreading a wedge of yellow over her work and her half-finished sandwich on its square of white, waxy paper. Lisa was twenty-one, and pregnant, and getting married. Why did it sadden her so? Why did she find herself longing for the days when the children were small?

Motherlove, she supposed. That mysterious force that could strike at unexpected moments and make nostalgia blossom and fill the heart. She longed, suddenly, to be with Lisa, to touch her, hold her.

Ignoring the work that needed attention, she leaned forward and dialed Lisa's number.

"Hello?"

"Hi, honey, it's Mom."

"Oh, hi, Mom. Something wrong? You sound a little down."

"Oh, just a little nostalgic, that's all. I thought if you weren't busy I might come over for a while and we could talk."

Thirty minutes later Bess had turned her back on her best design time and was entering the setting of last night's confrontation with Michael. When Lisa opened the door Bess hugged her more tightly and a little longer than usual.

"Mom, what's wrong?"

"I guess I'm just being a typical mother, is all. I was sitting there at the store, getting all misty-eyed, remembering when you were little."

Lisa gave a foxy grin. "I was pretty fantastic, wasn't I?"

Lisa had the gift for creating effortless laughter but as Bess released the sound she was wiping a tear from the corner of one eye.

"Oh, Mom . . ." Lisa curved an arm around her mother and led her toward the living room. "I'm getting married, not cloistered."

"I know. I just wasn't prepared for it."

"Dad wasn't either." They sat on the davenport and Lisa put her feet up. "So how did it go when the two of you left here last night? I figured you went off to talk about everything in private."

"We went out and had a cup of coffee and actually managed to be civil to one another for the better part of an hour."

"So what did you decide about Mark and me?"

Bess's expression became wistful. "That you're my only daughter, and you're only getting married once . . . at least I hope it'll only be once."

"That's why you really came over, isn't it, to make sure I'm doing the right thing."

"Your dad and I just wanted you to know that if for any reason you decide marriage to Mark isn't what you want, we'll stand behind you."

It was Lisa's turn to display a wistful expression. "Oh, Mom, I love him so much. When I'm with him I'm more than I was. He makes me want to be better than the me I was before, and so I am. It's as if . . ." Sitting cross-legged, Lisa gazed at the ceiling in her intense search for the proper words, then back at her mother, gesturing with both hands as if she were singing a heartfelt ballad. ". . . As if when we're together all the negative stuff disappears. I see people around me in a more charitable light; I don't criticize, I don't complain. And the funny thing is, the same thing happens to Mark.

"We've talked about it a lot . . . about that night when we met. When he walked into that pool hall and we looked at each other, we suddenly didn't want to be in a pool hall anymore but someplace pure, a woods maybe, or listening to an orchestra someplace. An orchestra! Cripes, Mom!" Lisa threw up her hands. "I like Paula Abdul but there I was, with all my senses open and new avenues looking inviting.

"Something happened . . . I can't explain it. We just . . ." Silence awhile, then Lisa continued, softly. "We just felt different. There we were, living that crazy bar scene, hanging around in noisy, smoky places and swaggering and showing off and being loud and obnoxious at times, and then our two crowds bumped into one another, and he smiled at me and said, 'Hi, I'm Mark,' and from that night on we never felt like we had to be phony with each other. We can admit our weaknesses to one another and that seems to make us stronger. Isn't it weird?"

On her end of the sofa, Bess sat very still, listening to the most stirring description of love she'd ever heard.

"You know what he said to me one day?" Lisa looked radiant as she continued. "He said, 'You're better than any creed I ever learned.' He said it was a line from a poem he read once. I thought about it awhile—actually I've thought about it a lot since he said it—and I realize that's what we are to each other. We're each other's creeds, and *not* to marry someone you feel that way about would be the greatest shame of all."

"Oh, Lisa," Bess whispered, and moved to take Lisa in her arms, this very young woman who had found a love to believe in the way every woman hopes she will one day. It was at once shattering and gratifying to learn that Lisa had grown up in a short span of time while she, Bess, had not been as attentive as she should have been. How humbling it was to realize that Lisa had learned something at age twenty-one that Bess herself had not at age forty. Lisa and Mark had discovered how to communicate, they had found the proper balance between praising each other's virtues and overlooking each other's shortcomings, which translated not only into love but into respect, as well. It was something Bess and Michael had never quite managed.

"Lisa, darling, if you feel that way about him I'm so happy for you."

"Yes, be happy. Because I am." While they were still hugging, Lisa added, "There's just one more thing I want to say." She set Bess away from herself and told her point-blank, "I know you're probably wondering how an educated young woman of the eighties could possibly be so stupid that she got pregnant when there are at least a dozen ways to prevent it. Remember when we went skiing up at Lutsen before Christmas? Well, I forgot my birth control pills that weekend, and we realized we might very well be making a choice if we made love. So we talked about it beforehand. What if we risked it and I got pregnant? He told me then that he wanted to marry me, and that if I got pregnant that weekend, it was fine with him, and I agreed. So, you see, Mom, we're not just handing you a pile of gas when we say we're happy about the baby. What you're worrying about . . . well, you just don't have to. Mark and I are going to be great . . . you'll see."

Bess tenderly touched her daughter's face. "Where have I been while you did all this growing up?"

"You were there."

"Exactly . . . there. Running my business. But I suddenly feel as if I spent too much time at it and not enough with you during the past few years. If I had, I'd have seen this relationship between you and Mark blossoming. I wouldn't have been caught so off guard last night."

"Mom, you handled it okay, believe me."

"No, you handled it okay, and so did Mark. Your dad was totally impressed by him."

"I know. I talked to him today. So did Mark's mother. She said she was going to call you, too. Did she?"

"Yes, she did. She's delightful."

"I knew you'd think so. So everything is set for Saturday night? No objections?"

"Now that I know how you feel, none."

"Whew! That's a relief. So Dad said you two talked about the rest—the dress, and all of us walking down the aisle together, and you'll do it, huh?"

"Yes, we'll do it."

"And I can wear the dress?"

"If it'll fit you, yes."

"Hey, Mom? I know what you're thinking about the dress, that it might put some kind of hex on my wedding or something, but that's really a lot of crap. It isn't dresses that make weddings work, it's people, okay?"

"Okay."

"I just like the dress, that's all. I used to play in it when you weren't home. You never knew that, did you?"

"No, I didn't."

"Well, that's what you get for putting something so irresistible off limits. Someday I'll tell you some of the other stuff that Randy and I used to do when you guys were gone."

Bess's grin became suspicious. "Like what?"

"Remember that sex manual you used to keep hidden between the spare blankets in the linen closet in your bathroom? The one with all the drawings of all the positions? You didn't think we knew it was there, did you?"

"Why, you little devils!"

"Yup, that's us. And remember that vase that disappeared and you could never find it again? That white one with the pink hearts around the top? We broke it one night when we were playing monster in the dark. We used to turn off all the lights and one of us would hide and the other one would walk like Frankenstein, with his arms out, roaring, and one night—*chink!*—over went your vase. We knew you'd be royally pissed if we told you, so we hid the pieces in a tomato-juice can we found in the garbage and pretended we didn't know anything about it. But I just knew, Mom, that one day you'd have more vases than the Monticello Flea Market, and sure enough, look at you now. You probably have twenty of them in your store as we speak."

How could Bess resist laughing at such flippancy?

"And all the while I was sending you to catechism classes and teaching you to be good, honest children."

"Well, we were, basically. Look at me today. I'm going to marry the boy I got into trouble and give his baby a name."

When Bess finished laughing, she said, "It's getting late. I should go. It's been a long day."

Rising from the sofa, Lisa said, "You work too hard, Mom. You should take more time to yourself."

"I take all I want."

"Oh, sure you do. But I have a feeling that when Mark and I have this baby we're going to lure you away from your little loft in the sky more often. Just feature that, would y'—my mom a grandma. What do you think about that?"

"I think my hair needs bleaching. The roots are beginning to show."

"You'll get used to the idea. What does Dad think about being a grandpa?"

"We didn't discuss it."

"Oo . . . I hear a cool note."

"You bet you do. Now that the emotional part is over I can tell you that was an underhanded trick you pulled last night."

"It worked though, didn't it?"

"We've drawn a truce for the duration of the wedding festivities, nothing more."

"Oh yeah? Randy said you were playing 'Homecoming' when he got home last night."

"Good heavens, have I no privacy at all?" The two of them moved to the apartment door.

"Think about it, Mom . . . Dad and you together again, coming to visit us and your grandchild. That'd be wild, huh? The two of you wouldn't have to fight about taking care of the housework and kids anymore, because we're all grown up and you have a housekeeper. And you're all done with college so he couldn't be barking at you about that. And he's got his own cabin now so you wouldn't have to stay behind when he goes hunting. And since he's all washed up with Darla—"

"Lisa, you're hallucinating." Bess drew on her coat with an air of finality.

"Yeah, well, think about it, I said." Lisa braced one shoulder against the wall.

"I *will not!* I'll treat him civilly but that's the extent of it. Besides, you're forgetting about Keith."

"Old bald-headed Keith the rag man? Don't make me laugh, Mom. You've been dating him for three years and Randy says you don't even spend nights with him. Take it from me, Bess, the rag man's not for you."

"I don't know what's come over you tonight, Lisa, but you're being intentionally outrageous." Bess opened the apartment door.

"I'm in love. I want the rest of the world to be, too." Lisa popped a kiss on her mother's mouth. "Hey, see you Saturday night, huh? You know how to get there?"

"Yes, Hildy gave me directions."

"Great. And don't forget my little brother."

Heading for her car, Bess had totally lost her melancholy mood of earlier. Lisa truly had a gift for making people laugh at their own foibles. Not that she, Bess, had any intention of reviving anything between herself and Michael. As she'd said, there was Keith to consider. The thought of Keith brought a frown: he wasn't going to be pleased about her breaking their date Saturday night.

She called him from the phone in her bedroom the moment she got her suit and hosiery off.

He answered after the fifth ring.

"Hello?"

"Keith, it's Bess. Did I get you away from something?"

"Just got out of the shower."

There wasn't and never had been any sexual innuendo following convenient lead-ins such as this. It was one of the things Bess missed in their relationship, yet she never felt compelled to start it and since he didn't, humorous and intimate repartee was missing.

"I can call back later."

"No, no it's fine. What's up?"

"Keith, I'm really sorry but I'm going to have to cancel our dinner date Saturday night."

In the pause that followed she imagined he'd stopped drying himself. "Why?"

"The Padgetts are having a dinner at their house so both sides of the family can meet."

"Didn't anyone ask you if you were busy?"

"Everyone else was able to make it. I hardly thought I could ask them to delay it for me alone, and given how short a time there is before the wedding, I thought it best if the two families met right away."

"I suppose your ex will be there?"

Bess massaged her forehead. "Oh, Keith."

"Well, won't he?"

"Yes, he will."

"Oh, fine, just fine!"

"Keith, for heaven's sake, it's our daughter's wedding. I can't very well avoid him."

"No, of course you can't!" Keith snapped. "Well, when you have time for me, Bess, give me a call."

"Keith, wait . . ."

"No . . . no . . ." he said sarcastically, "don't worry about me. Just go ahead and do what you have to do with Michael. I understand."

She detested this brittleness he adopted whenever he became jealous of her time with the children.

"Keith, I don't want you to hang up mad at me."

"I've got to go, Bess. I'm getting the carpet wet."

"All right but call me soon."

"Sure," he replied brusquely.

When she'd hung up, Bess rubbed her eyes. Sometimes Keith could be so insufferably childish. Did he always have to see these conflicts as a choice between her children and him? Once again she wondered why she continued seeing him. It would probably be best for both of them, she thought, if she broke it off entirely.

She dropped her arms and thought wearily of the design work she'd brought home and left downstairs on the dining-room table. She hated designing when she felt this way. Somehow it seemed her moroseness might creep into the design itself.

But she had three jobs waiting after this one, and customers eager to get her phone call setting up their presentations, and more house calls on her calendar in the days ahead.

With a sigh she rose from her desk and went downstairs to put in two more hours.

Chapter 4

On Saturday night Bess took pains with her hair. It was nearly shoulder-length, its shades of blonde as varied as an October prairie. She curled it only enough to give it lift, and pouffed it out behind her ears, where it billowed like the sleeves of a choir gown caught in the wind. Her makeup was subtle but applied with extreme care—twelve steps from concealer to mascara. The finished results enlarged her brown eyes and plumped her lips. She stared at her reflection in the mirror, sober, smiling, then sober once again.

Unquestionably she wanted to impress Michael tonight: there was an element of pride involved. Toward the end of their marriage, when she'd been caught up in the rigors of studying for her degree and maintaining a domicile and a family of four, he had said during one of their fights, "Look at you, you don't even take care of yourself anymore. All you ever wear is blue jeans and sweatshirts, and your hair hangs in strings. You didn't look like that when I married you!"

How his accusation had stung. She'd been burning the candle at both ends trying to achieve something for herself, but he'd failed to recognize that her output of time meant some cuts were necessary. So her hair had gone uncurled, her nails unpainted and she had forsaken makeup. Blue jeans and a sweatshirt were the easiest to launder, the quickest to grab, so they became her customary uniform. At the end of a six-hour school day she'd come home to face studying and housework while he'd grow obstinate about helping with the latter. He'd been raised in a traditional household where women's work was exactly that, where men didn't peel potatoes or wash laundry or run a vacuum cleaner. When she'd suggested that he try these, he'd suggested she take a few less credits per quarter and resume the duties she'd agreed to do when they got married.

His narrow-mindedness had enraged her.

Her continued lack of attention to herself and to the house eventually drove him out of it, and he found a woman with beautiful curled tresses, who wore high heels and Pierre Cardin suits to work every day and painted her nails and brought him coffee and dialed his clients for him.

Bess had seen Darla occasionally, most often at the company Christmas parties, where she wore sequined dresses and dyed-to-match satin pumps and lipstick that sparkled nearly as much as her dangly earrings. Had Michael simply left Bess, she might have acceded to maintaining a speaking relationship with him; but he'd left her for another woman, and a stunning beauty at that. The realization had galled Bess ever since.

After she'd gotten her degree, one of the first things she had done was lay out three hundred dollars for a beauty make-over. Under the tutelage of a professional she'd learned what colors suited her best, what clothing silhouettes most flattered her shape, what shades of makeup to wear and how to apply them. She'd even learned what size and shape of handbag and shoes suited her build and what style of earring most flattered her facial features. She'd had her hair color changed from muskrat brown to tawny blonde, its style lightly permed into the bon vivant wind-fluffed look, which she still wore. She'd grown her fingernails and kept them meticulously polished in a hue that matched her lipstick. And over a span of years she'd acquired a new wardrobe to which she added judiciously only those pieces which perfectly matched the color and style guidelines she'd learned from the professionals.

When Michael Curran got a load of her tonight there'd be no ketchup on her jabot, no shine to her makeup and no hair out of place.

She chose a red dinner suit with a straight skirt and an asymmetrical jacket sporting one black triangular-shaped lapel rising from a single black waist-button. With it she wore oversized gold door-knocker earrings that drew attention to her winged hairstyle and her rather dramatic jawline.

When the suit jacket was buttoned she pressed both hands to her abdomen and turned to view herself in profile. She needed to lose ten pounds—it was a constant struggle. But since her mid-thirties the pounds seemed to go on so much faster than they came off. She'd shaved off the four extra pounds she'd gained over the holidays but she had merely to *look* at a dessert to put it back on.

Ah, well—she was satisfied with one full hour's efforts at grooming, anyway. She switched out her bedroom light and went down two flights to Randy's room. When he was sixteen he'd chosen to hole up in an unfinished room on the walk-out level because it was twice as large as the upstairs bedrooms and two walls were backfilled with yard so the neighbors wouldn't complain about his drums.

They filled one corner, his prized set of Pearls—twelve pieces of gleaming stainless steel, including his pride and joy, three graduated sizes of rototoms, whose pitch could be changed with a simple twist of the revolving heads. The two concrete-block walls behind the drums were painted black. Fanned on one were posters of his idols, Bon Jovi, Motley Crüe and Cinderella. From an overhead strip a half-dozen canister lights picked out the drums. One of the remaining walls was white, the other covered with cork that gave the room the perennial smell of charcoal. The corkboard was hung with pictures of old girlfriends, beer ads, band schedules and prom garters. Since the room had no closet, Randy's clothes hung on a piece of steel pipe suspended from the ceiling by two chains. The floor was littered with several years' issues of *Car & Driver* magazine, dozens of compact discs, empty fast-food wrappings, shoes and overdue video rentals.

There was a compact disc player, a television, a VCR, a microphone and a fairly sophisticated taping setup. Among all this, the water bed—sporting disheveled leopard sheets—seemed almost incidental.

When Bess came to the door Paula Abdul was blasting "Opposites Attract" from the CD player, and Randy was standing before his dresser adjusting the knot in a skinny gray leather tie. He was dressed in baggy, pleated trousers, a silvery-gray double-breasted sport coat and a plaid shirt in muted shades of purple, gray and white. He'd put something on his hair to make it glossy and though he'd had it cut, as promised, it still hung to his collar in natural ringlets.

Coming upon him this way, while he was engaged in tying his tie, looking spiffy for once, brought a catch to Bess's heart. He was so good-looking, and bright, and charming when he wanted to be, but the path of resistance he'd chosen to take had put so many obstacles between them. Today, however, entering his room Bess felt a shaft of uncomplicated love. He was her son, and he was getting to look more like his father every year, and in spite of her animosity toward Michael, he was undeniably a handsome man. The aroma of masculine toiletries drifted to Bess as she entered Randy's room. She had missed such smells since Michael's departure. For that brief moment it was almost like having a husband and a happy marriage back.

Without glancing his mother's way, Randy said to the mirror, "I promised Lisa I'd have it cut, and I did but this is as short as I go."

She went to the CD player, glanced at the flashing control panel and shouted, "How do I turn this thing down?"

He came and did it for her, dropping one shoulder with unconscious masculine grace. The music ceased. Randy straightened and let a grin lift one side of his mouth while his eyes scanned her outfit and hair. "Lookin' vicious, Mom."

"Thank you, so are you. New clothes?" She touched his tie.

"It's a hot deal—the elder sister tying the big knot."

"Where'd you get the money?"

"I *do* have a job, Mom."

"Yes, of course you do. Listen, I thought we could ride over together."

"Yeah, sure, whatever you say."

"I left my car in the driveway. We may as well take it."

She let him drive, deriving a secret maternal pleasure from being escorted by her full-grown son, something she had fantasized about when he was a young boy, something that happened all too infrequently since he'd become a man. They took highway 96 to White Bear Lake, ten miles due west. The ride led them through snow-covered countryside, past horse ranches and long stretches where no electric lights shone. The lake itself appeared, a blanket of blue-gray in the thin light of an eighth-moon, and rimming it, like a necklace of amber, the lights from lakeshore homes. The lake shared its name with the town that lay on its northwest curve, paling the night sky with its halo.

As they were approaching the city lights, with a bay of the lake on their left, Mark said, "That's where the old man lives."

"Where?"

"In those condos."

Bess looked over her shoulder and caught a glimpse of lights receding behind them, tall skeletal trees and an imposing building she'd often admired when driving past.

"How do you know?"

"Lisa told me."

"Your dad will be there tonight, you know."

Randy glanced her way but said nothing.

"See what you can do to act natural around him, okay?"

"Yes, Mother."

"For Lisa's sake."

"Yes, Mother."

"Randy, if you say yes Mother one more time I'm going to sock you."

"Yes, Mother."

She socked him and they both chuckled.

"You know what I'm saying about your dad."

"I'll try not to punch his lights out."

The Padgetts lived on the west side of town in a middle-class residential neighborhood as flat as an elephant's foot. Randy found the house without a misturn and escorted his mother along the edge of a driveway filled with cars to a sidewalk that curved between snowbanks and led to the front door.

They rang the bell and waited.

Mark and Lisa answered, followed by a short woman shaped like a chest of drawers, in a blue dress with a pleated skirt and a white collar. She had brown hair, frizzled in a bowl-shape, and a smile that put six dimples in her cheeks and made her eyes all but disappear.

Mark said simply, with an arm around her shoulder, "This is my mom, Hildy."

And Lisa said, "This is my mom, Bess, and my brother, Randy."

Hildy Padgett had a grip like a stevedore's and a contralto voice.

"Glad to meet you. Jake, come over here!" she called, and they were joined by Mark's father, straight, tall, thin-haired and smiling, with a hearing aid in his left ear. He was wearing brown trousers and a plaid shirt, open at the throat and rolled up at the cuff. No jacket.

There would be—Bess saw—no dog put on by the Padgetts, not even at a wedding. She liked them immediately.

The living room stretched off to the left, decorated like a country keeping room with blue-and-white plaid wallpaper and a plate rail running the perimeter of the room, a foot below the ceiling. The furniture was thick and comfortable-looking and filled with people. Among them, standing near the archway to the dining room, was Michael Curran.

At the sound of the doorbell Michael turned to watch Bess come in, looking very voguish, followed by Randy, looking surprisingly tall in an outsized overcoat with baggy shoulders and a turned-up collar. The sight of Bess coming in escorted by their son caught Michael in a vulnerable spot. Lord, Randy had grown up! The last time Michael had seen him was nearly three years ago in a busy shopping center. It was Easter, Michael recalled, and the mall had been turned into a miniature farm, with children everywhere, petting baby goats and chickens and ducks. Michael had just bought a spring jacket and come out of J. Riggings to find Randy moving toward him in the foot traffic, talking animatedly with another boy about his age. Michael had smiled and headed toward him but when Randy spied him, he'd halted, sobered, grabbed his friend's arm and done a brusque right-face, disappearing into a convenient women's clothing store.

Now here he was, three years later, taller than his mother and shockingly good-looking. His face had filled out and resembled Michael's own, though Randy was much handsomer. Michael felt a paternal thrill at the sight of that dark hair so much like his; the eyes, mouth and cheeks that had at last taken on the mature planes and curves they would keep into middle age.

He watched Randy shaking hands, giving up his overcoat, and finally Randy's deep brown eyes found Michael's. His hand stopped smoothing down his tie. The smile dropped from his mouth.

Michael felt his chest constrict. His heart flopped crazily. They stood for a light-year, across the room from one another while the past rushed forth to polarize them both. How simple, Michael thought, to cross the room, speak his name, embrace him, this young man who as a boy had idolized his father, had followed like a shadow beside him when he mowed the lawn and shoveled the driveway and changed the oil in the car and said, "Daddy, can I help?"

But Michael could not move. He could only stand across the room with a lump in his throat, trapped by his own mistaken past.

Someone came between them—Jake Padgett, extending his hand in welcome, and Randy's attention swerved to him.

Bess moved into Michael's line of vision. They forced smiles while he committed himself to his spot in the dining-room archway. He might have moved forward to speak to Randy while Bess was near at hand to act as a buffer but the hurt of Randy's last snub returned, sharp and real as if it had happened only yesterday. Bess's admonitions the other night at Lisa's rang clearly in Michael's head—Randy needs a father, be one to him.

But how?

The living room was filled with people—the other four Padgett children, all younger than Mark, as well as a grandmother and grandfather—requiring a round-robin of introductions that seemed to shift people like fog. But Randy made sure he remained far enough from Michael to avoid the risk of having to speak. Bess, however, shook hands with one after another and eventually reached her ex-husband.

"Hello, Michael," she said, remote as if their brief truce had never happened.

"Hello, Bess."

They trained their eyes on the people and lamps across the room, avoiding the risk of lingering glances. They struggled for polite inanities, finding none. Covertly he assessed her clothes, hair, jewelry and nails—mercy, had she changed. As much as Randy, if not more.

Bess clamped a black patent-leather clutch bag beneath one elbow and adjusted an outsized gold earring, looking over the crowd while speaking.

"Randy's grown up, hasn't he?"

"Has he ever. I couldn't believe it was him."

"Are you going to talk to him or just stand here as if he's a stranger?"

"You think he'd talk to me?"

"You can give it a try."

A memory flashed past of Randy at two, padding into their bedroom on Saturday mornings and climbing aboard his chest in his feet pajamas. *'Toons, Daddy,* he would say, and Michael would open his bleary eyes and tip him down for a kiss, then the two of them would whisper awhile before sneaking out to turn on cartoons and let Mommy have a morning in bed. He wanted to kiss him now, wanted to pin his arms at his sides and take him in a fatherly embrace and say *I'm sorry I screwed up, forgive me.*

Hildy Padgett came from the kitchen with a tray of canapés. Jake was passing around cups of mulled cider. Lisa was showing the grandparents her small diamond ring, and Mark was with her. Randy stood across the room with his hands in his trouser pockets, knowing no one, glancing occasionally at his father but determinedly keeping his distance.

One of them had to make the move.

It required a heroic effort but Michael took the risk.

He crossed the room and said, "Hello, Randy."

Randy said, "Yeah," his eyes casting about beyond Michael's shoulder.

"I wasn't sure it was you, you got so tall."

"Yeah, well, that happens, you know."

"How have you been?"

Randy shrugged, still avoiding his father's eyes.

"Your mother tells me you're still working in a warehouse."

"So?"

"Do you like it?"

"What's to like? You get up in the morning, you go put in your hours. It's just something to do till I get in with a band."

"A band?"

"Yeah, drums—with a band, you know, like *rrupp pup pup rrr* . . ."

"You pretty good?"

For the first time Randy looked squarely into Michael's eyes. An insolent expression twisted his face, and he released a sarcastic snort. "Spare me," he said and walked away.

Michael's stomach felt as if he'd leapt off a second-story roof. He watched Randy's shiny black curls as the young man moved off, and felt the clench of disappointment and failure. His face grew warm and a fist seemed to be closing over his windpipe.

He glanced over at Bess and found her watching.

She's right. I'm a failure as a father.

Lisa came to rescue him, capturing his elbow and hauling him across the room. "Dad, Grampa Earl was wondering about your cabin. He used to be a big hunter and I was just telling him you got a ten-point buck this fall. He wanted to hear more about it."

Earl Padgett was a big man with three chins and a florid face. He had a voice like a truck collision and endless hunting stories upon which to use it. His gestures were wide and sweeping, and when he pointed an invisible gun he might as well have been wearing a camouflage hunting vest lined with rows of shotgun shells. The hunting stories drew in Jake as well as the Padgett boys, who'd been hunting since they were old enough to take gun-safety classes. Of the men in the room, only Randy remained aloof.

Michael listened and added his own hunting anecdotes, all the time aware of Randy visiting with Bess, his back turned on Michael.

He'd bought Randy a .22 when Randy was twelve, and had dreamed of teaching the boy all about the woods and wildlife, and taking him on hunting trips. But his divorce had quashed that dream. Now he stood among a circle of fathers and sons whose enthusiasm had been passed from generation to generation, and his heart broke for what he and Randy had missed.

Hildy Padgett came in and announced dinner.

In the dining room, Michael and Bess were directed to seat themselves side-by-side at one end of the table, while Hildy and Jake presided at the opposite end. Mark and Lisa took chairs in the center of one long side, and the others were staggered around. Michael automatically pulled out Bess's chair. Her poise faltered momentarily while she shot him a wry glance, then she submitted to propriety and accepted his gesture of courtesy.

While Michael was seating himself he caught Randy watching sourly from diagonally across the table.

In an undertone he said to Bess, "I don't think Randy likes seeing me with you."

"Probably not," she replied, flipping her napkin onto her lap, glancing surreptitiously at Randy. "Did he say something about it?"

"No, just glared at me when I pulled out your chair."

"On the other hand, Lisa seems overjoyed. I've assured them both it's all for appearances. So . . . here we go." She picked up her glass of water and saluted him. "Let's see if we can't keep up the charade for our children's sake." He returned her salute and they sipped their water. A platter of ham was served, followed by bowls of vegetables, warm rolls, butter, bacon-and-lettuce salad and glorified rice, all passed around family-style. Passing a bowl to Bess, on his left, Michael remarked, "If someone had told me a week ago that I'd be sharing a dinner table with you twice in one week I'd have said no way."

"We did this a time or two with our own families, didn't we?" She watched him load his plate with au gratin potatoes and said, "Hildy really hit you in the taste buds, didn't she?"

He took an immense helping and answered, "Mmm . . . I still love 'em."

He always had. Watching him loading up on his old favorites brought back a sharp flash of nostalgia. Her mother had always said, *That Michael is fun to cook for. He knows how to eat.*

Bess glanced away from his plate—damn, she was thinking like a throwback. But it was difficult to sit beside a man with whom you've shared thousands of meals, whose table mannerisms are more familiar to you than your own, without those familiarities imposing themselves. She found herself anticipating his moves before he made them—how he held his fork, where he laid his knife, the order in which he tasted his food, the particular way he stroked one corner of his mouth with the pad of his right thumb after taking a drink, how he rested a wrist on the edge of the table while he chewed. Certain quiet sounds peculiar only to him.

"Did you have that talk with Lisa?"

She turned to find him watching her, chewing, his lips politely closed. There was an intimacy to chewing that had never struck her more profoundly than at that moment. He still had beautiful lips. She looked away. "Yes, I did. I went over to her apartment the next night."

"Do you feel better now?"

"Yes. Infinitely."

"Look at her," Michael said, poising with an elbow on the table, holding a glass of iced tea.

Bess studied their daughter. She appeared jubilant, laughing with her intended, the two of them unquestionably happy.

"Look at *them*," Bess corrected. "She convinced me he's the right one for her. She almost had me in tears that night."

"And what about your wedding dress?"

"She's going to wear it."

Bess felt Michael's gaze on the side of her face and succumbed to the urge to meet his eyes. Webs of wistfulness drew them.

"It's hard to believe she's old enough, isn't it?" he said quietly.

"Yes. It seems like only yesterday we had her."

"Randy, too."

"I know."

"My guess is, he's watching us right now and wondering what's going on down here."

"Is something going on down here?"

He shocked her by replying, "You look great tonight, Bess."

She flushed and applied herself to cutting a piece of ham. "Oh, for heaven's sake, Michael, that's absurd."

"Well, you do. Is there any harm in my saying so? You've really changed since we divorced."

Her anger flared. "Oh, you're really smooth. You're without a wife—what? A month? Two?—and you're telling *me* how great I look? Don't insult me, Michael."

"I didn't mean to."

At that moment Jake Padgett stood up with a glass of iced tea and interrupted. "I think a toast is in order here. I'm not very good at this so you'll have to bear with me." He rubbed his left eyebrow with the edge of a finger. "Mark's our first to get married, and naturally we hoped he'd pick somebody we liked. Well, we sure got our wish when he brought Lisa home. We just couldn't be happier, and Lisa, honey, I know you're going to make him the happiest man in Minnesota when you marry him. We want to welcome you, and say how nice it is to have you and your family here with us tonight." He saluted Michael and Bess and nodded to Randy. "And so . . ." He raised his glass to the engaged couple. "Here's to a smooth road ahead for Lisa and Mark. We're behind you all the way."

Everyone joined in the toast. Jake resumed his seat and there passed between Michael and Bess a silent message, the kind husbands and wives of long standing can execute merely by the expression in their eyes.

Somebody should make a toast on our side.

You want to do it?

No, you.

Michael rose, pressing his tie to his shirt, lifting his glass.

"Jake, Hildy, all of you, thank you for inviting us. It's the proper way to start a young couple off, with the families united and showing their support. Lisa's mother and I are proud of her, and happy for her, and we welcome Mark as her husband-to-be. Lisa . . . Mark . . . you have our love. Good luck to you."

When the toast was complete, Michael sat down and Bess felt herself in an emotional turmoil. There wasn't a false word in his toast. It *was* the proper way to start the young couple off but how bittersweet, having their own immediate family reassembled for the first time amidst all these undercurrents. Earlier, when she'd watched Michael cross the room and approach Randy, her heart had leaped with hope. When Randy turned away, she had felt bereaved. Sitting beside Michael she'd been wafted first by nostalgia, then by bitterness and now, in the wake of the toasts, she simply felt muddled.

She was divorced and independent. She had proved she could live alone, build a business, keep a house and a car and a lawn and her own tax records. But the truth was, sitting beside Michael again, on this auspicious occasion, felt fitting. Having him stand and make a toast on behalf of them brought both a strong sense of security—imitation though it was—and a longing for what was gone: a father, a mother, their children, united as it had been in the beginning, as they had thought it would always be when they'd conceived those children who were now seated across the table.

Michael sensed himself being observed, turned and caught Bess regarding him. She glanced away self-consciously.

Coffee and dessert were served—a layered concoction of angel food, strawberries, bananas and something white and fluffy. She watched Michael watching Randy while he ate. Randy ignored his father and visited with the Padgetts' seventeen-year-old daughter on his left.

"That was a nice toast you gave," Bess offered.

Michael took a forkful of dessert, which he held without eating. "This whole thing is turning out to be tougher than I thought."

She resisted the impulse to lay her hand on his sleeve. "Don't give up on him, Michael, please."

Cognizant of social obligation, surrounded as they were by people they'd just met, they assumed untroubled faces and pretended to be politely chitchatting.

"It hurts," he said.

"I know. It hurts him, too. That's why you can't give up."

He laid down his fork, picked up a cup of coffee and held it in both hands, looking beyond it at his son.

"He really hates me."

"I think he wants to but it's costing him."

He sipped his coffee, left his elbows propped on the table. In time he turned to study Bess. "What's your stake in all this? Why all of a sudden the push to see Randy and me reconcile?"

"You're his father, nothing more complicated than that. I'm beginning to see what harm we've done by forcing the kids into this cold war we've waged."

He set down his cup, released a weary sigh and settled his shoulders against the back of the chair.

"All right, Bess, I'll try."

On the way home from White Bear Lake, Randy acted surly.

Bess said, "Do you want to tell me what's on your mind?"

He cast her a glance, returned his eyes to the road and went on driving.

"Randy?" she prodded.

"What's going on with you and the old man?"

"Nothing. And don't call him the old man. He's your father."

Randy tossed a glance out his side window and whispered, "Shit."

"He's trying to make amends to you, can't you see that?"

"Great!" Randy shouted. "All of a sudden he's my father and I'm supposed to kiss his ass when for six years you haven't kept it any secret that you hate his guts."

"Well, maybe I was wrong. Whatever I felt, maybe I shouldn't have imposed those feelings on you."

"I've got a mind of my own, Ma. I didn't need to pick up vibes from you to realize that what he did was shitty. He was screwing another woman and he broke up our home!"

"All right!" Bess shouted and repeated, more calmly, "All right, he was but there's such a thing as forgiveness."

"I can't believe what I'm hearing. He's getting to you, isn't he? Pulling out your chair and making toasts and cozying up to you over the dinner table just as soon as his other wife throws him over. He makes me sick."

Guilt struck Bess for having instilled such hate in her son without a thought for its effect on him. Bitterness such as he felt could stultify his emotions in dozens of other ways.

"Randy, I'm sorry you feel this way."

"Yeah, well, it's a pretty quick switch, isn't it, Mom? Less than a week ago you felt the same way. I'd just hate to see him make a fool of you a second time."

She felt a surge of exasperation with him for voicing what she'd thought, and with herself for being culpable. After all it was true she had felt flashes of cupidity at given moments tonight.

Let this be a lesson, she thought, and if you mend fences between yourself and Michael, keep your distance while doing it.

The following day was Sunday. There was Mass in the morning, prefaced by a battle to make Randy get up and go, followed by a lonely lunch for two—a pair of sad, bald, diet chicken breasts and baked potatoes with no sour cream for Bess and very little table conversation out of Randy. He left immediately afterward, said he was going to his friend Bernie's house to watch the NFC playoff games on TV.

When he was gone the house grew silent. Bess cleaned up the kitchen, changed into a sweat suit and returned downstairs, where the silent, familyless rooms held a gloom that was only amplified by bright day beating at the windows. She did some design work for a while but found concentrating difficult and finally rose from the dining-room table to wander from window to window, staring out at the wintry yard, the frozen river, a squirrel's nest in the neighbor's oak tree, the blue shadows of her own maple branches on the pristine snow. She sat down to resume her work but gave up once more, distracted by thoughts of Michael and their sundered family. She meandered into the living room, played middle C on the piano and held it till it dissolved into silence.

Once more she returned to the window to stare out with her arms folded across her chest.

In a yard several doors down a group of children were sledding.

When Randy and Lisa were little she and Michael had taken them one Sunday afternoon much like this one—a sterling, bright, blinding day—to Theodore Wirth Park in Minneapolis. They'd taken red plastic boat-shaped sleds, sleek and fast, and chosen a hill with fresh, unbroken snow. On their first glissade down the hill Michael's sled had slewed one hundred and eighty degrees and had carried him the remainder of the way backwards. At the bottom he'd hit a slight hummock, gone tail over teakettle and rolled to a stop looking like a snowman. He'd grown a beard and moustache that year; they and his hair were totally covered with snow. His cap was gone. His glasses were miraculously in place but behind them his eyes were completely covered with white.

When he'd finally sat up, looking like Little Orphan Annie, they had all rolled with laughter, collapsing on their backs in the snow and hooting themselves breathless.

Years later, when their marriage was losing its mortar, he'd said disconsolately, "We never do anything fun anymore, Bess. We never laugh."

In the yard next door all the children had run away and left one small bundled-up individual behind, crying.

You and me, Bess thought, left behind to cry.

She turned away from the window and went into the family room, where the fireplace was cold and the Sunday *Pioneer Press Dispatch* was strewn on the sofa. With a sigh she picked up the sections and began aligning them. Disconsolately she abandoned the job and dropped to a chair with the papers forgotten in her hand.

In silence she sat.

Wondering.

Withering.

Wasting.

She was not a tearful person, yet her aloneness had magnitude enough to force a pressure behind her eyes. It drove her in time to pick up the telephone and dial her mother.

Stella Dorner answered in her usual cheerful two-note greeting. "Hel-lo."

"Hello, Mother, it's Bess."

"Well, isn't this nice? I was just thinking of you."

"What were you thinking?"

"That I haven't talked to you since last Monday and it was time I called you."

"Are you busy?"

"Just watching the Minnesota Vikings get whipped."

"Could I come over? I'd like to talk to you."

"Of course. I'd love it. Can you stay for supper? I'll make some of those bar-becued pork chops you love with the onion and lemon on them."

"That sounds good."

"Are you coming right away?"

"As soon as I get my shoes on."

"Good. See you soon, dear."

Stella Dorner lived in a townhouse on Oak Glen Golf Course on the western edge of Stillwater. She had bought it within a year after her husband died, and had furnished it with sassy new furniture, declaring she hadn't been buried along with him and wasn't going to act as if she had. She'd continued her job as an on-call op-erating-room nurse at Lakeview Memorial Hospital, though she was nearly sixty at the time; had taken up golf lessons and joined a ladies' league at Oak Glen, the church choir at St. Mary's and the African Violet Society of America, which met quarterly in various places all over the Twin Cities. She went as often as she pleased to visit her daughter Joan in Denver, and once took a trip to Europe (on a Eurail Pass) with her sisters from Phoenix and Coral Gables; she often went on organized bus tours to places such as the Congden Mansion in Duluth and the University of Minnesota Arboretum in Jonathan; spent time at least once a week visiting the old folks at the Maple Manor nursing home and baking cookies for them. She played bridge on Mondays, watched *thirtysomething* on Tuesdays, went to bargain matinee movies most Wednesdays and got a facial every Friday. She had once signed up with a dating service but claimed all the old farts she'd been paired up with couldn't keep up with her and she didn't want any ball and chain around her foot.

Her townhouse reflected her spirit. It had three levels, long expanses of glass and was decorated in peach, cream and glossy black. Entering it, Bess always felt a shot of vitality. Today was no different. In the ten minutes since Bess's call, Stella had the place smelling like baking pork chops.

She answered the door dressed in a sweat suit the colors of a paint rag—a white background with smears of hot pink, yellow, green and purple, all strung together with black squiggles and dribbles. Over it she wore a disreputable lavender smock. She had coarse salt-and-pepper hair, styled only by gravity. It fell into a crooked center part and dropped in two irregular waves to jaw level. She had a habit of push-ing it back by making a caliper of one hand and hooking both temple waves at once. She did so as she greeted her daughter. "Bess . . . darling . . . this is wonderful. I'm so glad you called." She was shorter than Bess and reached up to hug her gingerly. "Careful! I don't want to get any paint on you."

"Paint?"

"I'm taking an oil-painting class. I was working on my first picture." She per-formed the caliper move on her hair once more while closing the door.

"How in the world do you find time?"

"A person should always find time for the things he likes." Stella led the way inside, where the west window light was strong but unreached yet by the afternoon sun, which lit the snow-laden golf course beyond. Facing the window was a long sofa upholstered in coral calla lilies on a cream background. One wall was filled with an ebony entertainment unit, where the football game was in progress on TV. The tables were ebony frames with glass tops. Before the sliding glass doors stood an easel with a partially finished rendering of an African violet.

"What do you think?" Stella asked.

"Mmm . . ." Removing her jacket, Bess studied the painting. "Looks good to me."

"It probably won't be but what the heck. The class is fun, and that's the object." Stella walked over and turned down the television volume. "Can I get you a Coke?"

"I'll get it. You keep on with your work."

"All right, I will." She pushed back her hair and picked up a paintbrush while Bess went into the kitchen and opened the refrigerator.

"Can I fix you one?"

"No thanks, I'm having tea." Beside Stella, a waist-high folding table held her mug and tubes of paint. She reached for the mug, drank from it while studying her artwork and called, "How are the kids?"

"That's what I came to talk to you about." Bess entered the room sipping her pop, slipped off her black loafers and propped her back against one end of the long sofa, drawing her feet up and resting her glass on her knees. "Well . . . part of what I came to talk to you about."

"Oh-oh. This sounds serious."

"Lisa's getting married . . . and she's expecting a baby."

Stella studied her daughter for several seconds. "Maybe I'd better put these paints away." She reached for a rag and began cleaning her brush.

"No, please don't stop."

"Don't be silly. I can do this any old time." The brush joined some others in a tin can of turpentine before Stella removed her smock and joined Bess on the sofa, bringing her cup of tea and hooking her hair back.

"Well . . . Lisa pregnant, imagine that. That'll make me a great-grandmother, won't it?"

"And me a grandmother."

"Spooky, isn't it?"

"Uh-huh."

"Which is the least important aspect of all this. I imagine you're in shock."

"I was but it's wearing off."

"Does she want the baby?"

"Yes, very much."

"Ah, that's a relief."

"Guess what else."

"There's more?"

"I've seen Michael," Bess told her.

"My goodness, you have had a week, haven't you?"

"Lisa set us up. She invited us both to her apartment to announce the news."

Stella laughed, throwing her chin up. "Good for Lisa. That girl's got style."

"I could have throttled her."

"How is she?"

"Happy and excited and very much in love, she assures us."

"And how is Michael?"

"Detached again, on his way to getting another divorce."

"Oh my."

"He said to tell you hi. His exact words were, 'Say hi to the old doll. I miss her.' "

Stella saluted with her mug—"Hi, Michael"—and sipped from it, studying Bess over the rim. "No wonder you wanted to talk. Where is Randy in all this?"

"Where he's always been, very resentful, shunning his father."

"And you?"

Bess sighed and said, "I don't know, Mother." She shifted her gaze to her knees, where it remained for a long time before she sighed, let her head drop back and spoke to the ceiling. "I've been carrying around all this anger for six years. It's very hard to let it go."

Stella sipped her tea and waited. Nearly a minute of silence passed before Bess looked at Stella.

"Mother, did I . . ." She paused.

"Did you what?"

"When we were getting the divorce you never said much."

"It wasn't my place."

"When I found out that Michael was having an affair, I wanted so badly for you to be angry for me. I wanted you to raise your fist and call him a bastard, take my side, but you never did."

"I liked Michael."

"But I thought you should be indignant on my behalf, and you weren't. There must have been some reason."

"And you're sure you're ready to hear it now?"

"Is it going to make me mad?"

"I don't know. That depends on how much you've grown up in six years."

"It was partly my fault, is that what you're saying?"

"It always takes two, honey, but when a man retaliates by having an affair, he's usually the one who gets all the blame."

"All right, what did I do?" Bess's voice grew defensive. "I went back to college to get my degree! Was that so wrong?"

"Not at all. But while you were doing it you totally forgot about your husband."

"I did not! He wouldn't let me forget about him. I still had to cook and do laundry and keep the house in shape."

"Those are superficialities. I'm talking about your personal relationship."

"Mother, there wasn't time!"

"Now there, I think you've put your finger on it." Stella let that sink in while she went to the kitchen to refresh her tea. When she returned to the living room, Bess was sitting with one elbow on the high sofa arm, her thumbnail between her teeth, staring out the window.

Stella resumed her seat and said, "Remember when you were first married how you used to ask Dad and me to take the kids occasionally so you and Michael could go off camping by yourselves? And the Christmas you bought him that shotgun that he wanted so badly, and hid it over at our place so he wouldn't find out? Remember all the trouble we went to, sneaking that thing into your house and hiding it on Christmas Eve? And then there was the April Fools' Day when you had that Fanny Farmer box delivered to his office and it was full of nuts and bolts."

Bess stared at the snowy golf course, her Coke forgotten.

"Those are the kinds of things that should never stop," her mother said.

"Was I the only one who stopped them?"

"I don't know. Were you?"

"I didn't think so then."

"You got awfully caught up in school, and after it was finished, in opening your store. When you'd stop over to see us you were always alone, never with Michael anymore, always rushing between two places. I know for a fact that you stopped having Dad and me over for meals, and that sometimes the kids would come over and act a little forlorn and abandoned."

Bess looked at her mother and remarked, "That's when Michael accused me of letting myself go."

"As I recall, you did."

"But I asked him for help around the house and he refused to give it. Isn't he partly to blame?"

"Maybe. But those kinds of things are a trade-off. Maybe he'd have helped you around the house if he hadn't fallen to the bottom of your priority list. How was your sex life?"

Bess looked out the window and answered, "Shitty."

"You didn't have time for it, right?"

"I thought once I got through school and had my own business, everything would fall back into place. I could get a housekeeper, maybe, and I'd have more time to relax with him."

"Only he didn't wait."

Bess got up and passed the easel to stand near the window with one hand on her hip. She drank her Coke, then turned to Stella. "Last night he told me I looked great, and do you know how angry it made me?"

"Why?"

"Because!" Bess flung up one hand. "Because . . . hell, I don't know. Because he's just sloughed off another wife and he's probably lonely and I don't want him crawling back to me under those circumstances. I don't want him crawling back to me at all! And Randy was watching us from the other end of the table! And I was upset with myself because I took an hour and fifteen minutes getting ready for that damned supper just to show him I could knock his socks off and . . . and . . . then when I did . . ." Bess covered her eyes with one hand and shook her head vehemently. "Hell, Mom, I don't know. It just seems like all of a sudden I'm so damned lonely and I'm caught in this wedding situation and I'm . . . I'm asking myself questions." She stared unseeingly outside and ended, more quietly, "I don't know."

Stella set her mug on the coffee table and went to her daughter. From behind, she finger-combed Bess's hair back to her nape, then massaged her shoulders.

"You're going through a catharsis that's been six years coming, that's what it is. All that time you've hated him and blamed him, and all of a sudden you're starting to explore your own fault in the matter. That's not easy."

"I don't love him anymore, Mother, I really don't."

"All right, so you don't."

"Then why does it hurt so much to see him?"

"Because he's making you take this second look at yourself. Here." Stella produced a wrinkled Kleenex and handed it to Bess.

It smelled like turpentine when Bess blew her nose in it. "I'm sorry, Mom," she said, drying her eyes.

"Don't be sorry. I'm a big girl. I can handle it."

"But coming here like this, spoiling your day."

"You haven't spoiled my day. Matter of fact, I think you've made it." Walking Bess back to the sofa with one arm around her shoulders Stella asked, "Feel better now?"

"Yes. Sort of."

"Then let me tell you something. It was all right for you to be angry at first, right after the divorce. Your anger is what got you through. Then you got efficient, businesslike, and threw all your energies into showing him you could make it on your own. And you did make it. But now you're going into another stage where you're going to do more questioning, and I suspect you might have a few more days like this. When you do, come over and we'll talk you through it, just as we did today. Now sit down, tell me about the wedding plans, and about Lisa's young man, and about what I have to wear to this shindig and if you think I might meet any interesting men there."

Bess laughed. "Mother, you're incorrigible. I thought you didn't want a ball and chain around your ankle."

"I don't. But you can only stand so much of hearing women's cackly voices before you need to hear a male one, and I've been playing an awful lot of bridge this winter."

Bess gave her mother an impulsive hug. "Mom, maybe I never told you this before, but you're my idol. I wish I could be more like you."

Stella hugged her back and said, "You're a lot like me. I see more of me in you every day."

"But you never get down."

"The heck I don't. But when it happens I just go out and join another club."

"Or look for a man."

"Well . . . there's nothing wrong with that. And speaking of the critters, how are you and Keith getting along?"

"Oh . . . Keith." Bess made a face and shrugged. "He got upset because I had to break a dinner date with him to go to the Padgetts' last night. You know how he is where the kids are concerned."

"I'll tell you something," Stella said, "since we're being honest with each other today. That man is not for you."

"Have you and Lisa been comparing notes or what?"

"Maybe."

Bess laughed. "Why, you two devils. If you think this wedding business is going to get me back together with Michael, you're wrong."

"I didn't say a word."

"No, but you're thinking it, and you can just forget it, Mother."

Stella lifted one eybrow and asked, "How does he look? He still as handsome as ever?"

"Moth-er!" Bess looked exasperated.

"Just curious."

"It'll never happen, Mother," Bess vowed.

Stella put on a smug expression and said, "How do you know? Stranger things have."

Chapter 5

That same Sunday morning Michael Curran awakened, stretched and stacked his hands behind his head, loath to stir and rise. His stomach grumbled but he remained, staring at the ceiling, which took on a rosy glow from the bright sunlight bouncing off the carpeting. The bedroom was huge, square, with triple sliding glass doors facing the lake, and a marble fireplace. The room held nothing more than a television set and the pair of mattresses upon which Michael lay. They were pushed against the north wall to keep his pillows from falling off.

The ten o'clock sun, reflecting off the frozen lake, made a nebula of light patterns on the ceiling, broken by strands of shadow from the naked elm trees beyond the deck. The building was absolutely silent; it was designed to be. No children were allowed, and most of the wealthy tenants had gone south for the winter, so he rarely crossed paths with anyone, not even in the elevator.

It was lonely.

He thought about last night, about his encounter with Randy. He closed his eyes and saw his nineteen-year-old son, bearing so much resemblance to himself, and so much animosity. The impact of seeing him came back afresh, bringing a replay of last night's convoluted emotions: love, hope, disappointment and a feeling of failure that made his chest feel heavy.

He opened his eyes to the ceiling designs.

How it hurt, being disowned by one's own child. Perhaps, as Bess had accused, he'd been guilty of withdrawing from Randy's life emotionally as well as physically, but wasn't Randy at fault, too, for refusing to see him? On the other hand, if Bess could have felt the cataclysm he'd experienced when he'd seen Randy walk into that house last night, she would have been forced to reconsider her words.

That boy—that *man*—was his son. His son, whose last six vital growing years had been lost to Michael, largely against his choice. If Bess had encouraged, or if Randy had not been brainwashed, he, Michael, would have been seeing Randy all along. There were things the two of them could have done together, particularly hunting and enjoying the outdoors. Instead, Michael had been excluded from everything, even Randy's high-school graduation. He'd known, of course, that Randy was graduating. When no announcement came he'd called Bess and asked about it, but Bess had replied, "He doesn't want you here."

He'd sent money, five hundred dollars. It was never acknowledged, either by written or spoken word, except for Lisa who, when Michael had asked, told him on the phone some weeks later, "He put it down on a thirteen-hundred-dollar set of drums."

A set of drums.

Why hadn't Bess seen to it that the kid went to college? Or a trade school? Something besides that dead-end job in a warehouse. After the way Bess had fought to complete her own college education he'd have thought she'd have taken a strong stand on the issue with her own kids. Maybe she had, and maybe it simply hadn't worked.

Bess.

Boy-o-boy, how she'd changed. When she'd walked into that room last night the craziest thing had happened! He'd actually felt a little charge. Yeah, it was crazy, all right, because Bess had a sharp edge to her now, a veneer of hardness he found abrasive. But she was his children's mother, and a transformed lady, and in spite of the way she carefully distanced herself from him, they shared a past that would forever intrude upon their lingering dissatisfactions with one another. He'd bet any money she felt it, too, at times.

Sitting next to each other at the dinner table, looking over at Lisa and Randy, how could either of them deny the gravity of memory?

As he lay in his unfurnished condominium with the Sunday sun shifting through the room, recollections of their beginnings played back through his mind—when Bess was in high school, and he, already a sophomore in college, had gone back for homecoming and had discovered her all grown up, an underclassman he didn't even remember. The first time he'd kissed her they were walking back to his car after a University of Minnesota football game in the fall of '66. The first time they'd made love was toward the end of her senior year on a Sunday afternoon when a gang of them had gone to Taylors Falls with picnic food, Frisbees and plenty of blankets. They'd been married a year later, with him fresh out of college and her with three more years to go. They'd spent their wedding night in the bridal suite at the Radisson Hotel in downtown Minneapolis.

Her mom and dad had given them the room as a surprise, and a bunch of her girlfriends had bought her a lacy white nightgown with a thin thing that went over it. He recalled how, when she came out of the bathroom wearing it, he was waiting in his blue pajama bottoms, both of them as hesitant as if it were their first time. He'd thought he'd never forget the details of that night but over time they'd become blurred. What he did remember, clearly, was waking the next morning. It was June and sunny and on the dresser sat a basket of fruit from the hotel manage-

ment, along with two fluted glasses from the night before, each half-full of bub-
bleless champagne. He'd opened his eyes to find Bess next to him, with her nightgown back on. He'd lain there wondering when she'd gotten up and put it on, and
if she expected him to wear his pajamas all night, too, and if, in spite of their pre-
marital sex, she'd turn out to be a prude. Then she'd awakened and smiled, indulged
in a quivering, all-over stretch, lain on her side facing him with her hands joined
near her knees, and he'd gotten a hard-on just looking at her.

When the stretch ended she'd said simply, "Hi."

"Hi," he'd answered.

They'd lain a long time, looking at each other, absorbing the novelty and wonder of sanctioned morning bliss. He remembered her cheeks had grown flushed and
supposed his had done the same.

In time she'd said, "Just imagine, nobody can ever send you home at one A.M.
again. We get to wake up together for the rest of our lives."

"It's wild, isn't it?"

"Yeah," she'd whispered, "pretty wild."

"You put your nightgown back on."

"I can't sleep without something on. I wake up and my arms are stuck to my
sides. What about you?" The sheet covered him to his ribs.

"I don't have that problem," he'd answered, "but I've got another one."

She had put her hand on his hip—he remembered so vividly what had followed,
for in all of his life to that point nothing had been as incredible as that morning. Sex
before marriage had been frequent for them but it had carried restraints, nevertheless. That sunny June morning when she had reached out for him those restraints
had dissolved. They *felt* married, they *belonged* to each other and there was a difference. The vows they'd spoken gave them license and they reveled in it.

He had seen her half-naked, nearly naked, had gotten her naked from the waist
down a lot of times. They'd made love in the sunlight wrapped in a blanket, in the
moonlight wrapped in shadows and in cars beneath streetlamps with their socks still
on. Even on their wedding night they'd left only the bathroom light on to shed a
dim glow from around a corner. But that morning, the day after their wedding, the
east sun had been streaming in a broad, high window, and she'd taken off his sheet
and he'd taken off her nightgown and they'd indulged their eyes for the first time.
In that regard they'd been virgins, and nothing he'd experienced before or since
had been any sweeter.

Their breakfast had been delivered on a rolling cart with white linen and a red
rose. Over the meal they had studied each other's eyes and reaffirmed that they'd
done the right thing, and that their joy was so intense it eclipsed any other they'd
ever felt.

About that day he recalled most vividly the overriding sense of consecration
they'd both felt. They had met in an era when more and more young couples were
declaring, *Marriage is dead,* and were choosing to set up housekeeping together instead. They'd discussed doing the same thing but had decided no, they loved each
other and wanted to commit for life.

After breakfast they'd made love again, then had bathed and dressed and walked
to St. Olaf's for Mass.

June 8, 1968, their wedding day.

And now it was January 1990, and he was rolling off his mattresses in an empty condo, dressed in gray sweatpants, aroused once again from his memories.

Forget it, Curran. Horn in. She doesn't want you, you don't really want her and your own kid treats you like a leper. That ought to tell you something.

He shuffled to the bathroom, switched on the light, flattened one palm on the vanity top, examined his face and harvested some sand from his eyes. He swigged a mouthful of cinnamon-flavored Plax, swished it around for the recommended thirty seconds and brushed his teeth with a full one inch of red Close-Up. Bess had always harangued him about using too much toothpaste. *You don't need that much,* she'd told him, *half that much is enough.* Now, damn it, he used as much as he wanted and nobody nagged. He brushed for one whole minute, rinsed, then bared his teeth to the mirror and thought, Look at these, Bess, pretty damned nice for a forty-three-year-old, eh?

His flawless teeth were of curiously little consolation this morning in his big, empty, silent condo.

He wiped his mouth, threw down the towel and went to the kitchen. It was tiled in white, had white Formica cabinets trimmed with blond oak and was connected to a family room with sliding glass doors at its far end, facing a small park with a gazebo. His entire pantry stock, on an oversized island in the middle of the kitchen, looked like a city block from 30,000 feet. Instant coffee, a box of Grape-Nuts, a loaf of Taystee bread, a jar of peanut butter, another of grape jelly, a half-stick of margarine smeared on its gold foil wrapper, a handful of paper sugar packets and a plastic spoon and knife he'd kept from Hardee's.

He stood awhile, staring at the collection.

Two times I've let women clean me out. When am I going to learn?

A quick-flash came along: the four of them—himself, Bess, Randy and Lisa—during those fun years when the kids were old enough to sit at the table and swing their feet without their toes touching the floor. Lisa, fresh from church, with her hair in pigtails and her elbows on the table, picking apart a piece of toast and eating it in tiny increments (all the while with her feet swinging wildly): "I saw Randy pick his nose in church this morning and wipe it on the bottom of the pew. *Yuuuuukkkk!*"

"I dint neither! She's lying!"

"You did, too! I saw you, Randy, you're *so gross!*"

"Mom, she lies all the time." (This with a whine that verified his guilt.)

"I'm *never* sitting in that pew again!"

Bess and Michael exchanging glances with their lips pursed to keep from hooting before Bess remarked, "Randy picks his nose in church, his dad does it when he's sitting at stop lights."

"I do not!" Michael had yelped.

"You do, too!"

Then the whole family breaking into laughter before Bess delivered an admonition about hygiene and handkerchiefs.

Sunday breakfasts were a lot different then.

In his White Bear Lake condominium, Michael poured some Grape-Nuts into a white plastic deli-food container, covered them with milk from the otherwise empty refrigerator, tore open a sugar packet, took his plastic spoon and returned to his mattresses, where he propped his pillows against the wall, turned on the TV and sat down to eat alone.

He wasn't up to either evangelists or cartoons, however, and found his mind returning to the perplexing stringball of family relationships he was trying to un-knot. For perhaps the ten thousandth time in his life he wished he had sisters and brothers. What would it be like to pick up the phone and say, "Hi, you got any coffee over there?" and sit down with someone who'd shared your past, and your parents, and some warm memories, and maybe a few scoldings, and the chicken pox, and the same first-grade teacher, and teenage clothing, and double dates and memories of Mom's cooking? Someone who knew all you'd put into your lifetime's struggles, and who cared about your happiness and how you felt today.

How he felt today was lonely. So damned lonely, and hurting some, and wondering where to go next in his life. How to be a father to Randy, and how to make it through this wedding, and what tack to take with Bess, and what to make of these nostalgic thoughts he'd been having about her. Even being a grandfather—he'd like to talk about that.

Alas, there was no brother, no sister, and he felt as cheated and isolated as ever.

He got up, showered, shaved and dressed, then tried working awhile at his desk in one of the other two bedrooms, but the silence and emptiness were so depressing he had to get out.

He decided to go shopping for some furniture. He sure as hell needed it, and at least in the stores there'd be people moving around.

He went to Dayton's Home Store on highway 36, thinking he'd simply pick a living-roomful and have it delivered, but discovered to his dismay that just about everything would have to be ordered and would take from six weeks to six months to arrive. Furthermore, he had no carpet samples, no wallpaper samples and no idea what he really wanted.

He went next to Levitz, where he walked the aisles between assembled rooms and tried to visualize pieces in his condo but found he had no concept of what would look good. Color, in particular, threw him, and size, of course, became a factor. He realized that all the places he'd ever lived in had been decorated primarily by women and that he had no eye for it whatsoever.

He went next to Byerly's grocery store, where he stared at the fresh chickens a long time, wondering how Darla had made that stuff called fricassee. He passed the pork chops—Stella was the one who knew how to make pork chops. They had onions on top, he recalled, and lemon slices, but how she got them red and barbe-cuey, he had no idea. Ham? Ham sounded simpler, though his foremost craving was not for it but for the mashed potatoes and ham gravy that went along with it, the way Bess used to fix it.

Aw, hell . . . he turned away and went back to the delicatessen, where he fixed a salad at the open salad bar and bought some wild-rice soup for his supper.

It was twilight when he headed home, a melancholy time of day with the sun setting in his rearview mirror and the empty condo ahead. He parked in the underground garage, took the elevator up and went straight to the kitchen, where he warmed his soup in the microwave and ate it seated on the cold tiles of the countertop.

The idea hit him while he was sitting there with his feet dangling a foot above the floor, eating soup out of a cardboard carton with a plastic spoon.

You need a decorator, Curran.

He knew one, too; knew a damned good one.

'Course, this could be nothing but an excuse to call her. He looked around, reconfirming that he hadn't so much as a kitchen table to eat at. Fat chance she'd believe he really needed his place furnished; she'd think he was nosing around for something else.

He could call another one. Yes, he could, he certainly could. But it was Sunday: you can't call an interior decorator on Sunday.

He stared at the view of the gloaming out the sliding glass door, picturing Bess. If he called her he'd look like a jerk. So he sat on the cold counter, beside the white telephone, tapping the plastic spoon on his knee.

It took him until eight o'clock to work up the courage to dial his old number. In six years it hadn't changed, and he remembered it by heart.

Bess answered on the third ring.

"Hi, Bess, it's Michael."

A long silence passed before she said, "Well . . . Michael."

"Surprised, huh?"

"Yes."

"Yeah, me too." He was sitting on the edge of his mattress with its messy blankets, fiddling with the material covering his right knee, wondering what to say next. "It was a nice supper last night."

"Yes, it was."

"The Padgetts seem like likable people."

"I thought so, too."

"Lisa could do worse."

"She's very happy, and after seeing Mark with his family I have no objection whatsoever to their marriage."

Each ensuing silence became more awkward. "So, how's Randy today?" Michael asked.

"I haven't seen much of him. We went to church and he left right afterwards to watch the game with his friend."

"Did he say anything last night?"

"About what?"

"About us."

"Yes he did, as a matter of fact. He said he hoped you wouldn't make a fool out of me again. Listen, Michael, is there something in particular you wanted, because I brought some work home to do this evening and I'd like to get back to it."

"I thought you wanted us to be civil to each other for the kids' sake."

"I did. I do but—"

"Then give me a minute here, will you, Bess! I'm making the effort to call you and you start slinging insults!"

"You *asked* me what Randy said and I told you!"

"All right . . ." He calmed himself. "All right, let's just forget it. I'm sorry I asked about him, and besides I called for something else."

"What?"

"I want to hire you."

"To do what?"

"To decorate my condo."

She paused a beat, then burst out laughing. "Oh, Michael, that's so funny!"

"What's so funny about it?"

"You want to hire *me* to decorate your condo?"

His mouth got tight. "Yes, I do."

"Are you forgetting how you railed against my going to school to get my degree?"

"That was then, this is now. I need a decorator. Do you want the job or not?"

"First of all, let's get one thing straight, something you apparently never caught the first time around. I'm not a decorator, I'm an interior designer."

"There's a difference?"

"Anybody who owns a paint store can call himself a decorator. I'm a U of M graduate with a four-year degree and I'm accredited by the FIDER. Yes, there's a difference."

"All right, I apologize. I won't make that mistake again. Madame Interior Designer, would you care to design the interior of my condo?" he asked snidely.

"I'm no fool, Michael. I'm a businesswoman. I'll be happy to set up a house call. There's a one-time forty-dollar trip charge for that, which I'll apply to the cost of any furniture you might order."

"I think I can handle that."

"Very well, my calendar is at the store but I know I have next Friday morning open. How does that sound?"

"Fine."

"Just so you'll know what to expect, the house call is primarily a question-and-answer period so that I can get to know your tastes, budget, life-style, things like that. I won't be bringing any samples or catalogs with me at this time. That'll all come later. During this initial visit we'll just talk and I'll take notes. Will there be anyone else living in the condo with you?"

"For God's sake, Bess—"

"It's part of my job as a professional to ask, because if there will be, it's best to have everybody present at this first consultation and get everybody's input at the start. It eliminates problems later when the one who wasn't there says, 'Wait a minute! You know how I hate blue!' Or yellow, or African masks or glass-top tables. Sometimes we hear things like, 'What happened to Great-Aunt Myrtle's lamp made out of the shrunken head?' You'd be surprised what rhubarbs can come up over taste."

"No, there won't be anyone else living here with me."

"Good, that simplifies matters. We'll make it Friday morning at nine, then, if that's agreeable."

"Nine is good. I'll tell you how to get here."

"I already know."

"You do?"

"Randy pointed it out to me."

"Oh." For a moment he'd flattered himself thinking she'd taken the trouble to look it up after he gave her his card. "There's a security system, so just call up from the lobby."

"I will."

"Well, I'll see you Friday, then."

"Yes." She ended the conversation without either stumble or halt.

"Good-bye, Michael."

"Good-bye."

When he'd hung up Michael sat on the edge of his mattress, scowling. "Whoa! Madame Businesswoman!" he said aloud, eyeing the phone.

The place seemed quiet after his outburst. The furnace clicked on and started the fan quietly wheezing through the vents. The night pressed black against his curtainless windows. The ceiling fixture sent harsh light over the room. He fell back with his hands behind his neck. A knot of jumbled bedding created an uncomfortable lump beneath him. He moved off it, still scowling.

This is probably a mistake, he thought.

When Bess hung up, she thought about the infamous decorating Doris Day had perpetrated on Rock Hudson's apartment in *Pillow Talk*. Ah, those red-velour tassels, those chartreuse draperies, that moose head, the orange player piano, beaded curtains, fertility gods, potbellied stove and the chair made of antlers . . .

It was tempting.

Definitely tempting.

The following evening Lisa went home to Stillwater to try on her mother's wedding dress. It was stored in the basement in a windowless space beside the laundry room, inside a plastic bag hanging from the ceiling joists. They went down together. Bess pulled the chain on a light switch and a bare 40-watt bulb smeared murky yellow smudge over the crowded cubicle. Its walls were the backside of the adjacent rooms, giving a view of two-by-fours and untaped Sheetrock. It smelled like fresh mushrooms.

Bess glanced around and shivered, then looked up at the row of shrouded garments.

"I don't think either one of us can reach. There's a step stool in the laundry room, Lisa, would you get it?"

While Lisa went to find the stool, Bess began moving aside boxes and baby furniture, a badminton net, a case holding a twenty-five-dollar guitar they'd bought for Randy when he was twelve, before he'd discovered his true love was drumming. Some of the cardboard boxes were labeled—*Baby Clothes, Lisa's Dolls, Games, School Papers*—representing many years' accumulation of memories.

Lisa returned and while Bess forced the legs of the stool into the tight space among the boxes, Lisa opened one of them.

"Oh, Mom, look . . ." Lisa took out a cigar box and from it drew a school picture of herself. In it she was missing both incisors and her hair was parted on one side, slicked to the opposite side and held in place with a barrette. "Second grade, Miss Peal. Donny Carry said he loved me and put those little heart-shaped candies on my desk every morning, with a different message on every one. *Be mine. Cool babe.* I was a real heartbreaker, wasn't I?"

Bess viewed the picture. "Oh, I remember that dress. Grandma Dorner gave it to you for Christmas and you always wore it with red tights and patent-leather shoes."

"Dad used to call me his little elf whenever I wore it."

Bess said, "It's cold down here. Let's get the dress and go upstairs."

Bess carried the bridal gown and Lisa took the cigar box, glancing through report cards, old, curled pictures and notes from her childhood friends as the two women climbed the stairs. Bess went outside on the front stoop, stripped the dusty plastic bag off the wedding dress and gave it a shake. She carried it upstairs to find Lisa in her old room, sitting cross-legged on the bed.

"Look at this one," Lisa said, and Bess sank down beside her with the gown doubled over on her lap. "It's a note from Patty Larson. 'Dear Lisa, Meet me in the empty lot after lunch and bring your Melody doll and all your Barbies and we'll put on a concert.' Remember how Patty and I used to do that all the time? We had these little penlights and we'd pretend they were microphones, and we'd set up all our dolls as our audience and sing our lungs out." Lisa extended her arms, clicked her fingers and sang a couple of lines from "Don't Go Breaking My Heart." She ended with a laugh that softened to a nostalgic note. "I remember once when we put on a show for you and Dad wearing some of her sister's dance costumes. We made up little tickets and charged you admission."

Bess remembered, too. Sitting beside Lisa, freeing the buttons on the back of her wedding dress, she remembered altogether too well those happier days, before her and Michael's troubles had begun. Though she could feel nostalgic at moments such as this, she was a realist who knew these flashes were momentary. She and Michael would never be husband and wife again, much as Lisa wished it.

"Why don't you try the dress on, honey?" she said gently.

Lisa set aside the cigar box and got off the bed. Bess stood behind her and forced twenty satin loops around twenty pearl buttons up the back of the dress while Lisa studied the results in the dresser mirror.

"It's going to fit," Lisa said.

"I was a size ten back then. You're a size eight. Even if you get a little tummy in the next few weeks there shouldn't be any problem."

Both of them studied Lisa's reflection. The dress had a beaded stand-up collar above a V-shaped lace bodice that ended with a point on the stomach. It had elbow-length pouf sleeves, a full satin skirt and train trimmed with beadwork and sequins. Though it was wrinkled, it hadn't discolored. "It's still beautiful, isn't it, Mom?"

"Yes, it is. I remember the day my mother said I could buy it, how excited I was. Naturally, it was one of the most expensive ones in the store, and I thought she'd say no but you know Grandma. She was always so crazy about your dad she'd have said yes to anything once she heard the news that I was going to marry him."

Without warning Lisa spun from the mirror and headed for the door. "Wait a minute!" she called as she disappeared.

"Where are you going?"

"Be right back. Stay there!"

Lisa thumped downstairs in her stocking feet and returned in a minute making a high-energy entrance, then dropping to the bed in a swish of wrinkled satin with a photo album on her lap.

"It was right where it always used to be in the bookshelves in the living room," she said breathlessly.

"Oh, Lisa, not those old things." Lisa had brought Bess and Michael's wedding album.

"Why not these old things? I want to see them."

"Lisa, that's wishful thinking."

"I want to see how you looked in the dress."

"You want to see things the way they used to be but that part of our lives is over. Dad and I are divorced and we're staying that way."

"Oh, look . . ." Lisa opened the album. There were Michael and Bess, close up, with their cheeks touching and her bouquet and veil forming an aureole around them. "Gol, Mom, you were just beautiful, and Dad . . . wow, look at him."

The photo caught at Bess's heart while she sat beside her daughter searching for the perfect balance in her response to Lisa. She had been bitter too long and was learning the hurt it had caused her children. At this turning point in her life, Lisa needed this foray into the past. To deny her the freedom of exploring it was to deny a certain part of her heritage. At the same time, allowing her to believe there was a chance of reconciliation between her parents was sheer folly.

"Lisa, dear . . ." Bess took her hand. Lisa looked into Bess's eyes. "Your dad and I had some wonderful years."

"I know. I remember a lot of them."

"I wish we could have made a happier ending for you but it didn't work out that way. I want you to know, though, that I'm glad you forced us to confront each other. It's making me take a second look at myself, which I needed, and even though your dad and I aren't getting back together, it feels much better to be his ex-wife without so much animosity between us."

"But Dad said you looked great the night of the dinner."

"Lisa, darling . . . don't. You're pinning your hopes on nothing."

"Well, what are you going to do, marry *Keith?* Mom, he's such a dork."

"Who said anything about marrying anybody? I'm happy as I am. I'm healthy, the business is going good, I keep busy, I have you and Randy—"

"And what about when Randy decides to grow up? What about when he moves out?" Lisa gestured at the walls. "You going to stay in this big old empty house alone?"

"I'll decide that when the time comes."

"Mom, just promise me one thing—if Dad makes a play for you, or if he asks you out or something, you won't get all pissed off and slug him or anything, will you? Because I think he's going to do it. I saw how he looked at you the other night, while you two were sitting down there at your end of the table—"

"Lisa—"

"—and you're still quite a looker, Ma—"

"Lisa!"

"—and as for Dad, he's one of the truly excellent men around. Even when he was married to that dumb Darla I thought so. You know, Ma, you could do worse."

"I'm not going to talk about it, and I wish you wouldn't."

Lisa left soon thereafter, taking the dress with her to drop at the dry cleaner's. After seeing her out, Bess returned upstairs to turn out the light in Lisa's old room. There on the bed lay the wedding album, bound in white leather and stamped in gold: BESS & MICHAEL CURRAN, JUNE 8, 1968.

The room still seemed to retain the musty smell of the bridal gown and the cigar box, which Lisa had left behind. A fitting smell, Bess thought, for the marriage that had turned to must.

She dropped to the bed, braced a hand beside the album and slowly flipped its pages.

Thoughtful.

Nostalgic.

Alternately relishing and ruing while the diametrically opposed wishes of her two children tugged her in opposite directions—Randy, the bitter; Lisa, the romantic.

She closed the book and fell back on the bed with one wrist across her waist. Outside somebody's dog yapped to be let in. Down in the kitchen the automatic icemaker switched on and sent the hiss of moving water up the pipes in the wall. Out in the world all around her men and women moved through life two-by-two while she lay on her daughter's bed alone.

This is silly. I have tears in my eyes and a pain in my heart that wasn't there before I entered this room. I've let Lisa put ideas into my head that are based on nothing but her sentimentality. Whatever she thought she detected between Michael and me the other night was strictly her imagination.

She rolled her head and reached out to touch the wedding album.

Or was it?

Chapter 6

She went to the beauty shop on Thursday and had her roots bleached, her ends trimmed and her hair styled. She painted her nails that night and spent nearly fifteen minutes deciding what to wear the next morning, choosing a wool crepe dress in squash gold with a tucked waist, tulip-shaped skirt and a wide belt with an oversized gold buckle. In the morning she finished it off with a variegated scarf, gold earrings and a spritz of perfume, then shot a critical glance at the mirror.

You're still quite a looker, Ma.

If, at given moments in her life, Bess Curran had considered herself a *looker,* she had not done so in the six years since Michael had put her down on that score. The insult lived on each time she looked in a mirror, and no matter what efforts she put into her grooming, at the final moment she always found some detail less than perfect. Usually it was her weight.

Ten pounds, she thought today. Only ten and I'd be where I want to be.

Aggravated with Michael for creating this perennial dissatisfaction and with herself for perpetuating it, she slammed off the light switch and left the room.

She arrived in White Bear Lake with five minutes to spare and approached Michael's condominium doubly impressed, observing it at close range in broad daylight. The sign said CHATEAUGUET. The driveway curved between two giant elms and led through grounds dotted with mature oaks. Closer to the building, a pair of venerable spruce trees stood sentinel beside the doors, taller than the four stories they guarded. The structure itself was V-shaped and sprawling, of white brick and gray siding, studded with royal-blue awnings. It had underground garages, white balconies, brass carriage lanterns and a lot of glass. On the uppermost floor, the decks and patio doors were topped by roof gables inset with sunburst designs.

But more, it had the lake.

One was conscious of it even from the landward side, and Bess found herself speculating on the view she'd discover when she got inside.

The foyer smelled like scented carpet cleaner, had tastefully papered walls, an elevator and a small bank of mailboxes along with a security phone. She picked it up and rang Michael's unit.

He answered immediately, "'Morning, Bess, is that you?"

"Good morning, yes it is."

"I'll be right down."

She heard the elevator hum before its doors split soundlessly and Michael stepped out, wearing gray/black pleated trousers with needle-fine teal stripes, a teal polo shirt with its collar turned up and a finely knit double-breasted sweater in white. His trousers had the gloss of costly fabric, and the polo shirt picked up the exact hue of the stripes. Since becoming an interior designer, Bess noticed things like that. She could spot cheap fabric at twenty paces and clashing colors at fifty. Michael's clothes were well chosen, even the tassled loafers of soft black leather. She wondered who'd chosen them, since Michael was all but color-blind and had always had difficulty coordinating his wardrobe.

"Thanks for coming, Bess," he said, holding the elevator doors open. "We're going up."

She stepped aboard and was closed into the four-by-six-foot space with him and the familiar smell of his British Sterling. To dispel the sense of déjà vu she asked, "How do you pronounce the name of this place?"

"Chateau-gay," he replied. "Back in the 1900s there was a big hotel here by that name, and it was also the name of a racehorse that won the Kentucky Derby years ago."

"Chateauguet," she repeated. "I like it."

They arrived at an upper hall shaped like the one below, and he waved her ahead of himself into the condominium whose door stood open to their right.

She wasn't three feet inside before exhilaration struck. Space! Enough space to make a designer drool! The entry hall was as wide as most bedrooms, carpeted in a grayed mauve. It was totally bare but for a large, contemporary chandelier of smoked glass and brass. Ahead, the foyer widened into a space where a second, matching chandelier created a rich corridor effect.

Michael took her coat, hung it behind a louvered door and turned back to her. "Well, this is it." He spread his hands. "These are guest bedrooms. . . ." Light came through two doors to their right. "Each one has its own bath." They were identical in size and had generous windows. One bedroom was empty, the other held a drafting table and chair. She glanced over the rooms as she followed Michael, carrying a clipboard, measuring tape and pen, leaving her purse on the floor in the foyer.

"Do these windows face due north?"

"More like northwest," he replied.

She decided to put off her note-taking and measuring until she'd moved through the entire place, to get a sense of each of its rooms in relationship to the whole. They advanced beyond the entry to an interior octagonal space in the center of which the second chandelier hung. It appeared to be the hub of the apartment, created of four flat walls and four doorways.

"The architect calls this a gallery," Michael said, stopping dead center in the middle of the octagon.

Bess turned in a circle and looked up at the chandelier. "It's very dramatic . . . or can be."

They had entered the gallery from the hall door. Michael indicated the others. "Kitchen, combination living room/dining room, and utility area and powder room off this small hall. Which would you like to see first?"

"Let's see the living room." She stepped into it to be washed in light and delight. The room faced south-by-southeast, had a marble fireplace on the northerly wall, another chandelier at the south end and two sets of sliding glass doors—a triple and a double—that gave onto a deck overlooking the frozen lake. Between the two doors the wall took a turn at an obtuse angle.

"It's just struck me, Michael, this place isn't rectangular, is it?"

"No, it's not. The entire building is arrow-shaped, and this unit is at the point of the arrow, so I guess you'd call it oblique."

"Oh, how marvelous. If you knew how many rectangular rooms I've designed you'd know how exciting this is." Though the two guest bedrooms were rectangular, this room was a modified wedge. "Show me the rest."

The kitchen was done in white tile and Formica with blond oak woodwork. It was combined with an informal family room, which had sliding doors giving onto the same deck that wrapped around the entire apartment on the lake side. The laundry area was in a wedge-shaped space beside a powder room, both leading off the gallery. The master bedroom led off the living room and shared its fireplace flue. Besides the fireplace, the bedroom had yet another set of glass doors leading onto the deck, a walk-in closet and a bathroom big enough to host a basketball game.

In the bathroom, the smell of Michael's cosmetics was as evocative as that of fresh-cut grass. A rechargeable razor sat on the vanity with its tiny red light glowing. Beside it lay his toothbrush and a tube of Close-Up. The shower door was wet and on a towel bar hung a horrendous beach towel with fireworks designs in gaudy colors on a black background. No washcloth. He'd always used his hands.

Shame on you, Bess, you're regressing.

In the bedroom her glance slid over his mattresses and returned for a second take, then moved on as if the sight of them lumped on the floor had not stirred old memories. He must have left Darla taking nothing. Even his blankets were new; the fold lines still showed. How ironic, Bess thought, I'll probably end up choosing his bedspread again. Already she was envisioning the room with the bed and window treatment matching.

"Well, that's it," Michael said.

"I must say, Michael, I'm impressed."

"Thank you."

They returned to the living room with its magnificent scope. "The way the building blends with the land, and how the architect utilized the mature trees, the contour of the lakeshore and even the little park next door—it all becomes a part of the interior design as well as the exterior. The outdoors is actually taken inside through these magnificent stretches of glass, while at the same time the trees lend privacy." Bess strode the length of the room, admiring the view through the windows while Michael stood near the fireplace with his hands in his trouser pockets. "It's interesting," Bess mused aloud, "clients are often surprised to learn that architects and interior designers rarely get along well at all. The reason is because very few architects design from the outside in the way this one did, consequently we're often called in to analyze the space use and handle the problems the architect left behind. In this case, that's not so. This guy really knew what he was doing."

Michael smiled. "I'll tell him you said so. He works for me."

From the opposite end of the room she faced him.

"You built this building?"

"Not exactly. I developed the property and arranged to have it built. The city of White Bear Lake came to me and asked me to do it."

"Ah . . ." Bess's eyebrows rose in approval. "I had no idea your projects had grown to this size. Congratulations."

Michael dipped his head, displaying an appealing mix of humility and pride.

She was no appraiser but the building had to be worth several million dollars, and if the city came to him and invited him to do the job, he must have established a sterling reputation. So both of them—Michael and she—had made great strides since their breakup. "Do you mind if we continue moving from room to room while we talk?"

"Not at all."

"It helps me recall where I've been and familiarize myself with the psychological impact of each room, how the light falls, the space there is to be filled and the space that should remain unfilled. It's kind of like kicking the tires on a car before you buy it."

They gave each other glancing grins and moved into the gallery, where they stopped directly beneath the chandelier. Bess braced her clipboard against her hip and said, "On with the questions. I've been doing all the talking and it's supposed to be the other way around during a house call. I'm here to listen to you."

"Ask away."

"Did you choose the carpet?"

She'd noted that the same carpet was used throughout, with the exception of the kitchen and baths. It wasn't a color she'd have expected him to like. From the gallery she could glance to the sunny or shadowed side of the condo and observe its subtleties change.

"No, it was here when I took over the place. Actually what happened was that this unit was sold to someone else, a couple named Sawyer, who intended it to be their retirement home. Mrs. Sawyer picked out the carpet and had it laid but before she and her husband could close on the place, he died. She decided to stay put, so I inherited the carpet."

"It's staying?"

"It should. It's brand-new and I'm the first tenant."

"You say that as if you have reservations."

He pursed his lips and studied the carpeting. "I can live with it."

"Make sure before we plan a whole interior around it, and be aware that color affects your energy, your productivity, your ability to relax, many things. You're as affected by color as you are by texture and light and space. You should surround yourself with colors you're comfortable with."

"I can live with it," he repeated.

"And I can tone it down, make it more masculine by bringing out its gray rather than its rose, perhaps using a deep gray and a pastel lavender as an accent, maybe bringing in some black pieces. How does that sound?"

"All right."

"Do you have a carpet sample I can take along?"

"In the entry closet on the shelf. I'll give you a piece before you leave."

"What are your thoughts on mirrored walls?"

"In here?" Michael looked up. They were still standing in the octagonal gallery.

"An interior space like this would benefit from them. It could be dramatic to relight the chandelier in four mirror panels."

"It *sounds* dramatic. Let me think about it."

They moved into the room with the drafting table. "Do you work here?"

"Yes."

"How much?"

"Primarily in the evenings. Daytime I'm in the office."

Bess wandered nearer the drafting table. "Do you work—" she began but the question died on her lips. Taped onto an extension lamp over the drafting table was a picture of their two children, taken when they were about seven and nine, in the backyard after a water fight. They were freckled and smiling and squinting into the hard summer sun. Randy was missing a front tooth and Lisa's hair was sticking up in a messy swirl where the force of the hose had shot it.

"Do I work . . . ?" Michael repeated.

She knew full well he'd seen her reaction to the picture, but she was a businesswoman now and personal byplay had no place in this house call. Bess regrouped her emotions and went on.

"Do you work every evening?"

"I have been lately." He didn't add, Since Darla and I broke up, but he didn't have to. It was obvious he sat here in this room regretting some things.

"Would you ever be needing a desk in this room?"

"That might be nice."

"File cabinets?"

"Probably not."

"Shelving?"

He wobbled a hand like a plane dipping its wings.

"In order of preference, would you place this room high or low in the decorating order?"

"Low."

"All right . . . let's move on."

They meandered to the other guest bedroom, and from there to the powder room, the gallery, the kitchen, ending up in the living room.

"Tell me, Michael, what's your opinion of art deco?"

"It can be a little stark but I've seen some I like."

"And glass—glass tabletops, for instance, as opposed to wood."

"Either is fine."

"Would you be entertaining in this room?"

"Maybe."

"How many might you want to seat at one time?"

"I don't know."

"A dozen maybe?"

"Probably not."

"Six?"

"I suppose so."

"Would that entertaining be formal or informal?"

"Informal, probably."

"Meals . . ." She moved to the end of the room where the chandelier hung, studying the change of light on the carpet, imagining it on furniture as she moved from the light-realm of one window to another. "Would you ever entertain at sit-down meals?"

"I have in the past."

"Will you use the fireplace or not?"

"Yes."

"Will you ever watch television in this room?"

"No."

"How about a tape player or CD player?"

"Probably I'd want that in the family room off the kitchen."

"Which do you prefer, vertical or horizontal lines?"

"What?"

She looked up at him and smiled. "That one usually throws people. Vertical or horizontal? One is restful, the other energetic."

"Vertical."

"Ah . . . energetic. Are you an early riser or a late riser?"

"Early." He always had been but she had to ask.

"And how about the tail end of the day? Do you watch the David Letterman show?"

"Do I what?"

"Are you a night person, Michael?"

He scratched his neck and grinned crookedly at the floor. "I remember a time when I was but it's funny how nature takes care of that for you when you reach middle age."

She smiled and went on to her next subject. "Give me your opinion of this chandelier." She looked up at the ceiling.

He wandered nearer and looked up, too. "It reminds me of grapefruit sections," he said.

She laughed. "Grapefruit sections?"

"Yeah, those pieces of smoky glass all standing on end like that. Aren't they shaped like grapefruit sections?"

"Skinny ones, maybe. Do you like it?"

"Mmm . . ." He studied it pensively. "Yeah, I like it a lot."

"Good. So do I."

She made a note about repeating smoked glass in the tables and another about café doors as she moved through a wide doorway into the family room/kitchen. In this room the view had curved away from the lake and focused instead on a tall stand of cottonwood trees—naked now in winter—and a small town park with a white gazebo. Thankfully there were no swing sets or playground equipment, which would be desirable for a young family, not for a building that catered to older, wealthier people.

"What happens in the park?" she asked.

"Picnics in the summer, I guess. That's about all."

"No band concerts, no boat launching?"

"No. Boats are launched over at the county beach or at the White Bear Yacht Club."

"Will you launch one?"

"Maybe. I've thought about it."

"A lot of sailboats on the lake, aren't there?"

"Yes."

"I imagine you're looking forward to watching them from both inside and out on the deck."

"Sure."

She made a note about vertical blinds and sauntered toward the kitchen island, where a jar of peanut butter, a loaf of bread and some throw-away containers created his bachelor's pantry. She glanced over the pitiful collection, then looked away because it brought a sharp desire to play housewife, and neither of them needed that.

"Will this be a working kitchen?" she asked, her back to Michael as she waited for an answer.

It took some time before he replied, "No."

She gathered her composure and turned to rest her clipboard on the island. "Are there any hobbies of yours I should know about?"

"They haven't changed since six years ago. Hunting and the outdoors but I go up to my cabin for that."

"Have you developed any allergies?"

His eyebrows puckered. "Allergies?"

"It has to do with fabrics and fibers," she explained.

"No allergies."

"Then I guess all that's left to ask about is the budget. Have you thought about a range you want me to work within?"

"Just do it the way you'd do it for yourself. You were always good at it, and I trust you."

"All of it?"

"Well . . ." He glanced around uncertainly. "I guess so."

"The guest bedroom, too?"

His eyes came back to her. "I hate empty rooms," he said.

"Yes . . ." she agreed, "and it is the first room a visitor sees when he steps into the foyer."

She had the illogical impulse to go to him, take him in her arms for a moment, pat his back and say, It'll be all right, Michael, I'll fill it with things so it isn't so lonely, though she knew perfectly well a home full of things could not substitute for a home full of people.

She looked down at her clipboard. "I'll need to take some measurements. Would you mind helping me?"

"Not at all."

"I've tried to sketch the layout of the unit but it's unusual enough to be difficult."

"I have some floor plans at the office that were done for the sales people. I'll send you one."

"Oh, that would be helpful. Meanwhile, shall we measure?"

They spent the next twenty minutes at opposite ends of a surveyor's tape, getting room and window dimensions. When they were all tidily written on her rough floor plan, she cradled the clipboard against her arm and reeled in the tape.

"What happens next?" he asked as they returned to the foyer, where he retrieved her coat and held it for her.

"I'll take all these dimensions and transfer them onto graph paper, room by room. Then I'll go 'shopping' through my catalogs and come up with a furniture plan, window treatments, fabric and wallpaper samples. I'll also have all the suggested furniture cut out to scale on magnetic plastic so they can be arranged on the floor plan. When all that is done I'll give you a call and we'll get together for the presentation. I usually do that at my store after hours because all my books and samples are there and it makes it easier without customers interrupting. Then, too, if you don't like something I've suggested we can go into other books and look for something else."

"So when will I hear from you?"

Her coat was buttoned and she drew on her gloves. "I'll try to get on it right away and get back to you within a week, since you're living in rather Spartan conditions. I don't see anything wrong with playing favorites and putting you ahead of some of my other clients, do you?"

She flashed him a professional smile and extended her gloved hand. "Thank you, Michael."

He took it, squeezing hard. "Aren't you forgetting something?"

"What?"

"Your forty-dollar trip charge."

"Oh, that. I initiated the trip charge merely to dissuade lonely people who only want company for an afternoon—and you'd be amazed how many of them there are. But it's obvious you need furniture, and you're not some stranger whose intentions I question."

"Business is business, Bess, and if there's a trip charge, I'll pay it."

"All right, but why don't I bill you for it?"

"Absolutely not. Wait here."

He went into the room with the drafting table, leaving her in the empty foyer. She watched him through the doorway, stretching her gloves on tighter. She picked up her clipboard, her purse, and watched him some more, then followed him into the room, where he was making out the check with one hand flat on the drafting table, his elbow jutting.

The photo was still there, compelling. She studied it over his angled shoulders and said quietly, "They were adorable when they were that age, weren't they?"

He stopped writing, looked at the picture awhile and tore out the check before turning to Bess. His gaze lingered on her, then traveled once more to the picture.

"Yes, they were."

The room remained silent while the two of them studied their son and daughter caught in a carefree day from their past. His gaze returned to Bess and she felt it on her cheek as one feels heat from a nearby fire, while she continued studying the picture.

"Michael, I . . ." Struggling for words, she met his eyes and felt a burning sense of imminence in the admission she was about to make. "I went to visit my mother on Sunday and we had a talk." She paused but he said nothing. "I told her how difficult it's been seeing you again, and she said that the reason is because you're making me take a second look at myself and my fault in the divorce."

Still he waited while she clung to her clipboard and willed the words forth.

"I think I owe you an apology, Michael, for turning the kids against you."

Something changed in his eyes—a quick transport of repressed anger, perhaps.

Though he moved not a muscle he seemed more rigid, while his hazel eyes remained steady upon hers.

She looked down at her glove. "I swore I wouldn't do this—mix business with anything personal but it's been bothering me, and today when I saw their picture here I realized that . . . well, that you loved them, too, and how it must have hurt you, losing them." She met his eyes once more. "I'm sorry, Michael."

He thought about it for passing seconds before speaking in a low, throaty tone. "I hated you for it, you know."

She shifted her gaze to the drafting table. "Yes, I know," she said quietly.

"Why did you do it?"

"Because I felt hurt, and wronged."

"But that was another matter entirely, what was between us."

"I know that now."

They stared at each other until the silence in the room seemed to be compressing them.

"Mother said something else." Again Michael waited for her to go on while she struggled for courage to do so. "She said that when I went back to college you fell to the bottom of my priority list and that's why you found another woman." Nothing changed on his face so she asked, "Is that true, Michael?"

"What do you think?"

"I'm asking you."

"Well, I'm not going to answer. I don't see any point, not at this late date."

"So it is true."

He handed her the check. "Thanks for coming, Bess. I really should get down to my office now."

Her cheeks were hot as she accepted his check and said, "I'm sorry, Michael. I shouldn't have brought it up today. It's not the appropriate time."

She preceded him into the foyer, where he opened the door for her then changed his mind and held it closed for a moment.

"Why did you bring it up at all, Bess?"

"I don't know. I don't understand myself lately. It seems as if there were so many things between us that were never settled, all these . . . these ugly emotions that kept roiling around inside me. I guess I just need to deal with them once and for all and put them behind me. That's what apologies are all about, right?"

His eyes lit on hers, hard as chips of resin. He nodded stiffly. "All right, fair enough. Apology accepted."

She didn't smile; she couldn't. Neither could he.

He found her a carpet sample and ushered her out, at a respectable distance, and pushed the elevator button. The door opened instantly, while he was still speaking.

"Thanks for coming."

She stepped on, turned to offer a conciliatory smile and found him already stalking back into his condo. The elevator door closed and she rode down-stairs, wondering if by her apology she'd made things better or worse between them.

Chapter 7

―⁓ⓥ⁓―

Randy Curran dropped into a lopsided upholstered rocker and reached into his jacket pocket for his bag of pot. It was almost 11 p.m. and Bernie's mom was out, as usual. She was a cocktail waitress so most nights they had the place to themselves. The radio was tuned to Cities 97 and they were waiting for "The Grateful Dead Hour." Bernie sat on the floor with an electric guitar on his lap, the amp turned off as he picked along with a Guns N' Roses song. Randy had known Bernie Bertelli since the eighth grade, when he'd moved to town right after his parents got divorced, too. They'd smoked a lot of dope together since then.

Bernie's place was a dump. The floors were crooked, and the walls had a lot of plastic knickknacks hanging on them. The shag carpeting was the color of baby shit and matted worse than the hair of the two old Heinz 57 dogs, Skipper and Bean, who were allowed to do pretty much anything they wanted anywhere in the house. Skipper and Bean were presently stretched out on the davenport, which in its younger days had been upholstered in some cheap nylon plaid but now was covered with a flowered throw with soiled spots the shapes of the dogs at either end. The coffee tables and end tables had screw-on legs and the drapery pleats sagged between all the hooks. Against one wall a pyramid of beer cans reached the ceiling, the top can wedged against the water-stained tile. Bernie's mom had put the top one there herself.

Randy never sat on the davenport, not even when he was high or drunk. He never got *that* high or *that* drunk! He always took the green rocker, a decrepit thing that looked as if it had had a stroke, because everything on it sagged to one side. The broken springs in the seat were covered with a folded rag rug to keep them from poking your ass, and the upholstered arms were covered with cigarette burns.

Randy fished out the Ziploc bag and his bat, a miniature pipe big enough for a single hit. Gone were the days of rolling smokes. Who could afford that anymore?

"This shit is getting expensive, man," he said.

"Yeah, what'd you pay?"

"Sixty bucks."

"For a quarter?"

Randy rearranged his expression and shrugged.

Bernie whistled. "Better be good shit, man."

"The best. Lookit here . . ." Randy opened the bag. "Buds."

Bernie leaned over, took a closer look and said, "Buds . . . wow, how'd you score that?" Everybody knew that buds gave you the most for your money— better than leaves or sticks or seeds. You could pack it tighter and get really loaded off a couple of hits.

Randy packed his pipe, missing the days when he'd tear off a Zigzag paper and roll a joint big enough to pass around. He'd seen a guy one time who could roll one with one hand. He'd practiced it himself at home a few times over a sheet of paper, but he'd dropped more than he'd rolled, so he'd settled for doing it deftly with two hands, which in itself was considered a mark of prowess among pot smokers.

Randy struck a match. The bat held less than a thimbleful. He lit up, took a deep drag and held it in his lungs until they burned. He exhaled, coughed and refilled the bat.

"Want a hit, Bernie?"

Bernie took a turn, coughing, too, while a scent like burning oregano filled the room.

It took two hits before Randy got the rush—the sweet chill that riffled through him and left him with a slow-growing euphoria. Everything became so exquisitely distorted. Bernie looked as though he was on the opposite side of a fishbowl, and the lights on the component set shimmered like a meteor shower that was taking ten years to fall. Someplace in the distance men coughed occasionally but the sound filtered down a long corridor, like shouting through a concrete culvert. The music from the radio became a major sensation that expanded his pores, his hair follicles, his fingers and his ability to perceive.

Words came to him and swirled through his vision as if they had mass and form—graceful, beckoning words.

"I met this girl," Randy said. "Did I say that already?" Seemed like he'd said it about one hour ago and it had taken till now for the words to drift down, landing on the dog Bean, bouncing off his red fur in slow motion, disturbing him so he rolled over onto his back with his paws up and his eyes closed.

"What girl?"

"Maryann. Some name, huh? . . . Maryann. Who names their kids Maryann anymore?"

"Who's Maryann?"

"Maryann Padgett. I had dinner at her house. Lisa is marrying her brother."

On the davenport Bean was snoring and his lip was fluttering. Randy became transfixed by the sight, which took on kaleidoscopic beauty, that dog lip, black on the outside, pink on the inside, flap-flapping in rhythm with his gentle snores.

"She scares the shit out of me."

"Why?"

" 'Cause she's a good girl."

Thirst came, exaggerated like everything else. "Hey, Bern, I got the dry mouth. You got some beer?"

The beer tasted like magic elixir, every sip a thousand times better than orgasm.

"We don't mess with good girls, do we, Bern?"

"Shit no, man . . . why should we?"

"Screw 'em and strew 'em, hey, Bern?"

"That's right. . . ." Two minutes later Bernie repeated, "That's right."

Ten minutes after that Bernie said, "Shit, man, I'm really fucked up."

"Me too," Randy said. "I'm so fucked up your nose even looks good. You got a nose like a goddamned anteater and I'm so fucked up your nose looks cute."

Bernie laughed and scattered sound down a jeweled corridor.

Many minutes later Randy said, "You can't get serious about girls, you know what I mean, man? I mean . . . hell . . . next thing you know you're marryin' 'em and you got kids and you're screwin' somebody else's old lady and walkin' out and your kids are bawlin'."

Bernie digested that a long time before he asked, "You bawl when your old man left?"

"Sometimes. Not where anybody could see me, though."

"Yeah, me too."

A while later Randy felt the lethargy lifting and the munchies coming on. He pitched forward in his chair and counted seven beer cans around him. He belched and Bean woke up, stretched and quivered, jumped off the couch and shook a fresh layer of dog hair onto the matted carpet. Pretty soon Skipper did the same. The two of them nosed at Bernie, whose eyes were as red as if he'd been fighting fires.

Randy gave himself some time, coming down. It was after midnight and the deadhead hour was in progress on Cities 97 and he had to be up at six. Actually, he was getting pretty tired of the Grateful Dead and of that stinking job at the warehouse. And of this pigsty of Bernie's and of the rising cost of marijuana. And of Bernie, who never could afford to buy his own. What the hell was he doing here in this lopsided rocking chair with the cigarette burns on its arms, looking at Bernie's big nose and counting the beer cans?

Who was he getting even with?

His father, that's who.

Problem was, the old man didn't really give a damn.

Bess received the floor plan from Michael on the Monday after she'd seen his condo. He'd mailed it, along with a note in his familiar handwriting, on a piece of notepaper with his company logo in blue at the top.

> Bess, Here's the floor plan for the condo, as promised. I've thought about the mirrors for the gallery. Go ahead and plan them in. I think I'll like them. I've been thinking about what you said just before you left and it makes me realize there were areas where I needed to change and didn't. Maybe we can talk about it some more. It was nice seeing you again. Michael.

She got a queer flutter at the sight of his handwriting. Funny about a thing like that, it was like studying his wet toothbrush and his damp towel, things he'd touched, held, worked with. She reread the entire message four times, imagining his beautifully shaped hand holding the pen as he wrote it. *Maybe we can talk about it some more.* Now that was a loaded suggestion, was it not? And had it really been nice for him, seeing her again? Didn't he feel the same tension she felt whenever they stood in the same room? Didn't he feel eager to escape, as she did?

———

Michael received a call from Lisa.

"Hey, Dad, how's it going?"

"All right. How's it going with you?"

"Busy. Cripes, I didn't dream there was this much stuff you had to do to plan a wedding. You free on Saturday afternoon?"

"I can be."

"Good, 'cause you men have to meet at Gingiss Formal Wear and pick out your tuxedos."

"Tuxedos, wow."

"You're gonna be a knockout, Dad."

Michael smiled. "You think so, huh? What time and where?"

"Two o'clock at Maplewood."

"I'll be there."

Randy hadn't thought about his dad being there. He walked into Gingiss Formal Wear at two o'clock the following Saturday afternoon, and there stood Michael, talking with Mark and Jake Padgett. Randy came up short. Mark spied him and came forward, extending his hand. "Here's our last guy. Hey, Randy, thanks for coming."

"Sure, no problem."

Jake shook his hand. "Hello, Randy."

"Mr. Padgett."

That left only Michael, who offered his hand, too. "Randy."

Randy looked into his father's somber eyes and felt a sick longing to go into his arms and hug him and say, "Hi, Dad." But he had not called Michael *Dad* in a long time. The word welled up and seemed to fill his throat, needing to be spoken, needing to be repressed. Michael's eyes so resembled his own it seemed like looking in a mirror while his father's hand waited.

At last he put his hand in Michael's and said, "Hello."

Michael flushed and gripped Randy's hand hard. Long after the contact ended Randy felt the imprint of his father's palm on his own.

A young blond clerk intruded. "Everybody here now, gentlemen? If you'll step this way."

They followed him into a rear room, carpeted and mirrored. Mark and his father went first, leaving Michael and Randy to exchange uncertain glances before Michael politely waved Randy through the doorway before him. The room held tuxedos in every conceivable color from black to pink, and smelled of a hot iron from a tailor's adjacent workroom. The clerk told Mark, "Sometimes the bride is in on this, too. Since yours isn't, I presume you've talked about colors."

"The bridesmaid's dress is coral. She said I could decide what color the tuxes should be."

"Ah, good. Then might I suggest ivory with coral cummerbunds—ivory is always tasteful, always elegant, and seems to be the trendy choice right now. We have several styles, the most popular are probably the Christian Dior and After Six."

The clerk prattled on while Michael and Randy remained intensely aware of each other, electrified by their encounter. With their emotions in turmoil they missed much of what was being said. They assessed jackets with satin lapels, pleated shirts, bow ties, cummerbunds and patent-leather shoes.

They removed their jackets, faced a wall of mirrors and had their measurements taken—neck, sleeve, chest, overarm, waist and outseam. They shucked off their pants and donned trousers with satin stripes up the sides, stood stocking-footed before a wall of mirrors and zipped up their flies, trading glances in the mirror before looking discreetly away.

They buttoned on pleated shirts, ruffled shirts, experimented with bow ties and thought about when they were a boy and a young father and Randy had put shaving cream on his face and shaved with a bladeless razor while his dad stood beside him and shaved with a real one; and times when they'd stood side-by-side and Randy had asked, wishfully, "Do you think I'll ever be taller than you, Dad?" And now he was, by a good inch—all grown up and capable of holding grudges.

"A forty-two long, sir," the clerk said. Michael slipped into a tuxedo jacket that smelled of dry-cleaning fluid, tugged the sleeves and collar into place while the clerk circled him, assessing the fit. Mark made some joke and Randy laughed. Jake said, "Never been in one of these monkey suits before, how 'bout you, Michael?"

"Just once." At his own wedding.

When the fitting was done they put on their street clothes again, zipping winter jackets as they shuffled from the store into the mall. Saturday shoppers moved past in twos and threes. The smell of baking cookies drifted through the hall from Mrs. Field's across the way. Mark and Jake headed straight toward the exit, leaving Michael and Randy to follow. Every step of the way Michael felt his chest contract as his chance slipped away. A question danced on his tongue while he feared Randy's rebuff.

Just before they reached the plate-glass doors, Michael spoke. "Listen, I haven't had lunch yet, have you?" He strove for an offhand tone in spite of the fact that his heart was in his throat.

"Yeah, I grabbed a burger earlier," Randy lied.

"You sure? I'm buying."

For a moment their gazes locked. Hope took on new meaning as Michael sensed Randy vacillating about changing his mind.

"No thanks. I'm meeting some friends."

Michael gave away none of the crushing disappointment he felt. "Well, maybe some other time."

"Yeah, sure . . ."

The gravity remained in both of them, exerting a force that distorted their heartbeats. But six years is a long time and some sins go beyond forgiving. So they left the shopping center by separate doors, went their separate ways and clung to their separate hurts.

Like a penitent toward Mecca, Randy drove straight into downtown Stillwater to his mother's store. He had no meeting with friends. He quite nearly had no friends.

He had only a deep need to be in his mother's presence after dashing aside his father's halting offer of conciliation.

Heather was at the counter when he walked in, and there were customers browsing.

"Hi, Heather, is Mom here?"

"Up here, darlin'," Bess called. "Come on up."

He shuffled upstairs, dipping his head to avoid bumping the ceiling when he reached the top, and found her among the jumble that looked capable of eating her alive.

"Well, this is a surprise." She swiveled to face him, sitting in a wooden captain's chair with her legs crossed and a black high heel dangling from her toes.

He scratched his head. "Yeah, I guess it is."

She studied him more closely. "Is something wrong?"

He shrugged.

She bent forward and began thrusting books aside, flopping heavy binders of fabric samples off the top of a heap, eventually unearthing a chair of sorts.

"Here . . . sit down."

He sat.

"What's wrong?"

He slouched back in the chair, crossed an ankle over a knee and poked at the blue rubber edge of his Reebok.

"I just saw Dad."

"Oh . . ." Her eyebrows arched. The word escaped her in an extended syllable as she, too, sat back in her chair, studying Randy. Her forearms rested along the worn wooden arms and in one hand she held a yellow pencil with her thumb folded over the red eraser. "Where?"

"We tried on tuxedos together."

"Did you talk?"

Randy spit on one finger and rubbed some dirt off the edge of his shoe sole. "Not really." He rubbed some more. "He wanted to buy me lunch but I said no."

"Why?"

Randy forgot his shoe and looked up. "Why! Shit, Mom, you know why!"

"No I don't. Tell me. If you said no and it's bothering you so much, why didn't you go with him?"

"Because I hate him."

"Do you?"

Their eyes locked in silence.

"Why should I go with him?"

"Because it's the adult thing to do. It's how relationships are handled, it's how wrongs are righted, and because I think you want to. But after six years it takes a little swallowing of pride, and that's hard."

Randy's anger flared. "Yeah, well, why should I swallow my pride when I never did anything to him. He's the one who did it to me!"

"Hold your voice down, Randy," she said calmly. "There are customers downstairs."

Randy whispered, "He walked out on me, I didn't walk out on him!"

"You're wrong, Randy. He walked out on me, not on you."

"It's the same thing, isn't it?"

"No, it's not. It hurt him very much to leave you and Lisa. He made many efforts to see you over the years but I made sure that didn't happen."

"But—"

"And in all these years I wonder if you've ever asked yourself why he walked out on me."

"What do you mean why? For Darla."

"Darla was the symptom, not the disease."

Disgusted, Randy said, "Aw, come on, Mom, who put that idea in your head? Him?"

"I've had a long examination of conscience lately, and I've discovered that your dad wasn't the only one at fault in the divorce. We were very much in love once, you know. When we were first married, when we had you kids—why, there was no family that was happier. Do you remember those times?"

Randy was sitting the way losers sit on the sidelines during the last thirty seconds of a championship basketball game. He stared at the floor between his Reeboks and made no reply.

"Do you remember exactly when it started to change?"

Randy said nothing.

"Do you?" she repeated softly.

He lifted his head. "No."

"It started when I went back to college. And do you know why?"

Randy waited, looking disconsolate, studying his mother.

"Because I didn't have time for your dad anymore. I came home at the end of the day and there was a family to take care of and housework to do, besides studying, and I was so set on doing it all that I let the most important thing go—my relationship with your dad. I'd get upset with him because he wouldn't help me around the house, and, yes, he was at fault for that but I never *asked* him nicely, we never sat down and talked about it. Instead, I made cutting remarks occasionally, and the rest of the time I zoomed around the house with my mouth tight, feeling like a martyr. Then it became a bone of contention between us. He refused to help me and I refused to ask him to, and pretty soon it was left up to you kids, and you weren't old enough to do it well, so most of the time things were in a mess. Now, if all that was going on in the rest of the house, what do you think was going on in the bedroom?"

Randy only stared at his mother.

"Nothing. And when nothing goes on in the bedroom it sounds the death knell to a relationship between a man and a wife. And that was my fault, not your dad's. . . . That's why he found Darla."

Randy's cheeks grew pink. Bess tipped her chair forward and rested her elbows on her lap.

"You're old enough to hear this, Randy. You're old enough to learn from it. Someday you'll be married, and at first it'll be a bed of roses, and then the humdrum starts in and you forget to do the small things that made that person fall in love with you in the first place. You stop saying good morning, and picking up his shoes when he forgets to take them to his closet, and bringing home the one special kind of Dairy Queen he likes. After all, it's out of your way and you're in a hurry. When he says, Do you want to take a bike ride after supper? you say no because you've had a rough day, so he goes alone and you don't stop to realize that if you'd gone with him it would have made your day a little better. And when he takes a shower before bed, you roll over and pretend to be asleep already because, believe it or not, you begin to consider sex work. You stop doing these things, and then the other one stops doing them, and pretty soon you're substituting criticism for praise, and giving orders instead of making requests, and letting sex fall by the wayside, and in no time at all the whole marriage falls apart."

A long silence passed before Bess sat back in her chair and went on ruminating quietly.

"I remember once, just before we broke up, your dad said to me, We never laugh anymore, Bess. And I realized it was true. You've got to keep laughing, no matter how hard times seem to be. It's what gets you through, and if you really stop to analyze it, one person trying to make another one laugh is a way of showing love, isn't it? It says, I care about you. I want to see you happy. Your dad was right. We had stopped laughing."

Bess set her chair in motion. The spring beneath the seat made a tick with each slight undulation while Randy studied her crossed legs. From downstairs came the *tt-tt-tt-tt* of Heather closing out the cash register for the day; then she turned on the lamps in the front window and called, "I'm going now. I'll lock the front door on my way out."

"Thanks, Heather. Have a nice weekend."

"You, too. 'Bye, Randy."

" 'Bye, Heather," he called.

When she was gone, the sense of intimacy doubled with all quiet below, and the overhead lights darkened. Only the dim light from Bess's desk lamp spread a brandy-colored glow on her abandoned work. She went on speaking in the same quiet tone as before. "I had a talk with Grandma Dorner a while back. It was after I saw your dad at Lisa's. I asked her to tell me, after all these years, why she'd never taken my side during the divorce. She verified all these things I've just told you and more."

Randy met his mother's eyes again as her tone took on sudden passion. Once more she leaned toward him earnestly.

"Listen to me, Randy. I've spent six years telling you all the reasons you should blame your dad, and now I've spent a few minutes telling you why you should blame me. But the truth is, you shouldn't blame anyone. Your dad and I both had a part in the breakup of our marriage. Each of us made mistakes. Each of us got hurt some. Each of us retaliated. You got hurt, too, and you retaliated. . . ." She took his hand. "I understand that . . . but it's time to reassess, dear."

He fixed his eyes on their joined hands, rubbing his thumb over hers. He appeared sheer miserable. "I don't know, Mom."

"If I can, you can." She squeezed his hand in encouragement.

He remained passive, disconsolate, answering nothing.

After some time, Bess swiveled toward her desk and began clustering her work, though she had little spirit for it. She scooped together a few papers, then swung back to Randy.

"You get to look more like him every day. It really does things to my insides sometimes when I turn and catch a glimpse of you standing the way he used to, or grinning the way he used to." She reached out and took both his hands loosely, turning them palms up within her own. "You got his hands," she said. "And his eyes." She looked into them and let a moment of silence pass before smiling gently. "Try as you might to deny you're his, you can't. And that's what hurts most, isn't it, honey?"

He made no reply but the expression in his eyes told her this day had made a deep impression on him.

"Well!" With forced brightness she sat back and checked her watch. "It's getting late and I have a little more work to do here while it's quiet."

"You going home then?"

"In about an hour."

"What's so important that it keeps you here on a Saturday night?"

"Actually, it's some work for your dad. I'm doing the interior design work for his new condo."

"When did all this happen?"

"I went to see it this week."

"Are you two getting back together or something?"

"No, we're not getting back together. He hired me to decorate his place, is all."

"Do you *want* to get back together?"

"No, but it feels better treating him civilly than it did being enemies. There's something about being hateful that deteriorates a person. Well, listen, honey, I really should get back to work, okay?"

"Yeah, sure. . . ." Randy rose and went down one step so he could stand erect. He turned back to his mother. "I'll see you at home, then. You fixing supper when you get there?"

A shaft of guilt struck Bess deep. "I'm afraid not. I have a date with Keith."

"Oh . . . well . . ."

"If I'd known you wanted to, I would have—"

"No, no . . . hell, I'm no baby. I can find supper by myself."

"What will you do tonight, then?"

"I'll probably go up to Popeye's. There's a new band playing there."

"See you at home in an hour or so."

When Randy was gone Bess turned back to her graph paper but sat staring at it with the pencil idle in her hands. Tonight was one of those rare nights when Randy truly wanted to be with her, and she felt devastated for having turned him down. But how was a mother to know? He was nineteen, she forty. They lived in the same house but went their separate ways. Most Saturday nights he wouldn't have stayed home if she'd cooked a five-course meal.

But all the commonsense self-rebuttal in the world would not assuage her guilt. A thought came to accompany it, to add weight to the burden she already carried:

if Michael and I had never divorced, we'd be there together on nights like this when Randy needs us. If we had never divorced, he wouldn't be going through this pain in the first place.

On the street a short distance from the Blue Iris, Randy slammed his car door, started the engine and sat staring at the windshield while it collected his breath and turned it to frost. The streets of Stillwater were deserted, the ice along the curbs was too dirty and pitted to reflect the red stoplights. Dark had fallen. By 6:30 the streets would be strung with cars as diners came out to enjoy the restaurants, but now at the close of the business day the whole town looked like the aftermath of a nuclear power leak—not a moving soul about. A semi lumbered up Main Street from the south. He could hear it coming, downshifting, rumbling. He watched it appear at the corner ahead and make a right-hand turn toward the lift bridge, heading east into Wisconsin.

He didn't want to go home.

He didn't want to go to Bernie's.

He didn't want to be with any girls.

He didn't want any fast food.

He decided to drive over to Grandma Dorner's. She was always cheery, and there was always something to eat over there, plus he liked her new place.

Stella Dorner answered his knock and swept him into her arms for a hug. "Well, Randy Curran, you handsome thing, what are you doing here on a Saturday night?"

She smelled like ritzy perfume when he hugged her. Her hair was combed fluffy and she had on a fancy blue dress. "Just came to see my best girl." When he released her she laughed and lifted her hands to her left ear to fit it with a pierced earring.

"You're a doggone liar but I love it." She turned a circle and her skirt flared. "There, how do I look?"

"You're a killer, Gram."

"I hope he thinks so. I've got a date."

"A date!"

"And he's darned good-looking, too. He's got all his hair, all his teeth *and* his gallbladder! A darned nice set of pecs, too, if I do say so myself."

Randy laughed.

"I met him at my exercise class. He's taking me dancing to the Bel Rae Ballroom."

Randy scooped her close and executed an Arthur Murray–style turn. "Stand him up and go with me instead."

She laughed and pushed him away. "Go find your own girlfriend. Have you got one, by the way?"

"Mmm . . . got my eye on one."

"What's the matter with *her?*" She gave his arm a love pat as she swung away, crescendoing as she walked toward her bedroom. "So how's everything with you?"

"Fine," he called, ambling into the living room. There were lights on all over the condo, with music playing on a component set and a painting on an easel by the sliding glass doors.

"I hear you're going to be in a wedding," Stella called from the far end of the place.

"How about that."

"And I also hear you're going to be an uncle."

"Can you believe it?"

"Do I look like a great-grandma to you?"

"Are you kidding? Hey, Gram, did you paint these violets?"

"Yes, how do you like them?"

"Jeez, they're good, Gram! I didn't know you could paint!"

"Neither did I! It's fun." The lights went off in the far bedroom, the bathroom, the hall, and Stella breezed into the living room, wearing a necklace that matched her earrings. "Did you find a band to play with yet?"

"Nope."

"Are you trying?"

"Well . . . not lately."

"How do you expect to find a band if you don't keep trying?" The doorbell rang and Stella said, "Oh, there he is!" She skipped once on her way to answer. Randy followed, feeling like the old one there.

The man who came in had wavy silver hair, shaggy eyebrows, a firm chin and a nice cut on his suit. His pecs didn't look too bad, either.

"Gil," she said. "This is my grandson, Randy. He just dropped in to say hello. Randy, this is Gilbert Harwood." The two shook hands, and Gil's grip was hearty. They made small talk but Randy could see the pair was eager to be going.

Minutes later he found himself back in his car, watching his grandma drive off with her date. Hungrier. Lonelier.

He headed back down McKusick Lane to the stop sign at Owens Street, where he sat observing the collection of cars around The Harbor across the street. He parked and went into the crowded beer joint, slid onto a bar stool and ordered a glass of tap beer. The place was smoky and smelled like the grill was in use. The customers were potbellied, gruff-voiced and had a lot of broken capillaries in their faces.

The guy beside Randy wore a Minnesota Twins billcap, blue jeans and an underwear shirt beneath a soiled, quilted vest. His forearms rested on the bar while he turned his head and glanced at Randy from beneath puffy eyelids. "How's it goin'?" he said.

"Good . . . good," Randy replied and took a swig from his glass.

They sat with their elbows two inches apart, sipping beer, listening to Randy Travis sing a two-year-old song on the jukebox, and the sizzle of cold meat hitting a hot grill in the kitchen, and occasional loud bursts of laughter. Somebody came in and the cold air momentarily chilled the backs of their legs before the door thumped closed. Randy watched eight faces above eight bar stools turn and check out the new arrivals before returning indifferently to their beers. He finished his own, got off the stool, fished a quarter from his pocket and used the pay phone to dial Lisa's number.

Her voice sounded hurried when she answered.

"Hey, Lisa, it's Randy. You busy?"

"Yeah, sort of. Mark is here and we're making spanakopita to take to an all-

Greek supper over at some friends' of ours. We're in butter and filo to our elbows!"

"Oh, well, listen, it's no big deal. I was just gonna see if you wanted to watch a video or something. Thought I could pick one up and come over."

"Gosh, Rand, sorry. Not tonight. Tomorrow night, though. I'll be around then."

"Yeah, well maybe I'll stop over then. Listen, have a good time tonight and say hi to Mark."

"Will do. Call me tomorrow, then."

"Yeah, sure. 'Bye."

Back in his car, Randy started the engine, turned on the radio and sat awhile with his hands hanging loosely on the wheel. He hiccuped once, then belched and studied the lights of the houses on either side of the Owens Street hill. What were they all doing in there? Little kids having supper with their folks. Young married couples having supper with each other. What would Maryann Padgett say if he called her up and asked her out? Hell, he didn't have enough money to take her anyplace decent. He'd spent that sixty bucks on pot earlier this week, and his gas tank was nearly empty, and the payment on his drum set was due, and payday wasn't until next Friday.

Shit.

He rested his forehead on the wheel. It was icy and brought a sharp stab of cold that concentrated in the back of his neck.

He lifted his head and pictured his dad's reflection in the mirror today beside his own while they'd zipped up their flies and experimented with tying bow ties. He wondered where they'd have gone if he'd said yes to lunch, what they'd have talked about, if they'd be together now.

He checked his watch. Not even seven yet. His mother would still be home, getting ready for her date with Keith, and he'd just be in their way if he got there before they left; and his mother would get that guilty look on her face for leaving him after he'd opened his big mouth at the store and asked if she was making supper.

Everybody had somebody. Everybody but him.

He reached into his pocket, found his bat and the Ziploc bag of marijuana and decided, To hell with it all.

Chapter 8

Bess and Keith ate at Lido's at a table beneath a potted tree trimmed with miniature lights. The minestrone was thick and spicy, the pasta homemade and the chicken parmigiana exquisite. When their plates had been removed they sat over wine and spumoni.

"So . . ." Keith said, fixing his stare on Bess. He wore glasses thick enough to magnify his eyes. His face was round, his sandy hair thinning, allowing the tree lights to reflect from his skull between the strands. "I've been waiting all evening for you to mention Michael."

"Why?"

"Isn't it obvious?"

"No, it's not. Why should I mention Michael?"

"Well, you've been seeing him lately, haven't you?"

"I've seen him three times but not in the way you infer."

"*Three* times?"

"I hardly thought I'd get through Lisa's wedding with*out* seeing him."

"The night Lisa set you up, and the night of the dinner at the in-laws." Keith ticked them off on his fingers. "When was the third time?"

"Keith, I don't appreciate being grilled like this."

"Can you blame me? This is the first time I've seen you since he came back on the scene."

Bess pressed a hand to her chest. "I divorced the man, are you forgetting?"

Keith took a sip of wine, lowered the glass and remarked, "You're the one who seems to be forgetting. I'm still waiting to hear about the third time you saw him."

"If I tell you, will you stop haranguing me?"

He stared at her awhile before nodding stiffly and picking up his spoon.

"I went to see his condo. I'm going to decorate it for him. Now could we just finish our spumoni and go?"

With his spoon poised over his ice cream, Keith asked, "Are you coming over tonight?"

Bess felt him watching her minutely. She ate some spumoni, met his eyes and replied, "I don't think so."

"Why?"

"I have a lot of work to do at home tomorrow. I want to get up early for church. And something's come up with Randy that's on my mind. I think I should be there tonight."

"You put everything and everybody else before me."

"I'm sorry, Keith, but I . . ."

"Your kids, your work, your ex-husband, they all come before me."

She said gently, "You demand a lot."

He leaned closer to her and whispered fiercely, "I'm sleeping with you, don't I have a right?"

He was so close she could detect the subtle color shadings in his green-brown eyes. She found herself unmoved by his resentment, grown very tired of fighting this fight. "No. I'm sorry, but no."

He pulled back and his lips thinned.

"I've asked you so many times to marry me."

"I've been married, Keith, and I never want to go through that again."

"Then why do you keep seeing me?"

She considered carefully before answering. "I thought we were friends."

"And if that's not enough for me?"

"You'll have to decide."

His spumoni had melted into a sickly green puddle. He pushed it aside, took a deep breath and said, "I think we'd better go."

They rose and left the restaurant politely. At the coat check, he held her coat. At the entry, he held the door. At his car, he unlocked the passenger door and waited while she got in. Inside his car they buckled their seat belts and headed for his place in silence. She had left her car parked at the foot of his driveway. He passed it and stopped before the garage door, which he got out to open. When he'd pulled inside, when the headlights were off and the engine silenced, Bess unsnapped her seat belt but neither of them moved. The beam from the streetlight stopped short of the car, leaving them in blackness. Beneath the hood the engine ticked as it cooled. The absence of warmth from the heater chilled Bess's legs. The absence of warmth in her heart chilled much more.

She turned to Keith and laid her hand on the seat between them. "Keith, I think maybe we should break it off."

"No!" he cried. "I knew this was coming but it's not what I want. Please, Bess . . ." He took her in his arms. Hampered by their heavy winter outerwear, the embrace was bulky. ". . . You've never given us a real chance. You've always held yourself aloof from me. Maybe it's something I've done and if it is I'll try to change. We could work things out, we could have a nice life together, I just know we could. Please, Bess . . ."

He kissed her heavily, wetting her mouth and spreading the taste of wine into it. She found herself slightly revolted and eager to be away from him. He released her mouth but held her head in both hands with his forehead against hers. "Please, Bess," he whispered. "We've been together for three years. I'm forty-four years old and I don't want to start looking for someone else."

"Keith, stop it."

"No . . . please, don't go. Please come inside. Come to bed with me . . . Bess, please."

"Keith, don't you see? We're a convenience for each other."

"No. I love you. I want to marry you."

"I can't marry you, Keith."

"Why? Why can't you?"

She had no desire to hurt him further. "Please don't make me say it."

As he grew desperate his voice became pleading. "I know why, I've known all along, but I can make you love me if you just give me the chance. I'll be anything you want . . . anything, if only you won't leave me."

"Keith, stop it! You're abasing yourself."

"I don't care. I'll even abase myself for you."

"But I don't want you to. You have a lot to offer a woman. I'm just not the right one."

"Bess, please . . ." He tried to kiss her again, groping for her breast.

"Keith, stop it. . . ." Their struggle became ferocious and she shoved him back, hard. *"Stop it!"*

His head struck the window. Their breathing beat heavily in the confined space.

"Bess, I'm sorry."

She grabbed her purse and opened her door.

"Bess!" he pleaded, "I said I'm sorry."

"I have to go," she said, scrambling from the car with her heart clubbing and her limbs trembling, welcoming the rush of cold air and the sight of her own car in the nearby shadows. She hurried toward it, running the last several yards after she heard his car door opening.

"Bess, wait! I'd never hurt you, Bess!" he called. Her car door cut off his last word as she slammed and locked it, then rummaged in her purse for her keys. The sound of all four automatic locks clacking down should have calmed her but she found herself shuddering and digging frantically, then peeling out of his driveway in reverse.

A quarter mile up the street she realized her hands were gripping the wheel, her back was rigid and tears were running down her cheeks.

She pulled to the curb, dropped her forehead to the steering wheel and waited for the tears and shakes to dissolve.

What had happened to her back there? She knew full well Keith would not hurt her, yet her revulsion and fear had been genuine. Was he right? Did his being her lover give him the right to expect more from her? She *had* always held herself aloof from him: this much was true. Her children *had* often come first, and she *had* frequently put him off in favor of business that could have been delayed.

Furthermore, she was beginning to suspect perhaps Michael did play a part in her rather sudden severing of ties with Keith. He had been the one calling out apologies as she'd run away, but perhaps it was she who owed them.

She thought of Michael too much during the week that followed. While she leafed through wallpaper and furniture catalogs she pictured his empty rooms and recalled their voices echoing off the white ceramic tiles of the empty kitchen. She saw his damp towel, his toothbrush, his mattresses on the floor—most often his mattresses on the floor. Though she was divorced from him it was impossible to divorce herself from the knowledge of him, and sometimes she pictured him moving about the rooms, in intimate disarray, the kind only a wife or lover can know, or in an equally intimate freshly dressed state, with his skin still flushed from a shave and his lips still shiny from the shower. She saw him in a suit with his tie in a Windsor knot, still in his stocking feet, picking up his change, money clip and flat, flat billfold that held little more than his driver's license and two credit cards (he hated bulging out his rear pocket). And last, before he donned his shoes, she saw him opening the penknife he always carried, standing in the bedroom beside the dresser and cleaning his fingernails. He did it every morning without fail; in all the years she'd known him she'd rarely seen him with dirt beneath his nails. It was part of the reason she so loved his hands.

She unconscionably worked on Michael's designs before seven others that had been in her files longer. She knew things he liked: long davenports a man could stretch out on, chairs with thick arms and matching ottomans, the *USA Today* with his breakfast, fires at suppertime, schefflera plants, things with rounded corners rather than squared, real leather, diffused lighting.

She knew things he disliked: scatter rugs, doilies, hanging plants, clutter, busy florals, the colors yellow and orange, twelve-foot telephone cords that got stretched out and testy, television playing at mealtimes.

It was hard to remember a job she'd enjoyed more or had designed with as much confidence. How ironic that she knew his tastes better now than she had when planning the house in which the two of them had lived together. Having carte blanche with his budget didn't hurt, either.

She called him on Thursday.

"Hi, Michael, it's Bess. I've got your design all worked up and wondered when you can come to the store and go over it with me."

"When would you like?"

"As I said before, I try to make the appointments at the end of the day so that we won't be interrupted. How's five o'clock tomorrow?"

"Fine. I'll be there."

The following day, a Friday, she went home at 3:30, washed her face, put on fresh makeup, touched up her hair, changed into a freshly pressed suit and returned to the store in time to lay out the materials for her presentation and dismiss Heather with ten minutes to spare.

When Michael came in the window lamps were lit, the place smelled like fresh coffee and at the rear of the store around the grouping of wicker furniture, the materials for Bess's presentation stood at the ready, fabrics draped, wallpaper books standing; textures, colors and photographs overlapped.

She heard the door open and he came in bringing the smell of winter and the sound of the five o'clock traffic moving on the street behind him. When the door sealed it off Bess went forward, smiling.

"Hello, Michael, how are you? I'll lock that now and turn over the sign." She had to shinny past him in the limited space between her floor stock. The profusion of tables, baskets and glassware filled up all but the most meager traffic paths. She locked the door, reversed the OPEN sign and turned to find him perusing the walls, which were hung with framed prints and wall decor clear up to the blue iris border strip just below the cove molding. He turned her way, still looking up, unbuttoning his coat and blocking the aisle. The store seemed suddenly crowded with his presence, its proportions so much better suited to women.

"You've done a lot with this place," he said.

"It's crowded, and the loft is unbearable in the summer, but when I think of getting rid of it I always seem to get nostalgic and change my mind. Something keeps me here."

His eyes stopped when they reached her and she became aware that he, too, had freshly groomed for this meeting: she could tell by the absence of four-o'clock shadow and the faint scent of British Sterling.

"May I take your coat?"

It was gray wool and heavy in her hands when he shrugged it off along with a soft plaid scarf. She had to say excuse me to get around him once more. Hanging the coat on the back of the basement door, she caught a whiff of scent from it, not simply a bottled scent but a combination of cosmetics and fresh air and his car and himself—one of those olfactory legacies a man leaves on a woman's memory.

She drew a deep breath and turned to conduct business. "I've got everything laid out here at the back of the store," she said, leading the way to the wicker seats. "May I get you a cup of coffee?"

"Sounds good. It's cold out there."

He waited, standing before the settee, until she set the cup and saucer on the coffee table and took an armchair to his right.

"Thanks," he said, freeing a button on his suit jacket as he sat. The furniture was low and his knees stuck up like a cricket's. He took a sip of coffee while she opened a manila folder and extracted the scale drawings of his rooms.

"We'll start with the living/dining room. Let me show you the wallpaper first so you can be picturing it as a backdrop for the furnishings as I describe them." Surrounded by samples, she presented his living room the way she envisioned it—subtle wallpaper of cream, mauve and gray; vertical blinds; upholstered grouping facing the fireplace; smoked-glass tables; potted plants.

"I seem to remember you liked our schefflera plant and watered it when I forgot to, so I thought it was safe to plan live plants into your furniturescape."

She glanced at him and found him considering the collected samples. He shifted his regard to her and said, "I think I like it. Actually, I like the sound of everything so far."

She smiled and went on, laying out her suggestions.

For the formal dining area a smoked-glass Swaim table on a brass base, surrounded by fully upholstered chairs.

For the foyer, a large mirror sculpture above a sassy Jay Spectre console table, flanked by a pair of elegant LaBarge side chairs upholstered in tapestry.

For the gallery, mirrored walls and a single faux pedestal directly beneath the chandelier, highlighting the sculpture of his choice.

A desk, chair, credenza, feather lamp and bookshelves for his drafting room.

For the guest bedroom, an art deco bed and dresser in cream lacquer, and a heavier concentration of lavender in the fabrics.

For the master bedroom, art deco once again—a three-piece suite in black lacquer from Formations, along with torchères and an upholstered chair. She suggested that the bedspread, wallpaper and vertical blinds all match.

She'd saved the coup d'état for last. For the family room, sumptuous Natuzzi Italian leather on a loose-cushioned sofa of cream that stretched out into forever and turned two corners before it got there.

"Italian leather is the finest money can buy, and Natuzzi is the best in the industry," she told him. "It's expensive but worth it, and since you gave me carte blanche on the budget, I thought you might enjoy the sheer luxury."

"Mm, I would." Michael studied the colored brochure of the curved sofa. She recognized the look of covetousness on his face.

"Exactly how much is 'expensive'?"

"I'll tell you later but for now submerge yourself in fantasy. The sticker shock will come at the end of the presentation, so if you don't mind waiting . . ."

"All right, whatever you say."

"The sofa is available in cream or black, and either color would fit but I thought we'd go with cream in the family room. Besides, black shows dust. Here, let me show you the entertainment unit I think would be really wonderful."

It was double wide and could be completely closed to reveal a solid, sleek surface of whitewashed oak.

"Whitewashing is being used a lot. It's rich yet casual, and I've repeated it in this ice-cream table and bentwood chairs for the adjacent informal eating area."

There were more wallpapers, fabric samples, wood swatches and photographs to be considered, as well as furniture layout. By the time she'd covered the highlights it was 7:30 and she'd lost his eye contact and could see that he was suffering data saturation.

"I know I've given you a lot to consider but believe it or not, there's still more. We've barely touched on the accent pieces—floor urns, wall decor, lamps and smaller case goods, but I think we've covered enough tonight. Most people do a room at a time. Doing an entire home is Olympian."

He leaned back, flexed his shoulders and sighed.

She laid a paper-clipped sheaf of papers on the table before him.

"Here's the bad news you've been waiting for. A breakdown, room-by-room and item-by-item with an allowance for additional small decor, which I'll select as I go—always with your approval, of course. The grand total is $76,300."

Michael looked as if he'd been poleaxed. "Holy old nuts!"

Bess threw back her head and laughed.

"You think it's funny!" He scowled.

"I haven't heard that expression in years. You're the only one I ever knew who said it."

Michael ran a hand over his hair and puffed out his cheeks. "Seventy-six thousand . . . Crimeny, Bess, I said I trusted you."

"That's including the Natuzzi sofa, which by itself is eight thousand, and a custom-made five-by-seven rug for in front of the living-room fireplace. We could drop those two items and save you almost ten thousand. Also the mirrored walls in the gallery are fifteen hundred. I went with some pretty classy designers, too—Jay Spectre, LaBarge, Henredon—these are makers who set standards in the industry."

"And how much am I paying you?"

"It's all there." She pointed at the sheaf of papers. "A straight ten percent. Most independents will charge you the wholesale price plus ten percent freight, and seventy-five dollars an hour for their design and consultation time. And believe me, those hours can mount up. It's also important to realize that the term 'wholesale price' is arbitrary, since they can say it's whatever they want it to be. My price includes freight and delivery, and my one-time trip charge, you'll remember, was only forty dollars, which I'll apply toward the cost of the job if you decide to go with me. You're welcome to compare, if you wish."

She sat back, collected, with her eyes leveled on Michael while he looked over the list. He studied it in detail, only the rustle of the turning pages marking the passing minutes. She rose, refilled his coffee cup and returned to her chair, crossing her legs and waiting in silence until he finished reading and closed the sheets.

"The price of furniture has gone up, hasn't it?" he asked.

"Yes, it has. But so has your own social status. You own your own firm now, you're very successful. It's only right that your home should reflect that success. I should think that in time you'll have more and more clients into your home. Decorated as I've suggested, it will make a strong statement about you."

He studied her without blinking until she wanted to look away but resisted. The light from the floor lamp on his far side put a luster of silver on the hair above his left ear. It painted his cheek gold and put a shadow in the relaxed smile line connecting his nose and mouth. He was an unnervingly handsome man, so handsome, in fact, that she had associated that handsomeness with unfaithfulness, so had intentionally chosen an unhandsome one in Keith. She realized that now.

"How much did you say that leather sofa's going to cost?"

"Eight thousand."

He considered awhile longer. "How long before I get this stuff?"

"The standard wait for custom orders is twelve weeks. Natuzzi takes sixteen because it's shipped directly from Italy and it comes over by boat, which takes four weeks by itself. I'll be frank with you and admit there's been some trouble over there lately with dock strikes, which could delay it even longer. But on the brighter side, sometimes we call the manufacturer and find out they have a piece already made up in the fabric we want and out it comes in six weeks. But figure twelve, on the average."

"And what about guarantees?"

"Against defects and workmanship? We're dealing with quality names here, not flea-market peddlers. They stand behind everything, and if they don't, I do."

"And what about the wallpaper and curtains? How long do I have to wait for them?"

"I'll place an order with the workroom immediately, and window treatments should be installed within six weeks. Wallpaper, much sooner. It's possible I could have paper hangers in here within two weeks, depending on their work schedule and the paper availability."

"You take care of all that?"

"Absolutely. I have several paper hangers who do my work. I contract them directly, so you never have to do any of that. All you have to do is make arrangements to have the door unlocked when they come to do the job."

Her estimate still lay on his lap. He glanced at the top sheet and his lower lip protruded.

She said, "I should warn you, I'll be in and out of your place a lot. I make it a point to check the wallpapering immediately after it's done, and I also accompany my installers when they come to put up window treatments. If there's something wrong, I want to find it myself instead of having you find it later. I also come out to see the furniture on site once it's been delivered, to make sure the color match is right. Do you have any problem with that?"

"No."

Bess began gathering up the floor plans and putting them into the manila folder. "It's a lot of money, Michael, there's no question about that. But any interior designer you hire is going to cost a lot, and I think I have one advantage any other wouldn't have. I know you better."

Their gazes met as she sat forward in her chair, with a stack of things on her knees, steadying them with both hands.

"You're probably right," he conceded.

"I know I'm right. The way you've always loved leather, you'll go crazy over that Italian sofa, and the rich rug in front of the fireplace, and the mirrors in the gallery. You'd love it all."

So would you, he thought, because he knew her well, too, knew these were colors, styles and designs she liked. For a moment he indulged in the fantasy that she had planned the place for both of them, as she had once before.

"May I have a while to think about it?"

"Of course."

She stood and he did likewise, while she bent to collect his cup and saucer. Michael checked his watch.

"It's almost eight o'clock and I'm starved. How about you?"

"Haven't you heard my stomach growling?"

"Would you want to . . ." He cut himself off and weighed the invitation before issuing it in full. "Would you want to grab a bite with me?"

She could have said no, she should put away all these books and samples, but in truth she'd need them for ordering if he decided to sign with her. She could have said she'd better get home to Randy, but at eight o'clock on a Friday night Randy would be anywhere but at home. She could have simply used good judgment and said no, without qualifying it. But the truth was she enjoyed his company and wouldn't mind spending another hour or so in it.

"We could go to the Freight House," she suggested.

He smiled. "They still make that dynamite seafood chowder?"

She smiled. "Absolutely."

"Then let's go."

She locked up and they left the Blue Iris with the lamps softly illuminating the window display. Outside the wind was biting, swaying the streetlights on their posts, whipping the electrical wires like jump ropes.

"Should we drive?" he asked.

"Parking is always horrendous there on weekends. We might as well walk, if you don't mind."

It was only two blocks but the wind bulldozed them from behind, sending their coattails skipping and Bess hotfooting it to keep from toppling on her face in her high-heeled pumps.

Michael took her elbow and held it hard against his ribs while they hurried along with their shoulders hunched. They crossed Main Street against a red light and as they turned onto Water Street the wind shifted and eddied as it stole between the buildings and formed whirlpools.

His hand and his ribs felt both familiar and welcome against her elbow.

The Freight House was exactly what its name implied, a red-brick relic from the past, facing the river and the railroad tracks, backing against Water Street with six wagon-high, arch-top doors through which freight had been loaded and unloaded in the days when both rail and river commerce flourished. Inside, high, wide windows and doors faced the river and gave onto an immense wooden deck, which in summer sported colorful umbrella tables for outside wining and dining. Now, in bitter February the corners of the windows held ice, and the yellow umbrellas were furled fast, like a flotilla of quayside sails. It smelled wonderful and felt better, being in out of the chill.

Unbuttoning his overcoat, Michael spoke to the hostess, who consulted an open book on her lectern.

"It'll be about fifteen minutes. You can have a seat in the bar if you'd like, and I'll call you."

They kept their coats on and perched on hip-high stools on opposite sides of a tiny square table.

"It's been a long time since I've been here," Michael remarked.

"I don't come here often, either. Occasionally for lunch."

"If I remember right, this is where we came to celebrate our tenth anniversary."

"No, our tenth we celebrated down in the Amana colonies, remember?"

"Oh, that's right."

"Mother took care of the kids and we went down for a long weekend."

"Then which one did we celebrate here?"

"Eleventh, maybe? I don't know, they sort of all run together, don't they?"

"We always did something special though, didn't we?"

She smiled in reply.

A waitress came and laid two cocktail napkins on the table. "What would you like?" she asked.

"I'll have a bottled Michelob," Michael answered.

"I'll have the same."

When the girl went away Michael asked, "You still like beer, huh?"

"Why should I have changed?"

"Oh, I don't know, new business, new image. You look like somebody who'd drink something in a tall stem glass."

"Sorry to disappoint you."

"It's not a disappointment at all. We drank a lot of beer together over the years. It's familiar."

"Mmm . . . yeah, a lot of hot summer evenings when we'd sit on the deck and watch the boats on the river."

Their beers arrived and after a skirmish about who would pay, they each paid for their own, then eschewed glasses in favor of drinking straight from the bottle.

When they'd each taken a deep swallow, Michael fixed his eyes on her and asked, "What do you do now on hot summer evenings, Bess?"

"I'm usually busy doing design work at home. What do you do?"

He thought awhile. "With Darla, nothing memorable. We both worked long hours and afterwards just sort of occupied the same lodge. She'd be gone, grocery shopping or having her hair done. Sometimes, when Mom was still alive, I'd go over to her house and mow her lawn. It's funny, because I had a yard service that took care of my own but after she had her stroke she couldn't handle the mower anymore, so I'd go over once a week or so and do it."

"Didn't Darla go with you?"

Michael scratched the edge of his beer label with a thumbnail. He worked up a little flap that was sticky on the backside. "It's a funny thing about second wives. That extended family bonding never seems to happen."

He took another swig of beer and met her eyes over the bottle. She dropped her gaze while he studied the way her lipstick held a tiny circle of wetness after she drank from her own bottle. Beneath the table she had one high heel hooked over the brass ring on the bar stool and her knees crossed. It made a pleasant shadow in her lap where her skirt dipped. Man-oh-man, she looked good.

"You know how it is," Michael continued. "A good Catholic mother doesn't believe in divorce so she never actually recognized my second marriage. She treated Darla civilly but even that took an effort."

Bess lifted her eyes. Michael was still studying her.

"I imagine that was hard for Darla."

"Yup," he said, and snapped out of his regardful pose as if nudged on the shoulder by an elder. "Aw, hell . . . water over the dam, right?"

The hostess came and said, "We have a booth ready for you now, Mr. Curran."

The backs of the booths went clear up to the ceiling, sealing them into a three-sided box which was lit by a single hanging fixture. While Bess spent some time perusing the oversized menu, Michael only flipped his open, glanced for five seconds and closed it again. She sat across from him, feeling his eyes come and go while he finished his beer and waited.

She closed her menu and looked up.

"What?" she said.

"You look good."

"Oh, Michael, cut it out." She felt a blush start.

"All right, you look bad."

She laughed self-consciously and said, "You've been staring at me ever since we came in here."

"Sorry," he said but went on staring. "At least you didn't get mad this time when I told you."

"I will if you don't stop it."

A waitress came to take their orders.

Michael said, "I'll have a grilled chicken sandwich and a bowl of seafood chowder."

Bess's eyes flashed up: she'd decided on the same thing. This used to happen often when they were married, and they would laugh at how their tastes had become so alike, then speculate on when they might start looking alike, the way people said old married couples did. For a moment Bess considered changing her choice but in the end stubbornly refused to be cowed by the coincidence.

"I'll have the same thing."

Michael looked at her suspiciously.

"You won't believe it but I'd made up my mind before you ordered."

"Oh," he replied.

Their seafood chowder came and they dipped into it in unison, then Michael said, "I saw Randy last Saturday. I asked if I could take him to lunch but he said no."

"Yes, he told me."

"I just wanted you to know I'm trying."

She finished her chowder and pushed the bowl back with two thumbs. He finished his and the waitress came and took away their bowls. When she was gone Michael said, "I've been doing some thinking since the last time we talked."

Bess was afraid to ask. This was too intimate already.

"About fault—both of ours. I suppose you were right about me helping around the house. After you started college I should have done more to help you. I can see now that it wasn't fair to expect you to do it all."

She waited for him to add *but,* and offer excuses. When he didn't she was pleasantly surprised.

"May I ask you something, Michael?"

"Of course."

"If I'm out of line just say so. Did you ever help Darla with the housework?"

"No."

She studied him quizzically awhile, then said, "Statistics show that most second marriages don't last as long as first ones, primarily because people go into them making the same mistakes."

Michael's cheeks turned ruddy. He made no remark but they both thought about their conversation throughout the rest of the dinner.

Afterward they divided the check.

When they reached the door of the restaurant, Michael pushed it open and held it while Bess passed before him into the cold. To her back he said, "I've decided to give you the job decorating my condo."

She came up short and turned to face him while behind him the door swung shut.

"Why?" she said.

"Because you're the best woman for the job. What do I do, sign a contract or something like that?"

"Yes, something like that."

"Then let's do it."

"Tonight?"

"Judging from how you handle yourself as a businesswoman, you've got a contract all made up back at the shop, right?"

"Actually, I do."

"Then let's go." He took her arm quite commandingly and they headed up the street. At the corner, when they turned into the wind it whistled in their ears and almost knocked them off their feet.

"Why are you doing this?" she shouted.

"Maybe I like having you poke around my house," he shouted back.

She balked. "Michael, if that's the only reason . . ."

He forced her to keep walking. "Just a joke, Bess."

As she unlocked the door of the Blue Iris, she hoped it was.

Chapter 9

February sped along. Lisa's wedding was fast approaching. The telephone calls from her to Bess came daily.

"Mom, do you have one of those pens with a feather at your store? You know . . . the kind for the guest book?"

"Mom, where do I buy a garter?"

"Mom, do you think I have to get plain white cake or can I have marzipan?"

"Mom, they need the money for the flowers before they make them up."

"Mom, I gained another two pounds! What if I can't get into the dress?"

"Mom, I bought the most beautiful unity candle!"

"Mom, Mark thinks we should have special champagne glasses engraved with our name and date but I think it's silly since I'm pregnant and can't even drink champagne anyway!"

"Mom, have you bought your dress yet?"

Since she hadn't, Bess set aside an afternoon on her calendar and called Stella to say, "The wedding is only two weeks away and Lisa threw a fit when she found out I don't have a dress yet. How about you? Have you got one?"

"Not yet."

"Do you want to go shopping?"

"I guess we'd better."

They drove into downtown Minneapolis, browsing their way from the Conservatory to Dayton's to Gavidae Commons, where they struck it lucky at Lillie Rubin. Stella, turning up her nose at the grandma image, found a hot little silvery white number with a three-tiered gathered skirt and perky sleeves to match, while Bess chose a much more sedate raw silk sarong suit in palest peach with a flattering tulip-shaped skirt. When they stepped out of their adjacent dressing rooms Bess gave Stella the once-over and said, "Wait a minute, who's the grandma here?"

"You," Stella replied, "I'm the great-grandma." Perusing her reflection in the mirror, she went on, "I'll be darned if I've ever been able to understand why the mothers of brides go to such great lengths to add fifteen years onto their age by buying those god-awful dowdy dresses that look like Mamie Eisenhower's curtains. Now *this* is how I feel!"

"It's very jaunty."

"Y' darned right it is. I'm bringing Gil Harwood along."

"Gil Harwood?"

"Do I look like a dancing girl?"

"Who's Gil Harwood?"

"A man who makes my nipples stand at attention."

"Mother!"

"I'm thinking of having an affair with him. What do you think?"

"Mother!"

"I haven't done any of that sort of thing since your father died, and I think I should before all my ports dry up. I did a little experimenting the last time Gil took me out, and it's definitely not his arteries that are hardening."

Bess released a gust of laughter. "Mother, you're outrageous."

"Better outrageous than senile. Do you think I'd have to worry about AIDS?"

"You're the outrageous one. Ask him."

"Good idea. How are things between you and Michael?"

Bess was saved from answering by the clerk, who approached and inquired, "How are you doing, ladies?" But she felt a flurry of reaction at the mention of his name and caught Stella's sly glance that said very clearly she knew something was stirring.

They bought the dresses and went on to search out matching shoes. When they were in Bess's car, heading east toward home, Stella resumed their interrupted conversation.

"You never answered me. How are things between you and Michael?"

"Very businesslike."

"Oh, what a disappointment."

"I told you, Mother, I'm not interested in getting tangled up with him again, but we did straighten out some leftover feelings that have been lingering since before we got the divorce."

"Such as . . ."

"We both admitted we could have worked a little harder at holding things together."

"He's a good man, Bess."

"Yes, I know."

Bess had little occasion to run into the good man between then and the wedding. The paper was hung in Michael's condo and though Bess went over to check it when the paperhangers were just finishing up, Michael wasn't there. She called him the next day to ask if he was satisfied.

"More than satisfied. It looks perfect."

"Ah, good."

"Smells like squaw piss, though."

Bess burst out laughing and even across the telephone wire felt a thrill of attraction that she'd been staving off ever since her last meeting with him. She had forgotten how genuinely funny Michael could be and how effortlessly he'd always been able to make her laugh.

"But you like it?"

"Yes, I do."

"Good. Listen, the invoices are starting to come in now on your furniture. So far it looks as though most things will be arriving in mid-May. No word yet on the Natuzzi from Italy but I'm sure that'll take longer. I'll let you know as soon as I hear."

"All right."

Bess paused before changing the subject. "Michael, I need to talk to you about the bills for Lisa's wedding. Some of them have already been paid and others are coming in, so how do you want to handle it? I've paid out eight hundred dollars already, so why don't you match it and add two thousand, and I'll add the same and Lisa can put it into her savings account and draw on it as she needs it? Then what's left over—if any is—we can split."

"Fine."

"I have the receipts for everything, and I'll be more than happy to send them to you if—"

"Heaven's sake, Bess, I trust you."

"Oh . . . well . . . thanks, Michael. Just send the check to Lisa, then."

"You really think we'll see any leftover money?"

Bess chuckled. "Probably not."

"Now you're thinking like a realist."

"But I don't mind spending it, do you?"

"Not at all. She's our only daughter."

The chance remark left the phone line silent while they reached back to their beginnings, wishing they could undo the negative part of their past and recapture what they'd once had. Bess felt an undeniable stirring, the urge to ask him what he'd been doing, where he was, what he was wearing, the kind of questions that signal infatuation. She quelled her foolhardiness and said instead, "I guess I'll see you at the rehearsal, then."

Michael cleared his throat and said in a curiously flat voice, "Yeah . . . sure."

When Bess hung up she tipped her desk chair back to its limit, drove both hands into her hair and blew an enormous breath at her loft ceiling.

Randy kept his car like the bottom of a bird cage. Whatever fell, stayed. The day of the groom's dinner and rehearsal he took the battered '84 Chevy Nova to the car wash and mucked 'er out. Fast-food containers, dirty sweat socks, empty condom packages, crumpled *Twin Cities' Readers*, unopened mail, unmailed mail, parking-lot receipts, a dried-up doughnut, empty pop cans, a curled-up Adidas, unpaid parking tickets—all got relegated to the bottom of a fifty-gallon garbage drum.

He vacuumed the floor, ran the mats through the washer, Armor Alled the vinyl, emptied the ashtrays, washed the windows, washed and dried the outside and bought a blue Christmas tree to hang from the dash and make the inside smell like a girl's neck.

Then he drove to Maplewood Mall and bought a new pair of trousers at Hal's, and a sweater at The Gap, and went home to put on his headset and play Foreigner's "I Want to Know What Love Is" and beat his drums and dream about Maryann Padgett.

The rehearsal was scheduled for six o'clock. At quarter to, when his mother asked if he wanted to ride to the church with her, he answered, "Sorry, Mom, but I've got plans for afterwards." His plan was to ask Maryann Padgett if he could drive her home.

When he walked into St. Mary's and saw Maryann, the oxygen supply in the vestibule seemed to disappear. He felt the way he had when he was nine years old and used to hang upside down on the monkey bars for five minutes, then try to walk straight. She was wearing a prim little navy-blue coat, and prim little navy-blue shoes with short, prim heels, and probably a prim little Sunday dress with a prim little collar, and talking to Lisa in prim, proper terms. She probably went to Bible camp in the summer and edited the school newspaper in the winter.

He'd never wanted to impress anyone so badly in his life.

Lisa saw him and said, "Oh, hi, Randy."

"Hi, Lisa." He nodded to Maryann, hoping his eyes wouldn't pop out of their sockets and bounce on the vestibule floor.

"Where's Mom?" Lisa asked.

"She's coming. We drove in separate cars."

"You and Maryann are going to be first up the aisle."

"Yeah? Oh, well, hey . . . how about that." *Bravo, Curran, you glib rascal, you. Really knocked her prim little socks off with that one.*

Maryann said, "I was just telling Lisa that I've never been in a wedding before."

"Me either."

"It's exciting, isn't it?"

"Yes, it is."

Inside his new acrylic sweater he was warm and quivering. She had this little pixie face with blue eyes about the size of Lake Superior; and pretty puffed lips and the teeniest, tiniest mole above the upper one but close enough that if you kissed her properly you'd kiss it, too; and not a fleck of makeup ruining any of it.

"Dressing up for first Communion is about as close as I've come to this," she remarked. The vestibule was crowded, and Lisa spied someone else she needed to talk to.

Left in a lull, Randy searched for something to talk about. "Have you always lived in White Bear Lake?"

"Born and raised there."

"I used to go to the street dances there in the summer during Manitou Days. They'd get some good bands."

"You like music?"

"Music is what drives me. I want to play in a band."

"Play what?"

"Drums."

"Oh." She thought awhile and said, "It's kind of a tough life-style, isn't it?"

"I don't know. I never had the chance to find out."

Father Moore came in and started getting things organized, and they all went inside the church and laid their coats in the rear pews, and sure enough, Maryann Padgett was wearing her Marion-the-librarian dress, some little dark-colored thing with a dinky white collar made of lace. Without mousse or squiggly waves in her hair, she was a throwback, and he was captivated.

Randy was standing in the aisle continuing to be dumbstruck by her when someone rested a hand on his shoulder blade.

"Hi, Randy, how's it going?"

Randy turned to encounter his father. He removed all expression from his face and said, "Okay."

Michael dropped his hand and nodded to the girl. "Hello, Maryann."

She smiled. "Hi. I was just saying, this is the first wedding I've ever been in, and Randy said it is for him, too."

"I guess it is for me, too, other than my own." Michael waited, letting his eyes shift to Randy but when no response came, he drifted away, saying, "Well . . . I'll be seeing you."

As Randy's expressionless gaze followed Michael, he repeated sarcastically, "Except for his own . . . both of them."

Maryann whispered, "Randy, that was your father!"

"Don't remind me."

"How could you treat him that way?"

"The old man and I don't talk."

"Don't talk! Why, that's awful! How can you not talk to your father?"

"I haven't talked to him since I was thirteen."

She stared at Randy as if he'd just tripped an old lady.

Father Moore asked for silence and the practice began. Randy remained put out with Michael for intruding on what had begun as a conversation with some possibilities. After the whole day of thinking about Maryann Padgett, cleaning up his car for her, dressing in new clothes for her, wanting to impress her, the whole thing had been shot by the old man's appearance.

Why can't he just lay off me? Why does he have to touch me, talk to me, make me look like a jerk in front of this girl when he's the one who's a jerk? I walked in here, I was ready to show Maryann I could be a gentleman, make small talk with her, get to know her a little and lead up to asking her out. The old man comes over and screws up the whole deal.

During the practice Randy was forced to observe his mother and father walking down the aisle on either side of Lisa, then sitting together in the front pew. There were times when he himself had to stand up front and face the congregation and could hardly avoid seeing them, side-by-side, as if everything was just peachy. Well, that was bullshit! How could she sit there beside him as if they'd never split up, as if it wasn't his fault the family broke up? She might say she had faults, too, but they were minor compared to his, and nobody was going to convince Randy differently.

When the business at the church ended they all went to a restaurant called Finnegan's, where the Padgetts had reserved a private room for the groom's dinner. Randy drove alone, arrived before Maryann and waited for her in the lobby. The door opened and she stepped inside, speaking with her father and mother, a smile on her face.

She saw him and the smile thinned, her speech faltered.

"Hello again," he said, feeling self-conscious waiting there with such obvious intent.

"Hello."

"Do you mind if I sit with you?"

She looked straight at him and said, "You'd do better to sit with your father but I don't mind."

He felt himself blushing—blushing, for Christ's sake—and said, "Here, I'll help you with that," as she began removing her coat.

He hung it up along with his own and they followed her parents into the reserved room, where a long table waited to accommodate the entire wedding party. Walking behind her, he studied her round white collar, which reminded him of something a Mennonite would wear, and her hair, dark as ink and falling in tiers to her shoulders, the tips upturned like dry oak leaves. He thought about writing a song about her hair, something slow and evocative, with the drums quiet at the beginning and building toward a climax, then ending with sheepskin mallets doing a cymbal roll that faded into silence.

He pulled out her chair and sat down beside her, at the opposite end of the table from his parents.

While they ate, Maryann sometimes talked and laughed with her father, on her right. Sometimes she did the same with Lisa or Mark, across the table, or bent forward to say something to her mother or one of her sisters, down the line. She said nothing to Randy.

Finally he asked, "Would you please pass the salt?"

She did, and flashed him a polite smile that was worse than none at all.

"Good food, huh?" he said.

"Mm-hmm." She had a mouthful of chicken and her lips were shiny. She wiped them with her napkin and said, "My folks wanted something fancier for the groom's dinner but this was all they could afford, and Mark said it was fine, as long as Mom didn't have to do all the cooking herself."

"You all get along really well, I guess . . . your family, I mean."

"Yes, we do."

He tried to think of something more to say but nothing came to mind. He grinned and glanced at her plate.

"You like chicken, huh?" She had eaten all of it and little else.

She laughed and nodded while their eyes met again.

"Listen," he said, his stomach in knots. "I was wondering if I could drive you home."

"I'll have to ask my dad."

He hadn't heard that answer since he was in the tenth grade and had just gotten his driver's license.

"You mean you want to?" he asked, amazed.

"I kind of suspected you'd ask me." She turned to her father, sitting back in her chair so Randy could hear their exchange. "Daddy, Randy wants to drive me home, okay?"

Jake touched his hearing aid and asked, "What?"

"Randy wants to drive me home."

Jake leaned forward, peered around Maryann to study Randy a moment and said, "I guess that would be all right but you have things to do early tomorrow, don't you?"

"Yes, Daddy, I'll get in early." She turned to Randy and said, "Okay?"

He raised his right hand like a Boy Scout. "Straight home."

When the meal was over there was a jumble of good-byes at the door. He held

Maryann's coat, then the heavy plate-glass door, and they walked across the snowy parking lot together.

"This one's mine," he said, reaching his Nova and walking around to open the passenger door for her, waiting until she was seated, then slamming it, feeling gallant and eager to extend every courtesy ever invented by men for women.

When he was sitting behind the wheel, putting his key in the ignition, she remarked, "Boys don't do that much anymore . . . open car doors."

He knew. He was one of them.

"Some girls don't want a guy to open doors for them. It's got something to do with women's lib hang-ups." He started the engine.

"That's the silliest thing I ever heard. I love it."

He felt all glowy inside and decided if she could be honest, so could he. "It felt good doing it, too, and you know what? Other than for my mother, I don't do it much, either, but I will from now on."

She buckled her seat belt, something else he rarely did, but he fished around and found his buried buckle and engaged it. He adjusted the heater, stalling for time, judging he'd have her at her doorstep in less than ten minutes. The floor fan came on and twisted the blue Christmas tree around and around on its string.

"It smells good in here," she said. "What is it?"

"This thing." He poked the tree and put the car into reverse and headed toward White Bear Avenue. It would have been more direct to take I-95 to 61 and go around the west side of the lake but he headed around the east side instead, driving twenty miles an hour in the thirty-mile zone through the residential district.

When they were halfway to her house he said, "Could I ask you something?"

"What?"

"How old are you?"

"I'm a senior. Seventeen."

"Are you going with anybody?"

"I don't have time. I'm in girls' basketball and track, and I work on the school paper and I spend a lot of time studying. I want to do something in either medicine or law, and I've applied to Hamline University. My folks can't afford to pay their tuition fees so I'll need a scholarship if I'm going to go there, which means I have to keep my grades up."

If he told her how he'd skated through high school she'd ask him to stop the car and let her out right here.

"How about you?" she asked.

"Me? Nope, don't go with anybody."

"College?"

"Nope, just high school."

"But you want to be a drummer."

"Yes."

"In a rock band?"

"Yes."

"And meanwhile?"

"Meanwhile, I work in a nut house."

"A what!" She was already amused.

"It's a warehouse, actually. I package fresh roasted nuts—peanuts, pistachios, cashews—it's a big wholesale house. Custom orders that go out to places all over America. Christmas is our biggest season. It really gets crazy in a nut house at Christmas."

She laughed, as people always did, but the comparison between their ambitions was pointed enough to sound ludicrous, even to him.

They rode in silence awhile before Randy said, "Jesus, I really sound like a loser, don't I?"

"Randy, I need to say something right up front."

"Say it."

"I'd just as soon you didn't say 'Jesus' that way. It offends me."

That was the last thing he'd expected. He hadn't even realized he'd said it. "Okay," he replied, "you got it."

"And as far as being a loser—well, that's all just a state of mind. I guess I've always thought if a person feels like a loser he ought to do something about it. Go to school, get a different job, do something to boost your self-esteem. That's the first step."

They reached her house and he parked on the street, leaving the engine running. There was a bunch of cars in the driveway—her parents', Lisa's, Mark's. The lights were on throughout the house. The living-room draperies were open and they could see people moving through the room.

Randy hunched his shoulders toward the steering wheel, joined his hands between his knees and looked straight out the windshield at a streetlight twenty feet away.

"Listen, I know you think I'm a jerk because I don't get along with my dad but maybe you'd like to hear why."

"Sure. I'm a good listener."

"When I was thirteen he had an affair and divorced my mother and married somebody else. Everything just sort of fell apart after that. Home, school. Especially school. I kind of drifted through."

"And you're still feeling sorry for yourself."

He turned his head, studied her awhile and said, "He screwed up our whole family."

"You think so?" He waited, eyeing her warily. "You aren't going to like what I have to say but the truth is, each of us is responsible for ourself. If you started sloughing off in school, you can't blame him for that. It's just easier if you do, that's all."

"Jesus, aren't we smug?" he replied.

"You said 'Jesus' again. Do it once more and I'm leaving."

"All right, I'm sorry!"

"I said you weren't going to like what I had to say. Your sister made it through. Your mother seems to have done all right. Why didn't you?"

He threw himself back into the corner of the seat and pinched the bridge of his nose. "Christ, I don't know!"

She was out of the car like a shot, slamming the door, leaping over the snowbank onto the sidewalk and heading for the house before he realized what he'd said. He opened his door and shouted, "Maryann, I'm sorry! It just slipped out!" When the house door slammed, he slugged the car roof with both fists and railed aloud, "Jesus Christ, Curran, what are you doing chasing this uptight broad!"

He flung his body behind the wheel, gunned the engine with the ear-splitting thunder of an Indy-500 ignition, peeled down the street fishtailing for a quarter of a block, rolled down the window, yanked the smelly Christmas tree off the radio knob, cutting his finger before the string broke, and hurled the thing into the street, cursing a blue streak.

He slewed around a corner at twenty-five miles an hour, came within inches of wiping out a fire hydrant, ran two stop signs and shouted at the top of his lungs, "Well, fuck you, Maryann Padgett! Get that? Fuck you!" He braked beside some strange house, got out his marijuana, had a couple good hits and waited for the euphoria to drift in and calm him.

He was smiling the last time he either said or didn't say, Yeah, fuck you, Maryann Padgett . . .

While Randy was escorting Maryann from the restaurant, Lisa was saying good night to her mother and father.

She gave Michael a hug first.

"See you tomorrow, Dad."

"Absolutely." He felt unusually sentimental and held her extra long, one of the last times he'd do so before she took another man's name. "I understand you're staying at the house tonight with Mom."

"Uh-huh. We moved all my stuff over to Mark's today."

"I'm glad. I like to think of you there with her tonight."

"Hey, Dad?" At his ear she whispered, "Keep up the good work. I think you're makin' points with Mom." She broke away and smiled. "See you at home, Mom. Good night, everyone!"

Michael hid his surprise while Lisa went out the door with Mark, leaving various stragglers behind. While helping Bess with her coat he remarked, "Lisa seems absolutely happy."

"I believe she is."

The rest of the Padgetts said good night and left. Michael and Bess were the last two in the place, standing near the plate-glass door, dawdling, putting on their gloves, buttoning their coats.

"It looks to me like something is cooking between Randy and Maryann," Michael remarked.

"They were together all night."

"I noticed."

"She's a pretty girl, isn't she?"

"I'll say."

"Why do mothers always make that remark first?" Bess said.

"Because they want pretty girls for their handsome sons, I guess. Fathers are no different. Hell, I'd just as soon see my kids end up with foxes instead of dogs."

Bess chuckled, meeting Michael's eyes while an unsettling quiet fell between them. They should go, should follow the others outside and say good night.

"She's very young, still in high school," Bess said.

"I noticed she asked her father's permission to go with Randy."

"Nice old-fashioned thing to see, isn't it?"

"Yes, it is."

A soft expression came into Bess's eyes. "They're a wonderful family, aren't they?"

"I thought it bothered you to be around wonderful families."

"Not as much as it used to."

"Why's that?"

She gave no answer. The restaurant was closing up. Someone was running a vacuum cleaner and their waitress came through, dressed in her winter coat, on her way home. They should walk out, too, sensibly, and end this cat-and-mouse game they were playing with their own emotions. Still, they stayed.

"You know what?" Michael said.

"What?" Bess said the word so softly it could scarcely be heard above the whining vacuum cleaner.

He'd intended to say, I wish I was going home with you, too, but thought better of it.

"I've planned a surprise for Lisa and Mark. I've ordered a limousine to pick them up tomorrow."

Bess's eyes widened. "You didn't!"

"Why? What's—"

"So did I!"

"Are you serious?"

"Not only that, I had to pay in advance for five hours, and it's nonrefundable!"

"So did I."

They began laughing. When they stopped they were smiling into each other's eyes. The restaurant manager came along and said, "Excuse me, we're closing."

Michael stepped back guiltily.

"Oh, I'm sorry."

They went out into the chill night air at last and heard a key turn in the lock behind them.

"Well," Michael said, his breath a white puff in the frigid air, "what are we going to do about that extra limo?"

Bess shrugged. "I don't know. Split the loss, I guess."

"Or treat ourselves. What do you say—wanna go to the wedding in a white limo?"

"Oh, Michael, what will people say?"

"People? What people? Want me to take a guess what Lisa would say? Or what your mother would say? Matter of fact, we could give the old doll a thrill and swing by her place on the way and pick her up, too."

"She's already got a date. He's picking her up."

"She does! Well, good for her. Anyone I know?"

"No. Somebody named Gil Harwood. Claims she's going to have an affair with him."

Michael reared back and laughed. "Oh, Stella, you're a real piss cutter." When his laughter subsided, he angled Bess a flirtatious grin. "Now, what about you?"

She grinned. "Do *I* want to have an affair? Michael, hardly."

"Do you want to ride in a limo?"

"Ohhhh . . ." She drew out the word coquettishly, as if to say, Oh, that's what you meant. "Do I want to ride in a limo? Certainly. Only a dummy would say no to an invitation like that, especially since the thing is paid for with her own money."

"Good." He grinned, pleased. "We'll let yours take Lisa and mine will come and pick you up. Four forty-five. We'll get there in time for pictures."

"Fine. I'll be ready."

They started toward the parking lot.

"My car's this way," he said.

"Mine's that way."

"See you tomorrow, then."

"Yup."

They turned and walked at a forty-five-degree angle away from one another. The night was so cold it made their teeth hurt. Neither of them cared. Reaching their cars, they unlocked their doors and opened them, then stood looking at each other across the nearly empty parking lot while the halogen lights turned everything the color of pink champagne.

"Hey, Bess?"

"What?"

It was a moment as sterling and clear as the silent city night around them, the kind of moment lovers remember years after it happens, for no particular reason except that in the midst of it Cupid seemed to have released his arrow and watched to see what mischief it might arouse.

"Would you call tomorrow a date?" Michael called.

The arrow hit Bess smack in the heart. She smiled and replied, "No, but Lisa would. Good night, Michael."

Chapter 10

To Lisa, spending her wedding eve in her childhood home seemed neat. Shortly after eleven, when she dropped her overnight bag on her bed, things were much as they'd been when she was a teenager. Randy was down in his room with his radio tuned low. Mom was in her bathroom cleansing off her makeup. It almost seemed as if Dad would shut off the hall light, stop in the doorway and say, "G'night, honey."

She dropped to the bed and sat looking at the room.

Same pale-blue flowered wallpaper. Same tiered bedspread. Same crisscross curtains. Same . . .

Lisa dumped her purse off her lap and radiated to the dresser. Into the mirror frame her mother had wedged her school pictures. Not just the second-grade one they'd laughed at the day she'd tried on the wedding dress but all thirteen of them, from kindergarten through twelfth. With her hands flat on the dresser and a smile on her face, Lisa studied them before turning to find, on the rocking chair in the corner, her Melody doll, and propped against its pink vinyl hand, the note from Patty Larson.

She picked up Melody, sat down with the doll on her lap and faced her closet doorway, where her wedding gown hung between the open bifold doors.

She was totally ready for this marriage. Nostalgia was fun but it failed to beckon her into those bygone days. She was happy to be altar-bound, happy to be pregnant, happy to be in love and happy she'd never taken up lodging with Mark.

Bess appeared in the doorway, dressed in a pretty peach nightgown and peignoir, rubbing lotion on her face and hands.

"You look all grown up, sitting there," she said.

"I feel all grown up. I was just thinking how absolutely ready I am for marriage. It's a wonderful feeling. And remember years ago when I asked you what you thought of girls moving in with guys, you said just try it and watch the shit hit the fan? Thanks for that."

Bess walked into the room, leaned over Lisa and kissed the top of her head, carrying with her the scent of roses. "I don't think I said it exactly like that but if the message stuck, I'm glad."

Lisa hugged her mother, her head nestled against Bess's breasts.

"I'm glad I'm here tonight. This is the way it should be."

When the hug ended Bess sat on the bed.

Lisa asked, "You know what I'm happiest about, though?"

"What?"

"You and Dad. It's so great to see you two sitting side-by-side again."

"We're getting along remarkably well."

"Any, ah . . ." Lisa made a hanky-panky gesture with a widespread hand.

Bess laughed quietly. "No. No *ah* anything. But we're becoming friends again."

"Well, hey, that's a start, isn't it?"

"Is there anything you want me to do for you tomorrow? I'm taking the whole day off so I've got time."

"I don't think so. It's hair in the morning and be at the church by five for pictures."

"Speaking of that, your father asked if he could drive you to the church. He said he'd pick you up here at quarter to five."

"Will you be here, too? And Randy? So we could all go to the church together?"

"I don't see why not."

"Wow, won't that be something . . . after six years. I can't wait."

"Well . . ." Bess said, rising. "It's early, and isn't that a miracle? I'm going to get a full night's rest and wake up bright and early with the whole morning to myself." She kissed Lisa's cheek. "Good night, dear." She looked into her happy eyes. "Sweet dreams, little bride. I love you."

"Love you, too, Mom."

The light over the kitchen stove was still on. Bess went down to turn it off. It was a rare occasion when Randy was home at this hour, so she indulged herself and continued down to the walkout level, where she knocked softly on his door. Music played low but no answer came. She opened the door and peeked inside. Randy lay on his side, facing the wall, both arms outflung, still dressed in the new clothes he'd worn earlier. On the opposite side of the room one dim lamp lit the top of his chest of drawers, and the ever-present lights on his component set spiked and fell like electronic graphs.

He always slept with the radio on. She'd never understood why or how he did so but no amount of nagging had changed his habit.

She approached the bed and braced a hand behind Randy while leaning over to kiss the crest of his cheek. So like his father he looked, young and innocent in slumber. She touched his hair; it even felt like Michael's, was the same dark color, the curl more pronounced.

Her son—so proud, so hurt, so unwilling to bend. She had seen Randy snub Michael tonight and thought him wrong. Her heart had gone out to Michael, and in that moment she'd felt a flash of bitterness toward Randy. Mothering was so complex: she didn't know how to handle this young man who hovered on a brink where an influence in either direction might decide his fate for years to come, possibly for life. She saw very clearly that Randy could be a failure in many regards. In human relations, in business and in that most important aspect of life, personal happiness.

If he fails, I'll be part of the reason.

She straightened, studied him a moment more, turned out the lamp and quietly slipped from the room, leaving the radio playing softly behind her.

When the door closed, Randy's eyes snapped open and he twisted to look back over his shoulder.

Whew, that was a close one.

He let his head drop to the pillow and rolled onto his back. He thought she'd come in to ask him some question, and all the while she'd been touching his hair he'd expected her to shake him and make him turn over. She'd have taken one look at his eyes and known, then he'd be out on his ass. He had no doubt she meant it the last time she'd warned him.

He was still loaded, the lights on the component set seemed threatening, as if they were attacking from the corner of his eye, and he was getting dry mouth and the munchies.

The munchies—God, they always got him, hard. And food never tasted so good as when he was high. He had to have something. He rolled from the bed and walked the mile and a half toward the door. Upstairs all was black. He felt his way to the kitchen, turned on the stove light and found a bag of Fritos. He searched the refrigerator for beer but found only orange juice and a covered jar of iced tea.

He drank some tea straight from the jar. It tasted like ambrosia.

Somebody whispered, "Hey, Randy, is that you down there?"

He nudged himself away from the cabinet and shuffled stocking-footed down the hall. Above him Lisa leaned over the rail.

"Hiya, sis."

"Whatcha got?"

"Fritos . . ." A long while later he added, "and iced tea."

"I can't sleep. Bring 'em up."

Climbing the stairs he mumbled, "Jesus, I hate iced tea."

Lisa was sitting Indian-fashion against her pillows, dressed in a gray jogging suit. "Come on in and shut the door."

He did as ordered and dropped to the foot of her bed, where he bounced forever, as if on a trampoline.

"Here, give me some," Lisa said, rolling onto her knees, reaching for the Frito bag. "Randy!" She dropped the bag and grabbed his face, pointing it toward herself. "Oh, Randy, you stupid ass, you've been smoking pot again, haven't you!"

"No," he whined. "Come on, sis—"

"Your eyes look like abortions! Gol, you're so damned dumb! What if Mom caught you? She'd throw you out."

"Are you going to tell her?"

"I should, you know." She looked as if she were considering it. "But I don't want to spoil my wedding day tomorrow. You *promised* me you weren't going to smoke that shit anymore!"

"I know but I just had a couple o' hits."

"Why?"

"I don't know." Randy fell to his back across the foot of Lisa's bed, one arm upflung. "I don't know."

She took the iced tea out of his hand, helped herself to a swig and stretched to set it on her bedside stand, then resumed her Indian pose and wondered how to help him.

"Man, do you know what you're doing to your life?"

"It's just pot; hey, I don't do coke."

"Just pot." She shook her head and sat awhile, watching him stare at the ceiling.

"How much you spend on it a week?"

He shrugged and flopped his head once.

"How much?"

"It's none of your goddamn business."

She stretched out a foot and rocked him. "Look at you. You're nineteen years old and you got a set of Pearls. Big deal. What else have you got? A decent job? A stick of furniture? A car anybody besides your mother paid for? A friend who's worth anything? Bernie, that anal aperture. God, I can't figure out for the life of me why you hang around with him."

"Aw, Bernie's all right."

"Bernie's a loser. When are you going to see it?"

Randy rolled his head and looked at her. She ate three Fritos. She leaned forward and put one in his mouth. She ate another one, then said, "You know what I think is wrong with you? You don't like yourself very much."

"Oh, listen to her, Lisa Freud."

She fed him another Frito. "You don't, you know. That's why you hang around with losers, too. Let's face it, Randy, you've dated some real pus bugs. Some of the girls you've brought over to my apartment, I mean I wanted to stretch a condom over my hand before I shook with them."

"Thanks."

She fed him two Fritos this time, then set the sack aside and brushed off her hands.

"You treated Dad like shit tonight."

"Yeah, well, you treat shit like shit."

"Oh, come off it, Randy, he's doing his damnedest to mend things between you. When are you going to be a big man and get past it? Don't you know it's eating you?"

"He's not what's bothering me tonight."

"Oh, yeah? Then what is?"

"Maryann."

"Struck out with her, too, huh? Good."

"Listen, I was trying. I was really trying!"

"Trying what? To get in her pants? You leave her alone, Randy, she's a nice girl."

"Boy, you really think a lot of me, don't you?"

"I love you, little brother, but I have to overlook a lot to do it. I'd love you more if you'd get your act together and give up that weed and get a job."

"I've got a job."

"Oh yeah, working in that nut house. What're you scared of, huh? That you're not good enough on those Pearls?" She stretched out one leg, put her foot on his ribs and wriggled her toes.

He rolled his head and looked at her.

"You gonna remember this in the morning?" she asked.

"Yeah, I'm all right now. I'm coming down."

"Okay then, listen, and listen good. You're the best drummer I've ever heard. If you want to drum, then by God, drum. But realize this—it's a high-risk job, especially when you go into it smoking grass. The next thing you know they'll have you on coke, then on crack, and before you know it you're dead. So if you're gonna be a musician, you get in with a straight band."

He stared at her a long time, then sat up. He drew one knee onto the bed. "You really think I'm good?"

"The best."

He grinned crookedly. "Really?"

She answered with a quirk of her head.

In time she said, "Okay, so what happened with Maryann? She didn't look too happy when she came charging into the house."

"Nothing happened." He dropped his gaze to the bedspread and ran a hand through his hair. "I cussed, that's all."

"I told you she was a good girl."

"And I apologized but she was already beatin' it inside."

"Next time watch your mouth around her. It won't hurt you, anyway."

"And I no sooner got inside the restaurant than she yelled at me for how I treated Dad."

"So other people notice it, too."

"I don't even know why I should like the girl!"

"Why do you?"

"I just said, I don't know."

"I'll bet I do."

"Yeah? . . . So tell me."

"She's no pus bag, that's why."

Randy chortled deep in his throat. He sat silently for some time before telling his sister, "The first time I saw her it was like wham! You know? Right there." He socked his chest. "Felt like I couldn't breathe."

Lisa gave a crooked grin. "Sometimes it happens that way."

"I put on my best manners tonight, honest, I did." He plucked at his sweater. "Even got these new clothes, and mucked out my car, and pulled out her chair at the table, and opened the car door for her but she's tough, you know?"

"Sometimes a tough woman is best. Same goes for friends. If you had tougher ones who demanded more of you maybe you'd be right for Maryann."

"You don't think I am?"

Lisa studied him awhile, then shrugged and reached for the nightstand. "I think you could be but it'll take some work." She handed him the Fritos and the iced tea. "Go get some sleep, and your eyes better not look like guts when you walk down that aisle tomorrow, okay?"

He smiled sheepishly. "Okay." He rose from the bed and shuffled toward the door.

"Hey," she said quietly, "c'mere." She raised her arms. He came around the bed and plopped into them. They rocked and hugged a moment with the crackly Fritos bag and the cold tea jar against her back.

"I love you, little brother."

Randy squeezed his eyes shut hard against the sting. He really believed her and wished himself more worthy.

"I love you, too."

"You've got to end this thing with Dad."

"I know," he admitted.

"Tomorrow would be a good time."

He had to get out of there or he'd be bawling. "Yeah," he muttered and fled the room.

The day Bess had predicted would be relaxed was anything but. There was her own hair appointment in the morning, followed by nails. There were two calls from Heather with questions from the store. There were the white satin bows to be hung on the pews at St. Mary's, and the caterers to be contacted with notice of three late RSVPs, and a slotted box to be prepared for guests to drop their wedding cards into, and some odds and ends to be carted over to the reception hall, and the hall itself needed checking to make sure the cake had arrived and the table arrangements were the right color, and the guest register was set up and—how had she forgotten!—a wedding card to buy! And nylons—lord, why hadn't she thought to check her nylons earlier in the week?

By quarter to four Bess was frazzled. Lisa wasn't home yet and she was worried about the limo. Randy kept asking for things—an emery board, some mouthwash, a clean handkerchief, a shoehorn.

"A shoehorn!" she shouted over the railing. "Use a knife!"

Lisa returned, the calmest one of the trio, and hummed while putting on her makeup and donning her gown. She dropped her shoes and makeup into her overnight bag, collected her veil and arranged everything in the front hall for removal to the car when her father came.

He rang the bell at precisely 4:45.

Upstairs, Bess was crossing her bedroom and inserting a pierced earring when she heard it ring. Her footsteps halted. Her stomach went fluttery. She hurried to a window and held back the curtain. There in the street were two white limousines, and downstairs, Michael was entering the house for the first time since he'd collected his power tools and left for good.

Bess dropped the curtain, pressed a hand to her rib cage and forced herself to take one deep breath, then collected her purse and hurried out. At the top of the stairs her footsteps were arrested by the sight below. Michael, smiling, handsome, dressed in an ivory tuxedo and apricot bow tie, was hugging Lisa in the front entry, his trouser legs lost in the billows of her white lace. The door was open; the late afternoon sun slanted across the two of them and for that moment, it seemed Bess was looking down at herself. The familiar dress, the handsome man, the two of them smiling and elated as his hug curled Lisa's feet off the floor.

"Oh, Daddy, *really?*" she was squealing. "Are you serious?"

Michael was laughing. "Of course. You didn't think we'd let you ride to church in a pumpkin, did you?"

"But two of them!" Lisa wriggled from his embrace and danced outside, beyond Bess's sight.

"Your mother had the same idea, so they're really from both of us." Through the open door and the fanlight above it, the westering sun spread gold radiance into the house and upon Michael as he watched his daughter, then turned to look back inside at the place he'd once called home. From overhead, Bess watched his gaze take in the familiar terrain—the potted palm in the corner beside the door, the mirror and credenza, the limited view of the living room to the left of the entry, partially obscured by Lisa's bridal veil, which hung on the doorframe, and the family room straight ahead. He took three steps farther inside and stopped almost directly below Bess. She remained motionless, gazing at his wide shoulders in the exquisitely tailored tuxedo, at his thick hair, the tops of his dark eyebrows, his nose, the silk stripe down his right trouser leg, his cream-colored patent-leather shoes. He, too, stood motionless, taking in his surroundings like a man who's missed them very much. What memories called to him while he stood there so still? What pictures of his children returned? Of her? Himself? In those few moments while she observed him she felt his yearning for this place as keenly as she had many times felt his kiss.

Two things happened at once: Lisa came in from outside and Randy arrived from downstairs, coming to an abrupt halt at the sight of his father standing in the front hall.

Michael spoke first. "Hello, Randy."

"Hi."

Neither of them moved toward the other. Lisa stood watching, just inside the front door. Bess remained where she was. After a pause, Michael said, "You're looking pretty sharp."

"Thanks. So are you."

An awkward pause ensued and Lisa stepped in to breach it. "Hey, Randy, look what Mom and Dad ordered—two limos!"

Bess continued down the stairs and Lisa smiled up at her. "Mom, this is just great! Does Mark know?"

"Not yet," Bess answered. "And he won't till he gets to the church. Grooms aren't supposed to see their brides before the service."

Michael looked up and followed Bess's descent, taking in her pale peach suit and matching silk pumps, the pearls gleaming at her ears and throat, her hair flaring back and touching her collar, the soft smile on her lips. She stopped on the second to the last step, her hand on the newel post. The town idiot could have detected the magnetism between them. Their gazes met and riveted while Michael touched his apricot cummerbund in the unconscious preening gesture men make at such times.

"Hello, Michael," Bess said quietly.

"Bess . . . you look sensational."

"I was thinking the same thing about you."

He smiled at her for interminable seconds before becoming aware that his children were observing. "Well, I'd say we all look great." He stepped back to include the two. "Randy . . . and Lisa, our beautiful bride."

"Absolutely beautiful," Bess agreed, moving toward her. Lisa's hair was drawn back by two combs and fell in glossy ringlets behind. Bess turned her by an arm. "Your hair turned out just lovely. Do you like it?"

"Yes, miracle of miracles, I do."

"Good. Well, we should go. Pictures at five on the dot."

Michael said, "May I get your coat, Bess?"

"Yes, it's in the closet behind you, and Lisa's, too."

Lisa said, "No, I'm not going to wear mine. It'll only wrinkle my dress. Besides, it feels like spring out there."

Michael opened the closet door as he'd done hundreds of times, got out Bess's coat while Lisa took her veil from the living-room doorway and Randy picked up her overnight bag.

"How are we doing this?" Randy asked as they headed outside toward the two waiting cars with their liveried drivers standing beside them.

Michael was the last one out of the house and closed the front door. "Your mother and I thought we'd ride in one, and Randy, you can escort Lisa . . . if that's okay with you."

The limousine drivers smiled, and one tipped his visored hat and extended his hand as Lisa approached.

"Right this way, miss, and congratulations. You've got a beautiful day for a wedding."

Lisa put one foot into the car, then changed her mind and leaned back out as Bess was preparing to step into the second car.

"Hey, Mom and Dad," she called. Bess and Michael both looked over. "Tell Randy not to pick his nose while we're in church. This time the whole congregation will be watching."

Everyone laughed while Randy threatened to push Lisa face-first into the limo as he would have when they were children.

The limo doors closed everyone inside and in the lead car, Lisa reached over and patted Randy's cheek. "Nice job back there, little brother. And your eyes look better today, too."

He said, "Something's going on between those two."

Lisa said, "Oh, I hope so."

In the trailing car, Michael and Bess sat on the white leather seat a careful space apart, employing discipline to keep their eyes off each other. They felt resplendent, wondrous, radiant! Not only in solo but in duet, down to their color-coordinated clothing.

When the temptation became too great, he turned his gaze on her and said, "That felt just like when we used to leave for church on Sunday mornings."

She allowed herself to look at him, too. "I know what you mean."

The limo pulled away from the curb while their eyes lingered. It turned a corner and the driver said, "The bride is your daughter?"

"Yes, she is," Michael answered, glancing up front.

"Happy day, then," the driver ventured.

"Very happy," Michael replied, returning his gaze to Bess while the day became charged with possibilities. The driver closed a glass partition and they were alone. The climate was right, seductive even, and the trappings romantic. Neither of them denied that the past and the present were both at work, wooing and weakening them.

In a while Michael said, "You changed the carpet in the entry hall."

"Yes."

"And the wallpaper."

"Yes."

"I like it."

She looked away in a vain attempt to recall common sense. His image remained in her mind's eye, alluring in his wedding finery of apricot and cream.

"Bess?" Michael covered her hand on the seat between them. It took a great deal of self-restraint for her to withdraw it.

"Let's be sensible, Michael. We're going to be bumping up against nostalgic feelings all day long but that doesn't change what is."

"What is?" he asked.

"Michael, don't. It's just not smart."

He studied her awhile, with a pleasant expression on his face. "All right," he decided. "If that's the way you want it."

They rode the remainder of the distance without speaking but she felt his eyes on her a lot and her own pulse so close to the surface of her throat she thought it must show. It felt exhilarating, and bewildering, and oh so threatening.

At the church the Padgett family had already arrived. The appearance of the limousines set off an excited reaction. Mark, dressed in a tux identical to Michael's and Randy's, saw his bride arriving and smiled disbelievingly as he opened the back door and stuck his head inside.

"*Where* did you get this?"

"Mom and Dad rented it for us. Isn't it great?"

There were hugs and thanks and exuberations exchanged on the church steps before the entire party went inside, where the photographer was setting up his equipment and the personal flowers were waiting in flat white boxes in the bride's changing room. A full-length mirror hung on the wall there, too, and before it, Bess helped Lisa don her veil while the Padgett ladies fussed with their own last-minute adjustments. Bess secured the hidden combs in Lisa's hair and added two bobby pins for good measure.

"Is it straight?" Bess asked.

"It's straight," Lisa approved. "Now my bouquet. Would you get it, Mom?"

Bess opened one of the boxes. The green tissue paper whispered back and her hands became still. There, nestled in the waxy green nest was a bouquet of apricot roses and creamy white freesias that exactly duplicated the one Bess had carried at her wedding in 1968.

She turned to Lisa, who stood with her back to the mirror, watching Bess.

"No fair, darling," Bess said emotionally.

"All's fair in love and war, and I believe this is both."

Bess looked down at the flowers and felt her composure giving way, along with her will to keep things sensible between herself and Michael.

"What a cunning young woman you've become."

"Thank you."

Sentiment welled up within Bess, bringing the faint blur of tears.

"And if you make me cry and ruin my makeup before the ceremony even begins I'll never forgive you." She lifted the bouquet from the waxy green paper. "You took our wedding pictures to the florist, of course."

"Of course." Lisa approached her mother and lifted Bess's chin, smiling into her glistening eyes. "It's working, I think."

Bess said with a quavery smile, "You naughty, conniving, conscienceless girl."

Lisa laughed and said, "There's one in there for Daddy, too. Go pin it on him, will you?" To the other women in the room, she said, "Everybody, take the men's boutonnieres out and make them stand still while you pin them on, will you? Maryann, would you do Randy's?"

Randy saw Maryann walking toward him dressed like some celestial being. Her black hair hung in a cloud against a dress the color of a half-ripe peach. It had short sleeves as big as basketballs, which caught on the tips of her shoulders and seemed to be held there by a sorcerer's spell. Her collarbones showed, and her throat, and the entire sweep of her shoulders above a very demure V-neck.

Maryann walked toward Randy, thinking that in her entire life she'd never met anyone as handsome. His cream-colored tuxedo and apricot bow tie were created to be modeled against his dark skin, hair and eyes. She'd never cared much for boys who wore their hair past their collars but his was beautiful. She'd never cared much for swarthy coloring but his was appealing. She'd never hung around with under-achievers but Lisa said he was bright. She'd certainly never gone with wild boys but he represented an element of risk toward which she gravitated as all habitually good girls will at least once in their lives.

"Hi," she said quietly, stopping before him.

"Hi."

His lips were full and beautifully shaped and had a lot of natural pigment. Of the few boys she'd kissed, none had been endowed with a mouth as inviting. She liked the way his lips remained parted while he stared at her, and the faint flare of pink that tinged his cheeks beneath his natural dark skin, and his long, black, spiky eyelashes framing deep brown eyes that seemed unable to look away.

"They sent me with your flower. I'm supposed to pin it on you."

"Okay," he said.

She pulled the pearl-headed pin from an apricot rose and slipped her fingers beneath his left lapel. They stood so close she caught the scent of his after-shave, and whatever he put on his hair to hold it in place and make it so shiny, and the new-linen smell of his freshly cleaned tuxedo.

"Maryann?"

She looked up with her fingertips still close to his heart.

"I'm really sorry about last night."

Was his heart racing like hers? "I'm sorry, too." She returned to her occupation with his boutonniere.

"No girl ever made me watch my mouth before."

"I probably could have been a little more tactful about it."

"No. You were right and I was wrong, and I'll try to watch it today."

She finished pinning on his flower and stepped back. When she looked into his face again a picture flashed across her mind, of him with drumsticks in his hands, and sweatbands on his wrists, and a bandanna tied around his forehead to catch the perspiration while he beat the drums to some outrageously loud and raucous song.

The image fit as surely as Mendelssohn and Brahms fit into her life.

Still, he was so handsome he was beautiful, and his obvious infatuation with her resounded within some depth of womanliness that had lain dormant in Maryann until now.

Today, she thought, for just one day I will bend my own rules.

Bess, too, had taken a boutonniere from the box and gone out in the vestibule to find Michael. Approaching him, she thought how some things never change. Males and females were made to move through the world two-by-two, and in spite of the Women's Movement, there would be tasks that remained eternally appropriate for one sex to do for the other. At Thanksgivings, men carved turkeys. At weddings, women pinned on corsages.

"Michael?" she said.

He turned from conversation with Jake Padgett and she experienced a fresh zing of reaction at his uncommon pulchritude. It happened much as it had when they were dating years ago. The moment his dark eyes settled on hers, embers were stirred.

"I have your boutonniere."

"Would you mind pinning it on for me?"

"Not at all." Performing the small favor for him brought back the many times she'd brushed a piece of lint off his shoulder, or closed a collar button, or any one of the dozens of niceties exchanged by husbands and wives. It brought her, too, the smell of his British Sterling at closer range, and the warmth of his body emanating from beneath his crisp lapel as she slipped her hand beneath it.

"Hey, Bess?" he said softly. She glanced up, then back at the stubborn stickpin that refused to pierce the wrapping around the flower stem. "Do you feel old enough to have a daughter getting married?"

The pin did its job and the boutonniere was anchored. She corrected its angle, smoothed his lapel and looked into Michael's eyes. "No."

"Can you believe it? We're forty."

"No, I'm forty. You're forty-three."

"Cruel woman," he said, with a grin in his eyes.

She backed up a step and said, "I suppose you noticed Lisa picked the same colors we had in our wedding."

"I wondered if it was just a coincidence."

"It isn't. Get ready for another one—she took our wedding pictures to the florist and got a bouquet just like mine."

"Did she really?"

Bess nodded.

"This girl is serious about her matchmaking, isn't she?"

"I have to admit, it did things to me when I saw it."

"Oh yeah?" He dipped his knees to bring his eyes level with hers, still grinning.

"Oh yeah, and don't get so smug. She looks absolutely radiant, and if you can look at her without getting misty I'll pay you ten bucks."

"Ten bucks I got. If we're going to bet, let's at least pick something that—"

Someone interrupted. "Is this the fellow who's been sending me Mother's Day cards for six years?" It was Stella, in her bright silvery tiers, coming at Michael with her arms spread.

"Stella!" he exclaimed. "You beautiful dame!"

They hugged with true affection. "Ah, Michael," she said, cheek-to-cheek with him, "if you aren't a sight for sore eyes." She backed up, commandeering both his hands. "Lord in heaven, you get better-looking every six years!"

He laughed and kept her hands in his larger, darker ones, then clicked his tongue against his cheek. "You, too." He looked down at her delicate satin pumps. "But is this any way for a grandma to dress?"

She kicked up one foot. "Orthopedic high heels," she said, "if it'll make you feel any better. Come on. You, too, Bess, I want you to meet my main man."

They had barely shaken hands with Gil Harwood when the bride appeared in full regalia. She stepped into the vestibule and both Michael and Bess lost communion with everything but her. They turned to her as one, and as she began moving toward them Michael's hand found Bess's and gripped it tightly.

"Oh, my God," he whispered, for both of them.

She was a pretty young woman, the synthesis of her mother and father, and as she moved toward them they were aware of many things—how nature had amalgamated the best features of both of them into her face and frame; how happy she was, smiling and eager for this wedding and her future life with her chosen; that she carried their first grandchild. But mostly they were aware of how carefully she had recreated aspects of their own wedding.

The dress rustled just as it had when Bess wore it.

The veil was a close match to Bess's own.

The bouquet might have been preserved intact from that day.

"Mom, Dad . . ." she said, reaching them, resting a hand on each of their shoulders and raising her face for a touch of cheeks. "I'm so happy."

"And we're happy for you," Bess said.

Michael added, "Honey, you look absolutely beautiful."

"Yes, she does," Mark spoke, coming to claim her.

The photographer interrupted. "Everyone, please! I need the wedding party at the front of the church right now. We're behind schedule!"

As Lisa moved away and the mélange of shifting began toward the front of the church, Michael's eyes found Bess's.

"Even though you warned me, it's still a shock. I thought for a second it was you."

"I know. It's very disconcerting, isn't it?"

During the next hour, while the photographer set up pose after pose, Michael and Bess seemed to be always together, whether in the picture or watching from the sidelines, intensely aware of each other's presence while recounting scenes from their own wedding.

Late in the photo session the photographer turned and called, "Now the members of the bride's family. Immediate family only, please."

There was a moment of hesitation on Michael's part before Lisa motioned him forward and said, "You too, Dad. Come on."

Moments later there they were—Michael, Bess, Lisa and Randy—on two steps in the sacristy of St. Mary's, the church where Michael and Bess had been married, where Lisa and Randy had been baptized, confirmed and received their first Communion, where they had gone as a family during all those happy years.

"Let's have Mom and Dad stand on the top step, and you two just in front of them," the photographer said, motioning them into position. "A little to your left . . ." He pointed to Randy. "And Dad, put your hand on his shoulder."

Michael placed his hand on Randy's shoulder and felt his own heart swell at touching him again.

"That's good. Now everybody squeeze in just a little tighter. . . ."

The photographer peered through his viewfinder while they stood close enough to feel one another's body warmth, touching where they were ordered.

And Lisa thought, Please let this work.

And Bess thought, Hurry or I'll cry.

And Randy thought, Dad's hand feels good.

And Michael thought, Keep me here forever.

Chapter 11

During the final minutes while guests milled in the vestibule and the bride and her mother were having their photo taken in the dressing room, Michael turned and saw two familiar faces coming toward him.

"Barb and Don!" he exclaimed, breaking into a huge smile. The surprise stunned him even as he hugged the couple, who had been best man and maid of honor at his own wedding. During his years with Bess they had been dear friends but in the years since the divorce, some queer misplaced sense of unworthiness had prompted him to let their friendship flag. He had not seen them in over five years. Hugging Barb, he felt his emotions billow, and shaking Don's hand brought such a sharp pang of fraternity, it simply wasn't enough: he caught him in a quick embrace that was returned with equal heartiness.

"We've missed you," Don said at Michael's ear, squeezing so hard Michael's bow tie compressed his windpipe.

"I missed you, too . . . both of you."

The words brought a shaft of regret for the years lost, of pleasure for the friends retouched.

"What happened? How come we never heard from you?"

"You know how it is . . . hell, I don't know."

"Well, this segregation is going to end."

There wasn't time for more. Others found Michael—former neighbors, aunts and uncles from both sides, some of Lisa's old high-school friends and Bess's sister Joan and her husband, Clark, who had flown in from Denver.

Soon the ushers seated the last of the guests. The vestibule quieted. The bride prepared to make her entrance. While Maryann arranged Lisa's train, Michael found a moment to whisper to Bess, "Don and Barb are here."

Surprise and delight lit her expression. She quickly scanned the heads of the seated guests but of course, they were facing front, and furthermore, it was time for the ceremony to begin. The ushers unfurled the white runner. The priest and servers waited up front. The organ rumbled. The strains of *Lohengrin* filled the nave. Bess and Michael took their positions on either side of Lisa and watched Randy head up the aisle with Maryann on his elbow.

When their turn came, they stepped out onto the white runner with their emotions running as close to the surface as at any time since the plans for this day had begun. Bess's knees shook. Michael's insides trembled. They passed the sea of faces turned toward them without singling out any. They gave up their daughter to the waiting groom, then stood side-by-side until the traditional question was asked: "Who gives this woman?"

Michael answered, "Her mother and I do," then escorted Bess to the front pew, where they took their places side-by-side.

In a day laden with emotional impact, this hour was the worst. Michael and Bess felt themselves moved by it from the time Father Moore smiled benignly on the bride and groom and told the gathered witnesses, "I've known Lisa since the night she came into this world. I baptized her when she was two weeks old, gave her her first Communion when she was seven and confirmed her when she was twelve, so it feels quite fitting that I should be the one conducting this ceremony today." Father Moore's gaze encompassed the assembled as he went on. "I know many of you who have come as guests today to witness these vows." His eyes touched Bess and Michael and moved on to others. "I welcome you on behalf of Lisa and Mark, and thank you for coming. How wonderful that by your presence you do honor not only to this young couple who are about to embark on a life-time of love and faithfulness to one another, but you express your own faith in the very institution of marriage and family, and the time-enriched tradition of one man, one woman, promising their fidelity and love to one another till death do them part.

"Till death do them part . . . that's a long, long time." The soliloquy went on, while Michael and Bess sat inches apart and took in every word. The priest told a lovely story about a very rich man who, upon the occasion of his wedding, so wanted to show his love for his bride that he imported a hundred thousand silk worms and upon the eve of his wedding had them released in a mulberry grove. In the pre-dawn hours the grove was laced with the efforts of their night's spinning, and be-fore the dew had dried on the silken threads the groom ordered that gold dust be sprinkled over the entire grove. There, in this gilded bower by which the rich man attempted to manifest his love, he and his bride spoke their vows just as the sun smiled over the horizon, lighting the entire scene to a splendiferous, glittering dis-play.

To the nuptial couple the priest said, "A fitting gift, most certainly, this gift the rich man gave his new bride. But the richest gold a husband can bring to his wife, and a wife to her husband, is not that which can be sprinkled on silk threads, or bought in a jewelry store, or placed on a hand. It is the love and faithfulness they bring to one another in the ongoing years as they grow old together."

From the corner of her eye Bess saw Michael turn his head to look at her. The seconds stretched on until she finally looked up at him. His expression was solemn, his gaze steady. She felt it as one feels a change of season on a particular morning when a door is flung open to reveal that winter is gone. She dropped her gaze to her lap. Still he continued watching her. Her concentration was besieged, and the words of the priest became lost on her.

She tried letting her gaze wander but always it returned to Michael, to the fringes of his clothing, which was all she'd allow herself to watch . . . to his knees . . . to the side seam of his tuxedo, which touched the edge of her skirt . . . to his cuffs, his elegant hands resting in his lap, the hands that had touched her so many times, that had held their newborn babies, and provided a living for them, and had rung the doorbell earlier today and had hugged Lisa and touched Randy so tentatively several times that she'd seen. Oh, how she still loved Michael's hands.

She emerged from her preoccupation to find everyone getting to their feet, and she followed suit, bumping elbows with Michael as he rose and jiggled his right knee to drop his pantleg into place. It was one of those little things that got her: Michael jiggling his pantleg down the way she remembered from a past when such a simple action meant nothing. Now it took on undue significance simply because it was happening beside her again.

They sat once more and Bess felt Michael's upper arm flush against hers. Neither of them drew away.

Father Moore spoke again, letting his eyes communicate with the congregation. "During the exchange of vows, the bride and groom invite all of you who are married to join hands and reaffirm your own wedding vows along with them." Lisa and Mark faced each other and joined hands.

Mark spoke clearly, for all to hear.

"I, Mark, take thee, Lisa . . ."

Tears rolled down Bess's cheeks and darkened two spots on her suit jacket. Michael found a handkerchief and put it in her hand, then, in the valley between them, where no one else could see, he found her free hand, squeezed it hard, and she squeezed back.

"I, Lisa, take thee, Mark . . ."

Lisa, their firstborn, in whom so many hopes had been realized, during whose reign as the center of their world they had been so unutterably happy. Lisa had them holding hands again.

"By the power invested in me by God the father, the son and the holy spirit, I now pronounce you man and wife. You may kiss the bride."

While Lisa raised her happy face for Mark's kiss, Michael's hand squeezed Bess's so hard she feared the bones might snap.

In consolation?

Regret?

Affection?

It mattered not, for she was squeezing his right back, needing that link with him, needing the firm pressure of their entwined fingers and their locked palms. She studied the back of Randy's head and said a silent prayer that his antipathy with Michael would end. She watched Lisa's train slide up three steps as she and Mark approached the altar to light the unity candle. A clear soprano voice sang "He has chosen you for me . . ." and still Michael's hand gripped hers, his thumb now drawing the pattern of an angel's wing across the base of her own.

The song ended and the organ played quietly as Lisa and Mark came toward their mothers, each carrying a long red rose. Mark approached Bess and Michael released her hand.

Over the pew, Mark kissed her cheek and said, "Thank you for being here together. You've really made Lisa happy." Shaking Michael's hand, he said, "I'll keep her happy, I promise."

Lisa came next, kissing each of them on the cheek. "I love you, Mom. I love you, Dad. Watch Mark and me and we'll show you how it's done."

When she was gone Bess had to use Michael's hanky once more. A moment later, as they were kneeling, he nudged her elbow and reached out a hand, palm-up. She placed the hanky in it and concentrated on the proceedings while he wiped his eyes and blew his nose, then tucked the handkerchief away in his rear pocket.

They celebrated the remainder of the Mass together, received Communion as they had in the past and tried to figure out what it had meant when they'd held hands during the vows while for the rest of the service they maintained a careful distance, touching no longer. When the organ burst forth with the recessional they were smiling, following their children from the church, Michael's hand holding Bess's elbow.

Lisa had insisted there be no receiving line at the church: it put a crimp in the festivities and made some people uncomfortable. So when the bridal party burst from the double doors of St. Mary's, their guests burst right behind them. The hugs and felicitations that happened on the church steps were spontaneous, accompanied by a quick shower of wheat and a retreat to the waiting limousines.

The bride and groom piled into the first car, the photographer snapped some pictures and Michael called, "Randy and Maryann, you can ride with us!"

Regretfully, Maryann replied, "I'd like to but I brought my own car."

Randy said, "I guess I'll ride with Maryann, then. See you there."

Bess touched Michael's arm. "I have to get Lisa's things from the changing room. I told her I'd bring them to the reception."

"I'll come with you."

They reentered the church and went to the brightly lit room where it was quiet and they were alone. Bess began collecting Lisa's street shoes, makeup, overnight bag. She was putting the smaller bag into the larger one when a great wave of melancholy struck. She released the handles of the duffel bag, covered her eyes and dropped her chin. Standing with her back to Michael she fished in the duffel bag for Kleenex while she felt a first sob building.

"Hey . . . hey . . . what's this?" Michael turned her around and took her gently in his arms.

"I don't know," she sniffled, with her hand between them, covering her nose with the tissue. "I just feel like crying."

"Ah, well, I guess it's allowed. You're her mother."

"But I feel like such a jerk."

"Doesn't matter. You're still her mother."

"Oh, Michael, she's all married."

"I know. She was our baby and now she doesn't belong to us anymore."

Bess gave in to the awful need to let the tears go. She put both arms around his shoulders and bawled. He held her loosely and rubbed her back. In his arms she felt less like a jerk. When her tears had stopped she remained against him. "Remember when she was little, how she used to put on shows for us?"

"And we thought for sure she was going to be the next Barbra Streisand."

"And how she always had to sit up on the cupboard when I was baking cookies and try to help me stir. Her head would always be in my way."

"And the time she tied her doll blanket around the light bulb in her playhouse and nearly burned the house down?"

"And the time she fractured her arm when she was ice skating and the doctor had to break it completely before he could put it in a cast? Oh, Michael, I'd sooner have had him break my own arm than hers."

"I know. Me, too."

They grew quiet, reminiscing. In time they became aware that they stood quite comfortably in a full-length embrace.

Bess drew back and said, "I've probably ruined your tuxedo." She brushed at his shoulder while his hands rested at her waist.

"We did all right by her, Bess." Michael's voice was quiet and sincere. "She's turned into a real winner."

Bess looked into his eyes. "I know. And I know she'll be happy with Mark, too, so I promise I'm done with these tears."

They remained awhile longer, enjoying the closeness, until she forced herself to step back. "I promised Lisa we'd make sure this room was cleaned up. Would you mind closing up the flower boxes while I fix my face?"

He dropped his hands from her and said, "Don't mind a bit."

When she got a load of herself in the mirror, Bess said, "Mercy, what a mess."

Michael looked back over his shoulder while packing up the floral tailings. Bess opened her purse and began repairing her makeup. Michael put the box on a chair by the door, zipped up Lisa's duffel bag and added it to the collection, then ambled back to Bess and stood behind her, watching in the mirror as she did mysterious things to her eyes.

"Don't watch me," she said, tipping her head to catch the light properly.

"Why?"

"It makes me nervous."

"Why?"

"It's personal."

"I've watched you do other things that were a lot more personal."

Her hand paused as she glanced at him in the mirror. He was exactly half a head taller than she. His bow tie and white winged collar showed above her shoulder, setting off his dark features and black hair to best advantage.

She went back to work, dotting green kohl beneath her eyes, smudging it with a fingertip, while he stood with his hands strung into his trouser pockets, defying her order and studying each move she made as though he enjoyed every minute of it. She tipped her head back and put mascara on her upper lashes, tipped it down to do the lower.

"I don't remember you going to all this fuss before."

"I took a class."

"In what?"

"Not a class, exactly. I had a beauty make-over."

"When?"

"Right after our divorce. Soon as I started earning money."

"You know what?" He let his lips hint at a grin and said quietly, "It worked, Bess." Their eyes met in the mirror while she made a grand effort to appear unruffled. When the effort failed, she dropped her mascara wand into her purse and snapped it shut.

"Michael, are you flirting with me?" She lifted her chin and fluffed at the hair behind her left ear.

He let the grin grow and took her elbow. "Come on, Bess, let's go celebrate our daughter's wedding."

The reception and dance were held at the Riverwood Club overlooking the St. Croix, out in the country on the Wisconsin side of the river. They rode there in the leather-wrapped privacy of the limousine, each on his own half of the seat, with not so much as their hems touching. Dark had fallen but as they descended the hill toward downtown Stillwater streetlights glanced into the car and swept across their shoulders, sometimes the sides of their faces. Occasionally they would let their eyes drift over one another, waiting for the sweep of lights to illuminate the other's face, and after it did, would turn their gazes out the windows with studied nonchalance.

They crossed the bridge to a whining note of tires on textured metal and left Minnesota behind as the car climbed the steep grade toward Houlton.

Finally Michael turned, letting his knee cross the halfway point on the seat.

"Bess?" he said.

She searched out his face on the other side of the seat. They had left the street-lights behind now and traveled through upland farm country.

"What, Michael," she said at last.

He drew a breath and hesitated, as if what he was about to say had taken great mulling.

"Nothing," he said at last, and she released her disappointment in a careful breath.

The Riverwood Club sprawled high above the banks of the river in a stand of knotty oaks. On the landward side it was approached by a horseshoe-shaped drive leading to an open-arms style entry reminiscent of a seventeenth-century Charlestonian mansion. The two arcs of its sweeping front stairs embraced a heart-shaped shrubbery garden filled with evergreens, trimmed at an angle to follow the descending steps. Above, six white fluted columns rose two floors, setting off the club's grand front veranda.

Michael helped Bess alight from the limo, took her elbow as they mounted the left stairway, opened the heavy front door, took her coat, checked it with his own and pocketed the number.

The entry held a chandelier the size of Maryland and a magnificent, free-flying staircase that led to the ballroom above.

"So this is what we're paying for," Michael remarked as they mounted the stairs, his knees lifting in perfect rhythm with Bess's. "Well, I don't know about you, but I intend to get my money's worth."

He started with the champagne. A fountain of it flowed just inside the entry to the ballroom, and beside it a cloth-covered table held a pyramid of stem glasses that a juggler would think twice about disturbing. Michael plucked one from the top and asked Bess, "How about you? Champagne?"

"Since we're paying for it, why not?"

With their glasses in hand they headed into the crowd to mingle. Bess found herself trailing Michael, stopping when he stopped, visiting with whom he visited, as if they were still married. When she realized what she was doing she drifted off in another direction, only to find herself searching him out across the room. Round tables with apricot-colored cloths circled a parquet dance floor. Above it, the mate to the entry chandelier hung in splendor, shedding whiskey-hued light over the gathering. Every table held a candle, their dozens of flames reflected in one entire wall of glass that looked out over the river, where the lights of Stillwater lit the sky to the northwest. It was a huge room, yet she could pick Michael out among the crowd within seconds of trying, his pale tuxedo and dark hair beckoning from wherever he stood.

She was studying him from clear across the room when Stella came up behind her shoulder and said, "He's easily the best-looking man in the place. Gil thinks so, too."

"Mother, you're incorrigible."

"Were you two holding hands during those vows?"

"Don't be absurd."

Heather came along with her husband in tow and said, "I loved the ceremony, and I *love* this room! I'm so glad you invited us."

They moved on and Hildy Padgett was there, saying, "Thank heavens I don't have to go through *that* every day."

Jake, beside her, said, "She cried all through the ceremony."

"So did I," Bess admitted.

Randy and Maryann showed up and began visiting with the group. Lisa and Mark appeared, holding hands, being hugged and kissed by everyone. Bess hadn't realized Michael had drifted up behind her until Lisa hugged him and said, "Wow, Daddy, you look good enough to be dessert. Speaking of which, I think they're ready to start serving dinner now. Mom and Dad, you're at the head table with us."

Once again Bess and Michael found themselves seated together while their food was served and Father Moore stood to say grace.

They dined on beef tips in wine sauce, wild rice and broccoli, relaxing even more with each other. The servers came around to refill their champagne glasses for the official toast.

Randy, as best man, stood to make it.

"Attention! Attention, everyone!" he said, buttoning his tuxedo jacket and waiting for the rustle of conversation to die. Several people clinked their glasses with spoons and the room quieted.

"Well, today I watched my big sister get married." Randy paused and scratched his head. "Boy, am I glad. She always used up the last of the hot water and left me with . . ." Laughter drowned out the rest of his recollection. He picked up again when he could be heard. "No, really, Lisa, I couldn't be happier for you. And you, too, Mark. Now you get to share the bathroom with her and fight for mirror time." Laughter again before Randy got sentimental. "Seriously, Lisa . . . Mark . . . I think you're both pretty great." He saluted them with his glass. "So here's to love and happiness, on your wedding day and for the rest of your lives. We hope you have plenty of both."

Everyone sipped and applauded, and Randy resumed his place beside Maryann.
She smiled at him and said, "That seems to come naturally to you."

He shrugged and said, "I suppose so."

"So you'll love it on stage when you get there."   ·

He drank some champagne and grinned. "What, you don't think I'll get there?"

"How can I know? I've never even heard you play."

They ate awhile, then he said, "So tell me about these sports you're in. I suppose you've lettered."

"All three years."

"And you get straight A's."

"Of course."

"And you edit your yearbook."

"School paper."

"Oh . . . school paper, sorry." He studied her and asked, "So what do you do for fun?"

"What do you mean? All that is fun. I *love* school."

"Besides school."

"I do a lot with my church group. I'm thinking of going to Mexico this summer to help the hurricane victims there. It's all being arranged by the church. Fifty of us can go but we all have to raise our own money to pay our way."

"Doing what?"

"We raise pledges."

The concept boggled him. Church group? Hurricane victims? Pledges?

"So what'll you do there?"

"A lot of very hard work. Mix concrete, put roofs back on, sleep in hammocks and go without baths for a week."

"Pardon me, but if you go without baths those Mexicans are going to want you out of there long before a week is up."

She laughed, covering her mouth with a napkin.

"You smell good tonight, though," he said in his flirtiest fashion, and her laughter died. She lowered the napkin, blushed and transfered her attention to her plate.

"Is that the line you use on all the girls?"

"All what girls?"

"I figure there must be plenty of them. After all, you aren't exactly Elephant Man."

He told her the truth. "The last girl I dated seriously was Carla Utley and we were in the tenth grade."

"Oh, come on. You don't expect me to believe that."

"It's true."

"The tenth grade?"

"I've taken girls out since then, but none of them were serious."

"So what else? You do a lot of one-night stands?"

He leveled his dark, long-lashed eyes on hers and said, "For a beautiful girl you sure are vicious."

She blushed again, which pleased him.

She was the prettiest, freshest, most inviolable creature he'd ever had the pleasure of spending an evening with, and he thought with some astonishment that it was going to be the first time in years he kissed a girl without thumping her into bed.

Someone started tapping a champagne glass with a spoon, and the entire phalanx of wedding guests caught the cue and filled the ballroom with chiming.

Mark and Lisa rose to their feet and performed the ritual with gusto. They gave their guests a good one—a lusty French kiss that lasted five seconds.

While Maryann watched the proceedings, Randy watched her. She appeared transported while she took in the kiss with her own lips slightly parted.

When the bride and groom sat down the crowd burst into applause. All but Maryann. She dropped her eyes self-consciously, then, sensing Randy's unbroken regard, flashed a quick, embarrassed glance his way. It lasted only long enough for Maryann to grow more flustered but as her glance fled away, for the merest fraction of a second her eyes detoured to his lips.

The meal ended. Milling began and a band started setting up. Michael pushed back his chair and said to Bess, "Let's go mingle."

They did so together, catching up with relatives they'd each lost through divorce, with old friends, new friends, neighbors whose children had played with Lisa and Randy in their elementary-school days—a hall full of familiar people who politely refrained from asking their status as a couple.

They came at last to Barb and Don Maholic, who saw them approaching and rose from their chairs. The men clasped hands. The women hugged.

"Oh, Barb, it's good to see you," Bess said emotionally.

"It's been too darn long."

"It must be five years."

"At least. We were so happy to get the wedding invitation, and what a beautiful bride Lisa is. Congratulations."

"She is, isn't she? It's hard not to get teary-eyed when you watch one of your kids get married. So tell me about yours."

"Come on. Sit down and let's catch up."

The men brought drinks and the four of them sipped and talked. About their kids. About their businesses. About trips and mutual acquaintances and their parents. The band started up and they talked a little louder, leaning closer to be heard.

In the background, the bandleader called the bridal couple onto the floor as the group struck into "Could I Have This Dance." Lisa and Mark walked out beneath the chandelier and as they danced, captured the attention of everyone in the room, including Bess and Michael.

The bandleader called, "Let's have the other members of the wedding party join them."

Across the hall, Randy turned to Maryann and said, "I guess that means us."

Jake Padgett stood and said to his wife, "Mother?"

Over Mark's shoulder, Lisa pointed and gestured to Michael: *ask Mother!*

He glanced at Bess. She had her forearms crossed on the table and was watching Lisa with a wistful smile on her lips. At the turn of Michael's head, she turned her own.

"Dance, Bess?" he asked.

"I think we should," she answered.

He pulled out her chair and followed her onto the dance floor, conscious of Lisa's wide smile as she watched. He winked at the bride and turned to open his arms to Bess.

She stepped into them wearing a smile, wholly glad to be with him again. They had danced together for sixteen years, in a fashion that attracted the admiring gazes of onlookers, which happened once again as they struck the waltz position, waited out the measure and stepped into the three-quarter rhythm with flawless grace. There might have been no lapse, so at ease were they together. They danced awhile, smiling, making wide sweeping turns, before Bess said, "We always did this well, didn't we, Michael?"

"And we haven't lost it."

"Isn't it great to do this with somebody who knows how?"

"Boy, you said it. I swear, *no*body knows how to waltz anymore."

"Keith surely doesn't."

"Neither does Darla."

They did it properly, with the accent on the first beat. If there'd been sawdust on the floor they'd have scraped a wreath of neat little triangles through it.

"Feels good, huh?"

"Mmm . . . comfortable."

When they'd danced for some time, Michael asked, "Who's Keith?"

"This man I've been seeing."

"Is it serious?"

"No. As a matter of fact, it's over." They went on waltzing, separated by a goodly space, happy and smiling at each other without any undercurrents. What each of them said, the other took at face value.

Bess inquired, "How are things between you and Darla?"

"Uncontested divorces go through the courts quite fast."

"Are the two of you talking?"

"Absolutely. We never stopped. We never cared enough to end it with a war."

"Like we did?"

"Mm."

"We were so bitter because we still cared, is that what you're saying?"

"I've thought about it. It's possible."

"Funny, my mother said essentially the same thing."

"Your mother looks great. What a pistol she is."

They chuckled and danced in silence until the song ended, then remained on the floor for another song, then another and another. Finally walking her off the floor after four numbers, Michael said at her ear, "Don't go far. I want to dance some more."

The music got louder and faster as the night wore on. There was a predominance of young people present, and more drifted in as the night got older. The band catered to their wishes. The slower ballads—"Wind Beneath My Wings," "Lady in Red"—gave way to the kind of songs that lured even doubtful middle-agers out onto the floor: "La Bamba" and "Johnny B. Goode." When the crowd had caught the fire and were heating up, the band threw in "The Twist," followed by "I Knew the Bride," which filled the dance floor and got everybody sweaty, including Michael and Bess, who'd been partners the entire night.

Moods were high. Michael said, "You mind if I dance one with Stella?"

"Heavens no," Bess replied. "She'd love it."

To Stella he said, "Come here, you painted hussy. I want to dance one with you."

Gil Harwood snared Bess, and at the end of the song the foursome switched partners.

"You having fun?" Michael asked as he reclaimed Bess.

"I'm having a ball!" she exclaimed.

They danced another fast, hot one and when it ended, Michael had curled Bess up against his side, puffing. "Come on, I gotta get rid of this jacket." He hauled her by the hand to the table where they'd left their drinks and draped his jacket over the back of a chair. They were taking quick gulps of their cocktails when the band struck up "Old Time Rock and Roll." Michael slammed his glass down on the table, said, "Come on!" and towed her back toward the dance floor. Behind him, she snapped his suspenders against his damp shirt and shouted above the music, "Hey, Curran!"

He turned and dipped his ear to catch what she was shouting in the din. "What?"

"You look pretty sexy in that tuxedo."

He laughed and said, "Yeah, well, try and control yourself, honey!" They elbowed their way into the crowd and launched themselves into the joie de vivre of the music once again.

It was easy to forget they were divorced, to join in the merriment, raising their hands above their heads and clapping while beside them old friends and family did the same thing and sang along with the familiar words. . . .

I like that old time rock and roll . . .

When the song ended they were flushed and exuberant. Michael stuck two fingers between his teeth and whistled. Bess clapped and thrust a fist in the air, shouting, "More! More!" But the set was over and they returned to Barb and Don's table, where all four of them collapsed into their chairs at the same time.

Sapped, exhilarated, wiping their brows, reaching for their glasses, they slipped back into the familiarity of their long-standing friendship.

"What a band."

"Aren't they great?"

"I haven't danced like this in years."

Barb's eyes glowed. "Gosh, it's good to see you two together again. Is this . . . I mean, are you two seeing each other?"

Michael glanced at Bess.

Bess glanced at Michael.

"No, not really," she said.

"Too bad. On the dance floor you look like you've never been apart."

"We're having a good time, anyway."

"So are we. How many times do you think the four of us went out dancing?"

"Who knows?"

"What happened anyway? Why did we all stop seeing each other?" Barb asked.

They all studied one another, recalling the fondness of the past and those awful months when the marriage was breaking up.

Bess spoke up. "I know one reason I stopped calling you. I didn't want you to have to take sides or choose between us."

"But that's silly."

"Is it? You were friends to both of us. I was afraid that anything I said to you might have been misconstrued as a bid for sympathy. And in a way, it probably would have been."

"I suppose you're right but we missed you, we wanted to help."

Michael said, "I felt pretty much the same as Bess, afraid to look as if I wanted you to take my side, so I just backed off."

Don had been sitting silently, listening. He sat forward, working the bottom of his glass against the tabletop as if it were a rubber stamp.

"Can I be honest here?"

Every eye turned to him. "Of course," Michael replied.

"When you two broke up, you want to know what I felt?" He waited but no one said a word. "I felt betrayed. We knew you two were having your differences but you never let on exactly how bad they were. Then one day you called and said, 'We're getting a divorce,' and selfish as it sounds now, I actually got angry. We had all these years invested in a four-way friendship, and all of a sudden—pouff!—you guys were dissolving it. The absolute truth of it is, I never blamed either one of you more than the other. Both Barb and I looked at your relationship through pretty clear eyes, and we were probably closer to you than anyone else at that time. Anyway, when you said you were getting divorced from each other it felt as if you were getting divorced from us."

Bess reached over and covered his hand. "Oh, Don . . ."

Now that he'd said his piece, he looked sheepish. "I know I sound like a selfish pig."

"No, you don't."

"I probably never would have said that if I hadn't had a couple of drinks."

Michael said, "I think it's good that the four of us can talk this way. We always could, that's why we were such good friends."

Bess added, "I never really looked at our breakup from your viewpoint before. I suppose I might have felt the same way if you'd been the ones divorcing."

Barb spoke in a caring tone. "I know you said you haven't been seeing each other but is there any chance you two might get back together? If I'm speaking out of line, tell me to shut up."

Silence fell over the group before Bess said, in the kindest tone possible, "Shut up, Barb."

Randy and Maryann had danced the entire night long, talking little in the raucousness, playing eye games. When the second set ended she fanned herself with a hand while he freed his bow tie and collar button and said, "Hey, it's hot in here. Want to go outside and cool off?"

"Sure."

They left the ballroom, walked down the grand staircase and collected her coat.

Outside, stars shone. The fecund smell of thawing earth lifted from the surrounding grounds and farmlands. Someplace nearby, rivulets of melted snow could be heard gurgling toward lower terrain. The air was heavy with damp that had left the painted floor of the veranda slippery.

Randy took Maryann's arm and walked her to the far end, where they stood looking out over the driveway while the evergreens below them threw out a pungent scent like gin.

Now don't say Jesus, he thought.

"You're a good dancer," Maryann said as he released her arm and braced his shoulder against a fluted pillar.

"So are you."

"No, I'm not. I'm just average but an average dancer looks better when she dances with a good one."

"Maybe it's you making me look good."

"No, I don't think so. You must get it from your mom and dad. They look great out there on the dance floor together."

"Yeah, I guess so."

"Besides, you're a drummer. It makes sense—good rhythm, good dancer."

"I never really danced much."

"Neither did I."

"Too busy getting straight A's?"

"You don't like that, do you?"

He shrugged.

"Why?"

"It scares me."

"Scares you! You?"

"Don't look so surprised. Things scare guys, you know."

"Why should my straight A's scare you?"

"It's not just them, it's the kind of girl you are."

"What kind am I?"

"Goody two-shoes. Church group. National Honor Society, I bet."

She made no reply.

"Right?" he asked.

"Yes."

"I haven't been around many girls like you."

"What kind have you been around?"

He chuckled and looked away. "You don't want to know."

"No, I guess I don't."

They stood awhile, looking out over the horseshoe-shaped drive, surrounded by the burgeoning spring night, a moon as thin and white as a daisy petal, and tree shadows like black lace upon the lawns. Once he looked over at her and she met his gaze, Randy with his ivory tuxedo sleeve braced upon the pale pillar, Maryann with her hands joined primly on the veranda railing.

"So a guy like me just doesn't . . . you know . . . make a play for a girl like you."

"Not even if you asked first and she said yes?"

Miss Maryann Padgett, in her proper little navy-blue coat, stood with her shoes perched neatly side-by-side, her hands on that railing, waiting. Randy drew his shoulder from the pillar and turned toward her, standing close without touching. She, too, turned to him.

"I've been thinking about you a lot since I met you."

"Have you?"

"Yeah."

"Well, then . . . ?" Her invitation was just reserved enough to make it acceptable.

He lowered his head and kissed her the way he used to kiss girls when he was in the seventh grade. Lips only, nothing wet, nothing else touching. She put her hands on his shoulders but kept her distance. He embraced her cautiously, letting her make the choice about the proximity of bodies. Close but not too close, she chose, resting against him the way chalk rests on a blackboard: a touch and it'll disappear. He offered his tongue and she accepted shyly, tasting the way she smelled— fresh, flowery, no alcohol or smoke. As kisses went, it remained chaste, but all the while sweetness coursed through him and he experienced a return to the innocent emotions of first kisses, knowing he wanted more of this girl than he either deserved or probably ought to dream about.

He lifted his head and kept a little space between them. Their fingertips were joined at arm's length.

"Pretty wild, huh?" He smiled, lopsided. "You and me, and Lisa and Mark?"

"Yeah, pretty wild."

"I wish I had my car tonight so I could drive you home."

"I have mine. Maybe I can drive you home."

"Is that an invitation?"

"It is."

"Then I accept."

She started to turn away but he stopped her. "One other thing."

"What?"

"Would you go out with me next Saturday? We could go to a movie or something."

"Let me think about it."

"All right."

He took a turn at turning away but she kept his hand and stood where she'd been. "I've thought about it." She smiled. "Yes."

"Yes?"

"Yes. With my parents' approval."

"Oh, of course." As if a parent had approved of him since he'd turned thirteen. "So what do you say we go dance some more?"

Smiling, they returned inside.

The band was blasting out "Good Lovin' " and the dancers were getting into it. His mom and dad were still on the floor, having a grand old time with their friends the Maholics and Grandma Stella and her date, who'd turned out to be a neat guy after all. Stella and the old dude were dancing the way old people do, looking ridiculous but enjoying it anyway. Randy and Maryann melded into the edge of the crowd and picked up the beat.

When the song ended, Randy heard Lisa's voice over the amplifiers and turned in surprise to see her standing on stage with a microphone.

"Hey, everybody, listen up!" When the crowd noise abated she said, "It's my special night so I get what I want, right? Well, I want my little brother up here— Randy, where are you?" She shaded her eyes and scanned the room. "Randy come up here, will you?"

Randy suffered some friendly nudging while panic sluiced through him. *Jesus, no, not without getting wrecked first!* But everyone was looking at him and there was no way he could slip outside and sneak a hit.

"A lot of you don't know it but my little brother is one of the better drummers around. Matter of fact, he's the best." She turned to the lead guitar man. "You don't mind if Randy sits in on one, do you, Jay?" And to the crowd, "I've been listening to him pounding his drums in his bedroom since he was three months old— well, that might possibly have been his heels on the wall beside his crib but you know what I mean. He hasn't done a lot of this in public, and he's a little shy about it, so after you hog-tie him and carry him up here, give him a hand, okay?"

Randy, genuinely embarrassed, was being encouraged to go onstage by a throng of his peers who circled him and Maryann.

"Yeah, Randy, do it!"

"Come on, man, hammer those skins!"

Maryann took his hand and said, "Go ahead, Randy, please."

With his palms sweating, he removed his tuxedo jacket and handed it to her. "Okay, but don't run away."

The drummer backed off his stool and stood as Randy leaped onto the stage and picked his way around the bass drum and cymbals. They did a little talking about sticks and Randy selected a pair from a quiver hanging on a drum. He straddled the revolving stool, gave the bass drum a few fast thumps, did a riff from high to low across the five drums circling him, tested the height of the cymbals and said to the lead guitar man, "How 'bout a little George Michael? You guys know 'Faith'?"

"Yo! 'Faith' we got." And to the band, "Give him a little 'Faith,' on his beat."

Randy gave them a lead-in on the rim and struck into the driving, syncopated beat of the song.

On the dance floor, Michael forgot to start dancing with Bess. She nudged him and he made a halfhearted attempt to do justice to both but the drumming won out. He bobbed absently while watching, entranced, as his son became immersed in the music, his attention shifting from drum to drum, to cymbal to drum, now bending, now reaching, now twirling a stick till it blurred. Some silent signal was exchanged and the band dropped off, giving Randy a solo. His intensity was total, his immersion complete. There were he and the drums and the rhythm running from his brain to his limbs.

Most of the crowd had stopped dancing and stood entranced, clapping to the rhythm. Those who continued dancing did so facing the stage.

At Michael's side Bess said, "He's good, isn't he?"

"My God, when did this happen?"

"It's been happening since he was thirteen. It's the only thing he really cares about."

"What the hell's he doing working in that nut house?"

"He's scared."

"Of what? Success?"

"Possibly. More probably of failure."

"Has he auditioned anywhere?"

"Not that I know of."

"He's got to, Bess. Tell him he's got to."

"You tell him."

The drum solo ended and the band picked up the last verse while on the floor Bess and Michael danced it out, reading messages in each other's eyes.

A roar of applause went up as Randy struck the cymbals for the last time and the song ended. He rested his hands on his thighs, smiled shyly and let the drumsticks slip back into the quiver.

"Good job, Randy," the band's drummer said, returning to the stage, shaking Randy's hand. "Who did you say you play with again?"

"I don't."

The drummer stopped cold, stared at Randy a moment and straddling his seat, said, "You ought to get yourself an agent, man."

"Thanks. Maybe I will."

On his way back to Maryann, he felt like Charlie Watts. She was smiling, holding his jacket while he slipped it on, then taking his arm, unconsciously resting her breast against it.

"You even look like George Michael," she said, still smiling proudly. "But I suppose all the girls tell you that."

"Now if I could only sing like him."

"You don't have to sing. You can play drums. You're really good, Randy."

None of the applause counted as much as her approval. "Thanks," he said, and wondered if it would still feel like this after twenty-five years of performing—the way Watts had been performing with the Stones all these years—the rush, the exhilaration, the high!

Suddenly his mother was there, kissing his cheek. "Sounds much better in a club than coming up the stairs." And his father, clapping his shoulder and squeezing hard, with a glint of immense pride in his smile.

"You've got to get out of that nut house, Randy. You're too good to squander all that talent."

If he moved, Randy knew, even half-moved toward his Dad he'd be in his arms and this stellar moment would be complete. But how could he do that with Maryann looking on? And his mother? And half the wedding guests? And Lisa coming at him with a big smile on her face, trailed by Mark? Then she was there and the moment was lost.

Jamming in somebody's basement had never been like this. By the time his praises had been sung by everyone who knew him and some who didn't, he still felt like a zinging neon comet and thought if he didn't smoke some grass to celebrate, he'd never have another chance to get the high-on-high. Christ, it'd be wild!

He looked around and Maryann was gone.

"Where's Maryann?" he asked.

"She went to the ladies' room. Said she'd be right back."

"Listen, Lisa, I'm kind of warm. I gotta go outside and cool off some, okay?"

Lisa mock-punched his arm. "Yeah, sure, little bro. And thanks again for playing."

He slumped his shoulders, gave her a crooked smile and saluted himself away. "Any time."

Outside, he returned to the shadows at the far end of the veranda. The earth still smelled musty, and the runnels were still running, and the thump of the drums could be registered through the soles of his shoes. He packed his bat, lit it, took the hit and held it deep in his lungs, his eyes closed, blocking out the stars and the cars and the naked trees. It didn't take long. By the time he left the veranda he believed he *was* Charlie Watts.

He went inside to find Maryann. She was sitting at a table with her parents and some of her aunts and uncles.

"Hey, Maryann," he said, "let's dance."

Her eyes were like ice picks as she turned and took a chunk out of him. "No, thank you."

If he hadn't been stoned he might have done the sensible thing and backed off. Instead, he gripped her arm. "Hey, what do you mean?"

She jerked her arm free. "I think you know what I mean."

"What'd I do?"

Everyone at the table was watching. Maryann looked as if she hated him as she jumped to her feet. He smiled blearily at the group and mumbled, "Sorry . . ." then followed her out into the hall. They stood at the top of the elegant stairway down which they'd walked together such a short time earlier.

"I don't hang around with potheads, Randy," she said.

"Hey, wait, I don't—"

"Don't lie. I came outside looking for you and I saw you and I know what was in that little pipe! You can find your own way home, and as far as Saturday night goes, it's off. Go smoke your pot and be a loser. I don't care."

She picked up her skirts, turned and hurried away.

Chapter 12

Bess and Michael reclined in the backseat of the limousine, a faint sense of motion scuttling up from the trunk and massaging the backs of their heads through the supple leather. Michael was laughing, deep in his throat. His eyes were closed.

"What are you laughing about?"

"This car feels like a Ferris wheel."

She rolled her head to look at him. "Michael, you're drunk."

"Yes, I am. First time for months and it feels spectacular. How 'bout you?" He rolled his head to look at her.

"A little, maybe."

"How does it feel?"

She faced upward again, closed her eyes and laughed deep in her throat. They enjoyed some silence, and the purring, easy-chair ride, the subtle euphoria created by the dancing and drinking and the presence of each other. In time, he spoke.

"You know what?"

"What?"

"I don't feel much like a grandpa."

"You don't dance much like a grandpa."

"Do you feel like a grandma?"

"Mm-mm."

"I don't remember *my* grandpa and grandma dancing like that when I was young."

"Me either. Mine raised irises and built birdhouses."

"Hey, Bess, come here." He clamped her wrist, tipped her his way and put an arm around her.

"Just what do you think you're doing, Michael Curran?"

"I'm feelin' *good!*" he said, exaggerating an accent. "And I'm feelin' *baaad!*"

She laughed, rolling her face against his lapel. "This is ridiculous. You and I are divorced. What are we doing snuggling in the backseat of a limo?"

"We bein' *bad!* And it feel so good we gonna keep right on doin' it!" He leaned forward and asked the driver, "How much time have we got?"

"As much as you want, sir."

"Then keep driving till I tell you to head back to Stillwater. Drive to Hudson! Drive to Eau Claire! Hell, drive to Chicago if you want to!"

"Whatever you say, sir." The driver laughed and faced full front again.

"Now where were we?" Michael settled back and reclaimed Bess, nestling her close.

"You were drunk and being foolish."

"Oh, that's right." He threw up his arms and started singing a chorus of "Good Lovin'," adding a few hip thrusts for good measure.

". . . gimme that good, good lovin' . . ."

She tried to pull away but he was too quick. "Oh no you don't. You're staying right here. We gotta talk about this now."

"Talk about what?" She couldn't resist smiling.

"This. Our firstborn, all married up and off someplace to spend her wedding night, and you and me only months away from becoming grandparents, dancin' our butts off while our secondborn plays the drums. I think there's some significance here."

"You do?"

"I think so but I haven't figured it out yet."

She settled beneath his arm and decided to enjoy being there. He kept on singing "Good Lovin' " very softly, mumbling the words so they barely moved his lips. Pretty soon she was mumbling softly in counterpoint.

He'd mumble, "Good lovin' . . ."

And she'd mumble, "Gimme that mmm-mmm-mmm . . ."

"Good lovin' . . ."

"Mm-mm-mm mm-mm-mmm-mmm . . ."

"Mm-mmm . . ."

"Mm-mm mm-mm-mm-mmm-mmm . . ."

He tapped out the drum rhythm on his left thigh and her right arm, then found her free hand and fit his fingers between hers, closed them and bent their elbows in lazy unison. She could feel his heartbeat beneath her jaw, could hear his humming resonate beneath her ear, could smell the diluted remnants of his cologne mingled with smoke on his jacket.

So quietly the sound of her own breathing nearly covered it up, he sang: "Good lovin' . . ."

"Mm-mm-mm mm-mm-mmm-mmm . . ."

Then nothing. Only the two of them, reclining on his half of the seat, holding hands and fitting their thumbs together and feeling and smelling one another while their arms wagged slowly down and up, and down and up . . .

He didn't say a word, just leaned forward, curled his hand around her far arm and kissed her. Her lips opened and his tongue came inside while she thought of the dozens of arguments she ought to voice. Instead she kissed him back, the leather seat soft against her head, his breath warm against her cheek, his taste as familiar as that of chocolate, or strawberry, or any of the flavors she had relished often in her life. And, my, it felt good. It was the familiarity of that first step on the dance floor magnified a thousandfold. It was each of them fitting into the right niche, melding to the right place, tasting the right way.

They kept it friendly, passionless almost, engaging themselves solely in the pleasure one mouth can give another.

When he drew away she kept her eyes closed, murmuring, "Mmm . . ."

He studied her face for a long moment, then reclined, removing his arm from around her, though she remained snug against his side with her cheek on his sleeve.

They rode along in silence, thinking about what they'd just done, neither of them surprised it had happened, only wondering what it portended. Michael reached over and touched a button, lowering his window a couple of inches. The cool night air whisked in, scented by fertile fields and moisture. It threaded across their hair, their lips, bringing a near taste of thawing earth.

Bess interrupted their idyll as if rebutting thoughts they'd both been having. "The trouble is," she said quietly, "you fit in so remarkably well."

"I do, don't I?"

"Mother loves you. All the shirttail family thinks I was crazy to get rid of you in the first place. Lisa would sell her soul to get us back together. Randy's even coming around little by little. And Barb and Don—it felt like slipping into an old, comfortable easy chair to be with them again."

"Boy, didn't it."

"Isn't it strange, how we both gave them up? I thought you were probably seeing them all along."

"I thought *you* were."

"With the possible exception of Heather down at the store, I really don't have any friends anymore. I seem to have forsaken them since we got divorced—don't ask me why."

"That's not healthy."

"I know."

"Why do you suppose you did that?"

"Because when you're divorced you always end up feeling like the odd man out. Everyone else has a partner to be with and there you are trailing along like a kid sister."

"I thought you had that boyfriend."

"Keith? Mmmm . . . no, Keith wasn't one I took around and introduced to many people. When I did, most of them looked at me funny and got me in a corner and whispered, 'What in the world are you doing with *him?*' "

"How long did you go with him?"

"Three years."

They rode awhile before Michael asked, "Did you sleep with him?"

She gave him a mock slap on the arm and put distance between them. "Michael Curran, what business is it of yours?"

"Sorry."

Away from him, she felt chilled. She snuggled back against his arm and said, "Close the window, will you? It's cold."

The window made a whirr and thump and the chill breeze disappeared.

"Yes," Bess said after some time. "I slept with Keith. But never at home and never overnight so the kids would know."

It took some time before Michael said, "You want to know something funny? I'm jealous."

"Oh, that's rich. *You're* jealous?"

"I knew you'd say that."

"When I found out about Darla I wanted to scratch her eyes out, and yours, too."

"You should have. Maybe things would have ended up differently."

They spent time with their private thoughts before Bess told Michael, "My mother asked me if we were holding hands in church today and I lied."

"You *lied?* But you never lie!"

"I know but I did this time."

"Why?"

"I don't know. Yes, I do." She pondered a while and admitted, "No, I don't. Why were we?" She tilted her head to look up at him.

"It seemed like the right thing to do. It was a sentimental moment."

"But it had nothing to do with renewing vows, did it?"

"No."

Bess felt simultaneously relieved and disappointed.

Soon, she yawned and snuggled against his arm once more.

"Tired?"

"Mmm . . . it's catching up at last."

Michael raised his voice and told the driver, "You can head back to Stillwater now."

"Very good, sir."

On the way Bess fell asleep. Michael stared out the window at the blur of snowless, grassless land lit by the perimeter of the headlights. The wheels dipped into a low spot in the road and Michael swayed in his seat, Bess along with him, her weight heavy against his arm.

When they reached the house on Third Avenue, he touched her face.

"Hey, Bess, we're home."

She had trouble lifting her head, as much trouble opening her eyes.

"Oh . . . mmm . . . Michael . . . ?"

"You're home."

She forced herself upright as the driver opened the door on Michael's side. He stepped out and offered his hand, helping her out. The driver stood beside the open trunk.

"Shall I help you carry the gifts inside, sir?"

"I'd appreciate that."

Bess led the way, unlocking the door, turning on a hall light and a table lamp in the family room. The two men carried the gifts inside and stacked them in the family room on the floor and the sofa. The front door stood wide open. Michael followed the driver to it and said, "Thanks for your help. I'll be out in just a minute."

He closed the door and slowly walked the length of the hall to the family room, where he stopped with the sofa and a long table separating him from Bess, who stood among the packages.

Michael's glance swept the room.

"The house looks nice. I like what you've done with this room."

"Thanks."

"Nice colors." His glance returned to her. "I never was much good with colors."

She took two precariously perched boxes off the sofa and put them on the floor.

"Are you coming over tomorrow?"

"Am I invited?"

"Well, of course you are. You're Lisa's father, and she'll want you here when she opens her gifts."

"Then I'll be here. What time?"

"Two o'clock. There was food left over so don't eat lunch."

"You need any help? You want me to come early?"

"No, all I have to do is make coffee but thanks for offering. Just be here at two."

"It's a deal."

A lull fell. They weren't sure if Randy was home or not. If so, he was down in his room asleep. From outside came the faint note of the limousine engine. Inside, the room was dim, the window coverings drawn high, the night beyond the sliding glass door absorbing much of the light cast by the single burning lamp. Michael's tie was in his pocket, his collar button open, his cummerbund a splash of color as he stood on the opposite side of the furniture from Bess, with his hands in his pockets.

"Walk me to the door," he said.

She came around the sofa at a pace suggesting reluctance to see the evening end. Their arms slipped around each other as they sauntered, hip-to-hip, to the door.

Reaching it, he said, "I had fun."

"So did I."

She turned to face him. He linked his hands on her spine and rested his hips lightly against hers.

"Well . . . congratulations, Mom." He gave a smile of boyish allure.

She returned it, accompanied by a throaty chuckle. "Congratulations, Dad. We got us a son-in-law, didn't we?"

"A good one, I think."

"Mm-hmm."

Would they or wouldn't they? The questions glimmered between them as they stood together with every outward sign indicating they wanted to, and every inward voice warning it was unwise: that once in the limousine had been dangerous enough. He ignored the voice, dipped his head and kissed her, open-mouthed, tasting her fully and without restraint. Where his tongue went, hers followed, into all the familiar sleek caverns they'd learned during long-ago kisses. She tasted as he remembered, felt the same, the contours of her lips, teeth and tongue as familiar as during the uncountable kisses of their younger years. Their lips grew wet and he could tell by her breathing she was as turned on as he.

When he lifted his head she whispered, "Michael, we shouldn't."

"Yeah, I know," he replied, stepping away from her against all his basic instincts. "See you tomorrow."

When he was gone she shut off the downstairs lights and climbed the stairs in the dark. Halfway up she paused, realizing he had offered to help her in the kitchen. She was smiling as she continued toward her bedroom.

———

At 1:30 p.m. the following day Randy found Bess in the kitchen. He was dressed in jeans and a distressed leather bomber jacket. She, dressed in green wool slacks with a matching sweater, was arranging cold turkey and raw vegetables on a two-tiered platter. The room smelled strongly of perking coffee.

"I don't think I can make it today, Mom."

She glanced up sharply. "What do you mean, you can't?"

"I mean, I can't. I gotta meet some guys."

"You're a member of the wedding party. What *guys* are more important than your sister on her wedding weekend?"

"Mom, I'd stay if I could, but—"

"You'll stay, mister, and call your *guys* and tell them you'll make it another time!"

"Mom, goddamnit, why do you have to pick today to become Mussolini?" He thumped a fist on the cabinet top.

"First of all, stop your cursing. Second, stop rapping your fist on the counter. And third, grow up! You're Lisa and Mark's best man. As such you have social obligations that aren't done yet. This gift-opening today is as much a part of the wedding festivities as last night was, and she'll expect you to be here."

"She won't care," he jeered. "Hell, she won't even miss me."

"She won't, because you won't *be* missing!"

"What's got into you all of a sudden, Ma? Did the old man tell you you ought to get tougher on me?"

Bess flung a handful of raw cauliflower into a bowl of ice water. It splashed onto her sleeve as she spun to face him.

"I've had just about all the smart remarks about him I'm going to take from you, young man. He's making an effort, a real effort where you're concerned. And if he *did* tell me to get tough on you, and if that *were* the reason I am—which I'm not saying is true—maybe he'd be right! Now I want you back downstairs, out of that leather jacket and into some kind of respectable shirt. And when our guests get here I'd like you to answer the door, if that wouldn't be too much trouble," she ended mordantly, turning back to the raw vegetables.

He went downstairs, leaving her facing the kitchen sink with her face burning and her pulse elevated.

Mothering! Whoever said it got easier as they got older was a damned liar! She hated the indecisiveness—should she have lashed out or not? Should she have given orders or not? He was an adult, so he deserved being treated like an adult. But he lived in her house, lived in it virtually scot-free at nineteen, when most boys his age were either attending college, paying rent or both. So she had a right to have expectations and make demands now and then. But did she have to take him on today of all days? Thirty minutes before a houseful of guests arrived?

She dried her hands, swiped the droplets of water off her sleeve and followed him downstairs. In his room the stereo was playing quietly and he was standing with his back to the door, facing the chain-and-metal bar that held his clothes, yanking off his shirt as if someone had called him a sissy. She went up behind him and touched his back. He got absolutely still, his wrists still caught in his inverted sleeves.

"I'm sorry I shouted. Please stay home this afternoon. You were wonderful on the drums last night. Dad and I were so proud of you." She slipped her arms around his trunk, gave him a swift kiss between the shoulder blades and left him standing there, his chin on his chest, his shirt still dangling from one wrist.

When the doorbell rang for the first time, Randy was there to answer it, dressed in a pressed cotton shirt and creased pants. It was Aunt Joan, Uncle Clark and Grandma Dorner, probably the easiest person to hug of all Randy knew, because with Grandma Dorner nothing was calamitous. She had a way of bringing everything into perspective. She hugged him in passing, said, "Nice job with those drumsticks," gave him her coat and continued toward the kitchen, asking what she could do to help.

Lisa and Mark came next, arriving at the same time as Michael, all of them swiftly followed by the Padgetts, who descended en masse. Randy's heart gave a little surge as he took Maryann's coat, but he might have been a hired doorman for all the truck she gave him. She handed him her coat, making sure it was off her shoulders so he need not touch her, turning away in conversation with her mother as they moved toward the family room, where a fire was burning in the fireplace and food was spread on the adjacent dining-room table.

He remained on the perimeter of the activity the entire afternoon, feeling like an outsider in his own home, standing back, watching and listening as gifts were opened and *oohed* over, studying Maryann, who never so much as glanced at him, watching his mother and dad, who remained carefully remote from each other at all times but whose eyes occasionally met and exchanged covert messages.

Damn weddings, he thought. If this is what they do to people, I'm never going to get married. Everybody goes crazy, they do things they wouldn't do for a thousand bucks on a normal day. Shit, who needs it?

When the giftwrap was shaped like a mountain and the table looked as though a grasshopper plague had just passed, the carry-through of weariness from three days of activity began to dull and slow everyone. Michael asked Lisa to play "The Homecoming" on the piano and she obliged. Half the guests left; half trailed into the formal living room while some of the women began repacking the gifts into their boxes and making neat stacks of them.

The music ended and the group thinned more. Randy caught Maryann just as she was about to leave and said, "Could I talk to you a minute?"

She found someplace to occupy her eyes: on her purse handle, untwisting it before threading it over her shoulder with a toss of her head. "No, I don't think so."

"Maryann, please. Just come in the living room a minute." He caught her sleeve and tugged.

Reluctantly she followed, refusing to meet his eyes. Outside, twilight had arrived. The room was dusky at the west end, where no lamps were lit. At the east end, the lamp on the abandoned piano made a small puddle of light. Randy led

Maryann around a corner, away from the prying eyes of the departing guests, and stopped beside an upholstered wing chair with a matching ottomon.

"Maryann, I'm sorry about last night," Randy said.

She ran a thumbnail along the welting on the high back of the chair. "Last night was a mistake, all right? I never should have gone outside with you in the first place."

"But you did."

She gave up her preoccupation with the chair and flung him a reprimanding glare. "You're a talented person. It's obvious you come from a home with a lot of love, in spite of the fact that your parents are divorced. I mean, look at this!" She waved a hand at the room. "Look at them, and how they've made a solid show of support throughout this wedding. I know a lot more about you than you think I do—from Lisa. What are you fighting against?" When he made no reply she said, "I don't want to see you, Randy, so please don't call or anything."

She left to join her parents on their way out the door. He dropped onto the ottoman and sat staring at the bookshelves in the far corner, where the gloaming was so deep he could not discern the spines of the volumes.

People were making trips out to Mark's van, carrying the wedding gifts. Lisa and Mark were leaving. He heard her ask, "Where's Randy? I haven't said good-bye to him." He hid silently, waiting out the moments until she gave up calling down to his room and left the house without a good-bye. He heard Grandma Dorner say, "Joan and I will help you clean up this mess, Bess." And his father, "I'll help her, Stella. I've got nothing waiting at home but an empty condo." And Stella again, "All right, Michael, I'll take you up on that. It's just about time for *Murder, She Wrote* and that's one show I don't like to miss." There were more sounds of farewell, and cold air circling Randy's ankles, then the door closed a last time and he listened.

His mother said, "You didn't have to stay."

"I wanted to."

"What's this, a new side to Michael Curran, volunteering for KP?"

"You said it yourself. She's my daughter, too. What do you want me to do?"

"Well, you can carry in the dishes from the dining room, then burn the wrapping paper in the fireplace."

Dishes clinked and footsteps moved between the kitchen and dining room. The water ran, and the dishwasher door opened, something was put away in the refrigerator.

Michael called, "What do you want me to do with this tablecloth?"

"Shake it out and drop it down the clothes chute."

The sliding glass door rolled open and, a few seconds later, shut. Other sounds continued—Michael whistling softly, more footsteps, more running water, then the sound of the fire screen sliding open, the rustle of paper and the roar of it catching flame; in the kitchen the clink of glassware.

"Hey, Bess, this carpet is a mess. Scraps of paper everywhere. You want me to vacuum it?"

"If you want to."

"Is the vacuum cleaner still in the same place?"

"Yup."

Randy heard his father's footsteps head toward the back closet, the door opening, and in moments, the whine of the machine. While the two of them were distracted and the place was noisy, he retreated from his hiding spot and slipped down
to his bedroom, where he put on his headphones and flopped onto his water bed
to try to decide what to do about his life.

Michael finished vacuuming, put away the machine, went into the living room
to turn off the piano light and, returning through the dining room, called, "Bess,
how about this table? You want to take a leaf out of it?"

She came from the kitchen with one dishtowel tied backwards around her waist,
drying her hands on another.

"I guess so. The catch is at that end."

He found the catch and together they pulled the table apart.

"Same table, I see."

"It was too good to get rid of."

"I'm glad you didn't. I always liked it." He swung a leaf into the air, narrowly
missing the chandelier.

"Ooo, luck-y," she said, low-voiced, waiting while he braced the leaf against
the wall.

"Not lucky at all, just careful." He grinned while they put their thighs against
the table and clacked it back together.

"Oh, sure. And who used to break bulbs in the chandelier at least once a year?"

"I seem to remember you broke a couple yourself." He hefted the table leaf.

She was grinning as she headed back to the kitchen. "Under the family-room
sofa, same place as always."

He put the table leaf away, snapped off the dining-room light and returned to
her side by the kitchen sink. She had kicked off her shoes someplace and wore only
nylons on her feet; he'd always liked the air-brushed appearance of a woman's feet
in nylons. He took the dishtowel from her shoulder and began wiping an oversized
salad bowl.

"It feels good to be back here," he said. "Like I never left."

"Don't go getting ideas," she said.

"Just an innocent remark, Bess. Can't a man make an innocent remark?"

"That depends." She squeezed out the dishcloth and began energetically wiping off the countertop while he watched her spine—decorated by the knotted
white dishtowel—bob in rhythm with each swipe she made.

"On what?"

"What went on the night before."

"Oh, that." She turned and he shifted his gaze to the bowl he was supposed to
be drying.

"That was Jose Cuervo talking, I think." She rinsed out her cloth and wiped
off the top of the stove. "People do dumb things at weddings."

"Yeah, I know. Wasn't this bowl one of our wedding gifts?" He studied it while
she went to the sink to release the water.

"Yes." She began spraying the suds down the drain. "From Jerry and Holly Shipman."

"Jerry and Holly . . ." He stared at the bowl. "I haven't thought about them in years. Do you ever see them anymore?"

"I think they live in Sacramento now. Last time I heard from them they'd opened a nursery."

"Still married, though?"

"As far as I know. Here, I'll take that." While she carried the bowl away to the dark dining room he took a stab at a cupboard door, opened the right one and began putting away some glasses. She returned, took off her dishtowel and began polishing the kitchen faucet with it. He finished putting away the glasses; she hung up her towel, dispensed some hand lotion into her palm and they both turned at the same time, relaxing against the kitchen cupboards while she massaged the lotion into her hands.

"You still like anything that smells like roses."

She made no reply, only continued working her hands together until the lotion disappeared and she tugged her sleeves down into place. They stood a space apart, watching each other while the dishwasher played its song of rush and thump, sending out faint vibrations against their spines.

"Thanks for helping me clean up."

"You're welcome."

"If you'd done it six years ago things might have turned out differently."

"People can change, Bess."

"Don't, Michael. It's too scary to even think about."

"Okay." He pushed away from the cabinet edge and held up his hands, surrendering to her wishes. "Not another word. It's been fun. I've enjoyed it. When is my furniture coming?"

He moved toward the front hall and she trailed him. "Soon. I'll call you as soon as anything arrives."

"Okay." He opened the entry coat closet and found his jacket, a puffy brown thing made of leather with raglan sleeves that smelled like penicillin.

"New jacket?" she asked.

Zipping it, he held out an elbow and looked down. "Yes."

"Did you stink up my closet with it?"

He laughed as the zipper hit the two-thirds mark and he tugged the ribbed waist down into place. "Cripes, a man just can't do anything right with you, can he?" His remark was made in the best of humor and they both chuckled afterward.

He reached for the doorknob, paused and turned back. "I don't suppose we ought to kiss good-bye, huh?"

She crossed her arms and leaned back against the newel post, amused. "No, I don't suppose we ought to."

"Yeah . . . I guess you're right." He considered her a moment, then opened the door. "Well, good night, Bess. Let me know if you change your mind. This single life can leave a man a little hard up now and then."

If she'd have had their glass wedding bowl, she'd have lobbed it at his head. "Jeez, thanks, Curran!" she yelled just as the door closed.

Chapter 13

The last of the March snows had come and gone, late blizzards battering Minnesota with fury, followed by the sleety, steely days of early April. The buds on the trees were swollen, awaiting only sun to set them free. The lakes were regaining their normal water level, lost through the past two years of drought, and the ducks were returning, occasionally even some Canadian honkers. Michael Curran stood at the window of his sixth-floor St. Paul office building watching a wedge of them setting their wings for a landing on the Mississippi River. A gust of wind blew the leader and several followers slightly out of formation before they corrected their course with a rocking of wings and disappeared behind one of the lower buildings.

He'd called Bess, of course, twice in the past month, and asked her out but she'd said she didn't think it was wise. In his saner moments he agreed with her. Still, he thought about her a lot.

His secretary, Nina, poked her head into his office and said, "I'm on my way out. Mr. Stringer called and said he won't make it back in before the meeting tonight but he'd see you there." Stringer was the architect of the firm.

Michael swung around. "Oh, thanks, Nina." She was forty-eight, a hundred and sixty pounds, with a nose shaped like a toggle switch and glasses so thick he teased her she'd set the place on fire if she ever laid them in the sun on top of any papers. She kept her hair dyed as black as a grand piano and her nails painted red even though arthritis had begun shaping her fingers like ginseng roots. She came in and poked one into the soil of the schefflera plant beside his desk, found it moist enough and said, "Well, I'm off, then. Good luck at the meeting."

"Thanks. Good night."

" 'Night."

When she was gone the place grew quiet. He sat down at a drafting table, perused Jim Stringer's drawings of the proposed two-story brick structure and wondered if it would ever get built. Four years ago he had purchased a prime lot on the corner of Victoria and Grand, an upscale, yuppie, commercial intersection flanked by upscale, yuppie residential streets lined with Victorian mansions that had regained fashionable status during the last decade. Victoria and Grand—known familiarly throughout the Twin Cities as Victoria Crossing—had in the late seventies sported no less than three vacant corner buildings, each of them formerly a car dealership. The Minnesota Opera Company had rented one old relic nearby for its practice studio and had spread the lonely sound of operatic voices up and down Grand Avenue for a while.

Eventually Grand had been rediscovered, redone, revitalized. Now, its turn-of-the-century flavor was back in the form of Victorian streetlights, red-brick storefronts and flower boxes, three charming malls at the major intersection, along with variety shops that stretched along Grand Avenue itself.

And one vacant parking lot owned by Michael Curran.

Victoria Crossing had everything—ambience, an established reputation as one of the premiere shopping areas in St. Paul, even buses coming off the nearby Summit Avenue Historic Mansion Tours, disgorging tourists by the dozens. Women had discovered its gift shops and restaurants, and met there to shop and eat. Students from nearby William Mitchell Law School had discovered its fine bookstores and came there to buy books. Businessmen from downtown, and politicians from the State Capitol, found it an easy ride up the hill for lunch. Local residents walked to it pushing their baby carriages—baby carriages, no less! Michael had been down there last summer and had actually seen two old-fashioned baby buggies being perambulated by two young mothers. At Christmastime the storekeepers brought in English carolers, served wassail, sponsored a Santa Claus and called it a Victorian Walk. In June they organized a parade, street bands and ethnic food stalls and called it The Grand Old Days, attracting 300,000 people a year.

And all that clientele needed parking space.

Michael offset the edges of his teeth, leaned on the drafting table with both elbows and stared at the revised blueprints—including an enlarged parking ramp—remembering the brouhaha at last month's Concerned Citizens' Meeting.

Our streets are not our own! was the hue and cry of the nearby homeowners, whose boulevards were constantly lined with vehicles.

People can't shop if they can't park! complained the businesspeople till the issue ended in a standoff.

So the meeting had adjourned and Michael had hired a public relations firm to create a friendly letter of intent, including an architect's concept of the building blending with its surroundings; the results of the market analysis with demographics clearly indicating the area could bear the additional upscale businesses; additional demographics showing that the proposed parking ramp would hold more cars than the flat lot presently there; and assurance that Michael himself, as the developer, would remain a joint owner of the building, thus retaining an avid interest in its aesthetic, business and demographic impact not only now but in the future as well. Nearly two hundred copies of the letter had been distributed to business owners and homeowners in the vicinity of the proposed building.

Tonight they'd hash it over again and see if any minds had changed.

The meeting was held in an elementary-school lunchroom that smelled like leftover Hungarian goulash. Jim Stringer was there along with Peter Olson, the project manager from Welty-Norton Construction Company, who was slated to do the building.

The St. Paul city planning director called the meeting to order and allowed Michael to speak first. Michael rose, arbitrarily fixed his eyes on a middle-aged woman in the second row, and said, "The letter with the drawing of the proposed building that you got this past month was from me. This is my architect, Jim Stringer, who'll be co-owner of the building. And this is Pete Olson, the project manager from Welty-Norton. What we want all of you to think about is this. We've already had soil borings done on the lot and the land meets EPA standards—in other words, no contamination. With that obstacle aside, the truth is, that lot is going to be built on eventually, whether you like it or not. Now you can wait for some shyster to come along, who's going to build today and be gone tomorrow, or you can go with Jim and me. He designed it, I'm going to manage it, we'll both own it. Would we put up something unsightly or poorly constructed, or anything that would clash with the aesthetics of Victoria Crossing? Hardly. We want to keep the same flavor that's been so carefully preserved because, after all, that's what makes the Crossing thrive. Jim will answer any questions about building design, and Pete Olson will answer those about actual construction. Now, since our last meeting, we've scaled down the number of square feet in the commercial building and increased the area for parking, and Jim's got the new blueprints here. That's our bid toward compromise but you people have to bend a little, too."

Someone stood up and said, "I live in the apartment building next door. What about my view?"

Someone else demanded to know, "What kind of shops will be in there? If we say yes to the building, we invite our own competition to put a dent in our business."

Another person claimed, "The construction mess will be bad for business."

Someone else said, "Sure, there'll be more parking spots but the extra businesses will bring in extra people and that means more cars on our side streets."

The discussions went on; most of the locals were outraged until after some forty-five minutes a woman stood up at the rear.

"My name is Sylvia Radway and I own The Cooks of Crocus Hill, the cooking school and kitchenwares shop right across the street from that lot. I was at the first meeting and never said a word. I received Mr. Curran's letter and did a lot of thinking about it, and tonight I've been listening to everything that's been said here, and I believe some of you are being unreasonable. I think Mr. Curran is right. That piece of land is too valuable and in too desirable a location to remain a parking lot forever. I happen to like the looks of the building he's proposing, and I think a half-dozen more tasteful specialty shops will be good for business all around. Another thing a lot of you haven't admitted is that when you moved here, you all knew Grand Avenue was a business street, whether you're a local resident or you own a business. If you wanted vacant lots, you should have been here in 1977. I say let him put up his building—it's darned nice-looking—and watch our property values rise."

Sylvia Radway sat down, leaving a lull followed by a murmur of low exchanges.

When the meeting ended, the concerned citizens had not yet voted to allow Michael's building but the tide of objection had clearly moderated.

Michael caught up with Ms. Radway in the school lobby just short of the door.

"Ms. Radway?" he called from behind her.

She turned, paused and waited as he approached. She was perhaps fifty-five, with beautiful naturally wavy hair of silver white, cropped in a soft pouf. Her face was gently grooved, roundish and attractive. The smile upon it looked habitual.

"Ms. Radway . . ." He extended his hand. "I want to thank you for what you said in there."

They shook hands and she told him, "I only said what I believe."

"I think it made a difference. They know you—they don't know me."

"Some people are against change, doesn't matter what it is."

"Boy, don't I know that. I run into them all the time in my business. Well, thanks again. And if there's anything I can ever do for you . . ."

She made her eyes wider and said, "If you take any cooking classes just make sure they're from The Cooks of Crocus Hill."

He thought about her on his way home, the surprise of her standing up in the meeting and speaking up on his behalf. You never know about people, he thought; there are a lot of good ones out there. He smiled, recalling her remark about cooking classes. Well, that was going a little far, but the next time he was up at the Crossing he'd stop in her store and buy something, by way of showing his appreciation.

That happened a week later. He had to meet a fellow from a land surveyor's office for lunch, and suggested Café Latte, which was just across the street from The Cooks of Crocus Hill. After lunch he wandered over to the shop. It was pleasant, with two levels and an open stairway, southern window exposure, hardwood floors and Formica display fixtures of clean, modern lines, everything done in blue and white. It smelled of flavored coffee, herbal teas and exotic spices. The shelves were loaded with everything for the gourmet kitchen—spatulas, soufflé dishes, popover pans, aprons, nutmeg graters, cookbooks and more. He passed some hanging omelette pans and approached the counter. Sylvia Radway stood behind it, reading a computer printout through half-glasses perched on the tip of her nose.

"Hello," he said.

She looked up and smiled like Betty Crocker's grandmother.

"Well, look who's here. Come to sign up for cooking class, did you, Mr. Curran?"

He scratched his head and winced. "Not exactly."

She picked up a jar off the counter and tipped her head back to read its label. "Some pickled fiddlehead fern, then?"

He laughed and said, "You're kidding." She handed him the jar. "Pickled fiddlehead fern," he read. "You mean people actually eat this stuff?"

"Absolutely."

He glanced at the assortment of jars and read their labels. "Chutney—what in the world is chutney? And pecan praline mustard glaze?"

"Delicious on a baked ham. Just smear it on and bake."

"Oh yeah?" he said, taking a second look at the glaze.

"Steam a few fresh asparagus spears with it, a couple new potatoes with the skins on, and you have a meal fit for a visiting dignitary."

She made it sound so easy.

"Trouble is, I don't have anything to steam them in."

She turned with a flourish of the palm, presenting the whole of her shop. "Take your pick. Metal or bamboo."

He perused the store and felt out of his league. Pots and pans and brushes and squeezers and things that looked as if they belonged in a doctor's office. "I don't cook," he admitted, and for the first time ever, felt foolish saying so.

"Probably because nobody's ever turned you on to it. We have a lot of men in our basics classes. When they start they don't know which end of a spatula goes up, but by the time they finish they're making omelettes and quick breads and poached chickens and bragging to their mothers about it."

"Yeah?" He cocked his head and turned back to her, genuinely interested. "You mean anybody can learn to cook, even a dodo who's never fried an egg?"

"The name of our beginners' class is 'How to Boil Water 101.' Maybe that answers your question."

When they'd both chuckled, she went on. "Cooking has become a unisexual skill. I'd say we probably have an even mix of men and women in our classes now. People are marrying later in life, men leave home, get apartments of their own and get tired of eating out all the time. Some get divorced. Some have wives who work full-time and don't want to do the cooking. Voilà!" She threw up her hands and snapped her fingers. "The Cooks of Crocus Hill! The answer to the yuppie quandary at mealtime."

She was such an excellent saleswoman, he didn't even realize he was being pitched until she asked, "Would you like to see our kitchen? It's right upstairs."

She led the way past a tall, fragrant display of coffee beans in clear plastic dispensers to an open stairway of smooth, blond varnished oak. On the second floor more stock was arranged on neat white Formica cubes. Beyond it, at one end of the building, they emerged into a gleaming stainless-steel and white-tiled kitchen. A long counter with blue upholstered stools faced the cooking area. Above it hung a long mirror angled so that any demonstrations in progress could be viewed from the retail sales floor. When Michael hesitated she waved him in. "Come on . . . have a look." He meandered farther inside and perched on one of the blue stools.

"We teach you everything from basic equipment to how to stock your kitchen with staples, to the proper way of measuring liquid and dry ingredients. Our instructors demonstrate, then you actually prepare foods yourself. I take it you're single, Mr. Curran."

"Ah . . . yes."

"We have a lot of single men registering for classes. College graduates, widowers, divorcees. Most of them feel like fish out of water when they first come in here. Some are genuinely sad, especially the widowers, and act as if they need . . . well, nurturing, I guess. But do you know what? I've never seen one leave unhappy that he took the class."

Michael looked around, trying to imagine himself struggling with wire whips and spatulas while a bunch of people looked on.

"Do you have an equipped kitchen?" Sylvia Radway asked.

"No, nothing. I just moved into a condo a few months ago and I don't even have dishes."

"I'll tell you what," she said. "Since you and I are going to be neighbors, I'll make you a deal. I'll give you your first cooking class free if you buy whatever kitchenwares you need from the shop. I won't sell you a thing that's unnecessary. If you enjoy it—and I have a hunch you will—you'll pay for any extra classes you want to take. How does that sound?"

"How long do classes last?"

"Three weeks. One night a week, or afternoon, if you prefer, three hours each class. If you enjoy them, the second series continues for an additional three weeks."

It was tempting. He hated that empty kitchen at home, and eating out all the time had long ago lost its appeal. His evenings were lonely and he often filled them by working late.

"One other thing, Mr. Curran . . . speaking from a purely objective point of view, just in case you're interested, today's women love men who cook for them. That old stereotype has definitely done a turnaround. It is often the men who woo the women with their culinary expertise."

He thought about Bess and imagined the surprise on her face if he sat her at a table and pulled a gourmet supper out of the kitchen. She'd get up and search the broom closet for the cook!

"All I have to do is buy a couple kettles, huh?"

"Well . . . I'll be honest. It'll take more than a couple kettles. You'll need a wooden spoon or two and some staples at the grocery store. What do you say?"

He smiled. She smiled. And the pact was made.

On the night of his first class, Michael stood in his walk-in closet wondering what a person wore to cooking school. He owned no chef's hat or butcher's apron. His mother had always worn housedresses around the kitchen, and often had a dish-towel slung over her shoulder.

He chose creased blue jeans and a stylized blue-and-white sweatshirt with a ribbed collar.

At The Cooks of Crocus Hill, the class numbered eight, and five of them were men. He felt less stupid to find the other four men present, even less when one leaned close and quietly confided to him, "I can't even make Kool-Aid."

Their teacher was not Sylvia Radway herself but a plain-faced Scandinavian-looking woman around forty-five, portly, named Betty McGrath. She had a cheer-ful attitude and a knack for teasing in exactly the right way that made them laugh at their own clumsiness and revel in each small success. After a brief lecture they were given a list of recommended kitchen supplies, then they made applesauce muffins and omelettes. They learned how to measure flour and milk, crack and whip eggs, mix with a spoon—"Muffins should look lumpy"—grease a muffin tin, fill it two-thirds full, dice ham and onions, slice mushrooms uniformly, shred cheese, pre-heat an omelette pan, test it for readiness, fold the omelette and get the whole works cooking at the proper time. They learned how to test the muffins for doneness, re-move them from the tin and serve them attractively in a basket lined with a cloth napkin, along with their nicely plumped omelette, all timed to end up on the table together—hot and pretty and perfect.

When he sat down to taste the fruits of his labor, Michael Curran felt as proud as the day he'd received his college diploma.

He furnished his kitchen with Calphalon cookware, oversized spoons and rubber scrapers. He bought himself some blue-and-white dishes and a set of silverware. He found to his delight that he enjoyed poking around Sylvia Radway's shop, buying a lemon squeezer for Caesar salad dressing, a French chef's knife for dicing onion, a potato peeler for cleaning vegetables, a wire whip for making gravy.

Gravy.

Holy old nuts, he learned how to make gravy! And cheese sauce on broccoli!

They did it the night of the second class, along with roasted chicken, mashed potatoes and salad. That night when the meal was done, the man who'd whispered he couldn't make Kool-Aid—his name turned out to be Brad Wilchefski—sat down at the table grinning and saying, "I don't believe this, I just damn well don't believe this." Wilchefski was built like a Harley biker and came close to dressing like one. He had frizzy red hair and a beard to match and wore John Lennon glasses. He looked like a man who'd be at ease walking around a campfire gnawing on a turkey drumstick and wiping his hands on his thighs.

"My old lady'd shit if she could see what I done," he said.

"Mine, too," Michael said.

"You divorced?"

"Yes. You?"

"Naw. She just took off and left me with the kid. Figured, what the hell, she was dumber'n a stump. If she could cook, I can cook."

"My wife always did all the cooking when we were first married, then she went back to college and wanted me to help around the house but I refused. I thought it was woman's work but you know something? It's kind of fun." It didn't occur to Michael that he hadn't even referred to his second wife, only his first.

Wilchefski chewed some chicken, tried some potatoes and gravy and said, "Any of the guys tease me and I'll serve 'em up their own gonads in cheese sauce."

Michael was amazed at how cooking had changed his outlook. Evenings, he left the office when everyone else did. He stopped at Byerly's and bought fresh meat and vegetables and hurried home to prepare them in his new cookware. One night he dumped some wine from his goblet into the pan when he was sautéing beef and mushrooms, delighting himself with the results. Another night he sliced an orange and laid it on a chicken breast. He discovered the wonders of fresh garlic, and the immediacy of stir-frying, and the old-fashioned delectation of meat loaf. More important, he discovered within himself a growing satisfaction with his life as it was and a broadening approval for himself as a person. His singleness took on a quality of peace rather than loneliness, and he began to explore other lone occupations that brought their own satisfaction: reading, sailing, even doing his own laundry instead of taking it to the cleaners.

The first time he took a load of clothes out of the dryer and folded them, he thought, Why, hell, that was simple! The realization made him laugh at himself for all the months he'd stubbornly refused to use the washer and dryer simply because he "didn't know how."

He hadn't seen Bess since the wedding but in mid-May she called to say the first of his furniture had arrived.

"What exactly?"

"Living-room sofa and chairs."

"The leather ones?"

"No, those are for the family room. These are the cloth-covered ones for the formal living room."

"Oh."

"Also, the workroom called to say the window treatments are all done and ready to install. Can we set up a date for my installer to come out and do that?"

"Sure. When?"

"I'll have to check with him but give me a couple of dates and I'll get back to you."

"Do I have to be there?"

"Not necessarily."

"Then any day is okay. I can leave the key with the caretaker."

"Fine . . ." A pause followed, then, in a more intimate voice, "How have you been, Michael?"

"Okay. Busy."

"Me too."

He wanted to say, I'm learning to cook, but to what avail? She had made it clear the kisses they'd shared had been ill-advised; she wanted no more of them or of him on a personal level.

They spoke briefly of the children, comparing notes on when they'd last visited Lisa, and how Randy was doing. There seemed little else to say.

Bess put a postscript on the conversation by ending, "Well, I'll get back to you about when to leave the key."

Michael hung up disappointed. What had he wanted of her? To see her again? Her approval of the strides he was making in his life? No. Simply to be in the condo when she came by with her workmen to bring furniture or trim windows. He realized he had been subconsciously planning to see her repeatedly during those times but apparently that was not to be the case.

On the day of the installation, Michael arrived home in the evening to find his living-room sofa and chairs sitting like boulders in a wide river, looking a little forlorn before the fireplace, but his windows sporting new coverings: vertical blinds and welted, padded cornice boards in the living room, dining room, family room and bedrooms; unfussy little things he immediately liked in the bathrooms and the laundry room.

On the kitchen counter was a note in Bess's handwriting.

Michael,

I hope you like the living-room furniture and the window treatments. I hung the custom bedspreads in your entry closet until your beds arrive. I think they're really going to look classy. The upholsterer who's covering the matching pair of chairs for your bedroom says those should be done next week. One of the vertical vanes in the living room (south window) had a smudge on it so I took it along and will return it as soon as the shop replaces it. I have shipping invoices on your guest-bedroom furniture and the family-room entertainment unit, which means they should be coming in next week, so I'll probably have to bug you to let me in again soon. It'll be exciting to watch it all come together. Talk to you soon. Bess.

He stood with his thumb touching her signature, befuddled by the emptiness created within him by her familiar hand.

He went to the entry closet and found the thick, quilted spreads folded over two giant hangers and got a queer feeling in his chest, realizing she'd been here, putting his house in order, hanging things in his closet. How welcome the idea of her in his personal space, as if she belonged there, where she'd been years ago. How unwelcome the thought of being no more to her than a client.

In those moments he missed her with a desolate longing like that following a lovers' quarrel.

He telephoned her, striving to keep his voice casual.

"Hi, Bess, it's Michael."

"Michael, hi! How do you like the window treatments?"

"I like them a lot."

"And the furniture?"

"Furniture looks great."

"Really?"

"I like it."

"So do I. Listen, things are going to be coming in hot-and-heavy now. I got some more invoices today from Swaim. All of your living-room tables have been shipped. Would you like me to hold them and bring them out all at once or keep bringing them out as they arrive?"

As they arrive, so I have more chances to bump into you. "Whatever's more convenient for you."

"No, I want to do whatever is more convenient for you. You're the customer."

"It's no bother to me. I can just leave word with the caretaker to let you in whenever you need to, and you can go ahead and do your thing."

"Great. Actually that does work out best for me because my storage space is really limited and at this time of year, after the post-Christmas rush, everything seems to be coming in at once."

"Bring it over, then. I'm only too glad to see the place fill up. Any sign of my leather sofa yet?"

"Sorry, no. I'd guess it'll be at least another month or more."

"Well . . . let me know."

"I will."

"Ah, Michael, one other thing. I can begin bringing in small accessories anytime. I just need to know if you want me to choose them or if you want to help. Some clients like to be in on these choices and others simply don't want to be bothered."

"Well . . . hell, Bess, I don't know."

"Why don't I do this. When I spot accessory pieces I think would fit, I'll bring them in and leave them. If there's anything you don't like just let me know and we'll try something else. How does that sound?"

"Great."

He grew accustomed after that to coming home and finding another item or two in place—the entry console, the living-room tables, a giant ceramic fish beside the living-room fireplace, a pair of framed prints above it (he loved how the snow geese on the right print became a continuation of the flock on the left), a floor lamp, three huge potted plants in containers shaped like seashells that suddenly made the living room look complete.

His divorce became final in late May and he received the papers feeling much as he did when a business deal was concluded. He put them away in a file drawer, thought, *Good, that's final,* and made out one last check for his lawyer.

He signed up for his third series of cooking classes and learned to plan menus and make a chocolate cake roll with fudge sauce. He met a woman in class named Jennifer Ayles, who was fortyish and divorced and relatively attractive, and who was looking for ways to alleviate her loneliness so had joined the class to fill her evenings. He took her to a Barry Manilow concert, and she talked him into using her son's golf clubs and trying golf for the first time in his life. Afterward at her house he tried to kiss her and she burst into tears and said she still loved her husband, who had left her for another woman. They ended up talking about their exes, and he admitted he still had feelings for Bess but that she didn't return them, or, maybe more accurately, wouldn't *let* herself return them and had warned him to stay away.

He bought a patio table and ate his evening meals on the deck overlooking the lake.

A torchère appeared in his bedroom and a faux pedestal in the center of his gallery with a note: *You sure you want me to pick out this piece of sculpture? I think this one should be strictly your choice. Let me know.*

He left a message with Heather at the Blue Iris: "Tell Bess okay, I'll look for the piece of sculpture myself."

Another time a message was left on his answering machine: "Get yourself some new sheets, Michael. Your bed is here! We'll deliver it tomorrow." He bought designer sheets that looked like blue-and-lavender rain had splashed across them driven by a hard wind, and slept in a fully decorated bedroom suite for the first time since separating from Darla.

And finally, in late June, the message he'd been waiting for: "Michael, it's Bess, Monday morning, eight forty-five. Just called to say your dining-room table is here and your leather sofa is on its way by truck from the port of entry on the east coast. Should be here any day. Talk to you soon."

He came home the following day at 4 P.M. and found her in his dining room removing the heavy plastic factory wrapping from his six fully upholstered dining-room chairs. A new smoked-glass table was centered beneath the chandelier, which was lit, even in the bright summer afternoon.

He stopped in the doorway and said, "Well . . . hello." It was the first time he'd seen her since Lisa's wedding.

She was on her knees beside an upturned chair, pulling oversized staples out of its four feet with a screwdriver and a pair of needle-nosed pliers. She lifted her head, used one whole arm to knock her hair out of her eyes and said, "Michael, I didn't think you came home this early."

He ambled inside and dropped his keys onto the glass top sofa table beside something that hadn't been there that morning—an arrangement of cream silk flowers stuck in a snifter full of clear marbles.

"I don't usually but I was clear up in Marine so I decided not to go back downtown to the office. How do they look?" he said of the chairs.

"So far so good." Only two chairs were unwrapped.

He removed his suit coat, tossed it onto the sofa and crossed to one of the sliding glass doors. "It's hot in here. Why didn't you open the doors?"

"I didn't think I should."

He opened the vertical blinds and both sets of wide doors, at the living and dining ends of the room. The summer air bellied in, then receded to a faint breeze that trembled the leaves of the new green plants and toyed with the vanes of the blinds.

He went to Bess. "Here, let me help you with that."

"Oh, no, this is my job. Besides, you're all dressed in your good clothes."

"Well, so are you." She was wearing a classy yellow sundress, its matching jacket draped over the back of the sofa beside his jacket.

"Here, give me those." He took the tools out of her hand, knelt and began pulling the remaining staples.

Still kneeling beside him, she looked at her hands and brushed them together with three soft claps. "Well . . . thanks."

"Something new over there." He nodded backwards at the silk bouquet.

She got to her feet, revealing black patent-leather pumps and giving off her customary aura of roses. "I kept it simple, only one kind of flower and very small, which tends to be a little more masculine."

"Looks nice. And if I get bored I can lay a string in a circle on the carpet and shoot marbles."

She laughed and began examining one of the unwrapped chairs. It was armless, with a solid upholstered back shaped like a cowboy's gravestone, covered in a subtle design of mauves and grays that reminded him of the seashore after waves have receded.

"Now these are smart. Michael, this place is coming together so beautifully! Are you pleased, or is there anything you don't like? Because the final okay has to be yours."

"No! No, I like it all. I have to hand it to you, Bess, you really know your business."

"Well, I'd better, or I won't have it long."

He finished with the chair and righted it, and she slid over another to be unwrapped while he reached up and loosened the knot in his tie and freed his collar button.

Setting back to work, he said, "You've got a suntan."

She lifted one elbow, glanced at it. "Mmm . . . a little."

"How did that happen?" He let his eyes flick to her, then back to his work. In all the years they'd been married she'd never taken time to lie in the sun.

"Heather's been scolding me for working too hard, so I've been knocking off a couple hours early once or twice a week and lying in the backyard. I have to admit, it's felt heavenly. It's made me realize that in all the years we've . . . I've lived in that house I never utilized the backyard the way I should have. The view from there is magnificent, especially with the boats out on the water."

"I've been doing the same thing from my deck." He nodded toward one of the sets of sliding glass doors. "I got myself that patio table and I sit out there in the evening and enjoy the water when I'm not on it."

"You're sailing?"

"A little. Fishing a little, too."

"We're slowing down some, aren't we, Michael?"

He lifted his gaze to find her studying him with a soft expression in her eyes.

"We deserve it, at our age."

He had stopped working. Their gazes remained twined while seconds tiptoed past and the screwdriver hung forgotten in his hand. Outside, a lawn mower droned, and the scent of fresh-cut grass came in, along with a faint breeze that ruffled the pages of a newspaper lying on the sofa. In the park next door children called, at play.

Bess studied Michael and recognized not age but a rekindling of feelings she had experienced years ago. In her imagination it was Lisa and Randy outside, and she and Michael thinking, *Hurry, while the kids are busy playing.* Sometimes it had happened that way—the rare hot summer day, the rare hot summer urge, the mad scramble with their clothing, the quickie with shirttails getting in the way, sometimes the two of them giggling, and the mad rush if the kids slammed the kitchen screen door before they had finished.

The memory hit like a broadside, while she became conscious of his attractiveness as he knelt beside the overturned chair, with his open collar casting shadows on his throat, and the breast pocket of his shirt flattened against his chest, and his trousers taut around the hips and his steady hazel eyes hinting he might be having much the same thoughts as she.

Bess's eyes dropped first. "I talked to Lisa yesterday," she said, breaking the spell and prattling on while they busied their eyes with more sensible pursuits.

He finished unwrapping the chairs while she folded and stacked the bulky packing material. When the entire dining-room set was in place, they stood at opposite ends of the table, admiring it in spite of the many blotchy fingerprints on the edge of the glass.

"Do you have any glass cleaner?" she inquired.

"No."

"I suppose it's futile to ask if you have any vinegar?"

"That I have."

She looked properly surprised, which pleased Michael as he went off to the kitchen to find it as well as a brand-new blue-and-white checked dishcloth and a roll of paper towels.

When he returned to Bess, she said, "You have to mix it with water, Michael."

"Oh."

He went away once more and returned in a minute with a blue bowl full of vinegar water. When she reached for it, he said, "I'll do it."

She watched him clean his new tabletop, watched him bend down at times while working at a stubborn smudge, catching a reflection across the glass. Sometimes his shirt would be stretched across his shoulder blades in a way that tightened her groin muscles. Sometimes the light from the chandelier would play across his hair and make her hands feel empty.

When he finished he returned the bowl to the kitchen while she went to the sofa table, confiscated the cream silk flowers and set them in the middle of the larger table. Once more they studied it, exchanging glances of approval.

"A raffia mat is all we need," she said.

"Mm . . ."

"Do you like raffia mats?"

"What's raffia?"

"Dried palm . . . you know, Oriental-looking."

"Oh, sure."

"I'll pick one up at the store and bring it out next time I come."

"Fine."

The table was polished, the chairs in place, the centerpiece centered; nothing more needed doing; they had no excuse to linger.

"Well . . ." Bess lifted her shoulders, let them drop and headed for her jacket. "I guess that's it, then. I'd better get home."

He was closer to the jacket and was holding it for her before she could reach it. She slipped it on and fluffed her hair free from the neck of the garment, picked up a black patent handbag and looped it over her shoulder. When she turned he was standing very near with his hands in his trouser pockets.

"How about having dinner with me on Saturday night?" he asked.

"Me?" she asked, her eyes wide, a hand at her chest.

"Yes, you."

"Why?"

"Why not?"

"I don't think so, Michael. I told you the other two times you called that I don't think it's wise."

"What were you thinking about a minute ago?"

"When?"

"You know when."

"Michael, you're so vague."

"And you're a damned liar."

"I've got to go."

"Running away?"

"Don't be ridiculous."

"What about Saturday night?"

"I said I don't think so."

He grinned. "You'll miss the chance of a lifetime. I'm cookin'."

"You!" Her expression of surprise lit him up inside.

He shrugged and raised his palms to hip level. "I took it up."

She had lost the ability to speak, giving him a distinct advantage.

"Dinner here, we'll christen my new table. What do you say?"

She seemed to realize her mouth was hanging open and shut it. "I'll have to hand it to you, Michael, you still have the ability to shock me."

"Six-thirty?" he asked.

"All right," she replied cockily. "This I've got to see."

"You'll drive over?"

"Sure. If you can cook, I can drive."

"Good. I'll see you then."

He walked her to the door, opened it and leaned one shoulder against the door-frame, watching her as she pushed the button for the elevator. When it arrived she began to step aboard, changed her mind and held the door open with one hand while turning to Michael. "Are you putting me on? Do you really know how to cook?"

He laughed and replied, "Wait till Saturday night and see," then went into his condo and closed the door.

Chapter 14

Michael's cream leather sofa arrived on Friday and Bess moved heaven and earth to find a transport service to deliver it to his place Saturday morning. She wanted it there, wanted to walk in and see it in place that evening, wanted to sit on it her-self with Michael in the room and rejoice with him over its sumptuousness. She was as giddy as if it were her own.

She was bound and determined that dressing for dinner with him was *not* going to take on the importance of a State visit. She wore white slacks and a short-sleeved cotton sweater of periwinkle blue with an unornamented gold chain at her neck and tiny gold loops in her ears. She'd had her hair cut and styled but that appoint-ment had been made before Michael's invitation had been issued. She polished her nails but that happened twice a week. She wore perfume but it, too, was as routine as checking a watch. She shaved her legs but they needed it.

The only thing she couldn't dismiss was the new lacy underwear she'd splurged on yesterday, when she'd *just happened* to be passing Victoria's Secret. They were powder blue, with a deep plunge on the bra and plenty of hip showing inside the panties, and they'd set her back thirty-four dollars.

She put them on, looked in the mirror, thought, *How silly,* and took them off. Replaced them with plain white. Cursed and put on the sexy ones again. Grimaced at her reflection. *You want to get tangled up with a man you've already failed with once?* On, off, on, off, three times before defiantly putting the blue ones on and leaving them.

Michael had thrown himself upon the mercy of Sylvia Radway and admitted, "I want to impress a woman. I'm cooking for her for the first time and I want every-thing to be the way women like it. What should I do?"

The result was a pair of candle holders with blue tapers, a bowl of fresh white roses and blue irises, real cloth place mats and napkins, stem glasses and chilled Pouilly-Fuissé, a detailed menu plan and Michael's nervous stomach.

At ten to six on Saturday evening he paced around the table he'd just finished setting, surveying the results.

Obvious, Curran, disgustingly obvious.

But he wanted to knock her socks off. Well, hell, he admitted, he wanted to knock off a lot more than her socks. So what was wrong with that? They were both single and uninvolved with anyone else. Still, roses. Lord, roses. And he'd tied the napkins around the foot of the stemglasses just the way Sylvia had shown him. Sylvia said women most certainly appreciated details like that, but now that he'd set the stage Michael studied this invitation to thump and figured Bess would be back in her car before he could say Casanova.

He checked his watch, panicked and hit for the bathroom to shower and change.

Because the table suddenly looked so obviously overdone, he himself purposely set out to look underdone. White pleated jeans, a polo shirt in big blocks of primary colors and bare feet in a pair of white moccasins. A gold chain around his wrist. A little mousse in his hair. A splash of cologne. Nothing out of the ordinary.

So he told himself while he meticulously combed his eyebrows, wiped every water spot off the bathroom vanity, put away every piece of discarded clothing from his bedroom, smoothed the bedspread, dusted the furniture tops with his hands, closed the vertical blinds and left the torchère on beside the bed when he left the room.

She called from the lobby at precisely 6:30.

"That you, Bess?"

"It's me."

"Be right down."

He left his condo door open and rode the elevator down. She was waiting on the other side of the door when it opened, looking as studiedly casual as he.

"You didn't need to come down. I know the way up."

He smiled. "Blame it on good breeding." She stepped aboard and he stole a glance at her, remarking, "Nice evening, huh?"

Her return glance was as cautious as his. "Beautiful."

In his condo a strong draft from all the open patio doors made a wind tunnel of the foyer. It wafted the smell of Bess's rosy perfume into his nostrils as she entered ahead of him. He closed the door and the wind immediately ceased. Bess preceded him through the foyer toward the gallery, where she paused.

"Nothing for the pedestal yet?" she asked.

"I haven't had time to look."

"There's a wonderful gallery in Minneapolis on France Avenue, called Estelle's. I was looking at some Lalique glass pieces there and also some interesting hammered brass. Might be something you'd like."

"I'll remember that. Come on in." He passed her and led the way toward the kitchen and the adjoining family room, stopping in the doorway and deliberately blocking her view. "You ready for this sofa?" he teased, looking back over his shoulder.

"Let me see!" she said impatiently, nudging him on the back.

With his hands on the doorframe he barricaded the way. "Aw, you don't really want to see it, do you?"

"Michael!" she exclaimed, giving his shoulder blades a pair of good-natured clunks with both fists. "I've been waiting four months for this! I can smell it clear from here!"

"I thought you hated the smell of leather."

"I do but this is different." She pushed again and he let himself get thrust forward out of her way. She headed straight for the Natuzzi, five pieces of swank off-white leather that took two turns on its way around the perimeter of the room, dividing it from the kitchen and facing the new entertainment unit. She dropped onto the sofa dead center and snuggled deep. The supple cushions rose to envelop her like a caress.

"Ah . . . luxury. Sheer luxury. Do you like it?"

He sat down at a right angle to her. "Are you kidding? Does a man like a Porsche? A World Series ticket on the first-base line? A cold Coors on a ninety-degree day?"

"Mmm . . ." She nestled down deeper and closed her eyes. Momentarily they opened and she said, "I'll confess something. I've never sold a Natuzzi before."

"Why, you phony. Here all the time I thought you knew what you were talking about."

"I did. I just hadn't *experienced* it." Abruptly she popped up and began examining the sofa, working her way along its length. "I didn't get a chance to look at it before it was delivered. Is everything all right? No tears? No marks? Anything?"

"Nothing as far as I could see. Of course, I haven't had much time to look." She reached his knees and detoured around them as she prowled the sofa, eyeing its stitching and curves and welting. When she'd finished she stood with hands akimbo, looking at the thing. "It really does stink, doesn't it?"

He burst out laughing, sitting with his arms stretched out at shoulder level along the tops of the cushions, feeling the soft leather. "How can you say that about an eight-thousand-dollar sofa?"

"I'm just being realistic. Leather stinks. It's as simple as that. So how do you like the dining-room furniture by now?" She walked toward the doorway leading from the family room into the dining room while he remained where he was, waiting for her reaction.

The sight of the table stopped her the way the ground stops a thrown bronc rider. "Why, Michael!" She stared at his handiwork while he studied her back. "My goodness . . ."

He got himself out of the sofa and went up behind her. "I did invite you for supper, remember?"

"Yes, but . . . what an elegant table," she said in disbelief. "Did you do all this?"

"Not without a little advice."

"From whom?" She ventured closer to the table but not too close, still caught in the throes of disbelief.

"A lady who owns a cooking school."

She gaped at him in amazement. "You went to cooking school?"

"Yes, actually, I did."

"Why, Michael, I'm stunned." Half-turning, she swept a hand toward the centerpiece. "All this . . . roses, blue irises . . ." He could tell she was surprised by his sentimentalism, but he recalled very clearly how she associated blue irises with her grandmother. Her lips closed and her expression became wistful as she continued admiring the flowers, then the matching linens, the stemware.

"Would you like a glass of wine, Bess?"

"Yes, I . . ." She looked back at him but seemed unable to put coherent thoughts together. "Please," she finished.

"Be right back."

In the kitchen he checked the glazed ham in the oven, turned on the burner under the tiny red potatoes, checked to make sure his fresh asparagus was still waiting beneath a lid, centered the cheese sauce recipe directly beneath the microwave, consulted his careful list of starting times and finally opened the wine.

Returning to the living room, he found Bess standing before the sliding door, enjoying the view, with the breeze riffling the hair at her temples. She turned her head at his approach and he handed her a goblet.

"Thanks."

"Shall we go out?" he suggested.

"Mmm . . ." She was sipping as she answered. He slid the screen open, waiting while she stepped onto the deck before him.

They sat on either side of a small white patio table, angled toward the lake in cushioned chairs that bounced at the smallest provocation. The setting was lovely, the evening jewel-clear, their surroundings those of evocative movies, but suddenly they found themselves tongue-tied. Everything had changed with that dining-room table: there was no question anymore, this was a stab at a new beginning. Subjects of conversation were strangely elusive after their easy-fire repartee upon her arrival. They watched some sails on the water, the rim of trees outlining Manitou Island, waves washing up at the feet of some nearby cottonwoods. They listened to the soft slap of water meeting shore, the particular click of the cottonwood leaves against one another, the sound of themselves drinking, the metallic *bing* of their gently bouncing chairs. They felt the warmth of summer press their skins and smelled the aroma of someone lighting a barbecue grill nearby, and that of their own supper stealing outside.

But everything had changed and they understood this, so they sat unnaturally hushed, experiencing the uncertainties of forging into that second-time-around.

Finally Bess broke the silence, turning to look at him as she spoke.

"So when did you take this cooking course?"

"I started in April and took nine classes."

"Where?"

"Over at Victoria Crossing, place called The Cooks of Crocus Hill. I'm doing some developing over there, and I just happened to meet the woman who owns the cooking school."

"It's funny Lisa didn't mention it."

"I didn't tell Lisa." From the first, if only subconsciously, he'd been planning this day, planning to shock Bess. Funny, though, now that tonight was here all sense of smugness had fled. He felt nervous and afraid of failure.

"This woman . . ." Bess looked into her wine. ". . . is she someone important?"

"No, not at all."

His answer wrought only the subtlest change in Bess, but he detected it in the faint relaxing of her shoulders, of her lips just before she sipped her wine, of her eyes as she lifted them to the distant sails on the water. Too, she set her chair barely bouncing again, sending up a rhythmic *bing, bing, bing* that eased some tension in his belly.

He crossed his feet on the handrail and said, "I've been trying to do more things for myself lately."

"Like the cooking?"

"Yes. And reading and sailing, and I've even gone to a couple of movies. I guess I just came to the realization that you can't always rely on somebody else to take away your loneliness. You've got to do something about it yourself."

"Is it working?" She looked over at him.

"Yes. I'm happier than I've been in years."

She watched him study the wine in his glass while a slow grin stole over his lips. "You probably won't believe it, Bess, but . . ." His gaze shifted over to her. "I'm even doing my own laundry." She didn't tease as he'd expected.

"That's wonderful, Michael. That's growth, it really is."

"Yes, well . . . times change. A person's got to change with them."

"It's hard for men, especially men like you, whose mothers filled those tradi-tional roles. You're in the generation that got caught in the cross fire. For the young guys like Mark it's easier. They grew up taking home ec class, with working moth-ers and a more blurred line between the obligations of the sexes, if you will."

"I never expected to like any of these domestic jobs but they're not bad at all, especially the cooking. I really enjoy it. Speaking of which . . ." He checked his watch and dropped his feet off the rail. "I've got some last-minute things to do. Why don't you just sit here and relax? More wine?"

"No, thanks. I'm going to be more sensible tonight. Besides, the view is heady enough."

He smiled at her and left.

She remained inert, listening to sounds drifting out from the kitchen—the clack of kettle covers, the bell on the microwave, running water—and wondered what he was making. The sun lowered and the lake looked bluer. The eastern sky be-came purple around the edges. Over on the public beach people began rolling up their towels and heading home. One-by-one the sails began disappearing from the water. The pastoral coming of evening, coupled with the wine and the sense of dis-solving friction between herself and Michael, brought on a welcome serenity in Bess. She dropped her head back against the wall and basked in it.

After a full five minutes she took her empty wineglass and went inside, past the dining-room table to the kitchen doorway, against which she lounged with one shoulder. Michael had put on an audiotape of something New Age and keyboard-ish, and was measuring Parmesan cheese into a bowl, a blue-and-white dishtowel over his left shoulder. The picture he made was still so unexpected she felt a momentary thrill, as if she'd met this attractive stranger only tonight.

"Anything I can do to help?"

He looked around and smiled. "Nope, not a thing. Everything's under control . . ." He laughed nervously. ". . . I think." With a wire whisk he whipped an egg, then opened the refrigerator and took out a salad bowl filled with romaine.

"Caesar?" she inquired.

"Class number two." He grinned.

She raised one eyebrow and teased, "Do you trade recipes?"

"Listen, you're making me nervous, standing there watching me. If you want to do something, go light the candles."

"Matches?" she asked, boosting off the doorway.

"Oh, hell." He searched four kitchen drawers, came up with none, pawed through another and frantically lifted a lid off a simmering kettle before stalking toward his office. Finding none there, either, he hurried back to the kitchen. "Will you do me a favor? Check the pockets of my suitcoats. Sometimes I pick them up at restaurants. I've got to get these vegetables off the stove."

"Where are your suitcoats?"

"Master-bedroom closet."

She walked into his bedroom to find it impeccably clean, the torchère softly glowing, the bed neatly made. The room itself was engaging. All the decor items she'd chosen blended together in a wholly pleasing way: wallpaper, blinds, bedspread, matching chairs, art prints, a floor urn. The gleaming black bedroom furniture had a rich sheen, even in the reduced lighting. She particularly liked a unique, masculine piece called a dressing chest, and the headboard, shaped like a theater marquee from the thirties. Beside the bed the cover of a *Hunting* magazine displayed a stag with its rack in velvet. Michael's pocket tailings lay atop the chest of drawers— billfold, coins, somebody's business card, a ballpoint pen but no matches. Though she had planned the room and been in it countless times while decor items were being delivered, now that it was in use and occupied by his personal items, she felt like a window peeper in it.

She opened his closet door, searched for the interior light and switched it on. The closet smelled like British Sterling and him, a mixture so potent with nostalgia she felt her face heat. His shirts hung on one rack, jeans on another, suits on the third. A row of shoes toed the mopboard, one pair of Reeboks with worn white sweat socks poked inside. A rack of ties hung to the left of the door; one had slipped off and lay on the floor. She picked it up and hung it with the others, an insidiously wifely reaction that struck her only after the deed was done, and she whipped around to make sure he wasn't standing there watching her. He wasn't, of course, and she felt foolish.

Searching his jacket pockets proved nearly as personal as frisking the man himself. In one she found half of a theater ticket—*Pretty*, it said; presumably he'd seen the current hit *Pretty Woman*. In another was a used toothpick, in another an ad he'd torn out advertising a piece of land for sale.

She found some matches at last and scurried from the closet as if she'd just watched a porn movie in it.

The wine glasses were filled and their salad bowls on the table when she returned to it. She lit the blue candles while he came in with two loaded plates.

"Sit down," he said, motioning with a plate, "there." When she was seated, he placed before her a plate of steaming, savory food—glazed ham, tiny red potatoes in parsley butter and asparagus with cheese sauce. She stared at it, dumbfounded, while he seated himself at the opposite end of the table and watched for her reaction.

"Holy cow," she said, still staring at his accomplishment. "Holy old cow."

He laughed and said, "Could you be more specific?"

She looked up to find two candles and an iris directly in her line of vision, cutting his face in half. She craned to one side to see around them.

"Who really cooked this?" she asked.

"I knew you'd say that."

"Well, Michael, can you blame me? In the days when I knew you your idea of a three-course meal was chips, dip and a Coke, if you were doing the cooking." She looked down at her plate. "This is incredible."

"Well, taste it, go ahead."

She untied her napkin from around the stem of the wineglass, spread it on her lap and sampled the asparagus first while he held his fork and knife and forgot to use them, watching closely again for her reaction.

She shut her eyes, chewed, swallowed, licked her lips and murmured, "Mmm, fantastic."

He felt as if he'd just landed a job as head chef at the Four Seasons. He put his knife and fork to use as she spoke again.

"Whatever have you done to this ham? It's incredible."

He peered around the centerpiece and abruptly clacked down his silverware on his plate. "Aw, hell, Bess, I feel like I'm on *Dallas*. I'm coming down there." He picked up his wineglass and slid his place mat down to her end of the table, taking a chair at a right angle to hers. "There, that's better. Now let's get this meal off to a proper start." He lifted his wineglass and she followed suit. "To . . ." He thought a while, their glasses poised. "To bygones," he said, "and letting them be."

"To bygones," she seconded as their glasses chimed. They drank with their gazes fused and afterward, with their lips still wet, lingered in their absorption with one another until Michael wisely broke it.

"Well, try the salad," he said, and did so himself.

She was filled with praise, and he with pride. They spoke of cheese sauce, and real estate ventures, and pecan praline mustard glaze, and the smoothness of the wine, and the film *Pretty Woman,* which they'd both seen. He told her about the Concerned Citizens' Meeting and his hopes for the corner of Victoria and Grand. She told him about the American Society of Interior Designers and her hopes that they would get legislation passed to require licensing, thereby prohibiting the unschooled interlopers of the industry from calling themselves interior designers.

He said, "Hear, hear! You've made me a firm believer in interior designers."

"You're pleased, then?"

"Absolutely."

"So am I." She proposed a toast. "To our amicable business association, and its most successful outcome."

"And to the condo . . ." he added, toasting the newly decorated room, ". . . a much brighter place to come home to."

They drank and relaxed over their empty plates. Dusk had fallen and the candlelight created a halo. The scent of the roses seemed to intensify in the damper air of evening. Outside, the calls of the gulls hushed while those of the crickets commenced. Beneath the table Bess removed her shoes. Above it both she and Michael toyed lazily with their wineglasses.

"You want to know something?" he said. "Ever since I divorced you I've longed to live back in our house in Stillwater. Now, for the first time, that's not true anymore, and it feels great. This place suits me. I walk in here and I have no desire to leave." He looked very self-satisfied as he continued in a quiet tone. "Want to know something else?"

She sat with one fist propping up her jaw. "Hm?"

"Since I've bought this place I've finally managed to get over the feeling that I was ripped off when you ended up with the house."

"You felt that way all these years?"

"Well, yeah, sort of. Wouldn't you?"

She pondered a while. "I suppose I would have."

"With Darla it was different. I moved into her place so it never really felt like *ours*. All of her stuff was in it, and when I left it I felt as if I was only letting her have what was rightfully hers all along. I just sort of . . ." He shrugged. ". . . walked out and felt relieved."

"It really was that simple, leaving her?"

"Absolutely."

"And she honestly felt the same?"

"I think so."

"Hm . . ."

In silence they compared that scenario to their own upon divorcing, all the bitterness and anger.

"Sure different from you and me," Bess said.

He stared at his wineglass and rotated it on the place mat, finally lifting his eyes to hers. "Feels good to leave all that behind us, doesn't it?"

"Why do you suppose we were both so hateful?" she asked, recalling her mother's words.

"I don't know."

"It would be interesting to hear what a psychologist would have to say on that subject."

"All I know is, this time when I got my divorce papers, I just put them away in a drawer and thought, So be it, another item of business closed."

Bess felt a pleasant shock. Her eyes widened. "You've got them? I mean, it's final?"

"Yup."

"That was fast."

"That's how it is when it's uncontested."

For a minute they studied each other, trying not to let their total freedom cloud judgment.

"Well!" he said, breaking the spell, pushing back from the table. "I wish I could say I prepared a breathtaking dessert but I didn't. I thought I was pushing my luck to make as much as I did, so Byerly's is responsible for the chocolate-mint creme cake." He picked up their plates and said, "I'll be right back. Coffee?"

"I'd love some but I don't think I have room for dessert."

"Oh, come on, Bess." He disappeared into the kitchen and called from there, "Indulge with me. Can't be more than . . . oh, hell, eight hundred calories in one piece of this stuff."

He returned with two plates of the most sinful-looking green-and-brown concoction this side of Julia Child's kitchen. Bess stared at it with her mouth watering while he went off after the coffeepot.

When he was seated again he dug in and she continued vacillating.

"Damn you, Michael," she said.

"Oh, come on, enjoy yourself."

"May I tell you something?"

She was glowering at him less than affectionately.

"What?"

"Something that's been aggravating me for six, closer to seven, years now? Something you said to me just before we got divorced that's burned me up ever since?"

He set down his fork carefully, disturbed by her quick change of mood. "What did I say?"

"You said I'd stopped taking care of myself. You implied that I'd gotten fat and seedy, and all I wore were jeans and sweatshirts anymore; and see what it's done to me? I'm ten pounds overweight and it might as well be fifty. I look at a dessert and feel like a glutton if I eat it, and no matter what I put on or how my hair looks, I'm still critical of myself; and in all these years I've never stooped to putting on a pair of jeans again, no matter how badly I've wanted to. There, now I've gotten it off my chest, and I'm going to see if it feels better!"

He stared at her in astonishment.

"I said that?"

"You mean you don't remember?"

"No."

"Oh God!" She covered her face, threw back her head, then pretended to pound on the table with both fists. "I go through six years of obsessive self-improvement and you don't even remember the remarks?"

"No, Bess, I don't. But if I made them, I'm sorry."

"Oh, shit," she said gloomily, dropping her jaw to a fist and eyeing her dessert. "Now what am I going to do with this?"

"Eat it," he said. "Then tomorrow, go buy yourself a pair of jeans."

She looked across the corner of the table at him and put on her puckered, disgruntled mouth, lips all turned inside like a stripped-off sock. "Michael Curran, if you knew all the misery you've caused me!"

"I said I was sorry. And there's nothing wrong with your shape, Bess, believe me. Eat the damned cake."

She glanced at the cake. Glanced at him. Felt one corner of her mouth threaten to grin. Saw both corners of his do the same. Felt her grin break, and then they were both laughing and gobbling dessert and it felt so damned comfortable at one point she actually reached across the table and wiped one corner of his mouth with her own napkin.

They finished, leaned back and rubbed their bellies and sipped coffee.

At her first taste she looked with surprise into her cup. "What next? Is this raspberry-flavored?"

"Chocolate-raspberry. Sylvia sells it at the shop, fresh-ground. She said it goes well with dessert and that it would be bound to impress a woman."

"Oh, so you set out to impress me, did you, Michael?"

"Isn't that obvious?" he said, rising with their dessert plates, escaping to the kitchen. She stared at the empty doorway for some time, then finished her coffee and followed him. He was rinsing plates and putting them in the dishwasher when she entered the room. She set their cups and saucers down beside him and remarked quietly, "We've covered a lot of ground tonight."

He continued his task without looking at her. "You named it earlier. Growth."

She rinsed their cups and handed them to him. He put them in the dishwasher. She wiped off a cabinet top and he ran water into the roaster in which he'd baked the ham.

"Tell you what . . ." He closed the dishwasher door. "Let's lighten up a little bit. Let's go out and take a walk along the lakeshore. What do you say?"

Leaning his hips against the cabinet, he dried his hands on a towel then handed it to her. She wiped hers, too, then folded the towel over the edge of the sink.

"All right," she said.

Neither of them moved. They stood side-by-side, studying each other, their backsides braced against the edge of the countertop. They were doing a mating dance and both knew it. They might very well suspect the outcome but when it came to stepping close and bringing the dance to its logical conclusion, both backed off. They had loved and lost once before and were terrified of the same thing happening twice; it was as simple as that.

They walked over to the public beach, speaking little. They stared at the path of the moon on the water. He sidearmed a rock into it, distorting the moon's reflection, then watched it reform. They listened to the soft lick of the waves on the shore, and smelled the tang of wet wood from a nearby dock, and felt the sand close in around their shoes and hold them rooted.

They looked at each other, standing a goodly distance apart, uncertain, desirous and fearing. Then back at the lake again, knowing relationships did not come with guarantees.

In time they turned and walked back, entered the lobby and rode the elevator to the second floor in silence. Back in his condo, Michael stopped off at the bathroom while Bess continued to the family room and flopped onto her back on the leather sofa, staring at the ceiling, one leg stretched out, the other foot on the floor.

I can stay or go, risk it or risk nothing. The choice is mine.

The bathroom door opened and he entered the family room, crossed it and stopped several feet from her, his hands in his rear pockets. For moments he remained so, in the pose of deep reflection and indecision, concentrating on her without moving.

Cautiously she sat up and dropped her other foot to the floor in a last-ditch decision for common sense.

Taking his hands from his pockets, he moved toward her smilelessly, as if his decision had been made. "I liked you better lying down," he said, grasping her shoulders and pressing her against the pliant cream leather as she had been. In one fluid motion he stretched half-beside, half-upon her and kissed her, a soft, lingering question after which he searched her eyes and held her rounded shoulder in the cup of his hand.

"I'm not at all sure this is the right thing to do," he said, his voice gruff with emotion.

"Neither am I."

"But I've been thinking about it all night."

"Only tonight? I've been thinking of it for weeks."

He kissed her a second time, as if convincing them both it was the right thing to do, taking a long, sweet time while temptation began its work. They let it build slowly, opening their mouths to each other, touching and holding one another tentatively, finally ending the kiss to embrace full-length, the way old friends do, needing time before taking one more step.

"What do you think?" he asked.

"You feel good."

"Ahh, so do you."

"Familiar."

"Yes." Familiarity had caught him, too, bringing with it a rightness he welcomed. When he kissed her again the friendliness had fled, replaced by a first show of fire and demand. She returned both and they held strong, heart-to-heart, with their legs plaited and urgency beginning. With their caress gone full-length, the kiss became lush and stormy, wholly immodest as the best of kisses are, with arousal at last admitted and moderation denied. They hove together, searching for a dearer fit, tasting coffee and concupiscence upon one another's tongues, reveling in it while past and present welled up and became enmeshed in this embrace—desire, hope, amity, past failures and fear of repeating those failures.

Their breakdown marked the end of a long abstinence for both of them; passion was swift and complete. He found her breast, cupped and caressed it briefly through her clothing before delving beneath. He shinnied down her body, pushed her sweater up and kissed her through her brassiere and pressed his face between her breasts while pinning her hips flat with his chest. She arched, and cradled his head as a murmur of delight slid from her throat.

He shot up, sitting on one heel, and made short work of her clothing, then his own. Down he flung her again, and she was eager to receive his open mouth upon her naked breasts and belly. He uttered a single word while working his way down her body, to her midriff, stomach, and the warm familiar flesh below.

"Remember?"

She remembered—ah, she remembered—the shyness the first time they had done these things, the years it had taken to perfect them, to feel comfortable doing them. She closed her eyes as his mouth touched her intimately. Her nostrils dilated as he nuzzled her, calling back other nights, other times when, with hearts hammering as now, they'd explored these primal forces and allowed themselves to enjoy them. In three years of intimacy with another man she had allowed no such license. But this was Michael, whose bride she'd been, whose children she'd borne, with whom such intimacies had once been learned.

In time she returned the favor while he lay back with his head against the soft leather cushions as she knelt on the floor in the wishbone of his legs.

"Oh, Michael," she said, "it's so easy with you. It feels so right."

"Do you remember the first time we did this?"

"We'd been married two years before we dared."

"And even then I was scared. I thought you'd smack me and go sleep in the spare room."

"I didn't, though, did I?"

He smiled down at her as she resumed her ardent ministrations. Moments later he reached down to touch her head. "Stop." He groped for his white trousers, which lay on the floor, drawing a foil packet from his pocket. "Do we need this?" he asked.

Smiling, she stroked him and said, "So you planned on this."

"Let's just say I was hoping."

"Yes, we need that. Unless we want to risk having a baby who's younger than our own grandchild." She watched him put on the condom as she had uncountable times before, hoping for a thousand future times.

"Wouldn't the kids have something to say about that?"

"Lisa would be overjoyed."

"She'd be overjoyed anyway. This is what she was scheming for all along." The tone of his voice became sultry. His hair was messed and his grin was teasing as he reached for her. "Come here, Grandma." He laid her where he wanted her and arranged her limbs to best advantage. "Let's christen this Italian leather properly."

She lifted her arms in welcome and they ended six—nearly seven—years of separation.

She looked up at his face as he entered her, and touched his temples where the silver hairs gilded the black, and drew him down flush upon her.

He made a sound, "Ahhh . . ." the way some men would after pushing back their plate after a satisfying meal. She'd been expecting it and it brought a smile. They held one another for a while without moving, letting familiarity and relief overtake them.

"It's wonderful," she said, "doing this with someone you know so well, isn't it?"

He pressed back to see her face and smiled softly. "Yes, it's wonderful."

"I knew you'd make that sound just now."

"What sound?"

"Ahh, you said, 'Ahh,' the way you always did."

"Did I always?"

"Always. At that moment."

He grinned as if this was news to him and kissed her lightly on the upper lip. Then her lower one. Then her full mouth while he began moving.

Her eyes closed, the better to enjoy what followed, and her hands rode low upon his hips.

Sometimes they kissed, softly, in keeping with veneration.

Sometimes they smiled for no single reason.

Sometimes he voiced questions, throaty and thick.

Sometimes she whispered a reply, gazing up into his eyes.

And once they laughed, and thought how grand they could do so in the midst of lovemaking.

When they reached their climaxes, Bess called out and Michael groaned, their mingled voices shimmering through the dimly lit rooms she had so newly trimmed for him. Ah, the dazzling disquiet of those few trembling seconds while they lost touch with all but sensation.

In the afterglow they lay on their sides, sealed to each other and the warmed leather. The welcome breath of early night drifted in to cool their skins. Moths beat against the screen. Through the archway the forgotten dinner candles washed the walls with amber light.

Bess's hair trailed over Michael's arm while his free hand idled over her breasts in a soothing, endless rhythm. She heaved a sigh of repletion and let her eyes close for a while. He knew these were the moments she savored best, afterward, when the souls took over where the bodies left off. Always she'd whispered, "Don't leave . . . not yet." He remained now, studying the faint tracery of creases at the corners of her eyes, the rim of her lips, which were so at rest they revealed a glimpse of teeth inside, the place on her throat where her pulse billowed and ebbed like the wings of a sitting butterfly.

She opened her eyes and found him studying her without the smile she'd expected.

"Just what do we think we're going to do about this?" he asked quietly.

"I don't know."

"Did you have any ideas before you came here?"

She wagged her head faintly.

"We could just keep having a torrid affair."

"A torrid affair? Michael, what have you been reading?"

He put his thumb beneath her lower lip and pulled down until her bottom teeth appeared.

"We're awfully darn good together, Bess."

"Yes, I know but be serious."

He gave up his preoccupation with her mouth and laid his arm along his hip. "All right, I will. How much do you think we've changed since our divorce?"

"That's a loaded question if I ever heard one."

"Answer it."

"I'm scared to." After a long pause she asked, "Aren't you?"

He studied her eyes for some time before answering, "Yes."

"Then I think what I'll do is just get up and put my clothes on and go home and pretend this never happened."

She rolled over and off him.

"Good luck," he said, watching her pick up her clothing and go. She used the guest bathroom off the gallery and felt reality return with every minute while she donned the brief blue underwear that had certainly done its job. Reality was the two of them, failures the first time around, starting up a carnal relationship again without rationalizing where it might lead. Dressed once more, she returned to the doorway to find him standing at the far end of the family room before the sliding glass door, barefooted, bare-chested, wearing only his white jeans.

"May I borrow a brush?" she asked.

He turned and looked back at her, silent for a stretch.

"In my bathroom."

Once again she went away, into his private domain, where she had probed once before. This time was worse—opening his vanity drawers and finding an ace bandage, dental floss, some foil packets of Alka-Seltzer and an entire box of condoms.

An entire box!

Looking at them, she found herself blush with anger. All right, so he was single, and single guys probably bought condoms by the dozen. But she didn't like being duped into believing this was an uncommon occurrence in his life!

She slammed that drawer and opened another to find his hairbrush at last. Some of his dark hairs were stuck in the bristles. The sight of them, and the feel of his brush being drawn through her hair, dulled her anger and brought a sense of grave emptiness, a reluctance to return to her lone life, where there was no sharing of brushes or of bathrooms or dinner tables or beds.

She did what she could with her hair, searched out mouthwash and used it, refreshed her lipstick and returned to the family room once more. He was still staring out at the darkness, obviously troubled by the same misgivings as she, now that the easy part was over.

"Well, Michael, I think I'll go."

He swung to face her.

"Yeah, fine," he answered.

"Thank you for supper. It was wonderful."

"Sure."

A void passed, a great terrifying void that reared up before both of them.

"Listen, Michael, I've been thinking. There are a few more empty walls in here, and you could use some more small items on the mantels and the tables but I think it's best if you find them on your own."

His expression grew stormy. "Bess, why are you blaming me? You wanted it, too. Don't tell me you didn't, not after those underclothes you were wearing. You were planning on it just as much as I was!"

"Yes, I was. But I'm not blaming you. I just think that we . . . that it's . . ." She ran out of words.

"What? A mistake?"

She remembered the condoms. "I don't know. Maybe."

He stared at her with a hurt look around his eyes and an angry one around his mouth.

"Should I call you?"

"I don't know, Michael. Maybe it's not such a good idea."

He dropped his chin to his chest and whispered, "Shit."

She stood across the room, her heart racing with fear because of what he had almost suggested. It was too terrifying to ponder, too impossible to consider, too risky to let it be put into words. They had changed a lot but what assurance was there? What fool would put his hand in the mill wheel after his finger had been cut off?

She said, "Thanks again, Michael," and he made no reply as she saw herself out and ran from the idea of starting again.

Chapter 15

When Bess got home the lights were on all over the house, even in her bedroom. Frowning, she parked in the driveway rather than waste time pulling into the garage, and had barely put foot inside the front door when Randy came charging down two steps at a time from the second story. "Ma, where you been? I thought you'd never get home!"

Terror struck. "What's wrong?"

"Nothing. I got an audition! Grandma's old dude, Gilbert, got me one with this band called The Edge!"

Bess released a breath and let her shoulders slump. "Thank heavens. I thought it was some catastrophe."

"Turns out old Gilbert used to own the Withrow Ballroom and he knows everybody—bands, agents, club owners. He's been talking to guys about me since Lisa's wedding. Pretty great, huh?"

"That's wonderful, Randy. When's the audition?"

"I don't know yet. The band's playing a gig out in Bismarck, North Dakota, but they're due back tomorrow. I've got to call them sometime in the afternoon. God, where were you, Mom? I've been hangin' around here all night, waiting to tell you."

"I was with your dad."

"With Dad?" Randy's ebullience fizzled. "You mean, on business?"

"No, not this time. He cooked dinner for me."

"*Dad* cooked dinner?"

"Yes. And a very good one at that. Come on upstairs with me and tell me about this band." She led the way to her bedroom, where the television was on and she could tell Randy had been lying on her bed. He must have been anxious, to have invaded her room. She snagged a robe and went into her bathroom, calling through the door as she changed into it, "So what kind of music does this band play?"

"Rock, basically. A mix of old and new, Gilbert said."

They went on talking until Bess came out of the bathroom with her face scrubbed, rubbing lotion on it while a headband held her hair out of the way. Randy was sitting on the bed, Indian-fashion, looking out of place in her boudoir, with its pastel stripes and cabbage roses, bishop sleeve curtains and chintz-covered chairs. Bess sat down in one and propped her bare feet on the mattress, crossing her terrycloth robe over her knees.

"Did you know about this?" Randy asked. "I mean, did Grandma tell you?"

"No. It's as much of a surprise to me as it is to you." From a skirted table Bess took a remote control and lowered the volume of the television, then pulled the band from her hair.

"Old Gilbert . . . can you believe that?" Randy wobbled his head in amazement.

"Yes, I can, the way he dances."

"And all because I played at that wedding."

"You see? Just a little courage and look what happens."

Randy grinned and slapped out a rhythm on his thighs.

"You scared?" his mother asked.

His hands stopped tapping. "Well . . ." He shrugged. "Yeah, I guess so, a little."

"I was scared when I started my store, too. Turned out good, though."

Randy sat looking at her. "Yeah, I guess it did." He fell pensive for some time, then seemed to draw himself from his thoughts. "So what's this between you and the old man?"

"Your dad, you mean."

"Yeah . . . sorry . . . Dad. What's going on between you two?"

Bess got up and walked to the dresser, where she dropped the headband and fiddled with some bottles and tubes before picking one up and uncapping it. "We're just friends." She squeezed some skin mask on her finger and put her face close to the mirror while touching selected spots.

"You're a lousy liar, you know that, Mom? You've been to bed with him, haven't you?"

"Randy, that's none of your business!" She slammed down the tube.

"I can see in that mirror and you're blushing."

She glared at his reflection. "It's still none of your business, and I'm appalled at your lack of manners."

"Okay! Okay!" He threw back his hands and clambered off the bed. "I just don't understand you, that's all. First you divorce him, and then you decorate his place, and now . . ." He gestured lamely as his words died.

She turned to face him. "And now, you will kindly give me the same respect I give you in personal matters. I've never asked about your sex life, and I don't expect you to ask about mine, okay? We're both adults. We both know the risks and rewards of certain choices we might make. Let's leave it at that."

He stared at her, torn by ambivalence about his father, one facet of him leavened by the possibility of her getting back together with him permanently; the other facet curdled by the idea of having to make peace with Michael at last.

"You know what, Mom?" Randy said, just before leaving the room, "You were never this touchy about Keith."

She studied the empty doorway when he was gone, realizing he was right. She dropped down and sat on the edge of the bed with her inner wrists together between her knees, trying to make sense of things. In time she flopped to her back, arms outflung, wondering what the outcome of tonight would be. She was being protective of herself because she was scared. That's why she had walked out on Michael, and why she had snapped at Randy. The risk of becoming involved was so great—hell, what was she saying? She was already involved again with Michael; to think anything else was self-delusion. *They* were involved, and more than likely falling in love again, and what was the logical conclusion of falling in love if not marriage?

Bess rolled to her side, drew up her knees, crossed her bare feet and closed her eyes.

I, Bess, take thee, Michael, for better or for worse, till death do us part.

They had believed it once and look what their gullibility had cost. All the anguish of breaking up a family, a home, joint finances, two hearts. The idea of risking it again seemed immensely foolhardly.

The audition was scheduled for Monday afternoon at two, at a club called Stonewings. The band had their equipment set up for their evening gig and were working on balancing sound when Randy walked in with a pair of drumsticks in his hand. The place was dark but for the stage, lit by canister lights from a ceiling strip. One guitarist was repeating into a mike, "Check, one, two," while another squatted at the rear of the stage, peering at the orange screen of an electronic guitar tuner.

Randy approached out of the darkness. "Hullo," he said, reaching the rim of light.

All sound ceased. The lead guitarist looked over, an emaciated man who resembled Jesus Christ as depicted on Catholic holy cards. He held a royal blue Fender Stratocaster with a burning cigarette stuck behind the strings near the tuning pegs. "Hey, guys," he said, "our man is here. You Curran?"

"That's right." Randy reached up, extending his hand. "Randy."

The man pushed his guitar against his belly and leaned over it to shake hands. "Pike Watson," he said, then turned to introduce the bassist. "Danny Scarfelli."

The keyboard man came over and shook hands, too. "Tom Little."

The rhythm guitarist followed suit. "Mitch Yost."

There was a sound-and-light man, too, moving around in the shadows, adjusting canisters from a stepladder.

Watson told Randy, "That's Lee out there, doing lights." He shaded his eyes and called, "Yo, Lee!"

Out of the darkness came a voice like a bastard file on babbitt. "Hey!"

"This is Randy Curran."

"Let's hear his stuff!" came the reply.

While the others drifted back to tuning and balancing, Watson asked Randy, "So what do you know?"

Randy's gesture flipped his drumsticks once, like windshield washers. "Anything. You name it—something with a shuffle beat or straight rock—doesn't matter."

"Okay, how about a little of 'Blue Suede Shoes'?"

"Great."

He had expected the simplest of songs, something everybody knew as well as they knew every nick and scratch on their own instruments. Simple songs were the best gauge of true talent.

The trap set was simple, five pieces—bass, snare, a floor tom, two ride toms and assorted cymbals, one, of course, a high hat. Randy settled himself behind them, found the foot pedals of the bass and a ride, rattled a quick riff across the skins and adjusted the height of a cymbal. He put both sticks in his left hand, drew the stool an inch forward, tested the distance again, looked up and said, "All set. I'll count it out, give you three for nothing and then we'll go into it on four."

Pike Watson blew smoke toward the ceiling, replaced the cigarette next to a tuning peg and replied, "Beat me, Sticks."

Randy tapped out the pickup beat on the rim of the snare and the band struck into the song with Watson singing lead.

For Randy, playing was therapy. Playing was forgetting anyone else existed. Playing was living in total harmony with two sticks of wood and a set of percussion instruments over which he seemed to have some sort of mystic control. It felt to Randy as if they put out sound at the command of his mere thought waves rather than his hands and feet. When the song ended, Randy was surprised, having little recall of playing it, measure-for-measure. It seemed, instead, to have played him.

He pinched the cymbals quiet, rested his hands on his thighs and looked up.

Pike Watson appeared pleased. "You got your chops down, man."

Randy smiled.

"How about another one?"

They played a little twelve-bar blues, then three more, typical musicians who, like the alcoholic, can never stop with just one.

"Nice licks," Scarfelli offered when they broke.

"Thanks."

Watson asked, "Do you sing?"

"A little."

"Harmony?"

"Yeah."

"Lead?"

"If you want."

"Well, shit, man, let's hear you."

Randy asked for the new Elton John hit, "The Club at the End of the Street," and although the band hadn't worked it up they ad-libbed expertly.

When the song ended, Watson asked, "Who have you played with?"

"Nobody. This is my first audition."

Watson raised one eyebrow, rubbed his beard and glanced at the others.

"What have you got for drums?"

"A full set of Pearls, rototoms and all."

"You must be into heavy metal."

"Some."

"We don't do much of that."

"I'm versatile."

"A lot of the club stages are smaller than this. Any objection to leaving a few of your Pearls at home?"

"No."

"Are you married?"

"No."

"Planning on it?"

"No."

"Got any kids?" Randy grinned and Watson added, "Well, hell, you never know anymore."

"No kids."

"So you can travel?"

"Yes."

"No other jobs?"

Randy chuckled and scratched the back of his head. "If you can call it that. I pack nuts in a warehouse." The whole band laughed. "If you guys take me on I'll be kissing that job good-bye."

"What have you got for wheels?"

"That's no problem." It was, but he'd face it if and when.

"You union?"

"No, but I will be if you say so."

"Whoever we hire will have to sit in on about six solid days of practices 'cause our drummer's leaving at the end of the week."

"No problem. I can blow off that pistachio palace in one phone call."

Pike Watson consulted the others with a glance, returned his gaze to Randy and said, "Okay, listen . . . we'll let you know, okay?"

"Okay." Randy lifted his hands, let them fall to his thighs, backed off the stool and shook hands all around. "Thanks for letting me sit in. You guys are great. I'd sell my left nut to play with you."

He left them laughing and stepped out into the midafternoon sun, longing for a hit of something to relax the tension. He tipped back at the waist, closed his eyes and sucked in half the blue sky; he jived toward his car, rapping out a rhythm against his thighs with one palm and the paired sticks. Sweet, the very sweetest—playing with real musicians. Hope pressed up against his throat and made his head buzz. He thought about spending the rest of his life playing music instead of weighing and packing nuts. The comparison was ludicrous. But it was a long shot; he realized that. The Edge had undoubtedly auditioned other guys with plenty of experience, guys who'd played with well-known bands from around the Twin Cities or beyond. What were his chances of competing with them?

He unlocked his car, slid in and rolled down the windows. No air-conditioning, so the interior was like a sauna, the vinyl seatcovers radiant, even through his jeans. Somewhere under the seat he'd left a fast-food container with part of an uneaten bun, and it smelled as yeasty as working beer.

He started the engine, turned the fan on, then off again when the blast of engine heat proved hotter than the motionless air had been. He put in a tape of Mike and the Mechanics and began pulling out of the parking lot.

Something hit the car like a falling rock.

Jesus, what was that?

He braked and craned around to find Pike Watson had thumped on the trunk to stop him. His bearded face appeared at the open window.

"Hey, Curran, not so fast."

"Was that you? I thought I ran over a kid or something." Randy turned down the stereo.

"It was me. Listen, we want you to be our rimshot."

Shock suffused Randy. It went through his body faster than a hit of marijuana. Felt better, too.

"You serious?"

"We knew before you went out the door. We just have this policy, we all talk it over, no one person decides. Wanna come back inside and get in a couple hours of practice?"

Randy stared, dumbfounded. He whispered, "Jesus . . ." and after a pause, "I don't believe this."

Watson wagged his head. "You're good, man. Believe it. But we've got only six days to work you into four hours' worth of music, so what do you say?"

Randy smiled. "Let me park this thing."

He parked the car and stepped onto the blacktop, wondering how he'd operate the foot pedals with his knees this weak, how he could do licks with his body trembling so. Pike Watson shook his hand as they headed back inside the club.

"You get that union card as quick as you can."

"Anything you say," Randy replied, matching him pace for pace as he headed toward paradise.

It had been three days since Michael's evening with Bess. At work, he had been withdrawn. In his car, he had ridden with the radio off. At home, he'd spent a lot of time sitting on the deck with his feet on the railing, staring at the sails on the water.

That's where he was on Tuesday evening when his phone rang.

He answered and heard Lisa's voice.

"Hi, Dad. I'm down in the lobby. Let me in."

He was waiting in his open door when she stepped off the elevator, looking quite ballooned, in blue shorts and a white maternity blouse.

"Well, look at you," he said, opening his arms as she hove up against him. "Getting rounder every day."

She rested a hand on her stomach. "Yup. Not unlike the St. Paul Cathedral." The church had a dome that could be seen for miles.

"This is a nice surprise. Come on in."

They sat on deck chairs, sipping root beer, watching evening slant in behind them and tint the tips of the trees golden. The water was jeweled and the smell of wild sweet clover drifted from nearby roadsides.

"How've you been, Daddy?"

"Okay."

"I haven't heard from you in a while."

"Been busy." He told her about the Victoria and Grand plans and the attendant hassle with the locals. He told her he'd been sailing some and had seen the new movie *Dick Tracy,* and asked if she and Mark had seen it. He mentioned his cooking classes and how he was enjoying his new skills.

"I hear you made dinner for Mother Saturday night."

"How did you hear that?"

"Randy called, about something else, actually, but he mentioned it."

"I suppose Randy wasn't too pleased."

"Randy's got other things on his mind right now. He auditioned for a band called The Edge, and they hired him."

Michael's face brightened. "Great!"

"He's blown away, rehearsing all morning with tapes and all afternoon with the band."

"When did all this happen?"

"Yesterday. Didn't Mother call you and tell you?"

"No, she didn't."

"But if the two of you were together on Saturday night . . ." Lisa let the suggestion hang.

"Things didn't go too well between us."

Lisa got up and went to the railing. "Damn."

Michael studied her back, her hair knotted in a loose French braid and tied off with a puckered circle of blue cloth.

"Honey, you've got to stop dreaming that Mom and I will get back together. I don't think that's ever going to happen."

Lisa flounced around to face him and rested her backside on the railing. "But why? You're divorced, she's free, you're both lonely. Why?"

He rose and caught her around the neck with one arm, turning her to face the lake. "It's not that simple. There's history between us that's got to be considered."

"What? Your affair? Mother can't honestly be hung up on that anymore, can she?"

Lisa had never used the word before. Hearing her speak it now, forthrightly, throwing it out for honest examination, Michael discovered the two of them crossing some new plateau as a father and a daughter.

"We've never talked about it before, you and I."

She shrugged. "I knew about it all along."

"But you never held it against me the way the others did."

"I figured you had your reasons." He wasn't going to delineate them at this late date. Lisa added, "All I ever heard was Mom's side of the story but I remember things weren't so super around our house at that time, and part of it was her fault."

"Well, thanks for the benefit of the doubt."

"Dad?" Lisa looked up at him. "Will you tell me something?"

"Depends on what the question is." She bore so much resemblance to Bess as she looked straight into Michael's eyes.

"Do you still love Mom—I mean, even a little bit?" she finished hopefully.

He dropped his arm from around her and sighed. "Oh, Lisa . . ."

"Do you? Because the way you were acting at my wedding, it seemed like both of you had some feelings for each other."

"Maybe we do, but—"

"Then, please don't give up."

"You didn't let me finish. Maybe we do but we're both a lot more cautious now, especially your mother."

"I think she loves you. A lot. But I can understand why she'd be scared to let you know. Heck, who wouldn't be when a guy has left you for another woman? Now, don't get upset that I said that. I *didn't* take sides when you left Mom but now I am. I'm taking both of your sides, because I want you back together again so badly, I just . . . I just don't even know how to say it." She turned to him with tears magnifying her eyes. "Give me your hand, Daddy."

He knew what she would do even as he complied. She placed his palm against her stomach and said, "This is your grandchild in here, some little thing who's probably going to come out looking like you and Mom in some way, right? I want him to have all the best advantages a child can have, and that includes a grandpa and grandma's house to go to at Christmastime, and the two of you together picking him up sometime and taking him to the circus, or to Valley Fair, or going to his school programs, or . . . or . . . oh, you know what I mean. Please, Daddy, don't give up on Mother. You're the one who left her; you've got to be the one to go back and convince her it was a mistake in the first place. Will you try?"

Michael took Lisa in his arms and held her loosely.

"It's dangerous to idealize things so."

"Will you?"

He didn't answer.

"I'm not idealizing. I saw you two together. I know there was something between you the night of my wedding, I just know it. Please, Daddy?"

It had been far easier to promise her he'd have her piano moved forever.

"Lisa, I can't promise such a thing. If things had gone better between us the other night . . ."

The note upon which the night had ended had made mockery of his and Bess's sexual encounter. Since then Michael had viewed his actions as foolish and willful. Lisa's remarks only ripened his disillusionment into confusion. If Bess loved him as Lisa suspected, she had a strange way of showing it. If she didn't, her way was stranger yet.

Lisa drew herself out of his arms, looking forlorn.

"Well, I thought I'd try," she said. "Guess I better go."

He walked her to the door and rode the elevator with her down to the lobby, where she stopped and turned to him.

"There's something else I'd like to ask you, Dad."

"Ask away."

"It's about when the baby's born. I wondered if you'd like to be there during the delivery. We're inviting Mark's folks, too."

"And your mother, too, no doubt."

"Of course."

"Another attempt to work us back together, Lisa?"

Lisa shrugged. "Sure. Why not? But it might be the only chance you get to witness the awesome spectacle. I know you weren't there when Randy and I were born, so I thought . . ." She shrugged again.

"Thanks for asking. I'll think about it."

When Lisa was gone, Michael's thoughts returned to Bess, plunging him into a limbo of indecisiveness.

Ever since Saturday night he'd passed telephones the way sinners pass confessionals, wanting to reach out and dial Bess's number and say he was sorry, he needed absolution. But to call her was to place himself in a position of even greater vulnerability, so he resisted the urge once again.

The following day, however, he dialed the house at eleven o'clock in the morning, expecting Randy to answer.

To his surprise, Bess did.

"Bess!" he exclaimed, lunging forward in his desk chair and feeling his face ignite. "What are you doing home!"

"Grabbing a sandwich and picking up some catalogs I forgot before I head out for a noon appointment."

"I didn't expect you to be there. I called for Randy."

"He's not here, sorry."

"I wanted to congratulate him. I hear he's found a job with a band."

"That's right."

"I suppose he's really excited, huh?"

"Is he ever. He's quit his job at the nut house and he's practicing here every morning and with the band every afternoon. Today, though, he's out shopping for a used van. Says he's got to have one to haul his drums in."

"Has he got any money?"

"Probably not but I didn't volunteer any."

"What do you think? Should I?"

"That's up to you."

"I'm asking your advice, Bess. He's our son and I want to do what you think will be best for him."

"All right, then, I think it's best to let him struggle and find his own way to get a van. If he wants the job badly enough—and of course he does—he'll work it out."

"All right, I won't offer."

A lull fell. End of one subject, opening for another . . .

Michael picked up a stapler, moved it to a different spot on his desktop, moved it back where it had been. "Bess, about Saturday night . . ." She said nothing. He depressed the head of the stapler four times, not quite hard enough to release staples. "All week long I've been thinking I should call you and apologize."

Neither of them spoke for a long time. His fingertips lingered over the stapler, polishing it as if it were dusty.

"Bess, I think you were right. That wasn't a very smart thing we did."

"No. It only complicates matters."

"So I guess we shouldn't see each other anymore, should we?"

Again, no answer.

"We're only getting Lisa's hopes up for nothing. I mean, it isn't going to lead to anything, so why do we put ourselves through it?"

His heart was drumming hard enough to loosen the stitches on his shirt pocket. Sweet Jesus, it was just like when they used to talk this way on the phone in college, longing to be together yet summoning willpower to do the right thing, which they inevitably failed to do once they were together.

When he spoke again the words emerged in a ragged whisper. "Bess, are you there?"

Her voice, too, sounded strained. "The damned awful truth is that it's the best piece of sex I've had since the last good one you and I had together when we were still married. I've thought about it so much since Saturday night, about all those years of learning it took to get it right together, and how comfortable and easy it felt with you. Did it feel that way for you, too?"

"Yes," he whispered hoarsely while beneath the desk he felt himself grow priapic.

"And that's important, isn't it?"

"Of course."

"But it isn't enough. It's the kind of reasoning teenagers use, and we're not teenagers any longer."

"What are you saying, Bess?"

"I'm saying I'm scared. I'm saying I've been walking around thinking of nothing but you since Saturday night and it scares the living hell out of me. I'm scared of getting hurt again, Michael."

"And you think I'm not?"

"I think it's different for a man."

"Oh, Bess, come on, don't give me that double-standard crap. My feelings are involved here just like yours are."

"Michael, when I went into your bathroom to look for a brush I found a whole box of condoms in the drawer. *A whole box!*"

"So that's why you got all huffy and walked out?"

"Well, what would you have done?" She sounded very angry.

"Did you notice how many were used?" When she made no reply he said, "One! Go back and count them. One, which was in my pocket before you got there that night. Bess, I don't fuck around."

"Oh, that word is so offensive."

"All right then, screw. I don't and you know it."

"How can I know it, when six years ago—seven—it's a good part of what broke up our marriage."

"I thought we'd been through all that and agreed that it was both our faults.

Now here we go again; we get together, we make love once and you're already slinging accusations at me. Hell, I can't fight this for the rest of my life."

"Nobody asked you to."

After a broad silence he responded in a sound of pinched anger, "All right. That's certainly clear enough. Tell Randy I called, will you? Tell him I'll try him again later."

"I'll tell him."

He hung up without a good-bye. "Shit!" He made a fist and banged the stapler. "Shit! Shit! Shit!" He banged it three more times, pumping out staples and jamming the contraption. He sat staring at it, scowling, his lips as straight and thin as a welt pocket. "Shit," he said again, quieter, spreading his elbows on the desk, joining his hands with the thumbs extended and pressed to his eyeballs.

What did she want of him? Why should he feel like the guilty one when she'd been as willing and eager as he last Saturday night? He hadn't done a damned thing wrong! Not one! He'd seduced his ex-wife with her total compliance, and now she was putting the screws to him for it. Damn women, anyway! And damn this one in particular.

He went up to his cabin the next weekend, got eaten up by mosquitoes, wished it were hunting season; got eaten up by deerflies, wished there were someone with him; got eaten up by wood ticks, wished he had a phone up there so he could call Bess and tell her what he thought of her accusations.

He returned to the city still fuming, picked up the phone on Sunday night and slammed it back into the cradle without dialing her number.

On Tuesday night he attended another "unreasonable citizens" meeting on the Victoria and Grand issue, came out of it angrier than ever because they wanted him to plant twenty-four good-sized boulevard trees all up and down Grand Avenue at a cost of probably a thousand dollars per tree (including concrete ironwork), which had nothing whatever to do with the building he wanted to put up but it appeared he was being legally extorted and would go along with it: twenty-four thousand dollars' worth of trees for his building permit and an end to their squawking.

He had tried to call and congratulate Randy three additional times, always without getting an answer, and that irritated him, too.

Every time he passed through the gallery, with its empty faux pedestal still waiting for a piece of sculpture, he railed against Bess for writing him off with the job unfinished.

She was at the root of his dissatisfaction with life in general, and he realized it.

Two weeks had passed and his disposition hadn't improved. Finally, one night in late July, when he'd overbroiled some fresh scallops for himself and gotten them rubbery, and had listened to roaring speedboats until he'd been forced to close the deck doors, and had picked up the television guide to find nothing but junk scheduled, and had sat at his drafting table for two hours without accomplishing a thing, he went into his bathroom, got the box of condoms, stormed down to his car, drove to her house, rang the bell and stood on her doorstep, waiting to tie into her.

After a delay the hall light came on, the door opened and there she stood, barefoot, wearing a thigh-length thing made of white terrycloth with an elastic neck hole and a tie at the waist. Her hair was wet and she smelled good enough to bottle and sell, which further piqued him.

"Michael, what in the world are you doing here?"

"I came to talk and I'm going to." He burst his way inside and closed the door.

She attempted to check her watch but her wrist was empty. Obviously she was fresh out of the shower. "It's got to be ten-thirty at night!"

"I really don't give a damn, Bess. Are you alone?"

"Yes. Randy's out playing."

"Good. Let's go into the family room." He headed that way.

"You go straight to hell, Michael Curran!" she shouted. "You come bursting into my house giving orders and bossing me around. Well, I don't have to put up with it. You can just get out and lock the door when you go!"

She caught her short skirt in her fingertips and headed up the stairs.

"Wait just a minute there, missus!" He charged after her, taking the steps two at a time, and caught her halfway up. "You're not going anywhere until you—"

"I'm not a missus, and take your hands off me!"

"That's not what you said that night in my apartment, is it? My hands were just fine on you then, weren't they?"

"Oh, so you came to throw that up in my face, did you?"

"No. I came to tell you that ever since that night everything's been horseshit. I walk around with a wad of anger in my throat, and I snap at people who don't deserve it, and I can't even get my own damn son to answer the phone so I can congratulate him!"

"And that's *my* fault?" She opened a hand on her chest.

"Yes!"

"What'd I do?"

"You accused me of screwing around, and I didn't!" He grabbed her hand and slapped the box of condoms into it. "Here, count 'em!"

She gaped at the box, dumbstruck.

"Count 'em! One missing, and that's all. I bought them that day! Count 'em, I said!"

She tried to give the box back to him. "Don't be absurd, I'm not going to count them!"

"Then how will you know I'm telling the truth?"

"It doesn't matter, Michael, because it's not going to happen again."

"The hell it isn't! I'm hornier than a two-peckered goat just standing here smelling you, and either you're by God going to count those rubbers or I will. You're not going to? All right, give them to me!" He grabbed the box and sat down on a step at her feet, opened it and started pulling them out. "One. Two. Three." He slapped them down on the carpet, counting clear to eleven, until they were scattered like petals at her feet. "There, you see?" He looked up at her, high above him. "One missing. Now do you believe me?"

She was leaning against the wall, covering her mouth with a hand, laughing.

"You should just see yourself; you look absolutely ridiculous, sitting there counting those things."

"That's what you damn women do to us men, you play around with us until we do things that make us look like blithering idiots. Do you believe me now, Bess?"

"Yes, I believe you but for heaven's sake, pick them up. What if Randy happened to come home early?"

He grabbed her bare ankle. "Come on down here and help me."

"Michael, let go."

He gripped harder and with his free hand lifted her hem. "What have you got on under there?"

She slapped her skirt to her thighs. "Michael, you damned fool, stop it."

"My God, Bess, you're naked under that thing."

"Let my ankle go!"

"You horny, too, Bess? I'll bet you are. Why don't you invite me up to our old bedroom and we'll take one of these things and put it to good use?"

"Michael, don't." He was rising to his feet, one condom in his hand, climbing the two steps to reach her, then flattening her against the handrail, to which she clung with both hands.

"Bess, there's a lot of sex between you and me just waiting to be made. I think we found that out that night at my place, so let's get started."

She was trying hard not to be swayed by him. He looked devastating with his hazel eyes snapping and his hair in need of cutting, and he felt inviting, too, so near and warm and seductive. "You get out of here. You're plum crazy."

He kissed her neck and ground himself against her, breast to hips. "I'm crazy all right, crazy about you, missus. Come on, what do you say?"

"And what then? A replay of the last two weeks? Because it hasn't been any more fun for me than it's been for you."

He kissed her on the mouth once, more the strike of a wet tongue than an actual kiss, and whispered a suggestion in her ear.

She giggled. "Oh for shame, you dirty old man."

"Come on, you'll like it."

He was still grinding, and she was still amused but weakening.

"You're going to crush my pelvis on this handrail."

"But you'll be moaning so loud you won't even hear it crack."

"Michael Curran, your ego exceeds anything known to woman."

"Doesn't it, though." He had her skirt up and a two-handed grip on her buttocks. Then he had his lips on hers, and his tongue in her mouth, and her arms went around his shoulders and he was touching her inside where she was all liquid heat. The kiss grew rampant. Their breathing grew stressed.

Against his lips she mumbled, "All right, you devil, you win."

He hauled her by the hand, up the steps, along the hall, leaving the foil packets scattered on the stairs, into their bedroom, strewing flotsam as they went—his shirt, her belt, his shoes, her white cover-up—and hit the bed naked, already tangled.

They were laughing as they bounced onto the mattress on their sides. Abruptly the laughter fled, replaced by a gaze of pure passion.

"Bess . . ." Michael whispered, "Bess . . ." rolling with her, wanting his mouth everywhere at once. "I missed you."

"I missed you, too, and I thought about this. I wanted it . . ." She sucked in a quick breath and exclaimed, "Oh!"

They were giving and greedy, tender and tensile by turns. With hands and mouths they savored one another's bodies, each the perfect recipient of the other. The bedspread grew mussed, two pillows fell to the floor, several others bolstered them randomly, and in time not so randomly.

He told her, "You smell the way I remember."

She said, "So do you . . ."

Ah, the smells, the tastes.

"Your hands," she said once, examining them. "How I've always loved your hands. Here . . . they belong here . . ."

Later, he murmured, "You still like this, don't you?"

"Ohhh . . ." she crooned, her eyes closing, ending on a whisper, ". . . yes."

What they shared was universal. Why, then, did it feel unique? Triumphant? As if no one before them or after them would share these same feelings? They answered these questions themselves, when he entered her, levered her as close as possible with one heel and clasped her against his breast with her face in the cay of his neck.

"I think I've fallen in love with you again, Bess," he whispered against her damp hair.

She went still, all but her heart, whose beat seemed to suddenly fill her entire body, the entire room, the entire world.

"I think I've fallen in love with you, too."

For that trembling, precious moment each was afraid to speak further, to move. His eyes were closed, his wide hand cradling the back of her head where her hair felt cool. Her mouth had made a damp spot just below his whisker line.

Finally he drew back, tenderly brushing the hair from her face.

"Really?" His smile was delicate, surprised.

"Really."

They kissed with exquisite tenderness, touching each other in places that mattered as much as those joined below—napes, faces, temples, throats—each touch a reiteration of the words they'd spoken.

"These last two weeks apart were horrible. Let's not ever do that to each other again," he whispered.

"No," she agreed, so softly the word drifted back into her throat.

Then all that had begun so ribaldly ended in beauty, a man and a woman, cleaving, rhythmic, then gasping at the moment of cataclysm and smiling when it was over.

Afterward, she whispered, "Stay," and found a place for his hand, and another where her sole seemed to belong.

Later, they lay back-to-belly. The bedside lamp was on and an insect worried the shade with a *tick-tick* of wings. Bess's hair had dried and spread a floral scent upon their shared pillow. The bedspread, now snarled beneath them, rode up in rills here and there, creating a barrier between their legs. Michael flattened it with his calf and found Bess's bare toes with his own, invited hers to curl around his and closed his eyes.

He sighed.

She studied his left arm, stretching forth from beneath her ear; his hand hanging limply over the edge of the mattress; the pattern of dark hair ending along the soft inner arm, where white skin began; his gold watchband; the inside of his relaxed palm; ringless fingers.

She felt his lips on her hair, his breath warming it. She closed her eyes to enjoy the wondrous impuissance, the sense of well-being.

After many minutes he said quietly, "Bess?"

She opened her eyes. "Hm?"

"Are you ready to hear that M word yet?"

She thought for some time before answering. "I don't know."

He curled his arm toward her face and she turned to look back at him behind her.

"I think we'd better talk about it, don't you?" he said.

"I suppose so."

They settled on their backs. He removed his arm from beneath her.

"Okay," he said, "let's get it out in the open instead of dancing around it the way we have been. Do you think we could make it if we married again?"

Even forewarned, Bess was startled by the word. She said, "I've been spending a lot of time lately wondering. In bed we could."

"And out of it?"

"What do you think?"

"I think our biggest problem would be trust, because each of us has had others and . . ."

"Other. Just one, for me, anyway."

"Yeah, for me, too. But trust will still be a big factor."

"I suppose so."

"We'll each be meeting people, doing business with people, sometimes even in the evenings. If I tell you I'm going to a city council meeting, will you believe me?"

He picked up her near hand and placed it atop his, matching the curl of her fingers to his knuckles.

"I don't know," she answered honestly. "When I found that box of condoms, I really thought . . ." They both studied their hands, fitting and refitting them together. "Well, you know what I thought."

"Yeah, I know what you thought." He deserted her hand to double both his behind his head. "But we can't always be counting condoms, Bess."

She chuckled and turned on her side to study him, laying one hand on the hollow beneath his ribs.

"I know. I'm just being honest, Michael."

"You don't think you can ever trust me again?"

She only studied him, wondering herself. Soon he spoke again.

"I've been thinking about a lot of other things. The fact that both of us are working now—I think I've come to terms with that, and I'd be willing to share the housework, and not even fifty-fifty. Sometimes it might be sixty-forty, other times forty-sixty. I realize now that when both people are working it's got to be a cooperative effort that way."

She smiled. "I have a housekeeper now."

"Does she cook for you, too?"

"No."

"Well, there, you see? We can take turns cooking."

Bess was getting sleepy. "Know what?"

"What?"

"I like being convinced. Go on."

"I've even given some thought to my hunting. I know you used to get upset when I'd leave you to go hunting but now I have the cabin and you can come along . . . light a fire in the fireplace, bring a good book . . . how does that sound?"

"Mmm . . ."

"It'd be good for you to get away from the store, relax a little more . . ."

"Mmm . . ."

Her hand below his ribs lay heavy and motionless.

"Bess, are you sleeping?"

Her breathing was regular, her eyelashes at rest upon her cheek. He braced up on one elbow and reached beyond her, caught the side of the bedspread and flipped it over her, then did the same on his side. She murmured and snuggled deeper. He put a hand on her waist, drew a knee up against her belly, nestled on his side with his forehead near hers and thought, I'll only stay for a half hour or so . . . it's so nice here beside her . . . if I leave the light on it'll wake me up again in a while.

Chapter 16

⁓⁓⁓

Randy got home at 2:15, pulled into the driveway and sat staring at the silver Cadillac Seville. *What the hell is he doing here?* He glanced up at his mother's bedroom window, found the light on, shook his head in disgust and slammed the van door behind himself.

Inside, the entry chandelier was aglow, as well as the lights in the upstairs hall. Something was scattered on the steps. He went up to get a closer look and discovered an empty box of condoms, along with its contents lying strewn all over two steps. He picked one up, studied it as it lay in his palm and glanced at the head of the stairs. He started up cautiously, passing a piece of clothing, and when he reached the top, peered around the corner along the hall. More clothing left a trail—a man's trousers, shoes, his mother's little white thing that she wore after her bath. At the far end of the hall her bedroom door was wide open and the light was on.

"Mom?" he called.

No answer.

He proceeded to the doorway, stopped just outside and called, "Mom, you all right?"

Again, no answer, so he stepped inside.

His mother and father were lying curled up together spoon-fashion, naked, with the bedspread haphazardly covering them to the hips. Michael's arm was looped over Bess's waist, his hand near her breast. From the looks of the room they'd had a wild one. Pillows lay scattered on the floor around the bed, which itself looked as though a twister had struck it. The empty packet from a condom lay on his father's side of the bed beside a soiled handkerchief.

Randy felt his face flame but just as he made a move to retreat, Michael came awake, lifted his head and discovered Randy in the doorway. He glanced sharply at Bess, still asleep, caught the edge of the bedspread and drew it up to cover her naked breasts. Once more he looked across the room at his son.

"Randy?"

"You got balls, man," Randy sneered, "coming here like this."

"Hey, Randy, just a min—"

But Randy was gone, his footfalls thundering angrily down the hall, down the steps.

Bess squinted awake and mumbled, "Michael? What time is it?"

"Two-fifteen. Go back to sleep."

She clambered onto her knees and began scraping the spread back. "Let's get under."

"Bess, Randy's home."

"Oh so what. So now he knows. Shut off the lamp and get under."

Michael shut off the lamp and got under.

In the morning he awakened to the sensation of being watched. He was. When he opened his eyes he found Bess with her head on the only pillow still remaining on the bed, her face turned his way, studying him.

"Hi," she said, looking quite pleased with herself.

"Hi."

"Where's your pillow?" His head was flat on the mattress.

"I seem to remember we threw it on the floor."

She smiled and said, "So we got caught, huh?"

"Did we ever."

"Did he come in here?"

"Uh-huh."

"Did he say anything?"

"He said, 'You got balls, man.' "

Her smile turned lurid. "Yeah, you do. Mind if I fondle them a little bit?"

He grinned, pushed her hand away and regretfully told her, "Listen, missus, our son's in the house, and he's royally pissed."

She gave up her pursuit and said, "So what are we going to tell him?"

"Hell, I don't know. You got any ideas?"

"How about, 'Forty-year-olds get horny, too'?"

"Cute. Very cute." Michael sat up on the edge of the bed, flexed his arms and stretched.

Bess braced her jaw on one hand and reached up to ruffle his tousled hair.

"He probably won't get up till nine or so."

"Then I'll stay till nine or so."

"You don't have to. I can talk to him."

"You're not the one he'll be angry with. It'll be me. I'm not leaving you here to do my dirty work while I slink off with my tail between my legs."

She let her palm ride down the center of his back. It was a good, straight back, still firm and tapered.

Michael looked back over his shoulder at her. "Did you ever think when we had him that we'd end up making excuses for something like this?"

She smiled.

He rose, fully naked, and she watched him move around the foot of her bed through the bathroom doorway on her left. He left the door open, which brought a smile to her lips and some pleasant memories of married life. After taking care of morning necessities, he leaned against the vanity top, inspecting his face, rubbing sandmen out of his eyes.

"You know how I knew you were having an affair?" she asked.

He said, "How?" opened a drawer, found her hairbrush and started using it.

"You started closing the bathroom door."

From her vantage point she saw the rear half of him, the front half cut off by the doorway. He stopped brushing, tipped back at the waist, peered into the bedroom and said, "Really?"

"Mm-hm." She was lying on her side, with her head cradled on a folded arm, wearing a soft smile. He left the bathroom and walked toward her, undeterred by his nakedness, dropped down to sit on the bed at her hip.

"There . . . you see?" He touched her nose with the back of the brush. "I left it open. Now doesn't that prove something?"

They smiled at each other a long time while he sat with one hand braced on either side of her, their bare hips separated by a single layer of sheet. It had rained during the night. The morning-cool air came through the open window bringing a faintly dank smell resembling mushrooms. Somewhere in a metal downspout droplets of water made a modulated *blip, blip, blip.* It was one of those sterling stretches of minutes that come along rarely in a relationship, certainly the most idyllic for Michael and Bess since their divorce. She hated to tarnish it.

"Michael, listen . . ." She rubbed her palms lightly up and down his arms. "I'm not going to lie to Randy and tell him you and I are getting married again, because it's just not true. I need some time to think things through. This . . . this affair we've started . . . well, it's just that, an affair, nothing more. If Randy has trouble adjusting to that, then so be it but I won't vindicate myself with a lie. Do you understand what I'm saying?"

He withdrew to the edge of the bed, turning his back on her. "Sure. You're saying I'm good enough for you in bed but not out of it."

She sat up, touched his back. "No, Michael."

He rose and found his underwear, stepped into it and followed the trail of clothing still decorating the hall and steps. When he returned he was half-dressed, carrying her white cover-up and a handful of condoms. He tossed them on the bed along with the empty box. "There." He buttoned his shirt and began stuffing it into his trousers with angry shoves. "Keep them handy, then, because I can promise you I'll be back. I won't be able to resist it but we'll be setting one hell of an example for our kids, won't we, Bess?"

"Michael, you came here! I didn't come to you, so don't blame me for what happened!"

"I want to marry you, damn it, and you're saying no, you'd rather have an affair; well what kind of—"

"That's not what I'm saying." She jumped up and grabbed her cover-up from the foot of the bed, flung it over her head. "I don't want to make the same mistake again, that's all."

"I can see the writing on the wall. We'll get together once, maybe twice a week, we'll make love, and afterwards we'll go through this same scene, me saying 'Let's make it honest' and you getting angry, and then both of us getting angry. Well, that's not what I want, Bess. I want what Lisa wants—the two of us back together for good."

She stood before him, a little angry, a little repentant, a lot afraid. No matter what they'd agreed about shared guilt during their first breakup, he'd been the philanderer and the hurt still clung.

"Michael," she said calmly, "I don't want to fight with you."

His shirt was on, his pants were zipped, his belt was buckled.

"Okay," he said. "I've called you twice. It's your turn next time. See how it feels to be the one who comes begging."

He strode toward the door.

"Michael . . ." The tone of her voice was tantamount to a reaching hand but he'd already disappeared around the door. She hurried to it and yelled down the hall, "Michael!"

He called back as he reached the top of the stairs, "Tell Randy I'll call him and explain."

Randy's voice came from below.

"You don't have to call him, he's here."

Michael's footsteps faltered, then continued more slowly to the bottom of the steps, where Randy stood, bare but for his blue jeans, which were zipped but unbuttoned. It startled Michael to see for the first time the dense pattern of hair on Randy's chest and around his navel, proof that he was as fully mature as Michael himself.

"Randy . . . I'm sorry we woke you."

"I'll just bet you are."

"I didn't mean it that way. I had every intention of talking to you about this. I wasn't going to skip out and leave it to your mother."

"Oh yeah? Well, that's the way it looked to me. Why don't you just leave her alone?"

"Because I love her, that's why."

"Love—Christ, don't make me laugh. I suppose you loved her then, too, when you had an affair with another woman and walked out on her. I suppose you loved me, and Lisa, too!"

Michael knew it would do no good to declare he did. He stood in silence. Randy replied as if Michael had answered.

"Well, that's some way to show your kids you love 'em. You want to know how it feels to have your father write you off? It hurts, that's how it feels!"

"I didn't write you off."

"Aw, fuck that, man, you left her, you left us! I was thirteen years old. You know how a thirteen-year-old thinks? I figured it must've been my fault, I must've done something wrong to make you leave but I didn't know what; then Mom finally tells me you had another woman and I wanted to find you and smash your face, only I was too little and skinny. Now here you are, crawling out of her bed—well maybe I should smash it now, huh?"

From the top of the stairs, Bess reprimanded, "Randy!"

His icy eyes looked up. "This is between him and me, Ma."

"You will apologize to him at once if for nothing more than your offensive language!"

"Like hell I will!"

"Randy!" She started down the stairs.

Randy's face wizened with disbelief. "Why are you taking his side? Can't you see he's just using you again? Comes down here saying he loves you—man, that's just bullshit! He probably said the same thing to that other floozy he married but he couldn't make that marriage stick, either! He's a loser, Ma, and he doesn't deserve you and you're a damn fool for letting him in here!"

She slapped Randy's face.

He stared at her in shock. Tears spurted into his eyes.

"I'm very sorry I had to do that. I've never done it before and I want you to know I hated it. But I cannot allow you to stand there berating your father and I. Neither one of us are blameless but there are proper, respectful ways in which to talk these things out. Now, I think, Randy," she said quietly, "that you owe us both an apology."

Randy stared at her. At Michael. Back at her before spinning and heading for his downstairs bedroom without another word.

When he was gone Bess put her hands to her cheeks and felt them burning. She turned to Michael, who stood forlornly, studying the toes of his shoes. She put her arms around him. "Michael, I'm sorry," she whispered in a shaken voice.

"It's been coming for a long time."

"Yes, I suppose so but that doesn't make it hurt any less."

She held him awhile. Though his arms automatically went around her, they applied no pressure, only hung there like limp ropes.

Finally he pulled back and said in a strange, choked voice, "I'd better go."

"I'll talk to him when he's settled down."

Michael nodded at the floor. "I'll . . ." He didn't know what he'd do. Take another cooking course. Buy another piece of land to develop. Choose a sculpture for his gallery. Pointless, senseless, frantic scrambling by a man seeking to fill his life with meaning when the only meaning in life can come from people, not things.

"I'll see you, Bess," he said, and left, closing the door quietly behind him.

In his room, Randy sat on the edge of his water bed, doubled forward, holding his head in both hands.

Crying.

He wanted a dad, wanted a mom, wanted love like other kids. But why did it have to be so painful, getting it? He'd been hurt so much by their divorce. Why shouldn't he be allowed to vent this fury that had been building in him since the eighth grade, when they'd split? Couldn't they see what jerks they were making of themselves, falling back together this way for convenience? It wasn't as if they talked about getting married again—the word hadn't been mentioned. No, it was just plain lust, which made his mother as guilty as his father, and he didn't want her to be. Damn Lisa for stirring this all up. She was the one—Lisa!—who insisted they end the cold war. Now this.

It had been bad holding things inside all these years but letting them out hadn't felt much good, either. Seeing the look of pain on his dad's face when he had yelled, "It hurts!"—that was what he'd wanted, wasn't it? To hurt his old man for once the way the old man had hurt him. Wasn't that what he wanted? So why was he doubled over here, bawling like a baby?

Goddamn you, Dad, why did you leave us? Why didn't you stick with Mom and work it out?

I'm so confused. I wish I had somebody to talk to, somebody who'd listen and make me understand who I'm angry at and why. Maryann. Oh God, Maryann, I respected you so much. I was going to show you I could be different than my old man, I could treat you like some princess and never lay a hand on you, and show you I was worthy of you.

But I'm not. I talk like a gutter rat, and smoke pot, and drink plenty, and screw any girl who comes along, and my own father doesn't love me enough to stick around, and my own mother slaps me.

Somebody help me understand!

Shortly, Randy's mother came to his door. She knocked softly. He swiped his eyes with the bedsheet, hopped up and pretended to be busy at the controls of the CD player.

"Randy?" she called quietly.

"Yeah, it's open." He heard her come in.

"Randy?"

He waited.

"I'm sorry."

He watched the knobs on the control panel blur as his eyes refilled with tears. "Yeah . . . well . . ." His voice sounded high, like when he was going through puberty and it was changing.

"Slapping you was wrong. I shouldn't have done it. Randy?"

He wouldn't answer.

She had come up silently and touched his shoulder before he realized she was there. "Randy, I just want you to know something. Your dad asked me to marry him again but I'm the one who said no."

Randy blinked and the tears dropped to his bare stomach, clearing his vision somewhat. He remained with his back to Bess, his chin on his chest.

"Why?"

"Because I'm afraid of getting hurt again, the same as you."

"I'm never apologizing to him. Never."

Her hand went away from his shoulder. She sighed. Time passed. Her hand returned, warm and flat on his bare skin.

"Randy, he loves you very much."

Randy said nothing. The damn tears plumped up again.

"I know you don't believe that but he does. And whether you believe it or not, you love him. That's why you're hurting so badly right now." Another pause before she continued. "The two of you will have to talk someday—I mean, really talk, without anger, about all your feelings. Please, Randy . . . don't wait too long, dear."

She kissed his shoulder and silently left.

He remained in his windowless room, willing away tears that refused his bidding. He touched a silver knob on his CD player, let his hand fall to his side. He imagined going to his father's place and knocking on his door and simply walking into his arms and hugging him hard enough to snap their bones. How did people manage to do that after they'd been hurt this bad?

The tape of The Edge was in the deck, the one he practiced with. He knelt down and replaced it with the rock group Mike and the Mechanics, fast-forwarded it to the song he wanted. Forward, back, forward again to the band between songs. The intro came on and he plugged in his earphones, put them on and sat at his drums, holding both sticks in his one hand, too bummed out to use them.

The words started.

Every generation
Blames the one before . . .

It was a song written by someone after his father had died. "The Living Years." A rueful, wrenching song.

And all of their frustrations, come beating on your door . . .
I know that I'm a prisoner to all my father held so dear
I know that I'm a hostage to all his hopes and fears
I just wish I could have told him
In the living years.

Randy sat through it all, listening to the plaintive call of a son who waited until it was too late to make his peace with his father. He sat with his eyes closed, his drumsticks forgotten in his hand, tears leaking from the corners of his eyes.

That evening, The Edge was playing at a club called The Green Light. Randy was unusually quiet while they were setting up. Through the cacophony of tuning and balancing he let the others go about their BS'ing without him. There was always a lot of give-and-take at this time, part of the ritual of getting up for a performance.

When the lights were set and the instruments ready, the filler tape playing for the crowd and the amplifiers humming softly, the guys put their guitars in their stands and went off toward the bar to get drinks. All but Pike Watson, who stopped by Randy, still sitting behind his drums. "Heya, Rimshot, you're a little low tonight."

"I'll be okay once we start playing."

"Got trouble with some of the songs? Hey, it takes time."

"No, it's not that."

"Trouble with your girl?"

"What girl?"

"Trouble at home, then."

"Yeah, I guess you could say that."

"Well, hell . . ." Pike let his thought trail away, standing with his hands caught on his bony hips. Brightening, he asked, "You need something to pick you up?"

"I got something."

"What, that jimmy dog you smoke? I mean something to really pick you up."

Randy came from behind the drums, heading for the bar. "I don't do that shit, man."

"Yeah, well, I just thought I'd offer." Pike sniffed. "Those drumsticks can get mighty heavy at times."

Randy had two beers and a hit of marijuana before they started the first set but the combination only seemed to make him lethargic and tired tonight. They played to a desultory audience, who acted as if the dance floor was off limits, and after the second set he tried more marijuana but it failed to do the trick. Even the music failed to lift Randy. The drumsticks felt very heavy, indeed. During the third break he went into the men's room and found Pike there, the only one in the room, sniffing a hit of cocaine off a tiny mirror through a rolled-up dollar bill.

"You really ought to try it." Pike grinned. "It'll cure whatever ails you."

"Yeah?" Randy watched as Pike wet his finger, picked up any stray powder and rubbed it on his gums.

"How much?"

"First hit is on me," Pike said, holding out a tiny plastic bag of white powder.

Randy looked at it, tempted not only to get out of this low but to spite his mother and father. Pike wiggled the bag a little bit as if to say, Go on, give it a try. Randy was reaching for it when the door burst open and two men came in, talking and laughing, and Pike swiftly hid the bag and mirror in his pocket.

After the night Randy discovered them in bed, Michael quit calling Bess, and though she missed him horribly, she, too, refused to call him. Deep summer came on: in Stillwater a time for lovers. They came by the hundreds, teenagers over from

Minneapolis and St. Paul, flooding the town in their souped-up sports cars; the town's own teenagers, cruising the length of the quay on Friday nights; college kids off for the summer, dancing to the canned music at Steamers; boaters down for the weekends, setting the river agleam with the reflection of their running lights; sightseers out for an evening, walking the riverbank, holding hands.

At night, the volleyball court in front of the Freight House was a maze of tan, young arms and legs. The riverside restaurant decks were crowded. The old lift bridge backed up traffic several times an hour letting boats beneath it. The antique stores did a landmark business. The popcorn wagon put out its irresistible smell. The wind socks in front of Brick Alley Books waved a welcome to the cars streaming down the hill into town.

One hot Saturday Bess was invited to a pool party at Barb and Don's house. She bought a new bathing suit, expecting Michael to be there. He wasn't; he'd been invited but had declined when he'd learned Bess was coming.

A man named Alan Petrosky, who introduced himself as a horse rancher from over by Lake Elmo, kept up an irksome pursuit until she wanted to dump him into the pool, cowboy boots and all.

Don and Barb noticed what was going on and came to rescue her. Don gave her a brotherly hug and asked simply, "How have you been?" She found tears in her eyes as she replied, "Very mixed up and lonely."

Barb caught her by a hand and said, "Come up to the bedroom for a minute where we won't be disturbed." In the cool green bedroom with the curtains drawn and the party sounds distant, Barb asked, "So how are things between you and Michael?" and Bess burst into tears.

She broke down and called him in early August on the pretext of advising him about some nice pieces of sculpture on display at a gallery in Minneapolis. He was brusque, almost rude, declining to ask anything personal or to thank her for recommending the gallery.

She submerged herself in work; it helped little. She told Randy she wanted to come out some night and hear him play; he said no, he didn't think the kind of bars he played in would be her style. She attended a shower for Lisa, given by Mark's sisters; it only reminded her she would soon be a grandmother facing old age alone. Keith called and said he missed her, wanted to see her again; she told him no, smitten by a wave of mild revulsion.

Life felt humdrum to Bess while, by comparison, it seemed everyone around her was living it to the fullest, having the gayest summer of their lives. She found a batik piece depicting sandpipers that would have been stunning in Michael's dining room, but she stubbornly refused to call him for fear he'd again treat her as if she'd just peed on his shoe. Worse, what if she herself broke down and suggested their getting together for an evening?

Sexuality—damn the stuff. Bess would have thought, considering impending grandparenthood, that she'd be immune. She was not. She thought of Michael in a sexual regard as often as in a nonsexual. She fully admitted the reason she'd been repulsed by the idea of reviving anything with Keith was because, by comparison to Michael, he was a vacant lot. Michael, on the other hand, was a lush orchard—

but hardly enough reason for a woman of forty to make a fool of herself gorging on ripe fruit. As she'd told him the night they'd last made love, they weren't teenagers anymore. Still, all the platitudes in the world couldn't prevent her from missing him immensely.

On August ninth Bess turned forty-one. Randy forgot all about it, didn't even give her a card before he left for a three-day gig in South Dakota. Lisa called and wished her a happy birthday but said she'd ordered something that hadn't arrived yet; it should be here by the weekend and they'd get together then. Stella was gone with three of her ladyfriends on a two-week vacation in the San Juan islands north of Seattle and had sent a birthday card that had arrived the day before, along with a postcard from the Burchart Gardens in Victoria, British Columbia: wish you were here.

Bess's birthday fell on a Thursday; she had appointments all afternoon long but rushed back to the store before Heather left for the day, asking if she'd had any calls.

"Four," Heather answered. But none were from Michael, and Bess climbed the stairs to her stifling loft telling herself she had no right to be disappointed. She was responsible for her own happiness, it was not the duty of others to create it for her.

Still . . . birthdays.

She found herself remembering certain ones while she'd still been married to Michael. The first one after they got married, when he'd taken her tubing on the Apple River and had pulled a Pepperidge Farm cake out of a floating cooler tied between them while they were bobbing down the stream on inner tubes, scraping their hinders on rocks and burning the tops of their knees and loving every minute of it.

The year she turned thirty, when he'd arranged a surprise party at Barb and Don's house and she'd sulked all the way there, thinking she was going to a birthday party for their daughter, Rainy, who was turning four the next day.

Another one—she'd forgotten exactly which. Thirty-two? Thirty-three?— when Michael had given her a particular bracelet she'd admired and had pulled it out of his vest pocket on their way out to dinner, the way rich men did in movies. It had been in a black velvet box, a simple gold serpentine chain, and she had it still.

No bracelets today, though. No black velvet boxes, no cards in the mailbox at home, nobody to float down a river with, or go out to dinner with, or surprise her with balloons and cheers.

She stopped at Colonel Sanders's on her way home and picked up two pieces of fattening chicken and some fattening potatoes and gravy and a cob of fattening corn and one of those little fattening lemon desserts, which she ate on the deck while watching the boats on the river and wishing she was on one of them.

Birthdays . . . oh, birthdays.

If there was any day when a lonely person felt more lonely, when a single person felt more single, when a neglected person felt more neglected, she wanted to know what it was.

With dusk approaching she puttered around the yard, plucking weeds in the rock-lined perennial beds she'd once tended meticulously but which had fallen into a state of neglect after she'd gone back to college. She broke a fingernail and got disgusted, went inside and took a long bath and gave herself a facial, examining her skin critically after washing the mask from it.

Forty-one—lord. And her skin getting a little droopy and soft like a maiden aunt's.

Forty-one and no gifts, no calls.

Tiny lines lurking at the corners of the eyes. A faint jowl beginning to show if she forgot to keep her chin high.

At 11 P.M. she turned off the television and lamp in her bedroom and lay with the windows open, listening to a thousand crickets and the bishop sleeves fluttering faintly against the sill, smelling the dampness of deep summer thread in from the yard, recalling nights like this when she was sixteen and went with mobs of kids to the drive-in theater. Always, there was company then.

The neighbors across the street came home, Elaine and Craig Mason, married probably forty years or more, slamming their car doors and talking quietly on their way into the house. Their metal screen door slammed and all grew quiet. Bess had stacked up her pillows as if knowing sleep would be reluctant, and reclined with her eyes wide open, intent upon the fretwork of shadows on the opposite wall, cast through the maples by the night light in the yard.

When the phone rang her body seemed to do an electric leap that shot her heart into fast time. The red light on the digital clock said 11:07 as she rolled over and grabbed the receiver in the dark, thinking, *Let it be Michael.*

"Hello, Bess," he said, his familiar voice at once raising a sting in her eyes.

"Hello." She went back against the pillows, touching the receiver with her free hand as if it were his jaw.

Outside, the crickets kept sawing away, their song throbbing in the summer night while on the telephone a lengthy silence hummed. She knew it meant he was not entirely pleased with himself for having broken down and called her after vowing he would not do so again.

"It's your birthday, huh?"

"Yes." She pointed one elbow to the ceiling, covering her eyes to stop them from stinging.

"Well, happy birthday."

"Thanks."

They remained silent for so long her throat began to ache. The crickets continued their rasping.

Finally Michael asked, "Did you do anything special?"

"No."

"Nothing with the kids?"

"No."

"Didn't Lisa come over or anything?"

"No. She said we'll get together soon, maybe this weekend. And Randy's playing out in South Dakota, so he's not around."

"Damn those kids. They should have done something for you."

She dried her nose on the sheet and forced her voice to sound normal. "Oh, what the heck. It's just one birthday. There'll be lots of others."

Please come over, Michael. Please come over and just hold me.

"I suppose so but they still should have remembered."

Another silence came and gripped them, and beat across the telephone wire. She wondered if he was in his bedroom, what he was wearing, if the light was on. She pictured him in his underwear, lying in the dark on top of the covers with one knee up and the balcony doors open.

"I ah . . . I got that mess straightened out down on Victoria and Grand." She formed an image of him watching his own fingernail scratching a groove into a sheet while he spoke. "Building's going to get under way soon."

"Oh, good!" she said, with false brightness. "That's . . ." Softer, she ended, ". . . that's good."

Why are we in separate bedrooms, Michael?

If she didn't invent some perky conversation soon, he'd surely hang up. She stared at the indigo leaf shadows on the opposite wall and searched for some clever dialogue to keep him on the line.

"Mom's gone on a trip to Seattle."

"Seattle . . . well." After a pause, "So she wasn't around today, either."

"No, but she sent a card. She's having a grand time with all her friends."

"She always seems to manage that, doesn't she?"

Bess turned on her side with the receiver pressed against the pillow, her position going slightly fetal while she coiled the phone cord around the tip of her index finger. Her chest felt ready to splinter into fragments. Oh God, she missed him so much.

"Bess, are you still there?"

"Yes."

"Well, listen, I . . ." He cleared his throat. "I just thought I'd call. Force of habit on this day every year, you know." He laughed. Oh, such a melancholy laugh. "I was just thinking about you."

"I was thinking about you, too."

He fell silent and she knew he was waiting for her to say, *I want to see you, please come over.* But the words stuck in her throat because she was afraid all she wanted to see him for were sexual reasons, and because she was so utterly lonely and it was her birthday, and she was forty-one and dreading the possibility of spending the rest of her life alone; and if he came over and they made love she'd be using him, and nice women weren't supposed to use men that way, not even ex-husbands, and then what would she say afterward, if he asked her again to marry him?

"Well, listen . . . it's late. I should go."

"Yes, me too."

She covered her whole face with one hand, her eyes squeezed shut, her lips bitten to keep the sobs from falling out, the telephone a hard knob between her ear and the pillow.

"Well, 'bye, Bess."

" 'Bye, Michael . . . Michael, wait!" She was up on one elbow, frantic, her tears at last running. But he'd hung up, leaving only the throb of the crickets to keep her company while she wept.

Chapter 17

Lisa called the Blue Iris at 11 a.m. on August sixteenth and said she had gone into labor. Her water hadn't broken but she was spotting and cramping and had contacted the doctor. There was no reason for Bess to come to the hospital yet; they'd call when she should.

Bess canceled two afternoon appointments and stayed in the store near the phone.

Heather said, "It brings back the days when you were waiting for your own kids to be born, doesn't it?"

"It really does," Bess replied. "Lisa took thirteen hours but Randy took only five. Oh, I must call him and tell him the news!" She checked her watch and picked up the phone. Her relationship with Randy had been bumping along since the day she'd slapped him. She talked, he grunted. She made an effort, he made none.

He answered on the third ring.

"Randy, I'm so glad you're still home. I just wanted you to know that Lisa's gone into labor. She's still at home but it looks as though this is the real thing."

"Yeah? Well, tell her good luck."

"Can't you tell her yourself?"

"The band's heading out for Bemidji at one o'clock."

"Bemidji . . ." Her voice registered dismay.

"It's not the end of the world, Ma."

"No, I suppose not, but I hate your having to travel so much."

"It's only five hours."

"Well, be careful, dear, and be sure you get some sleep before you head back."

"Yeah."

"And no drinking and driving."

"Aw, come on, Ma, jeez . . ."

"Well, I worry about you."

"Worry about yourself. I'm a big boy now."

"When will you be back?"

"Sometime tomorrow morning. We're playing in White Bear Lake tomorrow afternoon."

"I'll leave a note at home if the baby is here. Otherwise call me at the store."

"Okay. Ma, I gotta go."

"All right, but listen . . . I love you."

He paused too long before replying, "Yeah, same here," as if pronouncing the actual words was more than he could manage.

Hanging up, Bess felt forlorn. She remained with her hand on the phone, staring out the front window, feeling like a failure as a mother, understanding how Michael had felt all these years, wondering how to mend these fences between herself and Randy.

"Something wrong?" Heather asked. She was dusting the shelving and glassware, working her way along the west wall of the shop.

"Ohhh . . ." Bess released a deep sigh. "I don't know." After a while she turned to Heather and asked, "Do you have one child who's harder to love than the others? Or is it just me? Because I feel very guilty sometimes but I swear, that younger one of mine is so distant."

"It's not just you. I've got one who's the same way. My middle one, Kim. She doesn't like being hugged—never mind kissed—never wanted to do anything with the family after she reached age thirteen, disregards Mother's Day and Father's Day, criticizes the radio station I listen to and the car I drive and the movies I like and the clothes I wear and only comes home when she needs something. Sometimes it's really hard to keep on loving a kid like that."

"Do you think they eventually grow out of it?"

Heather replaced a bowl on the shelf and said, "Oh, I hope so. So, what's wrong between you and Randy?"

Bess shot Heather a glance. "The truth?"

Heather continued her dusting indifferently. "If you want to tell me."

"He caught me in bed with his father."

Heather started laughing silently, her mouth open wide, the sound at first only a tick in her throat until it crescendoed and resounded through the store. When the laugh ended she twirled the dustrag through the air above her head. "Hooray!"

Bess looked a little pink around the edges. "You're spreading dust all over the stuff you just cleaned."

"Oh, big deal. So fire me." Heather returned to her task, smiling. "I figured it was getting serious between you two. I knew you weren't spending all that time on business, and I for one am glad to hear it."

"Well, don't be, because it's only caused problems. Randy's been bitter about the divorce ever since it happened, and he finally told his father so but I stepped in and things got out of hand. I slapped Randy and he's been withdrawn and unaffectionate ever since. Oh, I don't know, Heather, sometimes I hate being a mother."

"Sometimes we all do."

"So what did I do wrong? His whole life long I loved him, I told him so, I kissed and hugged him, I went to school conferences, I did everything the books said I should but somewhere along the line I lost him. He just pulls farther and farther away. I know he's drinking, and I think he's smoking pot but I can't get him to admit it or to stop."

Heather left her dustrag on the shelf and went around behind the counter. She took Bess in her arms and held her caringly. "It's not always us doing something wrong. Sometimes it's them, and we just have to wait for them to grow out of it, or confide in us, or hit bottom."

"He loves this job so. His whole life long he's wanted to play with a band but I'm so afraid for him. It's a destructive way of life."

"You can't make his choices for him, Bess, not anymore."

"I know . . ." Bess held Heather tighter for a second. "I know." She drew away with glistening eyes. "Thanks. You're a dear friend."

"I'm a mother who's tried her damnedest, just like you but . . ." Heather raised her palms and let them drop. ". . . all we can do is love 'em and hope for the best."

It was hard to concentrate on work knowing Lisa was in labor. There were designs to be finished in the loft but Bess felt too restless to be confined upstairs. She waited on customers instead, tagged some newly arrived linens and hung them on an old-fashioned wooden clothes rack for display. She went outside and watered the geraniums in the window box. She unpacked a new shipment of wallpaper. She checked her watch at least a dozen times an hour.

Mark called shortly before 3 P.M. and said, "We're at the hospital. Can you come now?"

Bess barely took time to say good-bye before hanging up, grabbing her purse and running.

Lakeview Hospital was less than two miles from her store, up to the top of Myrtle Street hill and south on Greeley Street to the high ground overlooking Lily Lake. Though there were other hospitals closer to Lisa and Mark's apartment, her pregnancy had been confirmed by the physicians she'd known all her life, so she'd stayed with the familiar names and faces who practiced right here in town. Bess found it comforting to be approaching the hospital where Lisa and Randy had been born, where Lisa's broken arm had been set, where both of them had been given their preschool physicals, and countless throat cultures, and where their height and weight and periodic infirmities had been recorded and were still safely filed away in metal drawers. Here, too, the whole family had seen Grandpa Dorner for the last time.

The OB wing of the hospital was so new it still smelled of carpet fiber and wallpaper. The hall was indirectly lit, quiet, and led to a hexagonal nurses' station surrounded by a circle of rooms.

"I'm Lisa Padgett's mother," Bess announced to the nurse on duty.

The young woman led the way to a birthing room, where both the labor and birth would be carried out. Lisa and Mark were there, along with a smiley nurse wearing blue scrubs, whose nametag read JAN MEERS, R.N. Lisa was lying on the bed holding up a wrinkled patient's gown while Jan Meers adjusted something that looked like a white tube top around her belly. She picked up two sensors, slipped them beneath the bellyband, patted them and said, "There. That'll hold them." Their leads dropped to a machine beside the bed, which she rolled nearer.

Lisa saw Bess and said, "Hi, Mom."

Bess went to the bed, leaned over and kissed her. "Hi, honey, hi, Mark, how's everything going?"

"Pretty good. Getting me all hog-tied to this machine so we can tell if the baby changes his mind or something." To the nurse, Lisa said, "This is my mom, Bess." To Bess, "This is the lady who's going to put me through the seven tortures."

Ms. Meers laughed. "Oh, I hope not. I don't think it'll be so bad. Look here now . . ." She moved aside and rested a hand on the machine where an orange digital number glowed beside a tiny orange heart that flashed in rhythm with a sound like a scratchy phonograph record. "This is the fetal monitor. That's the baby's heart-beat you hear."

Everyone's eyes fixed upon the beating orange heart while beside it a white graph paper began to creep into sight, bearing a printout of the proceedings.

"And this one"—Ms. Meers indicated a green number beside the orange one—"shows your contractions, Lisa. Mark, one of your jobs will be to watch it. Between contractions it'll read around thirteen or fourteen. The instant you see it rising you should remind Lisa to start breathing. It'll take about thirty seconds for the contraction to reach its peak, and by forty-five seconds it'll be tapering off. The whole thing will last about one minute. Believe it or not, Mark, you'll often know there's a contraction starting before she will."

Ms. Meers had scarcely finished her instructions before Mark said, "It's going up!" He moved closer to Lisa, his eyes on the monitor. Lisa stiffened and he reminded her, "Okay, relax. Here we go now, remember, three pants and one blow. Pant, pant, pant, blow . . . pant, pant, pant, blow . . . okay, we're fifteen seconds into it . . . thirty . . . hang on, honey . . . forty-five now and nearly over . . . good job."

Bess stood by uselessly, watching Lisa ride out the pain, feeling her own innards seizing up while Mark remained a bastion of strength. He leaned over Lisa, rubbed the hair back from her forehead and smiled into her eyes. He whispered something and she nodded, then closed her eyes.

Bess checked the clock. It was 3:19 P.M.

The next contraction came fifteen minutes later and by the time it arrived, so had Mark's mother. She greeted everyone, giving Mark a quick squeeze.

"Is Dad coming?" Mark asked her.

"He's at work. I left a note on the kitchen table for him. Hi, Lisa-honey. Today's the day you get your waistline back. I'll bet you're happy." She kissed Lisa's cheek and said, "I think it's going to be a boy. I don't know why but I have the strongest feeling."

"If it is we're going to be in trouble because we haven't thought of a boy's name yet. But if it's a girl it'll be Natalie."

The contractions came and went. It was hard for Bess to watch Lisa suffer. Her child. Her precious firstborn, who had, as a youngster of five, six, seven, mothered her baby brother the way little girls do: held his hand when they crossed the street together; lifted him up to reach the drinking fountain; soothed and cooed when he fell down and scraped a knee. And now she was a grown woman and would soon have a baby of her own. No matter that the pain was the means to eventual happiness and fulfillment, watching one's own child bear it was terrible.

At moments Bess wished she'd decided to delay coming here until the baby was safely born, then felt guilty for her selfishness. She wished she were needed more, then felt grateful that Mark was the one Lisa needed most. She wished Lisa were a little girl again, then thought, No, how foolish; I really wish no such thing. She was enjoying having an adult daughter. Nevertheless, often during those minutes of travail, she pictured Lisa as a kindergartner, walking bravely up the street alone for the first time—absurd, how fragments of those bygone years kept insinuating themselves into this hour that was so far removed from the days of Lisa's childhood. Perhaps it was peculiar to the stepping-stones of life that at those times an underlying sadness was rekindled.

Sometimes when the contractions ended, both Bess and Hildy released their breaths and let their shoulders slump, then glanced furtively at each other, realizing they'd been copying Lisa's breathing pattern as if doing so could make it easier on her.

At 6:30 Jake Padgett arrived, and Bess left the birthing room for a while because it was getting too crowded. She walked down to the pop machine by the cafeteria, got a can of Coke and took it to the family room, adjacent to Lisa's birthing room, a spacious, restful place with comfortable chairs and an L-shaped sofa long enough to stretch out and nap on. It had a refrigerator, coffeepot, snacks, bathroom, television, toys and books.

Bess found her mind too preoccupied to be interested in amusements.

She returned to the birthing room at five to seven and watched two more contractions, before rubbing Mark's shoulder and suggesting, "Why don't you sit down awhile. I think I can do this."

Mark sank gratefully into a recliner and Bess took his place beside the bed.

Lisa opened her eyes and smiled weakly. Her hair was stringy and flat, her face looked slightly puffy. "I guess Dad's not coming, huh?"

Bess took her hand. "I don't know, sweetheart."

From his chair, Mark murmured sleepily, "I called his office a long time ago. They said they'd give him the message."

Lisa said, "I want him here."

"Yes, I know," Bess whispered. "So do I."

It was true. While she had watched Lisa laboring she'd wanted Michael beside her as strongly as ever in her life. It appeared, however, that he was avoiding the hospital, knowing she was there, just as he had the pool party at Barb and Don's.

By ten o'clock there'd been no change, and the anesthesiologist was called in to administer an epidural, which made Lisa woozy and a slight bit giddy. The baby was big, probably close to ten pounds, and Lisa was narrow across the pelvis. The epidural, it was explained, would not stop the contractions, only make Lisa unaware she was having them.

Mark was napping. The Padgetts had their eyes closed in front of the TV, and Bess went out to find a pay phone and call Stella, who said she wouldn't clutter up the proceedings but wanted to know the minute the baby was born, even if it was the middle of the night. After the phone call, Bess returned to the obstetrics wing and ambled around the circular hall. On the far side she wandered into the solarium, an arc-shaped room with a curved bank of windows overlooking the treetops and Lily Lake across the street. Only a glimpse of the night-dark water was visible and from inside, where climate was carefully controlled and trees were potted, it was impossible to tell if the night was warm or cool, still or noisy, if crickets were chirping, water lapping or mosquitoes buzzing.

The thought of mosquitoes brought the memories of warm summer nights when Lisa and Randy were little and the whole neighborhood resounded with the sounds of squeals from a dozen children playing starlight-moonlight and kick the can. When they were called for bedtime, the kids would whine, "Come on, Mom, just a little while longer, pleeeeze!" When they were finally coerced inside, their bare legs would be welted with bites, their hair sweaty, their feet dirty. Then she and Michael would bathe and dry them and put them in clean pajamas. How good they would smell then, with their faces shiny and their pajamas crisp. They would sit at the kitchen table and gobble cookies and milk and scratch their mosquito bites and protest that they weren't a bit tired.

But once in bed they'd be asleep in sixty seconds, with their precious mouths open and their sunburned limbs half above, half under the sheets. She and Michael would study them in the wedge of light from the hall as it picked out their lips and noses and eyelashes, and often their bare toes protruding from pajama legs rucked up about their knees.

Remembering, Bess felt her eyes grow misty.

She'd been standing a long time, staring out the window, weighted by the bittersweet tug of nostalgia, too weary to uncross her arms, when someone touched her shoulder.

"Bess."

She turned at the sound of Michael's voice and felt an overwhelming sense of relief and the awful threat of full-fledged tears.

"Oh, you're here," she said, as if he had materialized from her fantasy. She stepped into the calm harbor of his arms as she had longed to step into that shadowy bedroom where her younglings slept. The pressure of his embrace was firm and reassuring, the smell of his clothing and skin familiar, and for a minute she pretended the children were young again, they had tucked them into bed together and at last were stealing a moment for each other.

"I'm sorry," he said against her temple. "I'd flown to Milwaukee. I just got back and my answering service gave me the message." The strength of Bess's embrace surprised Michael. "Bess, what's wrong?"

"Nothing, really. I'm just so glad you're here."

His arms tightened and he let out a ragged breath against her hair. They had the solarium to themselves. The indirect lighting created a soft glow above the black windows. At the nurses' station beyond the door, all was quiet. For a while time seemed abstract, no rush nor reason to refrain from embracing, only the utter rightness of being together again, bolstering each other through this next stepping-stone in their daughter's life and their own.

Against Michael's shoulder Bess confessed, "I've been thinking about when the children were little, how simple everything was then, how they'd play games after dark with all the neighborhood kids and come in all full of mosquito bites. And how they looked in bed when they fell asleep. Oh, Michael, those were wonderful days, weren't they?"

"Yes, they were."

They were rocking gently. She felt his hand pet her hair, her shoulder.

"And now Randy is out on the road somewhere with some band, probably high on pot, and Lisa is in there going through all this."

Michael drew back but held Bess by the upper arms while looking into her eyes. "That's how it is, Bess. They grow up."

For a moment the expression in her eyes said she wasn't ready to accept it. Then she said, "I don't know what's come over me tonight. I'm usually not so silly and sentimental."

"It's not silly," he replied, "it's understandable on this particular night, and you know something else? Nostalgia looks good on you."

"Oh, Michael . . ." She drew away self-consciously and dropped into a chair beside a potted palm. "Did you stop by Lisa's room?"

"Yes. The nurse explained they gave her something to help her rest for a little while. She's been here since three, they said."

Bess nodded.

He looked at his watch. "Well, that's only seven hours. If I remember right she took thirteen getting here." He smiled at Bess. "Thirteen of the longest hours of my life."

"And mine," Bess added.

He sat down in a chair beside her, found her hand and held it on the hard wooden arms between them, rubbing her thumb absently with his own. They thought about their time apart, their stubbornness that had brought them both nothing but loneliness. They studied their joined hands, each of them grateful that some force outside themselves had brought them here and thrust them back together.

After a while Bess said quietly, "They said the baby is really large, and Lisa might be in for a hard time."

"So we'll stay, for as long as it takes. How about Stella? Does she know?"

"I called her but she decided to stay home and wait for the news."

"And Randy?"

"He knew she was in labor before he left. He'll be home tomorrow."

They waited in the solarium, alternately dozing and waking. Around midnight they went for a walk around the wing, discovering a new shift had come on, gazing into the empty nursery, passing the family lounge, where Jake Padgett was stretched out on the sofa, sound asleep. In the birthing room Hildy was the only one awake. She was sitting in the wooden rocking chair doing cross-stitch and waved at them silently as they paused in the doorway.

Lisa's new nurse came by and introduced herself. Marcie Unger was her name. She went into Lisa's room to check the digital readings, came back out and said, "No change."

By two o'clock things had picked up. Lisa's contractions were coming every five minutes and the anesthesiologist was called to cut off the epidural.

"Why?" Lisa asked.

"Because if we don't, you won't know when to push."

The birthing room came to life after that. Those who wanted to witness the birth were asked to don blue scrubs. Marcie Unger stayed beside Lisa every moment and Mark, too, holding Lisa's hand, guiding her through her breathing.

Jake Padgett decided to wait in the family lounge but Hildy, Bess and Michael donned sterile blue scrubs.

For Bess it was a curious sensation, looking up to find only Michael's attractive hazel eyes showing above his blue mask. She felt a momentary current the way she had when she was first falling in love with him. His eyes—stunning beyond all others she'd ever known—still had the power to kick up a reaction deep within her.

His mask billowed as he spoke. "How do you feel?"

"Scared, and not at all sure I want to go in there. How about you?"

"The same."

"We're just being typical parents. Everything will go fine. I'm sure of it."

"If I don't faint on the delivery-room floor," Michael said.

Her eyes crinkled. "Birthing room, and I'm sure you'll do just great."

"If we don't want to go in there, why are we doing it?" Michael said.

"For Lisa."

"Oh, that's right. That darned kid asked us to, didn't she?"

The interchange took the edge off their nervousness and left them smiling above their masks. Bess could not resist telling him, "If we're lucky, Michael, this baby will have your eyes."

He winked one of them and said, "Something tells me everything's going to be lucky from here on out."

When they entered the birthing room again, Lisa's knees created twin peaks beneath the sheet. The head of her bed was elevated at a 45-degree angle but her eyes were closed as she panted and labored through a contraction, her face glistening with sweat and her cheeks puffing as she breathed.

"I've g . . . got to p . . . push," she got out between breaths.

"No, not yet," Marcie Unger said soothingly. "Save your strength."

"But it's time . . . it's . . . I know it's . . . oh . . . oh . . . oh . . ."

"Keep breathing the way Mark tells you."

Beside her, Mark said, "Deeply this time, in and out, slow."

Bess's eyes sought Michael's and saw reflected there the same touch of anguish and helplessness she herself felt.

When the contraction ended, Lisa's eyes opened and found her father's, above the blue mask. "Dad?" she said with a weak smile.

"Hi, honey." His eyes crinkled with a smile as he moved to her side to squeeze her hand. "I made it."

"And Mom," she added in a whisper, searching for and finding her mother's eyes. "You're both here?" She gave a tired smile and closed her eyes while Bess and Michael exchanged another glance that said, This is what she wanted, this is what she set out to do. They took their places on Lisa's left while Mark and his mother stood on her right.

A second nurse appeared, all sterile and masked. "The doctor will be here in a minute," she said. She looked down into Lisa's face and said, "Hi, Lisa, I'm Ann, and I'm here to take care of the baby as soon as it arrives. I'll measure him, weigh him and bathe him."

Lisa nodded and Marcie Unger moved to the foot of the bed, where she removed the sheet from Lisa, then the end cushion of the bed itself, before tipping up a pair of footrests. She told Lisa, "These are for your feet if you want them. If not, fine." On the side rails she adjusted two pieces that looked like bicycle handles with plastic grips, and placed Lisa's left hand on one. "And these are for you to hang onto when you feel like pushing."

Mark said, "Here comes another one . . . come on, honey, show me that beautiful breathing. Pant, pant, pant, blow . . ."

Lisa moaned with each blow. In the middle of the contraction the doctor swept in, dressed like all the others in blue scrubs and skull cap. She spoke in a feminine voice. "Well, how are things going with Lisa?" Her eyes darted to the vital signs, then she smiled down at her patient.

"Hello, Doctor Lewis," Lisa said with as much enthusiasm as she could muster. Her voice sounded weak. "Where've you been so long?"

"I've been in touch. Let's see if we can't get this baby into the world and have a look at him. I'm going to break your water, Lisa. After that, everything will happen pretty fast."

Lisa nodded and rolled a glance at Mark, who held her hand folded over his own, smoothing her fingers.

While Dr. Lewis broke Lisa's water, Michael glanced away. The doctor was giving Lisa a monologue on what she was doing but Lisa made small sounds of distress. Under cover of the doctor's voice, Bess whispered to Michael, "Are you all right?"

He met her eyes and nodded but she could tell he was not, especially when he observed the faint pinkish fluid that ran from Lisa and stained the sheets beneath her. She found his arm and rubbed it lightly while from across the room she caught Hildy watching. Hildy's eyes smiled and the two women, who'd both borne children of their own, exchanged a moment of silent communion.

Lisa's next pushing contraction brought even greater sounds of distress. She cried out, and her body and face quaked as she clasped the handles and tried mightily to push the baby from herself.

The contraction ended with no results, and when it ebbed Bess bent over Lisa and said, "You're doing fine, honey," worried herself but hiding it. She lovingly wiped Lisa's stringy, wet bangs back form her brow and thought, *Never again, I'll never watch this again!*

She straightened to find Michael's eyebrows furrowed with concern, his breath coming fast, luffing his mask in and out.

The next contraction seemed worse than the last and racked Lisa even harder. Her head lifted from the bed, and Bess bolstered her from behind while Michael stared at the swollen shape of the baby's head engaged in the birth canal and repeated along with Mark, "Pant, pant, pant . . . push."

Still the baby refused to emerge, and Bess glanced at Michael's eyes to find them bright with tears. His tears prompted some of her own and she glanced away, wanting to be strong for Lisa's sake.

The doctor ordered, "Get the mighty vac."

Marcie Unger produced it: a tiny cone-shaped device at the end of a rubber tube and hand pump.

"Lisa," the doctor said, "we're going to give you a little help here. This is just a miniature suction cup we're going to put on the baby's head so the next time you push, we can pull a little, too, all right?"

"Will it hurt him?" Lisa asked, attempting to lift her head and see what was going on below.

"No," the doctor replied while Mark pressed his wife back against the bed, leaning over her, soothing her, urging her to rest as much as possible between pains. Bess did likewise from the opposite side of the bed, cooing comforting words, softly rubbing the inside of Lisa's knee.

Lisa murmured, "I'm so hot . . . don't touch me . . ."

Bess dropped her hand and felt Michael secretly grope for it in the folds of their blue scrubs. She gripped his hand and squeezed it all the while the tiny cone was inserted, and the hand pump worked by Marcie Unger, all the while Lisa moaned and wagged her head deliriously against the mattress.

With the next contraction the mighty vac began helping but midway through the suction broke and the cup flew free, spraying blood across six sets of scrubs and striking terror into the eyes of Mark, Hildy, Bess and Michael.

"It's okay," Marcie Unger reassured. "No harm done."

It seemed to take hours for them to get the suction cup reapplied.

But with the next pain, it worked.

Dr. Lewis said, "Here it comes . . ." and all eyes were fixed upon Lisa's dilated body. She pushed and the doctor pulled, and out of her swollen flesh emerged a tiny head with bloody, black hair.

Bess gripped Michael's hand and stared through her tears while he did likewise, both of them wonder-struck by what was happening before their eyes.

Between breaths Lisa managed to ask Mark, "Is it born yet?"

Dr. Lewis answered. "Halfway but one more push and it'll be here. Okay, Mark, help her through it."

The next pain did, indeed, bring the full birth. Michael and Bess watched it happen, still clinging to each other's hands, smiling behind their masks.

"It's a girl!" the doctor announced, catching the infant as it slipped forth.

Lisa smiled.

Mark cried, "Yahoo!"

Hildy rubbed Mark's back.

Bess and Michael looked at each other and found telltale dark splotches on their blue masks. Michael shrugged a shoulder to an eye and left another dark spot, and Bess felt her heart go light with joy.

The nurse named Ann came immediately with a soft blue towel, scooped the infant into it and laid her on Lisa's stomach. The doctor clamped the cord in two places and handed a pair of scissors to Mark.

"How about it, Daddy, do you want to cut the cord?"

The baby was wriggling, testing out its arms in the confines of the towel while Bess bolstered Lisa up so she could see the baby's head and touch it.

"Wow . . ." Lisa breathed, ". . . she's really here. Hey, Natalie, how you doing?" Then to the doctor, "Isn't she supposed to cry?"

"Not as long as she's breathing, and she's doing that just fine."

Lisa sank back and discovered there was more work to do—afterbirth to be delivered, and stitches to be tolerated.

Meanwhile, Natalie Padgett was being passed around from hand to hand—to her father, her grandmothers, her grandfather, whose dark eyes beamed above his mask while he, too, welcomed her with "Hi, Natalie." She was about as pretty as a baby bird, still plastered with afterbirth and working her head and arms with the diminutive motions of a slow-motion film, trying to keep her eyes open while her fists remained tightly shut.

Hildy said, "I'd better go tell the news to Jake." While she was gone Bess and Michael had one lavish minute to appreciate their grandchild themselves. She lay in the soft blue towel, squirming, held in Michael's wide hands, with Bess cupping the warm flannel around her tiny, smeared head.

The instinct to kiss her was irrepressible.

Tears kept welling in their eyes and blurring her image while a wellspring of love encompassed them both.

Michael said, "How awful that I missed this when our own were born. I'm so glad I was here this time." He passed the baby to Bess, who held her far too short a time before she was claimed by her father, then by Ann, for weighing and measuring. Hildy returned with Jake in tow, and the birthing room became crowded, so Bess and Michael left for a while, repairing to the family room next door. There, all was quiet and they were alone. They turned to each other, pulled down their masks and embraced, wordless for a long time, the birth they'd just witnessed melding with the birth of Lisa in their memories.

When Michael spoke his voice was gruff with emotion.

"I never thought I'd feel like this."

"How?" she whispered.

"Complete."

"Yes, that's it, isn't it?"

"A part of us, coming into the world again. My God, it does something to you, doesn't it, Bess?"

It did. It brought a lump to her throat and a yearning to her heart as she simply stood in Michael's arms, softly rubbing his shoulders through the ugly blue scrubs, disinclined to ever leave him again.

"Oh, Michael . . ."

"I'm so glad we're together for this."

"Oh, me too. It was awful before you got here. I kept thinking you weren't coming, and I didn't know how I'd get through it without you."

"Now that I've been through it, I wouldn't have missed it for the world."

They remained locked in an embrace until their emotions calmed and weariness made itself known, then Michael asked, against her hair, "Tired?"

"Yes. You?"

"Exhausted."

He set her away and looked into her face. "Well, I guess there's no reason for us to stay. Let's go see the baby once more and say good-bye to Lisa."

In the room next door the new parents created a heartwarming tableau with their clean, red-faced infant between them, wrapped now in a pink blanket, Lisa and Mark radiant with love and happiness. So radiant, it seemed a transgression to interrupt and bid them good-bye.

Bess did so first, leaning over Lisa as she rested in bed, touching her hair and kissing her cheek, then the baby's head. "Good night, dear. I'll see you later on this afternoon. Thank you so much for letting us be a part of this."

Michael went next, kissing them, too, deluged with the same emotions as Bess. "I didn't really want to come in here tonight but I'm so glad I did. Thank you, honey."

They congratulated and hugged Mark and left the hospital together.

Outside it was nearly dawn. Sparrows were beginning to cheep from the nearby trees. The sky had begun its fade from deep blue to lavender. The night dew seemed to have lifted into the air and hung damp all around. The visitors' parking lot was nearly empty as Bess and Michael walked across it with lagging footsteps.

As they approached Bess's car, Michael took her hand.

"That was really something to go through, wasn't it?" he said.

"I feel as if I had the baby myself."

"I bet you do. I never had one, and *I* feel like I just did!"

"The funny thing is when I was the one giving birth I don't think the wonder of it struck me so hard. I suppose I was too busy to dwell on that part of it."

"Same for me. Waiting in another room—I wish things had been different in those days and I could have been in the delivery room like Mark was."

They reached her car and stopped but Michael kept her hand. "Can you believe it, Bess? We're a grandpa and grandma."

She smiled up at him wearily and said, "A couple of very tired ones. Do you have to work today?"

"I'm not going to. How about you?"

"I was supposed to but I think I'll let Heather handle it alone. I'll probably sleep for a few hours then come back up to see Lisa and the baby again."

"Yeah, me too."

There seemed little else to say. It was time to part, time for him to go to his condominium and for her to go to her house on Third Avenue.

They had been through an exhausting night. Their eyes hurt. Their backs hurt. But they stood in the parking lot, holding hands until it made no sense anymore. One of them had to move.

"Well . . ." she said, "see y'."

"Yeah," he repeated, "see y'."

She pulled free as if someone were dragging her against her wishes, from the opposite direction. She got into her car while he stood with both hands crooked over the open door, watching as she put her keys in the ignition and started the engine. He slammed the door. She shifted into reverse and waggled two fingers at him through the window, wearing a sad expression on her face.

He stepped back as the car began to roll, slipped his hands into his trouser pockets and remained behind feeling empty and lost as he watched her drive away.

When she was gone, he sighed deeply, tipped his face to the sky and tried to gulp down the lump in his throat. He went to his own car, got in and stuck his keys into the ignition, then sat motionless with the engine unstarted and his hands hanging limply on the wheel.

Thinking. Thinking. About himself, his future and how empty it would remain without Bess.

It began deep down within him, a bubbling rebellion that said, Why? Why must it be that way? We've both changed. We both want, need, love each other. We both want this family back together. What the hell are we waiting for?

He started his engine and tore out of the parking lot doing a rolling stop at the stop sign, then wheeled out onto Greeley Street on Bess's trail, doing a good fifteen miles an hour above the speed limit.

At the house on Third Avenue he screeched to a halt and opened the car door even before the engine stopped running. Her car was already put away in the garage, the door was down. He jogged up the sidewalk to the front door, rang the bell, thumped on the door with his fist several times, then stood waiting with one hand braced on the doorframe at shoulder level. She must have gone upstairs already. It took her some time to get back down and answer.

When she did, surprise dropped her jaw.

"Why, Michael, what's wrong?"

He burst inside, slammed the door and scooped her into his arms. "You *know* what's wrong, Bess. You and me, living in two separate houses, being divorced from each other when we love each other the way we do. That's no way for us to act, not when we could be together and happy. I want that . . ." He gripped her harder. ". . . oh God, I want that so much." He interrupted himself to kiss her—hard, brief, possessive—before wrapping his arms around her firmly and holding her to his breast. "I want Lisa and Mark to bring that baby to our house and the two of us waiting with outstretched arms, and keeping her overnight sometimes, and all of us together on Christmas mornings after Santa Claus comes. And I want us to try to make up for what we did to Randy. Maybe if we start now we can turn him around." He drew back, holding her face in both hands, pleading, "Please, Bess, marry me again. I love you. We'll try harder this time, and we'll compromise, for both us and the kids. Can't you see, Lisa was right? This is the way it should be!"

She was crying long before he finished, the tears coursing down her cheeks. "Aw, don't cry, Bess . . . don't . . ."

She dove against him and threw her arms around his neck. "Oh, Michael, yes. I love you, too, and I want all those things, and I don't know what's going to become of Randy but we've got to try. He still needs us so much."

They kissed the way they'd wanted to in the hospital parking lot, sealed together full-length, earnest with passion while at the same time too tired to know if they were standing on their own power or supporting one another. Their lips parted, their gazes locked but even so, they floundered in their attempt to impart the depth of emotions coursing through them.

He kissed the crests of her cheeks, sipping up her salty tears, then her mouth, softly this time. "Let's get married right away. As soon as possible."

She smiled through her tears. "All right. Whatever you say."

"And we'll tell the kids today. And Stella, too," he added. "We're going to make her the second happiest woman in the whole USA."

Bess kept smiling. "The third, maybe . . . behind me and Lisa."

"All right, third. But she'll be smiling."

"She'll be doing cartwheels."

"I feel like I could do a few myself."

"You do? I'm falling off my feet."

"On second thought, so am I. Should we go to bed?"

"And do what? Get caught again by Randy? He's due home, you know."

Michael took her breasts in both hands and went on convincing her. "You'll sleep better afterwards, you always do."

"I won't have any trouble sleeping at all."

"Cruel woman."

She drew back and smiled lovingly. "Michael, we'll have plenty of time for that, and I really am tired, and I don't want to antagonize Randy any more. Let's do the sensible thing."

He caught her hands and stepped back. "All right, I'll go home like a good boy. Will I see you at the hospital later?"

"Around two or so, I thought."

"Okay. Walk me to my car?"

She smiled and walked with him, holding his hand, outside into the yard, where full dawn was staining the sky a spectrum of purples and golds and a faint breeze was stirring the tips of the maple leaves. The hydrangeas in front of the garage were heavy with great white blooms and the scent of heavy summer was rising from the warming earth.

At his car, Michael got in, closed the door and rolled down the window.

She leaned inside and kissed him. "I love you, Michael," she said.

"I love you, too, and I really think we can make it this time."

"So do I." He started the engine, still looking up into her eyes.

She grinned. "It's hell being mature and having to make sensible decisions. For two cents I'd drag you up to our bedroom and ravish you right now."

He laughed and said, "We'll make up for it, just wait and see."

She stood back, crossed her arms and watched him back out of the driveway.

Chapter 18

⟶ ⟵

The band quit playing at 12:30 a.m. It took them one hour to load up and over five hours to drive back from Bemidji. Randy got home at seven to find his mother still asleep and a note on his bed.

Lisa had a girl, Natalie, 9 lbs. 12 oz. at five this morning. Everybody's doing fine. I'm not going into the store but hope to see you at the hospital later. Love, Mom.

But the way it worked out he was unable to make it to the hospital that afternoon. He was still asleep when his mother got up, and she was gone from the house by the time he rose, groggy, at 12:15 to get ready for his afternoon gig, which started at two in White Bear Lake.

These town celebrations paid well. Every little suburb around the Twin Cities had them at some time during the summer: the Raspberry Festival in Hopkins, Whiz-Bang Days in Robbinsdale, Tater Days in Brooklyn Park, Manitou Days in White Bear Lake. They were all the same: carnivals, parades, bingo, beard-growing contests and street dances. Some of the dances took place at night but many, like today's, were scheduled for the afternoon. Bands liked the bookings not only because they paid well but also because the afternoon scheduling gave them a rare Saturday night off to catch a decent stretch of sleep or to go hear some other band play, which every professional musician loved to do.

White Bear Lake had a pretty little downtown—shady, with trees springing out of openings in the brick sidewalks; fancy, old-fashioned storefronts painted candy colors; flags hanging from the sides of buildings; a little town square.

The entire length of Washington Street was barricaded off, and a bandstand was set up at the south end, facing a turn-of-the-century post office building with its surrounding green grass and flower beds. While the band set up, little girls sat on the curb and watched, licking ice-cream cones or chewing licorice sticks. Pint-sized boys wearing chartreuse billcaps and hot-pink shorts maneuvered their skateboards back and forth, deftly jumping the thick electrical cables that snaked across the blacktop. From several blocks away the sounds of a carnival drifted over on the whims of the wind—an occasional tinkle of calliope music, the revving engines from the amusement rides. From nearer wafted the smell of bratwursts roasting on a pushcart in front of a ladies' wear shop midway along the block.

Randy stacked a pair of drums and lifted them from the rear of the van. He turned to find a boy of perhaps twelve years old watching. The kid was wearing sunglasses with pink frames and black strings. His hair was jelled up into a flattop, and his high-top tennis shoes had tongues nearly as big as the skateboard on his hip.

"Hey, you play those things?" the kid asked in a gruff, cocky voice.

"Yup."

"Cool."

Randy smiled at the kid and took the load up the back steps onto the stage. The boy was still there when he returned.

"I play drums, too."

"Yeah?"

"In the band at school."

"That's a good way to learn."

"Ain't got any of my own yet. But I will have someday though, and then look out."

Randy smiled and pulled another load of equipment to the rear of the van.

The kid offered, "Want me to help you carry some of that stuff?" Randy turned and looked the kid over. He was a tough-looking little punk, as tough-looking as it's possible to be at a hundred pounds, without much for muscles or whiskers or body hair. His Dick Tracy T-shirt would have fit Mike Tyson, and he had an I-don't-care way of standing inside it that reminded Randy of himself at that age, about the time his father had left: *Screw the world. Who needs it?*

"Yeah. Here, take this stool, then you can come back for the cymbals. What's your name, kid?"

"Trotter." He had a voice like sand in ball bearings.

"That's all? Just Trotter?"

"That's enough."

"Well, Trotter, see what you think about being a roadie."

Trotter was as good as his name, trotting up and down the steps, hauling anything Randy would hand him. Actually the kid was a godsend. Randy was zoned, operating on four hours of sleep and too much pot last night. God, how he needed to chill out for a solid sixteen hours but that hadn't been possible all week. Their traveling schedule had been horrendous, and they'd been rehearsing a lot, too. All that on top of setup and breakdown—which totaled two and a half, three hours a gig—left damned little time for Z'ing out. Now he faced four hours of playing when his feet would scarcely lift to carry him up the steps and his head felt like a bowling ball balanced on a toothpick.

With the help of the tough little groupie, the last of the equipment got to the stage.

"Hey, thanks, Trotter. You're okay." He handed the kid a pair of royal-blue drumsticks. "Here. Go for it."

The kid took the sticks, his eyes huge and filled with worship behind his shades. "For me?"

Randy nodded.

"Bitchin'," the kid marveled softly and moved off, already jiving to some silent beat.

"Hey, kid," Randy called after him.

Trotter turned, one of the sticks whirling like a propeller through his fingers. "Stick around. We'll send one out specially for you this afternoon."

Trotter saluted with one drumstick and disappeared.

Pike Watson came around the back of the stage carrying a guitar case.

"Who's the punk?"

"Name's Trotter. Just a kid with big dreams, wants to be a drummer someday."

"You give him the sticks?"

Randy shrugged. "What the hell, keep his dreams alive, you know?"

"That's all right."

"I didn't tell him he'd have to learn to sleep and drive at the same time if he wanted to play with a band."

"You droned, man?"

Randy shook his head as if to wake himself up. "Yeah. Major droned."

"Hey, listen, I'll do you a solid. I got some really good shit here." Pike tapped his guitar case.

"Cocaine, you mean? Naw. That stuff freaks me."

"How do you know? One little snort and you're goddamned Batman. You can stop trains and start revolutions. What do you say?"

Randy looked skeptical. "Naw, I don't think so."

Pike gave a mischievous grin. "I guarantee you'll forget you're tired." He spread his fingers and fanned them in slow motion through the air. "You'll play like freakin' Charlie Watts."

"How much?"

"Your first hit's on me."

Randy rubbed his sternum and tipped his head to one side. "I don't know, man."

"Well . . ." Pike threw his hands up and bounced a couple times at the knee. "If you're scared of flyin' . . ."

"What's it do to you—bad, I mean?"

"Nothin', man, *nothiiin'!* You get a little zingy at first—anxious, you know—but then it's strictly superfly!"

Randy rubbed his face with both hands and flexed his shoulders. He blew out a blast of breath that made his lips flop and said, "What the hell . . . I always wanted to play like Charlie Watts."

He snorted the cocaine off a mirror in the back of Pike's van just before they started playing. It made his nose sting and he rubbed it as he headed onto the stage. He felt wildly exhilarated and invincible.

They started the first set and Randy played with his eyes closed. When he opened them a moment later, he saw Trotter out in front of all the others on the street, sitting on his skateboard with his eyes riveted on Randy, playing along on his knees with the blue drumsticks. Yeah, it was hero worship, all right, and it felt sensational. Nearly as sensational as the high that was coming on. Some teenage girls stood at the front of the crowd, too, dressed in shiny biking tights with an inch of their tan, flat stomachs showing below their itty-bitty crop tops. One of them, a blonde with a spectacular mop of curly hair that exploded clear down past her shoulder blades, kept her eye on him without letup. He could spot them every time, the ones who were easy marks. All he had to do was return her gaze a few times, give the little hint of a smile she waited for and at break time stand nearby—not too close, just close enough for her to know he knew—and wait for her to sidle over. The conversations always went the same.

"Hi."

"Hi."

"You're good."

He'd let his eyes overtly explore her breasts and hips. "So are you. What's your name?"

After he'd learn it, he'd make sure he dedicated one song to her and that's all it took to get in her pants.

Today, however, the dedication was for Trotter. Randy put his lips to the mike and said, "I'd like to send this song out to one terrific little roadie. Trotter, this one's for you, kid." Trotter actually smiled, and while Randy rapped out the pickup beat to *Pretty Woman,* he truly forgot about the pretty woman standing behind the kid, and reveled in the genuine admiration he saw beaming up at him from the boy's face.

It happened as they began the second song. One minute Randy was watching the kid idolize him, and the next he was struck by an illogical shock of apprehension. His heart started racing and the apprehension became fear. He turned as if to seek help from Pike but all he saw was Pike's back, in a loose black shirt, diagonally bisected by a wide guitar strap as he stood with his feet widespread, playing.

Sweet Jesus, his heart! What was happening with his heart? It was pounding so hard it seemed to be lifting the hair from his skull. The kid was watching . . . no breath . . . hard to keep playing . . . people everywhere . . . had to make it to the end of the song . . . dizzying anxiety . . . oh-oh, pretty woman!

The song ending . . . "Pike!" . . . everything inside him vibrating . . . "Pike!" . . . and pushing outward . . . Pike's face, leaning close, coming between him and the crowd . . .

"It's all right, man. It always happens at first, you get a little uptight, scared-like. Give it a minute. It'll go away."

Clutching Pike's hand . . . "No, no! This'z bad, man . . . my heart . . ."

Pike, angry, ordering in a fierce whisper, "Let it ride, man. There's a couple hundred people out there watching us right now. It'll be better in a minute! Now give us a goddamn lead-in!"

Tick, tick, tick . . . the sticks on the rim of his Pearls . . . the kid watching from down on the pavement, playing along with the blue sticks . . . dizzy . . . so dizzy . . . kid, get outa here . . . don't want you to see this . . . Maryann, I wanted to change for you . . . his heart fluttering fast as a drumroll . . . everything tipping . . . tipping . . . the floor coming up to meet him . . . the crack of his head as he landed . . . the stool still tangled in his legs . . . looking straight up at the blue sky . . .

The band continued playing for several measures until they realized there was no more drumbeat. As the music dribbled into silence the crowd pressed forward, lifted up on tiptoe and murmured a chorus of concern.

Danny Scarfelli reached Randy first, leaned over him with his bass guitar still strapped over his shoulder.

"Jesus, Randy, what's wrong, man?"

"Get Pike . . . where's Pike?" Danny caught two of his guitar keys on the edge of a drum as he shot to his feet.

Randy lay in a haze of fear with the sound of his own heart gurgling in his ears. Pike's face appeared above Randy's, framed by the blue sky.

"Pike, my heart . . . I think I'm dying . . . help me . . ."

A jumble of voices.

"What's wrong with him?"

"Has he got epilepsy?"

"Call 911!"

"Hang on, Randy."

Pike leaped off the front of the stage and took off at a run. "Where's a phone? Anybody! Where's a phone!" Before the frantic question left his lips he saw a policeman coming toward him at a run, his silver badge bouncing on his blue shirt.

"Officer . . ."

The policeman ran right past him on his way to the stage, and Pike did an about-face to follow.

"Anybody know what's wrong with him?" the policeman asked, bending over Randy.

Pike said nothing.

The others said no.

Randy mumbled, "My heart . . ."

The man in blue grabbed the radio off his belt and called for help.

Randy lay ringed by faces, looking up at them, terror in his eyes. He grabbed a shirtfront: Danny's. "Call my mom," he whispered.

Blissfully unaware of the events happening at White Bear Lake ten miles away, Bess and Michael met at the hospital, stole one brief kiss in the hall, smiled into one another's eyes and entered Lisa's room together, holding hands. She and Natalie were there alone, the new mother asleep in her hospital bed, and the new baby making mewling sounds in a glass bassinet. The room was filled with flowers and smelled like oniony beef from the remains of Lisa's lunch, which was waiting to be collected.

Bess and Michael scanned the room from the doorway, then tiptoed to the bassinet and stood on either side of it, looking down at their new granddaughter.

They spoke in whispers.

"Oh, just look at her, Michael, isn't she beautiful?" And to the baby, Bess said, "Hello, precious, how are you today? You look a lot prettier than you did last night."

They both reached down and touched the baby's blankets, her downy cheek, rapt in her presence. Michael whispered, "Hi there, little lady. Grandma and Grandpa came to see you."

"Michael, look . . . her mouth is just like your mother's."

"Wouldn't my mother have loved her."

"So would my dad."

"She's got more hair than I thought. Last night it seemed as if she didn't have hardly any but today it looks quite dark."

"Do you think it would be okay if we picked her up?" Bess looked up into Michael's eyes. He smiled conspiratorially, and she slipped her hands beneath the soft pink flannel blanket and lifted Natalie from the bassinet. They stood shoulder-to-shoulder, inundated by love as pure and exquisite as any they had ever felt, stunned once again by a sense of completeness, by the idea of leaving their mark on the future through this child.

"Isn't it something, how she makes us feel?"

Michael kissed the baby's forehead, then straightened and smiled at her. "Wait till you're one or two or so. You'll come to our house to stay and we'll spoil you plenty, won't we, Grandma?"

"You bet we will. And someday when you're old enough, we'll tell you all about how your birth made your grandpa propose to me and brought us back together again. Of course we'll have to edit out the part about the condoms and how your grandpa threw them all over the steps but . . ."

Michael smothered his laughter. "Bess, these are delicate ears!"

"Well, she comes from a randy lot, and if—"

From behind them, Lisa spoke. "What are you two whispering about over there?"

They looked back over their shoulders. Lisa looked sleepy but wore a soft smile.

"Actually, your mother was talking about condoms."

"Michael!" Bess shouted.

"Well, she was. I told her Natalie was too young to hear such things but she wouldn't listen to me."

Lisa boosted herself up. "All right, what's going on between you two? I wake up and you're whispering and giggling . . ." She reached with both hands. "And bring my baby here, will you?"

Lisa pressed a button that raised the head of the bed, and they went to take her the baby, then sit one on each side of her and lean over simultaneously to kiss her cheeks.

"She was awake so we didn't think we'd get in trouble for picking her up."

"She's been a good girl . . . haven't you, Natalie?" Lisa fingered the baby's hair. "She slept five hours between feedings."

They talked about how Lisa was feeling, whom she'd called, who'd sent flowers (she thanked them for theirs), when Mark was expected to return, the fact that Randy hadn't called or stopped by, the probability of his visiting that evening, and Grandma Dorner, too. They admired the baby, and Bess offered reminiscences about Lisa's birth, and what a good sleeper she'd been, and what a lusty set of lungs she'd had when she decided not to sleep.

After all that, while they still sat one on either side of Lisa, Bess glanced at Michael and sent him a silent message. He captured her hand and, resting it on the bedspread covering Lisa's stomach, said, "Your mother and I have something to tell you, Lisa." He let Bess speak the words.

"We're going to get married again."

A radiant smile lit Lisa's face as she lunged forward, the baby still on her right arm, clasping Michael with her left as Bess, too, bent into the awkward, three-way embrace. The baby started complaining at being squashed between two bodies but they ignored her, allowing the moment its due, cleaving to one another, their throats thick with emotion.

Against Lisa's hair, Bess whispered simply, "Thank you, darling, for forcing two stubborn people back together."

Lisa kissed her mother's mouth, her father's mouth. "You've made me so happy."

"We've made *us* so happy." Michael chuckled, drawing a like response from the others as they drew back, all of them a little glisteny-eyed and flushed. They all laughed self-consciously. Lisa sniffed, and Bess ran the edge of a hand under her eye.

"When?"

"Right away."

"As soon as we can get it arranged."

"Oh, you guys, I'm *so* happy!" This hug was one of hallelujah, a near banging together of cheeks before Lisa held Natalie straight out and rejoiced, "We did it, kiddo, we did it!"

Stella spoke from the doorway. "May I get in on this celebration?"

"Grandma! Come in, quick! Mom and Dad have some great news! Tell her, Mom!"

Stella approached the bed. "Don't tell me. You're going to get married again." Bess nodded, smiling widely. Stella made a victor's fist. "I knew it! I knew it!" She kissed Bess first, because she was closer, then went at Michael with her arms up. "Come here, you handsome, wonderful hunk of a son-in-law, you!" She met him at the foot of the bed as he came around to scoop her up. "I thought that daughter of mine was crazy to divorce you in the first place." Released, she fanned her face and turned toward the bed. "Whoo! How much excitement can a woman stand in one day? All this and a great-grandchild, too! Let me see the new arrival—and Lisa, you little matchmaking mother, don't you look happy enough to float?"

It was an afternoon of celebration. Mark arrived, followed by the rest of the Padgetts as well as two women Lisa worked with, and one of her high-school friends. Bess and Michael's news was received with as much excitement as was their new granddaughter.

At one point Lisa asked, "Where are you going to live?"

They gaped at each other and shrugged.

Bess replied, "We don't know. We haven't talked about it yet."

Leaving the hospital at 4:15 P.M., Bess said, "Where *are* we going to live?"

"I don't know."

"I suppose we should talk about it. Want to come over to the house?"

Michael affected a salacious grin and said, "Of course I want to come over to the house."

They were driving separate cars but arrived at the house simultaneously. Bess parked in the garage and Michael pulled up behind her, went into the garage and waited beside her car while she switched off the radio and collected her purse and turned up the visor. As he opened her door and stood waiting, he found himself happier than he could recall being in years, for simply being with her, feeling certain that the last half of his life was going to be less tumultuous than the first. Everything seemed near perfect—the new baby, the marriage plans, the children all grown up, happiness, wealth and health; he found himself tempted toward smugness as he stood beside Bess's car.

From behind the wheel she looked up at him and said, "You know what?"

She could have announced that she'd taken a job as a palm reader and was going to travel the country with a carnival, and he wouldn't have objected at that moment, as long as he could tag along. Her face looked young and glad, her eyes content. "I couldn't guess."

She got out of the car. He slammed the door but they remained beside it, in the concrete coolness of the garage with its peculiar mixture of scents—mower gas and rubber hoses and garden chemicals. "I've discovered something about myself that surprises me," Bess told him.

"What?"

"That I really don't care about this house as much as I used to. As a matter of fact, I absolutely love your condo."

He couldn't have been more surprised. "Are you saying you want to live there?"

"Where do *you* want to live?"

"In my condo, but I thought for sure you'd have a fit if I said so."

She burst out laughing, draped her arms around his neck and dropped back against the side of her car, taking him with her. With his body fit to hers she smiled up into his eyes. "Oh, Michael, isn't it wonderful, getting older? Learning to sort out what's really important from what's petty and superficial?" She kissed him briefly and told him, "I'd love to live in your condo. But if you'd said you wanted to move back into the house, that would have been all right, too, because it's not so important *where* we live as that we live there together from now on."

He rested his hands on the sides of her breasts and said, "I've been thinking about that same thing, too. Are you sure you aren't saying you like the condo better just because you think it's what I want?"

"I'm sure. In more ways than one we sort of outgrew this house. It was grand while the kids were little but now it's—I don't know—a new phase of life, time to move on. There are a lot of sad memories here, as well as happy ones. The condo is a fresh start . . . and after all, we did decorate it together, to both of our tastes. Why, it makes perfect sense to live there! It's newer, it's got as wonderful a view as this does, nobody has to take care of the yard, it's still close enough for me to get to my store in fifteen minutes and for you to get to downtown St. Paul fast, and there's the beach and the parks, and—"

"Listen, Bess, you don't have to convince me. I'll be overjoyed to stay there. There's only one question."

"Which is?"

"What about Randy?"

She put her hands on his collarbone and absently smoothed his shirt. She let her hands fall still on his chest, lifted her gaze and said calmly, "It's time to cut Randy loose, don't you think?"

Michael made no reply. He had told her essentially the same thing that first night Lisa had tricked them into facing each other at her apartment.

"He has a job now," she went on. "Friends. It's time he got out on his own."

"You're sure?"

"I'm sure."

"Because it strikes me that even though parents think they ought to treat all their kids equally, it's not always possible. Some of them need us more than others, and I think Randy will always need more of our help than Lisa ever did."

"That may be true but it's still time for him to live in his own place."

They let a kiss seal their decision, sharing it leaning against the car with the late afternoon sunlight flooding in, and the sound of condensation dripping off the auto air conditioner, and the smell of gasoline coming from the nearby lawn mower.

When Michael lifted his head he looked serene. "This time I'm staying with you till he gets home, and we'll tell him together."

"Agreed." She smiled and threaded one arm around his waist, turning him toward the kitchen door.

They entered the house to find the phone ringing. Bess answered, unprepared in her radiant state for the voice at the other end of the line.

"Mrs. Curran?"

"Yes."

"This is Danny Scarfelli. I'm one of the guys in Randy's band. Listen, I don't mean to scare you but something's happened to him and he's not . . . well, I think it's pretty serious, and they're taking him by ambulance to the hospital."

"What? A car accident, you mean?" Bess's terrified eyes locked on Michael's.

"No. We were just playing, you know, and all of a sudden he's laying on the floor. He says it's something with his heart is all I know. He asked me to call you."

"Which hospital?"

"Stillwater. They've already left."

"Thank you." She hung up. "It's Randy. Something's wrong with his heart and they're taking him to the hospital in an ambulance."

"Let's go."

He grabbed her hand and they ran out the way they'd entered, to his car. "I'll drive."

All the way to Lakeview Hospital, they sat stiff-spined, fearful, thinking, Why now? Why now? It's taken us all this time to get our lives back on track, and we deserve some unconfounded happiness. Michael ignored stop signs and broke speed limits. Gripping the steering wheel with both hands, he thought, There must be something I should be saying to Bess. I should touch her shoulder, squeeze her hand. But he drove in his own insular parcel of dread, as silent as she, inexplicably reft from her by this threat to their child.

His heart? What could be wrong with the heart of a nineteen-year-old boy?

They reached the emergency room of Lakeview at the same time as the ambulance, catching a mere glimpse of Randy as they ran behind the gurney bearing him along a short hall to a curtained section of the area. An alarming number of medical staff materialized at once, speaking in brusque spurts, in their own indigenous lexicon, focused on the patient with unquestionable life-and-death intensity, ignoring Michael and Bess, who hovered on the sidelines, gripping each other's hands now as they had not in the car.

"Got a sinus tach here."

"What's his blood pressure?"

"One eighty over one hundred."

"Respiration?"

"Poor."

"How bad are the arrhythmias?"

"Bad. Heart is moving like a bag of worms in there. Very irregular and rapid. We put him on D5W."

Three patches were already pasted on Randy's chest, and a blood pressure cuff ringed his arm. Someone snapped leads to them, connected to monitors on the wall.

Intermittent beeps sounded. Randy's eyes were wide open as a doctor in white leaned over him. "Randy, can you hear me? Can you hear me, Randy? Did you take anything?"

The doc pulled back Randy's eyelids one at a time and studied the periphery of his eyes. A woman in blue scrubs said, "His parents are here."

The doctor caught sight of Bess and Michael, standing to one side, supporting each other. "You're his parents?"

"Yes," Michael answered.

"Are there any congenital heart problems?"

"No."

"Diabetes?"

"No."

"Seizure disorders?"

"No."

"Is he on any medication?"

"None that we know of."

"Does he use cocaine?"

"I don't think so. Marijuana sometimes."

A nurse said, "Blood pressure's dropping."

An alarm sounded on one of the machines, like the hang-up tone on a dangling telephone.

The doctor shouted, "This guy's coding! Page code blue!" He made a fist and delivered a tremendous blow to Randy's sternum.

Bess winced and placed one hand over her mouth. She stared, caught in a horror beyond anything she'd imagined, while her son lay on the gurney dying and a medical team fought a scene such as she'd witnessed only on television.

More staff came running, two more nurses, one who started a flowchart, a lab technician to help monitor the vital signs, a radiology technician who watched the monitors, an anesthetist who inserted a pair of nasal prongs into Randy's nose, another doctor who began administering CPR. "Grease the paddles!" he ordered. "We have to defibrillate!" With stacked hands, he thrust at Randy's chest.

Bess and Michael's interlocked knuckles turned white.

A nurse turned on a machine that set up a high electrical whine. She grabbed two paddles on curled cords and smeared them with gel. The doctor ordered, "Stand back!" Everyone backed away from the metal gurney as the nurse flattened the paddles to the left side of Randy's chest.

"Hit him!"

The nurse pushed two buttons at once.

Randy grunted. His body arched. His arms and legs stiffened, then fell limp.

Bess uttered a soft cry and turned her face against Michael's shoulder.

Someone said, "Good, he responded."

Through her tears and her terror, Bess looked back at the table, little understanding why these methods were used. Electrical current, zapping through her son's body, making it jerk and flop, that precious body she'd once carried within her own. *Please don't! Don't do that to him again!*

The room fell silent. All eyes riveted on a green screen and its flat, flat line.

Dear God, they've killed him! He's dead! There is no heartbeat!

"Come on, come on . . ." someone whispered urgently—the doctor, who'd made a tight fist and pushed it into the gurney mattress as he stared at the monitor. "Beat, damn it . . ."

The line stayed flat.

Bess and Michael stared with the others, linked by wills and hands, in near shock themselves from this quick plunge into disaster.

Tears leaked down Bess's face. "What is it? What's happening?" Bess whispered but no one responded.

The green line squiggled.

It squiggled again, lifting to form a tiny hillock on that deadly, unbroken horizon. And suddenly it picked up, became regular. Everyone in the room sighed and let their shoulders sag.

"All right, way to go, Randy," one of the medical team said.

Randy was still unconscious.

The lab technician, in a businesslike tone, with his eyes locked on the screen, reported, "We're back to an organized rhythm . . . eighty beats per minute now." The nurse with the clipboard checked the clock and made a note.

Bess looked up at Michael and her face sagged, as if made of wet newsprint. His eyes were dry and burning. He put both arms around her shoulders and hauled her close, cleaving to keep his knees from buckling while Randy began to regain consciousness.

"Randy, can you hear me?" Again a doctor was leaning over him.

He made a wordless sound, still groggy.

"Do you know where you are, Randy?"

He opened his eyes fully, looked around at the ring of faces and abruptly grew belligerent. He tried to sit up. "What the hell, let me outa—"

"Whoa, there." Hands pressed him down. "Not much oxygen getting to that brain yet. He's still light-headed. Randy, did you take anything? Did you take any cocaine?"

A nurse informed the doctor, "The cardiologist is on his way over from the clinic."

The doctor repeated to Randy, "Did you take any cocaine?"

Randy wagged his head and tried to lift one arm. The doctor held it down, encumbered as it was by the blood pressure cuff and the lead-in for an IV.

"Randy, we're not the police. Nobody is going to get in trouble if you tell us but we have to know so we can help you and keep your heart beating regularly. Was it cocaine, Randy?"

Randy fixed his eyes on the doctor's clothing and mumbled, "It was my first time, Doc, honest."

"How did you take it?"

No answer.

"Did you shoot up?"

No answer.

"Snort it?"

Randy nodded.

The doc touched his shoulder. "Okay, no need to get scared. Just relax." He lifted Randy's eyelids again, peered down, held up an index finger and said, "Follow my finger with your eyes." To the recording nurse he said, "No vertical nystagmus. No dilation." To Randy, "Are any of your muscles twitching?"

"No."

"Good. I'm going to tell you what happened. The cocaine increased your heartbeat to the point where there wasn't enough time during each beat for it to properly fill with oxygenated blood. Consequently not enough oxygen was getting to your brain so at first you probably felt a little light-headed, and finally you fell off your stool. After you got here to the hospital your heart stopped beating completely but we started it again. There's a cardiologist on his way over from the clinic right now. He'll probably give you some medication to keep your heartbeat regular, okay?"

At that moment the cardiologist swept in, moving directly to the gurney in brisk steps. The physician speaking said, "Randy, this is Dr. Mortenson."

While the specialist took over, the other doctor approached Bess and Michael. "I'm Dr. Fenton," he said, extending his hand to each of them in turn. He had grand gray eyebrows and a caring manner. "I imagine you both feel like you're going to be next on that table. Let's step out into the hall, where we can talk privately."

In the hall, Dr. Fenton took a second glance at Bess and said, "Are you feeling faint, Mrs. Curran?"

"No . . . no, I'm all right."

"There's no need to be heroic. You've just been through a stressful ordeal. Let's sit down over here." He indicated a line of hard chairs across from the emergency-room desk. Michael put his arm around Bess and helped her to one, where she sank down gratefully. When they were all seated, Fenton said, "I know you have a lot of questions, so let me fill you in. I think you heard what I was saying to Randy in there—he snorted some cocaine, which can do a lot of nasty things to the human body. This time it caused an abnormally high heart rate—ventricular tachycardia, we call it. When the paramedics answered the call, Randy had been playing the drums and had fallen off his stool. That's because there wasn't enough oxygen getting to his brain. When you saw him arrest, there was so much electrostimulus going through his heart it wasn't actually beating anymore, it was only quivering. When a heart does that we have to bring it to a complete standstill so its normal rhythmicity can return. That's why I struck his chest, and that's what we did when we defibrillated him. Once you do that the normal electrical pathway can take over again, which is what's happened now.

"You saw how Randy got a little belligerent when he was coming awake. That often happens when the oxygen is returning to the brain but he should rest easier now.

"I have to warn you, though, that this can happen again during the next several hours, either from the drugs or from the heart itself, which is very irritable after all it's been through. My guess is Dr. Mortenson will prescribe some medication to prevent fibrillation from recurring. The problem with cocaine is that we can't go

in there and get it out like we could poison, for example. We can only offer supportive care and wait for the effects of the drug to wear off. It stays in the system
long after the high is gone."

Michael said, "So what you're saying is, there's still a chance that he could die?"

"I'm afraid so. The next six hours will be critical. But his youth is a plus. And
if he does go into a fast rate, chances are we can control it with the drugs."

The cardiologist appeared at that moment. "Mr. and Mrs. Curran?"

"Yes, sir?"

Michael and Bess both stood.

"I'm Dr. Mortenson." He had steel-gray hair, rimless silver glasses and thick
hands with a generous peppering of black hair on them. His handshake was hearty
and firm. "Randy will be in my charge for a while yet. His heartbeat has leveled
off now—a little rapid but we've administered inderal, which should help stabilize
his heartbeat. If we can keep it reasonably steady for—oh, say twenty-four hours or
so—he'll be totally out of the woods. Right now the lab people are drawing his
blood gases. Our toxologist will do a drug screen and we'll be running a routine
battery of other tests as well—blood sugar, electrolytes—standard procedure where
cocaine is involved. We'll monitor him here in the ER for a while, then in a half
hour or so he'll be transferred to Intensive Care. He's actually very alert now and
asking if his mother is here."

"May we see him?" Bess asked.

"Of course."

She gave a timorous smile. "Thank you, Doctor."

Michael thought to ask, "Are there legalities involved, Doctor?"

"No. As I told Randy, we're not the police, neither do we report these cases
to the police. Because he's admitted to using cocaine, however, he'll be referred for
counseling, and a social worker will more than likely get involved."

"I heard him say he's never used it before. Is that possible?"

"Absolutely. You recall the death of the young basketball player, Len Bias, a
couple of years ago? Sadly enough it was his first time, too, but what he didn't know
was that he had a heart defect, a weakness too great to endure the effects of the cocaine. That's the trouble with this damned stuff. It can kill you half a dozen different ways, even the first time you let it in your body. That's why we have to educate
these kids *before* they try it."

"Yes . . . thank you, Doctor."

The ER medical staff was still watching Randy's monitors as Bess approached
the gurney, with Michael lingering several steps behind. A nurse in a traditional white
uniform and cap was filling a syringe with blood from Randy's arm. She snapped a
piece of rubber tubing off his biceps and said to him, "You've got nice veins." She
sent him a smile, which he returned halfheartedly, then closed his eyes.

Bess stood watching, willing her eyes to remain dry. The lab nurse finished
drawing her samples and left, pushing a tray containing rows of glass test tubes that
clinked like wind chimes as she moved away. Michael hung back while Bess moved
to the bed and bent over their son. He looked ghastly, sickly white, his eye sockets gaunt and his nostrils occupied by the oxygen prongs. The leads from his chest
draped away to the monitors. She remembered when he was one and two years old

how deathly afraid he'd been of doctors, how he'd cried and clung to her whenever she took him into the clinic. Again she struggled against tears.

"Randy?" she said softly.

He opened his eyes and immediately they filled. "Mom . . ." he managed in a croaky voice as the tears made tracks down his temples. She leaned down and put her cheek to his, found his hand at his hip and took it gingerly, avoiding the IV lead-in taped to its back.

"Oh, Randy, darling, thank God they got you here in time."

She felt his chest heave as he held sobs inside, smelled smoke in his hair and shaving lotion on his cheek, and felt his warm tears mingling with her own.

"I'm sorry," he whispered.

"I'm sorry, too. I should have been there for you, talked to you more, found out what was bothering you."

"No, it's not your fault, it's mine. I'm such a rotten bastard."

She looked into his eyes, so like his father's. "Don't you ever use that word." She wiped the tears from his temples but they continued to run. "You're our son and we love you very much."

"How can you love me? All I've ever been is trouble."

"Oh, no . . . no . . ." She smoothed his hair as if he were two years old again, then braved a wobbly smile. "Well, yes, sometimes you were. But when you have babies you don't say I want them only when they're good. You take them knowing that sometimes they'll be less than perfect, and that's when you find out how much you love them. Because when you've struggled through it, everybody comes out stronger. And that's how this is going to be—you'll see."

He tried to wipe his eyes but she did it for him, with a corner of the sheet, then kissed his forehead and moved back so Michael could take her place.

He moved into Randy's line of vision and said simply, "Hi, Randy."

Randy stared at his father while his eyes filled once again. He swallowed hard and said, "Dad . . . ?"

Michael braced a hand on Randy's far side, bent over and kissed his left cheek. Randy's arms went around his father's back and clung, trailing IV cords and blood pressure paraphernalia. He hauled Michael down as a sob broke forth, then another. Michael held him as fiercely as possible while attempting to keep his weight off the electronic leads taped to Randy's chest. For a long time they embraced in silence, only an occasional telltale sniffle giving away the difficulty they were having holding their weeping inside.

"Dad, I'm so sorry . . ."

"I know . . . I know . . . so am I."

Ah, sweet, sweet healing. Ah, welcome love. When they had filled both their hearts, Michael drew back, sat on one hip and rested an elbow alongside Randy's head. He put his hand on Randy's hair, looking down into his brimming eyes. "But this is the end of all that, huh? You and I have some time to make up for, and we're going to do it. Everything Mom just said goes double for me. I love you. I hurt you. I'm sorry and we're going to work on it, starting today."

Just don't die. Please don't die when I've just gotten you back again.

"I can't believe you're here when I treated you so shitty."

"Aw, listen . . . we just didn't know how to get past our own hurt, so we shut each other out. But from now on we're going to talk, right?"

"Right," Randy croaked. He sniffed and tried to run the edge of one hand beside his eyes.

"Let me help you. Bess, is there a Kleenex over there?" She brought some and passed a handful to Michael and watched as he ministered to his son much as he had when Randy was a toddler, drying his eyes, helping him blow his nose. The sight of the two of them, close and loving again, brought back fresh tears to her eyes.

At last Michael sat back. "Now listen . . ." he said to Randy. "Your mother has something to tell you." He stood and reached for Bess's hand, his eyes saying, *Just in case he doesn't make it through the next twenty-four hours.* He drew Bess forward and stood behind her, his hands resting on her shoulders. She slipped her palm under Randy's and told him quietly, "Your dad and I are going to get married again."

He said nothing. His eyes locked on hers for some time, then shifted to Michael's.

Michael broke the silence. "Well, what do you think?"

"My God, you've got guts."

Michael squeezed Bess's shoulders. "I guess you'd see it that way. We think we've grown up a lot in the last six years."

Bess added, "And besides that, we fell in love again."

A nurse interrupted. "We're going to move Randy to Intensive Care now. Then I think we'd better let him rest for a while."

"Yes, of course. Well, we just wanted you to know, darling. We'll be outside." Bess kissed Randy. "We'll talk about it more when you're out of here. I love you."

Michael, too, kissed Randy. "Rest. I love you."

Together they went out to the ICU waiting room to face the long vigil that would either take or give them back their son.

Chapter 19

During his critical twenty-four hours, time passed for Randy as phantasm. He would sleep as if for aeons and awaken to find the clock had moved a mere ten minutes. Faint sounds interposed themselves between sound sleep and full consciousness like a background score for his dreams. The *beep, beep, beep* of the blood pressure monitor announcing its new reading became his drumsticks on the rim of his Pearls, beginning a new song. The tinkle of test tubes when the lab technician returned became Tom Little's keyboards. The dim squish of rubber soles on hard floors became a rush of tail feathers on a woman who was dancing through his dream, dressed like a Las Vegas chorus girl in a bright pink flamingo costume while he played backup music with the band. She whirled and he caught sight of her face: it was Maryann Padgett. Somewhere in the room rubber wheels rolled across the floor and through his dream sped a skateboard and on it, the kid Trotter, going faster and faster, on a collision course with Maryann. Randy tried to call out, Trotter, don't hit her! but Trotter was watching his high-top tennies, jumping black electrical cables, unaware that he was going to wipe out and take her right along with him.

"Trotter, look out!"

Randy opened his eyes. His own voice had awakened him. His heart was thudding in fear for Maryann.

Lisa was standing beside his bed, holding a baby in her arms.

He smiled blearily.

"Hi," she said quietly.

"Hi," he tried but it came out so croaky he had to try again. "Hi. What are you doing here?"

"Came to show you your new niece."

"Yeah?" He managed a weak grin. Lisa wore her smug Ali McGraw smile, the one with the hard edge that scolded while telling him beyond a doubt how much she loved him.

So I'm going to die, Randy thought.

The realization brought little fear, only an incredible sense of well-being, of giving up the fight at last and doing so content in the knowledge that he was surrounded by love. There was no doubt in his mind he was right, otherwise they wouldn't have let Lisa bring that newborn baby in here.

He grinned and thought he said, "I'd hold her but I'd probably electrocute her with all these damned wires."

Lisa showed him the baby's face. "She's a beaut, huh? Say hi to your uncle Randy, Natalie."

"Hi, Natalie," Randy whispered. Jeez, he was tired . . . such effort to get words out . . . cute baby . . . Lisa must have made Mom and Dad so happy . . . Lisa always did. He, as usual, had screwed up again. "Hey, listen . . . sorry I didn't come to see you."

"Oh, that's okay. I had about eight midwives as it was."

His eyelids grew too heavy to keep open. When they dropped he felt Lisa kiss his forehead. He felt the baby blanket brush his cheek. He opened his eyes as she straightened and saw her tears glimmering and knew undoubtedly he was dying.

The next time he woke up Grandma Stella was there, in her eyes the same soulful expression as in Lisa's.

Then his mom and dad again, looking haggard and worried.

And then—too unreal to believe—Maryann, which made no sense at all, unless, of course, he'd already died and this was heaven. She was smiling, dressed in aqua blue. Did angels wear aqua blue?

"Maryann?" he said.

"I was here visiting Lisa, and she asked me to come down and see you."

Virgin mother Mary, she spoke. She was real.

He told her, "I'd pretty much given up on you." To his own ears his voice sounded as if he was in a tunnel.

"I'd given up on you, too. Maybe now you'll get some help. Will you?"

She wasn't an easy woman; rather, an exacting one, a throwback to a time when parents taught their daughters to seek a man who was pure in heart and mind. The crazy thing was, he wanted to be that kind of man for her. He didn't understand it but there it was. Lying on his hospital bed, dying, he promised himself that if by some miracle he was wrong and he got out of here, he'd smoked his last joint and screwed his last groupie and snorted his last coke.

"I guess it's time," he answered and closed his eyes because he was so tired not even Maryann Padgett's presence could keep him awake. "Hey, listen," he said from the pleasant darkness behind his closed eyelids, "you'll be hearing from me when I get my act together. Meanwhile, don't go falling in love or anything, will you?"

When Maryann Padgett returned to the ICU waiting room, his entire family was there. She went straight to Lisa.

"How is he?" Lisa asked.

"Weak but making jokes."

Worry sketched drooping lines down Lisa's face. "I got too involved in my new married life and stopped calling him."

"No," Maryann whispered, embracing her friend. "You mustn't blame yourself."

But at one point or another during their vigil, recriminations fell from everyone's lips.

Michael said, "I should have tried harder to get him to talk to me."

Bess said, "I shouldn't have encouraged him to audition all the time."

Gil Harwood said, "I shouldn't have put him in touch with that damn band."

Stella said, "I shouldn't have given him the money for that van."

By ten o'clock that night, everyone was exhausted. Randy's condition seemed stable, his heartbeat regular, though he remained in Intensive Care, where five-minute visits were allowed only once an hour. Michael said, "Why don't you all go home and get some rest."

"What about you?" Bess said.

"I'll stay here and nap in the waiting room."

"But, Michael—"

"No buts. You do as I say. Get some rest and I'll see you in the morning. Stella, Gil, you too, please. I'll be here and I'll call you if anything changes."

Reluctantly they went.

A nurse brought Michael a pillow and blanket and he lay down in the family lounge with the reassurance that they'd wake him if Randy showed the slightest change. He awakened after what seemed a very brief time, drew his arm from beneath the blanket and lurched up when his watch showed 5:35 A.M. He sat up, rubbed his face, finger-combed his hair, stood and folded the blanket.

At the nurses' station he asked about Randy.

"He had a very good night, slept straight through, and there was no sign of any more problems with his heart."

Less than twelve hours to go before he was totally out of the woods. Michael shrugged and stretched and went to find a bathroom. He splashed cold water on his face, rinsed out his mouth, combed his hair and tucked his shirt in. He'd had these same clothes on since yesterday afternoon. It seemed half a lifetime ago since he'd donned them and come up to the hospital, smiling, to meet Bess and to visit Lisa and the new baby. He wondered how they were. Poor Lisa had had a shock, learning about Randy, but she'd handled it like a trooper, getting permission to bring the baby down here to show Randy in case he died. Nobody'd said as much but they all knew that was the reason.

He stood in the doorway of Randy's room, watching him sleep.

Ten more hours. Just ten more.

He walked to the window and stared out, standing with both hands on the small of his back. What irony, both of his children in the same hospital, one bringing in a new life, the other with his life in the balance.

He thought about it as dawn lifted over the St. Croix valley and lit the river and the boats at anchor and the thick maples that rimmed the water and the dozen church steeples of Stillwater. Sunday morning in late August, and the townspeople would soon be rising and dressing for worship services, and the tourists would soon be flooding in to shop for antiques and buy ice-cream cones and walk the waterfront. And the boat owners would be awakening in their cabin cruisers and stepping out onto their decks and watching the mist rise off the St. Croix and deciding at which restaurant they'd eat brunch. At noon Mark would come to the hospital and take Lisa and Natalie home.

And four hours after that—please, God—Bess and I will do the same thing with Randy.

As if the thought penetrated his sleep, Randy opened his eyes and found his father standing at the window.

"Dad?"

Michael whirled and moved directly to the bed, taking Randy's hand.

"I made it."

"Yeah," his father said, his voice breaking with emotion. If Randy didn't know he needed ten more hours to be out of the woods, Michael wasn't going to disillusion him.

"You been there all night?"

"I slept some."

"You've been here all night."

Moving his thumb across the back of Randy's hand, Michael gave a quarter smile.

"You all thought I'd die, right? That's why Lisa brought the baby for me to see, and why Grandma came, and Maryann."

"That was a possibility."

"I'm sorry I put you through that."

"Yeah, well, sometimes that's what we do to people who love us—we put them through things without really meaning to."

They took a while to study each other and to reaffirm silently that they were done trying to put each other through anything and were ready to take the next step toward a wholesome relationship with one another.

"Where's Mom?"

"I made her go home and get some sleep."

"So you two are getting married again."

"Is that okay with you?"

"You guys in love?"

"Absolutely."

"Then it's okay."

"We'll have some things to work out."

"Like?"

"Getting you well again. Deciding where we'll live."

"I can live anyplace."

You'll live with us, Michael vowed silently, realizing his and Bess's plans to cut Randy free would have to be waylaid for a while. The idea brought him great hope and a sense of impending peace. "Just so you know—we're not abandoning you. Not this time."

"You didn't abandon me before. That was all in my head but the shrinks here are going to get my head on straight again."

Michael bent low over his son, looking into his eyes. "We'll be there for you. Whatever you need, whatever it takes. But now, I'd better go. Five minutes is up and that's my limit. Anyway, I need a shower and a shave and a change of clothes." Michael stood. "I'll call your mother, then take a run home. But I'll be back in a couple of hours, okay?"

Randy looked up at his tired father, whose rumpled clothes and shadowy growth of whiskers bore witness to his night's vigil. It struck Randy in that moment how damned hard it must be to be a parent, and how little he'd considered the fact until now. *I must be growing up,* he thought. It made him feel expansive, and a little scared, taken in the light of the events of the past twelve hours. *What if I have a kid someday and he puts me through this?*

"Dad?" he said.

Michael sensed whatever was coming would be of import. He waited silently.

"You didn't give me hell for using the cocaine."

"Oh, yes I did. A dozen times while you were fighting for your life. I just didn't say it out loud."

"I won't do it again, I promise. I want to get well and be happy."

Michael put his hand on Randy's hair. "That's what we all want, son." Then he leaned over and kissed Randy's cheek and told him, "I'll be back soon. I love you."

"I love you, too," Randy said.

And with those words another fragment of pain dissolved. Another window of hope opened. Another beam of sunlight radiated into their future as Michael leaned down to hug his son before leaving.

Randy was released from the hospital shortly before suppertime that day. His mother and father walked him out into the sunshine of late afternoon, into a setting crowned by a cobalt-blue sky and a world where people moved about their pursuits with reassuring normality. Down at the public beach on Lily Lake some families were lighting barbecues and calling to their kids to be careful in the water. At the ball diamond across the street, a group of little boys were playing kittenball. A couple of blocks north, on Greeley Street, Nelson's Ice Cream Parlor was doing its usual landmark business, lining the concrete step out front with a row of lickers of all ages. Out on the river the drawbridge was raised, backing up traffic clear up to the top of Houlton Hill. The day-trippers were pulling their boats behind their packed cars, heading back toward the city, and the residents of Stillwater were sighing, looking forward to winter, when the streets would once again become their own.

"Where to?" Michael asked, sitting behind the wheel of his Cadillac Seville.

"I'm starved," Bess replied. "Would anyone like to pick up some sandwiches and eat them down by the river?"

Michael turned to glance at Randy in the backseat.

"Sounds fine with me," Randy said.

And so they took the next halting step in their journey back to familyhood.

Six weeks later, on an Indian summer's day in mid-October, Bess and Michael Curran were married in a simple service in the rectory of St. Mary's Catholic Church. The ceremony was performed by the same priest who'd married them twenty-two years before.

When he'd kissed his stole and draped it around his neck, Father Moore opened his prayer book to the correct page, smiled at the bride and groom and said, "So . . . here we are again."

His remark brought smiles to the assembled faces. To Bess's, which shone with happiness. To Michael's, which radiated hope. To Lisa's, which might have been touched ever so slightly by smugness. To Stella's, which seemed to say, It's about time. To Randy's, which held a promise. And even to Natalie's as she lay on her daddy's arm and studied the glistening silver frames on the eyeglasses of Gil Harwood.

When the priest asked, "Who gives this woman?" Lisa and Randy answered, "We do," bringing another round of smiles.

When the bride and groom repeated the words ". . . until death do us part," their eyes shone with sincerity that had depth far beyond the first time they'd spoken the words.

When Father Moore said, "I now pronounce you man and wife," Lisa and Randy exchanged a glance and a smile.

When their mother and father kissed, Lisa reached over for Randy's hand and gave it a hard squeeze.

The small wedding party went to dinner afterward at Kozlak'a Royal Oaks, overlooking a beautiful walled garden decorated with pumpkins, cornshocks and scarecrows. The personalized matchbooks awaiting them at their table and reserving it for them said *Mr. and Mrs. Curran.*

Spying them, after he'd seated Bess and was taking a chair himself, Michael picked up one of the books and folded it into her hand, saying, "Damn right, once and for all." Then he kissed her lightly on the lips and smiled into her eyes.

There were, as in all relationships that matter most, wrinkles that needed smoothing for all of them in that bittersweet autumn. There was Randy's intense counseling, his loss of a way of life, of friends, of drug-dependency, and his search for inner strength and positive relationships. There was family therapy, and the painful resurrection and obliteration of past guilts, fears and mistakes. There was Lisa's anger when she learned her mother and father were selling the family house. There was Michael and Bess's frequent frustration at living with an adult son when in truth they were impatient to have total privacy. There were Michael and Bess themselves, the husband and wife, readjusting to married life and its constant demands for compromise.

Ah, but there were blessings.

There was Randy, coming home one day and bringing a new friend named Steve, whom he'd met in therapy and who wanted to start a band that would be drug-free and would play for school kids to spread the message "Say no!" There was Michael, turning one day from the kitchen stove as Randy asked, "Hey, Dad, think you could teach me how to make that?" There were suppers for three, with three alternate cooks, and Randy eating healthily at last. And days when Lisa and Mark would come breezing in with the baby, calling, "Yo, Grampa and Grandma and Uncle Randy!" And the simpler homely joys of Bess shouting, "All right, who put my sweatshirt in the dryer and shrunk it!" And of Michael, breaking a radiator hose on his way home from work and calling home to hear Randy volunteer, "Hang on, Dad, I'll come and get you." And of Randy learning to change his niece's diapers and describing what he found inside them in phrases that had the entire family in stitches. And one day when Randy finally announced, "I got a job at Schmitt's Music selling instruments and giving drum lessons to little kids. Pay sucks but the fringe benefits are great—sitting around jamming whenever the place isn't busy."

And one day Bess went out to the County Seat and bought herself a pair of blue jeans.

She had them on when Michael came home from work and found her in the kitchen making Parmesan cream sauce for tortellini—it was her turn to cook. The pasta was boiling, the roux was bubbling, and she was mincing garlic as he stopped in the kitchen doorway and tossed his car keys onto the cabinet top.

"Well, lookit here . . ." he said in wonder, ". . . what my bride is wearing."

She smiled back over her shoulder and twitched her hips.

"How 'bout that. I did it."

He ambled toward her, dressed in a winter trench coat, cocked one hip against the edge of the cabinet and perused her lower half. "Looks good, too."

"Y' know what?" she said. "I really don't care if they do or not. They *feel* good."

"They do, huh?" He boosted himself away from the cabinet and put both hands on her, splayed and inquisitive. "Let's see . . ." He rubbed her, back and front, all over her tight blue jeans, kissed her over her shoulder and murmured against her mouth, "You're right . . . feels very good."

Giggling, she said, "Michael, I'm cutting up garlic here."

"Yeah, I can smell it. Stinks like hell." He turned her fully around and caught her against himself with a two-handed grip on her buttocks. Her arms crossed behind his neck, the paring knife still in her right hand.

"How was your day?" she asked, when they'd shared a nice long kiss.

"Pretty good. How was yours?"

"Crappy. This is the best part of it so far."

"Well, good," he said. "I can make it even better if you'd care to turn off those burners and put down that paring knife."

"Mmm . . ." she murmured against his lips, dropping the paring knife on the floor, reaching out blindly to the side, groping for the control knobs on the stove.

At the other end of the condo the door opened.

Michael dropped his head back and said quietly, "Oh, shit."

"Now, now," she chided gently, "you wanted him back, didn't you?"

"But not when I have a hard-on in the middle of the kitchen at suppertime."

She giggled again. "Just keep your coat buttoned awhile," she whispered at the same moment Randy stepped to the kitchen doorway.

"Mom, Dad . . . hi. Hope we're not disturbing anything. I brought someone home for supper." He drew her forward by a hand, a pretty young woman with dark hair and a smile that had put a boyish look of eagerness on Randy's face. "You remember Maryann, don't you?"

Two parents turned, joy on their faces, their embrace dissolving as they reached out to welcome her.

NOVEMBER OF THE HEART

Chapter 1

―――⟶∗⟵―――

White Bear Lake, Minnesota
1895

The dining room of Rose Point Cottage hummed with conversation. Eighteen people sat around its immense mahogany table in the glow of the gaslight chandelier, supping on a third course of asparagus ice surrounded by pickled nasturtium seeds, dinner rolls shaped like swans and butter chips molded into the image of water lily leaves. The table, spread with Irish linen bearing the Barnett family crest, was set with Tiffany silver flatware and Wedgwood Queen's ware. Its centerpiece held precisely fifty Bourbon Madame Isaac Pereire roses from the cottage's own gardens, their overpowering scent scarcely diluted by the nine p.m. breeze fluttering in the lakeside windows.

The walls of the room were decked in William Morris paper spreading grape clusters and acanthus leaves across a burgundy background. The woodwork, crafted of ruby-rich cherry wood, climbed to shoulder level and surrounded the nine-and-a-half-foot windows with wide, ornate moldings from which, at each corner, a hand-carved cherub grinned down upon the gathering.

At the head of the table presided Gideon Barnett, a thickset man with a graying walrus moustache and chins as stacked as thick, poured pudding; at the foot sat his wife, Levinia, overfed too, with large breasts carried as high as a full-bellied sail. She wore her hair to suit her station, like a diadem high upon her head, the sides rolled back in a perfect silver coil, secured by combs and one silk organza rose. The four Barnett children, ages twelve to eighteen, had been allowed at the table tonight, as well as the aunts, Agnes and Henrietta, Gideon's spinster sisters, who were permanent fixtures in the Barnett family. Also present were the elite coterie, members of the White Bear Yacht Club, friends of the Barnetts who—like they—had migrated from Saint Paul to their seasonal cottages here for the summer.

The supper was to have been a victory celebration: The Minnetonka Yacht Club, amid much hoopla and publicity for the burgeoning sport, had challenged the White Bear Yacht Club to a three-year series of regattas. The first had been run today. In a society where sailing had become an obsession and its participants nearly rabid in their zeal to excel, the afternoon's defeat had left as bitter an aftertaste as a lost lawsuit.

"Damn!" Commodore Gideon Barnett exploded, thumping a fist on the table. "It's unthinkable that one of us didn't win!" He was still wearing his white duck trousers and blue sweater with *WBYC* in big white letters across his breast. "The *Tartar*'s faster than the *Kite* and everyone knows it!" Barnett banged the table again and his goblets chimed together.

At the foot of the table Levinia lofted her left eyebrow and shot him a reproving glance: The stemware was Waterford, from a matched set of twenty-four.

"We should have changed sail plans!" Gideon continued.

"Changed sail plans?" replied his friend Nathan DuVal. "She already carries six hundred and seventy feet of sail. That's about all a seventeen-footer can handle, Gid, you know that."

"Then we should have made them out of silk and saved weight. Didn't I say all along we should have tried silk?"

Nathan went on with much more forbearance than Gideon. "The problem's not with the sail, Gid, it's with the drag. The *Tartar* seems bottom-heavy to me."

"Then we'll reduce the drag! By next year—mark my words!—we'll reduce the drag and win that second race!"

"The question is how."

"How?" Gideon Barnett threw up both hands. "I don't know how, but I for one refuse to lose ten thousand dollars to those damned Minnetonka sandbaggers, not when it was *they* who challenged *us* to these three years of races!"

Levinia said, "Nobody forced you to place so large a bet, Gideon. You could as easily have made it a hundred dollars." The betting, however, was as keenly enjoyed as the races themselves, and the members of the club cheerfully put up their collected ten thousand dollars.

A servant stepped to Gideon's right elbow and inquired quietly, "Are you through with your asparagus, sir?"

Gideon flapped a hand and barked, "Yes, take it away." To his wife, he railed, "Every man at this table has an equal stake in these regattas, Levinia, and none of us wants to lose, especially not to *that* bunch, with all the newspapers in America watching what happens, and Tim here photographing the event." He referred to Tim Iversen, a club member and a successful photographer, who had chronicled the formation of the yacht club itself from its beginnings. "The money aside, I'm the commodore of this yacht club, and I detest losing. So the question remains—how do we come up with a boat that'll beat theirs?"

Gideon's daughter Lorna had been biting her tongue long enough. From halfway down the table she spoke up. "We could hire the Herreshoff brothers to design and build one."

Every eye in the room swerved to the pretty eighteen-year-old who sat with her brown eyes fixed upon her father. Her auburn hair was combed in a "Gibson girl" pompadour, its intentional droop and neckline squiggles so much more alluring than her mother's braided crown. She had worn it so ever since the previous summer, when Mr. Charles Dana Gibson himself had been a guest at Rose Point Cottage, and had indulged her with long interludes of conversation about the personification of his "girls" and the message they conveyed: that women could have freedom and individuality while remaining feminine. In the wake of Gibson's visit, Lorna had not only changed her hairstyle, she had eschewed her elaborate silks and bustles for the more casual shirtwaist and skirt, which she wore tonight. As she faced her father, her brown eyes seemed to sparkle with challenge.

"Couldn't we, Papa?"

"The Herreshoff brothers?" her father repeated. "From Providence?"

"Why not? Certainly you can afford them."

"What do you know about the Herreshoff brothers?"

"I can read, Papa. Their names are in practically every issue of *Outing* magazine. Do you know of anyone better?"

Lorna Barnett knew full well her father disliked her interest in the unladylike sport of sailing, to say nothing of tennis. If he had his way she would sit through this entire meal biting her tongue, as a lady ought. Lorna regarded true ladies, however, as unmitigated bores. Furthermore, it salved her secret sense of retaliation to realize that her father blamed himself for her newfound attraction to sports, which Mr. Gibson had so encouraged. After all, it was her father who'd invited Gibson to Minnesota. No sooner had the young artist arrived, with his radical views on liberating American females, than Lorna had adopted the habits and dress of Gibson's "boy-girl." Gideon had blustered, "This is outrageous! A daughter of mine slapping around a tennis court with her ankles flashing! And coercing her friends to form a female contingent of the White Bear Yacht Club. Why, any fool knows a woman's place is in a drawing room!"

Now, at a dinner party before all his friends, Gideon's daughter had the temerity to suggest a solution to their woes.

"Do you know of anyone better?" she repeated when he continued glowering at her.

Support came, however, from young Taylor DuVal, who was seated next to Lorna.

"You'll have to admit, Gideon, she has something there."

Gideon drew his eyes from his daughter to Taylor, who at twenty-four already resembled his father in both appearance and business acumen, a dapper and bright young man who would surely go places. Around the table glances were exchanged among the men—Gideon, Taylor, Nathan, Percy Tufts, George Whiting and Joseph Armfield—the most powerful and persuasive cartel not only of the White Bear Yacht Club, but of the Minnesota financial scene in general. They read like the *Who's Who* in Minnesota, their vast wealth earned in railroading, iron ore mining, flour milling and, in Gideon Barnett's case, lumbering. Lorna was right: They certainly could afford to hire the Herreshoff brothers to build them a winning sloop, and if their wives objected . . .

But the wives wouldn't object. Levinia's chiding meant little. She and all the other wives in her social circle enjoyed the notoriety brought about by their husbands' yachting. It was considered chic, privileged and newsworthy enough to get the women's photographs in the newspapers right along with the men's. Every wife present realized she was measured primarily by the length of her husband's shadow, and none would have voiced the slightest objection to the commissioning of a sailboat by the best-known boat designers in America.

"It could be done. We could commission them," Barnett said.

"Those New Englanders know how to build boats, always have."

"They'd know about the relative merits of silk sails, too."

"We could telegraph them immediately, tomorrow!"

"And have a scale drawing in hand by the end of the summer, and the boat itself by next May, in time for the yachting season."

The disgruntlement of earlier had been displaced by excitement as the men went on discussing possibilities with bright expressions on their faces.

Meanwhile, around the table the third-course dishes had been removed. A server approached Levinia's elbow and announced quietly, "Your main course, ma'am."

Levinia looked up, twin creases between her eyebrows, while the man simply stood there with a covered gold-rimmed plate in his hand. "Well, put it down, for heaven's sake!" she ordered in an undertone.

From three inches above the tabletop Jens Harken dropped the heated plate. The domed silver cover bounced to one side and rang out like a bell buoy.

Levinia looked up. She, like every other wife there, might be nothing more than her husband's shadow in most regards, but the one place she reigned was at the head of her own household staff. Abashed that her prowess as a hostess should be compromised by that staff's incompetence, she inquired sharply, "Where is Chester?"

"Gone home, ma'am. His father is ill."

"And Glynnis?"

"Ill, ma'am, with a bad tooth."

"And who are you?"

"Jens Harken, ma'am, the kitchen odd-jobs man."

Levinia's face had turned scarlet. On the night of an important dinner party, the kitchen odd-jobs man! The housekeeper would hear about this! She scowled at the outsized young fellow, trying to recall if she'd ever seen him before, then ordered, "Remove the cover."

He whisked it away to reveal roasted teal in a surround of alternating Jerusalem artichokes and brussels sprouts. Around these an arabesque of oven-browned mashed potatoes formed a perfect oval frame.

Levinia examined the work of art, selected a fork, poked at the duck, nodded to Jens and said, "Proceed."

Jens went sedately through the swinging door. On the other side he broke into a run, carrying him the length of a ridiculously long hall, through a second swinging door and finally into the kitchen.

"Hell's afire, fourteen feet of passageway just to make sure smells don't drift into the dining room? Rich people are crazy!"

Hulduh Schmitt, the head cook, thrust two plates into his hands and ordered, "Go!"

Eight more times he ran the length of that passageway, careening to a halt just before reaching the dining room doorway, trying to hide his breathlessness as he entered and placed the dinner plates before the diners. On each trip he overheard bits of conversation about today's regatta and why Barnett's sloop, the *Tartar,* had lost, and how they could make sure one of their next year's entries would win, and whether it was the drag or the sails or the distribution of sandbag ballast or the hired skipper that had caused the afternoon's loss. Oh, they were a zealous lot, all right, bitten by the sailing bug so badly it had spread over them like a rash, this desire to best the Minnetonka club.

And Jens Harken was the one who knew how they could do it.

"Hulduh, find me a paper!" he ordered, bursting through the kitchen door with the last two silver plate covers.

Hulduh removed her mouth from the double-sided bombe mold into which she'd been blowing in an effort to free the ice cream. "A paper? What for?"

"Just find it, please, and a pencil, too. I'll work tomorrow, my day off, if you just find it fast and don't ask questions."

"Sure, and lose my job," remarked the German woman, giving one more puff into the mold, then guiding a perfect fluted cone of ice cream onto a waiting almond-flavored meringue nest. "What would you be wanting with a pencil and paper? Here, put this one in the ice cave," she ordered the second kitchen maid, who took the dessert and placed it, on its saucer, in a metal box full of crushed ice, then closed its lid.

Jens dropped the domed plate covers into the zinc sink and zipped across the hot kitchen to take the cook's two puffy red cheeks into his hands.

"Please, Mrs. Schmitt, where?"

"You're a nuisance, Jens Harken, and a big one at that," she scolded. "Can't you see I've got ten more ice creams to unmold here before the missus rings for dessert?"

"We'll help you, won't we? Here, everybody—" Jens motioned to the first and second kitchen maids, Ruby and Colleen. He picked up a bombe mold out of the ice chest. "How much should we blow?"

"Ach, here, you'll ruin it, and it'll mean my job!" Mrs. Schmitt snatched the copper mold from his hand and began unscrewing its stem base. "On the wall, the list for the housekeeper, you can use the tail end of that, but I don't see what's so important it needs writing in the middle of the most important dinner of the year."

"You're right! It could turn out to be the most important dinner of the year, especially for me, and if it does I promise you my eternal love and gratitude, my dear and lovely Mrs. Schmitt."

Hulduh Schmitt succumbed to his charm, as always, with a flap of the hand and a tinge of additional color in her cheeks. "Oh, go on with you," she said, then covered the screwhole with a small piece of muslin and continued her blowing.

Jens neatly ripped off the tail end of the paper and printed in well-formed letters: *I know why you lost the race. I can help you win next year.*

"Mrs. Schmitt, wait! Give me that plate." He snatched a dessert plate from her hands, placed the note on it and covered it with one of her fluffy, tan meringue nests, letting a corner of the note show. "There. Now put the ice cream on top."

"Of that paper? You're the one who's crazy. We'll both lose our jobs. What does it say?"

"Never mind what it says, just blow into that mold and get the ice cream on this."

Mrs. Schmitt got stubborn. "Nossir, Jens Harken, not on your life. I'm the cook. What goes out of this kitchen is my responsibility, and there ain't no desserts going out of here with notes underneath them."

He saw that unless he told her, she'd remain adamant. "All right, it's for Mr. Barnett. I told him I know how he can win that regatta next year."

"Ah, boats again. You and your boats."

"Well, I don't intend to be a kitchen handyman forever. One of these days someone will listen to me."

"Oh, sure, and I'm gonna marry the governor and become first lady."

"He could do worse, Mrs. Schmitt," Jens teased. "He could do worse." Mrs. Schmitt got that flat-chinned look he knew too well. When he saw he was getting nowhere, he promised, "If it backfires I'll take all the blame. I'll tell them I was the one who put the note in there even after you warned me not to."

In the end, Levinia Barnett herself decided the issue by yanking the satin bellpull in the dining room and tinkling the brass bell above the kitchen doorway. Mrs. Schmitt looked up at it and grew flustered. "See what you do! All this talk and I don't have the ice creams ready. Go, go! Take the first ones and hope I got enough hot breath to keep them coming steady to the end."

In the dining room, Levinia kept a hawk's eye upon the odd-jobs man, Harken, as he brought in the desserts. After his first faux pas he performed the remainder of the serving without mishap. The ice-cream molds still had sharp edges in spite of the summer heat, and each was delivered and placed on the table with the inconspicuous motions she expected from her help. The peach ice cream was covered with a thin layer of apricot ice and filled with sweetened strawberries. The meringues were crisp, appropriately tanned, and the plates beneath them chilled. Surely the ladies present could find no fault with the food.

As if divining her hostess's thoughts, Cecilia Tufts praised, "What an exquisite dessert, Levinia. Where *ever* did you find your cook?"

"She found me over fourteen years ago, when she very cleverly had some of her special tortes delivered to me by messenger. She's been with me ever since, but lately she's been making sounds about quitting—she's well over fifty already. But I don't know what I should do without her."

"I know what you mean. Anyone bright enough to know their elbow from a soup bone seems to be going into service as a governess these days, and one can scarcely find kitchen help capable of—"

"Levinia!" It was Gideon, interrupting from the opposite end of the table. His consonants snapped like sails taking wind. His mouth was as tight as a bowline knot. "May I speak to you a moment?"

At the tone of his voice, Levinia's heart gave a thump. She looked up across the low-sprawling roses to find Gideon telegraphing disapproval with every angle of his body. A mouthful of apricot ice seemed to slip down her throat of its own volition while she wondered frantically what could be amiss.

"Now, Gideon?"

"Yes, now!"

He pushed back his chair while Levinia's blood rushed up her neck and she touched a linen napkin to the corner of her mouth.

"Excuse me," she murmured, leaving the table and following her husband into the servants' passage. The servants' passage, of all places, while her closest lady friends looked on! The narrow, windowless hall was dimly lit by a single gas wall sconce and held the faint stench of boiled brussels sprouts, which, thankfully, had not escaped into the dining room before the vegetables themselves were served.

"Gideon, whatever—"

"What in the *deuce* is going on here, Levinia!"

"Keep your voice down, Gideon, I'm already dying of mortification at being summoned to the servants' passage by my own husband in the middle of a dinner party! We have a library and a morning room, either of which would—"

"I make enough money to keep you in silks and ice creams and two fancy houses! Must I oversee the kitchen staff as well?" Into her hands he thrust a note. It had a strawberry stain on its edge and stuck to his thumb when he tried to release it.

She pulled it from his skin and read it while he informed her acidly, "It was *in my dessert.*"

Her eyes shot up. "In your dessert? Surely not, Gideon."

"It was in my dessert, I tell you, obviously put there by someone in the kitchen. The kitchen is your domain, Levinia. Who's in charge of it?"

"I . . . why . . . w . . ." Levinia's mouth hung open. "Mrs. Lovik." Mrs. Lovik was the housekeeper, whose job it was to hire all the kitchen and cleaning staff.

"She goes!"

"But Gideon—"

"And so does the cook! What's her name?"

"Mrs. Schmitt, but Gideon—" He was storming down the passageway toward the kitchen, leaving her little choice but to follow.

"And whoever wrote this note also goes, if it's neither of them, and I can scarcely believe a cook or a housekeeper would have the temerity to suggest they know how to win a regatta that the entire White Bear Yacht Club couldn't win." He rammed open the kitchen door with Levinia at his heels and bellowed, "*Mrs. Schmitt! Who is Mrs. Schmitt?*"

There were four people in the room and only three were cowering. Gideon pinned his eyes on the one who wasn't, the dolt who had dropped Levinia's plate earlier. "I repeat! *Who is Mrs. Schmitt?*" he roared.

A woman shaped like her own bombe mold, with a face as red as the coals in her kitchen range, whispered, "I am, sir."

Gideon skewered her with his eyes. "Are you responsible for this?"

Her starched white cap trembled as she gripped one hand with the other upon the soiled paunch of her white floor-length apron.

Jens spoke up. "No, she's not, sir. I am."

Gideon snapped his attention to the offender. He let his disdain impart itself fully, for ten long seconds, before speaking. "Harken, is it?"

"Yes, sir."

The man neither trembled nor quailed but stood beside the zinc sink with his shoulders erect and his hands at his sides. His handsome face was shiny with sweat, a trickle of which ran from his left temple to his jaw. He had a direct gaze, blue eyes, fair hair and the shaved face Levinia demanded in all her male help.

"You're fired," Gideon declared. "Collect your things and leave immediately."

"Very well. But if you want to win that regatta, you'd better listen to me—"

"No, you're going to listen to me!" In a flash Gideon crossed the slate floor and thrust his index finger into Harken's chest, hard. "I own this house; you work in it! You don't speak to me unless spoken to. Neither do you embarrass my wife and myself by delivering missives in the dessert when we are entertaining half the residents of White Bear Lake! And you sure as hell don't give *me* advice on how to race boats! Is that understood?"

"Why?" Jens replied calmly. "You want to win, don't you?"

Gideon spun away with his fists clenched, forcing Levinia to leap aside. "Have him out of here within the hour, Schmitt, and yourself right behind him. Your week's pay will be sent to you."

Harken jumped after him and grabbed his arm. "It's got nothing to do with canvas sails or poor skippers or too much ballast. Mr. DuVal is right. It's got to do with drag. The sloops you've been racing have to cut *through* the water. What you need is a skimmer that'll sail *over* it. I can design it for you."

Barnett turned slowly, a superior expression on his face. "Oh, you're the one. I've heard about you."

Harken dropped Barnett's arm. "Yes, I imagine you have, sir."

"Every yacht club in Minnesota has turned you away."

"Yessir, and some on the east coast, too. But one of these days someone's going to listen, and when he does his boat is going to sail circles around the fastest sloop ever built anywhere in the world."

"Well, I'll say this for you, boy. You've got gall, offensive as it is. What I want to know is what you're doing working in *my* kitchen?"

"A man's got to eat."

"Well, eat somewhere else. I don't want to see you anywhere near this place ever again!"

Barnett stalked back into the passage with his wife plucking at his sleeve. The door swung closed. "Gideon, stop this instant!"

Her shout was heard clearly in the dining room, where Lorna watched her parents' guests exchange uncomfortable glances. Indeed, everything that followed could be heard clearly as the guests stopped eating and Lorna fixed her eyes on the passageway door.

"Gideon, I said stop!"

When he refused, Levinia grabbed his elbow and forced the issue. Gideon relented with an air of long-suffering.

"Levinia, our guests are waiting."

"Oh yes, this is a fine time for you to remember our guests, after you've turned me into an object of ridicule before them and the help! How dare you, Gideon Barnett, undermine me with my own staff! I will not have Mrs. Schmitt dismissed simply because you're offended by one of the kitchen staff. She's the best cook we've ever had!" She squeezed his sleeve so hard she inadvertently pinched him.

He winced and yelped, "Ouch! Levinia, we can't have the staff—"

"We can't have the staff witnessing you overriding my decisions. If they think I'm not in charge of my own domicile, their respect for me will vanish; then how shall I be expected to order my own kitchen staff? I insist on going back in there and telling Mrs. Schmitt she can stay, and if you don't like it—"

The argument had grown louder and louder until Lorna, now blushing herself, could sit by quietly no longer. Whatever were Mama and Papa thinking to strike up an argument in the kitchen passage in the middle of a dinner party!

"Excuse me," she said quietly, and rose from the table. "Please continue eating, everyone."

She hit the swinging door with both hands just as Gideon was shouting, "Levinia, I don't give a damn—"

"Mother! Father! What on earth is going on!" Lorna halted, scowling, as the door swung shut behind her. "All of your guests are staring at this door and shifting on their chairseats! Don't you realize they can hear every word that's being said? I can't believe you two are out here fighting over the kitchen staff! What's gotten into you?"

Gideon tugged at the waist of his sweater and resumed an air of dignity. "I'll be there in a moment. Go back in and suggest that they retire to the parlor, and play them something on the piano, will you, Lorna?"

She stared at the two of them as if they'd gone mad, then left the door swinging once again.

When she was gone Gideon said in a much quieter tone, "All right, Levinia, she can stay."

"And Mrs. Lovik, too. I'm not the least inclined to spend my summer training a new housekeeper."

"All right, all right . . ." He raised both palms in surrender. "They can both stay, but tell that . . . that"—he pointed a quivering finger at the kitchen—"upstart in there to get his hide out of my house within the hour or I'll have it upholstering one of the chairs, do you understand?"

With a sniff and a lift of her nose, Levinia swung away.

In the kitchen, everyone was speaking at once. When Levinia pushed open the door the babble ceased. The maids, washing dishes at the sink, let their wrists hang limp against it. Each bobbed her knees once. Harken and Mrs. Schmitt, near the ice chest, halted an argument and self-consciously closed their mouths. The room was a good ninety-five degrees, steamy and strong-smelling yet from the brussels sprouts. Levinia had the fleeting thought that she'd rather eat raw food than cook it here.

"My husband spoke precipitously, Mrs. Schmitt. I do hope you won't take offense. The food tonight was splendid, and I very much hope you'll stay."

Mrs. Schmitt sniffed once and shifted her weight to the opposite leg. With the skirt of her soiled apron she dried the sweat from beneath her nose. "Well, I don't know, ma'am. My mother's getting on toward eighty and all alone since my father died. I've been thinking it might be time I gave up this hard work and went to take care of her. I have a little money put by, and to tell the truth, I'm getting on my-self."

"Why, nonsense. You're just as spry as the day I hired you. And look at the magnificent dinner you just prepared without the slightest hitch."

Mrs. Schmitt did something she'd never done before: She sat down in her mistress's presence. She plopped her heavy form onto a small stool and her spare flesh seemed to droop over its edge like a soufflé when the oven door is opened.

"I don't know," she said, shaking her head tiredly. "I get dizzy these days, blowing into those ice-cream molds. And all the hurrying . . . Some days my heart gets palpitations."

"Please, Mrs. Schmitt . . ." Levinia joined her hands together like an opera singer delivering an aria. "I just . . . Well, I don't know what I'd do without you, and now in the middle of the summer out here in the country, I cannot think where I'd find anyone to replace you."

Mrs. Schmitt's fleshy forearm in its rolled-up sleeve rested on the scarred wooden table in the center of the room while she studied her employer and considered.

Levinia's hands gripped each other tighter.

Mrs. Schmitt glanced at Ruby, at Colleen, still gaping, motionless, at the sink, and with a *flap-flap* of one hand and not so much as a word, sent them scuttling back to work.

Levinia said, "Perhaps an extra three dollars a week would convince you."

"Oh, that'd be nice, ma'am, it surely would, but it wouldn't ease the work none, especially with him going." The cook thumbed over her shoulder at Harken.

"I'd be willing to put on an extra kitchen maid."

"To tell the truth, ma'am, I don't want to train a new one any more than you do. I'll take the extra money, and I thank you, ma'am, but if I stay, he stays. He's a good worker, the best I've ever had in the kitchen, and he's willing. Like tonight, filling in when he wouldn't have had to. And he does the heavy work, lifting and carrying and washing vegetables, and pretty soon the canning starts, as you know. Those boilers get heavy."

Levinia's corset stays seemed to bond themselves to her ribs. She regarded Harken with her sternest expression and made a sudden decision. "Very well, but I want you to stay out of my husband's sight, and you must promise me, Harken, that you'll never—*never!*—again do anything like you did tonight."

"No ma'am, I won't."

"And you are to stay strictly to the kitchen and the vegetable gardens, is that understood?"

Harken gave a slight bow in answer.

"Then it's settled. And, Mrs. Schmitt, in the morning I'd like you to prepare the coddled eggs on spinach boats that Mr. Barnett loves so much."

"Coddled eggs it is, ma'am."

Without further word, Levinia left the kitchen. All the way along the length of the stuffy, ill-lit passageway she felt her heart thunder at the realization that she had defied Gideon's wishes. He'd be incensed when he found out, but the kitchen was her domain—hers! He had his politics, and his business, and his yachting and hunting, but what did she have besides the pretty compliments from her peers when perfect ice-cream molds and exotic vegetables came out of the kitchen?

At the door to the dining room she paused, adjusted her corset, patted her forehead, discovered it was beaded with sweat from that insufferable kitchen, found a handkerchief in a hidden pocket of her skirt, wiped it dry, patted her hair and went in to face her guests.

The dinner party was ruined, of course. Though the guests tried valiantly to pretend they'd heard nothing of what was said in the kitchen passage, they'd heard most of it. The women, ever competitive when it came to hostessing social gatherings, exchanged sly, silent, superior messages while treating Levinia as if she'd just heard her dressmaker had died.

At the piano, Lorna observed her mother's reentry, Levinia's forced calm while ordering Daphne and Theron up to bed. She was still rattled, Lorna could tell, and having trouble disguising it. Whatever had caused the set-to? Had the handsome blond server prompted it? Who was he, anyway? And who had been responsible for his serving in the dining room when he hadn't been trained to do so?

To draw attention away from her mother, Lorna said, "Come on, everybody, let's sing 'After the Ball.' "

Immediately Taylor DuVal moved up behind Lorna, rested his hands on her shoulders and began singing robustly. Taylor was a good sport, always willing to do whatever Lorna suggested. The others, however, barely peeped, so Lorna shut the key cover and left the hostessing to her mother, suggesting she and Taylor step out onto the veranda.

Immediately her sister Jenny jumped up and announced, "I'm coming, too!"

Lorna got disgusted. A sixteen-year-old sister could be such a pest. Only this summer Levinia had allowed Jenny to stay up later with the adults on occasions such as this, and she'd been hounding Taylor ever since. Not only did she make moon eyes at him every chance she got, she ran back and told Levinia everything that was talked about.

"Isn't it your bedtime?" Lorna asked pointedly.

"Mother said I could stay up until midnight."

Lorna checked with Taylor. Behind Jenny's back he shrugged and feigned helplessness.

Lorna hid a smile and said, "Oh, all right, then, you can come along."

The veranda crossed the entire front of the house and wrapped around two corners. Wicker chairs, tables and chaise longues were scattered upon it, splashed by the light from the parlor and morning room windows. It smelled of roses and must, from the climber on the south trellis and the cushions that had been in storage all winter.

The estate itself was situated on the eastern point of Manitou Island, with White Bear, the lake, spreading in a cloverleaf shape to the north, east and south around it, and White Bear, the village, spread along the northwesterly shore of Snyder's Bay, behind it. The house was set back seventy-five feet from the water, with the yard fanning out flat all around it, giving way to gardens, both formal and utilitarian, and a glasshouse, where a full gardening staff kept Levinia in flowers and the family in both summer and winter produce.

Now, on this warm summer evening, the fruits of their labors scented the night. It was June, with the gardens in full bloom and the imported Italian fountains gurgling background music. The moon had risen and lay golden as a trumpet across the water. In the distance the naphtha launch *Don Quixote* could be heard, *splut-splut-splutting* its way back toward the town dock with a load of concertgoers from the Ramaley Pavilion across the lake. Nearer lay the dim finger of Rose Point's own dock and, beside it, a mast, scarcely swaying in the soft lap of waves.

The romantic setting, however, was wasted tonight. Jenny gripped Lorna's arm the moment they reached the shadows. "Tell me what happened in the kitchen, Lorna! Did Papa go back there? What was it all about, anyway?"

"We mustn't discuss it in front of Taylor. Jenny, where are your manners?"

"Oh, never mind me," Taylor said. "I'm just an old family friend, remember?"

"Come on, Lorna, tell me."

"Well, I don't know everything, but I know this much—Papa wanted to fire the cook and Mama wouldn't let him."

"The cook? Why? Everybody loved the food tonight."

"I don't know. Papa's never been in the kitchen in his whole life, much less in the middle of a dinner party, and Mama was livid with him. They were shouting at each other fit to kill."

"I know. We could hear it in the dining room, couldn't we, Taylor?"

Lorna recounted what she'd heard, but the sisters could make no sense of any of it. Lorna found herself as baffled by the scene as Jenny was, but before they could discuss it further Tim Iversen wandered out to the veranda, interrupting their speculation. He lit his pipe as if he meant to stay awhile and the conversation shifted to the photographs he'd taken of the regatta that day and what newspapers might run them.

Soon others drifted out of the house to join them, and the two sisters found themselves with no further opportunity to discuss the altercation during dinner.

Lorna was still puzzling over it when the party broke up. She and Jenny went upstairs together, leaving Gideon and Levinia to wish their last guests good night.

"Has Mama said anything about that scene in the kitchen?" Jenny whispered as they climbed.

"No, nothing."

"So you still don't have any idea what it was about?"

"No, but I aim to find out." Upstairs, Lorna kissed her younger sister's cheek. " 'Night, Jen." They went to their separate rooms—Jenny into the one she shared with Daphne, and Lorna into her own. Inside, it was hot in spite of the high ceilings and ample windows. She removed her earrings and lay them on her dressing table, then her shoes, which she left beside a chair. Fully clothed, she sat down to wait for the sounds of activity to grow quiet in the hall. When she was sure Papa,

Mama and Jenny had finished traipsing back and forth to the bathroom, she opened her door and listened a moment, then slipped out.

All was quiet. The hall lamps had been extinguished. The aunts had come up a little earlier and were undoubtedly asleep.

In the dark, she tiptoed past the main central staircase to the crooked servants' stairway at the very end of the hall. It led from their third-floor bedrooms directly to the kitchen, accessible from the second-floor hallway through a door that was always kept closed.

Lorna opened it now and turned up her nose at the stale smell of brussels sprouts. In spite of it, she descended.

When she opened the kitchen door and peeked inside she found four people still there: two maids, the cook—Mrs. Schmitt—and the fellow Harken, who had dropped Mama's plate tonight. The maids were putting away the last of the dishes. Mrs. Schmitt was slicing ham and Harken was sweeping the floor. Goodness, he was a treat for the eyes, she thought, watching him a moment before he knew she was there.

Finally, realizing how improper it was to admire the help, she said, "Hello," and everyone stopped dead still.

Mrs. Schmitt remembered her manners first. "Hello, miss."

Lorna stepped inside and closed the door softly behind her. "What time do they let you go to bed, anyway?"

"We're done now, miss, just finishing up."

On the wall hung a hexagonal clock the diameter of a dishpan. Lorna glanced at it.

"At twelve-forty?"

"Tomorrow's our day off, miss. Soon as breakfast is over we can leave to go to church ourselves. All we have to do is get the cold buffet foods ready for the other two meals first."

"Oh . . . yes, of course . . . Well . . ." Lorna flashed a smile. "I had no idea you worked such long hours."

"Only on party days, miss." The room fell silent. The two kitchen maids stood with their hands full of clean copper kettles. Harken had stopped sweeping and stood with his hands draped over the broom handle. Ten seconds of discomfort passed.

"Is there something I can get you, miss?" the cook finally asked.

"Um . . . oh . . . oh, no! I was just wondering what . . . well . . ." Lorna realized her mistake immediately. The question she'd come down to ask was beyond all impertinence, even to the kitchen help. How could she inquire of these tired, sweaty people what they had done wrong tonight to set her father off? "It's very warm upstairs. I wondered if you have any fruit juice down here."

"We haven't squeezed the juices for morning yet, but I believe there's a little judy left over, miss. Could I get you a cup of that?"

Judy contained champagne and rum; Lorna had never been allowed to drink it.

"It's mostly green tea and mint, miss," the cook added.

"Oh, well, in that case, yes . . . a cup would be grand."

The cook went off to get it. While she was gone, Harken spoke up. "If I may be so impertinent, miss, I imagine that you're wondering what all the commotion was about in the kitchen earlier."

For the first time she looked square into his eyes—they were as blue as the spots behind one's eyelids after watching a bolt of lightning.

Harken looked right back, for she was too pretty to deny himself the pleasure.

"It was me they were angry with," he admitted forthrightly. "I put a note in your father's ice cream."

"A note? In my father's ice cream?" Lorna's mouth dropped open in amazement while Jens resumed sweeping. "Did you really?"

He cast her a quarter glance, very brief. "Yes, ma'am."

"*You* put a note in *my* father's ice cream?" The corners of her mouth began to twitch. When she burst out laughing, the kitchen help began exchanging uncertain glances. She covered her mouth with both hands and filled the room with sound, finally managing, as her chortles subsided, "My father, Gideon Barnett?"

Harken had stopped sweeping to openly enjoy this very improper exchange with her. "That's right."

"What did it say?"

"That I know how he can win the regatta next year."

She controlled her grin but let her eyes grow mischievous. "And what did he say?"

"You're fired."

"Oh, my . . ." She sobered with an effort, realizing the poor young fellow probably found the situation less than amusing. "I'm sorry."

"No need to be. Mrs. Schmitt saved me. She said she wouldn't stay on without me."

"So you're not fired after all?"

He shook his head slowly.

She studied him with an inquisitive look. "Do you really know how my father could win the regatta next year?"

"Yes, but he wouldn't listen."

"Of course not, my father doesn't listen to anyone. You took a terrible chance, trying to give him advice."

"I know that now."

"Tell me—how can he win the regatta?"

"By changing the shape of his boat. I could do that for him. I could—"

Mrs. Schmitt returned with a cup of liquid as clear and pale as a peridot.

"Here you are, miss."

"Oh, thank you." Lorna took it and held it in both hands. Somehow, with the cook standing close, propriety reared its head and told Lorna she ought not be standing here discussing her family business with the kitchen help, no matter how interested she was in sailing. She cast a glance at the two maids, who still remained motionless, awestruck by her presence. Suddenly she realized she was keeping them from getting to bed.

"Well, thank you again," Lorna said brightly. "And good night."

The maids bobbed at the knees and blushed.

"Good night, Mrs. Schmitt."

"Good night, miss."

And after the faintest pause . . . "Good night, Harken." She threw one more glance into his very blue eyes. Outwardly, he neither smiled nor flustered but showed only the respect a kitchen servant should have for his betters. He simply nodded good night, but as she walked away his eyes scanned her rear profile from head to heel and his hands took a firmer grip on the broom handle. It was none of his business, but a man would have to be flat-out unconscious not to wonder. As she reached the servants' stairway and put her hand on the doorknob, his words stopped her.

"Might I ask, miss, which one you are? There are three of you, we are told."

She paused and looked back over her shoulder. "I'm Lorna. The oldest."

Lorna, the oldest, he thought, keeping the admiration from showing in his eyes. "Ah," he said quietly. "Well, good night, then, Miss Lorna. Rest well."

She rested, however not at all well. How could she, when a kitchen servant's very blue eyes got between her and sleep? When that very same servant had had the temerity to slip a note to Papa and tell him how to win a regatta? When she herself was dying to know how to win a regatta? When the night's events had caused the most notorious set-to between Papa and Mama that *all* their friends were bound to be talking about tomorrow morning? When she had tasted her first judy and gotten the slightest bit flushed and fanciful from it? And taken over Mama's hostessing duties for even such a short and wonderful while, and played the piano for the guests, and exchanged secret messages with Taylor on the veranda, and felt sure that if they'd found a moment alone Taylor would have kissed her?

How could a young woman of eighteen sleep on a warm summer night when life was pushing at her bosom like a wing pushes at a chrysalis before it unfolds?

Chapter 2

In the master suite of Rose Point Cottage, Levinia donned a great white tent of a nightgown with long, full sleeves, and in spite of the heat buttoned it to the throat before stepping from behind her dressing room screen, properly attired for bed. Mattie, her maid, waited beside the dressing table.

Wordlessly Levinia sat down. Mattie removed the silk organza rose and combs and brushed Levinia's hair, then plaited it loosely in a single thick braid. When the end was tied, she inquired, "Will there be anything else, ma'am?"

Levinia rose, still regal in spite of relinquishing her crown. She rarely thanked the help: Their pay was their thanks. Furthermore, thanks spawned complacency, and complacency spawned laziness. She tipped up her lips in a smile never quite realized, and said, "Nothing more, Mattie, good night."

"Good night, ma'am."

Levinia posed as erect as a holy statue until the door closed, then whipped up her nightgown and indulged in a frenzy of scratching at the deep red ruts left in her belly by her corset stays. She scratched until her skin grew raw, muttering bland expletives, then rebuttoned the waistband of her cotton pantaloons, extinguished the gaslight and entered the bedroom.

Gideon was sitting up in bed smoking a cigar, looking as if he wanted to grind it out in the center of her forehead.

The mattress was high; she always felt conspicuous climbing up onto it when he was watching. "Must you smoke that detestable thing in here? It smells like burning dung."

"It's my bed, Levinia! I'll smoke in it if I want to."

She flounced onto her side, presenting her back, and jerked the sheet to her armpits, though even her feet were sweating. She'd be hanged if she'd lie on top of the sheet. Every time she did he came poking and prodding, expecting to do *that* again. She wondered for the ten thousandth time how old a man had to get before he grew tired of it.

He went on sullying the air above her head with that rank weed, because he knew how she hated it, and because he'd been bested by her tonight, which he hated.

All right, she thought, *two can play the same game.*

"I think you should know, Gideon, that Mrs. Schmitt refused to stay unless I kept Harken on, so I said he could stay, too."

Behind her he choked and coughed.

"You . . . did . . . *what?*"

"I told Harken he could stay. If that's what it takes to keep Mrs. Schmitt, that's how it'll be."

He gripped her shoulder and flattened her onto her back. "Over my dead body!"

She glared at him, her hands clutching the sheet to her chest. "You embarrassed me tonight, Gideon. You made us laughingstocks, raising such a furor in the middle of a dinner party, and all because nobody can tell you what to do. Well, *I'm* telling you, because it's the only way I can save face in front of my friends. The word will leak out—it always does. Our servants will tell the DuVals' servants, and theirs will tell the Tufts' and pretty soon the whole island will know that Levinia Barnett cannot command her own household staff. So Mrs. Schmitt stays and Harken stays, and if you're going to make a fuss about it and blow that stinking smoke all around the bedroom just because I have the upper hand for once, I'll be happy to go into the dressing room and sleep on the chaise."

"Oh, you'd like that, wouldn't you, Levinia? Then you wouldn't have to touch me, even in your sleep!"

"Let me go, Gideon. It's hideously hot."

"It's always hideously hot, isn't it? Or you're hideously tired, or you're afraid the children will hear, or my sisters will hear. There's always some excuse, isn't there, Levinia!"

"Gideon, what's gotten into you?"

Holding both her wrists crossed on her chest, he shucked down the sheet, reached beneath her nightie and began freeing the waist button on her pantaloons.

"I'll show you what's gotten into me!"

"Gideon, please don't. It *is* hot, and I'm very tired."

"I really don't care if you are or not. Once every three months I think a man has a right, Levinia, and tonight your three months are up."

When she realized there was no putting him off, she stopped resisting and lay like a hickory branch, her trunk stiff and her legs where he shoved them, enduring the ignominy that accompanied marriage vows. Midway through the ordeal he tried to kiss her, but sealing wax couldn't have made Levinia's mouth any tighter.

When the graceless debacle ended, Gideon rolled over, sighed and slept like a baby, while Levinia lay at his side with her mouth still pinched and ice in her heart.

In the room they shared, Agnes and Henrietta Barnett, too, used a dressing screen. Henrietta changed first. Henrietta took it as her God-given right to do things first; after all, she'd been born first. She was sixty-nine to Agnes's sixty-seven and had been keeping Agnes out of trouble their whole lives long. That wasn't about to change now.

"Hurry up, Agnes, and turn out that lamp. I'm tired."

"But I have to brush my hair first, Etta." Agnes stepped toward the dressing table, tying her nightgown at the throat. Henrietta reclined against two stacked pillows, closed her eyelids and tolerated the rosy gaslight against them while listening to Agnes putter around in her usual poky fashion, wasting time at the dressing table and keeping *everyone in the room* awake.

Agnes sat down, removed the celluloid pins from her rusty-gray hair and began brushing. A mosquito came and buzzed at the round globe of the gaslight, but she paid it no mind, stroking, stroking, tipping her head to one side. Her eyes were pale blue, with brows as finely arched and tapered as they had been in her twenties, though they, too, were fading from their earlier rich mahogany to gray. She was thin in both face and body, fine-boned, with delicate features that had attracted many a second glance over the past forty years. Recently her voice had developed a delicate tremble and her eyes wore an expression to match it.

"I think young Mr. DuVal is smitten with our Lorna."

"Oh, bosh, Agnes. You think every young man is smitten with every young woman he's seen with."

"Well, I think he is. Did you see them go out onto the veranda together tonight?"

Henrietta gave up and opened her eyes. "I not only saw them, I heard them, and for your information it was she who invited him outside and I intend to speak to Levinia about it. I don't know what the world is coming to when a girl of eighteen acts so bold! It's simply not acceptable!"

"Our Lorna's not a girl, Etta, she's a young woman already. Why, I was only seventeen when Captain Dearsley proposed to me."

Henrietta threw herself over to face the opposite wall and gave her pillow a plump. "Oh, you and your Captain Dearsley; how you do prattle on about him."

"I shall never forget how he looked in his uniform that night, with the gold braid on his epaulettes shining in the moonlight, and the . . ."

Henrietta joined in. " '. . . And the gloves on his hands as white as a swan's back.' If I hear that one more time, Agnes, I swear I shall be sick to my stomach." She glared over her shoulder. "Now turn down the gas and come to bed!"

Agnes went on brushing her hair dreamily. "He *would* have married me if he'd come back from the Indian wars. Oh, he would have. And I would have had a house this fine, and servants, and three sons and three daughters, and I would have named the first one Malcolm and the second one Mildred. Captain Dearsley and I had spoken about children. He wanted a big family, he said, and so did I. By now, of course, our Malcolm would have been in his forties and I would be a grandmother. Just imagine that, Etta: me a grandmother."

Henrietta twitched in exasperation.

"Ah, me . . ." Agnes sighed. She set down her brush and began tying her hair back in a single tail.

"Braid your hair," Henrietta ordered.

"It's too hot tonight."

"A lady braids her hair at night, Agnes. When will you learn that?"

"If I had married Captain Dearsley, I'm sure there should have been many nights I would not have braided my hair. He would have asked me to leave it down and I would have." When her hair was tied, Agnes turned out the gas lamp, went to the window that looked out over the glasshouse and the side yard, where Levinia's prize rose garden spread an intoxicating scent upon the night. She lifted aside the curtain, listened to the fountain patter, breathed deeply, then padded barefoot to the carved bed and lay down beside her sister, where she'd been lying for as long as she had memory.

Through the wall they heard the muffled sounds of voices from the room next door. "Oh my," Agnes said softly, "it sounds as if Gideon and Levinia are still fighting." Abruptly the rumble ceased and a rhythmic thumping began against the common wall.

Henrietta lifted her head and listened a moment, then turned to her side and pulled a pillow over her ear.

Agnes lay on her back staring at the night shadows, listening to the sounds and smiling wistfully.

In a room across the hall Jenny Barnett sat cross-legged on her sister Daphne's bed. They were dressed in their nightclothes and the lantern had been extinguished. Jenny had already forgotten about Mama and Papa's quarrel and was rhapsodizing on her favorite subject.

"Lorna is so lucky." Jenny flopped to her back, one hand flung up to pluck at her hair, one leg over the edge of the mattress, its bare foot wagging. "He's *sooo* handsome."

"I'm going to tell."

"Oh no you won't, because if you do I'll tell about you smoking corn silk out behind the glasshouse."

"I did not!"

"You did too. Theron saw you and he told me. You and Betsy Whiting."

"I'm going to kill that Theron!"

Jenny continued swinging her foot. "Don't you just love Taylor's moustache and beard?"

"I think moustaches are dumb."

Jenny rolled onto her belly and lay her cheek on her doubled hands. "Not on Taylor they're not." She heaved a huge sigh. "Gosh, I'd give anything to be Lorna. Theron says Taylor kissed her down in the rose garden last week after they got home from the chautauqua."

"Oh, yuk. You wouldn't catch *me* kissing Taylor DuVal! You wouldn't catch me kissing any boy! Boys are disgusting."

"I'd kiss Taylor. I'd even kiss him with my mouth open."

"With your mouth open! Jenny Barnett, you'll go to hell for talking like that."

Jenny sat up, cross-legged. She let her head loll back until her hair fell clear down to her waist, joined her hands and stretched them straight toward the ceiling, thrusting out her young breasts under her round-yoked nightie. "No I won't. Sissy told me that when you grow up everybody kisses like that. They even put their tongues in each other's mouths."

"I'm telling Mama you said that!"

Jenny let her arms fall and braced them on the mattress behind her. "Go ahead, tell her. Sissy says *everybody* does it." Sissy Tufts was Jenny's best friend, the same age as she.

"Well, how does Sissy know?"

"Sissy's done it. With Mitchell Armfield. She said it was terribly exciting."

"You're lying. Nobody would do such a putrid thing."

"Oh, Daphne . . ." Jenny eased off the bed, shoulders back and toes pointed like a ballerina crossing a stage toward her prince. "You're such a child." She fainted onto the window seat, where the moonlight flooded in thick as cream. Like a dying diva, she wrapped both arms around an updrawn knee and dropped her cheek upon it.

"I am not! I'm only two years younger than you!"

On her buttocks, Jenny pivoted a half-circle, imagining strings playing Tchaikovsky. "Well, all I know is, if some boy wants to kiss me I'm going to try it. And if he wants to put his tongue in my mouth I'll try that, too."

"Do you really think Lorna did that with Taylor?"

Jenny gave up her dancing, drew both feet onto the window seat and folded both hands over her bare toes.

"Theron saw them through his spyglass."

"Theron and his dumb spyglass. I wish Aunt Agnes had never given it to him. He carries it everywhere, and pulls it out and points it at my friends and makes this cackly laugh and says 'The eye knows' in a weird voice. Honestly, it's so embarrassing."

They sat awhile, thinking about how dumb twelve-year-old brothers could be, wondering when kissing would start for them.

In time Jenny interrupted the silence. "Hey, Daph?"

"What?"

"Where do you suppose your nose goes when you kiss a boy?"

"How should I know?"

"Wouldn't you think it would get in the way?"

"I don't know. It never gets in the way when the aunts kiss me."

"But that's different. When boys kiss you they do it longer."

After the two pondered silently awhile, Jenny said, "Hey, Daph?"

"What?"

"What if some boys tried it with us and we didn't know what to do?"

"We'd know."

"How do you know we'd know? I think we should practice."

Daphne caught her sister's drift and was having none of it. "Oh no, not me! Go find somebody else!"

"But, Daph, you're going to kiss boys someday, too. Do you want to be a dumb dodo who doesn't know the first thing about it?"

"I'd rather be a dumb dodo than practice kissing with you."

"Come on, Daphne."

"You're crazy. You've been gawking at Taylor DuVal too much."

"We'll make a pact. We'll never tell anyone else as long as we live."

"No," Daphne said stubbornly. "I'm not going to do it."

"Supposing it's David Tufts who tries to kiss you for the first time and you bump noses and make a fool out of yourself if he tries to put his tongue in your mouth."

"How do you know about David Tufts?"

"Lorna's not the only one Theron's used his spyglass on."

"David Tufts would never try to kiss me. All he ever does is talk about his bug collection."

"Maybe not this summer, but sometime he might."

Daphne considered awhile and decided there might be the slightest bit of merit in what Jenny said. "Oh, all right. But I'm not hugging!"

"Of course not. We'll do it like Sissy and Mitchell did. They were sitting on the porch swing when it happened."

"So what should I do? Come over there and sit by you?"

"Sure."

Daphne left the bed and joined her sister on the window seat. They sat side by side, with their bare toes touching the floor and their hair backlit by moonlight. They looked at each other and giggled, grew silent and uncertain, neither of them moving.

"Do you think we're supposed to close our eyes or what?" Daphne asked.

"I suppose so. It would be too embarrassing to do it with them open, like looking into a fish's eye when you're taking him off the hook."

Daphne said, "Well, let's do it, then. Hurry up. I feel stupid."

"All right, close your eyes and tip your head just a little."

They both tipped their heads and puckered their lips like sausage casings that have burst while cooking. They touched lips briefly, then backed up and opened their eyes.

"What did you think?" Jenny asked.

"If that's what kissing is like, I'd as soon look at David Tufts' bug collection."

"It was pretty disappointing, wasn't it? Do you think we should try it again and touch tongues?"

Daphne looked doubtful. "Well, all right, but dry your tongue off real good first on your nightie."

"Good idea."

They both pulled at their nighties and energetically dried their tongues, then quickly tilted their heads, scrunched their eyes shut and kissed the way they thought it ought to be done. After two seconds of contact, a snort of laughter came through Daphne's nose.

"Stop that!" Jenny scolded. "You blew boogers on me!" But she was laughing, too, hard enough to rock her backward, pulling them apart.

Daphne spit into a wad of nightgown and scrubbed her tongue as if she'd eaten poison. "Oh, ish! That was horrible! If that's what kissing is like, I'd rather *eat* David Tufts' bug collection!"

They laughed so hard they clutched their stomachs and doubled up, rolling on the window seat in the moonlight. Curled against the pillows, with their feet drawn up into the warm air stealing through the open windows, they became two young sylphs treading the brink of womanhood, hesitant to step in, knowing they would soon and trusting that when it happened they'd be ready. Their sprigged gingham nightgowns created two puddles of blue light on the darker blue cushion as they lay in relaxed coils, hushed now and tired, their attempt at kissing already mellowing into a humorous recollection they would recount for their own children well into their dotage. In time Jenny ventured to the stars outside, "I guess it only works if you do it with a boy, huh?"

"I guess," Daphne agreed, staring, too, at the stars.

Down on the lakeshore soft waves licked the sand. Frogs made the night pulse with their dissonant songs. From the gardens below lifted the smell of Mama's roses and the babbling of the fountains. Off in the distance the theater train could be heard chugging softly, bringing a load of summer people back from Saint Paul. In their blissful innocence, Jenny and Daphne drifted off to sleep, on their tongues not the taste of lovers' kisses, only that of starch from their own nightgowns.

In his room, with the lantern still hissing, surrounded by nautical paraphernalia, Theron Barnett lay on his back in a bed whose headboard and footboard were shaped like ships' wheels. His skinny right ankle rested on his updrawn left knee, and his nightshirt was shinnied around his hips. In his right hand he held a brass spyglass, extended full-length. He was driving it through the air, making flatulent sounds of propulsion with his mouth. He had studied the Civil War this past winter and was fascinated by the fight between the *Monitor* and the *Merrimack*.

"Vrrrtt!" Imitating an engine, he made his spyglass dive and rolled with it until his arms were hanging over the side of the bed and he was facing the floor with his chin screwed into the edge of the mattress. He raised both bare feet and flailed them some, crossed them, hummed a little and *thupped* the spyglass closed and open, closed and open. Abruptly he shot up and knelt in the middle of his bed, squinting one eye, peering through the brass piece at his wallpaper. A brigantine with furled sails loomed up in his sights.

"Ship ahoy! The brigantine *Theron* ten degrees off the larboard bow!" He had no idea what his words meant. He swung his spyglass around the room and found an entire army surrounding his ship. "Man the guns! All hands on deck!" Artillery fire hit his ship and he fell over, his eyelids shut and twitching, his fingers loosening on the spyglass.

As he sprawled across his wrinkled bedspread, he heard giggling from his sisters' room next door. He stood on the bed, reached for the high bracket and extinguished his gas lantern, hurried to the window seat and pushed the curtain back, training his spyglass on his sisters' bay window, which projected from the house on the same plane as his own. But their window was dark and all he could make out were white curtains and black window glass.

Disappointed that he, Black Barnett, the feared and hated Yankee spy, would witness no skulduggery tonight, he left his spyglass on the window seat and padded, yawning, to his bed.

The Sunday morning ritual at Rose Point Cottage began with breakfast at eight, followed by church at ten. Lorna awakened at six-thirty, shot up, checked her clock and flew out of bed.

Mrs. Schmitt had said the help were free as soon as breakfast was finished, which meant she had to corner Harken before eight if she wanted any questions answered.

At seven forty-five, all dressed and combed for church, Lorna once again entered the kitchen from the servants' rear stairs. Glynnis, the dining room serving maid, was back, coming out of the butler's pantry with a stack of clean plates. Mrs. Schmitt was coddling eggs; the red-headed kitchen maid was squeezing spinach dry in a tammy cloth, the other was mincing herbs on the chopping block. Harken was down on one knee on a piece of canvas, chipping ice with an ice pick. "Excuse me," Lorna said, once again arresting all motion.

After a first jolt of surprise, Mrs. Schmitt found her tongue. "I'm sorry, miss, breakfast isn't quite ready. It'll be on the sideboard at the crack of eight, though."

"Oh, I haven't come for breakfast. I want to speak to Harken."

Harken dropped a shard of ice into a cut-glass bowl and rose slowly, drying a hand on his trousers.

"Yes, miss?" he said politely.

"I want you to explain to me how my father can win the regatta next year."

"Now, miss?"

"Yes, if you don't mind."

Harken and Mrs. Schmitt exchanged glances before her eyes grazed the clock. "Well, I'd be happy to, miss, but with Chester still gone and breakfast expected at eight, I should be helping Mrs. Schmitt."

Lorna, too, checked the clock. "Oh, yes, how silly of me. Perhaps later, then? It's ever so important."

"Of course, miss."

"After church?"

"Actually . . . ah . . ." He cleared his throat and shifted his weight from one foot to the other. He folded a thumb over the pointed end of the ice pick.

Mrs. Schmitt returned to coddling eggs and put in, "It's his day off, miss. He was planning to go fishing. Girls," she said to the maids, "finish them herbs and spinach now, hurry."

The two girls began packing spinach into boat-shaped molds and Lorna realized she was holding things up. To Harken she said, "Oh, of course, and I wouldn't dream of using up your day. But I do so want to hear more about your plan. I'd only take up a few minutes of your time. Are you fishing here on the lake?"

"Yes, miss. With Mr. Iversen."

"With *our* Mr. Iversen? You mean Tim?"

"Yes, miss."

"Why, that's perfect! I'll just sail the catboat over to Tim's as soon as we get back from church, and we can talk for a few minutes and you'll still get in a full afternoon of fishing. Would that be agreeable?"

"Yes, of course, miss."

"All right, then. I shall see you at Tim's the minute I can get away."

When Lorna had gone, Mrs. Schmitt shot Harken a sideward glance. She was whipping cheese sauce, her double chin flapping like a turkey wattle. "You'd best look out what you're doing, Jens Harken. You nearly lost your job once this week; this'll sure do the trick. And this time I won't be able to save you."

"Well, what should I have done? Refused her?"

"I don't know, but she's the gentry and you're the help, and them two never mix. You'd best be remembering that."

"We're not exactly sneaking out to meet in secret. After all, Iversen will be right there."

Mrs. Schmitt snorted and whacked her wooden spoon down. "All I'm saying is watch your p's and q's, young man. You're twenty-five and she's eighteen and it don't look good."

At breakfast Lorna was vaguely disappointed to see that Glynnis was serving their coffee instead of Harken. Papa and Mama were particularly silent this morning. Jenny, Daphne and Theron seemed lethargic after being up later than usual last night. Aunt Henrietta was busy telling Aunt Agnes how much food to take and to be careful of the spicy sausage as too much of it would give her dyspepsia. Aunt Agnes, as usual, was busy discoursing with the help.

"Why, thank you, Glynnis," she said when Glynnis served her coffee. "And how is your tooth today?"

Levinia glared at Agnes, who missed it and smiled up at the young woman in the white mobcap and apron. She was no more than eighteen and had pitted skin and a nose resembling a nicely risen muffin.

"Much better, mum, thank you."

"And have you heard from Chester?"

"No, mum, not since he left."

"How unfortunate that his father is ill."

"Yes, mum, though he's old. Seventy-seven, Chester says."

Levinia cleared her throat, lifted her cup and whacked it down on her saucer. "My breakfast will be cold if you don't move on with that coffeepot, Glynnis."

"Oh yes, mum." Glynnis colored and hurried along with her duties.

When she'd left the room, Henrietta scolded, "Mercy sakes, Agnes, I wish you'd control your urge to visit with the help. It's quite embarrassing."

Agnes looked up innocently. "I don't know why it should be. I was just asking after the poor girl's tooth. And Chester has been with us so many years. Don't you care about his father being ill?"

Levinia said, "Of course we care, Agnes. What Henrietta is saying is that we don't discuss it with the help over breakfast."

Agnes replied, "You don't, Levinia, but I rather enjoy doing so. That Glynnis is ever such a nice young girl. Please pass the butter, Daphne."

Levinia's left eyebrow went up as she and Henrietta exchanged glances.

Lorna went to the sideboard and helped herself to fresh strawberries, taking a second look at the ice in the cut-glass bowl beneath them, recalling Harken on his knees chipping it with an ice pick a quarter hour ago. Returning to the table, she said, "If nobody's using the catboat, I'd like to take it out after church. May I, Papa?"

Gideon hadn't spoken a word through the entire meal. He did so now, with his eyes on his plate as he cut and stabbed a piece of sausage. "I don't condone women sailing, Lorna, and you know that." He popped the sausage into his mouth, leaving grease on his moustache.

Lorna stared at it, fighting for composure. If he had his way, she would remain in stays forever, sitting in the shade watching life sail by the way Mama did. She could fight him, but persuasion worked best with Papa. As long as he thought the final decision was his, the females in the family had a chance of getting their way.

"I'd stay close to shore, and I'd make sure I wore my bonnet."

"Why, I should think you'd wear your bonnet," put in Aunt Henrietta. *"With a sharp hatpin!"* Aunt Henrietta never stopped warning her nieces they must always wear a sharp hatpin. It was their only weapon, she held, though Lorna often wondered what man in his right mind had ever done anything to cause Aunt Henrietta to believe she needed a weapon. Furthermore, what man might do so to Lorna out in the middle of White Bear Lake on a bright Sunday afternoon?

"I'll make sure it's sharp," she agreed with feigned meekness. "And I'll be home at whatever time you say."

Gideon wiped his moustache and studied his daughter while reaching for his coffee cup. She could see he was in a rancid mood.

"You can take the rowboat."

They'd had a tremendous tiff when he'd learned—via Theron's tattling—that she had coerced one of the boys, Mitchell Armfield, into teaching her to sail his catboat.

"The rowboat," she wailed. "But Papa—"

"It's the rowboat or nothing. Two hours. And you'll take a life preserver with you. Why, if you capsized in those skirts they'd take you down like an anchor."

"Yes, Papa," she agreed. To her mother she said, "If it's all right, I thought I'd take a hamper and eat on the boat."

Sunday was the day this was most feasible on brief notice, with only a skeleton staff on duty and the day's noon and evening meals made up of cold foods.

"Very well," Levinia agreed. "But I *do* worry about you out on the water all alone."

"I could go along!" Theron put in hopefully.

"No!" Lorna cried.

"Please, Mother, can I?" Under the table Theron eagerly clapped his knees together.

"Mother, I took him into town with me this week when I'd rather have gone alone, and he tagged along with Taylor and me the other night to the band concert. Must I take him again?"

"Lorna's right. You can stay home this time."

Lorna breathed a sigh of relief and hurried to finish her breakfast before the others finished theirs. "I'll go tell Mrs. Schmitt." She gulped the last of her coffee, then hurried out before anyone could change his mind.

Jens Harken was in the kitchen when Lorna stuck her head into the room yet again. He was kneeling before the icebox, pulling out the drip pan from below it. When the door from the passageway swung open he looked up and met Lorna's gaze. His eyes were as blue as she remembered, his face as handsome, his shoulders as wide.

He stood, bearing the swaying water in the wide pan, and nodded silently in greeting as he headed for the back door to sling it into the herb garden.

"Mrs. Schmitt?" Lorna called, craning to peer around the edge of the door. Mrs. Schmitt came hurrying in from the butler's pantry, counting a handful of silverware in Chester's absence.

"Oh, miss, it's you again."

"Yes." Lorna flashed a smile, realizing that requests such as she was about to make cut into the few free hours the kitchen staff was allotted each week. Harken had returned and knelt to replace the drip pan.

"I was wondering if you'd pack me a hamper before you leave. Just a few things from the noon buffet that I can take on the boat."

"Certainly, miss."

"You can leave it at the back door and I'll come around and get it before I go."

"Very well. And I'll be sure to put in a couple of those currant cakes you like so much."

Lorna was nonplussed. Never in her life had she told Mrs. Schmitt she loved currant cakes.

"Why, how ever did you know?"

"The staff talks, miss. I know most of the foods you fancy, as well as the favorites of the others in the family."

Again Lorna smiled. "Why, thank you, Mrs. Schmitt, I'd love some currant cakes, and you have a nice afternoon off, will you?"

"That I will, miss, and thank you, too."

She left without another glance at Harken, though even after the door swung shut she was inappropriately aware of the fact that his forearms, below his rolled-up sleeves, had looked like knots in a piece of oak firewood, and his eyes had strayed to her more than once as he moved about his kitchen work.

She set out at noon with the hamper. Upon her head her leghorn bonnet was dutifully secured with a hatpin, freshly sharpened. Down her back streamed pale blue ribbons that matched the stripes in her sateen skirt. For her feet she had carefully chosen a pair of white canvas Prince Alberts, whose elastic gussets eliminated the need for troublesome buttonhooks. Twenty feet from shore she released the oars, reeved her skirts and tugged off the shoes, followed by her lisle stockings and garters, which she stowed in the picnic hamper. Reclaiming the oars, she took a bearing on the shoreline behind her and set out for Tim Iversen's place across the lake.

Tim Iversen was one of those rare people liked by everyone. By dint of his occupation, he had managed to breach the line separating the upper and lower classes, for as a photographer he worked for both. He wasn't rich by anyone's standards, yet he'd had a self-made log cabin on White Bear Lake since before the wealthy had built their fancy summer homes there. He called his cabin Birch Lodge and kept open house in it for any and all comers. He not only yachted with the wealthy, he hunted, fished and socialized with them as well, and he'd been chronicling it all in photographs since the rich had decided to make White Bear their playground.

Similarly, the working class found a friend in Tim. He had come from humble beginnings and refused to shun them. Furthermore, he was unpretentious and unpretty: As a youngster he'd lost his left eye in an accident involving an arrow made from a corset stay, and wore a glass eye. His remaining eye, however, served him well as a photographer of both classes. Not only had he set up a studio in Saint Paul, but he was garnering national acclaim as a stereophotographer, traveling the world over with a double-lensed stereo camera, producing side-by-side pictures for the stereoscope that had taken its place in every parlor of America and had created a national pastime.

Iversen's camera was nowhere in sight, however, as Lorna approached his dock. Instead, he and Harken, with their trouser legs rolled up, were manning opposite ends of a seine in the shallows along his shoreline. A goodly distance out, she stowed her oars and donned her shoes and stockings. Rowing once more, she glanced over her shoulder and found Tim waving. She waved back. Harken, with the net in his hands, only watched the boat come on.

When it reached the dock the two men were waiting in knee-deep water to stop it. Harken took the painter to pull the boat against the dock while Tim greeted, "Well, this is a pleasant surprise, Miss Lorna."

She stood up and caught her balance as the boat rocked.

"It's no surprise at all, Mr. Iversen. I'm sure Harken told you I was coming."

"Well, yes, he did"—Iversen laughed and vaulted onto the dock to offer Lorna a hand—"but I know your father's views on ladies yachting, so I suspected you'd have trouble getting away."

"As you can see, I had to settle for the rowboat," Lorna replied, taking Iversen's hand and stepping from the boat. "And I had to promise to be back in two hours."

Until now she had avoided glancing at Harken. She did so as he stood in the water, tying up the boat below her.

"Hello," she said quietly.

He lifted his face to squint up at her. His blond head was bare. His trousers were wet nearly to the crotch. The collar was missing from his wrinkled white shirt and its shoulders were dented by red suspenders. He gave a final tug on the knot.

"Hello, miss."

"I've interrupted your seining."

"Oh, that's all right." He flung out a glance that never quite reached the abandoned net and bucket. "We can finish later."

She strode the length of the bleached dock, followed by Iversen, who left wet footprints. Harken waded alongside and below her. They converged on the sandy shore, where the sun beat down and the placid water scarcely moved against it. The afternoon was hot and still. All around the sound of katydids created a piercing syllable that never ceased. In the nearby woods even the maples looked wilted. Along the shoreline overhanging willows appeared to be dipping their tongues to drink.

Lorna asked Tim, "Did Mr. Harken tell you I've come to talk about how to win a regatta?"

"Yes, he did, but did he tell you he's taken his idea to about half a dozen members of the White Bear Yacht Club and they've all told him he's crazy?"

She turned her gaze on the tall blond man again. "Are you, Mr. Harken?"

"Maybe. I don't think so, though."

"Exactly what do you propose?"

"A revolutionary new boat design."

"Show me."

His eyes met hers directly for the first time while he wondered why a pretty young thing like she wanted to know about boats. And could she understand? He'd sketched his ideas for yachtsmen far more experienced than she, and they'd failed to believe his reasoning. Furthermore, if her father found out about this clandestine meeting, he'd lose his job for sure, as Hulduh Schmitt had warned. But there she stood, looking up at him expectantly from the shadow of a straw bonnet, with a faint sheen of sweat on her brow and a hint of it dampening the armpits of her ham-shaped sleeves. From the waist down she was as slim as a buggy whip, while above she'd inherited her mother's generous breasts. A man would have to have *two* glass eyes not to notice all that plus her pretty face. Jens Harken, however, knew his place. He could easily keep propriety intact and treat her with the deference expected of the kitchen help, but he could not so easily cast aside the opportunity to talk about his boat to one more person. The boat would work. He knew it as surely as he knew he should not be standing on this lakeshore in his bare feet beside Miss Lorna Barnett in her pretty striped skirt and beribboned hat. But who knew which person might make the difference? It could turn out to be even so unlikely a one as this bored rich girl, who might possibly be doing nothing more than amusing herself with the kitchen help. On the off chance that her intentions were more honorable, he decided to show her.

"All right," he answered, retrieving his pail of minnows. He took three steps into the water, sent the minnows and lake water shimmering through the air, then filled the bucket once more. "Look out," he warned Lorna before swashing the water across the sand, creating a smooth, wet blackboard. From a nearby bush he snapped off a twig and returned to Lorna's side, where he squatted down with his weight on one heel.

"You sail a little, right?" he inquired as he began sketching.

"Yes, a little. Whenever I can sneak out to do it."

He smiled but kept his eyes fixed on the sand. "This is the kind of boat your father is sailing now. It's a sloop, and you know how a sloop is shaped underneath. . . ." He sketched a deep lower fin. "This keel configuration means that all this area from here . . . to here"—he sketched the waterline—"is displacing water. At the same time, when they're used for racing, they're carrying more and more sail, and to counterbalance that, there's more and more iron and lead being bolted onto the keel for ballast. And when even *that* won't keep them from tipping, they take on sandbags and the crew shifts them from side to side whenever she heels, you see?"

"Yes, I know all about sandbagging."

"All right now, imagine this . . ." He dropped both knees to the sand and began avidly sketching a second boat. "A scow, a light little thing with a virtually flat bottom that skims over the water instead of plowing through it. A planing hull versus a displacement hull, that's what we're talking about. We cut down on the sail area so we don't need all that weight on the hull. A thirty-eight-footer that would weigh, say, eighteen hundred pounds with a displacement hull would weigh only about five hundred fifty with a planing hull. We'd save all that weight."

"But if you don't use lead ballast, what'll keep it from tipping?"

"Shape." He shot Lorna one quick glance—animated now—and drew a third picture. "Imagine it shaped like a cigar that somebody stepped on. It'll be only about three feet from the top of her deck to the bottom of her hull."

"So shallow?"

"Not only that, we do away with the long bowsprit—we don't need it anymore to hold the tacks of those ridiculously big sails. We'll use much smaller sails."

"But won't it nose into the water, being down so close to it?"

"No."

"You'll have a hard time convincing my father of that."

"Maybe so, but I'm right. I know I am! She might be shallow-hulled, but she'll still have a belly"—he pointed to the flattened cigar—"and because of her planing characteristics she'll have plenty of natural lift. When she's on a downwind run, the bow will lift instead of dip; and when she's sailing close-hauled she'll be heeled up so that very little wetted surface is in the water, versus the old design, where the hull is fully in the water, creating such a tremendous drag."

He paused for breath and sat back, hands on his thighs, looking straight into Lorna's eyes. His own, caught in the bright summer sun, became as brilliant as the sky behind him, and his breath seemed short from excitement.

"How do you know all this?"

"I can't say how. I just do."

"Have you studied?"

"No."

"Then how?"

He looked away, threw down the stick he'd been drawing with and brushed his palms together. "I'm Norwegian. I think it's in our blood, and besides, I've been sailing since I was a boy. My father taught me, and his father taught him."

"Where?"

"In Norway at first, then here when we immigrated."

"You immigrated?"

He nodded. "When I was eight."

So that accounted for his lack of accent. He spoke well-modulated English, but as she gazed up at his profile she saw very clearly the clean-lined Nordic features of his face—straight nose, high forehead, shapely mouth, blond hair and those discommoding blue eyes.

"Does your father agree with you?"

He gave her a glance, making no reply.

"About the boat, I mean," she added.

"My father's dead."

"Oh, I'm sorry."

He picked up the stick again and absently poked it into the sand. "He died when I was eighteen, in a fire at the boatworks where he worked in New Jersey. Actually I worked there, too, and I tried to convince them to listen to me, but they laughed at me just the way everybody else did."

"And your mother?"

"She's dead, too, before my dad. I have a brother, though, back in New Jersey." His smile returned, slightly mischievous this time. "I told him I'd come to Minnesota and find somebody to listen to me, and when I got rich and famous designing the fastest boats on the water he could come here and work for me. He's married with two little babies, so it isn't as easy for him to pull up stakes and move. Someday I'll get him here, though, mark my words."

They were both on their knees, intent upon each other with little sense of passing time. His hand was motionless upon the stick that protruded from the sand. Hers rested quietly on her thigh. His eyes were in full sunlight. Hers were shaded by the brim of her straw bonnet. She was wholly feminine in her high-necked white shirtwaist with its immense sleeves. He was wholly masculine in his wrinkled shirt, suspenders and bare feet. For just a moment they became two exceedingly comely people admiring each other for the sheer enjoyment of it.

Then propriety intruded and Harken dropped his eyes. "You're soiling your skirt, Miss Lorna."

"Oh." She looked down. "It's just sand. It'll brush off when it dries. So . . ." She leaned toward the drawing and outlined it with one fingertip. "Tell me, Mr. Harken, how much would it take to build this?"

"More than I have. More than I can convince the yacht club to put up."

"How much?"

"Seven hundred dollars, probably."

"Oh, that *is* a lot."

"Especially when they believe it'll tip right over on its side and sink."

"I must confess, some of that was hard for me to understand. The part about wetted surface. Explain it to me again so I can convince my father."

His expression opened in surprise. "Are you serious?"

"I'm going to try."

"You're going to tell him you were here, talking to me?"

"No. I'm going to tell him I was here talking to Mr. Iversen, and that he believes it'll work."

Harken's lips formed an unspoken O that remained a moment before he ventured, "You're a brave young lady."

She shrugged. "Not really. Tell me, Mr. Harken, have you ever heard of the novelist Charles Kingsley?"

"No, I'm afraid I haven't."

"Well, Mr. Kingsley holds that today's women suffer from a bevy of health problems, all of them caused by the three S's—silence, stillness and stays. I choose to reject all three and stay healthy, that's all. My father doesn't like it, but occasionally he gets tired of upbraiding me and I get my way. Who knows, perhaps this will be one of those times. Now, once more, Mr. Harken, explain your boat."

He had been doing so for some time when an explosion sounded nearby. They both started and looked up. There stood Iversen, surrounded by a cloud of smoke, withdrawing his head from beneath the black hood of his Kodak camera, which was standing on a tripod in the sand.

"Mr. Iversen, what are you doing!" Lorna cried.

"I have a hunch that those drawings in the sand might prove to be historic someday. I've simply recorded it for posterity."

She rose to her knees and lifted one hand in alarm. "Oh, but you mustn't."

Iversen smiled. "Don't worry. I won't show your father. At least not until the boat is built and Jens has sailed it across the lake without sinking. Beyond that, I can't promise."

Lorna relaxed and sat back on her heels. "Well, all right. But you must promise to keep the photograph hidden now. You know how my father is. After last night he isn't exactly congenial toward Mr. Harken, and if he thought for a minute that I was here discussing it with him, he'd have apoplexy. I'll need to convince him that you're behind Harken and that you believe this new boat will work. All right?"

"I *am* convinced his boat will work."

Lorna looked from Iversen to Harken to Iversen again. "Well then, why haven't you said so?"

"I have. They don't listen. You know what kind of a sailor I am." He had a reputation for losing every race he entered and on one occasion actually came in swimming behind his boat, claiming he could push it faster than sail it. He'd even good-naturedly named his boat the *May-B*.

Lorna clambered to her feet and approached Iversen. "Well, will you try again? With me? And with Harken if Papa will speak with him?"

"I guess I'd do that."

"Oh, thank you, Mr. Iversen, thank you!" Impulsively, she gave him a hug, then remembered herself and assumed a pose of demureness. "Oh, I'm sorry. Don't tell Mother I did that."

Iversen laughed.

"Or Aunt Henrietta, either." When Iversen's laughter once again faded, a lull fell. "Well!" Lorna said, throwing out her arms, then joining her fingers at her skirt-front. "I have a hamper and I'm starved. Would you gentlemen care to join me for a light repast?"

"Mrs. Schmitt's cooking?" Iversen replied, his eyebrows rising. "And me a bachelor? You needn't ask twice."

Harken had risen to his feet and stood beside the sketches, saying nothing. Lorna looked back at him. "Mr. Harken?" she invited much more quietly.

She had no idea what a lovely sight she made, with the sun slicing across her heart-shaped chin and her blue bonnet ribbons trailing down behind. No one need tell Harken it was as far from acceptable as anything could get to have a picnic with her. But Iversen was here with them, and it was only one stolen hour about which her father—she hoped—would never learn. Furthermore, after today Jens Harken would return to his kitchen and Lorna Barnett to her croquet games on the east lawn and neither of them would even bother to remember this odd, implausible encounter on a hot June afternoon.

"That sounds good," Harken answered.

Chapter 3

Iversen got an Indian blanket which they spread in the shade beneath the birches near his cabin. The three of them sat cross-legged while Lorna produced from her hamper sliced ham, buttered rolls, deviled eggs, fresh strawberries, pickled watermelon rind and currant cake. She arrayed the foods at the rim of her skirt, which surrounded her like a collapsed tent of blue-and-white stripes.

"Ah, it's much nicer here, isn't it?" she said.

Harken tried to admire the food instead of her, but it was difficult. She lifted her arms and removed a hatpin, then the hat itself, tossing it onto the grass and wildings at the edge of the blanket. She gave her neck a little twist of freedom. "Ah, the shade is wonderful." Once again she lifted her arms to do an all-around tucking job on her looped-up hair. The pose threw her breasts into relief and brought her immense white sleeves up about her ears. The cameo at her throat disappeared beneath her chin while her tapered and tucked shirtwaist strained against her ribs.

She dropped her arms and looked up, catching Harken's eye. Immediately he looked away.

"Well!" she said, rubbing her palms together and leaning forward to assess the food. "Strawberries, ham, eggs . . . Gentlemen, what would you like first?" Holding a saucer, she gazed at Iversen.

"A little of everything."

She filled the saucer and handed it to him, leaning across her skirts, making them crackle.

"And you, Mr. Harken?"

"A little of everything except pickled watermelon rind."

"Oh, but they're quite exquisite." She selected eggs and berries while he watched her hand, with its little finger elevated, move over the colorful foods.

"You wouldn't think so if you'd helped Mrs. Schmitt can them. Makes the kitchen stink something terrible."

She was licking off a thumb and forefinger, which came out of her mouth slowly as she handed him his plate. "You helped can these?"

"I help with most of the canning. I wash the fruits and vegetables and do the lifting. Those boilers are pretty heavy for the women. Thank you, miss."

He accepted the plate and began eating while she considered the pickled watermelon rinds, realizing she had no idea what a boiler looked like, or how heavy it must be, or what all went into creating so simple a food as this.

"What else do you do?"

He met her eyes and spoke levelly. "I'm the kitchen odd-jobs man. I do what I'm asked."

"Yes, but what else?"

"Well, this morning was the gardener's day off, so at five-thirty I picked the strawberries, and after that—"

"At five-thirty!"

"Mrs. Schmitt believes that they're sweetest if they're picked before the sun dries the dew on them. Then, after I washed the berries I filled the woodbox for her, and built a fire, and helped polish the silver from last night, since Chester isn't back yet, and I squeezed oranges, and fetched a new block of ice from the icehouse and cracked some for under the berries, and put the rest in the icebox, and emptied the drip pans, and fetched the hamper from the storeroom and ran a hose over it, and swept the kitchen floor after breakfast, and hosed down the back stoop, and watered the herb garden. Oh, and I helped Mrs. Schmitt pack the hamper."

Lorna stared at him in stupefaction.

"You did all that this morning? On your day off?"

Harken's cheek was puffed out with a mouthful of bread and ham. He swallowed and said, "My day off starts when the breakfast work is done."

"Oh, I see. Still, all that before I was even out of bed."

"Early morning's the best part of the day. I don't mind getting up early."

She thought a moment, then inquired, "Why didn't the gardener's day off start after breakfast?"

"I believe he has a special arrangement with your mother, miss."

"A special arrangement? What sort of special arrangement?"

Harken toyed with the food on his plate, reluctant to go into detail about the absurd lengths to which the ladies went in their quest for one-upsmanship.

Iversen answered. "You know what a tremendous competition there is among the ladies out here, Lorna, when it comes to gardens."

"Well . . . yes?"

"And you know that Smythe is from England."

"Yes. His father gardened for Queen Victoria herself. I remember how Mother crowed about it when she hired him."

Harken explained, "Part of their agreement when he came here to work for her was that Smythe would have each weekend off from eight o'clock Saturday night until dawn on Monday morning."

"Oh, I see. So you pick the fruits and vegetables on Sundays."

"Yes, miss."

"And my mother takes the credit for growing the best produce and flowers in White Bear Lake, even though she does none of the work. I'll confess to both of you, I've always found it utterly silly the way the women compete to have the most spectacular gardens when they don't do any of the work themselves."

"It's no different with the men and their yachting," Harken said. "They own the boats but hire the skippers."

"Only for the really important regattas, though, like yesterday," Lorna said.

"And only because the Inland Lake Yachting Association allows it," Tim put in.

"Still, wouldn't you think they'd want to skip themselves?" Harken put in. "I would if I owned a boat."

"I guess you're right. There's really not much difference between Mama hiring a gardener and a boat owner hiring a skipper."

Iversen told them, "There's talk about the ILYA changing the rule, though, and demanding that the men who own the boats must skip them."

This brought about a lively discussion of the pros and cons of hired skippers, followed by a rehash of yesterday's regatta.

Lorna leaned forward, selected a strawberry and bit into it. "Now you, Tim"— she pointed at him with half the berry—"you've earned your reputation on your own."

"You mean on the *May-B*? Now, Miss Lorna, I'll thank you not to spoil a pleasant afternoon by reminding me of that."

They all laughed, and Lorna said, "I'm talking about your photography, not your sailing. Tell me, is it true that your boxed sets of stereophotos are going to be sold by Sears and Roebuck?"

"It's true."

"Oh, Tim, you must be so proud! And to think of your work being viewed in practically every parlor in America! Tell us about the pictures, and the places where you took them."

He described the Chicago World's Fair, which he'd photographed two years earlier, and spectacular places like the Grand Canyon and Mexico and the Klondike. He lit a pipe and settled himself against a tree while Lorna nibbled on a piece of currant cake and asked him where he might go this winter when he closed his little cabin for the season. He said perhaps to Egypt to photograph the pyramids.

She breathed, "The pyramids . . . oh my . . . ," and broke off another piece of currant cake and ate it, unaware of the fetching picture she made, rapt at Tim's stories, surrounded by a mound of crisp skirts, nibbling cake whenever she wasn't too mesmerized to forget it was in her hand.

Harken sat Indian fashion, elbows to knees, splitting a blade of grass, admiring her profile, her mannerisms, her quick laughter and naturalness. In time she said to Iversen, "Perhaps you'll go to New Jersey. Mr. Harken has a brother there."

She turned and smiled at Harken, catching him off-guard. He forgot to look away, and she chose not to. His thumbnail quit splitting the grass and they both became caught in an awareness that seemed to hum through their heads like the song of the katydids around them. The dappled shade, the post-picnic lassitude, the pleasant conversation—all had combined to steal wariness away and beg them indulge themselves in an exchange of silent curiosity that breached all class distinction. They simply looked their fill, admiring what they saw, filing away details to take out and explore later, when they lay in separate rooms on separate floors—the color of eyes, the curve of hair, the outline of mouths, noses, chins. Iversen leaned against his tree trunk, puffing his fragrant briarwood pipe and watching the two of them. Even his presence failed to end their folly, until finally his pipe burned out and he rapped out the dottle against a tree root.

With a start, Lorna emerged from her absorption with Harken to realize how long they'd ignored Tim. She reached for the first diversion she could find: the round tin.

"A piece of cake before I put it away?" She extended it to Iversen.

"No, thank you, I'm full."

"Mr. Harken?" She hadn't known offering a man cake could seem so intimate, but it felt that way, his being help with whom she'd never before associated.

"No, thank you, that was for you," he said, and forced himself to look away. His gaze settled on Iversen, whose mustachioed mouth wore a pleasant if knowing expression behind the empty briarwood pipe. Harken, too, realized it was time to call an end to this folderol.

"Well, Tim, are we going to catch those fish or not?"

Lorna moved as if she'd been stuck by a pin. "Gracious, I've been keeping you." On her knees, she began closing tins and jars and piling things back in the hamper.

"Not at all, Miss Lorna." Harken rolled to his knees to help her, placing the two of them in closer proximity than they'd been since they'd knelt over the drawings on the beach. She had a scent—warm, willowy, womany—that reached him as she moved about, putting her hat back on, driving the hatpin into place, closing the hamper, getting to her feet and swatting at her wrinkled skirts. She reached for the hamper but he reached, too.

"I'll get it," he said, expecting Iversen to rise and join them. When he didn't, Harken said, "Well, are you going to sit there all day, or are you going to see the lady back to her boat?"

Iversen got to his feet and said, "I'll put the blanket away." He took one of Lorna's hands. "Goodbye, Miss Lorna." He kissed it and said, "Good luck with your father."

Jens and Lorna left Tim shaking out the Indian blanket as they turned and walked, shoulder to shoulder, from the cool shade into the hot sun, across the shifting sand, onto the long wooden dock.

There were things he wanted to say, but knew he could not. She had said she must be home in two hours, yet more than two hours had passed and she seemed in little hurry. She walked like a woman reluctant to reach her boat. Turning his gaze, he granted himself one last study of her face. Downcast, it was, her chin lowered, creating a delicate pillow underneath and a puffed profile of her lips. Pinpricks of sunlight pierced her flat-brimmed bonnet and freckled her ear and jaw.

At her boat she stopped and turned, fixing him with a look so direct it could not be avoided. It entered his eyes and fragmented when it reached his chest, like a school of minnows when a rock is dropped among them.

"It's been a wonderful afternoon," she said gently, with an unmistakable note of regret at their parting. "Thank you."

"Thank *you*, Miss Lorna, for the picnic."

"I only brought it. You prepared it."

"My pleasure," he replied.

"I shall send word to you when I've spoken to my father."

He nodded silently.

Five seconds passed, motionless, bringing a faint weightlessness to both their stomachs.

"Well, goodbye," she said.

"Goodbye, miss."

She gave him her hand, and for the short spell while she stepped down into the rowboat, they knew the touch of each other's skin. Hers was soft as chamois, his tough as leather. She sat and he handed down the hamper. He knelt to untie the bow line, then reached down for the gunwale as if to push her off. Before he could do so she looked up and her bonnet brim nearly touched his chin. Their faces were very close while he knelt, motionless, above her.

"Will you be picking the strawberries tomorrow morning, then?" she inquired.

His heart gave a kick as he answered, "Yes, miss, I will."

"Then I shall have some for breakfast," she replied, and he pushed her away.

He stood on the dock watching while she rowed out stern first, then expertly turned the boat until she faced him. For a full five pulls on the oars she locked gazes with him, finally looking away to call, "Goodbye, Mr. Iversen," raising one hand and waving.

From the shadows of the trees, Tim called, "Goodbye, Miss Lorna!"

She neither smiled nor waved at Harken, nor could he make out her eyes in the shadow of her bonnet brim. Somehow he knew they were fixed on him, and he stared at her diminishing face until it was too far out to make out her features.

He thought of her that night as he lay on his narrow cot in his tiny third-floor room with its single window facing the vegetable garden. Tim had said only one thing when Harken had returned from seeing Miss Lorna off at the dock. He'd taken the pipe from his mouth, looked squarely at Jens with his one good eye, and said, simply, "Be careful, Jens."

Jens Harken would be careful, all right. In spite of all the ogling they'd done today, he wasn't fool enough to pursue even the most innocent exchange between himself and Lorna Barnett. He valued his job too much, and the proximity it gave him to men who could afford yachts and had the free time to sail them. But what in the world was she up to, trifling with the kitchen help that way? Undoubtedly she had suitors who'd be as rich as her old man someday, fluttering around the place and signing her dance cards. Richly dressed, boat-owning, acceptable young swains whom her mother greeted with a lifted cheek, her father with offers of expensive brandy when they entered the parlor.

One of them had been sitting beside her last night during dinner, Jens was sure. So what could he make of today?

She didn't seem the flirtatious type, indeed her fascination with him seemed to have grown apace as the day progressed, just as his had for her: even more reason to follow Tim's advice. A slow-growing allurement held more dangers than a quick flirtation. He'd be better off encouraging the little kitchen maid Ruby, who'd shown overt interest in him recently. Ruby's frizzy red hair and freckles put him off, however, whereas Miss Lorna's hair was a deep, rich mahogany color, with a pattern of new growth around her face. Stepping from the boat, she'd been warm, and the fine whorls had clung to her temples and neck and had teased her ears. He'd always thought fine ladies spent the bulk of their summers devising ways to keep cool. Instead, she had rowed across the lake in the heat, had removed her hat and smoothed her hair and had shared a picnic with one for whom she should at the very least have shown total indifference, at the very most, disdain. That's how it usually was: The rich disdained those they employed.

Disdain, however, seemed wholly absent from Miss Lorna Barnett's demeanor today.

Lying in his servants' quarters, remembering, Jens tried to put her from his mind. His sheets felt sticky. He tossed over, flipped his pillow to the cool side and shut his eyes, but she was there again in memory, stepping down into the boat, taking the picnic basket from his hands, lifting her heart-shaped face and inquiring if he would be picking the strawberries for her breakfast tomorrow. He recalled her biting into one, then pointing it at Tim as she spoke—a glorious, unaffected creature with eyes brown as acorns and a beguiling smile, which she'd shown less and less as the afternoon progressed.

Was she, too, lying in bed restless, recounting the afternoon's events?

M iss Lorna Barnett most certainly was. She lay on her back with her hands stacked under her head, staring at the faint shadows delineating the ceiling medallion that surrounded her gaslight. When she'd set out in the boat today she hadn't half suspected what the afternoon would bring.

Jens Harken.

She thought about his given name, the name she dare not say, for to call him by it would be to cross a demarcation line that even she, with her independent spirit, would never breach. But simply to think it brought pleasure.

Jens Harken, a kitchen odd-jobs man . . . Merciful heavens, whatever had possessed her?

She had gone to Tim's merely to learn more about boats, for they fascinated her, and even though she wasn't allowed to sail yet, she would one day. When she did she'd organize the women into a yachting club of their own, and if they could sail revolutionary new boats that skimmed the water, why shouldn't they? If her papa was too obstinate to listen to Harken's ideas, she wasn't.

Papa—that stubborn, stubborn man. She had thought at first she would delight merely in getting him to change his mind for once and listen to Harken, perhaps end up in his good graces if Harken's plan worked and the White Bear Yacht Club eventually won the regattas. But her goal had taken on a new aspect once she'd knelt in the sand and watched Harken's wide, strong hands drawing boats in the sand. How could he know all that without any formal training in naval architecture? He had convinced her his plan would work simply by the strength of his conviction. In all the time they'd spent together today she was certain the only minutes he'd lost sight of the difference in their stations was when he was slashing at the sand and talking about keel configurations. When she'd looked up into his face and asked him how he knew all that, he'd answered, "I don't know," and she'd thought, *Why, he really doesn't!* That was the moment when her fascination for him took wing.

She had knelt beside him, gazing up into his intent blue eyes and thought, *He can do this crazy thing. I know he can.* And upon the heels of that thought came another. *Oh dear, how incredibly handsome he is.*

His eyes, his face had captivated her time and time again today, try though she had to remain disinterested. Such a nice straight nose, and clear skin and a wonderful mouth, so visible without facial hair. She was accustomed to beards: All the men she knew wore beards, so Harken's shorn face had presented an almost startling novelty, apart from his handsomeness. He was muscular, too, from lifting all those blocks of ice and heavy boilers and who knew what else in the kitchen.

How long had he been here? Had he worked for them in town last winter? Had he worked here at the cottage last summer? The summer before? Why hadn't she thought to ask him? She suddenly wanted to know everything about him, about his mother and father and his trip across the ocean, and his childhood and his years on the East Coast, and especially she wanted to know how long he'd been in their kitchens, touching the foods she was served and the silverware she put in her mouth.

The thought seemed to bring her to her senses.

Abruptly she shot up in the dark, dropped her feet over the side of the bed and scratched her scalp with both hands, roughing up her hair in frustration. Lord, if only those crickets would stop. And the humidity drop. And a breeze come up! She lifted her hair from her hot nape, released a great sigh and let her shoulders slump.

She had to stop thinking of Jens Harken now. If she wanted to get spoony over a man, the one to get spoony over was Taylor DuVal. He was the one Mama and Papa intended for her to marry. She'd known it for quite a while already, even though they hadn't said so. Furthermore, twenty-four hours ago it was Taylor she couldn't wait to kiss on the front veranda. Tonight it was the kitchen help. But she'd better get that idea square out of her head!

She fell onto her side, mounding up the pillow beneath her cheek, bending one knee and pulling her nightdress up to let the air on her legs.

But she couldn't sleep. And she couldn't stop thinking of Jens Harken.

She overslept the next morning and missed breakfast. The dining room was silent and empty when she entered it, no linen on the table, no strawberries on the sideboard picked fresh by Jens Harken. The room smelled of a recent dusting with lemon oil. A new arrangement of flowers was centered on a lace runner, testifying to the fact that Levinia had been up long enough to arrange them. Lorna glanced at the passageway door to the kitchen: She could walk back there and ask for something— a logical excuse to see Harken, but a dangerous habit to form.

Instead she went into the morning room and found her mother there at her oak secretary, writing correspondence. The room, unlike the dining room, shimmered with morning light. It was decorated in shades of ivory and peach, with chintzes instead of jacquards, and French doors instead of casements. They were opened to the sunny east veranda, letting in a welcome breeze.

"Good morning, Mother."

Levinia looked up briefly, then continued writing.

"Good morning, dear."

"Where is everybody? The house seems deserted."

"Your father's gone back to the city. The aunts are on the back veranda in the shade and the girls went off to Betsy Whiting's. I'm not precisely sure where Theron is. He had his spyglass, though, so he's probably up in a tree somewhere getting his clothing dirty."

"Will Father be back tonight?"

"No, not until tomorrow."

"Oh Criminey, why not?"

"I've asked you not to use that vulgar expression, Lorna. What's so important that it can't wait a day?"

"Oh, nothing. I just wanted to talk to him." She headed for the door but Levinia stopped her.

"Just a moment, Lorna. I want to speak to you."

Lorna turned back and began explaining, "Mother, I know I said I'd be back in two hours yesterday, but it was so nice on the lake and—"

"It's not about that. Close the doors, dear."

Nonplussed, Lorna stared at her mother a moment before closing the pocket doors and crossing the room.

"It's about Saturday night," Levinia said. Her hard-edged lips looked as if they could cut glass.

"Saturday night?" Lorna lowered herself to the edge of a sofa.

Levinia sat back in her chair. "I noticed it, and Aunt Henrietta noticed it, so certainly others around the room did, too."

"Noticed what?"

"That you invited Taylor out onto the veranda." Lorna was already rolling her eyes before her mother went on, "Lorna, it simply isn't done."

"Mother, there were at least fifteen people in the room!"

"All the more reason for you to mind your manners."

"But, Mama—"

"You're the oldest, Lorna. You set the example for your sisters to follow, and frankly, dear, in this last year I've been growing more and more concerned about your flinging propriety to the winds. Now, I've talked to you about it before, but as Aunt Henrietta said—"

"Oh, blast Aunt Henrietta!" Lorna threw her hands in the air and popped to her feet. "She put a bug in your ear, I suppose. What's the matter with that woman?"

"Shh! Lorna, hold your voice down!"

Lorna lowered her voice but squared off to face her mother. "You know what Aunt Henrietta's problem is? She hates men, that's what. Aunt Agnes told me so. Henrietta had a beau she was engaged to, but he threw her over for someone else and she's hated men ever since."

"Be that as it may, she was only thinking about your welfare when she brought up the subject of you and Taylor."

"Mother, I thought you liked Taylor."

"I do, dear. Your father and I both like Taylor. As a matter of fact we've had frequent discussions about what a perfect husband Taylor would be for you."

Here it was, what Lorna had suspected.

Her mother's eyes dropped to the desktop while she lifted her pen horizontally and repeatedly touched it to her ink blotter. "I've never mentioned it before, but you're eighteen now and Taylor has been paying a lot of attention to you this summer. But Lorna, when his mother and father are in the room and you entice him onto the veranda—"

"I did not *entice* him! It was stiflingly hot in the house and the men were stoking up their cigars. And anyway, Jenny was with us every second."

"And what lesson does it teach Jenny when you take the lead in these amorous tête-à-têtes?"

"Amorous . . ." Lorna was so incensed her mouth dropped open. "Mother, I do not engage in amorous tête-à-têtes!"

"Theron has seen one of them through his spyglass."

"Theron!"

"The other night, when you and Taylor came home from the band concert."

"I'd like to ram that spyglass down Theron's gullet!"

"Yes, I'm sure you would," Levinia said, cocking her left eyebrow, dropping her preoccupation with the pen.

Lorna sank onto the arm of a sofa and said straight out, "Taylor kissed me, Mother. Is there anything wrong with that?"

Levinia folded her hands tightly on the desktop. "No, I suppose there isn't. One must expect young swains to do that, but you must never . . ." Levinia stopped and studied her joined hands as if searching for the proper phrase. She cleared her throat. Her face had turned bright scarlet, her knuckles white.

"Must never what, Mother?"

Staring at her hands, Levinia said, barely above a whisper, "Let them touch you."

Lorna, too, felt herself coloring. "Mother!" she whispered, abashed. "I wouldn't!"

Levinia met her daughter's eyes. "You must understand, Lorna, this is very difficult for a mother to say, but it's my duty to warn you. Men will try things." She reached out and touched Lorna's hand urgently. "Even Taylor. As fine a young man as he is, he'll try things, and when he does, you must withdraw immediately. You must come into the house or . . . or insist on leaving for home at once. Do you understand?"

"Yes, Mother," Lorna answered obediently. "You may trust me to do exactly that."

Levinia looked relieved. She sat back and relaxed her hands on her lap. The flush began fading from her face. "Well then, that unpleasantness is taken care of. And in the future, may I rely on you to let Taylor be the one to do the inviting during this courtship?"

"Mother, I'm not sure he's courting me."

"Oh, bosh, of course he is. He's simply been waiting for you to come of age. Now you are and I suspect things will advance quite fast this summer."

There seemed little more to say. Considering that the conversation had clearly defined Levinia's and Gideon's approval of Taylor DuVal, the room held a lingering tension.

"May I go now, Mother?"

"Yes, of course. I must finish my letters."

Lorna walked slowly to the pocket doors, rolled them open and exited the morning room in a state of total confusion. What exactly had Mother been saying? That kissing was acceptable within bounds? That men would try to press those bounds by touching? Touching where? Mother's warning had been so vague, yet her blush spoke more clearly than her implications, suggesting that nothing further could be said on the subject.

One thing, however, was sterling clear. If Mother was displeased over Lorna's suggesting she and Taylor step onto the veranda, she would positively detonate if she learned Lorna had set up an assignation with a kitchen handyman and had had a picnic with him.

Lorna made up her mind she would steer clear of the kitchen and keep herself out of a potential pickle.

The remainder of Monday passed with stultifying uneventfulness. The range of activities available to those of the female gender left Lorna bored and restless. One could garden, fill scrapbooks, collect shells, butterflies or birds' nests, read, stitch, go shopping, have lemonade on the veranda, attend chautauquas or play the piano.

Lorna thought a game of tennis sounded much more exciting, but her friend Phoebe Armfield had taken the train into Saint Paul to shop, and Lorna's sisters were at Betsy Whiting's. As for sailing, Lorna was afraid to sneak out in the catboat after returning late yesterday. There was the rowboat, of course, but without Tim and Jens Harken waiting on the opposite shore it seemed pointless. After a light noon dinner (during which she wondered if Jens had picked and washed the vegetables) Lorna napped in the hammock. She played croquet with her sisters on the lawn in the late afternoon, and caught Theron in his room just before supper, issuing a warning that if he spied on her any more she was going to store his spyglass in his thorax.

He cackled and singsonged, "Lorna's sparking Taylor! Lorna's sparking Taylor!" and clattered down the front stairs when she tried to catch and throttle him.

Finally, in the early evening, Phoebe Armfield came to Lorna's rescue. She walked over from her parents' cottage four houses down the shoreline and said, "Come over and see what I bought today."

Walking west along the shaded road that bisected the island, Lorna exclaimed, "I'm so glad you came! I thought I would die of boredom today!"

The Armfields' summer retreat was no more a "cottage" than the Barnetts'. It had seventeen rooms on fifteen acres: Phoebe's father was the second generation of a mining empire which had accumulated its original wealth selling iron ore to the steel foundaries during the building of the railroads.

Phoebe's room was perched in a turret with a view of the lake to the north. The doors of her armoire were thrown open and hung with new frocks, which Phoebe modeled for her friend, one for an upcoming moonlight sail, which the yacht club had organized, and another for a dance aboard the excursion steamer *Dispatch* the following weekend.

"I'm going with Jack." Jackson Lawless was a young man who stood to inherit his father's hardware holdings in Saint Paul. The Lawless family's cottage was located in Wildwood, across the lake.

"Are you going with Taylor?" Phoebe asked, swirling about with the dress pressed to her front. She was a petite girl with hair the color of cinnamon apples, and a bubbly disposition.

"I don't know. I suppose."

"What do you mean, you suppose? Don't you *like* Taylor?"

"Of course I do. It's just that it seems as though he's everywhere our families are, his and mine. If I didn't like him, there'd be no way to escape him."

"Well, if you don't want him just let me know. I think he's cute, and Daddy says he's smart, too. He'll take his father's millions and double them in no time."

"Phoebe, do you ever get tired of having a father who has millions?"

Phoebe halted in mid-swirl and stared at Lorna in astonishment. She hooked the hanger over the top of the armoire door and rocketed onto the bed, making it bounce.

"Lorna Barnett, what's gotten into you? Are you saying you'd rather be poor?"

Lorna fell backward, staring at the crocheted tester above Phoebe's bed.

"I don't know what I'm saying. I'm in a mood, that's all. But just think of it, if we didn't have all this money, would our fathers care who we chose for friends, or whether or not it was ladylike to sail and play tennis? I'm so sick and tired of being told what to do by my father. *And* my mother!"

"I know. So am I." Phoebe became suddenly gloomy. "Sometimes I get like you. I want to just *do something!* To assert myself and make them realize I'm eighteen years old and I shouldn't have to live by all their silly rules."

Lorna studied her friend, suddenly bursting with her secret. Smugly she divulged, "I did something."

Phoebe came out of her torpor. "What? Lorna Barnett, tell me! What did you do?"

Lorna sat up, her eyes bright. "I'll tell you, but you must promise not to tell another living soul, because if my father found out he'd put me in a convent."

"I promise I won't tell." Phoebe crossed her heart and pressed forward eagerly. "What did you do?"

"I had a picnic with our kitchen handyman."

Phoebe's eyes and mouth formed three O's and stayed that way until Lorna put a finger beneath her chin and pushed.

"Close your mouth, Phoebe."

"Lorna, you didn't!"

"Oh, it's not the way it sounds. Tim Iversen was there, too, and we talked about boats; but Phoebe, it's so exciting! Harken thinks he can—"

"Harken?"

"Jens Harken, that's his name. He thinks he can design a boat that will revolutionize yacht racing. He says it'll beat anything on the water, but none of the yacht club members will listen to him. He actually went so far as to put a note in my father's dessert on Saturday night, and Papa got so angry he created a deplorable scene."

"So that's what it was all about! Everyone on the island is talking about it."

Lorna filled in the rest of the story, from her mother's and father's argument in the kitchen passage to her plans to intercede with her father on Harken's behalf.

When she finished, Phoebe asked, "Lorna, you aren't going to see him again, are you?"

"Goodness no. I told you, I'm just going to encourage Papa to listen to him. And besides, Mother spoke to me this morning about Taylor. She and Papa think he'd be the perfect match for me."

"And of course he is. You've told me so yourself."

Lorna, however, looked thoughtful. Her gaze rested on the crocheted bedspread as she unconsciously hooked it again and again with a fingernail and let it pull away.

"Phoebe, may I ask you something?"

"Of course . . ." Phoebe became concerned at Lorna's quick reversal of mood and touched her friend's hand. "What is it, Lorna?"

Lorna continued staring at the spread. "It's something Mother said to me this morning and it's . . . well, it's very confusing." Lorna raised her disturbed gaze and asked, "Has Jack ever kissed you?"

Phoebe blushed. "A couple of times."

"Has he ever . . . well, touched you?"

"Touched me? Of course he's touched me. The first time he kissed me he was holding me by my shoulders and the second time he put his arms around me."

"I don't think that's what Mother meant, though. She said that men would try to touch women—even Taylor—and that if he tried I must immediately come into the house. Mother was terribly embarrassed when she said it. Her face was so red I thought she might pop her collar button. But I don't know what she meant. I just thought maybe . . . well, maybe you'd know."

Phoebe's expression had turned sickly. "Something's going on, Lorna, because my mother had the same kind of talk with me one day this spring, and she got the same way, all red in the face and looking everywhere in the room but at me."

"What exactly did she say?"

"She said that I was a young lady now, and that when I went out with Jack I must always keep my legs crossed."

"Keep your legs crossed! What does that have to do with anything?"

"I don't know. I'm just as confused as you are."

"Unless . . ."

The flabbergasting thought struck them both at once. They stared at each other, unwilling to believe it.

"Oh no, Lorna, that's not possible." They considered awhile before Phoebe asked, "What did your mother say again?"

Neither of the girls realized they were whispering.

"She said that Taylor might try to touch me and I must not let him. What did your mother say?"

"She said when I'm with Jack I must keep my legs crossed."

Lorna put her fingertips to her lips and whispered, "Oh dear, they couldn't have meant there, could they?"

Phoebe whispered, "Of course they didn't mean there. Why would a man do such a thing?"

"I don't know, but why did our mothers blush?"

"I don't know."

"Why are we whispering?"

Phoebe shrugged.

After some more silent rumination, Lorna suggested, "Maybe you could ask Mitchell sometime."

"Are you crazy! Ask my brother!"

"No, I guess that's not such a good idea."

"He can teach us to sail whenever we can sneak out to do it, but I'd go to my grave ignorant before I'd ask him anything about something like this."

"All right, I said it wasn't such a good idea. Who else could we ask?"

Neither of them could think of a soul.

"Somehow," Lorna ventured, "this is all tied up with kissing."

"I suspected the same thing, but Mother never warned me not to kiss."

"Neither did mine, even when she found out I had been. That little pissant Theron was spying on me and Taylor and he told Mother. That's what started all this."

"Lorna, have you ever seen your mother and father kissing?"

"Heavens no. Have you?"

"Once. They were in the library and they didn't know I had come around the doorway."

"Did they say anything?"

"Mother said, 'Joseph, the children.' "

" 'Joseph, the children'? That's all?"

Phoebe shrugged.

"Did he touch her?"

"He was holding her by the tops of her arms."

Silence again while the girls stared at their skirts, then at each other, coming up with nothing. First Lorna turned onto her back. Then Phoebe followed suit.

They stared upward a long time before Lorna said, "Oh, it's so confusing."

"And mysterious."

Lorna sighed.

And Phoebe sighed.

And they wondered when and how the mystery would be solved.

Chapter 4

The moonlight sail was rained out, forcing Lorna to postpone the talk with her father until Saturday night, when both she and Tim Iversen would be attending the dance aboard the steamer *Dispatch*.

She dressed in a gown of rich silk organdy in vibrant petunia pink. Its basque was trimmed with white point guipure lace and was shaped by graceful bretelles that erupted into billows upon her shoulders and met in points at the center waist, both front and back. The skirt, fitted in front, broke into pleats that fell behind and caught her heels in a miniature train as she crossed her bedroom to her dressing table.

The children's maid, Ernesta, was positively abysmal at dressing hair, especially at creating the new "Gibson girl" poufs, which Lorna herself had practiced for long hours before mastering, so Ernesta had been dismissed to see after Theron's supper while Lorna was preparing for the dance.

Jenny and Daphne had drawn up stools and sat flanking Lorna while she put the finishing touches on her hair. The younger girls watched, transfixed, while, with curling tongs, Lorna created a haze of fine corkscrews around her face and nape. She pulled at them, frowning as they sprang back, then with a wet fingertip touched a bar of soap and stuck two curls to her skin.

"Gosh, Lorna, you're so lucky," Jenny said.

"You'll be allowed at the dances, too, as soon as you're eighteen."

"But that's two whole years," Jenny whined.

Daphne crossed her wrists over her heart and faked a swoon. "And who will she *drooool* over when Taylor DuVal is already married to you?"

"You just shut up, Daphne Barnett!" Jenny retorted.

"Girls, stop it now and help me pin this in my hair." Lorna held up a cluster of silk sweet peas trimmed with wired teardrop pearls. Jenny won the honors and secured it in Lorna's hair while Lorna donned pearl earbobs and atomized her throat with orange-blossom cologne.

The final results awed even Daphne, who crooned, "Gosh, Lorna, it's no wonder Taylor DuVal is sweet on you."

Rising, Lorna petted Daphne on both plump cheeks, nearly touching her nose to nose. "Oh, Daph, you're so sweet." The two younger girls adulated their older sister as Lorna made her taffeta-lined train whistle across the floor to the free-standing cheval mirror. Posing before it, she pressed her skirt flat to her belly and twisted to see what she could of her train.

"I guess that'll do."

Jenny rolled her eyes and crossed the floor, playfully aping her older sister, lifting an invisible skirt, dipping her shoulders gracelessly. "La-dee-da . . . I guess that'll do." Turning serious, she added, "You'll be the prettiest girl on that boat, Lorna, and don't pretend you don't know it."

"Oh, who cares about being pretty anyway? I'd rather be adventurous and sporting and interesting. I'd rather be the organizer of the first women's yachting club in the state of Minnesota or hunt wild tigers in the velds of Africa. If I could do that nobody would say, 'There goes Lorna Barnett, isn't she pretty?' They'd say, 'There goes Lorna Barnett, who sails as well as the men and hunts with the best of them. Did you hear she has a dozen loving cups on her mantel and the head of a tiger mounted above it?' That's what kind of woman I'd like to be."

"Well, good luck, because Papa would mount *your* head above the mantel if he found out you'd ever gone to Africa hunting. In the meantime, I guess you'll just have to settle for being Taylor DuVal's dance partner."

Lorna took pity on Jenny and petted her cheeks, too. "You're sweet, too, Jenny, and I'll tell Taylor that if you were eighteen years old you'd let him sign your dance card several times tonight, how is that?"

"Lorna Barnett, don't you *dare* tell Taylor such a thing! I'd positively die of mortification if you uttered one single word to him!"

Laughing, taking her ivory fan, waggling three fingers in farewell, Lorna swept from the room.

In the hallway she encountered Aunt Agnes just stepping out of her room.

"Oh my, it's little Lorna. Stop a minute and let me have a look." She took Lorna's hands and held them out from her sides. "Land, don't you look radiant. All grown up and off to the dance."

Lorna executed a twirl for her. "On the boat."

"With that young man Mr. DuVal, I expect." Aunt Agnes's eyes grew twinkly.

"Yes. He's meeting me at the dock."

"He's a handsome one, that one. I expect when he sees you he'll want to fill every spot on your dance card."

"Shall I let him?" Lorna teased.

Aunt Agnes's expression grew mischievous. "That depends on who else asks. Why, when I was being courted by Captain Dearsley I made certain I always danced with others, just to keep him guessing, though no one could dance like he." With a rapturous expression, she closed her eyes and tilted her head. One hand touched her heart, the other drifted into the air. "Ah, we would waltz until the room fairly spun, and the gold fringe on his epaulettes would sway and we would smile at each other and it would seem the violins were playing for us alone."

Lorna took Captain Dearsley's place and waltzed Aunt Agnes along the upstairs hall, humming "Tales from the Vienna Woods." Together they swirled, smiling,

Lorna's gown rustling, both of them singing, "Da-dum, da-dum, da-dum . . . da daaa . . ."

"Oh Aunt Agnes, I'll bet you were the belle of the ball."

"I once had a dress very nearly the color of yours and Captain Dearsley said it made me look exactly like a rosebud. The night I first wore it he was dressed all in white, and I daresay every woman at the dance wished she were in my shoes."

They waltzed on. "Tell me about your shoes. What were they like?"

"They weren't shoes, they were slippers. White satin high-heeled slippers."

"And your hair?"

"It was deep auburn then, swept up into side clusters, and Captain Dearsley said at times it picked up the color of the sunset and shot it back at the sky."

Someone ordered, "Agnes, let that girl go! Her parents are waiting for her in the porte cochere!"

The waltzing stopped. Lorna turned to find her aunt Henrietta standing at the top of the stairs.

"Aunt Agnes and I were just reminiscing."

"Yes, I heard. About Captain Dearsley again. Honestly, Agnes, Lorna isn't the least bit interested in your witless fantasies about that man."

"Oh, but I am!" Aunt Agnes had clasped her hands as if about to wring them together. Lorna commandeered them for one more squeeze. "I wish you were coming to the dance tonight, and Captain Dearsley, too. Taylor would sign your dance card, I'm sure, and just imagine—we could exchange partners for a waltz!"

Aunt Agnes kissed her cheek. "You're a darling girl, Lorna, but this is your time. You just run along now and have a grand evening."

"I shall. And what are you going to do?"

"I have some flowers to press, and I thought I just might wind up the music box and listen to a disc or two."

"Well, have a nice evening. I shall tell Taylor that a little rosebud sent her hello." She bowed formally from the waist. "And thanks ever so much for the waltz." As she whisked by Henrietta, who wore her perennially scolding expression, Lorna said, "When Aunt Agnes cranks up the music box, why don't you ask her to dance?"

Aunt Henrietta made a sound as if she was clearing her nostrils, and Lorna went down the stairs.

She rode to the dance with her parents in their open landau. The ride took mere minutes, for Manitou Island itself was a scant mile long and covered only fifty-three acres. It was connected to land by a short arched wooden bridge, three blocks beyond which began a string of stunning lakeside hotels, giving way to the town of White Bear Lake itself.

Crossing the Manitou Bridge, the horses' hooves created a melodious echo, which turned blunt as the carriage swung southwest onto Lake Avenue. The evening was glorious, eighty degrees and golden. Beneath the trees contouring the lakeshore winsome ribbons of shadow stretched eastward toward the azure water. Overhead, white gulls hung like kites, while out on West Bay sailboats skimmed.

Lorna was watching them when Gideon, in formal black, with his hands crossed on the head of a brass walking stick, remarked, "Your mother tells me that she spoke to you about Taylor."

"Yes, she did."

"Then you know our feelings regarding him. I'm given to understand you're to be under Taylor's escort at the dance tonight."

"Yes, I am."

"Excellent."

"But that doesn't mean I won't dance with others, Papa."

Gideon glowered and his moustache bounced as he replied, "I don't want you doing anything that will give Taylor the idea you don't want to marry him."

"Marry him? Papa, he hasn't even asked me."

"Be that as it may, he's an ambitious young fellow, and a good-looking one, too, I might add."

"I'm not saying he isn't ambitious or good-looking. I'm saying you and Mother are putting words in his mouth."

"The man has been dancing attendance on you all summer. Don't worry, he'll ask."

Since tonight was not the time she wanted to irritate her father, Lorna prudently let the subject drop as they approached their destination.

The *Saint Paul Globe* had recently reported that the village of White Bear Lake was home to more wealth than any other town in the United States of America. When the Barnett landau pulled up, the scene that greeted them might well have illustrated the article. The members of the yacht club had chartered the steamer *Dispatch* for the dance. It waited beside the Hotel Chateaugay dock, where a crowd had already gathered beneath the roof of the dock gazebo.

Across the street the hotel itself reigned over Lake Avenue with its commanding view of the water. Turreted and gabled, it was painted white with green shutters and had a vast veranda that overlooked a finely shaded lawn dappled with hammocks and iron benches. Tonight the scene was studded with the jeweled hues of ladies' frocks, while their escorts in penguin colors paid dotage at their sides. On the street liveried carriage drivers drew up matched pairs and set wooden carriage blocks on the cobbles for the alighting gentry. The sound of hoofbeats mingled with the measured burps of the *Dispatch*'s engine, while liveried footmen hurried to scrape into their tin carry-aways any offensive nuggets dropped by the horses before the ladies' noses became offended or their trains tainted. From the upper deck of the *Dispatch* came the music of violins and oboes as a small orchestra struck into "The Band Played On," the signal for boarding.

Taylor spotted Lorna the moment she alighted. He left his parents and came from the shade of the hotel lawn wearing a broad smile.

"Lorna," he said, "how lovely you look." Taking her gloved hand, he bowed and kissed it. Like a proper gentleman, he immediately released it and greeted her parents.

"Mr. Barnett, Mrs. Barnett, you're both looking splendid this evening. Mother and Father are over on the lawn."

When the elder Barnetts had sashayed away, Taylor reclaimed Lorna's hand. "Miss Barnett." His eyes wore an especially appreciative light. "You look as delicious as an ice-cream sundae, all pink and white and smelling delectable, I might add."

"Orange blossom. And you're looking and smelling wonderful yourself."

"Sandalwood," he rejoined, and they both laughed as he offered his elbow.

He was an attentive partner, and undeniably attractive. As they boarded the *Dispatch* Lorna noted more than one gaze returning to them. Taylor's dark brown beard and moustache were trimmed to perfection, little disguising his firm jawline and attractive mouth. His nose had a faint crookedness that seemed to disappear in bold sunlight, but had its own engaging appeal when hit by shadows from a certain angle. His eyes were hazel and his brown hair parted just off-center, combed back above well-shaped if extraordinarily large ears. He did look attractive tonight, in his dress blacks with a white winged collar pushing up firmly against his throat.

Lorna told him, "My aunt Agnes sends her fondest hello. She wishes she could be here tonight."

"She's a darling."

"She and I had a waltz in the upper hall before I left."

He laughed and said, "If I may be permitted, you, Miss Lorna Barnett, are a darling, too."

Arm in arm, they boarded the boat.

Phoebe was already aboard with Jack Lawless and came to brush Lorna's cheek and say hello. When Taylor took Phoebe's hand in greeting she pinkened but declared, "I swear you two do turn heads." She smiled briefly at Lorna, much longer at Taylor. "But even so, I hope you won't forget, Taylor, that the rest of us plain Janes would like a dance sometime tonight."

Taylor replied, "All I need is a sharp pencil." He caught the one dangling from Phoebe's dance card while Jack, in return, signed Lorna's and suggested they all repair to the upper deck, where the band had struck into "Beautiful Dreamer."

Upstairs, the seven P.M. sun was blinding. A forward bell clanged twice and a moment later a thump and lurch sent the boat under way. The stutter of the engine quickened. The smoky blue smell of naphtha exhaust lifted momentarily, then the craft eased away from shore and the air freshened. The breeze fluttered Lorna's curls and ruffled her skirt. She shaded her eyes and searched for Tim, spotting him finally when the launch turned eastward and eased the golden glare.

"Tim!" she called, waving and moving toward him.

"Good evening, Miss Lorna," he greeted, removing the pipe from his mouth, his good eye assessing her squarely while the other seemed to look out over the aft rail.

"Oh, Tim, I'm so glad you're here."

"I told you I'd be here, didn't I?"

"I know, but plans can change. We'll talk to my father tonight, won't we?"

"My, you are impatient, aren't you?"

"Please, Tim, don't tease me. Will you do it tonight?"

"Of course. Jens is as impatient as you are to see what Gideon will say."

"But listen, Tim, let's not speak to him until the sun goes down and it gets cooler, because Papa hates the heat. And by that time he'll have drunk a couple of mint juleps, which will have taken the edge off his everlasting urge to dissent. Agreed?"

Tim leaned back from the waist, smiling at her speculatively.

"Do you mind if I ask, Miss Lorna, what stake you have in this? Because, as I remarked earlier, you seem unduly impatient to reverse your father's opinion of young Harken."

Lorna's eyes took on the roundness of professed innocence. Her lips opened, closed, then opened again. She tried valiantly to remain composed and keep her cheeks from coloring. Finally she replied, "Suppose he's right and his boat beats everything on the water?"

"You're sure that's the only reason you're pursuing this?"

"Why, of course. What other possible reason could there be?"

"Could I be wrong, or did I detect a faint attraction between the two of you on Sunday?"

Lorna's cheeks most definitely flared. "Oh, Tim, for goodness' sake, don't be silly. He's kitchen help."

"Yes, he is. And I feel obliged to remind you of that, because I am, after all, a friend to both your father and Jens Harken."

"I know. But please, Tim, don't mention anything about the picnic."

"I promised I wouldn't."

"You know my father," she said, squeezing his sleeve in appeal. "You know how he is about us girls. We're nothing to him but fluffy empty-headed matrimonial material to whom he gives orders which he expects to have obeyed without incident. Just once, Tim, just *once* I'd like my father to look at me as if he knew I had a brain in my head, as if he knew I had wishes and aspirations that go beyond catching a husband and running a house and raising children the way Mama's done. I'd like to sail. Papa won't let me sail. I'd like to attend college. Papa says it's unnecessary. I'd like to travel to Europe. He says I can do that on my honeymoon. Don't you understand, Tim? There is no way on this earth for a woman to gain an advantage on Papa. Well, maybe—just maybe—I might change that if he listens to Harken and finances his boat. And if it should win, might Papa not at long last consider me in a new light?"

Tim covered her hand on his sleeve with his own. The bowl of his pipe was warm against her knuckles as he gave her hand a squeeze.

"When you're ready to talk to Gideon, you give me a little whistle."

She smiled and let her hand slide from Tim's sleeve, and thought what a truly nice man he was.

She danced with Taylor and Jack, and Percy Tufts and Phoebe's father; with Taylor again, and once with Tim, and yet again with Taylor and with Phoebe's brother, Mitchell, who inquired how her sailing was coming along and offered to take her out for another lesson anytime she wanted. Though Mitchell was two years her junior, she detected an interest in her that went beyond nautical instructions, and found herself surprised by it, for she'd always thought of him as Phoebe's little tag-along brother, much as she'd thought of Theron. Mitchell had, however, grown tall, his shoulders had broadened, and he was doing his best to begin growing a beard, which presently had the appearance of a mouse with mange. When he released her and turned her over to Taylor, he gave her hand a secret squeeze.

The sun set behind a bank of violet clouds with brilliant pink and gold edges. The air cooled. The *Dispatch* cruised leisurely around all three petals of the clover-shaped lake, and the gentlemen's cigar coals burned red as lava against the fallen night.

Again Lorna danced with Taylor while her father observed with an expression of smug approval on his face. She smiled up at her escort for Gideon's benefit, wondering all the while if a flat-bottomed boat could keep upright, and how long it would take to build one, and if Jens Harken knew what he was talking about, and what he was doing at Rose Point Cottage at this moment, and if he had some young kitchen maid he was wooing, and where he might take her to do so.

Across Taylor's shoulder she noted that Tim Iversen had moved over to Gideon and struck up a conversation. When the dance ended she requested, "Leave me with Papa, would you, Taylor? And come back to get me after two songs or so?"

"Of course." As he walked her toward Gideon, under cover of darkness, his fingers rode the notch above her hip and his hand kneaded the shallows of her spine, alarmingly close to her right buttock. It shot blood to her cheeks and sent strange impulses racing along her spine. She started when he spoke close to her ear. "You don't mind if I ask his permission to drive you home, do you?"

"Of course not," she replied, certain that this was some of the touching her mother had warned her about, and surprised that it had begun right under her father's nose. She had expected such things occurred only under the most dark and clandestine of circumstances.

"Mr. Barnett," Taylor said, delivering her to her father. "Do you have any objection to my driving Lorna home tonight?"

Gideon removed a cigar from his mouth and cleared his throat. "No objection whatsoever, my boy."

"I'll be back," Taylor said quietly, and disappeared.

Tim told Lorna, "Your father and I were talking about next year's regatta."

Bless your heart, Tim, Lorna thought.

Gideon said, "It seems Tim here has got wind of that harebrained scheme our kitchen handyman came up with about how to build a faster boat. Seems the two of them have done some sailing together."

"Yes, I know. Tim and I talked about it on Sunday."

"So I heard. Clear across the lake you rowed."

"It was such a heavenly day, I couldn't resist. And I had enough food for two, so I shared my picnic with Tim and we got to talking about Harken's ideas."

Tim took over. "The fellow says the scow will plane, Gideon. And it makes a lot of sense to me that if it doesn't have to cut through so much water it'll be faster than the sloops by far. If I were you, I'd give Harken a listen."

"When everybody else laughed him away?"

Lorna put in, "But supposing, after they did, that you were the only one who'd listen, and Harken's scheme worked. You are, after all, the commodore of this yacht club. If his boat does what he says it will do, you could be immortalized."

Gideon puffed on his cigar and pondered. He loved being reminded he was commodore, except when being reminded as he'd been by last week's newspapers, which listed him as commodore of the losing yacht club. Those articles, accompanied by Tim's pictures, had undoubtedly been featured as far away as the East Coast, for the country was closely watching the heartland and following the formation of the Inland Lake Yachting Association, which was still in its infancy.

"Papa, listen," Lorna reasoned. "Look around you. There's more wealth on this very launch than can ever be spent in your lifetime. What good is all that money if you don't enjoy it? You won't even miss the piddling few hundred dollars it'll cost to finance the building of this boat. And if it capsizes, so what? Harken said—to Tim, that is—that it won't sink. It'll have a cedar hull instead of a metal-clad one, and the masts will be hollow, so they'll float. And he says that if she did go over, a five-man crew could right her like nothing, even without sandbags!"

They let silence drift awhile before Tim added, "He says a thirty-eight-footer will go eighteen hundred pounds instead of the usual twenty-five hundred. Can you imagine what a boat that light could do with a little wind, Gideon?"

"All we're suggesting, Papa, is that you talk to him."

"He can explain it a lot better than I can, Gid."

"And if you don't think his ideas have merit, don't put up the money. But he's your best chance to win next year and you know it."

Gideon cleared his throat, spit over the rail and flicked his ashes into the water. "I'll think about it," he told the two of them, and whisked the air with his fingers as if brushing crumbs from his lap. "Now go away and quit pestering me, Lorna. This is a dance. Go on and dance with young Taylor."

She grinned and curtsied playfully. "Yes, Papa. So long, Tim."

When she was gone, Gideon remarked to Tim, "That girl is up to something, and I'm damned if I know what it is."

The *Dispatch* docked at a quarter past eleven. Gas lanterns illuminated the gazebo as the yacht club members disembarked and broke into smaller groups. Some of the older set decided to take aperitifs and desserts at the Hotel Chateauguet. Lorna's and Taylor's parents went off with them. Lorna bid good night to Phoebe, and Taylor took her arm.

"The carriage is over here," he said.

"Do you have to come back and get your parents?" she asked.

"No. We took separate rigs."

They sauntered along the street beneath puddles of gaslight. Behind them the chugging of the naphtha launch quieted for the night. In the yard of the hotel the hammocks hung empty like cocoons whose inhabitants had flown. The smell of the lakeshore mingled with that of horses as they passed the row of sleeping animals still hitched to their conveyances. Several rigs went past, hoofbeats fading into the darkness as Taylor handed Lorna into the buggy, stepped to the side of the horse and tightened her bellyband, then boarded the rig himself.

"It's a little cool," he said, twisting around and reaching behind them. "I think I'll put the bonnet up." A moment later the light from a half-moon was cut off and the scent of leather freshened as the bonnet spread above their heads.

Taylor took up the reins and flicked them, but the horse set off at a lethargic walk.

"Old Tulip is lazy tonight. She doesn't like being awakened from her nap." He looked down at Lorna. "Do you mind?"

"Not at all. It's a heavenly night."

They plodded back to Manitou Island at the pace Tulip herself set, sometimes riding in deep shadow, sometimes turning into a plash of moonlight that turned Lorna's bodice lavender. On the island itself they passed beneath an allée of old elms that cut off any wink of light from overhead. The single road bisected the island, dividing its properties into northshore and southshore sites, each with its grand cottage and surrounding lawns viewed from the rear side through deeply wooded backlots. They passed the Armfields' but turned off the road well short of Rose Point, into a trail so narrow the spokes of the carriage wheels fanned the underbrush.

"Taylor, where are we going?"

"Just up ahead, where we can see the water. Whoa, Tulip."

The buggy stopped in a small clearing, facing the moonlight, with a bit of lakeshore visible through the willows ahead, and the backside of an outbuilding to their left. Somewhere in the nearby dark a horse whinnied.

"Why, we're out behind the Armfields' stable, aren't we?"

Taylor set the brake and tied the reins around its handle.

"Yes, we are. If we peered really hard through the trees we might even see Phoebe's bedroom light."

Taylor relaxed and stretched one arm along the back of the tufted leather seat while Lorna leaned forward, searching for Phoebe's light.

"I don't see it."

Taylor smiled and brushed her bare shoulder with the back of one finger.

"Taylor, there are mosquitoes out here."

"Yes, I suppose there are, but there are no little brothers or sisters." Indulgently he drew her back into the carriage, took her left hand and began patiently removing her glove. He did the same with her right and, when it was bare, held it in his own and searched her face.

"Taylor," she whispered, her heart racing, "I really should go home."

"Whenever you say," he murmured and shut out the moonlight with his head as his arms circled her and his mouth descended to take a first kiss. His beard was soft, his lips warm, his chest firm as he drew her against it. She put her arms around him and felt herself tipped and twined just so, until their fit became exquisite and Taylor opened his mouth wider. The heat and wetness of his tongue sent all thoughts of mosquitoes and Phoebe's light from her mind. He moved his head, slewing it in some canny motion that created magic within their joined mouths. Above her hip his right hand rested, kneading in counterpoint to his searching tongue. Somewhere in the distant rim of consciousness a bullfrog barked, and nearer, beneath the bonnet hood, the predicted mosquitoes arrived, buzzing, buzzing, landing, being brushed away while the kiss went on and on.

Its reluctant ending left them breathless, with their foreheads and noses touching.

"Am I forgiven for stealing you away into the woods?" he asked, nipping at her lips.

"Oh, Taylor, you've never kissed me like that before."

"I've wanted to. I knew from the moment you got out of your father's carriage tonight that I'd bring you here. How long do you think our parents will spend over dessert?"

"I don't know," she murmured.

His mouth descended once again, and hers lifted to meet it. With the second kiss his hands moved over her ribs and back as if chafing her warm after a thorough chilling. This, she supposed, could be none of the touching her mother had warned about, for it felt sublime and left her with no desire to run into the house.

Taylor ended the kiss himself, upon a grunt of amiable frustration, while thrusting both arms around her waist and reversing their positions, so she cut off the moonlight from his face. Listing to one side, he sprawled across the buggy seat and bent her forward atop his breast. "Lorna Barnett," he said against her neck, "you're the prettiest creature God ever put on this earth and you smell good enough to eat."

He licked her neck, surprising her and bringing out a giggle.

"Taylor, stop that." She tried to shrug him away, but his tongue made a hot wet spot and raised the scent of her orange-blossom perfume like a soft southern breeze through the soft northern night. She quit resisting and closed her eyes. "That must"—she struggled for breath—"taste awful." She tipped her head to accommodate him and felt a thrill shoot its warning from her middle. He bit her lightly, as stallions nip mares in the spring, and took her earlobe between his lips and suckled it before moving round to her lips again.

"Simply awful . . ." he murmured, transferring the taste of her own perfume from his tongue to hers. Where he led, she followed, opening her mouth to revel in exciting sensations. Kissing with open mouths . . . What a wondrous and mesmerizing convention. His hand on her side opened wide and his thumb moved across the silk of her bodice, its tip grazing the underside of her breast, sending delightful shivers everywhere.

She freed her mouth and whispered shakily, "Taylor, I must go home . . . please . . ."

"Yes . . ." he whispered, pursuing her mouth with his own, his thumb clearly stroking the underside of her breast. ". . . So must I."

"Taylor, please . . ."

He was showing signs of resisting when a mosquito came and took a drink out of his forehead. When he slapped it Lorna righted herself on the buggy seat, putting space between them though her skirt remained caught on his pantleg.

"I don't want my mother and father to beat me home, Taylor."

"No, of course not." He straightened up and ran both hands over the sides of his hair. "You're right."

She drew her skirt aright and tugged her bodice down all around, touched her hair and asked, "Am I mussed?"

With his hand he turned her face his way. His gaze, wearing a likable grin, went all around her hairline and came to rest on her mouth. "No one will guess," he answered. When she would have withdrawn, he held her as she was, swaying a thumb across her chin. "So very shy," he said. "I find that immensely attractive." He kissed the end of her nose. "Miss Barnett," he teased, "you may find me hanging around your doorstep a lot this summer."

She gazed up at him with the wonderment of a young woman led for the first time into the seductive realm of carnality, overcome by it and by him for being the first to teach her.

"Mr. DuVal," she replied without guile, "I certainly hope so."

Chapter 5

————— ⚬⚬⚬ —————

On Tuesday afternoon following the dance aboard the *Dispatch,* a small drawstring bag containing Levinia Barnett's loose change was delivered to the kitchen with orders that the coins were to be washed in soap and water. Jens Harken was busy doing so when the housekeeper, Mary Lovik, swept in.

She was a spare woman with a face like a waffle, fluted by its severe expression that reduced her mouth to a third its normal size and gave her unforgiving eyes the look of a weasel. She wore a white hat shaped like a soufflé, distinguished from those of the other female help by its pleats and diminutive size. Her hair was black, her dress gray and her apron starched so stiffly it gave off a *whang* like sheet metal when she walked.

Mrs. Lovik never moved amid her underlings without an air of self-importance. In the echelon of household help, she presided at the top, along with Chester Poor, the butler; everyone else fell beneath her, and she took contrary pleasure in reminding them at every turn.

"Harken!" she bellowed, flapping back the kitchen door and sweeping inside. "Mr. Barnett would like to see you in his study."

Harken's hands went motionless in the soapy water. "Me?"

"Yes you! Do you see anyone else in this room named Harken? Mr. Barnett doesn't like to be kept waiting, so get up there immediately!"

"Yes, ma'am. As soon as I finish these coins."

"Ruby can finish. Ruby, finish washing and drying Mrs. Barnett's change, and make sure every penny gets back to her."

Harken dropped the coins into the dishpan and reached for a towel to dry his hands.

"Do you know what he wants, Lovik?"

"It's *Mrs.* Lovik to you, and most certainly I don't know what he wants, though if he dismisses you over your outspokenness about the matter of the boats I shouldn't be at all surprised. Mrs. Schmitt! Has your help nothing better to do than stand and gape when someone walks into this room? Girls, get to work. Ruby, your apron is filthy. See to it that it's changed immediately. Harken, move!"

No sooner had Harken moved than Mrs. Lovik lambasted him again as he was about to push through the swinging door. "For pity's sake, turn your cuffs down and button your collar. You can't go into the master's study looking like kitchen riffraff."

Buttoning his collar and pushing the door with his backside, he replied, "But I am kitchen riffraff, Mrs. Lovik, and he knows it."

"I don't much care for your back talk, Harken, and I may as well tell you this, too—that if it were left up to me, you'd have been gone the very night you pulled that disrespectful stunt with the master's ice cream."

"But it wasn't up to you, was it?" He gave her a shameless grin, waved an arm toward the dining room passage and said, "After you, Mrs. Lovik."

She *whanged* along in front of him, with her snout in the air and her white cap bobbing. Officiously, she led the way to the foot of the main staircase and waved him on.

"Upstairs. And make sure you go back to the kitchen immediately when the master has dismissed you."

Upstairs.

Lord in heaven, they were some stairs. He'd never been up them before nor seen the gleaming mahogany handrail nor the cherubs on the newel post. The naked little fellows held up a gaslight and smiled down at him as he ascended upon a Turkish runner of blue, red and gold. Above, an arched window with a leaded-glass header looked down over the yard, and a second pair of cherubs held up another gaslight. Reaching it, he came to a T, where he stopped and looked left and right. Doors opened off the hall in both directions, with no clue as to which led into Mr. Barnett's study.

He chose left, coming first to a bedroom, where an old gray-haired lady sat asleep in a rocking chair with a book on her lap. He remembered serving her dinner that night in the dining room. He tiptoed past and peered into a bathroom with white-and-green granite tile on the floor, a china toilet with an oak water tank high on the wall above it, a pedestal sink and a huge sleigh-shaped bathtub with lion-paw feet. It smelled flowery and had a sunny window with a white curtain. Next he came to a boy's room, its wallpaper covered with windjammers on a blue background, its bed rumpled. Already he realized he'd chosen the wrong wing, but went on nonetheless, deciding to glance into the last rooms—more than likely the only chance he'd ever get.

He reached a doorway and stopped dead still.

There was Miss Lorna Barnett, sitting on a chaise longue reading a magazine. His stomach fluttered once at the sight of her. She was caught in the crossfire of light from two windows, and her hair was untended, her feet bare, her knees forming an easel for her magazine. She wore a pale lavender skirt and a white shirtwaist with a high stovepipe collar that was unbuttoned in the warm afternoon, wilting down over her collarbones. Her room was airy, with a view of the lake and the side garden. It was trimmed in the same pale blue as the striped skirt she'd worn a week ago Sunday.

She looked up when he stopped in the hall. Surprise clutched them both and turned them momentarily to statues.

"Harken?" she whispered, wide-eyed, coming to life muscle by muscle, lowering her knees and self-consciously covering her feet with her skirt. "What are you doing up here?"

"I'm sorry to disturb you, Miss Lorna, but I'm looking for your father's study. Upstairs, I was told."

"It's in the other wing. Second to the end on your right."

"Thank you. I'll find it."

He began to move away.

"Wait!" she called, throwing her magazine aside, dropping her feet to the floor.

He waited on the hall runner while she came and stood just within the doorway of her room. Her skirt was wrinkled and her shirtwaist limp. Her toenails showed below her hem.

"Has Father asked to see you?"

"Yes, miss."

Her eyes grew excited. "To talk about the boat, I'll bet! Oh, Harken, I'm sure of it."

"I don't know, miss. All Mrs. Lovik said was that I was to get myself up to the master's study and try not to look like kitchen riffraff while I was doing it." He glanced down at his trousers with damp spots on the belly, at his coarse white cotton shirt with black suspenders slicing it in thirds. "Seems I do, though." He lifted his wrists and let them fall.

"Oh, Mrs. Lovik." Lorna flapped a hand. "She's such a sour apple. Don't pay any attention to her. If Papa asked to see you we've got him thinking, and I'm sure it's about the boat. Just remember, there's nothing Papa wants so badly as to win. Nothing. He's simply not used to losing. So be convincing and maybe we'll see your boat built yet."

"I'll try, miss."

"And don't let Papa intimidate you." She pointed a finger to enforce her order. "He'll try, but don't let him."

"Yes, miss." He held his smile to a properly subdued one. How childishly enthusiastic she was, standing there improperly dressed, with her hair looking like burgundy wine splashed against a wall. It was dark and rich and stood out everywhere as if she'd been running her fingers through it while reading. Her state of dishevelment did little to disguise her natural beauty, which shone through without benefit of hats or curls or corset stays. He remembered she had said she'd forsaken the latter, and found himself charmed by the knowledge that she'd done the same with her stockings and shoes today. She was, without a doubt, the prettiest female he'd ever known.

"Well, I'd best not keep your father waiting."

"No, I guess not." She put two hands on the doorframe and leaned her top half out into the hall to point. "Down there. The one that's closed."

"Yes. Thank you." He headed away.

"Harken?" she whispered.

He stopped and turned.

"Good luck," she whispered.

"Thank you, miss."

When he got to Gideon's study door he looked back along the hall and found her head still poking out. She waggled two fingers at him, and he raised a palm to her, then knocked. She was still watching when Gideon Barnett ordered, "Come!"

Jens Harken entered a room with high, deep windows standing open behind a comma-shaped desk. At it Gideon Barnett sat, flanked by bookshelves on either side. The study smelled of cigar smoke and leather even though a brisk afternoon breeze flapped the heavy scarlet draperies at the windows. The room was a blend of light and dark, the light coming from the afternoon sun that slanted in obliquely, missing the desk itself but striking the spines of some books and one corner of the gleaming hardwood floor. The dark hovered in the sunless corners, where brown wing chairs surrounded a low table shared by a globe, a scattering of leather-bound books and a black lacquered humidor.

"Harken," Barnett said dourly in greeting.

"Good afternoon, sir." Harken came to a halt before the desk, remaining on his feet though there were four vacant chairs in the room.

Gideon Barnett let him stand. He stuck a cigar into his mouth and held it firmly with his teeth, drew his lips back and silently studied the blond man before him. The smoke lifted up and out the window. Barnett kept puffing, testing the man's mettle, waiting for the usual fidgeting to begin. Instead Harken stood at ease, his hands at his sides, his belly wet from some menial work he'd been doing in the kitchen.

"So!" Barnett finally barked, removing his cigar. "You think you know how to build boats."

"Yes sir."

"Fast boats?"

"Yes sir."

"How many have you built?"

"Enough. In a boatworks in Barnegat Bay."

Gideon Barnett hid the fact that he was impressed: Barnegat Bay, New Jersey, was a hotbed of sailing. The boating magazines were filled with articles about it. He pursed his lips, twirled his wet cigar tip around and around between them, and wondered what to make of the young whippersnapper who refused to be cowed by him.

"But have you ever built one of these things you're ranting about?"

"No sir."

"So you don't know if she'll capsize and sink."

"I know. She won't."

"You know," Barnett scoffed. "That's some flimsy conjecture to put money on."

Harken neither moved nor replied. His face remained impassive, his eyes steady on the older man's. Barnett found himself irritated by the fellow's unflappability.

"Some people around here are putting pressure on me to hear you out."

Again Harken said nothing, raising a commensurate urge in Barnett to fluster him.

"Well, say something, boy!" he burst out.

"I can show you on paper if you understand hull design."

Barnett nearly choked on his own spittle, squelching the urge to throw the damned whelp out on his tailbone. Kitchen help intimating that *he,* Gideon Barnett, commodore of the White Bear Yacht Club, didn't understand hull design! Gideon threw down a pencil atop a stack of oversized white paper on his desktop. "Well, here! Draw!"

Harken glanced at the pencil, at Barnett, at the pencil again. Finally he picked it up, flattened one hand on the paper and began drawing. "Would you like me to come around there, sir, or will you come around here?"

A muscle in Barnett's jaw grew rigid, but he relinquished his position of superiority and walked around the desk while Harken continued drawing, one hand braced on the desk.

"The first thing you've got to understand is that I'm talking about two totally different kinds of boats here. I'm no longer talking about a displacement hull. I'm talking about a planing hull—light, flat, with very little wetted surface when it's heeled up." He went on sketching, cross-sectioning, comparing two yachts with two completely different outlines, explaining how the bow would lift when planing downwind, how the drag would be reduced when she was heeled up. He spoke of length and weight and natural lift. Of discarding the bowsprit, which would no longer be necessary because the sails would be much smaller. He spoke of gaff-rigging and sail plans and how much less they affected the scow's speed than did the overall boat shape. He spoke of a flat-bottomed sailboat without a fixed keel, something that had never been built before.

"So if there's no keel, where's your ballast?" Gideon asked.

"The crew acts as ballast, and there'll be no more need for sandbagging."

"And they alone can keep it from capsizing?"

"No, not alone. The boat will have bilgeboards." Again he drew. "Instead of one fixed keel, we use two bilgeboards—sideboards, if you will—that can be dropped or raised as needed. You drop the leeboard when you're heeling, to prevent side drift, and just before tacking you change boards—up with one and down with another. See?"

Barnett thought awhile, studying the drawings.

"And you can design it?"

"Yes sir."

"And build it?"

"Yes sir."

"Single-handedly?"

"Pretty much. I might need one other man to help when I'm bending the ribs and applying the planking."

"I don't have a man to spare."

"I'll find one if you'll pay him."

"How much would it cost?"

"The whole boat? In the neighborhood of seven hundred dollars."

Barnett considered awhile. "How long would it take you?"

"Three months. Four at the most, including the work on the interior structure and the painting. I'd need tools and a shed to work in, that's all. I can build my own steam box."

Barnett stared at the drawings, snubbed out his cigar in an ashtray and walked to the window, where he stood looking out at the lake.

"The only thing I wouldn't make are the hardware and the sails. We'd farm out the sailmaking to Chicago," Harken told him, bringing Barnett's head around. "The boat can be done by fall and the sails made over the winter. I'll rig it myself. By next spring, when the season starts, she'll be seaworthy." Harken dropped his pencil and stood erect, facing Barnett and a glimpse of blue water behind him.

When Barnett said nothing, Harken went on. "I've sailed a lot, sir. My father sailed, and his father before him, and his father before him, clear back to the Vikings, I imagine. I know this plan will work as surely as I know where my love of water comes from."

The room fell silent while Barnett went on scrutinizing the younger man. "You're pretty confident, aren't you, boy?"

"Call it what you will, sir, I know that boat will work."

Barnett joined his hands behind his back, rose onto his toes once, settled back onto his heels and said, "I'll think about it."

"Yes sir," Harken replied quietly. "Then I'd best get back to the kitchen."

All the way to the study door he could feel Barnett's eyes burning into his back, could sense the man measuring him, could feel his reluctance to place faith in one of his underlings. Also he felt the depth of Barnett's obsession to be best at whatever he undertook. Miss Lorna had said her father hated losing, and that was obvious. Jens Harken wondered, should he be given the go-ahead to build this boat and it was as fast as he believed it would be, how a winning Gideon Barnett might repay him.

He took the straightest route back, noting that Miss Lorna's door was closed, tarrying not a moment. In the kitchen everyone was sitting around the table taking an afternoon breather over white cake and mint tea. They all jumped up and began babbling at once.

"What did he say? Is he going to let you build it? Did you go up to his study? What's it like?"

"Hold it, hold it!" He held up his hands to calm the excitement. "He said he'll think about it, nothing more."

The anticipation slid off their faces.

"I've got him thinking, though," Jens offered as consolation.

"What was his study like?" Ruby asked.

While he was describing it, the door from the servants' stairway burst open and Miss Lorna Barnett breached the kitchenhold again.

"What did he say, Harken?" she demanded, breathless, still wrinkled, but with her buttons closed and her shoes on. She came full into the room, crossed it and stood among the kitchen help near the scarred worktable in the center of the room, for all the world looking as if she'd been working among them all day. Her eyes were bright as sunstruck tea, her cheeks flushed from her run down the stairs, her lips open in excitement.

"He asked me if I could build a fast boat and I said yes. He asked me to sketch it on paper, and when I did he said he'd think about it."

"Is that all?" Her excitement vanished, then changed to vehemence. "Oh, he's so stubborn!" She rapped the air once with her fist. "Did you try to convince him?"

"I did what I could. I can't twist his arm, though."

"Nobody can. My father is immovable when he wants to be." She sighed and shrugged. "Ah, well . . ."

The room grew quiet, uncomfortably so. None of the kitchen help knew quite how to react to the presence of one of the family among them.

Mrs. Schmitt thought to say, "We have some cool mint tea, miss, and white cake. Would you care for any?"

Lorna glanced at the table and replied, "Oh, yes, it sounds good."

"Ruby, fetch a glass. Colleen, go out and get more mint. Glynnis, get a tray. Harken, chip some ice for Miss Barnett, please." Everyone bustled around, following orders, leaving Lorna to stand by herself beside the table, watching. Glynnis went into the butler's pantry and returned with a gold-rimmed plate and silver tray. The second kitchen maid, Colleen, washed the mint and bruised it in a mortar and pestle. Jens Harken found an ice pick and made it flash through the air—an arresting sight that caught and held Lorna's regard while ice chips scattered like diamonds onto the slate floor. While Ruby held a glass an ice shard slid from his fingertips into it. Mrs. Schmitt was carefully arranging everything on the tea tray when she discovered Lorna still standing beside the table, waiting.

"I can send Ernesta up to your room with it, miss, or out onto the veranda, if you prefer."

Lorna glanced at Harken, then at the table and inquired, "Couldn't I eat it right here?"

"Right here, miss?"

"Why, yes. It looks as if all of you were sitting here. Can't I join you?"

Mrs. Schmitt wiped the surprise from her face and answered, "Why, if you want to, miss, yes."

Lorna sat down.

Mrs. Schmitt brought the tray forward and set the whole works—gold-rimmed plate, silver fork, long-handled spoon, cutwork linen napkin, crystal glass and silver tray—upon the beaten tabletop, where the kitchen staff's ordinary tea things had been abandoned: thick white plates, plain glasses and dull forks still stuck into unfinished pieces of cake. The centerpiece of the table consisted of a lard pot, salt bowl, a tall crock full of butcher knives, a brass dispenser holding string for tying up vegetables and the supper's cucumbers waiting to be sliced.

The room fell silent.

Ruby hesitantly set the pitcher of tea on the table and backed away.

Lorna slowly picked up her fork while a circle of faces watched, not a soul in the room moving toward their chairs. She cut into her cake and paused, feeling more out of place than ever in her life. She looked up and sent Harken a silent message of appeal.

"Well!" He came to life, clapped his hands once and rubbed them together.

"I could use another piece of that cake myself, Mrs. Schmitt, and a little more tea, too." He pulled out a stool next to Lorna's and mounted it from behind, cowboy-fashion, while reaching enthusiastically for the pitcher to pour himself a drink.

"A piece of cake it is," the head cook replied, and everyone took Harken's lead, filling the room with life once again. Ruby brought mint for him and inquired, "Don't you want ice?"

"Naw, this is fine." He refilled glasses on his side of the table, then passed the pitcher on, and soon they were all returned to their own places, taking their cues from him as he began chattering.

"So, how is Chester's father? Has anyone heard?"

"A little better. Chester says he's got his appetite back."

"And your mother, Mrs. Schmitt. I imagine you're going home to see her on Sunday?"

They talked, and ate cake, and passed a pleasant ten minutes while Lorna, internally attuned to his every motion, sat beside Jens as he downed three-quarters of a glass of tea in one tilt of the head, and ate a huge piece of cake. Afterward, he rolled up his shirt sleeves and leaned both elbows beside his empty plate and burped softly behind his curled hand. He teased Glynnis about a large sunfish she claimed to have caught, and leaned back to smile at Ruby when she came around and re-filled his glass, and in doing so accidentally nudged Lorna's shoulder. He asked Mrs. Schmitt when she was going to make sauerbraten and dumplings again, and she teased him about a fish-loving Norwegian asking for such heavy, sour German food, and they laughed good-naturedly. Straddling his stool, laughing with Mrs. Schmitt, one of his widespread knees bumped Lorna under the table. "Sorry," he said quietly, and withdrew it.

In time Mrs. Schmitt pushed back her chair and looked at the clock. "Well, there's cucumbers to soak, and cardoon to wash, and potato crulles to get cut. Time moves on."

They all stood, and Lorna said, "Well, thank you very much for the cake and tea. It was delicious."

"You're most welcome, miss. Anytime." Mrs. Schmitt picked up her own empties.

Once again movement bogged down, everyone uncertain of what protocol demanded when Mrs. Schmitt had ordered them back to work before the young miss had taken her leave. Lorna gave Mrs. Schmitt a smile, let it speed across the others and headed toward the door to the servants' stairway. Jens made sure he got there first and opened it for her. Their eyes met for the merest second as she passed through, and she gave a smile so guarded it barely moved her lips.

He nodded formally. "Good afternoon, miss."

"Thank you, Harken."

When the door had closed he found everyone but Ruby back at work. She was holding some vegetables at the zinc sink, riveting him with a disapproving stare. When he walked past her she leaned back and murmured, "So why didn't she ask her father what he said to you? Makes more sense than herself running down here to ask you."

"Mind your own business, Ruby," he replied, and walked outside to bring in the cardoon which waited in a wheelbarrow beside the back door.

The following weekend, the White Bear Yacht Club set up a local race for its own members. Twenty-two boats entered. Gideon Barnett donned his official blue yacht club sweater and skipped his *Tartar* into a second-place finish.

Afterward, in the clubhouse over a glass of rum, he grumbled to Tim Iversen, "I lost a hundred dollars to Percy Tufts on that damned race."

Tim puffed his pipe and replied, "Well, you know the answer to that."

Gideon stewed awhile and said, "Don't think I'm not considering it."

He considered until the following evening, when he spoke to Levinia about it. They were in their bedroom, ready to retire. Gideon was standing before the cold fireplace dressed in his short-legged union suit, smoking a last cigar of the day when he announced out of the blue, "Levinia, you're going to have to hire a new kitchen handyman. I'm going to set Harken to building a boat for me."

Levinia paused in the act of climbing into bed. "Not if Mrs. Schmitt threatens to quit again."

"She won't."

"How can you be so sure?" Levinia climbed onto the high mattress and settled herself against the pillows.

"Because it's only temporary. It'll take him only three, four months at most, then he'll be back in the kitchen, where he belongs. I intend to speak to him in the morning."

"Oh, Gideon, it's such a nuisance."

"Take care of it, nonetheless." He stubbed out his cigar and joined her in bed.

Levinia thought about objecting further but, fearing a reprise of what had followed the last time she'd crossed Gideon, she swallowed her aggravation and steeled herself to the fact that she'd have to go through the tiresome ritual of finding temporary help.

The following morning at nine Jens Harken was again summoned to Gideon Barnett's study. This time the room was brighter, flooded with molten sun. Barnett, however, trussed up in a three-piece suit with a gold watch fob dangling across his belly, looked as gruff and stern as ever.

"All right, Harken, three months! But you build me a boat that'll beat those damned Minnetonka sandbaggers and anything on this lake, is that understood?"

Harken repressed a smile. "Yes sir."

"And when it's done you'll go back to the kitchen."

"Of course."

"Tell Mrs. Schmitt I'm not taking you away forever. I don't want any more blowups out of her."

"Yes sir."

"You can set up shop in the shed behind the glasshouse and gardens. I'll leave word with my friend Matthew Lawless that you'll be coming into his hardware and that you're to be given carte blanche buying any tools you need. Take the train into

Saint Paul as soon as you've checked out of the kitchen. Steffens will drive you to the station. The hardware is on Fourth and Wabasha. As for lumber, same goes there—carte blanche here in town at Thayer's. You know where that is, don't you?"

"Yes sir. But if it's all the same to you, I prefer to pay for some of the lumber myself—whatever I'll need for the molds."

Barnett looked taken aback. "Why?"

"I'll want to keep them when they're finished."

"Keep them!"

"Yes sir. I hope to build a boat of my own someday, and the molds are reusable."

"Very well. Then about drafting tools . . ." Barnett scratched his brow, thinking.

"I have those, sir."

"Oh." Barnett dropped his hand. "Yes, yes of course. Well then." He put on his fiercest scowl and stood erect. "You answer strictly to me from now on, is that understood?"

"Yes sir. May I hire someone to help me when the time comes?"

"Yes, but only for the weeks it's absolutely necessary."

"I understand."

"You can eat your meals with the kitchen help the same as always and I'll expect you to work the same hours you did before."

"Sundays, too, sir?"

Barnett looked piqued by the request but replied, "Oh, all right, every Sunday off."

"And as far as going into town immediately, I'd rather have a look at the shed first, sir, if I may."

"Then let Steffens know when you'll need him."

"I will. And the train fare, sir?"

Barnett's mouth became pinched, his face ruddy. His upper lip appeared to tremble beneath his great drooping moustache.

"You will push and push until a man has all he can do to keep from throwing you out of the house, won't you, Harken? Well, I'm warning you, kitchen boy . . ." He pointed at him with a finger coiled tightly around a cigar. "Don't exceed your bounds with me or that's exactly where you'll find yourself." From his waistcoat pocket he withdrew a coin and dropped it onto his desktop. "There's your train fare, now go."

Harken picked up the fifty-cent piece, thinking he'd be damned if he'd dish out of his own pocket to make this rich man richer. He had plans for every fifty cents he could manage to save and they didn't include working in a kitchen until he was as old as Mrs. Schmitt. Furthermore, he understood something else about his employer: A man in his position wanted the esteem of his peers, and the household staff spread rumors. Being known as one who ordered his employees to take a train ride at their own expense would have left a curious if ironic dent in Gideon Barnett's pride.

Harken pocketed the silver coin without the slightest embarrassment. "Thank you, sir," he said, and left.

In the kitchen the news was greeted with a mixture of exuberance and worry.

Colleen, the little Irish second maid, teased, "Ooo, and aren't we rubbing elbows with the gentry now, hirin' out to build their playthings."

Mrs. Schmitt bemoaned, "Three months! Where do they think I can find somebody worth his salt to help me for three months? We'll end up doing it all ourselves."

Ruby chided, quietly, aside, "First upstairs in their study, next roaming around free on their grounds. Better be careful, Jens, you're not in their class and she knows it. So ask yourself why she's making eyes at you."

"You're dreaming, Ruby," he replied, and walked out the kitchen door.

Already he felt reborn, striding through the herb garden into the summer day. Lord, had herbs ever smelled so pungent? Had the sun ever been more dazzling?

He was a boatbuilder again!

He skirted the formal flower gardens, where the help was not allowed, and the picking gardens, which smelled strongly of petunias. Beyond them lay the glasshouse, where in winter fruits and vegetables were forced and in spring seedlings started. Behind the glasshouse a screen of columnar poplars circled the sprawling, meticulously tended vegetable garden. Cutting through it, he noticed the head gardener, Smythe, in the distance, wearing a straw hat, working between two rows of straw wigwams half again as high as himself. Though Smythe was a sour old fellow, Harken himself was in such a merry mood he couldn't resist calling, "H'lo, Smythe. How are your Baldwins this morning?"

Smythe turned and offered a limited smile as Harken approached and stopped to visit. "Ah, Harken, quite productive, I should say." Smythe had never smiled fully in his life, Harken was convinced. His correct British demeanor would not allow it. He had a long face with droopy eyelids and a nose as long and bumpy as one of his own white radishes. "I believe I'll have several quarts for herself by midweek."

The kitchen staff was well acquainted with Smythe's prized Baldwin blackcurrants and the mistress's predilection for them. He had devised a system of retarding the fruit by covering it completely with the outsized straw cones and removing them to let the sun ripen the berries only when Smythe or Levinia desired them ripened. By so doing he had prolonged their season a full two months.

"Mind if I try one?" Harken plucked a dark berry and popped it into his mouth before Smythe could reply. "Mmm . . . tasty. Yessir, Smythe, you really know what you're doing back here."

Smythe had cultured his expression of disapproval to a fine art. "*Miss*-ter Harken! You know the Baldwins are not for the kitchen help. The mistress has made that very clear."

"Oh, sorry," Harken replied blithely, "but right now I'm not the kitchen help. I'm heading for that shed back there in the trees to build the master a new sailboat. You'll be seeing me cut through here a lot this summer. Well, I'd better get to it." He headed on and threw back over his shoulder, "Thanks for the Baldwin, Smythe."

In jovial spirits he strode along through the rows of peculiar vegetables that gave evidence of the wealthy's desire to have the best and most unusual—Jerusalem artichokes, broccoli, leeks, fancy French climbing beans, salsify, scorzonera and the giant cardoons which resembled celery as tall as a man. He passed the more common ones—potatoes, turnips, carrots and the everlasting spinach, of which it seemed he'd washed haylofts full. *Three months,* he thought. *I don't have to wash any of that damned stuff for three whole months! And if this boat turns out to be the speed demon I believe it will, I might never have to wash it again!*

He passed fruit trees and hazelnut bushes, and a raspberry patch where the birds were pillaging. He helped himself to a handful and was eating them as he passed through the far screen of poplars into the cool of the woods beyond.

The shed was a long old clapboard structure that appeared never to have been painted. It had a pair of creaking crossbuck doors that turned back to reveal a crude plank floor, open rafters above and only two small, dirty windows on either side. There was a decrepit cutter inside with a broken trace, and some sacks of potatoes with sprouts growing up through the burlap, a rusty iron park bench, newspapers, barrels, bushel baskets and a variety of other flotsam that gave evidence of mice, squirrels and chipmunks having taken up residence. But as far as Jens Harken was concerned, it was paradise. It was cool, it smelled earthen, there were no sinks or iceboxes or hot, steaming kettles or imperious housekeepers ordering him what to do. No spoiled mistresses sending their dirty coins down for washing so their fingertips need not touch commoners' dirt. No horseradish to grate so tears streamed down his face, or teals to pluck or coppers to polish or rabbits to skin.

For three months he could work in this paradise, doing what he loved to do best, with only animals for company and the chirping of birds in the trees outside.

He walked the length of the building, looking up, checking out the rafters, which would need to be sturdy enough to support a winch. He decided where he'd run the stovepipe out the wall. It was July now. By September he'd need heat, and whether or not he finished in three months, the snow would be flying. He checked the grimy windows and found that with a little persuasion and a couple of sturdy clunks they would raise. The breeze blew in and brought the green smell of the woods. He imagined it filling sails, his sails, on a sleek, keelless beauty that would leap when it took the wind and disturb the water so little there would scarcely be a wake or a bow wave. His fingers itched to feel a plane in his hand and a length of spruce ripping and curling away as he fashioned a mast. He longed to smell a batch of white oak softening in a steam box, and hear his own hammer nailing ribs over a frame, and know the exquisite pride of watching a product of his own ingenuity take shape beneath his hands.

He stood with his elbows locked, the butts of both hands on the shoulder-high windowsill, and looked out into green trees and wild columbine and squirrels' nests. He thumped the gritty sill once with both hands and said with conviction, "Watch me. Just watch me."

Chapter 6

⟶⟿

The ride into town was heady for its sheer freedom. Summoning Steffens and the carriage, riding in the seat reserved for the privileged, Harken vowed one day he would own a carriage of his own and a fine bay to draw it. Boarding the train at the White Bear Beach Station, he reveled in being abroad at the time of day he'd normally be helping in the kitchen with the midday meal preparations. Alighting thirty minutes later amid the bustle of the downtown Saint Paul depot and making his way to the Lawless Hardware Store, he realized that Gideon Barnett, curmudgeon though he was, had given him the opportunity he'd been waiting for, and it was up to Jens Harken to make the most of it.

He selected the best tools money could buy, from the sandpaper paddle on which he'd sharpen his pencils to the four-horsepower electro-vapor engine that would drive his saw. After arrangements were made for delivery, he spent an enjoyable hour walking the downtown streets, resisting the smell of spicy Polish sausages steaming in a street vendor's wagon, saving his nickel and eating the cold beef sandwich he'd brought from home, peering into windows, watching the streetcars and admiring an occasional silk bustle. The city was exciting—there was no doubt about it—but when he boarded the train for White Bear Lake, his anticipation made the allure of Saint Paul pale by comparison.

Back in White Bear, he walked from the depot to the lumberyard and ordered what he'd need to tide him over until his boat plans were complete, then walked the remainder of the way out to Manitou Island, skirting the lake, where few sails were visible on this midweek afternoon, but enjoying the view nonetheless.

At Rose Point he changed into rough clothes, scavenged for cleaning supplies and went out beyond the gardens to turn a shed into a boatworks.

Reaching his domain, opening the double doors wide, stepping into the long, deep coolness of the building, he felt again the ebullience of that morning, the determination to make something important happen here. He carried out the musty old potatoes and newspapers, burned a pile of junk and pushed the other castoffs into a corner. He raked the mice nests and acorn shells outside, swept the floor and began washing the windows. He was standing on a barrel in the midst of the job when the voice of Miss Lorna Barnett scolded from the great doorway.

"Harken, where *ever* have you been?"

She was standing with both hands on her hips, only a silhouette in the late afternoon light that filtered through the woodsy backdrop behind her. Her sleeves were big as bed pillows and her skirt shaped like a bell with a short train. He could make out a rim of pink outlining her clothing, and the bird's-nest shape of her hair, but beyond that he was blinded to any details.

"Your father sent me to town, miss."

"And didn't tell me a thing about it. By the time I got up he was already gone himself, and nobody seemed to know where you were. You're going to build the boat, aren't you?"

"Yes, miss, I certainly am."

She planted her feet wide, made two fists and punched them straight at heaven. *"Eureka!"* she yowled at the rafters.

A laugh pealed out of Harken as he dropped off the barrel, threw his scrub rag into a bucket of water and his drying rag over his shoulder. "I felt like doing the same thing when he told me."

She strode inside, her skirts sweeping the dirty floor. "You're going to do it here?" She came to a halt inches from him, breaching the shadows, bringing her face into detail, and pretty detail it was.

"That's right. He gave me the go-ahead to buy anything I need at the Lawless Hardware Store and at Thayer's Lumberyard. I went into town to order tools. Miss Barnett"—he glanced down at her hems—"you're getting your skirts filthy walking on this dirty floor. I swept it, but it's still none too clean."

She picked up her hems and gave them a whack. "Oh, who cares!" The dust flew as she dropped her clothing back into place, spreading the scent of orange blossoms into the dank old building. "I don't know why I wear these silly skirts with trains anyway. Mr. Gibson says they're out."

"Who's Mr. Gibson?"

Her expression grew artificially pained. "Oh, please, Harken, I didn't come here to talk about skirt lengths. Tell me more about what Papa said!"

Though she was an enchanting creature, he stepped away, putting a proper distance between them. "Well, he said that I have three months to build the boat and then I go back to the kitchen."

"What else?" She pursued him, eager-eyed, keeping close.

"Nothing else."

"Oh, Harken, that can't be *all!*"

"Well . . ." He thought awhile, then added, "He said I should tell Mrs. Schmitt it was only temporary because he didn't want any more blowups in the kitchen."

Lorna laughed, a measure of grace notes that transformed the rough building and made Jens Harken indulge in a covert assay of her. She was dressed in pink-and-white candy stripes today, with a white lace stand-up collar and cuffs and a form-fitting bodice that dipped down at the waistline in a tiny point and made her look as curvy as fruit. Furthermore, whenever he moved away, she advanced, without apparent compunction. Finally he stopped retreating and stood his ground, the two of them an arm's length apart.

"May I ask you something, miss?"

"Why, of course."

"Why don't you go to your father to ask these questions?"

"Oh, phoo!" She flapped both hands. "He'd answer me as if he were giving an order for tainted food to be buried and spoil the whole thing. You see, he resists you all the way."

"So I've noticed."

"Besides, I like you." She smiled up at him point-blank.

He gave a self-conscious laugh, looking first at the floor, then at her.

"Are you always this honest?"

"No," she replied. "I spend a lot of time with Taylor DuVal. Do you know Taylor? No, I suppose you don't. Well, anyway, I suppose you could say we're courting, but I've never told him I like him."

"But you do?"

She thought a moment. "After a fashion. Taylor doesn't believe in things, though, not the way you believe in your boat. His family is in flour milling, and frankly, it's a very tedious subject—the wheat crop, the projected market prices, the source of cotton bags. Of course, when we're together we talk about other things, but they're rather repetitive—my family, his family, what dances are coming up at the yacht club, and what chautauquas are coming up at the Ramaley Pavilion."

"Does he race?"

"His family does. They own the *Kite.*"

"I've seen her. She's keel-heavy."

Lorna's eyes glinted with good-humored mischief. "But then, aren't they all, compared to what you propose to build?"

They stood awhile, smiling at each other, sharing the anticipation of building the boat and watching it sail for the first time, wondering for one reckless moment what might happen between now and then. A fly buzzed in some sunstream near the open doors and a transient breeze made a gentle mission through the trees, then went away.

Lorna Barnett was as charming a creature as he'd ever met. She seemed as down-to-earth as any of the kitchen staff, and as unpretentious. He decided to trust her.

"May I tell you something, Miss Lorna?"

"Anything."

"Once this boat races, I never intend to put foot in a kitchen again."

"Good for you, Harken. I don't think you belong there, either."

They stood close enough for Lorna to see the determination in his eyes and for Jens to see the corroboration in hers; close enough for him to smell the orange-blossom cologne in her clothes and for her to smell the vinegar water in his window rag; close enough to become aware of impropriety and disregard it.

"What will you do?" she asked.

"I want to own my own boatworks."

"Where will you get the money?"

"I'm saving. And I have a plan. I want to bring my brother from New Jersey so the two of us can run it together."

"Do you miss him?"

He answered with a click of the cheek and a wandering gaze that seemed full of memories. "He's my only family."

"Do you write to him?"

"Nearly every week, and he writes back."

She gave a conspiratorial smile. "Will *you* have something to tell him this week, huh, Harken?"

He smiled, too, and for a while they shared the moment of victory, commingled with an underlying sense of how much they were enjoying each other. The stretch of silence lingered, became an expanse of awareness in which they admired once again the mere visage of one another, for the first time ever in total privacy. Outside, the woods were still, not even a bird chirping. At the far end of the building the fly still buzzed, and the tea-green light threw leaf shadows along the crude floor and up the inside of one wall, making lacework of the grayed studs and the dirt-coated clapboards. Deeper within, where Jens and Lorna stood, the light from the half-washed window brightened only one side of their faces. Hers was smooth and curved, cupped high by the tight lace neckband that nearly touched her earlobes. His was dusty and angular, foiled by the open neck of a rough blue chambray shirt.

When they'd been silent and watchful too long, Jens spoke quietly. "I don't think your father would approve of you being here."

"My father is gone to the city. And my mother is napping with a cool cloth on her forehead. And furthermore, I have always been an unwieldy daughter and they know it. I'll be the first to admit, I haven't given them an easy time raising me."

"Why doesn't that surprise me?"

She grinned in reply. They were infinitely conscious of their aloneness as silence settled again and there seemed no acceptable way to fill it.

She looked down at her hands. "I suppose I should go. Let you get back to work."

"Yes, I suppose so."

"There's something I must say first, though, about yesterday."

"Yesterday?"

Her gaze lifted once more to his. "When I came to the kitchen and had cake with you. I realized, after it was too late, how uncomfortable I had made everyone. I just wanted to thank you, Harken, for understanding."

"Nonsense, miss. You had every right to be there."

"No." She touched his arm with four fingertips on the bare skin just above his wrist, a touch as brief as the sip of a hummingbird. Realizing her mistake, she withdrew quickly and curled the fingers into a tight fist. "I told you I'm unwieldy. Sometimes I do things I wish I hadn't. And when Mrs. Schmitt set down that silver tray with my cake on it, and the best silverware, and the good linen . . . well, I'd have given anything to be somewhere else. You knew it, and you did your best to ease my embarrassment. I simply didn't think, Harken. Anyway, thank you for your quick reaction."

He could have gone on insisting she was mistaken, but both of them knew she was not.

"You're welcome, miss," he replied. "I must admit, I feel a little more comfortable talking to you out here, away from the others. They . . ." He ended the thought abruptly, leaving her with the impression he wished he'd never begun.

"They what?"

"Nothing, miss."

"Of course it was something. They what?"

"Please, miss."

She touched his forearm again, this time insistently. "Harken, be honest with me. They what?"

He sighed, realizing there was no way he could sidestep her demand. "They sometimes mistake your intentions."

"What have they said about my intentions?"

"Nothing specific." He colored and looked away, pulling the dirty rag from his shoulder.

"You're not being honest with me."

When his eyes returned to her they wore the studied passivity of the trained household help. "If you'll excuse me, Miss Lorna, your father gave me a deadline, and I really should be getting back to work."

It had been a long time since Lorna Barnett had grown that angry, that fast. "Oh, you're just like him!" She rammed her fists onto her hips. "Men can be so infuriating! I can make you tell me, you know! You are, for all practical purposes, my employee!"

Jens was so taken aback by her sudden imperiousness he stood stunned and speechless. For a fleeting instant shock overtook his face, followed immediately by disappointment and a quick plummet back to reality. "Yes, I know." He turned away before she could see the patches of color ascend to his cheeks. Squatting, he recovered his rag from the bucket, wrung it out and, without further word, climbed back onto the barrel and resumed washing the window.

Behind him, Lorna's anger had collapsed as fast as it came. She found herself mortified at her thoughtless outburst. She took a step toward him, looking up.

"Oh, Harken, I didn't mean that."

"It's quite all right, miss." He could feel the heat climb his neck. How ridiculous he must have looked to her, losing sight of his station and allowing his attraction for her to show.

She advanced another step. "No, it's not. It just . . . just came out, that's all . . . please . . ." She reached out as if to touch his leg, then withdrew her hand. "Please forgive me."

"There's nothing to forgive. You were quite right, miss."

He would neither look at her nor stop going at the windowpane. His rag squeaked across the glass as he dried it and hid from her.

"Harken?" The appeal in her voice was lost on him. He stubbornly continued his work.

She waited, but his intention was clear, his hurt was clear, the barrier between them was as palpable as the shed walls. She felt like a quick-triggered misguided fool, but had no idea how to mend the hurt she'd caused.

"Well," she said in a small, remorseful voice, "I'll leave you be. I am sorry, Harken."

He need not turn to know she was gone. His body seemed to have developed sensors that prickled whenever she approached his sphere. In the silence following her leave-taking, the sensation withered, dulled, leaving him standing on the wooden barrel with the butts of both hands drilled against the lower window ledge and the rag hanging motionlessly from one. He turned his head, stared out across his left shoulder at the sunlit dust through which her petticoats had swept a trail. His gaze returned to the scene outside the window, a woodsy collection of sticks and leaf mold and greenery. He heaved an enormous sigh and stepped down slowly off the barrel. There he stood in the afternoon stillness. Motionless. Hurt. So she was just like her parents—aristocracy—and he'd best not forget it. Maybe what Ruby had hinted was right: Lorna Barnett was a bored rich girl playing games with the help simply to amuse herself.

With sudden vehemence, he pitched the rag into the bucket, spraying dirty water onto the floor, where it darkened the dusty planks. Then he kicked the barrel and sent it rolling.

For the rest of the day he was crotchety and malcontent. That evening he took Ruby out for a walk and kissed her in the herb garden when they got back to the kitchen door. But kissing Ruby was like kissing a cocker spaniel puppy—sloppy and difficult to control. He found himself anxious only to dry off his mouth and get her paws off his neck.

In his bed afterward he thought of Lorna Barnett . . . in pink-and-white stripes and orange-blossom cologne, with excited brown eyes and a mouth like ripe berries.

The woman had damned well better stay away from his shed!

She did exactly that for three days; on the fourth she was back. It was nearing three P.M. and Jens was sitting on a barrel, working at a makeshift table made of planks and sawhorses, drawing a long curved line on a piece of stiff manila chart paper.

He finished and sat back to study it, then felt eyes on him. He looked to his left and there she stood, still as a statue in the open doorway, wearing a big-sleeved blue shirtwaist, with her hands clasped behind her back.

His heart did a double take. His spine slowly straightened. "Well," he said.

She remained motionless, hands still clasped behind her. "May I come in?" she asked meekly.

He studied her awhile, pencil in one hand and a celluloid ship curve in the other.

"Suit yourself," he replied, and went back to work, poring over a numerical chart to the right of his partially finished drawings.

She moved inside with careful, measured footsteps to the opposite side of his table, where she stood before him in her pose of penitence.

"Harken?" she said very quietly.

"What?"

"Aren't you going to look at me?"

"If you say so, miss." Obediently he raised his eyes. Immense tears shimmered on her lower eyelids. Her bottom lip was puffy and trembling.

"I'm very, very sorry," she whispered, "and I'll never do that again."

Aw, sweet lord, did the woman not know what effect she had upon him, standing so girlishly with her hands clasped behind her back and tears the size of grapes making her eyes look devastating? Of all the things he'd expected, this was the last. The sight of her made his heart quake and his belly tense. He swallowed twice; the lump of emotion felt like a wad of cotton batting going down. *Miss Lorna Barnett,* he thought, *if you know what's good for you you'll get out of here as fast as your feet will carry you.*

"I'm sorry, too," he replied. "I forgot my place."

"No, no . . ." She brought a hand from behind her back and touched his chart paper as if it were an amulet. "It was my fault, trying to force you to say things you didn't want to, treating you like an inferior."

"But, you were right. I work for you."

"No. You work for my father. You're my friend, and I've been miserable for three days thinking I had ruined our friendship."

He refrained from saying he'd been, too. He had no idea what to say. It was taking a tremendous effort to remain on his barrel and keep the table between them.

Very softly, she said to the drawings, "I think I know what the kitchen help is saying. It wasn't too hard to figure out." She looked up. "That I've been flirting with you, isn't that right? Amusing myself with the help."

He fixed his eyes on his pencil. "It's just Ruby, but don't let it bother you."

"Ruby is the redheaded one, isn't she?"

He nodded.

"She particularly disliked my being there the other day. I could tell."

When he made no response, she asked, "Is she your girlfriend?"

He cleared his throat. "We've gone walking on our days off."

"She is."

"I suspect she'd like to be. That's all."

"So I embarrassed you, too, by showing up in the kitchen and insisting on having cake there."

"My father always said, one person doesn't embarrass another, one can only do that to himself. I told you, you had every right to be there and I meant it."

After an impacted silence during which he studied the chart paper, and she studied him, Lorna Barnett declared quietly, "I'm not amusing myself with you, Harken, I'm not."

He looked up. She was standing straight, eight fingertips resting on the edge of his rough table, the curve of her breast as smooth and flowing as if he'd drawn it with one of his own Copenhagen curves, her hair plumped up with a few tendrils floating loose around her face. That face—what a face—so sincere and pretty and vulnerable he wanted to take it between his two hands and kiss its trembling lips until they smiled once again.

Instead he could only say quietly, "No, miss."

"My name is Lorna. When will you start using it?"

"I've used it."

"Not Miss Lorna. Lorna."

In spite of the fact that she waited, he refused to repeat her name. That last formality was a necessary barrier between them, kept intact by Jens for both their good.

Finally she said, "Am I forgiven, then?"

Once again he could have insisted there was nothing to forgive, but they both knew she had hurt him.

"Let's just forget it."

She tried to smile but it didn't quite work. He tried to tear his eyes from her but it didn't quite work. In silence they confronted this unwise, unbidden attraction that was welling between them. It was drawn on their faces as plainly as the lines on his chart paper. He realized one of them had to be sensible and, as always, was the first to look away.

"Would you like to see my drawings?"

"Very much."

She came around and stood at his elbow, bringing along her familiar orange-blossom scent and the starchy blue presence of her clothing in his peripheral vision, her full sleeve so near his ear.

"They're not done yet," he told her, "but you can get an idea of the basic shape of the boat."

She reached for a loose piece of paper containing a rough sketch he'd done in about twenty minutes for her father.

"This is what it'll look like?"

"Roughly."

She studied it a moment then set it aside and took in the much larger, more precise drawing on which he was working. It was tacked down on the table.

"Do you always draw them upside down?"

"That's the way I'll build it, so that's the way I draw it."

"You'll build it upside down?"

"On these . . . here, see?" He pointed to one of several lines that vertically bisected the profile drawing of the boat. "There'll be one of these forms about every two feet down the length of the boat, and they'll stand on feet that'll support the whole thing. They're called cross sections or stations, and they form the basis of the mold. They'll be what determines the shape of the entire boat. Like this . . . see?"

He drew in the air with both hands but could tell she couldn't visualize it.

"It's hard to see from this one-dimensional drawing, but I'll do a fore-to-aft cross section, too, that will show each station. Then it'll be easier to see."

"How long will it take you?"

"To finish the drawings? Another week and a half or so."

"And then you can start building it?"

"No. Then I can start lofting."

"What's lofting?"

"Lofting? That's . . ." He stopped to think. "Well, it's fairing up a boat."

"What's fairing up?"

"Fairing up is making sure it doesn't have any lumps or bumps, making sure it has a good smooth even shape." *Like you,* he thought. "Like fruit," he said. "The surface of the hull has got to run smooth from any one spot to any other spot. Then she's fair."

Lorna Barnett looked down at Jens Harken, at the profile of his head and neck, at his black suspenders running in a tight curve from front to back, at the line his shoulder and arm made as he leaned his elbow on the table and concentrated on the chart paper.

Fair, she thought, *oh, yes, very fair indeed.*

Tempted to reached out and run a hand over that fine head and those solid shoulders, she decided she'd best get herself out of this shed and put some distance between them. Furthermore, she could see he wasn't getting much done with her interrupting. "Well, I'd better leave you to your work." She left his elbow and moved around the table. "May I come back again?"

Any other question would have been easier to answer. He wanted to say, No, stay away, but he could no more have denied her the right and himself the pleasure than he could have worked in a kitchen for the remainder of his life.

"I'll look forward to it," he replied.

She came frequently, dropping in to bother him not only when she was present, but after she'd left. She would inspect his drawings and ask questions, perch on the iron bench and chatter, watch him sometimes in silences so reaching they felt like strokes upon his flesh. She came one Friday when the drawings were nearly completed, and after inspecting his progress meandered around to the park bench. She spread its rusty seat with a piece of chart paper, sat down, pulled up her knees and wrapped them with both arms.

"Do you like band music?" she asked, out of the blue.

"Band music? Yes, as a matter of fact, I do."

"Mr. Sousa is coming tomorrow."

"Yes, I saw the posters."

"No, I mean he's coming here tomorrow, to Rose Point. Mother is hostessing a reception for him after the concert tomorrow night, then he's to be our overnight guest."

"So you're going to the concert."

She rested her chin on her knees. "Mm-hmm."

"And Mr. DuVal will be there?"

"Mm-hmm."

"Well, I hope you have a very nice time."

"Are you going?"

"No. I save my money."

"Ah, that's right. To start a boatworks."

She let him draw for a while, studying him, then abruptly changed the subject again. "When will you actually start building the boat?"

"Oh, another couple weeks or so."

"I'll help you."

She was a safe enough distance away that he could allow himself a protracted study of her. She wore pale yellow today. Her skirt had fallen over the edge of the bench like an inverted fan. Her breast was tucked fast against her thigh, and her hair looked soft as meadow grass. "Have you ever stopped to think what would happen if your father decided to walk out here and found you with me? I expect him to, you know, to check on the drawings."

"He'd be very angry, and he'd scold me and I'd argue that I have every right to be here, but he wouldn't fire you because he wants the boat too badly, and you're the only one who can build it for him."

"You're pretty sure of that, aren't you?"

"Well, aren't you?"

"No."

She only mused and lay her cheek on her knee, watching him unbrokenly.

"Is your brother like you?" she asked.

"No."

"What's he like, then?"

"He plods when I run. He stays behind in the East, where it's safe and he has a job, while I come out here, where there are none. But he knows boats."

"He worries about fair lines like you do?"

Jens merely shook his head as if to say, Girl, I can't keep up with you.

"Does he look like you?"

"People say so."

"Then he's handsome, isn't he?"

Jens colored. "Miss Barnett, I don't think that's appropriate for—"

"Oh, listen to him! Miss Barnett, in that tone of voice. And now I'm going to get preached to, I can tell."

He left his barrel, circled the table, took her by the calves and swung her feet to the floor. "Up!" he ordered. "And out! I have a boat to design!"

She got to her feet and walked backward to the door with him herding her. "Well, may I help you?"

"No."

"Why not? I'll be here anyway."

"Because I said so. Now get going, run off to Mr. DuVal, where you belong, and don't come back."

She turned, tossed her head, said with a great deal of assurance, "You don't mean that," and strode out the door. When she was gone he took a big deep swig of air, blew it out and energetically scratched the back of his head with eight fingers until his hair stood out.

"Jesus," he whispered to himself.

As she'd done once before when he'd stumbled upon her in her bedroom, Lorna Barnett stuck only her head back around the door, keeping everything else out of sight.

"Maybe I'll bring a picnic next time," she said.

"Oh, that's all I need!" he bellowed. "For you to go asking Mrs. Schmitt for—"

He was talking to thin air. She was gone at last, leaving him standing frustrated, tousle-headed and half-priapic in the middle of the cavernous shed.

On Saturday night, one hour before Mr. John Philip Sousa himself would raise his baton at Ramaley's lakeshore pavilion, the Barnett household was aflutter. The entire family was going to the concert, including the aunts.

In their room, Henrietta was scolding Agnes, "Don't be silly, you cannot go without gloves. It simply isn't done."

In Theron's room, Ernesta was parting his hair down the middle and greasing it back with brilliantine while he jiggled and squiggled and twisted to look behind him for his spyglass.

In their room, Daphne was teasing Jenny, "I suppose you're going to make goggle eyes at Taylor DuVal and make a dope of yourself again tonight."

In the master suite, Gideon happened to walk in on Levinia when she was only partially dressed. She shielded herself with a dressing gown and scolded, "Gideon, you could at least knock when you come in!"

In her room, Lorna needed help getting her dress buttoned up the back. Since Ernesta was busy with Theron, she went to the aunts' room.

"Aunt Agnes, will you please button me up the back?"

"Of course I will, dearie. What a lovely frock! Why, if you don't look like a regular little buttercup I don't know who does. Will young Mr. DuVal be there tonight?"

"Of course."

Across the room, Henrietta pursed her lips and put in, "Then be sure your hatpin is sharpened, Lorna."

They rode the steam launch *Manitoba* across the lake, boarding downtown at the Williams House Hotel and arriving at Ramaley's pavilion a good half hour before concert time. The pavilion itself was the most imposing structure on the lake, châteauesque in design, with turreted corners topped by finials, and a busy roofline broken by spires, pinnacles and gables. Its open-arms steps lifted to a quartet of doors topped by an elaborate plaster cartouche above which towered a roof peak shaped like a candlesnuffer. The second floor was a ballroom, surrounded by French doors giving onto pillared porticoes, while its third floor, circled by twenty-foot-high Renaissance arched windows, was devoted entirely to an auditorium. The auditorium seated two thousand and was lavishly appointed with red velvet and gilt.

The Barnetts entered their private proscenium box and seated themselves on opera chairs, all but Gideon, who'd gone backstage to deliver a personal welcome to Sousa.

The aunts grinned, whispered to each other and pointed with their folded fans at familiar faces. Daphne and Jenny peeped over the balustrade and giggled when young men tipped their heads in salute. Theron peered through his spyglass and said, "Wow, I can see the hair in that fat woman's nose!"

"Theron, put that down!" his mother scolded.

"Well, I can! And it's a big nose, too. Gosh, her nostrils are big as hoofprints, Mama, you should just see 'em!"

Levinia gave Theron a whack on the back of his head with her fan.

"Ouch!" He lowered his spyglass and rubbed his noggin.

"When the music begins you may use that thing. Not before."

He slumped in his chair and muttered, "Jeez."

"And watch your tongue, young man."

Taylor DuVal came in and greeted everyone in the box, kissing all the ladies' hands and taking a look through Theron's spyglass. Theron leaned close to him and, shielded from his mother, pointed and whispered, "There's a fat lady down there in a blue dress and you can see the hair in her nose."

Taylor took a look and whispered back, "I think I see some in her ears, too."

To Lorna, he said, with a special, private smile into her brown eyes, "I'll see you during the intermission."

The concert was inspiring. Sousa's original American music raised the hair on Lorna's arms and made her insides tremble. It brought thunderous applause and smiles to everyone in the audience.

At intermission in the lobby Taylor said to Lorna, "I've missed you."

"Have you?"

"I certainly have. And I intend to make up for it later at your house."

"Taylor, shh. Someone might hear you."

"Who's going to hear? Everyone's busy talking."

He took her hand and laid it over his palm and ran his own over it time and again, as if smoothing a curled page. "Did you miss me?"

She hadn't. "A lady wouldn't answer that," she replied.

He laughed and kissed her fingernails.

The reception at Rose Point was attended by fifty of White Bear Lake's elite. The dining room was festooned with red, white and blue flowers. A cake shaped like a bass drum was emblazoned with an American eagle clutching golden arrows in its claws, surrounded by the aurora borealis. The tea was flavored with rose geraniums and the finger sandwiches were fanciful enough to be mistaken for jewelry. The crowd was noisier than usual, their mood enhanced by the presence of the gentle but fiery patriot whose fame was spreading beyond America's shores since he'd resigned his post as conductor of the United States Marine Band and begun touring the world. In his goatee, oval spectacles and white uniform with three medals on his chest, Sousa bowed over Aunt Agnes's hand while Lorna watched from a distance. "Watch Aunt Henrietta," Lorna told Taylor. "As soon as Sousa turns away she'll say something to dampen Aunt Agnes's joy."

Sure enough, Henrietta's mouth drew tight as a drawstring purse as she delivered some stern reprimand to her sister. Agnes's fluttering immediately ceased.

"What makes people like that?"

"Lorna, your aunt Agnes is a bit daffy. Henrietta simply keeps her in line."

"She is not daffy!"

"The way she's always mooning about her young Captain Dearsley? You don't think that's daffy?"

"But she loved him. I think it's very sweet how she remembers him, and Aunt Henrietta can be so cruel. I've told Mother I believe she hates men. One of them spurned her when she was young, so she has nothing good to say about any of them."

"And how about you?"

When she made no reply, Taylor said, "I think I've upset you, Lorna. I'm sorry. Tonight of all nights, I didn't mean to do that."

Taylor was standing directly behind Lorna. In the lee between their bodies she felt him caress the center of her back. Shivers radiated up her arms, along with surprise, for they stood in the crowded hallway, her father only a few feet away in the archway to the morning room and her mother at the far end of the dining room. Such audacity right under her parents' noses. Taylor asked, "Do you think we'd be missed if we went out into the garden for a few minutes?"

Curiously, she thought of Harken at that moment, Harken, who occupied her thoughts most of the time she was away from Taylor. "I don't think we should."

"I have something for you."

She glanced back over her shoulder, her temple almost bumping Taylor's chin. His dark beard was beguiling, his eyes and lips smiling down at her—this man her parents wanted her to marry. "What?"

In the secret space between them his fingertips seemed to be finding and counting her vertebrae within her dress. "I'll tell you in the garden." She was a young, nubile woman, susceptible to each subtle nuance of courtship, to its touches and its flatteries and its very suggestibilities.

She turned and led the way toward the door.

Outside, Lorna walked beside him along the graveled paths between her mother's prized roses, around the splattering fountain, beyond the picking beds with their fragrant night-scented stocks and chrysanthemums and marigolds. When she stopped in the moonlit path, visible from many windows, he caught her elbow and said, "Not here."

He took her to the farthest side of the garden, into the glasshouse, where it was damp and private and smelled of humus. They stood on a flagstone walk between rows of clay pots holding shoulder-high blackberry canes being propagated by Smythe for winter bearing.

"We shouldn't be in here, Taylor."

"I'll leave the door open, so if anyone comes looking for us we'll hear them." He took both her hands and held them loosely. "You look pretty tonight, Lorna. May I kiss you . . . at last?"

"Oh, Taylor, you put me in a predicament. What exactly do you think a lady should answer?"

He turned her right hand palm-up and kissed the pads of four fingers. "Then don't answer," he said, and placed both her hands on his shoulders. His own went to her waist as his head dipped down and cut off the starlight shining through the glass roof. His lips met hers discreetly, warm and closed within the sleekness of his beard, hinting at opening, not quite doing so. He kept the kiss brief, then stepped back and reached inside his suit jacket to the watch pocket of his waistcoat. From the pocket he withdrew a small velvet pouch.

"I've known for some time that our parents would be very much in favor of you and me marrying, Lorna. My father spoke to me about it nearly a year ago, and since that time I've been watching you grow up, admiring you. Unless I'm mistaken, your parents would be as much in favor of our marriage as mine are. So I've bought you this . . ." From the pouch he emptied into his palm a piece of jewelry that gave a golden wink as it fell. "It's not a betrothal ring, because I think it's a little soon for that. But it's the next thing to it, and it comes with my sincere intention to ask for your hand when we both believe we've come to know each other well enough. So this is for you, Lorna."

He put it in her hand, a tiny gold bow from which was suspended a delicate oval watch.

"It's beautiful, Taylor."

"May I?"

What could she say? That she'd been flirting with their kitchen handyman lately in a shed behind the garden? That she'd been thinking of him much more often than of Taylor? That she'd been trying to get him to kiss her and he wouldn't?

"Oh, yes . . . of course."

He took the watch from her hand and pinned it on her bodice, exceedingly careful to avoid touching her breast, his very carefulness seductive in its own right. The faint brush of his fingertips on her garments, and the garments on her skin provoked a sensual reaction along the surface of her breasts. When the watch was in place she touched it with her fingertips and looked up into Taylor's shadowed face.

"Thank you, Taylor. You're a very sweet man."

He took her chin between thumb and forefinger and tipped it up. "I'm sure you know, Lorna, that I'm falling in love with you." He kissed her once more, starting gently, waiting until he sensed her reserve yield to curiosity, only then becoming more exacting. His lips opened and he drew her flush against his length in an embrace such as Lorna had recently been imagining with Harken. How many times had she stood near him, every meeting of their eyes a collision, willing him to break down and kiss her this way, hold her against his long body and answer so many vague questions about which she'd wondered? Only, he hadn't. Now here was Taylor, with his tongue in her mouth, his left arm clamped firmly around her waist, and his right hand, finally, wholly, covering one of her breasts. In all her life no single touch had ever radiated as this one did, to regions far removed from the touch itself, like a snagged thread puckering distant points. No wonder Mother had warned her.

They both regained propriety at once, ending the kiss suddenly, their chins downturned, heads close while their breathing evened.

No apologies came from Taylor.

None came from Lorna.

The last two minutes had been too momentous to warrant apologies. Finally they stepped apart, Taylor finding and keeping Lorna's hands.

Belatedly, she said, "We must go back in now, Taylor."

"Yes, of course," he whispered thickly. "What are you doing tomorrow?"

"Tomorrow? I . . ." Tomorrow was Sunday. She'd been planning to row over to Tim's and see if she could find Harken there again.

"Will you go sailing with me?"

At her pause, Taylor encouraged, "I'll sail over and pick you up at your dock at two o'clock. What do you say?"

Harken, she realized, was an impossibility. Not only was he remaining stubbornly polite and subservient, if he ever broke down and satisfied both their curiosities, where could it lead? Even he realized what was best when he'd sent her packing with an admonition to fly to Taylor, where she belonged.

Lorna heard herself answer the way circumstances dictated she answer.

"All right. Shall I ask Mrs. Schmitt to pack us a picnic?"

Taylor smiled. "It's a date."

Chapter 7

———— ❧ ————

The watch from Taylor raised a stir among Lorna's family. Everyone took it for a betrothal gift in spite of her protestations it was not. Her mother smiled smugly and said, "Wait till I tell Cecilia Tufts." Her father set no limit on her sailing time with Taylor. Her brother said, "I told you Taylor and Lorna were sparking." Daphne got starry-eyed while Jenny looked glum, realizing it was only a matter of time before she lost her idol completely and irrevocably. Aunt Henrietta issued her warning about wearing a hatpin on the boat. And Aunt Agnes said, "Aren't you lucky. I never got a chance to go sailing with Captain Dearsley."

Taylor picked up Lorna at two o'clock. They spent the entire afternoon on the water in Taylor's catboat. Lorna was in her glory crewing for Taylor, though the boat had only a single sail. He let her handle the rudder, and sometimes the winch during tacking. They sailed from Manitou Island into Snyder's Bay, then east to Mahtomedi and from there around West Point, up the Dellwood shore, where they passed Tim's cabin. But no one was about. Then south again toward Birchwood, off whose shore they reefed the sail and ate their picnic lunch bobbing on the water. Lorna had no need to use her hatpin, nor would it have been possible, for she'd removed her hat well over an hour earlier and sat with the sun on her face.

While they ate, the wind freshened, and as they crossed the lake yet again Lorna, exhilarated, pointed her nose to the wind like a figurehead on the prow of a great windjammer. Her dress front was damp and her hair tangled as they sailed the rim of the fishing bar in North Bay, where several rowboats were anchored and their occupants dozed in the late afternoon sun with cane poles in their hands.

Lorna picked him out immediately by the set of his shoulders and the overall familiarity of his form. Even in a wide straw hat, with his lower half hidden by the boat, she knew who it was. He was with another man, a stranger Lorna had never seen before.

Oddly, she could tell he spotted her at the same moment she did him. Even across the blinding water she had a sense of connection with him at the precise moment they recognized each other.

She smiled, stood and waved broadly above her head. "Jens! Hello!"

He waved back. "Hello, Miss Lorna!"

She cupped her mouth. "How are they biting?"

He leaned over the side of the boat and lifted a stringer of good-sized fish. "See for yourself!"

"What are they?"

"Walleyes!"

"My favorites!"

"Mine too!"

"Save one for me!" she joked, then sat down as the catboat sailed out of range and left Harken only a bump with wavy edges against the shimmering water.

Watching her smile after the boat, Taylor inquired, "Who was that?"

"Oh." She recovered quickly. "That was Harken, our kitchen handyman."

Taylor studied her closely. "You called him Jens."

Too late Lorna realized her slip and tried to make light of it. "Yes, Jens Harken, the one who's building the boat for my father."

"And just where might you be eating fish with him?"

"Oh, Taylor, don't be silly. I didn't mean it literally."

"Ah," Taylor said. But Lorna could tell he was not convinced. Furthermore, after the encounter with Jens her day seemed to go flat. Her zest for sailing lost its headiness, her damp clothes seemed cloying and she began to feel the sunburn on her face.

"If it's all right with you, Taylor, I'm ready to go home."

Taylor studied her so intently she turned away and reached for her hat to escape his scrutiny. She flattened it on her wind-whipped hair and rammed the pin home. "I think I've got a sunburn and Mama is going to kill me if she sees me in this wet dress."

"Then maybe we should wait until it dries."

"No, please, Taylor. I don't want to get a chill."

Finally he answered, "Whatever you say," and headed back toward Manitou Island.

Jens Harken cleaned the fish and left them in the icebox with a note asking Mrs. Schmitt to fry them for the staff's breakfast the following morning.

At five-thirty A.M. when he walked into the kitchen she was filling his request, dipping the fish into buttermilk and cornmeal while Colleen fetched lard for the skillet and Ruby set the table.

"Morning," Jens greeted.

Mrs. Schmitt replied, "Maybe."

He came up short and glanced from Ruby to Colleen to the streaked bun on the back of Mrs. Schmitt's head. "You're in a fine mood this morning, I see."

She went on coating the fish. "I hope you went out to get these fish alone."

"As a matter of fact, I didn't."

"Jens Harken, you ain't got the sense God gave a tree stump if you had that girl along with you!"

"What girl?"

"What girl, he says. Lorna Barnett, as if you didn't know."

"I did not have Lorna Barnett with me!"

"Then what was she doing ordering a picnic for two yesterday?"

"How should I know? She's got friends, hasn't she?"

Mrs. Schmitt gave him *that look*. It nearly pulled her eyeballs out of her left ear and said, *Don't you lie to me, young man!*

"I had a new friend with me, Ben Jonson, if you must know. I met him at the lumberyard, and he's about my age, single and has his own fishing boat, so the two of us went out together."

Mrs. Schmitt slipped a metal spatula under a fish fillet, whupped it over, sending up a lardy sizzle, and said to the frying pan, "Well, that's better."

Ruby, however, continued shooting daggers at Jens from the corner of her eye while thudding plates onto the table as if she were dropping anchors.

He ignored her and said to Mrs. Schmitt, "Fry it all. I'll take the extra out to the shed to eat at noon. That way I won't have to come back here, where all the old hens are waiting to peck my eyes out."

She'd come. He knew as surely as he knew the shape of his own hands that she'd come to explain why she'd been sailing with Taylor DuVal. The man in the catboat had been DuVal, Jens was sure, a damned handsome fellow in a fancy yachting cap with a white crown, black visor and gold braid trim—the kind of a fellow she belonged with.

It was a drizzly day the color of pewter. The rain had begun well before dawn and continued into the late morning, a steady garden soaker. On the roof of the shed intermittent plops sounded as the moisture collected on leaves and dropped in syncopated beats. On the two small windows, droplets coalesced before tumbling in zigzag rivulets down the panes.

Inside, the place was dry and fragrant, lit by a gas lantern, filled with new lumber: white oak, mahogany, spruce and cedar. The cedar above all raised an aroma so rich and redolent it seemed edible. It stood to one side, stacked on wood slats.

Jens had spent the morning on his knees, nailing sheets of fir onto the floor, creating an expanse of pale grain a full thirty-eight feet long and then some. It had brightened the room considerably, spreading its peachy glow toward the murky rafters and broadcasting its fresh-milled smell. Around the edges of the new wood the old floor formed a frame of dirty gray. Upon it he'd left his thick boots and worked stocking-footed, measuring, marking, tacking down a black rubber batten much longer than himself on the unsoiled sheets of fir.

He heard the door squeak and looked up.

As he'd expected, Lorna Barnett came inside and closed the door behind her.

"Hello," she said from two-thirds of a building away, so far her voice echoed.

"Hello."

"I'm back."

Back and wearing something sleek below, puffed at the sleeves that showed off a set of fair lines as pretty as any boat he'd ever seen. He let his smile answer, remaining on his knees with one hand draped over the head of a hammer and its handle braced on his thigh.

"Gracious, it smells good in here," she remarked, sauntering toward him.

"New lumber."

"So I see." She walked around the edge of the fir past the stacked lumber. "And new lamps." She looked up at them while coming to a halt at a point nearest where Jens knelt.

"Yes." He sat back on his heels and studied her as she moved from shadow into light. Her skirt was patterned with blue morning glories, her shirtwaist solid white. Her face, lifted briefly to the lantern, turned his best intentions to foolhardiness.

"Looks like you got a little too much sun yesterday," he remarked.

She touched both cheeks. "I'd have been all right if I hadn't taken my hat off, but I couldn't resist."

"Does it hurt?"

"Yes it does, actually, but I'll live." She glanced at a series of dots he'd drawn on the clean wood, connected by the long graceful curve of the black batten.

"What are you doing?"

"Lofting, at last."

"So this is lofting . . . fairing up the boat, right?"

"Right."

"Making sure it has no lumps and bumps, right?"

"Right."

"Making sure it's smooth as fruit."

Jens only smiled.

"How does it work?"

Explaining was much safer than admiring her, so he struck in. "Well, I do a full-scale drawing of the boat—a side profile first—and then a fore and aft drawing of all the cross sections sort of nested together. When I'm all done there'll be a whole series of dots on the floor. When I connect any of those dots with the batten it'll show me if all the curves are fair. If they're not, let's say one of them bulges by even an eighth of an inch, that station of the boat will be hideous when it's done. So I change the curve of the mold in that spot and fix it *before* I make the mold."

"Oh."

He could see she didn't understand his verbal explanation, but the curve of the batten on the floor was unmistakable.

"Well, go ahead," she said, "don't let me stop you."

He laughed softly and replied, "You already have. I might as well have my dinner." He pulled out a pocket watch and checked it. "Hoo! Where did the morning go? Last time I looked it wasn't even nine yet." Actually, he'd been starved for over two hours but had put off eating on the chance she'd get here beforehand: It was a matter of some fish she'd asked for. "Do you mind if I eat while we visit, Miss Lorna?"

"Not at all."

He left his hammer and tacks, rose and crossed the fir planking in stocking feet to fetch a tin from atop the stack of lumber and remove its lid.

"Care to join me?" he asked, returning to Lorna, extending the tin.

She peered inside. "What's in there?"

"Fried walleye."

"Why, it is!" Her face blossomed in surprise: eyebrows up, cheeks rounded, smile anchored by a bite on her bottom lip. "It's the fish you caught yesterday!"

"You said to save some for you."

"Oh, Jens, what a surprising man you are! You really brought some for me?"

"Of course." He gestured toward the rusty park bench. "Would you care to sit?"

She looked around and said, "All right, but not there. Let's sit in the boat instead."

"In the boat?"

"Certainly, why not? We can have our first picnic in it before it's even on the water."

He chuckled and said, "Whatever you say, Miss Lorna. Hold on while I find us a tablecloth." While he went off to get a piece of chart paper she removed her shoes and left them beside his boots.

"Oh, you don't have to do that," he called. "The wood will get dirty eventually anyway. I just like to enjoy it clean for a while."

"If *you* take off your shoes, *I* take off my shoes." Her heels made hollow thumps on the floor as she crossed it. Her shoes, perched beside his boots, made an intimate picture as he passed them to put the chart paper down in the curve of the batten and set the tin of fish upon it. He enjoyed the sight of her dropping down Indian fashion, her flowered skirt flaring like a morning glory. Her shirtwaist had the usual huge sleeves, lots of skinny pin tucks up the front and a good thirty buttons holding it closed clear up past her throat. Just above her left breast was pinned a tiny pendant watch he'd never seen before, drawing attention to that lush curve. He pulled his eyes away from it and dropped down facing her.

"Help yourself."

She reached into the tin, plucked out a piece of fish and flashed him a smile.

"Our second picnic," she said.

He, too, helped himself and the two of them, riding an imaginary boat upon a sea of fragrant fresh-cut fir, ate cold fish with soggy breading and thought no fare had ever tasted finer, for they were together, as they loved to be, talking, smiling, exploring with their eyes.

"You really did get a sunburn," he said. "Your poor little nose looks like a signal light."

"It kept me awake most of the night."

"Did you put anything on it?"

"Buttermilk. But it didn't do much good."

"Try cucumbers."

"Cucumbers?"

"That's what my mother used to put on us when we were boys. Ask Mrs. Schmitt for one, or just pick one out of the garden on your way back to the house."

"I'll do that."

He studied her face critically, the sunburn an excuse to do so for a protracted length of time. "It's probably going to peel, anyway."

She touched her nose self-consciously. "And I'll look like a scaly old scrub pine."

"Mmm . . . I don't think so. I don't think you'll ever look like a scaly old scrub pine, Miss Lorna."

"Oh, won't I?" Her expression turned saucy over the backward compliment. "What will I look like, then?"

Their eyes locked in good humor. He bit, chewed and swallowed, enjoying this mildly flirtatious wordplay as much as she. Finally, with a one-sided grin, he ordered, "Eat your fish."

They finished their first pieces and started on seconds.

"Was that your Mr. DuVal with you yesterday?" Jens asked.

"It was Mr. DuVal. It was not *my* Mr. DuVal."

"I figured it was him. He was the one sitting beside you the night I served dinner in the dining room. He's a fine-looking fellow."

"Yes, he is."

"A decent sailor, too."

"I'll bet you're better."

"You've got to have a boat before you can be a sailor."

"You will have, someday, when you own your own boatworks. I know you will." She licked off a finger.

"So you and DuVal had a picnic yesterday, did you?"

"Lordy, that kitchen staff is gossipy."

"Yes, ma'am, they are. Trouble is, they thought you were out there having a picnic with me."

"What!"

"Mrs. Schmitt likes to mother me, but yesterday she outdid herself. She gave me a proper scolding about taking you out fishing with me and how inappropriate it was. But don't worry—I set her straight. I told her it wasn't me. I was with somebody else."

"And are you going to tell me who he was or not?"

"A new friend, Ben Jonson. I met him at the lumberyard when I went in to order all this wood. It was his boat."

"A new friend—good. My best friend is Phoebe Armfield. I've known her since we were little girls. Tell yours I'm glad he invited you. The fish were delicious."

Again she licked off her fingers, looked around for something with which to wipe her mouth but found nothing. Still sitting cross-legged, she doubled forward, fished for a hem of her petticoat and used that.

Surprised, Jens laughed, looking down at the back of her head. "Miss Lorna, what would your mother say?"

"What mother doesn't know won't hurt her. Or me." She flipped down her skirt and said, "Thank you. I'm sure I shall never forget this wonderful picnic."

He smiled into her eyes. She smiled into his. As always, he was the one to keep things light between them.

"So tell me, how was Mr. Sousa's concert?"

"Rousing. Patriotic."

"You met him?"

"Absolutely. He has splendid bearing and wears tiny oval glasses with gold wire rims and a miniature moustache and goatee that looks quite stunning with his uniform. It was white, by the way, with gold trim, and a captain's hat. Oh, and white gloves, which I never saw him remove, even once, not even when he ate finger foods. Mama's soiree was a great success."

"And Mr. DuVal was there, too?"

"Yes," she replied, finding Jens's eyes and keeping them. "Mr. DuVal is everywhere I go, it seems." Nearly whispering, she added, "Except here."

It took Jens a beat to recover and reply sensibly, "That's to be expected; after all, you're courting."

"Not quite."

"You're not? But you told me you were."

"I may have said that, and I may spend a lot of time with him, but don't say we're courting! Not yet!" As she spoke, her voice became more agitated. "It's enough that my family is all saying so, but then I suppose they have good reason. . . . Oh, Harken, I don't know. I'm so confused."

"About what?"

"This." She touched the watch above her breast. "It's from Taylor, you see." Jens gave the watch a second look and felt jealousy billow. "He gave it to me Saturday night after the concert and said it's not a betrothal gift, but everyone in my family thinks it is. And I don't want to be betrothed to Taylor yet, don't you see?"

Jens said what he thought he ought. "But he's fine-looking, and wealthy, and one of your class. He treats you well, your parents approve of him. It makes good sense to marry a man like that."

He knew even before she spoke, from the sincere and troubled softening about her eyes, that her following words would be better left unsaid. She said them quietly, looking straight into Jens's eyes.

"But what if there's someone I like better?"

Time reeled out while her admission bore down on them both. He could have reached out and simply taken her hand and the course of their lives would have changed. Instead, he chose the prudent road, replying, "Ah, well, then that's a dilemma, Miss Lorna."

"Harken—"

"And you'd better do some long hard thinking before you pass up an opportunity like DuVal."

"Harken, please—"

"No, Miss Lorna." He reached for the tin and shifted in preparation for rising. "I've said my piece, and it's good advice, I think. But in the future I think it might be better if you talked to someone else about this." He picked up the tin and carried it away.

She followed him with her eyes. "Who?"

"How about your friend Phoebe?"

Lorna rose, got her shoes and sat on the park bench to pull them on. "Phoebe is no good. She's so smitten by Taylor herself that she hasn't got an ounce of objectivity in her body. All she ever says is, 'If you don't want him, I'll take him.' "

"Well, there . . . see? He's a good catch."

Jens turned from placing the tin on the stack of lumber and found Lorna coming toward him. She didn't stop until she was so close he could have rearranged her hair with his breath.

"You can be very exasperating, do you know that?" she said.

"So can you."

"You don't like it when I come here?"

"Of course I do. But you know the problem as well as I do."

She studied him at close range, her deep brown eyes importuning him for the kiss he wisely had decided never to give. When she saw she was getting nowhere, she glanced aside, absently studying the stacked lumber awhile. Raising her eyes abruptly, she astonished him by asking, point-blank, "Aren't you ever going to kiss me, Harken?"

He released a breath containing sound: half laugh of surprise, half self-protection.

"Sure," he said, "the day they let me join your father's yacht club."

He began to turn away but she stopped him with a hand on his arm. Five little suns seemed to rest where her fingers did, burning their shape into his flesh.

Nothing moved. Not he, not she, not the earth, not time. Everything halted in anticipation.

"I've considered ordering you to do so, but I tried that once before and it didn't work so well."

He bent down and kissed her so lightly and briefly it was over before either of them had a chance to close their eyes.

"Harken, don't," she chided. "I'm not a child. Don't treat me like one."

They stood in the throes of temptation, the blood caught in their throats, the moment sensitized by the realization that kisses between them were strictly taboo. Yet they had breached that taboo a dozen times already by meeting, picnicking, becoming friends. What paltry dictum carried any weight when balanced against what they already felt for one another?

"All right," he said. "Once, and then you go."

"And then I go," she agreed.

He knew once he did it he'd be doomed, but he put his hands round her starchy sleeves nevertheless, and took a single fateful step that brought the tips of her breasts against his suspenders. His head tilted at the very heartbeat in which hers did. Their eyes closed, their lips joined, bringing rampant stillness to all but their hearts. Above her elbows his grip tightened and the angle of his head deepened. They opened their lips and tasted for the first time, trespassing into the texture and wetness of each other until some lovely motion began, one head swaying above another while all around them the rain serenaded and the perfume of cedar flavored the shed.

One kiss. Only one.

They made it last . . . and last . . . and last . . . until all within them ached at the idea of ending it.

A bump sounded on the shed roof. They startled apart, looking up as a squirrel landed and skittered across the shingles.

They looked down into each other's eyes, their mouths still parted, breaths tripping fast, Lorna's bodice rising and falling rapidly like the belly of a sleeping kitten while Jens continued gripping her sleeves, rubbing the white cotton with his thumbs.

When she spoke her voice sounded reedy.

"Someday, when I'm as old as Aunt Agnes, I shall tell my grandchildren about this moment, just as she's told me about her lost love, Captain Dearsley."

Jens smiled and traversed her face with his eyes—lips, cheeks, eyelids, hairline, where the dark mass of her hair drooped, framed by flossy stragglers.

"You have romantic notions, Miss Lorna, that are very unwise."

She studied him with a blissful expression in her eyes, as if his kiss had transported her above a temporal plane.

"How was I to know," she returned, "unless you kissed me?"

"Now you know. Are you any happier?"

"Yes. I am infinitely happier."

"Miss Lorna Barnett"—he wagged his head—"you're an impetuous young woman and you make it hard for a man to turn you out." He dropped his hands from her sleeves. "But I must." Gently, he added, "Go on now."

She sighed and looked around as if coming back to earth. "Very well, but on second thought, I just might talk to my friend Phoebe. She may not have any judgment where Taylor is concerned, but she *is* my best friend, and if I don't talk to someone about this, I feel I shall burst."

What in the world could he do with a woman like her? She laid out her feelings like a grocer displaying his finest produce, proud of its bright color and freshness, inviting him to pick it up, squeeze and judge for himself.

"Do you think that's wise?"

"Phoebe can be trusted. We've shared a lot of secrets before."

"All right, but just remember, this isn't going to happen again. Agreed?"

With her lower lip caught between her teeth she studied his blue eyes. "I'm not going to make any promises I can't be sure to keep."

He simply gazed at her, wondering how it was possible an ordinary man like himself could put such a lovestruck expression on the face of a beautiful, privileged girl like her.

"Walk me to the door?"

She plodded with reluctance in every footfall. He followed at her shoulder, wishing she could stay the rest of the afternoon and keep him company while he worked, wishing for the first time ever that he was a rich man. At the doorway she paused and turned.

"Thank you for the fish."

"You're welcome, Miss Lorna."

"There you go with your Miss Lorna again. Doesn't it matter that you've just kissed me?"

He put a wealth of feeling into his reply. "It matters a great deal."

She captured his eyes while they both felt the tug of parting wrenching them in two directions. He could see very clearly she wanted to kiss him again. He wanted to kiss her, too. He opened the door a shoulder's width and they stood in a shaft of outside dampness while raindrops made *blip-blips* on the carpeted forest floor.

He wanted to say, Come back again, I love having you here, talking about the boat with you, sharing my dreams with you; I love your hair and eyes and smile and a dozen other things about you.

Instead he said, "Don't forget those cucumbers."

She smiled and replied, "I won't."

The last he saw of her she was running down the path holding her skirt up to her knees.

Lorna Barnett found herself surprised by her unwillingness to divulge anything to Phoebe Armfield about her tête-à-tête with Jens Harken. She hugged the knowledge to herself and retired early that night to draw it out and examine alone in the darkness. Lying flat on her back with coins of salady-smelling cucumber covering her face, she brought it all back. In memory, the entire afternoon took on a rich texture comprised of wood and rain, simplicity and honesty. What pleasure she had found in the plebeian pastime of sitting cross-legged in the middle of a fresh-wood floor and picnicking on leftover fish. What joy she had taken in facing Jens Harken at close range and watching his facial expressions run a range of responses, from laughter to thoughtfulness to admiration. And finally, when the kiss had ended, the same naked yearning she felt.

Her mother would be mortified if she knew.

Lorna was not—she was discovering—like her mother. She was a sensitive and sensual human being to whom Jens Harken had become a man, not hired help but someone respectable, likable, admirable, even, who dreamed a dream and acted upon it. Her physical attraction to him did not merely breach the barriers of class distinction; it negated them. When they were together they were simply a man and a woman, not a poor man and a rich woman. To be in his presence created happiness. To watch him work fascinated. To listen to him speak was as arresting as listening to John Philip Sousa's marches.

She found herself stunned by her intense reaction to his simplest physical aspects. His face, of course, his handsome Norwegian face; but also his hands, neck, the veins along his inner arms, his crossed suspenders, even the belled toes of his stockings—looking at any of them created a tempest of feelings within her, simply because they were part of him. When he moved, each angle of his limbs became in her eyes balletic, each turn of his head perfection. Even his clothing seemed to rustle differently than other men's.

And kissing him—oh . . . oh . . . kissing him was delight of unimagined magnitude. He had smelled like the shed, all cedary and woodsy, almost tasted that way, and when his tongue had touched hers it felt as if he'd drawn all the warm peachy glow from their surroundings into that one spot and transferred it inside her. She grew desirous simply thinking about it. Lying in her bedroom, one floor below his, she made up her mind that nothing short of incarceration could keep her from kissing him again.

Jens Harken had discovered it was far easier to escort Lorna Barnett out of his shed than out of his head. For the remainder of the afternoon she beset him, smiling from his memory, tipping her face up to be kissed, leaving it tipped when the kiss ended.

Damned adorable, incorrigible girl.

In his own room that night she was still there inside his head, very nearly inside his heart. To keep her from making further inroads in that direction, he wrote to his brother.

Dear Davin,

I think I've made some headway at last. I've finally got someone to finance the flat-hulled boat I've talked about for years—my employer, Mr. Gideon Barnett, would you believe. He's set me up in a shed, let me buy tools and wood, and I'm already doing the lofting. He still thinks I'm crazy, I believe, but he's willing to gamble his money on the off chance that I'm not. He's given me three months, even though the boat won't race until next summer. When it does, be ready to come out here. It'll win and win big, and the whole country will hear about it, and you and I will be in business. I've been saving every cent I can. I hope you have been, too. We'll need it if we want the Harken Boatworks to become a reality. When it does we'll have something to start with, because I've paid for the materials for the mold myself, so I can keep it afterwards, which is more than we had when I was out East.

I wish you were here now so we could talk about the boat design and work on it together. I've met a new friend named Ben Jonson, and I think I'll ask him to help me when it comes time to bend the ribs. He's a Norsky, as you guessed, and nobody can fair up a boat like us Norskies, yes, little brother? He works at the lumberyard where I bought my lumber, but work slows down there in the fall, when building season is over, so I think he'll be able to help me. He took me fishing on Sunday and we caught us a nice mess of walleyed pike, which are plentiful here.

Oh, by the way, I shared some of the fish with a lady.

I shared some of the fish with a lady. It was as much as Jens Harken trusted himself to say. The onslaught of feelings Lorna Barnett had stirred up in him demanded that he say that much, for, like her, he felt he would burst if he didn't tell someone. But he'd tell no more.

When the letter was sealed and the light off, he lay once more in his attic bedroom, much as she lay in hers below him, resurrecting her image and the pleasure of spending time with her, kissing her.

He closed his eyes, laced his fingers across his chest and realized something momentous. Up until now when he'd dreamed about building a fast boat, he'd dreamed of building it for himself, for the pleasure of watching it fly with the wind, and for the eventualities it would bring about: a business of his own and his brother, Davin, at his side with more customers than they could accommodate.

Now, for the first time, he dreamed of winning for her, so that he would be worthier in her father's eyes and would garner the respect of other men like her father, and would no longer be ordered back to a kitchen.

He pictured the regatta with himself skipping—always himself skipping—and Lorna Barnett on the shore, standing with the other parasolled women, cheering him on as he planed downwind with the bow of the boat lifted and the sails bellied. He pictured the boat shooting past the home buoy, and heard the applause of the crowd from the clubhouse lawn as he brought her in, and imagined Tim Iversen taking his photograph for the yacht club wall, and Gideon Barnett shaking his hand, saying, "Well done, Harken."

One kiss had enlarged his dreams to this extent. Yet he knew in his heart all this was not possible. He was not a yacht club member and probably never would be. Neither would he probably ever skip this boat, for they hired skippers with winning records and brought them from all over the country in their efforts to win the big races. He had no record, no boat of his own, no wealth, no status.

And absolutely no right to be falling in love with Gideon Barnett's daughter.

Chapter 8

————✦————

Those were the sun-strewn days of July. The weather turned hot, the rain disappeared and the gardens flourished. Levinia's roses flaunted themselves. Smythe's berries became grandiose. The lawns surrounding Rose Point Cottage seemed to hum daily with the whir of mowers, followed by the herbal scent of shorn grass. Out in the boat shed beneath the vaulty trees, the great double doors remained open fourteen hours a day, welcoming the summer breeze inside along with Miss Lorna Barnett whenever she chose to come.

She waited four days to return. On the day when she did, she went first to find her mother in the picking gardens, where Levinia was collecting long blue spikes of delphiniums in a flat basket hung over her arm.

"Mother . . . good morning!" Lorna called.

Levinia looked up, squinting from beneath the brim of a wide straw bonnet. She wore green gloves and held pruning snips.

"Good morning, Lorna."

"Isn't it a glorious day?" Lorna scanned the skies.

"It's going to be beastly hot, and you should have a bonnet on."

"Oh, I'm sorry, Mother. I forgot."

"Forgot? When you're still peeling from your last sunburn? Next you'll get freckled, and then how will you get rid of the ugly things?"

"I'll try to remember next time."

"What have you there?"

"Cookies. I smelled them baking and went down to the kitchen to investigate. Cinnamon and apple. Would you like one?"

Lorna opened the white napkin. Levinia pulled off one glove and helped herself.

"I'm taking the rest out to Mr. Harken in the shed, if it's all right with you."

"Gracious sake, Lorna, I don't like you loitering around the help that way."

"I know, but he sometimes works right on through lunch, and I thought he might like a little tideover. Is that all right, Mother?"

"Well . . ." Levinia glanced dubiously toward the vegetable garden and the woods beyond, back at Lorna and the napkin in her hand. "That's not our good linen, is it?"

"Oh, no. It's one for the staff's use, and I'll be sure to tell Harken to return it to the kitchen when he's done."

Again, Levinia threw an undecided glance toward the shed. "Well, I guess so, then."

"I've been going out occasionally and visiting with him and checking the progress on the boat. It's quite fascinating, actually. He's drawing it out full-scale, right on the floor. Would you like to come with me?"

"To that musty old building? Heavens no. Besides, I have bouquets to arrange."

"Well then, I guess I'll just go alone." Lorna sent her gaze in an appreciative arc across the gardens. "Mother, your flowers are truly breathtaking this summer. May I take one of these?"

"Help yourself . . . but, Lorna, you won't stay out in that shed very long, will you?" Levinia looked worried.

"Oh no." Lorna selected a delphinium and sniffed it. Surprisingly, it had no smell. "Just long enough to see how the work is going and give these cookies to Mr. Harken, then I thought I'd walk down along the shore to Phoebe's house. She's invited me for lunch on the veranda."

"Oh, how nice." Levinia looked relieved. "Tell her hello from me, and her mother, too. What time will you be back, then, dear?"

Backing away, Lorna shrugged. "Not late. By three for sure, then if it's not too hot I might try to talk Jenny into a game of tennis. Goodbye, Mother."

Levinia watched after her daughter, in her hand the cookie with a single bite taken from it. "Now, remember," she called, "you won't stay long!"

"No, Mother."

"And next time wear your hat."

"Yes, Mother."

Levinia sighed and watched her willful daughter disappear.

Lorna cut around the glasshouse, skirted the vegetable garden and entered the woods. She heard the engine even before she reached the shed. *Pup . . . pup . . . pup:* little explosions with long pauses between. She listened a moment, then continued along the short path to the sharp right curve that would deliver her to Harken's doorway. There at the curve, she paused to inspect herself. Juggling the cookies and delphinium in one hand, she checked her hair, running a palm over the smooth pouf to two fat ornamental hair brooches that protruded from her Gibson droop like pearl-headed chopsticks. She tugged at her skirt, looking down her midriff at the green-and-white stripes meeting like arrows down her center front. She touched the grosgrain cravat bow at her throat.

At last, satisfied, she transferred the delphinium to her right hand and stepped to the doorway of Harken's domain.

He was sawing a piece of wood, unaware of her presence. Waiting out the piercing shriek of the saw, she pleasured herself with the sight of him in a very faded shirt that had probably once been the color of tomato juice. It was so worn and thin that it draped from his limbs like jowls from an old jaw. With it he wore the usual black suspenders and black trousers. He worked bare-headed, and the rim of his hair was wet with sweat, darkened to the color of year-old grain.

The saw stopped whining but the engine continued its intermittent *pup . . . pup*. Whistling softly, he examined the piece of wood he'd just cut, running his fingertips over its sawn edge.

"Hello, Jens."

He looked up. His fingers stopped examining. Their ill-advised kiss was there between them as if it had just happened, demanding remembrance while they both knew it must be forgotten.

"Well, look who's here."

"Bearing gifts, too." Lorna went inside, approached him with her napkin-nest and flower, while he waited beside his sawing rig. "It was my turn. Cinnamon-apple cookies today, fresh from Mrs. Schmitt's oven . . . and something to match your eyes."

She offered him the delphinium first. He looked at the flower, at her, hesitated while the allure they possessed for each other smote them both with lovestruck quietude. Beside them the engine made another *pup*. He reached out to accept her gift: Its delicate blue petals painted a striking contrast to his soiled hand and faded work clothes.

"What is it called?"

"A delphinium."

"Thank you."

The flower did, indeed, match his blue eyes. It took an effort for Lorna to drag her gaze from them and recall she'd brought something more. "And here are your cookies." She put the napkin in his wide hand.

"Thank you again."

"I can't stay today. I'm going to Phoebe's for lunch on the veranda, but I just wanted to come by and see how you're doing."

He turned away, walked to the engine and touched something that shut it off. "I'm doing fine," he said, from a safer distance. "And see what I've got. Your father allowed me to buy this wonderful electro-vapor engine."

"Electro-vapor."

"Four-horsepower."

"Is that a lot?"

"You bet. It takes a spark from this little battery here and runs on illuminating gas."

"On illuminating gas . . . my."

"All I have to do is turn the switch and I can saw wood without using any elbow grease. Isn't that some miracle?"

She gave her attention to the engine. It had a big flywheel with long pulleys connecting it to the saw. He'd walked the length of those pulleys to put distance between them.

"My, yes, quite a miracle. I see you've done some cutting with it already." Across the floor where the battens had lain the last time she was here five molds stood, two feet apart, shaped like upside-down cross sections of the boat. Already she could see how they'd define the shape of the hull. He had been cutting another when she'd interrupted.

"You're making progress."

"Yes."

"I wish I could watch you work awhile, but I'm afraid I have to go. I'm supposed to be at Phoebe's by noon."

"Well . . . thanks for the cookies. And the flower."

"You're welcome."

She studied him for a very long moment, from a good ten feet away and, just before turning to leave, said, "Yes, I was right. They are very much the color of the delphinium."

At Phoebe's house, Lorna was directed to the cool seafoam-green summer room, where Mrs. Armfield was writing letters, seated on a chair by an open French door with a portable desk on her lap. She offered both hands, then her cheek for kissing. "Lorna, how nice to see you. I'm afraid Phoebe's not feeling too well today, but she told me to be sure to send you up to her room."

Upstairs, Phoebe lay curled on her bed, hugging a pillow to her abdomen.

"Phoebe . . . oh, poor Phoebe, whatever is wrong?" Lorna swiftly crossed to the bed and sat down beside her friend. She combed Phoebe's hair back from her temple.

"What's wrong every month at this time. Oh, I just hate being a girl sometimes. I get such bad cramps."

"I know. Sometimes I do, too."

"Mother had the maid bring me some warm packs to put on my stomach but they haven't helped at all."

"Poor Phoebe . . . I'm sorry . . ."

"I'm the one who's sorry. I've ruined our luncheon plans."

"Oh, don't be silly. We can have lunch any old time. You just rest and tomorrow I'm sure you'll feel better. If you do, should we have lunch then?"

They made the plan, and Lorna left her friend still coiled around the pillow.

She took the less-used shoreline rather than the road back to Rose Point property, silently thanking Phoebe for giving her an excuse to return to the boat shed, armed with her mother's reluctant approval, and the realization that nobody was expecting her back at the house till midafternoon. Picking her way through the woods, approaching him, she felt again the wondrous exhilaration that accompanied every trip she made to Jens Harken. He would put up barriers, she knew, but she understood why.

He was gone, however, when she got there. The delphinium she'd given him was lying on the sill of the north window, where the breeze ruffled its petals. The cookies were gone, but the napkin lay folded in fourths on a stack of lumber. The engine was quiet, the flywheel still. She walked near them, stooping at the stack of sawdust beneath the sawblade, picking up a handful, lifting it to her nose and letting it drift back down—fragrant, wispy evidence of his morning's labor. She examined his work in progress, running her fingertips over pencil lines he'd drawn on wood, and edges he'd cut with the saw, much as he did after he made them. She recalled his excitement over having such fine tools with which to work. She moved through the space he'd moved through, touched the things he'd touched, breathed the smells he'd breathed, and discovered that this mundane setting had been transported, in her eyes, simply because he'd been in it.

She sat on the iron bench and waited. He returned after thirty minutes, and she heard his approaching footsteps just before he reached the open double doors.

He stepped inside and halted, discovering her there. As always, a force field seemed to generate around them.

"Phoebe is ill," she told him, "and no one is expecting me till three o'clock. May I stay?"

He neither answered nor moved for the longest time. Standing as he was, with the light behind him, Lorna could not make out his features. But his pause was clear enough: It was caution, pure and simple.

"Why don't you go ask your parents and see what they say?"

"I already did. I asked my mother before I brought you the cookies."

"You asked your mother!"

"She was picking delphiniums in the garden and I stopped by and told her I was bringing the cookies to you and asked if I could have a flower."

"And she said yes?"

"Well . . . I'll have to admit, she didn't know I was bringing the flower to you."

"Miss Lorna, you know I love to have you here, but I don't think it's a good idea for you to come so often."

"Don't worry. I won't make you kiss me again."

"I know you won't because I'm not going to!"

"I just want to watch."

"You distract me."

"I'll be as quiet as a mouse."

He laughed aloud. She laughed, too, realizing what a magpie she was.

"Well, maybe not quite that quiet," she admitted. "But please let me stay anyway."

"Suit yourself," he finally conceded.

There was no more kissing. When she left, he did not invite her back again. But the next time she came, the rusty iron bench had been painted.

So began the parade of visits when Lorna would take up her station on the bench and keep Jens company while he worked. She came most often in the early afternoon, when her mother napped, sometimes bringing delectable tidbits of food she and Jens could share, sometimes sharing some sweet he brought from his noon dinner in the kitchen, explaining that the kitchen staff ate different desserts from the family. These—he thought—were often better than the fancy things served in the main dining room, which tended to be more looks than sugar.

Oh, how they would talk. Lorna especially. She would cross her ankles Indian fashion on the seat of the bench and chatter about her life. If she'd been to a chautauqua or a concert or a play, she described it in detail. If there was a soiree afterward, she would describe the food. He asked her who Mr. Gibson was, the one she'd once alluded to so briefly, and she told him about the previous summer, when the famous artist had been their houseguest and had influenced her so profoundly she'd changed her dress and hairstyle. They spent a long time discussing whether Lorna herself more closely fit into the category of Gibson's "boy-girl" (who was a sport and would enjoy losing her life on a runaway horse more than gaining the attentions of a lovesick man) or "the convinced" (who set a certain goal and pursued it without taking a single side step). They decided that if anyone was "the convinced" type, it was Harken himself, since he had left his only family to pursue his goal as a boatbuilder.

Jens spoke of his brother, Davin, and how he missed him. "I've written and told him all about this boat I'm building, and he's nearly as excited as I am. He says if it wins the regatta next year, he'll get here if he has to crawl all the way, so we can set up business together."

"I cannot wait to meet him. Did you tell him about me?"

"I told him I fed you fish."

"That's all?"

"That's all."

"Tell me what your parents were like," she said one day.

He told of a stern patriarch and a hard-working housewife who left their families behind to build a better life for their sons in America. He told of working with his father at the boatworks, prying answers out of the reticent man, who could never understand where Jens's questions came from, nor find the wherewithal to answer in a manner that would satisfy the curiosity of a young boy whose passion for boats soon outstripped his father's knowledge of them.

"So you truly didn't learn all you know about boats by working in the boatworks."

"No. Some of it just comes from in here." Jens tapped his temple. "I picture a boat and I know how it will act in the water."

Watching him work on the present one, she believed this fully.

He said to her one day, "It must be nice to have so much family, to have even your aunts live with you. I would like that."

"You only think you'd like that. There are so many people in our family it's hard to find any privacy." Lorna went on to tell Jens about her aunt Henrietta, who always seemed to know when she was going out and accosted her with humorous if aggravating reminders to always carry a sharp hatpin as a weapon. She told about Aunt Agnes's long-lost love, Captain Dearsley, and how Agnes's devotion to him had never waned, but shone like a hopeless beacon through the old woman's lonely years of being admonished and reprimanded by her older sister.

"I love my aunt Agnes," Lorna told Jens. "But I merely tolerate my aunt Henrietta. I've often thought that if I could have one wish in my life it would be to bring back Captain Dearsley for Aunt Agnes."

"You wouldn't wish for something for yourself?"

"Oh no. I have my whole life before me to work toward my wishes. Aunt Agnes is old, though, and it must be sad to see your life running out and never have love and children and a home of your own."

"So to you wishes are something you work toward, they're not pipe dreams?"

That set off a whole new avenue of discussion, which led eventually to the subject of luck and whether or not it was granted by fate or created by each person for himself.

During those days of discussion the work on the boat progressed. The cedar cross sections were completed and set in their proper relationship to one another along the length of the shed, like slices of salmon on a cutting board. These were strung together by a backbone and two side stringers made of spruce, laid in notches cut into the cross sections to receive them.

Ah, those cedar-scented, green-dappled days of deep summer. While they progressed, Lorna and Jens nurtured one another as confidantes and friends. As lovers, though, they stood fast in their resistance to each other, upholding their agreement not to kiss again. Until the day Lorna brought a bowl of the prized blackcurrants, sugared and creamed and smuggled out of the house in a Sevres china sauce dish folded inside a boating magazine. Jens saw her arrive and left his work to meet her.

"Look what I've brought!" She unveiled her prize. "Ta-daa!"

"Blackcurrants?" Jens laughed robustly. "If Smythe ever found out he'd pop a gasket."

"Aaand . . ." Lorna drew out the word like a fanfare, then proudly produced one silver spoon.

"Only one?" Jens asked.

"One is all we need."

They dragged the iron bench out to the very verge of the wide doorway and sat with their bodies inside, heels out, ankles crossed, eating blackcurrants and cream and sugar, taking turns with the spoon until, at the end, Lorna scraped every last vestige of purple juice from the side of the bowl and held it up to feed to Jens.

"You eat it," he told her. "It's the last of it."

"No . . . you," she insisted.

He was sitting with one wrist hooked casually over the backrest of the bench beyond Lorna's shoulder, the rest of him outwardly relaxed. She held the spoon in the air, waiting, her brown eyes locked with his blue ones, bent upon giving the last taste to him. Finally, his head dipped forward and he opened his mouth. She caught a glimpse of his tongue and watched, fascinated, as his lips closed around the spoon . . . and the spoon rearranged them . . . then lingered . . . lingered . . . inside his mouth . . . while that single shattering kiss came back to beguile them.

Finally she slipped the spoon free. It made a soft clink settling into the bowl, the bowl no sound at all nestling into the folds of Lorna's skirt. The only sound they heard was that of magnified heartbeats and breathing—their own—while a fine and unwelcome tension built and budded between them. For days they had been good, and careful, and discreet, and politic. But it had failed: They could not be merely friends when it was lovers they wanted to be.

Long before he moved, they both knew he would.

His arm left the bench and carried her toward him in one definite sweep as she lifted her face to his descending one. His fingers curved into her warm armpit as she reached up for his neck. There was no pretense of reserve, no coquettish or polite first affectation. Their kiss was lush, intimate, dense from the moment of contact. It involved tongues and teeth and a very stubborn gravity that seemed unwilling to allow them close enough, skewed as they were on the bench. It tasted of blackcurrants and temptation and lasted longer than the flavor of the berries, which they took from each other's tongues. It ended with Jens drawing back to rid them of the bowl and spoon before reclaiming her again. She went against him eagerly, her freed hands spreading on his back like sun on a prairie. Their mouths opened. They caressed the allowable spots—ribs, backs, napes, waists—while those crying out to be touched went unsatisfied. When at last the kiss ended they drew apart, smileless, their breaths beating on each other's faces, in plain view of anyone who happened to come around the curve in the path.

He broke free and ordered, "Come with me," led her by one hand from the bench, inside, where the wall hid them. There in the shadows, he drew her home against him and she went gladly, up on tiptoe, her arms thrown round his shoulders. Length to length, they kissed, discovering the wonder of fitting together as they'd so often imagined. The minutes stretched into the shadowy stillness of the afternoon while his hands played over her back, down her sides, bearing down upon her hips before sliding up till the butts of them rested against the side-swells of her breasts, very near indiscretion.

He lifted his head and their eyes met.

"Lorna," he said. Simply Lorna.

"Jens," she replied, experiencing the same urge to speak his name.

For some time they merely gazed, having reached this plane at last.

"Could I say it now?" he wanted to know.

"Yes . . . anything."

"You're the most beautiful woman I've ever known. I thought so from the first night you came into the kitchen."

"And I thought you were the handsomest man. It's been very hard not saying so."

"It's been very hard not saying a lot of things."

"Say them now."

"Beautiful girl, do you know how many times I've thought about doing this?"

"Kissing me?"

"Kissing you, holding you, running my hands over your fair lines." With his palms still at the sides of her breasts he stretched out his thumbs and stroked, narrowly missing two most sensitive spots.

"How many?"

"Fifty, a hundred, a thousand. So many that it kept me awake nights imagining it."

"Me too. You've truly ruined my sleep."

"I'm glad."

She took the next kiss, rising up on tiptoe and opening her mouth with an invitation he gladly accepted, delving into it fully. Their sleek tongues moved in ballet, deep, shallow, deep again. He bit her upper lip in pantomime, then licked as if to heal the unrealized hurt, and centered the kiss once more. In the midst of it, he moved his hands, slid them inward and covered both her breasts, held them gently.

Against his cheek she quit breathing.

Against his mouth, hers went lax. "Oh . . ." she whispered, and "Oh . . ." again, then stood very still with her eyelids closed and her arms over his shoulders. His caress was slow and easy, knuckles turned outward as if holding a globe, giving her time to acclimate to his touch. When she had, he explored with his thumbs.

Her eyelids flickered open. The tip of her tongue showed between her teeth. Her breasts rose and fell in his hands, marking the rhythm of her taxed breathing. He went on making small circles over those pleasure spots until a shudder quaked through her, then he put his arms around her again and gathered her close.

He spoke against her hair. "It's not safe here."

"Then we must meet someplace where it is."

"Are you sure?"

"Yes. I've been sure long before today. Oh, Jens." She gripped him tighter, feeling as thwarted and threatened and frustrated as he, unaccustomed to making plans for this sort of thing, uncertain, even, if *this sort of thing* was what they were agreeing to. There was a faint sense of transgression, an even greater one of inevitability. They felt bonded by both.

"Can you wait until Sunday?" he asked.

"If I must, but I feel as if I shall die when I walk away from you."

"There's a stretch of woods south of Tim's, where the beach is poor and rocky and nobody comes. Meet me there. I'll borrow Ben's boat. One o'clock?"

"One o'clock."

"And, Lorna?"

"Yes, Jens?"

"If you know what's good for you, you'll wear a very sharp hatpin."

On Sunday it was sunny. Lorna took a picnic. And a blanket. She wore blue and stuck a nine-inch cloisonné hatpin, freshly sharpened, into her hat. She rowed across the lake and found Jens's boat already there, on a rocky section of shoreline with a bit of a bluff leading up to the woods above. As she approached, he appeared from the trees and came down a path to wait on the shoreline, wearing a black Sunday suit and a black derby. She glimpsed his attire over her shoulder while he stood with his weight borne on one hip, the opposite leg cocked, his foot on a rock.

"Hello," he called, while she stowed the oars and the boat drifted in.

"Hello." He was waiting to take her bow line and tie it to a willow bush. The boat bumped and scraped along scarcely submerged rocks as Lorna stood up and steadied herself. She stepped over the seat to hand him the blanket and hamper, then poised before taking his waiting hand and making the leap to shore. He landed her safely, swinging her half behind him and planting her gracefully on the uneven ground.

He kept his hands at her waist. She kept hers on his shoulders. They stood immobilized by each other's presence and this summer day's bounty of time.

She took in his appearance, very different in the formal Sunday clothes, the suit over a white shirt and black tie, the hat that changed the overall shape of his face. Such a surprise it was.

He took in her appearance, pleased she'd chosen the same blue striped skirt she'd worn the day of their first picnic, the same billowing white sleeves, the same straw hat with its blue trailers.

"Hello," he said again, softer, smiling almost shyly.

She answered with a shy laugh and a very, very soft, "Hello."

Of the tens of things they'd planned to say or do at this moment, none came to mind, only to stand beneath the beating sun, resplendent in their newfound feelings for each other.

There were boats on the water within visible distance. He bent to retrieve the blanket and hand it to her. Carrying the hamper himself, he led her by the hand up the bank, where rocks and wild grasses made the footing precarious.

"Careful, it's steep."

When she began skittering backward he hauled her up to safety until they reached at last a plateau above, where the woods was heavy enough to hide them yet provided a view of the water to the west. There, beneath the birches and maples, they spread her tartan plaid blanket and pretended picnicking was what they had come here for.

There were glimpses, though, stolen and admiring. He caught her at one—it had turned into an outright stare—just as he straightened from setting the hamper on the blanket. They stood on the grass with the prepared place between them.

"Is something wrong?" he asked.

"I've never seen you in a suit before."

He looked down his front.

"It's a very old suit. My only one."

"Or a hat."

He removed it and stood with it in his hands, a courtesy he'd never before had the opportunity to show. "It's Sunday."

"No . . ." she said, "don't take it off. I like it on you."

"Very well." He put it back on, using two hands, tipping it ever so slightly off level. "For you."

She studied him, letting her glance drift from the derby to his freshly shaved face to his necktie, which formed a thick knot between the tips of a rounded shirt collar. His jacket, which was fully buttoned, appeared to be slightly too snug and short in the sleeves, as if he'd grown since it was purchased. To Lorna, it only emphasized his pleasing proportions.

"I suppose a lady shouldn't say a man looks breathtaking."

Jens couldn't restrain his smile. "No, I believe it's the man who tells the lady that." He removed the smile and added, "You look breathtaking, Miss Lorna. I hope you'll take it as a compliment when I say that I've always admired your fair line in those big sleeves and skinny skirts."

"You have?" She looked down and plucked at her sleeves as if to put more air in them. "I shall take it as my favorite compliment, even though the sleeves are forever catching on doorways and touching dusty things and getting crushed. And the skirt is only skinny in the front. In the back it's quite full . . . see?" She whirled, presenting her back—shapely, too—with the skirt poufing, the boned shirtwaist hugging and the blue bonnet ribbons trailing. When she faced him once more, her cheeks were pink. "Fair line, indeed," she teased with a smile.

He could think of nothing except how badly he wanted to kiss her, but the picnic should be had first, and some polite conversation shared, and things like the weather and the local fishing and the progress on the boat commented upon lest he appear indecently eager.

"Would you sit down, please, Miss Barnett, so I can sit down, too?"

"Oh, my goodness, I didn't realize." She knelt and watched his tall form bend and fold and find a comfortable, relaxed pose, his weight on one buttock with one foot extended and the other knee raised, one palm spread on the blanket behind him.

They looked at each other. They looked at the water.

"We couldn't have asked for a nicer day, could we?" he remarked.

"No, it's perfect."

"Lots of fishermen out."

"Yes."

"And lots of sails too."

"Mm-hmm."

"It feels good to be out of that shed for a day."

He'd covered the niceties, though he knew he'd done so too expressly for strict politeness. Their eyes were drawn to each other again, expressions painted by the unsaid.

"Shall we have our picnic right away?" she asked.

"That's fine. What have you got in there?"

She opened the hamper and began spreading things out on the blanket. "Cold chicken with a special mushroom ketchup, Jerusalem artichokes wrapped in bacon, almond tarts and glacé pineapple pears."

"You'll spoil me."

"I should love very much to spoil you." She made the remark while occupied with the foods, filling a plate. "However, I think it would take more than glacés and Jerusalem artichokes to rid you of your predilection for cold fish. This is what I love about our picnics. Mine are exotic and yours are satisfying. So we learn a little bit about each other, don't we?"

She handed him the plate with a flash of a smile and began filling one for herself. He watched her, admiring each motion, each feature, her delicate fingers, long throat in its cylinder of white, so many, many buttons up her center front, the way her hair ballooned beneath her bonnet brim, the delicate puff of her chin when it was tucked down.

"Did you ask Mrs. Schmitt to pack the hamper?" he inquired.

"Yes, I did."

"What did she say?"

She went on filling her plate but her diction became clipped. "She isn't paid to *say* anything. Furthermore, I don't answer to Mrs. Schmitt and neither do you. Did you borrow your friend's boat?" She hit him with a direct look.

"Yes, I did."

"What did you tell him?"

"The truth. That I was meeting a girl."

"Did he ask who she was?"

"He knows."

"He does?"

"He found the blue delphinium on the windowsill and asked how it got there. I'm no good at lying." A stretch of silence scintillated between them, rife with hinted truths about their feelings and the significance of these clandestine meetings. At length, Jens went on. "I want you to know, Lorna, that if we're ever discovered, if word ever gets to your mother and father and they confront me with it, I'll tell the truth."

She looked him straight in the eye and replied, "So shall I."

They each held a plate filled with excuses. Across the top of the picnic hamper their gazes declared very clearly that this willful postponement of kisses was becoming more than either could tolerate.

Jens set his plate on the grass. He reached across the hamper and commandeered hers, set it aside, too, along with the hamper and tins. Next, he removed his hat. "It's such a pretty little lunch," he said, "but I'm not the least bit hungry."

Lorna's cheeks blazed pink and her heart knocked as Jens knelt before her, his eyes steady on her upturned face, his pose filled with intention while she sat primly on her heels, her hands joined in her lap. He gripped her arms, crushing her starched sleeves, and drew her up . . . up . . . into his embrace. She went joyously, into a kiss of greatest import, for it was the first they had willed—mutually—long before this day arrived, this hour, this minute. In their beds alone at night, they had willed it. Trudging through the hours of the days, they had willed it. Rowing to this trysting spot in separate boats, they had willed it. Now at last it happened, callow as it began, for he'd had to bend down and dip his head beneath her hat brim to reach her lips. Joined like a wishbone, with their mouths softly engaged, they said their true hello. Jens parted Lorna's lips with his tongue, felt the tip of hers come shyly to meet it and stroked it: *Come hither, don't be afraid, let me woo you.*

Some gulls flew by, squawking. Some flies buzzed over their plates. In the distance a steam whistle blew. They heard none of this, heard only the voices in their heads that said, *At last, at last.*

The earth sighed. . . . Or was it the breeze? The summer trembled, or was it their touch? Two glad lovers neither knew nor cared as Jens blindly lifted his hands to her hat, found the pin and removed it, then the hat itself from her head. Lorna reached up reflexively, interrupting the kiss, just as the hat sailed away to join his on the grass. Her chin dropped down and she touched her hair with the same momentary shyness of earlier, feeling for any strand loosened by the departing straw. He took her face in his hands and lifted it to his intense regard.

Only summer was there to witness as they itemized and idolized—eyes, noses, lips, chins, shoulders, hair, eyes again.

"Yes," he said, "you're as perfect as I remember."

His head lowered, his arms surrounded her, drawing her flush against his black Sunday suit. At last they were body to body, mouth to mouth. All they'd been wishing they felt: fully-matched desire. He held her low across the spine, waltzlike, against his sturdy hips. His knees remained widespread. Her skirts puddled around them. She clung to his shoulders.

They twisted till their fit became grassy—two blades blown by the same wind—and the kiss became a wild suckling of mouths, wet and unrestrained in that awful burst of impatience between arousal and denial. She felt her mouth freed and exulted, "Jens . . . Jens . . ." while their arms crushed one another and beyond his shoulder she saw the birch branches swaying overhead.

"I can't believe this," he told her in a stranger's voice, a voice constricted with desire.

"Neither can I."

"You're really here."

"And you're really here."

"I thought this afternoon would never come, and when it did, I was sure I'd wait here for nothing."

"No . . . no . . ." She drew back and gave his mouth a brief and darting kiss, then another to his cheek. "How could you think that? I've always come to you, haven't I?"

"You know I'd come to you if I could." He captured her hands, kissed both her palms, then pressed them to his chest.

"Yes, I do know that now." She knelt with her hands spread flat upon him, upon his woolen jacket that felt warm and scratchy and marvelously exotic for belonging to this special man.

"Every time you come to the shed and I look up and find you standing there in the doorway, this happens to me."

"What?"

"This." He pressed her right hand even harder against him.

"This?" Looking into his blue eyes she slipped three fingers beneath his lapel and centered her hand over his clamoring heart. His white shirt was smooth with starch, his suspender textured, the flesh beneath it solid as hickory, and ever so warm. *Th-thup, th-thup, th-thup:* His heart felt as if it might bruise her palm.

"Oh . . ." she breathed, kneeling very still, concentrating. "Just like mine . . . for hours after I see you."

"Really?" he said softly, while absorbing the thrill of her hand inside his jacket. "Let me feel."

When she made no reply he laid his hand carefully on her heart—a big, rough boatbuilder's hand on the closely tucked fine white lawn of her blouse. He counted the heartbeats that seemed to have accelerated to the same pace as his own. He watched acceptance find and dwell in her eyes. And finally he let the hand drop gently to cover the fullest part of her breast. She closed her eyes and teetered. Her fingers clutched his shirtfront. Her breath came in tiny patters that pushed her flesh against his palm in rapid beats.

She thought, *Oh, Mother . . . Mother . . .*

Then, *Oh, Jens . . . Jens . . .*

She felt his mouth come down upon hers, and the shift of his body as he took her with him off her knees onto her back. His weight came down, too—a great, wonderful, welcome weight securing her beneath him—while his hand continued shaping and reshaping her breast, his mouth shaping and reshaping her mouth.

Below, his body beat a rhythm upon hers, his foot hooked her left knee and drew it aside, creating a cradle within which he lay.

When the kiss ended she opened her eyes to see his face framed by green leaves and blue sky. The rhythm below stopped . . . a pause only, before resuming . . . slower . . . It stopped again. No smiles. Only pure involvement with the tensions in their bodies, recognizing them, allowing them, saying so with their eyes. His hand moved slower on her breast, exploring lightly while he looked down at it, then placed breathy kisses on her nose, eyelids and chin.

He found her hand, carried it to her own waist. "Unbutton this," he whispered, and pushed himself back to kneel with one knee on either side of her right leg, pressing her skirts intimately against her. He sat back heavily upon her leg, removing his jacket while she began freeing the thirty-odd buttons of her shirtwaist.

Thirty buttons were a lot: He finished first and loosened his necktie, then said, "Here . . . let me," and bent forward to take over her task. His eyes followed his fingers; hers followed his eyes. When he reached her chin she raised it to clear the way. The last button fell free, leaving a hesitation beat while both of them struggled for breath. He put both hands inside her bodice and spread it wide, exposing her collarbone and throat, her white chest and her whiter shift with its shoulder straps edged in lace and a new set of buttons.

He undid these, too, but left the panels overlapped, her breasts still covered as he tipped forward, braced a hand beside each of her ears, closed his eyes and began touching his open lips to her collarbone . . . throat . . . chin . . . putting space between his mouth and her skin until she was unsure if she was being kissed or only breathed upon. Something warmed the underside of her jaw—lips? breath?—and tarried just above her left breast until she thought she must certainly either be touched there or die.

She became touched. There . . . upon her breast, which he gathered in a hand, shift and all, as he toppled to one side, collecting her against him and slipping an arm between her and the ground. Her breast was full, heavy, supple. He held it like a pear in his palm, then explored it through white cotton—its full, resilient perimeter, its aroused tip. Momentarily, he abandoned it to rub her shift back from her shoulder, exposing the single breast to summer shadows and his enamored gaze. Its aureole was copper-hued and stood like a gem in a high mount. Its orb was covered with a haze of ultrafine hair.

"My mother said . . ." she murmured behind closed eyes, and let the fragment trail as his wet mouth stole rational thought and made of her breast a lovely thing filled with life, warmth, need. From it a river seemed to unleash, some shimmering, sparkling flow running to the nether reaches of her body.

Then the shift was down at her waist and his open mouth had left one breast wet and moved to another as her shoulders arched up to meet him.

"Oh . . ." she breathed, her hands in his hair, "this is wicked, isn't it, Jens?"

He lifted his head and kissed her mouth. His was wet beyond the perimeter of his lips. "Some people would say so. Does it feel wicked?"

"No . . . oh no . . . I've never felt this way before."

"Your mother warned you against this—is that what you were going to say?"

"Don't talk, Jens. Please . . . just . . ." Her fingers were laced through his thick blond hair as his face loomed above hers. She circled the helix of his ears with her thumbs, and gently drew his head down. And it all began again, all the smoldering, kissing, wetting, grinding introductions that led only to frustration which Lorna did not fully understand. Jens did, though. When it reached a peak he could no longer handle, he guttered, "Lorna, we've got to stop," and rolled off her abruptly. He lay on his back, panting, with one wrist over his eyes.

"Why?"

"Just be still," he said, and reached over to grip her thigh through her skirts, his fingertips nearly at her groin. "Just be still."

She rolled her head to study him but his eyes were closed beneath his wrist. He gripped her leg hard. She looked up at the trees and tried to catch her breath, all the time aware of his hand and where it was. Someplace in the woods a squirrel chattered. Beside her Jens's chest rose and fell like a fevered man's. His hand began moving, up and down, rubbing her own underwear against her leg, his fingertips forcing petticoat and skirts and pantaloons to brush a hidden part of her that sent out startling reactions. Was this a caress? This tight, tight grip that moved first up and down, then sideways, twisting?

She had no idea what to do, say, think. She lay as still as if asleep, only stiffer, quite afraid, while all the feelings inside her seemed to rush to the private swell of flesh near his fingertips.

His wrist remained over his eyes. His sleeve touched her bare right arm.

I must go, she thought, but before she could voice the words his hand went away. He lay motionless for some time. Finally his head turned and she felt herself being studied at close range. She concentrated on the overlapped leaves above, delicate serrated edges shifting and changing the pattern of the blue backdrop behind them. Moments and moments passed before Jens finally spoke, giving her the impression he'd done some hard thinking before doing so.

"Do you know what all this leads to, Lorna?"

"Leads to?" She was afraid to look at him since he'd touched her that way.

"You don't, do you?"

"I don't know what you mean."

"Your aunt Henrietta's warning about the hatpin. Do you know what it means?"

Confused, she kept silent.

"I suspect your mother warned you about all this wickedness."

"She didn't say it was wicked."

"What did she say?"

With no answer forthcoming, Jens took Lorna's chin and made her meet his eyes.

"Tell me what she said."

"That men would . . . would try to touch me, and when they did I must immediately go into the house."

"She's right, you know. You should be heading back to the house right now."

"Are you telling me to go?"

"No. I'm telling you it would be best for you. But I want you here with me every minute you can stay."

"Oh, Jens, I really don't understand."

"You've never done this before, have you?"

She colored and would have sat up, but he was too quick, keeping her where she was.

"You have!" he said with some amazement, leaning over her to see straight down into her eyes. "With DuVal?"

"Jens, let me up."

"Not until you've answered me." He took her chin. "Was it with DuVal?"

Forced to meet his eyes, she found lying difficult. "Well . . . a little."

"A little?"

She found some spunk. "All right, yes."

"He kissed you there, the way I did?"

"No, he only . . . you know . . . touched me, sort of . . . like you did in the shed."

"Touched you."

"But I always did what my mother said—I went in the house right away."

"You were very wise."

"What's wrong, Jens? I shouldn't have done this with you and now you're angry with me, is that right?"

"I'm not angry with you. Get up." He took her hands and made her sit. "I'm not angry—you mustn't think that. But it's time you got dressed."

For the first time guilt assailed her. She hung her head as she threaded her arms through her shift and drew it together to cover herself. He saw and took pity, untwisting one strap on her shoulder, then sitting back and watching as she began the slow process of closing thirty-three buttons: He counted them this time. Lifting her sagging chin, he placed a soft kiss on her mouth. "Don't look so forlorn. You haven't done anything wrong." His words did little to remove the sudden glumness from her face. It remained downcast while he touched the fine curls at her forehead. "Your hair's come down. Do you have a comb?"

"No," she said to her knees.

"I have." He withdrew one from a pocket. "Here."

She wouldn't look at him all the while she found her scattered hairpins on the blanket, combed her hair up and did simple things to it. When she'd restored it to its bird's nest shape, she handed him the comb.

"Thank you," she said so meekly he scarcely heard.

He retrieved her hat, watched her pin it on and searched for some way to make her happy again.

"Should we have our picnic now?" he asked.

"I'm not very hungry."

"I am," he replied—anything to see her smile return.

"Very well." Obediently, she turned to get their plates. The food was crawling with ants. Not only crawling: swimming. To Lorna's dismay her eyes had filled with tears. She kept her head turned to hide them, trying to control her voice. "I'm afraid our picnic is r . . . ruined. The ants are all . . ." She tried for one more word. ". . . All ov . . ." She swallowed hard, but the tears kept coming, and her throat had closed up. A sob broke forth as she went limp, doubling forward to drop the plates blindly on the ground. There she slumped, the plates pressing the backs of her hands to the grass.

Immediately Jens went to his knees, turning her into his arms. "Oh, Lorna, what is it? Don't cry, sweetheart, don't cry . . . you'll break my heart."

She clung to his neck. "Oh God, my God, Jens, I love you."

He closed his eyes. He swallowed. He crushed her to his breast while she sobbed out broken words. "I love you so m . . . much that nothing else m . . . matters anymore, only seeing you, b . . . being with you. Oh Jens, what's g . . . going to happen?"

He had no answers. All of these days leading up to this moment he'd needed none because the words had gone unspoken. Now they were in the open, joined by more which spilled forth from Lorna. "To think that this spring when I came out here to the c . . . cottage I didn't even know you existed, and now your v . . . very existence is the most important thing in my life."

"If we stopped this right now—"

"No! Don't say it! How can I stop this when it's all that matters? When I have been more alive since I've met you than ever before? When my days begin with thoughts of you and end with desire for you. When I lie in my bedroom and think of you above me and imagine myself sneaking up the servant's stairway and finding your room."

"No! You must never do that, Lorna, never!" He pulled back and held her sternly by the sleeves. "Promise me!"

"I won't promise. I love you. Do you love me, Jens? I know you do. I've seen it in your eyes a hundred times, but you're not going to say it, are you?"

"I thought . . . if I didn't say it, it might be easier."

"No, it will be no easier at all. Say it. If you feel it, say it. Give me that much."

Her challenge hung in the air between them until at last he said, almost defeated, "I love you, Lorna."

She dove against him and held him as if to keep him near her forever. "Then I'm happy. For this one moment, I'm happy. I think I knew this could happen right from the first. From the night I walked into the kitchen and demanded to know what had happened to set my father off. When you admitted you'd put the note in his ice cream I began admiring you on the spot."

"Damn that note anyway," he despaired.

"No," she breathed. "No. It was meant to happen, this was meant to happen. Can't you feel it?"

They shared some quiet time, holding each other, but in his soul Jens knew heartbreak lay ahead for both of them. He sat back and held her hands loosely, rubbing her knuckles with his thumbs. "What about DuVal?" he asked. "What about the watch he gave you, and your parents' wish that you marry him? And the fact that I'm the kitchen help?"

"Never!" Her fierce expression demanded no more rebuttal. "Never again, Jens Harken! You're a boatbuilder, and one day you'll have a business of your own, and people from all over America will come to you to have you build boats for them. You've told me so."

He put a hand on her jaw, silenced her lips with a thumb. "Ah, Lorna,

Lorna . . ." He sighed, long and wearily. He looked off into the woods. A long time passed.

She broke the sad silence, asking, "When can we meet again?"

He seemed to pull his thoughts from the middle distance and drew her to her feet. Tenderly, he looked into her eyes.

"Think about it. Think if you really want to, and all the times you'll cry if we keep seeing each other, and all the sneaking and lying we'll have to do. Is that what you want, Lorna?"

It wasn't, of course. Her eyes told him so.

"You said you wouldn't lie," she reminded him.

"Yes, I did, didn't I?" The unspoken truth said they'd both do so if forced to. Each of them disliked knowing this about themselves.

"It's late," he said. "You have to get going."

Tears brimmed in her eyes as she shifted her gaze to the plates, still crawling with ants.

"Yes," she whispered lifelessly.

"Come, I'll help you put the picnic away."

They knelt and spilled their lovely food into the grass, stowed the plates and folded the blanket in forlorn silence. He took the hamper, she the blanket, and they walked back to the crest of the footpath. He led the way down, steadying her with one hand as she followed. At the boats, he stowed things, freed the painter for her, then turned. They stood facing each other on the gray rocks.

"I didn't even ask you how your boat is coming," she said.

"Fine. Just fine. I'll be steaming the ribs soon."

"May I come and watch?"

He tipped his face to the sky, closed his eyes and swallowed.

"All right," she relented. "I won't. But tell me you love me one more time, just so I can have it to remember."

He kissed her first, covered her delicate jaws with both hands and held her mouth firmly in place beneath his, trying to put into the kiss all the heartbreak he, too, felt. Their tongues joined in sad goodbye while above them the sun blazed and beside them the blue water glinted. "I love you," he said, and watched her leave with tears in her eyes.

Chapter 9

Returning home after her tryst with Jens, Lorna felt grateful it was Sunday. A cold supper buffet meant she need not face her parents over a formal dinner table. She had no appetite anyway, and spent the supper hour alone in her room, sketching Jens's name in rococo letters surrounded by roses and ribbons and forget-me-nots.

She dipped her pen and began adding a bluebird. With only one of its wings complete, she dropped the pen, covered her face with both hands and pressed her elbows to the dressing table.

Did he mean never to see her again? Was that his ulterior meaning when he'd said, Think if you want to, Lorna. . . . Think of all the times you'll cry and all the sneaking and lying we'll have to do.

She was so close to crying now.

This was love, then, this aching, forlorn dolorousness within. She had not suspected it would affect one so wholly, that it would take a life whose course had always been set and cast it adrift this way; that it could turn a gay nature into a gray one.

She drew his name again, trimmed in flowers with drooping heads. On the flowers she put faces raining teardrops. When her own threatened, she hid the sketches inside one of her summer hats and put the cover back on the bandbox.

She wandered the house listlessly. Her sisters were looking through scrapbooks. Theron had gone to bed. Gideon was smoking a cigar on the back veranda. Levinia and Henrietta were absorbed in a game of backgammon. Intent upon the board, they failed to look up when Lorna wandered to the morning room doorway. She stood a moment, watching the two women, who looked as if they were piqued with each other's recent plays, then returned upstairs and knocked softly on Aunt Agnes's door.

Agnes answered, "Come in," and put down her book face first on the bedcovers.

Lorna wandered in and found her aunt against her pillows with the coverlet turned back across her lap. Like a little girl lost, she inquired, "What are you reading?"

"Oh, just one of my old favorites from *Harper's. Anne,* it's called."

"Perhaps I shouldn't disturb you."

"Oh, heavens, don't be silly. I've read that old story a hundred times. Myyyy my, my, my, my, my . . . What is this?" Aunt Agnes pulled a long face. "You do look the very picture of dejection. Come here, child." She held out one arm and Lorna fell across the bed into its shelter.

"Tell your old aunt Agnes what's wrong."

"Oh . . . nothing. And everything. Growing up, minding Mother, these quiet Sunday nights."

"Ah, yes, they can get long for us single women, can't they? Where is that young man of yours? Why aren't you doing something with him?"

"Taylor? Oh, I don't know. I just don't feel like it tonight."

"Did you have words with him? Could that be the reason you're so glum?"

"No, not exactly."

"What about your sisters, and Phoebe—where are they?"

"I just didn't feel like being with them."

Agnes accepted this and stopped probing. Gloaming settled outside the window while Lorna lay ensconced by the comforting smells of starched cotton, violets and camphor.

After a while, Lorna said, "Aunt Agnes?"

"Hm?"

"Tell me about you and Captain Dearsley . . . what it was like when the two of you fell in love."

The old woman retold her timeworn stories, about a man in a white uniform with swaying gold-braided epaulettes, and dress military balls, and a woman overcome by love.

When the narrative ended, Lorna lay as before and stared across her aunt's breast at the roses and ribbons climbing the wallpaper.

"Aunt Agnes . . ." She composed her words carefully before going on. "When you were with him, did you ever feel tempted?"

Agnes thought, *Ah, so that's what this is about.* Wisely, she refrained from voicing the remark. Instead she answered truthfully, "It is the nature of love to tempt."

"Did he feel tempted, too?"

"Yes, Lorna, I'm quite certain that he did."

A long spell passed while the two communicated in silence. Finally Lorna spoke aloud. "When Aunt Henrietta warns me to make sure I wear a hatpin, what is she really warning me about?"

It took some seconds before Agnes responded. "Have you asked your mother?"

"No. She wouldn't answer me honestly."

"Have you and your young man been spooning?"

"Yes," Lorna whispered.

"And it has gotten . . . personal?"

"Yes."

"Then you know." Agnes hugged her niece tighter. "Oh, Lorna, darling, be careful. Be so very, very careful. Women can end up in terrible disgrace if they do those things with a man."

"But I love him, Aunt Agnes."

"I know. I know." Agnes closed her wrinkled eyelids and kissed Lorna's hair. "I loved Captain Dearsley, too. We went through all the same things you're going through right now, but you must wait till your wedding night, then there are no bounds to restrict you. You can share your body without shame, and when you do there shall be only the greatest joy for you both."

Lorna tipped her face up and kissed her aunt's cheek. It was downy and softened by age. "Aunt Agnes, I love you. You're the only one in this whole household I can talk to."

"I love you, too, child. And—believe it or not—you're the only one I can talk to, too. Everybody else thinks I'm dottier than a case of chicken pox, just because I enjoy my memories. But what else have I got besides your mother's short shrift, and Henrietta's constant belittling, and your father—well, I'm grateful for the home he gives me, but he treats me like I'm an idiot, too. Never asks my opinion of anything that matters. You, though, child. You're the special one. You have something more valuable than all the money and power and social standing it's possible to achieve in this world. You have a love of people. You care about them, and that's what makes you special. Many's the day I've said a prayer of thanks for you in this house. Now . . ." Agnes slapped Lorna's rump. "I think I hear my sister coming. She'll have some cutting remark to offer if she finds you wrinkling her side of the bed. You'd better get up."

Before she could, Henrietta came in. She halted at the sight of Lorna clambering off the bed, then closed the door.

"I should think, young woman, that you'd know better than to climb on someone else's bed in your shoes. And you, Agnes, should know better than to let her."

To make up for Henrietta's barb, Lorna knelt on one knee and stretched across the bed to kiss Agnes's cheek.

"Love you," she whispered. Passing the other aunt, whose mouth looked as if she were spitting out a cricket, Lorna said, "Good night, Aunt Henrietta."

The following day—only one day after Lorna's picnic with Jens—her mother had scheduled a croquet match. She had done so two weeks before, making it impossible for Lorna to avoid attending. Levinia had planned the event for early evening, a get-together for the young people, she said: Croquet at six P.M. followed by a twilight supper on the lawn.

That evening when the guests arrived, the grass looked plush in the long shadows. Against its emerald nap, the men's white trousers and the women's pastel skirts appeared paler, richer. Even the white wickets and stakes made a show against it. Tables for four dotted the south edge of the lawn. Each was draped with pristine battenberg lace, drawn up at the hems by nosegays of pink roses and white orchids with ribbons trailing down to lie curled on the grass. Upon each table a hurricane candle awaited the dusk, its glass globe ringed by flowers matching those below. The scene was sumptuous in every detail, with the lake in the background and the ladies all in wide-brimmed hats, these, too, laden with flowers.

Lorna wore one, a new white one with yards of gauzy tulle twisted round and round its crown like the work of a thousand spiders, and in this haze, a trio of lavender cabbage roses matching her trim-waisted dress.

She had overcome her blue mood of the day before and was actually enjoying the croquet match. Some of the very young set were included—Jenny, of course, and her friends Sissy Tufts and Betsy Whiting. Jackson Lawless and Taylor were there, as well as Phoebe and her brother, Mitch. There were sixteen in all, creating two even teams playing on two parallel courts. Mitch had ended up on Lorna's team and had been flirting with her ever since the game began, suggesting they go sailing once more before it was time for him to return to school in the city. She had laughingly refused for the third time when Mitch gave his blue-striped ball a solid rap that sent it smack up against hers.

Swaggering over, grinning, he studied her red-striped ball with wicked intent in his eyes. "Well now . . . I could be generous and leave you where you are . . . or I could send you to kingdom come. Which one will it be?"

"Mitch, you wouldn't!"

"Why wouldn't I? Maybe if you'd have been nice and said yes you'd go sailing with me, I might take pity on you."

"Oh, Mitch, please . . ." She began to fawn over him. "Look how close you are to that wicket. Why, with your two free shots you could be through it and halfway to the next wicket!"

Instead, he lined up to send her ball to kingdom come. She gave him a jostle that toppled him off-balance, and he pushed her aside to get back at her ball. A good-natured scuffle ensued.

"Brat!" she teased.

From across the court Taylor called, "Lorna, is he going to send you?"

"I think so! Will you come and beat him up if he does?"

"Here goes." Mitch butted the balls, anchored his own with a foot and—*crack!*—sent Lorna's red striped one rolling off the lawn, across a graveled walk and into a privet hedge bordering the gardens.

Lorna turned to watch it go. "Mitch, you big bully. Wait till—"

The words died in her throat. Coming toward her along the edge of the garden through which he was not allowed to walk was Jens Harken. He still wore his work clothes, the knees white with sawdust, the shirt sleeves rolled to the elbow. Obviously he was heading toward the kitchen for his supper. He stopped when he saw her. The two of them stared, transfixed.

Behind her, Taylor came to deliver mock punches to Mitchell, then drop a possessive hand on Lorna's shoulder. "I fixed his wicket, Lorna," Taylor said.

She had no delusions about how this tableau appeared to Jens: A privileged rich girl, cavorting with her peers on the verdant croquet court while behind them the tables, festooned with flowers and lace, awaited the hour when the hired help would bring out a fancy meal. Then the young men in their white linen suits would seat the young ladies in their expensive hats and gowns while the candles held back the gloaming. In the midst of all this frolicked she, the woman who had yesterday professed to love Jens Harken, wearing a small gold watch on her breast, caught in the midst of playful antics with—among others—the handsome young flour-milling heir her parents expected her to marry.

Staring at Jens Harken through the late summer twilight, Lorna wanted to drop her mallet and run to him, reassure him: What you've witnessed means nothing; it's how we live, but not always how we want to. I'd rather be with you in the boat shed than here at this soiree my mother arranged. I'd rather be watching your hands shape wood than holding it with my own, rapping a silly ball around the grass.

"Lorna?" Taylor said behind her, squeezing her shoulder. "I think it's your turn."

She glanced back to find his eyes fixed on Jens, who moved on toward the house.

From the other croquet court someone called, "Hey, DuVal, what are you doing over there? You're playing on this court!"

"Yeah, Taylor, get back here!"

"Lorna?" he asked, frowning. "Is something wrong?"

"No!" she answered too brightly, wishing he'd go away, drop his hand from her shoulder, stop studying her eyes so closely. "Just that I've got to try to get this ball out of the privet hedge now, that's all." She shrugged away from his touch and said with false gaiety, "Thank you for defending me."

But who would defend her before Jens Harken? Who would tell Jens how she hurried to the privet hedge to hide the fact that her eyes were gleaming with tears? He would think—with good reason—that she was plying her womanly wiles on two men at once. Three, even, for there had been Mitchell, a full two years younger than she, with whom she'd been involved in a playful scuffle just as Jens came along the path. Why would it not look as if she was playing the role of the consummate flirt? Furthermore, why would a poor, struggling boatbuilder believe a woman with such a privileged life would find it the slightest bit constricting?

"Supper! Supper, everyone!" On the far side of the lawn, Levinia was waving a handkerchief. "You'll have to call this last game a bye!"

Gideon stood behind her, his forefingers and thumbs in his vest pockets as he observed the young people. On the tables behind them the candles had been lit. Compotes of fruit had been delivered to each place setting, the facets of the crystal stemware catching the candlelight and scattering it around the scene like fallen stars.

"Come along now! Put those mallets down!"

Taylor slipped up behind Lorna and captured her elbow, tucking it firmly against his ribs. "Come along now," he gently mimicked Levinia, taking Lorna's mallet from her hand. "Put those mallets down and come to supper with the fellow who thinks you're the prettiest girl on the croquet court. Unless, of course, you were planning to sit with Mitchell Armfield, who is—in case you hadn't noticed—still wet behind the ears."

Here was Taylor, commandeering her elbow. And there was her father, watching. And her mother, whose only achievements were measured by the successes of her supper parties. And all around were Lorna's peers, laughing and happy and unaware of the drama that had just occurred at the edge of the garden where the kitchen handyman cum boatbuilder had confronted the society belle whom he had secretly kissed and caressed just yesterday.

Trapped in a social web from which there seemed no escape, Lorna allowed Taylor to escort her to the table.

Sleep came reluctantly that night. She felt she owed Jens an explanation, an apology. The nights had grown cooler and smelled of chrysanthemums, the harbingers of autumn. Not long now and September would arrive, and with it chill nights, then frost, threatening the water pipes in the house and sending the family back to Saint Paul for the winter. When they returned to the Summit Avenue house, Jens Harken would be left behind to complete the boat he had begun. What then? Would this summer's rendezvous be relegated to nothing more than a memory—best forgotten—of a tryst between a misguided young girl and a lonely immigrant who found temporary pleasure in each other's company?

It felt like more.

It felt like love.

It *was* love; thus today demanded both explanation and apology.

The following morning immediately after breakfast Lorna headed straight for the boat shed. She smelled it long before she reached it: wood scent so heavy in the air she was sure her clothing would smell of it when she returned to the house. She reached the open double doors and found herself face-to-face with the reason why: Inside, Jens had rigged up a steam box for bending the ribs of the mold. It was fired up, loaded and sending out small plumes of white mist at the smallest breaks in the pipes. Standing before the steam box, inspecting the operation, was her father. Beside him was Ben Jonson, whom she recognized from the fishing boat. Photographing the events for the yacht club wall and any newspaper interested was Tim Iversen.

Gideon saw Lorna the moment she saw him.

"Lorna, what are you doing here?"

"I came to see the progress on the boat. After all, if it hadn't been for me it wouldn't have been designed. Good morning, Mr. Iversen. Good morning, Mr. Harken." Not for nothing did Lorna possess some of Gideon's own backbone: She entered the shed as cool-headedly as if she'd fully expected her father to be there. "I don't believe we've met," she said to Jonson. "I'm Lorna Barnett, Gideon's daughter."

He slapped the cap off his head and accepted her handshake. "Ben Jonson. I'm happy to meet you, Miss Barnett."

"Do you work for my father?"

"Not exactly. I work at the lumberyard, but things are slacking off over there now that the season's ending, so I'm taking the morning off to help Jens bend these ribs."

"I hope you don't mind if I watch."

"Not at all."

Gideon interrupted. "Does your mother know you're out here?"

Lorna's voice said, "I don't believe she does." Her eyes said, *Hadn't you noticed, Father—I'm eighteen years old?*

"This is men's work, Lorna. Go back to the house."

"To do what? Press flowers? With all due respect, Father, how would you like to be told to go back to the house when there's a boat being built that may change yachting history, right out here in our very own shed? Please let me stay."

Tim interrupted. "While you're deciding, Gid, do you mind if I take a picture? I've got the camera all ready." He moved toward his tripod and black hood. "In the annals of the White Bear Yacht Club it could be important someday—boatbuilder, boat owner and boat owner's daughter, who convinced him the idea had merit. Don't forget, Gid, I was there when she asked you."

"Oh, all right, take your infernal picture, but make it quick. I've got a train to catch."

Tim took that infernal picture, and a lot more, and Gideon Barnett forgot about catching the train into town because the actual ribbing process was about to begin, and he was as fascinated with it as was his daughter. Jens had made his steam box out of a large-diameter metal pipe, plugged at one end by a wooden stopper, at the other by rags, fed by steam from a hot water boiler. The boiler created a quiet sizzle and took the faint touch of chill off the morning as Jens explained his work.

"An hour in the steam box is all it takes to expand the grain of the wood enough to make it pliable. When that white oak comes out of there it'll be as limp as a noodle, but it won't stay that way for long. That's why I needed Ben today. The mold is all ready, as you can see. . . ." He turned toward it. "The notches are all cut in the stringers." There were three longitudinal stringers. "And the boardboxes are in and the gunwale on. Now all we need is those ribs. What do you say, Ben"—Jens and Ben exchanged a bright-eyed look of eagerness—"you ready to play hot potato?"

The two men donned gloves and Jens removed the rag from the end of the pipe. A cloud of fragrant steam billowed out. The moment it cleared, he reached in and pulled out a length of white oak. It was an inch thick and an inch wide and, indeed, as white and limp as a cooked noodle. Ben took one end, Jens the other, and together they hurried to fit it across the boat, from gunwale to gunwale, into three clean notches waiting to receive it.

"Woo, she's a hot one!"

Working one on either side of the frame, they smoothed it in, removed their gloves and nailed it to each of the three stringers. With their knees they bent it down over the gunwale, cut it off with handsaws and nailed it to the gunnel on each side. The entire process had taken a matter of a few minutes.

"When we're done ribbing 'er up, the fair lines will show almost as clear as on the finished boat, and I guarantee you, Mr. Barnett, she'll be as fair as a boat can be. Another rib coming up," Jens announced, and withdrew a second one from the steam box, flopped it over the mold, and the two men repeated the process: fit, nail, trim, nail. Every six inches along the cross sections: fit, nail, trim, nail.

Their gloves got wet and they handled the hot ribs gingerly. Sometimes they yelped. Sometimes they blew on their reddened fingers. Their knees got wet and, more than once, burned.

Lorna watched, wholly fascinated as the shape of the boat appeared, rib by rib. She watched this man she loved, tugging off gloves with his teeth, wielding a hammer, cleaving with a saw, sweating as he advanced along the length of the mold, leaving a fragrant, white skeleton behind. She observed his pleasure in his work, the deftness and skill of his every movement, his keen sense of oneness with Jonson as they toiled in tandem. The two men matched motions until they'd perfected their timing and each of them finished a rib at the same moment. A look would pass between them as they'd step back from the newly applied rib, a look of satisfaction and concord that recognized—each in the other—purpose, talent and mutual skill.

Then, amidships, Jens would squat on his heels, peer along the snowy oaken ribs and view the fair line from this angle, that, and another. He would walk to the opposite end of the frame and peer outward toward the open doorway—port side, starboard side—bringing Lorna an even clearer understanding of the importance of all those dots on the floor during lofting. Their exactitude, transferred finally into three dimensions, brought satisfaction to the Scandinavian boat designer.

"Yup, she's fair," he'd murmur, more to himself than to anyone else in the shed.

In less than two hours the entire mold was ribbed up. Gideon Barnett was still there, watching. Tim Iversen had taken many photographs. Lorna Barnett had watched the entire process and was still waiting to be recognized in any way by Jens Harken.

He walked to the far side of the building and came back with a long batten.

Against the mold, Jonson held one end while Harken held the other. "This is her sheer line," he told Barnett. "Not much boat in the water, is there?"

"Not much," Barnett agreed, "but will she heel over and sink, that's the question."

Harken turned away but there was an undeniable note of superior knowledge in his question: "What do you think?"

Barnett bit his tongue. Actually, the longer he watched this Harken, the more he came to believe, as did the cocky young boatbuilder himself, that this craft would do what he said: It would make every other one in the water look like an albatross.

Into the void, Iversen spoke, removing his pipe from his mouth.

"What do you intend to name her, Gid?"

Gideon transferred his gaze to Tim's good eye. "I don't know. Something fast— like the *Seal,* maybe, or the *Gale.*"

"How about something faithful instead?" Tim's eye skimmed Lorna, then returned to Gid. "Like Lorna here, who believed in it well before you did. I think it would be fitting if this yacht were named after your daughter. What's your middle name, Lorna?"

"Diane."

"How about the *Lorna D?* It's got a nice ring. I like the hard *D* with the soft *A.*" Tim puffed a couple of times on his pipe, sending a fruity tobacco aroma to mingle with that of steamed wood. "The *Lorna D.* What do you think, Gid?"

Gideon pondered some. He bit on the left corner of his beetling moustache. He studied Lorna, who was assiduously avoiding studying Jens, and had been all morning.

"What do you say, Lorna? Do you want this yacht named after you?"

She thought of Jens, here in this shed, shaping the *Lorna D* day after day with his big, wide, capable hands, running them over the boat's fair lines, making her swift and sure and responsive.

"Do you mean it?"

"Divine justice, I suppose you'd call it. Especially if she wins."

"Those are your words, not mine." Even chiding her father, Lorna found it impossible to keep the excitement from shining in her eyes. "I'd love it, Papa, and you know it."

Gideon realized how true it was when he heard his daughter call him Papa, which she hadn't done much since she'd matured. Only when he was very much in her favor did the word escape her lips.

"Very well. The *Lorna D* it is."

"Oh, Papa, thank you!" She pranced across the shed and hugged his neck while Gideon cocked forward at the hips and searched for a place to rest his hands, ever in a quandary when his girls showed affection in such a way. He loved his daughters—of course he did—but his way of demonstrating it was by issuing gruff, authoritative orders, the way a proper Victorian father ought to, and by footing the bills for their expensive soirees and clothing. Returning hugs while other men looked on was beyond Gideon Barnett's pale. "Damnation, girl, you're going to tear my collar right off its buttons."

By the time Lorna released him, Gideon was flustered and harumphing.

"May I tell my friends?" Lorna asked.

"Your friends . . . well . . . hell, I don't care."

"Then it's official?" Lorna tipped her head to one side.

Gideon flapped a hand. "Go ahead, tell them, I said."

"And may I bring them here to see it?"

"And overrun the place?" Gideon blustered.

"Not all of them, just Phoebe."

"I swear, you young females are getting to act more like tomboys than anything I ever saw. Oh, all right, bring Phoebe."

"And I shall want to come often to check on the *Lorna D*'s progress. You don't mind, do you, Papa?"

"You'll be in Harken's way."

"Oh, fiddle. There were three of us here today, plus a camera, and we weren't in his way, were we, Harken?" She fired the challenge straight at Harken's eyes. It was the first solid contact they'd exchanged since she'd entered the shed.

His glance quickly veered to her father. "I . . . ah . . ." He cleared his throat. "No, I don't mind, sir."

"Very well, but if she gets to be a pest, throw her out. I swear to God, I don't know what I'm doing, letting a girl hang around a boat shed. Your mother will have a conniption." While upbraiding himself, Gideon tugged at his watch fob and slid a golden hunter out of his vest pocket. "Damnation, it's nearly noon. I've got to get into town before it's time to come back home! Harken, see me about a check when you're ready to order the sails from Chicago. And Jonson, what do I owe you for helping out today?"

"Nothing, sir. My pleasure, just to work on a boat again."

"Very well, then. I'm off. Lorna, you too. Do me a favor and give your mother at least a crumb of time spent at ladylike pursuits this afternoon."

"Yes, Papa," she replied meekly.

"I'll be leaving, too," Tim said. "Thanks for letting me horn in and take pictures. You'll see them soon, Jens."

With nothing resembling a personal farewell, Lorna took her leave with the others.

When they were gone the shed grew quiet. Ben and Jens worked for a while cleaning up the place, sweeping up the sawdust and the stub ends of the ribs from the floor, hammering in a nail more securely here and there on the mold. Moving around it, Jens whistled softly through his teeth: "Oh, Fetch the Water," an old Norwegian folk song. He touched the oak ribs in many places, pinched them, tried to jiggle them, but found them firm.

"They've already taken the mold," he remarked.

"Yup."

Jens put away some nails. Hung up a hammer. Ben's eyes followed him. Speculating. Jens whistled another verse. Ben leaned back against the mold with his arms and legs crossed. "So . . ." he said, "is she the one you met on Sunday?"

Jens's whistling stopped. His head snapped up. "What makes you ask a thing like that?"

"You didn't look at her once in all that time she was here."

Jens went back to work. "So?"

"A girl that pretty?"

"You think she's pretty?"

"Prettier than the sunset on a Norwegian fjord. Brighter, too. I had trouble keeping my eyes off her."

"So?"

"So, she didn't look at you, either. Until she tricked her father into agreeing to let her come out here whenever she wants to. And now you're whistling 'Oh, Fetch the Water.' "

"You know, Jonson, you must've gotten too close to that steam. Maybe it boiled your brains a little bit, huh? What in the world has 'Oh, Fetch the Water' got to do with Lorna Barnett?"

Jonson began singing the old love song in Norwegian, very softly, wearing a three-cornered grin that followed his friend around the boat shed till the last lines:

> But when it is the one I love
> Then life is surely worth the living.

By the time he finished, Jens had quit creating busyness to occupy his hands. He stood beside the stove with its coals dwindling, staring at the cooling boiler and steam box.

"You're right." He shifted his gaze to Ben. "We've got some feelings between us, Lorna and me."

"Aw, Jens," Ben said sympathetically, his teasing gone. "You haven't."

"We didn't mean for it to happen, but there you are."

"I figured something like this that day she stood up in the boat and waved to you. Just the way she did it—like she wanted to jump in and swim over."

"She's a fine girl, Ben, as fine as they come, but independent. She started hanging around here, asking questions about the boat, then about me and my family. Pretty soon we were talking like old friends. Then one day she asked me to kiss her." Jens ruminated awhile before shaking his head at the floor. "Worst mistake I ever made, kissing her."

Jens found two pieces of sandpaper and handed one to Ben. They both began sanding the ribs.

Ben said, "I imagine if her old man knew, you'd be out of here on your ass, and that'd be the end of your boatbuilding."

"Yup."

"You should have known, Jens. Our kind, we kiss the kitchen maids."

"I tried that." The two men exchanged wry glances. They went on sanding. "Ruby, her name is."

"Ruby."

"A redhead with freckles."

"And?"

The sandpaper rasped on. "Remember when you were a boy and you got a new puppy? You'd go off to school all day long, then when you'd come home that little thing was so happy to see you he'd lick you up one side and down the other. Well, that's what kissing Ruby was like. I just kept wishing I had a towel."

Both men laughed. A while later Ben asked, "So how far has this thing gone with you and the girl whose father would tack your hide to the door if he knew about it?"

"Not as far as you're thinking. But it could if we keep seeing each other. I decided last night that we're not going to. It's over. It's got to be, because she doesn't belong in my world any more than I belong in hers. Lord, Ben, you should have seen her last night. . . ."

Jens described the scene he'd come upon while walking back to the house for supper, sparing no details, not even about Lorna's relationship with Taylor DuVal. ". . . And there she stood with DuVal's hand on her shoulder and his watch on her breast, right where my hand had been the day before. Now you tell me—what business have I got with a woman like that anyway?" Speaking the words, Jens felt anger and hurt well up within. "If she comes around here again I'm ordering her point-blank to *get out!* Finishing this boat and getting a boatworks of my own mean more to me than Lorna Barnett anyway."

He wanted to mean it. All during that afternoon after Ben left, while Jens worked on the mold alone, while he listened to the monotonous *shh-shh* of sandpaper on wood, and felt the heat rise against his palm, and registered the shape of each rib through his callused hands, he wanted the boat to mean more to him than Lorna. But every thought of her brought longing. Every memory brought wishes.

At seven o'clock he closed the shed doors, put a stick through the hasp, then stood a moment, listening to the soprano section of crickets tuning up. An evening chill had arrived, gathering dampness from the earth. He drew on a plaid wool jacket. Turning down his collar, he looked at the sky—peachy in the west, violet overhead, overlaid by leaves and branches already blackened to silhouettes. He moved down the worn path toward the poplars. Over the vegetable gardens the bats were out, fluttering past as quickly as illusions. The tomato bushes smelled tangy. Some of the early-bearing vegetables had already been pulled up—pea vines, beans—and new ones undoubtedly started by Smythe in the glasshouse for the family's winter use in town. Jens's face collected a spiderweb that seemed suspended in midair: a sure sign of approaching fall.

He was unaware of Lorna's presence until she brought him up short with a "Psst." She stood between the poplars, as straight and still as they, camouflaged by their foliage and the deep shadows of evening. Around her shoulders she wore a short knit cape, gripped in both hands at her throat. "I've been waiting for you."

"Lorna . . ." He left the path and blended into the poplar shadows with her. "You've got to stop doing this."

How comely she looked with the dusk shading her skin faintly blue, and her eyes gleaming like polished agates as they found and held him with an expression of bald adoration. "I know I should stop, but I can't seem to." In a whisper, she appealed, "What have you done to me, Jens Harken?"

His heart began a crazy dance and all his good intentions fragmented. She moved at the same moment as he, a loved-starved lunge that opened her cape and closed it around both their shoulders as they clung and kissed. His tongue was swift and sleek in her mouth, opening it, invading it, spreading the flavor of wood and desire and frustration that had been increasing during their past two encounters of maneuvering around each other with false indifference. She kissed him as one ending a long deprivation, her tongue darting and licking and demanding a fulfillment of which she was ultimately ignorant. He clasped her body hard and took a spraddled stance into which he could mold and hold her. His hands dropped down, caught her buttocks within her skirts and bent her forward along his frame while he tipped back and made a bow of his body. Her toes lost purchase and dangled above the grass as she lay cast over his body, her breasts and belly yielding to his.

When he set her down they were breathless, their eyes avid and burning with impatience. They spoke in a rush.

"You were angry with me today," Lorna said.

"Yes, I was."

"About last night?"

"Yes, and about you coming to the shed when your father was there, about DuVal. About everything!"

"I'm sorry about last night. I didn't want to be with him, but I didn't know how to get out of it. My mother planned the whole evening and I had no choice."

"You belong with him."

"No. I don't love him. You're the one I love."

He held her by the head and looked into her face with an expression of aggravated frustration on his own. "You belong with him and that's what makes me the angriest, because I know it's true, and nothing can change it. Your world and his are the same, don't you see? Sousa as your houseguest, and discussions with Mr. Gibson, and croquet suppers on the lawn. That's a world I'm not allowed in. I can only live it by listening to you tell me about it."

When he'd finished she stared at him and whispered, "You haven't said you love me."

"Because it hurts too much." He gave her head one shake. "Because every time I do you believe a little stronger that it can work, and it can't. You took a big chance today, coming out here when your father was here."

"But now I have his permission, don't you see?"

"Not to do this. Don't fool yourself, Lorna."

"Oh, Jens, please don't be angry with me anymore. You still are—I could tell when you kissed me."

"You're so damned innocent," he railed, and kissed her again, the same as before, his entire body torn between inveighing and inviting. He moved his hands over her, touching her gingerly when he wanted to touch her passionately. "My hands are dirty. . . . I've been working all day."

"No . . . no . . . ." She captured one and plunged her face into its palm, kissing it. "I love your hands. I love them on your work. I love them on me. They smell like wood." She spread his palm on her face, as if it were a balm she would apply to heal herself.

The simple act of affection turned his heart over. He bent and scooped her up in his arms and carried her back along the path to the boat shed, through the woods where full dark had fallen. She curled her arms around his neck and put her mouth against his jaw, where a day's growth of whiskers abraded her lips.

"Will you be missed?" he asked, bearing her along with her hip bumping his stomach.

"My mother and father are at the Armfields' playing loo."

At the shed he set her on her feet and removed the stick from the hasp. He opened the door a narrow space. "Go inside and put some wood on the coals. I'll be right back."

"Where are you going?"

"Just do as I say, but don't light the lamps."

He ran into the dark woods, elbows up to deflect branches as he jogged in the opposite direction from the house, toward the northerly lakeshore. Reaching it, he stripped and plunged headlong into the water, gasping when he emerged into the brisk night air. He scrubbed everywhere, the best he could without soap, then stood on the bank and gave a canine shake of limbs and head before donning his trousers and snapping his suspenders up over his bare shoulders. Into his shirt he rolled his boots and remaining clothing, then returned through the woods to the shed and the woman who waited.

Inside, all was black but for two glowing spots: the open stove door and Lorna's face as she hunkered before it with both arms wrapped around her knees.

The shed door creaked.

"Jens?" she whispered, startled, her head snapping around toward the black end of the building.

He closed the door and answered, "Yes, it's me."

Her shoulders wilted with relief as she peered into the inkiness and watched him emerge from it, clothed in nothing but trousers and black suspenders. She rose slowly, as if spellbound, her eyes riveted on his naked chest, its golden fleece picked out by the flickering firelight.

"I took a quick bath," he said, shivering visibly, running his wadded-up clothing over his trunk, then casting it aside.

"Oh," she said, glancing away, unnerved by his unexpected appearance in such a state.

He reached up with both hands and fingercombed his wet hair, then dried his palms on his trousers and stood before her, ruffled all over with goose bumps. Her eyes returned to the golden V of hair on his chest and the nipples within it, then veered off shyly. "You must be freezing." She began to turn away as if to give him her place before the open stove door.

He caught her arm at the crook of her elbow, in a grip so tight it would have stopped her had his words failed.

"Lorna . . . don't turn away." His fingers left wet spots on her sleeve. She returned to him in the slow movements of a lover facing her chosen one at the momentous confluence of two lives. He pulled the knit cape from her shoulders and discarded it in the shadows somewhere at their feet. Her eyes were wide upon Jens's, then closed as he drew her into a tender embrace and kissed her with cold, wet lips and a warm, wet tongue. Her arms rose to his shoulders, her sleeves stuck to his damp back and her bodice to his damp chest. His flesh was puckered with goose bumps as she opened her hands on it. A cold droplet fell from his hair onto her face. Another followed . . . and another . . . and the trio ran in a rivulet down her cheek. The kiss gained motion, became a graceful swan dance of heads and hands. She gripped the edges of her cuffs to stretch her sleeves taut, then began blindly drying his back. He dipped his knees and clasped her to him, then surged up against her, wholly aroused. One of them shuddered . . . or was it both? Was it from the cold or from the quick release of suppression, neither could tell.

He found buttons along her back and began releasing them—down to her shoulder blades only before tugging the hem of the shirtwaist from her waistband and stripping it up over her head. Hairpins fell to the wooden floor as she emerged with her hair disarrayed and her eyes wide and bright with expectation.

Her shift was made of soft white lawn and was shirred by a blue ribbon into a scooped neck with buttons below. He gathered the garment into his two hands, and her breasts along with it, looking into her eyes as his thumbs changed her to the shape of desire.

"Are you afraid when I touch you this way?" he asked.

"I was at first."

"And now?"

"Now . . . oh, now . . ." She relaxed against his caress and let herself be swayed by it. He lifted one breast high and bent to it, kissed it through the thin lawn, and bit it gently. He treated the other to the same blandishment, then held both in his hands and smiled down into her blissful face.

"There are other ways a man touches a woman. You don't know about them, do you?"

"No . . ." she whispered.

"Here . . ." He dropped one hand down the front of her skirts and rubbed it softly against her pubis. "Like this"—he curled his fingers until they conformed to her hidden shape—"and like this . . . It's part of loving. Do you know why?"

She shook her head, once again mesmerized by his voice and touch.

"To make babies."

"B . . . babies?" She started and pulled back, her eyes disbelieving.

"Sometimes. Sometimes just for pleasure."

"Babies? When you're not married?"

"I didn't think you knew, and I wanted to warn you that could happen."

Suddenly her mother's warning became startlingly clear. She pulled away from him sharply, feeling cheated, foiled. All the lovely billowing feelings she held for Jens seemed like a mean trick nature had played on them both.

"I cannot have a baby. My mother and father would . . . would . . . Oh, gracious, I don't know what they would do." She looked genuinely horrified.

"I've frightened you. I'm sorry." He took her arms lightly and drew her near once more. "You're not going to have a baby, Lorna, it doesn't happen that easily. It takes more than touching, and even then, it doesn't happen all the time. And it won't happen at all if we stop in time."

"Oh, Jens . . ." She fell against him and doubled her arms around his neck. "I'm so relieved. You scared me. I thought I should have to go back to the house when that's the last thing I want to do." Her grip tightened, her plea became impassioned. "I want to stay here with you, until dawn if I could, and on into tomorrow, and the tomorrow after that. There's no other place I want to be than right here in your arms. If that isn't love I cannot imagine what is. Oh, Jens Harken, I love you so much that everything in my life has changed."

Her outpouring led to another kiss—a frantic seeking that dragged his open mouth across her face, and hers across his, to rejoin and reclaim and resurrect the passion interrupted earlier. Mouth to mouth, hand to breast, body to body, they strained ever nearer love's ineluctable conclusion. He lifted her skirt in both hands, found his way beneath it to her hips and bracketed them in a grip that drew her flush against him and tipped her to an obliging angle. Like waves against a shore, he taught her to move, and there, where their bodies hove together, urgency spread. He kissed her roughly, a lusty mingling of two wet mouths, then caught her lower lip between his teeth and held it as if to say, *Be still,* while sliding one hand down her shift with its long placket running from front to back. He gripped her firmly, through the damp white overlapped lawn, as if she were a handful of turf he might lift from the earth and fling over his shoulder. By his teeth and one hand, he held her, rocking the butt of that hand gently, rhythmically, until her mind went hot with colors—splendid sunrise colors that seemed to infuse her core and limbs. In time those limbs became limp, then jolted once in untutored surprise as he slid his hand inside her shift and found his way within her body.

"Oh, Jens . . ." she whispered as his touch went deeper and her head hung back.

"Lie down," he whispered, and supported her while lowering them both to the fragrant wooden floor, where he'd once lofted a boat that was named after her. Beside it now, he came to know her shape, as he knew the shape of the *Lorna D.* Over her his hands curved, as they'd curved over the white oak mold that hovered above them. Within her, warmth flowed, as warmth had flowed from the wood it-self when he'd sanded it smooth earlier that day. He touched her in myriad inti-mate ways, beckoning, until her hips rose from the hard spruce floor to seek more and more.

He turned her skirts back and braced on one elbow beside her, watching de-sire distort her features as her throat lifted toward the rafters overhead, and the mea-ger firelight painted the periphery of her face. Her eyes were closed, her arms flung wide, her shoulder blades scarcely touching the floor.

"Lorna, Lorna . . . beautiful creature . . ." he murmured, "this is how I've imag-ined you."

Her eyelids fluttered open as his touch left. He opened the few buttons on her bodice and turned it back, exposing her breasts. There, he kissed her, adored her, washed her with his tongue and shaped her with his lips. Again, he reached low to touch her intimately. At his return her eyelids closed and she cooed, a soft throaty sound while coiling half onto one side, her arms and one leg forming an arabesque around him.

There came that moment when he felt compelled to seek her eyes once again, his own lit by mere pinpricks of light from the dying fire beside them. "I love you so much," he whispered.

"I love you, too. I shall always, always love you, no matter what."

He put his parted lips very lightly upon hers and whispered, "It's all right if you touch me, too." He could tell from her stillness she wasn't sure where and how. "Anywhere," he invited.

She touched his bare chest and he abandoned her mouth to watch her eyes follow her hand. Timidly it explored, learning as it went: the texture of the golden hair, the firmness of his ribs, the silken hair again, diffidently avoiding his nipples.

"You're all golden. Like a Viking. Sometimes I think of you that way—as my golden-haired Norwegian Viking, sailing in on a great ship to sweep me away." She caught his head and drew it down for a kiss, and returned her hand to its preoccupation with his naked chest, slipping beneath a suspender and riding it to his jutting shoulder.

"Push it down," he whispered against her mouth. "It's all right . . . push it down."

She pushed the suspender over his shoulder. It fell limp upon his arm.

"Now the other one," he whispered, and shifted his weight, giving her access.

The second suspender fell and her hands played over him—shoulders, throat, ribs and chest, until all his senses reached outward toward her and all below yearned to be couched within her. He caught her hand and carried it downward, urging, "Don't be shy . . . don't be scared . . . here . . . like this . . . ," and she came to feel his warmth and hardness for the first time through a layer of scratchy wool. He cupped her hand beneath his and shaped it like himself. He uttered her name, the name he so loved—"Lorna . . . Lorna . . ."—and moved both their hands, teaching, beseeching, until hers moved of its own accord. In time he opened four buttons and slid her hand into the warm, dark secrecy awaiting within. At the moment of intimate encounter they were lying on their sides, each with an ear upon a bent arm, staring into each other's eyes.

His closed at her touch, and his breast rose and fell as if from hard labor.

"Oh," she said, the word a note of wonder and discovery at his heat and shape. "Oh . . . I had not dreamed . . ." He taught her what instinct had not, made of her hand a sheath and returned his own hand to her waiting body. Together, so bound, they reveled in the wondrous beck and call of their young bodies, their young love. They kissed sometimes. Other times they murmured inarticulate sounds composed of passion and promise and puissance that issued from their throats while splendid desire rose and demanded its due. At the breaking point, he knocked her hand away and turned upon her, kneeling, hauling her over his lap and supporting her from beneath until her body bowed like a wind-filled sail, her head and shoulders barely grazing the floor. Through the barrier of wool and lawn, they mimicked the consummation of love, until those flimsy, false, frail obstacles called clothing could no longer be tolerated.

He fell to all fours above her and ordered between racked breaths, "Lorna, open your eyes." She did, and looked up at him from the halo of dark hair that lay tangled on the rough floor. "Do you understand now? Me . . . inside you . . . that's how it happens; but if we do it you could end up with my baby. I don't want that to happen."

She caressed his face, beside his mouth, with one hand.

"I love you. . . . Oh, Jens, I love you so much. . . . I didn't know it would be like this."

"We can stop, or we can take a chance that it won't happen from just one time."

"Stop? Oh . . . I . . . please . . . please, Jens, no . . . will it happen?"

"I don't know. Maybe not. I . . . oh God, Lorna, I love you, too. . . . I don't want to hurt you or get you in trouble."

"The only way you could hurt me would be if you ever stopped loving me. Please, Jens, teach me the rest."

He crooked his elbows, bringing his face down to hers. He kissed her mouth in love and apology and desire, then said, "Wait . . . ," and reached back into the dark for his roll of clothing. One tug and the boots went tumbling and thumped to the floor. "Lift up," he ordered, "I'll put this under you." Beneath her hips he spread his shirt. "You're going to bleed, but don't be scared. It only happens the first time."

"Bleed? But, Jens . . . your shirt . . . Jens, it will get all—"

His kiss cut off her concerns. "Lie still . . ." he whispered, and placed himself just within her, while their hearts beat in frantic anticipation and all the world waited.

"Jens," she whispered, gripping his shoulders.

"Be still."

"Jens . . . oh . . ."

"It might hurt some. . . . I'm sorry. . . ." In a whisper, "I'm sorry."

With a gentle thrust he bound them, body and soul.

She caught her breath and arched up, as if prodded between the shoulder blades. He lay utterly still, watching her face, wishing away her hurt, until she slowly relaxed and opened her eyes to find him bearing his weight on strong arms above her.

"All right?" he asked.

She released a breath and nodded.

"I wish I had a fine featherbed for you right now," he told her as he began moving, "and a soft pillow that we could lie on, and some flowers from the picking garden—some of those blue delphiniums, maybe, like you brought me that time, and a rose or two for the good smell. I would put them on your hair, and watch your face put the flowers to shame. Aw, Lorna . . . sweet, darling Lorna . . . we're as close as two people can be now, and for the rest of our lives we'll be changed because of this minute."

She tried to keep her eyes open, but they became weighted by pleasure. "I think"—she struggled for breath between words—"that I should be the proudest . . . woman in the world . . . to have your baby . . . and that I . . . Oh, Jens . . ." She gasped and arched up high against him, her head tipped back at a sharp angle. "Oh, Jens . . . oh . . . ohahhhhhhh . . ."

At the moment of her cry, he withdrew and spilled his seed on his own shirt, atop her virgin blood, in the hope that she would never have to suffer disgrace because of him. Then he fell, depleted, upon her heaving chest. Her breath beat at his ear and their heartbeats played in counterpoint. He rested heavily upon her while her fingers ran up his skull again, and again, and again.

Beside them, the fire had dwindled to coals.

Above them, the skeleton of the boat loomed.

All about, the stillness of the late-summer night kept their secret. They thought about their future—the certain parting that lay ahead—and beyond, the hazy afterward and the forces that would try to keep them apart, the impossibility of being so after this.

"I would do it again," she said. "I would do this shameful, wonderful, incredible thing again with you, knowing full well what might happen if I do. Does that make me bad?"

He levered the brunt of his weight from her and looked down into her beautiful brown eyes. "It makes you mine, the way no wedding vows could, the way no promises could. How will I ever say goodbye to you when they take you back to town?"

"Shh . . ." She covered his mouth with her index finger. "Don't speak about that. That won't happen until the frost comes and the pipes are in danger of freezing up. We have at least five weeks till then. Maybe six, if we're lucky."

"Mid-October. Is that when you usually move back to the city?"

She nodded solemnly. "But I don't want to talk about it." She clasped him close, already in slight desperation. "Please, Jens, let's not talk about it."

"All right, we won't." He held her awhile, suspecting that there were tears in her eyes, though the room had grown too dark to see. "Stay where you are," he said, and slipped into the darkness, found some wood tailings and dropped them into the stove. Waiting for them to ignite, he pulled up his trousers and buttoned them, but left his suspenders hanging at his sides. When the wood flared he turned back to Lorna and drew her up by one hand. In the lambent orange light, he sat beside her and touched her face.

"I'm sure you don't know . . ." These things were hard to say, in spite of the intimacy they'd just shared: these less than romantic facts of life.

"Don't know?"

He drew a deep breath and faced what must be faced. "If your monthly doesn't come you must tell me right away. Promise."

"My monthly?" She, too, grew embarrassed, threaded her arms into her shift and drew it together to cover herself.

He told her, "If it's ever late it could mean you're going to have a baby, and if you are you must come to me and tell me right away, and we'll figure out what to do. Promise me."

"I promise," she said to her lap.

They sat awhile silently, imagining it, hoping it would never happen that way. Lorna slowly buttoned her shift. When she reached the top button he brushed her fingers aside and tied the blue bow, his fingers thick and clumsy on the fine, smooth silk. When he was done they sat on, facing one another, each occupied with his own approaching sadness.

Jens took both Lorna's hands loosely.

"I love you," he said. "I want to marry you, but it'll take some time. If we asked your father now he'd throw me out. Next year, if things go the way I plan, I'll have my own boatworks, and I can take care of you then. Could you be happy on a boat-builder's wages, Lorna?"

She stared at him in stunned amazement. "Yes," she uttered as if coming out of a stupor. "Oh, yes!" she exclaimed, and flung both arms around him. "Oh, Jens, I was so afraid you wouldn't ask. I thought that maybe . . . maybe after what we just did . . . I don't know what I thought."

He took her by both arms and pressed her back so he could see her face.

"You thought maybe I would do that to you, then act as if it had never happened?"

"I don't know. It only struck me afterwards, when we were lying so quietly together—I should not want to lie that way with any other man. I couldn't after doing it with you, but if you didn't ask me to marry you, then what?"

"I am asking. Will you marry me, Lorna Barnett, as soon as my boat wins that race, and I have my own boatworks with plenty of customers to make us a decent living?"

She beamed. "Yes, I said. Nothing can stop me. Not my father, not my mother, not Mr. Taylor DuVal, not all the social expectations they've set for me, because between you and me it simply must be. Especially after tonight."

"Oh, Lorna . . ." He clasped her to him. "I'm going to work so damned hard for you, and I might never get as rich as your father, but I'll give you a good life, you'll see."

"I know you will, Jens."

"And we'll have babies, and teach them to sail, and take them on picnics; and when they're old enough I'll teach them to build boats with me."

"Yes," she breathed, "yes."

They sat back and held hands and smiled at each other some more.

"Now you'd better get dressed so you can get back to the house before your parents get home."

"When will I see you again?"

"I don't know."

"Tomorrow. I'll bring Phoebe to see the boat."

"The mold. It's not a boat yet."

"Yes, the mold. I'll bring Phoebe, all right?"

"All right. But I'm not promising I can keep the truth from showing. I'll probably grab you on the spot and kiss you whether Phoebe's there or not."

She slapped him playfully on the chest. "You will not. You'll be perfectly proper, just as you were today."

"It'll cost me, though."

"Good," she teased, and touched his lower lip with an index finger.

After moments her hand slid down and rested on his chest, then captured his. Time was moving on: They knew they must part, but stole one more minute, holding hands like innocent children, adoring each other, sating themselves for the separation ahead.

"You have to go," he said softly.

"I know."

"Let me help you with your dress."

He pulled her to her feet and buttoned the back of her shirtwaist while she held her hair aside. When the garment was closed up to her nape, he put his hands at her waist.

"Lorna, about DuVal . . ."

She dropped her hair and turned. "I'll speak to my mother about him immediately. Papa will be a little more difficult, so I'll start with Mother, and get her used to the idea that he's not for me. The sooner they understand that I'm not going to marry him, the better."

Jens looked relieved.

"And I promise," Lorna added earnestly, "that I shall never wear his watch again. That promise I can keep from this moment forward, and I shall. I vow on my love for you."

He squeezed her hands and told her with his eyes how very grateful he was for her promise.

"Fix your hair," he said.

"Oh, dear." She reached up to it. "I forgot my comb. Do you have one?"

He shrugged—"Sorry"—and tried futilely to arrange it with his fingers.

"Oh, it's no use. It'll need much more than fingers."

She scraped at it while he knelt to find her hairpins on the dimly lit floor.

"How about these? Will they help?"

She did the best she could, bending forward at the waist and flopping the heavy, dark fall forward, then grasping it in both hands and trying to reconstruct the nest-and-pouf while he watched.

Each motion, each pose went into his treasured storehouse of memories, to be drawn out later, in the lorn hours of midnight, while he slept in the room above hers.

"I've never told you before—I love your hair."

Her hands stalled, putting in the last pin. She dropped them slowly, filled with love so pure and fine it seemed her very heart had left her body to dwell in his.

"I would like to watch you someday," he went on, "put it up in that pretty bird's nest you wear. I picture you doing it—when I'm alone in my room at night. Every time I imagine it you're dressed in the white-and-blue outfit you wore the first day, with huge sleeves that lift up around your ears when your arms go up, and your breasts lift, too, and your waist is as thin as a sapling. And I put my hands on it so that when you lower your arms they come around my neck, and you say my name. Jens . . . just Jens, the way I love to hear you say it. And that's the simple dream I have of you."

She smiled, and in the darkness felt her cheeks heat with joy.

"Oh, Jens, what a lovely man you are."

He chuckled, suspecting he'd waxed too romantic for manly ways, yet it was the truth, something he'd wanted to tell her all summer.

"When I'm your wife," Lorna said, "you can watch me every morning."

Her hair was up. Her dress was buttoned. The hour was late.

"I must go," she said.

He laid her knit cape upon her shoulders. They walked to the door. He pushed it open and it creaked a farewell song. Outside, they held each other one last time, silent, wishful. He drew away, caught her by the sides of her neck and kissed her forehead for several heartbeats, then stepped back and let her go.

Chapter 10

Phoebe was duly impressed by both the *Lorna D* and its builder. She exclaimed the moment the two girls were alone, "He's the one!"

Lorna crossed her lips with a finger. "Shh!"

"But he's the one you told me about. The one you had the picnic with, and you're sweet on him, aren't you?"

"Phoebe, be quiet! I'll be in real trouble if anyone hears you."

"Oh, who's going to hear me out here in the garden. Come on, let's go sit in the gazebo, where we can talk. If anybody comes around we'll see them."

They sat in the gazebo on the wooden benches with their backs to the lattice-work, soaking up the afternoon sun that had grown much less intense as August became September.

"All right," Phoebe demanded, "what's going on between you and that handsome Norwegian boatbuilder? Tell me right now!"

Lorna spoke as if giving up. Her inflection lacked all girlish giddiness when she replied, "Oh, Phoebe, promise you won't tell?"

"Cross my heart."

"I'm in love with him, Phoebe. Heart and soul, forevermore, in love with him."

Lorna's seriousness, her quietness, her straightforward manner conveyed as much as her words. From that first revelation, Phoebe believed her.

"But Lorna." She, too, lost her flighty manner. "What about Taylor?"

"I've never loved Taylor. My parents are just going to have to understand that I can't see him anymore."

"They'll never understand. They'll be very upset."

"Yes, I suppose they will, but it wasn't my fault, Phoebe. I saw Jens the first time and something happened inside here." Lorna touched her heart. "From the very first time we spoke there was a certain knowledge between us, as if we were fated to meet and be more than passing acquaintances. We both felt it, long before we spoke of it or . . . or kissed."

"He's kissed you?"

"Oh, yes. Kissed me, held me, whispered endearments to me, as I have to him. When we're together it's impossible not to do those things."

Phoebe, looking troubled, took Lorna's hand. "Then I'm afraid for you."

"Afraid?"

"He's a commoner, an immigrant; he has no family or money or social position. They'll never let you marry him, never. From the moment they find out they'll do everything in their power to see that it doesn't happen."

Lorna gazed off across the garden. "Yes, I imagine they will."

"Oh, Lorna, you're going to get hurt."

Lorna sighed and closed her eyes. "I know." She opened them again. "But please don't warn me not to see him anymore, Phoebe. I couldn't stand that. I need at least one ally I can trust, one who'll believe that what I'm doing is right . . . for me and for Jens."

"You can trust me, Lorna. You have my promise I'll never try to change your mind about him, because I can see it's true that you love him. You've already changed because of it."

"Changed? Have I?"

"There's a serenity that I've never seen before."

"A serenity . . . yes, I suppose so. That's how I feel inside . . . as if all my life I've been peering through a dusty window, frustrated because I could not see clearly, and finally someone has washed it clean. Now here I stand, gazing through at the world in all its bright, sparkling colors, and I wonder, How could I not have noticed before how beautiful everything is? Oh, Phoebe . . ." Lorna turned to her friend with a radiant face. "It's impossible to describe how it feels. How when I'm away from him everything around me seems gray and lifeless, then when I step into his presence all of life abounds once more. It becomes splendid, and meaningful. And when he speaks, his voice is more than just . . . just vocal intonations. It's a refrain. And when he touches me I know why I was born; and when he laughs I am happier than when I laugh myself; and when we part . . ." Lorna leaned her head back against the lattice and turned her face toward the distant boat shed. "And when we part . . . it is the November of my heart."

The girls sat in the silent sun, stricken—both—by Lorna's poignant soliloquy. In the gaillardia patch insects droned. Out beneath an oak tree at the far side of the yard Smythe raked up acorns. From the house Aunt Agnes came toddling through the flower beds, her hat left behind, her hair shining in the sun as she stretched forward to whisk a net at a butterfly.

"Here comes Aunt Agnes," Lorna said, melancholically.

"Catching butterflies for her collection."

The old woman swiped again at a cosmos blossom and placed her prey in a brass cricket box.

"Poor Aunt Agnes, pressing flowers and collecting butterflies, pining her life away for her dear lost love."

Agnes spied them, raised her hand and waved. The girls waved back.

"All she ever wanted in her life was her beloved Captain Dearsley."

"Then she'd understand how you feel about Jens."

The girls rolled their heads and exchanged gazes. The unsaid scintillated between them: Lorna would need such understanding in the days ahead.

"Yes, I believe she would."

September suddenly turned hot. The migratory monarchs came through and Aunt Agnes mounted several. Theron, Jenny and Daphne—as well as Mitch Armfield—took the train daily into the city to attend school, returning in the late afternoon and complaining about the heat on the train, the heat in their schoolrooms, the heat in their bedrooms. Lorna blessed each eighty-five-degree day, for it meant no plans were yet in the offing for the family's return to the house on Summit Avenue in Saint Paul.

Taylor invited her to take the theater train into the city to see May Irwin in *The Widow Jones,* but Lorna declined with the excuse that she was not in the least inclined to watch the buxom, boisterous blonde gambol around the stage singing this new profanity called ragtime. Taylor suggested perhaps another show, another night, then inquired why he hadn't seen her wearing the watch he'd given her. She touched her bodice and told a bald-faced lie. "Oh, Taylor," she said, "I'm so sorry. I lost it." That night she went out to the end of the dock and flung the watch into the lake.

Her mother planned a dinner party for twelve and placed Lorna's place card next to Taylor's. Lorna came along as Levinia was putting the finishing touches on the dining room, and switched hers to the opposite end. Levinia pursed her entire face and said, "Lorna, what in the world are you doing?"

"Would you be terribly disappointed, Mother, if I sat next to someone else?"

"Someone else—whyever, Lorna?"

Willing her face to remain pale and inscrutable, Lorna gripped the back of a rosewood chair and faced Levinia across the elegantly appointed table. "I suppose you won't believe me if I tell you that Taylor and I are not well suited."

Levinia looked as if her underwear had just come up missing. "Twaddle!" she exploded. "You're suited and I won't hear another word to the contrary!"

"I haven't any feelings for him, Mother."

"Feelings! What have feelings to do with it! Your marriage to Taylor will put you in a house as grand as our own, and you'll move among the cream of society. Why, I daresay it won't be a year or two before Taylor will even have a summer home out here."

"Is that what you married Father for? A grand house, and a place in society and a summer home on White Bear Lake?"

"Don't you be impertinent with me, young lady! I'm your mother and I—"

"And you what? You love Father?"

"Hold your voice down!"

"I am holding my voice down. You're the one who's shouting. It's a simple question, Mother. Do you love Father? I've often wondered."

Levinia's face had turned as maroon as the papered walls. "What's gotten into you, you insolent child?"

"The realization that when Taylor touches me I want to run in the house."

Levinia gasped. "Oh dear . . ." She came rushing around the table, leaving her stack of place cards behind, whispering, "Oh, gracious dear, this is distressing. Lorna, he hasn't taken advantage of you, has he?"

"Taken advantage?"

Levinia seized her daughter's arm and shepherded her toward the morning room, where she closed them in with the pocket doors.

"I warned you about men. They're all the same in that regard. Has he . . . well, has he . . . you know . . ." Levinia stirred the air with one hand. "Has he done anything untoward when you were alone together?"

"No, Mother."

"But you said he's touched you."

"Please, Mother, it's nothing. He's kissed me, that's all." Lorna spoke with conviction, for she knew now, fully well, that what she and Taylor had done together truly was nothing.

"And embraced you?"

"Yes."

"And that's all? You're sure that's all?"

"Yes."

Levinia wilted onto a settee. "Oh, thank goodness. Nevertheless, given what you've told me, I think it's time we set a wedding date."

"A wedding date! Mother, I just told you, I don't want to marry Taylor!"

Levinia went on as if Lorna hadn't spoken. "I'll speak to your father at once, and he will speak to Taylor, and we'll get the plans nicely under way. June, I should think, here in the garden when the roses are in bloom. We always have lovely weather in June, and the yard can hold as many or more than Saint Mark's. Oh dear . . ." She pinched her lower lip and gazed toward the window. "The best of the summer vegetables won't be ready yet, but I'll speak to Smythe and see if he can force them this winter. Yes, that's what I'll do—and the raspberries, too. Smythe can do magic with anything that grows, and we'll have dinner on the lawn. Oh!" She pointed at Lorna. "And the vows will be spoken in the gazebo, of course. I'll have Smythe plan some early-blooming flowers for around it—something showy since the clematis won't be in bloom yet—and of course your sisters will be bridesmaids, and you'll want Phoebe, too, I'm sure. Lorna? . . . Lorna, where are you going? Lorna, come back here!"

Lorna ran straight to Jens, panic-stricken and needing the reassurance of his arms around her, only to find two of her father's friends there, members of the yacht club, looking over the boat mold and asking questions about its design. She did an about-face in the path and ran to find Aunt Agnes. Agnes, unfortunately, was napping in her room with an afghan pulled over her thin shoulders, and Lorna had too much heart to awaken her. She ran downstairs and was slamming out the front door when Levinia called from the morning room doorway, "Lorna, where are you going?"

"To Phoebe's!" she shouted, and streaked as if a tornado were at her heels.

Phoebe—bless her soul—was home, playing the piano in the parlor when Lorna burst in.

"Phoebe, I need you."

"Lorna, hello . . . Oh dear, what's wrong?"

Lorna slid onto the piano bench and flopped into her friend's arms. "I'm scared and angry and I want to tie my mother to her stupid gazebo with her own clematis vines and leave her there for the winter!"

"What's happened?"

"I told her I didn't want to marry Taylor, but she said she's going to set a date anyway. Phoebe, I won't marry him! I won't!"

Phoebe held Lorna fast and searched for any rejoinder that wouldn't sound placative. Since all did, she held them inside and let Lorna rage.

"I won't end up like my mother. I just couldn't live my life like that. Phoebe, I asked her if she loved my father, and she couldn't even lie about it. She just didn't answer. Instead, she started running off on a tangent, planning my wedding, talking about Smythe and r . . . raspberries and J . . . June in the gaz . . . gaz . . ." Lorna broke into tears.

"Don't cry . . . Oh, Lorna, please, darling, don't cry."

"I'm not crying. Well, yes, I am, but I'm as angry as I am distraught." Lorna sat back and made fists in her lap. "We're nothing, Phoebe—don't you see? What we want, what we feel, who we love is dismissed simply because we're women, and worse yet, women who belong to rich men. If I wore trousers I could say marry me or don't marry me and nobody would bat an eye. Instead, look what they do to us—parcel us off as social chattel. Well, I won't be parceled off! You'll see, I won't!"

Phoebe was trying hard not to laugh, biting her lip because Lorna looked so fierce and pretty at the same time.

"All right, laugh if you want!" Lorna scolded.

Phoebe did. She released a frisson that relieved all the tension in the room. "I can't help it. You should see yourself. You should hear yourself. Why, if I were your parents I'd be scared half to death to tangle with you. Does this Jens Harken know what a hellcat he's getting?"

Phoebe could not have chosen a more perfect comeback. Lorna succumbed to her humoring.

"You've guessed, of course. He *has* asked me to marry him—or did he? Telling you now, it hardly seems as if either one of us asked. We simply agreed, as though it had to be. But he's got to finish the *Lorna D* first, and it's got to win that regatta so he'll have established a reputation. Then Father will see that he's going to be somebody. Oh, he is, Phoebe, I just know it."

"So all you really need to do is hold your mother off until next June, when the regatta will be run."

"But she's talking about a June wedding."

Phoebe ruminated awhile. "Maybe you could promise her an August one."

"I can't lie anymore. I've already lied once. I threw Taylor's watch in the lake and told him I lost it."

"Forget I suggested it."

Lorna sighed. She turned to the piano keys and played a minor chord, letting it ring through the parlor until it became a memory.

"Life is so complicated," she lamented, dropping her hand to her lap, staring at some black notes dancing along some white staff paper on the music holder of the piano.

"And growing up is so hard."

When Lorna and Phoebe were children they sometimes played duets together. The aunts would applaud and ask for another rendition, and the parents would brag about how bright and talented their daughters were. Times had been so simple then.

"Sometimes I wish I were twelve again," Lorna replied.

They sat on, pondering the difficulties of being eighteen. After a while Phoebe asked, "Did you talk to your aunt Agnes?"

"No. She was sleeping."

"Talk to her. Confide in her. Maybe she'll intercede for you with your mother."

The thought terrified Lorna. She dropped her head into her hands and her elbows made the piano go *Daang!* There she sat, miserable. Suppose Aunt Agnes did just that and her mother told her father, and her father dismissed Jens. Suppose Lorna herself came right out and declared she was in love with Jens Harken. It wouldn't surprise Lorna if her mother advanced the wedding date even farther.

Similar thoughts struck Phoebe. She herself was walking out with Jack Lawless when the one she had eyes for was Taylor DuVal. The day could very well come when her mother and father would set down edicts about whom she would marry, and it very likely would be Jack.

"Tell you what . . ." she said, rubbing Lorna's bowed back, jostling her affectionately. "How about if I go to your mother and tell her I'll marry Taylor, and the sooner the better. Would you untie her from the gazebo and let her plan *my* wedding feast? I don't think there's a woman in White Bear Lake who could do it any better."

Lorna laughed and slung her arms around Phoebe, and they sat on the piano bench with no more answers than they'd had when Lorna had arrived.

That evening she told her mother she wasn't feeling well and shunned the dinner party. Theron stuck his head into her room around eight o'clock and said, "You sick, Lorn?"

She was sitting on her window seat in her nightgown with her knees against her chest. "Oh, hi, Theron. Come on in. No, I'm not too sick, not really."

"Then how come you're not down at the party?" He came and sat at her feet with one buttock cocked on the padded seat.

"I'm just sad, that's all."

" 'Bout what?"

"About grown-up things."

"Oh." His expression grew thoughtful, then he screwed up his face in conjecture. "Like finding good help and the price of commodities?"

She reached forward and tousled his hair, smiling in spite of herself. "Yeah, something like that."

"Hey, I know!" he exclaimed, suddenly bright. "Wait here!"

Off the window seat he shot, and ran out the door. Lorna heard his heels thumping down the hall to his room, a pause, then the slam of a door before his footsteps returned. He whipped around the doorway, breathless, and charged to the window seat. "Here." He thrust his spyglass into her hands. "You can use this for a while. Nobody can feel sad when they can have the birds right in their room, and sleep in the trees and sail in a big ship. Here, I'll pull it out for you." He did, and handed it back. "Just stick it up to your eye and close the other one. You'll see!"

She followed orders and the moonlit dock jumped into her room. "Shiver me timbers," she said, and scanned around to Theron's face. "There's a pirate in my room. Captain Kidd, I believe."

He giggled, and she felt better.

"Thanks, Theron," she said sincerely, lowering the brass piece, smiling at him affectionately. "It's just what I needed."

He got embarrassed then and didn't know what to do. He scratched his head with stubby nails and left his hair standing up like hard-crack taffy. "Well, I guess I gotta go to bed."

"Yeah, me too. See you tomorrow. Sleep tight . . . and don't let the bedbugs bite."

His face got disgusted. "Aw, come on, Lorn, that stuff's for babies."

"Oh, sorry."

He headed for his room.

"Thanks again, Theron."

At the door, he turned and sent a last loving look at his spyglass. "Hey, Lorna, don't leave it outside overnight or anything. And don't get any sand in it."

"I won't."

"How many nights you think you'll need it?"

Till the regatta next summer, she thought. "Oh, two or three should be enough."

"Okay. I'll come back for it, but don't leave it where Jenny or Daph can find it."

"I won't." With the telescope she saluted.

"Well, see ya," he said, and left.

When he was gone she held the spyglass in her lap until the brass grew warm across her palm. She studied it, this gift of love, and found tears in her eyes. Finding good help and the price of commodities—she smiled through her tears. Did he even know what a commodity was? Dear, sweet Theron. Someday he would grow up and become a man, more like Jens than Papa, hopefully. She became overpowered by the tenderest, most touching love she had ever felt for her brother. Suffused by it, she sat on her window perch a long time, discovering something she had not known until now: that love feeds upon itself, multiplying as it is given. Just as her love for Jens had opened her senses to her physical surroundings, it had opened her heart to a truer love for those around her. Even for Mama, with her misguided priorities, and Papa, with his bluff, unaffectionate demeanor. She loved them, truly she did, but they were wrong, wrong, to dictate her affections. Father, of course, would go along with Mother when she said it was time to set a date for Lorna's wedding. And at the yacht club and at afternoon teas they would speak about it with Taylor's parents, and it would be treated as preordained that Lorna should be Taylor's wife.

How could she change their minds? It would be difficult, but she knew she must try, and she intended to do so tonight.

She was still awake when the dinner party ended, lying in bed, listening to the sounds of her parents ascending the stairs, using the bathroom and retiring to their room for the night. Slipping from her bed, she donned a wrapper and went to their room.

Her knock was followed by a surprised silence, then her father's voice, "Yes, who is it?"

"It's Lorna, Father. May I come in?"

He opened the door himself, dressed in his trousers over a short-sleeved summer union suit with his suspenders trailing. Levinia, she saw, was already in bed. The scent of cigar smoke was strong in the room.

"I must talk to both of you."

This was a room into which she rarely stepped, as an adult. She had never understood why until this moment. Levinia was clutching the covers to her chest, though she was covered to her ears in white cotton.

Lorna closed the door and stood with her spine against the knob, holding it behind her.

"I'm sorry I didn't come down to dinner tonight, and I'm sorry I lied. I was not feeling ill. I simply didn't want to be with Taylor."

Gideon spoke up. "Your mother has told me about this preposterous declaration you've made, that you don't want to marry him. Girl, what in blue blazes has gotten into you!"

"I don't love him, Father."

Gideon's eyes narrowed to pinpoints while he stared at her in derision. Then he snorted and spun away. "That is the singularly most asinine statement I've ever heard."

"Why?"

"Why!" He spun back to her. "Girl, if I have to tell you you're dumber than I think! I'm in total agreement with your mother. Taylor DuVal worships the ground you walk on. He's ambitious, and bright, and will have earned a fortune in his own right by the time he's thirty, just as his father did before him. He's part of our social circle, and his parents are as pleased as we are about the two of you keeping company. Now, the matter is settled! You're marrying him in June at whatever function your mother plans!"

Lorna stared at him, helpless, angry, her insides trembling.

"Papa, please . . . don't—"

"The matter is settled, I said!"

She compressed her lips. Hard. Tears built. Spattered. Spinning, she flung open the door and slammed it so hard the ash fell from Gideon's cigar in the ashtray. Everyone in the house heard her footsteps pounding down the hall, then her own door slamming as she careened toward her bed and bounced onto it, face down, weeping her heart out.

Ten minutes later she was still sobbing when Jenny crept in and approached the bed uncertainly. Lorna was unaware of her presence until Jenny stroked her hair softly.

"Lorna? . . . Lorna, what happened?"

"Oh, Jennneeeeee . . ." Lorna wailed.

Jenny clambered onto the bed and Lorna curled into her sister's arms.

"They're making me marry Taylor, and I don't want to."

"But Taylor's so handsome. And nice."

"I know. Oh, Jenny, I wish I admired him the way you do, but I love someone else."

"Someone else?" Jenny whispered, more awed by this news than by Lorna's weeping and door slamming. "Gosh."

"Someone they wouldn't approve of."

"But who?"

"I can't tell you, and you mustn't tell them. They don't know about it yet. I know I'm a coward not to come right out and tell them, but they're so . . . so forceful and righteous about it, ordering me around and . . . and telling me what I have to do. You know how they can be. But I just can't stand it anymore."

Jenny went on petting Lorna's hair. Never in her life had the older sister been succored by the younger. First Theron, now Jenny: They had come, sensing they were needed, and Lorna was deeply touched by their caring. Momentarily one more voice whispered timidly out of the dark.

"Jenny? What's the matter with Lorna?"

Daphne materialized like a child-spirit floating toward the bed from the doorway.

"She's had an argument with Mother and Father. Go back to bed, Daphne."

"But she's crying."

"I'm all right, Daph." From the sanctuary of Jenny's lap, Lorna reached out a hand. Daphne came to take it and lean against the edge of the bed. "Truly I am."

"But you never cry, Lorna. You're too old."

"A person is never too old to cry, Daphne, remember that. And I feel ever so much better now that you and Jenny and Theron have visited me."

"Theron was here?"

"Before his bedtime. He brought me his spyglass."

"His spyglass . . . gee . . ." Breathless wonder haloed the word.

Jenny asked, "Are you feeling better now, Lorna?"

"Oh, yes . . . thank you both. Now I think you'd better go back to bed before you get in trouble with Mother, too."

Jenny plumped Lorna's pillow, and Daphne gave her a quick kiss on the mouth. "I'll play tennis with you tomorrow, Lorna," she offered.

"And I will, too," Jenny added.

"I'd love that. Thank you. You're both dear sisters."

"Well, good night, Lorna."

"You sure you won't cry any more, Lorna?"

"I'll be just fine."

They lingered in the dark, unsure if they should abandon her yet, finally tiptoeing away as if she were an infant they had just rocked to sleep.

In their absence, Lorna's world grew dreary once more. The love shown by her siblings created a deep and touching afterglow, but it was tinged by an inexplicable sadness different from that of earlier. It was the sadness of the lovelorn who, when sundered from their beloved, find tears in all things happy.

Jens . . . Jens . . . you're the only one who can make me happy. You're the one I want to be with, laugh with, cry with, love.

She heard the old Chesterfield clock chime in the downstairs hall. Not a soul in the house astir.

A quarter hour.

A half hour—was it one-thirty? Two-thirty?

The three-quarter hour . . . in the deep of night.

No one to hear.

No one to know.

She lay flat on her back with her hands locked, pressed hard between her breasts, her heart pounding in trepidation. Jens . . . Jens . . . sleeping above me in your tiny attic room.

No one to hear.

No one to know.

Her bed was high. It seemed to take a long time for her feet to find the floor. When they did, she took neither wrapper nor slippers, but went barefoot, straightaway, across her room, down the hall and up the servants' stairway with its narrow walls and high risers and the trapped smell of the day's cooking. She had been up here several times and knew the layout: three rooms on the right, three on the left, all squashed beneath the roof like hair under a dunce's cap. Jens's was the middle door on the left.

She opened it without knocking, slipped inside and closed it deftly without making a sound. Inside, she stood motionless, her heart hammering, listening to Jens's breathing from the amorphous white shape of the bed. It stood to her left, against a wall. Beside it a single eyebrow window bent the shingles up scarcely enough to offer a breeze when dropped inward on its hinges. The room was very hot and smelled like a sleeping man—of warm breath and warm skin and the faint stuffiness of worn clothing. His clothing hung on hooks to her left: dark streamers against the lighter wall, created by the trousers and shirt he'd worn today.

His bed was single. His left arm cantilevered off it, its wrist pointing toward her as he lay on his side. He snored lightly, a sound resembling a curtain flapping against a window casing in a back breeze. Did he dream of sailboats? Of steamed wood? Of her?

She approached the bed and squatted beside it on her heels, next to his outstretched arm.

"Jens?" she whispered.

He slept on. In her life she had never approached the slumbering form of a man. His shoulders were bare. His chest, too, down to the waist, where a sheet covered him. The underside of his outflung arm appeared pale and vulnerable. She touched him there, with four hesitant fingertips, on the soft, warm, unflexed muscle of his biceps.

"Jens?"

"Hm?" His head came up and stayed so, his body registering the awakening before his mind did. "Whss . . ." he whispered, confused. "What is it?"

"Jens, it's me, Lorna."

"Lorna!" He sat up abruptly. "What are you doing here?"

"I came to be with you . . . to talk . . . I have some terrible news."

He took a moment to clarify his mind, glancing over to the eyebrow window, rubbing his face.

"Sorry . . . my mind is fuzzy. What happened?"

"They're going to marry me off to Taylor. Mother says she's going to set a date—next June. I pitched Taylor's watch in the lake, and pleaded with them, and told them I don't love him, but they're dead set against me, and angry to boot. They say I'm going to marry Taylor whether I like it or not. Oh, Jens, what am I going to do?"

"What time is it?"

"I don't know exactly. Close to two, maybe, or three."

"If you get caught here they'll crucify you . . . and me, too."

"I know that, but I won't get caught. They all just went to sleep about an hour ago. Jens, please, what are we going to do? I cannot marry Taylor after lying with you, but I'm afraid to tell them the real reason yet."

"Of course you can't." He raked back his hair, tugging the sheet closer to his hips and waist, casting around in the dark for good judgment in the midst of this muddled midnight morass. He had no more answers than she. "Here"—he reached for her arm—"come on up here."

She sat on the edge of his bed facing him while he gripped her arms through the sleeves of her cotton nightgown. "I don't know what we're going to do, but it's not this. We're not going to put you at risk by meeting up here where anyone could find out about it. You're going back down to your room and we'll take it a day at a time."

Plaintively she asked, "Would you marry me now, Jens?"

He dropped his hands from her warm, resilient flesh and tried not to think of it beneath a single layer of loose white cotton. "I can't marry you now. What would we live on? Where? Everybody I know knows your father. He'd make sure no one would hire me, and besides, I thought we agreed I wasn't going to be a kitchen handyman anymore. I'm going to be a boatbuilder. I can't do that until the *Lorna D* is finished."

"I know," she whispered, dropping her chin guiltily.

With the edge of a finger he tipped it up. "Right now there's no danger. They aren't saying you have to marry him tomorrow."

She told him calmly, "They had a dinner party tonight. I was supposed to sit next to him. Do you know what it's like to sit next to one man, pretending you're amused and attracted by him, while you love someone else? I've been doing that most of the summer, and I cannot do it anymore. It's dishonest. It's unfair to Taylor, and to you, and to me. And I love you too much to continue the pretense, Jens."

They sat in silence, linked only by a short stretch of sheet that flowed between his hip and hers, aggrieved by their love and its attendant heartbreak, wishing at times they had never met. They thought about addressing her parents, facing them with the truth. They knew such an act would be folly, for along with the right to love they both wanted a good life, and speaking to her parents now would nearly guarantee anything but.

"Have you ever thought," he asked, "how much simpler our lives would be if you'd never come back into the kitchen that night?"

"Many times."

"And then you feel guilty for thinking it."

"Yes," she whispered.

"Me too."

They let some silence pass. He sat with one hand propped on the mattress behind him. Reaching across his hip, he took her hand.

"If this ever works out, and we have children of our own, we're never going to dictate who they can love."

Their thumbs played a sad game of roundabout. Minute upon minute disappeared, and the sadness became supplanted by temptation, no matter what he'd said. They were two in love, in a warm attic bedroom, dressed in little, fighting memories of the first time they'd made love. They sat a long time, linked by only their fingers, while images of a more intimate link trespassed in their minds. They studied their joined hands, scarcely visible in the unlit room, while their thumbs circled . . . circled . . .

Then stopped.

He looked up first. At her face, or the place where it bowed low in the darkness. She looked up, too, as if in answer to his silent call. They sat helpless, hapless, in the tug of this merciless seduction perpetrated upon them by their own bodies. Such pounding. Such rushing. Such persuasion they felt.

Such knowledge of wrong, of right, of risk.

An admission left his lips, a word, uttered in a pleading whisper: "Lorna . . ."

And with it they moved.

Mouth to mouth, breast to breast, they ended the separation and yearning, and silenced the voices of common sense in their heads, falling from grace with all but each other. Over he took her, in a desperate tumble, and shifted her legs down along his own almost roughly. They kissed, matching their mouths, and rolled, matching their lengths, and lifted knees and opened legs and confirmed suspicions that there was nothing more than one sheet and one nightgown separating their skins.

"My beautiful Lorna," he praised, filling his hands with her breasts, then her hips, and finally her nightgown, hauling it out of their way. It caught on her left arm and became part of their rolling embrace.

"I tried not to come," she whispered beneath the onslaught of desire. "I stayed in my room willing myself to go to sleep . . . not to think of you . . . not to leave my bed. . . ."

His touches on her naked skin were swift and well aimed. "I tried, too . . ." He was touching her, inside, before the pillow changed shape beneath her head. She arched back and caught him behind a hip with her heel, her lips drawn back and her eyes closed. He grabbed the sheet and kicked it to the foot of the bed while she searched low and caressed him. Sharing those first impatient pleasures, they gave their bodies license, letting muscle and sinew celebrate this call to life. And all those days and hours of longing came into play—a summer's worth of looking away, looking toward, warning themselves one thing, feeling another. Their sexual encounter in the boat shed became part of tonight as well, its lessons well enjoyed and mulled, brought forth now to be repeated and elaborated.

"You . . ." he quite growled, a man overcome, ". . . driving me crazy night and day. Why didn't you stay away, you rich man's daughter?"

"Ask the moon to stop turning the tides. . . . Why didn't you turn me out, you poor boatbuilder's son?"

In answer he only growled, rolled flush upon her and entered her body to be caught from behind by both her heels.

Tensile and silent, they arched. And breathed through clamped teeth.

Those minutes of conjunction became fine in both their flamboyant and meditative moods. They discovered some rarified truths: that a cataclysmic first joining soon gives way rather than burn out too soon; that the ensuing expanse of lush, lazy caresses fills a need equally as vital; that it is hard to whisper when one feels like shouting exuberances to the heavens; that though a man's intentions may be noble, his actions don't always carry through. When they were wrapped in shudders and Jens had his hand clapped over Lorna's open mouth to keep her from calling out, he asked the moon to stop turning the tides, but the moon only smiled, and Jens remained in Lorna's body till the final slump and sigh.

Chapter 11

September aged. The brief spate of hot weather cooled and dawn began shrouding the lake with mist as its chill air kissed the warm water. The choiring of frogs ceased. The rusty creaking of Canada geese took its place, lifting faces skyward. In the marshes along the shoreline the cattails had exploded into powder puffs, forlorn now that the red-winged blackbirds had deserted them and headed south. At sunset the skies burned in vivid hues of heliotrope and orange as refracted light shimmered off the dust of harvesttime. The air became fragrant with leaf smoke and wheat chaff, and at night the moon donned a halo, warning of colder weather ahead.

In the boat shed the planking had begun. Daily now, the steam box hissed, loaded with fragrant cedar, perfuming the place with humidity and flavor so heavy and rich the sparrows pecked at the windowpanes as if begging to be let inside. Six inches wide and a half inch thick: steam it, glue it and screw it into place, then overlap that plank with another and another. The boat became a reality, a thing with a real fair line and a sheer line. The planking was completed and the caulking began:

strips of cotton batting forced into the plank butts with a sharp-edged disk roller, waiting for water to swell and expand them and make the craft seaworthy. The countersunk screw holes were filled with wooden plugs. Then came the part Lorna loved best.

From the first time she watched Jens planing, she thought it the most arresting motion she'd ever seen. With the tool in both hands he would twist and lean and lunge, his shoulders slanted at an oblique angle, shifting and flexing as he labored with a love as true as any she'd ever seen a person display for his work. He whistled a lot and dropped often to a squat, eyeballing the length of the boat with one lid closed. On the balls of his feet he would balance among the curled cedar shavings that were as blond as his hair and from which it seemed to take its fragrance.

"When I was a boy," he said, "I caught plenty of hell from my father if I tried to get by without fairing up a boat good with the hand plane before sanding 'er down. My dad . . . he was a fussy one. Sometimes even before we started planing, when we'd be making the mold, he'd see one station that was bulging, and he'd say, 'We got to rework that one, boys,' and we'd groan and complain and say, 'Aw, Dad, it's good enough.' But now I thank my lucky stars that he made us do it over till it was right. This boat here . . . this little beauty will have a fair line the wind won't know is there."

Lorna listened, and observed, and admired the fine articulation of muscle on Jens's arms and shoulders as he moved and moved. She thought she could go on forever watching this man build boats.

She told him, "That time I came into the kitchen when you were all eating cake and Mrs. Schmitt asked you to chip some ice for my tea . . . You squatted down and started chipping away with that ice pick, and a little space appeared between your waistband and your shirt. It was shaped like a fish and I couldn't take my eyes off it. You were wearing black trousers and a very faded red shirt—I remember thinking it was the color of an old tomato stain that's been washed a lot. And your suspenders cut right down through the middle of that bare piece of skin, and while you were chipping, the pieces of ice went sailing over your shoulder to the floor. Then finally you got a big piece off and cupped it in your hands and let it slip off your fingertips into my glass . . . and you dried your hands on your thighs." Jens had stopped planing and stood looking at her. "Watching you push that hand plane," she concluded, "does the same thing to my insides."

Wordlessly he put down the tool and crossed the room to her, took her in his arms and kissed her, bringing the smell—the near taste—of cedar along with him.

When he lifted his head his expression still wore a hint of astonished surprise. "You remember all that?"

"I remember everything about you from the first moment we met."

"That my shirt was red and faded?"

"And crept up . . . back here." She touched him in the Y of his suspenders, drawing three light circles with her middle fingertip.

"You're a very naughty girl, Lorna Diane." He grinned. "Here." He found a piece of sandpaper for her. "Put yourself to use. You can sand behind me." She smiled and kissed his chin, then together they returned to the *Lorna D* to labor side by side on this boat that symbolized their future.

She went often to his room during those last weeks before the family moved back to the city. After they'd made love they would lie entwined, whispering in the dark.

"I've made a decision," he told her one night. "When the *Lorna D* is done, I'll come back to town to work in the kitchen until spring."

"No. You don't belong in a kitchen."

"But what else can I do?"

"I don't know. We'll think of something."

Of course, they thought of nothing.

The members of the White Bear Yacht Club beached their crafts and turned their interests to hunting. Wild ducks and geese began appearing on the supper table at Rose Point Cottage. The second week in September, Levinia began to make lists of what should stay and what should go. Then in the third week of September an unseasonably early frost came and killed all of her roses. Gideon and his cronies decided they were leaving for a five-day hunting trip to the Brule River in Wisconsin, and Levinia announced at supper that she was having the pipes drained the following morning and everybody should have their things packed and be ready to go back to town in the afternoon.

That night when Lorna went to Jens's room their lovemaking held a desperate undertone. They clung harder. Spoke less. Kissed a little too frantically.

Afterward, lying in his arms, she asked, "When will the boat be done?"

"Two months. That's longer than your father gave me, but I can tell I'll never finish in one more month."

"Two months . . . how shall I stand it?"

"By remembering that I love you. By knowing that somehow, someday, we'll be together as man and wife." He kissed her to seal the promise, holding her head firmly between his hands, then lifting his head as they searched each other's sad eyes.

"So you'll come back to town when the boat is done?"

"Yes."

They had argued further about it and decided it was best, only till next summer.

"And you'll be staying at the Hotel Leip till then?" Most of the lake hotels closed in the winter, but the Leip reduced its rates and stayed open as a boardinghouse.

"Yes. Your father's paying my room and board. You can write to me there."

"I will. I promise. And you can write to me, but send the letters to Phoebe. Use her middle initial, *V,* so she'll know it's for me. Now, I'm getting too sad talking about us being apart, so tell me about the *Lorna D.* Tell me what you'll do next and next and next between now and winter, when I'll see you again."

He spoke in a monologue, his words meant to hold eventualities at bay for as long as possible. "A lot more hand sanding, then I'll paint the outside. Green, of course. It's got to be green. Then cut the planking even with the ribs and release the boat from the mold. Then I'll start the work on the interior structure. I'll have to laminate the center backbone, and put on the deck beams over the internal framework, and cover them with cedar planking. Then more planing and fairing, of course, and after that I'll cover the deck with canvas. Next comes a mahogany wood molding to cover the nails that are holding the canvas on. Then there's molding to be put on around the cockpit—mahogany, too. Then I drill the rudder hole and install the shaft, and put on the deck hardware and—"

She flung herself into his arms, cutting off his words, holding her sobs captive in her throat.

"So much work," she whispered. "Will you have time to be lonesome for me the way I will be for you?"

"Yes, I'll miss you." He rubbed her naked spine. "I'll miss your showing up in the doorway with delphiniums and blackcurrants, and your incessant questions, and the smell of your hair and the feel of your skin and the way you touch me and kiss me and make me feel like I'm a vital piece of this universe."

"Oh, Jens, you are."

"Since I've fallen in love with you I am. Before that I wasn't sure."

"Of course you were. Remember how you used to tell me you were certain you could build the fastest boat ever? And how you'd change the face of inland racing? Your self-confidence was one of the first things I admired about you. Oh, Jens, I'm going to miss you so much."

They clung, and counted off the minutes of the escaping night, and dreaded parting.

"What time is it?" she'd ask at intervals, and Jens would get up, turn the face of his watch to the eyebrow window and read it by the negligible moonlight that oozed in.

"Three-twenty," he answered the first time.

Then, "Nearly four."

And finally, "Four-thirty."

Returning to his narrow bed, he sat beside Lorna and took her hand. One of them had to be sensible. "You have to go. The kitchen staff will be getting up soon, and we can't risk you running into one of them in the hall."

She sprang up and flung her arms around his shoulders, whispering, "I don't want to."

He put his face to her neck and held her, impressing this moment in his memory to sustain him through the months ahead, thinking, *Let her be safe, and not pregnant, and keep her in love with me this much until I can be with her again, and don't let them talk her into marrying DuVal, who is so much better suited to her kind than I am.*

They kissed one last time, each of them trying to be strong for the other, Lorna failing.

He had to put her from him. "Lorna . . . where is your nightgown?" he asked gently. "You've got to put it on now."

She rummaged in the dark and found it but sat with her head hanging, the garment slack in her hands. He took it from her lifeless fingers and found its neck hole, and held it for her. "Here . . . put it on, darling."

She lifted her arms and the gown collapsed around her. He settled it into place and fastened all but the top two buttons, dipping his head and kissing her between her collarbones before buttoning them, too.

"Just remember . . . I love you. You mustn't cry now, or your eyes will be red in the morning, and what will you say when they ask about it?"

She flung herself upon him. "That I love Jens Harken and I don't want to go back to town without him."

He swallowed the lump in his throat and stood, forcing her arms to slide free of his neck.

"Come," he said, "you're making this awfully hard for me. Another minute and you'll have me in tears."

Immediately she obeyed—she could do for him what she could not for herself—leaving the bed and walking beside him to the door. There he turned and pulled her gently into his arms.

"It'll be the fastest, finest boat ever," he promised. "And it will win you for me—you'll see. Think about that when things get you down. And remember, I love you and I *will* marry you."

"I love you, too," she managed as her long-held weeping broke forth.

Their mouths collided in one last smeared, tormented kiss while she clambered barefoot onto the tops of his feet. His eyes stung. The kiss became anguish.

Finally Jens tore himself away, gripped her arms firmly and ordered, "Go."

A grievous pause punctuated by her soft sobs in the dark, and she was gone, leaving only a rustle of cotton and a vast emptiness in his heart.

Levinia spurted, in the midst of their leave-taking nine hours later, "What in heaven's name is wrong with you, girl? Are you sick?"

"No, Mother."

"Then put that hat on and get moving! Mercy sakes, you act as if you have Addison's disease!"

To Lorna, returning to the Saint Paul house felt like going to prison. It was her home, but so much less homelike than the cottage at White Bear Lake. Situated on Summit Avenue among the crème de la crème of Saint Paul's mansions, Gideon Barnett's town house had been erected as a monument to his success. The address in itself was one of superlative prestige, for the list of property owners along Summit included those with the oldest money in Minnesota—industrialists, railroad barons, mining executives and politicians who need only take a short carriage ride down the hill to be at the State Capitol. The house itself was constructed of gray granite mined at Saint Cloud, Minnesota, from one of Gideon Barnett's own mines; it had been erected by German stonemasons brought to America expressly for the job by Barnett himself. It was Gothic, burly, a massive pile of dinge with cubelike lines broken primarily by a high square tower at the center front, which housed the main stairway. Its doors were elaborately carved, with ornate bronze hardware shaped like gargoyles baring canine teeth. As a baby, Lorna had closed her eyes and burrowed her face against her mother's shoulder when being carried into the house to avoid confronting those scary beasts.

Inside, the place was overburdened with treacle-colored woodwork and mahogany furniture whose legs were as thick as human waists. It was accessorized by joyless pieces like malachite urns, French bronzes, stuffed stags' heads (Gideon's hunting trophies) and dark, busy Kirman rugs. Its immense chandeliers hovered overhead like the wrath of God, while its fireplaces—all eight of them—hove at the house's inhabitants like great, gaping maws. Add to all this windows set too deep to allow enough light inside, and there waited a place darksome enough to not only match but to augment Lorna's heartsickness.

She lived with that heartsickness daily, from the time she opened her eyes in her thick-posted satinwood bed to the time she appeared at supper in the gloomy dining room with its shroudlike wallpaper swallowing up all the light from the ugly chandelier worked in the shape of Indians bearing bows and arrows.

She felt as if she had left her heart at Rose Point Cottage and in its place lay a lifeless mass she carried around as one would a purse with no money, something that merely rode along without being opened to anyone. A week went by and Lorna remained listless and quiet. Two weeks, and Levinia grew concerned. She came, eventually, to press Lorna's forehead in search of fever. "Lorna, what is it? You haven't been the same since we came home from the lake."

"It's nothing. I miss the gardens, and the bright house, and the wide open air, that's all. This house is so dominating and dark."

"But you haven't been eating, and your color has been so sallow."

"I tell you, Mother, it's nothing. Really."

"Say what you will, I'm concerned. That day we were leaving Rose Point I made some remark about Addison's disease to get you going, but I've been watching you ever since, and yesterday I actually looked up Addison's in our *Health and Longevity* book. Lorna, you have many of the symptoms."

"Oh, Mother . . ." Lorna flounced to the other side of the room, displaying more energy than she had in two weeks. "For heaven's sake!"

"Well, it's true. You've been in a state of prolonged languor. Your appetite is capricious, and you seem to show a special repugnance to meats. Have you been vomiting, too?"

"No, Mother, I haven't been vomiting. . . . Now, please . . ."

"Well, don't get so upset with me. Every other symptom fits, and they say the vomiting comes only in more advanced cases. Nevertheless, I think we should take you to see Dr. Richardson."

"I'm not going to Dr. Richardson. I've just been a little tired is all."

Levinia considered, then rose to her full height as if she'd made a decision. "Very well. If you're not sick, it's time you end this moping and join the human race again. Dorothea DuVal has invited the two of us to lunch at her house this coming Thursday and I've accepted. She and I believe it's time to begin making wedding plans. Next June isn't that far away, you know."

"But Taylor and I aren't even officially engaged!"

"Yes, I know. But Dorothea says you will be soon."

The empty purse of a heart Lorna believed she carried showed it had a rich cache of objections that jingled around, wanting to be spilled: exasperation at her mother's refusal to listen, anger at both Levinia and Dorothea for railroading her this way, gut denial that any such wedding would ever take place.

Realizing, however, that her objections would again be overridden if voiced, she surprised Levinia by answering calmly, "Whatever you say, Mother."

She left the room and went directly to seek out Aunt Agnes, finding her in the music room with the lace curtain flipped back to let in extra light. The old woman was sitting in a sewing rocker beside a piecrust table doing some fancywork.

"Aunt Agnes, may I talk to you?"

Agnes removed a pair of spectacles and laid them on the table beside her thimble keep.

"Of course. I can do this anytime."

Lorna closed the pocket doors and drew a low footstool near her aunt's chair.

"Aunt Agnes," she said, curling her shoulders and propping her elbows on her knees, looking up into a pair of kind blue eyes. "I must trust you with the most important secret of my entire life."

"If you do, I shall honor that trust to my grave."

Lorna touched the backs of Agnes's shiny, mottled hands. "Remember when I talked to you about the man I love? Well, that man isn't Taylor DuVal. He is someone Mother and Father will strongly object to. He's one of their employees, Jens Harken—the one who's building the boat for Father. Until he began on the boat he was our kitchen odd-jobs man, but it doesn't matter to me at all—I love him as deeply and as truly as you loved Captain Dearsley. I want to marry him."

Aunt Agnes's eyes grew tender. She reached out both hands, her fingers permanently crooked and knotted, and took Lorna's face as if to place a kiss upon it. Instead, she spoke lovingly. "Dear child, then you have found it. You're one of the lucky few who've been blessed by it."

Lorna smiled. "Yes, I am."

Agnes dropped her hands. "And you're willing to fight for it—you'll have to be, because Gideon and Levinia will snarl and yelp and lay down laws."

"They already have. Mother and Dorothea DuVal are meeting over lunch on Thursday to start making wedding plans. They want me there, too. I've told and told Mother I don't want to marry Taylor, but she simply won't listen."

"Because she and your father were not blessed like you and I. They don't understand."

"What should I do?"

"Can this young boatbuilder support you?"

"No, not yet. In another year, maybe."

"Have you broken it off with Taylor?"

"No. I've just been avoiding him in the hope that he'll get the hint."

"Mmm . . . not a very honorable way to conduct yourself."

"I know," Lorna whispered.

"Nor a very effective way. If you want him to stop calling—and giving your mother ideas—tell him so. If you must, tell him you love another man. It will hurt him, but who of us hasn't been hurt by love? Hurt serves its purpose—it intensifies our joy when it finally arrives. So the way I see it, the first step is to sunder your tie to young Taylor in an absolutely clear-cut fashion. Mothers have been able for centuries to force their daughters to the altar, but they haven't been so successful with sons. If neither of you wants the marriage, perhaps those two meddlesome women will desist. The sooner you speak to Taylor the better."

This time it was Lorna who took Agnes's face between her hands. She kissed the old woman squarely on the mouth and told her sincerely, "I can see why Captain Dearsley loved you so much. Thank you, dear Aunt Agnes."

The following day Lorna dressed for the weather and took the streetcar down the hill into Saint Paul's business district, to the offices of the DuVal Flour Milling Company, which hovered at the base of a forest of tall grain elevators on the west shore of the Mississippi River. The place was dusty and smelled pleasantly oatsy, its air astir with fine particles of grain.

Taylor, wearing leather sleeveguards, was working at a desk within a glassed-in office when Lorna was announced. His surprise showed plainly: He shot to his feet and glanced up eager-eyed, searching her out on the other side of the glass. She waved inconspicuously. He smiled and came striding around his desk, removing the sleeveguards and leaving them behind as he swept through his door.

"Lorna," he said, reaching out with both hands. "What a surprise this is!"

"Hello, Taylor."

"I couldn't believe it when Ted said your name. I thought he was joking."

"So this is where you learn your father's business."

"This is it." He gestured. "Dusty, isn't it?"

"Pleasantly so." She looked to her right. "And that is your office."

"With its very dusty window."

"Could we go inside a minute, Taylor?"

Her tone took the smile from his face and turned it somber.

"Of course." He touched her elbow and followed, closing the door behind them. From a wooden armchair he removed a flat of grain samples, then dusted the seat and placed it beside his desk.

"Please . . . sit down."

She did, gingerly, with her back several inches away from the vertical ribs of the backrest. He sat, too, in a well-used wooden swivel chair, whose springs twanged loudly.

When they quieted, so did the room.

Into that uneasy silence Lorna spoke. "I came to talk to you about something very important, Taylor. I'm sorry to do it here in the middle of your workday, but I simply didn't know what else to do."

He sat waiting, his forearms resting on an open ledger as large as a tea tray. He was dressed in a gray striped suit, a white shirt with a high, round collar and a black tie. For the dozenth time she wondered why it had not been possible for her to fall head over heels in love with this man: He was so perfect.

"Has your mother spoken to you recently—about us?" she inquired.

"Yes, as a matter of fact, she has. Just last night."

"Taylor, you must know that I think a great deal of you. I admire you, and . . .

and I've had a lot of fun with you. This summer when you gave me the watch, you said it was intended as a token of your intention to marry me. Taylor"—she stumbled and looked down at her gloves—"this is so hard to say . . ." She raised her eyes to his. "You're a fine man, an honest man, a hard-working man, and I'm sure you'll make a wonderful husband, but the truth is . . . I'm so very, very sorry, Taylor . . . I don't love you. Not the way I think a woman ought to love the man she's going to marry."

Taylor's moustache lowered slightly on the left side, as if he'd caught his upper lip between his teeth. He sat motionless, his hands flat on the ledger page, separated by four inches of blue-lined paper. His calmness rattled Lorna: She chattered on to cover her discomposure.

"Our mothers have their heads together and they want me to join them tomorrow over lunch, to make plans for our wedding. Taylor, I beg you . . . please help me convince them this is not the right thing to do, because if you don't they're going to forge right ahead and plan a wedding that should not take place."

Taylor moved at last. He tipped back his chair, blew out an immense gust of breath and scrubbed one hand down over his face. It covered his mouth and chin while he studied her with troubled eyes. Finally he dropped his hand and admitted, "I suppose I'd guessed." He lined up the ledger with the edge of the green blotter, very precisely—something to occupy his eyes. "You've been avoiding me much of the summer, though I didn't know why. Then I noticed you weren't wearing the watch. I guess that's when it struck me. I just kept hoping you'd change . . . that one day you'd be the way you were those first nights we were alone together. What happened, Lorna?"

He looked so hurt she felt cruel and glanced aside.

He tipped his chair forward and joined his hands on the ledger, speaking earnestly. "Did I do something wrong? Did I change some way?"

"No."

"Did I offend you with my advances?"

She looked at her lap and whispered, "No."

"Then what is it? I deserve to know. What changed your mind?"

Her eyes had taken on a faint sheen of tears. In spite of them, she faced him squarely. "I fell in love with somebody else." Disbelief seemed to render him speechless. He stared at her while in the anteroom four workers stitched flour bags and a cat stalked for mice. Through the floor came the faint rumble and vibration of the nearby mill wheels grinding.

Lorna told him, "I'm being honest with you, Taylor, because I *am* guilty of hurting you—it's true—but I want you to know I never intended to do so."

He became animated at last, gesturing wide. "*Who* could you possibly have been seeing that I don't know about!" His cheeks had grown ruddy above his beard.

"I'm not allowed to divulge that. To do so would be to betray a confidence."

"It's not that young whelp Mitchell Armfield, is it?"

"No, it's not Mitch."

"Then who?"

"Taylor, please. I cannot tell you."

She watched his ire grow, though he tried to curb it. "Obviously your parents don't know about him." When she refused to reply, he continued speculating. "Which means it's someone they don't approve of, right?"

"Taylor, I've been truthful with you, but in the strictest of confidence. I must ask you not to reveal what we've said here today."

Taylor DuVal left his chair and stood at the dusty glass, knuckles to hips, facing the workroom, where clerks and seamstresses moved about their daily business, all making money for him, money this woman could have shared—a life of luxury this woman could have shared. And he would have been good to her! Generous to a fault! He'd given her a betrothal watch while she'd been two-timing him. Two-timing him, for God's sake! He wasn't such a bad catch. As she'd said, he was honest, hard-working and loyal—by God, he'd been scrupulously loyal to her! And if it came down to it, he was pretty easy on the eye. So, to hell with her. If all that wasn't enough for the woman, he didn't need her!

"All right, Lorna." He turned brusquely. "You'll have your way. I'll speak to my mother and tell her my future plans have changed. I won't bother you again."

She stood. He remained across the room.

"I'm sorry, Taylor," she said.

"Yes . . . well . . . don't be. I won't be unattended for long."

Lorna colored. It was the truth, she knew. He was far too plum a catch for the ladies to ignore, once they realized he was on the marriage market.

At the news, Levinia went into a decline. She took to falling back into chairs with her eyelids closed, speaking in a puling voice and sprinkling iris water into her handkerchief, then pressing it to her nose while her eyes brimmed once more.

Gideon swore a blue streak and called Lorna a stupid twit.

Jenny wrote to Taylor, expressing her apologies for the broken engagement and offering a friendly ear should he need someone to talk to.

Phoebe beamed and asked, point-blank, "So now he's fair game?"

Aunt Henrietta hissed, "Ungrateful girl, someday you'll regret this."

Aunt Agnes opened her arms and said, "We romantics must stick together."

Lorna wrote to Jens:

My Dearest One,

Bleak are these days without you, though I have some news to cheer us both. I have taken command of my own life and have severed my relationship with Taylor DuVal, once and for all.

Jens wrote back:

My Beloved Lorna,

This boat shed without you is like a violin without strings. No music happens here anymore. . . .

Lorna wrote:

Jens, my darling,

    Never have so few weeks felt like so many. I don't know if it's being separated from you that causes this lethargy, but I have been feeling so lifeless, and even food has lost its appeal. Mother fears it's Addison's disease, but it isn't. It is simply loneliness, I'm sure. She wants me to go to the doctor, but the only cure I need is you. . . .

Jens wrote:

Dearest Lorna,

    I grew terrified when I read your letter. If you're ill, please, darling, do as your mother suggests and visit the doctor. If anything should happen to you I don't know what I'd do. . . .

Lorna's lethargy persisted. Food, especially the odor of cooked meat, seemed to turn her stomach. Most upsetting, that symptom of Addison's which signaled its advancement—vomiting—happened one morning, and in its wake, Lorna, too, grew terrified.

She went straight to Aunt Agnes.

Agnes took one look at Lorna's blanched face and flew across the room. "Good heavens, child, what's wrong? You look as though you left all your blood in a jar in your room. Sit down here."

Lorna sat, shaken. "Aunt Agnes," she said, clinging to her aunt's hands, lifting her terrified eyes. "Please don't tell Mother, because I don't want to scare her yet, but I think I really do have Addison's disease."

"What! Oh, surely not. Addison's disease—why, what gave you that idea?"

"I looked it up in the *Health and Longevity* book and it's just as Mother suspected. I have all the symptoms, and now I just vomited, and the book says that means it's in its advanced stages. Oh, Aunt Agnes, I don't want to die."

"Stop it this minute, Lorna Barnett! You're not going to die! Now tell me about these symptoms."

Lorna described them, still clinging to Agnes's hands. When she finished, Agnes sat down beside her on the chaise.

"Lorna, do you love me?" she asked.

Lorna blinked, then stared, digesting this unexpected question. "Of course."

"And do you trust me?"

"Yes, Aunt Agnes, you know I do."

"Then you must answer a question, and you must answer it truthfully."

"All right."

Agnes squeezed Lorna's hands tighter. "Did you do with your young boatbuilder what a bride does with her groom on her wedding night?"

Lorna's cheeks flared. Her gaze dropped to her lap as she answered in a guilty whisper, "Yes."

"Once?"

Again a whisper. "More than once."

"Have you missed any of your fluxes?"

"One."

Agnes whispered, "Dear God." Quickly, she took control of her emotions. "Then I suspect this isn't Addison's, but something even worse."

Lorna feared asking.

"Unless I miss my guess, you're in a family way, dear."

Lorna spoke not a word. Her hands slipped from Agnes's, and one rested on her heart. Her gaze turned toward the window and her lips formed a silent O. She had two thoughts: *Now they'll have to let me marry him,* and, *Jens will be so happy.*

Agnes rose and paced the room, pinching her mouth. "I must think."

Lorna murmured, "I'm going to have Jens's baby."

Agnes said, "The first thing we must do is find out if it's true, but I see no reason for your mother to know unless it is. So here's what we'll do. I shall find a doctor, perhaps one in Minneapolis who wouldn't know us, and I'll take you there myself. We'll tell your mother that you and I are going out for tea and shopping, and we'll take the train. Yes, that's it. We'll take the train. Listen, dearling, it'll take me some time to arrange, but I'll do so as quickly as possible. Meanwhile, eat lots of fruits and vegetables and drink milk if nothing else will stick with you."

"Yes, I will."

"I must say, you don't look as upset as most young girls in your predicament would be."

"Upset? But don't you see—they'll have to let me marry him now. Oh, Aunt Agnes, this is the answer to our prayers!"

Agnes cranked her face into a whorl of creases that could have meant a dozen different things. "I don't believe your mother will think so."

To Lorna's surprise, on the day they went to the doctor Aunt Agnes told a pack of lies worthy of a patent medicine salesman. First she made Lorna don her own engagement ring, which had not been off her finger since Captain Dearsley had put it there in 1845. Then, when arriving at the doctor's office, she gave her name as Agnes Henry, and Lorna's as Laura Arnett. When the doctor confirmed that Lorna was carrying a child who would be born probably next May or June, Agnes told him she was absolutely delighted because, as "Laura's" legal guardian, she considered the baby her first grandchild. Too, she confided that Lorna's husband would be in for the delight of his life, since the two of them had been trying for two years already, with no success till now. She paid the doctor in cash, thanked him with a smile and said they would be back in two months, as recommended.

Over lunch at Chamberlain's, Lorna remarked, "You surprise me, Aunt Agnes."

"Do I?" Agnes sipped her coffee with one finger raised, a faint tremble in her hand.

"Why did you do that?"

"Because your father is a wealthy socialite and the word would spread like wildfire if it got out. He and your mother would know before your lunch is digested . . . or thrown up, as the case may be."

Lorna's heart filled with love. "Thank you."

"You have a right to see your young man first, so the two of you can confront your parents together. If he loves you as you say, and if you have a solid plan to marry, your parents' shock might only last twenty-five years, instead of fifty. At least, if it had happened to me and Captain Dearsley, that's how I'd have wanted it to be."

Lorna's eyes glowed. "Oh, Aunt Agnes, I'm so happy. Imagine, I'm carrying his baby right now. I'm not looking forward to facing Mother and Father—that's bound to be a horrible scene—but once it's over, I'm sure they'll help us."

That night, when Agnes said her bedtime prayers, she included a very, very brief one of contrition for her lies, and a much longer one asking that for once in their lives her brother and his wife might put their daughter's feelings first, before considering the petty, snobbish reaction of their own social circle.

Chapter 12

After the family left Rose Point Cottage, it wore an abandoned look, its windows covered from within, its verandas cleared of wicker, gardens mulched for winter, docks drawn up onto the lawn and masts gone from the lakeshore. Even more noticeable, the silence: no carriages coming and going, no doors slamming, fountains burbling, boat whistles shrilling; no voices from the water or the croquet court or the gardens. Only Smythe, puttering about his glasshouse, tipping and burying the roses for winter and swaddling the berry canes in warm wraps.

Jens saw the gardener occasionally through the trees, whose leaves had fallen, the Englishman slightly stooped, wrapped in a muffler over his black jacket. Sometimes the sound of wheels would carry across the back lot as Smythe pushed his garden cart along the gravel paths.

Mornings and evenings, Jens made the forty-minute walk to and from the Hotel Leip, observing the shortening of days, noting the frantic activity of the squirrels, the thickening of the morning frost, adding a sweater beneath his jacket, heavier gloves on his hands. In the boat shed he would build a fragrant fire of cedar scraps, and add maple stovewood that burned slow and hot and made the air smell like a smokehouse. On the fender of the stove he'd put a potato, and eat it, piping, for his lunch, often studying the floor where the marks from his lofting still outlined the spot where he and Lorna had picnicked during those days of first acquaintance. On the windowsill her delphinium remained—dry, crisp, but blue as the skies of summer that had watched them fall in love.

Tim came sometimes, bringing his pipe smoke and easy smile, taking a photograph or two, leaving the place lonelier than ever when he departed.

Jens completed the bottom of the boat, varnished and dried it, then began work on the interior structure. He laminated the center backbone, constructed two bil-geboards, put them in place and began the framework of the deck beams. Over it he nailed cedar planking, then once more spent time planing, sanding, fairing. Running his hands over the *Lorna D* he might have been running them over the woman herself, so vivid were his memories of touching her, loving her, rubbing her back in the suspended serenity of afterlove. Often, bending to his work, he re-heard her words: *Watching you push that hand plane does things to my insides.* He would smile wistfully, recalling the day she'd said that, what she'd worn, how her hair was arranged, how she'd studied him while he worked, and described the clothes he'd worn one time while he was chipping ice. It had struck him fully that day—she re-ally loved him. Why else would she have clung to such detailed memories of that inconsequential kitchen scene?

Fairing up the boat without her he felt a great, hollow loneliness inside.

Her letters said she missed him, that she felt ill from missing him, that all she needed was to see him again and her lethargy would vanish. *Let it be nothing more,* he thought, *nothing but loneliness.*

October waned and turned nasty. A rim of rime appeared at the edge of the lake and the first snow fell. The deck planking was complete and Jens needed a pair of extra hands to help him stretch a layer of canvas over it. He called upon Ben. One blustery day the two of them were working together in the cozy shed. The wood stove was stoked; the strong smell of paint and turpentine permeated the place. They had painted the deck to dripping wet and were stretching the canvas over the sticky paint, tacking it all around the outside edges.

Ben spit the last tack into his left hand and began hammering with his right. "So . . ." he said. "What do you hear from Lorna Barnett?"

Jens missed a beat with his hammer. "What makes you think I'd hear from Lorna Barnett?"

"Aw, come on, Jens. I'm not as ignorant as I might look. Ever since the fam-ily went back to town you've been gloomy as a November wake."

"It shows that much, then?"

"I don't know who else notices, but I sure do."

Jens stopped working and flexed his back. "She's a hard woman to forget, Ben."

"They usually are when you think you're in love."

"With us it's more than thinking."

Ben shook his head. "Then I pity you, you poor sap. I wouldn't be in your shoes for all the boats in the White Bear Yacht Club."

Ben's pessimism took hold of Jens. He grew silent and morose, wondering if he and Lorna were deceiving themselves, if they'd ever fight their way free of her parents' tentacles and actually get married. Suppose they did, would she be happy as the wife of a boatbuilder who could never give her the riches to which she was accustomed? Perhaps he'd be most kind to release her, send her back to DuVal, where she'd be assured of wealth, prestige and her parents' approval.

These black thoughts persisted, turning Jens wretched within himself. They robbed him of sleep at night and peace during the day, left him feeling fickle and unsteadfast, unworthy of Lorna's faithfulness, which rang forth clearly from her every letter.

He had reread those letters until he knew them by rote. He missed her, pined for her, needed a glimpse of her, a smile, a touch to see him through these times of separation and misgiving.

After the canvas was stretched and dried Jens worked alone applying the coaming around the cockpit: steaming it, clamping it on, tamping it into place with a mallet and securing it flush with the underdeck. He'd chosen the finest Honduran mahogany, as smooth beneath his fingertips as sterling silver, only warmer. Working it brought him great satisfaction, its grain close and its color warm as human blood. On a day in early November he was standing in the cockpit, a brace and bit in his hands, drilling a hole through the maroon wood when the hinges creaked and the door opened.

He swung around just as a blue coat and bonnet appeared. With her back to him, a woman closed and latched the cumbersome door.

"Lorna?" His heart burst into double time as she turned to face him. "Lorna!" He dropped the tool and vaulted over the side of the boat.

He ran.

She ran.

They collided off the starboard bow in a jubilant and frantic embrace. The impact swung them around, bruised their mouths, braided them into one. They drew back to see each other. "Sweet savior, you're here!" He grasped her head and stamped kisses everywhere, so untempered they bumped her about like a rough boat ride. His thumbs skewed her eyebrows as he kissed her mouth disbelievingly again and again.

"Jens . . . let me see you . . . Jens . . ." She took a turn beholding his face, touching it, exulting, "My love . . . my love . . ."

He held her fast against his body, nearly crushing her ribs. "Lorna, what are you doing here?"

"I had to see you. I simply couldn't wait another day."

"I think you saved my life." He closed his eyes and smelled her, ran his hands over her. She smiled and clung while they rocked from side to side.

"Where did you tell them you were going?"

"To Phoebe's."

"You took the train out?"

"Yes."

"How long can you stay?"

"Till three."

He withdrew a watch from his pocket—ten forty-five—and when he'd put it away, chuckled. "I'm still in shock. Let me see if you're real."

She was real, all right, and warm, and compliant as they kissed again, hoarding each other and making up for five weeks' separation. When the kisses ended her coat was unbuttoned and he was cupping her breasts through her thick winter suit.

"I missed you so much," she murmured.

"I missed you, too, like I hadn't imagined I could miss anyone." His eyes squeezed shut upon the memories of his weakheartedness. How could he have believed for a moment that he could turn her away? Send her to another man?

She admitted unabashedly, "I missed your hands on me."

He drew back and adored her upturned face, too rapt for smiles. "Did you get my letters?" he asked.

"Yes. Did you get mine?"

"Yes, but I worried so. Are you all right now?"

"I'm fine. Really, I am. Come . . ." She took his hand and led him to the wrought-iron bench, which was pulled up near the stove. "I have something to tell you." They sat close, knees to the heat, holding hands like minuet dancers. She studied his knuckles as she told him calmly, quietly, "It seems, Jens, that I'm in a family way."

She felt his fingers go slack, then tense. "Oh, Lorna," he whispered. She watched his breath grow ragged, his face blanch, then he gripped her in an awkward embrace, their knees intruding. "Oh, Lorna, no." He swallowed convulsively against her ear.

"Aren't you happy?"

When he made no reply, terror swelled her chest.

"Jens . . . please . . ."

His death grip relaxed. "I'm sorry," he said in a raspy, terrified voice. "I'm sorry. I'm . . . I just . . . God in heaven . . . pregnant. Are you sure?"

She nodded, growing more fearful by the moment. She had expected reassurance. She had expected concern. She had expected a tender hug and a caring expression in his eyes while he said, "Don't worry, Lorna. Now we can get married."

She had not cried since hearing the news, but her tears threatened while he sat with a sickly expression on his face.

"Oh, Jens, say something. You're scaring me to death."

He set her back and held her by both arms. "I didn't want it to happen this way, not . . . not with you in disgrace. Do your parents know?"

"No."

"You're absolutely sure it's true?"

"Yes. I've seen a doctor. Aunt Agnes took me."

"When is it due?"

"May or June, he wasn't sure."

Jens rose and began pacing, his brow furled, his gaze distant. She grew more disillusioned with each step he took. The stove threw out cloying heat. The smell of paint and glue began making her dizzy. Sweat broke out beneath her arms and on the back of her neck. Fear congealed into one sickening lump that lay in her stomach like a helping of bad fish.

She took control of her emotions and ordered, "Stop that, Jens, and come here."

He spun in his tracks and halted.

"It never occurred to me to be scared . . . until now," she said, forcing calm into her voice.

His preoccupation vanished. He rushed to her and dropped down on one knee. "Forgive me. Oh, sweetheart, forgive me." He took her hands and kissed them in apology, leaning over her lap. "I didn't mean to scare you. It was the shock, that's all. . . . I'm trying to figure out what to do. Did you think I was wondering how to get rid of you? Never, Lorna, never. I love you. Now more than ever, but we have to do the right thing. We have to . . . Aw, Lorna, sweetheart, don't cry." He touched her face tenderly, swiping at her tears with a thumb. "Don't cry."

She lunged into his arms, another awkward embrace with Jens kneeling and she curling above him. "I haven't until now, honest, Jens, but you scared me so."

"I'm sorry, oh, darling girl, of course you were scared with me charging back and forth like a mad bull and not saying a thing about the baby. Our baby . . . Lord in heaven, it's hard to believe." He opened her coat and touched her stomach reverently. "Our baby . . . here, inside you."

She covered his hands with her own and felt their warmth seep through her clothing. "It's all right. You can't hurt anything."

He stretched his hands wider, staring at them and the flattened plaid wool of her suit jacket. He lifted his gaze to her face.

"Ours," he whispered.

She dropped her forehead to his and they both closed their eyes.

"You're not disappointed?" she whispered.

"Aw, girl, no. How can I be?"

"When I found out I said to Aunt Agnes right away, Jens will be so happy. Now they can't keep us apart."

He sat back on one heel and took both her hands. Earnestly, he said, "We must go to your parents and tell them immediately. This is their grandchild. Surely they'll give us their blessing when we tell them we love each other and want to get married right away. I'll find us a place out here—it'll be small, but inexpensive: So many places are empty for the winter, and in the spring my brother will come, and we'll open our boatworks immediately. Why wait for the regatta? The word about the *Lorna D* has spread, and there are plenty of yacht club members who'll be waiting in line to have me design a boat for them. We won't be rich, not at first, but I'll take care of you, Lorna, you and the baby, and we'll have a good life, I promise."

She cupped his face and smiled into his dear blue eyes.

"I know we will. And I don't need to be rich, and I don't need to have a fancy house. All I need, Jens Harken, is you."

They kissed with renewed tenderness, almost as if each was kissing their unborn child and sealing a pact with him. Jens drew Lorna to her feet and wrapped both arms around her. They stood a long time, peaceful, hopeful, embracing with their baby pressed firm against its father's belly.

"So tell me . . . just how have you been feeling?"

"Mostly tired."

"Are you eating properly?"

"As properly as I can. Meat makes me sick, though, even the smell of it."

"Fruits and vegetables?"

"Yes, they still taste good."

"Thank heavens for old Smythe and his glasshouse. I'd like to run and find him right now and tell him thank you."

Lorna smiled against his shoulder. "Oh, Jens, I love you."

"I love you, too."

"Do you suppose we'll have lots of babies?"

"I'm sure of it."

"What do you think this one will be?"

"A boy. A boatbuilder like his papa."

"Of course, how silly of me to ask."

"The second one can be a girl, though, a little dark-haired beauty like her mother, and after that I'd take a couple more boys, because by then the boatworks will be thriving, and someday we'll call it Harken and Sons."

She smiled again, imagining it and loving the image of her future life.

Finally Jens drew back. "Did you rent a coach to bring you out here from the depot?"

"Yes, but I dismissed him."

"How do you feel about a forty-minute walk in the snow?"

"With you? Foolish question."

"Then here's what I think we should do. We'll walk back to the Leip and you can wait in the lobby while I take a bath and change into my Sunday suit. Then we'll take the train into town together and we'll talk to your mother and father right away, tonight. Once we get that behind us I can begin making plans for where we'll live, and you can begin making plans for the wedding."

"What about money?"

"I've saved every penny I could since I've been here. I've got enough put by to see us through the winter, maybe even longer."

She didn't ask if any would be left to start his business: one giant step at a time.

They walked arm in arm through a day with a marbled sky of gray and white. What little snow had fallen resembled marbling, too, lying in veins of white upon the frozen tangle of spinach-colored grass beside the road. Some crows had spotted an owl and scolded it, circling a tree in the distance. A wagon came by, loaded with casks that resounded like timpani as they thumped against one another. The driver raised a red-mittened hand and received a wave in return. Where the road neared the lakeshore the wind became icier and bore the musty scent of muskrat houses and decaying cattails. Near town, the expensive hotels had traded their June resplendence for the bleaker aspect of winter, their abandoned park benches, gazebos and lawns mere reminders of the gayer season. At the Leip an American flag clapped in the wind, shortened by two twists around its standard. Inside, a black potbellied stove warmed the lobby, which was otherwise deserted. Jens took Lorna to a horsehair chair near the stove.

"Wait here. It won't take me long. I'll see if I can get you something hot to drink while you wait."

He went to the desk and rang the bell but nobody came. "Be right back," he told Lorna, and went into the kitchen, which was also abandoned. Winter board at the Leip included breakfast and supper: Now, at midday, no meals were in progress or promised. He opened a reservoir on the stove, found some lukewarm water inside and took a pailful with him on his way back through the lobby.

"I'm sorry, Lorna. Nobody's around."

"Oh, I'll be fine. It's warm here by the stove. Don't worry about me."

"If anyone comes, tell them you're waiting for me."

She smiled. "I will."

Nobody came. She read a newspaper during the thirty minutes Jens was gone. He reappeared, freshly shaved, dressed in his Sunday suit, a heavy wool coat and his black bowler.

"Let's go."

So formal. So somber. In keeping with their mission today.

On the train to Saint Paul they clasped hands on the seat beneath Lorna's coat but found little cheerful to say to each other. Outside, a wispy snow began and the countryside became pale, as if viewed through a bride's veil. They crossed a trestle over the Mississippi River and slowed beneath the wooden canopy of the downtown depot.

From the depot they rode a hansom cab to Summit Avenue, still clasping hands, Lorna's fingers curled over the edge of Jens's palm—tighter and tighter—while he smoothed them repeatedly as if to stroke away her mounting dread.

On Summit Avenue, as they approached the great gray hunk of stone where they would confront her parents, Lorna said, "No matter what happens in here tonight, I vow I will walk out of this house with you."

He kissed her mouth briefly as the horse's hooves came to a halt beneath the porte cochere. Lorna reached for her reticule, but he laid a hand on her arm. "You're my responsibility now. I'll pay."

He paid the cabbie while the horse shook its head and jingled its harness, then the rig pulled away, leaving them before the door with its bare-toothed gargoyles. Lorna refused to acknowledge them. She looked up at Jens instead.

"Mother will probably be in the drawing room, and Father doesn't get home until around six o'clock. I don't want to approach them till they're both here. Would you mind terribly waiting in the kitchen? I'll come for you as soon as Father is home."

Inside the massive entry hall their luck ran out. Just as they entered, Theron, believing himself alone, came sliding down the banister, his hand squealing on the polished wood. Lorna glanced balefully at Jens and decided in this case offense was the best defense. As her brother hurtled off the end of the railing and landed with a thud, she scolded in a whisper, "Theron Barnett!"

Theron spun around in surprise.

"Mother would blister your backside if she caught you doing that."

Theron covered his rear flank with joined hands. "You gonna tell?"

"I should but I won't—not if you don't tell on me."

"Why? What'd you do?"

"Sneaked out to see the boat."

"You did!" His eyes grew great. "How does she look?"

"Ask Mr. Harken."

"Oh, hi, Harken. Is the boat all done?"

"Just about. All but the hardware and rigging. Had to come in and talk to your father about those."

"He ain't here."

"He's not here," Lorna corrected.

"He's not here," Theron repeated.

"I know," Harken replied. "I'll just visit in the kitchen awhile, how's that?"

"Can I come with you?"

It took great effort for Jens to resist telegraphing a silent question to Lorna. Quickly he reasoned that if the boy was with him for an hour he wouldn't be in the drawing room reporting Jens Harken's presence to the mistress of the house.

"Sure, come on," he said, reaching for the lad's head, steering him ahead of himself. "I'll tell you all about the *Lorna D.*"

In the kitchen, Hulduh Schmitt looked up and threw both hands in the air. *"Mein Gott!"* she exclaimed, followed by a spate of German while she waddled across the floor and grasped Jens in a breasty hug. "What are you doing here, boy?"

"Reporting to Mr. Barnett on the progress of the boat."

Everyone accepted his explanation. The kitchen maids came to say hello, Ruby hanging back coyly to be the last and offer an especially personal smile of welcome, which left Jens wondering how it was possible he'd ever found her attractive enough to kiss. He shook hands with his stand-in, a flat-faced fellow named Lowell Hugo, whose breath stank of garlic. To celebrate Jens's visit, Mrs. Schmitt authorized the tapping of a precious gallon bottle of last summer's homemade root beer, and they sat around the center worktable taking a rare fifteen minutes from their duties to visit and ask dozens of questions about the boat, and its prospects for winning, and Jens's plans if it did, and his lodging out at White Bear, and if he'd seen Smythe, and how the gardener was faring, and if the old Englishman was as irascible as ever.

After forty-five minutes, when Jens was beginning to worry about Theron's continued presence, the children's maid, Ernesta, came sweeping in, breathless and distraught. "Oh, there you are, bothering the kitchen help again! Your mother will be coming up to your room any minute to inspect your schoolwork and if you know what's good for you, you'll be there!"

Off Theron went, with Ernesta's fingers prodding the back of his neck.

Shortly after six P.M. Lorna appeared, wearing a form-fitting dress of forest green taffeta with an ivory collar and cuffs, her hair freshly combed and her cheeks unnaturally pink.

"Harken," she said formally, "my father would like to see you now."

"Ah . . ." He left his chair. "Very well, Miss Barnett."

She turned her back on him. "Follow me."

He did precisely as ordered, three steps behind her whispering taffeta that seemed to resound through the granite foyer like the rising of an entire church congregation at the entrance of the minister. Someone was playing the piano in the music room. As they passed its open doorway, Daphne looked up from the sheet music, and the two aunts from their tatting, but Lorna kept her eyes straight ahead on the doorway of the library. As luck would have it, Jenny happened along the upper hall at that moment and paused at the head of the stairs to watch in surprise the two passing below.

Lorna fixed her eyes on the library entrance and led Jens to it. Inside, Gideon Barnett sat in a brown leather wing chair with his knees crossed, holding a cigar between his teeth and a newspaper on his lap. The room smelled of burning things: the expensive tobacco, the birch in the fireplace and illuminating gas—faintly sooty. It held hundreds of leather-bound volumes reaching clear to the ceiling, with its ornate molding, center medallion and five-globe chandelier. On the table beside Gideon another single gas globe illuminated his newspaper. On the wall above a hide settee a mounted stag head held two guns across its antlers.

Gideon's gaze shot up the moment Lorna and Jens paused in the doorway.

"Hello, Father."

He removed the cigar from his mouth in slow motion, making no reply. His eyes flicked from Jens to Lorna.

"Where is Mother?" she asked.

"Upstairs with the boy." The boy was Theron.

"I thought she'd be down by now."

Barnett's stare became riveted on Harken. He pointed with the wet end of his cigar. "What's he doing here?"

"I invited him. We need to speak to you and Mother."

"You *invited* him?" Finally Gideon's attention snapped to Lorna. His eyes bulged and his color began to rise. "What do you mean, you *invited* him?"

"Please lower your voice, Father." Lorna turned and said to Jens, "Wait right here. I'll go find Mother."

Halfway up the stairs, Lorna met Levinia coming down. The older woman's face was ruched with worry. She descended hurriedly, clutching her skirts in one hand and the handrail in the other. "What's wrong? Jenny said that boatbuilder is down here with you."

"Could we talk in the library, Mother?"

"Oh dear," Levinia's voice trembled and her breasts bounced as she hastened after her daughter. Once again Lorna caught a glimpse of Jenny at the top of the stairs but chose to ignore her.

In the library, Gideon was on his feet, pouring himself a bourbon from a crystal decanter. Jens waited where Lorna had left him. Levinia circled wide around her ex–kitchen helper, as if he were someone brought in off the streets and not yet deloused.

"Gideon, what is it?"

"Deuced if I know."

Lorna closed the pocket doors to the hall. To her right, a second set of pocket doors—closed—led to the adjacent music room, where the piano music had stopped. She experienced a moment of grave doubt: Her father would soon be shouting while the remainder of the family would likely be poised beyond those doors, bent forward at the waist.

She stationed herself beside Jens. "Mother, Father, would you both please sit down?"

"Like hell I will," Gideon rumbled. "I sense disaster here, and I always meet disasters on my feet. Now get on with it, whatever it is."

Lorna looped her hand loosely through Jens's arm.

"Jens and I would very much like—"

Jens pressed her fingers to silence her. Then he took over.

"Mr. and Mrs. Barnett, I know it will come as a surprise to you, but I've come here to tell you that I have fallen most deeply in love with your daughter and I respectfully ask your permission to marry her."

Levinia's mouth fell open.

Gideon's expression turned thunderous. "You've what!" he bellowed.

"Your daughter and I—"

"Why, you impertinent young whelp!"

"Father, it isn't only Jens asking, it's me, too."

"You shut your mouth, young woman! I'll deal with you later!"

"I love him, Father, and he loves me."

"The kitchen handyman! Jesus Christ, have you lost your mind!"

In the music room Aunt Agnes began playing "Witch's Revel" in fortissimo: Lorna recognized her missed notes and deplorable technique.

"Oh, Lorna," Levinia moaned. "Is this why you threw Taylor aside?"

"I know all the arguments you two are going to give me, but none of them matter. I love Jens and I want to marry him."

"And live on what? Where?" Gideon shot back. "On a handyman's salary in his bedroom on the third floor? Wouldn't that look just ducky? Is that where all our friends should come to call on you for afternoon tea?"

"We'll live in White Bear Lake, and Jens intends to open up a boatworks there."

"Don't you mention the word boat to me!" Gideon roared, his face rubicund and trembling. "All this started because of that boat, and *you* . . ." He stabbed a finger at Jens. "You underhanded sonofabitch! Sweet-talking my daughter while I gave you advantages I wouldn't have *dreamed* of giving anyone else! Why, I wouldn't let her marry you if you were Christopher Columbus himself!"

Levinia touched her lips and wailed, "Oh, I knew something was wrong. I just knew it. So many times I tried to find you and couldn't—you were out there in that boat shed with him, weren't you?"

"Yes," Lorna replied, still pressed to Jens's sleeve. "I spent a lot of time with Jens last summer. I got to know him as well as any friend I've ever had—better. He's honest, and brilliant, and hard-working and kind, and he loves—"

"Oh, stop . . ." Gideon pulled a disgusted face. "You're making me sick."

"I'm sorry to hear that, Father. I should think it would matter a great deal to you that the man your daughter wants to marry is one she loves very much, and who loves her equally as much."

"Well, it doesn't! What matters is that you're not marrying any kitchen handyman, and that's final!"

Jens spoke up, moving behind Lorna and resting his hands on her shoulders. "Not even if she's carrying his baby, sir?"

Gideon reacted as if he'd been poleaxed. Levinia covered her mouth and let out a squeak. Beyond the wall a tortured "Witch's Revel" still clanked.

"My God in heaven," Gideon finally breathed, his color receding. Then to Lorna, "Is it true?"

"Yes, Father, it is. I'm carrying your grandchild."

For a moment Gideon appeared defeated. The starch left him and his shoulders slumped. He ran a hand through his hair and began pacing. "Never in my worst nightmares did I imagine one of my daughters shaming us this way! Sinning with a man . . . laying with him and baldly admitting it! Don't you ever call the spawn of your sin my grandchild! Dear God, we'll be outcasts!"

Levinia's knees buckled and she wilted to a wing chair. "Lord have mercy, the disgrace. What will I tell my friends? How shall I ever again hold my head up in public? And you—don't you realize decent people will shun you after this? They'll shun our whole family."

"Mother, you're overdramatizing."

Gideon recovered first. His shoulders squared, his fists clenched and the color returned to his face. "Take her upstairs," he ordered his wife.

"Father, please, we came here honorably to speak to—"

"Take her upstairs, Levinia, and lock her in her room! Harken, you're fired."

"Fired—but—"

"Father, you can't do that! We came to you for help and instead you—"

"Levinia, take her upstairs!" Gideon roared. "And lock her in her room, where her brother and sisters cannot see her or speak to her. Harken, I want you out of my sight before I count to three, or so help me God, I'll take the gun from that rack on the wall and kill you where you stand."

Levinia, becoming terrified, caught hold of Lorna's arm. Lorna struggled free. "Father, I love this man. I'm going to have his baby, and no matter what you say, it's my right to marry him!"

"Don't you speak to me of rights! Not after you've lain with him like some . . . some common slut! You gave up all your rights when you did that—the right to this family, to this house, to my support and your mother's concern. Now you'll live without all that and see how you like it! And you'll start by going upstairs without a whimper, because, by the Almighty, if your sisters get wind of this disgrace you've brought upon us, I'll take it out on your hide, pregnant or not! Now go!"

"No, Father, I will not," she replied defiantly, moving closer to Jens, finding his hand.

"By the devil, you will!" Gideon raged. "Levinia, take her this moment!"

Levinia clutched Lorna's arm. "Upstairs!" she ordered.

"No, you can't make me! Jens . . ." She was crying, reaching for Jens with one outstretched arm while Levinia dragged her away by the other. "Lorna . . ." He caught her hand.

Gideon barked, "Get your hands off her, you filthy swine. You've touched her all you're ever going to! I want you out of my house and off my property, and if you ever try putting foot anywhere on it again I'll have the law on you, and don't think I haven't got the connections to do it!"

"No! Jens, take me with you," Lorna pleaded.

Levinia tried force once again. "Girl, don't you defy your father!"

Lorna swung around and gave her Mother a shove. "Leave me alone, I don't have t—" Levinia stumbled back against a chair leg and nearly fell. Her hair jounced to one side and sat off center.

Gideon stormed across the room and struck Lorna once. The blow snapped her head to the side and left her cheek red, her eyes wide and stunned.

"You will go with your mother at once!" he roared.

She gaped at him through shimmering tears, pressing a palm to her cheek.

"Why, you bastard!" Jens lunged and grabbed Gideon's coat front. "You'd strike your own daughter!" He shoved the older man into an upholstered chair with enough force to teeter it backward. Gideon rebounded in one motion, coming at Jens with furor and fists.

"You filthy low-life scum! You got my daughter pregnant!"

"And I'll kill you if you touch her again!"

The two were ready for mortal combat when Levinia's voice called for common sense.

"Stop it! Stop it, everyone! Listen to me, Lorna . . ." She swung nose to nose with her daughter. "See what this has started already? Fisticuffs, enmity, rage. And you're at fault! You, who were taught right from wrong from the time you were in pinafores. Whether or not you see this as a disgrace, it is. You think you can walk out of here with him and everything will be all right! Well, it won't be! You have two fine and unsoiled young sisters but what you've done will reflect on them the moment you leave this house. It will reflect on us. They will have no suitors and we will have no invitations. Our friends will titter behind their hands and blame us for what you've done. We'll be disgraced right along with you because good girls simply don't perform the sinful act it took to get you in this condition! You don't seem to realize that. It's sinful! Shameful! Only the lowest creatures disgrace themselves as you have."

Lorna had dropped her chin and was staring at the carpet through her tears. Levinia went on pressing her advantage.

"What shall I say to your friends? To Taylor and Phoebe and Sissy and Mitchell? Shall I say to them Lorna went off to marry the kitchen helper whose bastard she's carrying? Don't fool yourself for a moment that they won't be shocked. They will be, and their parents shall forbid them to keep company with you, just as I would if it were one of them who were in this trouble."

In a cool, controlled tone, Levinia reiterated, "This is a bastard you're carrying, Lorna. A bastard. Think about that. Think about all it implies and if you want your child to go through life carrying that label of disgrace, for he will be disgraced time and again if you keep him."

The room had grown silent. Jens retained a light hold on Lorna's arm. "Lorna . . ." he said softly, uncertain of what to do.

Levinia said, "I'm asking you to be sensible. To go upstairs and give your father and me time to discuss this situation, to decide what is best for all concerned."

Lorna lifted her brimming eyes to the man she loved. "Jens," she whispered brokenly, "m . . . maybe . . ."

He held her wrist with one hand and rubbed her elbow with the other, up and down, up and down while their eyes remained locked in a sad soliloquy of silence.

"Maybe we all need to . . . to think things through," she whispered. "I'm going to need their help as well as yours in the months ahead. Maybe I should . . . should go with my mother now."

He swallowed once. His Adam's apple made a slow rise and fall. "All right," he whispered. "If that's what you want."

"It isn't what I want. It's what's wisest."

He nodded, dropping his eyes to her sleeve because they were at last filling with tears.

"I'll see you soon. I'll find you," she said.

He nodded again, drew her to him by both arms and kissed her cheek.

"I love you, Lorna," he whispered. "I'm sorry this had to happen."

"It'll be all right," she replied. "I love you, too."

They stood in a tiny universe of their own until Gideon straightened his clothes, moved to the hall door and wordlessly rolled it open.

He stood back while Lorna submitted to her mother's guiding hand and allowed herself to be ushered from the room. Just before they reached the doorway Levinia ordered in an undertone, "Get rid of those tears."

From somewhere deep within, Lorna found the gumption to do as ordered. She sniffed and dried her face with the backs of her hands as she walked into the hall and encountered her sisters and brother, wide-eyed, hovering near the newel post, and Aunt Henrietta lingering in the door to the music room, where, at the piano, Aunt Agnes had finally desisted and quit trying to cover the sound of the squabble with her terrible playing.

Levinia feigned a put-upon air. "All this fuss over sailing, if you can imagine. Honestly, who ever heard of a woman in a regatta anyway?"

Lorna marched past her siblings without meeting their glances, conscious of Jenny's gaze assessing her wet eyelashes and the dark tear splotches on her taffeta dress. Behind her she heard murmured goodbyes and knew Jens was leaving. She heard the outer door opening and closing and fortified herself with the silent promise that nothing could keep them apart as long as they loved each other.

In her bedroom Lorna moved stiffly to her bed and sat down, staring at an eye-level flower on the wallpaper. Levinia closed the door, dropping darkness upon them, making no move to light the lamp beside Lorna's bed.

She spoke with absolute authority. "I'm not going to lock you in. I know I don't have to, because you'll wait here until your father and I have had a chance to talk. Don't speak to anyone, do you understand?"

"Yes, Mother," Lorna answered dully.

"And don't even think about running away with that . . . that penniless, uncouth *immigrant!*"

"No, Mother."

Silence awhile before Levinia disparaged, "Well, I hope you're satisfied with yourself. Some example you've set for your sisters to follow, isn't it?"

Lorna made no reply. She kept thinking of the word *bastard* and wondering if it was true that her sisters would be shunned by all the young men they knew.

"If word of this leaks out, no decent man will ever speak to you again, to say nothing of marrying you. Women who fornicate give up all chances of that. God forgive you, I don't know how you could do such a filthy, base thing. Your father and I will never be able to hold up our heads in polite society again. You've sullied the name of this entire family, and I must say, the shock is probably going to be more than I can stand. But I shall bear up—I swear I shall—until we can think of what to do about this sorry state of affairs. Now you wait here like your father ordered, young miss, is that understood?"

"Yes, Mother."

The door closed behind Levinia and her footsteps faded down the hall. Lorna sat motionless in the dark, both hands wrapped around her unborn child, wondering where its father would go, what he would do, and when she would see him again.

Chapter 13

The train ride home found Jens tormented for having left Lorna. But what else could he have done? The almighty Gideon Barnett! Jens should have known better than to trust the man to react sympathetically to any plea for understanding. He should have taken Lorna and married her and told her parents afterward!

The fact remained he had not. He'd done the forthright, the honorable thing. With these disastrous results.

What should he do next? Storm the house? Abduct his bride? Elope with her? Confront Barnett and beat the hell out of him? (How satisfying that would be.)

The fact was, Jens Harken had no idea what to do next, so he went back to the Hotel Leip to lie awake until well after four A.M. and gnash his teeth about it.

In the morning he'd made two decisions: to remove his boat mold from Gideon Barnett's shed, and to speak to Tim Iversen about storing it at his place. He washed, dressed and went downstairs for breakfast, only to receive the news that if he was to eat, he'd pay for it himself: Gideon Barnett had already slammed the door on any further financial subsistence.

He ate, paid and took the train back to Saint Paul. From the depot he walked to Iversen's photographic studio on West Third Street. Though visiting it for the first time, he found it with no difficulty and entered to discover the place looked as much like a greenhouse as a photo studio. Plants flourished everywhere: filling the box window facing the street, in pots on the floor, in fern stands at the rear. Geraniums bloomed, violets rioted, potted trees thrived and ferns cascaded. Amongst these, George Eastman's patented Kodak cameras were offered for sale in a glass case while at the far end of the room, against a curtained wall, small furniture awaited subjects for the next picture. Near the front window, Iversen himself toyed with a stereo camera containing two lenses set three inches apart.

He craned around—sharply, to accommodate his single eye—at the sound of the bell on the door. Immediately he smiled, came forward and took the cold pipe from his mouth.

"Well, if it isn't my friend Harken. What in blazes are you doing here? Did you lose your boat?"

"As a matter of fact, I did. That's what I came to talk to you about."

"This sounds dour. What's happened? Come here . . . come, come . . . take your coat off and warm up by the stove."

Removing his coat, Jens followed Tim to an oval heater stove against the west wall of the room. Tim poured a cup of coffee and scraped two chairs forward.

"Well, I might as well give it to you straight," Jens said, accepting the cup and seating himself. "Barnett gave me the sack and the boat along with me."

Tim paused in the act of filling his pipe. "You don't say. What got into him?"

"I asked his permission to marry his daughter."

Tim's one good eye settled on Jens and probed while he struck a match, puffed, blew a cloud of fragrant smoke and waved out the flame.

"Aye, I can see how a request like that would set Gid off. He's stopped progress on the *Lorna D,* you say?"

"Yup. He wants me off his property for good, says if I put foot on it ever again he'll sic the law on me. Well, I got off, but I won't leave my boat mold behind. I paid for the materials to make it and he agreed that it would be mine once the *Lorna D* was finished. My only problem now is finding a place to store it. I came to ask if I could put it in your cabin till I can find a place of my own."

"I don't see why not. It's not being used for anything else right now."

"Thanks, Tim."

"And what about you? I don't imagine Gid is footing the bill for you up at the Leip anymore either."

"Nope. He cut me off before I could get down to breakfast this morning. Must've sent a telegram to get word there that fast."

"So what are you going to do?"

"I don't know. I'm not broke, but the money I've saved I intended to use to open my own boatworks. My plan was to wait until after next year's big regatta, but it looks as though I don't have much choice. I'll have to start my business now."

Tim grinned with the right side of his mouth and his one good eye. "Sometimes it takes adversity to spur a man to action. So what about Lorna? You still intend to marry her?"

"You bet I do. Nobody's going to take her away from me. Nobody!"

Tim crossed his arms, stuck the pipe back in his mouth and said around its stem, "It's odd, but I feel partially responsible for your predicament."

"You?"

"I saw what was happening between you and Lorna and I abetted it more than once."

"It would have happened with or without the picnic at your place. Lorna and me . . . well, it's strong between us, Tim, real strong. As if fate planned us to be together. And we will be, but first I've got to get established as a boatbuilder. I figure old man Barnett didn't do me so bad after all. There's been so much talk about the *Lorna D* that everyone in White Bear Lake knows my name by now. I've got about four hundred and twenty dollars of my own, and the rest I'll get a bank loan for. I should be able to find somebody willing to take a risk on me. One more favor I need to ask of you—could I have just one or two good photographs you took of the boat last time? I might not have much money to put up, but I've got a good head, and damned good boat sense, and when I show those photographs to a banker, he'll see for himself that I'm a good risk."

"One or two good photographs, huh?" Tim puffed on his pipe, striping the air with wispy gray fragrance. He puffed and thought, and thought and puffed, and finally said, "Come over here."

He led Jens to the camera he'd been puttering with near the front window. "See this?" He placed his hand affectionately atop the black box, which stood on a shoulder-high tripod. "You might say this is my *Lorna D."* He gestured to include the rest of the shop. "All of that—portraits—that's what I do out of obligation. This is what I do out of love. Travel the world taking my stereo camera with me, capturing all the places the ordinary man can never see any other way than in his living room looking through his stereoscopic viewer. Did you know I've been to the Klondike? Imagine that. And Mexico and Palestine and the Chicago World's Fair two years ago. Next week I'm leaving for Sweden and Norway, then at the end of the winter I'll be in Italy and Greece. And from all those places I'll bring home my little twin pictures, and do you know what I'll do with them? I'll not only sell them here, I've got a contingent of salesmen who are making me money all over the United States selling them door-to-door, to say nothing of Sears and Roebuck mail-order catalogues. I'm a rich man, Jens, as you've probably guessed. But I've got no wife, no family, nobody to spend all that wealth on." Tim paused for a breath.

"Now you come along. And I think you're a damned smart man who's designed a damned smart boat that's going to show a few of my good friends they should have paid attention to you when you asked them to. You need backing. I have money. So here's what I propose.

"You go ahead and take your mold out of Barnett's shed, but don't leave it in my cabin for long. The cabin, by the way, is yours until next spring, when I come back from my travels. It's colder than the devil—you'll be growing a beard to keep your face warm at night—but you can hug the stove when you have to, and cook your own meals, and pump your own water, and what more does a man need? When I get back in the spring I'll want it back—without a bunkmate, thank you.

"Meanwhile, find a decent building for the Harken Boatworks—rent one, buy one, whichever you prefer—and put your mold to work. You invest three hundred dollars, and I'll invest the rest and you start building those squashed cigars with sails and I suspect within two years—one, maybe—you'll have the busiest boatworks in the state of Minnesota. We'll set it up so that when you begin making a profit you can either buy me out or pay me back, with a little interest for my trouble. Now, what do you think about that?"

Flabbergasted, Jens only stared at his friend.

"Well, say something," Tim said.

"I can't. I'm speechless."

Tim chuckled deep in his throat, went to the stove, removed a lid and rapped out the dottle from his pipe, then slipped the pipe into his pocket. Turning back to Jens, he wore the smile of a man who enjoys seeing others thunderstruck. "Well, what do you think, mister boatbuilder? Shall I set up a bank account for you?"

"You'd do that? You'd do everything for me?"

"Mmm . . . not quite everything. I can't get your girl back for you. You're going to have to do that yourself."

"The hell you can't. This will do it! Don't you see? All I needed was a way to support her, and you're giving me that."

"Don't underestimate her father, Jens. You'll play billy hell trying to change his mind, even if you become as rich as Barnett himself, because he grew up rich, you see. You were beneath him when he met you, and beneath him you'll remain. No, I wouldn't plan on marrying his daughter unless you do it against his wishes, and that could be disastrous for your business. His best friends will be your best customers."

"What about you? You're his friend. Don't you fear his retribution?"

"Not particularly. I, too, grew up poor, and I don't want to marry one of his daughters. If he snubs me, I can tolerate that. As for my business—well, I just got done telling you I have the support of Sears and Roebuck, as well as my friend George Eastman, whose cameras I sell exclusively in Minnesota. Sure, word will get around the yacht club circle that I backed your business, but if there's one thing that crowd respects it's people who know how to make money. When they see your enterprise succeed, they'll congratulate us both."

"All but Gideon Barnett," Jens concluded.

"All but Gideon Barnett."

On that doomful note, their discussion ended, yet in spite of it Jens felt borne by hope. What a friend he'd found in Tim Iversen. What a genuine, good, foresighted man. Jens found himself overcome with gratitude. He felt the way a parent feels when another has saved the life of his child: No thanks are adequate. He attempted them nonetheless, clasping Tim affectionately while bidding goodbye.

"I cannot thank you enough. You're a good, good friend and I will make you happy you took a chance on me. I'll work hard to make my boatworks succeed. You'll see."

"You don't have to tell me that. I know a man with a dream when I see one, and they're the best kind, the wisest ones to invest in. I know, because I was one myself and someone helped me. Old feller name of Emil Zehring, who was a friend of my dad's. He's dead now, so the only way to repay him is to pass on the tradition, which I hope you'll do one day, too, when someone younger and needier than yourself needs a boost."

"I will. I promise."

"Well then, what are you waiting for? Go! Get that boatworks started so I can get my money back!"

Leaving Tim's, Jens found himself smiling. Yes, his life had taken on new promise. All would be perfect, if only he could marry Lorna. He had no delusions, however, about the welcome he'd get if he went to the door with the gargoyles and asked to see her. Instead, he decided to write to her with his good news, sending the letter through Phoebe, as earlier agreed, and set up a secret meeting.

That night he wrote:

Darling Lorna,

So much has happened since I saw you twenty-four hours ago. I hardly know where to begin. First, let me tell you I love you and that our future looks rosier than ever before. Last night was the worst day of my life—yours, too, I think—but we cannot let it deter us, especially after what happened today.

I went to see Tim, and unbelievable as it seems, he's going to set me up in business. I'm writing this from his cabin. Not only has he given me the use of it for the winter, he's putting up whatever money I need to start the boatworks. I've already walked the length and breadth of White Bear Lake searching for an empty building that would do, but everything is filled up with boats in winter storage. So I've found a lot that's for sale and tomorrow Tim is coming out to look at it and if he likes it, we'll build a new building on it that will be the home of Harken Boatworks. It's not far from Tim's cabin, between it and the yacht club, on a nice stretch of land that will need a little clearing first, but I don't mind that. I've got a strong back and a good axe, and that's all a Norwegian needs to survive. I've decided to build the place myself and save all that labor cost. Ben is going to help me, as the lumberyard in town has laid him off until spring. Another piece of good news is that Ben has found a sawmill we can use to make our own boards, so we'll save on lumber costs, too. It will be a lot of work but I don't mind. By spring the building will be up and ready well before the baby comes, so that by the time he gets here I'll be an official boatbuilder. What do you think about that?

I guess you can tell I'm pretty excited.

Everything we want is going to come true. The only hard part will be that we'll have to get married without your mother and father knowing. Lorna, it broke my heart to see her herding you out of the room like some criminal. For me, getting shouted at and called names didn't hurt near as bad as watching you get treated that way. I see that I was wrong in guessing they'd treat us kindly when they found out about the baby, so we'll never do that again. From now on, all our plans will be secret. Now, Lorna, sweets, we're going to have to meet so that we can make some arrangements. I've thought a lot about it today, and I think that what you should do is come out on the 10:30 a.m. train next Friday. Buy a ticket for Stillwater instead of White Bear Lake. Too many people know you in this town, and I don't want your father getting wind of this. When you get to White Bear, I'll board the train and we'll go on together to Stillwater to the courthouse there, and get our marriage license. Stillwater's got so many churches we can pick which one we want to get married in, and afterwards we can live at Tim's for the winter, then in spring, when the boatworks is done, it'll have a loft we can use for our home until we get on our feet and can afford to build a real house somewhere. I know it's a big step down for you, living in a log cabin and a loft above a boatworks, but it won't be forever. I'll work harder than you ever saw a man work, to get you the kind of things you deserve, sweetheart, and someday your dad will eat his words.

I just read what I wrote and on second thought maybe we better make it next week Tuesday when you come out on the train, to give this letter time to reach Phoebe and Phoebe time to get it to your place and you time to get some excuses dreamt up for leaving the house.

Well, Lorna Diane, that's what we're going to do. I hope my plans are all right with you. We're going to be so happy. I love you so much, darling girl, and our baby, too. Give the little feller a pat on the head and tell him it's from his papa and that in my spare time this winter I'll be making him a cradle with wood from our own land (at least it will be someday).

Now, don't be sad. Smile and think of me and of next week when we'll be Mr. and Mrs. Jens Harken

> Your loving future husband,
> Jens

He posted the letter the following day and went ahead with his plans. Tim thought the lot looked fine. It had some good trees on it that could be harvested and it was close to his cabin, so he could check on his investment readily come spring, when it was open for business.

They bought it.

Jens rented a freight wagon and went out to the boat shed at Rose Point to get his molds. Finding the door already padlocked, he broke the lock, took what was his and left with only one regret: that he'd never get the chance to finish the *Lorna D,* which looked forlorn in the shadows of the sprawling old shed that had already begun to smell stale from disuse. One last time he laid a hand on the boat's flaring side and said, "Sorry, old girl. Maybe I'll see you on the water sometime."

Out at Tim's, he hauled his precious mold inside the cabin—contrary to Tim's suggestion—and leaned the pieces against the wall of the main room, where they were out of the weather and he could look at them nights and picture the boats that would someday be formed around them.

At the new land, he and Ben set up a sawmill and began felling trees. They rented a pair of big, muscular Percherons from a nearby farmer and set to work making lumber, much to the delight of both men: two young Norwegians with the tang of new-cut wood in their nostrils, and sawdust on their boots, and horses to talk to.

Jens thought a man would have to be in heaven itself to be any happier.

On Tuesday he arose early, heated water and washed his flannel bedsheets and hung them over the boat molds to dry. He heated a second batch of water and bathed every inch of his hide, put on clean woolen underwear, his Sunday suit, a warm jacket and a cap with earlaps and walked four miles into town to meet the ten-thirty train.

He waited as it pulled in, his heart lifting half his gullet into his throat with each beat. While the train slowed, he shifted from left foot to right, right to left, scrunching his cold hands into fists inside his mittens and curling his cardboard train ticket in his palm. He watched the coach windows pass, searching them for Lorna's smile and wave, wondering which car she'd be on.

When the air brakes hissed and the couplings clanked, and with the depot platform vibrating beneath his feet, he waited where he was, expecting her to appear on the steps of one of the last cars and wave him in.

He waited and waited. Three passengers got off. The porter removed their luggage from the train and they carried it away. The station agent came out with a pouch of mail and stood a moment in friendly conversation with the porter. Up ahead, the steam whistle wailed and the porter called, " 'Booooooard!" then bent to pick up his portable step.

Jens shouted, "Just a minute! I'm boarding!"

He ran and mounted the steps in two leaps, his heart banging hard. The first car turned up no Lorna. As he entered the second, the whistle sounded and the train began moving, rocking him back on his heels. He clutched a seatback and waited out the momentum, then proceeded into the next car and the next, his dread growing with each passing seat. When he reached the coal car, he turned around and backtracked, clear to the caboose, getting his ticket punched midway.

Lorna was nowhere on board.

They were a third of the way to Stillwater by the time he sank into a seat and gave in to the trembling fear in his stomach. He sat staring out the window, swaying listlessly while the half-snowy November landscape swept by the window. At crossings, the train whistle would keen. A woman across the aisle from him asked if he was all right, but he didn't hear her. He saw a fox once, running along on a distant hillside with its tail straight out behind itself, but the animal failed to register as Jens stared and stared and wondered and wondered.

At Stillwater he went into the station and purchased a ticket for Saint Paul, then sat beside a hot iron stove, too preoccupied to realize he was sweating inside his warm winter outerwear. The inbound train came through shortly after noon. By one forty-five P.M., he was standing on the sidewalk before Gideon Barnett's house on Summit Avenue, glancing from the servants' entrance to the front one, wondering which was best to take. If he went in through the kitchen he'd surely get questioned by his friends, and he was in no mood to pretend blitheness.

He chose the front entry and raised a hand to the bronze gargoyle knocker with its bared canine teeth.

The door was answered by Jeannette, one of the downstairs maids, whom he recognized.

"Hello, Jeannette," he said. "I've come to speak to Miss Lorna. Would you mind going to get her for me?"

Jeannette, never cordial to him, was even less so today. Her mouth pursed. She held the door open so narrowly only one of her eyes showed.

"Miss Lorna is gone."

"Gone! Where?"

"I'm not at liberty to say, nor to allow you inside. Word's come down."

"But where is she?"

"Off to school somewhere, that's all we heard, and as you know, it's not our place to ask questions."

"School—in the middle of November?"

"As I said, it's not our place to question."

"But, doesn't anybody know?"

"None of the help, no."

"How about Ernesta, she must know. She's Lorna's maid."

Jeannette's single visible eyebrow quirked superciliously.

"The young miss is gone, I said, and Ernesta don't know no more than I do. Good day, Harken."

She shut the door in his face.

Feeling as if he were moving through a nightmare, he went around to the kitchen door. It was half below ground level, down a set of concrete steps.

Mrs. Schmitt said, "Oh, it's you again."

He minced no words. "Do you know where Miss Lorna is?"

"Me? Ha."

"Do you know when she left?"

"How would I know—the cook who never sees nothing but these four kitchen walls."

"Ask the others—somebody must know."

"Ask them yourself."

He was just about to do so when from the opposite side of the kitchen a door opened and Levinia Barnett flew inside, obviously informed by Jeannette of Jens's presence. She crossed straight to him and pointed out the door. "You've been dismissed, Harken. Now get out of my kitchen and quit slowing down my staff."

Jens Harken had been pushed to his limits. He'd been denigrated, shouted at, called names, turned out, treated like tripe. And now this woman—this detestable, manipulative, insufferable witch—was withholding from him the whereabouts of the woman who was carrying his child.

He grabbed Levinia Barnett's wrist and hauled her outside through the servants' entry. She let out a yelp and began swatting and clawing at his face. "Let me go! Let me go!" He slammed the door while she screeched, "Help! My God, somebody help me!" He crossed her forearms and shoved them hard against her breasts, flattening her against a concrete wall. Her silk dress caught on the concrete and pinioned her against it like a thousand porcupine quills.

"Where is she?" Jens barked. "Tell me!"

Levinia screamed again. He pushed her harder against the wall. One of her sleeve seams ripped. Her screaming stopped and her eyes bulged. Her skinny lips flopped open in fear.

"Listen to me, and listen good!" He loosened his hold. "I don't want to hurt you. I've never manhandled a woman in my life, but I love your daughter. That's my baby she's carrying. When I—"

The kitchen door opened and the new man, Lowell Hugo, stood there bug-eyed and going about a hundred and thirty pounds. Jens could have driven him into the ground like a tent stake with one bong on his pointy little head.

"Let her go!" Hugo demanded in a wimpy voice.

"Get back in there and shut the door!" Jens put one hand on Hugo's chest and shoved him six feet into the kitchen. Hugo tripped on the threshold and fell on his rump.

Jens dragged Levinia Barnett along the wall and slammed the door himself.

"Now listen and listen good! I'm not a violent man, but when you take away Lorna and my baby, I fight back. I love her. She loves me. You don't seem to understand that. Now, one way or another we're going to find each other, and if you don't think she'll be looking for me as hard as I'm looking for her, you don't know your daughter very well. So you can give your husband this message—Jens Harken was here, and he'll be back. As many times as it takes until I find his daughter." He released her cautiously, taking one step backward. "I'm sorry about your dress."

Levinia Barnett had gone so limp with fright she appeared to be hanging on the wall by the silk threads alone.

The kitchen door whapped open and Hulduh Schmitt emerged, brandishing a rolling pin.

"Get away from her!" Hulduh yelled, and cracked Jens a good one on his right temporal bone. He got an arm up to deflect the blow but its force dumped him back against the cement steps. He scuttled backward, on all fours.

"You get out of here or I'll give you another one!" Hulduh yelled, coming for him.

He turned and ran.

Behind him the kitchen help swarmed around their queen, caught her as her knees buckled and carried her back into the kitchen.

Within one hour, in the walnut-walled offices of Gideon Barnett's lumber empire, a stir escalated.

"Sir, you can't go in there! Sir!"

Jens Harken paid little heed, stalking through the corps of Barnett's underlings, peering into one glass office after another until he spotted Barnett himself, looking fat and walrus-y behind his desk, while two men sat on chairs before it.

Jens opened the door without knocking and stood like a warrior just inside the room.

"Tell them to leave," he ordered.

Barnett flushed above his thick gray moustache as he rose slowly to his feet. "Gentlemen," he said without a glance at either of them, "if you'll excuse us for a minute."

The two men rose and went away, closing the door behind them.

With distaste written on every muscle of his face, Barnett hissed, "You . . . low-life . . . immigrant . . . trash. I should have expected something like this from you."

"I came to ask you how much a woman's silk dress is worth, because I just ruined one of your wife's." Jens withdrew some bills from his pocket and laid twenty dollars on the desk. "You'll hear about it as soon as you get home, I suppose, probably sooner. This low-life immigrant trash who's in love with your daughter and who's the father of her baby just tried to force your wife to tell him where you've hidden her. You'll want to have me arrested, of course, so I came by to tell you where the law can find me. I'll be at Tim Iversen's cabin for the rest of the winter, or if not there, just a half mile or so north of there, putting up my own boatworks. Just listen for the saw—you can hear it for a couple of miles. But before you send the sheriff, think of this. Arrest me and there'll be a trial, and at that trial I'll tell them why I was at your house questioning your wife. I'll tell them I was fighting for Lorna and for our baby. And someday when I find her, and she never speaks to you again, you'll ask yourself if it was all worth losing a daughter over . . . and a grandchild along with her. Good day, Mr. Barnett—sorry I interrupted your meeting."

Chapter 14

In her room the night Gideon and Levinia learned she was in a family way, Lorna had waited—less obediently than apathetically. They had wielded the mightiest weapon of all: shame. Against her father's furor or her mother's reproach Lorna might readily have rebelled. But humiliation had done its dirty work.

Belittled, spiritless, she sat in the dark feeling for the first time ever like a sinner. Until her mother's denunciation Lorna had considered her love for Jens a hallowed thing. It had made of her a better person rather than a small one: benevolent where she might have been petty; generous where she might have been stingy; complimentary where she might have been critical; patient where she might have been intolerant; cheerful where she might have been morose.

Cheerfulness, however, had been snuffed out by Levinia's tirade. After her mother left the room, Lorna sat at the foot of her bed staring at the undrawn draperies, too dispassionate to get up and close them or light a lamp. She sat instead in the dark, enumerating the number of ways her family might be hurt if she ran away with Jens. Was it true? Would they and she be shunned forever by their former friends? Would her sisters be sullied by her reflected shame? Would her mother's friends whisper behind her back and her father's business associates avoid him? Would she herself lose Phoebe's friendship? Would her child suffer the name "bastard" for his entire life?

She considered the word *fornication* again and again. Never before had she put such a name to the act that had seemed so resplendent between herself and Jens. She'd considered it a wondrous manifestation of the love they felt for each other, a fitting celebration of that love.

Levinia, though, had called it low, base, filthy.

Shameful.

The night deepened and Lorna remained alone. Despondent. No dinner tray was delivered. None of her family came near. The piano kept silent. Jens left and stillness lurked in his wake. The house exuded a clandestine air as of whispered secrets being discussed behind closed doors. After a long, long time Lorna tipped to one side and drew her feet onto the bed. Fully clothed, she lay with her knees updrawn, eyes open, not even a pillow beneath her head. In time she slept, roused partially and shivered, slept again, awakened sufficiently to loosen her dress, remove her shoes and climb beneath the covers.

She awakened near eight A.M. to the sound of three knocks on her door.

"Your breakfast, miss."

A tray thumped the bottom of the door. Footsteps tiptoed away. Light shone through the west-facing windows, which gave the morning a questionable quality of dulled luminosity. A cold backdraft threaded down the fireplace, smelling of charcoal. Lorna lay supine, resting the back of a hand on her forehead, wondering where Jens was, what he would do to support himself now that Gideon had fired him, if he would come to the house again trying to see her, if he'd write to her, what would happen to each of them, if he had spent the night in the same blunt agony as she.

As shamed as she.

She collected her breakfast tray but ate nothing, drank only a cup of tea and a glass of some dark maroon juice that activated her saliva glands and made the inside of her mouth feel rough.

She lit a fire and stared into it, picturing Jens's face. Writing in her journal, she fell asleep with her head on her arm, sitting at her tiny writing desk. Downstairs a door closed, awakening her. Outside, horses' hooves pattered. Shortly before noon Lorna's bedroom door opened without any knock and Aunt Agnes slipped inside. She came straight to the desk and wordlessly embraced Lorna, holding the younger woman's head in both arms as if it were a load of Turkish towels gathered from a clothesline.

Aunt Agnes's dress smelled of her familiar musty rose dusting powder, a scent Lorna had always associated with loneliness. With her head on Aunt Agnes's breast, she tried not to cry. "Mother says I'm not supposed to speak to any of the family."

"Typical of Levinia. She can be such an imperious ass without half trying. Forgive me, Lorna, but I've known her longer than you so I feel I've earned the right to speak my mind. You can love her, but don't you ever—ever!—admire her!"

Lorna smiled wanly against Aunt Agnes's dress front, then drew back. "What's going to happen?"

"I don't know, but something's afoot. They know better than to let me in on it, but I can listen at keyholes better than anyone else in this family, and believe me, I will." The tremble in Agnes's voice, usually slight, was more pronounced today.

"Thank you for playing the piano last night when all that was going on in the library."

"Oh, child . . ." Agnes petted her niece's hair. It was all ascraggle and framed a face so laden with sorrow it shredded the older woman's heart. "He wanted to marry you, didn't he?"

Two oversized tears appeared in Lorna's lovelorn brown eyes, answering Agnes's question.

"And they sent him away, those merciless hypocrites." Angry, earnest, she continued, "By the memory of Captain Dearsley, I hope they suffer as they're making you suffer! What right have they? And rights aside, how could anyone who calls himself a Christian turn away the father of his own grandchild?"

Lorna plunged against her aunt again, wrapping both arms around her spare frame. It felt so good to hear voiced the thoughts she herself had submerged all night, thinking them wicked each time they surfaced. During those silent minutes in her aunt's arms Lorna thought how sad that she could not approach her mother this way. It should have been Levinia in whose arms she poured out her most intimate feelings about the expected child, her love for Jens, and their future. But Levinia's arms had never been welcoming, nor her breast a comfort as Agnes's was.

"I spoke to your mother this morning," Aunt Agnes said. "I told her I know about your condition and asked her what's going on. She said it was none of my affair and admonished me to keep my lip buttoned, so I'm afraid, dear one, that I'm to be kept in the dark. Short of coming to console you, there's little I can do."

"Oh, Aunt Agnes, I love you."

"I love you, too, dear heart. You are so like me at your age."

"Thank you for coming. You *have* helped—more than you know."

Agnes stood back and smiled down. "He's a fine young man, your handsome Norwegian boatbuilder. There is something about the cut of his shoulder and the angle of his chin that reminds me of my own fine captain. Be assured, Lorna, that if there is anything I can do to see the two of you together, I shall do it. Anything at all."

Lorna rose and kissed her aunt on both cheeks. "You're the rose in all these thorns, dear Aunt Agnes. From you I learn the very best lessons, the ones I carry closest to my heart. But you must go now. No sense in getting Mother more upset if she finds you here."

Aunt Agnes's visit was the only contact Lorna had with anyone until late afternoon, when Ernesta came to her room carrying an empty trunk.

"Ernesta, what is it?"

"I've been ordered to help you pack, miss."

"Pack?"

"Yes, miss. Only one trunkful, the mistress said. She says you're going to college at last, and that your father's made special arrangements to get you in at the beginning of the second semester. Isn't *that* wonderful. I wish I could go to school. Only went through the sixth grade, but where I come from that was something. It got me this job, 'cause I could read my letters whereas some others I grew up with never learned that much. Now, what'll you be wanting to take? The mistress said to ask you what you'd like."

Woodenly, Lorna gave orders while inside she frantically wondered what was going to happen to her. When the packing was finished and Ernesta gone, Levinia came in, dressed in a traveling suit the color of a gun barrel. She stood the full width of the room from Lorna, with her fingers laced compactly at stomach level, her expression pinched and punitive. "Your father has made arrangements for you and me to take a trip. The train leaves at seven-fifteen. See that you're dressed properly and ready to leave the house at a quarter to."

"Where are we going?"

"Where this disgrace can be handled in a discreet manner."

"Mother, please . . . where?"

"There's no need for you to know. Just do as I say and be ready. Your sisters and brother will be in the library to bid you goodbye. They are to be given to understand that you're going off to school, and that your father pulled plenty of strings to get you there at this odd time of year, primarily as an assuagement for refusing to let you skip the boat in the regatta next summer. If you play your part convincingly, they'll believe it, especially after all the times you harangued your father to let you attend college. Just keep that maudlin look off your face and remember, you and your lax morals prompted these drastic measures; your father and I did not."

Saying goodbye to Jenny, Daphne and Theron proved excruciating: pasting a false smile on her lips while they studied her in bewilderment, disbelieving her story and wondering what was amiss. She kissed them all and said to Daphne, "I'll write." To Jenny, "I hope Taylor sits up and takes notice of you at last." And to Theron, "Do your studies and someday it'll be you going off to college." Gideon kissed her stiffly on the cheek. He said, "Goodbye," and she replied likewise, with little semblance of affection.

Steffens drove Levinia and Lorna to the Saint Paul depot, where Levinia purchased two tickets to Milwaukee and they boarded a private compartment in which the seats faced each other. Levinia closed the velvet privacy curtains on the door, removed her hat, stored it beneath her seat and perched herself like a stuffed owl. Lorna sat opposite, fixing her absent gaze on the window during the interminable minutes before the train began to roll.

Once it did, they watched the lights of the city dwindle into an indigo night studded by starlight and a one-quarter moon.

Finally Lorna turned to regard her mother. "Why are we going to Milwaukee?"

Levinia leveled her eyes on Lorna. Censure had settled in them and would remain—Lorna was certain—until either this child or Levinia herself was in the grave.

"You must understand something, Lorna. What you have done is not only a vile sin, it is in some states actually against the law. Anyone who even suspects your situation will judge you by it for the rest of your life. One does not live down bearing an illegitimate child. One survives it the best one can and hides the fact so as not to ruin the rest of one's life and the lives of one's family. Your sisters must be considered. Their reputations could suffer because of you, and if not their reputations, certainly their tender young sensibilities. Your father and I don't like sending you away, but we saw no other way. He has . . . acquaintances, shall we say, apart from our social circle, who put him in touch with the proper church authorities through whom he found a Catholic abbey of Benedictine nuns who'll—"

"Catholic?"

"Who'll take you in during the period of—"

"But, Mother—"

"Who'll take you in during the period of confinement. You'll have good care, and seclusion, and the help of the good nuns and of a doctor when the time comes."

"So I'm to be stuffed away in a stone turret and treated like a profligate, is that it?"

"You don't seem to understand, Lorna, your father paid dearly to get them to agree to this arrangement. He made a ridiculously large donation to a church that isn't even his, so I'll thank you not to take that tone with me! We needed somewhere to put you, and we needed it fast. And frankly, I don't think it'll do you a bit of harm to be sequestered with a group of God-serving women who value purity and have taken vows of chastity. If our own religion had any such group your father would have approached them. Since they don't, Saint Cecilia's will have to do."

"I'm to be sequestered?"

"How naive you are. Women who've gotten themselves in the family way outside the bonds of marriage simply do not parade themselves around in public. This is what happens to them; they are hidden away so that decent people need not face the embarrassment of confronting them out in polite society."

"And what about the baby? Will I be allowed to keep it?"

"Keep a bastard? And do what with it? Bring it home for your two young and impressionable sisters to learn about? For your little brother to explain away to his friends? Live with your father and me and raise it under our roof? You can't honestly expect us to put ourselves in such a position, Lorna."

They rode in silence for some time, Lorna staring into the dark, heartsick and afraid. Occasionally she'd wipe tears away to clear her vision. Levinia made no move to comfort her. Eventually the older woman spoke again.

"While you're with the nuns I'm sure you'll have plenty of time to realize it would be disastrous for everyone concerned if you kept it. The church knows good families who are looking for children to adopt. There is no other answer."

Lorna wiped her eyes again.

Outside, the nightscape sped by.

Milwaukee by moonlight lay beneath a haze of coal smoke. Ahead, the network of railroad tracks looked like shooting stars as the train slowed and rounded a curve. It traveled for some time within visible distance of Lake Michigan, where wharves and moored ships crippled the shoreline. Ribbons of fog drifted landward, and as the train nosed through them they eddied about the windows. The station itself was murky, nearly deserted, and smelled strongly of creosote. Descending the train steps, Lorna glanced uncertainly toward the depot. A brick apron stretched between her and it, the bricks sheeny with fog, caught in the beams of two lanterns whose topaz light was dulled by the weepy weather and the film of smoke on their glass globes.

"This way," Levinia said.

Following her mother, Lorna felt the chill air creep along her skin. What she was doing, where she was going seemed unbelievable, yet even the foreboding weather was in keeping with her situation: Following Levinia's briskly striding form through the dark, unknown city, shrouded by fog and secrecy, Lorna became duly convinced of the magnitude of her sin, and with that conviction came a heavy load of guilt.

Levinia tipped a porter to fetch Lorna's trunk and summon a coach. It arrived behind a horse whose hide gleamed wet and in whose mane sleet had begun to freeze. A side lantern swung on its bracket as the driver stepped down and opened the coach door.

"Evening, ladies. Nasty night to be out." His breath smelled of liquor as they stepped past him into the murky confines of the conveyance. The door closed behind them. The coach dipped and rocked as Lorna's trunk was loaded on the boot, then the driver reopened the door and thrust his face inside.

"Where to, mum?"

"Saint Cecilia's Abbey," Levinia answered.

"Right. Make use of that lap robe. You'll need it tonight."

The lap robe was heavy and scratchy as wet hay. Levinia and Lorna shared it, seated hip to hip on the musty leather seat while the horse stepped out and their heads jerked backward.

The air inside the coach became cloying and the windows clouded from their breath. Several times Lorna wiped hers off with the edge of a hand to see brick buildings sliding past, then houses and boulevard trees, and once a pair of bicycles leaning against a stone building.

They traveled for over an hour with the sleet continuously pecking at the roof and windows. Levinia fell into a doze, her head canted to one side, bobbing as if her neck were broken. Glancing at her occasionally, Lorna considered how the vulnerability of sleep had the ability to either endear or repel. When it had been Jens she'd watched in slumber, she had been bewitched by tender feelings at the sight of his unguarded face transformed by laxity. Watching her mother, however, Lorna found Levinia's open lips and sagging chins faintly repulsive.

Finally, the driver's voice came muffled from outside.

"We're just about there, ladies. About five minutes more."

Levinia's head snapped to. She smacked her lips, coming awake. Lorna cleared her window. Outside, the moon had disappeared and sleet had turned thicker, whiter. It seemed they were beyond the city, for the land rolled beneath barren fields, then became host to a barren woods. A stone wall appeared and when they'd traveled along it for perhaps a hundred yards, the coach turned right, crunched over coarser gravel for several more feet, then came to a stop.

The coach door opened. The driver's head appeared and his breath smelled ranker than before. "Anyone expectin' you?"

"Just ring the bell on the gate," Levinia replied.

The coach door closed and the horse shook its harness, then the driver cranked a thumb-bell that reported with so little resonance Lorna felt certain no one would answer. The bell rang three more times before a thick, waddling figure appeared on the opposite side of the gate, garbed in black, carrying an umbrella.

"Yes? What can I do for you?"

"Got two ladies here want to come inside," they heard the coachman reply.

Levinia opened the door and stuck her head out. "I'm Mrs. Gideon Barnett. I believe you're expecting me."

"Ah." The nun withdrew a key from inside her robes and said to the coachman, "Drive them on up to the building at the far side of the courtyard."

He tipped his black hat and climbed aboard. First one gate squeaked long and lugubriously, then another sang the same song. The coach pulled through and stopped. "Won't you ride up, too, Sister?" came the cabbie's voice.

She replied in a heavy German accent, "Thank you, no. I'll follow. This snow smells fresh and the night air is very bracing."

Lorna glimpsed the nun as they pulled past her: a great round loaf of a woman with a black blanket folded over her head, anchored on her chest with one hand while she waddled up the ascending path beneath her black umbrella. Inside the stone wall a ring of evergreen trees seemed to hold the world at bay. The gravel drive was flanked by denuded hardwood trees and flower beds lain waste by winter. A building appeared: U-shaped, three-storied, made of dark stone, faced on the ground level by an arcaded gallery following the building's contour. On the upper stories windows placed as regularly as pickets in a fence looked down darkly on the courtyard below.

At the central door the coach stopped and the driver went behind to get Lorna's trunk. Levinia stepped out. Lorna stepped out.

Levinia told the driver, "You'll wait, please. I'll return as quickly as I can."

They stood in the wet, falling snow while the fat nun labored up the drive beneath her umbrella, which was nearly the same circumference as her black, swaying robes. She was puffing as she reached them and ordered in the same guttural German accent as before, "Go . . . go . . . get out of the wet."

Together, the three of them entered beneath the hooded walkway and approached an immense arched door made of black wood with a leaded glass window shaped like a cross. Through its amber and red glass shone the faintest light, as if a single candle burned inside.

The nun led the way. "Come in," she said, her voice echoing from the high stone walls of a vaulted entry.

The sound of the closing door reverberated as if a dozen others had followed suit along the upper corridors that hung in shadow. The area held a line of ladderback chairs pushed against one wall, a single huge obese-legged table holding three burning tapers in a brass candelabrum, and on one wall a wooden crucifix bearing a bronze image of the dead Christ. Stairs led off the entry to either side, and another stone archway fed into impenetrable shadows straight ahead.

"Mrs. Barnett, I'm Sister DePaul," the old nun said, letting the blanket slip from her head to her shoulders.

"Sister, it's very good to meet you."

"And you are Lorna." Her voice sounded as if she were gargling with stones in her throat. Her fleshy face pushed through her white wimple and drooped beyond its tight edges like bread dough over the edge of a crock. The simple gold ring on her left hand appeared to be cutting into her pudgy finger.

"Hello, Sister." Lorna offered no hand for shaking nor did the nun. The fat woman directed her words at Levinia.

"Father Guttmann let us know you were coming and arrangements are all made. She will have good care and good food and plenty of time to reflect. This will be good for her. Her room is all ready, but you must say your goodbyes here. Lorna, when you have bid goodbye to your mother I'll be waiting just there"—she pointed beyond the dark arch—"and we will get your trunk upstairs together."

"Thank you, Sister."

Left alone, Lorna and Levinia seemed unable to endure eye contact with each other. Lorna stared at her mother's left shoulder. Levinia toyed with her pigskin gloves, stacking and restacking them as if they were twenty instead of two.

"Well," Levinia said at last. "You be obedient and don't give them any trouble. They're doing us a big favor, you know."

"When will I see you again?"

"After it's born." Levinia had always referred to the baby as "it," except for the one time she'd called it a bastard.

"Not until then? How about Father? Will . . . will he come and visit me?"

"I don't know. Your father is a busy man."

Lorna's gaze shifted to the crucifix. "Yes . . . of course . . . of course he is." Too busy to waste time on a pregnant daughter who was carefully hidden away and needed nothing more than creature comforts for the next six or seven months.

"When it's born, you can come back home, of course," Levinia said.

"Without it . . . of course."

To Lorna's rank amazement, Levinia's stern facade crumbled. Her lips—hard moments before—trembled, and her eyes filled with tears. "Dear God, Lorna," she whispered, "do you think this is easy for your father and me? We're trying to protect you, don't you understand? You're our daughter. . . . We want the best for you, but something like this follows you your whole life long. People can be cruel, more cruel than you can imagine. While you're blaming us and calling us heartless, stop to realize for just one minute that it is our grandchild you're carrying. We shall not come out of this without scars of our own."

Levinia's outburst revealed a vulnerability Lorna had never before seen. She had not suspected her mother's susceptibility to hurt over this impasse. Until now she had considered Levinia merely dictatorial and hard, separating her from Jens for selfish reasons. In that one moment, when tears appeared in Levinia's eyes, Lorna realized her mother had been harboring a welter of emotions she had carefully hidden until now.

"Mother . . . I . . . I'm sorry."

Levinia clutched Lorna to her breast and held her, struggling to compose her voice. "When a mother has a child, she imagines that child's future will be ideal. She never plans for catastrophes like this. So when they happen, we just . . . we just . . . struggle along the best we know how and we tell ourselves that one day our children will see that we made the decision we thought was best for everyone." She patted Lorna's shoulder blade. "Now, you take care of yourself, and tell the sisters the minute you go into labor. They'll telegraph your father and I'll come straightaway." She kissed the crest of Lorna's cheek—hard—and hurried out before her tears became a greater embarrassment.

When the door closed, Lorna found herself surprised by her mother's emotional display. Odd that the outburst should come as a shock, but it dawned on Lorna, standing beside the door through which Levinia had just left, that for some people it takes a cataclysmic event to loosen their heartstrings and allow them to manifest the love they otherwise hide.

Sister DePaul came laboring in and picked up the candelabrum. "I'll take you to your room." She grasped one handle of the trunk and Lorna the other. "Ooph! So heavy. You'll find you won't have use for so many clothes here. Here we live simple and quiet and spend time in prayer and contemplation."

"I'm not Catholic, Sister. Did anyone tell you that?"

"You don't have to be Catholic to pray and contemplate."

The upper hall stretched into blackness divided into increments by symmetrically placed doors. Halfway along, Sister DePaul opened one on the right. "This is yours."

Lorna entered and looked around. A bed, a table, a chair, a window, a crucifix, a prie-dieu: prayer and contemplation in a monastic cell of immaculate white, representing purity, she surmised.

They set down the trunk; the nun lit a candle on a square bedside table, then turned.

"We have Mass at six o'clock and breakfast at seven. You're welcome at Mass anytime you might want to go, but of course it's not required. After Mass tomorrow someone will come to show you the way to the refectory. Sleep well."

Minutes later, in total darkness, lying flat on her back on a hard cot no wider than a baby's crib, Lorna rested her hands on her stomach and attempted to believe there was a fetus within her that had prompted this galvanic change in her life. The sheets were coarse and smelled cleaner than rain, the blankets woolen and heavy. The bedspread was stiff but textureless. The baby within all this covering, within her deceptively flat stomach, was no bigger than a teacup. Or was it there at all? How could it be when there was so little physical evidence of its existence? This entire day viewed in retrospect seemed like a drama being played out on a stage, with Lorna as its protagonist. She felt as if she could rise at will and leave this bed, this abbey, this stage, and end the scene whenever she chose. She could board the train and ride back to Jens and say, I took part in the strangest play—everyone was plotting to keep me away from you, and the baby away from us both. But I'm back, and I'm happy, and we can get married now.

Her mother's parting tears, however, struck fantasy from her mind and put reality firmly in place. Levinia's tears had made Lorna admit for the first time the very real stresses the conception of this child had brought to bear upon her parents. She considered all her mother had said about the eventual cruelty of people to a child born out of wedlock, and the stigma forever attached to the family of that child. Until now she had been idealizing, premeditating the day when she and Jens and their baby would be a family, as if social censure was of no importance. But it was. With one giant leap toward maturity, she realized she'd been denying it until now.

In the morning a soft-spoken, seraphic nun named Sister Marlene came to show her down to breakfast. Sister Marlene's lips tipped up at the corners in a permanently benevolent expression—not a smile, not a grin, more a radiance emanating contentment and inner peace. She walked, stood, waited with her wrists doubled upon each other inside the oversized black sleeves of her habit. She called Lorna "Dear Child."

"Dear Child," she said, "be not afraid. God will take care of you as he takes care of all his children." In the hall: "This way, Dear Child. You must be very hungry." And in the refectory: "Sit down, Dear Child, while Mother Superior says Grace."

Mother Superior had a face with more sags than a Monday wash hung out on a crowded clothesline. She was white as an altar cloth, bowing over her folded hands without once glancing at Lorna. She led the other women in the sign of the cross, and together they intoned a meal prayer that was strange to Lorna's ears. They were not singing, yet their voices blended as pleasingly as hymnsong. Everyone moved slowly here, holding back their ample sleeves to keep them from getting in the food when they reached beyond their plates. The food was simple: spicy links of wurst, pungent cheese, coarse white bread, saltless yellow butter, cold milk, hot coffee.

Sister Marlene made the necessary introduction. "Our young guest is Lorna. She came last night from Saint Paul, Minnesota, and will be with us until perhaps early summer. She is not Catholic, so our ways will seem strange to her. Sister Mary Margaret, when breakfast is done would you please show the Dear Child where the kitchen and the dairy are—she'll be wanting fresh milk often, I'm sure."

Though Sister Marlene spoke in perfect English, most of the others spoke with a German accent or, when conversing among themselves, in German itself. To Lorna's surprise, they laughed often, and occasionally appeared to be teasing one another. Each of them spoke to her at least once during the meal, giving her name and imparting a bit of information about life at the abbey, or what the cooks had planned for supper, or where and when Lorna should leave her dirty laundry. Nobody demanded she either attend Mass or pray with them when the meal ended. Nobody mentioned the expected child.

The abbey nestled among wooded hills with farms visible in the distance. Lorna's room faced opposite the central courtyard, looking west across a frozen stream and a landscape patched with forest and meadows that rose toward the horizon, where a pair of horses could occasionally be seen inside a split-rail fence. She spent many hours studying the scenery beyond her window, sitting on her hard ladder-back chair with her chin and forearms on the stone sill.

Saint Cecilia's Abbey, it turned out, was a place of prayerful and contemplative retreat for both retired nuns and nuns from the surrounding states on extended sabbaticals. Prayer and contemplation: Like the nuns, Lorna spent much time on both. It was a peaceful expanse without pressure. She was neither blamed nor chastised for her condition. She was merely accepted by the women, whose very serenity seemed to seep within herself the longer she was among them. Most of them were like Sister Marlene: They moved quietly and smiled as if with some inner tranquility, so different from Gideon and Levinia Barnett. They occupied themselves with the simplest activities—dipping candles, crocheting lace, making altar cloths, baking communion hosts. Their austere living conditions removed all sense of competition, which had been so strong a force among the circle in which Lorna had grown up. She found a great relief in simply *being,* without having to be what somebody else wanted: wittier, prettier, from the richer family, among the right class, wearing the prettiest dress, charming the most promising men.

At Saint Cecilia's Abbey she was simply Lorna Barnett, God's child.

November became December. In the common room, plaster statues of the infant Jesus, Mary and Joseph appeared on a bed of hay. The common room became her favorite place, with its diamond-paned windows overlooking the courtyard in one direction and the countryside in the other, and the infant Jesus smiling benevolently at anyone who entered. She studied him soulfully, asking him questions about the right thing to do. He returned no answers.

The common room held an ancient piano, set before the rear windows with their view of the snow-covered hills. Lorna played it often, its metallic scintillation sounding much less like a piano than a harpsichord. The nuns would enter and sit in silent appreciation, occasionally requesting a song. Sometimes one of them would fall asleep listening.

Sister Theresa taught her the care of houseplants.

Sister Martha let her knead bread.

Sister Mary Faith taught her to stitch.

December became January and Lorna's girth surpassed that of her clothing: She made two simple garments that looked little different from the nuns'—brown homespun dresses that hung from shoulder to ankle in a line broken only by the single hillock of her stomach.

January became February and the nuns skated on the frozen stream behind the compound. Their cow, a beautiful biscuit-brown creature named Prudence, gave birth to a beautiful biscuit-brown calf named Patience. Lorna often sat in the stable with the animals, the air warm and fecund, the structure crude, reminiscent of the boat shed where she and Jens had spent the summer with the *Lorna D.*

She had not written to him, for each week without fail her mother sent a letter admonishing her to give up the idea of seeing Jens Harken again, to accept the fact that she must give up the baby, to ask God's forgiveness for the shameful thing she'd done, and to pray that nobody they knew put two and two together when this was all over.

Lorna wrote to nobody except Aunt Agnes. To Aunt Agnes she poured out all her personal ache over the painful decision that lay ahead, and admitted that she'd avoided writing to Jens in order to give herself time to evaluate all that her mother had said and make the decision that would prove least painful for everyone concerned. She asked Aunt Agnes, *What have you heard of Jens?*

The reply said that he was using Tim's place for the winter and had built a boatworks nearby, where he had begun work on another boat, though she didn't know for whom.

Lorna read the words over and over again, sitting at her window staring at the linen landscape. In her throat a lump lodged. Upon the snow she saw his face. In the wind she heard his voice. In her imagination she saw their newborn child.

But one thought kept recurring and prevented her from contacting Jens.

Suppose my mother is right.

Chapter 15

⟶ ◦≫ ⟵

Af ter Lorna's banishment, an even greater strain than usual separated the master and mistress of the granite house on Summit Avenue. The children were asking a lot of questions about why Lorna was attending a *Catholic* college, and whenever Levinia tried to describe the abbey to Gideon, his mouth got small and he claimed he was busy.

One night shortly before Christmas, Levinia was waiting in the master bedroom when Gideon entered to prepare for bed. The city house, built well before the lake cottage, had no running water or bathroom facilities. She waited while he stepped behind the screen and used the toilet chair. The cover clacked shut and Gideon emerged with his suspenders drooping like overturned rainbows.

"I'd like to talk to you, Gideon," she said.

"About what?"

"Sit down, Gideon . . . please."

He stopped unbuttoning his shirt and came to sit opposite his wife on a small, uncomfortable chair beside the oval heater stove which had been installed in place of the fireplace grate.

"I thought you'd gone to bed already before I came up."

"No, I was waiting for you. We must talk about Lorna."

"Lorna's taken care of. What more is there to say?"

He moved to rise but she bent forward and stayed him with a touch on his hand. "You feel guilty—I understand. But we did what we had to do."

"I don't feel guilty!"

"Yes, you do, Gideon, and so do I. Do you think I liked leaving her there? Do you think I don't worry that someone will find out about it in spite of all the precautions we took? We did it so her future wouldn't be ruined, and we must both remember that."

"All right! All right!" Gideon threw up his hands. "I agree, but I don't want to talk about it any more, Levinia."

"I know you don't, Gideon, but has it struck you that it's our grandchild she's carrying?"

"Levinia, goddammit, I said enough already!" He leaped from his chair and strode toward his humidor.

It took a lot to make Gideon Barnett curse.

It took even more to make his wife stand up to him.

"Come back here, Gideon! And please don't light one of those reprehensible things. I have something to say and I'm going to say it. Furthermore, I don't intend to do so to your back!"

Surprise turned him around. He glared at her as she sat stiff-backed in the small tufted chair, dressed in her voluminous cotton nightgown with her hair still pinned up in tight daytime sausages. Leaving the cigars in the humidor, he returned to the matching chair and sat.

"I think you'll agree that I rarely ask for much from you, Gideon, but I'm going to ask now, and before you vociferate I think you ought to give it some consideration. The child is a bastard, there's no disputing that, but he's a bastard from our blood lines. I shouldn't like to think there's a grandchild of ours living in some . . . some *hovel* somewhere, perhaps cold and hungry. Maybe even sick." She paused as if regrouping, then went on. "Now, I've thought it all over and I know of a way we can see that he's cared for, and nobody need ever know. I'd like your permission to speak to Mrs. Schmitt."

"Mrs. Schmitt?"

"She's been threatening to quit for years, using her poor ailing mother as an excuse. I think she could be trusted."

"To do what?"

"To raise the child."

Gideon jumped up. "Now wait a damned minute, Levinia!"

"It would cost you money, I know."

"It's *already* cost me money!"

"Of which you have plenty. I'm asking you to do this for me, Gid." She had not called him Gid since their salad days. It stopped him in his tracks and returned him to the chair, where he dropped with a sigh while she went on speaking with absolute conviction. "Nobody would suspect a thing if Mrs. Schmitt were to quit now. She would be gone from here for several months before Lorna returned, and since she's been so outspoken about her mother's ill health, it'll be understood that was the reason she left. In return for taking the child, we would of course make sure she and her mother were well provided for for the rest of their days."

Some pensive quiet passed. Gideon remained in his chair, Levinia in hers, while their thoughts ranged backward to Lorna's childhood, forward to that of their grandchild's. During those silent moments the grandparents grew despondent with the weight of unwanted responsibility and worry.

At length, Gideon asked, "How old is Mrs. Schmitt?"

"Fifty-three."

"That's old."

It was the first hint Gideon had given that he, too, had been concerned about the child's welfare.

"Do you have any better ideas?" Levinia inquired, with one eyebrow arched.

Elbows to knees, Gideon studied the floor and shook his head. Finally he raised his gaze to Levinia. "You'd be willing to give up Mrs. Schmitt after the way you fought to keep her last summer?"

"Yes," she answered simply. Her voice broke into a whisper as she reached out and gripped the back of his hand. "Oh, Gid . . . he'll be our grandchild. How do we know where he'll end up if we let him be given away for adoption?"

After years of near physical estrangement, he turned his hand over and clasped hers.

"You never intend to let Lorna know?" he asked.

"Absolutely not, nor anyone else in this household. And Mrs. Schmitt will be sworn to secrecy."

They sat on awhile, faintly uncomfortable with their hands joined and their purposes suddenly unified.

"One thing," he said. "The child must never know."

"Of course not. It's for our peace of mind and nothing more."

"Very well." Gideon released Levinia's hand. "But I'll tell you something, Levinia." He studied some distant point while his face hardened. "I'd like to kill that damned boatbuilder. I mean every word of it. I'd like to kill the sonofabitch."

In the days after Lorna disappeared, Jens thought he'd lose his mind. He felt helpless, godforsaken and afraid. Where had they sent her? Was she all right? Was the baby all right? Had they killed it? Would he ever see it? Had they convinced her never to see him again? Why didn't she write?

He went back to the Barnetts' Summit Avenue house several times, only to be turned away at the door.

Tim was gone and there was no one he could talk to. He didn't confide in Ben, because it would mean divulging the fact that Lorna was pregnant. When days went by and no word came from her his despondency redoubled.

He spent Christmas like any other day, working on his building, constructing stairs to a loft he wondered if Lorna would ever see.

January turned bitter. He wrote to his brother, baring his heart with the truth about the expected child and the disappearance of the woman he loved.

In February the boatworks was complete. He moved his mold over from Tim's cabin and began construction of a scow commissioned by Tim himself, to be christened *Manitou*. But somehow his heart wasn't in it.

In March, bitter blizzards blocked him in for days at a time. He walked to town several times but found nothing at the post office from Lorna.

In April, five months after her disappearance, he received a letter in a strange handwriting. He opened it on the sidewalk in front of the post office, unprepared for the news it brought.

Dear Mr. Harken,

Given a set of circumstances of which I'm fully aware, I thought it my beholden duty to inform you of the whereabouts of my niece Lorna Barnett. She has been sent by her parents to the Abbey of Saint Cecilia on the outskirts of Milwaukee, Wisconsin, where she is being cared for by nuns. You must understand that Lorna's parents have placed and continue to place upon her a great burden of guilt. Bear that in mind if you are tempted to judge her.

                                        Kindest regards,
                                        Agnes Barnett

Standing in the late morning sun with the letter quivering in his fingers, he reread it. His heart thundered. Hope sluiced through him. Love and longing came, too, those emotions he had schooled himself to submerge during the past few months. He lifted his face to the sun and concentrated on its redness behind closed eyes. Already its warmth felt warmer. The spring air seemed fresher. Life seemed fairer. He reread the *Abbey of Saint Cecilia on the outskirts of Milwaukee,* realizing with a leaping heart that his decision was already made.

At Saint Cecilia's Abbey spring had arrived. The northerly winds had shifted to the southwest, and the surrounding fields had emerged from their blanket of white. The smell of thawing earth lifted over the abbey walls, while out in the field to the west a foal appeared with the mare. In the courtyard tulips sprouted. The song of the chickadee changed from the whistle of winter to the salutation of spring.

On an afternoon in late April Lorna was in her room napping when Sister Marlene knocked on her door.

"You have a visitor," the nun said.

"Someone to see me? Here?" Lorna had not known visitors were allowed. "Who?"

"I didn't ask his name."

"A man?" She pushed herself up straighter and dropped her feet over the edge of the bed. The only men she'd ever seen here were Father Guttmann, who came daily to say Mass, and a country doctor named Enner, who called occasionally to examine her.

"He's waiting for you outside in the gallery."

The door closed silently behind Sister Marlene, leaving Lorna sitting with one hand pressed to her bulbous stomach, her emotions in turmoil. Her father or Jens? They were the only men who might come to see her here. Undoubtedly it would be Gideon, fulfilling his parental duty, for Jens had no idea where she was.

But suppose he'd found out. . . . Suppose . . .

She pushed herself off the cot with both hands and waddled across the room, poured water into a pitcher, washed her face and stood a moment with her wet palms covering her flushed cheeks, her heart racing crazily. The room held no mirror: She dampened the sides of her hair and combed it by feel, clubbing it back into a plain tail at the base of her neck as she'd been wearing it since she'd come here. She exchanged her wrinkled brown dress for another, equally as plain, equally as brown, equally as coarse, wishing for the first time that she had something more colorful. Opening her door, she moved awkwardly down the stairs, her locomotion a queer combination of the sedate slowness of the nuns combined with the awkward hitch of a pregnant woman whose feet are no longer visible from above.

The central hall was empty but the front door stood open with a bright cone of afternoon sun fanning across the speckly granite floor. All within Lorna seemed to well up and push against her thudding heart as she stepped outside into the arcaded gallery and looked to her right down its length.

Sister DePaul was out for her usual midafternoon prayer-stroll, reading from her German prayer book while navigating the perimeter of the courtyard gallery.

Lorna glanced the opposite way . . . and there was Jens, hat in hand, rising from a wooden bench in the shadow of the gallery roof.

Her heart felt as if it would leap from her body. Relief and love swooshed through her as she started moving toward him with knees that suddenly felt unstable. He was wearing his Sunday suit and his hair was freshly cut, a little too close to his head. His face looked afraid and uncertain as he watched her approach in her drab maternity dress with her belly leading the way. She moved toward him in a morass of emotion—the need for him doing moral warfare with the repeated denigrations and warnings of her mother.

"Hello, Jens," she whispered, reaching him.

He could tell by her utter calmness the nuns and her parents had conditioned her to their way of thinking. They had stripped her of her beauty. Hair, clothing, somberness—none seemed fitting for the Lorna Barnett he remembered. Her spirit was gone, and her glee at seeing him. In its place was an obeisance that terrified him.

"Hello, Lorna."

They stood a respectable distance apart, aware of Sister DePaul strolling prayerfully nearby.

"How did you find me?"

"Your aunt Agnes wrote to me and told me you were here."

"How did you get here?"

"I took the train."

"Oh, Jens . . ." Her expression held a fleeting moment of pained love. "All that way . . ." She paused, then said softer, "It's good to see you," in that trained, martyred way.

"It's good to—" He stopped. Swallowed. Unable to go on. He wanted to draw her into his arms and whisper against her hair, tell her how glad he was to see her, and how he'd imagined all kinds of things, and how lonely and awful the winter had been without her, and how relieved he was that she was still carrying his baby. Instead, he stood apart, distanced from her by a new shield of untouchability that surrounded her as surely as if she, too, wore a habit.

"Why didn't I hear from you?" he asked.

"I . . . I didn't know where to write."

"Where did you think I'd go with you in a family way? You could have found out if you'd wanted to. Didn't you stop to think how worried I'd be?"

"I'm sorry, Jens. There was nothing I could do. They made the plans in secret and Mother packed me off on the train. I didn't even know where I was going until we were under way."

"You've been here five months, Lorna. You could have at least let me know you were all right."

Sister DePaul turned a corner and encroached.

"It's cold under here," Lorna said. "Let's sit in the sun."

They walked, untouching, from the shadows beneath the arches to a wooden bench drenched in afternoon sunlight. There, at the edge of the courtyard, they sat.

"You've grown . . ." he remarked, laying his hat on the seat, letting his eyes pass down her roundness, which raised such an emotional response within him he was sure she could hear his heart clubbing.

"Yes," she replied.

"How do you feel?"

"Oh, I feel fine. I sleep a lot, but otherwise, just fine."

"Do they take good care of you here?"

"Oh yes. The nuns are kind and caring, and there's a doctor who stops by periodically. It's lonely but I've come to learn the value of isolation. I've had a lot of time to think."

"About me?"

"Certainly. And about myself, and the baby." Quieter, she added, "About our mistakes."

His growing trepidation took a swift turn to anger when he thought of how her parents had manipulated their lives. "That's exactly what they want you to do, think of this as a mistake. Can't you see that?"

"They did what they thought was best."

"Sure," he replied sardonically, letting his eyes wander away from her.

"They did, Jens," she appealed.

"I've been alone a lot, too, but I can't say I've found any value in it!" He shifted, as if at some painful memory. "Jesus, I thought I'd lose my mind when you disappeared."

"So did I," she whispered.

They were both close to tears, and tears would not do with Sister DePaul so near at hand. So they swallowed them and sat stiffly beside each other, locked in an impasse not of their making, miserable, in love, watched by the nun. After some moments of awful silence, Lorna tried to redeem the situation.

"What have you been doing?"

"I work a lot."

"Aunt Agnes told me you've started your own boatworks at last."

"Yes, with Tim Iversen's backing." His eyes returned to her but he withheld the warmth from them. "I'm building a boat for him that'll run in the regatta in June. Tim says if I finish it in time, I can skip it."

"Oh, Jens, I'm so happy for you." She touched his arm and they both thought about the *Lorna D,* unfinished in a shed on Manitou Island, and those carefree days while it was being built. "You'll win, Jens, I'm sure you will."

He nodded, withdrawing his arm under the guise of sitting up straighter. "That's what I came to tell you after they took you away—that Tim was going to back me and everything was going to be all right and we could get married right away. But they wouldn't let me in. They treated me like offal on their boots. Now . . ." He fixed his eyes on a rose bed still locked in winter barrenness. Old memories swept over him while he ached as if those thorny roses were wrapped around his very heart. "Damn them to hell."

A cloud passed before the sun, its shadow trailing over them, bringing a momentary chill before it sailed on, leaving them in warmth.

He wanted to turn her into his arms and beg her to leave this place with him.

Instead, he sat his distance while Sister DePaul made another circuit inside the plaster arches, her lips moving in silent prayer.

"My parents want me to give up the baby for adoption."

"No!" he exploded, turning his tortured expression on her.

"They say the church knows childless couples who are looking for babies."

"No! No! Why do you let them put such ideas in your head?"

"But, Jens, what else can we do?"

"You can marry me, that's what!"

"They've made me see the price we'd pay if we did that. Not only us, but the baby, too."

"You're just like them! I thought you were different, but you're not. You've got these stupid rules you live by, and you put what other people think before what you feel!"

Her anger flared, too. "Well, maybe I've grown up a little since all this happened! Maybe I reasoned like a child then, thinking you and I could simply do whatever we wanted without a thought for the consequences."

"How can you talk to me about consequences! The consequences are a baby that's as much mine as it is yours, and I'm willing to take you out of here today, and marry you and give you a home, and to hell with what people say. But you're not, are you?"

Without a physical movement he sensed her withdrawing even further.

"What we did was a sin, Jens."

"And giving away a baby isn't?"

Tears came into her eyes and her mouth shrank as she looked away from him. She had been at peace before he came here. Like the nuns, she had learned acceptance and humility, and had spent time praying for forgiveness for what she and Jens had done. She had decided that giving up the baby was best for everyone. Now she was disturbed, distraught, questioning everything again.

Jens turned to her with love and hurt in his eyes. "Come with me," he urged. "Just walk out of here."

"I can't."

"Can't or won't? They can't keep you here against your will. You're not one of them."

"My father has paid a great deal of money to keep me here."

Jens jumped to his feet and towered over her. "Damn it! You are like him!"

Sister DePaul glanced at them and stopped walking.

"Jens, remember where you are!" Lorna whispered.

He lowered his voice and the nun resumed her prayers. "You care more about your reputation than about your own child."

"I haven't said I'm going to give it up."

"You don't have to. I can see you've fallen right into line with their way of thinking. Get rid of the kitchen handyman and get rid of his kid, then nobody has to know, isn't that right?"

"Jens, please . . . this hasn't been easy for me."

"Easy for you?" He had trouble holding his volume in check. "Have you given one moment's thought to what it's been like for me? Not knowing where you were, why you didn't meet me at that train, if they cut the baby out of you, if you were lying somewhere dying of fever from some butcher's knife? I'm here begging you to marry me and you're saying no, and you want me to cry because this hasn't been easy for you?"

He turned away, struggling to control his anger, struggling with the fact that he had no redress in the face of her refusal to go with him; hating her parents, and—fleetingly—her. He contended with his emotions for the better part of a minute, facing the cloistered world of Saint Cecilia's, taking in little of it—not the sprouting tulips, nor the barren rosebushes, nor the nun who created intermittent black flashes behind the arches. He labored in silence until he'd regained control and could speak more calmly.

"Do you want to know something funny?" he said, his back still to Lorna. "I still love you. There you are, sitting on that bench, saying you're going to stay here and let them take our baby instead of leaving with me and doing the right thing, and I still love you. But I'll tell you something, Lorna . . ." He turned back to face her, picked up his hat, put it on his head. "You give away our baby and I'll hate you till my dying day."

Torn, aching, trapped between two forces, she watched him walk away, into the stringy shadows of the bare elms by the gate, where his carriage waited. Sister DePaul had stopped praying and stood watching from the shadows of the gallery while the uncaring afternoon sun rained its warmth upon the sad creature Jens left behind.

"Goodbye, Jens," she whispered with tears in her eyes. "I love you, too."

Jens left the abbey hurt, so hurt.

Angry.

Frightened.

Searching for a vent for his roiling emotions.

By the time he reached the Milwaukee depot he'd made a decision: He might be nothing more than a kitchen handyman to the whole Barnett bunch, but he'd show them! And he'd do it where the whole damned world would find out.

Before boarding the train for home, he sent a telegram to his brother, Davin. *Come quick. I need you. Boatworks all ready.*

Back in White Bear Lake everything seemed to happen at once. Spring turned unseasonably hot. The summer people returned to their cottages. Tim came home from his winter sojourns. The yacht club opened. Sailing resumed. Everywhere, every day, everyone spoke of the upcoming mid-June regatta: The obsession was revived.

Tim reported that Gideon Barnett had stubbornly refused to have the *Lorna D* completed, so Tim's *Manitou* would be the one all eyes would be watching. Jens worked like a dervish on the *Manitou,* toiling away his frustration and anger while Tim commenced picturetaking, as he'd done the previous summer, chronicling it all for the yacht club wall.

On a day in mid-May when the lilacs and plum trees were blooming, and the town of White Bear was busy with commerce, and the trains once again were running every half hour, Jens went to meet the one bringing his brother, Davin.

He waited beside the tracks, studying the passing windows as the train pulled in, its steel drivers slowing, plumes of steam billowing aloft until it clanked to a final stop. The porter stepped out, followed by a woman carrying a basket, leading a boy by the hand. Then Davin himself . . . and Jens was running toward him with open arms. The two of them embraced with glad lumps in their throats, smacking each other's backs, smiling so hard their cheeks hurt, blinking against the sting in their eyes.

"You made it! You're here!"

"I'm here!"

They drew back, inspected each other and laughed with happiness.

"Ah, brother, look at you!" Jens clasped his younger brother by the muttonchops and wobbled his head around. Davin was blond, slightly shorter and slightly burlier than Jens. "You've finally got enough beard to shave, I see!"

"Well, I hope so. A married man with two babies—one you haven't even seen yet! Cara, come here!"

"Cara is here?" Surprised, Jens turned to find his sister-in-law waiting with a child in her arms, holding another by the hand. She was plump and smiling and wore her blond hair in a braided nest the way their mother always had. "Cara, darlin'!" He'd always liked her. They hugged as best they could with the one-year-old between them. "That big lummox never told me you were coming!"

"Jens . . . it's so good to see you."

Davin explained, "I just couldn't leave her behind."

"I'm glad you didn't! And who is this?" Jens reached for the towheaded baby who'd been balancing on his mother's arms. He lifted the toddler high overhead.

"This is little Roland," Davin answered proudly. "And that's Jeffrey. Jeffrey, you remember your uncle Jens, don't you?" Jeffrey smiled shyly and leaned his head against his mother's hip. Roland began to bawl and got returned to Cara. Jens gave his attention to Jeffrey, who'd been in diapers the last time he'd seen him.

"Jeffrey, that can't be you. Why, look how you've shot up!"

Family! Suddenly they were here, filling Jens's lonely world with a less lonely future. He and Davin exchanged some more affectionate whaps and bantering before Davin said, "I know you weren't expecting Cara and the boys, but we talked it over and decided where I go, she goes, no matter what uncertainties are waiting at the other end. We'll put up in a hotel until I can find us a place."

"Oh no you won't. I've got the loft, and it's big enough to hold us all."

"But that's your place, Jens."

"Do you think I'd let you out of my sight now that we're back together? We've got some catching up to do! There'll be time for you to look for a place after you've been here awhile."

Thus it happened suddenly—in the span of a week Jens's empty loft became a home. To his meager furnishings were added those Cara and Davin had brought, and to these more that the two brothers built or purchased. At breakfast there were hot biscuits and bacon, and one child in a high chair and another on a stool. While the brothers worked downstairs, there were footsteps overhead, and the sounds of the children's voices, and sometimes Cara's, singing to the boys, sometimes scolding. Between the trees around the building clotheslines appeared, and on them diapers blew in the summer breeze. In the heat of the day, while the young ones napped, Cara would come downstairs with iced coffee and lean against the workbench, visiting while the men drank, relishing the togetherness as much as the break.

Best of all, deep into the evenings there was a brother to talk to and plan with. That first night, after the babies and Cara were bedded down three abreast in Jens's own bed, he studied them, then said to Davin, "You're a lucky man."

The two were sitting on a pair of bent willow chairs with a kerosene lamp on the table at their elbow. Davin, too, studied his sleeping family, then shifted his regard to his brother.

"So what about this woman of yours? Where is she?"

When Jens had told him, Davin pondered long and silent before asking quietly, "What are you going to do?"

"What can I do? Wait and hope she comes to her senses."

"And marries you?"

When Jens made no reply, Davin reasoned, "It would be hard for her. She's high society. People would wag their tongues. They'd call the kid a bastard, and call her worse."

"Well, sure they would, but if it was Cara and you, she'd do it. Hell, look how she followed you out here, with no home to come to, no real assurance that this boatworks is going to pay off. That's how it ought to be when you love somebody."

"You say her parents live somewhere right across the lake?"

Jens blew out a breath of frustration and answered, "Yes, and I know what you're going to say next—they'd probably never speak to her again, right?"

Davin studied his brother, his face flat and thoughtful, offering little encouragement. He spoke, at length, as if he'd reached a dour conclusion.

"You should have taken her out of that convent."

"Yeah . . . how? Dragged her by the hair?"

"I don't know how, but if it was my baby I'd have put her in the carriage with me and gotten her out of there."

Jens sighed. "I know. But they've got her convicted and found guilty and they've convinced her that she's committed this unforgivable sin that will absolutely ruin her life if people find out about it, and she believes them. She doesn't sound or act anything like the girl I used to know. Hell, I don't even know if she loves me anymore."

Davin could do nothing but squeeze his brother's arm.

Jens sighed again and looked off toward the bed where Cara and the children were peacefully sleeping, wishing it were Lorna and two of their own. He told Davin, "This has been the best year of my life and the worst. Getting this at last . . ." He gestured to their surroundings. "And falling in love with her, and now the baby coming, and neither one of them mine . . ." He shook his head despondently, then said with much feeling, "What I do know is that I'm damned glad to have you here, Davin. I needed you for more than just helping me build a boat."

The two brothers worked on the *Manitou* eighteen hours a day. Jens told Davin right from the start, "You're sailing this thing with me."

"Are you sure they'll let me?"

"It's Tim Iversen's, and Tim is the lousiest sailor this yacht club's ever seen, but the rules allow him to hire his crew. We'll sail 'er together—you'll see."

The first day Tim came by to meet Jens's family, Cara talked the men into ending work early and invited Tim to supper. Before the meal ended, Tim cocked his head to one side—the better to give the stocky Norwegian a look-over with his one good eye—and said, "What do you know about sailing?"

Davin smiled, shot a grin toward his big brother and replied, "I taught him all he knows." It wasn't strictly true, but the two Harkens exchanged good-humored glances.

"Then you'll crew for Jens?" Tim inquired.

"I'd be proud to, sir." And the matter was settled.

Two alone, however, could not sail the *Manitou*.

"We'll need a crew of six, including the skipper," Jens said. "They'll act as ballast, you know."

"Six, eh?" Tim replied.

"And I think one of them should be you."

"Me!" Tim laughed and shook his head. "Thought you wanted to win."

"The name of this boat isn't the *May-B* anymore. Considering those tubs you've been sailing, it's no wonder you lost and got teased in the bargain. Stick with me and we'll change your reputation in a single race."

Tim scratched his head and looked sheepish. "Well, I can't say it doesn't sound tempting."

"I had in mind to let you fly the spinnaker."

Tim's real eye got bright and his cheeks pink at the thought of skimming across a finish line in the lead, with the giant sail bellied out full before him. "All right, you've twisted my arm."

"Good! Then I need to talk to you about the rest of the crew. With your permission I'd like to ask my friend Ben Jonson to be the pole setter and jiber, and one of Ben's friends, Edward Stout, to be the board man. They both know what they're doing and they're familiar with the boat design. And there's a young fellow I've had my eye on, tall, well-built kid who sails like he was born with a tiller in his hand. Mitch Armfield. I thought I'd ask him to tend the mainsheet."

"You're the skipper," Tim replied. "Whatever you say."

"It'll be a winning crew," Jens promised.

"Then get them together."

Cara went around the table filling coffee cups. Jens took a sip of his hot brew, then sat back with his gaze leveled on Tim. "One other thing . . . Do you have any objections to launching the *Manitou* at night?"

"Why?"

"Well, I'll tell you . . ." Jens glanced from Tim to Davin, then back to Tim. "I've got a plan, but to make it work, none of the other yacht club members can see the *Manitou* sail until the day of the race. We've got to take them completely by surprise."

"You're pretty sure of what she's going to do, aren't you?"

"Absolutely. So sure, in fact, that I'm willing to put money on it." Jens rose and went to the end of the loft near his own bed. He returned with a stack of money, which he placed on the table. "I have one last favor to ask of you, Tim. I'm not a member of the yacht club, so I can't place any bets. But I'm prepared to wager every penny I've saved—nearly two hundred dollars—that the *Manitou* will win. Will you place the bets for me?"

While Tim studied the money, Jens added, "I hear there are still those who think our boat will capsize and sink. The odds will be in our favor."

"Four to one right now," Tim added, "and probably going up once they see that flat little thing on the water."

"So you can understand why none of them must see her run before the first race."

"Perfectly."

"Will you do it?"

Tim covered the money with his hand. "Of course I will."

"And the first person I pay off when I win is you," Jens promised.

"It's a deal," Tim replied, as the two shook hands.

Jens had had many moments of misgiving about inviting young Mitch Armfield to crew for him. They all stemmed, however, from the boy's social class, not from his ability to sail.

The day Jens approached the Armfield house and knocked on the door with his hat in his hand, he hoped to high heaven he was doing the right thing.

A white-capped maid answered the door, bringing flashbacks of getting thrown out of the Barnett house. The woman was polite, however, and asked him to wait in a summery room with potted palms and rococo furnishings.

Young Armfield came jogging down the stairs less than a minute later and entered smiling. "Harken?"

"Yessir," Jens said, extending his hand toward Mitch's outstretched one. "Jens Harken."

"I remember—you used to work for the Barnetts."

"That's right."

"Lorna used to talk about you. And now you've got the boatworks."

"My brother and I—that's right. We're sailing Tim Iversen's boat, the *Manitou,* in the challenge cup against Minnetonka. You've probably heard about it."

"Heard about it! That's all everybody's been talking about around here."

"I came to ask if you'd crew for us."

Armfield's astonishment flashed across his face. "You mean it? Me?"

"I've been watching you. You've got good boat sense. You're quick and limber, and you love sailing as much as I do. Unless I'm mistaken, you've been doing it since you were a boy."

"Well, gosh, Mr. Harken . . ." Mitch ran a hand through his hair, surprised, delighted. "I'd be happy to. I'm just so surprised I don't know what to say."

"What you've just said is enough. You'll be tending the mainsheet."

"Yes sir."

"We plan to launch her at the end of next week. Think you could be at Tim's place Friday evening?"

"You bet!"

"Good. And one other thing—I know it's an odd request, but we don't want an audience when she sails the first time."

"Oh, absolutely, whatever you say." Armfield had heard Harken's detractors declaring the boat would turtle the first time the wind hit it. No wonder they didn't want an audience, just in case the boat went bottom up. "Friday evening."

The two shook hands and Jens left feeling he'd secured the best man for the job.

On the day of the launching, with one week to spare before the race, the crew of the *Manitou* assembled at Harken Boatworks. Tim took photographs of the craft from every angle, of its builders standing beside it, and—with Cara's help—of himself among the crew that would sail it for the first time. Together they guided the boat down the ways that had been laid of stripped logs, the double tracks leading straight from the wide doors of the boatworks down the incline to the shore.

When the *Manitou* took to the water and floated for the first time, they all cheered. Jens felt a pride unlike any he'd known before. Her fair lines were as gently curved as distant hills, her sheer line equally as pleasing, and she displaced so little water. Floating, she looked as pretty as a work by an old master.

On the dock, Cara, holding Jeffrey, said to her son, "Someday, when you're as old as your papa, even older, you'll be able to tell people that you watched him and your uncle launch the first flat-bottomed boat ever raced, and after people saw her sail the sport was never the same again."

Jens boarded, felt this work of his dreams buoy him up for the first time and knew a keen impatience to be under sail.

"Davin, you're tending the jib. Ben, you'll be setting and jibing the spinnaker pole. Edward, you understand how the sideboards work. Just listen for my orders, I'll tell you when to raise and lower them. Mitch, you've tended enough mainsheets to know what to do. Tim, just keep the lines untangled and fly that spinnaker when I tell you to."

Jens seated himself at the tiller.

At last—at long, long last—he gave the order he'd dreamed of giving since he was a boy of eighteen.

"Hoist the main." Up went the mainsail bearing the number W-30.

"Hoist the jib."

The sheets whirred through the blocks and the sails made sounds like quiet hiccups as the first puff of wind caught the canvas. The bow lifted. The boat came alive beneath their feet. No lag, no drag, no delay. She leaped to their command the way a well-trained dog obeys an order to fetch.

At the tiller Jens beamed and called, "Feel that!"

"I feel it, brother!" Davin rejoiced. "I feel it!"

"Glory be!" Tim exclaimed in disbelief. "I don't believe it!"

"Believe it!" Edward yelled.

"She flies!" Mitch put in, while Ben let out a whoop of excitement.

They skimmed over the water, exhilarated, joyous, laughing, fists in the air.

Trimming the jib, Davin called, "How does she feel on the helm?"

"Light as a feather and balancing out beautifully!" came Jens's reply.

Mitch asked his skipper, "How much do I dare trim the sail?"

"Let's find out. I'll point her up and all you guys hike out!" Jens steered the boat closer to the wind. "Okay . . . hike!" All five men leaned their bodies over the weather rail as the *Manitou* heeled higher. There they hung while the night wind freshened. The boat swept over the water and the dark waves whispered on the hull beneath them.

"We'll leave the rest of them floundering at the starting line!" predicted Mitch.

Indeed, it seemed so. The *Manitou* did precisely what Jens had said it would do. As he feathered the boat into the wind, she settled down; as he bore off, the heel increased and she accelerated. She was the perfect blending of quickness and balance.

"She's unbelievable!" Jens rejoiced.

"Smooth as silk!" Davin called back.

"Try tacking 'er, Jens," Edward suggested.

"Coming about! Drop the sideboard!"

When Jens pushed the tiller, Edward worked the boards—dropping the port, raising the starboard—and the *Manitou* performed splendidly. Jens pointed her up and she swung through the wind and sailed off on a new tack. They flew through the night, the crew and the boat responding to the skipper's orders, getting the feel for one another and the immediacy of the craft itself. The moon rose and they left a silver wake spinning diamonds out of moonshine. They sailed to Wildwood Bay, where Tim hoisted the spinnaker and they ran with the wind home, exuberant, smiling, dampened by nightspray and loving the very feel of their wet shirts against their hides.

Back at the dock they furled the sails reluctantly and took their time drying down the deck. When there was nothing left to do but call it a night, they spoke to the boat in terms a lover might use.

"You're quite a lady."

"Good night, sweetheart."

"I'll be back and you be ready."

"Don't forget who stroked you best."

Amid a sense of ebullient camaraderie, the crew bid good night to one another. When the others had gone, leaving Jens with hearty claps on the back, he walked the length of the dock with one arm draped over Davin's shoulders.

"She'll shame everything else off the water," Davin said.

"There's not a doubt in my mind," replied Jens. "And we'll win that cup and the purse along with it."

Climbing the loft stairs toward their beds, they both knew they'd lie awake into the wee hours, their hearts going a little crazy with anticipation.

Jens had promised himself he wouldn't think of Lorna on the day of the regatta. But when he awakened at four A.M. her memory was strong and forceful. Since visiting the abbey he'd pushed her from his thoughts time after time. Today, however, her image would not be banished. She hailed him from times past, in poses that tore at his heart while he wondered why he put himself through this today of all days.

She was so much a part of this day, though, had been since the night she'd stepped into the kitchen and questioned him for the first time about his knowledge of boats and boatbuilding.

Had she had the baby? Where was she this morning? Was the baby still with her—either born or unborn?

He pictured her standing on the yacht club lawn with the baby on her arm when he sailed over the finish line victorious. He imagined her smile, her wave, her hair, her clothing, a tiny blond head near her own . . . a welcome . . .

When the ache got too immense to bear, he thrust back his bedcovers and rose, determined to make it through the next twelve hours without dwelling on her or the baby again.

The day dawned fair with the wind at eight to ten knots. Jens felt an undeniable clench of satisfaction at dressing for the first time in the uniform of the White Bear Yacht Club: white duck trousers and the official club sweater, blue with white letters.

As he stood with his hands on the initials across his chest he realized that within the hour he would confront Gideon Barnett, dressed the same as he. The thought brought a surge of bitter resentment, followed quickly by another of satisfaction. Barnett had entered his own boat, the *Tartar,* in today's A-class race and was skipping it himself. Given all that had passed between them, Jens would take immense satisfaction at whipping Barnett at his own game. The fact that he would do so in the uniform of Barnett's elite club would only make the win that much sweeter.

He combed his hair and left the loft with a word to Davin. "See you at the boat. Sail well."

Precisely one hour before race time Jens entered the White Bear clubhouse for the skippers' meeting. It was held on the second-floor porch overlooking the water. Though a number of skippers had gathered, Jens's attention was riveted on just one: Commodore Gideon Barnett, as walruslike as ever, speaking to the race judge in a grating voice, wearing his white commodore's cap with the gold braid above the visor.

At Jens's approach Barnett looked up and fell silent. His mouth thinned. His jaw set. Jens met the older man's cold regard with an inspection several degrees colder. Not so much as a nod tempered the enmity between the two.

"Skippers . . ." the race judge intoned, and Gideon looked away. "Today's course will be . . ."

Jens knew the course as well as he knew every plank in his boat. He felt an almost surreal detachedness as he stood among the skippers, getting his instructions for running the race, knowing them before they were spoken.

Barnett looked at him only once more, when the meeting ended and the skippers headed outside. His glare held unmitigated hatred while his eyes said, You may be wearing that sweater, kitchen boy, but you'll never be a member.

Outside, spectators had gathered in amazing numbers. There must have been a good two hundred people. Jens walked through them heading for the crew of the *Manitou* who had assembled, smiling and confident, on the yacht club lawn. They had sailed their boat five out of the past seven nights and as a team had become meshed and efficient.

On his way toward them Jens grinned in reply to the disparaging remarks thrown his way.

"You gonna sail that loaf of bread, Jens, or eat it?"

"Who stepped on your cigar, Harken?"

"Better to leave a skimming dish like that in the kitchen!"

Jens merely greeted his crew. "Good morning, men. Let's board and sail!"

The crowd was still snickering when the crew of the *Manitou* carried their spinnaker aboard.

Heading down the dock beside Tim Iversen, Jens asked quietly, "Did you place my bets?"

"Yours and a few of my own."

"At four to one?"

"Five to one."

He stepped onto the boat experiencing a blend of exhilaration and confidence. Let them snicker. In ten minutes his craft and crew would wipe the smiles from their faces.

He gave the order to hoist the main, and up it went, smaller than some of the others, but more effective, Jens knew. He sensed their snickers turning to murmurs when, with twenty boats jockeying for a place on the favored end of the starting line, the *Manitou* proved herself maneuverable beyond anything they'd ever seen. From clear out on the water the hue was audible, "Watch W-30, watch W-30!"

The five-minute gun sounded. The crew was tense with anticipation. Jens felt his pulse thrusting hard against his ribs. He steered the *Manitou* near the *Tartar* and caught a glimpse of Gideon Barnett's set face. He caught glimpses of skippers' faces from the Minnetonka club, too, the M's on their sails identifying their club. But none of them mattered—only Gideon Barnett, the man who'd done him out of a wife and child.

A minute to go, and Edward held his watch in his hand, counting down the seconds to the gun. "Five . . . four . . ." Hearts surged, and Jens experienced that single damned last-second doubt: What if something goes wrong and the *Manitou* fails us today?

"Three . . . two . . ."

The starting gun sounded.

Jens pushed the tiller and ordered, "Hike!"

The *Manitou* surged forth while her competition hunkered as if dead in the water.

They plowed.

She skimmed.

They lagged.

She flew.

On the shore, murmurs of astonishment lifted. In the boats left behind, curses sounded.

"Let's show 'em what she can do, boys!"

Jens's crew cantilevered their bodies over the purling water and gave the spectators a show they'd never forget.

The call "Hike! Hike!" drifted shoreward on the wind and the spectators began cheering. Before any of her deep-keeled competitors struggled its first boat length, the *Manitou* was a quarter of a leg ahead. She rounded the weather mark with the second-place boat so far behind, its sail numbers were unreadable. The entire crew of the *Manitou* laughed for sheer joy.

"Waa-hoo!" Mitch cheered.

"Yee-ha!" Edward Stout joined in.

"They'll talk about this day till kingdom come!" Davin rejoiced.

"Damned shame so many of them are going to lose their money," Jens remarked with a glint of victory in his eye.

"You boys better be ready to build boats," Tim told them, "because everybody in the country's going to want one like this."

"You ready for that, Davin?" Jens shouted to his brother.

"Damn right!"

Ben asked them both, "You ready for all those reporters when we get back to shore?"

"Been waiting my whole life for 'em," Jens replied.

By the time Tim hoisted the spinnaker their closest competitor was a dot on the horizon. On the last windward leg the *Manitou* met the second-place boat, number M-14, coming downwind with one whole lap to go, followed closely by Gideon Barnett's W-10.

When W-30 crossed the finish line the roar from the crowd drowned out the judge's gun.

The crew were regaled like heroes. Spectators on the dock jostled for elbow-room as the *Manitou* tied up. A man was knocked into the water. Women were holding on to their hats. Reporters were shouting questions.

"Is it true you built boats in New England?"

"Will you sail the same boat next year?"

"Will you build one of your own?"

"Is it true you're not members of this yacht club?"

"What's the official time on this race?"

"Mr. Harken, Mr. Harken . . ."

Jens replied, "If you don't mind, we're hungry, boys, and Mr. Iversen's offered to buy dinner for the whole crew."

On his way toward the clubhouse, still hounded by reporters, Jens remained the center of attention. He stalked along feeling as if his body possessed a spinnaker of its own that was filled and billowing! Everyone reached for him, touched him, patted his back, treated him like their hero.

Suddenly, through the crowd, he caught a glimpse of Levinia Barnett.

His stride faltered and his glory dimmed.

She was standing back with a group of family and friends. Her eyes were fixed upon him, steely, arctic. Her rigid jaw was held level with the earth. She stared at him for three hateful heartbeats, then turned her back.

The thought rushed in unbidden: Lorna should be here, and the two of them should be married, and the baby should be here, too, and his boat should have been the *Lorna D*. If it had been, and if he and Gideon Barnett had sailed on the same crew, and if Lorna had been waving from the shore with the baby on her arm, and her mother smiling beside her . . . Ah, what a soul-sweet day this would have been.

But Lorna had been banished in shame. His baby was being stolen from him. Gideon and Levinia Barnett had coldly snubbed him today. And the *Lorna D* sat moldering in a shed, the reminder of what could never be.

He turned from the ramrod set of Levinia Barnett's back and took his bitterness along as he headed toward the consolation prize of collecting his winnings and eating his first meal ever inside the White Bear Yacht Club.

Chapter 16

Two days after the regatta, Lorna received a letter from Aunt Agnes with the news of Jens's illustrious victory. "He blew past everyone like a hurricane, leaving them gaping in disbelief, their crafts laboring as if sailing through mud, while his leaped forth as if upon a sea of mercury. He rounded the first buoy before the others had gotten halfway to it, and passed them all on his second way around the course. The cheers when he crossed the finish line were so uproarious they could be heard on the opposite shore. By the time the second-place boat crossed the same finish line, your Jens had tied up the *Manitou* and was in the clubhouse eating dinner with Mr. Iversen and being congratulated and interviewed by newspaper reporters from as far away as Rhode Island."

He's done it, Lorna thought, sitting in her room at the convent with the letter in her fist. Her face wore a wistful smile as she stared through her tears at the distant green hills and imagined blue water and white sails. How terribly she'd wanted to be there, to see his boat beat all the others, to watch that low, sleek courser distinguish Jens forever in the realm of yachting.

Her eyes returned to the letter.

"Your father, as commodore, was supposed to present the cups to the winners, but after the race he seemed to develop gastritis and turned the job over to the mayor."

So her father's pride was wounded. It somehow mattered so much less than Jens's victory.

She should have been there to see it. She'd had a hand in starting him out and had been through so much of it with him when he was designing the *Lorna D*. All those days of watching him work, of listening to his dreams, of encouraging them, falling in love. She should have been there.

Instead she was hidden inside this stone fortress, gravid with his child.

Outside, summer lay ripe upon the rolling hills and forests. In a crested field that sloped eastward, a crop of rye—blue-hued and shushing—undulated like the Caribbean before the hot summer wind. Staring out over it, longing, Lorna ran both hands over her distended belly . . . lightly . . . lightly . . . grazing it as if the one inside could feel her external touch. Her burden had grown immense, thrusting down so firm and wide her knees pointed outward. How overwhelming to realize this was her child . . . hers and Jens's . . . striving toward life. The baby had become for Lorna much more real in the last month, with elbows and heels that thudded the walls of her womb, and occasional hiccups that brought a smile of love to her lips. Sometimes at night he rolled around in his liquid world and awakened her as if to make her question herself and the answer she had given Jens. She would lie with her hands upon the subtly shifting shape within and try to imagine giving this baby up once she'd held and kissed it.

And she knew, beyond a doubt, she could not do that to herself or to the child's father.

Aunt Agnes had called him *your Jens*. He was not her Jens, but she wanted him to be, wanted it yet as she'd wanted it in the days when their intimacy had first flowered. She carried her love for him like a great stone that lodged in her chest and made breathing, moving, living a constant toil.

From the moment he'd walked away angry, declaring he'd hate her, that stone had grown heavier. Give up his child? And him? How could she? He was right: To give away this child—one conceived in love—would be heinous and unforgivable. It had taken the threat of losing the man she loved to make her realize she could do no such heartless thing. She would keep the baby and would marry Jens Harken. If it meant giving up her family forever, that's what she'd do. She'd been a fool not to leave with him when he'd asked her.

Her labor began three nights later. Awakened by a cramp, she lay waiting it out, staring at the night outside to gauge the time, discovering the moon had already begun its descent. When the first pain eased she rose and stood at her window with a hand on the ledge, waiting for another of verification. It seemed to take an hour, but when it came it brought an unquestionable clench and warning. She bent forward and flattened her hands on the window ledge and rode it out, Jens's face in her imagination to help her through it.

Afterward, she donned a wrapper and went to Sister Marlene's room, knocked softly and waited. The door was opened by a stranger, a beautiful young woman with wavy dark hair flaring out from her cheeks and forehead, her face lanternlit to a luminous coral glow.

"Sister Marlene?"

The young nun smiled at her uncertainty. "Yes, Lorna?"

Lorna continued to stare, struck dumb.

"You've never seen me with my habit off—is that it?"

"You have hair!"

The nun smiled again, the same serene smile as that on the statue of the Virgin Mary in their chapel.

"Has your time come, Lorna?"

"Yes, I think so."

Sister Marlene moved calmly, turning back into her room to set the lantern down and free her hands to don a robe. "Have you been awake long?"

"An hour, maybe less."

"Is it getting close?"

"No, I think it's just started."

"Then we should have plenty of time. I'll awaken Mother Superior and tell her. When Father Guttmann comes for five-thirty Mass we'll tell him and he'll contact the doctor. Your mother asked to be telegrammed, too."

"Sister, I have to ask you something."

"Yes?"

"Did she talk to anyone here about my giving the baby away?"

"Yes, she spoke to Mother Superior."

"But I'm not giving it away. I've decided I'm going to keep it."

Sister Marlene came forward bearing the lantern. By its light she touched Lorna comfortingly on the cheek, as if bestowing a blessing. "God has his ways, and sometimes they're not easy, as this will not be for you. But I cannot believe a child would be better off without its mother. I believe he will bless you for this choice you've made."

The messages were sent with the good Father when he left the convent shortly after dawn. The day progressed with agonizing slowness, a full nine hours of Lorna resting in her room while desultory pains waned and ebbed with great irregularity. Not until three in the afternoon did her travail begin in earnest. Dr. Enner arrived, examined her and declared it would be some time yet.

"S . . . some time?" Lorna asked, breathless after a contraction.

"These first babies can be stubborn."

For another two hours the pains worsened. Each felt longer and closer to the last while Lorna lay on her narrow cot believing surely this was the moment of birth, wondering where Jens was, if he somehow knew this was happening today, if she'd live through this. Sister Marlene stayed at Lorna's side, ever serene, ever attentive. "Rest," she would murmur between pains, while during them she would wipe Lorna's brow or offer her hands for gripping. Once, when the pain grew grievous, the nun murmured, "Think of your favorite place," and Lorna thought of the lake with the sailboats out and the spray from the bow cool on her hands hanging over the coaming, and Jens at the tiller with the sun on his blond hair and neck, and

Queen Anne's lace blooming along the shoreline and the willows trailing their boughs in the water. Another pain smote, and when Lorna opened her eyes Levinia was there, leaning above her.

"Mother?"

"Yes, Lorna, I'm here."

She smiled weakly. "How did you get here so fast?"

"There's nothing in America as dependable as a train. The doctor says it won't be long now."

"Mother, I'm so hot."

"Yes, yes of course you are, dear. The nuns will take good care of you and I'll be waiting outside."

When Levinia went away Lorna turned her weak smile on Sister Marlene. "I really didn't think she'd come." An intense contraction clutched her and she moaned softly, lifting her knees and twisting to one side. The doctor tied leather straps to the footboard of her bed and threaded her legs through them, advising her it would soon be time to push. The nuns, she saw, had rolled back their ample sleeves to the elbow and had pinned their veils back with common pins, joining them between their shoulder blades. Their ears made white bumps within their pristine wimples, and she wondered foggily how they could hear with that starched cloth covering their ears so tightly. During the next quarter hour there were helping hands, and cool cloths, and gushes of liquid, and her own growl, and a great trembling over the entire length of her body, and muscles straining to the quivering point, and her head rising off the mattress, and her voice calling, "Jens, Jens, Jeeeeeeeeens!" A slithering forth, followed by some relief, and a gentle female voice saying, "He's here. It's a boy."

Then a respite and a warm, wet weight on Lorna's belly, and the corners of the ceiling slipping sideways into figure S's as her tears welled and dribbled in warm streams onto her earlobes. Her own hands, reaching downward, and someone supporting her head as she touched the slimy red creature whose spindly arms and legs were doubled over like carpenters' rules.

"Oh, look . . . look at him . . . what a miracle."

"It is a miracle, indeed," Sister Marlene pronounced softly at Lorna's ear before lowering her head to a pillow. "Now rest a minute. You deserve it."

Later, when the cord was cut and the afterbirth taken, and Lorna had heard her son squall for the first time, Sister Marlene placed the infant, wrapped in white flannel, in Lorna's arms.

"Oh, Sister . . ." Lorna's tears welled again as she saw his features for the first time, distorted from the rigors of birth beyond comparison to anyone. "Look at him. Oh, precious little thing, I don't even have a name for you." She kissed his bloody forehead and felt him wriggle in his wraps. "Whatever shall I call you?" She lifted her eyes to the nun's and whispered, her chin shaking, "Oh, Sister . . . his father should be here."

Sister Marlene only smiled and rubbed Lorna's hair back from her brow.

"I wanted to marry him, you know, and my parents wouldn't let me."

Lorna thought she saw a suspicious brightness in the corners of Sister's eyes, but her eternal tranquility remained, superseding any other emotions she might be feeling.

"Well, I'm going to," Lorna vowed. "I should have followed my heart to begin with, and Jens would be with me now. With us." She returned her attention to the baby, touching his chin with a fingertip, which he followed with his seeking mouth. "Has my mother asked to see him?"

"I don't believe so, but she's waiting to see you." The nun reached for the baby. "I'm sorry to take him, but I must give him a bath, and you, too."

Lorna was bathed, garbed in clean white and lying on fresh sheets when Levinia entered her room. The baby had been taken elsewhere for his bath, so the room was quiet and stark as a cell once more. Though Levinia closed the door silently, she need not have bothered, for Lorna was lying awake waiting.

"Did you see him, Mother?" she asked.

Levinia turned, startled by Lorna's lucidity.

"Lorna dear, how are you feeling?"

"Did you see him?"

"No, I didn't."

"Mother, how could you not want to? He's your grandson."

"No. Never. Not in the sense you imply."

"Yes. In every sense. He's your flesh and blood, *my* flesh and blood, and I cannot give him up."

"Lorna, we've been through all that."

"No, *you've* been through all that. You told me how it would be, but you never asked me how I wanted it to be. Mother, Jens was here. He came to see me."

"I don't want to speak of that man!"

"I'm going to marry him, Mother."

"After all that your father and I have done for you, and after he came to our house and threatened me, how dare you even suggest such a thing!"

"I'm going to marry him," Lorna repeated determinedly.

Levinia turned heliotrope and quelled her urge to shout. Quietly she remarked, "We shall see about that," and left Lorna alone.

Outside the office of the Mother Superior, Levinia took a moment to compose herself. She drew and exhaled two deep breaths, pressed her palms to her flushed face and adjusted the veil on her oversized gray silk hat. When she knocked and stepped inside, her heart was still jumping in outrage, but she hid it well.

"Mother Superior," she said coolly, advancing into the room.

"Ahh, Mrs. Barnett, how good to see you again. Please sit down."

Mother Superior was approaching eighty and had a huge face with two chins and a giant German nose. The wire bows of her spectacles seemed to have grown into her temples, like barbed wire into a tree. Her hands were fleshy and liver-spotted as she deposited a fountain pen in its holder and braced her knuckles on the blotter as if to push to her feet.

"Please don't get up," Levinia said, taking one of the two leather-seated chairs facing the old nun's desk. Seated, she rested a silk-covered pocketbook on her knees and withdrew from it a check made out in the amount of ten thousand dollars, consigned to Saint Cecilia's Abbey. She placed the check on the blotter before the nun.

"Reverend Mother, my husband and I are both very grateful for the gracious care you've given our daughter these past few months. Please accept this as a token of our gratitude. You cannot know how it has eased our minds to know that Lorna was in a place like this, where she could be at peace and heal from this . . . this unfortunate interruption in her life."

Mother Superior looked down at the check and hooked it off the blotter with short, blunt fingernails. "Bless you both," she said, holding the check in both hands, reading and rereading it. "This is most generous."

"Bless you too, Sister. You'll be happy to know we've found a good, God-fearing family to take the child and raise it."

Mother Superior's eyes flashed up to Levinia's in some surprise. "I hadn't heard that. We have families, too."

"Yes, I'm sure you have. But as I said, the arrangements are all made, so I'll be taking the infant with me today."

"Today? But so soon."

"The sooner the better, don't you agree? Before his mother grows attached to him. I've brought a wet nurse with me who is waiting at a hotel in Milwaukee, so there's no need to worry about his welfare in any regard whatsoever."

"Mrs. Barnett, forgive me, but Sister Marlene has given me to understand that your daughter hadn't decided whether to give the child up or not."

Levinia impaled the nun with unsmiling eyes. "A girl of her age, in her state, is incapable of making a rational decision about something as important as this, wouldn't you agree, Sister?" She let her gaze drop to the generous check. "I understand that the money will be used to build a new wing on a nearby orphanage. I must say I'm relieved to think that this baby need not ever live in a place like that."

The old nun laid the check down, knuckled the blotter and pushed to her feet. "I shall see that the infant is properly dressed for travel and brought to you here." In her aging rheumatic gait she left the room with her right shoe squeaking.

"No, Mother Superior, you must not do it!" Sister Marlene's face flared as brilliant red as a blood spill against her white wimple.

"Sister Marlene, you will follow orders!"

"But Lorna told me she wants to keep the baby and marry his father—the young man who came to visit her here; you remember, don't you?"

"The decision is made. The child goes with his grandmother."

"Not by my hand."

"Are you *defying* me?"

"I'm sorry, Mother Superior, but it would be the greatest sin of all."

"Enough, Sister!"

The younger nun clamped her lips shut and fixed her eyes on Mother Superior's flat, bound chest.

"Get the infant."

Softly, dropping her gaze to the floor, Sister Marlene replied, "I'm sorry, Sister, I cannot."

"Very well. Go to your room. I shall speak to you later."

In her monastic cell with its single cot, white bedspread, white walls and curtainless window, Sister Mary Marlene—née Mary Marlene Anderson of Eau Claire, Wisconsin, who at age seventeen had borne a bastard child and had it taken from her this same way, and had been sent by her parents to this convent to repent and had stayed to live out her life—removed the rosary from her waist, held it in her right hand and raised her eyes to the simple brown wood crucifix on the wall. "Lord, forgive them," she whispered with tears in her eyes, "for they know not what they do."

Penitently she dropped to her knees, then lay down flat on her face on the cold stone floor, her limbs extended, duplicating the shape of the crucifix. Lying so, she silently prayed for forgiveness, and transported herself to a sublime vale far beyond this earthly one with all its pain and suffering and sorrow.

She was still lying prone when Lorna's scream vaulted through the building. It echoed along the barren stone halls in tenfold those that had accompanied the birth of her child. It raked the ears of eighteen black-clad virgins who had never known either the joy or the woe of procreation, and of the one prone woman who remembered both.

"Noooooooooooooooo!"

They let her scream, let her run from room to room, jerking doors open, slamming them, shrieking, "Where is he? Where is he?" over and over again. Terrified, they hunkered against the walls, gawping, these obedient nuns who had chosen a life of contemplative prayer and seclusion, who had just watched Mother Superior be struck down when Lorna had bounded from her bed, screaming.

Sister Mary Margaret and Sister Lawrence helped Mother Superior to her feet, mumbling in terrified voices, "Oh dear, oh dear . . . Sister, are you all right?" The old woman's glasses were broken and she could neither straighten fully nor readily draw breath.

"Stop her," Mother Superior whispered as they lowered her carefully to a chair.

No one stopped Lorna, however. Not until she reached Sister Marlene's room. She flung the door back, found the nun lying prone as a postulant, and screamed, "Where is my baby? Where is he, you wicked heathens?" She kicked Sister Marlene on her left hip and fell to her knees, pummeling the nun with both fists. "May God damn all of you, you pious hypocrites! Where!"

Sister Marlene rolled away, reared up and caught three cracks to the face before subduing Lorna with a cinch hug. "Stop it!" Lorna struggled to inflict more damage, flailing uselessly. "Stop it, Lorna, you're hurting yourself."

"You let my mother take him! Damn you all to hell!"

"Stop it, I said! You're bleeding!"

The younger woman suddenly collapsed in the nun's arms, weeping, drooping, her weight going slack. They knelt together, a tangle of black and white and the single, spreading, brilliant patch of scarlet seeping through Lorna's gown.

Lorna whimpered, "Why did you do it? Why?"

"You must go back to bed. You're bleeding badly."

"I don't care. I don't want to live."

"Yes you do. You will. Now come with me." Sister Marlene struggled to draw Lorna to her feet, to no avail. Lorna's body remained limp. Her coloring had grown waxy. Her gaze became bleary, fixed on Sister Marlene's face.

"Tell Jens . . ." she whispered weakly. "Tell him . . ." Her eyelids closed and her head sagged back against the nun's arm.

"Sister Devona, Sister Mary Margaret! Anyone! Come and help me!"

It took a minute before two nuns came to the doorway and peered timidly inside.

"She's unconscious. Help me get her back to bed."

"She knocked Mother Superior off her feet," Sister Devona whispered, still shocked.

"I told you, she's unconscious! Now, help me!"

Hesitantly, the pair entered the room to do as ordered.

Lorna emerged from a black well into the silver haze of a late afternoon. The day was bright and glittery, the sky white, not blue, as if in the aftermath of a hot summer rainstorm. A fly buzzed somewhere in the room, then landed and hushed. The air felt gummy and heavy upon her face, her blankets, her arms. Something bulky pressed against her genitals, which ached and felt sticky.

Suddenly she remembered.

I had the baby and they took him away.

Tears heated her eyes. She closed them and turned her face to the wall.

Someone braced a hand on the bed. She opened her eyes and turned to look. Sister Marlene, with her serenity returned, leaned over Lorna with one hand pressed to the mattress. On her face two bruises bulged like strawberries. Her black veil was perfectly ironed and draped symmetrically over her shoulder tips. A smell of cleanliness emanated from her, of clean laundry, and fresh air, and sinlessness.

"Lorna dear . . ." she said. "You're back." Upon her delicate frame she made a sign of the cross.

"How long have I been asleep?"

"Since yesterday afternoon. Nearly twenty-four hours."

Lorna shifted her legs restlessly and Sister Marlene removed her hand from the bed.

"It hurts."

"Yes, I'm sure it does. You tore yourself when the baby was born, and afterwards, running. We were afraid you might bleed to death."

Lorna lifted the blankets from her hips. An earthy-bloody-herbacious smell drifted forth. "What's down there?"

"A comfrey poultice to help you heal. It will help your torn flesh bond faster."

Lorna lowered the covers and lifted apologetic eyes to Sister's. "I kicked you and hit you. I'm sorry."

Sister Marlene smiled benignly. "You're forgiven."

Lorna closed her eyes. The baby had been taken. Jens was not here. Her body ached. Her life seemed pointless.

The fly began buzzing again. No other sound intruded into the overwhelming convent quiet. Sister Marlene sat with the patience only a nun could muster . . . waiting . . . waiting . . . giving Lorna all the time she needed to acclimate to what had happened.

When finally Lorna opened her eyes, having swallowed repeatedly and mastered her urge to weep, Sister Marlene told her in a voice placid with acceptance, "I, too, gave birth to a child when I was seventeen years old. My parents were devout Catholics. They took it away and sent me here and I've been here ever since. So I understand."

Lorna slung an arm over her eyes and burst into noisy weeping. She felt Sister Marlene's hand take her own.

And squeeze.

And squeeze.

And go on squeezing.

She clung to it, weeping behind her arm, her chest heaving, her stomach bucking, until her keening seemed to rebound upon itself and detonate the viscous summer day.

"What will I do?" she wailed, drawing into a ball, covering her slimy face with one hand, feeling her flesh pull where it had begun healing. "Oh, Sister . . . What will I dooooooo?"

"You will go on living . . . and you will find reasons to persevere," the nun answered, petting Lorna's matted hair, remembering with great sadness the handsome young man who'd come here to find her, and her own young man those years ago.

Lorna left Saint Cecilia's eleven days after the birth of her son, garbed in one of three new gowns Levinia had left. Mother Superior gave her an envelope bearing a train ticket and enough additional cash for the carriage back to Milwaukee and dinner aboard the train. Also in the envelope was a note from Levinia.

Lorna, it said, *Steffens will be waiting at the station to drive you to the Summit Avenue house or Rose Point, whichever you prefer. The entire family will be at Rose Point, as usual at this time of year. Love, Mother.*

Lorna made the return trip in a state of malaise, focusing on little, assimilating none of what she saw and smelled and touched en route. Her body had healed sufficiently to make the ride reasonably comfortable. Occasionally, when the train rocked, she felt a twinge down low that revived memory more than pain. Sometimes, from her train window, she saw in fields mares with foals that called back the view from her room at Saint Cecilia's. Between Madison and Tomah a woman boarded with a little blond boy about three years old, who peeked at Lorna around his coach seat and smiled shyly, breaking her heart. The money for her meals went untouched. She sat through the dinner hour without noticing either hunger or thirst; indeed, she had grown accustomed to living without liquids during the awful days when her breasts filled with milk and were bound and dissuaded from producing it. They hung now, slightly larger than before, slightly less resilient, useless pendants used only to rest her wrists beneath. It was how she thought of her body, when she thought of it at all—a useless, emptied vessel.

At Saint Paul the porter had to rouse her from her reverie and remind her to disembark.

Steffens was waiting, doffing his hat, greeting her with a formal smile. "Welcome home, Miss Lorna."

"Thank you, Steffens," she replied woodenly, then stood waiting as if she had no idea where she was.

"How was school? And your trip to Chicago?"

It took her a while to absorb the lie her parents had disseminated about her whereabouts since the end of the school term.

"It was fine . . . just fine."

When he'd helped her board and loaded her trunk, he inquired, "Where to, Miss Barnett?"

She thought awhile and murmured to the middle distance, "I don't know."

Steffens turned in his seat and studied her curiously. "The family's all out at the lake, miss. You want I should take you there?"

"Yes, I guess so. . . . No! . . . Oh dear . . ." She touched her lips and felt her eyes fill with tears. "I don't know." Around them the bustle of the train depot created a din of voices, rumbling wheels, hissing steam and clanging bells. In the midst of it, Steffens awaited her bidding. When she continued silent and vacuous, he offered, "I guess I'll take you out to the lake, then. Your sisters and brother are out there, and your aunts, too."

Lorna at last snapped from her muzziness. "My aunts—yes. Do take me to the lake."

She arrived in the late afternoon, when a game of croquet was in progress. Daphne was on the court with a group of her friends. Levinia was sitting at an umbrella table with Mrs. Whiting, drinking lemonade and watching. The aunts were on a glider in the shade of an elm tree. Henrietta was fanning herself with a palmetto fan and Agnes was doing punchwork embroidery, stopping occasionally to fan herself with the hoop. Down by the dock Theron and a friend were scooping minnows with hand strainers.

Nothing had changed.

Everything had changed.

Henrietta noticed Lorna first and arched her back, waving with the fan high overhead. "Lorna! Hello! . . ." and to everyone at large, "Look, Lorna is back."

They all came, the croquet players dropping their mallets, Theron clanking a minnow bucket against his knee, Levinia bussing Lorna's cheek, Aunt Henrietta clucking and babbling, Mrs. Whiting hanging back smiling, Aunt Agnes squeezing Lorna the longest, with moist, tacit affection, while over her shoulder Lorna searched the Dellwood shoreline where Jens's boatworks must be, making out at this distance only an undulating line of trees.

Daphne exclaimed, "Oh, Lorna, you got to go to Chicago! Is your new frock from there?"

Lorna looked down at the dress about which she cared so little. "Yes . . . yes, it is." She hadn't the enthusiasm to add that she had two others.

"Oh, Lorna, you're so lucky!"

Theron said, "Gosh, we thought you'd never get back." He'd grown a good three inches during her absence.

The young people offered smiles and hellos and Levinia said, "There's cold lemonade."

Lorna asked, "Where's Jenny?" and Daphne answered, "Out sailing with Taylor."

So things *had* changed.

Certainly for Lorna they had. She declined the invitations to join the croquet game, and to dip for minnows with Theron and his friend, and to sit on the glider, and to drink lemonade. She was tired from the trip, she said, and thought she would go to her room for a little rest.

There, the windows were open, the curtains fluttering, and Aunt Agnes—sweet, thoughtful Aunt Agnes—had picked a bouquet of every variety in the garden and left it with a note written on blue deckle-edged paper: *Welcome home, dear. We missed you.*

Lorna dropped the note, removed her hat and laid it on the window seat. She sat beside it and stared out across the water, wondering where he was, if he sensed she was home, when she would see him, how she would tell him about the baby. Below, the girls' voices drifted up in arpeggios of laughter from the croquet court, and she thought, Yes, laugh while you may, while you're young and carefree and the world seems nothing but good, for all too soon your childhood fantasies end.

Gideon came home on the six o'clock train but stayed clear of Lorna.

Jenny returned from sailing and bounded straight into Lorna's room to hug her and exclaim that she was truly in love with Taylor, and Lorna didn't mind if she was being courted by him, did she?

Mother came along and tapped on the door, reminding, "Supper at eight o'clock, dear."

With great difficulty Lorna put in the expected appearance, encountering her father for the first time, garnering another stiff kiss on the cheek, fielding her siblings' questions about her nonexistent school and shopping trip, avoiding Aunt Henrietta's eagle eye that said very clearly *Lorna has changed!*, listening to Levinia prattle on and on about the diminished quality of the food since Mrs. Schmitt had retired, biting her tongue to keep from asking Aunt Agnes if she'd seen Jens, realizing she herself didn't belong here anymore but accepting that there was no place else for her to go.

In the evening, when the family had dispersed, Lorna cornered her mother and father in the morning room, entering it silently and standing between the open pocket doors for some time before speaking. Her father's face was hidden behind a newspaper. Her mother was sitting in a chair by the French doors, staring out at the lake. Lorna made her presence known by announcing, "If you don't want to risk the children hearing this, you'd better close those doors."

Levinia and Gideon started as if arrows had whizzed past their ears. They exchanged glances while Lorna rolled the pocket doors closed, then Gideon rose and shut the French doors and remained beside Levinia's chair. It struck Lorna they had probably been expecting her: On a balmy summer evening such as this, when they stayed home they usually sat on the veranda in the wicker.

"I thought I should tell you how I feel about you stealing my baby."

Levinia replied, "We did not steal your baby. We made arrangements for its adoption."

"By whom?"

"The church doesn't tell you that."

"You stole my baby without even asking me."

"Lorna, be sensible. What would you have done with it? How could we possibly have allowed you to bring it back here—can't you see how your sisters adore you? How they admire you and want to be like you?"

Lorna ignored the oft-repeated refrain. She told her parents with absolute dispassion, "I want you both to know that I have lost all feeling for you because of what you've done. I'll live here for now, because I've nowhere else to go. But I'll marry the first man who asks me in order to get away from you. I hope you're both very happy with the outcome of your malevolent deed."

Calmly, imitating Sister Marlene, Lorna left the room.

A different mood prevailed when Aunt Agnes slipped into Lorna's room near eleven o'clock that night. The two women clasped each other and struggled to calm their pitifully pounding hearts.

"It was a boy," Lorna managed in a ragged whisper. "They took it from me against my wishes. I never even saw him w . . . washed . . . only with blood on his little f . . . face. I don't even know what color his hair was."

"Oh, my precious, wounded child."

While Lorna cried against her shoulder, Aunt Agnes asked, "Does Jens know?"

"No. I have to tell him." Lorna pulled back, swabbing her eyes with a cotton hanky. "Have you seen him, Aunt Agnes?"

"No. I've spoken to Tim, though, and the business is flourishing. Since the regatta everyone wants a boat from Harken Boatworks. You know where it is, don't you?"

Lorna gazed toward the window. "Yes. I've spent many weeks imagining it there."

She went the next day, dressed in the blue-and-white-striped skirt she'd worn the very first time she'd shared a picnic with Jens. Solemn-faced, she put a pin through her straw hat, staring at her countenance in the mirror, finding a dour woman where a carefree girl had stood one year before. She took the catboat, asking no permission, unshakably certain that Gideon wouldn't have the gall to forbid her the "unladylike sport of sailing" after all she'd been through. The few lessons she'd sneaked from Mitch Armfield left her ill-prepared to handle the one-man boat. If she capsized and drowned, so be it: The possibility brought not the slightest quiver of dread, given the reaction she was expecting from Jens. Indeed, drowning would be preferable to being shunned by him.

She found his place with no trouble. It was visible from clear out in North Bay, its new wood still blond and bright against the green backdrop of shoreline. So big, she thought, approaching it, admiring its high roof and grand proportions. She had intended to remain as calm as Sister Marlene, but catching sight of Tim's boat, the *Manitou,* tied up to a startlingly long dock, and the boatworks itself with its loft windows open above, and its wide, west-facing crossbuck doors doubled back to the late morning light, and the ways stretching down from them straight to the water, Lorna felt a rush and race within. It was coupled with a keen longing to be living here with him, in this place they had both dreamed of. Oh, to watch their child steady himself against his father's leg, and learn to walk between those ways down to the water's edge, and to design and build and sail yachts the way Jens could teach him.

Lorna tied up to the dock and walked its length, eyeing the *Manitou* as she passed it, feeling a great surge of nostalgia because it looked so much like the *Lorna D.* Approaching the beach, she glanced up and realized, to her dismay, that there were diapers drying in the wind.

Dear lord, he's found the baby!

She paused, rooted, staring at them until common sense brought a more believable if shattering probability: He's married some widow.

She forced her feet to move . . . up the dock to the newly cleared beach, across the sand to the wooden skids, between the skids, closer and closer to the sound of sandpaper scuffing and the light tap of a hammer.

In the double doorway she stopped. The building was as high, wide and venerable as a church inside, with dappled light falling through open windows and doors, and the new wood of the building itself still as bright as ripe grain. It smelled the same—aromatic cedar, glue and sawdust.

Three men were working on a new boat—Jens, Ben Jonson and a square-built stranger.

The stranger noticed her first and quit sanding.

"Well, hello," he said, straightening.

"Hello," she replied.

Jens and Ben quit working and straightened, too.

"Can I help you?" the stranger asked.

Her eyes left him and found Jens while Jonson offered, "Hello, Miss Barnett."

Jens said nothing. He stared at her for five flinty seconds, then returned to his sanding. From upstairs came the smell of cooking and the sound of children's voices, magnifying Lorna's dread.

"You're Lorna," the stranger said, coming forward with his hand extended. "I'm Jens's brother, Davin."

"Oh, Davin," she said, relieved. "Well, my goodness, I didn't know you'd come. It's good to meet you."

"I imagine you've come to see Jens."

Jens went on sanding, ignoring her.

"Yes . . . yes, I have."

Davin let his glance dance back and forth between the two of them. "Well . . .

listen . . . smells like Cara's got some dinner ready upstairs, and I for one could use a break. How about you, Ben?"

Ben set down his hammer and wiped his hands on his thighs. "Yeah, sure. Sounds good."

To Lorna, Davin said, "We've heard a lot about you. I'm sure Cara would like to meet you before you leave. Maybe you'd have time to go up and have a cup of coffee with her."

She gave him her best Sister Marlene smile, though everything inside her was jelling and quivering. "You're very kind," she said, and meant it, liking him on sight, this man who under happier circumstances might have become her brother-in-law.

"Well, let's go, Ben," he said, and the two clumped up a railed stairway to her left.

In their absence Lorna waited by the door for some acknowledgment from Jens. He continued sanding, presenting his back. The sight of it, so familiar and broad, rocking into his work, constricted her throat. She approached him timorously and stopped five paces behind him.

"Hello, Jens," she said plaintively.

Nothing.

The armpits of his blue chambray shirt were damp. His black suspenders were covered with sanding dust.

"Aren't you even going to say hello?"

Nothing.

She stood like a schoolgirl reciting a verse, feet primly planted, hands joined behind her back, aching with despair and mortification and the terrible need to have him turn to her and speak kindly.

"It's a grand building . . . everything you ever wanted. And your brother here working for you, and Ben, too. My goodness, you must be happy."

"Yeah, I'm real happy," he replied bitterly.

She swallowed the lump that rose into her throat and tried again. "I hear you won the regatta in grand fashion."

He straightened and turned, shoulders back and chest flared, slapping the sand-paper against his thigh to free it from dust.

"I'm a busy man, Lorna. What is it you want?"

"Oh, Jens . . ." she whispered, her voice breaking, "please don't . . ." Her chest hurt and tears rode the rims of her eyelids. "Because I don't think I can . . . oh, God . . . it's been so terrible these last few weeks." She closed her eyes and the tears spilled. She opened them and whispered, "I had a boy, Jens." The sandpaper stopped flapping. "I only saw him once before they took him away from me. My parents took him without asking me and gave him away."

From above came children's voices and the scrape of chairs.

Jens said, "I don't believe you. You gave him away."

"No, Jens, no . . . I didn't." Lorna's face contorted. "My mother came, and when she left, the nuns told me the baby was gone, too, and nobody will tell me where."

"You'd like me to believe that, wouldn't you!" He was so angry a white line appeared around his lips. His trunk jutted toward her and for a moment she thought he would strike her. "Well, I know better. You had your mind made up when I came there to visit you. It was plain as the nose on your face that they'd talked you into it, and you could see that your life would be a whole lot simpler if you didn't have to explain away some bastard baby you'd have to bring home, so you just scuttled it, didn't you? Just . . . just sloughed it off on somebody else and the problem was taken care of! Well, listen to this, and listen good!" He grabbed her left forearm and doubled it hard against her breast. "The sorriest day of my life was the day I met you. It's brought me nothing but misery ever since. Little miss rich bitch, sniffing around the kitchen, sniffing around the boat shed, and sniffing around my bedroom, looking for some big damned stupid peckered-up fool to cure your itch. Well, I sure cured it, didn't I? But you've got enough money to fix even that, haven't you?" His face was thrust close, filled with disgust. "Aaah . . ." He gave her a sudden shove. "Get out of here. I've got nothing to say to you."

She landed with her hip against a stack of lumber. A shard of pain shot down her leg as she stared at his back through her tears. He spun away and fell to sanding again with fierce, vehement strokes.

She rubbed her bruised arm, repeated in her mind a dozen denials, knowing he would listen to none. He only sanded . . . and sanded . . . and sanded . . . trying to sand away his anger, his hurt, her. Every stroke seemed to wear away a thin layer of her heart until she felt its wall would burst. When she could bear his enmity no longer, she gathered herself away from the stacked lumber, whispered, "You're wrong," and fled.

When she was gone Jens gave up sanding and straightened his back, bone by bone. He listened to her footsteps run down the dock, watched her tiny sail carry her west, away from him. After several minutes his shoulders sagged and he sank back against the boat mold, letting his body double upon itself as he slid to the floor. There, gripping his head, with the sandpaper caught in his hair, Jens Harken wept.

Chapter 17

Oh, that bitter, doleful summer while Jens lived across the lake and Lorna seemed incapable of living at all. She existed, little more. She placed one foot before another and moved about when occasion demanded; placed food in her mouth when her body sent out warning signals; spent insomnious hours watching moonshadows from her bed and sunrises from her window seat; wrote countless pages in her journal; composed the beginnings of nearly one hundred poems, the ends of none. She declined all invitations.

Only one activity brought her a measure of peace.

Sailing.

She neither asked permission nor received admonition for using the catboat. Gideon grew conditioned to finding it gone at all hours of the day. The residents of the lake became accustomed to seeing her out in the pink mists of morning with her sail up before there appeared to be any wind; and in the hard white sun of midday with the catboat keeled up and her hanging over its side; and in the gentler breeze of evening—drifting, sail reefed, lying back staring at the sky so the craft appeared unmanned.

Levinia said, "You're growing thin as a rail and so appallingly tanned. Please stay out of that sun."

Theron said, "You never let anyone go out with you. Couldn't I go just once, pleeeeeease?"

Phoebe Armfield said, "Lorna, I miss doing things with you."

Jenny said, "Is it because of Taylor that you're so blue? Do you still have feelings for him? If you still love him, you've got to tell me."

Gideon said, "No man will ever marry that girl. They think she's queer the way she sails around the lake mooning, day in and day out."

Aunt Agnes said, "Don't pay any mind to what anyone says. I acted the same way after Captain Dearsley died."

Lorna found solace in Aunt Agnes, who knew the details of her tragedy, and whose commiseration became balm to her wounded soul. They shared their innermost feelings, Lorna's recent heartbreak bringing forth Agnes's earlier one like pentimento upon an aged painting. The brushstrokes of Agnes's loss seemed to bleed through and superimpose themselves upon Lorna's present canvas, which was painted with loneliness and despair.

The two women went for long walks upon the beach and sat in the garden reading John Milton and William Blake. They took tea on rainy days in the gazebo, and on hot days picked switches of fresh lavender to fan away the flies while reciting poetry aloud to each other on the wickered veranda.

And so the summer passed.

Jens saw her often, recognized the little catboat when it came into the bay and sailed back to windward carrying her away once more. He would stand in the open door of the boatworks, tools forgotten in his hand, and watch her go, and wonder where his son was, what he looked like, what name he'd been given, and who was caring for him. He would think about any future children he might have and how they would never know their older brother existed somewhere in the world.

His son and Lorna Barnett.

His deepest despair and his utmost happiness forever embodied in the sight of a woman in a boat, skimming past, reminding him of what he wanted to forget.

Tim said, "Here, I thought you might like these," and gave Jens photographs of Lorna and himself documenting that idyllic, honeyed summer while the *Lorna D* was being built. He put them among his clothes, between his folded winter underwear in a trunk at the foot of his bed. Sometimes at night, lying with his hands doubled beneath his head, he would think of getting them out and looking at her, but remembrance brought bitterness and a wish for what could not be, so he'd focus his thoughts on other things and will her out of his memory.

He would succeed for a day or two at banishing her image, then he'd catch sight of her sail again, or hear her father's name, or glimpse one of the steam excursion crafts crossing the lake from the big hotels and wonder if she was aboard with the moneyed crowd whose laughter could be heard on the stillest of evenings as they headed toward the yacht club for dinner, or the Ramaley Pavilion for a play. Often music drifted from the water after dark, and the lanterns from some craft broadcast the ostentatious display of a dance in progress right out there in the middle of the water. Jens would stand on the end of his dock evaluating the chasm between himself and Lorna Barnett, and feel hurt well up at her unwillingness to challenge social pompousness when he'd asked her to marry him. *Dance then,* he thought bitterly, watching the lights on the water blink and bob. *Dance with your rich partners and forget you ever gave my baby away!*

The *Manitou* remained moored at his dock, bringing curious yachtsmen to view it almost daily. Often prospective customers would want to sail it, so Jens and Davin would get up a crew to take them out, coursing the length of the lake, passing the narrows off the east end of Manitou Island, where Rose Point Cottage gazed out over the water with its French doors thrown open and its emerald lawns spread like a velvet gown down to the water's edge. Once he passed a croquet game in progress, and another time what appeared to be a large-scale ladies' tea beneath a white gauze awning that had been erected on the lawn. Both times, after a single glance, he kept his eyes resolutely fixed upon his course, avoiding an inquisitive study of the girls with their long skirts trailing and their giant hats towering.

His business flourished. Orders came in for more yachts than he could build in a year, coupled with so many inquiries about boat repair that he hired Ben's friend Edward Stout to do repair work only. His second boat took to the water, christened *North Star,* commissioned by club member Nathan DuVal. It and the *Manitou* won every weekend race in which they took part. Reporters came from Chicago, Newport and New Jersey to interview Jens and write articles about his outlandish, unbeatable design and its impact upon the inland-lake racing scene. Quotes were printed and reprinted about the first race, when the crew of the *Manitou* were already in the yacht club having dinner before the second boat crossed the finish line.

A boatworks in Barnegat Bay, New Jersey, and another in South Carolina wrote and offered Jens jobs designing for them. He replied no to both but saved the letters, tucking them away in his trunk, using them as an excuse to cast a glance at the photographs of himself and Lorna Barnett.

Then one day Tim came over and said, "I've brought some news. Gideon Barnett is finishing the *Lorna D* and intends to put her in the water before the season is over. Speculation has it he's going to run her in next year's big regatta against Minnetonka."

Gideon Barnett had, indeed, hired a local man to finish the hardware and rigging of the *Lorna D.* When it was complete, he approached his daughter and told her, "I'm going to put the *Lorna D* in the water. Would you like to crew on her the first time she sails?"

Lorna was sitting on a chaise longue on the veranda desultorily buffing her nails. She paused and looked up at Gideon.

"No, thank you."

"But that's what you've always begged for, and you've been sailing the catboat all summer. Why not the *Lorna D*?"

"It's too late, Father."

Gideon's eyebrows beetled and his cheeks turned florid. "Lorna, when are you going to give up this infernal self-absorption you've been indulging in and join the human race again?"

"I don't know, Father."

Gideon wanted to shout that Levinia and he were getting mighty sick of her continuing this persecuted air and shutting them out of her life. Guilt sealed his lips. He turned and left her behind in the sultry air of late August.

It was inevitable the two boats would meet. It happened on a day in late September, when Jens and his crew had taken the *Manitou* out for a pleasure sail—a dark day with the wind up and the pebbled clouds lumped across the sky like scree. They met in the passage between the point and the peninsula, the *Manitou* sailing south, the *Lorna D* north. Approaching each other, the skippers of the two boats locked glances. They sat at the tillers of their respective yachts with eyes as turbulent and stormy as the clouds behind them, watching each other pass. Tim raised a hand in greeting but Gideon made no response, only glared from behind his great graying eyebrows, while Jens did the same. Had they been aboard warships, cannonballs would have flown. Lacking cannonballs they sent merely hate, and the certainty that the next time they met, their yachts would be going in the same direction.

In late October, the Barnett family closed up Rose Point and packed itself off to the city for the winter. Before leaving, Lorna stood a long time at the tip of the peninsula, looking northeasterly toward Jens's, wrapped in a winter coat with her arms crossed, her flossy hair fluttering loose from its twist and stinging her forehead. The wind slapped her coattails against her thighs and whipped the water's edge into creamy furrows. Out over the waves two gulls bucked a headwind and mewed at the gray billows below. Lorna thought of their child, four months old now, smiling and cooing for someone else.

"Goodbye, Jens," she said with tears in her eyes. "I miss you."

With winter just around the corner, the city house was as drear as the weather. Lorna's siblings were in school all day. Levinia worked diligently on benefits and balls, encouraging Lorna to get involved, receiving only refusals, though she volunteered some time at the lending library on Victoria Street. She loved the library work, which got her out of the house and put her in an environment of quiet and study, suiting her present mood. The holiday season brought a plethora of entertainment, which Lorna avoided whenever possible. Some houseguests came from the state of Washington, among them a thirty-one-year-old bachelor named Arnstadt, who showed overt interest in Lorna from the first moment he met her. He was involved with the railroads in some way, and her father did big lumber business with the railroads. It seemed Arnstadt was rich and available on the marriage market: She could perhaps fulfill her threat to marry the first man who asked her.

But when he took her hand in the library one night, she yanked it back as if scorched, got tears in her eyes and hurriedly excused herself to run to her room and wonder if ever again in her life she could allow herself to be touched by any man besides Jens Harken. . . .

Phoebe came to visit over the Christmas holidays, wearing an engagement brooch from a man named Slatterleigh, who was a rising star in Mr. Armfield's business firm. In early January came the announcement of other upcoming nuptials: Taylor DuVal finally popped the question to Jenny, the wedding to take place the next summer. Levinia went into raptures planning the grandest social event of her matriarchal career.

Life flourished all around Lorna, while she lived in as insular a bubble as she could manage, shutting it all out and her pain all in.

Then one day in late February she returned from a stint at the lending library to find Aunt Agnes rushing toward her across the echoey front entry.

"Come upstairs quickly!" the old lady whispered urgently.

"What is it?"

Agnes crossed her lips with a finger and grabbed Lorna's hand, hauling her upstairs with her coat still on. In Agnes's own bedroom she closed the door and turned to her niece with eyes as bright as polished sapphires.

"I think I've found him."

"Who?"

"Your baby."

Lorna quit tugging at her scarf. "Oh, Aunt Agnes . . ." she whispered, while a thunderclap of hope slammed through her body.

"Come here." Agnes took her hand and toted her to a rosewood secretary between a pair of windows. She picked up a small white paper and thrust it into Lorna's hands. "I think he's been with Hulduh Schmitt all the time at this address."

Lorna read, *Hulduh Schmitt, 850 Hamburg Road, Minneapolis, Minnesota.*

She looked up sharply. "But why would she have him?"

"I don't know, but I suspect Levinia and Gideon had a fit of conscience after all and talked her into taking him to raise."

"But how did you find out? What makes you think—"

"I've been systematically ransacking your father's desk ever since they sent you away." Aunt Agnes looked bright-eyed and smug.

"You haven't!"

"I most certainly have. It took me some time to figure it out, though. You see, I was looking for the name of someone from some church or orphanage—some stranger's name, or some documents of adoption. Here I was, overlooking Mrs. Schmitt's name all these months until it finally hit me—he started paying her while you were gone, but he's still doing it! I asked myself why, when she's no longer employed here. It all adds up, Lorna, doesn't it?"

Lorna's heart was thudding so hard her face turned cherry. Still dressed in her coat, she gripped her aunt's hands. "Oh, Aunt Agnes, do you really think so?"

"Well, don't you?"

"It could be, couldn't it?" Lorna paced, excitedly. "Mother came there and the baby disappeared. While I was away, Mrs. Schmitt retired. It all makes sense."

"And who would have suspected anything after Mrs. Schmitt harped for years about quitting? Why, summer before last, when this whole affair between you and Jens started, half of White Bear Lake heard about the fuss Levinia put up in the midst of a dinner party over the idea of losing her cook. Everyone knew it would happen sooner or later. I say they paid her off to quit when she did, and she's got your little boy now."

"I've got to go find out." Lorna reread the address. "Immediately . . . tomorrow!" She lifted excited eyes to her aunt. "If it's true, I'll never be able to thank you enough."

"If it's true, that will be all the thanks I need."

They both smiled, imagining it, then Aunt Agnes sobered.

"If you find him, what will you do?"

A haunted look came into Lorna's eyes. "I don't know." She dropped onto the chair before the secretary, stared at a crystal pen holder and repeated, quieter, "I don't know."

If it was true, what could she do? Take the child? Raise him alone? Go to Jens and tell him? Every solution spawned a dozen more quandaries to which she truly had no answers. First she would find Hamburg Road and hope that Aunt Agnes's suspicions proved true.

She went by streetcar the following day, leaving her family believing she was volunteering at the lending library again. Changing cars twice, she traveled west toward Minneapolis, and through it to its far western reaches, disembarking at a place called Ridley Court, where she asked instructions in a chocolate shop, and once again from a man driving a Washburn and Crosby wagon loaded with flour barrels. Her walk terminated, after a good half hour, on a gravel road, where the houses were wideset and situated beside open country, with small barns and sheds in their backyards. Evidence of livestock wafted in the air, though she saw none. There were backyard pumps, and front yard pickets, and woodpiles stacked against sheds.

Number 850 was made of yellow brick, a modest house, narrow, with a deep overhanging roof supported by decorative white bargeboards that needed painting, just as the surrounding fence did. The gate squeaked as she opened it and navigated a plank walk between piles of snow. When she was midway up the walk a dog rose from a braided rug on the doorstep in the sun and barked at her twice. She paused and he came loping down the path, his tail wagging, to circle her and sniff at her rubber overshoes. He was shaggy and as yellow as the house, with a fluffy tail and a foxy face.

"Hello, boy," she said, offering her gloved hand for sniffing.

He looked up at her and wagged, and she proceeded toward the house with him accompanying.

At the door trepidation reared and sent her heartbeat thumping. If Aunt Agnes was right, the next few minutes could change her life forever. Poised to knock, she paused like a diver breathing deeply and measuring the distance down. Her throat felt constricted and the tops of her arms tingled as if her sleeves were too tight.

She knocked and waited.

The dog ambled to one side and ate a mouthful of snow. Drips fell from icicles on the eaves, drilling deep holes into the snow on either side of the door. Off in the unseen distance a crow scolded. An interior door opened and sucked the outer door against its frame. Through a thick lace curtain Lorna saw someone approach. Then the door opened and there stood Hulduh Schmitt, holding a dishtowel. When she saw Lorna her mouth and jowls went slack.

"Well . . . Miss Lorna."

"Hello, Mrs. Schmitt."

The dog went in but the two women remained motionless, Lorna in a red plaid coat with matching tam-o'-shanter, and Mrs. Schmitt in a great white starched apron just as she'd worn in the Barnett kitchens.

"May I come in?" Lorna inquired.

Mrs. Schmitt considered a moment, then seemed to resign herself, stepping back and waving Lorna inside with the dishtowel. "You might as well. You're here now."

Lorna stepped into an unheated entry no larger than a pantry.

"Go on inside," Mrs. Schmitt ordered, and followed her guest into the main body of the house, closing the door behind them. It was warm inside and smelled of freshly baked bread. Steep stairs climbed straight ahead against the right wall, and a stretch of hall separated the stairwell from two rooms on the left, the frontmost one a parlor visible through a wide archway.

An aged voice called from the room beyond it, in German.

In German, too, Mrs. Schmitt shouted a reply. "My mother," she explained to Lorna.

They could hear the old woman scolding the dog, probably for having wet feet. Lorna looked into the parlor, then back at Mrs. Schmitt.

"Is he here?" she asked simply.

"How did you find out?"

"Aunt Agnes figured it out."

"Your mother and father swore me to secrecy."

"Yes, I'm sure they did. Is he here?"

Hulduh thought about the generous monthly stipend that eased her retirement and provided for her mother. The fleeting thought brought not the slightest inclination to lie to Lorna Barnett about the child she'd brought into the world. Hulduh raised her hands in surrender and let them fall. "He's in the kitchen. This way."

The place was immaculately clean, filled with stolid old furniture and trimmed with crocheted doilies. The downstairs had only two rooms: the parlor at the front—it held an empty crib—connected by a doorway to the oversized kitchen at the back. In the latter, an ancient white-haired woman sat on a rocking chair shaking a homemade stocking doll before a beautiful blond baby. He sat suspended in a curious little hammocky seat which hung from a ring-shaped frame equipped with casters, his little feet—in booties—tiptoeing the floor. His hand was reaching toward the toy when Lorna entered the room—a chubby hand on a chubby arm with five perfect little outstretched fingers which closed upon the doll with the questionable coordination of an eight-month-old. At her appearance, he forgot the doll and looked toward the doorway: soft pale curls, eyes as blue as a Norse midnight, pudgy peachy face, and an innocent mouth as perfect and bowed as a cherub's. His perfection dulled all Lorna's surroundings. She moved toward him as if down a shaft of heavenly light.

"What's his name?"

"Daniel."

"Daniel . . ." she whispered, floating toward him.

"We call him Danny."

Lorna's eyes remained riveted on his fair little face as she dropped to her knees before his rolling chair, shy, yearning, uncertain. "Hello, Danny."

He stared at her, unblinking, his eyelashes curved and fine, a shade darker than his hair. He had so much of Jens in his features and so little of her.

She reached . . . took him slowly from the chair, his hand trailing the limp doll while he stared at her face and his legs and arms stuck out straight as a stuffed teddy bear's. "Oh, my beautiful one . . ." she whispered, as she brought his soft small body to her breast and placed her lips against his temple. ". . . I've found you at last."

She closed her eyes and held him, simply held him, allowing the moment to heal and hearten. He began babbling—"Mum-mum-mum"—and flailing the doll against her arm while she remained motionless, her eyes closed, transported to a plane of absolute maternal grace. He smelled milky and bready, like the room, and felt too soft for this world. She had not known love could feel this way, filling her so superabundantly that all the previous emotions of her life felt paltry by comparison. In that single moment of holding, feeling, smelling him, she was rendered complete.

She sat back on her haunches and stood him on her thighs, feeling her gaiety billow now that she knew he was here and really hers. He put a finger in one corner of his mouth, distorting it, showing two tiny bottom teeth, while continuing to flail the doll. Suddenly he seemed to realize he held it and grew animated, bobbing on his stubby legs and smacking her softly on the mouth with a wet hand. Laughing, she chased it with her lips, tipping her head back.

"He's so beautiful," she said to the two old women.

"And smart, too. He can say 'hot' already."

"Hot. Can you say 'hot,' Danny?"

His eyes got exuberant and he pointed a stubby finger at the big iron range. "Hottt."

"Yes, the stove's hot."

"Hottt," he said again, directly at Lorna's face.

"Smart boy! Is he good?" she asked.

"Oh yes, an angel. Sleeps all night long."

"And healthy?"

"Yes, that too, though he's been a little fretful lately 'cause he's teething."

"Are you teething? Getting pretty new teeth? Aw, mercy, but you're beautiful." She hugged him and swimbled left to right while joy sluiced in to replace her first awe. "Sweet, sweet boy!" And to the world at large, "I can't believe I'm holding him."

"He's drooling on your coat, Miss Lorna. Wouldn't you like to take it off?"

"Oh, I don't care! Let him drool! I'm just so happy!"

The dog, who'd been drinking across the room, gave himself an allover shake and came across the hardwood floor with clicking toenails and a friendly nose for the tot. Danny bounced and let out a shriek of welcome, lunging toward the animal.

"Oh, he loves old Summer. They're the best of pals."

The baby doubled over Lorna's arm and got the dog by the ruff, making burbling sounds, grabbing handfuls of hair.

"Noooo," Hulduh Schmitt warned, coming quickly to take the two chubby fists from the dog's fur. "Be nice to old Summer. Danny, be nice." He opened both fists and patted the dog clumsily, looking up at Hulduh for approval.

"That's a good boy."

They were simple displays—hot, nice—but to Lorna, prodigious, these first demonstrations of her baby's intelligence. During the while she remained she learned that Danny could stand on wobbly legs beside a chair while holding the seat, and point to his nose, and identify both Tante Hulduh and Grossmutter, and would point at them with a sausagey index finger when asked to.

Hulduh Schmitt said, "Mother and I were going to have our afternoon coffee, and there's fresh bread if you'd care to stay."

"Yes, please, I'd love it."

She set the table with well-used dishes designed with tulips and roses on an ivory background. Once long ago they'd been rimmed with gold but only faint chips of it remained. She apologized for not using a tablecloth. They were afraid, she explained, that the baby would accidentally pull it off someday and scald himself with their coffee. Indeed, while the women enjoyed their drinks and ate fresh bread and butter and peach sauce, Danny crawled around the claw-footed table, and played with wooden spoons on the floor, and pulled at the women's long skirts, and faked a little crying when he wanted to get up on a lap. The dog had retired to the back door rug and lay on his side, asleep. Once Danny crept over and poked at Summer's black lip and babbled. The dog raised its head, blinked once and went back to sleep. Hulduh got up and washed the baby's hands and put him in his rolling chair, where a circle of playthings were tied on with yarn.

The ancient woman spoke no English but smiled at the baby with her wrinkled eyes and wrinkled lips, and followed his every move, even over the rim of her coffee cup. Sometimes she'd bend over as best she could, to adjust his clothing, or give him the tiniest piece of soft buttery bread, or mutter something loving or instructive in her native tongue, and he'd go *whap! whap! whap!* with some toy against his chair, and the old grandmother would smile down at him, then at Lorna.

Once she asked Lorna a question; its meaning came through no matter the language barrier, as the old one pointed her gnarled finger first at Lorna, then at the child: "You are his *Mutter*?"

Lorna nodded and spread one hand on her stomach, the other on her heart, with a soulful expression on her face.

The baby grew tired of his rolling chair and was allowed to maneuver around on his own once more. He toppled over and clunked his head on the table foot and Lorna shot to rescue and embosom him. "Oh, noooo, don't cry . . . it's all right . . ." But he cried and strained toward Hulduh Schmitt, and the old woman took him on her ample lap, where he settled down and got his face wiped off, and received a sip of her creamy, sugary coffee off the end of a spoon. Then he rested his head against the starched white bib of her apron and stuck a thumb in his mouth and stared at the wainscot. "He's tired. He didn't nap long."

Lorna wondered how long a nap was required by an eight-month-old. And what one did if he fell down and *really* split his head open. And how a person learned everything she needed to know about mothering if her own mother chose to shun her.

Danny's eyelids began drooping and his lower lip lost its grip on his thumb. Mrs. Schmitt took him into the parlor and tucked him to sleep in his crib.

Returning, she refilled their cups and asked, "Now that you've found him, what do you intend to do?"

Lorna set down her cup very carefully and looked the old cook in the eye. "He's my son," she replied quietly.

"You want to take him, then."

"Yes . . . I do."

Hulduh Schmitt's face seemed to grow puffy and pale, perhaps even slightly afraid. She glanced at her mother, who was nodding off in the rocking chair.

"They'll stop the money if you do. My mother is old and I'm the only one she's got."

"Yes, I . . . I'm sorry, Mrs. Schmitt."

"And the baby is happy here with us."

"Oh, I can see that. I can!" Lorna laid a hand on her heart. "But he's my son. He was taken from me against my wishes."

The old cook's face registered shock. "Against your wishes?"

"Yes. My mother came when he was born, and they told me they were taking him away to have his first bath, only I never saw him again. When I asked to see him, he was gone and so was Mother. Now, that isn't right, Mrs. Schmitt, it just isn't right."

Mrs. Schmitt covered Lorna's hand on the table. "No, child, it isn't. Nor was I told the truth. They said you didn't want him."

"Oh, but I do. It's just that I must . . ." Lorna swallowed and glanced toward the parlor. "Well, I must find a place for him, and a way to take care of him. I must . . . I must speak to his father."

"You'll pardon me, miss, but I can't help asking—might that be young Jens?"

Lorna's expression grew sad. "Yes. And I love him very much, but they wouldn't hear of my marrying him." She ended bitterly, "His family doesn't have a summer place on the lake, you see."

Mrs. Schmitt studied the creamy skin on the surface of her coffee dregs. "Ah, life. It's so hard. So much sorrow. . . . So much."

They thought of it while the baby napped and the old woman quietly snored, her head bobbing and jerking occasionally.

"I can't take him with me today," Lorna said.

"Well then, that's something, anyway." Longing already showed in the old woman's eyes.

It was Lorna's turn to lay her hand on Mrs. Schmitt's. "When I get settled and have a place, you can come and see him as often as you wish."

But they both knew it was unlikely, considering Mrs. Schmitt's age, and the length of the walk and the streetcar rides, and the old woman who couldn't be left alone for long.

"When I take him . . ." Lorna hesitated, unable to brush aside the nagging sense of responsibility she felt for the two women's welfare. "Will you be able to make it all right without the extra money?"

Mrs. Schmitt pulled her chins in, her shoulders back and said to her coffee cup, "I've got a little put by."

When Lorna rose to leave, the grandmother awakened, dried the corners of her mouth and looked around as if wondering where she was. She saw Lorna and gave a sleepy smile, nodding goodbye.

"Goodbye," Lorna said.

On her way through the parlor she kissed the downy head of her son. "Bye-bye, dear one, I'll be back," she whispered, and quailed at the thought that she must once again visit his father.

Chapter 18

The next day dawned bitter cold and windy. Dressing for her trip to White Bear Lake, Lorna took extreme care, selecting far different clothing from the last time she went. Then, she had worn the girlish outfit meant to evoke nostalgia. Now she felt far from girlish, far from nostalgic. She had suffered, matured, learned. She would face Jens as a woman fighting for happiness at the most significant juncture of her life. She dressed in a somber wool suit covered by a heavy black sealskin coat with a matching muff and a plain wool bonnet.

The countryside from the train window looked indistinct, as if viewed through lace. Snow slanted across the landscape, dissecting it into blurred diagonals that shimmered and shifted as the train rumbled through it. Woods, fields, frozen streams—all appeared grayed and vague.

The railroad car was cold. Lorna crossed her legs, tucked her coat tightly around them and watched her breath rime the window. Projecting to her meeting with Jens, she wondered, *What will I say?* But one did not rehearse dialogue as grave as this. She was no longer the moony, lovestruck jo who had courted the kitchen helper and hauled picnic lunches off to forbidden peccadillos with him. She was a mother—foremost—and a wronged one at that.

Danny's precious face appeared in her memory with its wheat-white hair, watercolor-blue eyes and his father's features. Love rose in a remarkable swell that filled her eyes with tears and pushed fear through her veins at the thought of never having him.

At the station she rented a sleigh and driver to take her around the north shore of the lake to Dellwood. Tucked beneath a fur lap robe with the snow stinging her face, she scarcely heard the endless note played by the runners on the snow, nor the bells on the harness, nor the *whuf-whuf-whuf* of the horse's breath. Her senses were all turned inward to thoughts of Jens and Danny and herself.

She made out Jens's building as they approached it through the needles of white, a giant New England barn of a place, painted the same green as most yachts, with HARKEN BOATWORKS painted in white on its huge triangular side. Beneath the sign immense sliding doors hung on a metal track. To the left of these a smaller door held a sign, saying, "Open."

"Here you are, miss," the driver announced, pulling up.

"I'd like you to wait, please."

"Yes, ma'am. I'll just tie Ronnie up. Now, you take your time."

How many times since meeting Jens Harken had she approached a door with trepidation beating in her throat? The door of the servants' steps leading down to the kitchen. That of the shed where he'd built the *Lorna D.* The door of his own bedroom to which she'd sneaked in the dead of night to spend stolen hours in his bed. The open double doors on the opposite side of this very building last summer, when she'd had to tell him that Danny had been stolen. And yesterday, the door of that yellow brick house with the dog out front and the hope that she'd find their son inside.

Now she faced another, and the same apprehension she'd felt on all those occasions had multiplied a hundredfold, clubbing at her vitals, warning that if this failed, her life would ever after be shadowed by the loss of this man she loved.

She drew a deep breath, lifted the black metal latch and stepped inside.

As always the place in which Jens Harken worked beleaguered her with memories and brought the past sweeping back—damp fir, fresh planed cedar and burning wood. She saw a boat half finished and another that seemed to be under repair. At the far end of the cavernous building someone was whistling in a warbling fashion. Others were speaking and their voices carried as in a church. Jens's enterprise had grown: Six men toiled now over boats, molds, sails and rigging. One of them noticed her and said, "Someone to see you, Jens."

He was bending a rib with his brother, Davin, and looked over his shoulder to find her at the door.

As always, there passed that first impact of stunned motionlessness before he could mask his face with indifference.

"Take over here, Iver," he said to one of his workers, and left his station to come to her. He wore a red plaid flannel shirt, open at the throat, rolled up at the cuffs, showing the placket and sleeves of his winter underwear. His hair was longer than she'd ever seen it, curling away from a side part, whisking around his ears. His face was the mold from which their son's had been cast. He kept it devoid of all expression as he stopped before her.

"Hello, Jens."

"Lorna," he replied smilelessly, removing his wet leather gloves, letting his eyes scan her face for only the briefest second before dropping to the gloves.

"I wouldn't have come, but it's important."

"What?" The curt word left little chance of mistaking his enmity.

"Could we talk somewhere privately?"

"You've come to say something—say it."

"Very well. I've found our son."

For the space of a heartbeat he looked stupefied, but he recovered swiftly and donned his stoic face again. "So?"

"So? That's all you've got to say is so?"

"Well, what do you want me to say? You're the one who—"

The door opened and her driver came in, shimmying his shoulders from the cold, closing the door behind him.

"Afternoon," he greeted when he saw them nearby.

"Afternoon," replied Jens, tight-lipped and unbiddable.

"Bit nippy out there." The driver looked from one to the other, aware that he'd stepped into something tense. "You don't mind if I wait in here where it's warm, do you? I'm driving the lady."

Jens nodded sideways toward the stove. "There's coffee on the fender and mugs on the pegs. Help yourself."

The driver went away unwinding a plaid scarf from around his neck.

"Come on," Jens ordered, stalking away and leaving Lorna to follow. He led her into his office, a ten-by-ten cubicle jammed with sailing paraphernalia surrounding a messy desk. Slamming the door, he rounded on her.

"All right, so you found him. What do you want me to do about it?"

"For starters, you might ask about his welfare."

"His welfare! Ha! Now's a fine time for you to be lecturing me about his welfare, after you gave him away!"

"I did not give him away! They took him and hid him out with Hulduh Schmitt in the country on the other side of Minneapolis!"

"Hulduh Schmitt!" He glowered.

"She's had him all this time. My parents are paying her to keep him."

"So what do you want me to do, go to Hulduh's and steal him back for you? Go into town and beat up your daddy? I tried that once and I got put out on my ass!"

"I don't expect you to do anything! I just thought—"

He waited a beat before replying sardonically, "You just thought I might beg you to marry me again and we could go collect him and make a cozy little threesome, hiding from all your high society friends for the rest of our lives, is that it?" She blushed while he raged on. "Well, let me tell you something, Lorna Barnett. I don't want to be anybody's husband on suffrance. When I marry a woman she's got to accept me unconditionally. I'm not high society but I'm no lowlife, either. When I came to that abbey and asked you to marry me I came offering you a damned decent future, nothing you'd have to hang your head about. I expected you to fight for me, to tell your parents once and for all to go to the devil, and to stand up for your rights . . . for *our* rights! But no, you whimpered and curled up and decided you just couldn't face the names they might call you if you showed up at the altar pregnant with my baby. Well, so be it. You wouldn't have me then—I won't have you now."

"Oh, you think it's so easy, don't you!" she spit, lowering her head like a she-cat facing a tom. "Big, bullheaded Norwegian he-man with your pride all hurt and your chin jutting out! Well, you try living with parents like mine! You try getting them to give just one inch on anything! You try falling in love with the wrong man and ending up—"

"The wrong man! That's for sure!"

"Yes, the wrong man!" she yelled louder. "And ending up carrying his bastard, and being shipped off to Timbuktu and manipulated and lied to and told over and over and over again what hell your life will be if people find out about it. You try living in an abbey with a gaggle of neuter women, who pray for your salvation in whispers until you want to scream at them to go get a little lusty themselves and see how they handle it! You try having two younger sisters and being reminded in every letter from your mother how you'll horrify them if word of your pregnancy leaks out, and how you'll ruin their chances of finding a decent husband because your shame will rub off on them. You try getting it through some man's thick Norwegian skull that at least *some* of this is not your fault, that you're human just like everyone else, and you fall in love and you make mistakes and you get hurt and you try your best to make things right, but you can't always do that so easily. You try it, Jens Harken!" Her insides were trembling by the time she finished.

He held up two fingers beneath her nose. "Twice I asked you to marry me—twice! But what did you say?"

She slapped his fingers away. "I said what the circumstances forced me to say!"

"You said no, because you were ashamed of me!"

"I was not! I was scared!"

"So was I." He tapped his chest. "But that didn't stop me from fighting for you! And that's some pretty damned flimsy excuse for how you acted!"

"Oh, you're so self-righteous you make me sick! I found Danny again, didn't I? I found him and I told Mrs. Schmitt I'm going to take him, and I will—with or without you I will, and I'll raise him if I have to do it by myself!"

"Oh, that's some big talk from a girl who's scared of her mommy and daddy's shadow. You told *me* you were going to raise him, too, but when it came right down to it you knuckled under to the Barnett commandment: Honor thy father and mother, even if they're wrong as hell and ruining your life!"

She stepped back, her mouth cinched. "I can see I made a mistake by coming here."

"You made the mistake when you decided not to meet that train. And a bigger one when you said no at the abbey. Now you can live with it."

She pulled decorum around herself like a fine fur stole and spoke levelly. "It strikes me, Jens, that I really never knew you. I knew one side of you, but it's more than that a wife's got to live with. You're more like my father than you can imagine, and that's the last sort of man I'd want to marry!"

She sallied out and slammed the door.

He stared at it through popping eyes for ten full seconds before dropping to his spring-mounted desk chair. First he glared at the cubbyholes before him, then gripped the top of his head with both hands and rammed the chair back as far as it would go, slurring her to the ceiling. He snorted aloud and let the chair spring forward, depositing him at the kneehole of the desk. A drawer was open to his right. He gave it a whack, attempting to slam it shut. It stuck. He whacked it again . . . harder! And harder still, hurting his hand! "Goddamn sonofabitch!" he railed, kicking the drawer so violently it countersank itself in its fitting.

Then he rocketed from the chair, rubbing his hands down his face while his turmoil fermented with anger, self-disgust, frustrated love and the heart-whumping news that his son's name was Danny and he could be reached in a couple of hours' ride.

He held out for three weeks, thinking, What good would it do to see the baby, he'd only want to take him, father him, never return him.

In the end paternal passion won out.

Mrs. Schmitt answered the door, not a hair different from when they'd worked together in the kitchen at Rose Point.

"Well . . ." she said, "I should have known you'd show up eventually."

"Been a long time, huh, Mrs. Schmitt?"

"You might as well come in, too. All the rest of his relatives have. It's beyond me why they thought I could keep him a secret."

He followed her inside and she awakened the baby from his nap. When Jens saw Danny the first time—oh, what a feeling! Stars seemed to be bursting and burning within him. Suns seemed to be glowing where once only his heart had been. He took the bleary-eyed child from Mrs. Schmitt's arms, held him high and kissed him, and soothed him when he cried, still shaky from sleep and discombobulated by his premature rousing. Jens held him on his arm—a warm little snail smelling of urine—and bounced him gently, strolled awhile, kissing his forehead and calming him in a remarkably short time.

He stayed the afternoon, meeting the old German woman who spent most of her time in the kitchen rocker; eating streusel, drinking coffee, acquainting with his son.

Hulduh Schmitt said, "His mother told you where he was, I suppose."

"Yes."

"Actually, I expected you sooner."

"I didn't know if I should come or not. Pretty hard to walk away from him."

"She says the same thing every time she leaves." Jens made no reply, only studied Hulduh Schmitt's droopy cheeks with a younger droop on his own.

"She comes every Thursday," Hulduh added.

"I was afraid she might have taken him already. She said she was going to."

"She wants to, but what's she going to do with him? A girl so young with no man to support her. The way I see it, that's your job. You ought to marry that girl, Jens Harken."

"Ehh . . . that wouldn't work out, her being the old man's daughter and me starting out as their kitchen help. We should have seen that right from the start."

Mrs. Schmitt nodded, though her expression remained dubious. "Well, he's a fine little boy, and I love him to high heaven. I'm not denying that the money I get from the Barnetts makes my life a lot easier, but as far as I'm concerned, it's a crime Danny ain't with his own mama and papa."

The following Thursday Mrs. Schmitt said, "Your man was here."

Lorna's head snapped up before she forced herself to show disdain. "Took him long enough."

"Left some money under his coffee cup. I told him your father pays me more than fair, but he left it anyway. I thought you should have it."

"No, he gave it to you."

"Your father pays me once. It wouldn't be fair to take money twice for the same job. Here . . ." She waggled her hand. "Take it."

Lorna looked balefully at the folded bills Mrs. Schmitt held out. Her anger smoldered. Damned bullheaded Norwegian ass! And that's where he could stuff it as far as she was concerned. It was nothing but conscience money, anyway.

In the end she snapped it out of Mrs. Schmitt's fingers and tucked it into her waistpocket.

"When was he here?"

"Tuesday."

"Is he coming back?"

"Next Tuesday, he said."

The following Tuesday Mrs. Schmitt said, "I gave the money to your woman."

"It was meant for the baby," Jens said.

"Oh, was it? Well, I didn't know. Miss Lorna took it anyhow."

When Jens left there were more folded bills beneath his coffee cup.

Through the remainder of that late winter Mrs. Schmitt grew accustomed to seeing them on their chosen days—Tuesdays and Thursdays—and her heart went out to the two of them, who seemed unable to find a way to mend their differences and become a family.

April came and Lorna continued badgering everyone who would listen to open up a new paid position at the lending library which she hoped to fill, meanwhile squirreling away the money from Jens.

May knocked, and the cottage owners of White Bear prepared to estivate there once again. On the day before the Barnett family was to leave for the summer, adding all those additional miles to her trips to visit Danny, Lorna went to see him one last time.

By now she was accustomed to rapping on the door and letting herself in, which she did as usual that warm spring day, knocking first, then calling, "Hello, every-one!" as she went through the hall and front room. She could hear the hand agitator going on a washing machine and realized Hulduh had probably not heard her call.

She stepped into the kitchen and there stood Jens holding Danny while Hulduh washed clothes.

She came up short, her heart performing some wild dance in her breast.

"Oh," she said, blushing, "I didn't know you were here."

"I thought you always came on Thursdays."

"Well, I usually do, but my family is leaving for the lake tomorrow and I'm going along. Since it'll mean extra train time to see Danny after this . . . well . . ." Her explanation faded into silence.

He blushed, too. He did! Standing there holding their son on his muscular arm, the two of them as blond and alike as golden lab puppies in a litter, Jens Harken blushed.

The baby saw Lorna and got excited. "Mama, Mama!" he jabbered, bucking in his father's hold, reaching for her. She set down her package and rushed forward, smiling, taking him from Jens's arm for the first time ever.

"Hello, darling! Mmm . . ." She kissed his cheek and whirled once, devoting all her attention to him while the two old women looked on, Grossmutter from her rocker and Hulduh from her wooden washing machine, where she was working the agitator with a long wooden handle.

Hulduh said, "He missed you since you were here last time. He said Mama every day."

"Did you say Mama?"

"Mama," the baby repeated.

"I've brought you something wonderful. Look!" She sat down at the kitchen table with Danny in her lap and began untying the package. He lunged at the white paper circled with store string and slapped it a couple of times with his pudgy hands, burbling baby talk that made no sense. "Here, let me open it so you can see." She was struggling with the string and the rambunctious baby when Jens came to her rescue, saying, "Here, let me hold him while you do that."

As he plucked Danny off her lap Lorna looked up and her eyes met Jens's. The impact went through her like a wish. She was aware for that fleeting second of his freshly shaved face and his cedary smell, his crisply ironed shirt, blue blue eyes, his very beautiful mouth and the fact that they were sharing their baby for the first time ever. And on some existential level she was aware of the rhythm of the wooden agitator going *shup, shup, shup* somewhere in the room.

Softly, Jens told her, "Open it," and to their son, "Look, your mama's brought something for you."

His voice, calling her Mama, seemed to addle her hands. They grew clumsy while her face took color. She finally broke the string and produced a small white teddy bear with black button eyes, nappy fur and a real leather nose.

Danny reached for it eagerly as Jens returned him to Lorna's lap. The baby studied the toy, babbled, "Buh-duh," looked up at his mother for affirmation and claimed it for his own while his mother and father looked on.

"I bought it with your money," Lorna told Jens, keeping her eyes downcast. "I hope you don't mind."

"No, I don't."

"I've never bought him anything before."

"Neither have I."

She wanted to meet his eyes but was afraid. Her feelings were running very close to the surface and kept a faint blush on her cheek. They concentrated on the baby while Mrs. Schmitt gave up agitating for wringing, and wringing for rinsing, and finally Lorna had the sense to offer, "Oh, here, Mrs. Schmitt, let me help you!"

"Aw, no, you just play with the baby. You get little enough chance."

"Why, don't be silly! While you're washing his diapers? It's the least I can do." She gave the baby to Jens, removed her hat, rolled up her sleeves and helped Mrs. Schmitt slosh the batch of diapers up and down in a galvanized washtub, then guide them through a wringer while the older woman operated a hand crank. When the batch was done, lying like pressed snakes in the oval clothes basket, Lorna asked, "May I hang them?"

"Well, it don't seem right, you in your pretty dress. And look, you've got it all wet."

Lorna brushed at her skirts. "Oh, I don't mind—really, I don't. And I'd love to hang the diapers."

"Well, all right, if you really want to. Clothespins are in a bag on the end of the clothesline."

With the clothes basket on her left hip, Lorna escaped Jens's rattling presence and stepped out the back door into the warm spring sunshine of a cloudless blue day. There, she could breathe deeper and regain common sense. This was a chance meeting, not an assignation. She, Jens and Danny were sundered individuals, not a family. It was silly to pretend otherwise.

The yard spread out to the west, where a small red barn and privy divided it from some grassland beyond. Farther to the west a section of thick woods created a deeper line of green. The dog, Summer, was napping in the sun beside the stone foundation of the barn, lying in a sandy nest he'd scratched among some freshly sprouted irises. Between the house and the barn a dirt path was worn in the grass. To the right of it a garden patch was already tilled, giving off a faint tinge of manure. A wooden wheelbarrow stood beside it filled with seed potatoes. Against the barrow leaned a hoe and a hand cultivator. To the left of the path the clothesline stood halfway down the yard, nestled between two immense clumps of blooming lilac bushes.

Lorna set down the basket and picked up a diaper, flat and stiff from the wringer. Never in her life had she hung clothing on a line. Where she came from, servants did that. But she'd seen the maids hanging towels and did as they had: She found two corners and gave the first diaper a snap, hung it . . . and another . . . and found she enjoyed it immensely, the wind tugging at her hair and the damp gauze filling like a sail, lifting against her face, bringing the smell of fresh lye soap. There was a sense of peace in the scene—the dog asleep in the sun, the lilacs scenting the air, some sparrows fluttering into the lilac bushes to explore and Lorna . . . handling her son's diapers.

She was hanging the third one when Jens came out the back door and started down the path. At his approach, she turned her back and bent over the wicker basket to pick up another diaper. When she straightened, he was standing beneath the T-shaped clothespole, gripping it loosely above his head with both hands.

She snapped the diaper and hung it.

Finally he said, "So you come here every week."

"As Mrs. Schmitt informed you."

"I usually come on Tuesdays, but I have to go to Duluth this Tuesday." She made no reply. "Fellow up there is commissioning a boat." Still she made no reply.

She hung up another diaper while Jens tried to pretend he wasn't watching her. Finally he gave up the pretense and pinned his gaze on her profile as she raised her face and arms to place two clothespins above her head. Her breasts—fuller than before the baby's birth—showed distinctly against the backdrop of green field. The profile of her lips and mouth had become—if anything—prettier during the two years he'd known her. Her face was that of a mature woman now, not a girl. The wind had tugged a strand of her hair loose and fluttered it gently along her jaw. A diaper billowed toward her shoulder and she pushed it away absently while reaching for another. He thought about the child he'd left in the house, coming from within the two of them.

"He's the prettiest thing I've ever seen," Jens said sincerely, softened by the presence of the three of them together for the first time ever.

"He's going to look just like you."

"That'd be something, wouldn't it?"

"Probably be bullheaded just like you, too."

"Yeah, well, I'm Norwegian." He frowned at the distant woods for a long time. Finally he dropped his hands and dusted his palms together, searching for something to say. A good half minute passed without anything coming to mind. He shifted his feet and muttered, "Damn it, Lorna . . ."

She shot him a look. "Damn it, Lorna, what?" The crack of a diaper punctuated her words while the set of her jaw grew belligerent. "I suppose you're upset about me taking your money."

"No, it's not that!"

"Well, what then?"

"I don't know what." After some agitated silence he asked, "Do your folks know you come out here to see him?"

"No. They think I'm working in a lending library."

"You see? You still won't admit anything to them. You're still living under their thumb."

"Well, what do you expect me to do!"

"Nothing," he said, and started back toward the house. "Nothing."

She kicked the clothes basket out of her way and went after him. "Damn you, Jens Harken!" She clunked him between the shoulder blades with her fist. "Don't you turn away from me!"

He spun around in surprise. She was standing defiantly with both hands on her hips, a clothespin clenched in one, and tears in her stormy brown eyes. She had never looked more beautiful.

"Ask me!" she ordered. "Damn you, you bullheaded Norwegian, you ask me!"

But he would not. Not until she realized that she had still never put him first before her parents. She could love him as long as nobody else knew, but that wasn't enough for him.

"Not until you defy them."

"I can't afford to! Even the money from you isn't enough for Danny and me to live on!"

"Then make your peace with them."

"Never!"

"All right then, we're at a stalemate."

"You love me! Don't tell me you don't!"

"That was never the issue. The issue was did you love me?"

"Did I love you! Jens Harken, I was the one who did all the pursuing. Are you going to stand there and deny it? *I* came to the kitchen! *I* came to the boat shed! *I* came to your room!"

"Until you got pregnant, then you tried to hide it and me from everyone you knew. You're still trying to hide it. How do you think that makes me feel?"

"How do you think it makes me feel, having to sneak off into the country to see my own son because I haven't got a husband?"

"You still don't understand what it is you've got to do, do you?"

"Besides stand here and make a fool of myself? No . . . no, I don't!"

He couldn't help it: He grinned. The situation was pitiful but she looked splendid, standing there in the dirt path with her hair blowing and her temper fired. Sweet Jesus, how easy it would be to take three steps and grab her waist and plunk her right up against the front of himself, where she belonged, and kiss the daylights out of her and say, Let's take Danny and go.

And then what? Live a life of lies, maybe telling people the child was adopted—anything so she could save face?

He'd have her come public with the truth, or nothing.

So he stood there grinning, because she looked so fetching, and he wanted her so badly, and she'd just admitted she loved him and felt like a fool for it.

"What are you grinning at!"

"You."

"Well, stop it!"

"You said it, I didn't. If you're feeling like a fool maybe there's a good reason."

Without warning she fired a clothespin. It pinged off his forehead and landed in the grass.

"Ouch!" he yelped, lurching back, scowling. "What the hell was that for?" He nursed his forehead.

"I wouldn't marry you now if my parents asked me to!"

He backed up a step and dropped his hand. "And since we both know that will never happen, we're right back where we started before this argument began." He turned and headed back toward the house. Ten feet up the path, he paused and did an about-face. "I suggest you stick to Thursdays from now on."

She fired another clothespin. It flew past his shoulder and dropped harmlessly to the ground behind him. In the wake of her paltry effort to hurt him they stood for five terrible heartbeats, staring at each other defiantly.

"Grow up, Lorna," he said quietly, then turned and left her alone in the sunny yard.

When the kitchen door closed behind him it seemed to unleash her tears. She swiped them away with her sleeve and marched back to the clothesline to hang the last diaper. She plucked it from the basket, gave it a snap and was lifting her hands toward the clothesline when the torrent struck. It hit with the force of a spring flood—tears and sobs wrenching her entire body until she went as limp as the gauze in her hands. She let it happen, sorrow and self-pity spilling out and wallowing into the green and gold spring day. She dropped to both knees and doubled forward, knotting the cool damp diaper in her fists as she rocked mindlessly.

And cried . . . and cried . . . and cried . . .

And scared the sparrows away.

Chapter 19

The days following her encounter with Jens left Lorna truly miserable. Seeing Danny at last with his father had left within her a living picture of the three of them that she embroidered in her imagination until it became more real than reality. In it, she, Jens and Danny lived in the loft above the boatworks; the diapers on the line were Danny's; at noon she cooked Jens dinner; in the evening the three of them sailed; at night she and Jens slept together in a great wooden bed.

Realizing this would probably never evolve, she cried often.

The next time she went to Mrs. Schmitt's, Jens was absent and her reunion with Danny seemed lacking and sad. Her days had grown empty and pointless and seemed to be leading into nothing but more of the same.

Then one day she was in a mercantile store in White Bear Lake and ran into Mitch Armfield.

"Lorna?"

At the sound of her name she turned and found him in the aisle behind her.

"Mitch," she said, smiling. "My goodness, Mitch, is that you?" He'd grown so much in the past two years. He was tall and strapping and already wearing a summer tan, a handsome young adult where a blushing boy had been before.

He grinned and spread his hands. "It's me."

"Where's the skinny young boy who used to want to teach me to sail?"

"Still sailing—how about you?"

"Still sailing, too, but mostly in the catboat alone."

"So we notice. Seems like you're never around anymore."

"I am. I just . . ." She let the thought trail, glancing aside and absently touching some fancy tea towels.

He waited politely, but when she remained silent, he spoke. "Everybody says where's Lorna when we go on the moonlight sails and over to the pavilion for concerts. Especially Phoebe."

Lorna looked up and asked wistfully, "How's Phoebe?"

"Phoebe's all right . . . but she misses you terribly."

"I miss her, too. We used to do so much together."

Mitchell's face became intent with thought before he inquired, "May I be honest, Lorna?"

"Why, of course."

"You broke Phoebe's heart. After you went away to school you never wrote to her, or called on her when you got back. She thought she must have done something to hurt you, but she didn't know what it was. Was she right?"

"No . . . oh no," Lorna replied heartfully, touching Mitch's sleeve. "She was my dearest friend."

"Then, what happened?"

Lorna could only stare at him and drop her hand from his arm. Time lengthened, and Mitchell pressed his point. "I know she missed you a lot when she became engaged and began making wedding plans. She said the two of you used to be the closest of confidantes about things like that. I know she'd love it if you could be again."

"So would I," Lorna whispered.

Sincerity shone from her face. Her eyes held a deep sadness that keyed in Mitchell a responsive sympathy. Whatever Lorna's reason for abandoning her friendship with Phoebe, it had hurt her as much as it had hurt his sister.

Mitchell extended his hand.

"Well . . . it was nice running into you. May I tell Phoebe I did?"

"Absolutely. And please give her my love."

He squeezed Lorna's hand affectionately. "I'll do that."

The conversation lingered on Lorna's mind for the remainder of the day. That night it stole her sleep and she arose from bed in the wee hours to sit on her window seat staring out across the dark water, analyzing why she'd cut herself off from Phoebe. It was senseless, really, to deny oneself the comfort of true friendship at a time in life when it was most needed. Was it shame that had held her aloof? Yes, she supposed it was. Her mother had said people would be shocked and horrified, and that she, Lorna, would be ostracized for bearing a baby out of wedlock. But would *Phoebe* be horrified? Would she cut off Lorna's friendship? The answer was no. Deep down in Lorna's heart she didn't believe her lifelong friend would act that way. Curiously enough, it was Lorna who'd done the ostracizing and she had no explanation why.

The following day Lorna awakened weary and puffy-eyed from lack of sleep. Inside, however, she was flustered with anticipation. Her decision had been made near four in the morning, and she rose hurrying, as if too long had been wasted already.

Anxious to see Phoebe once again, she declined breakfast, selected clothing, held a cold compress to her eyes, pouffed her hair up in a "Gibson girl" nest, dressed in a green-leafed skirt and a white shirtwaist, and at ten-thirty that morning presented herself at the door of the Armfield cottage. When Phoebe descended the stairs at the maid's summons and found Lorna waiting, her footsteps faltered. Her face withered as if she might break into tears, then she rushed down the last three steps into Lorna's arms.

"Oh, Lorna . . . Is it really you?"

"Phoebe, darling, yes, yes . . . I'm back."

They held each other and thrived for the moment on nostalgia. They grew misty-eyed, happy, and healed.

At last Phoebe drew back. "Mitch said he spoke to you, but I didn't dare hope."

"He certainly did, and made me see the light. We're overdue for a good long talk and I think it's time we had it."

The two went upstairs arm in arm, into Phoebe's room, where nothing had changed. The view out the turret was as splendid as ever, and the crocheted tester above Phoebe's bed the same one Lorna had flopped back and studied during many confidential girlhood exchanges.

"It's so good to be here again!" she exclaimed, walking to the window and looking out for a minute before turning to face the room and her friend. "I can't even remember the last time."

"Summer before last."

"Ah yes, summer before last, the year I first met Jens. So much has happened to me since then."

"Will you tell me?"

"Yes . . . everything."

"Come . . . sit." Phoebe stood her bedpillows up against the headboard and made herself a place at the foot of the bed. They both removed their slippers and sat cross-legged, facing each other.

Lorna smiled and said, "You first. I have a feeling your story is much happier than mine."

"All right. He's handsome and kind and outrageous and hard-working, and the first time I saw him I felt as if my guts got wrapped around my windpipe and choked me every time I tried to swallow."

Lorna laughed and said, "Your Mr. Slatterleigh."

"Dennis, yes."

"You're truly in love, then."

"So truly that I feel as if I'm dying every time he says good night and walks away."

"Oh, I'm so happy for you. When's the wedding?"

"Not soon enough. The last week in June. I wanted you to be one of my bridesmaids, but I was afraid to ask you. Then the time came for making plans and ordering gowns and you had become so withdrawn and stand-offish . . ."

"I know. And I'm so sorry for that, Phoebe. Mitch said you thought you'd done something to hurt my feelings but it wasn't that at all. It was me . . . just me . . . and my situation, that's all."

"What situation?"

Lorna's face took on a faraway expression. She gazed into the distance. "I've often wondered if you didn't figure it out—after all, you knew me so well." Her eyes returned to Phoebe. "We knew practically everything about each other's personal feelings."

"It was Jens Harken, the boatbuilder, of course."

"Yes . . . of course. We fell in love that summer he was building the *Lorna D.*"

"And?"

"And I had his baby."

Phoebe neither gasped nor cringed. She released a breath as if she'd been holding it in preparation for the revelation. Then she bent forward and offered both her hands for holding.

Lorna accepted them.

"So you weren't away at school."

"No, I was at an abbey near Milwaukee with a bunch of nuns." The whole story tumbled out with no detail omitted. Reaching the part about her painful meeting with Jens at Mrs. Schmitt's house the previous week, Lorna was trembling and battling tears. "And so . . ." she ended, ". . . he left me there in the yard."

Phoebe asked, "Did you mean it when you said you wouldn't marry him if your parents asked you to?"

"No," Lorna replied in a small voice. "I was upset so I blurted out the first thing that came into my mind. Marrying him is all I dream about."

She dreamed about it again for a passing moment while Phoebe watched the expression change in Lorna's eyes.

"I remember something you told me once, long ago, that first summer you met him. Remember the day we were sitting in the garden and you first confessed to me that you loved him? You were so sure of it, and your face became so serene when you told me. Then you said something that I never forgot. You said being with him made life suddenly feel more meaningful, and that when he left you it was the November of your heart."

"Did I say that?"

"Yes, you did, with such a beautiful and martyred look in your eyes. I was so sure that someday you'd find a way to be together with him, in spite of anything your parents might do or say. It seemed that you *should* be married to him. I've never stopped thinking so."

"Oh, Phoebe, I want to be . . . so much."

"Then do something about it."

"Do what? He's over there, and I'm over here and my parents haven't changed their stand one bit—"

"Of course they haven't. And if you wait around for them to do so, you'll wait your life away. Jens was right when he said that if you loved him enough you'd defy them. If it were me, I would."

"Defy your parents?"

"For the man I love? Absolutely."

"But, Phoebe, Jens said—"

"Yes, Jens said, then you said, then he said and you said, and you both were so upset and angry and stubborn that you weren't making sense. The fact remains that you love each other. You have a baby you want to call your own. Your parents have preached shame and fear and you fell for it, hook, line and sinker. Instead of telling *them* to go fly a kite, you told Jens to."

"I did not, Phoebe! How can you say that?"

"Well, it amounts to the same thing. You chose your parents over him, didn't you?"

"No I didn't!"

"Oh, Lorna, stop deluding yourself and listen to what Jens is saying. As long as you keep hiding the truth, and hiding the baby, and hiding your love for him, you're saying he's not good enough to meet your family's standards. If you want him, show him! Get Danny from Mrs. Schmitt's house and . . . and march up to your mother and father and say, 'Look, you can accept my baby, and accept my choice of a husband, or I'm walking out of your life forever.' "

"I did tell them that once."

"Yes, but did you follow it up or were you only blowing hot air? You're still living with them, aren't you? You haven't given them any ultimatums, have you? Well, if I were you, I'd do it! I'd . . . I'd . . ." Phoebe had grown more and more animated as she preached. She was on her feet, stirring the air with both hands and pacing beside the bed. "I'd take Danny out someplace in public where—"

"In public?"

"Yes, in public, like . . . like the regatta, maybe, and I'd—"

"The regatta?"

"—hold him on my arm and point to his father's boat—"

"Don't be silly."

"—and say, 'See your father sail? See the boat he built? He's the most famous boatbuilder in America, and I'm here to let the world know I've made my choice!' "

Silence fell in Phoebe's room. The idea was so outrageous it left both women breathless. They stared at each other, smitten by vivid images of Lorna doing such a brash thing.

Lorna whispered. "Would you really, Phoebe?"

"I don't know." Phoebe dropped to the bed. "I was just rambling, imagining . . . trying to find some answer for you."

"But *would* you?"

Phoebe gazed at Lorna. Lorna gazed back. Neither of them blinked.

Phoebe asked, almost secretively, "Gosh, Lorna, would *you?*"

It seemed too reckless to ponder, but ponder they did until their cheeks turned pink with excitement.

"It would be something, wouldn't it, Lorna? You, with Danny on your arm . . ."

"While my father skipped the *Lorna D* . . ."

"And your mother watched from the yacht club lawn . . ."

"And Jens skipped—what boat is he skipping this year?" Lorna's exhilaration was clear.

"The *Manitou.*"

"The *Manitou.*" After a beat of silence, Lorna asked, "Is he expected to win?"

"Nobody knows. Rumor has it there'll be ten flat-bottomed boats entered, including your father's. But rumor also has it that Jens has made some modifications to Tim's boat, only he's not saying what they are, and nobody else can even guess. Harken's the expert, everybody agrees."

"He'll win," Lorna said confidently. "I know he will. It's in his blood to win."

"And what about you?"

Lorna flopped to her back as she had so many times before, her wide eyes fixed on the tester.

"Jens wanted me to defy them. That would certainly do the trick, wouldn't it?"

Phoebe piled onto her knees, crawled over and looked directly down into Lorna's face. "You aren't seriously considering it, are you?"

"I don't know."

"Merciful heavens, you are!"

"You have to admit, the shock value would almost be worth the disgrace. And I have been spineless. And I do want to marry Jens Harken."

Phoebe flopped beside Lorna and for a full minute they lay in silence, staring upward, considering this outlandish idea.

At length Lorna mused, "I'd need one friend on my side. Would you stand beside me if I did it?"

Phoebe found Lorna's hand and squeezed it hard. "Of course I would." She considered a moment and gathered her courage before divulging, "I'm going to tell you something I haven't told another living soul." She turned her head, met Lorna's eyes and admitted, "The only difference between you and me is that you got caught and I haven't."

Perhaps it was Phoebe's admission that she, too, had lain with a lover, perhaps the fact that Lorna had been denied enough happiness that her time had come to claim it. Whatever the reason, within hours of her talk with Phoebe, she decided she would do this brash, unheard-of thing.

The regatta was only a week and a half away. She thought of little else, night and day from the time Phoebe put the idea into her head. She imagined herself with Jens and Danny, a mother and father and their child, a family at long last.

She imagined her own parents witnessing their reunion and her courage faltered.

She imagined living the rest of her life in this present limbo and her courage revived.

On her next visit to Mrs. Schmitt she took a package containing a little navy-blue-and-white sailor suit. When she laid it on the table the words were difficult to say.

"When I come next week, I'd like you to have Danny dressed in this. I'll be coming on Saturday, earlier than usual, and I'll be taking him with me."

"So the time has come."

Lorna covered Mrs. Schmitt's shiny, worn hand on the tabletop. "I'm sorry to take him away from you. I know you love him, too."

"So you don't plan to bring him back, then."

"No. Not if . . . well, if everything works out the way I hope."

"You and Harken."

"Yes. I hope so. He's a stubborn man but . . . we shall see."

Mrs. Schmitt removed her spectacles and cleaned them on her apron skirt. "Well, that's the way it ought to be, whether I'll miss the little one or not. The three of you being apart just ain't natural."

"I'll try to send you money when I can."

"Don't you worry about me. I've got a—"

". . . A little put by . . ." Lorna joined in. "Yes, I know. Still, I'll do what I can."

It was the first of many hurdles she would have to vault on her way to claiming happiness, but claim it she would, and with that goal in sight, she counted down the days.

The Saturday of the regatta had not yet dawned when Jens awoke, well before sunup. Carrying a mug of coffee, he left the sounds of somnolent breathing behind him in the loft and went outside into the rush of predawn wind and the sound of his own footsteps clunking on the dock.

The *Manitou* tossed restlessly on the water, giving an intermittent *thud-thud* that jarred the pilings and sent Jens's coffee swinging in his cup.

He sipped it down an inch and stepped aboard a deck that was sheeny with early morning dew, balancing, loose-kneed, shifting with the faint roll as the waves slapped the hull. He walked the length of the boat, touching things . . . wood, rope, canvas, metal . . . sipping his coffee. A sip . . . a touch . . . a sip . . . a touch . . . coffee and rigging . . . the wind already at ten knots and promising a good day for sailing. Only a thin pale line of clear sky showed above the eastern horizon, boding a stony-gray morning ahead. Between the hull ribs, collected water rocked with the rhythm of the swaying boat. He knelt to sponge it, then dried the dewy deck.

Times like this he felt close to his father, wishing the old man were here to see what he'd accomplished, to offer his deep, unruffled voice with its common sense and soothing tones.

Jens sent a thought to him: *Today's the day, Pa. Wish us luck.*

At dawn the sun poked through the narrow break between the clouds, beaming a false sunrise that gilded the tree-tips and mast-tips and the hair of Davin, who came ambling down the dock barefoot, carrying a coffee mug, too, with yesterday's wrinkled shirt thrown on over his trousers.

"You're up early," Davin greeted.

"Couldn't sleep."

"Yeah, I know what you mean. I didn't get to sleep myself till well after midnight. Just laid there thinking."

After a spell of silence Jens asked, "You think about Pa at all?"

"Yup."

"I wish he was here."

"Yup, me too."

"He taught us good, though, didn't he?"

"Sure did."

"Taught us to believe in ourselves. Win or lose today, we've got that."

"You want to win awfully bad, though, don't you?"

"Well, don't you?"

"Of course, but it's different for me. I haven't got Gideon Barnett trying to get even with me for getting his daughter pregnant."

"There's a lot riding on this race, that's for sure."

"Do you think there's any chance his boat can win?"

"Of course there is. I designed it, so it's going to be damned fast, and so is the *North Star,* but the moderations we made on the *Manitou* are going to make the difference." He had replaced the large single rudder with two smaller ones, which gave her quicker reaction on a turn.

"What about the Minnetonka club—you worried about any of their boats?"

"No, mainly the *Lorna D.*"

Davin clapped a hand on Jens's shoulder. "Well, tinkering around down here won't make the time go any faster. Come on upstairs and let's get Cara to make us some hot breakfast."

With race time set for noon, the morning seemed to crawl. Jens ate little but took time dressing, relishing as always the official yacht club sweater and vowing that one day he'd be more than an honorary member. Tim walked over from his cabin, all spiffed up in his whites, too, and grinning. "So, after today, can I take my boat home and keep it there?"

Jens had taken plenty of ribbing from the men about wanting the boat here the last few days "to make necessary modifications." Everyone knew there were no more to be made: They'd been done weeks before.

Davin had said, "If that boat was a woman she'd be hotter than Dutch love from all that stroking."

Ben had said, "We'll have to put a new coat of varnish on the splashboard if he polishes it any more."

Tim said, "Maybe I should offer to sell it back to him. Might make myself a pretty profit."

The rest of the crew arrived. Cara and the children boarded the *Manitou* for a ride over to the yacht club lawn, from where they'd watch the race. The ride over proved swift and wet, for the wind had increased to fifteen knots and threw spray over the bow.

When they arrived the B-class races were in progress. A crowd was already gathered on the lawn and milling along the dock, inspecting the boats tied there. When the spectators identified sail number W-30 approaching, a spate of applause went up. "Listen to that. They've got your number, Jens," Cara teased with a glint of pride in her eye.

Jens gave her a preoccupied smile that faded quickly as he scanned the other scows tied up at the dock. Immediately he picked out the *Lorna D* and Gideon Barnett among the crew, cleaning his deck and checking rigging. At the sound of the applause, Barnett straightened and peered out over the water to see who was approaching. Jens could tell the instant he read the sail number, for he spun away and became busy, giving some order to his crew.

The *Manitou* docked. Cara and the children alighted. Jens checked his watch—a quarter hour to go before the skippers' meeting and already there were chorus girls singing on the beach, and reporters and spectators galore. He checked the club flag fluttering from the tip of the cupola, gauging the wind and the scudding gray clouds to the south and west, the water surface, which was pilled and choppy. His crew hauled the spinnaker onto the lawn to fold and pack. Jens stayed behind to check the rigging, which he'd already done several times this morning. Still, it felt reassuring to be with the boat, keeping his hands busy.

Pins in the side stays.

Halyards untwisted.

Lines properly coiled.

He glanced up the lawn. Ladies with their petticoats luffing were holding their brightly colored hats on their heads. Children raced in and out, playing tag amid their mothers' skirts and eating lollipops. The chorus girls ended a song and a barber shop began one. He spied a contingent of spectators from Rose Point—Levinia Barnett and the two old aunts, Lorna's sisters and her brother (peering through a spyglass)—all of them milling among the society crowd who'd undoubtedly come to cheer for the *Lorna D.* Lorna herself was conspicuously absent.

Jens suppressed his disappointment and found things to keep himself preoccupied. He leaned over the stern to pull weeds from the rudders. He answered the questions of three young lads who stood on the dock with admiration in their eyes.

"You build this yourself, mister?"

"How long'd it take you?"

"My dad says I can have a boat someday."

Time for the skippers' meeting, and his crew came carrying the spinnaker aboard. He merely nodded to them—all the men tense now and introspective.

Approaching the Barnett group on his way toward the clubhouse, Jens felt their regard ricocheting his way but kept his eyes straight ahead, realizing that what he needed least during this final hour were distractions.

He had nearly reached the clubhouse when he caught a flash of something familiar at the edge of his peripheral vision. A color, an outline, a bearing—something made him turn to look.

And there stood Lorna.

With . . . with . . .

Dear God, she had Danny on her arm! Danny and Lorna were actually here at the regatta, where every person she knew would be watching!

For a frozen moment he stared. Then took a step toward them and halted while shock, euphoria and exultation exploded within him. His son and his woman, standing not twenty feet away, watching him! She was dressed in peach and Danny in a blue-and-white sailor suit, tugging fussily at a sailor hat that was tied under his chin.

Lorna pointed with an index finger and Jens read her lips.

There's Papa.

Danny quit fussing with the hat, focused on his father and beamed.

"Papa," he squealed, squirming as if to get down and run to Jens.

A lark in Jens's breast fluttered and sang. Never had he wanted to approach someone so badly in his life, but this was not the time. The seconds ticked away toward the scheduled skippers' meeting, and being late for it meant jeopardizing his chance to win if he missed the course instructions.

Someone came up the plank walk behind him. The footsteps halted and Lorna's face sobered. Jens looked around to find Gideon Barnett staring at his daughter and grandson. A murmur went through the crowd while Gideon's face turned gray as an old sail. Jens sensed when word reached Levinia, for a surge of motion parted the spectators. In that moment, while all factions recognized Lorna's presence and began counting back the months, it seemed the entire crowd held its breath.

Then a single young woman came forward with a smile.

"Lorna, hi! Where have you been? I've been looking for you." Phoebe Armfield stepped through the crowd, exuding an overt show of friendship. "Hi, Danny!" Not a soul would have known she'd never seen the baby before as she marched forward and kissed both him and his mother on the cheek.

Lorna's eyes reluctantly left Jens and he moved on toward the clubhouse with Gideon ten paces behind.

Inside, on the upper porch, it was hard to keep his mind on the race judge—a stern, officious man in white trousers, blue blazer and a tie, holding a blackboard in his hands.

"Skippers, welcome! Today's course will be a triangle, finishing to windward after two and one-third times around the course. We'll have a ten-minute assembly gun, a five-minute warning gun, and then the starting gun. Any premature starters will have to recross the starting line."

While the judge did his job, Jens felt Gideon Barnett's eyes skewering him from behind. Ten skippers were present, five from each yacht club, and all had entered scows. It would be a far different race from last year's.

The meeting ended. "Good sailing, gentlemen. Man your boats."

Amid skippers murmuring the standard refrain, "Sail well . . . sail well . . . ," Jens turned to find Barnett already stalking from the building ahead of him.

Outside, his eyes immediately veered to Lorna, seeking a cue—to go to her or directly to his boat, which did she want? Some friends of her age had gathered around her—he recognized faces from the yacht club crowd, plus one of the old-maid aunts, who was taking the baby from her arms. As Jens paused uncertainly with his crew waiting on board and his heart juddering, she left the others and came toward him.

He stood mute, quite nearly aching, waiting like some imbecile while she came straight on and stopped so close before him that her skirt blew across his ankles. She took his seasoned hand in her much softer one and said simply, "Sail well, Jens."

He squeezed her hand and felt as if his chest would explode.

"I will . . . for you and Danny," he managed.

Then he was stalking toward the *Manitou*. Surging! Sweeping! Ascending to some plane where only gods exist!

On board, he sensed his crew was fully aware of the human drama being contraposed with the nautical one soon to begin. They were soft-spoken, soft-smiling, non-questioning, taking their cue from his brother, Davin, who only said, "What do you say, skipper, shall we get this tub under sail?"

When Jens took his place at the tiller and gave the order to cast off, the crew of the *Manitou* understood they were racing under the orders of a skipper who had already won something far more important than an A-class race.

"Hoist the main! Hoist the jib!" There was a new note of alacrity in Jens's voice as he gave the command.

Mitch raised the mainsail, Davin the jib, and W-30 slid out among its competitors into the intermittently choppy waters of North Bay. They took her out toward the starting line on a broad reach, sailing leisurely downwind. Ten boats, sleek and speedy, cruised up and down, the sailors eyeing their competition and testing the wind in search of the favored end of the starting line. Every skipper cast his eye out for distant sails, gauging the wind shifts, checking the flag on the clubhouse roof and the telltales fluttering on their sails, looking for wind streaks on the water, anything to give him an edge at the moment the starting gun sounded.

The race officials manned a rowboat on either end of the starting line, surveying the milling fleet. Splotches of blue began appearing among the gray-bellied clouds, revealing even higher cirrocumulus clouds above.

"Looks like some mackerel sky showing up there," Jens remarked. "That could mean a high front, so watch for veering winds."

At the sound of the ten-minute warning gun, Jens ordered, "Edward, have your watch ready at the five-minute gun."

Edward got it out and stood ready.

Only necessary words were spoken after that as the crew of the *Manitou* continued reaching—sailing back and forth, back and forth—behind the starting line. Their shirts were already damp, their muscles tense, their gazes constantly scanning all the other boats, the *Lorna D* and the *North Star* among them.

The five-minute gun cracked. Edward checked his watch.

"Watch M-32," Davin said at the jib. "He's passing to leeward."

Jens steered the *Manitou* around the Minnetonka entrant and went on reaching. A moment later he picked his spot on the line and murmured to Davin, "We're going for the weather end. Trim! Let's get down there fast while the line is sagging." Then five of the others—six, seven—maneuvered in closer and closer, so close that their booms were swinging over their competitors' decks.

With one minute to go eight boats nosed toward the starting line separated by mere inches. Still Jens hung back, his sails luffing and the *Manitou* flat in the water. From his left he saw a boat heading up and heard the voice of Gideon Barnett shout, "Right of way! Right of way! Take it up and give me room!"

Recognizing the bluff, Jens held steady.

Fifteen seconds to go and chaos seemed to reign. Suddenly the wind freshened. Men shouted. Waves splashed. A Minnetonka skipper yelled, "We're going to be early! Ease the sails!"

Edward counted, ". . . Ten . . . nine . . ."

Amid the shrieking of wind through the rigging, boats heeled up and sails were trimmed. Bodies cantilevered over the weather rails as the boats gathered speed for the start.

Suddenly an opening cleared on the line.

"Trim in, Davin, there's a hole below me!"

". . . Eight . . . seven . . ."

"Trim! Trim!" Jens shouted.

Davin trimmed the jib. Mitch trimmed the main. The sails took full wind and Jens steered down as the boat picked up speed.

". . . Six . . . five . . ."

The *Manitou* heeled.

"Hike! Hike!"

". . . Four . . . three . . ."

The crew scrambled to the high side, angling their bodies so far over the water that their backs nearly touched the deck of the boat beside them.

". . . Three . . . two . . ."

The gun sounded as the *Manitou* leaped forward across the starting line.

"Keep 'er balanced!" Jens yelled, and they were under way, a nose ahead of the pack. A Minnetonka boat, M-9, dropped a length behind in the *Manitou's* wind shadow, followed closely by W-10, which tacked off for clear air. They sailed with the strategy of chess players, crossing each other all the way up the lake, using headers and lifts like pawns in a game.

Approaching the windward mark, Edward shouted, "W-10 has picked up a wind shift off of Peninsula Point. He's coming in on a full plane!"

From the *Lorna D* someone shouted, "Starboard!" asking for the right of way.

The *Lorna D* skimmed past and rounded the windward mark in first place with the *Manitou* inches behind her transom.

"Coming about, watch your heads!" Jens yelled. The boom swung as they cleared the mark. "Hoist the spinnaker!"

Ben set the pole, Tim hoisted, and a moment later their chute flew. With a smart crack the spinnaker filled and the boat leaped forward, chasing the *Lorna D*.

Ahead lay the turning mark, an orange buoy bobbing on the waves. Jens steered toward it with Barnett's boat close above him, and the picture of Lorna and Danny in his mind.

Mitch shouted, "There's a big puff astern!"

Jens swung around and saw busy black water. He turned down into it and felt the boat surge.

As he came abeam of the *Lorna D,* Jens yelled, "I need buoy room!"

Across ten feet of waves, he glimpsed Barnett's determined face, then the *Lorna D* dropped behind.

It was back and forth, back and forth for two more legs, one boat passing the other, calling for its rights and receiving them.

The *Manitou* led the race rounding the leeward mark, and the *Lorna D* led rounding the weather mark, with the *North Star* bringing up third place.

Off Peninsula Point bending wind shifts created tricky going as the land distorted the wind flow. Mitch continually played the mainsheet, and Davin the jib.

Approaching the leeward mark for the last time, faces were grave and wills determined. Jens and his crew were behind by a boat length. *For her, Barnett,* Jens thought, looking over the forward rail at Barnett's back. *For Lorna and the baby I'm going to win this race, then before you and society and God and the world I'm going to march up that yacht club lawn and claim them!*

"He's coming in wide. Let's dip inside!"

As the *Lorna D* took a wide swing around the buoy, Jens shouted, "Trim!" and ducked into the opening to round the mark first.

"Pull in the main! Hike for all you're worth!"

With the wind steady and strong off their bow, they headed upwind for the last time. Nose to nose they flew through the water. It was a game of inches. Laying the finish line, both skippers knew the race would be won by boat speed, not tactics or wind shifts.

"Hike for all you're worth! Hang by your toenails!" Jens hollered.

The crew hung so far over the weather rail that the waves were splashing over their throats. They tasted lake water on their lips and triumph close at hand as they pulled a length ahead. When they got close enough to see the cannon on the judge's deck, Jens shouted, "We're fetching the line! Hang on!"

Jens could hear the crowd cheering from shore. Could feel the power of the boat streaming up through the tiller. Could see the yacht club buoy beyond the line of hard, shivering bodies hanging over his weather rail and clinging to the lines. Water sprayed their faces as they looked over their shoulder at the *Lorna D* two full boat lengths behind. They headed straight for the flotilla of spectator boats dotting the water, saw the judge standing in his boat holding the string that would fire the cannon.

Teeth to the wind, they streamed across the finish line as the gun sounded.

"First place, W-30!" the judge shouted, drowned by the roar of the crowd. Though he called out the rest of the boat numbers as they came in, they were lost on the crew of the *Manitou*. Elation ruled them. Victory blotted out everything else.

They eased the sails . . . and their tense muscles . . . and let the rejoicing begin, meeting their skipper with open arms.

"We did it! We did it!"

"Nice job, Jens!"

A special hug from Davin. "You did it, big brother."

"We did it!"

And from Mitch Armfield, "Good job, skipper. Thanks for having me aboard."

"You're a hell of a sailor, Mitch. Couldn't have done it without you."

It seemed too immense to believe, now that it was all over. They had done this improbable thing that had started with a note in Gideon Barnett's ice cream dessert two years ago. It was over for the crew, who were only now realizing how tense, aching, wet and shivering they'd been; but for Jens there was so much more.

Under eased sail, he steered the boat toward a peach dress waiting on the shore. He picked her out with no trouble, partway up the grass, standing in full sunlight. She still held Danny on her arm, her free hand waving high above her head, and her friend Phoebe beside her.

Ah, that smile, that welcome—it was all that mattered. Not the trophies waiting on the cloth-covered table beneath an elm tree; not the crowd pressing to the water's edge and filling the dock with congratulations on their lips; not the photographers, or the brass band, or the rich club members waiting to order boats from him.

Only Lorna Barnett and the message she'd conveyed by bringing their child here today.

He kept them in his sights until his arrival at the dock forced his attention elsewhere. There were orders to be given, a boat to be secured, sails to be dried. During docking, spectators boarded and climbed all over the *Manitou,* asking questions, shaking the crew's hands, offering praise. Jens answered, complied, thanked, with Lorna ever on the edge of his vision and each moment tightening an emotional winch between them. The crew tied up the *Manitou* to the dock. Jens coiled the lines, got slapped on the back dozens of times, caught sight of the *Lorna D* tying up, its skipper and crew going through similar motions. The *North Star* arrived and the others continued straggling in. Two reporters vied for his attention.

"Mr. Harken, Mr. Harken . . ."

"Excuse me, gentlemen," he said, stepping around them, "there's someone I must see first."

She was standing uphill, her eyes the stars by which he navigated. He caught her gaze and held it, weaving through the throng while congratulations rained upon him, unheard now. He felt the beat of his own heart, like a sail filling and refilling, carrying him toward his heart's victory and the dark intensity of her unbroken regard as she watched him approach.

When he reached her the crowd receded into virtual unimportance. Among the hundreds of people beneath that June sun they recognized only each other.

His big hands closed around her arms just above the elbows and they beamed into each other's eyes.

"Oh Jens," she said, "you did it."

"I did it. . . ." He kissed her full on the mouth, one swift, hard, stamp of possession with Danny between them.

"Papa?" Danny was patting him on the cheek.

"And who's this? Why, it's Danny. Come here and give us a kiss."

Danny was too excited. "Ribe a boat?" He pointed toward the dock.

"He wants to ride the boat," Lorna interpreted.

"Y' darned right you'll ride a boat. We'll make you one that's just your size and we'll have you sailing it yourself as soon as you can swim."

Danny had quit staring at the boat in favor of staring at his father. Jens kissed Danny on his beautiful rosy mouth and rested his big, rough hand on the boy's blond head. "Lord, what a day," he murmured, and kissed him again on the hair, letting his eyes close.

Struggling to recover from a surfeit of emotions, he turned his attention once more on Lorna, who said, "You remember Phoebe, don't you?"

During Phoebe's congratulations someone said, "Two pretty women and where's mine?" It was Davin, arriving at the same moment as Cara and the children.

"She's right here, you big blond Viking. Oh, I'm so proud of you!" Cara gave her man a kiss. "And you, too." Another kiss for Jens as the round of celebration grew appropriately congested with baby Roland on his mother's arm, transferring to his father's, and Jeffrey pulling on his mother's skirt and Jens still holding Danny.

Finally Jens found time to say, "You've met my brother, Davin . . . and here's Cara . . . Cara, come here, darlin'." Jens put his arm around her shoulders while she smiled shyly. "This is Lorna . . ."

It went without saying: Their futures were inexorably entwined. The two women exchanged smiles and hellos rife with friendly curiosity. Then Davin and Lorna did the same while his big hand engulfed her much smaller one. He held it firmly, smiling into her eyes, and said, "Well this is some day. I'm not sure what I'm the happiest about."

Jeffrey was pulling on Jens's leg. "Lift me up! Lift me up!"

"Ho, it's Jeffrey!" Jens managed to pick him up. With a boy on each arm he said, "Look here now, this is your cousin, Danny. I wouldn't be surprised if the two of you sail in a race someday, just like your daddy and I. And you'll be winning, too, just like we did."

The round of babble and new faces suddenly became too much for Danny. His face crumpled and he began crying, reaching for his mother. The adults all laughed, relieving some of the tension.

A quavery female voice said, "I demand to be introduced to the winning skipper. I've waited long enough."

They all turned to find Aunt Agnes waiting, looking sprightly at Jens.

When she was holding Jens's hand, the pair created an endearing contrast, she no higher than his elbow, delicate, graying and somewhat bowed; he so tall, tan and strapping, robust with youth. Looking up into his windburned face, she said in her quaky voice, "I was not wrong—there is a striking resemblance to my own Captain Dearsley. I'm sure, young man, that this is the happiest day of your life. I want you to know it is also the happiest day of mine."

Lorna's sisters approached timidly, hanging back. Theron came with them, so fascinated by Danny that he went right to him, his eyes riveted on the baby. "Gosh, Lorna, am I really his uncle?"

"Yes, you are, Theron."

"What's his name?"

"Danny."

"Hi, Danny. Wanna come to your uncle Theron? I'll show you my spyglass."

The baby put out his arms and went to Theron as if he'd known him since birth. Theron threw a smile of pride around the group, while Jenny and Daphne inched forward.

Lorna, with a lump in her throat, said, "It's time you all met Jens."

The story would be told and retold for decades, about the day Jens Harken met Lorna Barnett's family, and she his, out on the yacht club lawn after he'd sailed his winning boat across the finish line to take the three-year White Bear/Minnetonka Challenge Cup. How she came there bringing his baby dressed in a little blue-and-white sailor suit, and how Jens and Lorna kissed in broad daylight before several hundred spectators. And how Gideon and Levinia Barnett watched from a distance just after Gid had lost the race in a boat named after his daughter. And how Jens Harken had at one time been kitchen help for the Barnett family. And how the day of the regatta began cloudy but ended up sunny, as if the couple's new life were being granted a heavenly blessing. And how Gideon Barnett, after stubbornly refusing to award Harken the cup the previous year, finally bent enough to do the honors.

The boats had all come in. The band had at last silenced. Shade dappled the single cup left standing on the white-draped table beneath the big elm.

Commodore Gideon Barnett placed it in Jens Harken's hands.

"Congratulations, Harken," Barnett said, offering his hand.

Jens took it. "Thank you, sir." It was a firm grip that lingered a beat longer than necessary, turning bitterness into doubt. Barnett's face was stern, Jens's wiped of all traces of vainglory. This man was his child's grandfather. Gideon's features and abilities and perhaps even his temperament would be passed down through their bloodlines for generations to come. Surely there was some way to resolve this bitter hatred.

The handshake ended.

"I'd like the cup to remain at the club, sir. That's where it belongs."

Barnett appeared momentarily nonplussed. He recovered quickly to reply, "The club accepts it. That's good of you, skipper."

"I'll keep it for today, though, if that's all right."

"Of course."

Jens turned and lifted the loving cup high above his head. The roar of applause seemed to ripple the curtain on the table behind him. He saw Lorna and Danny waiting . . . and Levinia Barnett standing off in the distance, looking very unsure of herself . . . and he sensed Gideon Barnett's rancor showing its first signs of cracking. There had been an undercurrent as the two of them shook hands and exchanged their first civil words in nearly two years. They had done it before a mob of people; surely they could do it again someday in private. It would take time, though, time and forgiveness and a swallowing of pride on both their parts.

Stepping from the dais, Jens put thoughts of Gideon and Levinia Barnett behind him as he headed for their daughter. But time was still not their own. Everyone had to touch the loving cup, then the crew had to drink champagne from it and have their pictures taken by Tim's big black-hooded camera with the cup held high above their heads. After that, Jens submitted to being interviewed by a circle of photographers, but throughout the questions and answers his eyes kept returning to Lorna. The baby had fallen asleep on her shoulder. Still on her feet, swaying with the slumbering child, her cheek against his golden hair, Lorna kept her eyes fervently pinned upon Jens.

He finally put an end to the hubbub. "Gentlemen, it's been a long day." He held up his hands, staving off more questions. "Now I've got some celebrating of my own to do. If you'll excuse me . . ." He said goodbye to his crew, shaking each man's hand, ending with Davin.

Quietly, Jens told him, "I may not be home tonight."

"Listen, Jens, Cara and I . . . well, we feel bad, taking up your house when you've got your own family to—"

"Don't say another word. There's time for that later. The woman hasn't even said she'll marry me yet. But if you'll let go of my hand, I intend to go ask her."

Davin squeezed Jens's knotty upper arm and said, "Go on, then."

At last Jens turned toward Lorna.

She was waiting for him, still swaying gently with Danny asleep on her shoulder. A wet spot had formed beneath the baby's open mouth on her peach-colored dress, turning the sateen to deep apricot. The wind, long since subsided, had loosened her auburn hair from its great drooping nest. The sun had burned her cheeks and forehead. Two years had turned her into his greatest reason for living.

"Let's get out of here," he said, reaching her. "Should I take him?"

"Oh, yes, please . . . he's gotten so heavy."

He handed her the loving cup and took the slumbering baby, whose eyes fluttered open briefly, then closed against Jens's shoulder.

"I left a bag of diapers over there under a tree."

They detoured to collect it, then walked—three at last—toward the gravel driveway with Jens's right hand resting on Lorna's shoulder.

"Where are we going?" Lorna asked.

"Somewhere alone."

"But where?"

He hailed a rig and driver, helped her board. "The Hotel Leip," he ordered, climbing in, then turned to question Lorna quietly, "All right?"

Her eyes answered before her lips. "Yes."

She set the loving cup on the floor between their knees. He settled the baby in the crook of his left arm and took her hand with his free one, studying it in his own—hers diminutive, slightly freckled from the summer sun; his wide and horny and red-burned from the wind. Her fingers were slim as evening shadows while his were thick and coarse as rope. He lifted her hand to his lips and kissed the back of it, overcome at last, now that he could allow his emotions sway.

"My God," he whispered, letting his head fall back against the leather seat, his eyes closed. "I can't believe you're here." He rested so awhile, with her hand clasped tightly within his own, rubbing her soft skin with his thumb, listening to the *clip-clop* of the horse's hooves and the steady rasp of wheels on gravel. The air felt cool on his windburned face. The baby's wet diaper was soaking through his pants. He thought if he were asked to describe heaven he would ever after describe this moment. He opened his eyes. Lorna's face was turned sharply away with a handkerchief pressed to her mouth.

He lifted his head and cooed, "Hey, heeey . . . ," touching her far jaw to make her turn. "Are you crying?"

His words released one quiet sob and brought her coiling against him with her cheek on his sleeve. "I can't help it."

"The time for crying is over."

"Yes, I know. It's just that . . ." She had no reason. She sniffled again and dried her streaming eyes.

"I understand. I'm feeling the same way. We've been through so much hell it's hard to accept heaven."

"Something like that . . . yes."

They rode awhile in silence, passing under an arch of beech trees that threw green and gold streaks eastward as evening approached. They could smell the lake—wet rocks and weeds and water-cooled air mixed with a tincture of horse—and feel the warm sun on their left cheeks, the evening cool on their right. A rock flew up and hit the underside of the carriage. A meadowlark trilled from their right. A dog barked somewhere in the unseen distance. The metal of the loving cup had warmed against their knees.

In time Jens said, "Your father shook my hand, though," as if the subject of Gideon had been under earlier discussion.

"Yes, I saw."

"And he congratulated me . . . and you know what?" Jens looked down and Lorna looked up. "It's going to take some time, but I think we'll mend those fences. I could tell. Something was different. Something was . . ." He left the thought dangling.

"Something was making him question his own stubbornness."

"It seemed that way."

"That something was Danny," she said.

They both looked down at their sleeping son.

"Yes, probably so."

In time Jens asked, "Your father didn't say anything to you today?"

"No."

"Your mother either?"

"No."

He squeezed her hand and laid it against his heart.

"But it hurt them not to, I could tell. And the girls, and Theron, and your aunt Agnes . . . didn't they love Danny, though?"

"Yes, they certainly did."

He had no further consolations to offer.

At the Hotel Leip he said to the desk clerk, "We'll need two rooms."

"Two?" The young man with a protuberant Adam's apple and receding chin looked from the sleeping baby in Jens's arms to Lorna, then back to Jens.

"Yes, two, please."

"Very well, sir. Happy to oblige, especially with all the regatta guests leaving town again."

Jens signed the register first, then handed the pen to Lorna.

Lorna & Daniel Barnett, she signed.

The clerk plucked two keys from two hooks on the wall and came from behind his cubbyhole. "Bags, sir?"

Lorna handed him the cloth diaper bag with its looped handles. He looked down at its contents, easily visible within the open top, but led them without further questions to their rooms.

Lorna took Danny into the first. Jens went on to the second. Within a minute he returned to Lorna's, entering without knocking, closing the door with extreme care not to click the latch. She had laid Danny on the bed and was beginning to loosen his clothing.

"Wait a minute . . ." Jens whispered. "Don't wake him up yet."

She straightened and turned to face him. He dropped his keys on her dresser, then slowly crossed the room and stood before her. He took her head lightly in both hands, his thumbs lightly stroking the crests of her cheeks while their eyes partook of each other. Her lips were parted, her breath quick and reedy.

"Jens . . ." she whispered at the moment his head began tipping and his arms gathered her in.

At last, at last, the kiss they had so longed for. Since he'd seen her standing on the clubhouse lawn, since she'd seen him sail the *Manitou* to the yacht club dock, this moment had been glimmering like a promise on their horizon. They met in full length—mouths, breasts, hips seeking and finding mates. With hands and bodies and throaty murmurs they claimed what had been denied them so long. Their starved hearts pressed close. Her hands opened upon his back, rubbed his ribs, burrowed in his hair. He cupped her head, her disheveled knot filling his palm and falling further awry as their ardor brought the sweetest of swaying and refitting. Enough, enough—they could not get enough of this first taste and touch. To reclaim was not enough: The kiss became a struggle to achieve the impossible, to imbibe each other and so become a part of the other's heart and blood and muscle. They twined, curved one to the other, until like two meeting waves they seemed to lose distinction and become one.

He tore his mouth free, held her head in both hands and spoke into her open mouth.

"Will you marry me?"

"Yes."

"When?"

"Right now, tomorrow, as soon as the law will let us."

"Ah, Lorna, Lorna . . ." Squeezing his eyes shut he clasped her hard against him. "I love you so much."

"I love you, too, Jens, and I'm so sorry I hurt you. I've been just miserable without you." She drew back, took his face in her hands and touched her lips to his mouth, cheek, eye, mouth, speaking between strewn kisses. "So miserable . . . so wrong . . . so much in love that my life became meaningless without you . . . And then that day I saw you at Mrs. Schmitt's, saw Danny with you . . . Oh, dear, dear heart, I thought I should rather die than watch you walk away."

"Shh . . . later . . . we'll talk later. Come here." He scooped her up and sank into an upholstered chair with her across his lap. Their mouths were joined before their weight settled, and his hand made free swipes over her breast, hip, belly. Up to her throat and hair, where he began searching out what hairpins remained. It was clumsy going with his left arm pinned beneath her, so she reached up to help, dropping four pins onto the floor, shaking her head once till the hair fell free, then looping her arms around his neck and kissing him as if he were a peach that she had just peeled. In the midst of the kiss he tried opening the buttons up the back of her dress, which again proved awkward.

He ended the kiss impatiently. "Sit up. I can't reach."

She sat up and straddled his lap in a billow of peach-colored skirts, with her elbows on his shoulders and her fingertips in his hair. While he tended her buttons, she tended his mouth—full, beautiful, soft Norwegian mouth that had kissed her lips and breasts and stomach in those secret days of summer passion, and would kiss them again and again into the anniversaries of their years.

The buttons up her back were opened. He freed his mouth to say, "Your wrists." What exquisite torture to look into each other's eyes and bank fires while she sat erect and offered first one wrist, then the other for his chapped fingers to attend. She lifted her arms and he swept the dress away, working it over her breasts and making of her hair a galaxy of shooting stars.

"Your sweater," she whispered, when the dress had fallen. And he took a turn submitting to his lover's wishes.

When his sweater had joined her dress, he unbuttoned her chemise and bared her to the waist, then slid his hands beneath her armpits and tipped her forward to kiss her breasts—soft, pear-shaped, florid breasts that had been offered for kissing a dozen times before. He washed them with his tongue, and held them in his wide, rough hands, her chin tipping back, her eyes closing and her body beginning to rock to the primal rhythm set free within them both.

He stopped kissing her, still cupping her breasts. "These—what about these when they took the baby away? I've wondered so many times."

She drew her heavy head up and opened her eyes. "They bound them," she answered, "and after a few days the milk stopped coming."

"Then who fed Danny?"

"My mother brought a wet nurse."

In silence he absorbed her answer, his thumbs grazing her nipples, saddened by thoughts of that heartbroken, tormented time.

"That must have hurt."

"It doesn't matter anymore."

As if to wipe it from his mind, he growled deep in his throat and circled her ribs in a huge bear hug that buried the side of his face against her naked skin.

"Don't think about it tonight," she whispered, ringing his head with both arms and riffling her fingers along his scalp. "Not tonight, Jens."

"You're right. Not tonight. Tonight is just for us." He drew back, gripping her lightly, kneading the sides of her breasts with the butts of his hands. "So unbutton your petticoat," he whispered, "before our baby wakes up."

She followed orders and he rose, swinging her to the floor, her clothing collapsing like reefed sails till it caught on her hip. He brushed it down and it dropped to her ankles with a quiet swish.

"You're more beautiful than ever." There were changes—wider hips, a pouf to her stomach that had been absent before Danny's birth. He touched her there.

"No fair," she whispered. "I'm anxious, too."

Smiling, he worked off the remainder of his clothes, then took her down upon them, crushing her dress, his trousers, their underwear, caring little that they had no featherbed. Having each other was enough.

They touched, stroked, caressed, whispered endearments, made promises as eloquent and lasting as any they would speak in a marriage ceremony.

"I'll never let you get away again."

"I'll never go."

"And when our next baby is born I'll be beside you."

"And our next and our next."

"Oh, Lorna Barnett, how I love you."

"Jens Harken, my dearest, dearest one, I love you, too. I shall love you till my dying day and spend every day till then proving it."

When he placed his body within hers, he trembled and closed his eyes. She drew in a shaken breath and released it in a near sigh. They felt exalted as he beat a rhythm upon her, and smiles broke forth, quiet smiles of rightness as he folded his fingers tightly between hers and pressed the backs of her hands to the floor.

"Supposing you get pregnant tonight," he said.

"Then Danny will have a brother."

"Or a sister."

"A sister would be fine, too."

"Especially if she looked like you."

"Jens . . ." Her eyelids were closing. "Oh, Jens . . ." Her lips dropped open and he knew the time for talking was over. Time now to take their share of ecstasy, to store it up for the less than ecstatic times when babies were sick, or tempers short, or work hours long or loved ones troublesome—there would be those troubled times, they both knew. Yet they would take each other, in sickness and in health, in good times and bad, till death did they part, knowing that their bond of love would be strong enough to see them through. For ever waiting, beyond the troubled times, would be this, life's most wondrous recompense.

He shuddered, and groaned in broken syllables, spilling within her.

She arched and whimpered and cried out in repletion, and he muffled the sound with his mouth.

In the sweet reflux that followed, as he lowered his weight upon her and felt her arms loop loosely around him, he saw their life together spinning into the future of bright, shining hours undershadowed by occasions when tears would gather. He accepted both, knowing that's what true loving was about. He rolled to his side and held her close with one heel. He strummed her hair back from her face and touched her cheek lovingly.

"We're going to do just fine," he whispered.

She smiled, one arm folded beneath her ear. "I know we are."

"And we're going to try very hard with your mother and father."

"But if it doesn't work with them—"

He touched her lips to silence them. "It will."

She removed his finger. "But if it doesn't work we'll still be happy."

"I asked you to defy them for me and you did, but I'm not sure I should have asked such a thing of you. My mother and father are dead. Yours are the only ones we've got left—right or wrong, the only ones—and I want you to know that today or tomorrow or whenever we say our vows I'll be adding a silent one to you to do my best to win them over. Not for me, but for you . . . and for our children."

"Oh, Jens . . ." She captured him and drew him close. "You're such a good man. How can they help but see it?"

They rocked together on their lumpy bed until a sound came from up above: The first frightened whimper of a baby awakening alone in a strange place.

"Oh-oh," Jens whispered.

The whimper quickly turned to gusty bawling.

"Hey, Danny darling, Mommy's here!" There followed a less than graceful scuffle of lovers trying to disengage with the least amount of mess and the greatest amount of haste before their baby fell off the bed. "Look!" Lorna's head popped up as she made it to her knees. "Here's Mommy . . . and Daddy, too!" Jens popped up beside her, still tangled in clothing and struggling with things that made Lorna giggle.

Danny stopped crying and stared, his eyes still puffy from sleep, and a single tear caught on the lower lashes of each.

"Well, hi, darling boy. Did you think you were all alone? Oh, no, Mommy and Daddy would never leave you alone." Still kneeling, she leaned across the bed to kiss and comfort him. Danny, struggling to make sense of it, continued staring, first at her, then at Jens.

Jens leaned on his elbows and gave Danny's stockinged foot a kiss.

"Hello, little man," he said. "Sorry, but I was busy making you a brother."

Lorna whapped Jens on the arm. "Jens Harken!"

He raised his eyebrows and feigned innocence. "Well, I was, wasn't I?"

She laughed and told Danny, "You mustn't listen to everything your Daddy says. He's got an outrageous streak that'll do your tender ears little good."

Jens put one arm around Lorna's bare waist and slid her belly along the edge of the mattress till their bare hips bumped.

"Oh yeah? Who started this, you or me? You're the one who came courting. You're the one who wouldn't leave me alone. You're the one who showed up at the regatta today, bringing this child, and put him to sleep right on the bed, where he was bound to wake up and see what's been going on here on the floor."

She grinned smugly. "And you're mighty glad I did."

He returned her grin. "You bet I am."

For a moment they basked in happiness, then they each put an arm around their son's wet bottom and pulled him into their embrace.

FAMILY BLESSINGS

Do not stand at my grave and weep
I am not there, I do not sleep.
I am a thousand winds that blow,
I am the diamond glints on snow,
I am the sunlight on ripened grain,
I am the gentle autumn rain.
When you awaken in the morning's hush,
I am the swift uplifting rush
   of quiet birds in circled flight,
I am the soft stars that shine at night.
Do not stand at my grave and cry,
I am not there, I did not die.

—Anonymous

Chapter 1

━━━⌒⌒━━━

For Christopher Lallek life couldn't have been better. It was payday, his day off, all the junk was scraped out of his old beat-up Chevy Nova, and his brand-new Ford Explorer had come into Fahrendorff Ford. It was an Eddie Bauer model, top of the line, with a four-liter V-6 engine, four-wheel drive, air-conditioning, tilt wheel, compact digital disc player and leather seats. The paint color was called wild strawberry, and it was wild, all right, wilder than anything he'd ever owned. Within an hour the papers would all be signed and he'd be slipping behind the wheel of his first new vehicle ever. All he needed was his paycheck.

He swung into the parking lot of the Anoka Police Station, cranked his old beater in a U-turn and, out of long practice, backed the car against the curb beside two black-and-white squads parked the same way near the door.

He sprang out whistling "I've Got Friends in Low Places" and took a happy leap onto the sidewalk, scanning the sky from behind a pair of mirrored sunglasses strung with hot-pink Croakies. Perfect day. Sunny. Couple of big white fluffy clouds in the east. Eighty degrees now shortly before noon, and by the time all the guys met at the lake it would be pushing ninety and the water would feel great. Greg was going to stop and price oversized inner tubes; Tom was bringing his Jet Ski; and Jason had the use of his folks' speedboat for the day. Some of the guys would bring beer. Chris would pick up a couple of six-packs of soda and some salami and cheese, maybe a pint of that herring in cream sauce that he and Greg loved so much, and drive out there in his shiny new truck playing his new Garth Brooks CD—hey, hell of a deal.

He unlocked the plate-glass door and walked into the squad room, still whistling.

Nokes and Ostrinski, both in uniform, were standing beside the computer table, looking sober, talking.

"Hey, what's new, guys?"

They looked up and fell silent, watching him poke a hand into his mail cubicle, come up with an envelope and rip it open. "Payday at last—hot damn!" He swung around, scanning the check, then slapped it against his palm. "Eat your heart out, boys, my new Explorer came in at last and it's all dealer-prepped and ready for pickup! If you want to go outside and administer last rites to my old Nova—" It struck him suddenly that neither Nokes nor Ostrinski had moved. Or smiled. Nor had they said a word since he'd come in. From the patrol room two more uniformed officers came silently through the doorway, looking equally as solemn as the two already there.

"Murph, Anderson . . ." Christopher greeted, wary now. He'd been a police officer for nine years: He recognized this silence, this somberness, this stillness too well.

"What's wrong?" His eyes darted from man to man.

His captain, Toby Anderson, spoke in a grave tone. "It's bad news, Chris."

Christopher's stomach seemed to drop two inches. "An officer went down."

"Afraid so."

"Who?"

Nobody spoke for ten seconds.

"Who!" Chris shouted, his dread mounting.

Anderson replied in a low, hoarse voice. "Greg."

"Greg!" Christopher's features registered bald-faced surprise, followed by disbelief. "Wait a minute. Somebody's got their wires crossed here."

Anderson only shook his head sadly. His gaze remained steady on Christopher while the others studied their shoes.

"But you're wrong. He's not on duty today. He left the apartment no more than an hour ago to come over here and get his check, then he was going to the bank, then he had to stop by his mother's house, and as soon as I picked up my Explorer we were going to buy a water tube and go out to Lake George."

"He wasn't on duty, Chris. It happened on his way here."

Christopher felt the truth shoot through his nerves to his extremities and turn them prickly. He felt his head go light.

"Oh, shit," he whispered.

Anderson spoke again. "A pickup ran a red light and hit him broadside."

Shock created havoc inside Christopher and hammered his features into hard, unaccepting lines. He dealt with tragedies daily, but never before with the death of one of the force. Certainly not with the death of a best friend. He stood in the grip of conflicting reactions, his human side sending heat and weakness streaming through his insides, while the trained lawman maintained an analytical exterior. When he spoke his voice came out patchy and gruff. "He was on his motorcycle."

"Yes . . . he was."

Anderson's pause, his throaty voice precluded the need for details. Christopher's throat closed, his chest constricted and his knees began trembling, but he stood his ground and asked the questions he'd ask if Greg were some stranger, little realizing that shock had him operating as if by remote control.

"Who responded to the call?"

"Ostrinski."

Christopher's eyes found the young police officer, who appeared pale and shaken. "Ostrinski?"

Ostrinski said nothing. He looked as though he'd been crying. His lips were puffy and his face pink.

"Well, go on . . . tell me," Christopher insisted.

"I'm sorry, Chris, he was dead by the time I got there."

Out of nowhere came a hot smack of anger. It sent Christopher whirling in a half circle, flinging a chair out of his way. "God*damn* it!" he shouted. "Why Greg?" Beset by passion, he lashed out with the most simplistic blame. "Why didn't he ride with me! I *told* him I didn't mind taking him by his mother's house! Why did he have to take his motorcycle?"

Anderson and Ostrinski reached out as if to comfort Christopher, but he recoiled. "Don't! Just . . . just let me . . . I need . . . give me a minute here . . ." He spun away from them, marched two steps to an abrupt halt and exclaimed again, "Shit!" Fear roiled within him, spawned by a shot of adrenaline that turned him hot, cold, trembly, made him feel as if his entire body could no longer fit inside his skin. Working as a cop, he'd seen reactions like this dozens of times and had never understood them. He'd often thought people hard when their response to the news of death took the form of anger. Suddenly it was happening to him, the quick flare of absolute rage that made him storm about like a warrior rather than cry like a bereaved friend.

As swiftly as the anger struck, it fled, leaving him shaken and nauseated. Tears came—hot, stinging tears—and a hurt in his throat.

"Aw, Greg," he uttered in a strange, cracked voice. "Greg . . ."

His fellow officers came up behind him and offered support. This time he accepted the touch of their arms and hands on his shoulders. They murmured condolences, their voices, too, strangled by emotions. He turned, and suddenly Captain Anderson's arms were around him, big burly arms trained in the martial arts, clasping him hard while both men strained to withhold sobs.

"Why Greg?" Chris managed. "It's just so damned unfair. Why not some . . . some dealer selling coke to school kids or some parent who's beating on his k . . . kids twice a week? Hell, we got a hundred of 'em in our files."

"I know, I know . . . it's not fair."

Christopher's tears streamed. He stood in his captain's grip, his chin pressed to Anderson's crisp collar with its fifteen-year chevrons, listening to the bigger man swallow repeatedly against his ear, feeling the captain's handcuff case pressing his belly while the other officers stood nearby feeling useless and vulnerable.

Anderson said, "He was a good man . . . a good officer."

"Twenty-five years old. Hell, he'd hardly even lived."

Anderson gave him a bluff thump on the shoulder and released him. Christopher lowered himself to a chair and doubled forward, covering his face with both hands. Visions of Greg flashed through his mind: earlier this morning in the apartment they shared, shuffling out of his bedroom with his brown hair standing on end, scratching his chest and offering the usual bachelor good morning: "I gotta pee like a racehorse. Outa my way!" Then plodding from the bathroom to the kitchen, where he stood holding the refrigerator door open for a good minute and a half, staring inside, asking, "So what time're you going to get the new Explorer?" Reaching inside for a quart of orange juice and drinking half of it from the carton, belching and finally letting the door close.

He couldn't be dead! It wasn't possible!

Only one hour ago he was standing by the kitchen cupboard eating a piece of toast, dressed in bathing trunks and a wrinkled T-shirt that said MOUSTACHE RIDES FREE! "I gotta stop by my Mom's," he'd said. "The end busted off one of her garden hoses and she asked me to put a new one on."

Greg was always so good to his mother.

Greg's mother . . . aw, Jesus, Greg's poor mother. The thought of her brought a fresh shot of dread and grief. The woman had been through enough without this. She didn't need some strange police chaplain coming to her door to break the news.

Christopher drew a shaky breath and straightened, swiping a hand under his nose. Somebody handed him some hard napkins from the coffee room. He blew his nose and asked in a husky voice, "Has the chaplain informed his family yet?"

"No," Captain Anderson answered.

"I'd like to do it, sir, if that's all right."

"You sure you're up to it?"

"I know his family. It might be easier coming from me than from a stranger."

"All right, if you're sure you want to do it."

Chris drew himself to his feet, surprised at how weak he felt. His body was trembling everywhere—knees, stomach, hands—and his teeth were juddering together as if he'd just stepped into subzero cold.

Anderson said, "You okay, Lallek? You look a little unsteady. Maybe you'd better sit back down for a minute."

Chris did. He hit the chair as if he'd been bulldozed, closed his eyes and drew several deep breaths only to feel tears building once more.

"It's just so hard to believe," he mumbled, clutching his head and shaking it. "An hour ago he was standing in the kitchen eating toast."

Ostrinski said, "And yesterday when he went off duty he was talking about you guys going out to the lake."

Chris opened his eyes and saw Pete Ostrinski through a wavery pool of tears, a six-foot-four giant, only twenty-five years old, wearing a stricken expression. "Hey, Pete, I'm sorry, man. You're the one who responded to the call and here I sit blubbering when you took the biggest shock."

Ostrinski said, "Yeah," choked on the word and turned away to dry his eyes.

Chris took a turn at comforting, rising to drape an arm across Pete Ostrinski's shoulders and give his thick neck a squeeze.

"Is he at the morgue already?"

Ostrinski could scarcely get the words out. "Yeah, but don't go over there,

Chris. And whatever you do, don't let his mother go. He was broken up pretty badly."

Chris squeezed Ostrinski's shoulder once more and let his hand drop disconsolately.

"This is going to kill his mother."

"Yeah . . . mothers are tough."

Their records technician, a woman named Ruth Randall, had been standing silently in the doorway leaning against the door frame as if uncertain what to say or do, just as they all were. The door from the parking lot opened and closed and another on-duty uniformed officer arrived. "I just heard," Roy Marchek said, and the crowded room fell utterly silent. Every person in it dealt with tragedies on a daily basis and had, of necessity, become somewhat inured to them. This death, however—one of their own—hit them in a way that made the impersonal dealings of past police calls feel like cakewalks.

The outside door opened again and the police chaplain, Vernon Wender, arrived. He was a man in his forties, with erect stature, thinning brown hair and silver-rimmed glasses. Captain Anderson nodded a silent hello as Wender stepped past Ruth Randall and moved into the squad room among the men.

"We've lost a good one," he said in a respectfully subdued voice. "A terrible tragedy." A stultifying silence passed while everyone struggled with their emotions. "The last time I talked to Greg he said to me, 'Vernon, you ever think about how many people hate their jobs? Well, not me,' he said. 'I love being a cop. It feels good to be out there helping people.' Maybe you'll all feel better if you dwell on that. Greg Reston was a happy man." Wender let some seconds tick away before adding, "I'll be here all day long if any of you need to talk . . . or pray . . . or reminisce. I think we'd all feel a little better if we said a prayer right now."

Throughout the prayer Christopher lost touch with the chaplain's words. He was thinking of Greg's family, especially his mother, and the shock that lay ahead for her. She was a widow with two other children—Janice, twenty-three, and Joey, fourteen—but Greg had been the oldest, the one she'd relied on most since the death of her husband nine years ago. "A strong woman," Greg had called her countless times, "the strongest woman I know . . . and the best." In all his life Christopher Lallek had never heard anyone praise a mother the way Greg Reston had praised his. The relationship between them had been one of mutual respect, admiration and love, the kind that brought a hollow lump of envy to Christopher's stomach as he'd heard about it over the past couple of years since Greg had joined the force. Greg and his mother could talk about anything—sports, money, sex, philosophy, even the occasional hurt feelings that crop up in the best-balanced families. Whatever it was, those two had discussed it, and afterward Chris would hear about it from Greg. He knew more about Mrs. Reston than many people knew about their own mothers, and because of it he had acquired a vicarious admiration and respect for her such as he'd never had for his own parents.

The prayer ended. Feet shuffled. Somebody blew his nose. Chris drew a deep, shaky sigh and said to Wender, "Greg and I are . . . were roommates. I'd like to tell his family."

The chaplain squeezed his arm and said, "All right, but are you sure you're okay yourself?"

"I'll make it."

Wender dropped his hand and nodded solemnly.

Outside, the sun was still radiant. It hurt his burning eyes. He covered them with his dark glasses and got into his car, scarcely noticing the hot upholstery beneath his bare legs. He started the engine then forgot to put the car in gear. *He's not really dead. He's going to pull in beside me and come over here and lean his hands against the car door and say, "See you out at the lake."*

Only he wouldn't.

Never again.

Christopher had no awareness of passing time, only of a lump of sorrow so overwhelming it controlled every atom of his being. Sluggishly he put the car in gear and pulled out onto the street, functioning within a haze of emotions that removed him from the mundane process of operating an automobile. He searched for Greg's face as he'd last seen it, struggling to recall the absolute final glimpse he'd had of his friend. Greg had been going out the apartment door—that was it—dressed for the beach with a red bill cap on his head, an apple in one hand and his keys in the other. He'd anchored the apple between his teeth while opening the door, then had taken a bite and said with his mouth full, "See you in an hour or so."

A bill cap instead of a helmet.

Swimming trunks instead of jeans.

A T-shirt instead of a leather jacket.

Not even any socks inside his dirty white Nikes.

Chris knew only too well what happened to the victims of motorcycle accidents who failed to wear proper gear.

Skulls crushed . . .

Bones laid bare by the hot blacktop . . .

Skin burned . . .

Sometimes their shoes were never found.

A car horn shook Christopher back to the present. The world swam beyond his tears. He'd been driving at ten miles an hour in a thirty-mile zone and had just gone through a stop sign without slowing. Hell, he was in no condition to be operating a vehicle. He'd be the next one to kill somebody if he didn't look out.

He dried his eyes on his shirt shoulders and speeded up to thirty, trying to push the horrifying images from his mind. He had to get his emotions pulled together before he reached Mrs. Reston's house.

The thought of her brought a billow of dread. A mother—God almighty, how do you tell a mother a thing like this? Especially a mother who's lost a child before?

She had lost her secondborn to SIDS—Sudden Infant Death Syndrome—when Greg had been so young he'd scarcely remembered it. But she'd talked about that time with Greg, after he'd gotten older. It had been her philosophy that Greg had admired so and set out to duplicate. She'd held that nothing was as important as the happiness of her marriage and her family, and to let either be undermined by extended grief would have been unpardonable. She'd had a responsibility to be a happy

mother and wife for her husband and surviving son, and she'd done so by immediately trying to get pregnant again. The result had been Greg's younger sister, Janice, two years his junior. Nine years later Joey had been born.

Then at age thirty-six, Greg's mother had been widowed, losing a husband she'd
loved immensely. He had died of a brain aneurysm after lingering for three days in
a hospital bed. But Mrs. Reston had shown the same grit as before. Left with three
children who needed her, no career, and a measly $25,000 in life insurance, she had
refused to curl up with grief and self-pity. Instead, she'd consulted a vocational counselor, taken some business courses, spent a year in a trade school, bought herself a
florist shop and established a firm foundation for supporting her children for as long
as need be.

Strong? The woman was the Rock of Gibraltar. But even rocks can crack under
intense pressure.

Driving to her house through the noon heat on this tragic late June day,
Christopher Lallek wondered how to break the news that she'd lost another child.
There simply was no good way.

Her house wasn't far from the station, just two miles or so. After spending most
of the drive oblivious to his surroundings, Christopher became startlingly alert as
he turned onto Benton Street. It was a shaded avenue that followed a bend of the
Mississippi River, with older, well-maintained houses on both sides. Hers was several blocks off Ferry Street, facing southwest, across the street from the river. It was
a nice old rambler, white with black shutters and a beige brick planter full of red
geraniums flanking the front step. The maples in the yard were mature and as perfectly round as lollipops, as if they'd had professional pruning their entire lives.
Around their trunks pink and white petunias bloomed inside circles of brick. The
grass was neatly mowed but drying near the curb where an oscillating sprinkler
fanned desultorily back and forth. It threw water across Christopher's windshield
and his left elbow as he pulled into the driveway and stopped before an oversized
detached garage. The garage door was up. One stall was empty; the other held her
car, a five-year-old blue Pontiac sedan with some rust surrounding a bumper sticker
that said FLOWERS MAKE LIFE LOVELIER.

Chris turned off his engine and sat awhile, staring into the garage at the testi-
mony of her life: rakes and hoes, a garden cart, a bag of charcoal, her dead husband's
workbench with tools still hanging above it, an old yellow bicycle hanging from
the rafters, probably Greg's.

A new swell of grief struck and he pinched the bridge of his nose while an invisible winch seemed to tighten around his chest. He felt as if he'd swallowed a tennis ball.

Damn you, Greg, why didn't you wear a helmet?

He sat awhile, crying, dimly registering the thought that Mrs. Reston
shouldn't leave her garage door open this way; anybody could walk right in and
steal anything in sight. Greg used to scold her for it but she'd laughingly reply, "I've
known every person on this block for twenty years and nobody locks their garages.
Besides, who'd steal anything from me? Who'd want that junk out there? If they
need it that badly, let them come in and take it."

But Christopher was a police officer who knew the dangers of leaving doors unlocked, just as Greg had.

Who would warn her to lock up from now on? Who would remind her to have the oil changed in her car? To replace her furnace filter? Who would fix her hoses?

Christopher dried his eyes, put his sunglasses back on, drew a fortifying breath and opened his car door.

Outside, the heat from the blacktop driveway beat up through the soles of his blue rubber thongs. It struck him suddenly what he was wearing—a man shouldn't bring news like this dressed in beach clothes. He closed up three shirt buttons and was rounding the hood of his car when he encountered the garden hose lying coiled on the driveway waiting for Greg to replace its end.

Everything inside him mounded up volcanically again.

Oh hell, would every reminder of Greg bring this awful affliction? Sometimes the force of it seemed as if it would send his ribs flying in two directions like a pair of gates bursting open. His life would be a series of reminders from now on; would every one bring this terrible desolation and urge to cry?

He stepped around the coiled hose and continued toward the front door.

It was open.

He stood awhile, looking through the screen, summoning courage. Inside, from some distant room, a radio softly played an old Neil Diamond song. The front hall led straight to the rear of the house, where a kitchen table stood before an open sliding glass door. A sheer drapery was being sucked and blown against the screen. Beyond it he could see a deck and a big backyard, shaded by trees, where he was supposed to come with Greg for a Fourth of July picnic. He made out the silhouettes of other things: a bouquet on the table, a sweater hanging on the back of a chair, a soda can and purse atop a stack of books, as if she was getting ready to go someplace.

Deeper in the house a faucet ran, then stopped. A female voice sang a line along with Neil Diamond, then disappeared as if around a bedroom doorway off to his right.

He stood in the shade of a small entry roof with a wall jutting to his right and the strong-smelling geraniums poking up out of the planter at his left.

The button for the doorbell was black, mounted in a pitted brass casing.

In his entire life Christopher Lallek had never dreaded doing anything as much as ringing that doorbell.

He knocked instead—somehow a knock seemed gentler—knocked and waited with the tennis ball still filling his throat.

Lee Reston shut off the water, polished the faucet, hung up the towel and gave her head a little shake, watching in the bathroom mirror as her plain brown hair fell into its customary place. Sometimes she thought about letting it grow, doing something different with it, but she'd never felt comfortable with fuss. Her hair parted where it would and hung in a short, simple Julie Andrews cut, a blow-and-go hairdo that suited her just fine and seemed to go well with the childish freckles that plagued her whenever summer came. She gave a yank on the knot holding her wraparound denim skirt at the waist, glanced at her plain white blouse and twirled both of her tiny gold stud earrings in her ears the way she'd been instructed when she'd had them pierced many years ago.

Singing a line from "Cracklin' Rosie," she shut off the bathroom light and zipped around the corner into her bedroom, took a shot of hand lotion from a dispenser on her dresser and was rubbing it in when she heard a knock on the front door.

"Coming!" she yelled, glancing at her wristwatch. Five to twelve already and she was due at the shop at noon. Ah, well, her sister Sylvia was there handling things. She and Sylvia didn't watch clocks on one another.

She cut through the living room on her way to the front door wondering if she'd have to buy a new rubber hose. That darned Greg had promised three times already that he'd come over and fix it, but no luck yet.

Rounding the living room archway into the front hall she was surprised to find her son's apartment mate on the step.

"Christopher!" she greeted, smiling, opening the screen door. "What are you doing here? I thought you and Greg were going to the lake. Come on in."

"Hello, Mrs. Reston."

"He's not here, if you're looking for him. He promised he'd come over today to put a new end on my hose, but he never showed up. He still might though. You can wait for him if you want."

He stepped inside, wearing bathing trunks and a wild orange-and-green Hawaiian-print shirt, his hairy legs bare, his feet in rubber thongs. As she looked up she saw her distorted reflection in his mirrored sunglasses, which were looped from ear to ear by a hot-pink string.

She stood before him, still working the flowery-smelling lotion into her hands, impatient to be off to work.

"I understand you can join us for the Fourth. That's great. We're going to try injecting a turkey with garlic juice and doing it on the grill. Then if we can stand one another's breath for the rest of the day we'll play some volleyball and bocce. How does that sound?"

He didn't answer. In very slow motion he removed his sunglasses and lowered them gently to the limits of the hot-pink string. She could see immediately he'd been crying.

"Christopher, what is it?" She took a step toward him.

He swallowed once and his Adam's apple drifted down like an ice cube dropped into a drink.

"Mrs. Reston . . ."

She knew things about this young man that he didn't know she knew, about his pitiable childhood and the parents who'd treated him as if he were a mistake they never should have made.

"Christopher . . ." She touched his arm, prepared to let Sylvia work alone a little longer. "You need to talk?"

He cleared his throat, caught both her hands and gripped them hard. They were still sleek from lotion and smelled like honeysuckle.

"Mrs. Reston, I have some terrible news." He'd decided the best way to say it was straight out, avoiding any prolonged limbo. "There's been a very bad accident. Greg is dead."

Her face changed neither shape nor line. Her eyes either. "Greg?" she repeated in a perfectly normal voice, as if the message he'd delivered was too bizarre to be believable.

"I'm so sorry," he whispered.

For the longest time she didn't move, only stood before him while the shock waves rippled in and changed her life. Finally she covered her mouth with both hands and stared at Christopher while tears made her rust-colored eyes gleam like polished copper. "Greg," she uttered in a squeaky, distorted voice.

"He was on his way over here. A car ran a red light and hit him broadside. He was dead by the time our squad car reached the scene."

"Oh my God," she whispered, her hands dropping slowly. "Not Greg . . . oh no, not Greg."

Involuntary spasms replaced her indrawn breaths, each one accompanied by a tick in her throat. Her mouth opened and stayed open in a wide, silent call. It erupted at last in a dolorous, elongated syllable as Christopher caught her in his arms and felt his sunglasses bruise his chest. He pulled them free and held her as hard as human arms can hold. Her keening took on a pitiful tone like a child playing a high, uncertain violin note—"No . . . no . . . noooooo . . ."—squeaky, sliding off-tune near Christopher's ear with her face pointed toward heaven. Finally, when it seemed her lungs would burst from lack of air, she broke into wretched, full-scale weeping that racked her body. He held her firmly, feeling her weight deliver itself into his safekeeping until her knees finally buckled and she hung on him.

"Not another one . . ." she mourned. "No . . . not another one."

His heart broke. Surely it did, for he felt the splintering deep within, putting pressure on his bones, his belly, his lungs.

"H . . . he . . . w . . . was . . . c . . . coming . . . ov . . . er . . . to . . . fix . . . my . . . ho . . . ho . . . h . . ." She could not complete the word.

"Yes . . ." he whispered in a strangled voice. "He was coming to fix your hose." She began quaking terribly, and he lowered her to the floor. It was hardwood, cool against his bare knees as he held her from tipping sideways. She drooped with her forehead against his throat, against the bare triangle of hair and skin above his ridiculous Hawaiian shirt, to which she clung, sobbing and sobbing, rocking and rocking, pushing so hard against him that he swayed backward with each lunge.

"He tr . . . tried to f . . . fix it o . . . o . . . once but he b . . . bought the wr . . . wrong-sized end."

"I know . . ." he said, "I know . . . ," rubbing her back, aching from pity, wishing he could spare her this, bring Greg back, bring her other dead baby back, or her husband to help her through this ordeal. Instead, here he knelt and did his best at comforting, not quite a stranger but certainly not a friend, merely a young man she'd met a few times in passing to whom she'd been kind because he worked and lived with her son.

They knelt together so long his shirtfront grew soaked. His knees began aching. She was still weeping and rocking and keening. He gripped her arms and set her on the floor, leaned her back against the hall wall and sat with an arm around her while she wept against his chest.

Wept and rocked. Rocked and wept. Until the blue denim of her skirt was dotted with dark spots.

"I'll be right back." He propped her against the wall, then hurried off to hunt for Kleenex, which he found in the kitchen and took back to her. He sat down again, put the blue flowered box on her lap, pulled out three tissues for himself and three that he stuffed into her hand. It lay limp on her lap while she sat like a muscleless lump, propped against the wall. He put an arm around her and gave her all the time she needed, resting a cheek on her hair and stroking her arm, wiping her face now and then, and his own, dropping the used blue Kleenexes on the floor beside them.

Out on the street a car passed. The sprinkler splattered across the end of the driveway ten times . . . fifteen . . . twenty . . . . Her head felt hot in the hollow of his shoulder. Her bare arm stuck to his.

Finally she let out a ragged sigh and rolled her head upright, running the heel of her hand up her forehead. He removed his arm from around her and wondered what to do next. She blew her nose hard and discarded the Kleenex.

"Oh God," she whispered, as if unsure she had strength for more than remaining slump-shouldered against the wall. Her eyes closed and residual sobs jerked her body.

"Where's Janice?" he asked.

Tears seeped from between her eyelashes and she bit her lip to hold in some squeaking sobs. She drew her knees up, crossed her arms on them and buried her head, her shoulders shaking.

He put a hand on her shoulder blade. "Where is she?" he whispered.

"In S . . . San Fr . . . Francisco."

"San Francisco?"

"With her fr . . . friend K . . . Kim."

That's right. Greg had said his sister was going out west for a week's vacation. "How about Joey?"

"Joey's up at G . . . Gull Lake with the Wh . . . Whitmans."

"Someone will have to call them."

Her shoulders shook as she remained bowed over. He didn't know what to do: forget the details or begin handling them, let her cry or encourage her to stop, get help or leave her alone.

"Your sister—is she at the store?" he asked.

She nodded into her arms.

He went onto one knee beside her, looking down on her short disheveled hair, which was brown with copper highlights. "Would you like me to call her to come and be with you?"

"N . . . no." She lifted her head at last and swiped below her eyes with her open hands. "No, I'll call her." She sniffed once, hooked the Kleenex box and began rising unsteadily. When she rocked on her heels he reached out to help her, rising with her, waiting with a grip on her arm while she hung her head, drying her eyes once more.

At last she gave him a forced, quavery smile. Without returning it, he draped his arm around her shoulders and walked her slowly toward the kitchen. There was a phone on the counter but the table seemed safer. He pulled out a chair and guided her onto it, then sat down himself, on the chair with her sweater slung over the back. Her purse, Coca-Cola and books were still stacked on the table, a reminder of the happy, normal routine he had interrupted.

"We don't have to call anybody yet. Just take your time."

She propped her head with one hand and turned her face to the sliding door, where the curtain still luffed in the warm summer air.

He waited in silence, so wrapped up in her grief he had momentarily set his own aside.

"Do I have to go and identify him?" she asked, turning her puffy face to him.

"No. His driver's license did that."

She closed her eyes and sighed in relief, opened them and asked, "Did you see him?"

"No."

"Do you want to?"

"I don't know."

"Do you know if he was smashed up badly?"

"I didn't ask." Literally speaking, it was the truth. He hadn't asked.

"Was he in his car?"

He rose and tried three cupboard doors before finding glasses. He filled one with ice from the freezer and returned to the table, popped open the Coke can and filled the glass for her.

"Was he in his car?" she repeated, stoic and insistent, ready to go on to the next step.

Christopher went to stand at the sliding glass door with his back to her, his feet spread wide and his bare toes digging into the spongy blue rubber of his thongs. "No. On his motorcycle."

After a brief silence while she absorbed the news, her high, peculiar violin voice played some short, muffled, staccato notes. He turned to find her with the drink untouched, both elbows propped on the table, both hands covering her face. He moved behind her and bracketed her neck with both hands, just to let her know he was there, just the touch of someone who cared.

"You don't have to see him at all. What purpose will it serve?"

"I don't know . . . I have to . . . I'm his m . . . mother . . . oh God oh God oh God . . ."

"You need your family here. Should I call your sister . . . or your mother?"

"I'll c . . . call." She mopped her face and gained enough control to rise wearily, pushing off the tabletop with both hands.

He watched her walk into the U-shaped work area of the kitchen and pick up a white phone. The dial tone hummed for fifteen seconds before she dropped the receiver into the cradle without dialing and doubled over the counter.

He went to her immediately and said, "I'll call. Who?"

She seemed incapable of making the decision. "I don't know," she squeaked, beginning to cry again. "I d . . . don't kn . . . know. I don't want to p . . . put them through this."

"Here." He took her back to the table. "Just sit down and I'll take care of it. Where's your phone book?"

"In the d . . . drawer . . . over th . . . there."

He found her personal phone book in the second drawer he tried, and looked up the number of her flower shop. When he'd dialed she looked back over her shoulder at him, holding a blue Kleenex plastered over her mouth with one hand, her eyes red and running.

"Absolutely Floral," a woman answered.

"Is this Mrs. Eid?" he asked.

"Yes, it is."

"Mrs. Eid, are you there all alone or is there someone there with you?"

Her voice became suspicious. "Who is this?"

"I'm sorry, this is Christopher Lallek. I'm a friend of your nephew Greg Reston. I'm at your sister's house and I'm afraid I have some very bad news. Greg has been killed in a motorcycle accident."

He pictured Mrs. Eid with her mouth wide open during the silence, then dropping into a chair when she whispered, "Oh my God."

"I'm sorry to give you the news so abruptly. Is someone there with you?"

She had begun to cry and was muffling the sound with her hand. Throughout the conversation his eyes had not left Mrs. Reston. She rose from her chair and came around the cabinet to take the receiver.

"Sylvia? . . . Oh, Sylvia . . . I know . . . oh God . . . yes . . . no, no . . . neither one of them . . . yes . . . oh, yes, please . . . thank you."

She needed his arms again and turned into them after hanging up. "She's coming," she whispered, and clung. The smell of her hand lotion became fixed in his memory while they stood in the kitchen waiting for her sister. Other impressions were stored away, too. The exact angle of the afternoon light falling through the trees in the backyard. The way the curtain kept flapping. The distant burping of a lawn mower being started. The smell of freshly cut grass. The sight of a bouquet of flowers blurring, then clearing, then blurring again as his eyes filled and refilled, familiar garden flowers whose names he did not know. A photograph of Greg stuck into the corner of a framed print on a blue-papered wall. The beads of condensed moisture running down the side of an iced glass of Coke the way Greg's mother's tears rolled down her face. The feel of her denim skirt against his bare legs. Her hot face stuck to the side of his neck and his own shirt plastered to his skin by their combined tears. A note on her refrigerator door that said *Give Greg the leftover lasagna.* Another that said *Janice, NW Flight 75, 1:35.* The ceaseless drone of that mower. The radio playing Vince Gill's mournful "When I Call Your Name."

Greg's mother whispering brokenly, "Oh, he loved this song."

Chris replying, "Yes, I know. He played it all the time." They both had loved the song; they'd both owned the CD.

Sorrow spilling upward in Christopher and Lee Reston as they realized how many such sad reminders lay in the days, months and years ahead.

They heard the car pull in and separated. Her forehead was marked with an oval red spot where it had stuck to his neck, crossed by a deeper red crease from his hot-pink Croakies.

Footsteps pounded up the sidewalk. The front door opened and Lee ran toward it, trailed by Christopher, who stood back and watched the first of many sorrowful embraces he would witness in the coming days. He saw her tears begin again and swallowed down his own.

"Oh, Lee . . ." As her name was spoken in sympathy he thought, *It's too much for one woman—a baby, a husband, now a full-grown son.*

"Why, Sylvia, why?" she wailed.

Sylvia could only answer, "I don't know, honey, I don't know."

The two sisters clung and wept together.

"Oh, Greg . . . Greg . . ." The name escaped Lee Reston as a lament, a long woeful call to her beloved boy who would never hear his name spoken again.

Christopher Lallek, standing by listening, watching, felt his desolation deepen with every passing minute. He was thirty years old, but was experiencing the cruel impact of true grief for the first time in his life. He was stunned by how lost and uncertain he felt. All the past concerns of his life seemed paltry and inconsequential when weighed against the awful finality of death. How consuming and powerful it was, robbing one of the will to think, to move, to force one's limbs to bend toward the next eventuality.

If he felt so, how must she feel, the mother?

She withdrew from her sister's embrace and Sylvia Eid drew back to find Christopher hovering nearby. Through her tears she managed to speak the words "You're Christopher." He found himself clinging to the strange woman with an intensity he would not have imagined yesterday. He, who held people at bay, who radiated toward no one—least of all strangers—was locked breast to breast with a woman he'd scarcely spoken to before.

They gave each other momentary solace, then turned back to the one who needed it more. Each with an arm around Lee, they urged her toward the living room and sat her on the sofa between them—an odd spot at noon on a weekday, but the place that seemed fitting for mourning. Lee Reston clung to her sister's hand, repeating the chant that Christopher would hear over and over again in the next three days.

"He was . . . he was coming over here to . . . to put a new end on a hose for me."

Why did it start his tears again? Because it was a reminder of how blithely he had taken life for granted until an hour ago? Because it was a reminder of how Greg had cared for his mother? Because it was one of those simple everyday things that speaks of love and devotion so much more loudly than words?

The women made it over another emotional hurdle, then Sylvia asked, "How did you find out?"

"From Christopher. He came over as soon as he heard."

Sylvia looked over at him with reddened eyes. "How did you find out?"

"I . . ." He had to clear his throat and start again. "I went into the station to pick up my paycheck and they told me."

Lee Reston looked up through her tears. She squeezed the back of his hand. "What a horrible shock that must have been for you. And then you had to . . . to come over here and tell me." He looked down at her hand covering his and relived the shock, but found some control deep down within that kept his hand steady and his eyes dry. He turned his hand over, linked his fingers with hers and whispered hoarsely, "He loved you so damned much."

She let her eyes close, battling for control; opened them to reveal large, rust-colored irises brimming with tears. "Thank you," she whispered, squeezing his hand tenaciously.

In that moment while they sat connected by grief and sympathy for each other some ineffable bond was forged.

He had given her what she needed to make it through the next hour.

She had recognized that he'd had the toughest job of all, coming here to break the news to her.

"I'll be here for you . . . whatever you need," he promised, and the promise went as deep as his love and grief for her son.

"Thank you, Christopher," she said, squeezing his hand even harder, appreciating him fully for the first time, admitting how comforting a man's presence was and that she'd undoubtedly call on him again and again throughout the terrible days ahead.

Chapter 2

Lee Reston felt as if she were moving through a phantasm, at moments so steeped in grief it rendered her incapable of anything more than weeping. At other times she'd operate almost as if outside herself, facing the next dread and unavoidable duty.

Janice must be called.

"Janice . . ." Merely speaking her name brought tears welling, along with a great unwillingness to shatter her daughter's world a moment sooner than necessary.

"I'll call Janice," Sylvia offered.

"Thank you, Sylvia, but Janice should hear it from me."

"Oh, Lee, why put yourself through it?"

"I'm her mother. I'll do it."

There was within Lee Reston a vein of implacability so strong it sometimes amazed even her. To escape in a faint, to collapse uselessly would have been totally out of character. What needed facing, she faced. Always had, always would. Sylvia was here, and the young man, Christopher. She would rely on their support and do what must be done.

She did, however, allow Sylvia to dial the phone. Lee's hand shook as she took the receiver, and her legs felt rubbery. A chair was nudged behind her knees—a sudden blessing—and she withered down to it.

Janice sounded agonizingly happy. "Mom, hi! What a surprise! Five more minutes and we'd have been out the door. We're going to Fisherman's Wharf today!"

Oh, Janice, my beloved daughter, how I wish I didn't have to do this to you.

"Honey, I'm afraid I'm going to have to ask you to come home. I have some very sad news. Janice, dear, I'm so sorry . . . there's been a very bad motorcycle accident." Saying it for the first time was like hearing it for the first time: shock and horror coupled with a sense of unreality, as if it were someone else speaking the words about her son. "Our sweet Greg is dead."

"Oh no . . . no . . . nooooo. Oh, Mom . . . Oh God . . . no . . ."

She gripped the receiver in both hands, wanting to be there with Janice, to hold her, cradle her, help her through this. Instead they were separated by 2,000 miles and she could only listen to her daughter weep. "No, no, it can't be true!"

"Oh, Janice, darling, I wish I were there with you." Through those terrible minutes on the phone, Lee was vaguely aware of Sylvia's arm surrounding her shoulders and Christopher standing nearby.

"Janice, you'll have to . . . to get the first . . . first fl . . . fl . . ." She broke into tears and tried to stifle them so Janice wouldn't hear. Sylvia turned her into a hug and Chris took the receiver.

"Janice, this is Christopher Lallek. I'm here with your mother and so is your aunt Sylvia. I'm so sorry . . . yes, we're all in shock."

Her voice was broken and distorted by weeping. She asked questions and he answered—the difficult ones a mother should not have to repeat. Afterward he said, "Janice, put Kim on the phone." Realizing Janice was too overwrought with shock to function well, he spoke to the other young woman about changing plane reservations, told her to call back and that he'd be out at the airport himself to pick up Janice whenever she came in. With these details handled, he returned the phone to Mrs. Reston and listened to a painful goodbye.

"J . . . Janice? . . . Yes . . . me too . . . Please hurry."

Hanging up, Lee felt depleted. Still, she said, "I may as well call Joey too and get it over with."

"Let me," Sylvia pleaded in a whisper. "Please, let me."

"No, Sylvia. This one I have to do, too. And the mortuary. Then I'll let you and Christopher do the rest."

As it turned out, the Whitman family couldn't be reached. It was a hot summer afternoon: They were probably out on the lake.

Lee said, "We'll keep trying them." She stared at the telephone, which seemed both friend and enemy. She'd been through this before; she knew what must be done but resisted making the move to pick up that instrument once more and order a caretaker of dead bodies to take care of her son's. *Dear God . . . on his motorcycle.* The image struck with horrendous force but she buried it behind a memory of Greg hale and smiling as he drove his cycle out of her driveway, lifting a hand in farewell, shouting, "Thanks for the good grub, Ma. You're a helluva cook!"

Other memories came, of the day Bill died, and their three-month-old baby, Grant. She shuddered and summoned a picture of her two remaining children, thinking, *I'm lucky, I'm lucky, I've still got them. I'll be strong for them.*

Keeping their images clearly before her, she dialed the mortuary. She did fine until the question "Where is he?"

Suddenly reality dropped and crushed her. "Why . . . where?" she repeated, casting her eyes around as if searching for the answer in the paint on the walls. "I . . . I don't . . . oh, goodness . . ."

Immediately Christopher came and took the phone. He spoke in a clear, authoritative voice. "This is police officer Christopher Lallek of the Anoka Police Department, a friend of the deceased. May I answer any questions?"

He listened and said, "Mercy Hospital morgue."

"At ten-thirty today."

"A motorcycle accident."

"Yes."

"Yes, I think so."

"910-8510."

"Faith Lutheran."

"Yes, if she doesn't have one we have one at the police department."

"If it would be all right I think she'll need a little time to make that decision. Some of the family members haven't even been informed yet."

"Yes, tomorrow would be better."

"I think nine would be fine. Thank you, Mr. Dewey."

When he'd hung up he wrote Walter Dewey's name and number on a pad beside the phone and told Lee, "You'll need to meet with him, of course, but tomorrow is time enough. He suggested nine o'clock and I said I thought that would be fine. Meanwhile you don't have to worry about making any other arrangements. He'll take care of everything."

"Greg is at the morgue already?"

"Yes. At Mercy Hospital. When the department responds to a fatality that's where they're taken. Mr. Dewey will handle everything."

It struck Lee again how glad she was to have Christopher Lallek here. He, too, must still be in the throes of shock, but he was hiding it well, taking over some of the unpleasant tasks as a husband would if she still had one . . . or as a grown son would. Whenever she was near crumbling, he stepped in and relieved her without being asked to. She recognized that having him here—not only a masculine presence but also Greg's best friend—moving around her kitchen, lifting her burdens in whatever way possible, was much like having Greg himself here.

She left Sylvia and went to him. "Christopher," she said, putting her hands on the short sleeves of his wild Hawaiian shirt. "Thank you. I'm sorry I broke down and left that to you."

"You've got a right to break down, Mrs. Reston. This is one of the worst days of your life."

"Of yours too," she said understandingly.

"Yes . . . it is. But . . . ." He looked at the notes on her refrigerator door. "I think he'd want me to help you any way I could, so if you don't mind, I'll stick around."

She hugged him hard and they listened to each other gulp down wads of grief.

She rubbed the center of his back with both hands as if he were her own son, and for the briefest flash it felt like holding Greg again.

The telephone rang.

Sylvia answered while the other two watched and listened.

"Yes, Kim. Northwest flight three fifty-six . . . Seven fifty-nine. I've got it." She wrote it down and listened for a while. "I'm sorry your vacation has been ruined, but it's so kind of you to come back home with her. She'll need your support, I'm sure." After another pause, she said, "Seven fifty-nine, yes. I'm not sure which one of us will be there to pick you up, but somebody will. Please tell her her mother is doing all right. We're still here with her and she'll have someone with her every minute. Yes. Yes. All right, see you then."

When she'd hung up, Sylvia said, "Kim is coming home with Janice, so try not to worry about her, Lee."

That was only the first call of many. The afternoon wore on, bringing the reality of the staggering number of telephone calls necessitated by an unexpected death. Sylvia and Christopher took turns making them—to Sylvia's husband, Barry, who showed up at the house within fifteen minutes after receiving the news; to Lee's mother and father, who broke into noisy weeping and needed much calming before the conversation could be continued; to the next-door neighbor and dear friend Tina Sanders, who came immediately, too. To the flower shop. To the Whitmans' again and again and again with no response.

The house began filling with people. Neighbors arrived asking what they could do. Sylvia began organizing them with calling lists. While they were writing down names and telephone numbers the oddest impulse came over Lee. She turned, lifted her head and actually opened her mouth to ask the question *Did anyone call Greg yet?* Just like on any normal day. Startled, she caught herself before phrasing it, and the reality of his death struck her afresh. She stood in midst of a circle of women who were poring over her phone book, wondering how it could be possible she'd never call Greg again, never hear him laugh, never see him walk into this kitchen and open the refrigerator door looking for leftovers, never see him marry, have children. Could it really be true that his death had prompted all the hubbub around her?

Someone brought in a thirty-six-cup percolator and soon the house was filled with the smell of coffee. Someone else brought in a platter of sliced fruit, then a coffee cake appeared. Lee's parents arrived needing more consolation than they were able to give, and she found herself giving the support despite the fact she still needed it so badly herself. But for them the news was fresh. There was a fleeting moment when she was holding her mother, feeling the older woman's sobs quaking them both, that Lee thought, *I've got to get out of here! I can't stand this a minute more!* But the door opened and someone else came in. Someone else who needed to shed first tears on Lee's shoulder, and grip her in a desperate embrace. In the midst of the growing gaggle of mourners Christopher found Lee and quietly told her, "Mrs. Reston, I've got Joey on the phone."

Her heart began pounding and her limbs felt suddenly leaden. She went dutifully to the phone and he followed, then stood with his back to her as if shielding her from the others in the room while she faced this next heartrending duty. "Joey?"

"Hi, Mom, is something wrong? How come Chris called me?"

"Joey, honey, this is the hardest thing I've ever had to tell you. It's . . ."

While she paused to steady herself he said in a panicky voice, "Is somebody hurt, Mom? Is Janice okay?"

"It's not Janice, Joey . . . it's Greg."

"Greg?" His voice cracked into a high falsetto. "What happened?"

"Greg had a motorcycle accident, honey."

He said really softly, "Ohhh."

"Greg is dead, honey."

He said nothing for the longest time. When he spoke, his voice sounded the way it had a year ago when it was first changing. "Dead? But . . . but how can he be?"

"I know it's hard to believe but it's really true. It happened this morning."

"But . . . but he was gonna take me and the guys to Valley Fair next week."

"I know, dear, I know."

"Aw Jeez, Mom . . ." He was trying not to cry, but the falsetto and the broken phrasing gave him away. "It's not fair."

She whispered, "I know, Joey."

"How we gonna get along without him?"

"We will . . . you'll see. It'll be hard, but we've still got each other. And lots of people who love us. Aunt Sylvia is here with me now, and Grandpa and Grandma and a lot of the neighbors, and Christopher, and Janice is coming home tonight. But I need you here too, okay?"

He barely got out, "Okay."

"I love you. And we're going to be okay. You'll see. We're going to make it through this."

"Okay. Mrs. Whitman wants to talk to you now."

Mrs. Whitman sounded terrified. "Dear God," she said. "We'll leave immediately. We'll have Joey home as soon as we can get him there. Oh, Lee, I'm so sorry."

Lee hung up the phone and dried her eyes to find Chris still shielding her from the rest of the room. He turned and said quietly, "That was a tough one."

"Yes."

"Does someone need to drive up there and get him?"

"No, they're bringing him back."

"You're sure? Because I'll go. I'd be happy to."

Gratitude flooded her. She laid a hand on his arm. "I know you would, but no. They're leaving immediately. But, Chris, if you meant it when you said you'd go to the airport to get Janice and Kim, I'd really appreciate it."

He covered her hand and squeezed it. "Of course I meant it."

"Because if I went out to get Janice, I might not be here when Joey gets home, and I—" She could feel her emotions cracking again but he forestalled another breakdown.

"Don't say another word. I'll be there when her plane touches down. Now how about you? You making it okay? Do you want some coffee or something?"

"No thank you, Christopher, but have some yourself."

"No, I couldn't eat a thing. Feel like it'd come back up."

It was late afternoon. The neighbors had begun returning with hot foods, sandwiches, salads. The front screen door seemed to open and close incessantly and the murmur of voices filled the place.

Sylvia came into the kitchen and said, "Lloyd is here, Lee."

"Lloyd. Oh, Lloyd." She immediately moved toward the front hall, where her father-in-law had just come in. His hair was as silver as the rims of his glasses. A trim man of medium height, he had the gentlest face of any human being she'd ever known, with features that even in sorrow looked accepting and kind.

"Lee," he said. Nothing more. Only folded her in his arms and held her for the longest time while they both relived the day they'd grieved this way for Bill, his son. Odd how she loved this man. More than her own father, for she felt more at ease with him, could talk to him more honestly, could bare her soul with him. He wasn't Bill—she had never mistakenly substituted him for Bill—but in Lloyd Reston's arms she felt closer to her husband than anywhere else. It felt as if Bill were here with her now, fortifying her, as Lloyd said quietly, "Life is so full of sorrow, and we've had our share, haven't we, little one? But we'll weather this one, too. We know we can because we've done it before."

When he pulled back there were tears in his eyes and on his cheeks, but he demonstrated none of the histrionics of her own mother and father, and she found this calming.

"Do the children know?"

"Yes. They're on their way."

"Good." He squeezed her shoulders. "You'll feel better once they're with you. Are there too many others? Are we overwhelming you?"

"No. They all mean well, and they need to gather because it's scary for them, too. It might not be their son, but they all realize it could be someday. Let them stay."

Her pastor arrived, Reverend Ahldecker, and as she was being consoled by him she looked out through the screen door to see Christopher, alone in the front yard, turning off the lawn sprinkler, which had been running in one spot all day. He gathered in the hose, coiling it between the shrubs by the front door. His chin was resting on his chest and his motions were slow and methodical. There were tears running down his face.

His sad solitude touched her deeply. Alone out there, winding up the hose, crying the tears he withheld in the house while offering his support to her. Time and again he had sensed when she needed him, and now it was time to return the favor.

"Excuse me, Reverend Ahldecker, I'll be right back."

She went outside, closing the screen door silently. Approaching him from behind she slipped her arms around his waist, spread her hands on his chest where his sunglasses still hung and laid her cheek between his shoulder blades. His shirt was hot from the late afternoon sun. His heartbeat was steady but his breathing irregular, caught at intervals by swallowed sobs. At her touch, his hands fell lifelessly to his side, the hose still trailing from his fingers. They stood so for long moments, the sprinkler head dripping water onto the sidewalk and splashing their ankles. Neither of them noticed. Neither of them cared.

Their shadows, from behind, stretched along the wet concrete like gray cutouts. Evening was approaching. From a telephone wire nearby a mourning dove called. Some distance away, another answered—like the two of them, calling and answering each other's mourning throughout this bizarre and unspeakably sad day.

At last Christopher drew in a great sigh and expelled his breath with a shudder. "I loved him, you know? And I never told him."

"He knew it. And he loved you, too."

"But I should have told him."

"We tell people those things in countless ways. Last week he said you brought him two cinnamon tornados from Hans's bakery. And I recall times when you washed his car just because you were washing your own, and drove out to give him a jump start when his battery was dead, and returned his video rentals so he wouldn't have to pay an overdue charge. Those are all ways in which we say I love you. He knew it. Don't ever think he didn't."

"But I should have said it."

"Don't be so hard on yourself, Christopher. I'm sure he knew."

"No one ever taught me how to say it. I never had . . ."

He cut the remark short and her mother's heart went out to him for the love he'd never had at home.

"Did he ever say it to you?"

Christopher dropped his gaze to the green rubber hose, scratching it absently with a thumbnail. "No."

"But do you doubt it?"

He shook his head.

"Let me tell you something, Christopher." She stepped back, turned him around and looked up at him. "From the time you two became roommates, he never once took leftovers from here without asking if I had enough for you, too. 'He's never had much home cooking, Mom,' he'd say, 'so put in extra for Chris.' And I did, and he'd take them for you because that was one of his ways of saying he loved you. And there was never a holiday he wasn't worried about you being alone. That's why he invited you here to be with us. And didn't he fix something on that disreputable old car of yours just a couple of weeks ago? Some fuse for the air conditioner or something? I know he did, so don't you waste a minute of your precious life regretting that you never told him. Because he knew it just like you knew it."

Christopher sniffed and wiped his nose with the edge of one hand. Lee found a tissue in her skirt pocket and handed it to him.

"If it'll make you feel better, promise yourself that from now on you'll tell people how they matter to you. If you love someone, tell him."

He blew his nose and nodded at the sidewalk. "I will."

"All right," she said. "Feeling better now?"

He blew out a deep breath. "Yeah. Thanks."

"I've been through this before, you know. I'm an old hand at handling grief, and I know that there's a good year or more of it ahead for both of us. I also know that it doesn't always strike you conveniently when you're off duty, or during daylight hours, or in the privacy of your own home. Grief is an ill-mannered bastard. It strikes you when you least expect it to. When that happens, just remember, Christopher, I'm here and you can come to me anytime, night or day. And somehow we'll muddle through. Okay?"

He nodded again and murmured, "Thanks, Mrs. Reston."

"And now you have to leave for the airport, and I have to speak to Reverend Ahldecker."

She braved a smile. There wasn't a trace of makeup left on her face. Her skin was red and roughened by all the tears and tissues that had worried it that day. Studying her, Christopher saw the resemblance to Greg in the shape of her eyebrows and lips.

"I can see why he loved you so much, and admired you. You're very wise and very strong."

She gave him a gentle shove toward his car and said, "Go on now, before you start me crying again."

At Twin Cities International Airport, Northwest flight 356 taxied to a stop at Gate 6. Janice Reston reached in the overhead compartment for her carry-on bag and waited leadenly for the door to be opened and the passengers to bump their way up the aisle ahead of her.

She wondered if her mom was waiting inside the terminal, or Aunt Sylvia and Uncle Barry. Maybe Grandpa and Grandma Hillier. She had cried throughout most of the flight from San Francisco, staring out the window while the sun moved around behind the plane and reflected off its silver wing. Kim had dried her eyes often, too, then had opened a book that lay unread on her lap while she clasped Janice's hand and Janice had talked through her grief.

Now, walking up the jetway and into the airport she was surprised to see Christopher Lallek waiting at the top of the ramp.

"Chris," she cried, and dropped her canvas bag as he came forward to scoop her into his arms.

"Janice . . ."

"Oh, Chris, how can it be true?"

She clung to him, her arms doubled around his neck while weeping assailed her once more. He held her so firmly only her toes grazed the floor while passengers threaded their way around them and Kim looked on with fresh tears in her eyes. Janice had imagined being in Chris's arms since the first time she'd met him two years ago, when Greg had joined the Anoka police force and the two had begun sharing an apartment. Never had she imagined him holding her for such a reason. He was thirty, she only twenty-three. He'd always treated her like Greg's kid sister, old enough to be in college and out on her own, but far too young to date. Suddenly, in the space of a few hours, death had stepped in and trivialized age differences. Their mutual bereavement brought them together simply as two people who had loved someone they'd lost. Only that loss mattered while they clung and grieved.

They separated and Chris extended his hand. "Hi, Kim. I'm Christopher Lallek. I'm sorry you had to end your vacation so soon after you got there."

Kim's face, too, looked puffy and red. "There was no question of my staying once I heard the news."

He picked up Janice's carryon and they walked three abreast toward the luggage return.

In his car, heading north to Anoka, Kim sat in back, Janice in front. He answered Janice's questions and reached over to rub her shoulder when she was forced to dig in her purse for Kleenex again and again.

"How's Mom holding up?"

"Like the Rock of Gibraltar, cheering up everybody who comes in the door instead of the other way around. Greg always said she was a strong woman and I've seen it today. I know she'll feel better when you get home though. The hardest thing she did was call you and your brother."

"Is he home yet?"

"He wasn't when I left. The Whitmans were heading back from the lake though to bring him."

They rode along thinking awhile, about their own feelings, and Lee's, and those of a fourteen-year-old boy who had been left the only male in the family. The muffler on Chris's old car was nearly shot; its thunder reverberated in their heads while the rush of hot wind from the partially opened windows moved their hair. The fuse had blown on the air conditioner shortly after Greg replaced it, but Christopher had decided it wasn't worth replacing with the new Explorer soon to arrive. The new Explorer—hell, he hadn't given it a thought since noon. The dealer had probably called his apartment all afternoon wondering what had happened to him. Funny how the new vehicle had lost all importance in light of today's tragedy. The sun was dropping toward the horizon. The outline of downtown Minneapolis appeared veiled in a shimmery pearlescent haze then fell behind them as I-94 curved around it and continued north.

Christopher fixed his eyes on the tar and drove without conscious awareness of changing lanes, working a signal light, maintaining speed. The two women stared out their side windows and Janice thought about how everything had changed since yesterday. How her life would never be quite the same again. All those memories she and Greg had shared of growing up together; there was nobody to reminisce with now, especially about the time before Daddy had died. Joey was so much younger his memories were separate from Janice's. It was Greg she'd played with, had gone to high school with, had cheered for when he ran the 440 and talked with about dating and the boys she'd liked, the girls he'd liked.

His kids would have been her kids' cousins. They'd have played together as they grew up, and would have shared holidays. She'd have baby-sat them sometimes when he and his wife wanted to get away alone. All their kids would have been at each others' birthday parties, graduation parties, weddings. Staring out the car window she felt suddenly cheated and angry. All that time and love invested in someone else's life and now he was gone, and with him so much of her future!

Abruptly she felt guilty for the thought. *How can I be angry? And with whom? Greg? Mom? Dad? The baby that died and didn't have to go through all this heartache and isn't here for me now? Myself for going off to San Francisco instead of spending the last couple of days with him?*

She dropped her head back against the seat and said, "Do you feel angry, Chris?"

He glanced over at her. "Yes."

"With whom?"

"With Greg, for not wearing a helmet. With fate. Hell, I don't know."

She felt better then, knowing he'd experienced the same feeling as she—selfish as it seemed.

"I keep thinking about how he never got a chance to get married . . . to have kids."

"Yeah, I know."

"And Mom and all of us. I mean—damn it!—think about birthdays! Think about Christmas!" She had begun to cry again. "They're gonna b . . . be awful!"

She was right. He could only reach over and take her hand.

He thought he had never witnessed anything more pathetic than the reunion of Lee Reston and her children. He stood by, watching the three of them form a knot of sorrow, and would truly have given a good portion of his own life in exchange for the restoration of Greg to them.

He heard their weeping, witnessed their ungainly three-way hug, watched the mother's hands stroke her children's heads while their faces were buried against her. He moved away to give them privacy, went into the backyard and sat down on the deck steps leading to the lawn. It was a pretty lawn, deep, reaching 200 feet back toward a row of arbor vitae that divided it from the neighbor's house beyond. At the near end shade trees spread. At the far end flower borders with serpentine edges meandered around three edges of the property surrounding an open stretch of grass that served as a volleyball court during family picnics. He'd been at a couple of these. They lingered in his memory as lucky days, some of the luckiest of his life. Hot dogs and laughter and family and friends—all the things he'd missed in his own life. And Greg had brought him into it all. They'd welcomed him as they'd welcome one of their own—"Beer's over there. Pop's over there and anybody who doesn't help himself to the food goes hungry without sympathy!"

Fourth of July was probably off. He supposed there'd be no picnic here this year. He'd asked his captain for the day off clear back in April. He'd probably go in and volunteer for duty that day so one of the married guys could be with his family. Hell, he had nothing better to do. He was used to volunteering for holidays. Better than sitting around feeling sorry for himself.

He remembered one Fourth of July when he was twelve, thirteen maybe. Junior high and he'd joined the band, asked to play the tuba because there was no money for instruments at his house, and the school provided tubas and drums. He'd chosen tuba and could remember its weight on his shoulder, the feeling of that big cup-sized mouthpiece against his lips, and the surge of excitement when he'd marched down the street with that big brass bell above his head for the first time. There'd been a favorite march: the Klaxon, that was it, and—damn!—how it had stirred his blood when they'd played it. Pum, pum, pum, pum: He and the bass drum setting the rhythm as the band strutted down the street. The band director, Mr. Zatner, said the junior band had been invited to march at a parade in the small town of Princeton and they'd all been issued satin capes, maroon on one side, black on the other, and were told to wear black trousers and white shirts.

He went home with a knot in his gut because he knew he'd have to ask his parents to buy him a pair of black pants. They lived in a sleazy apartment above an appliance store a half block off Main. A warped, weathered open stairway led up to it from the alley where the smell of rotting vegetables hung heavy in the warm months from the garbage dollies of the Red Owl store next door. A few times, when there was nothing in the apartment to eat, he'd hung around the back door of the grocery store when the produce people were weeding out the bad stuff.

"Hey, need some help?" he'd asked, and the man in the soiled white apron had said, "Hey, this is one for the record! A kid offering help? Sure, why not?"

They'd tossed away some discolored cauliflower, some fancy kinds of lettuce that looked black and slimy, and bunches of broccoli that looked fine to Chris. Trouble was, he hated broccoli. They came to oranges—soft in spots but far from moldy.

"Hey, these look good yet," Chris had said.

"Not good enough to sell."

"Mind if I eat one?"

"Don't mind at all. Here, have two. Have three." Chris caught the three oranges as the man tossed them his way.

That day he took home oranges, wilted carrots and something called spaghetti squash, which tasted like fodder when he peeled and cooked it. His little sister, Jeannie, complained, "But I don't like it!"

"Eat it!" he'd ordered. "It's good for you and it's another nine days before the old man gets his welfare check."

But they both knew the old man and old lady had to buy their booze first. They bought most of it in a dive the kids referred to as "The Hole," a block from the apartment, down one level from the street, a dank, smoky basement bar where the old man went as soon as he got up in the morning, and where the old lady joined him straight from work. She was a fry cook in a truck stop out on Highway 10, gone from the apartment before the kids woke up in the morning, most nights stumbling home after they'd gone to bed.

Both the old man and old lady were at The Hole the day Christopher came home with the knot in his gut about the black slacks. He boiled Jeannie some macaroni and mixed it with Campbell's tomato soup and after she went to bed, he waited up for his parents.

They came in around midnight, arguing as usual. When they stumbled in, stinking like a barroom floor, the old man wavered in his tracks and spoke with slack lips anchoring a smoking cigarette.

"What the hell you still doing up?"

"I gotta talk to you."

"At midnight, for Chrissake! Punk like you oughta be in bed."

"I would be if you'd have gotten home at a decent hour!"

"You're some smart-ass kid, you know that! Don't tell me when to come home and when not to! I still wear the pants in this family!"

He sure did. They were filthy and smelled bad, like all the rest of him, and hung like a hammock below his protruding beer belly.

"I need some money for a pair of slacks."

"You got jeans."

"Black ones."

"Black ones!" he exploded. "What the hell you need black ones for!"

"For a band uniform. We're marching in a parade and everyone needs to wear white shirts and black slacks."

"A parade! Jesus Christ, they think I got money to fork over every time a parade comes to town! Tell your band director to come over here and tell me to my face that I got to foot the bill for any goddamn band uniform! I'll tell him a thing or two!"

His mother spoke up. "Shh, Ed, shut up for God's sakes! You're gonna wake up Jeannie!"

"Don't tell me to shut up, Mavis! This is my goddamn house! *I can yell as loud as I want to in it!*"

"Dad, I need the money."

"Well, I haven't got it!"

"You had enough to get drunk tonight. Both you and Ma."

"You just watch your mouth, sonny!"

"It's the truth."

"There's nothin' wrong with a man having a little drink or two, and I don't need any smart-ass kid like you tellin' me when I've had enough!"

"Ed, don't start in on him."

"You always stick up for him, goddamn it! Smart-ass kid's got no respect for his elders, that's what. Anytime a smart-ass kid tells his own father—" He belched unexpectedly, his slack lips flapping, the bags under his eyes nearly doing the same.

"I'll be the only one without black slacks."

"Well, that's just too bad, ain't it! Goddamn government bleeds a man for taxes to build schools, then they come beggin' for more! You can wear the jeans you got on, and if that ain't good enough for 'em, screw 'em."

"Dad, please . . . everyone's wearing maroon-and-black capes and my blue jeans will look—"

"Capes!" Ed's head jutted forward. "Capes! Jesus Christ, what're they turning out over there, a bunch of sissies! Capes!" He bellowed with laughter, the buttons over his belly straining as he bent back. With a jeering stare at his son, he straightened, pulled the cigarette from his mouth and squashed it out in an ashtray. "I got no money for sissy uniforms and you can tell your band director I said so."

Christopher and Jeannie shared a dinky bedroom with space for little more than their narrow twin beds and one beat-up chest of drawers. Though he got under his covers without turning on the light, he knew she was over there wide awake. Sometimes she pretended to be asleep when their parents were fighting, but not tonight.

"I hate them," she said matter-of-factly.

"You shouldn't say that."

"Why? Don't you?"

He did, but he didn't want his feelings to infect her. Girls were different. Girls needed their moms, especially—a lot longer than boys did.

Jeannie startled him by declaring, "I'm getting out of here as soon as I'm old enough."

Hell, she was only nine. She should be living a carefree life instead of plotting her escape from her family.

"Jeannie, don't say that."

"But it's true. I'm going to run away."

"Aw, Jeannie, come on . . ."

"And when I do, I'm never coming back, except maybe once or twice to see you. You're the only good thing around here."

He lay with a lump in his throat, unable to rebuke her with any amount of conviction, for he'd had the same thoughts himself.

The following week, Mavis slipped him twenty-five dollars. "Here's for those black slacks," she said.

"Thanks," he said without any warmth. He deserved decent clothes, and food on the table, and parents at home and sober now and then. Every kid deserved that much. If it weren't for him Jeannie'd have gone to school even tackier than she did. He made her comb her hair and eat some toast and put on her jacket every morning while the old man snored in his alcoholic stupor and his mother fried eggs at the truck stop to earn enough money for their endless boozing.

Twenty-five dollars slipped into his hand now and then couldn't make up for two drunken parents who didn't have time to raise their kids.

"Your dad didn't mean anything by it. He's had it hard, you know—falling off that loading dock and busting up his back. He was a different man before that happened."

He'd heard this so often, but he didn't buy any of it. Other people had strokes of bad luck in their lives and overcame them. Other moms realized that nine-year-old girls needed somebody to wash and iron their clothes and be home to cook them supper and wish them goodnight at bedtime. Ed and Mavis were alcoholics, plain and simple, and she was no better than the old man. They didn't beat their kids, but they didn't have to: Neglect did it for them.

Christopher Lallek marched in that Fourth of July parade dressed in new black jeans. But no parents were there watching from the curb, and the joy of playing the Klaxon had somehow dimmed after his father's disparaging remarks about sissies. The following year he dropped band from his schedule and took Home Ec instead. He figured if he had to cook for himself and Jeannie for the next five years he'd at least learn how. And in Home Ec class he got a free meal now and then.

Christopher sat on the steps of a redwood deck, remembering. Dark had fallen and the first stars were gleaming in the southeast sky. Crickets were singing in Mrs. Reston's garden. Behind him, light glowed through her kitchen door while on her refrigerator hung a note about leftover lasagna. His stomach growled, reminding him he hadn't eaten all day, but he had no urge to do so. He should get up and go home, leave this family to themselves, but he didn't know how he could handle walking into his apartment with all its reminders of Greg. Greg's clothing in the closet, his CDs in the living room, his mail on the kitchen cabinet, his shampoo in the shower, his favorite juice in the refrigerator.

Sweet Jesus, he'd give anything if he had a mom and dad to go to, someone whose house he could walk into and be hugged and held and loved and cared about the way this family cared about one another. Someone who'd turn down the bed in their spare room and come to him as he lay in it and comb his hair back with their fingers and say, "It's going to be all right, son. You lost a friend but you still have us. We love you."

He'd never heard the words from them. Never. He'd never said them to a living soul, not even to Jeannie before she left or to Greg before he died. It was true what he'd told Mrs. Reston: He'd never been taught how.

They still lived in town, Ed and Mavis, in a trashy subsidized housing project where he was called regularly to handle domestics and disturbances of the peace. Last time he'd seen them was maybe three years ago. The old man had a grizzled beard and smelled as bad as ever, sitting in a rocker and sipping cheap whiskey straight from a pint bottle. The old lady had been drinking beer and watching soap operas, the place so filthy only a torching could improve it. He'd been called there to break up a fight in another apartment, and who knows what had prompted him to knock on their door. He wished he hadn't. Nothing had changed. Nothing was going to change.

Behind him, Lee Reston said, "Christopher? What are you doing out there alone in the dark?"

He sighed and rose from the hard wooden step, flexing his back, looking up at the stars.

"Remembering."

She slid open the screen and stepped out, crossing her arms and facing the sky just as he did.

"Yes," she said, then both of them held silent awhile, thinking about the night ahead, the days and months ahead. The crickets went on scraping away and the stocks in the garden gave off a pungent perfume. The moon had risen and dew was forming on the grass, which was growing at this very moment.

Life went on.

They must, too.

"It's time I go," he said.

"Where?"

"Back to the apartment."

"Oh, Christopher . . . shall I . . . would you like someone to . . ."

"It's okay, Mrs. Reston. I'll have to face it sometime. Your children are here now and you need some time alone with them. The captain has cleared me till after the funeral, for as long as I need, actually, so I'll be there at the apartment tomorrow. You'll need some of his clothes, his mail, his car keys . . . whatever. If you want me there when you come to get them just say the word. If you'd rather have me gone, that's okay, too. Now you'd better get some rest. You've had a rough day."

She crossed the deck, her feet clad in nylons, shoes left behind somewhere, and stood above him with her arms crossed and her hair backlit by the kitchen light. "You don't have to go back there yet. You can sleep on the sofa in the living room and we'll go together tomorrow."

For a moment he was tempted. The scene he envisioned earlier flashed through his imagination, of her combing his hair back as he lay on a pillow, of her calm voice saying, "It's okay, Christopher, I'm here and I love you. You're going to be just fine." But she had her family now, and her own grief to work through; she didn't need him hanging around tonight—someone else to worry about and soothe.

"Thanks, Mrs. Reston, but I'll be just fine. You go on back inside and be with your kids. I'll see you tomorrow."

She watched him head around the side of the house toward his car. Just as he reached the corner she called, "Christopher?"

He stopped and looked back at her. The moon had risen and by its light she made out the rim of his short regulation haircut, the busy Hawaiian print on his shoulders, his bare legs and feet, still in the rubber thongs he'd been wearing this morning when he'd been heading for the beach for a day of fun.

"Thank you for all you did today. I couldn't have made it without you."

"Thank you, too," he said, "for letting me stay. I'd have gone crazy if I couldn't have been here with all of you."

He began to move again but she called "Just a minute!" and disappeared inside the kitchen. Momentarily she returned carrying a tinfoil-wrapped square in her hand. She thumped softly down the steps in her stocking feet, the light following her left side as she crossed the grass to put the packet in his hands. "You haven't eaten all day. Warm this up in your microwave . . . promise?"

"I will. Thanks."

It was cold on his palm, chilled from her refrigerator. He didn't have to open it to know it was lasagna.

Chapter 3

⌐⌐⌐

In his car, Christopher set the tinfoil packet on the seat, started the engine and with the greatest reluctance headed home.

Home was an apartment in a complex called Cutter's Grove where he and Greg had lived for two years. What had attracted Chris to the buildings at that time was the fact that they were brand-new and he'd be the first renter in his unit. Ask him and he'd admit he had a colossal hang-up about cleanliness. Not only was the apartment going to start clean, anybody who shared it was going to keep it that way!

When he learned that the new guy on the force was looking for a place to live, he'd approached Greg and told him truthfully, "I grew up in filth. I had two alcoholic parents who didn't give a damn whether there was food on the table, much less whether or not the joint got cleaned. So if you don't intend to do your share of KP duty, say so now. It'll save us a lot of friction later on."

Greg had replied, "I grew up with a mother who was widowed at thirty-six and had to leave the house and work from that time on. There were three of us kids left at home. Every Thursday morning she'd roust us out of bed at six o'clock and make us clean until seven, then that night after supper we had to finish the job so the place was shipshape for the weekend. If we didn't do our share of the work around the house we lost all privileges—and that included pocket money and using the car. How's that, Lallek?"

They had assessed each other, grinned, shaken hands and begun a friendship.

When Christopher unlocked the apartment door and turned on the light all was in order, as usual. To his right the kitchen was neat. Straight ahead, the living room was, too. It was decorated—actually decorated—in off-white and cocoa brown. They had agreed when moving in that there was no reason two bachelors had to sit on beer kegs and prop their feet on wooden reels that had formerly held telephone cables. So the place had taken on a personality—with a great big cream-colored sofa and oversized pillows, a pair of overstuffed club chairs, a snazzy brown leather chair with matching ottoman, a monstrous entertainment center that covered one whole wall and a few odds and ends to make the place homey: a fig tree beside the sliding glass doors (donated by Greg's mother, along with a few smaller green plants), a couple of framed posters on the wall, some brass lamps, Danish teakwood tables and on one wall their collection of bill caps. They both liked bill caps and had decided right away to put up a couple of expandable crisscross racks and hang them up where they were easy to grab.

Christopher had remembered right—the red Minnesota Twins cap was gone from the rack. He wondered where it was now and what it looked like. Greg's favorite green one was still there though, the one his grandpa Reston had given him for his last birthday. It said PEBBLE BEACH on it and Greg had always claimed it was shaped the way a bill cap ought to be shaped. Chris shuffled slowly to the rack, took down the green cap and held it a long time. He went to the leather chair and sat down with the sluggish, labored movements of an old man, and put the tinfoil packet on the ottoman and the Pebble Beach cap on his head. He closed his eyes, tipped back against the chair and let memories of Greg flutter over him like film across a screen: playing ball in the summer police league, waterskiing, eating hot dogs—the man had been crazy about hot dogs—riding in his black-and-white cruiser, sitting in the patrol room with his feet up on a table bullshitting with the guys, working around the apartment, turning up the radio when a song came on that he liked, especially anything by Vince Gill.

Memories, memories . . . hell, but they hurt.

In time Christopher rose, put the lasagna in the refrigerator and headed down the hall to the far end of the apartment. Outside Greg's bedroom doorway he lingered a long time, standing in the murky shadows, working up the courage to turn on the bedroom light and face the emptiness. Finally, he did . . . and stood leaning against the door frame coming to grips with the finality of Greg's absence. That gun and holster on the chest of drawers would never be strapped on Greg again. The department badge would never be pinned on, not the tie clasp or the radio, none of the police paraphernalia he'd worn for the past two years. He'd never sleep in this room, wear the uniforms in the closet, look at the family pictures in frames on the dresser, finish reading the Robert B. Parker book with the bookmark sticking out of it, pay the bills that were propped against a mug on his dresser, turn on that radio, put on those earphones, yell from this room, "I'm starved! Let's go out and get a hot dog someplace!"

He used to do that and Chris would yell back, "You and your hot dogs! Gimme a break, will ya, Reston?"

The hot dog jokes never ceased.

For Christmas last year Greg had given him a gift certificate from Jimbo's Jumbo Dogs, a dumpy hot dog wagon on Main Street that had become a town fixture. When you ate one of those gut-rotters with everything on it you tasted it for two days and everyone around you smelled it for three. Many was the time they were cruising in the black-and-white and as they approached Jimbo's, Greg would say, "Pull over."

"Aw, no," Chris would say. "Jeez, come on, not today!"

"Look at it this way: We'll save on Mace," Greg had replied the last time it had happened.

Chris moved into the room, still wearing the green cap. He felt it coming—the welling up, the thick throat, the hot, tight chest and the burning eyes. And he let it in. Let it slam hard and double him over as he squatted on the floor with his back against Greg's bed, his knees drawn up while he held the sides of the green cap against his skull and bawled as he'd never bawled in his life. Great whooping, heaving, terrible sobs that wailed through the room and probably up through the ceiling into the apartment above. He didn't care. He let it out, let its force control and wilt him, taking him one step closer to accepting Greg's death.

It felt terrible.

It felt brutal.

It felt necessary.

"Goddamn it!" he shouted once, then went on weeping until he was spent.

Afterward, he stayed where he was, on the floor, drooping, blowing his nose, wearing Greg's cap, wondering again why the good ones got taken and the slime kept on beating and raping and robbing and dealing and neglecting their kids.

He sat there with his head throbbing at one o'clock in the morning, turning Greg's cap around and around in his hands, caught periodically by a jerky after-spasm, feeling weariness steal in and turn him defenseless. He sighed twice—deep, shuddering sighs—looked around the room and wondered why it was said that crying like this made you feel better.

He felt like shit.

Felt as if his head were going to explode and his eyeballs burst like popcorn.

And he admitted to himself that maybe a little bit of the reason he'd wept so hard was—at long last—for himself, for the child he'd been, the loneliness he'd lived with and the painful memories that today had put him through.

At Lee's house everyone was gone. The children had dressed for bed, where they were reluctant to go alone. As it had been for all of them when Bill had died, the dread of aloneness had returned.

"Come into my bed," she invited, and they did, gladly.

They lay three abreast, sleepless, with Lee in the middle, an arm under each of them.

It took a long while before Joey hesitantly confessed his greatest guilt.

"Hey, Mom?"

"Yes, dear?"

"When you called . . . I didn't mean what I said. I mean, it was stupid, what I said."

"What did you say?"

"That Greg was gonna take me and my friends out to Valley Fair next week. Like that's all that mattered to me, you know what I mean?"

She flexed her right arm and curled him closer.

"Oh, Joey, have you been worrying about that all this time?"

"Well, it must've sounded pretty selfish."

"No, no, Joey honey—don't you worry about it. It was just a human reaction, that's all. It's hard to believe news like this, and when it comes we simply . . . well, we express our disbelief. You know how it is—we go along day by day taking our routine for granted and all of a sudden something like this happens and we think of the most common things and say, 'Gosh, how can it be true when the person we lost left unfinished business?' I remember when your dad died I kept saying, 'But we were going to go on a trip to Florida together.' And today when Christopher came and told me the news I kept blubbering about Greg not having fixed the end of my garden hose yet. So you see, I did the same thing as you. When we hear that someone we love has just died, we don't *think,* we just *react,* so don't worry about it."

Janice said, "Wanna know what I thought about all the way home on the plane?"

"What?"

"About how much I'd been cheated out of when Greg died, because he'll never get married and have kids and have a wife who'll be my sister-in-law, and how awful Christmas is going to be from now on, and that my birthdays will never be the same without him there."

"I think every one of us had those thoughts today."

They lay awhile, studying the faint night-light that picked out shadowed objects in the room—moonbeams through a curtain, the bulky presence of furniture, the dresser mirror reflecting the blue-black expanse before it.

Lee's arms were growing numb. She took them from beneath her children but kept Janice and Joey close to her sides. "Now I'll tell you what I thought—several times today. And when it happened I felt so terrible . . . so . . . well, let me tell you.

In the midst of all the planning and the telephoning and people coming and going I'd catch myself thinking, 'Did anybody call Greg yet?' And then it would strike me—Greg's dead. He won't be coming. And I'd feel so strange and terribly guilty that I could have forgotten he'd died, that he was the reason for all the commotion."

Janice admitted, "The same thing happened to me."

Joey said, "Me too."

They took comfort from the fact that once again they'd apparently pinpointed a human reaction, then Janice whispered timorously, "Nothing's ever going to be the same."

Her mother replied, "No, that's for sure. But we owe it to ourselves to keep our lives full and good and as happy as possible, in spite of Greg's absence. It's what I had to tell myself a thousand times after Daddy died, and it got me through. When things start to get you down I want you to think of that. Your happiness is imperative, and you must work hard at having it."

In time they grew drowsy. They each slept sporadically, tossing frequently; ultimately, they made it through the first night without Greg.

In the morning they forced themselves to do the things they must: bathe, eat, answer the phone . . . again . . . and again . . . and again. Between the incoming calls, Lee made one of her own, to Lloyd.

"Hello, dear," she said. "It's Lee."

"Little one. It's good to hear your voice, shaky as it is."

"I need to ask you a favor, Lloyd."

"Sure, anything."

"Will you come with me to the funeral director's this morning?"

"Of course I will."

"I don't want to put the kids through that. Sylvia would have come and so would my folks, but I'd rather be with you."

"That's the nicest thing you could have said to an old man at this hour of the morning. What time should I pick you up?"

With Lloyd at her side she felt a sense of calm once again, as if Bill were there with her. Dear, kind Lloyd, the eye in the middle of the storm—how grateful she was to have him in her life.

She had dealt with Walter Dewey before and knew what to expect: a man compassionate yet businesslike, asking the questions his occupation required him to ask.

Death certificate statistics first—birth date, birthplace, progenitors' names, social security number. Facts were easy. The more difficult questions followed—what day they wished to have the services, the visitation time, did they want an organist, a soloist, did they have a cemetery plot, what about flowers, lunch after the ceremony, printed memorial folders? Did they want an open or closed casket? Did she have a recent picture of Greg? Who would act as pallbearers?

At this point Lee seemed beleaguered so Lloyd stepped in. "Young Lallek spoke to me about it yesterday. It seems there'll be law-enforcement officers from all over the state at Greg's funeral. When one of their ranks dies, that's how it is. Would you want some of his fellow officers to act as pallbearers, Lee? There seems no question they'd be honored if you'd let them."

"Yes . . . oh, yes. And wouldn't Greg like that. He loved being a policeman so."

Lloyd squeezed her hand, smiled his benevolent smile. "And if you'd permit a doting grandpa—I thought about this last night when I couldn't sleep—I'd love to give a eulogy."

If it were possible to love Lloyd Reston more Lee would have done so, but all her married life she had loved him for exactly the qualities he was displaying now—lovingness combined with unflappable calm. She had learned so much from this man.

In answer to his question she smiled and turned her hand over to squeeze his. "I know your grandson would approve. Thank you, dear."

They went into a room full of caskets and tried to be analytical rather than emotional. Lloyd finally pointed at a gunmetal silver one and said, "I think I like that one. It's about the same color as that first car of Greg's that I financed for him when he graduated from high school."

They left the funeral director's with a promise that they would call back with the names of the pallbearers for the obituary and would return later that day with a set of Greg's clothing.

There was no avoiding it any longer. This above all pierced the heart—facing the place where he had lived, made happy plans for the future, stored the artifacts of his day-to-day life.

"Well, Dad," Lee said when they were back in Lloyd's car. "I guess it's time to face Greg's apartment."

He reached across the seat and took her hand. "Nobody ever said being a parent was easy. You have to weigh the responsibilities against the rewards. This is one of them. Maybe it'll help to think about all the joy he brought to your life. Remember that time when he and Janice were little and they decided to make you and Bill an anniversary cake? The cake turned out just fine, but, as I remember, they didn't know what *confectioners'* meant so they used plain sugar in the frosting."

"And we ate it." Lee grimaced at the recollection.

"And that Mother's Day when he built you that little birdhouse."

"I still have it."

"I predicted then that that kid was sure to end up being a carpenter. He was awfully handy with a hammer."

"Remember when he was in high school track? Gosh, how I used to enjoy going to those meets."

They went on reminiscing until they reached Greg's apartment. When the engine was cut, they sat looking at the building, loath to approach it.

Lloyd asked, "Do you want me to come in with you?"

"Yes," she whispered. "Please."

Christopher answered their knock, freshly shaven, his hair neatly combed, dressed in jeans and a polo shirt. Lee took a look at his puffy eyes and knew he'd had one hell of a night.

"Hi," she said simply and took him in her arms. They remained together for as long as they needed, remembering yesterday and how they'd been the first two to know, to console each other, to face the calamity. He smelled like fresh aftershave and felt sturdy yet vulnerable as Lee rocked with him, her eyes closed and her heart heavy.

When they parted Chris said, "Hi, Lloyd, how are you?" The two men patted each other's shoulders.

"Well, I've been better," Lloyd answered. "I imagine you put in a bad night yourself."

"Yessir, the worst."

Lee said, "You should've stayed at the house with the kids and me."

"Maybe," he replied. "Maybe. But all I'd have done was put off facing this place. There'd still be tonight, and tomorrow and the next day."

He had, Lee knew as she studied him, the most difficult task of any of them, since he'd been closest to Greg. Even she—mother though she was—had not lived with Greg for over two years. This place was where his absence would be felt most.

"Did you eat my lasagna?" she asked.

"Yes, this morning." He put a hand on his flat stomach and managed a smile. "It was good."

She glanced around the kitchen, reluctant to move farther into the apartment, coming up with one more item of business to delay it a few minutes.

"May I use your phone, Christopher? I'd like to call the shop."

"Sure."

He and Lloyd moved into the living room while she dialed Absolutely Floral. Sylvia answered.

"Sylvia, you're there?" They employed four designers who came in at staggered hours.

"I thought I'd better come down and see how things were going."

"Everything okay?"

"Just fine. The girls are handling everything. Don't worry about a thing. Did you sleep at all?"

"Not much. Lloyd and I have already seen the funeral director and we've set the funeral for Monday at two P.M. We decided not to have a reviewal."

"Honey, I would have come with you."

"I know, so would Mom and Dad. Lloyd came. We did just fine . . . really. But there is something you can do for me at the shop, Sylvia."

"Anything. Just name it."

"I'd like you to call Koehler & Dramm and order three dozen calla lilies, some freesias, gardenias and sword ferns. Everything white and green. Make sure we've got sprengeri and tall myrtle, too . . ." She paused and added, "For Monday."

"Lee, you're not going to arrange it yourself."

"Yes, I am."

"But, Lee . . ."

"He was my son. I want to do it, Sylvia."

"Lee, this is silly. Why not let one of the girls do it? Or me? I'll be happy to."

"It's something I must do, Sylvia, please understand. Lloyd is going to give the eulogy; I'm going to arrange the casket flowers."

It took a while before Sylvia agreed. "Very well. Full or half?"

"Full. We've decided to leave it closed."

Sylvia sighed. "All right, Lee, I'll do it right away."

"Thanks, Sylvia."

"Oh, Lee? I thought you'd want to know. The orders are flooding in for Greg. I think I'll stay here and help the girls, but if you need me, just call and I'll come over, okay?"

"I'll be just fine. I'm here at Greg's apartment with Lloyd and Christopher, and the kids are at home."

"Okay, but call if you need me . . . promise?"

"I will. Thanks, Sylvia."

When Lee hung up and went into the living room she knew the two men had overheard, though they'd been talking softly all the time. She was grateful that neither one said a word to try to dissuade her. Instead they each put an arm around her and stood looking up at the collection of caps on the wall.

Christopher said, "He was wearing his red Twins cap, but his favorite one is still here. It's the one you gave him last year, Lloyd."

Lloyd nodded, and they all realized it was time to pull themselves out of the maudlin mood. Lee moved away from their arms toward the fig tree. "The ficus looks good." She poked a finger in the soil. "So does the pothos . . . and the grape ivy." They made her want to cry, these dumb plants, simply because he'd never water them again. No, it was more than that: They'd been a symbol of his independence, gifts she'd given him when he went out on his own to start his adult life in his first apartment. Only two years he'd had them . . . only two.

"Oh, this is stupid!" she said, angry with herself for starting to cry again. "They're just plants! Just dumb plants!"

"It's not stupid," Christopher said. "I feel the same way every time I look at them . . . and at his hats, and his CDs . . . everything. It's not stupid."

"I know," she said, mollified. "But I'm so tired of crying."

"Yeah," he replied softly, "we all are."

"I might as well face his closet—is that what you're saying?"

He nodded silently and led the way. At the doorway to Greg's room he stepped back and let her enter first. Lloyd had remained behind in the living room.

She took in the room and said, "Was he always this neat?"

"He said you forced him to be. Something about Thursday-morning cleaning."

"Lord, how he hated it."

"Didn't hurt him a bit though."

Chris moved to the dresser. "He got a couple pieces of mail yesterday." He handed them to her. "And I went through his bills this morning. The ones we share for the apartment are taken care of. These are for other things."

She glanced at them.

"This one's for his motorcycle," she said and broke down again.

He held her while she cried, held her hard and motionless, his own eyes dry, her hands clutching the back of his shirt with the envelopes bent in one. "Oh God," she whispered. "Oh God . . ."

It struck him while he stood strong for her, how often he'd held this woman in the past twenty-four hours, closer and longer than he'd held any woman for years. Being relied on by her felt fitting, and each time she turned to him he found his own sorrow eased. The process of grieving was so new to Christopher. He'd seen strangers grieve in the course of his nine years on the force. He'd had psychology courses on handling traumatized victims and their equally traumatized families, but this was the first time true grief had ever touched him. No grandparents, extended family or dear friends of any kind had ever been part of his life, so there'd been no tearful funerals for him. He doubted that when his own parents died he'd care much at all.

This though—this was tough.

Lloyd came to the door holding the green bill cap. His eyes met Christopher's over Lee's shoulder. He waited patiently, his face a map of sadness.

Finally he shuffled into the room and sat down on the bed.

"I've been thinking," he said, almost as if to himself. "The casket's going to be closed. Greg loved this cap the best. And he hardly ever wore dress suits when he was alive. What do you say we bury him in jeans and one of his favorite T-shirts and this cap? Lee, dear, what do you think about that?"

She drew herself out of Christopher's arms and fished for a tissue in her pocket. Wiping her eyes, she managed a snuffly laugh. "In blue jeans and that cap? Oh, Lloyd, you're priceless."

"Well, what do you think?"

"I think that's a wonderful idea."

"Then let's pick a shirt. Chris, which one did he wear most?"

After that it wasn't so hard, opening the closet door, leafing through Greg's clothes. They had interacted as a team, one supporting the other as emotions demanded, and by the time they left the apartment they recognized they'd done a fine job of conquering another hurdle.

Lee said to Chris, "You're coming with us back to the house. You can't stay here alone."

"Thanks, but actually I have to go to the Ford dealer and pick up a new Explorer I ordered. I was supposed to pick it up yesterday, but . . ." He shrugged. "I called the dealer and told him I'd be in to get it today."

"Then you'll come over later?"

He hesitated, afraid of spending too much time over there, getting in the family's way.

"Listen, I don't think—"

"Christopher, I insist. What are you going to do here? And besides, the neighbors have been bringing in so much food. Come on."

"All right. I will."

"Oh, I almost forgot. Will you do something for me?"

"Anything."

"Will you speak to your captain and express my thanks to him for offering to have the members of the police force act as pallbearers? Ask him to pick six of them—whomever he thinks. Greg liked a man named Ostrinski, and someone named Nokes."

"Ostrinski and Nokes, sure."

"And you, Christopher . . ." She touched his hand. "If . . . if you want to, I'd be pleased to have you act as pallbearer. But only if you want to."

"I'd have been hurt if you hadn't asked. Besides, he'd expect it, and so would I if it were the other way around."

She squeezed his hand and released it. "I need the names of the other men as soon as possible so they can be listed in the obituary."

"I'll take care of it all, Mrs. Reston. I'll speak to the captain and call Walter Dewey myself—how's that?"

"That would be a big help, thank you. It seems . . ." She felt a renewed surge of gratitude at having him to rely on. "It seems as if I've been leaning on you very heavily, Christopher. Forgive me. You've really helped—I want you to know that. Whenever you're around, things just seem—well, I feel better."

She smiled and he felt better than he had since awakening that morning.

"Me too."

When she was gone he drove over to the station and spoke to the captain, called Walter Dewey, then took care of an unpleasant detail that he didn't want Lee Reston to have to handle: He drove to the impound lot to pick up Greg's key ring. Toby, who ran the lot, knew him and knew he and Greg had been roommates.

"I'm sure sorry, Chris," he said as he handed over the keys.

"Yeah," Chris said, clearing his throat. "He was a good man and a good friend."

Toby clapped a heavy hand on his shoulder and they commiserated in silence.

"I imagine the motorcycle is a loss."

"Yes, it is."

Chris nodded, studying the oily dirt of the yard. "That's good." He hadn't looked around for the machine, nor would he. "I guess that's good, otherwise his mother would have to have it fixed and sell it. This way she'll never have to deal with it at all."

Toby squeezed his shoulder and dropped his hand.

"Family must be takin' it pretty hard."

Chris nodded. Sometimes it was hard to know what to say.

"Well, take 'er easy, okay?" Toby said.

"Yeah, thanks."

The weather had grown muggy. To the east the sky was blue as an Easter egg. To the west the clouds looked like a dirty old hen who'd rolled in the dust. Thunder rumbled in the distance. Nearer, one could almost smell the first wetted-down dust, that summery scent that came just before the rain.

It was approaching 4 P.M. when Christopher drove his spanking new wild-strawberry Ford Explorer out of the parking lot of Fahrendorff Ford. The dust-rain smell whipped in the open windows and mingled with that of new vinyl and an engine burning away the residual factory oils from its metal housing.

This should have been a rip-roaring happy moment. He and Greg had looked forward to it for two months, ever since he'd ordered the vehicle. They had made plans to take a trip in it this fall, maybe down to Denver, where they'd go up into the mountains and search out some old abandoned ghost towns where gold mines had played out. They'd also talked about going up to Nova Scotia to see its rugged coastline, or even wait until winter and drive down to Florida. Whatever place they chose, they were going to take the Explorer.

Suddenly Chris was sick and tired of all these mawkish thoughts. He was cruising along Coon Rapids Boulevard when he shouted at the thin air, "Hey, Greg—look! I got it!" He smiled and let some gladness seep in, let himself enjoy this milestone he'd anticipated for so long. "You there, Reston? Hey, lookit this. I've really got it at last and damn your 'nads for not being here with me! I'll get you for this, you little pecker-head! I'm gonna go to Denver anyway, just you wait and see! And you're gonna be sorry as hell you didn't stick around to go with me!" The Explorer had a faint tick in the right door panel. He'd have to have the dealer look into that. "So how is it up there, Reston? They got hot dogs with everything on 'em? Well, good! You keep 'em up there, okay?"

He drove along feeling unexpectedly happy, realizing something for the first time: that until now he had not accepted Greg's death. With acceptance came a measure of peace and the ability to get on with life. He had no doubt there'd be more bad days, bad hours, maybe even longer stretches when he'd miss Greg terribly, but he'd just learned one way to handle them. Get on with what needed getting on with, and give yourself the right to enjoy what ought to be enjoyed.

He drove over to the police station to show the boys. Out of long practice, he checked the call reports from the last shift—suspicious person, domestic, disturbing the peace, lockout, animal complaint, same stuff as usual. He had a cup of coffee, answered sympathetic questions about the Restons and the funeral plans, and went back out to enjoy his Explorer.

It was raining as he headed over to Lee Reston's house. His new windshield wipers worked great, made a different sound than the ones on the old beater. He put a Vince Gill compact disc in the player and drove slowly, singing along softly when he knew the words, enjoying the quiet snicker of the rain on the metal roof, the occasional ranting of thunder, healing a little.

Vince came on singing "When I Call Your Name" and took the cheer out of the afternoon.

At Mrs. Reston's, several cars stood in the driveway; he parked behind them and ran through the rain to the front door.

Janice answered his knock and opened the screen door. "Come on in. Hi. How are you today?"

"Better. How about you?"

"Tired, sad, sighing a lot."

"Yeah, it's rough." He glanced toward the kitchen where the lights were on and people were gathered around the table. "It looks like you've got plenty of company. I probably shouldn't have come."

She put her arm around his waist and drew him forward. "Don't be silly. This is no time to be alone. Come on . . . join the rest."

Beneath a hanging light fixture people were leaning on their elbows looking at photo albums containing snapshots of grandparents, aunts, uncles, cousins, friends. The counter was arrayed with hot dishes, bowls of salad, platters of sandwich fixings, muffins, cookies and four different cakes in aluminum cake tins.

"Hi, Christopher," Lee greeted from across the room. "Glad you came back. I guess you know everyone except these three. They all went to high school with Greg. This is Nolan Steeg, Sandy Adolphson and Jane Retting."

He nodded to them all while Janice added, "Jane dated Greg when they were in high school. She spent a lot of time over here." She gave the girl a hug from behind; Jane looked as if she'd been crying.

They continued examining the pictures, exclaiming, "Oh, there he is with that terrible cap he used to wear everywhere! Remember how you couldn't get him to take it off at bedtime, Lee?"

"He always loved caps."

"And hot dogs."

"And raw cookie dough."

"Oh, look, there he is at a track meet."

"For somebody only six feet tall he could really run."

"Nolan, look at this one—where was this taken?"

"Taylors Falls. A bunch of us guys used to go over there and take our shirts off and play Frisbee in our cutoffs and see if we could pick up girls."

"My son . . . picking up girls?" Lee said in mock horror.

"My boyfriend . . . picking up girls?" Jane echoed in mock horror.

"He wasn't perfect, you know."

Lee said, "Well, we thought so, didn't we, Jane?" and the two of them shared a sad smile.

The examination of photos went on while Lee worked her way around the table and asked Christopher, "Are you hungry? There's plenty to eat. Let me get you a plate and you can help yourself."

He ate some goulash, some chicken-and-rice casserole, Italian salad, two turkey sandwiches and three pieces of cake, all the while standing, looking over everyone's shoulders at pictures of Greg he'd never seen before. Four times he refused to accept chairs that were offered. Janice handed him a glass of milk. He peered over heads at the open albums. There was Greg as an infant; a two-year-old blowing out birthday candles; holding his new baby sister on his lap; going off to his first day of kindergarten; around age seven, missing his front teeth; with Janice and Joey; the whole family beside a fishing boat holding up their catches; standing spraddle-legged with a basketball under one arm, beginning to stretch out in height; with four grandparents in front of Faith Lutheran Church, probably on his confirmation day; lying flat on the grass with some other boy's head on his stomach, the two of them laughing, wearing prank sunglasses one foot wide; carrying his mother piggyback, her arm raised as if holding a horsewhip; with a group of four teenage boys, one of them Nolan, leaning against somebody's car; dressed in a tux with Jane at his side in her prom formal; with Lee on his high school graduation day; standing beside a black-and-white cruiser in his new uniform and badge; playing volleyball last Fourth of July, balancing the ball on five fingertips with his other arm slung around Christopher's shoulder while Christopher's arm hooked Joey around the neck.

A wave of envy struck Christopher: What a charmed life Greg Reston had had. It wouldn't be so bad to die, having had so many happy memories. Greg had had so much family love, friends, every occasion of his life marked by photographs that preserved them forever, lovingly stored in a photo album by a mother. Now here she was, sharing them with everyone again, helping them heal, passing out food and refilling glasses, touching shoulders as she moved around the table.

He gazed at her and thought, *What a woman*. She caught his eyes and smiled. He looked away quickly, back down to the picture of himself and Greg just as the page was being turned.

He had exactly four photographs of himself as a child, and he didn't know who'd taken them, but to the best of his recollection there'd never been a camera around his house. Of elementary school pictures he had none. He was one of the kids who never brought money to pay for the photo packet when the teacher passed them out. Instead, they went back to the photographer.

His graduation picture he'd paid for himself, for by then he was working in the produce department of the Red Owl, earning fairly decent money.

He took his plate to the kitchen sink and rinsed it off.

Lee Reston came up behind him and said, "Here, let me do that."

"It's done. Should I put it in the dishwasher?"

"Yes, please."

He did so. When he straightened and turned she was near, the two of them isolated from the others by an arm of the kitchen cabinets that divided the working area from the eating area.

"Thank you for taking care of the pallbearers today."

"No need to thank me. I was glad to do it."

"About Greg's things in the apartment . . ."

He shook his head. "Take all the time you need. There's no hurry."

"But you'll probably want a new roommate."

"I haven't decided that yet. It's too soon."

"All right," she agreed quietly. "But I should probably get his car out of the garage."

"I got his keys for you . . . here." He fished them out of his pocket. "But there is no hurry. Nobody cares if it sits there for a few days. His rent is paid up till the first."

She studied the keys in her palm and a veil of sorrow descended over her face again.

"Really, Mrs. Reston," he repeated, "there's no hurry. Take your time getting everything."

Janice overheard and came up to join them. "Mom . . . are you talking about Greg's car?"

Lee cleared her throat and replied, "Yes. I told Chris we should probably get it out of the garage over there. He got the keys for us."

"I was hoping I could use it for a while. It's a lot more reliable than mine."

"Of course you can."

"Mine's been burning oil, and if the front tires last another month I'll be surprised. It would really be a lifesaver."

"Sure, dear, go ahead and use it. Maybe we can even have the title changed over to you and sell yours instead of his."

"I was thinking the same thing, but I didn't want to . . ." Janice shrugged and grew glum. "Well, you know."

Lee squeezed her arm. "I know. But something will have to be done with all his belongings eventually anyway."

"Thanks, Mom."

Christopher said, "If you want me to take the keys I can run it over here anytime. One of the cops can follow me and give me a ride back. Or I can come and get you, Janice, whenever you say."

"I could ride back home with you tonight and get it."

"Sure. That'd be okay. It's raining though."

"I've driven in the rain before. You sure this is okay with you, Mom?"

"Of course it is. It's one more detail taken care of. Go ahead and get it."

"Do you want to go now?" Janice asked Chris.

"Anytime."

"Just let me get my purse."

While Janice was gone he said to Lee, "Is there anything else you need me to do?"

"Oh, Christopher, you've been so helpful already. No, you just go." She walked him to the door, where Janice joined them. "I hope for all our sakes that we can all get some sleep tonight. Janice, be careful driving home in the rain. And, Chris . . ." She gave him one of the hugs she shared so freely, an affectionate, motherly brushing of cheeks that said goodnight and thanks. "You're so kind . . . so thoughtful. Thank you for being here." He wondered if she knew how much he liked the way her hand lingered on his neck before he turned away to open the screen door for Janice.

"Oh, just a minute!" Lee said, and hurried to the kitchen, where a drawer rolled open and tinfoil tore. Momentarily she returned with a neatly folded silvery packet. "It's chocolate cake. For morning."

"Thanks, Mrs. Reston."

In the Explorer, in damp shirts, he and Janice headed for the apartment with the rain-spotted tinfoil between them.

"Your mother is wonderful," he said.

"Everybody always says that. All my high school friends wished she was theirs."

"Does she ever get down?"

"Not very often. She has this saying: It is out of adversity that strength is born. But I don't think Greg's death has really hit her yet."

"It will when she stops supporting everyone else and has some time alone. That's when it really hit me—when I got back to the apartment last night."

She reached over and placed her hand on his bare arm, and let silence roll down the rainy streets with them.

In time she dropped her hand and seemed to realize something. "Christopher! Is this vehicle brand-new?"

"I just got it this afternoon."

"And you didn't say anything?"

He shrugged.

"I thought it smelled new. And it's still got cardboard liners on the floors."

"You're the first one to ride in it."

She gazed at his profile. In the center of this sadness came a moment when pure life zinged through her like a shock of electricity. She had always loved his face, from the first time she'd seen it, a handsome face with clear, tanned skin that always looked freshly scrubbed. Highlighted by the dash lights, his nose, lips and forehead formed an attractive silhouette. In these days when men shaved designs into their heads, or wore their hair in ugly crew cuts or below the ear, his vigorous short hair with its slight curl gave him an all-American look that only added to the overall appearance of squeaky cleanness.

"There've been times when I imagined riding somewhere in a car with you. Too bad the occasion isn't happier."

He had felt her gaze and let her subtle implication pass. "Greg and I had planned to take it to Denver in the fall, maybe to Nova Scotia."

"Funny how every path leads back to him."

"I guess that's natural. When someone dies suddenly he leaves unfinished business."

"We talked about that last night, Mom, Joey and I. We all slept in Mom's bed together and we talked about a lot of our feelings."

He featured Lee gathering her kids in beside her. The picture fit.

"I'll bet she never in her life yelled at you, or swore at you or smacked you."

"Swore at us, no. But we got yelled at when we deserved it. And I got smacked once when I was about five or six years old. I called my uncle Barry a dumb shit."

Chris burst out laughing.

Janice went on. "I must have heard someone else say it—I don't know. And right now I can't even remember what it was that bugged me so about Uncle Barry, but whatever it was I didn't like it, so I called him a dumb shit and Mom slapped my face and made me apologize. Afterwards she hugged me so hard I thought she'd crack my ribs, and she cried too and said she was sorry but I must never talk that way to anybody again."

Where Chris came from the parents called the kids dumb shits and meant it. And afterward there were no tearful apologies.

"You're a lucky girl. She's one fantastic mother." He made a sharp left turn that took them into the parking lot of Cutter's Grove apartments. "Here we are." He wound between the buildings and activated the door of an underground garage. Pulling to a halt beside Greg's white Toyota, he shut off his engine and asked, "Are you gonna be able to handle it?"

"I told you I've driven plenty of times in the rain."

"I'm not talking about the rain."

"I can handle it," she replied in a whisper. "I'm my mother's child." She gave in to impulse, leaned over and kissed him on the jaw. "Thanks for everything, Christopher. My mother said she didn't know what she'd have done without you, and the same goes for me."

The next moment she was out of his vehicle, unlocking the door of Greg's car.

Chapter 4

The following morning the rain was gone and the sun promised a torrid day ahead.

Christopher awakened at 6:35 and listened to the silence in the apartment. *What am I going to do today?* The wake this afternoon, but between now and then the hours would stretch like a Dalí painting, empty, dry, distorted.

He rolled over and switched on the radio.

Lorrie Morgan was singing about Monday, which was never good anyway. The deejay came on with news about road repairs that would narrow I-694 down to a single lane for the remainder of the summer. The weather report predicted a high of 89 today, clear skies and extreme humidity. The announcer said, "Watching your grass grow might actually be exciting on a day like today."

He thought of Lee Reston's grass and wondered when it had last been mowed. Everybody running around like chickens with their heads cut off, and the house overrun with people, and who, in their despair, gave a damn about whether or not the grass got mowed? It was Joey's job, he supposed, but Joey was having as tough a time as the rest of them dealing with Greg's death.

Chris got up and hit the shower.

At ten to eight, when Lee Reston shuffled to the front door and opened it, she heard noises coming from the garage. She went outside barefoot, onto the cool concrete sidewalk, tightening the belt of a knee-length kimono, peering around the corner of the house to find Christopher Lallek with the garage door raised, pouring gas into her mower. He was dressed in cutoff shorts, a sleeveless blue T-shirt and a hot-pink bill cap that matched the strings on his sunglasses.

"Christopher?" she said, surprised. "What are you doing here?"

"Mowing your lawn."

"Oh, Christopher, you don't have to do that."

"I know what pride you take in your lawn, Mrs. Reston, and there'll be lots of company coming the next couple days."

"Joey can mow it."

"Joey's got all he can handle right now."

"Well . . . all right, but have you had breakfast?"

He gave her a small smile. "I had a piece of chocolate cake."

"Well, at least come in and let me give you some coffee." She led the way into the house while he watched her bare feet from behind. She had shapely calves for a woman of her age, and very small feet.

"The kids are still sleeping." She held the screen door open and he followed her inside.

"How about you?" he asked. "Did you sleep?"

"Oh, a little. You?"

"I did, yes. Woke up early though, and the radio said it's going to be a scorcher later on, so I thought I'd come over and do the lawn while it's still cool."

She poured coffee into two thick blue mugs and they sat down at the table.

"I'll bet you'll be glad when tomorrow is over," he said.

"Going back to work is beginning to sound good."

"You must be getting a little tired of having people in your house."

"At moments, yes."

"Listen, I wasn't going to come in, I was just going to—" She pressed him back into his chair when he began to rise.

"No. Not you. I like being with you. Whenever I am, the disaster seems less disastrous. This is nice, just the two of us sitting here quietly." Beneath the table she crossed her ankles and propped her heels on a chair seat.

It was shady in the kitchen at this time of day. She hadn't turned on any lights. The room was rather a mess, the counter still covered with cake pans, Tupperware, loaves of bread and neglected mail. Beside the sink a roaster was filled with water, soaking the remnants of somebody's offering. The photo albums were closed and piled on the table along with a bunch of stacked clean coffee cups that someone hadn't known where to put away. The sliding door was open, bringing in the cool, dewy freshness of morning. Out on the lawn a pair of robins cocked their heads, enjoying a healthy breakfast after the previous night's rain.

"I feel the same way," he said. "When I'm over here, I'm closest to Greg. But I don't want to make a pest of myself."

"Tell you what. If you do, I'll let you know."

He sipped his coffee and let his eyes smile at her over the rim of the cup.

"Everybody at the station asked how you were when I was over there yester-day."

"Everybody I know seems to be wondering how I am. Can I tell you something? Without meaning to sound ungrateful for people's good intentions, there was a moment yesterday when the phone rang again, and I heard that question again, and I thought I'd scream and run out of here. I just wanted to hang up and say, 'Leave me alone! How do you think I am!' "

"Well, you'd better get used to it, because from what I've seen of the people you know, they're going to keep calling for a long, long time."

"I must sound ungrateful. What would I have done without all the wonderful people who came and brought love and hugs and food the last two days?"

"Aw, come on, don't be so hard on yourself. You're not ungrateful, you're just human. It's a tough question to answer on the best of days—how are you." He took another sip of coffee and they listened to the birds singing.

"So, how *are* you?" he asked.

They both laughed.

Afterward they felt themselves grow a notch more relaxed with each other.

"Gosh, that felt good." She roughed up her hair with four fingers, the sleeves of her silky kimono falling to her shoulders. "Haven't done that in a long time."

"Me either. Mostly I have long lapses when my mind hardly works. How about you?"

"Same here. You find yourself staring at nothing."

He scratched at his mug with a thumbnail and said, "I did something yesterday that I was quite proud of, though."

"What?"

"I spoke out loud to Greg."

"Really?" She propped her jaw on an upturned palm. "What did you say?"

"I said, 'Hey, Greg, I finally got my new Explorer!' And then I said, 'Damn your 'nads for not being here with me to ride in it!' "

She laughed softly and got a little teary-eyed at the same time.

"We had talked about taking a trip in it this fall, maybe to Denver, maybe to Nova Scotia."

"I didn't know that. But that's . . ." She wagged her mug back and forth across the tabletop, then looked up again. ". . . That's what I value about being with you right now. Talking with you is like talking with him. Getting tidbits about his life that I wasn't privy to in the last couple months. He was always fascinated by Nova Scotia."

"Yeah, I know," Chris said, studying the contents of his mug. "Then yesterday, after I got mad at him I asked him if there were hot dogs up there. . . ." He looked up at Lee. "And afterwards I felt so much better. You ought to try it."

She took her mug in both hands and, resting her elbows on the table, studied the yard while he studied her. Her kimono was flowered and crossed at the breast. Above it hung a tiny pearl surrounded by a gold swirl and two small diamonds, suspended on a fine gold chain around her neck. Her neck was thin and long. Her chest was slightly freckled.

He looked away, finished off his coffee and rose. "Well, I'd better get to work."

"Sorry," she said, rising, too. "I got melancholy on you. I didn't mean to."

"Don't apologize, Mrs. Reston. Not to me."

In silence they studied each other. The coffee machine clicked on and sizzled, rewarming the pot. Outside the birds sang. At the other end of the house a toilet flushed.

"All right," she agreed quietly.

"And one more thing. You should keep your garage locked. Anybody could come in and start your mower."

Her mouth hinted at a smile. "You sound just like him."

"I know. Us damn cops never let up, do we?"

He headed for the door and she trailed after him.

"Thanks for the coffee."

"Thanks for mowing."

"The best thing is to keep busy."

"Yes, I've found that out."

He went out and she caught the screen door as it closed, stood with her fingers caught idly on its handle, watching him go down the steps. At the bottom he did an about-face and stood below her, looking up. Strings dangled from his lopped-off jeans onto his thighs. The hair on his sturdy arms and legs was bleached by the sun. His bare feet, in dirty sneakers, were set wide apart.

"I'll tell you something, Mrs. Reston." He slipped his sunglasses on, the pink Croakies flaring back behind his neck. "I've never lost anyone before. I've never been to a funeral. It's damned scary."

He turned and headed for the garage before she could answer.

Thirty-five minutes later he was mowing the backyard when Janice came out the sliding door with a glass of ice water. He glanced up and remembered it was Sunday: She was wearing a pale peach dress and white high-heeled pumps. He went on maneuvering the machine around the edge of the flower beds until she approached. He killed the motor, pushed his cap back on his head, accepted the glass and said, "Thanks."

She watched him drink the ice water, his head tipped back, a trickle of sweat sliding from his short-trimmed sideburn. "Ahhh," he growled, finishing, backhanding his mouth and returning the glass. "Thanks."

"You're welcome. It's really nice of you to do this."

"Keeps me busy."

"Don't make light of it. Mother really appreciates everything you've done for us."

"Yeah, well it goes both ways. Your family's pretty special."

She smiled.

"Did I wake you with the mower?" he asked.

"No. I had to get up and get ready for church anyway. Do you want more water?"

"No, thanks . . . that was great." He nodded at the flower beds. "She do all this?"

"Yes. In her spare time. We keep saying to her, 'Mom, how can you spend all that time in the garden after working with flowers at the shop all day long?' but she just loves it."

He studied some tall blue spiky flowers while she studied him and wondered if he'd ever notice her. He hadn't for two years. Now that Greg was gone Chris wouldn't be around anymore, and she'd never been comfortable with flirting. Furthermore, this wasn't the time for such thoughts.

"Do you go to church, Chris?" Janice asked.

"No."

"Mom said to tell you you can come with us if you want. We can wait for a later service."

"No thanks, I'll just . . ." He gestured toward the mower. "Finish the mowing."

"All right." She fired the ice cubes off the lip of the glass onto the grass and turned toward the house. Halfway there, she called back over her shoulder, "Anytime though. It's an open invitation."

"Thanks."

He watched her walk away in her peachy summer dress with the sun showing the outline of her slip through the skirt, her legs looking firm and polished, her white high heels adding a pleasing curve to her ankles. He watched her, feeling the uneasy regret of a man who knew full well a woman found him attractive though she failed to stir him in the least.

Disquieted, he turned back to work.

A while later, with the mower still buffeting his ears, he saw Mrs. Reston step onto the deck, dressed in a short-sleeved brown-and-white suit and high heels with a purse slung over her wrist. She waved; he waved and watched her walk the length of the deck toward the garage. A moment later, between the two buildings, he saw them drive away for church.

When he got home the light was blinking on his telephone answering machine. He pushed the message button and Lee Reston's voice came on.

"Christopher, this is Lee. I just wanted to tell you one thing. Funerals aren't bad, Chris. If you think about it, they're really for the living."

He tried to bear that in mind that afternoon as he showered, shaved and dressed in a suit and tie for the wake of his best friend. But when he was in the Explorer with the air-conditioning turned on high, driving toward Dewey's Funeral Home, the stream of cold air couldn't quite dry the sweat on his palms.

The funeral home was one of the prettiest buildings in town, on a shaded corner, looking like a stately southern mansion with white pillars and Palladian windows. Walking toward it, he felt a knot of dread in his stomach. Inside the shadowed building, it was nappy and gloomy, the windows mostly covered to hold out the summer light. But where one might expect to hear recorded organ music, he heard instead—very softly as a background to murmured voices—the sound of Vince Gill's album "I Still Believe in You."

His mouth twisted into a disbelieving half-smile as he smoothed his tie and stepped toward a lectern holding a memorial book. Lee's mother and father were there signing, then whispering together, scowling as they cast their eyes toward the ceiling as if in search of the speakers.

He caught a snatch of their conversation ". . . what in the world she was thinking of!"

"I can just imagine what Aunt Delores will say."

He signed and followed them toward a cluster of people, watching Lee separate herself from them to come forward and greet her parents.

"Hi, Mom. Hi, Dad. I know what you're going to say, but please . . . let's celebrate his life, not his death."

"Oh, Lee, people are whispering."

"Who?" she said, gazing straight into her mother's eyes, gripping Peg Hillier's hands in both of her own. "I talked it over with the kids and it's our choice. It makes our memories happier."

Peg withdrew her hands. "All right, have it your way. Orrin, let's go say hello to Clarice and Bob."

When they'd moved on, Christopher took their place. He and Lee hugged briefly.

"I walked in and heard that music and all of a sudden I could swallow and breathe again. Thanks."

She smiled and squeezed his fingers. "Did you get my message?"

"Yes."

"Then why are your palms damp and trembling?"

He released her hands, making no reply, still uncertain of protocol.

"There's no reason to be afraid."

"I don't know what to do."

"Go up and say hi to him, just like you did in your Explorer. That's all."

He glanced at the casket and felt his insides seize up. She rubbed his sleeve then gave him a gentle nudge. He approached the coffin with his heart racing, dimly aware of the multitude of flowers surrounding the dais like a forest, so strong-smelling it seemed there wasn't enough pure oxygen left to sustain life. He stood between two huge bouquets, looking down at the framed photographs of Greg that smiled up at him from atop the closed metal box. There were two: one in his police uniform and cap, the other a very informal shot of him in a striped polo shirt and the green Pebble Beach cap.

Christopher put his hand on the smooth metal beside the picture. "Hi," he said quietly. "Miss ya."

How inconsiderate life was. It taught you how to deal with everything but the most important parts—marriage, parenthood, death. These people just stumbled through, making plenty of mistakes along the way. Christopher felt himself stumbling and wished again for family, someone whose hand he could hold, who would understand with no further words at this moment.

He dropped his hand from the casket and discovered he felt better.

Behind his shoulder someone said "Hi."

He turned and there stood Joey, disconsolate, his hands in his suit pockets.

"Hi," Chris said, and slung an arm around Joey's neck.

They stood there listening to Vince Gill. Gazing at Greg's picture. Choking on the smell of flowers.

Finally Joey hung his head, whacked at the tears in his eyes and whispered, "Shit."

Chris tightened his affectionate headlock and dropped his cheek against Joey's hair.

"Yeah, that's for sure."

Janice drifted up on his left, twined an arm around his elbow and rested her cheek on his sleeve.

On the far side of the room, Lee Reston accepted a hug from her aunt Pearl and uncle Melvin. As they left her with pats and murmurs, she turned to watch them move away and caught sight of Christopher with Janice and Joey at his side.

What a fine young man he was. Thoughtful beyond mere good manners; considerate of people's feelings; dependable in tens of ways. He had been a role model for Greg when the two of them met—older, more mature, out on his own already. When Greg joined the force Christopher had taken him under his wing and taught him, in a practical fashion, the best way to deal with suspects and perpetrators as well as the many personalities on the force.

He'd taught Greg how to survive on a day-to-day basis, too: how to balance a checkbook, establish credit, live on a budget, keep income-tax records, maintain a car, buy groceries, run a washing machine. Greg had left home and fallen in with a man who had helped him mature in so many ways.

Christopher Lallek—sensible, reliable, willing.

Even the kids sensed it and leaned on him. He was what Greg had been—a cop, a caretaker of a community, one to turn to in emergencies—and all of them had turned to him perhaps more than they ought since Greg's death. But his willingness made one reach toward him, as Joey and Janice were doing now. They might very well be using him as a substitute for the brother they'd lost, but what harm would it do? If they radiated toward him, let them. It was no different for them than it was for Lee: saying goodbye to Greg came easier over stories of his life, which Christopher had shared most recently.

Nonetheless, his vulnerability touched her deeply. How uncharacteristic his uncertainty had been when he'd stared at her with daunted eyes and admitted, *I don't know what to do.* Her mother's heart had reached out to him. It did so again as he stood with his arms around her children, once again the strong one for their sakes.

"Lee . . ." Someone else had come to pay their condolences and she turned to the business at hand.

Nearly two hours later, as she finished bidding goodbye to the last callers, Christopher spoke behind her.

"Mrs. Reston?"

She turned, feeling drained and anxious to go home.

"Would you mind if I took Joey for a little while?"

"No, of course not. Where are you going?"

"I thought I'd take him for a ride in my new Explorer, maybe let him drive it a little, cheer him up some."

"Oh, Christopher, yes, do."

"You'll be all right? Janice will be with you?"

"I'll be fine. I'm going to go home and collapse."

"You're sure? I realize moms need their kids at a time like this, and I don't want to—"

She touched his hand. "Take him. It's just what he needs today."

"Okay." He smiled and stepped back. "And don't worry, I'll bring him back in good shape."

Joey agreed, without much enthusiasm, but once they were out in the summer air, with the late afternoon sun dappling the boulevard, Christopher sensed Joey growing more interested.

"It's new?"

"Brand-new." Chris removed his tie and got the truck moving. "Greg and I were gonna take it out to the lake day before yesterday."

Joey threw him a dubious glance. "How can you talk about him so easy?"

"What else you gonna do? Pretend he didn't exist?"

"I don't know, but I can't talk about him at all without starting to bawl."

"So what's wrong with that? Bawling's okay. I bawled plenty in the last couple days. So did a lot of other cops."

Joey looked out his far window and said nothing.

They were riding along the shady streets of Anoka, heading toward Main. "You hungry?" Chris asked.

"No."

"I am. Mind if I stop for a burger?"

No response. He went through the drive-in window of the Burger King and ordered two cheeseburgers, two fries and two Cokes. Once the food was smelling up the truck, Joey turned to watch Chris unwrapping his sandwich.

"I guess I am sorta hungry," he admitted.

"Help yourself."

Eating burgers and fries, they cruised down Main Street onto Highway 10, then headed north toward Ramsey township. In no time at all they were out in the country between cornfields and stretches of woods, where silos stuck up on the horizon and the hot crackle of summer could be felt expanding things all around. Grains bowed in the breeze and crows flapped across the blue sky. On a barbed-wire fence hung a sign advertising hybrid corn. Along a farm driveway a child rode a bicycle. A woman was putting a letter in her rural mailbox and putting up the red flag. A young boy about Joey's age was sitting on a lawn chair in the shade of a pickup truck with a sign that said FIRST CROP GREEN BEANS. A farmer on a tractor was mowing weeds in the ditch ahead of them, spreading the sweet green scent of grass and clover.

That damned old life again—just rolling on.

"How old are you?" Chris asked.

"Fourteen—why?"

"So you haven't got your driver's permit yet."

"You're a cop—you should know."

"Sure I do. Wanna drive?"

Joey's eyes got wide. His back came away from the seat. "You kidding?"

"No, I'm not kidding."

"Won't you get in trouble?"

"What do you intend to do, wreck the thing?"

"No—heck, no—I'd be careful."

"All right then . . ." Chris pulled onto the shoulder. When the gravel stopped rasping, he got out and circled the truck. Joey slid across the front seat and Chris climbed into the passenger seat.

"Adjust the seat if you need to, and the mirror, too. Have you driven before?"

"A little."

"Ask, if there's anything you don't know."

Joey drove cautiously but well. He gripped the wheel too hard and sat with his shoulder blades six inches away from the backrest, but he stayed on his half of the road and kept the speedometer steady at fifty.

Chris reached over and turned on the radio.

"You like country?"

"Yeah."

Travis Tritt was singing "Trouble."

About seven minutes later Joey asked, "Could I turn onto that road?" It was narrow, gravel.

"You're driving."

Brooks & Dunn started in on "Boot Scootin' Boogie."

About five minutes after that, Joey asked, "Can I turn again?"

"You're driving."

They listened to one by Reba McEntire and one by George Strait before Chris asked, "You know where you're going?"

Joey dared remove his eyes from the road for the first time. "No."

Chris chuckled and hunkered down in the seat with a knee wedged against the dashboard. "Sounds good."

They ended up in a little ghost town called Nowthen, got their bearings and made their way back to State Highway 47, where Chris had to take over the wheel. Back in Anoka, Main Street was all but deserted, except for the hot dog wagon, which never seemed to have any business. Passing it put Greg sharply back into both their minds. Chris drove the length of Main and swung past the police department, glancing at the squads backed up near the door. Joey glanced, too, and again Greg was in their thoughts.

Joey remained silent until Chris pulled up at the curb in front of the Reston house. For once there weren't a half dozen cars in the driveway—just Lee's, Janice's and Greg's. Chris reached over and turned down the radio. Joey sat despondently, staring out the windshield and saying nothing.

Finally he said, "I think he came to every game I ever played in. I just keep thinking all the time, Who'll come to my games now?"

"I will," Chris told him.

Joey turned only his head. He studied Chris glumly but made no reply. His eyes looked sheeny.

Chris dropped a hand on his shoulder. "You're gonna do okay, kid. You've got a hell of a family. Stick close to them and they'll get you through."

He saw movement at the front door as Lee stepped near it and looked out through the screen. She stood with her arms crossed like a worried mother who was trying not to be. Even from this distance one could almost sense her relief at Joey's return.

Joey got out and slammed the truck door. Chris lifted a palm in greeting and she did the same, then opened the screen door to wait for her son.

It's got to be tough, Chris thought, *to give your kids their freedom after you've lost two, trying not to worry every minute they're out of your sight.*

He thought about it a lot as he drove home, the picture she made, waiting in the front door with her arms crossed and no smile on her face.

Lee and Sylvia had decided to close Absolutely Floral on Monday, the day of the funeral. Lee was alone when she went in that morning to make the casket spray, which was how she wanted it. Dressed in a lavender smock and listening to Dvořák on the tape player, she arranged one of the most beautiful sprays she'd ever done. It was pungent yet pure, made of fragrant gardenias and clean-lined callas. As she worked she wiped tears on her shoulder.

She could not have verbalized why she had to put herself through this. She was his mother—that was all—and this was her trade, working with flowers. This was one last favor she could do for her son before putting him in the ground.

When the spray was finished she telephoned Rodney, their delivery man, and said quietly, "Okay, Rodney, you can come and get it now."

When he came she unlocked the back door and said, "Hello, Rodney."

Though he was mentally handicapped, Rodney did a fine job of delivering flowers. His lips were pressed firmly together, zipped up tightly to keep him from breaking into tears: It was the first time he'd seen her since Greg's death.

He took off his bill cap and worried it with both hands. "I'm sure sorry, Miss Lee."

"We all are, Rodney," she said, placing a hand on his shoulder. "Thank you."

When he'd taken the spray and left she turned off the tape player and sat down heavily on a stool in the back room between the walk-in cooler and the metal-topped designing table. So peaceful with no customers or employees about, only the buckets of blooms and greens and the familiar herbal smell of cut stems. Lord, it was good to be alone at last. She rested a forearm on the table, glanced down at her hand and noted that it was stained again; after three days away from flowers it had been rather pleasant to have soft, white hands if only for a single day. Now the stains were back. She rubbed at one with a thumb . . . rubbed and rubbed . . . until her vision suddenly wavered. She reached into her smock pocket for a Kleenex and wiped her eyes. Immediately they filled again, faster than before. And finally, there amid the flowers and quiet, truly alone for the first time since Greg's death, she fell across the metal tabletop and let the storm of emotion happen.

She cried his name, "Greg . . . Greg . . . ," and wept noisily, until her face and the tabletop were messy and the metal had turned warm beneath her skin. She let her body lie limp on the shiny steel and allowed her heart's sorrow to spill forth in a rash of self-pity. *It's not fair . . . not fair! All that time and love I put into raising him and now he's gone. All that planning for his future only to be robbed of it on its very threshold.*

When her crying ceased she lay awhile with her cheek in a puddle, resting between the residual sobs that slowly subsided.

Finally she pushed up, wiped her face, and the table, sighed deep and long and sat awhile, gazing around the flower shop, letting some restorative thoughts in to replace the victimized feelings.

Suddenly Greg seemed very close, as if he'd been nearby waiting for her to calm.

"Well, I had you for twenty-five good years, didn't I, hon?" she said aloud. "And what the heck—better twenty-five good ones than a hundred bad ones. Plus I've still got Janice and Joey . . . and dozens of others who'll be gathering for the funeral in less than three hours."

The funeral. She drew a deep breath and rose from the stool. Well, the truth was she'd just conducted her own private funeral for Greg. The one she'd face at two o'clock would be easy by comparison.

The funeral of Greg Reston was attended by 350 law-enforcement officers from all over the state of Minnesota. Their squad cars filled two entire parking lots and more. They made an impressive sight, filing into the church two by two, dressed in their official uniforms of pale blue, navy, brown, and the pure white that designated captains and chiefs. They had come from Twin Cities suburbs and small, distant communities, from police departments, the State Highway Patrol and sheriff's departments representing every one of the eighty-seven counties. Striding in with stately dignity, their badges crossed by black mourning bands, they filled pew after pew until Grace Lutheran Church took on the blurred hues of an impressionistic landscape.

Lee Reston watched them arrive and felt a riffle of astonishment. So many! So impressive! Then, out of all those faces, all those uniforms, one in navy blue stepped forward to distinguish himself.

"Hello, Mrs. Reston." Christopher removed his visored hat and held it under his left arm. His appearance, in full uniform, gave Lee another start, accustomed as she was to seeing him in civilian clothes. The full regalia—navy blue uniform, tie, name tag, badge, belt, gun—added inches to his stature, years to his age and an uncommon dignity to his bearing. It caught her square in her pride and struck within her a new recognition of his manliness.

"Hello, Christopher." They shook hands very formally, Christopher maintaining a military bearing. Their eyes said an empathetic hello, but between them passed a silent message of support that went deeper than the casual sympathies of most mourners who'd weep today and forget next week. The handclasp lengthened while Lee recognized a strength within him to which she responded in an unprecedented way. It was more than bereaved mother to bereaved friend: It was woman to man.

He released her hand and said, "Hello, Janice . . . Joey." Though he'd greeted all three, he directed his following remark straight at Lee. "When Greg died our chaplain came in and talked to us. He said something that I forgot to tell you about. He said the last time he talked to Greg, Greg told him how much he loved being a cop, and how sorry he felt for guys who hate their jobs so much they detest going to work every day. He told Vernon Wender, 'I love my job because I like helping people.' I thought you'd want to know that today. He was very proud of being a cop."

"Thank you, Christopher."

He cleared his throat and glanced at the assembled men nearby. "Let me introduce you to the other officers who are acting as pallbearers." When he'd done so, and she'd shaken all their hands and accepted their condolences, Christopher spoke to her in the same formal manner as earlier.

"Your son was very well liked on the force, Mrs. Reston."

"I'm . . . well, I'm overwhelmed . . . so many of you here today."

"They came from all over the state."

"But so many."

"That's how it is when a peace officer dies."

"But I thought that was only if he died in the line of duty."

"No, ma'am."

A void fell. In the midst of it their eyes met and recognized that his formal attitude felt peculiar after the past three days of close contact.

"Are you going to make it okay today?" he asked, more like his familiar self.

Lee forced a rigid smile and nod.

"Janice? Anything I can do, just say so. Joey . . . I enjoyed our ride yesterday. Anytime you need to do that again, you call me. Maybe next time we can do it in a squad car while I'm on duty . . . with me driving, of course."

He smiled at Joey, who managed a limp smile in return. Then Christopher went away to greet other family members, with the decorum of a man in uniform.

For Lee, the funeral service passed not as a series of hazy impressions, as she'd expected, but as very distinct ones observed by a clearheaded woman who'd done her deepest mourning and was now mourning more for those around her.

Christopher maintained his stiff demeanor while bearing the coffin along with five of his fellow officers, his eyes straight ahead, his visor level with the floor, his shoulders erect. She watched him and thought of her own son in uniform, proud to wear it, liked by those he served with. In those thoughts she found very little sadness.

The white flowers she had arranged covered two-thirds of the coffin; everyone cried harder to learn Lee herself had arranged them.

Grampa Lloyd gave a eulogy with a smile on his face, and made everyone laugh aloud with recollections of Greg as a boy.

Janice and Joey held her hands all through it.

Reverend Ahldecker had a summer cold and sneezed several times in the middle of his prayers.

Sally Umland played the organ as flawlessly as an organ can be played, but Rena Tomland was away on summer vacation, so the soloist—a stranger—was rather mediocre.

Lee's mother—bless her misguided heart—had bought a new black suit for the occasion and was looking with judgmental if tearful eyes at all the summer colors on the women around her.

There was no denying that the presence of so many law-enforcement officers added a measure of pride that filled Lee and strengthened her throughout the service. Afterward, the procession of cars stretched for a mile and a half, every vehicle gleaming, directed through town by on-duty police officers who halted traffic at intersections, then removed their hats and placed them over their hearts as the cortege passed.

At the cemetery the law-enforcement officers circled Greg's grave and created a corridor to it through which Chris and the other pallbearers carried the casket. Graveside prayers were intoned, a bugler played taps, then six officers drew and discharged their pistols in a final goodbye salute.

Dust to dust: It was done.

The cars drove away, one by one. The family lingered, friends touched them, murmuring, dabbing at eyes. An old aunt plucked a gardenia from the casket spray as a keepsake. People held hands, walking slowly to their cars, appreciating life, the blue sky and beautiful earth, perhaps each other more than they had in recent days.

Lee put her arms around her children. She walked between them toward the car, sensing perhaps inappropriately the feeling of her high-heeled shoes sinking into the grass. It was a sensation peculiar to funerals: What other occasion put a woman in high heels on grass? She wondered how she could dwell on such a ridiculously unimportant thing at the saddest moment of her life. Moments of strife were like that though; they brought with them their own little escapes. While she thought of her high heels her eyes were dry.

There followed two hours in the church hall amid the smell of percolating coffee, a macaroni-tomato hot dish and Jell-O laced with bananas. Again Lee was overcome by the number of those who had come to pay last respects today.

High school friends of Greg's, policemen and their wives, customers from her store, former business acquaintances of Bill's, people from whom she bought floral supplies, members of the Faith Lutheran congregation whom she scarcely knew, grade school and high school friends of Janice's and Joey's, some along with their parents. Greg's high school track coach was there, as well as his ninth-grade English teacher, who brought along a poem Greg had written when he'd been her student. Even some people who said he'd been their paper boy when he was twelve years old.

"I can't believe it," she said over and over again, accepting their sympathies, their handclasps and their genuine caring. "I can't believe it. All these people."

"He touched a lot of lives," her mother said.

And he would go on touching them for years to come. There was his old girlfriend, Jane Retting, who'd never stopped calling him. And Nolan Steeg, who approached Lee timidly and asked if he could have some little memento of Greg, any small thing that had belonged to him. And Janice, who would continue to drive his car. Joey, who wanted his tape and CD collection. His grandparents, who kept Greg's picture on their living room wall. And Christopher Lallek, who would return to the apartment the two men had shared.

When the church hall emptied, he was one of the last remaining, collapsing metal folding chairs and carrying a few dirty coffee cups to the pass-through window for the hot, tired cooks.

Lee was standing near the door with a cluster of family members who were discussing details of dividing the work that remained: recording the offerings, addressing thank-you cards, distributing flowers to retirement homes. Peg Hillier handed a book and a small white box to Lee and said, "This is the memorial book and the rest of the memorial folders. What do you want to do with the sympathy cards that haven't been opened? Do you want us to take them or do you want to?"

She glanced at Chris, standing apart, waiting, still dressed in his crisp navy blue uniform with the black-crossed badge. She wanted to rush to him and say, "Take me for a ride in your new truck so I don't have to face one more detail or hear one more sad voice or make one more decision! Just take me out of here!"

Instead, she answered her mother, thanked her relatives, expressed her appreciation to the church circle ladies who were finishing the kitchen cleanup and left the building with a bunch of unopened sympathy cards, plus the gift cards from perhaps twenty floral arrangements.

As she emerged into the late afternoon sun, she breathed a sigh of relief. Joey and Janice were sitting on the grass in the shade with a bunch of their and Greg's friends—Kim, Nolan, Sandy, Jane, Denny Whitman. She looked around for Christopher but he was nowhere in sight. His Explorer was gone, too. An unexpected siege of disappointment swamped her. She had no right to feel let down; what would he want to hang around this gloomy group for? He'd done more than his share and had been on hand practically every minute since Friday afternoon.

"Did Christopher leave?" she called to the young people.

Janice answered, "Yes. He said to tell you he was sorry he didn't get to say goodbye, but you were busy."

"Oh."

"He said he'll call you soon."

Lee turned away to hide her disappointment. She'd been thinking about going home and putting a couple of lounge chairs on the deck and maybe even opening up a couple of beers and sitting beside him without saying one damned word. She had no idea why, but out of all who'd offered, his was the only company she wished for tonight. Not her own kids', not her parents', neighbors', friends'. When they were around she was forced to talk, give hugs, put out food, pick up empty glasses, watch them get falsely cheery and morose by turns, rub shoulders, listen to them. All she wanted was simple quiet and someone to share it with.

But those were her children over there, and she couldn't say to them, *Leave me alone for a while*.

"Are you ready to go home now?" she called.

"Sure, but is it all right if these guys come too for a while?"

Lee withheld a sigh. They needed their own support system, too, and these young people were thoughtful to provide it.

"Fine," she answered.

They picked themselves up from the grass, brushing wrinkles from their clothes, and she realized it would be some time before routine would return to normal and her life would be her own.

Chapter 5

As Christopher drove home through the hazy golden evening, the tail end of rush hour seemed mistimed: He'd lost sight of the fact that it was Monday and people were going about their regular pursuits, stopping for a loaf of bread, filling their gas tanks, waiting in left-turn lanes. The last four days had effectively removed him from routine, making it seem as if the rest of the world was out of step with the sloweddown pace of his life and the lives of the people about whom he cared. Passersby seemed callous, though he knew full well they had no way of knowing that Greg Reston was dead and he was a man in mourning.

The thought of facing the empty apartment took five miles an hour off his speed. He pictured the Reston kids, surrounded by their friends, visiting on the green grass. He'd considered going over and joining them, but he was too old. He didn't fit in there. The one he'd really wanted to stay with was Lee, but he was too young and didn't fit in there either. Besides, he'd nearly worn out his welcome. He wasn't, after all, one of her family.

With nowhere else to go, he drove home.

Inside, the apartment was quiet and stuffy. He opened the sliding glass doors and stepped out onto the deck, which overlooked the picnic area of Cutter's Grove Park with mere glimpses of the Mississippi River visible beyond a thick stand of verdant woods. The sun was still high, lighting the green treetops and the roof of the park shelter. A couple of mothers were giving a birthday party for a bunch of small kids. Crepe-paper streamers were stretched from the poles supporting the shelter roof. Smoke drifted from the barbecue grills. A bunch of preschoolers were blowing bubbles the size of basketballs and their voices carried up to him. "Look at that one! Look at that one!"

His mother had never given him a birthday party that he could remember.

He went back inside, loosening his tie, unbuttoning his shirt, pulling it out of his trousers, opening the refrigerator and overlooking Greg's orange juice in favor of a Sprite. He popped the top, took a swig from the can and noticed that the red message light was lit on his answering machine.

He pushed the button, listened to it rewind and swigged again as a twelve-yearold voice came on.

"Hey, man, what the hell happened to you! You said we was gonna do something this weekend. You said you'd call and we'd maybe go swimming or something. Shit, man, you're just like all the rest of 'em; never mean what you say. Well, don't bother calling me no more. I got better things to do than sit around waiting for some lyin' no-good pig to call and dish me shit." *Click!*

Judd.

Hell, he'd forgotten about Judd. Chris's hand, holding the Sprite can, dropped tiredly to his side as he stared at the machine.

Judd Quincy, age twelve, male, black, shoplifter, runaway, truant, vandal of school property, bicycle thief, neglected son of two known druggies, a reflection of Christopher Lallek at that age.

The poor little bastard. No question he was one. His mother and "dad" were white. Judd was pale brown. Maybe that was why the old man kicked the shit out of him now and then, and out of the mother, too.

He picked up the receiver and dialed.

"Yeah, say it," the kid answered.

"Judd?"

A pause, then, "Shit, man, whaddyou want?"

"Got your message."

"Yeah, so what."

"So, give me a break, huh?"

"Give you a break! Man, you lied! I sit around this dump all weekend long thinking I'm going out to the lake. Nobody calls. I look like a jerk, man! My friend Noise he says maybe I'm makin' you up! He don't believe no cop would give a fuck about a dipwad like me."

"You back to using that word again?"

"Why the fuck not?"

Chris stared at the floor, rubbing his forehead, picking his way carefully. "Something happen, Judd?"

"Something always happening here. This the most happenin' place you ever seen."

"Something worse than most days?"

"Why don't you just stick it, man! Go on out to the lake with your honky friends!"

"What'd they do, Judd?"

"Didn't do nothin', I told you!"

"So you're okay, then?"

"What do you care?"

Chris decided on a new tack. "Well, I'll tell you what . . . I need a friend right now."

The concept of being needed stopped Judd's attitude. Kids like him knew, from the time they were old enough to think, that they'd never been wanted, much less needed.

"You weirding me out, cop."

On top of everything else, Judd was having an identity crisis. Half the time he talked like a semi-educated white kid, the other half he broke into black rap.

"You got an hour?" Chris asked.

"Do what?"

"Ride. I'll come and pick you up."

"Not here."

"Wherever you say."

Judd thought some. "Seven-Eleven, same like always."

"Seven-Eleven. Give me five to get out of my uniform."

When Chris pulled up in the parking lot of the 7-Eleven, Judd had his shoulder blades against the front window and the sole of one sneaker flattened to the brick wall below it. His hands were buried to the elbows in the pockets of black-and-chartreuse knee-length Zubaz. He had on a faded, stretched-out purple body shirt that would have fit Michael Jordan. His hair was black and curly with a lightning bolt shaved into his skull above his left ear—inexpertly, as if with a home razor.

Judd watched the Explorer roll in, leaving his butt against the wall to show that it didn't mean jack-shit to him if anybody got a new red truck with fancy running boards, a visor and chrome wheels. As the vehicle approached, Judd didn't move, only rolled his eyes to keep up with the truck and its driver.

Chris pulled to a stop and looked at Judd out of the open driver's window.

"Yo," Chris said.

"What you talkin' like a black boy for?"

"What *you* talkin' like a black boy for?"

"I be black."

"You might be, but no sense talking like a dumb one if you ever want to get anywhere in this world. Get in."

Judd pushed himself off the wall and made sure his heels dragged with every step on his way to the truck.

He got in, slammed the door and slouched into his corner, letting his knees sprawl.

"Buckle up. You know the rules."

"Bad-ass cop."

"That's right. Now buckle up."

He did. And started complaining and jabbing a finger with his face all scrunched up. "I could turn you in for dat, you know. Teachers in school can't even make us change how we talk. It's the rules. We got our culture to preserve."

"I'm not your teacher, and if you ask me, you're preserving the wrong side of your culture, and furthermore, who you gonna turn me in to?"

"Somebody."

"Somebody." Chris rolled his eyes and shook his head sardonically.

"Yeah, somebody. Your captain, dat who."

"*Dat who?* Listen to you, talking like a dummy! I told you, if you want to get out someday and make something of yourself and have a truck like this and a job where you can wear decent clothes and people will respect you, you start by talking like a smart person, which you are. I could hack that oreo talk if it was real, but the first time I picked you up for doing the five-finger discount over at the SA station, you talked like every other kid in your neighborhood."

"Man, you don't know jack-shit about my neighborhood, so what you talkin'!"

"The hell I don't. How many times a month do you think I have to bust asses over there?"

"I'm twelve years old. You not supposed to talk to me like dat."

"Tell you what—I'll make you a deal. I'll talk to you nicer if you'll talk to me nicer. And the first thing you do is stop using that F word. And the second thing you do is start pronouncing words the way your first-grade teacher taught you to. The word is *that*, not *dat*."

Judd let his mouth get punk-disgusted, rolled his face toward the window and made some breathy sound like "Sheece . . ."

"I know you're doing it to get even with your dad."

"He's not my dad."

"Maybe not, but he pays the rent."

"And buys the cheese and snow."

Cheese and snow meant marijuana and cocaine.

"Is that what went on this weekend?"

Judd grew animated again, his bony knees jutting, his head leading the way as he retorted, "You gonna diss on me the rest of this ride, then you can just let me off!"

"Is that what went on this weekend?" Chris demanded.

Judd crumpled into his corner and looked out the window. "So what you gonna do? Put me in foster care again?" he said disparagingly.

"That what you want?"

Judd's answer was only rebellious silence. There were some who'd been in and out of foster homes so many times they grew cynical about it. Caught in the middle, these poor kids longed for nothing as much as security. It was not to be found, however, in being bounced into a foster home for two or three days while social services came out to their home to do a pep talk and offer a job to the parents, who'd rather live on welfare and get a free ride. The result was always the same. The parents would pledge to reform, straighten up for a day or two, then be back on drugs and alcohol before the week was out.

"All right, I'll tell you," Judd conceded. "They had a party Saturday night. Bunch of their friends come over. They got high and started doing a bone dance in the living room—"

"Bone dance?"

"Yeah. You know." Judd fixed Chris with a look that blended indifference and challenge. "That *word* you won't let me say. Then somebody tried to change partners and this fight breaks out. The old man hits the old lady and one of her teeth goes flyin', and she starts hittin' him back."

"Anybody hit you?"

"No."

"You sure?"

Judd refused to answer.

"What did you do?"

"I went out the window. Went to the Seven 'Leven and called you like you said. But you weren't home. Where the hell were you, man?"

"I was burying my best friend."

If Judd had been any other twelve-year-old his head would have snapped around. But Judd was Judd, and he had little energy to spare on other people's problems. Surviving took all the energy he had. He merely turned his head Chris's way and asked, "Who?"

"Greg. He died in a motorcycle accident on Friday."

Judd contemplated the news. His face remained impassive but there were things going on behind his unblinking eyes. After some time he withdrew even his glance, turning back to the view out the windshield.

"Man, that sucks."

Chris said nothing.

They rode awhile before Judd said, "So you bummed out or what?"

"Yeah. I miss him. It's bad in our apartment without him there."

They rode some more while Chris sensed Judd pondering the idea of the death of a friend, changing subtly, losing some of his defiance. He had no frame of reference, however, for dealing with grief or doling out compassion, so he only repeated, "Man, that sucks."

In a while Chris asked, "You hungry?"

Judd shrugged and looked the other way. Chris pulled through a drive-in window and got a double order of chicken McNuggets, a side salad, four packets of sweet-and-sour sauce and two small cartons of milk. They went to the Round Lake boat landing and sat on a picnic table, watching sunset stain the water.

"Sorry I wasn't there Saturday night," Chris said.

"That's bad, about your friend."

"I've got to get over it though. Nobody said life was fair."

"Nobody I ever knew."

"Still, we've got to keep on keepin' on, you know what I mean?"

Judd ate another nugget and nodded.

"Eat the salad, too. It's good for you. And drink all that milk."

Judd tipped his head and swallowed three times, then swiped his mouth with the back of a hand. "This friend—he got people who treat him good, or he like you and me?"

"He's got a good family. The best."

Judd's head bobbed as he studied his badly worn high-top sneakers planted a foot apart on the picnic bench.

"Want to know something?" Chris said. He let a few beats of silence pass, leaning forward on his knees like a basketball player on the bench. "When I was your age I used to be jealous of the kids who had decent parents. I used to treat them like worms, not talk to them—you know? Problem was, the only one it hurt was me because I didn't have any friends. Life is a bitch without friends. Then I grew up and realized that it was nobody's fault my parents were alcoholics. I could go on carrying a chip on my shoulder or I could shrug it off. I shrugged it off and found out that there are some fine people out there in the world. I decided I was going to be a fine person, too, and not do like my old man and old lady did. And that's why I became a cop."

They sat in the twilight thinking about it while Judd finished his food. In time they walked back to the truck with Chris's hand curled around Judd's skinny neck. Just before they reached the Explorer, Judd said, "This some bitchin' ride, man. Gonna have me one like it someday."

The following day Christopher returned to work. He was scheduled on the dogwatch, 11 P.M. till 7 A.M., and reported with a full half hour to spare, as required. In the locker room the radio speaker crackled from the wall while metal doors clanged and officers exchanged small talk. Nokes came over and hung a hand on Chris's shoulder.

"How you doin', Chris?"

"The locker room seems strange without him."

"Yup, it sure does." Nokes squeezed his neck and shuffled to his own locker to get dressed.

With twenty-nine sworn officers on the Anoka force, Chris wasn't always scheduled on the same shift as Greg, but often enough the two of them had stood back to back in the aisle between the lockers, exchanging small talk and wisecracks that were missed tonight.

Chris got into his bullet-proof vest and shirt, then knotted his tie before the tiny mirror on his locker door where most people kept family pictures. His held only one snapshot of himself and Greg by a black-and-white squad car. He loaded his belt with the paraphernalia of his profession: silent key holder, radio in a leather holder, stream light, Cap-stun, rubber gloves, handcuffs in their leather holder, a 9mm Beretta in its holster and two extra magazines. When he was completely dressed, twenty-six pounds of gear hung on his body, and tonight he felt every one of them.

Fifteen minutes before the shift change, he reported to the patrol room for roll call and sat down with the four others who were coming on duty to watch the updates on LETTN—the Law Enforcement Training Television Network. Today, however, the large-screen TV got sporadic attention. Instead the men, their voices subdued, exchanged remarks about the funeral and Greg's absence, asked Chris questions about the Reston family and whether or not he was going to get a new roommate. Somebody passed him the roll-call book and he took his turn acquainting himself with information on missing persons, stolen vehicles and arrest warrants faxed to the department from the jail since he'd been gone. When roll call ended, Chris wandered into the communications room, greeted the dispatcher and checked the past four days' shift reports, which listed every call answered by the department. Though only twenty miles from Minneapolis, the city of Anoka, population 17,000, had far less crime than the big city, and needed a much smaller police force to fight it.

On Saturday night the department had responded to a total of twenty-three calls; Sunday night only seventeen. Same things as usual: suspicious person, disturbing the peace, simple assault, disorderly conduct. After scanning the clipboard, Chris hung it back on the wall, realizing that apart from the fact that memories of Greg lingered throughout the familiar rooms of the police station, it felt good to be back, occupied once more.

He collected his hat from the patrol room table and said, "I'm outta here, guys."

"Me too," Nokes said, and together they headed out to their squad cars.

He spent the night as he'd spent hundreds of others, guarding the sleeping city. Sometimes he prowled. Sometimes he sat, listening to channel one crackle ceaselessly with the voice of the county dispatcher. He and Nokes both responded to a domestic and found the apartment door open, the TV on and nobody home. He got bad-mouthed by two other apartment tenants when he knocked on their doors to ask questions. Back in his squad car, he cruised until a call from the dispatcher sent him to check out an alert from a motion alarm, which he discovered had been tripped by a falling ceiling panel. He sat in the parking lot of Carpenter's Hall beside a shadowy pine tree and watched cars come over the Mississippi River bridge from Champlin, tracking speeds on his radar. He watched the two red lights on his radar screen and listened to the sound of the signal change as the cars swept abreast and passed him.

He thought about how close he was to Benton Street. Nine blocks away Lee Reston probably lay in bed—asleep or awake? Resting after the past four exhausting days or wide-eyed, in the company of sad memories? He started his engine and rolled out of the Carpenter's Hall parking lot, onto Ferry Street, then left on Benton. A dark, sleeping neighborhood with nothing more than a pair of cat's eyes gleaming at him from beneath a clump of shrubs before it shot across the street. He slowed to a crawl as he approached her house. The lights were off, the garage door was down. Janice's old car was parked in the driveway. Greg's Toyota was nowhere in sight, probably in the garage.

Are you sleeping? he thought. *Or are you lying awake wishing you were? Are you wondering whose headlights are sliding down Benton Street so slowly at this hour of the morning? Well, don't worry. It's just me, keeping watch. Did you work today at your shop or stay home and write thank-you cards? I see you closed your garage door. That's better. Now you keep it closed every night, okay? How are the kids doing? I suppose they're a help to you, reasons for you to make it through another day. I could use a little of that. It was sad in the locker room tonight, Greg's locker closed and locked and no Greg clanging the door open and lipping off. I suppose we'll all get used to it, but it'll take time, won't it?*

At 3 A.M. he ate a full meal at Perkins Restaurant.

At five, when the sky had begun going pinkish in the east, he checked her street again.

At six he cruised it one more time and discovered an oscillating sprinkler fanning back and forth over her front lawn: She was up. Was she having coffee in the kitchen the way the two of them had a couple days ago? It took an effort to roll past without stopping to ask for a cup.

At seven he left his bullet-proof vest in his locker and went home to bed.

The phone rang at 1:30 that afternoon and woke him up.

"Hello, Chris, this is Lee."

"Lee . . ." He twisted around to peer, one-eyed, at the digital clock. "Hi." His voice sounded like somebody scraping paint.

"Oh, no . . . did I wake you?"

"That's okay. No problem."

"I'm sorry. I should have called the station for your schedule before I dialed. Did you work last night?"

"Yeah, dogwatch, but that's okay." He settled on his back and wedged a pillow beneath his head, squinting at the bars of sunlight just beginning to peek through the blinds.

"I really am sorry."

"I usually get up around two anyway. Don't give it another thought." He dredged some sandmen out of his eyes, thinking she could call and wake him every day and he wouldn't mind. "There's stuff I want to do this afternoon anyway. I've got a little rattle in one of the doors on my Explorer and I want to take it in and see if they can get it out of there."

"Everybody got a ride in your Explorer but me. How do you like it?"

"Love it. I'll take you for a ride sometime and you can see for yourself. Joey really liked it, too."

"So I understand. You let him drive."

"I hope you don't mind."

"No, of course not. If it were one of his friends I'd be madder than heck, but with you—one of our men in blue—how can I object?"

"We talked a little . . . about Greg. Got some feelings out in the open."

"He needed that very badly, to talk to a man."

"How's Janice doing?"

"She's very blue and sleeps a lot. I think she'll have more trouble than Joey will, getting over this."

"And you—I won't make the mistake of asking how you're doing. *What* are you doing?"

"Trying to face the idea of going back to work again. It's hard when your thoughts are so scattered. I can't seem to concentrate on anything. But I'll have to go back soon and relieve Sylvia. She's been pulling double duty. Today I'm facing a stack of post-funeral business items that seems endless. That's what I'm calling about. Greg's things."

"I told you there's no rush. You don't have to get them out of here until you're good and ready."

"I know, but it's hanging over me like a storm cloud. I want to get it done with and put it behind me. I thought, if it's okay with you, I'd come over on Sunday. My shop is closed that day and Janice and Joey should both be around to help me."

"I'll still be working the night shift so I'll be here all day. You can come anytime you want."

"You said you usually get up around two?"

"Give me till noon."

"Five hours of sleep? Christopher, that's not enough."

"All right, how about one o'clock?"

"Two is better. I don't want to mess up your sleeping schedule. You cops get little enough of it as it is."

"All right, two. What are you going to use to haul the furniture in?"

"Jim Clements next door said I could use his pickup."

"You okay driving it or do you want me to come over and drive?"

"Jim offered, too, but I'll be just fine. See you Sunday at two."

"Fine."

"And, Christopher?"

"Hm?"

"Please go back to sleep. I feel so bad I woke you."

She planned to ask the kids at supper that night if they'd help her. Before she could do so, Joey announced that Denny Whitman had asked him to drive up to the lake that day with his family.

"Oh," she said, halting in the midst of setting a bowl of scalloped potatoes on the table. "I sort of made plans for the three of us to go over to Greg's apartment and pack up his things that day. I was counting on both of you to help me." She sat down at her place and Joey began filling his plate.

"On Sunday?" he complained. "Couldn't we do it on Saturday so I could still go up to the lake with the Whitmans? They're only going for that one day."

Lee hid her disappointment and reminded herself he was only fourteen. At that age kids had a lot to learn about their parents' needs, especially in a situation like this. The Whitmans had undoubtedly invited him with the best of intentions, realizing that he needed diversions now more than ever.

"Janice?" she said, glancing at her daughter.

Janice put down her fork and shifted her gaze out the kitchen window while her eyes filled with tears. On her plate, her favorite food in the world was scarcely touched. "Mom . . . I . . . I'm just not ready for that yet. Can't we put it off for a while?"

Lee set her fork down, too.

Janice added, "And anyway, I'm supposed to work on Sunday." She clerked at The Gap store at Northtown Shopping Center. "I'm afraid if I don't go back pretty soon I might lose my job, and I need the money for college. Can't we put it off for a while?"

Lee took Janice's hand and held it on the tabletop. "Of course we can," she said quietly. "Christopher says there's no rush at all."

Janice blinked and her tears fell. She withdrew her hand from Lee's, swiped beneath both eyes, retrieved her fork and filled it with chunks of potato and ham, then stared at it for some time before the fork handle clinked against her plate. "Mom, I'm just not hungry tonight." She lifted her brimming eyes to Lee. "The scalloped potatoes are great—honest. But I think I'll just . . . I don't know . . . go to my room for a while."

"Go ahead. The potatoes will keep till another day."

When Janice was gone Lee and Joey fought the feeling of abandonment, but it won. Joey had eaten only half of his dinner when he, too, said, "Mom, I'm not very hungry either. Could I be excused?"

"Sure," she said. "What are you going to do?"

"I don't know. Maybe go over to the ballpark, watch a couple games."

"All right. Go on," she said understandingly.

He rose and stood by his chair uncertainly. "Want me to help you with the dishes?"

"I can do them. Give me a kiss." He pecked her on the cheek while she patted his waist. "Have a good time and be back by ten."

"I will."

He left the house and she sat at the table, listening to him raise the kickstand of his ten-speed bicycle, then whir away on it until its clickety-sigh disappeared down the driveway. She sat on, lonely beyond words, willing herself to get up and put away the leftovers, rinse the plates, load the dishwasher. These were healthy pursuits that would help lift her spirits. But she was so tired at that moment of falsely trying to lift those spirits. Instead she remained at the table, her chin braced on a palm, staring out the window at the backyard. She could go pull a few weeds in the garden, stake up the delphiniums, which were blooming heavily, pick a bouquet for the kitchen table. She could call her mom or Sylvia, ask Janice if she'd like to go to a movie, go outside and wash the car, get into it and return the various cake pans and Pyrex dishes that people had left here and never come back to collect. She could scribble a few thank-you cards.

She sighed, weary of being the strong one for everyone else's benefit, wishing someone else would take over the duty for just this one evening. She sat on at the table, overcome by a lassitude so enormous it seemed insurmountable.

She turned her head and stared down the front hall at the sunshine bouncing off the white siding and lighting the front entry. Such a sad time of day, suppertime, when you were sitting at a table alone. Jim Clements's truck rolled past; he was a construction worker and just getting home from work. Two young girls in bathing suits rode past on their bicycles. Their ten-year-old chatter filled Lee with sadness. Everybody busy, heading for someplace, to do something with someone.

She was still sitting there morosely when a black-and-white squad car rolled past her line of vision and pulled into her driveway. She was up and out the front door before she realized she felt rescued.

She got outside in time to see Christopher, in full uniform, getting out of the car. His unexpected appearance filled her with sudden happiness.

He slammed the door but left the engine running, and came around the front of the car. She moved toward him eagerly, energized by some new reaction she had not expected. She had always rather clumped him with Greg's friends and thought of him as a boy. But the police officer approaching her was no boy. His navy blue uniform granted him a stature, a respectability, a maturity that caught her unaware. His visored hat was anchored low over his eyes. His uniform shirt, pressed to perfection, was tucked in smoothly, holding chevrons, pins and badges of all sorts. His tie was neatly knotted beneath his tanned chin. The heavy black leather holders on his belt lent him additional authority while his bullet-proof vest added girth to his overall shape.

They met at the front of the car, beside the hot, running engine.

"Hi," he said, removing his sunglasses and smiling.

"Hi." She stuck both hands into the front pockets of her white shorts. "I didn't expect to see you today."

"Some mail came for Greg." He handed it to her.

"Thanks." She glanced down and leafed through four envelopes. "I guess I'd better go to the post office and fill out a change-of-address form. I'll have to add it to the list. I'd forgotten how much paperwork has to be done when someone dies." She looked up again. "I thought you were working the eleven-to-seven shift."

"I'm supposed to be, but one of the guys asked me to exchange shifts with him today." The radio on his belt began crackling out a dispatch, and he reached down without looking to adjust its volume. Greg used to do the same thing. She could never figure out how they could decipher the stuttering radio and carry on a conversation at the same time. "I just passed Joey back there. Said he was heading over to the ballpark."

"Summer leagues," she replied. "Much better than hanging around the dreary house."

"How about you? You just hanging around the dreary house?"

"I'm going back to work pretty soon. I figure I've let Sylvia carry the load long enough. Christopher, about Sunday though . . ."

He waited, standing with his feet planted firmly in thick-soled black regulation shoes.

"The kids can't help me that day. Joey wants to go up to the lake with Denny, and Janice just needs some time yet before she can face the job. So we'll have to do it some other time."

"I'll help you," he said.

"But you've helped so much already."

"I was planning to help anyway. If you want to go ahead, the two of us can probably handle it all ourselves. If you want to wait for the kids to be there with you—well, that's fine too."

"It's not an easy job," she told him. "I've done it before, after Bill died, and it can be devastating."

"Then we could spare the kids, couldn't we?" After a beat he added, watching her very closely, "But I imagine sometimes you get a little tired of sparing the kids and wish they'd spare you."

How intuitive, she thought. For a man so young, he could read her with amazing accuracy. Sometimes when she had such thoughts she felt guilty, but hearing him put voice to them filled her with a sense of relief and excused her of the guilt.

"How did you know?" she asked.

On his radio a voice came through, sputtering like arcing electrical current. "Three Bravo Eighteen."

"Just a minute," he told Lee, plucking the radio from his belt and nearly touching it to his lips. She had never before noticed what beautifully sculpted lips he had. "Three Bravo Eighteen."

The crackly voice said, "Eight two zero west Main Street. Apartment number G-thirty-seven. Report of loud voices. Possible domestic in progress. No one to be seen."

"Copy," he said, then to Lee, "Sorry, I've got to go." He slipped his sunglasses back on. "Let me know about Sunday. In my opinion you should wait for your kids, but if you decide to go ahead we can get it done in three hours. Then you can stop dreading it."

She nodded and found herself following him to the door of the squad car, waiting while he got in and scribbled the address on a legal pad beside him on the front seat. He reached for the dash radio to report his car number and the time. "Three Bravo Eighteen en route. Eighteen-oh-nine." He replaced the radio on the dash, put the car into reverse and said out the open window, "You look tired. Get some sleep." A simple farewell, but with a familiarity that unexpectedly stirred a reaction deep within her. It was the kind of blandishment a husband might toss out, the kind that implied caring that went much deeper than the words.

She crossed her arms and watched him leave. She'd seen Greg do it dozens of times, slinging an arm along the top of the seat and craning around to look through the rear window as he pelted backward at ten miles an hour. The car bounced off the concrete apron at the end of the driveway, and he lifted a hand in farewell as he roared away down the street.

Long after he had disappeared she stood in the driveway looking after him.

She returned to work later that week to the blessed balm of routine. Opening the store at 8 A.M., brewing coffee, watering all the arrangements in the cooler and checking their care cards to see what day each was made—the familiar motions brought ease, though often she found herself staring into space. Sylvia asked often, "How are you doing, sis?" Their hired arrangers, Pat Galsworthy and Nancy Mc-Faddon, also showed concern, but Lee found herself answering by rote, rather than expressing what she really felt: that she was absolutely dreading Sunday, when she had to face Greg's possessions.

By Sunday she had put a full nine days between herself and Greg's death, but it helped little in light of the duty that lay ahead. She awakened early, with four hours to spare before church. At six-thirty she was out in the backyard, kneeling on a green rubber pad, pulling quack grass from between the daylilies and wishing it were tomorrow morning and today was behind her.

By two o'clock the temperature had risen to eighty-five degrees and had five more to go. She put on some faded green shorts and a misshapen cotton shirt, forcing herself to move, step by step, get the truck from next door, drive it across town and face the place where her son had lived. She left the truck in the hot parking lot and struggled up to his apartment with a bunch of nested cardboard boxes bumping against her bare leg. Christopher answered the door wearing cutoff blue jeans and a white T-shirt. Gloria Estefan was singing quietly on the radio. No country music today to remind her of Greg.

"Hi," Christopher said, taking the boxes from her, sobered as she was by what they had to do today.

"Hi," she answered, remaining on the threshold.

"Hell of a thing to have to do on a beautiful day like this, isn't it?"

He saw her battling self-pity, but it won and her face began to crumple. The boxes hit the floor and suddenly she was in his arms, being held hard against his sturdy chest. After a moment he said, "I think you should have waited for your kids."

"No, I'll be all right. I promise I will." She withdrew and took a deep breath.

"You sure?"

She nodded hard, as if convincing herself.

He'd known this moment would be difficult for her and had done all he could to make it easier. "I've got his bed all taken apart and I've sorted through our CDs and got all of his put into one box."

She sniffed once, ran a hand beneath her nose and said, "Good. Let's get to work then."

They went directly into Greg's bedroom, where his mattress and box spring were leaning against the wall.

"I washed his bedding and put it in that bag." He pointed. "And the stuff wrapped in newspaper is everything that was on his wall and on top of his chest of drawers—pictures, certificates from the department. His shoot badge and merit badges and all that stuff are in here." He squatted and touched a shoe box. "I took care of returning his gun to the department, and his cuffs and radio and whatever had to be turned in." He lifted his gaze to her before rising slowly to his full height, his palms to his thighs like an uncertain suitor. "I hope I did the right thing. I thought it would make it easier on you."

She touched his bare arm in gratitude. "It does."

They went to work, she turning to Greg's closet, he carrying the bed frame out into the beating heat and loading it on the pickup.

When the contents of the closet were boxed, they carried them out together, followed by the heavy chest with its drawers still full, the mattress and box spring, lugging them down two flights of stairs and onto the bed of the pickup. By the time they finished they were sweating profusely and wiping their foreheads.

Back inside, the air-conditioned halls felt heavenly. In the apartment the venetian blinds were closed on the west windows. The radio was still playing and Lee turned on the kitchen faucet.

"How about a Sprite?" Christopher asked, opening the refrigerator door.

"Sounds good."

He found two cans, two handfuls of ice, and had the soda glugging into a pair of glasses when he turned around . . . and stopped pouring.

Lee was tilted over the sink, scooping handfuls of water onto her face and neck, stretching the collar of her knit shirt and running her hands into it. The hair on her nape was wet, stuck together into short brown arrows. Her green shorts had sneaked up in the back, revealing a rim of white underwear. She turned off the single-lever faucet and began drying her face with both palms. He snatched a hand towel and touched it to her left arm.

"Thanks," she said, grabbing it blindly, turning to him with her face covered, pat-pat-patting at her skin the way men didn't. By the time her eyes appeared above the towel he was pouring their drinks again.

"Hot out there," she said.

He handed her a glass. "This will cool you down."

She took it and drank. He did the same, keeping an eye on her over the rim of his glass. Her face was red from exertion, the hair around it standing out at angles. Her white shirt was damp to the first button.

He pulled a short black comb out of his rear pocket. "Here," he said, handing it to her.

"Oh . . . thanks." She used it without the slightest self-consciousness, and without the need for a mirror, then handed it back to him.

"You want to go through the kitchen next?" he asked.

"I suppose." She looked up at the cabinets. "What's in here?"

"An electric popcorn popper." He opened a bottom door. "He bought the toaster when the old one went kaflooey, and a set of glasses he said we needed. He brought a few dishes from home, I think—these green ones here, and that pitcher. But most of the dishes and silverware I already had when he moved in. We shared the cost of the groceries, but we had an agreement that we'd each buy our own steaks whenever we wanted them. There are a couple of his in the freezer yet. Rib eyes, I think."

He'd been opening and closing cupboard doors as he spoke. When he finally stopped, she said, "Listen, Christopher, this is silly. I'm not going to take his groceries, and these are all things you can use. The few dishes he took from home were just old junk, no family heirlooms, I can assure you. I have no need for anything."

"Not even the popcorn popper?"

"I have one."

"Or the toaster?"

"Keep it."

"How about the rib eyes?"

"You can bring them over on the Fourth of July. Everyone's bringing their own. I've changed my mind about doing the turkey. That was Greg's favorite."

"You mean you're still going to have the picnic?"

"I suppose we could pretend we died right along with him, but I'm not very good at acting like that, are you?"

"No."

"A picnic will be good for us. Play a little volleyball again, get some barbecue smoke in our eyes, go out to the park and watch the fireworks. You'll be there, won't you?"

"I wouldn't miss it."

They raised their glasses and drank again, filling a void that had inexplicably jumped between them as soon as the room grew silent.

"Well," he said, clacking his empty glass on the counter. "I'm going to go sort through the stuff in the bathroom. Why don't you take a look at the living room?"

She went into the room where the radio still played. On the sunny side of the apartment it felt warmer, in spite of the closed blinds. A box of tapes and CDs sat on the floor before the open glass doors of the entertainment unit. The potted tree she'd sent from the shop as a moving-in gift looked healthy, its branches weeping above one end of the sofa. On the wall the crisscross wooden rack held twenty-odd caps, with two pegs empty.

She stood with her thumbnails poking into her thighs, gazing up at it, daunted by it, feeling the suffocation begin, damning it when she'd thought she'd make it through today with flying colors. She steeled herself and selected a cap—a white one with a large maroon A above the bill: Anoka. From his high school days. She carried it to the bathroom doorway and stood for a moment watching Christopher drop things into a black duffel bag balanced on the small vanity top. Quietly, she said, "I'm not sure which ones are his."

Chris stopped pulling things from the drawers and turned to look at her. Her mouth was trembling and her rusty eyes looked vulnerable. She put the cap on her head, dropped one shoulder against the door frame and stuck her hands into her front shorts pockets. "This is a test," she said. "Get through the afternoon without breaking down and bawling . . . because he's never coming back."

"Yeah, I know." His voice broke a little. He was holding Greg's toothbrush and toothpaste in his hands. "This is a hell of a job, too. His hairbrush, razor, aftershave—" Angrily he threw the handful into the duffel bag and braced both hands against the vanity top like a runner stretching. "God, this room even smells like him."

It struck her how self-centered she'd been, considering only her sorrow, not his. "Oh, Christopher, I'm sorry." She moved into the small room, pulling the cap from her head, holding it in one hand while laying the other on his back. "You miss him, too," she whispered. Abruptly he straightened, spun and embraced her. In that white-tiled room with its nostalgic scents of male cosmetics, they closed their eyes while the mirror reflected the two of them locked together, drawing strength from one another, she with Greg's cap still in one hand.

"No, I'm the one who's sorry," he whispered. "I shouldn't have said that. It's hard enough for you without remarks like that."

"But it's hard for you, too, and if we can't be honest with each other about our feelings . . ." She didn't know how to finish.

"God, what a pair we make, huh? Stumbling along and hugging each other every five minutes like this is the end of the world."

"I did so well all week, I thought I could make it through today without this happening. But the caps in the living room . . . somehow I just couldn't handle them."

She opened her eyes and saw herself in the mirror, in Christopher's arms. His head was bent over her far shoulder, his hands clasped on her spine. Their stomachs and bare legs touched and though she realized most hugs of commiseration would remain more guarded, she stayed where she was.

He broke the contact first, drawing back and ordering, "Here, give me the cap." He squeezed the bill into a nice curve, put it on her head and turned her to the mirror, standing behind her with his hands on her shoulders. "There. Look at that. It's a mother in a bill cap and there's not a damn thing wrong with it, okay? Matter of fact, you look pretty good in it. You ought to wear one more often."

He grinned, coaxing a responsive smile from her. She raised both hands and tipped the cap back a little, then grabbed a big, deep, restorative breath and blew it out fast. "All right, I can get through it now. How about you?"

"Me too. Let's get it done and get the truck over to your house. One thing though." He dropped his hands from her shoulders and his mood changed.

"What?" She turned to look up at him.

"There's this kid I know. He's sort of teetering on the brink—not much hope at home, no family life to speak of, both parents druggies trading in their food stamps for money so they can buy their next fix. If you don't mind, I'd like to give him one of Greg's caps. This kid respects cops. He'd like to think he doesn't but he does. A cap could make a difference."

"Sure. Give him any one you want. Give him two."

They got the caps sorted and the bathroom items divided and sifted through some of Greg's papers that were stored in a kitchen drawer. About the living room furniture, Christopher said, "I had some, and we bought some together, but I'd like to keep it all. I have receipts and I'll pay you a fair price for his half of its value. That is, if it's okay with your kids. If they want anything, it's theirs."

"For now, let's leave it here."

"You should take the fig tree though," Christopher said.

"Oh, come on, I can get a dozen more like it wholesale any day I want to. It belongs in that corner."

"All right," he said, "I accept. If you had taken it I'd just go to your store and buy one exactly like it anyway. Thank you."

They shut off the radio, carried the last load out and worked together lashing down the mattress and box spring so they wouldn't blow off. Christopher had put on his sunglasses. Lee's eyes were shaded by the visor of Greg's cap. Heat waves zigzagged off the blacktop.

Christopher tied the last knot and asked, "You okay driving this truck with all that stuff on it?"

"I'm okay."

"All right. I'll be behind you."

He followed her to her house and they unloaded everything into her garage. Janice would be moving back to the U of M campus when school resumed in the fall, and she'd use Greg's bed and leave her own room intact for weekend visits.

By the time they finished and returned the truck to Jim Clements, they were hot and sweaty.

Christopher asked, "Do you know how to swim?"

"Sure."

They were standing in the shade of the garage roof with the overhead door wide open.

"You want to go? Cool off a little bit? We could drive over to the public beach on Crooked Lake."

"Gosh, that sounds good."

She went in, put on a suit and oversized shirt and came back out wearing thongs and carrying two towels.

"Let's go."

He drove.

She clambered into his Explorer and said, "Wow, I like this."

"So do I."

"Did you get the rattle fixed?"

"Yup."

They talked all the way to the lake. About cars. And her business. And how she'd chosen the name Absolutely Floral because it would appear first in the yellow pages, and how Sylvia said Lee was crazy to want a name like that, but her psychology had worked—most of their first-time business came from the yellow pages.

At the lake the beach was crowded. They stripped off their shirts, ran in among children playing in the shallow water and swam out to a diving board. They dove some, swam some, hung on the side of the float and talked some. About surfing, which he'd been watching on TV, and Hawaii, where neither of them had ever been but always wanted to go. They recounted where they'd each learned to swim when they were kids, who they'd swum with. A volleyball plopped into the water ten feet from Chris. He pushed off the raft to return it and they found themselves involved in a game of waterball with a bunch of fun-loving strangers.

They laughed.

And tired.

And worked up a roaring appetite.

When he pulled the Explorer into her driveway she said, "I have some leftover spaghetti I could nuke."

He said, "You're on," and shut off the engine.

She scooped out two servings and warmed them while he fixed ice water and got forks from the drawer she pointed at. Unceremoniously she handed him a plate and a napkin, remarking as she sat down, "Don't tell my mother how I served this."

"What's wrong with this?"

"No place mats, no table setting, letting you get your own water and fork, me in this disgusting shirt and thongs throwing you your plate. My mother would have a shit fit. She's stuck on propriety. One doesn't do the unexpected or the unconventional. Her favorite phrase is 'What would people say?' "

"Shit fit?" He was wearing a smile. His face was shiny from the water and his hair had fallen neatly into place without apparent help from him. "You actually said 'shit fit'?"

She stopped winding spaghetti to meet his amused eyes. "What? I can't say that?"

"It doesn't bother me, it's just that I never heard you say anything like that before. I always thought of you as Mrs. Perfect. Perfect mother, perfect lady, perfect . . . you know what I mean."

"Me?" Her eyes grew big and her mouth dropped open. "I'm far from perfect. What in the world makes you say a thing like that?"

"The way Greg talked about you. In his eyes you could do no wrong."

"I cuss now and then. Does it bother you?"

"No, it makes you human, makes me more comfortable around you. Now what were you saying about your mother?"

"Oh, just that she lives according to Emily Post. Tables set properly, joining the right clubs, dressing properly for dinner, sending thank-you cards, playing Grieg at funerals, not Vince Gill."

"I overheard her remark about that."

"I'm sure. What did she say?"

His eyes grew mischievous. "If I remember right, she said, 'What will people say?' "

Lee grinned and they dug into their spaghetti.

"So what about your mother?" she asked. "What's she like?"

He stopped chewing, stopped winding spaghetti and took a drink of water before answering, "Nothing like yours, believe me."

"You won't tell me?"

He pondered awhile, his eyes leveled on her, before deciding to confide. "She's an alcoholic. So is my father."

"Were they always?"

"Always. She worked as a fry cook on the early morning shift at a truck stop; he didn't work at all that I remember. Claimed he'd hurt his back somehow and couldn't. Most days, by the time I got home from school they'd be down at this place I always called The Hole, pickling their gizzards. Not only didn't she set tables properly, she never set them at all. Any cooking that was done was pretty much left up to me. And I'll guarantee you she never sent a thank-you note in her life—

I don't know what the hell she'd have to thank anybody for. She didn't have any friends except the drunks who hung out at that bar. So don't be too hard on your mother. You could have done a lot worse." He said it amiably and she accepted it.

"What about sisters and brothers?"

"One sister."

"Older or younger?"

"Four years younger."

"Where is she now?"

"Jeannie is somewhere on the west coast. She moves around."

"Do you ever see her?"

"Not very often. She ran away when she was fifteen and has been married and divorced three times since then. Last time I saw her she weighed about two hundred fifty pounds and lived off the welfare system, just like our folks did. Jeannie and I don't have a lot in common."

"And your parents? Where are they?"

"They live over on the other side of town in a squalid apartment complex called Jackson Estates. They haven't changed much except that they do their boozing at home now because it's hard for them to get up and down the stairs."

"I've upset you, asking about them."

"No, not really. I gave up expecting them to change a long time ago."

"They must be very proud of you."

"You don't understand. They're not the kind of parents who get proud. To do that you have to get sober first. They haven't been sober in thirty-five years."

"I'm sorry, Christopher," she said quietly.

They finished eating their spaghetti and meatballs. They had progressed through a day running a range of emotions, from low to high, now low again. What they had shared left them undeniably closer, so close, in fact, that he grew uncomfortable as they sat in her cozy kitchen, relaxed in their chairs and exchanging gazes that lasted longer and longer.

He got up and refilled his water glass.

"You want some more?" he asked.

She nodded. That's how it was getting to be between them, comfortable one moment, uncomfortable the next. A man filling a woman's water glass because she was getting to look a little too good to him, and Emily Post and her mother would undoubtedly have a few choice remarks about that.

He drank his water standing up, then reached for their dirty plates. "Well, let's clean this up so I can get out of your hair."

"I'll clean it up."

"No way. I'll help."

They were both clearing the table when Janice came home from work. She walked into the kitchen and dropped her car keys on the table.

"Christopher, hi! What are you doing here?"

"Your mom fed me supper."

A beat of awareness caught and held Janice, pulling the smile from her face. "You helped her move Greg's things, didn't you?"

"Yes."

"I saw them in the garage." She turned to Lee. "Mom, I'm sorry I didn't help."

"It's okay, sweetie." She gave Janice a kiss on the cheek. "It's all done now."

"No, it's not okay. I should have been there. I'm really sorry."

"Christopher helped, so don't say another word about it."

Lee went on swishing a plate under the hot water while Janice studied her, then Chris, then Lee again.

"You sure?"

"I'm sure. You hungry?"

The question convinced Janice her transgression was minor. "Mmm . . . sorta." She nosed along the cabinet to the bowl of cold spaghetti sauce, still in its Tupperware storage dish. With two long rose-colored fingernails she plucked out a meatball. "Boy, it's sweltering out there." She turned, taking a bite, resting her spine against the cabinet edge. "I was thinking about going somewhere for a swim. You interested in going along, Chris?"

He was dressed in his T-shirt again and his cutoffs were nearly dry.

"Actually, your mom and I already did that."

Janice swallowed the last of her meatball with a slight gulp. "You did?" She glanced inquisitively between the two of them.

After an awkward beat of silence Lee offhandedly opened the dishwasher door and said, "It was hot dragging that furniture around. We just cooled off and then grabbed some supper. Do you want me to warm some for you?"

"Mom," Janice said with an air of gentle chiding, "I'm twenty-three years old. You don't have to warm up my supper anymore."

Lee smiled at her daughter, drying her hands on a towel. "Force of habit."

Christopher pushed his chair under the table and said, "Well, I'd better go. I have to work tonight. Thanks for the supper, Mrs. Reston."

"It was the least I could do. Thank you for everything you did today."

He moved toward the door and Janice said, "I'll walk you out." Lee felt a peculiar spurt of resentment at Janice for blithely usurping her place with Christopher. The feeling struck suddenly, then retreated under duress as she told herself her place was not with him. Still, they'd been together all day, working on a decidedly difficult task, and she felt abandoned, watching the two of them walk outside. They looked so young and perfect together.

By his truck door Janice paused, preventing him from getting in. She was dressed in a simple pullover pink blouse and a short jeans skirt. Her tan, bare legs ended in unadorned white flats. She stood on the sides of her heels with her toes curled up off the blacktop, her head tipped to one side. "Thank you for helping her, Chris. I was really a rat not to do it, but I was bummed."

He looked her straight in the eyes, holding his key ring over his index finger. "Sometimes we've got to do things whether we're bummed or not. I didn't mind doing it, but you're right. You and Joey should have helped her today. She needed you."

Janice stared at the chrome edging around his windshield, her mouth contracting.

"Hey, don't cry," he said, touching her chin.

She struggled not to but there was evidence of tears.

"Just be there for her a little more, okay? This is a rough time for her. She carries the brunt of it, taking care of all the details—funeral, cars, paperwork. You know that she wouldn't criticize you in a million years, but she's got feelings too, yet she always puts your feelings first."

"I know," Janice whispered.

They stood awhile in the slanting sun. "You mad at me for saying what I think?"

She shook her head, still staring at the chrome molding.

"You got any objections to me coming around now and then to take her mind off things?"

She shook her head again.

"Okay then . . . see you on the Fourth of July?"

She nodded at the molding.

She was still standing in the driveway holding onto one elbow with the opposite hand when he waved farewell and drove away.

Chapter 6

Serious crime was the exception rather than the rule in the city of Anoka. There were relatively few times when its police officers felt their lives threatened. Now and then a robber was apprehended, or the SWAT team was called out on a drug bust, but for the most part, Christopher Lallek and his fellow officers took their duties in stride.

At 6:20 A.M. on a hazy, hot morning in the first week of July, Christopher was sitting in his squad car yawning. He checked his watch—forty minutes to go—and shifted his stiff rump on the car seat. Glancing up at the movement of vehicles rolling by on Highway 10, he noticed a '78 Grand Prix weaving in and out of traffic.

Immediately he came alert, switched on his reds and pulled out into the westbound lane. He could tell the moment the driver saw the flashing reds because he increased speed and made a reckless lane switch. The inbound lane held more traffic than this one, but the westbound flow was heavy enough to put starch into Christopher's spine and tighten his grip on the wheel.

He caught up with the Grand Prix and followed close on his tail, watching for the driver to look into his rearview mirror.

The driver ignored him.

He gave the siren a short hit and got ignored some more.

He turned on the siren full blast and felt his ire mount as the driver continued pretending the black-and-white wasn't there. He picked up the radio, reported his position and the Grand Prix's plate number and, finally, after a good half mile saw the smart-aleck respond, pulling to a stop on the right shoulder.

Sizzling with temper, Christopher got out of his squad and approached the rusted red vehicle.

The driver had his window down and was slumped slightly toward the wheel. He was perhaps twenty-eight or thirty years old, needed a shave and a haircut, and looked as if he'd been on an all-night bender.

Chris glanced into the car, looking for open bottles, and asked, "Could I see your license, please?"

"Whaffor?" His breath could have cured leather.

"Just show it to me, please."

"If you wanna see my license, tell me what I done wrong."

"Do you have a license?"

The guy shrugged and turned a baggy-eyed expression of disdain Chris's way.

"The license, sir."

" 'S been revoked," the guy mumbled.

Christopher put a hand on his shoulder and said, "Get out of the car, please."

The driver sneered, "Screw you, prick," and tromped on the gas. The edge of the back window glass struck Christopher's arm and carried him six feet down the highway. Even as the pain shot through him he was spun free and found himself running to his squad.

Door slamming! Heart pumping! Siren squealing! The black-and-white fishtailed and sprayed gravel and weeds twenty feet behind him. He grabbed the radio and forced his voice to remain calm. "Two Bravo Thirty-seven. He took off on me, westbound on ten! I'm in pursuit!"

The dispatcher acknowledged and verified the time. "Two B Thirty-seven. Copy WB on ten: oh-six-two-five."

The speed of his pulse seemed to increase with the speed of the car. Fifty, sixty, seventy miles an hour. He focused his senses and suppressed all natural alarm.

On the radio, a voice: "Three union thirty-one, I'm eastbound on ten, approaching Ramsey Boulevard. Will intercept there." That was a Ramsey car, coming to assist.

Eighty miles an hour, ninety, adrenaline pumping. Up ahead the Ramsey squad, its cherry light flashing, pulled into the left lane. The Grand Prix roared past it with colossal disdain. Christopher pinned his eyes on the road while the Ramsey squad—off his fender at ten o'clock—rocketed down the highway with him. Sweat popped out on his forehead, trailed down his trunk, sealed his body armor against his skin. His palms turned slick. It was work to control the force on the wheel.

He spoke at intervals into the radio, reporting his progress.

"Crossing westbound ten and Armstrong . . . Westbound ten, passing the weigh scale . . ." Familiar landmarks turned into a blur behind him.

A new radio voice said, "Elk River thirty-six thirteen, in position at Highway 169 turnoff westbound on ten, along with SP Unit 403."

Jesus. That made four units. Five counting the suspect . . . at a hundred and ten miles an hour. He shut down his mind to a single track and drove while the damned idiot in the Grand Prix threatened the lives of all the motorists on the highway pretending he was Mario Andretti. For nine miles Christopher drove, anticipating the sharp left curve at the base of the power plant in Elk River. The river itself was on their left. Ahead lay the underpass with its deadly concrete pilings where 169 crossed above 10.

Up ahead he saw the maroon state patrol car and the navy blue Elk River vehicle with its golden elk emblem on the door. There were more flashing reds. Cars scuttled out of the way, left and right.

He reported his position and hung up the radio to lock both hands on the wheel.

The five vehicles converged. Sirens screamed like jet blasts. Red lights flashed everywhere and speeding cop cars filled Christopher's peripheral vision. And somehow as they approached the big curve the four squads had the Grand Prix in a box!

Under the overpass! Into the curve! River water on the left! Huge green hill on the right! Roaring engines and cars inches apart, halfway into a lazy S-curve at ninety miles an hour. Chris's car got bumped. The world tipped and righted itself. On his far right the Ramsey squad lost ground in some loose gravel on the shoulder and fell behind. They hit the second curve and suddenly the suspect's car shot off to the right, into the ditch, up a rise, lost its back bumper and sideswiped a huge tree. The back bumper—a missile now—sailed straight on and wedged itself into the V of the tree's two huge trunks. Hubcaps rolled and bounced. Grass, dirt, dust flew into the air as if a bomb had exploded. The Grand Prix landed on its wheels. The four squads converged on it, bumping over rough grass. Officers out and running. Doors left gaping. Radios clattering. Red lights everywhere. Observers stopping on the shoulder above to stare at the spectacle in wonder.

Christopher ran to the driver's window, his adrenaline pumping like an uncapped gusher. The suspect was alive and cussing a blue streak, kicking the dash, hammering the steering wheel.

"Are you hurt?"

"Sonofabitch!"

Chris tried his door but it was jammed.

"Can you get out?"

"Goddamn it! Look what you did! Motherf—"

He reached in and grabbed the driver's shirt. "Get out. Do it now!"

The driver fought and slapped, refusing to follow orders. Chris and the Ramsey officer reached in and forcefully pulled him out through the window. The Elk River officer had drawn his gun and had it pointed in a two-hand grip at the suspect's head. The state trooper backed him up.

"On your face!" Chris shouted.

Down went the suspect and out came the cuffs.

"Goddamn sonsabitchin' pigs! Whorin' no-good suck-ass cops!" The driver lay facedown in the dirt, calling them every name in the book. Christopher grabbed a handful of red shirt and yanked the jerk to his feet, then propelled him toward his squad car with plenty of upward pressure on the cuffs.

"In the car, asshole!" he shouted, letting off the first steam.

Anger carried him through the rest of his duties. Locking the suspect in the caged backseat. Thanking the assisting officers. Reporting to the dispatcher. Killing his reds and maneuvering the car out of the ditch. Driving the nine miles back to Anoka and going through the booking procedure once he got there.

Forty-five minutes after it was over, the shakes began.

He was on his way home when everything inside him started quivering like a tuning fork. His hand trembled like an old man's as he reached for the button to activate his garage door. Inside, when he'd parked and shut off the engine, his knees felt rubbery as he got out of the Explorer and went upstairs to his apartment. All the way up he felt as if he were falling apart, muscle by muscle. He had trouble getting the key into the lock. When he'd finally managed it, he had trouble getting it out again.

In his apartment he walked around aimlessly from room to room, stripping off his uniform and leaving it scattered. He washed his face in cold water, dried off, went to the refrigerator and opened the door to find he had no purpose in opening it. The walls seemed to press in on him.

He took a thirty-minute run, showered, drank a glass of tomato juice and fried himself an egg sandwich, which he couldn't eat. He closed the blinds, stretched out on his back in the middle of the bed . . . and stared at the ceiling.

The movies liked to glamorize high-speed chases, but he wondered how many movie directors had ever been involved in one. He could still feel the heat in his neck and face. His heart refused to slow down. A pain had settled between his shoulder blades. He was horizontal, but instead of growing more relaxed, he felt like poured concrete—as if he were "setting up."

He forced his thoughts to something else. Lee Reston working with her flowers in a good-smelling shop on Main Street. Judd Quincy and his plan for the Fourth of July. Lee Reston and the garden hose he'd intended to fix for her. Janice Reston and the overt interest she was showing in him. Lee Reston cooling her face with the running water at his kitchen sink.

He checked the clock after forty minutes.

After an hour.

An hour and a half.

By ten-thirty he knew perfectly well he wasn't going to sleep. He felt as if he were on amphetamines.

He rolled to the edge of the bed and sat up with both hands curled over the edge of the mattress. He roughed up his scalp, leaving the hair in furrows. He stared at the mopboard on his left, the nightstand on his right, rewinding the film that had been reeling through his mind for the past two hours: the chase . . . Lee Reston . . . the chase . . . Judd Quincy . . . Lee Reston . . . Lee Reston . . . Lee Reston . . .

No question, he thought of her too much, and not always within the context of mutual grieving. Well, hell, it didn't take Freud to figure out he'd developed a mother complex over her. It was natural, the way she hugged him, rubbed his back, fed him leftovers and relied on him for a few of the difficult tasks as she would rely on a son.

Which is what brought the broken hose back to mind.

A distraction!

He bounded off the bed, brushed his teeth, put on a pair of jeans, a police department T-shirt, sneakers and a gold cap and went down to the garage to make sure his tool box was in the Explorer before heading over to Benton Street.

She wouldn't be home; that was good. He'd been hanging around there too much, but this was different. He'd just sneak in and sneak out and leave the hose repaired. Anything to work off this excess of energy.

He was right. She wasn't home. Neither was Janice. Both of their cars were gone, but the garage door was wide open again. Damn woman needed a week on the force to find out how many open garages get pilfered. The front door of the house was open, too, and Christopher could see right in through the screen, so he figured maybe Joey was around.

He parked in the driveway, took a jackknife out of his pocket, cut off the end of the hose and went to a hardware store to buy a replacement.

Once again at her house, he sat on the front step in the partial shade to do the repair job. It was pleasant there. The concrete was cool. Some ants were busy doing commerce in the cracks of the sidewalk. About five kinds of birds were singing. The neighborhood always seemed populated by birds because it was older and had so many mature trees. The red geraniums in the planter gave off their peculiar peppery smell.

He sat there whistling, working, failing to realize that the jumping nerves from the chase were finally beginning to calm. He went to his truck to look for a pair of pliers and discovered he'd left them in the apartment when he was taking Greg's bed apart. So he went into the garage to look for a pair.

The workbench there was amply outfitted with tools. It looked as if Bill Reston had been a tinkerer. Neat, too. There were banks of tiny plastic drawers stocked with fastidiously separated screws, bolts, washers and nails. On the wall above the bench every tool had its spot on a pegboard, though it was obvious that in the years since his death those that were used didn't always get replaced. Some were strewn on the bench itself, along with a ball of string, barbecue tools and a few gardening tools in a bucket. The whole area had grown dusty.

He looked up at the pegboard again, finding himself fascinated by these telltale hints of the man Lee Reston had once been married to. Tin snips, glass cutters, wood clamps . . . ah, and a common pair of pliers.

He was sitting on the step clamping the new end on the hose when a voice behind him said, "Hey, Chris, what're you doing here?"

He swung around and found Joey standing in the screen door in gray sweat shorts with sleep-swollen eyes.

"Fixing your mother's hose. You just get up?"

"Yeah."

"Everybody else gone to work?"

"Yeah."

Chris returned to his task and said, "This yard could use some mowing."

"You just mowed it."

"That was more than a week ago. Think you better do it today. You got gas?"

"I don't know."

"Well, go check, will you?"

"I just got up."

"Doesn't matter. Go check anyway."

Joey came outside, barefoot, and went off to the garage. In a minute he returned and said, "Not much."

"I'll go get you some, give you a little time to wake up. Then when I get back you'll mow for your mother, right?"

Joey mumbled, "Yeah, I guess so."

The hose was all fixed. "Okay. See you in a bit."

He got the gas can from the garage, filled it at the Standard Station on the corner of Main and Ferry, then returned to the house. The front door was still open, but Joey was nowhere in sight.

He leaned on the door frame and called inside, "Hey, Joe?"

Momentarily the boy appeared, looking unenthusiastic about the whole deal. Instead of combing his hair he'd put on a baseball cap. However, he was wearing socks and grungy Adidas and eating the first of six slices of peanut-butter-and-jelly toast he had piled on his hand.

"Got that gas," Chris told him. "And I filled the mower."

"Grmm . . ." Joey stepped outside. His mouth was too full to talk.

"Hey, listen . . ." Christopher scratched his head and tilted the bill of his cap way down. The two stood side by side with their toes hanging off the top step, Chris studying the house across the street and the glimpse of river in its backyard while the smell of peanut butter floated around their heads. "I know your mother always made all you kids do your share around the place, and I know it's hard with Greg gone, but nothing's changed. You've still got to help her . . . maybe even more. Give her a little break sometimes. Don't make her ask." He glanced at Joey from the corner of his eye. "Okay?"

Joey considered a moment, consulting the concrete sidewalk below them where the hose had left a wet spot shaped like a dotted *J*.

"Yeah, okay," he said, when his mouth was empty.

"Great," Chris said. "And when you're done with the mowing, will you put the sprinklers on?"

"Yeah, sure."

"Thanks, Joey." He clapped him between the shoulder blades and left him to get the work done.

Lee called that afternoon and woke him shortly after five.

"Don't tell me I've done it again," she opened when he'd mumbled hello.

"Mrs. Reston . . . that you?"

"Who else consistently ruins your sleep by ringing your phone?"

He stretched. "Rrrr . . ." After a chesty waking-up growl he asked, "What time is it?"

"Ten after five. You told me you sleep till two when you're on the night shift."

"Couldn't get to sleep this morning. I had a high-speed chase."

"Oh, no. Not one of them." Obviously, Greg had talked to her about how hairy high-speed chases were, and how they affected nearly every cop who'd ever donned a uniform. "Did you catch him?"

"Not before he drove in the ditch and got his back bumper stuck four feet up in the air in a tree."

She chuckled.

"Of course, he blamed us."

"Was he drunk?"

"What else? They're the worst ones."

"Well, I'm sorry you had to start your day like that."

"The adrenaline's worn off now that I've slept. Hey, what can I do for you?"

A beat of silence passed before she said, "Thanks for fixing the hose."

"You're welcome."

"And for getting the gas."

"You're welcome."

"And for lighting a fire under Joey. I've no doubt you're the one who's responsible."

"Well, I might have made a remark or two."

"Subtle."

"Well, I *can* be subtle, you know."

"You must have talked to Janice, too. I've noticed a change in her."

"They're both good kids. They just got a little too wrapped up in themselves and sort of forgot how hard it's been for you."

"What can I do to repay you?"

"You really want to know?"

He sensed her surprise before she answered, "Yes."

"Would you mind if I brought a guest with me to your Fourth of July picnic?"

"Not at all."

"It's Judd Quincy. The kid I told you about?"

"The one from the bad home?"

"Yeah. It struck me this morning when I was lying here wide awake thinking about everything in the world but sleep—Judd's probably never even seen a functional family, much less been among them for a holiday. A kid's got to see how it *can* work before he can believe it's possible. He's going to grow up just like his parents unless somebody shows him there's a better way. I can't think of a family in America that'd be a better role model than yours."

"Why, thank you, Christopher. Of course . . . bring him." Her voice had grown warm with understanding.

"And it's okay if he gets Greg's rib eye?"

"Absolutely."

"But listen—let's get this straight before we get there. Judd's on *my* volleyball team."

"Now, wait a minute. You're getting mighty pushy here."

"Well, the kid's built like a used bar stool. All legs and spokes and about as loose in the joints as they come. You don't think I'm gonna let him play on somebody else's team, do you?"

"Well, I think the hostess should get a handicap. We'll have to discuss it more after I've seen him."

"Okay, it's a deal."

Chris lay on his pillow smiling at the ceiling, his wrist cocked above the receiver.

"Well . . ." she said. Then nothing.

"Yeah, I'd better get up."

"And I'd better throw together some sandwiches. Joey's playing ball tonight and I've got to go watch." After a pause, she asked uncertainly, "Want to come?"

"Can't. Got a game of my own."

"Oh, that's right. The police team."

"Yeah."

"First base, right?"

"Right."

"Who's playing center field now?" That had been Greg's position.

"Lundgren, I think. This is my first time back since . . ."

After a pause, she filled in the blank.

"Since Greg died."

"I'm sorry."

"We've got to learn to say it."

"I know, I know. The thing is I have been saying it. I don't know why I pulled back this time."

She put on a cheerful voice. "Well, listen . . . good luck tonight, huh?"

"Thanks. Same to Joey."

"See you on the Fourth."

"Yes, ma'am."

"Eleven o'clock?"

"We'll be there."

He called Judd and said, "Hi, what's doing?"

"Nada."

"Wanna go to my game tonight? I'll pick you up at the usual spot. Six-thirty."

"Sure. Why not."

At six-thirty that evening Judd was holding up the front wall of the 7-Eleven as usual. Chris wheeled up and the kid got in.

"Heya," Chris said.

"Heya."

"Got a deal for you."

"I don't do deals."

"You'll do this one. It's a Fourth of July picnic with these friends of mine."

The kid couldn't quite maintain his indifference in the face of the news. His head made an eighth turn left and his eyes did the rest.

"Picnic?"

"Yeah. Steak fry. Backyard volleyball. A few pops. Fireworks afterwards over at Sand Creek Park. What do you say?"

"Shit, man, why not?"

"You're gonna have to can the talk like that though. These are nice people."

Judd shrugged. "It's cool. I can do that."

"All right." From the front seat Chris picked up a white bill cap with the maroon letter A. "This is for you."

"For me?"

"Yeah. It was my friend Greg's. His mother said I could give it to you. It's her house we're going to on the Fourth."

Hesitantly, Judd took the cap.

"I'll tell you something," Chris said, "you wear that, you wear it with respect. He was a good cop. He stood for something. When you've got that cap on your head I don't want you stealing bicycles or selling parts or doing any of that crap. Deal?"

Judd considered the cap for a long moment before agreeing. "Deal."

"And one more thing."

"What's that?"

"We've got to get you a new pair of tennies. If you're going to be on my volleyball team I don't want you stumbling over those tongues. Cost us points, you know?"

Judd looked down at his fried tennis shoes, then over at Chris. Realizing he was in danger of showing some emotion here, he settled his shoulders against the back of the seat with his usual unimpressibility.

"New tennies I can handle."

They were almost at the ballpark before he spoke again. "Air pumps?" he asked, cocking a glance at Christopher.

"Air pumps!" Chris exploded. "Gimme a break, kid! You know how much those things cost?"

The kid gave his shoulders a little shrug-n-shimmy then let them droop as if to say, *Air pumps, hell, who needs Air pumps.*

When they reached the ball field and were leaving the truck, Judd hooked the Anoka cap on his curly head with the bill cantilevered over his left ear.

Fourth of July came on the way a Fourth of July ought to. Fair, dry, hot. By the time Christopher pulled up at the curb in front of Lee Reston's house the driveway was full of cars, and music was blaring from the backyard. There was red, white and blue bunting hung above the open garage door and twisted around all the trees in the front yard, where a croquet field was set up. The American flag was waving from its standard on the front stoop post, while below it smaller flags were stuck into the dirt between the geraniums.

Christopher and Judd slammed the truck doors and headed for the backyard. Christopher was wearing a white T-shirt and a horrendous pair of shorts in blinding neon colors. Judd was wearing cutoff jeans, a saggy body shirt, Greg's white cap with the bill sticking out over his left ear and a pair of one-hundred-dollar Air pumps.

For the first time since Christopher had known the kid, his heels weren't dragging.

They stepped into a backyard stippled by maple shade extending clear across the rear of the house and deck where Lee's dad, Orrin Hillier, was dumping charcoal briquettes into a number of portable barbecue grills. From the speaker that had been propped in an open window of the house, band music blasted—raucous marches that made an ex-tuba player itch to have fifteen pounds of brass coiled over his shoulder. Just below the deck in the scattered shade, Janice, Kim, Sandy Adolphson and Jane Retting were wiping off the lawn chairs while Lloyd Reston and Joey unwound a volleyball net in the sunny rear yard between the U-shaped flower beds. Lee's mother, Peg, was out in the flower bed on the left, snipping flowers with a scissors. Sylvia Eid turned from flipping a plastic cloth over a picnic table and hollered, "Get one of those delphiniums, too, will you, Mom? That'll make it red, white and blue." There were some people Chris had met only briefly at the funeral, neighbors, cousins and in-laws. One woman was filling a vase from the garden hose. A man came along and stepped on it, intentionally stopping the water flow, and she took off chasing him, laughing, calling him names, slinging water from the vase that caught him on his left ankle and got his sock soaked. Lee slid open the screen and stepped from the kitchen with a can of lighter fluid.

"Here it is, Dad. And some matches." She was dressed in white Bermuda shorts and a T-shirt printed with a waving American flag. Handing the matches to Orrin, she caught sight of the new arrivals and her face broke into a smile. "Christopher, you made it!" She came down the deck steps.

Hearing Christopher's name, Janice swung around, dropped her rag in a bucket and abandoned the job to come over and welcome him with obvious enthusiasm.

Lee pecked Christopher on the jaw and said, "Glad you came." She stuck out a hand and said, "Hi, Judd. I'm Lee Reston."

Janice said, "Hi, Chris. Hi, Judd, I'm Janice." After shaking his hand she gave Christopher's clothing the once-over. "Cow-a-bunga! Would you look at those shorts! What circus did you get them from?"

"You covet them, I'm sure." He put his hands on his waist and looked down. "Judd here's been telling me I need a little color in my wardrobe. Bought 'em specially for today."

Lee said, "I'd introduce you around, Judd, but everybody will do that themselves. Pop's over there in the coolers. Doritos and Mexican dip on the table over there to hold you over till steak time. Be careful of the one with the little flag sticking out of the middle. It's extra hot. Christopher, you can put your steaks in the cooler till the coals are hot, then would you two mind giving Lloyd and Joey a hand with the volleyball net?"

"Be happy to."

Across the yard Kim called, "Hi, Chris! Who you got there?"

"This is Judd, and he's going to be on *my* volleyball team!" Everyone offered hellos as they moved toward the volleyball net, which by this time was stretched out to its full length on the grass while Joey shook a bunch of aluminum poles out of a cardboard box.

Lloyd came to meet them. "Well, this must be Judd. Nice to meet you. Joey . . . look here."

Joey quit chiming the poles together and approached the new boy with the diffidence of a fourteen-year-old.

"Hi," he said, hanging back a little. "I'm Joey."

"I'm Judd."

After a second of hesitation the two shook hands. Joey said, "Wanna help with these poles?"

"Sure," Judd said.

And so the picnic began.

Orrin touched a match to the briquettes, sending the smell of hot charcoal across the yard. "The Stars and Stripes Forever" came from the speaker, and Janice's friends started an impromptu parade. Lee found an old baton in Janice's room and everybody took turns trying to twirl it. Peg Hillier did surprisingly well and admitted she'd been a majorette in her youth. While she was twirling, dressed in pedal pushers and a loose shirt that covered her slight potbelly, Orrin's eyes got quite avid and he whispered to Joey, "You know, when your grandma was a senior in high school every boy in the class wanted to date her. I was the lucky one." Judd overheard and took a second look at Peg. She threw the baton into the air and missed it. "Try it again, Peg!" "Go for it, Grandma!" everyone shouted. On the third try she succeeded in catching it and the entire crowd cheered. When the song ended she laughed at herself, pressed a palm to her chest and fanned her face with the other hand. Orrin took her by both shoulders and whispered something into her ear, after which she laughed again and gave the baton back to the younger girls.

Joey lugged a box of bocce balls out of the garage and a game started up, going from front yard to back to front again with nobody paying attention to court rules.

Lee came out of the garage with a baseball bat, shouting, "All right, everybody! Time to choose sides for the volleyball game! Christopher and I will be captains!"

She marched toward Christopher and sent the bat on a vertical ride through the air. He caught it low on the barrel, just beneath the trademark, still surprised by her announcement.

"You count knobs?" she asked, slapping a right-handed grip just above his while firing him a mischievous look of challenge.

"Darn right." He gripped it with a right.

Left.

Right.

Left.

Right.

Clear up the bat till only the knob was left. She put a cat claw on it and said smugly, "Me first. I choose Judd."

"Oh, you are really underhanded," he murmured with mock scorn, then shot back, "Joey!"

"Dad."

"Mrs. Hillier." Everybody did a woo-woo number because there were still lots of guys left. "Well, we can't have a husband and wife on the same team!" Christopher claimed. "Too much scrapping! Besides, she twirls a mean baton. I'll bet she's going to be good."

"For heaven's sake, call me Peg," she said, joining his squad.

"Barry."

"Janice."

"Sylvia."

"Hey, I thought we couldn't have a husband and wife on the same team!"

They had a pleasant time haranguing back and forth during the remainder of the choosing up. They had just finished when Nolan Steeg sauntered into the backyard, tall, lean and muscular.

"Hey, we get Nolan!"

"No, we get Nolan!"

Nolan puffed out his chest and spread his arms wide. "Am I wanted?" he hammed. "Take me . . . take me!"

It turned out his cousin, a redheaded kid named Ruffy, was up for the week, and stepped into the backyard right behind Nolan, so each side took one of the power players.

They played a stupendously bad game, with lots of people letting the ball drop two feet in front of their faces. They got into arguments about the out-of-bounds markers and finally laid out four tennis shoes to represent the corners of the court. Lee yelled "Oh, noooo, not the flowers!" the first time the ball headed that way. Then they all watched the ball snap off a yellow lily. Lloyd retrieved the ball, high-stepping into the flower bed and putting the lily behind his left ear with a "Sorry, honey" as he returned to the game. The next time the ball headed for the gardens about four voices chorused *"Oh, noooo, not the flowers!"* After that it became the battle call that inevitably raised laughter as the gardens took a battering and Lee, shrugging good-naturedly, turned her palms up to the sky.

Judd could leap like a pogo stick and every time he got on the front line Lee's team would score. Joey was pretty good at spiking too, and the game picked up momentum. Peg Hillier made a save on the sideline and garnered high fives from her teammates when the point had been made. And twice while Lee and Christopher were playing on their front lines directly opposite each other, they banged chests while going for the ball at the same time. The second time, he knocked her down and stepped on her left ankle when he landed.

Immediately he came under the net. "Sorry. You okay?" He offered her a hand up.

"Yeah, I'm fine." Hopping on one foot, she added, "You big lug."

"You sure?" He brushed some dry grass off her back.

"I'm gonna get you for this," she threatened in the best of humor. "So get back over to your own side of the net."

The game ended when the redheaded cousin named Ruffy accidentally broke wind—very loudly—while going after a tough return on game point, making everyone laugh.

"It's time we put the steaks on," Lee said, heading for the deck, wiping her brow. Someone turned on the garden hose and it got passed from hand to hand for drinks. Beer and soda cans popped. "Who'll take care of the sweet corn?"

Barry and Sylvia did. From a tub of saltwater they fished ears of corn, still in their husks, and slapped them, sizzling, onto one of the grills. They turned them wearing asbestos mitts, while Orrin and Lloyd took over the grilling of the steaks, raising an aroma that made everyone's mouth water. A parade of helpers carried bowls of food from the kitchen. The sun had shifted and tables needed moving into the shade.

Orrin announced, "I think some of this steak is done."

Sylvia stripped the corn husks off the first perfect yellow ear and swabbed it with a paintbrush from the butter kettle. "Corn's ready!"

The slow procession started around the buffet table, past the corn station and over to the grills where the steaks were raising curls of fragrant smoke.

"Anyone want iced tea?"

"Here, Mom, I'll do that." Janice came to take the cold pitcher out of Lee's hands and distribute paper cups.

Lee was nearly the last one to fill her plastic plate with potato salad, baked beans, pickles and steak. She carried it to one of the two long picnic tables where Chris sat with Joey, Judd and some others. "Hey, skootch over," she said, nudging him with her hip. He pulled his plate over and she slid onto the bench beside him.

"How's the corn?" she inquired.

"Mmm . . ." He was butter from dimple to dimple. He grinned at her and chewed another mouthful with his elbows propped on the tabletop. She took up the same pose and went to work, nibbling along a row of buttery yellow kernels. He reached for a salt shaker, sprinkled his corn, and as he settled back into place, his warm bare arm slid down along hers.

They both pulled apart, concentrated on their corn and tried to pretend it hadn't happened.

Across the table Judd and Joey were comparing notes on the music they liked—rap versus country.

From a table nearby, Janice called, "Mom, these baked beans are terrific."

"So is the potato salad," Christopher added. "Bachelors don't get a treat like this very often."

"Even ones who know how to cook?" she inquired.

"I cook pretty simple things, mostly."

"My mother taught me how to make potato salad. She's got a secret."

"What?"

"A little sweet pickle juice in the dressing." Lee raised her voice. "Isn't that right, Mom?"

"What's that?" At another table, Peg turned in her chair and looked back over her shoulder.

"Pickle juice in the potato salad."

"That's right. But yours is every bit as good as mine, honey."

Lloyd came around refilling iced tea glasses. He patted Lee's shoulder. "Nice picnic, dear."

From another table one of the cousins called, "Hey, Aunt Lee?"

"What, Josh?"

"Is it really true that when you were eleven years old you drove Grandpa's car through the window of the dime store?"

Lee dropped her empty corn cob and covered her head with both arms. "Oh my God."

"Did you, Aunt Lee?"

She came up blushing. "Daddy, did you tell him that?" she scolded.

"Did she really, Grandpa?"

"Well now, Josh, I told you it wasn't exactly *through* the window, just a few feet into it."

Christopher smiled down at Lee's right ear, which was as red as the zinnias in her garden.

"What's this?" he teased quietly.

"Daddy, I could crown you!" she blustered.

Christopher teased, "It's no wonder you didn't get upset about Joey driving. At least he waited till he was fourteen. And he didn't do it on the main street of town."

Somebody said, "Hey, what about the time when my dad peed through the screen. Tell 'em, Dad."

It was Orrin Hillier's turn to be put on the hot seat. He laughed and pretended embarrassment, but everyone convinced him to tell the oft-repeated story. "Well, it was when we were kids, and we lived on the farm and I slept with my brother, Jim. Our room was on the second floor, of course, and one summer we got the idea that when we had to get up and go in the middle of the night we could save ourselves the trouble of walking all that way outside to the outhouse by just whizzing through the screen. We got by with it for quite a while, but don't you know, the next year in the spring when my dad was changing the storm windows, he noticed that one of the screens was all rusting out in a perfect circle, about, oh"—he measured off a distance from the ground with one hand—"about wiener high to a couple of snot-nosed boys. And we sure caught it then."

"What happened?"

"We had to shell corn. He put us out in a corncrib with one of those old hand-crank shellers and said, 'Go to work, boys, and don't stop till the crib is empty.' Well, he took pity on us around suppertime, when I suspect my mom stuck up for us, but let me tell you, I've never had blisters like that before or since."

Christopher had been watching Judd's eyes while the story was being told. He had hiked one foot up beneath him on the picnic bench and stretched his neck to see over the heads around him. Like any child of twelve, he had watched the storyteller and listened with his empty fork forgotten against his teeth. He had laughed when the others laughed. He had experienced firsthand the flow of familial lore from one generation to the next, and the fascination showed on his face.

When the story ended he said to Joey, "I thought grampas were like, you know, soybean people, but yours is definitely primo."

Joey smiled and said, "Yeah, I think so too."

They had watermelon for dessert, followed by a watermelon seed spitting contest, which Sylvia won. She received a box of sparklers as her prize.

They played more volleyball, bocce and croquet, and when evening set in ate leftovers, then began cleaning up the yard and the kitchen. By the time they headed for Sand Creek Park, Lee hadn't one item left to fold up, wash or pack away.

Joey said, "Hey, Chris, can I ride with you and Judd?"

"Sure."

"You got room for me, too?" Lloyd asked.

"You bet. Jump right in."

Lee rode with her parents, Janice with all the girls. The cavalcade left the house when the sun was sitting on the rim of the world and the neighborhood resounded with an occasional volley of firecrackers.

At Sand Creek, a huge multifield baseball complex, the surrounding unpaved parkland had been pressed into use as parking lots. The cars, entering bumper to bumper, raised a fine haze of dust that settled like a lanugo on the vehicles as they pulled in. The sky had lost color, faded like an iris left in water too long. The warmth of the day lifted from the sandy earth, met by a press of coolness beginning above. Crayon-colored lights, subdued by dust, blinked and gyrated in the distance where a carnival beckoned. Its enticing clamor drifted across the field, interspersed with the occasional report of firecrackers. Children ran among the cars. Adults walked. The oldest of them carried webbed lawn chairs.

Joey and Judd jogged ahead, raising puffs of dust, talking animatedly as they headed for the carnival and its promise of excitement.

Ambling after them, Lloyd remarked to Chris, "Those two seem to be hitting it off quite well."

"Better than I expected."

Lee called from behind them, "Hey, you two, wait for us."

And that's how Lee ended up beside Christopher, where she seemed to stay the remainder of the night, while Lloyd faded back and fell in beside Lee's folks.

"Want to walk over to the carnival?" Lee asked the older ones.

Her mother replied, "No, I think I've had enough excitement for one day. I'll just settle down on a blanket and wait for the fireworks." Orrin and Lloyd agreed.

"Mind if we go for a while?" Lee asked.

"Of course not. Have fun," her mother replied.

"We'll find you later."

They ambled through the dusty grass toward the red, blue and yellow bars of moving neon, toward the smell of popcorn and Pronto Pups and the sounds of carnival engines and calliope music. All day long they'd been with others; their footsteps slowed as they shared this first time alone.

"Thanks for today," he said, "and especially for letting Judd come."

"You're welcome. I was glad to have you both."

"I don't think he's ever experienced anything like it before. He doesn't have any grandparents that I know of. I was watching his eyes when your dad was telling his story, and the kid was transfixed."

"The rest of us have heard that old story so often we know it by heart."

"That's exactly the point. I wanted him to see how a real family works, and you all certainly gave him a firsthand look."

"Well, you can bring him anytime."

"He and Joey seemed to warm up to each other eventually. They were talking and laughing together quite a bit by the end of the day."

He glanced down at her as they reached the periphery of the carnival. She had put on fresh lipstick before leaving the house, and walked with a sweater folded over her arm. The lights of the carnival stained her face and danced across her eyes, which suddenly grew sad as the sights and sounds amplified. Instinct told him she was remembering Greg, a childhood Greg, perhaps, a little boy begging for one more ride, for money for another treat. In all his life, how many times had Greg Reston been brought here on the Fourth of July by his parents? Year after year until it became tradition. Now the tradition continued without him.

She stopped walking as they reached the midway, stood staring at it while his heart hurt for her.

"Do you want anything?" he offered—a paltry offering, but what else had he?

She shook her head and walked a few steps away, presumably to hide her tears.

He moved up behind her and put a hand on her shoulder. "You brought him here every Fourth when he was a kid, didn't you?"

She nodded stiffly and spoke only after a long silence. "You can go through a day like today and do pretty well. Then you face something like this and it's as if you . . . you expect to see him running toward you through the crowd."

"Eight years old, I bet."

"Eight, nine, ten . . . asking for more money for the rides. I think it's the smells that do it. It happens more often when there's a familiar smell around than at any other time. Have you noticed that?"

"It's still that way in the bathroom at our apartment. It seems worse in that room than anyplace else. Like his after-shave is imbedded in the walls."

They stood motionless, his hand on her shoulder, while people milled past and a man in a white apron and a white paper hat twisted a white paper cone full of pink cotton candy.

"Let's take a ride," he suggested.

"I don't feel much like it."

"Neither do I, but let's do it anyway."

She turned, looked back over her shoulder and his hand fell away. "I don't feel like it, Christopher."

"How about on the Ferris wheel?"

She looked at it and realized he was suggesting the right thing to get them over this emotional stone upon which they'd stumbled. "Oh, all right, but I'm afraid I won't be very good company."

He bought a string of tickets, used four and they boarded the Ferris wheel. Her eyes were dry but she looked as if only determination kept them that way. They sat without touching, their bare legs stretched out and crossed at the ankles while the machine took them backward in lurches and starts as others boarded below.

"I've been reading about grief," Christopher told her. "It says that facing places the first time will be hardest and that you shouldn't try facing them all at once. You're supposed to give yourself time. Don't try to be a hero about it."

"I'm not trying to be a hero," she said.

"Aren't you? You made the flowers for his coffin. You went right into his bedroom and cleaned it out. You went right ahead and planned the Fourth of July, the same as always. Maybe you need to cool it for a while and not be quite so strong. Hell, Lee, I've watched you and you blow my mind. All the while I'm admiring your strength, I'm wondering how you do it. I think tonight it's finally catching up with you."

Her anger flared out of nowhere. Her rust-colored eyes flashed his way. "How dare you criticize me! You haven't been through it! You don't know what it's like!"

"No, I haven't. Not like you. But nobody's asking you to be Superwoman."

The Ferris wheel moved and green lights picked out the tracks of tears on her cheeks. Regret shot through Christopher and made his ribs feel too tight.

"Aw, Lee, come here . . . I didn't mean to make you cry." He took her in his arms and cradled her head against his shoulder. "I didn't mean to hurt you. I was trying to get you to see that you can take on too much too soon, and nobody expects it of you. Just give it time, huh?"

Abruptly she huddled against him, her hand folded over his shoulder, gripping it as she wept. They stayed that way while the wheel carried them up into the darkening sky where they seemed to hang like the only two beings on earth. They lurched to a stop and their seat swung. Below, the light and sound seemed far away. Above, the first stars had made their appearance.

He rested his mouth against her hair. It smelled of her and dust and barbecue smoke.

"Lee, I'm sorry," he whispered.

"You're right," she admitted brokenly. "I *have* been acting like Superwoman. I should have waited till the kids could help me with his room. And I should have let well enough alone when we finished the picnic at the house today. Maybe if I hadn't come here I would have made it without doing this again." She sniffed and pulled back, drying her face with her hands. He kept one hand around her nape, his elbow resting on the back of the seat.

"You feel better now?"

She nodded fiercely, as if to convince herself.

"And you're not mad at me?"

She wagged her head twice. "No."

With a slight pressure on her neck he forced her to turn her face, then bent down and kissed her between the eyes. The Ferris wheel moved to its apex and jerked to a stop again. His hold remained loose upon her neck as their eyes met, and lingered, and they wondered about this curious relationship blossoming between them.

"Okay, then, let's enjoy the ride."

She gave him a feeble smile as the Ferris wheel began its steady circling, returning them to the light and sight of activity below. He released her neck but found her hand and, linking their fingers tightly, turned the back of his hand to his bare knee. They rode that way, staring at their joined hands until they realized faces were looking up at them from below, and anyone they knew could be among the crowd. Prudently, he released her hand and they finished their ride in silence, touching no more, but sharing a physical awareness of each other that could be explained only one way.

After their ride, Joey found them and asked his mom for money. Christopher gave him the string of extra tickets and said, "Give half to Judd."

"Gosh, thanks!"

Judd said, "Yeah, thanks, man."

"And meet us back at the car right after the fireworks!" Lee called at their departing backs.

Full dark had fallen as they headed for the baseball fields where everyone was waiting for the display to begin. The park was huge. They had no idea where the others were, and after ten minutes of looking they gave up.

"Want to sit here?" he asked when they found a reasonably good-sized patch of grass surrounded by strangers.

"Why not?"

She spread her sweater and said, "I'll share it."

They dropped onto the small island of white knit, their hips touching, giving themselves that much forbidden contact. When the fireworks started they stretched out their legs, crossed their ankles and braced on their palms behind them.

Spangles of peridots seemed to burst up above, followed by diamonds, rubies, sapphires. Their arms aligned, like earlier at the picnic table. Tonight, however, under cover of darkness, when they touched, they stayed, skin to skin with their faces turned skyward like the hundreds of others surrounding them.

Up in the sky a boom and a whistle . . . another starburst of glitter, blue and red this time . . . pop, pop, pop! . . . and voices in chorus.

"Ohhhhhhh . . ."

"Christopher?" she said, very quietly.

"Hm?" He swung his face to her profile, just beyond their joined shoulders.

"You're very good for me," she said, keeping her eyes on the sky.

Chapter 7

⁓⧫⁓

A couple of weeks after the Fourth of July, Janice came home from work one night at 9:45. It was hot in the house and she looked tired as she came down the hall and dropped one shoulder against the open doorway of Lee's bedroom.

"Hi, Mom."

"Hi, honey." Lee was sitting up in bed reading, wearing a pair of short yellow pajamas. "Busy at the store?"

Janice ran a hand through her hair and gave her head a shake. "Not very. Gosh, it's so hot in here, Mom. I wish you'd get air-conditioning."

"Why don't you take a lukewarm shower? That'll make you feel better."

Janice pulled her blouse out of her skirt and unbuttoned it. She lifted her left foot and took off a white flat, hung it over an index finger and did the same with the right, then propped herself against the door casing once more.

"Mom, could I ask you something?"

"Of course." Lee patted the mattress and rested her magazine on her legs. "Come here."

Janice sat on the bed with one knee crooked up, the other foot on the floor. "Mom, what do you do when you've tried everything within the range of good taste to get a guy to notice you . . . only he doesn't?"

"Some guy in particular?"

"Yes . . . Christopher."

Lee sat absolutely still for five seconds, then closed her magazine and put it on the nightstand, giving herself a brief grace period in which to concoct a response. Leaning against the pillows again, she said quietly, "Oh, I see."

"Mom, he treats me like a kid sister and I just hate it."

"There's quite a bit of difference in your ages."

"Seven years, that's not so much. You and Daddy were five years apart."

Lee considered Janice's reply. "That's true. Two more isn't so terribly lopsided."

"Then why doesn't he pay any attention to me? I've tried dropping hints, but he doesn't pick up on them. I've looked in the mirror and I'm not a troll or anything. I've acted like a lady around him, engaged him in conversation, complimented him, dressed nicely, tried in every way I know how to let him know I'm interested and old enough to take it seriously. So what is it?"

"I don't know what to say."

"You're with him a lot. Does he say anything about me?"

"He asks how you are. He's concerned about you just like he is about all of our family."

"Concerned," Janice repeated with a grimace, staring at her white flats as she held them sole to sole in her lap. "Hooray." She sat there looking dejected. Out in the yard crickets were carping. In the living room Joey was watching TV with the volume turned low. Janice's voice grew quiet with sincerity. "I've had a crush on him since the first time Greg introduced him to us. It was at the police station, and he was dressed in his uniform, just pulling up in a squad car. Honest, Mom, he stepped out of that car and my heart just . . . just *flew* into my throat. I'm sure he knows. Kim says I look at him like he's fresh-buttered popcorn."

She raised her disillusioned eyes to Lee and they laughed. Once. Not too cheerily.

Lee opened her arms. "Come here, honey."

Janice stretched across the bed and nestled in the crook of Lee's arm.

"We women have a rotten deal, don't we?" Lee rubbed Janice's hair with her jaw.

"Not anymore. Lots of women ask men out on dates."

"Then why haven't you?"

Janice shrugged. Lee stroked Janice's hair back from her temple and let it fall again and again. It was beautiful hair, mid-back length, auburn, naturally wavy. She had inherited her hair from Bill's side of the family. "I guess I want him to ask me."

At that moment Joey interrupted. "What are you two doing?" He appeared in the doorway and leaned against it where Janice had been. He was dressed in a gray T-shirt and shorts, and filthy white socks with the toes belled out like light bulbs.

"Talking," Lee replied.

"Yeah, I bet I know about what. Janice has got a crush on Chris, hasn't she?" He started to cackle softly, in falsetto.

Janice rolled her head and told her brother, "You know, Joey, it might not hurt you to get a crush on somebody. Maybe you'd grow up a little and pay some attention to your personal hygiene. You've got half the ball diamond on your shirt and I can smell you clear over here."

Lee said, "Could we have a little privacy here, Joe?"

"Yeah, yeah . . . I'm going to bed."

"After you take a shower."

He made a disgusted face and rolled away from the door frame with his shoulders artificially slumped. A minute later the shower started down the hall.

Janice drew herself up and sat with her back to Lee.

"Kim says I should just call him up and ask him to do something. Go to a movie or something. What do you think, Mom?"

"Honey, it's up to you. When I grew up girls didn't do things like that, but I realize times are different now."

"The thing is, I'm scared he'll say no again, then I'll feel like a jerk."

"Again?"

"That one night I asked him if he wanted to go for a swim, but he'd already gone with you. This time though, I'd ask him earlier in the week for a Friday or Saturday night. Maybe make some dinner plans at some place casual." She looked back over her shoulder wistfully. "What do you think?"

Lee studied her daughter and felt a swell of maternal sympathy. Janice was such a pretty girl. How could any young man brush her off? "I think mothers should stay out of decisions like this."

Janice remained on the crumpled sheets in her crumpled blouse staring at her bare knees. Finally, she gave a rueful laugh. "Well, hell, Mom, you're no help at all," she said, and pulled herself off the bed.

Half an hour later when the house had finally grown quiet, Lee lay in the dark with the pillows mounded under her ear, considering her reaction to what Janice had said. When Janice had mentioned Christopher's name she'd felt a spurt of panic. Or had it been jealousy? How ridiculous. *Either one* was ridiculous, given Christopher's age. He was fifteen years younger than herself and she had no business considering him anything more than a friend. Yet she did. What set him apart was how she'd come to rely on him. He was wise beyond his years, perhaps made so by virtue of his chosen work or his unhappy youth.

In the month since Greg's death she had seen Christopher perhaps a dozen times. It was obvious she was using him as a substitute for Greg. She understood this clearly and supposed her reaction was typical. Any mother who'd lost a child would seek the company of those closest to that child to get over the hurdle of first loss. When the young people were around—any of them—she could talk about Greg with less pain. The girls came by occasionally, and Nolan had even stopped in the flower shop one day, just to say hello.

Then what was so different about Christopher?

She flopped over on her back. The sheets felt sticky and she wondered why she hadn't taken the trouble to have air-conditioning installed after the shop had proven itself and she'd no longer had to watch every penny. Those damned crickets could drive a person crazy. She switched to her side and stretched one leg onto a cool part of the bedding with the top sheet between her legs.

What was so different about Christopher?

He wore a uniform and drove a black-and-white police car. When she saw it pulling into her driveway she had the momentary illusion it was Greg pulling in, Greg stepping from behind the wheel, Greg in that neat navy blue uniform with badges all over the chest. Mercy, Christopher's coloring was even like Greg's. Brown hair, blue eyes, tan face. He had the same stocky build. The police department had a weight room over behind Perkins restaurant where they worked out all the time, and to Lee every fellow on the force had the thick-necked, toned, muscular shape that spoke of a man keeping fit because someday his life might depend on it.

So what about holding hands with Christopher on the Ferris wheel?

That was comfort, nothing more.

And the kiss between the eyes?

More comfort.

And the compulsion to touch his bare arm?

She tossed a while longer.

No more iced tea after eight o'clock at night if this is what it did to her! She rolled to her other side and stared at the moonlit window, listening to the rasp of crickets and a faint susurrus of leaves as a night breeze filtered past. Then silence. Utter silence, in which she lifted her head off the pillow and looked around the darkened room.

Silly single woman who'd given up those jitters years ago! What in the world had gotten into her tonight? Then she heard it, faintly . . . in the distance . . . a siren . . . so far away even the crickets started up again.

Was he still working night shift? Had he had any more high-speed chases? There . . . see? She didn't even know the answers to these things because she hadn't seen him for two weeks. Wasn't that proof there was nothing untoward about those few moments they'd held hands on the Ferris wheel?

She spent two more weeks without seeing him. During that time she devoted part of every day to settling Greg's business affairs. She'd been fighting with the bank for weeks and was on the phone at the flower shop yet again with someone named Pacey, finding it difficult to get over the loss of Greg when she had to fight these battles daily to clear up his affairs. "But I told you, Mr. Pacey, it's not going through probate. He didn't own enough property to make it worth the trouble."

"In that case my hands are tied."

"Good lord, it's only a four-hundred-dollar savings account!"

"I understand that, but unless he was a minor you have no jurisdiction over his assets, and of course, he was no minor."

"But do you realize, Mr. Pacey, that even after I sent you a copy of his death certificate your computer still sent me another monthly statement? I just want to close it out so that doesn't happen again."

"I'm sorry about that, Mrs. Reston. It sometimes takes a while for the paperwork to be entered into the computer."

"And what about his motorcycle payment? The same thing happened there. I came into the bank over a month ago to let you know he was dead and that his motorcycle was insured. Today I got a notice claiming his payment was overdue and there's a late charge tacked on!"

After a puzzled pause, he asked, "What day did you say you came in?" When she told him, he said, "Just a minute, please," and put her on hold.

She had developed a headache. It seemed to intensify while she stood listening to Barry Manilow sing in her ear. Handling Greg's business affairs became a constant reminder of him—looking at his handwriting in his checkbook register, finding notes he'd made on papers in his files, unearthing evidence of plans he'd had for the future. When snags like this came up—and it was often—she found it harder to cope. Sometimes, after a conversation with someone like Pacey over some tie-up she couldn't control, she'd have herself a brief cry, fueled largely by exasperation.

She was still on hold when the shop door opened and Christopher walked in, dressed in his police uniform. At the same moment, Mr. Pacey returned.

"Mrs. Reston?"

"Yes." Her eyes followed Christopher as he came inside and smiled at her.

"Your son certainly had paid off his car, but the trouble is he used it as collateral against a loan he took out for a motorcycle."

"I know that, Mr. Pacey! I told *you* that the first time I came in! My trouble is that I can't transfer ownership of the car to my daughter without the registration card, and you won't release that without the motorcycle being paid for, and the insurance company is paying for the motorcycle, not me, but they haven't issued a check yet."

She heard him draw a breath of strained patience. "Then wouldn't it be a lot simpler, Mrs. Reston, just to go through probate?"

Her voice was trembling as she said, "Thank you, Mr. Pacey," and slammed down the receiver with such force the bell tinged in the phone.

Christopher stood watching her across the length of the shop. He looked totally out of place amid a tiered display of potted yellow mums and blue hydrangeas. She stood behind a Formica counter with both hands pressed flat upon it, striving to calm herself.

Frustration won out.

She made a fist and thumped it on the counter as hard as she could. "Damn it!" She squeezed her eyes shut.

"What's wrong?" He picked his way between cut flowers and revolving stands of greeting cards to the opposite side of the counter. He rested his forearms on it, bending at the hip and bringing his face down to the level of hers. "Bad day?"

She swung around, presenting her back, hands caught on the edge of the counter, blinking hard at the ceiling.

"Why is it that every time you see me, I'm crying again? I swear I go through *days* without crying, and you walk in here and I'm at it again."

"I don't know," he replied quietly. "Seems to be a rhythm to it, doesn't there? I've sort of been on a downer again myself, so I just thought I'd stop by and see how you're doing."

She turned back to face him, managing a self-deprecating smile. Looking at him in his visored hat and crisp collar and tie, she felt her frustration begin to dissipate. "Oh, hell, I don't know."

"What was that all about on the phone?"

"The joys of settling an estate."

"Ah, I see." He was still bent over the counter, forearms resting on it. The gold band of a wristwatch peeked from under his left cuff. A single bow of a pair of sunglasses was hooked into a pen hole of his shirt pocket. His pose tightened his collar and stretched taut the skin of his neck, which was cinched by a carefully knotted tie held in place by an APD tiepin. As usual, the sight of him in uniform seemed to add ten years to his age and make him her peer.

"Wanna do something?" he asked quietly. "Go to a movie? Walk? Talk? Forget it for a while?"

"When? Tonight?"

"Yeah. I'm on days."

She had an inspiration. "Could we take Janice?"

"Sure," he said without hesitation, straightening and tugging up his leather belt with all its heavy accessories. "Joey too if you want. What should we do?"

"A walk sounds best. A brisk, hard, long walk."

"How about the paved trail west of the Coon Rapids dam?"

"Perfect."

"Should I pick you up?"

"Sure."

"What time?"

She checked her watch. "I'm through here at five-thirty. How about six? I'll pick up some sandwiches to take along."

"Perfect."

"See you then."

She called home immediately. The phone rang nine times and nobody answered. She called The Gap at Northtown. Someone named Cindy told her Janice wasn't scheduled to work that day, which Lee already knew. She called Kim's house. Kim's mother said the two girls had gone down to the university to do some preregistration for fall quarter. She didn't know what time they'd be back.

"Well, if you talk to her, tell her not to eat supper and to meet me at the house at six."

"Will do."

Sylvia had the day off, so Lee locked up the shop herself, swung by the Subway sandwich shop and picked up four combination sandwiches containing everything but the kitchen sink. At home she charged into the house, calling, "Joey, you here?"

"Yo!" he hollered from the depths of his room.

"Wanna go walking with Chris and me?"

"Where?"

She was passing his bedroom door, unbuttoning her waistband as she answered. "Walking trails over by the dam." He was lying on his bed reading a *Hot Rod* magazine.

"Hey, yeah! Only, would it be okay if I took my Rollerblades instead? That walking stuff is heinous."

She laughed and said louder, closing her bedroom door, "I don't care, but hurry and get ready. He'll be here at six. Did Janice come home yet?"

"Haven't seen her all day."

Well, Lee had tried.

She changed into a pair of faded purple knit shorts with a matching T-shirt, put on tennis socks and a pair of Adidas, ran a brush through her hair, wiped her face with a Kleenex, slapped on some fresh lipstick and was shutting off the bathroom light when Christopher knocked on the front door.

"Ready?" he said when she came around the corner into the front hall.

"Yup."

"Where are the kids?"

"Joey's coming." She raised her voice. "Hey, Joe? You all ready?"

He came barreling down the hall and did a Tom Cruise stocking-slide onto the shiny front hall floor, carrying his Rollerblades.

"Where are your shoes?" Lee said.

"I don't need shoes. I'm gonna skate."

She pointed with an authoritative finger at his bedroom. "Get! Your! Shoes!"

Grumbling, he went back to get them. When she turned around Chris was snickering.

"Gnarly adolescent boys!" she whispered. While Joey was gone she jotted a note for Janice and left it on the kitchen table. *Gone walking with Joey & Chris. Sandwich for you in fridge. Home early. Love, Mom.*

"Shut the front door when you come out, Joey!" she called, following Christopher outside, letting the screen door slam behind them. "What kind of sandwiches?" he asked, showing pointed interest in the white sack as they walked toward the Explorer.

She hefted the bag. "Salami, ham, cheese, mayo, black olives, lettuce, tomato, onions, Oil of Olay, sassafras root, watercress, potato dumpling, peanut butter, sauerkraut and pigs' ears. What do you mean, what kind of sandwich? You expect a person to remember what they put in those things over there?"

Laughing, he opened the front door of the Explorer for her. "Sorry I asked."

She clambered in the front, leaving the back for Joey. He came out a minute later and they were off, with the windows down and the evening breezing against their ears.

"Thanks for suggesting this, Christopher, it feels so good." She lifted her elbows and face, shut her eyes and ruffled her hair with both hands. "If I have to talk to one more banker or insurance representative or gravestone salesman, I think I'm going to scream."

Christopher glanced at her askance, caught her in profile with her elbows and breasts outlined against the far window. When she broke her pose, he quickly returned his attention to the road. "None of that tonight. The purpose of this walk is to forget all that. Deal?"

She flashed him a smile. "Deal."

The stultifying heat of July had burned itself out and left a more temperate August. By the time they reached the dam it was 6:30 and pleasantly warm. The sky appeared hazy, as if viewed through a steamy window, its colors opaque melon and lavender, while the sun burned through in orange so muted one could look at it with the naked eye. The air smelled of summer's end—drying crops and crisping weeds and the graininess of dust and harvest.

At the dam the Mississippi thundered over the lowered gates, and cars with bicycle carriers were lined up door to door in the angled parking slots. Serious cyclists, in their helmets and gloves, were resting against the guardrails, still seated on their bikes, watching fishermen working the more placid waters above the boil.

Joey grumbled while he put on his Rollerblades. "See, I told you I didn't need shoes." When he finished, he said, "I'm hungry. Can I have my sandwich, Ma?"

"Sure." She fished it out of the sack and handed it to him over the back of the seat while he hung his feet out the open door. "Just make sure you don't leave the paper somewhere along the trail. Have you got a pocket?"

"Yeah, yeah."

He stood beside the truck, wearing a blue baseball cap, scissoring back and forth on his blades, peeling the paper down and taking a first bite big enough to stuff an entire Thanksgiving turkey, then talking with his cheek bulging. "Hurry up, you guys!" In the last year his nose seemed to have mushroomed and lost its boyishness while the rest of his features hadn't quite caught up. His hands had grown to the size of Maine lobsters.

Standing beside him, Lee observed her son and wondered how to get him from fourteen to nineteen in the shortest time possible. She loved him, but this crude, gangly adolescent stage was really the pits.

She leaned across the truck seat and looked in the sack. "You want your sandwich now, Christopher?"

"I'd rather walk on an empty stomach, if you don't mind." He was busy finding his sunglasses, threading the earpieces into their hot-pink string.

"Me too. We'll eat after."

"Better yet, I've got a fanny pack under the seat. We could take the sandwiches along and eat at a picnic stop."

"Sounds good."

Christopher slipped on his sunglasses, locked the truck and carried the blue nylon bag around to Lee's side. She filled it and he buckled it around his waist with the zippered pouch at the rear.

By then Joey was already thirty yards away, swaying gracefully on his Rollerblades, eating his sandwich, caring about little else.

She watched him and said, "Lord, if only he were that graceful on his own feet."

"The miracle is, they actually outgrow it."

"Meanwhile I'm raising the hormonal hurricane. I never knew noses could grow so fast."

They were laughing as they struck out on their walk, heading west along the North Hennepin Trail. It took them through open grassland dotted by brown-eyed Susans and wild asters, between fields of ripe corn where pheasants foraged, through copses of trees that sliced them with intermittent shade. It curved around small marshes where red-winged blackbirds sent forth their distinctive summer call. It passed the remnants of distant farms and an occasional newer house, which looked misplaced next to all that preserved parkland. Bikers occasionally surprised them from behind, passing them in swift puffs of wind, pedaling hard. Other joggers and walkers met them head-on, nodding or speaking winded hellos. Sometimes Joey was visible, sometimes not. He went and returned at will, zooming back at them along the blacktop trail with his blue cap reversed, adding further insult to his adolescent bad looks.

In time Lee squinted at the empty blacktop path that caught the setting sun and turned it to liquid gold. Joey had gone on ahead; the trail stretched for miles, clear out to Elm Creek Park Reserve in the town of Maple Grove.

"I wonder where the hormonal hurricane is," she said.

"Don't worry. He'll be back."

"Are you ready to turn around yet?" she asked.

"Anytime."

They reversed directions, turning their backs on the glare and checking their watches.

"A little over an hour already," Christopher noted. "You tired?"

"Darn right I'm tired, but it feels good."

"Do you do this regularly?"

"Irregularly. In the summer. How about you?"

"I work out regularly in one way or another. Summers a little more outside. Winters, I work out a little more in the weight room, especially after a bad day at work."

They needed their breath for walking, so talking ceased as their shadows grew long on the trail in front of them. The air cooled and frogs began croaking. At a place where the trail crossed a blacktop road a picnic table sat in a clearing. Beside it were bike stands, a garbage can and a drinking fountain. Lee used the fountain first while Christopher waited, standing behind her, watching the curve of her backside as she bent forward to drink. He was growing—he'd discovered—more and more familiar with her curves. She straightened and turned, backhanding her mouth and smiling behind her hand.

He leaned on the fountain with both hands, elbows jutting, sunglasses hanging free and tapping the side of the fountain. She watched the side of his neck as he swallowed, the rhythmic beat of his pulsating skin just below one ear, the line of his backbone beneath his T-shirt, ending where the fanny pack projected from the small of his back. It had been a long time since she'd studied a man's outline in the particular way she found herself studying Christopher's.

He straightened with the sound men make—"Ahh!"—masculine and throaty, a sound she hadn't heard much around her house for many years. With a forearm, he wiped his brow.

"Sandwiches, sandwiches!" she said, clapping twice like a bedouin calling for dancing girls.

"Get 'em out," he said, presenting his back.

She worked the zipper, keeping her eyes on it and nothing else—silly woman, admiring a man fifteen years her junior!—and fished out their supper. At the picnic table they sat down on opposite sides, unwrapped their sandwiches and ate.

And studied each other with mayonnaise in the corners of their mouths. With their hair imperfect and wet around the edges. And their complexions ruddy and unsmooth from exertion. Wearing some of the oldest clothes they owned. Experiencing a comfort level they found with few others.

"So . . ." she began, wiping her mouth on a hard paper napkin printed with an orange-and-black logo. "Any more high-speed chases?"

"No, thank heavens."

"So what's new at the department?"

"I've been made a firearms instructor."

"Wow . . . congratulations."

"Just one of several."

"Still . . . an instructor. Does this mean you'll have to make room for another badge on your chest?"

"Not a badge, just a little pin."

"What does a firearms instructor do?"

"The correct title is range officer. I have to set up quarterly qualification shoots with our duty weapons at the shooting range."

"Where's that?"

"Little park maintenance building behind Perkins."

"The one where the weight room is?"

"Yes."

"I've been in there. Greg took me in once, showed me how the targets move on the metal tracks and put a pair of ear protectors on me and shot off a few rounds. So you have to give the tests?"

"I can design them, too. Next month we're going to be having a gamma shoot that the whole county will participate in."

"What's a gamma shoot?"

"It's done with a gamma machine—it's sort of a simulator."

"And you design the shoots on the simulator?"

"No, the ones I design are done differently."

"How?"

"Well, I'm working on one now. The officers will have to start in the basement and run up three flights of stairs, down a hall, open a door and shoot out six red balloons from a field of twenty-four multicolored ones in two minutes."

"Two minutes?" It seemed long to her.

"Have you ever tried shooting off six accurate rounds in two minutes? Especially when you're breathing like a steam engine and your adrenaline is pumping? If you're on a SWAT team, maybe you've got a gas mask on. Or maybe it's a low-light situation and your reds are flashing, changing the color of everything around you. It's not easy. Even worse, in the test I've designed, they'll have to do it six times, on six different lanes."

"You dreamed this up yourself?"

He shrugged. "There are films and books to give you ideas, and I've been through a lot of qualifying shoots myself in nine years on the force."

"You must be good."

"As good as some, not as good as others. I tend to get less rattled than some of the guys. At least until it's all over . . . then the shakes begin. Like that day of the chase."

He talked about that awful time after all high-risk situations when the adrenaline stops pumping and the shakes set in. How hard it is to concentrate after that, to sleep, to return to normal routine.

"That's why I came and fixed your hose. Couldn't sleep . . . just had to work off that excess energy." A lull fell. Sometimes when this happened—as now—they found themselves studying each other's eyes a little too enjoyably. "So . . . enough about my life. What's going on in yours?"

"Well . . . let's see." She pulled herself from her absorption with him. "School will be starting soon. Right after Labor Day for Joey, two weeks later for Janice. She's had to pay her own way, so it's taking her longer than usual. She was at the U doing some preregistering today. Next week Joey starts football practice, and I'll have to think about taking him out to do some school shopping. His nose isn't the only thing that's been growing this summer. His ankles are hanging out of every pair of jeans he owns." She folded her waxed paper and put it into the sack, then looked off across the open field to the south where twilight was settling. "I hate to see Janice go back to school. The house will seem so empty."

"Will she live in a dorm?"

"Yes."

"So you'll have to move her back. Do you need help with that?"

"I can borrow Jim Clements's truck again."

"Let me know if you need a strong back."

"Thanks, I will."

They sat in silence awhile. A sparrow came and pecked at some crumbs around the garbage can. A gray-haired man and woman came by and said hello. When they'd moved on, Christopher sat with a question in his mind, afraid to pose it, afraid that if he did he might spook Lee and that would be the end of these pleasant times with her. But they'd become friends, good friends. They'd talked about their personal feelings time and again, so what was wrong with talking about this? *Ask her,* an inner voice urged. *Just ask her.* Instead, he rose and threw their trash into the garbage can, gathering courage. Returning to the picnic table, he straddled a bench and rested one arm on the tabletop, looking off at the grass.

"Could I ask you something?"

"Ask."

He turned to watch her face. "Do you ever go out on dates?"

"Dates?" she repeated, as if the word were new to her.

"Yeah, dates." He rushed to explain. "You know, Greg talked a lot about you, but I never heard him mention any guys in your life." He allowed a stretch of silence, then asked, "So do you?"

"No."

"Why?"

"Because when Bill died my kids were enough for me. I just never felt the urge."

"Nine years?" he questioned. "You never dated anybody in nine years?"

"Boy, you've really got your figures down, don't you?" Before he could react to her observation she went on. "They've been busy years. I went to school and started a business. Joey was only five when Bill died. The others were fourteen and sixteen. I didn't have time for dating. Why do you ask?"

He glanced at the grass again. "Because it seems to me it'd be good for you. The way you were today in the shop when I came in, frustrated to the point of tears, handling all this stuff you've had to contend with since Greg died. Seems to me dating would be a distraction. It'd be good for you. Somebody to talk over your feelings with, you know?"

She said quietly, "I seem to talk my feelings over with you," then rushed on as if catching herself at an indiscretion. "And I have my family, the kids . . . I'm not lonely. What about you?"

"Do I date?"

"That's the question here, I believe."

"Now and then."

"Who are you dating now?"

"Nobody special. Girls are sort of put off when they find out you're a cop. I guess they're afraid to get serious because they think you're going to get blown away or something . . . I don't know. It's a stressful lifestyle, especially on wives, they say. Ostrinski keeps trying to get me to go out with his sister-in-law. She's divorced, has a couple of kids, had a bad marriage to a guy who lied to her for four years while he played around with anybody and everybody, including one of her best friends. I finally told Ostrinski, okay, I'll take her out. Saturday's the day, but I'm not looking forward to it."

"Why not?"

"Two kids, an ex-husband, all this past history she's trying to get over . . ." He gave a rueful shake of the head.

"Sounds like me," Lee remarked.

"You aren't saying your husband—"

"Oh, heavens no. We had a great marriage. Maybe that's why I haven't dated. What I had was so perfect it'd be hard to . . ."

"Hey, you guys, here you are!" Joey came swooping off the path, panting, bumping over the grass, dropping both palms flat on the picnic table, smelling execrable. "Gol, you know how far I went?"

"Clear to South Dakota, judging by what time it is," his mother replied.

"You mad, Mom?"

"Actually, Christopher and I were talking so hard I hadn't even noticed it's nearly dark."

"Jeez, am I relieved. Guess what? I ran into this girl I know . . . Sandy Parker? And she's having an end-of-the-summer party at her house the last week of vacation and I'm invited."

"A party? With girls? And you want to go?"

"Well, Sandy's not like the other girls. She likes to Rollerblade and fish and stuff like that." He swung his hat bill around to the front and used it as a handle to scratch his head. "I can go, can't I, Ma?"

Lee and Chris pushed up off the table. "You can go." The three of them headed back toward the blacktop trail where Joey immediately pulled ahead. "Wait by the truck for us, okay?" she called after him.

For the short remainder of their walk, and all the way back to Anoka, Lee and Christopher found little to say. He was going out on a date next Saturday and they both knew it was an antidote for the him-and-her situation they'd been nurturing since June: the two of them with their mismatched ages, beginning to enjoy each other's company a little bit too much.

Joey jabbered all the way back to the house, unaware of the deflated moods of the two with him. Back at home, Christopher walked them to the door then waited while Lee unlocked it and Joey passed them in his stocking feet, carrying both his shoes and his skates, his stockings filthy.

She watched the screen door slam behind him and muttered, "I give up."

Neither she nor Christopher laughed as they would have earlier in the evening. Somehow their mood had dulled.

"Joey, come back here and thank Chris!" she called.

He reappeared in the entry hall and said through the screen door, "Oh yeah . . . hey, thanks, Chris. It was fun."

"Sure thing. 'Night, Joey."

He disappeared and a moment later the bathroom door slammed. Lee stood on the step above Chris, telling herself she had no right to react this way to his dating a young woman his own age.

"Yes, it was fun. Thank you. You rescued me again and I needed it."

"So did I."

Joey came banging out of the bathroom and flashed past on his way into the kitchen where the cupboard and refrigerator doors started opening and closing. Lord, it was hard to sort out these feelings with a teenager banging around.

"Well, listen . . ." Lee said. "Have a good time Saturday night. Give the woman a chance. Who knows . . . she might turn out to be somebody you like a lot."

He dropped his foot off the step and stood in what she'd come to think of as his *cop pose,* weight distributed evenly on widespread feet, shoulders back, chest erect, chin level with the earth. His key ring was looped over his index finger and he gave it a jingle, then snuffed it in a tight fist.

"Yeah, right," he said, deep in his throat. "Who knows."

He'd already turned away before saying, "Good night, Mrs. Reston."

Chapter 8

On Saturday night Christopher, Pete Ostrinski, his wife, Marge, and sister-in-law, Cathy Switzer, had a date to go bowling. Summer leagues were done, winter leagues hadn't started: the lanes would be half empty.

Pete and Marge lived in a nice new house over in the Mineral Pond addition on the east side of town: split entry with two bedrooms up, finished, two down, unfinished. The seams still showed between the rolls of sod in the front yard, and inside, the place smelled like new carpet and paint.

Pete answered Christopher's knock and walked him up into the living room, where toys shared equal space with furniture and the two women were waiting. He kissed Marge on the cheek. When introductions were performed, Cathy Switzer rose from her chair and shook Christopher's hand; her palm was damp. She was blonde, sharp-featured, relatively attractive in a bony way, but when she smiled her gums showed.

"Hi, Chris," she said. "I've heard a lot about you."

He smiled. "That makes two of us."

Pete said, "Marge has got some drinks out on the patio," and they trailed after him, attempting to make conversation. Outside, drinking a Sprite while the others drank margaritas, Christopher covertly assessed Cathy Switzer.

Her hair was fluffed up into a huge arrangement of disheveled corkscrews that must have taken her some time to accomplish. He quite hated it. She had tiny breasts, skinny hips and an unearthly thinness that gave her the frail look of a matchstick. Plainly thought: She didn't look healthy.

He remembered Lee's admonition to give the woman a chance, and remarked, "Pete tells me you work for a plumbing supply."

"Yes, in the office. I'm going to school two nights a week though, to get my realtor's license."

So she had goals and ambition.

"And you bowl on a league, I hear."

The conversation bumped along like all conversation on all blind dates has bumped along for aeons. The baby-sitter came home from the park with the kids, providing a welcome diversion just before the foursome left for the bowling alley in Pete's car.

Cathy Switzer—it turned out—brought her own ball.

The first time she delivered it down alley number five, Christopher expected to see her skinny little arm snap off at the elbow. Instead, she went into a downswing in perfect form, right leg crossed behind left, shoulders canted in a perfect follow-through, and put enough backspin on the ball to throw pins halfway to the scoring table, had the setter not descended to scrape them away, still whirring.

Naturally, she got a strike.

Everybody clapped, and Cathy blushed as she returned to her seat next to Chris.

"Nice," he said, grinning at her askance.

"Thanks," she said with a pleasing balance of pride and humility.

They had a lot of fun, playing three games, all won by Cathy in her size seven blue jeans with her top-heavy hair, matchstick arms and her gums that showed when she smiled. Afterward they drove down to Fridley to T. R. McCoy's for some burgers, fries and malts, and sat in a rainbow of neon with Fats Domino's "Walkin' " on the jukebox and James Dean smiling down off the walls beside a '59 Merc.

"I like this place," Cathy said. "Mark and I used to—oops!" She covered her lips with four fingers. "Sorry," she whispered, dropping her eyes to the black Formica tabletop.

"That's okay," Christopher said. "Mark's your ex?"

She looked up at him like Betty Boop and nodded.

"The divorce has been final for nine months, but I still slip and mention him sometimes when I'm not supposed to."

Across the table Marge said, "The ass."

Pete nudged her arm. "Marge, come on now, not tonight."

"All right, sorry I called the ass an ass."

Things got tense after that and they decided to call it a night. When they got back to Pete and Marge's house it turned out Cathy had no car, so Christopher offered to drive her home. In his truck he turned on the radio and Cathy stayed buckled onto her half of the seat.

"You like country?" he asked when the music came on.

She said, "Sure."

While Willie Nelson tried his darnedest to sound less than pitiable, she said, "Sorry I mentioned my ex."

"Hey, listen . . . it's okay. I imagine you were with him for a few years. You've got two kids, I hear."

"Yeah, Grady and Robin. They're five and three. He never comes to see them. He married my best friend and he's busy with her kids now."

He wondered what to say. "That's tough."

"You're only the second guy I've been out with since my divorce. The first one never called back."

"Probably because you took him on the pro bowling tour."

She laughed and said, "Mark hated it when I bowled. It was okay for him to go running all over the country taking my best friend to bed, but he didn't like it when I went out with the girls from work to our bowling league."

He began to regret telling her it was okay to talk about this guy.

"What hurts worst," she went on, "is that a lot of the stuff he'd never do with me and the kids, he does with her and her kids. I know because I talk to his mother, and sometimes she slips and mentions things." She talked nonstop about her ex-husband, barely pausing to give directions to her townhouse. When they got there, she said, "Oh, are we here already?"

"Wait there," he said, got out, pocketed his keys and went around to open her door.

"It's been a long time since a guy has done that for me," she said. "That kind of stuff stopped long before Mark divorced me. That's sort of how I knew something was going on."

He trailed along after her to a concrete walk that took two turns between buildings and led them to a ground-floor door without an outside light. There she took one step up and turned to him.

"Well, I've enjoyed it," she said. "Thanks a lot for the bowling and the burgers and everything."

"I enjoyed it, too," he said. "Especially the bowling, even though you beat everything in sight. It's fun to watch somebody do something that well."

"You're sweet," she said.

"Sweet?" he repeated with a chuckle. "I'm a lot of things, but sweet I don't think is one of them."

"Well, you put up with me crying on your shoulder all night about Mark. That's sweet, isn't it?"

"Hey, listen," he said, taking a step backward. "Good luck. I know it's hard losing someone that way, but I hope everything works out for you and your kids."

She stood in shadow so deep he couldn't make out her face. He had the impression her hands were stuck into the tight front pockets of her jeans, and her puffy hair created a faint nimbus in the dark around her head.

Suddenly he took pity on her. "You know, Cathy, you ought to get over him. Somebody who treats his wife and family like that doesn't deserve any tears."

"Who says I cry about him?"

He saw himself getting in deeper than he wanted with this deluded woman and backed away another step. "Listen . . . I've got to go. Good luck, Cathy."

When he got a yard down the sidewalk she stopped him. "Hey, Chris?"

He turned.

"Would you . . ." She paused uncertainly. "Come here?"

He knew what was coming and experienced little joy in the presumption. Nevertheless he again took pity on her and moved to the base of the stoop, which put their heads on the same level.

"Listen," she whispered, and he heard her swallow as she put her hands on his collar. "I know you're not coming back again either, and that's all right . . . I mean, really it is!" She spoke anxiously. "I mean, I talk too much about Mark and I know that. But before you go, would you mind very much if I kissed you? I mean, it's been a long, long time since he left, and I know you don't like me or anything, and I don't want you to go away thinking I ask strange guys to kiss me all the time. You're a cop, like Pete, and I trust you . . . I mean, I know you think this is a pretty dumb thing to ask, but it's been . . . I've been . . . I've been so lonely . . . and . . . and it would be the sweetest thing you could do for me if you'd just stand there and . . . well, I don't care . . . pretend I'm somebody else if you want . . . and let me kiss you."

Something in his heart twisted. Lonely he understood. Lonely was Judd Quincy waiting with his foot against the wall of the 7-Eleven store. Lonely was little Chris Lallek waiting for his mom and dad to come home so he could ask them for money for a band uniform. Lonely was this skinny, divorced woman laboring under the delusion that she didn't love her philandering husband anymore.

He didn't wait for her to kiss him. He kissed her—an honest, full-mouthed French kiss, holding nothing back. She felt like a bundle of kindling wood in his arms, and he put from his mind the way her gums showed when she smiled, and how unnatural her hair looked, all tortured up three times bigger than her narrow little face.

He'd kissed enough women that he felt the universal pull of all that went along with it; he gave himself over to that universality, to the pre-mating ritual of running hands over backs, and tongues over tongues, and fitting two bodies together so that the line of one obscures the other.

It stopped when Cathy ran her hands down the rear pockets of his jeans and made a place for him between her thighs. His sympathy didn't extend quite that far.

He pulled her arms from behind his neck, stepped back and gripped both her hands hard.

"Listen," he said throatily. "I gotta go. You take care of yourself now."

"Yeah. You too."

When their hands parted and she stayed on her stoop, he couldn't help but breathe a sigh of relief.

Odd, for a woman he hadn't particularly liked, she stayed on his mind a lot the next couple of days. Then he realized why: He was comparing her to Lee Reston. She had a Dolly Parton hairdo, not Lee's short, unaffected cap, which took wind and weather as it would. She had a profile like an eleven-year-old girl, not the rounded curves of maturity. She had a bony, emaciated face instead of a full, healthy one. And those gums—ye gods. Had he really French-kissed her? Well, hell, the kiss hadn't been so bad if he really stopped to think about it. Cathy Switzer's greatest shortcoming was simple enough for Christopher to understand: She wasn't Lee Reston.

Damn, but that woman stayed on his mind a lot. Not a day went by that he didn't think of her and manufacture excuses to see her, which he most often decided not to act on.

Several days passed after his date without either seeing or speaking to Lee. Then one day he was standing in his kitchen scooping ice cream into a bowl when someone slipped a piece of paper under his door. He reacted like a policeman: leaped and yanked the door open suddenly, to confront whoever was on the other side.

And there was Lee, leaping back in fright.

"Christopher!" She pressed her heart. "Lord, you scared me! I didn't think you were home. I thought you were working days."

"It's my day off." He looked down the hall both ways, then at the envelope on the floor. "What's this?"

"Something of yours I found stuck between Greg's papers. I think it's an insurance card. I must have picked it up when I was taking some things out of your kitchen drawer."

He opened the envelope and perused the item. "Oh yeah . . . I was looking for this."

"Sorry." She shrugged.

"You could have mailed it."

"I know. I was passing by."

He studied her in her green canvas skirt, white blouse and slip-on shoes, her healthy middle-age robustness so different from Cathy Switzer. He had done the right thing; he'd tried a date, tried meeting someone new, but it had only served to point out how much he enjoyed the woman standing before him in the hall.

"Wanna come in?" He stepped back and motioned toward the kitchen.

"No. I've got to go home and fix supper for Joey."

"Oh. Well, okay then." They stood awhile coming to terms with her correct decision before he dropped one shoulder and said, appealingly, "Well, hell, you can come in for a minute, can't you?"

"What were you doing?" She bent forward from the waist, going up on tiptoe to peek around the open door.

"Having a bowl of ice cream."

"At suppertime?"

"Yeah. You want one?"

She settled back down on her heels. "No, I really have to go."

"All right then," he said, accepting her decision, but wishing if she was going to go, she'd go, because they both knew it wasn't what she wanted to do. "Say hi to Joey. I gotta go," he added with a hint of irritation, "my ice cream is melting."

"Well, you don't have to get mad at me." If someone were to point out how childish they sounded they both would have made loud protestations of denial.

"I'm not mad at you."

"All right then, could I change my mind about the ice cream?"

He waved her in, shut the door and followed her into the kitchen, where he took out a glass dish and scooped out ice cream. "You want topping?" He opened a cupboard door and hung a hand from it while taking a tally of its contents. "There's chocolate, caramel and . . ." He picked up a moldy bottle of something, turned and made a perfect shot into a garbage can next to the stove. "I guess there's just chocolate and caramel."

"Caramel," she said.

He drizzled some straight from the jar, caught the stalactite with a finger and sucked it off. Recapping the bottle, he put it away, found spoons, then brought the two sundaes to the kitchen table.

"Sit down," he ordered.

"Thanks."

They ate in silence until half their ice cream was gone. Then Lee asked, "So how was your blind date on Saturday?"

"Great," he answered. "She owned her own bowling ball."

A stretch of silence passed before Lee asked, "So, are you going to see her again?"

"Why do you ask?" He watched her carefully, but she refused to meet his eyes.

"I was just wondering, that's all."

He got up and took their bowls to the sink, rinsed them both and put them in the dishwasher. When he finished, he stayed clear across the room from her, catching his hips and both palms against the edge of the countertop, studying her back while she remained at the table waiting for his answer. After an uncomfortable stretch of silence he sighed—an enormous effort to relieve the tension in his shoulders—and spoke resignedly.

"No," he told her.

She twisted around in her chair and stared at him but said nothing.

"She was pathetic," he added, pushing off the cabinet and returning to the table, where he took the chair at a right angle to her. A fingernail clipper lay on the table. He picked it up and let it slide between the pads of his thumb and index finger time and time again, turning it end for end each time his fingers touched the table.

"She was a skinny pathetic little thing who got dumped by some jerk who had an affair with her best friend, then married her."

"Could we give her a name, please?" Lee requested.

He looked up at her and the fingernail clipper stopped sliding. "Cathy," he said, "Cathy Switzer."

Lee sat with her arms crossed on the table, motionless, studying him.

He threw down the fingernail clipper and went on. "She talked about him all night long. Couldn't stop. How he never liked her to go bowling. How he never came to see his kids anymore. How the first guy she saw after the divorce never came back after one date. And when I walked her to her door she said over and over how she knew she'd talked about him all night long and that I was never going to come back either. Then she asked me to kiss her." He let his eyes wander to Lee and settle there. His voice lost its rough edge. "She said she was lonely, and that she trusted me because I was a cop, and would I just kiss her once and that she didn't care if I pretended she was someone else."

The silence seemed to run itself out into minutes before Lee asked, "And did you?"

It took some time for him to answer, time during which their glances collided and held.

"Yes," he finally said, so low it sounded like someone else had spoken in a faraway room. Their stillness, both with arms crossed on the table, remained absolute. The ambivalence of her question remained: Did he kiss the woman, or did he pretend she was someone else? He thought it best not to fill in the entire truth. The strain in the room got to him, however, and he realized it was the same for her. They had both been dancing around their feelings for each other, afraid to admit them, afraid of this vast difference in their ages and the unwritten rule of propriety it posed. They could go on pretending friendly indifference forever, but he knew and she knew that feelings had begun stirring between them, and one of them had to get it out in the open, because it was hell holding it inside. But there were things she should know first, things he'd told rarely in his life that were important for her to hear.

"I think it's time I told you a little more about myself, Lee. Bear with me, if you will, because some of this you've heard before, and it's rather a long story, but until you hear it all, you can't understand where I'm coming from."

Christopher shifted in his chair, making the wood snap and creak. He picked up the nail clipper again and squeezed it in his palm, concentrating on it as if it were a scientific experiment. "I've told you some of what it was like when I was growing up. How my mom and dad left me to take care of my little sister. All they cared about was where their next drink was coming from. Groceries didn't matter. If there were any in the house, fine. If not, hell with it.

"There was this grocery store two doors down from the apartment where we lived. The Red Owl. I found out what time of day they cleaned out their produce department and I used to make sure I was back there in the alley when this guy named Sammy Saminski used to bring all the wilted stuff out and put it in the dumpster. Some of it was pretty good yet, edible. Sammy would let me take it home. He was a smart guy, Sammy. Didn't take him long to figure out Jeannie and I were living on the stuff. So eventually he started bringing out better stuff. I knew it was still plenty good yet, but I took it anyway. And that's why I learned to cook, so there'd be something on the table for Jeannie and me.

"Mavis and Ed, they might come stumbling in at ten o'clock, maybe midnight— we never knew. How they survived is a mystery to me because I never saw them eat. Just drink and fight, that's all. She used to call the cops on him every once in a while and that's when I first got the idea I'd like to become one, because when I saw that officer walk in in his clean blue uniform I thought for sure he was going to take Jeannie and me away and put us in someplace better, and it was the only time in my life I ever felt safe. It didn't last long though, because instead of taking us, they took the old man. He'd stay in the clink a day or two, and while he was gone Mavis seemed to be around a little more taking care of us. But then Ed would be back out, and he and Mavis would take up their drinking again as if she'd never called the cops in the first place.

"One time when she called them, he had the DTs. He was standing in front of a medicine chest pulling back his lips and looking in the mirror, and he thought there were worms eating his teeth. I can remember Mavis yelling, 'Ed, Ed, there's nothing there!' And he raved, 'Can't you see 'em, Mavis, the goddamn things are eating my teeth!'

"That was one of the worst times I remember. Jeannie and I were both crying. Hell, we didn't know what was going on. And that policeman came and I wanted so damn bad for him to take us out of there. But he didn't." Christopher stared at the fingernail clipper in his hand, then seemed to pull himself from the past and shift his weight on the chair. He settled his back against it and went on.

"Sammy Saminski got me on the payroll at the Red Owl when I was fourteen. He lied about my age. By the time I graduated from high school I was managing the produce department and I'd saved enough money to put myself through two years of vocational school. When I could, I'd give some to Jeannie. She hoarded it away without telling me, and when she was fifteen years old, she ran away."

Christopher cleared his throat. "I think I told you once before that my parents still live here in Anoka. Still drink. Still fight. I don't have anything to do with them."

He looked at Lee—dear, sweet Lee—and decided he didn't care if she saw love in his eyes. He was damned tired of trying to hide it.

"And then you come into my life. And do you know what you are to me? You're all the things they weren't. You're everything a mother should be. You're kind and loving and caring; you're there for your kids no matter what they need. You earn a living and provide for them. They can talk to you about anything, and you love them—you genuinely love them, and they love you back. And all of a sudden I'm right in there being treated like I'm one of them. Then Greg dies and I feel like I've taken his place. And you know what? I love it."

His volume had lowered to a coarse whisper. "Then this woman Saturday night . . . she asks me to kiss her and she says it's okay if I pretend she's someone else. And you know who I was thinking about, don't you, Lee?"

"Christopher, stop!" She jumped up, crossed the room, faced the kitchen sink with her back to him.

"I'm so damned mixed up, Lee."

"Stop, I said!" He could hear terror in her voice.

"You don't want to hear this."

"I don't want to lose your friendship and that's what'll happen if you go on with this."

"Yes, I know. That's why I'm scared."

"Then drop it. Now. Before any more is said."

He considered awhile, waiting for her to turn and face him. When he realized she would not, he whispered, "All right."

She turned on the water. Took a drink. Turned off the water. Set down her glass. All these motions having nothing to do with thirst. Neither of them had looked at the other since she'd leaped from her chair.

She said quietly, "I've got to go."

An aeon seemed to pass while neither of them moved. Then he asked a question.

"How old are you?"

She made a sound—chortle? grunt? he wasn't sure which—and moved to the door, opened it before she spoke.

"Old enough to be your mother."

She went out and left him sitting on his kitchen chair.

Left behind, he remained right there, brooding, disappointed, angry with himself for reading her wrong and opening his mouth, fearing their friendship would end now. Well, what the hell, she was probably scared, too, and she had a lot more at stake than he did.

After twenty minutes he shot to his feet, found his truck keys, drove to the police station, stalked into the squad room and went directly to the computer in the corner. It was on, its screen a quivering green.

He pushed QMR and waited. Nokes sauntered in eating an apple and said, "What the heck are you doing?"

"Looking something up."

"On your day off?"

He slowly turned his chair seat around and gave Nokes a wincing look of long-suffering. "Nokes, haven't you got anything better to do than stand around here crunching that apple in my ear?"

Nokes shrugged and walked down the hall to the communications room.

Query Motor Vehicle was waiting when Christopher turned back to the screen, asking him to put in his initials before it would give out any information.

He entered his initials and the machine sounded a *beep,* giving him the go-ahead.

He typed in her license plate number, pushed the code button and swung around in his chair to listen for the printer in the communications room. It began clattering and he walked down the hall to the room where tonight's dispatcher and records technician, Toni Mansetti and Ruth Randall, were sitting on their respective chairs doing their jobs. Nokes had hooked his buns against a table edge, crossed his legs and was finishing his apple while lazily watching a couple of split-screen televisions that monitored the city parking ramps across the street.

The printer stopped clattering and Christopher reached over Ruth Randall's shoulder to rip the sheet off.

He left the communications room reading the info from the Minnesota Bureau of Driver's Licenses.

Lee Therese Reston
    1225 BENTON STREET   ANOKA 55303
    SEX/F. DOB/091848. HGT/506. WGT/130. EYE/BRN
    PHOTO #: 8082095102.
    NO VIOLATIONS
    NO HIT
    QDP NAM/RESTON, LEE THERESE. DOB/091848

He read the last item again: Date of birth: 9-18-48.
She was forty-four years old.

Lee had left Christopher's apartment just as upset as he was.

How dare he! she thought, lying awake in the dark that night. How dare he wreck the fragile balance they'd managed during these past couple of months! She needed him, treasured the times they spent together, because she could talk to him about things nobody else seemed to understand. She could be herself—sorrowful or gay— and he accepted whatever mood she was in.

How dare he ruin that by intimating he had other-than-friendly feelings toward her? Anything else was unthinkable, given their ages and his relationship to this family as a whole. Why, Janice had a crush on him! Joey thought he was the neatest thing since pointed footballs, and every other person in the entire family knew how much time he spent around here.

Good god-afrighty, imagine the gasps if anybody got wind of this.

Especially Mother.

August turned the corner into September and Christopher stayed away. Joey started football practice, then school. Lee arranged her working schedule so that she could go to his junior high games in the late afternoons once each week.

At the shop huge bronze and maroon football mums started coming in. The arrangers began putting miniature cattails and preserved gold maple leaves in their fresh bouquets. A new batch of FTD containers came in, shaped like mallard ducks.

Janice moved into her dorm at the university, and Lee stubbornly withheld Christopher's offer of help, pressing her lazy son (who rammed his body against football dummies every afternoon for two hours but said he was too tired to help move the furniture) into duty instead. The three of them—Joey, Janice and Lee—spent a beautiful Sunday afternoon in mid-September lugging Greg's mattress, box spring and bed onto Jim Clements's pickup truck and hauling it thirty miles into the city, then up two flights of stairs at the dormitory.

Janice bid them goodbye with a hug and a promise. "Don't feel so bad, Mom. I've got my car so I'll come home a lot on weekends."

That was, very possibly, the worst week of Lee's life. She began to understand why a lonely woman would ask a strange man to kiss her even though she knew perfectly well he was never going to ask her on a date again.

Such splendid fall days.

Such beautiful fall nights, and after supper—lo!—Joey would come out of the bathroom smelling like deodorant with his hair freshly combed and wearing clean sweat socks *and* shoes.

"A bunch of us kids are going to walk uptown and get a Coke," he'd say. And a bunch of them—boys and girls together—would come in a group and spirit him away. Later, at a very respectable hour, they'd be back in the yard, hanging around the front steps talking and laughing in the moonlight. One of them, she overheard, was named Sandy Parker.

Lee began to feel like a useless old woman.

Then on September eighteenth (a day she'd been dreading as much as she'd dreaded her first root canal) at precisely 10:32 A.M. (she would forever recall the time because she was so used to tracking delivery times, she actually tracked this one made *to* her) Ivan Small, the delivery man for her biggest competitor, Forrest Floral on Fourth Avenue, entered her shop bearing an arrangement of American Beauty roses so huge it made Ivan look like a walking bouquet.

"Mizz Reston?" he said from behind his burden, then set it down on the counter and stepped to one side so he could see her. "I don't know what's going on, but we got an order to deliver this to you here at your shop."

"Are you kidding?" she replied.

"God's truth. Forty-five of them," he said. He wore an expression like the lion in *The Wizard of Oz.*

"Oh God." She covered the bottom of her face and felt herself begin to blush while Sylvia, Pat and Nancy stood in wonderment.

"They're from Mom and Dad," she said hopefully. "Or Lloyd. I'll bet they're from Lloyd."

"There's a card." Ivan plucked it from the foliage and handed it to her.

So help me God, if it's from Christopher and Sylvia reads his name over my shoulder, I'll drive over him with his own cop car!

The card said: *Your secret is out.*

Now she'd have some fancy explaining to do.

"Thank you, Ivan," she said. "Oh, wait!"

She opened the cash register and got out five dollars, and felt ridiculous tipping somebody else's flower delivery man at the door of her own shop.

Ivan accepted, said, "Thank you, Mizz Reston," and left.

The second the door closed, all three women asked, "Who are they from?"

"I don't know," Lee lied.

"Well, have you been . . . *dating* anyone?" Sylvia actually seemed to trip over the word.

"Heavens no."

"Then how do you explain it?"

"Your guess is as good as mine."

She took them home and put them in the middle of the kitchen table where never in all her years as a florist had she brought this many roses at one time. The damn fool! These things ran thirty-six dollars a dozen at retail. He'd paid well over one hundred dollars, not counting tax and delivery, for an item she could have gotten from her supplier for half that.

She couldn't help being charmed. Sitting there on her kitchen chair squeezing her mouth, she held in a laugh, but soon it escaped, lilting through the room and making her heart feel light.

"Lallek, you young fool," she said aloud, "what am I going to do with you?"

Joey came home from football practice and actually paused for a full fifteen seconds on his way to the refrigerator.

"Wow, Mom, did you bring them home?"

"They're not throw-aways from my store, if that's what you mean."

"Where'd they come from then?"

"I don't know." She had put the card in her billfold on her way home. "There are forty-five of them."

"One for every hamburger I'm going to eat as soon as Janice gets home and we take you out to eat."

"Are you serious, Joey? Janice is coming home?" She leaped from the chair, the roses forgotten.

"That's right, so get changed. We're going to take you out to the restaurant of your choice. As long as the bill doesn't run over twenty dollars."

Janice came bounding in with a great big hug. "Happy birthday, Mom! Did Joey keep my secret? . . . Gosh, did you bring those flowers home?"

"I've been wondering if they're from Grampa Lloyd. I don't think Mom and Dad would spend that kind of money."

"Grampa Lloyd, huh?" Janice headed toward the bathroom, looking at the flowers over her shoulder. From behind the closed bathroom door she called, "Wasn't there any card?"

Lee Reston pretended she didn't hear, and by the time they were in the car heading for the Vineyard Café, the card was forgotten.

Chapter 9

She was afraid to call him. Two weeks passed. Three. Then on an afternoon in early October Lee stood on the bleachers of Fred Moore Middle School with a sparse collection of other parents. Down below a game was in progress. Up above weather was churning. A morose layer of low gray scud clouds tumbled along before a pushy wind. Debris, caught in the chain link fence, flapped against it like a playing card against bicycle spokes. The field was wet; they'd had rain the night before. Even from here Lee could see she'd have fun trying to get the stains out of Joey's uniform.

He was a defensive lineman, a position that garnered little glory in most games, especially from moms of ninth graders without men beside them to explain what was happening. But suddenly the line broke and she saw her clumsy son spurt through like O.J. Simpson through an airport, eluding tackles, sidestepping arms, running an abbreviated U-turn and hauling the opposing quarterback smack off his pins!

She stuck her pinkies between her teeth and whistled. "Hey, way to go, Joey!" She whistled again, this time without the fingers, brandishing one fist in the air. She yelled at the top of her lungs, "You could show those Vikings a thing or two!"

On the street above the field, Officer Christopher Lallek parked his black-and-white squad, turned up the collar of his navy blue winter jacket and slammed the door.

Down below, white and blue jerseys darted around like dots on a video screen. He threaded his way inside the chain link fence and giant-stepped down the bleachers, searching for Joey's number. There it was, number eighteen, blue. He was halfway down the steps when the kid made a damned good sack, and the Fred Moore parents sent up some noise. He glanced along the bleachers to his right and there was Lee. She was dressed in a thick blue denim jacket almost to her knees. Her collar was up. Her cheeks were red. And she had two fingers stuck in her mouth, whistling.

Smiling crookedly, he clumped onto the metal bench and moved toward her. She raised a fist and yelled, clapped some, then jammed her hands into her pockets and hunched her shoulders against the wind.

His footfalls made the metal bench clang.

She turned and saw him approaching. The hunch dropped from her shoulders and her eyes grew bright, though her mouth was hidden behind a generous upturned collar.

"Hi," he said, stopping beside her.

It took her a while to answer while their eyes made up for lost days and their pulses got unruly.

"Hi."

The wind ruffled her hair. It buffeted their backs and pushed them from behind.

"Haven't seen you for a while," he ventured.

"No." She finally looked away, back to the football field.

"So how's the game going?" He, too, turned his attention below.

"Fred Moore is behind but Joey just made a great play."

"I saw it. Saw you whistling, too. Pretty impressive. I don't know many women who can whistle like a cattle drover."

They grinned at each other askance, with their collars still hiding their mouths. Another play broke below and she hollered, "Get him! Get him!"

The teams huddled and Christopher returned to studying Lee.

"So, how've you been?"

"Gettin' older," she replied smugly, keeping her eyes steadfastly on the field.

"Yeah, so I heard."

They watched two whole plays before she said, "I got your flowers." She turned, her eyes filled with humor. "I didn't know whether to thank you or ram 'em up your nose holes."

"To the best of my recollection, you didn't do either."

"How'd you find out?"

"Ran your plate number through Motor Vehicle Registrations. Lee Therese Reston, September 18, 1948."

"All right, so now you know and maybe you'll understand why I got upset that day."

"Hey, listen. Can we just forget that day? It won't happen again."

She turned back to the field and began alternating feet to warm them up. She was wearing black leggings that disappeared into black patent-leather boots with fur around the ankles.

He watched for her reactions while he said, "I missed you."

She stopped stamping, going motionless for a moment with her hands in her pockets and her eyes on the field. "I missed you too," she said, then swung her face to him. "And I never got so many roses in one bunch in my entire life. Thank you."

"My pleasure," he said.

They spent some seconds enjoying the fact that they'd reconnected before she let her mouth quirk. "You damn fool. I could have gotten them for you at half the price, wholesale."

He reared back and laughed. "Wouldn't have been half as much fun though, would it?"

The ref's whistle blew and they remembered why they were there. The play stopped, however, and the teams went back to their huddles.

"So," she said as if their past contretemps had not happened, "you want to come over Saturday night and have some pot roast with Joey and me?"

With that simple question his life became happy again. "You don't have to ask me twice."

They grinned at each other in anticipation until his radio crackled and he reached for it.

"One Bravo Seventeen."

The dispatcher came back, giving him a staticky message.

"Copy," he replied, and to Lee, who hadn't comprehended a word the dispatcher had said, "Teenage runaway. Gotta go check it out. What time on Saturday?"

"Six-thirty."

He touched his hat, walked two steps away, then came back. "You gonna make gravy?"

"I take it you like gravy?"

"Never learned how to make it myself."

"What's a pot roast without gravy?"

His lingering smile said the last thing he wanted to do at that minute was check out a teenage runaway. "See you."

She swiveled and watched him respond to duty, his thick-soled black shoes making the metal bleacher tremble beneath her feet, the crease in his navy trousers breaking behind the knees, his jacket puffed out above the waist, the leather holders full of heavy paraphernalia hanging thick from his belt, even in back. He turned left, bounded up the steps, taking them two at a time. She watched him climb to the top, turning her back to the field while he shouldered his way around the opening in the chain link fence and walked briskly to his squad car. Opening the door he glanced down, saw her following his progress and raised a hand in farewell.

She saw his smile and waved back, watching until the black-and-white pulled away, amazed at how his return into her life lent it a buoyancy that had been lacking since she'd spooked and cut him out of it. All right, so she might be making a mistake, but Lord it felt good to be looking forward to a night with him again.

On Saturday evening one of those bleak October rains was falling when Christopher arrived at Lee's house. Joey answered the bell and said, "Hi, Chris."

"What do you say, Joe?"

"Saw you at my game Wednesday."

"Sorry I couldn't stick around. I got a call. But I saw your sack. Man, you really nailed him!"

"I got him again in the last quarter, too! Jeez, you should've seen that guy. Took him the whole time-out to get back on his feet, and then after that his linemen were really on me. This one big bruiser . . ."

Lee stuck her head around the kitchen corner and despaired of getting a word in edgewise. She wagged two fingers at Christopher while Joey went on babbling excitedly, moving toward the kitchen with their guest, walking backward without realizing it.

For Christopher, returning to this place, to these people, to these homey comforts filled his heart with a sense of belonging. The table was set for three. Some bronze-colored flowers decorated the middle of it. The kitchen was bright and cozy with the rain beating against the sliding door and the curtains drawn against the dark. The smell in the place made his mouth water—beef and cooked onions, coffee, fragrant steam rising from kettles on the stove. And, of course, there was Lee wearing carpet slippers and a blue sweat suit, moving about, getting a meal ready while her son rambled on as he would with a father or a big brother.

". . . and the coach said, 'Tear their legs off!' and I think I almost did. Hey, Mom, Chris was there when I made my first sack! He saw it!"

"Yes, I know. Hi, Christopher." She was thickening gravy at the stove, and neither of them gave away their gladness at being together.

"Smells good in here."

"You bet your badge. I didn't eat much today. Hope it's okay if I put it on right away. Joey, will you fill the milk glasses?"

Christopher asked, "Can I do something?"

"Sure. You can put this salt and pepper shaker on the table." She handed him the pair. "Then reach up onto the top shelf behind me and get down two bowls for the potatoes and the carrots."

Such plain family activity, but moving around the room together, Christopher and Lee felt a subtle shift in their relationship. Perhaps, for the moment, they simply indulged in playing house. He got down the bowls, she filled them, then put them in his hands. Women set tables differently than men, he noticed. Not only bronze flowers, but bearded wheat sticking out of them, and place mats and a pair of rust-colored candles. She handed him matches and he lit them. There was a jumble of activity—Joey with the milk, Lee opening the oven door, finding pot holders, running water into empty kettles, handing Chris another bowl of food to set on the table.

Then, at last, the three of them sat down to a tableful of steaming foods that Norman Rockwell surely must have painted dozens of times. Roast beef, mashed potatoes, rich dark gravy, bright orange carrots, sweet peas in a thick white sauce, a tossed green salad and something brown, moist and unidentifiable in a casserole dish so hot it burned Christopher's fingers.

"Ouch!"

"You okay?"

"Yeah." Mesmerized, he reached again . . . for the spoon this time. "What's this?"

"Corn-bread stuffing with pork sausage."

"Oh my Go-o-o-d." He drew out the word as if singing a canticle.

They feasted for the better part of an hour while the raindrops tapped against the window like a thousand impatient fingers, while the warmth from the oven suffused the room, and a fourteen-year-old boy amused them all with tales of football and school pranks. They laughed and had refills and Joey asked Christopher what was the first bust he ever made. Christopher wore a self-deprecating grin as he replied that the very first day of work he was watching the crosswalk by Lincoln Elementary when he'd spied a seven-year-old urinating against the corner of the school building. Scared the kid half to death when a great big police officer in an official blue uniform stood above him and gave him a lecture. Forever after, everybody at the station snickered when they recalled that on his first day on the force Chris Lallek busted a seven-year-old for peeing on the school building.

The three at the table laughed and felt relaxed with each other. Lee said,

"There's apple cobbler and ice cream." Christopher expanded his chest and rubbed his stomach. "I couldn't hold one more morsel . . ." He released his breath and added, ". . . But give me an extra scoop."

When his dessert was gone, Christopher said, "That's the best meal I've had since the last time I ate at your house. Thanks, Lee."

"It's nice to cook for a man again." It was true. Joey was merely an eating machine. He'd eat metal bolts if they were sautéed in butter. But cooking for a man was different, and there was no denying she'd put extra effort into tonight's meal.

They worked together cleaning up the kitchen, rinsing dishes, loading the dishwasher. Lee was washing off the top of the stove when she paused and said, "Christopher, I know I shouldn't take advantage of you, but would you do me a favor?"

"Name it."

"I put a couple of rugs in the washer the other day and it walked halfway across the basement floor, then afterwards it was sagging way down on one corner. Would you mind leveling it for me?"

"Don't mind at all."

"Joey, will you go downstairs with Chris and show him where?"

Her laundry room was all finished off and brightly lit. A pair of her panty hose hung from a towel bar on a plastic clothespin. Chris thought about taking them off her sometime. Joey got one of his dad's levels and they jostled the machine onto two legs and screwed the other two this way and that until the machine sat level.

Christopher was dusting off the knees of his jeans when she came to the laundry room doorway rubbing lotion into her hands. "Ah, you fixed it. Thank you so much." She walked past him, plucked the panty hose down and folded them. "Most things I'll tackle on my own, but that's one I won't. Thanks again."

She led the way back upstairs. "Anybody for a game of Parcheesi?"

They began a game of Parcheesi, but midway through it Joey got a phone call—obviously from a girl. His voice cracked from contralto to soprano and back again while he said, "Oh, hi, I thought you were going out with your family to your aunt's house tonight . . . Yeah, but just a minute." He covered the mouthpiece with his hand. "Hey, Mom, would you hang this up when I get in your bedroom?"

She complied, and returned to the kitchen table, crooking a knee onto her chair seat while standing beside it. "He'll be on for two hours. The telephone is his newest toy. You want to keep playing or should we watch TV?"

"What do you want to do?"

"Watch TV. I'm tired. I worked today."

"Me too. I'll help you put this away."

When the Parcheesi game was boxed, they went into the living room and she tucked herself into a corner of the sofa while he stretched out on his back on the floor.

"Hey, there are chairs," she said.

"No, this is fine." He tipped his chin up and looked at her backward, then concentrated on the screen.

"All right, stubborn." She tossed him a sofa pillow that landed on his face. He tucked it beneath his head and said, "Thanks."

A situation comedy flickered through its tired scenes before them. She flicked channels with the remote control. The rain kept pummeling the windows behind the closed curtains. In the bedroom, Joey laughed, then his voice returned to a distant murmur. Lee lowered the volume on the TV. Occasionally her eyes would wander to the figure stretched out across her living room floor, to his flat stomach and crossed ankles and everything in between. Guiltily, she looked away and returned her attention to the television.

But it swerved back to him of its own accord.

"Hey, Christopher?" she said.

"Hm?"

"I've been thinking a lot about the story you told me . . . about your growing up." He lay very still with his hands behind his head. "I'm glad you told me. It makes me understand your relationship with Judd."

"I didn't tell you so you'd feel sorry for me."

"I know that. But I'm glad you did just the same. Your parents . . . they sound like very sad creatures." She waited but he said nothing. "Do you think it would make any difference if you tried to make peace with them?"

"No, I don't."

"Have you ever tried?"

"Drop it, Lee."

"But they're your parents."

He sat up and swung around to face her. "Hey, listen," he said calmly. "We've got to get one thing straight. Don't crusade with me about them. I know it's hard for you to swallow, but I hate them. And with just cause. In my book, a parent doesn't *inherit* the right to respect from his children, he *earns* it. And mine missed the chance years ago."

"But surely everybody deserves a second chance."

"I said, drop it, Lee." She could hear the tight control in his voice.

"But, Christopher, family is so important and they're your—"

"As far as I'm concerned, they're dead."

"Why, Christopher, that's an awful thing to say!"

He leaped to his feet, threw the pillow onto the sofa and headed for the front coat closet.

She was up and after him instantly. "Christopher, I'm sorry." She caught his arm before he reached the front hall. "I'm sorry," she repeated. "It's just that . . ."

He spun on her. "It's just that you live in a dream world, Lee." She had never seen his mouth like that, curled in upon itself in a hard, flat-cheeked face. "You think that just because your mom twirls a baton at a Fourth of July picnic and your dad grills steaks you can somehow get the whole world to do that? Woman, you are *so* naive! You were born into this ideal family, and you raised an ideal one of your own, but they're not all like that. There are millions of Judds in this country—poor, hungry, neglected, scared to death because they don't know what's going to happen to them the next day. And so they turn to drugs and gangs. They become pushers and rapists. Well, I'm one of the few lucky ones who got out—no thanks to my parents. So don't ask me to forgive them, Lee. Don't ever ask that of me, because I won't."

She took his face in her two hands and whispered, "So much anger. I've never seen it before."

He jerked away, twisting his head up and to one side. "Don't!"

She dropped her hands. "I'm sorry," she whispered.

He got his jacket out of the closet. "No, I'm the one who's sorry. I spoiled this perfectly nice Saturday night after you went to so much trouble cooking for me and everything. And I had a good time talking to Joey and . . ." He'd put his jacket on and zipped it up. At the top of the zipper his hands stalled while he looked at her beseechingly. "I'm sorry I ruined it, that's all."

"I shouldn't have brought up the subject of your parents. I promise I won't again, okay?"

He took some gloves out of his pocket and flapped them toward the bedroom. "Okay if I go say goodbye to Joey?"

She stepped back and said, "Sure."

He went down the hall and leaned into her bedroom, glimpsing it for the first time—perfume bottles on a dresser, open closet doors with dresses hanging inside. Joey was lying on top of a blue-flowered bedspread that was all messed up beneath him. The bottom of one enlarged sock was pointed straight at the doorway, propped on top of a knee. Two pillows were piled beneath his head. They, too, had blue floral cases.

"Hey, Joey . . . see ya. Gotta go."

"Already?" Into the phone Joey said, "Just a minute."

Christopher flourished the pair of gloves. "Thanks. I enjoyed it. I'll try to stop by one of your games again before the season is over."

"Yeah, sure . . . hey . . . glad you came."

At the front door Lee was still waiting. He paused before her. Their eyes met, parted, met again. He became preoccupied with stacking and restacking his leather gloves.

"I'm not mad at you," he said. "It's just that . . . well, I'm a little frustrated." He gave in and looked directly into her autumn-colored eyes. They were much the same hue as the flowers she'd put on their supper table. They were eyes he thought of so much when he was away from her, eyes whose mood he'd learned to read so well. When he spoke, his voice came out in a gritty near-whisper. "What are we doing, Lee?"

"Healing," she said.

"Is that all?"

She looked away. "Please, Christopher."

He sighed and tapped his gloves on his palm, then slowly drew them on. So she wanted to pretend this was a platonic relationship. Hell and high water, the idea of it scared him worse than his feelings for her.

"Can I call you again?" he asked.

"I don't know," she said. "This is getting too complicated for me."

"Well, let me add a new wrinkle," he said, and without planning to, he leaned down and kissed her on the mouth, a kiss short enough to prevent immediate trouble but long enough to portend great long-range trouble ahead: This was no son's friend pecking a mother-figure on the cheek. She was still standing with her lips open in surprise when he said, low, "Sorry," and walked out without giving her a chance to speak.

He expected her to call and she did, though not until after eleven that night. He figured Joey must have been on the line all that time and it was the first chance she had to use it.

He was already in bed, lying awake in the dark thinking of her when the phone rang. He rolled over, felt for the receiver and said, "Hello."

"Hello," she returned, then nothing.

He cleared his throat and said, "Now I suppose *you're* mad at *me.*"

"Don't you ever do that again with my son in the house!"

"Why?"

"Oh, for heaven's sake, Christopher, what's the matter with you?"

"What's the matter with me? I don't know whether to treat you like my mother or my lover—that's what's the matter with me! So what do you want me to do? Do you want me to keep the hell out of there? Because I can do that, you know!"

The line got quiet for the longest time. Then she whispered, "Shit." He could almost see her leaning her forehead on the heel of one hand.

"Are you crying?"

"No, I'm not crying!"

He commenced rubbing his eyes, then sighed so hugely it sounded like a horse whickering.

"God, Lee, I don't know," he said, dropping his hand to the mattress. His answer took on more impact because no one had asked the question.

They stayed silent for so long his ears began to ring.

Finally she said, "You know what you just said . . . I mean about not knowing how to treat me? Well, the same is true for me and how to treat you. It's the creepiest thing I've ever been through in my life. You walk in here, and it's like Greg walking in. Only I can distinguish very clearly between you and Greg. You're . . . well, you're very different. You're Christopher, and when I'm with you the strange thing is, I hardly ever even think of Greg anymore. Then you go away and I'm deluged by guilt feelings, like I'm some . . . some pervert. I mean, I've read my psychology, too, you know! And my Greek mythology! I know about the Oedipus complex!" She had grown more agitated and sounded as if she were arguing with herself.

"Guilt feelings about what?"

"Oh, come on . . . this isn't some situation comedy we're playing in. This is real life, and you're not going to trick me into saying things I don't want to."

He said not a word, listening to the faint hum along the telephone wire and feeling their uncertainties stretch in both directions.

Finally she said, "Listen . . . I don't think we should see each other for a while.

I've been reading about grief, too, and I'm smart enough to see the similarities be-tween the way I'm acting and what they warn you against doing."

He took in the words, let them settle like a rock in his heart, then said thickly, "Okay . . . if that's the way you want it."

Her voice sounded sheer miserable. "It's not the way I want it. It's the way it's got to be."

"Yes, I understand."

More trembling silence, then she said, "Well . . . it's late. We've got church in the morning."

"Sure."

"Well . . . goodbye."

"Goodbye." Neither of them hung up. When they did, that would be it—their relationship would be over. So they clung to their receivers and the sound of each other's breathing for a few seconds longer. He pictured her in her blue-flowered bed. She pictured him in his mannishly plain one.

Finally, he said, "Thanks again for the supper. I practically felt like Ozzie Nel-son."

She couldn't find the wherewithal to laugh. Nothing seemed funny at that mo-ment. It felt as if nothing ever would again.

" 'Bye, Christopher."

" 'Bye, Lee."

This time he hung up, then lay in the dark wondering if her eyes were sting-ing like his.

For Lee, facing the future without him seemed a cruelty she didn't deserve. It was the abysmal time of year between the first frost and the holiday season, when the prospect of hibernating away indoors for the next six months only dampened her spirits further.

Janice got so busy at college Lee rarely spoke to her unless Lee was the one to initiate the call. Then the conversations were rushed and most often ended by Jan-ice: "Gosh, sorry to run, Mom, but so-and-so is waiting for me and we're running late, as usual."

Joey was smitten by first love. Many evenings after supper he'd spiff up like the froggie goin' a-courtin', and would walk a mile over to Sandy Parker's house, leav-ing Lee to find her own diversions. Occasionally Joey and Sandy would spend time at her house, monopolizing the living room where they made goo-goo eyes at one another in between tickling sessions on the sofa that were so embarrassing for Lee she'd finally leave them to themselves and hide away in her bedroom reading her *Flowers&* magazine.

Orrin and Peg Hillier set out on an extended trip to New England that would take them south along the entire Atlantic seaboard. They planned to be back in time for Thanksgiving.

Lee had only to call anyone she knew to have a companion for the evening. She went to Donna and Jim Clements' for supper twice, out to the movies with Sylvia and Barry, even to the Rum River Boutique with Nancy McFaddon one evening. There were parent/teacher conferences for Joey at the junior high, and final fall gardening in the backyard, and baked goods to be made for the annual autumn bake sale at church.

However, most evenings Lee spent alone.

One night shortly after ten o'clock she had turned off the lights and was standing at a front window in her pajamas, rubbing lotion into her hands and admiring a big harvest moon, when a black-and-white squad car cruised by so slowly she thought for a moment the driver had probably been able to see her standing in the dark window. She had no doubt it was Christopher. The white door of the car was picked out clearly by the blue-white moonlight, and his speed was so slow she was certain it could be no one else.

Dear God, she got a rush.

Standing there with her hands going motionless she felt her face heat, felt a reaching within, as if an inner voice beyond her control were calling to him.

He didn't stop, of course, just cruised past so silently she felt shaken by the realization that he'd been watching her house at night.

When she went to bed she lay flat on her back with the covers clamped tightly beneath her armpits, flattening her breasts, as if lying motionless and plank-stiff could negate the yearning she'd felt at the window a moment ago.

You've made the right decision, she told herself. *An affair with him would be disastrous. Scandalous. Imagine what people would say.*

Funny, her admonition did little to get her to sleep or to fill the gaping void in her life or to get Christopher off her mind through the days and nights that followed.

She remained firm in her resolve not to see Christopher again as the rains of mid-October turned into the frosts of late October, that stunning time of year when it was so hard to be alone. The world donned its gilded raiments. It burnished apples, turned pumpkins orange in the fields and dried corn upon its stalks.

The town began preparing for Halloween. Since 1920, when its civic leaders had put on its first Halloween celebration to divert old-time pranks such as putting wagons on roofs and overturning outhouses, Anoka had dubbed itself the Halloween Capital of the World. This year, as every year, events happened one upon another. There was a Fiddler Jamboree; the Pumpkin Bowl in which the Anoka Tornadoes played their archrivals, the Coon Rapids Cardinals; a senior citizens' card party, a round-robin horseshoe tournament and Bingo; a pumpkin pie bake-off; a lip-sync contest; and the Gray Ghost 5K Run and One-Mile Fitness Walk. The Knights of Columbus sponsored a haunted house out at the fairgrounds; merchants participated in a Moonlight Madness sale; and students from the Anoka Senior High painted all the store windows downtown. The events were to be culminated in the Friday afternoon kiddies' parade and the Saturday afternoon Grand Day Parade followed by the crowning of Miss Anoka at the senior high.

The entire celebration was supremely good for retail business.

And made one hell of a lot of extra work for the police force.

Being a downtown merchant, and dealing in the products she did, Lee found herself in the thick of it.

It seemed everybody wanted potted chrysanthemums for their doorsteps, wind socks shaped like ghosts or a pile of pumpkins to carve into jack-o'-lanterns. More homeowners decorated their yards than didn't, and the town took on a festive air with ghost effigies hanging from front-yard trees and doorways hung with black skeletons. Beside lampposts, hay bales, scarecrows and pumpkins appeared. And at Absolutely Floral, dried autumn wreaths for front doors nearly outsold fresh-cut flower arrangements.

On the day the high school seniors came to paint their front window, Lee and Sylvia were busy taking care of some older flowers at the rear of the store. The place smelled like hot apple cider from an electric pot near the front where a sign said HELP YOURSELF. The teenagers were painting the glass, drinking cider and having a wonderful time. The bookkeeper was upstairs in the office doing his biweekly work, and two customers were browsing through the display area where Pat Galsworthy was answering questions for them. Lee was taking care of the unpalatable task of changing the water in a canister of multicolored stocks, a member of the radish family that gave off such a hot radishy smell it burned her eyes.

"Lord, this stuff is foul," she said, transferring the stocks to fresh water, emptying out the old and filling the used container with chlorine bleach and water.

Sylvia went on washing out a container and said, "Mom called yesterday. They were in Brattleboro, Vermont. Did she call you?"

"Not since Tuesday."

"She said it's beautiful there."

"I know. She said they're having trouble moving on."

"Did she talk to you about Thanksgiving?"

"No."

"She wants to have it at her house this year."

"Fine."

"She said that by the time they get back she'll be anxious to cook again and they'll get here in plenty of time for her to make preparations."

"Great. I'm glad I don't have to do it. I'm really not in the mood this year."

"She's going to want us each to bring something, of course."

"She'll ask me to do pies, I'm sure. She loves my pies."

"I'm taking my broccoli casserole and wild rice. Oh, by the way, she said I should tell you to ask Chris."

Lee was pouring Hi-lex water from one container to another. The stream stopped as she looked up at her sister. Sylvia didn't notice and went on talking. "She and Dad really like him. Did you know that when Greg died he even sent them a sympathy card? Mom just can't get over that. And I *know* he really impressed her when he chose her for his volleyball team on the Fourth of July. Have you talked to him lately?"

As Sylvia looked up, Lee snapped back to washing the containers.

"No, I haven't."

"Well, give him a call and tell him he's invited for Thanksgiving dinner."

"Yeah, sure . . . I will."

"So, how's Joey doing with his little heartthrob?" The talk moved on and the subject of Christopher was dropped. The teenagers finished their window painting and came back to thank the owners for letting them do it. Sylvia went to the cooler and sent them each away with an orange carnation. The bookkeeper came downstairs and said he'd finished all his posting and needed some signatures. Lee dried her hands and signed. Sylvia and Pat Galsworthy began getting the store ready for closing. When Pat had said goodbye and left the two sisters alone, Lee turned off the radio and looked across the room at Sylvia, who was donning her coat. She opened her mouth to speak and knew that if she said she didn't want to invite Christopher for the holiday, Sylvia would look at her in stunned amazement and ask "Why?"

She clapped her mouth closed, got on her coat and the two went out the back door together into a swirl of dried leaves that were dancing and rustling like a whirlpool in the close quarters between the buildings. Sylvia had already reached her car before Lee called from beside her own, "Sylvia . . . about Thanksgiving . . ."

Sylvia turned, holding her car keys, waiting.

But Lee had no logical excuse for eliminating Chris from their holiday plans. Suddenly she found herself extemporizing.

"I have a new vegetable recipe I'd like to try. Would you mind making the pies this year?"

Sylvia looked doubtful. "Mom will be disappointed. I can't make crust nearly as well as you."

"Well, maybe I can make the pies and the casserole, too."

"Let's wait till Mom gets home and talk over the menu then."

Chicken! Lee thought when she'd gotten into her car. She sat without starting the engine, gripping the wheel and going nowhere, frustrated and feeling like a jerk for cutting Christopher out when he so looked forward to being with the family on holidays. She was made more miserable by the fact that she was planning a lie, for when the time came she'd tell everybody that Christopher had to work on Thanksgiving day.

The morning of the Grand Day Parade Anoka got crazy well before noon. Thousands of people flooded in, coming to shop, eat lunch and get a good spot on the curb along the parade route. Cars inched along on every side street, looking for parking spaces. Children in costume, hand-towed by their mothers, passed the store windows in droves. Lee looked out between the tempera-painted corn shocks and saw people setting up lawn chairs on the sidewalk out front. Inside, the place was a madhouse. One or two real customers were honestly doing business, but the rest were only creating chaos. Some woman with a bawling baby was looking at greeting cards and wrinkling them when the baby threw itself backward in her arms. A bunch of little boys had discovered the free apple cider and were running in and out, using up her paper cups and bringing their friends in to empty the hot pot. An older woman with a frantic look on her face limped in and asked, "Could I use your toilet, please?" A representative of the Miss Anoka Pageant came tearing in, demanding, "The corsages for the queen candidates—I need them, quick!" The phone rang incessantly. Customers lined up at the checkout counter. The door opened again and the backdraft blew over a wire stand holding a potted cyclamen plant.

At one o'clock, Lee clasped her head and said, "Enough already! Let's lock this place up!"

With a feeling of relief they locked the door, put on their jackets and went out to join the throng on the curb waiting to see the color guard come marching down Main Street to the drumbeat of the Anoka High School band.

Ah, sweet relief! It was a heavenly day, and so good to be outside. Overhead, the sky was deep blue, mottled here and there with puffy white clouds. The temperature on the bank sign read forty-seven degrees, so the sun felt splendid through Lee's denim jacket. Down at the river crossing, the Rum River was frothing over the dam. Along Main Street all the businesses had put out orange-and-black flags, American flags, flags with the school colors and some whose designation was merely decorative.

A police car came inching by, and Lee's heart lurched. But it was someone else at the wheel, not Christopher.

A few yards up the curb some teenagers had gathered and were laughing and jostling each other. One of them threw a basketball-sized pumpkin as high into the air as he could. It hit the blacktop and splattered ten yards, sending people jumping back, then brushing at the orange strings of pumpkin guts hanging from their clothes. Some laughter went up, along with some cursing and complaining.

At the corner of the block Christopher had pulled up his squad car at an angle, cutting off traffic on a cross street. He'd been standing at the front of the car with the flashing reds on, watching the crowd when the pumpkin hit the pavement.

Immediately he headed that way.

He walked along the concrete gutter in front of the gathered crowd, unhurried but authoritative.

Reaching the three rowdy teenage boys, he asked, "You guys throw that?"

One of them said, "Shit no, man. An old lady did. She went that way, didn't she, Kevin?"

Kevin said, "Oh, yeah, way down that way."

Christopher remained calm. "You're going to have to clean it up."

One of the boys said, "Screw you."

An onlooker yelled, "It flew clear over here!"

A block away, the color guard was approaching, followed by the band— seventy pairs of white shoes stomping through all that pumpkin hash. "Now!" Christopher ordered. "Because if that band gets here first, I'm going to start taking names, and I'm sure a lot of these people would be interested in sending you their dry-cleaning bills."

One of the teenagers relented. "What are we supposed to pick it up with?"

Someone handed over a newspaper. The three boys took the paper, went out into the street, scraped up the pumpkin slime with their hands and piled it into the newspaper while Officer Lallek stood by with his thumbs hooked into his belt, watching.

They came running back to the curb just as the American Legion color guard came by with the flags. Behind them, the band was blaring. Christopher pointed down the block in the direction of his patrol car. "There's a garbage receptacle down there."

Grumbling, the boys went toward it.

From the curb in front of her store, Lee Reston had seen it all. She might have willfully cut Christopher out of her life, but the sight of him—particularly in uniform, performing his duties—still had the power to switch her heart into overdrive. There was so much noise that she hadn't heard his voice, but she'd watched without once pulling her eyes from the scene. He looked as strikingly attractive as ever. The color guard passed and she forgot to stand at attention. The band approached and she forgot to watch their synchronized footsteps. Instead, she watched the visor of Christopher's hat above the heads between them, hoping he would turn her way and find her standing there. He removed his hat and placed it over his heart as Old Glory waved past.

He watched the flag.

She watched him.

He stood erect and respectful, raising such a turmoil within her that it felt as if the drums were beating deep in her breast.

The color guard passed and Christopher replaced his hat, leaned over to say something to a small child in the crowd. He laughed, touched the child's head, then straightened, glancing down the street while the band came on, their brass blaring.

As if he sensed himself being studied, he turned and looked over his left shoulder in Lee's direction. Their gazes collided. Neither of them smiled, but he began coming toward her with the same unruffled pace at which he'd approached the boys who'd thrown the pumpkin.

Flustered, she turned her attention to the band, watched their ranks passing by as even as cornrows. The march ended and the drum section took up a street beat—*throom, thr-thr throom!*—tenors and bass drums answering the snares with such booming vigor it battered the eardrums.

Then Christopher was before her and she could no longer keep herself from looking up at his smooth-shaven face. His mouth moved. He must have said hello, though the drums covered it up. She said the word, too, though it was lost in the reverberations around them. Their attraction for each other and denial of it were in the forefront of their encounter, coloring it with polite distancing while the entire city of Anoka and her sister looked on. Finally he realized how long he'd focused on Lee, and touched his hatbrim in a polite hello to Sylvia and Pat Galsworthy. A boy on a BMX bike was doing wheelies, threatening to wipe out the rear corner of the band. "Gotta go," he said, and escaped under the guise of duty.

Against her will, Lee's eyes followed him as he motioned the boy over closer to the curb, then answered a greeting from someone in the crowd with whom he stood talking, Christopher with one foot on the street, one on the curb.

Further contingents of the parade passed by—the grand marshal, kids in costume, the Shriners on their purring Harleys, more kids in costume.

Lee pretended to watch the movement in the street, but all the while she kept Christopher in her peripheral vision. He visited with people. He touched kids on their heads. He caught some candy thrown by a clown and gave it to one of them. He plucked up his radio and put it to his mouth, scowled westward up the street, then turned purposefully and headed back toward his car. Passing Lee, he gave her only a glance, and then he was gone.

The parade kept coming—endless kids in costume, the Forest Lake band, the Hopkins band, a float holding the school cooks from Coon Rapids Senior High, more floats, more bands, the football team on a flatbed truck and the cheerleaders waving pompons, the royalty from the Miss Anoka Pageant—but long before the big red city fire trucks rolled by with their air horns deafening, signaling the parade's end, it had ended for Lee Reston.

Chapter 10

She didn't call him about Thanksgiving.

On November eighteenth her parents got back into town and Peg called right away. She wanted Lee to make the pumpkin pies and was planning on twenty-three for the holiday meal. She said, "Chris is coming, isn't he?"

"I'm not sure. I think he has to work."

Peg said, "Oh, what a shame."

Lee hung up, burdened by an enormous load of guilt.

On the Tuesday before Thanksgiving, Peg and Orrin Hillier were at the Red Owl store shopping for their Thanksgiving turkey when Peg turned into the frozen-food aisle and nearly collided with Christopher, just off duty, still dressed in his blues and shopping for his supper.

"Christopher! Well, for goodness sake, it's you!"

"Hello, Mrs. Hillier."

She gave him a hug, which he returned, holding his frozen chicken divan away from her back. He and Orrin shook hands. They stood and talked awhile, about Orrin and Peg's trip to New England, the stupendous fall colors they'd seen and the covered bridges of Vermont. They praised the architectural splendors of Charleston and the fine golf courses of Myrtle Beach.

Then Peg said, "I was so sorry to hear you couldn't make it to our house for Thanksgiving dinner."

Unsure of what was going on, Christopher covered his surprise well. "I'm sorry to miss it, too. You know how a bachelor loves home cooking."

"I was hoping you'd get the holiday off, but Lee said you have to work."

Out of nowhere he blurted the truth. "Not until three."

"Not until three! Why, then, it's settled. We eat at one and you'll be there."

He smiled. "Thanks, Mrs. Hillier. In that case, I will."

"The mulled cider will be hot at eleven, so come early."

"Your family is so good about including me. I just can't thank you enough."

Peg Hillier looked pleased and patted his shoulder. "Nonsense," she said. "You're like one of the family yourself." As proof, he received a grandmotherly hug of farewell.

On the day before Thanksgiving, Lee arranged an elegant centerpiece for Rodney to deliver to her parents' home. It was a lavish mixture of apricot ranunculus, kalanchoes and an abundance of sprayed pomegranates, all tied together with dark trailing ivy and wired bicolored grosgrain ribbon. She put it in a low, gleaming oval of polished brass and signed the card *Happy Thanksgiving and welcome home. Love, Sylvia and Lee.* All the while Lee worked on it she was recalling last Thanksgiving when the family had gathered at her house and Greg had still been alive. How many months since he'd died? Five, yet on given days she was still assaulted by anguish at the realization that he was gone forever. She supposed it was natural that holidays would be the worst.

Lee put the last twist on the wired ribbon and was standing back assessing the arrangement when Sylvia came over to the arranging table and said reverently, "Wow." They stood for a moment admiring the color, balance and texture of the creation.

"It's a masterpiece." Sylvia draped a wrist over Lee's shoulder. "I wish I could arrange something like that just once in my life."

Lee put her arm around Sylvia's waist. "And I wish I was better at the business side of business. It's why we work together so well, isn't it?"

"Mom's going to love it."

"Mm."

To Sylvia, Lee seemed unusually quiet and subdued. "Something wrong?"

Lee only stared at the flowers.

"You thinking of Greg?" Lee got tears in her eyes and Sylvia gripped her shoulder, pulled her over and put her temple against her sister's.

"It's just that it's Thanksgiving . . . the first one without him. We're supposed to give thanks for all our blessings, but I'm not feeling especially blessed right now."

"I know," Sylvia whispered. "I know."

They stood awhile, staring at the flowers, which had paled in importance. In a quiet, lost voice, Lee admitted, "I've been so lonely, Sylvia."

"Oh, honey," Sylvia said sadly.

Lee blinked, scraped the tears off her cheeks and shook herself. "Oh, shoot, I don't know what's the matter with me! I do have plenty to be thankful for, and lots of it is right here at this minute." She gave Sylvia a hug. "Thanks, sis. I feel better now. Just getting it off my chest makes me feel better."

That night at home, Lee tallied up other blessings for which she should be grateful. It snowed that night, a light, fluffy blanket of white. Janice came home from college, Joey stayed home, and the three of them had a lot of fun making four pumpkin pies and an artichoke casserole together.

They awakened on Thanksgiving morning to a pearl-gray sky and a world garbed in ermine. The snow had stopped falling and no wind blew. Still in her nightclothes, Lee looked out the window and said, "Yesss!"

They dressed in their finery, went to church, and from there straight out to the Hillier home.

Peg and Orrin lived several miles north of Anoka beside the Rum River on four very pricey acres covered with red oaks. The trees looked rich beyond description in their new dressing of white. Contrasted against the snow, the black, knurled branches created a stark, stunning tableau like a pen-and-ink drawing. The driveway was long and curved, wending between the oaks on its way to a sprawling, single-level house of salmon-colored brick that had once been featured in a photo layout in *Better Homes and Gardens*. Both inside and out, the place radiated class and good taste. When the house was being custom-built, Peg Hillier had personally chosen every fixture and feature, working not only with the builder, but also with a Minneapolis decorator whose clientele list included officers of the 3M corporation, doctors from the Mayo Clinic and members of the Minnesota Orchestra.

When Lee and the kids arrived, Peg came to answer the door herself, still an impeccably groomed woman in spite of the faint roundness at her middle. "Darlings. Happy Thanksgiving." They all exchanged kisses and hugs, juggling pies and a casserole dish while Orrin came to take their coats and offer hugs, too.

Peg said, "We're having drinks in the study so go right on in."

Lee said, "I had to stop and pick up the ice cream on the way and the carton was a mess. I've got to wash my sticky hands, then I'll be right with you."

In the bathroom a clover-leaf-shaped whirlpool tub was surrounded by carefully placed pots of leafless corkscrew sticks and immense baskets of black and white towels. While Lee washed and dried her hands she heard Sylvia's laugh and a rustle of voices raised in greeting. She opened a drawer, found her mother's brush and ran it through her hair. The doorbell rang. Someone else arrived and voices blended, then faded off toward the study. Sylvia's little granddaughter, Marnie, came running down the hall and into the bathroom, her patent-leather shoes slapping against the tile.

"Hi, Auntie Lee," she said.

"Hi, Marnie!"

"I got a new dress!" It was frosted with lace and ruffled as a tutu.

"Ooo, is it ever pretty!"

"Mommy said to blow my nose." She went up on tiptoe but couldn't reach the tissue box on the vanity counter. Lee helped her and the child chattered all the while . . . about her new white tights and how her mom had brought along her snow pants and boots today so she and her brothers could go out and play in the snow later.

Lee snapped off the light and the two of them left the bathroom together.

"Want to go see the flowers?" Lee asked.

The child nodded and offered her hand.

They cut across one end of the entry hall where a great-aunt and uncle were arriving, and moved on toward the rear of the house where the side-by-side dining room and living room looked out over a view that was the house's greatest asset. Roosting high over the river, the building's entire eastern exposure was made of

glass, and the view beyond it was splendid today with the water still tumbling between the white wooded banks where squirrels and blue jays added a touch that no
decorator, whatever her credits, could have provided.

The tables—two of them butted—were spread in unabashed resplendence,
stretching across the archway and spanning both rooms, which were carpeted in
palest taupe and decorated with a lot of white upholstery on straight-lined functional furniture. The tables were spread with white damask and set with Bavarian
bone china chosen by the decorator to complement the traditional decor.

If there was one thing Peg prided herself on, it was good taste.

Marnie was dancing around, holding one foot up behind her, touching the backs
of chairs, too young to be impressed by the lavish layout of finery that glittered and
shone before the long, bright windows.

Lee checked the flowers: They looked truly worthy of a Peg Hillier table setting. She wandered along, passing several place settings, noting that her mother had
paid her usual attention to every detail. Who but Peg Hillier used place cards anymore?

"Did you make those flowers?" Marnie asked, still dancing on one foot.

"Yes, I did."

"They're pretty."

"Thank you."

Marnie scampered off. Lee took one last look at the flowers and turned toward
the sound of happy chatter coming from the study. It was a large room at the front
of the house with a brass-screened fireplace where a festive fire burned. Relatives
sat on the brown leather sofas or stood in groups chatting with the usual exuberance of arrival time. Peg stood beside a skirted round table ladling hot cider into a
crystal cup, adding a cinnamon stick and handing it to . . .

Christopher Lallek!

Lee felt her face go red and her chest constrict.

He took the cup and napkin, smiled and thanked Peg, then put it to his mouth
to sip while turning toward Janice, who was talking and smiling up at him, already
holding a cup of her own.

She said something and he laughed, then drank again. Over the rim of his cup
he saw Lee for the first time, standing stricken in the doorway. Of the two, he managed far more poise than she. No one would have guessed there was the slightest
strain between them as he lowered the cup—smile intact—and said to Janice, "Oh,
there's your mother."

Lee moved into the room toward him—what else could she do?

Janice turned and said, excitedly, "Mom, why didn't you tell me Christopher
was coming?"

"I thought he had to work."

"Not until three, it turned out," he said, then leaned to kiss her cheek. "Happy
Thanksgiving, Mrs. Reston. I'm glad I could make it after all."

"So am I," she responded, finding that deep in her heart it was true. Lord, how
she'd missed him. They had parted at her request, but she'd come to believe that
request—prompted by forces other than what she felt for him—was one of the most

misguided of her life. She had said to him once that she was not a lonely woman, then yesterday to Sylvia she'd said just the opposite. Her loneliness had begun, she realized now, since he had come into her life and then been exiled from it.

He was dressed in gray wool trousers, white shirt, blue floral tie and a finely knit shawl collar sweater of navy blue. He was well proportioned, fit, trim, and wore clothing well. So rarely had she seen him in anything other than his uniform or jeans. Shorts in the summer, of course, but his clothing today lent him a new aspect that brought to Lee feelings she hadn't experienced since Bill was alive.

It was sexual attraction, pure and simple. And for the first time, she admitted it.

She watched him with her family. Every person in the room knew him. Everyone liked him. But what, exactly, would their reaction be if she started dating him? *Really* dating him.

Janice looked radiant. She stood beside him, looking up, adoring, offering small talk that often made him laugh. Once she touched his arm; it was only briefly, but Lee understood what kind of feelings women put into touches like that. It was flirtation of the subtlest kind. Studying the two of them as they stood talking, Lee admitted to herself what a beautiful couple they made. He, at thirty, so healthy and well groomed. She, at twenty-three, with her dark wavy hair and perfect skin; not a wrinkle beside her mouth or eyes; in the full flush of youth. Lord in heaven, Lee didn't understand this. How could such a bizarre attraction have happened? Why herself? Why not Janice, who was so much more suitable?

Peg called from the kitchen that she needed help, and Orrin rounded up a few of the women to fill wineglasses and carry bowls. He himself went along to carve the turkey and dig the stuffing from inside the bird.

As Lee circled the table with the wine decanter, she noted what she'd missed earlier: Christopher's place card at a chair between her own and Janice's.

Without asking, she went to the refrigerator, found some cranberry juice and filled his glass with that.

The placement of guests began amid far less than the usual shuffling and shifting, due to Peg's carefully calligraphic place cards. Christopher found himself between the two Reston women and politely seated them both, pulling out their chairs before taking his own.

Orrin said, "Let's all join hands now for a prayer."

Around the table everyone formed a ring. Lee took Joey's hand, on her left, and Christopher's, on her right. His hand was smooth and warm. She was momentarily conscious of her own being rough and dry from too many prickly flower stems and too many dunkings in chlorine water. She was more conscious of a current flowing between them during the warm, firm contact of flesh that seemed to link more than their hands.

Orrin bowed his head.

"Dear Lord, on this day of thanksgiving we give special thanks for everyone around this table, for their health and prosperity and happiness. We thank you for the bounty you've given us, and ask that you watch over us all in the year to come. We also ask that you look after Greg, who's missing from this table this year, but is there with you . . ." Lee felt Christopher's fingers tighten on her own and returned the pressure. ". . . and that you help each of us accept his absence and not question your reason for taking him. Give special strength to Lee, Janice and Joey in the year ahead. Until we gather again next year at this time . . . thank you, Lord, for everything."

Few at the table lifted their heads immediately after the prayer. Neither did Christopher release Lee's hand but held it under the tablecloth a moment longer and looked over at the tears in her downturned eyes.

"I'm glad to be here," he whispered, giving her hand an extra squeeze before finally releasing it.

Oh, that meal. That beautiful, awful, high-tension meal, with Christopher so close she could smell the wool of his sweater, and touch his sleeve, and watch his hands moving over the silverware, all the while pretending none of it meant anything out of the ordinary. The family probably attributed her unusual quiet to Orrin's prayer, though everyone recovered from it nicely and began chattering.

She forced herself to speak to Christopher lest the others wonder at her reticence.

"Your glass is filled with cranberry juice," she said.

"Thank you."

"So you're on mid-shift today."

"Yes. Three to eleven."

"Will it be busy?"

"Tonight it will. Lot of college kids home for the weekend, getting together at bars. You know kids and alcohol."

Askance, she watched him put away a helping of potatoes and gravy that covered half his plate.

"So how about you?" he asked. "Tomorrow's the biggie, huh?"

"That's right—biggest shopping days of the year, tomorrow and Saturday. I'm not looking forward to it."

"And after that you're into the Christmas rush."

"That's already started. In my business we have to start preparing permanent Christmas arrangements so they're ready to sell on Thanksgiving weekend."

They talked about superficialities only, locking away what really mattered and behaving like Greg's friend and Greg's mother with Janice and Joey near enough to hear every word they said.

At two o'clock Chris checked his watch and said to Peg, "I'm sorry to do a hit-and-run, but I have to be at roll call in thirty minutes, dressed like a cop." He pushed back his chair and rose, holding back his tie. "That means a stop at home first."

Peg looked disappointed. "So soon? But you haven't even had your pie."

"Someone else can have my piece. I'm so full."

"I'll send one with you."

"Oh, no, that's not necessary. Everything was so delicious."

They went on exchanging dialogue while he moved away from the table and Peg rose to disregard his polite refusal of the pie. Orrin stood and those around the table bid Christopher farewell. After a moment of indecision, Lee got up too and went with him to the foyer while Orrin got his gray wool chesterfield coat and plaid scarf, holding them as Christopher slipped them on. Peg emerged from the kitchen with a triangular piece of tinfoil.

"Here's your pie. A Thanksgiving dinner just isn't complete without pumpkin pie. Lee made it."

"Thank you," he said. "I see where Lee gets her compulsion to send leftovers home with everybody. And thank you for another wonderful holiday." He kissed Peg's cheek, shook Orrin's hand and kissed Lee's cheek.

She opened the door and said, " 'Bye."

" 'Bye, and thanks again."

She lined the edge of the door with one hand while watching him walk down the wet driveway to his Explorer, which waited in a turnaround some distance away.

The wind had come up and lifted the end of his scarf as he opened the truck door and waved before getting in. He always did that—waved that way—and Lee was struck with warm familiarity watching him do so again.

As usual, from the moment he drove away the ebullience went out of the day.

Lee and the kids stayed till 6:30 P.M., then Janice said she wanted to get home and change clothes: She, too, was going out with a bunch of friends that night.

At home, Joey and Lee changed into sweat suits and turned on the TV while Janice switched on the radio in the bathroom and spent time redoing her makeup and hair. Jane and Sandy came by for her at 8:30, leaving Lee and Joey watching an old rerun of a Waltons Thanksgiving movie.

At 9:15 the doorbell rang.

Lee glanced over at Joey, sprawled on the sofa, and discovered he was sound asleep.

She got up from her chair and went to answer.

Christopher stood on the front step, dressed in uniform, his squad car parked in the driveway behind him with its engine still running and the parking lights on.

She opened the storm door and he held it that way while she stood on the level above him in her sweat suit and slippers.

"I want to talk to you," he said—no smile, no softness, just a statement of fact. "Could you come out to the car for a minute?"

"Joey is here."

"Tell him where you're going and come outside, please."

"Can't we talk in the house?"

"No, not with Joey there."

Suddenly, things inside her began trembling. How indomitable he was to face this head on, far more than she, who had eluded the confrontation in various temporizing ways.

"All right," she said, "let me get my jacket." She opened a coat-closet door and called into the living room, "Joey, Christopher is here. I'm going out in the car to talk to him a minute."

He shifted onto his left side, facing the back of the sofa, and mumbled something while the TV played behind him.

Outside, she preceded Christopher down the walk to his squad car. He opened the passenger door and waited while she got in. Inside it was warm, the heater blowing. A multitude of gear formed a barricade between his half of the seat and hers. A rifle stood barrel-up beside her left knee. On the dash a large radio, glowing with red lights, was mounted beside a larger speaker pointed at the driver's seat. On the seat itself a wooden cup holder was secured in place with space behind it for a bunch of notebooks that were wedged upright. Behind the driver's seat a glass partition divided the front from the back, while behind her a steel mesh partition did the same.

He got in and slammed the door. On the radio, the county dispatcher's voice crackled intermittently. He reached up and lowered the volume, then took off his hat and wedged it behind the speaker. Resting his left wrist on top of the steering wheel, he turned to look at her.

After an uncertain stretch of silence they both spoke at once.

"These past few weeks—" he said.

"I'm sorry about—" she said.

They both clipped off their remarks.

She picked up first. "I'm sorry about the Thanksgiving invitation."

"This isn't about that. I understand perfectly well why you didn't call and ask me."

"It was selfish of me. I'm sorry."

"Apology accepted. Now let me say what I came here to say." He sat back, looking straight out over the steering wheel at her garage door, which was closed for once. "These past few weeks have been bad. I don't like the way things were left between us. I've been miserable, how about you?"

"Lonely." She, too, looked straight out over the dash.

He turned to study her profile, dimly outlined by the pale lights from the dash. The radio light put a ruby haze on the tips of her eyelashes and rouged her cheeks. Her mouth looked somewhat sullen. "I know all the reasons we shouldn't keep seeing each other, but somehow when I add them up they don't seem to matter much. The plain truth is, I want to see you again, and I want it clear that I'm not coming around looking for leftover lasagna, or for sympathy, or to fill in for your son. I want us to be together without all that baggage between us, but I'm working midshift right now so the timing is crummy. My next night off is Sunday. Would you go out to a movie with me?"

"What would I tell Joey?"

"Tell him the truth."

"Oh, Christopher, I can't do that."

"Why not?"

"You know why not."

"You didn't hesitate to tell him we were going walking together last summer, or swimming, or riding on a Ferris wheel."

"But the difference was, he went with us most of the time."

"No, the difference is in how *you* perceive us, not in how *he* will. If you tell him you're going out with me, he'll accept it. Just lay it out there, plain and simple."

"I'm scared," she said.

He let out a mirthless nasal huff, rested his elbow on the window ledge, pinched his bottom lip and looked off to his left.

"Well, I am!" she said defensively.

He rolled his head to face her. "Yeah, this is pretty scary, going out to a movie." His tone became more assertive. "Don't make anything of it. Just tell him, 'Chris and I are going out to a movie. See you later,' and walk out with me."

She thought about it awhile and surprised herself by agreeing. "All right, I will."

She seemed to have surprised him, too. He said, disbelievingly, "Really?"

"Yes, really."

He reached for the radio volume though she hadn't even heard the word "Bravo" signaling a call for the Anoka officers.

". . . reporting a vehicle going north on southbound lane of Main."

He plucked his mike from the dashboard and said, "Forty-one to base. Did you copy if that was West Main or East Main?"

"East Main."

"Ten-four," he said, then to Lee. "I've got to go."

She opened her door and the dome light came on. "I'll see you Sunday."

"I'll call with the time."

"Okay." She got out.

"Hey, Lee?"

She leaned down and looked across the seat at him.

"Good pie. I had it on my break."

She smiled and slammed the door.

On Sunday night she didn't have to worry. Janice went back to her own place in the late afternoon; Joey got listless and called Denny Whitman, then announced, "I'm gonna go over to Denny's house and play video games. Can you give me a ride?"

"Sure," she said, giving herself clear sailing, even as far as getting ready was concerned.

With the house to herself, she experienced a sense of ambivalence about what to wear, how much to fuss, whether or not to wear perfume. Lord in heaven, she was going on a date for the first time in twenty-six years. She was terrified!

She put on a pair of blue jeans (an effort to reduce the significance of this event) and a pullover sweater, the same makeup she wore to work every day and the same amount of perfume. Her hair? Well, her hair came as it was. She tugged at it, calling up a memory of Janice's long, young mane, and wondered again how a man of Christopher's age could prefer her over her daughter.

He arrived at the time they'd arranged, and she hurried to the door with a queer tight feeling in her chest, blushing maybe the tiniest bit, wondering what in the world she was letting herself in for.

He was wearing jeans and a red down-filled jacket and acted much less flustered than she.

"Hi," he said, stepping inside and closing the door with the small of his back. "All ready?"

"If you don't mind, I'd like to call Joey first. He's at Denny Whitman's play-ing video games. I'm not sure if he needs a ride home or not."

"Okay."

While she dialed on the kitchen phone and spoke to Joey, Christopher ambled in behind her and sauntered around the room, looking at this and that, slapping a pair of leather gloves against his thigh. He glanced at a Pyrex baking dish holding leftover peach cobbler on the stove, and at a note on the refrigerator door that said *Pick up watch at jeweler's.* He bent over the kitchen table and read a school an-nouncement Joey had brought home about upcoming teachers' workshop days.

Plainly, he heard her say, "I'm going to a movie with Christopher, but we should be back by nine-thirty," and after a pause, *"The Firm."*

He was watching her and listening quite pointedly when she answered Joey's question about what they were going to see. She spoke for a minute longer, then hung up and told Chris, "Denny's dad will bring him home."

To his credit, Christopher refrained from saying I told you so.

In the front hall he held her denim jacket while she slipped it on; at his truck, he opened her door . . . just like a real date.

During the movie he sat low on his tailbone with both elbows on the armrests. Sometimes their elbows touched. There was a kiss on-screen, and throughout it Christopher and Lee kept their eyes riveted on the scene and wondered what the other was thinking.

In the truck afterward he asked, "Did you like it?"

"Yes. Did you?"

"Not as well as the book."

"Oh, it was better than the book!"

The discussion lasted all the way home. When they got there the lights were on just as she'd left them. Joey's bedroom was in the rear so they couldn't tell if he was home yet or not.

"Do you want to come in and have a piece of peach cobbler and ice cream?" she asked.

"Sure."

They got out and went inside.

Pulling off her jacket she called, "Joey? Are you here?"

No answer.

She threw the jacket on a living room chair and went back to his room to find it dark. When she returned to the kitchen Christopher had hung his jacket on the back of a chair.

"He's still gone. He knows he's got to be home by ten or he's in trouble." It was 9:45.

She got out two sauce dishes, put peach cobbler in them, set them in the mi-crowave and took ice cream from the freezer. When she tried to scoop it out, her muscles bulged, but nothing else moved.

"Can I help?" he asked.

She gave him the ice-cream scoop and opened a drawer to find spoons.

The buzzer went off on the microwave and she carried the two bowls to him, waited while he added the ice cream, then took the desserts to the table while he put the ice cream away in the freezer.

They did all this without ever so much as brushing against each other.

They sat down. The house was intimately quiet—no radio, no television, no Joey moving around anywhere.

She picked up her spoon and gouged into the cobbler, then glanced up to find Christopher intent on her, sitting motionless, his wrists resting against the edge of the table beside his bowl. His blue eyes were steady, smileless, sure.

He said, "Let's get this over with," and took the spoon from her hand, put it back in the bowl and drew her toward him around the corner of the table. She let herself be pulled sideways onto his lap while his arms came around her and his face lifted to kiss her. There was no subtle foolery, no dissembling, not from the first. The kiss was wholly sexual, wet and filled with motion. He tilted his head back, opened his lips and stroked her teeth and tongue. She looped her arms around his neck and let it happen . . . and happen . . . until her heart seemed to expand against her ribs, leaving little room for her lungs to fill and empty. They tasted and stroked each other in the way each had imagined many times, in a whorl of sleek tongues and moist lips, while a full minute slipped away, and then two. In the middle of that time, he shifted her on his lap, dropping her to one side, bending above her until they were twisted together like a pair of tree trunks from a long-ago storm.

It ended lingeringly, with an easing of his hold and a slow unwinding of their bodies until her face was again above his. Their lips parted but stayed close. Their breathing was strident. His hands rested lightly on her sides.

He spoke first, in a voice half-trapped in his throat. "I wasn't sure I could choke down those peaches without getting this out of the way first."

"Me either," she answered, and slipped from his lap to return to her chair.

They picked up their spoons and each ate a bite of warm cobbler and cold ice cream. The air around them seemed smothering, as if it contained too little oxygen for their needs. She glanced up and saw him watching her, his elbows on the table and his spoon leaving his lips. Suddenly, the nine years' dearth of physical affection seemed to catch her like the crack of a whip. It coiled around her body, knocked the spoon from her hand and hauled her from her chair back to his.

It happened so fast. One moment she was safely seated. The next she was standing above him with her hands on his face, lifting it, bending above it and picking up where they'd left off moments ago. And ten seconds after that—without a break in the kiss—she had thrown one leg over his lap and straddled him, striking the table edge with her hip, then taking a ride with him as he pivoted his chair at a sharper angle away from the table.

His arms slid low, pulling her flush against him. She embraced him from her high vantage point, kissing his warm supple mouth while his hands slid around the backs of her thighs and cupped them gently from behind, near the bend of her knees. They shared the flavor of peaches and cream from within each other's mouths, and that sleek fit of two tongues mating, of lips sliding in an endless quest. They had put this off so long it felt like a reward which they shared. They did so, however, sitting smack in view of the front door, while her mind clamored, *Don't come in yet, Joey, please don't come in!*

When things got too crazy inside her, she drew back, as one drugged, realizing she had to get off his lap. "I have to—"

His open mouth cut off the words. His arms snapped her back where she'd been and his shoulder blades came away from the chair. They'd played the song and dance so long that they explored now with exquisite relief, tasting each other and letting their feelings carry the reckless moment. It fled her mind how young he was, for this close, age had no significance. It fled his mind how old she was, for it had never mattered to him nearly as much as it had to her. Kissing, they were merely man and woman, and very facile ones at that.

They ended the kiss mutually, if reluctantly.

Though their mouths parted, their eyes refused. They sat beguiled, breathing hard, a little stunned, his hands still cupping the backs of her thighs in her tight blue jeans.

"Joey could come," she whispered, and slowly swung her leg off him, his right hand trailing around her kneecap, lingering there until she reluctantly backed off and returned to her chair.

They centered themselves before their peach cobbler, which was now surrounded by a lake of melted ice cream. She picked up her spoon and watched the white liquid drip from its tip. She looked up at him.

"Do you know how long it's been since I've done that?"

"No, but I'd like to."

"Nine years."

"Are you kidding? That's not natural."

She shrugged.

"You never kissed anyone since your husband died?"

"A few times I did, a year or so after he died. But never like this. Always testing myself to see if I could, then afterwards feeling as if I wanted to hurry home and brush my teeth."

"And what do you feel like now?"

"I feel . . . a little scared. A little surprised. But brushing my teeth is the farthest thing from my mind."

He gave a smile that was quickly spirited away by the gravity of what had just happened, the call of their bodies for more, the near certainty that this was only the beginning. They sat as they were, with the house's emptiness beating around them, their food forgotten, studying each other in an elaborate silence.

Finally Christopher pushed his chair back and said, "I think I'd better go." His voice sounded like someone else's, throaty with suppressed emotion. He rose and threaded his arms through the sleeves of his jacket, fitted the zipper together and raised it to pocket level. He took out his gloves but held them without putting them on.

She sat on the edge of her chair, tipped forward from the hip, her hands spread on the tight thighs of her blue jeans, looking up at him.

"Thanks for the cobbler," he said. "Sorry I didn't finish it." He looked down at his gloves, then back over at her. "Well, to be honest, I'm really not that sorry."

She grinned timorously and rose as he turned toward the front hall, navigating its length with dilatory footsteps. At the door, he turned back to her.

"Do you want to do something . . ." His pause might have been a shrug. "Whenever? It's hard right now. Our schedules are pretty conflicting."

"Let's just wait and see," she said. "Things are going to get busy at the shop and we'll be staying open evenings between now and Christmas. I think we're going to put on a couple of temporaries for the season, just to clerk for us, but still, my hours will be uncertain."

"Sure," he said, understanding the need to progress cautiously.

"Well," he said, opening the door. "I'll call."

"Yes, do that."

Their belated caution kept them from considering a goodbye kiss. What had happened on the kitchen chair was enough to send him, if not scuttling, most certainly retreating to give thought to what they had initiated here tonight.

Chapter 11

———❦———

Secrecy came hard for Lee Reston. What she had done surprised and shocked her. She needed desperately to talk about it with someone she could trust. She ran through the list of possibilities. Sylvia? Sylvia was, for all her dear qualities, a staunch prude. She never talked about anything regarding sex. She and Barry were the kind of couple who rarely touched in public and generally demonstrated so little affection for one another Lee had often wondered what they did in their bedroom.

Mother? Mother was so totally out of the question it was absurd to consider her. Propriety was the ultimate force in Peg Hillier's life, and discussing straddling a man fifteen years your junior on a kitchen chair during a first necking session would have drawn only a metaphoric standing in the corner from the older woman.

Janice? Oh, mea culpa, mea culpa. What Lee had done, when measured against Janice's confessed feelings for Christopher, was reprehensible. Merely thinking of Janice made Lee feel like the town harlot. What kind of mother was she anyway?

What about the women who worked for her? She felt it was inadvisable to blur the line between employer and employee with off-hours friendship. It made leadership difficult in negative times.

If only Joey were older. Unfortunately, Joey was at the age where he thought snapping a girl's bra was foreplay. It would be many years yet before she could talk about the birds and the bees with Joey.

Lloyd? She nearly succumbed to the idea that Lloyd might be a guiding light in this impasse, but she felt awkward broaching the subject with the father of her late husband.

Ironically, the only one she could possibly trust with such intimate stuff was Christopher himself, and right now she felt it wiser to keep her distance from him.

She had discovered that something he'd said Sunday night was too true for comfort: going as long as she had without kissing a man was unnatural. Now that she'd broken the fast, she was tempted to gorge.

She became distracted at work. On the day after her date with Christopher she and Sylvia were discussing the price of red carnations, which always shot sky-high at holiday time. Sylvia had said she wished they'd pre-booked more the previous month, when the best discounts had been available.

Lee came out of a fog to realize Sylvia had asked her a question.

"Oh, sorry. What was that?"

Sylvia was studying her with a pucker between her eyebrows. "Lee, what in the world is the matter with you today?"

"Nothing. What did you say?"

"I said, do you think we should hire a couple of high school students to cut up Christmas greens and put them in plastic bags?"

"Of course. Good idea. Why pay designers' wages for work like that? Oh . . . and, Sylvia?" Lee paused, giving her full attention to her sister in an effort to erase the frown from her face. "Order a lot of incense cedar, will you? You know how I love the smell of it."

Sylvia said, "Do you feel all right today?"

"I feel fine."

"Then pay attention to what you're doing. You just put those evergreen boughs in the cooler with the carnations."

Lee looked and, sure enough, she'd done exactly what Sylvia had said. There sat a bucket of boughs which, if left in the same cooler, would put the carnations to sleep.

She took the evergreens out and said, sheepishly, "Sorry."

She had been daydreaming about straddling Christopher's lap and kissing him till her jaws ached.

Two days went by and he didn't call. Her shop was on Main Street. The police department was a block off Main on Jackson, meaning the black-and-white cars drove by constantly, coming and going on calls. She seemed to have developed sensors that lifted her head every time a squad car rolled by. Most times there was a smattering of greenery between her and the window, impossible to see through, but sometimes she caught a glimpse of a squad car through it and imagined him behind the wheel. Other times the cars went out on flashing red with their sirens shrilling, and the sound would quicken her heart.

A week after Thanksgiving she was watering some plants in the window when she caught a flash of black-and-white, looked up, and there he was, cruising past on duty. He waved. She waved . . . and stood with the watering pitcher forgotten in her hand, her heart doing a circus act against her ribs while she watched the police car roll down Main Street out of sight.

Only minutes later the phone rang beside the cash register at the rear of the store.

"Lee, it's for you," Sylvia called.

"Thanks." Lee set down her watering pitcher and went to the back counter. "Hello?"

"Hello," Christopher said. "You look pretty good in that front window."

She had no idea what to say, so she said nothing, just stood there like a dummy trying to keep her face pale.

"Oh, somebody's there, right?"

"Yes."

"Do you ever get days off in the middle of the week?"

"Sometimes. Now, during the Christmas season when we're open nights, we stagger our hours a little more. What did you want?"

"Some help with a Christmas tree. I've never had one before but I thought I'd put one up this year. Will you help me pick out some decorations?"

Sylvia asked, "Who is it?"

Without covering the mouthpiece, Lee said, "It's Christopher. He wants me to give him a little advice on buying tree ornaments." Into the phone, she asked, "Isn't there any chance of doing it in the evening?"

Sylvia interrupted. "Lee, just a minute."

"Just a minute, Chris."

Sylvia's expression said she felt guilty for what she was about to ask. "I need a day off, too, to do some Christmas shopping. Go ahead and make your plans. I'll fill in for you if you fill in for me. We'll both go nuts if we don't get away from here a little."

Lee asked Chris, "What day did you have in mind?"

"Any day. I'm off next Tuesday and Wednesday though, if you wanted to make a day of it."

"Tuesday?" she asked Sylvia. When her sister nodded, she said, "Tuesday's good, Chris."

"I'll pick you up at your house at ten."

"Fine."

When Lee had hung up, Sylvia lamented, "I don't know how I'm going to get everything done before Christmas. It's the same thing every year. I've been meaning to talk to you about a day off, but things have been so crazy around here I felt guilty to ask."

"You're right though. We'll both go bonkers if we don't get away now and then."

Lee realized something that afternoon that had not struck her before. People were unsuspicious of her comings and goings with Christopher simply because they saw him as a boy, not a man. Because it was inconceivable that a woman of her age would be engaged in any kind of romantic liaison with a man of thirty, their antennae never went up. Furthermore, he had been her son's friend. They saw him, perhaps, as he'd been at the beginning: a son figure who got along well with the family and had been adopted by them because he had none of his own. The concept was simple: familiarity as camouflage.

She found it difficult to digest the fact that on a workday morning in the middle of the week, she was playing hooky from the shop, dressing in play clothes and waiting to go off on a lark with a man who had filled her thoughts with adolescent musings for the past two weeks. Yet she was. There was her very own reflection in the bathroom mirror looking brighter-eyed than usual, her cheeks with so much color she disdained blusher while putting on her makeup. It had been so many years since she'd felt this exhilaration at the thought of being with someone, since she'd examined her mirrored image with some male's projected opinion guiding her judgment of what she saw: a middle-aged woman, reasonably trim, reasonably pleasant-looking, with plain, plain hair, wearing black stretch pants and an aqua-blue turtleneck beneath an oversized thick-knit cotton shirt done in blocks of black, yellow and aqua. She spent a brief worry over whether or not the outfit was too coedish; nothing looked sillier than a woman her age trying to look as though she were eighteen.

Giving herself approval on all but the color spots in her cheeks, she shut off the light.

He arrived promptly. Because she feared her reaction to meeting him the first time after their tryst on the kitchen chair, she was slamming the front door behind her while his Explorer was still bumping over the end of the driveway. He managed to get one foot on the ground while she was halfway down the sidewalk, and waited there in the lee of the open truck door as she reached the other side and got in.

He got in, too, and smiled her way. *Dear God,* she thought, *don't let him lean over and kiss me right here in broad daylight with my neighbors home up and down the street.*

He didn't.

He put the truck in reverse and said, "Where we going?"

She said, "Lindstrom, Minnesota."

"Lindstrom, Minnesota?" It was an hour away.

"If you want to."

"What's there?"

"Gustaf's World of Christmas. Two charming turn-of-the-century houses, side by side on the main street of town, where it's Christmas all year long. I haven't been there for a long, long time, but as I recall, it incites the child in you, plus they have Christmas decorations from all over the world. I think you'll enjoy it."

He shifted to drive, and she felt his eyes linger on her as the truck began rolling down the street. She flashed him a smile, which seemed to be what he was waiting for before settling into his duty as driver.

The day suited their purpose. It was dove-gray with crystal etchings. Overnight, hoarfrost had formed and was drifting from the trees in glisteny falls. On the boulevards snow piles stood knee-high; toddlers with scarves over their faces slid down them on sheets of blue plastic. Christmas music was playing on the truck radio, and the heater threw out a steady current of warm air.

They left the city behind and bore east into open country.

Christopher said, "I need to buy a Christmas tree. Do you think I should get a fake one or a real one?"

"A real one. Those fake things are abominable. Besides, they don't have any smell."

"So you like the smell of pine?"

"I love it. This is my favorite time of year in the shop because it smells so intoxicating. Just about every arrangement we make has evergreens in it, and we get in a new batch nearly every day. They come in huge boxes and they have to be snipped into usable lengths, and when you're cutting them—especially the incense cedar—there's nothing else like it in the world. Incense cedar has a real lemony smell mixed with the pine. And it stays fragrant forever."

"I never heard of incense cedar. I wouldn't even know what it is."

"You would once you smelled it. We buy lots of other varieties though, too— white pine, balsam, fir, arborvitae, juniper. Juniper is the worst to work with. It really makes a mess of your hands."

He glanced down at her hands, but they were covered by gloves.

"Sylvia just flat refuses to work with it. But Sylvia doesn't do as much arranging as I do. She's the businesswoman. I'm the arranger."

"Did she say anything about your going with me today?"

Their eyes met briefly before he returned his attention to the highway. "No. All she said was that she needs a day off too, to start on her Christmas shopping."

No more was said on the subject.

Christopher said, "Tell me more about what you do every day."

He was the rare person who asked a question, then listened to the answer. As she talked about her shop, she realized that in her life as a mother of three busy offspring, years had gone by since she'd been around anyone genuinely interested in her day-to-day affairs. With Joey and Janice, she was expected to be interested in theirs, but the truth was they rarely asked about hers.

She described an ordinary day in the florists' business: waiting on customers, designing arrangements, throwing out old stock, scrubbing buckets, getting in new flowers, stripping their lower leaves, the various ways they needed hardening before being used in arrangements. She told him that half their flowers came from South America, where pesticides were used more liberally than in the States, and that she occasionally worried about the amount she was absorbing through her hands. Hands, she said, absorbed them more readily than you'd think. He glanced at her hands, but she still had her gloves on.

She described the boxes that came from Colombia by way of Miami, where agents ran metal rods through them, looking for cocaine, so the cartons arrived looking as though they'd been shot full of bullet holes. She told him how much fun it was going to trade shows, and that her next one was coming up in January at the Minneapolis Gift Mart. She said business was very good this winter: They'd just gotten a standing order from a Methodist church for twenty dollars' worth of loose flowers every Saturday, and orders like that were bread and butter because they didn't cost any arranging time, and the bill always got paid. She and Sylvia would have to hire a new designer soon, she said, because Nancy was pregnant and going to quit. He asked how you know a good designer. She replied that you can always tell a good one by her hands: Good ones never wear gloves and work with a Swiss army knife instead of scissors. Christmas time, she said, was especially hard on the hands because of the sap in the evergreens and all the turpentine it took to get rid of it.

He said, "Let me see your hands."

She said, "No."

"You have a thing about your hands, but I've never noticed anything wrong with them."

"They're always a mess."

He said, "A new side of Lee Reston—self-conscious about her hands."

She said, "That's right."

And he didn't ask again.

The yard at Gustaf's was decorated with life-size wooden reindeer wearing willow wreaths around their necks, trailing red-and-green-plaid ribbons.

Inside, it smelled of mulberry. Lights twinkled everywhere. Christmas carols tinkled forth in myriad tones: Swiss bells, carillons, jingle bells and chimes. Ceilings, walls and floors were Disneyesque with holiday trimmings for sale. Balls and bells, toy soldiers and tinsel, tree lights and yard ornaments and a room with so many miniature painted wooden trinkets it felt like walking into a shop in Oslo. Dolls with porcelain faces sat in miniature rocking chairs. Santas of all descriptions beamed upon the colorful array with rosy cheeks and mischievous eyes. A clerk dressed like one of Santa's helpers smiled and said, "Merry Christmas."

"Merry Christmas," they replied in unison.

"Ask, if I can help with anything."

"We will."

They explored every magical room of the old house.

Christopher found a Santa beard and hooked it on behind his ears. "Ho ho ho," he boomed in his best basso profundo. "Have you been a good little girl?"

"Not exactly," she replied, giving him a saucy glance. The words slipped out before she realized how flirtatious they were.

He took off the beard and put it back on the wall, and she knew he was going to touch her shoulder, say something intimate about what had passed between them the last time they were together. To forestall him, she slipped into another room. He came right behind her, hustling around the corner to find her facing the doorway wearing a white mobcap, holding a stuffed white teddy bear to her cheek, singing, "All I want for Chrith-muth ith my two front teeth."

Moments later she discovered him holding up a personalized stocking at least two feet long, pointing at it with his eyebrows raised. Across the top of it was printed CHRIS.

She found a pair of the ugliest earrings in the world, shaped like red electric Christmas lights, and held them up to her ears. "Would you believe they actually light up?"

They laughed and she put them back where they belonged.

The next time she turned around he'd found some mistletoe and was holding it above his head, wearing a rowdy smile.

"Oh, no," she reprimanded. "Nothin' doing. Not in the middle of a public place."

"Oh—what?" he asked innocently, looking around. "You need a kitchen chair?"

"Christopher!" she scolded in a whisper.

He put the mistletoe back in a wooden sleigh and sauntered over to her, putting himself between her and any further progress through the shop. "Touchy subject?" he inquired.

"Not exactly. Well, yes, sort of. I mean, I don't know. I'm just a little amazed at myself for what I did."

"Any regrets?" he asked.

She shook her head slowly, looking up at him at such close range it would have taken only the smallest movement for them to be kissing again right here in Gustaf's World of Christmas.

They chose his tree decorations after that—multicolored miniature lights, gold tinsel garland, some oversized gilded jingle bells, and glass balls that appeared to have snow falling inside them when the light refracted off their transparent surface. They bought a tree stand and a fat red candle surrounded by holly, and a box of delicate ribbon candy, which he claimed he'd never seen before in his life and which totally fascinated him.

They hauled their booty to the truck and he asked, "Are you hungry?" It was 1:30 in the afternoon.

"Ravenous."

He looked up and down the main street of Lindstrom, Minnesota, and said, "Let's take a walk . . . see what we can find."

They found the Rainbow Café, where coffee was served in thick white mugs, and napkins were stored in metal dispensers on the tables, and the locals were telling jokes over coffee at a long Formica bar.

She ordered a Denver sandwich and he opted for a hot beef, mounded with potatoes and gravy, of course.

Afterward, they found a tree lot next to a bank building and bought two fragrant green Norway pines, which they tied on the top of the Explorer before heading back to Anoka.

They rode without talking until well after the truck got warm and cozy. He turned the radio on softly and she sat low on her tailbone with one knee up on the dash. He looked over at her, relaxed, with her fingers linked over her stomach. Her nails were clipped short and the cuticles looked stained and ragged. It only made her more real to him.

"What time does Joey get home?"

She checked her watch and said, "Right about now."

He asked, "Do you have to go home?"

Her head was resting against the back of the seat. She rolled it to face him and they jiggled along the road in the tightly sprung vehicle for another five seconds. He noted that at some time since they'd finished their lunch she'd put on fresh lipstick. She noted that his hair, much like hers, always seemed to look the same. After a whole day of being on the go, shaking snow off of Christmas trees, tying them onto the roof of the truck in the wind, his hair sprang up and away from his face as perfectly as ever. She absolutely loved his hair.

Did she have to go home?

"No," she answered.

She thought he'd never look back at the highway.

He took her to his apartment complex, pushed an activator for an automatic door and drove into an underground garage. The door rumbled shut behind them, they parked, and he said, "If you'll get the packages, I'll get the tree."

When he'd untied it from the roof of the truck she said, "It'll make a mess unless you put it in the stand down here."

"Oh," he said—a novice. "Right."

It took some tools, but he had them in the truck, and after ten minutes he had the tree in the stand and he carried it while she opened doors in front of him. At his own door he handed her the keys and said, "Both locks."

She opened them both, thinking how different she was from Christopher in this regard. She who left her garage door up night and day and often never locked her house; he—the policeman—who recognized the value of a dead bolt.

Inside, he set the tree down and said, "Be right back. Take off your jacket and make yourself at home."

He went to the bathroom and came back out to find her talking to Joey on the kitchen telephone.

"Hi, hon, it's Mom."

"Oh, hey, Mom, I'm glad you called. Are there any of those meat roll-up things left that we had for supper the other night?"

"They're in the refrigerator in a square plastic container with a yellow cover."

"Oh, great! Jeez, I'm starved. We had tripe for school lunch today. Hey, what time are you coming home?"

She looked up and found Christopher standing in the living room doorway, sucking a piece of ribbon candy, watching and listening. "I should be there by eight." Their eyes met and held.

"Good, then I don't have to wait to eat, right?"

"Right. Go ahead and warm up the beef rolls. Zap a potato with it too, if you want. There's sour cream in the fridge."

"Okay. Yeah, that sounds good."

"Well, I'll see you around eight then, okay?"

"Yeah, sure, unless I go over to Sandy's."

"Home by ten, mister, right?"

She could imagine him rolling his eyes. He'd been creeping over the mark lately. "Yeah, right."

"Okay then, 'bye."

When she'd hung up, Christopher asked, "Everything okay?"

"Fine. He had tripe for lunch, but it seems he survived the ordeal."

Christopher chuckled and said, "Come and help me decide where to put this thing."

They lit lamps against the dusky afternoon, turned on the radio and studied his living room furniture.

"Where do you think?" he asked.

They cleared a spot in front of the sliding glass door and pushed the sofa into the exact center of the room facing it. It looked unorthodox, but the view of the tree was great, and with the stereo components on the wall behind the sofa, the sound came through beautifully, too.

Dumping their purchases from the packages, Christopher asked, "What goes on first?"

"Lights," she said, and while he began pulling the tree lights out of their boxes, she said, "Christopher, didn't you *ever* do this at home?"

"Nope," he said, tending to what he was doing.

She heard the brusque note of defensiveness and decided this was no time for unhappy memories. "Well, plug them in first so you can see what you're doing. I think it works best to start at the top and work your way down. How's the ribbon candy?"

"Spicy. Have a piece."

The tree was six feet tall, so he strung the top ones while she did the bottom, and they both sucked the hard candy. They got out the tinsel garland next, while Kenny Rogers came on the stereo with a sentimental song about a married couple playing Santa on Christmas Eve. Lee gave Christopher the end of the garland and said, "Start up at the top." He draped it from branch to branch while she did the same below, weaving back and forth, and somehow she got in his way. The gold-spangled garland caught on her mouth while she was dipping beneath his arm, and as she tried to swing free, it caught on the turtleneck of her shirt, pulled out of his hands and off the last branch he'd decorated.

"Oops, look what I've done. Sorry."

"Hey, there's more on you than on the tree."

She looked up and he saw a single golden filament caught on her lipstick, glistening there like a fragment of a fallen star.

"Hold still," he said, and reached out to remove it with a fingertip. It stuck to her glossy lipstick and he had to use a fingernail to free it, while she stood as still as an hour hand, holding her lips open, looking up at him.

They'd delayed it all day. They'd been responsible, clear-thinking, non-libidinal adults while they were out in public. They had refrained from ardent gazes, touches, intimate exchanges and all the tens of things in which two healthy, red-blooded, attracted people might well have indulged. But her lips were open . . . and he'd touched them with one finger . . . and the kisses they'd shared two weeks ago had remained in their thoughts ever since . . . and around them a gravelly voice was singing about the greatest gift of all.

He dipped his head and put his mouth on hers so tenderly not a hair on her head moved. The golden garland, still in his hand, draped onto the floor where it pooled and glistened like the dropped belts of angels. They remained just so, lips scarcely joined, each tipping slightly toward the other until she teetered a bit and touched his chest to regain her balance. He opened his eyes, caught her hand with his and carried it to his mouth to kiss its roughened knuckles.

Into her eyes, he said softly, "Let's finish this first."

They finished festooning the tree, never touching, politely handing one another ornaments, realizing full well it was only six o'clock.

When the ornaments were hung and the floor was littered with Christmas scree, she knelt to pick up loose pine needles and cardboard boxes and cellophane. He turned off the lamps and went to stand behind and above her, touching the top of her head. "I'll do that tomorrow. Come here." At her delay in rising, he doubled forward, running a hand down her arm to make her drop the cardboard box full of pine needles. "Come here," he whispered again, and pulled her to her feet, then led her to the sofa.

There, he stretched out on his side and drew her down beside him. The cushion gave and she rolled lightly against him. He put a hand on her waist, tipped his head and gave them both the only Christmas gift they wanted at the moment. He wet her lips and abraded her tongue with his own and wiped out all the pent-up longing of that day, and the days before it, and the nights they'd lain awake in their separate beds wondering when this would happen again. They took the sweetest of time, exchanging a candy-flavored kiss that stretched on . . . and on . . . and on . . .

When they opened their eyes they saw red, green, blue and gold lights pieing the walls, the furniture, their clothing and hair.

"Can we talk about it now?" he asked, still with his hand on her waist.

"Talk about what?" she whispered.

"About what we've been feeling since that night. What we've been feeling all day today. What made you resist getting up from your knees and coming over here a minute ago."

A beat passed before she confessed, "Guilt."

"About what?"

"What I did on that kitchen chair."

"You didn't do anything wrong."

"Didn't I?"

"I shouldn't have teased you about it today. I'm sorry. I didn't know it was bothering you so much."

"I've thought about how others would see it—my mother, my daughter, my sister. I think they'd call it seduction."

"It went both ways."

"But I'm fifteen years older than you."

"So you're not allowed to express your emotions?"

"I shocked myself."

"You shocked me, too, but I loved it."

"It's been a very long time, you see, and kissing you was suddenly so irresistible. This is irresistible . . . lying here this way. You were right, it's unnatural to go without . . . without this kind of physical affection for so long. It's been two weeks since we kissed on that kitchen chair, and I haven't been able to think of anything else since."

"And so you feel guilty?"

"Of course, don't you?"

"No. You're female. I'm male. What's there to feel guilty about?"

"Our ages, for one thing."

"I figured that was coming."

"And my long drought, for another. I imagine women can do some pretty dumb things when a younger man pays them some attention after years of none at all."

"Is that all I am to you . . . a younger man paying you some attention?"

"No, you know you're not."

"So what's your big problem with us? All we're doing is kissing."

"You were Greg's friend."

"And that's the first time his name has been mentioned all day long. Do you realize that?"

She hadn't. Her eyes told him so.

"Hey, don't go guilty on me again. It's a healthy sign, you and me spending an entire day together and all we concentrated on was having fun. I thought we did rather well at it, myself."

"We did. I loved it."

"And you don't think it's significant that we never talked about Greg once?"

"Yes, I do. But it's only been six months since his death, and maybe I'm . . . maybe . . ."

"Go on, say it. Maybe you're still going through some grief process and this is part of it."

"Well, maybe it is."

"Maybe. Then again, maybe it's not. And if it is, so what? We're talking about it, it's out in the open. If that's what this is for either one of us, we'll find out soon enough. The glow will wear off and we won't feel so much like being together anymore. Personally, I don't think that's going to happen though."

"Which will be disastrous, too."

"Why?"

"Because Janice has a crush on you."

"I know that."

She picked her head up off his arm. "You do?"

"I've known that for a long time."

"And you'd still do this with me?"

"I never gave her one iota of encouragement. Ask her."

She laid her head back down and admitted, "I don't have to. She's already confided in me."

"There, you see? Now what other hang-ups do you have here?"

"You make it so simplistic."

"It is. All I set out to do was lie here for a while and kiss you and enjoy my first Christmas tree, and maybe make the two of us feel a little less lonely for a while. That's pretty simplistic." His voice turned soft, seductive. "It's just my mouth . . ." He moved closer. ". . . on your mouth."

And what an incredible mouth he had. He was so good at using it, suckling her lips, setting his head in motion and encouraging her to do the same. He kissed her the way she hadn't been kissed since courting days, in the lingering, juicy, slow, sexy way that says, *If this is what we're settling for, let's make it good.* His sweet blandishments worked. She freed her mind of thought and let sensuality pull her into its lair, following his lead and immersing herself in the texture and taste of him. Long liquid kisses led to a dearer fit of their bodies down below. He lifted a knee and she made space for it between her own, welcoming the high, hard pressure he exerted as he lifted it against her warmth.

He made a pleasured sound, "Mmm . . . ," and moved his hand up her back, pressing circles on it, touching her nape, her shoulders, riding his palm flat and hard down her vertebrae to the bend of her spine.

It had been so long since she'd lain with a man, fit herself against one, felt his arousal against her stomach. So long since she'd run her hands over firm, hard shoulders, into short, springy hair. His hair—ah—the feel of it was so different from her own, and when she sifted her fingers through it his scent lifted, the peculiar and individual essence she would ever after recognize as his.

It was as he'd said—this was so unutterably good, she had no desire to desist. His moist lips left hers and wandered her face, dropping kisses where they would— upon her cheek, eyebrow, hairline, nose—dampening her skin, sometimes letting the tip of his tongue mark its passing. He pressed his mouth to her neck, drew three circles with his tongue, bringing forth the scent of the perfume she'd sprayed there that morning.

At last he pulled back and looked into her face.

She opened her eyes and saw his at close range, with the tree lights reflected in them.

"My, you're good at that," she murmured.

"So are you."

"A little out of practice."

"Wanna practice some more?" He grinned.

"I'd love to . . . but my arm is falling asleep." It had been pinned under him for fifteen minutes.

"I can fix that," he said, and rolled on top of her, putting a hand under her back and plumping her over two inches at a time until he lay flush atop her in the center of the couch.

They studied each other's eyes, searching for consent.

"Lee, I meant it," he whispered. "Just kissing, if that's all you want."

"What I want and what I'll allow myself to do are two different things."

He kissed her mouth, bearing his weight on his elbows, crooking one knee along the side of her hip.

When the kiss ended she twined her arms around his neck and drew him down, his face falling above her shoulder.

She sighed. "Oh, Christopher, you feel so good on me I could stay here all night."

"Good idea," he said, intentionally shattering the spell that was getting too tempting. "Should I call Joey or will you?"

She laughed but her stomach refused to lift beneath his greater weight.

"Laugh some more," he said, muffled, near her ear. "Feels great."

Instead she grew still, closing her eyes and appreciating these minutes of closeness, and the realization that she was still desirable, still sexual, with a man again and enjoying it.

"Lee?" he said near her ear.

"What?" she murmured, lazily finger-combing the back of his hair.

He lifted his head and bore his weight on his elbows. "Promise me you won't pull the same tricks you pulled on me at Thanksgiving."

She said, "I'm so sorry for that."

"I want to be with you on Christmas."

"You will be, I promise. But how are we going to keep from giving ourselves away?"

"Trust me. You didn't know how I felt about you until a few weeks ago, did you?"

"I had my suspicions."

"When?" he exclaimed, as if accusing her of fibbing.

"As long ago as the Fourth of July."

"The Fourth of July!"

"When we were sitting side by side eating corn on the cob. And when we banged into each other playing volleyball. And on the Ferris wheel. A woman senses these things before a man does."

"Why didn't you say something?"

"I never would have if you hadn't said something first."

"Why?"

"Because of all the reasons we talked about earlier—the difference in our ages, what my kids would think, the fact that we're still both in mourning and emotionally vulnerable. There are so many reasons they make me question my sanity now."

With his elbows at her shoulders he put his thumbs in the hollows of her cheeks and pushed gently. He watched her lips press into a false pout and relax as his thumbs retreated. He studied her eyes, locked on his and happy, in spite of her words.

When he spoke, his voice was deep with candor and honesty. "Any mother fixation I ever had on you is gone. Do you believe me?"

She studied his face, wiped clean of smiles and teasing. She felt a thrill and a warning inside, that what they'd begun could lead to hurt for both of them if they let this get out of hand. She hooked his neck and brought his mouth close enough to kiss. Once. Fast.

"Yes. And now I must go."

"Why?"

"Because I like this too much. I like you too much. You feel too good and I've had too much fun today and I'm getting so mixed up." His eyes seemed to be studying her as if putting great thought into what she said. "And because I'm afraid of what we've started here. Aren't you?"

Again he considered before answering, "No, I'm not. Not like you." Then he sat back and worked his way off her, grabbed her by both hands and hauled her up. "Come on. I'll take you home."

Chapter 12

The following Saturday night Lee closed the store at nine after a grueling day spent mostly on her feet. The demand for fresh-cut flower arrangements had become so great she and Sylvia had decided to hire an additional designer now and have her stay on when Nancy quit after the holidays. The new designer was named Leah. She was Asian, and brought to Absolutely Floral a fresh, new visual aspect in flower arranging. Many of her arrangements were minimalistic, asymmetrical and stunning. Lee had watched her work, caught Sylvia's eye and known within ten minutes she was the one they wanted. They had offered her ten dollars an hour, compromised at eleven when she asked for twelve, and believed they were getting a bargain.

However, even with the additional designer, and with Rodney making extra delivery runs each day, they could scarcely keep up with poinsettias for churches, centerpieces for Christmas parties and gift bouquets, both personal and business. There had been three weddings today as well, plus the foot traffic in the store, which got so bad Lee had called Joey over for a few hours just to help bag green plants and carry them out to the cars, take tailings out to the trash, scrub buckets, polish the showcase doors and keep the floor swept in the designing area. She had kept him there till five o'clock, then had given him fifteen dollars and a kiss as thanks before he walked out the door saying, "A bunch of us are going to do something tonight so I won't be home when you get there."

Now it was 9:15 and Lee arrived home nearly exhausted. Her feet hurt, her legs hurt, she had cut her hand on her Swiss army knife and that hurt. She'd been pricked by so many juniper sprigs her hands had developed a puffy red rash. The constant hammering of woody stems had given her a headache. At this time of the year and at Valentine's Day, the banging went on hour after hour until the place sounded like a carpenter's shop instead of a florist. Sitting in the silent house the absence of sound was so abrupt it seemed felt rather than heard.

She threw her coat across one kitchen chair and plunked down on another to scan the mail, too tired to open the two envelopes mixed in with the junk. She yawned, stared absently at Joey's note lying beside the potted pothos on its red plaid runner. *Mom, a bunch of us are going bowling together, then over to Karen Hanson's for sloppy joes. Home by 10:30.* His curfew time was ten, but she was too tired to quibble over trivialities. It was the Christmas season, and he'd come to the shop to help her without complaining: She'd give the kid a break.

She heated up a can of Campbell's tomato soup, put it in a mug and took it, steaming, to the bathroom where she filled the tub, sank into bubbles to her armpits and leaned back, sipping when she remembered to, mostly letting the mug wobble back and forth on her knee while she dozed.

She awoke with a start when the soup spilled down her leg and stained the water orange. Groaning, she sat up, washed, dried, powdered herself from stem to stern and crawled into some warm, soft pajamas. In the living room, she turned on a single lamp and the television, lay down on the sofa and covered herself with an afghan to wait for Joey.

Some time later she awoke again, startled, disoriented after sleep so sound that the hour, day and all basic reason momentarily eluded her. On the screen Raymond Burr was holding forth in an old Perry Mason rerun. It was Saturday night. She was waiting for Joey. Time was . . . she checked her watch . . .

Ten to twelve!

She threw off the afghan and sat up, heart racing from the discombobulating effects of her startled awakening and the sudden plunge into fear for Joey. He was never late! Never! Ten or fifteen minutes lately, since his hormones had started rampaging and little Sandy Parker had come on the scene.

If he was late, there was something wrong.

Oh God, not another one!

The thought skittered through her brain while it was still short of oxygen from getting vertical too fast. She swayed a bit and sat back down to regain her equilibrium. As surely as she knew he hadn't come in, she knew he was dead. It was Greg all over again, and baby Grant. Oh God, a third one, and she'd have only one left. Panic sluiced through her as she rose and ran to his room to find it empty, the bed rumpled but still made from morning, his work clothes from today lying in a heap on the floor beside a pair of hand weights and a carrying case of CDs.

"Joey!" she shouted, turning frantically into the hall, then hurrying toward the kitchen. "Joey, are you here?"

The light was still on over the stove the way she'd left it. There were no empty dishes in the sink, no evidence of recent snacking.

"Oh God . . . oh God . . ." she despaired under her breath, checking her watch against the kitchen clock. "Where can he be?"

It was midnight when she dialed the number for the Anoka police station— not 911, which was routed through a county dispatcher, but the direct line into the station on Jackson Street.

A woman answered and Lee struggled to keep the panic out of her voice.

"This is Lee Reston. I'm Greg Reston's mother, was Greg Reston's mother, I mean. I know this sounds silly, but my fourteen-year-old son, Joey, is missing. I mean, he didn't come home when he said he would, and he's *always* on time. *Always*. I'm just wondering if by any chance there's been any . . . well . . . report of anything . . . or word of him . . . anything you know of."

"Hi, Mrs. Reston. This is Toni Mansetti. No, I'm sorry. Nothing at all. But I'll certainly put it on the radio and alert the officers on duty."

"No!" she exclaimed, struck by the nebulous illogic that as long as she kept it unofficial he was okay. Then quieter, "No. It's probably something perfectly explainable and he'll come walking in any minute. He was with a bunch of kids so he's probably just fine."

"His name is Joey and he's fourteen?"

"Yes."

"Can you give me a description?"

"Oh listen, no, no, I don't want . . . he'll be . . . just forget it."

"Are you sure?"

"Yes, I'm . . . thank you, Toni. I'm sure he'll show up any minute."

When Toni Mansetti got off the phone she went into the squad room but none of the on-duty officers were around. Christmas season was a violent time of the year and Saturday nights were the worst. Suicides, burglaries, robberies and lots of drunks. Domestics broke out over ridiculous reasons: whose in-laws couples were going to spend Christmas with, who spent too much money on Christmas presents, who was flirting with whom at the company Christmas party. Money shortages, alcohol and loneliness kept 911 ringing more often than at any other time of year. Of the five officers on duty, none were in the squad room when Toni Mansetti checked.

Back at her radio, she called Ostrinski, who was cruising. He picked up immediately.

"Pete, this is Toni. I just had a call from Greg Reston's mother. She sounded a little panicky and said her fourteen-year-old son isn't home yet from some teenage get-together, but she didn't want me to declare him missing. Keep your eyes open though, will you?"

"Ten-four. Toni, is Lallek around there yet?"

"No, he got off at eleven and left right afterwards."

"Do me a favor, will you? Give him a call at home and apprise him of the situation. He's close to that family and I think he'd want to know. He's just like the rest of us, has a hard time sleeping when he gets off mid-shift. He'll probably still be up."

"Copy, Pete. Will do."

Chris had gone to bed but was lying awake when his phone rang. He rolled over, grabbed it in the dark and said, "Yuh."

"Chris, this is Toni down at the station. We just had a call from Greg Reston's mother saying her fourteen-year-old son, Joey, is missing. We're going to keep an eye out, but Ostrinski thought you'd want to know."

Chris was already out of bed, stretching the phone cord while reaching for his clothes. "What are the details?"

"All she said was that he was with a bunch of friends and that he didn't come home when he said he would. She hung up before I could get a description out of her. She sounded panicked."

"He's about five feet seven, short brown hair a little wavy, no glasses, probably wearing a red jacket with white sleeves—no letter. He looks a lot like Greg. Home address is 1225 Benton Street. Put it on the radio, okay, Toni? And thanks for calling. I'll get over there right away. She'll be going crazy worrying."

"You want me to send a squad over, too?"

"Not yet. I'll call in if I want one."

"Copy. Good luck, Lallek."

Christopher was not a praying man, but a prayer went through his mind, directed at Lee Reston. *Hang on, Lee, I'm coming, I'm coming. He's going to be okay. He's not going to be dead like your other two, but I know what you're going through, so hang on, babe, till I can get there and help you through this!*

While he drove to her house disregarding every driving law he'd ever learned, he found his heart ramming in fear for her and what he knew was going through her mind.

At 12:15 when Lee saw car lights turning into her driveway, she opened the door and went out onto the icy concrete step barefoot, in her pajamas.

The engine and lights were cut, a door slammed and Christopher came striding up the sidewalk.

The sight of him was a gift of greater value than any she'd ever received in her life. His presence—his sturdy, commonsense, trained presence—lifted a portion of the weight from her heart. He knew, always knew when she needed him. It was uncanny.

"Have you heard from him yet?" he asked well before he reached her.

"No. Oh, Christopher, I'm so scared."

She had come halfway down the sidewalk to meet him. He swept her forward in one arm toward the storm door, which had already grown frosty with the inner door open. "Get inside. My God, you haven't even got any shoes on."

The tears she'd held at bay while alone began stinging her eyes now that he was here to carry some of the burden of worry. "He's never done this before. He's always had a curfew and always obeyed it without complaining."

Inside, he shut the doors and she rocketed into his arms. "I'm so glad you're here. How did you find out?"

"The station called me." He hugged her briefly, then gripped her arms to press her back. "Tell me where he was going, what time he left, who he was with."

"He said he was going bowling with a bunch of kids. He left the shop around five o'clock—he'd helped out there this afternoon because we were so busy. After bowling, he said they were all going over to Karen Hanson's house. She's one of the girls he hangs around with. There's a whole bunch of them who always do things together. Here, he left a note."

She led him to the kitchen table. While he read the brief note she told him, "They're all a bunch of really good kids."

"Do you know these Hansons?"

"Yes. I already called there and Karen's mother said the kids went home about ten-fifteen." The tens of dire possibilities implied by the words brought more unwanted tears, but he remained clearheaded and practical.

"Walking?"

"Yes. Different parents give them rides whenever they ask, but a lot of times they just walk in a big group. I never thought to ask him if he needed a ride tonight. He knows that all he has to do is call though and I'll come and pick him up."

"Have you looked in his room?"

"Yes. Nothing."

He headed back there and she followed, stood in the doorway with her arms tightly crossed while he switched on the light and assessed everything slowly. She wondered what his trained eye might pick out that she'd missed, and felt another rush of gratitude for his understanding how hard it would be for her to go through this alone.

"Are these the clothes he was wearing earlier today?"

"Yes."

"Anything missing that you can see?"

"No. Just his jacket, the one he usually wears."

Christopher continued assessing the room while she felt compelled to explain her parental breach.

"I suppose you're wondering why I didn't call earlier, but I came home from work at nine and I was so tired I took a bath and fell asleep on the couch. When I woke up I couldn't believe it was nearly midnight and he wasn't home."

Christopher switched off the light and they went back to the kitchen. "I don't think there's anything to worry about yet. These things happen a lot—kids are reported missing and they just come home later than usual, that's all." He gave her a hug and rubbed her back.

"But he would have called. He knows how I worry."

"How can he know if you've never had to before?"

"Because he knows me, that's all. He wouldn't . . ."

The front door opened and Joey walked in, dressed in his red wool jacket with white leather sleeves, his cheeks rosy from walking in the winter night.

Anger and relief battled in Lee. She marched toward him, demanding, "Where have you been!"

One-handed, he freed his jacket snaps. "With the gang."

"Do you know what time it is!" she bellowed.

He hung his head some while he opened the front closet and hung up his jacket but gave no other sign he shared her concern over the hour.

"It's almost twelve-thirty at night!"

"It's the first time I've ever been late. I don't see what the big deal is."

Lee scarcely controlled the urge to smack him on the side of his head.

"The big deal is that I was worried half out of my mind, that's what the *big deal* is! While you were nonchalantly *hanging out with the gang* I was wondering if you were alive or dead! Calling parents' houses and asking if you were there, finding out you'd left at ten-fifteen. Where have you been since ten-fifteen?"

"At Sandy's," he answered, so quietly she could barely make out the words.

"At Sandy's," she repeated disparagingly. It was then she saw the hickeys on his neck and everything suddenly became clear. The room got uncomfortably silent. Into that silence, Christopher spoke.

"You're okay then, right, Joey?"

Joey shrugged, looked sheepish and mumbled some wordless reply.

Lee stood by feeling guilty for hearing the question she herself should have thought to ask, but she was so angry with the kid, it took an effort to keep from striking him.

To Lee, Christopher said, "I'd better call the station," and moved toward the kitchen telephone. Nobody else spoke while he dialed and said, "Yeah, Toni, this is Chris Lallek. All clear on Joey Reston. You can radio the squads he's home and he's all right."

When he hung up, Joey's face became a mixture of disbelief and embarrassment.

"You had the *police* looking for me?" he said to his mother, his voice cracking with chagrin.

"You don't seem to realize, young man, that things happen to kids your age when they wander around the streets late at night."

"But, gol, Mom . . . the police."

She was about to tear into him again when Christopher said, "Well, now that he's home okay, I'll be going." He walked past Lee and when he got to Joey, curled a hand over his shoulder in passing. "She's right, you know. And you had her awfully scared."

Joey's lips hung open and he stared at the floor, but said nothing.

When Christopher opened the door, the sound seemed to jar Lee from her absorption with her anger. She went to him and stood very close, saying, "Thank you, Christopher, again and again." She banked the strong urge to hug him, but with Joey nearby she could only put a hand on his jacket sleeve. "I can't tell you what it meant to me to see you walking up that sidewalk."

"Anytime," he answered. "See you." Before he left, he said, " 'Night, Joey."

Joey said, "Yeah, g'night."

In Christopher's absence, the silence in the front hall seemed to reverberate. Joey headed for safety, for once bypassing the refrigerator in favor of his room. He hadn't made it to the head of the hall before his mother spoke in the sternest voice possible.

"Joey, come in the living room."

She led the way and sat down stiffly on the sofa, waiting. He followed, walking in that peculiar fashion adopted by guilty teenagers, with their napes high and their chins low. He perched on the edge of a chair at Lee's right, leaning forward with his elbows on his knees, studying the carpet between his tennis shoes.

"All right, let's talk about it," Lee said.

"Talk about what?" The glance he gave her skittered away again in a millisecond.

"About what you were doing at Sandy's house."

"Nothing. Just watching TV."

"And that's how you got the hickeys on your neck—watching TV?"

It was obvious he hadn't known they were there. He blushed and his hand went up to his shirt collar.

"Were Sandy's parents home?"

It took a while before he shook his head guiltily, still staring at the floor.

"Where were they?"

"At some Christmas party."

Silence again . . . a long, long silence in which Lee's trembling stomach finally began to calm and her anger to dissipate. She leaned forward and reached across the arm of the sofa to cover both of Joey's hands with one of hers. When she spoke her voice held a low hiss of appeal.

"Don't ever do that to me again."

He blinked hard as if tears had formed in his downcast eyes. "I won't."

"I know you think I'm being ridiculous, but since Greg, if I get a little overprotective and jumpy, you'll just have to bear with me. I've never said it before, but it's very hard to be a mother and lose one of your children and not worry every time the others are out of your sight. I've tried really hard to balance my fears with rationalization, but tonight was horrible. Just horrible."

He kept blinking hard at the carpet.

"And don't think I don't understand about what went on tonight, because I do. I've been fourteen and I know how hard it can be to leave your friends when you're having a good time. But, Joey, you and Sandy are only fourteen . . . that's so young."

"Mom, we weren't doing anything, honest."

"Weren't you?"

He met her eyes defiantly. "Just kissing, that's all."

"Standing up or lying down?"

He rolled his eyes and head in disgust. "Jeez, Mom, come on."

"From ten-thirty till twelve-thirty?"

He looked at a far corner of the room and refused to speak.

"Listen," she said, relaxing into a more confidential pose, "there isn't a parent in the world who doesn't face this conversation with every one of her kids, and there isn't a parent in the world who hasn't had to face it with her own parents. I'm not oblivious, you know. I've seen the signs. My goodness, you've grown up practically overnight, and I understand that with that growth comes curiosity, first love, experimenting . . . am I right?"

Joey lurched to his feet and said, "Mom, can I go to bed now?"

"No, you can't," she replied calmly. "If you're old enough to lay down with a girl and get hickeys, you're old enough to make it through this conversation."

Joey sat back down, elbows to knees, linked his fingers loosely and fit his thumbnails together.

She steeled herself and took the plunge, saying the big word. "You've known about intercourse for a long time already; I know because I told you about it myself. Now you're finding out what leads up to it. But, Joey, it's dangerous. Thinking you can indulge in a little foreplay and only go so far can backfire on you, and the next thing you know you're a father."

He met her eyes directly, at last. "Mom, we didn't do that; why won't you believe me?"

"I do believe you, but listen to me anyway. What I'm saying is that now, at your age, the best thing to do is to stay with the group. Be with Sandy—I'm not saying you don't have the right to have a girlfriend—but keep yourselves out of situations where you're alone. I could give you a sermon on condoms, but you get those at school and on TV and in newspapers and just about everywhere you look these days. Right now, I think you need to be a fourteen-year-old boy, maybe kissing girls on doorsteps, okay?"

He nodded halfheartedly. She reached out and tipped up his chin.

"And from now on, if you're going to be late, you call me."

"I will."

"And you'll give some thought to the other?"

He nodded.

"Okay, then, I think it's time we both got some sleep."

She pushed off the couch while he remained in his chair, still dejected. "Come on," she said, refashioning his hair with her fingers. "It's not the end of the world."

He jerked his head away from her touch, sullenly avoiding her gaze.

"All right," she said, "I'm off to bed. Goodnight."

In her room she turned off her bedside lamp and got under the covers but lay looking at the thin thread of light beside her nearly closed bedroom door. The living room lamp snapped off. The bathroom door closed, the toilet flushed, water ran, and in his bedroom she heard Joey's shoes thump to the floor as he took them off.

She had closed her eyes when his voice opened them again. "Hey, Mom?"

"Yes?"

She could see the line of his body cutting off the light along the edge of her door. He pushed it open and stood slump-shouldered, the hall light outlining the hair she had rearranged earlier. "I'm really sorry I scared you," he said. "I never thought about what you said before, I mean, how you worry about us when we're out of your sight. I didn't mean to do that to you."

Her throat began filling instantly.

"Come here," she said.

He walked around the foot of the bed to *her side,* where she'd never stopped sleeping after Bill died, even though it was farther from the door. She put up her arms and he sat on the edge of the mattress, bending over her.

"I love you," she said as they hugged, "and that's the important message in everything that's happened tonight. If I didn't love you I wouldn't care about where you are or what you're doing."

"I love you too, Mom."

And with those words, the knot of sadness dissolved in her throat.

Christopher called the next day, right after church.

"How's everything with Joey?" he asked.

"We had a talk and things came out all right."

"I could see it coming, that's why I thought it was best if I got out of there."

What a kind and caring man he was. It struck Lee again, as it had over and over when she'd lain in bed last night, that whatever her needs, he was always there for her. Turning to him had become so natural for her that it was hard to imagine her life without him. Not only had he come on the run last night, now he was calling the way a true friend would, concerned once more for both her and Joey.

"Christopher, I can't thank you enough for coming. I'd forgotten how stressful it is to handle a teenager without a partner. When I saw you coming up the walk, I felt . . ." She found it hard to put into words. Even now the thought of him brought a welcome reprise of the relief and gratitude she'd felt last night.

"What?" he prodded.

"Relieved. So relieved to dump my worries on someone else for once. And so often you seem to know how I need you, and you show up as if by magic. It always feels right when I . . . I turn to you. I guess I rely on you too much, but just to have you there . . . it means so much to me, Christopher."

"I like being there for you."

The line grew quiet while their feelings extended beyond those of friends into that winsome world of near-lovers.

After a while he cleared his throat. "I've thought about you a lot since Tuesday. Could I see you today? I thought, if you don't have any other plans, I'd take you and Joey out to brunch somewhere."

Disappointment deluged her. "I'm sorry, Christopher, but Lloyd is here. I was just going to start making some chicken for dinner."

"Bring him along. I'd like to see him again, too."

Lee looked toward the wall dividing her from the living room where Lloyd was reading the Sunday paper and Joey was playing a video game on TV.

"All right. I'll ask him." She raised her voice. "Lloyd? Joey? Either one of you interested in going out to Sunday brunch with Christopher?"

Joey came around the corner in his church clothes. The mention of food once again brought him running. "Yeah, sure . . . where?"

She covered the mouthpiece. "I'm not going to ask him where," she whispered. "That would be rude."

Lloyd called, "That sounds good to me."

She told Christopher, "They both said yes, and that goes for me, too. I'll put the chicken in the refrigerator and cook it tomorrow night."

"How about over at Edinburgh?"

"I've never been there, but I hear it's fabulous."

"I'll pick you up in thirty minutes."

At Edinburgh Country Club, they were seated by a window that looked out across the snow-covered golf course. In the middle of the room an ice carving of a dolphin formed the centerpiece for the main buffet. Around them, in tables of all sizes, extended families were brunching likewise. Everywhere Lee looked she saw grandparents, parents and children: Three generations out for a family get-together, dressed in Sunday clothes, talking and laughing. The four of them—herself, Christopher, Joey and Lloyd—looked as if they were another of those families. For a while she indulged in the fantasy that they were, that she and Christopher were a pair who'd left their home for a pleasant Sunday meal among others. Last night they had handled a crisis over Joey together, and today here they were, like those around them, putting the incident behind them and going on with life.

She sat across the table from Christopher, listening to him talking with Lloyd about the canine units of the Anoka police force, then listening while Lloyd told about a black labrador he'd had when he was a boy on the farm. Joey got into the conversation, too, with an anecdote about his friend's dog who had once chewed the crotches out of all the family's underwear in the dirty-clothes basket.

Everyone laughed, and the waitress came to replenish their coffee.

Lloyd said, "Well, I think I'm going back for more of that fettuccine."

Joey said, "Me too, Grampa. But first I'm gonna have some bread pudding with caramel sauce."

Left alone, Christopher and Lee watched them go. "I like Lloyd," he said.

"So do I."

Christopher's eyes veered back to the woman across the table, catching her watching him steadily, wearing an unmistakable look of admiration. Maybe even love.

"Was your husband like him?"

"I suppose so, in some ways. But Bill was less patient, maybe even a little more judgmental than Lloyd. I think he got that from his mother."

"I'm surprised to hear you say that about Bill."

"Why?"

"Because you told me once you'd had a perfect marriage."

"A perfect marriage doesn't mean the people in it are perfect. Usually it means that they both overlook each other's imperfections."

He thought about that awhile, then asked, "So, didn't you get along with your mother-in-law?"

"I got along with her just fine. But she was judgmental. When Bill died she said I was crazy not to pay off the house with the insurance money so I'd be secure. She thought I shouldn't go to school, shouldn't start a business—what if it failed and all that. Then when Sylvia decided to quit her job with an accounting firm and come in with me, Ruth said it would never work out. Two sisters working together every day—she said we'd be at each other's throats in no time. But we've managed just fine. We each have our fortes and we stick to them. She takes care of the business and I take care of the arranging."

Joey returned to the table with a mountain of the restaurant's signature dessert, which he dug into, doubled over the plate. "Hey, Christopher, guess what," he said with his mouth full.

"What?"

"My birthday is next month and I'm going to be fifteen. That means I can get my driver's permit."

"Your mom better look out then."

Lloyd returned and the talk moved on to a variety of subjects.

Eventually, Christopher checked his watch. "I hate to break this up, but it's after one-thirty and I've got to report for roll call in an hour."

Joey said, "Do I have time for just one more piece of dessert? I didn't get a chance to try that chocolate fool stuff with all the nuts in it."

Lee said, "Go get one, quick, and take it with you in a napkin." Observing him hurry away, Lee remarked, "The bottomless pit," and they all rose, chuckling.

Chris took them home. They thanked him before he drove away, and Lloyd said he thought he'd go home right away, too; he was tired and his Sunday cross-word was waiting for him. He drove off only moments after Chris did.

Lee spent the afternoon wrapping Christmas gifts and making popcorn balls, listening to Christmas music on the stereo and enjoying the arrival of a gray twilight that brought a light snow along with it. In the midst of that dusky time of day someone knocked on the front door and she answered to find Christopher there again, this time in uniform with his trusty radio in its leather sleeve on his belt.

"Hi," she said, opening the storm door and letting him in. "Back so soon?"

He held up a napkin with a square grease stain on the bottom. "Joey forgot his chocolate fool in my truck."

"Oh, thanks," she said, taking it from him and carrying it toward the kitchen.

He followed and stopped beside the table, perusing it and the disorderly room. There was a difference between it and the dirty rooms of his youth. This disorder had a homely warmth to it.

"Wrapping gifts, huh?"

"I have been, but I'm about to put this junk away. I've got a backache from bending over too long. Want a cup of coffee or something?"

"No, but what's that I see over there?"

She looked where he was pointing and couldn't help smiling at his boyish pose, the back of his hand to his nose, the index finger straight out. "Why, I believe those are popcorn balls. Could it be you want one?"

He answered with his eyebrows, Groucho Marx style.

"Help yourself." While she began putting away Christmas wrap, he peeled the plastic covering from a pink popcorn ball and bit into it.

"Mmm . . ." It stuck to his teeth and he had to work his jaw to manage chewing. "Did you make them?"

"Aha. Family tradition."

"Mmm . . ."

He leaned against the cabinet, chewing the sticky treat, watching her clean off the table, wipe it with a dishcloth, find a Christmas centerpiece and put it there, then get a broom and begin sweeping. She was wearing a pair of blue jeans and an oversized sweatshirt emblazoned with the words MAD ABOUT MINNESOTA! On her feet she wore white socks with dirty bottoms, reminiscent of her son's. All the while she moved around the room he was remembering lying on his couch kissing her last Tuesday.

"Where's Joey?"

"Sleeping off last night. He's been lost to the world most of the afternoon."

He put the popcorn ball down on the cabinet, sucked off a thumb and finger, went up behind her, took the broom from her hand and angled it against the edge of the table. "Come here," he said, and led her by the hand into the work area of the kitchen where they couldn't be seen from the bedroom hall. "I didn't get a chance to do this this morning, and it's been driving me crazy." He put his arms around her and kissed her, standing in the middle of the messy kitchen with the popcorn popper and dirty kettles and syrup bottles littering the sink and countertop, and bits of ribbon and wrapping paper littering the floor. She gave him no resistance, doubling her forearms behind his neck and leaning against his chest in its metal-bound bullet-proof vest. The kiss began friendly, as if it might be brief, but they started swaying in unison and opened their mouths, and everything felt so lovely that they kept on swaying and soon they were gyrating their heads. He ran his hands up beneath her sweatshirt and over her bare back just above her waistband. Even when his radio crackled and he reached down to adjust the volume, they continued the kissing and swaying.

"Is that for you?" she asked against his mouth.

"No."

They went on pleasuring each other with their mouths until it seemed absurd to continue without doing more; yet they were doing no more.

At last she freed her mouth, but left her arms where they were. "This is so exciting," she teased with a crooked smile. "It's like hugging a brick wall."

"Gotta wear 'em when we're on duty," he said of his flak vest, "but if you want to hug me without it, just name the date and time and I'll be there."

"Tuesday night, seven o'clock. Joey usually goes to the movies because it's dollar night."

"Can't. Gotta work."

"Wednesday night, seven o'clock. Joey *doesn't* go to the movies but what the hell—let's shock him."

"Can't. Gotta work."

She was sort of hanging on him, her mouth pasted with a saucy smile.

"Fine squeeze you are. Get a woman to proposition you, then you dream up excuses."

"How about Tuesday noon at my apartment? I'll fix you lunch."

The word "nooner" flashed through her mind. "Seriously?"

"Mm-hm. Something light that won't make you logy." He grinned suggestively, still rubbing his hands over her warm, smooth back while her chin drilled his chest and he arched back to look down at her.

"It's a date," she said, and slipped from his arms.

The word came to her again and again. Is that what it was going to be? A nooner? Was he anticipating it the way she was? Fearing its complications? Living with this uncertainty about what would happen once they had uninterrupted privacy?

On Tuesday morning, just before shutting off the bathroom light and heading for work, she gazed at herself in the mirror in wide-eyed wonder. Good God, she was heading for a romantic liaison at high noon! There was no other explanation for her preparations. Why else had she shaved her legs, and put on perfume, and scrubbed her fingernails until the flesh tore beneath them? And shaved under her arms and put on her best underclothes, and made sure her pantyhose had no runs, even though they'd be hidden beneath her slacks?

Could it be she was planning to take them off?

No, she was not! She was merely covering all bets.

The morning seemed to crawl. Of all plants to work with, she ended up arranging dyed heather, and it stained her fingers so badly they looked inked. Before she left the store at noon she went into the bathroom and gave them the scrubbing of their lives, then applied some strong-scented almond-oil lotion, as much of it as her hands would absorb. She also refreshed her lipstick and brushed her hair.

"Hey, Syl?" she called, moving through the store. "I might be gone a little longer than usual. Any problem?"

"No. I'll be here. See you when you get back."

Parking in Christopher's parking lot, heading into the building, knocking on his door, she felt as if she were heading toward some nefarious dealings. She was meeting a man for lunch. So what?

So there were butterflies in her stomach and she was fidgeting with her hair when he opened the door.

"Hi."

"Hi."

Her cheeks might have turned the faintest bit pinker.

"You really came. I wasn't sure you would."

"Why not?"

"I don't know. I just wasn't sure."

He stepped back and she walked in, left her boots by the door, let him take her jacket and hang it.

"Hungry?" he asked.

"Ravenous. What are we having?"

"Egg-salad sandwiches and tomato soup."

"I love tomato soup! And egg salad, too."

"Well . . . everything's ready." He gestured to his kitchen table. "I just have to pour the soup. Sit down."

The dishes were some of her old green ones. The sandwiches were plump with egg salad between thick-sliced nine-grain bread, with curly red lettuce showing around the edges. Each sandwich was cut in half and accompanied by a little pile of tiny dill pickles. The silverware was mismatched. Paper towels substituted for napkins. The centerpiece was the fat red candle and holly ring he'd bought the day they were together at Gustaf's. The candle was lit though it was a bright, sunny day.

He put two bowls of steaming tomato soup on the table and sat down.

"Christopher, this is lovely."

"Nothing fancy, like I promised."

"Curly red lettuce."

"I learned about different kinds of lettuce when I worked at the Red Owl store."

"And a centerpiece."

"Largely because of you. If I remember correctly, you were the one who said it's impossible to be lonely with a candle glowing in the room. That's why I bought it."

"I think I recognize the dishes."

"I'm sure you do."

"I got them when Bill and I were first married. It was back before the price of gas flew sky-high. Gas stations used to offer premiums to get customers to come in. A free dish with every fill—that's where these came from."

"They serve the purpose."

"Yes, they do. They make me feel right at home."

They both smiled, biting into their sandwiches and getting egg salad caught on the corners of their mouths.

She asked how Judd was doing, if he'd seen him lately. Christopher said he made sure he saw him every week. This week he'd taken him to the police weight room and let him work out a little.

She asked about Christmas, if there'd be any sort of holiday for the boy at home. He told her that parents like Judd's usually got guilt pangs at holiday time and did *something* for their kids. He also said it was high drug- and alcohol-use time of year, so one never knew what could erupt.

She asked him if he'd ever thought about becoming Judd's foster parent.

"No," he answered. "I'm there for him when he needs me, and he knows that. He understands that life dealt him a tough hand, but that he's got to play it out. I'm only there to help him do that. But I've never wanted to have kids of my own, either adopted or otherwise. I've known that since I was twelve years old, forced into the role of parenting my sister."

They sipped their hot soup, ate their sandwiches. He looked at her hands, holding the bread.

"What's that on your fingers?"

She dropped the sandwich and hid the hand in her paper towel on her lap. "Dye. I was working with heather this morning. It's sprayed with this awful stuff that stains just like ink."

He reached over, found her wrist in her lap and carried it up to the tabletop. "You don't have to hide your hands from me, okay? They're honest hands. I like them."

They finished their food and he said, "Sorry, no dessert. It's too hard to keep in shape eating desserts, and fat cops can't run fast when they need to . . . so . . . this is it."

"I don't need dessert either. This was just perfect."

She rose with dishes in her hand. He took them from her. "Leave them. That's my job."

She was his guest, she realized, and conceded. "All right."

He picked up the soup bowls to rinse while she wandered into the living room and found herself unable to resist testing the soil in every flowerpot there, then looking into the Christmas tree stand to discover it nearly dry.

"Christopher, shame on you. You'll burn the place down if you don't keep your tree watered." She went to the kitchen and asked, "Do you have a coffeepot I can fill it with?" At the kitchen sink she filled the pot, and returned to the living room. On hands and knees, pouring, she realized there was only one gift beneath his tree and wondered who it was from.

He shut off the water and came into the room just as she finished pouring and sat back on her heels. The coffeepot was taken from her hands and discarded to one side as he sat down beside her on one hip, a hand braced on the carpet.

"The gift is for you," he said. "I want you to open it."

"For me?"

He nodded. "Open it."

"But it isn't even Christmas yet, and I don't have anything for you."

"You're here. That's all the gift I need. Open it."

The box was wrapped in silvery-blue foil with a gauzy silver ribbon. The package was shaped like a necktie box. She opened it as eagerly as a child.

Inside she found a plain white business envelope. From inside that she pulled two plane tickets and a color brochure from Longwood Gardens in Kennett Square, Pennsylvania. She barely gave the tickets a glance, but opened the brochure and avidly ran her eyes over photographs of trailing wisteria, statuary, glass houses and profuse blooms of many kinds. On second glance, she saw the tickets were to Philadelphia.

"A trip?" she said, raising excited eyes. "You're giving me a trip?"

"For two. Next summer, in July, when everything's in bloom. You can take whoever you want. I thought you might like to take Sylvia, or maybe even Lloyd."

"Oh, Christopher . . ." She looked down at the beguiling color brochure again and read aloud, "Longwood Gardens . . . a setting of perfect serenity, with its winding paths, temples, passionate bursts of color . . ."

"I went to a travel agent and she helped me pick which one. She said this is one of the best, and I didn't think you'd ever done anything like that before. I thought it was time you did."

"Oh, Christopher . . ." When she lifted her face there were tears in her eyes. She flung both arms around his neck, the brochure crackling against his shoulder. "All my life I've wanted to do something like this."

He hugged her back, smiling at her response, which was exactly the one he'd hoped for. "I'll bet you'll meet a lot of people there with blue fingers, and not one of them will be apologizing."

She kissed him, kneeling in the crook of his hip, tipping her head sharply to one side while his arms spanned half her circumference. Her heart was hammering from excitement over his gift. When she pulled back, she looked square into his eyes and said, "Nobody's ever given me a gift I liked this much. Nobody reads me like you do, Christopher Lallek. How is it that you read me so well?"

"I don't know."

"It's like you see into my head sometimes! If somebody asked me to name the perfect gift for me, I couldn't even name it myself, yet you knew what it was."

He only smiled.

Hugging him, she looked at the brochure over his shoulder. "This cost you a bundle, and I know I should object, but I'm not going to. I want to go too badly! Longwood Gardens! My God, Christopher, you're too good to be true!"

She kissed him again, both of them so perfectly happy at that moment it could only be celebrated thusly: with open mouths that fit less than passionately because they were both smiling; with appreciative hands that ran over one another's sweaters; with sheer joy in being together, and alive, and having one another to spend this improbable sunny December lunch hour with.

He fell to his back, taking her with him, and she reveled in lying across his chest, down one half of his body, letting herself kiss and kiss and kiss him, unable to get enough of the delightful pastime after so many, many manless years. Oh, the warm, liquid interior of his mouth, how good it felt again. And the sturdiness and texture of a strong male body—it, too, filled her with a sense of coming back to a pleasure long abandoned. The kiss changed tone and the glossy brochure in her hand became extraneous. She put it on the rough plush of the carpet and slid it away till it *tinked* against the coffeepot, freeing her hand to slide into his hair. Her right leg lay between his legs and she knew perfectly well what she felt down there; she raised her knee and pressed against it, against the hard, aroused flesh of a man whose desire for her came as a great joy. He raised his knee, too, between her legs, and his head off the floor, rolling them partially onto their sides. He gripped her from behind, hands spread wide on her woolen slacks, catching the curve of her buttocks, thrusting against her while she gave them both some added leverage by putting the sole of her foot on the backside of his calf. He was wearing denim jeans, stiff and heavy through the nylon covering her foot. There had been times after Bill died when she'd wondered if she'd ever do this again, times she'd lain alone in the dark and longed for someone to touch this way, to make her feel alive and sexual.

"Oh, Christopher," she whispered against his mouth, "you feel so good. Everything about you. Hair, muscle, even whiskers. It's been so long since I've felt a man's face this way." She rubbed hers against it, seeking texture from his freshly shaved skin, kissing him wherever she pleased. His hands slid up inside her sweater and cupped her breasts. She shuddered, arched and grew very still, her eyes closed while she absorbed all the wondrous sexual feelings reeling back after all the years. "It's been so long. Sometimes I'd wonder if I might dry up and lose my ability to do this. Now here you are, making me feel it all again after so many years. It's all rushing back, making me feel like a woman. And, ohhh, it feels good."

"What do you want?" he asked in a husky voice while she kissed his face everywhere. "Do you want to make love?"

"I can't. I want to but I can't. I don't have anything and it's—"

"I do."

"You've been planning this."

"We've both been planning this."

"Maybe I have." Her hands were in his hair, but both their eyes were closed. "I thought about the word 'nooner' ever since Sunday night, but if I went and got a contraceptive and brought it along, I would have been . . . you know. I couldn't make myself do it. Christopher, I'm forty-five years old."

"And hornier than you've been since your husband was alive."

"I've got to get back to the shop."

"Yeah, you feel like you're heading back to the shop." Their eyes were still closed. He was caressing both her breasts, sending rivers of feeling from them clear down her limbs. Their legs were still plaited with the sole of her foot wedged behind his calf. He reached behind her as if to unsnap her bra.

"Don't . . . please. This is far enough. Please, Christopher . . . please . . . I'm too tempted."

He returned to caressing her through her bra. "We're going to end up in bed eventually anyway, and you know it."

"My God, I'm being seduced." She had thrown her head back and he was kissing her throat.

"Yes, you are."

"By a boy of thirty."

"Thirty's no boy."

"No, I can feel that."

"So what do you say . . . Mrs. Robinson?"

She smiled and opened her eyes, drawing her head down to meet his gaze eye-to-eye. He was smiling, too, teasing her. They lay on their sides on the carpet, reading one another's faces at close range . . . her rust eyes, his blue ones.

"I just realized I'm doing exactly what I lectured Joey not to do last Saturday night. How do I think I'm ever going to keep on resisting you if we keep this up? Some mother I am, preaching out of one side of my mouth and flirting out of the other, but, damn it, Christopher, you feel so good, I just can't say it enough. But if we go to bed—what then? Where does it lead? What if someone finds out?"

"You've got a lot of hang-ups, you know that? Maybe all it will lead to is us having a good time together, but what's wrong with that? Enjoying each other *in* bed seems to me a natural extension of how we enjoy each other out of bed. Furthermore, we're both single. We're both beyond the age of consent. We both want it a lot."

"Boy, you can say that again." She rolled from him and sat up, feeling shaky and liquid and sensitized. With their legs still tangled she propped an elbow on her knee and rubbed her messy hair back from her face. "All right, suppose we do go to bed. I live in a modern-day world with modern-day problems. I'd want to know something about your past sex life."

He sat up, too—his legs lolling open—and caught one of her feet, put her smooth sole against his genitals and held it there, lightly, with one hand, caressing her through her nylons.

"If a condom isn't enough for you, just say the word and I'll be at a doctor's office tomorrow morning having an AIDS test."

She might live in a modern-day world, but his remark dropped her chin and left her staring at him. Nothing he'd said today had affected her more than these words: what an act of faith for a man to do such a thing.

"You mean it, don't you?"

"Of course I mean it. We'll start with a clean slate."

She stared at him, struck with a fresh new fear: She thought perhaps—dear God, how could it be?—she was falling in love with him. With a man fifteen years her junior.

He went on calmly, "The last time I went to bed with a woman was about two years ago. We dated for about six months, then she moved to Texas on a job promotion. Before that there were four, I think, going way back to high school. I've never been what you might call a ladies' man. Mostly I've been a loner."

She reclaimed her foot from his genitals and sat on it. She took his hand in both of hers, examining it while spreading the fingers wide, then closing them repeatedly.

After some thought, she looked up into his clean, handsome face.

"I need some time to think about this, Christopher. It still doesn't seem right."

"Because I'm younger?"

"Partly."

He looked down at his hand in hers, its fingers opening and closing. "Well, that I can't change. I'll always be younger, and there'll always be those who might accuse you of robbing the cradle. I know that."

A dejected silence fell. She put her hand on his shoulder. "I love my gift very, very much. Of all the people I've ever known in my life, I've never known one as intuitive as you. Not even Bill, and I mean that."

He looked up and gave her a three-cornered smile. "Well, that's a start anyway, isn't it?"

She, too, smiled. "Now I really do have to go back to work. May I use your bathroom first?"

"Sure."

She took her purse along, brushed her hair and applied fresh lipstick. When she came out he was getting her jacket from the closet. He held it while she slipped it on, then turned her by her shoulders to face him.

Angling his head, he gave her a goodbye kiss, gentle and lingering.

When it ended she touched his mouth with the pad of one forefinger. "Thank you for the lunch."

"You're welcome. Anytime."

"And for the tickets."

He only smiled in reply and kissed her finger.

"Christmas Eve," she said quietly, backing away. "Eleven o'clock. I'll wait up for you." One last word came out in a whisper. " 'Bye."

Chapter 13

Chris was scheduled to work both Christmas Eve and Christmas Day from three to eleven. That shift, on that particular night, was known to be unusually busy with emergency calls, though most of them were not true emergencies: The calls came from lonely people without friends or family who, rather than face Christmas Eve alone, manufactured ailments and went to emergency rooms. There they found people to talk to, someone to pay attention to them, human hands that touched and cared.

Those on duty at the station had come to expect calls from old Lola Gildress, who smelled so bad they had to leave the squad car doors open for a while after dropping her off. Frank Tinker's gallbladder acted up every year, too. He called every patrolman "sonny" and offered them his snuffbox for a pinch, needed a pop can to spit into while he rode in the squad car and always asked them if they'd mind swinging down along Brisbin Street on their way to the hospital. There, he turned rheumy eyes to a two-story house where he'd lived as a boy in a family of six, all of them gone now but him. Elda Minski called, too, as usual, and flounced out of her front door wearing a flea-bitten fox stole, vintage 1930, and a horrendous sequined turban on her bald head, eager to repeat her story of escaping the Russian Revolution and coming to America to sing opera on the same stages where Caruso and Paderewski had performed. The one they all waited for, though, was Inez Gurney, a sweet old woman curled over like a bass clef, who toddled out of her house taking baby steps—the largest she could manage—carrying a tin of German butter cookies for anyone kind enough to wish her Merry Christmas.

Christopher answered Inez's call this year.

When he knocked on her door she was all ready and waiting, wearing a home-knit cap that tied under her chin and ancient rubber boots with zippers up the front and fur above the ankles. The heels of the boots never left the ground when Inez walked.

He touched his hat visor and said, "Emergency call, Mrs. Gurney?"

"Gracious me, yes, but there's no need to hurry." Her *S*'s whistled through false teeth that had outgrown her shrinking gums. "I'm actually feeling a little better. If you'll give me your arm, young man, and carry this . . ."

He took her red tin with the painting of a holiday wreath on top, and escorted her down the path to the squad car.

"I thought the doctors might enjoy a taste of my German butter cookies." She said the same thing every year. "And, of course, you're welcome to sample them yourself. My-oh-my . . ." She tried to look up at the sky but her osteoporosis wouldn't allow it. "Isn't this some heavenly night though? Do you suppose we can see the Star of Bethlehem?"

"I imagine we can, but I wouldn't know which one it is. Would you?"

He stopped in the path to give her time. Again she tried to look up, bending her knees and angling her stiff old body. "No, I suppose not, but when I was a girl my papa taught me to find Cassiopeia and Orion and all the constellations. We lived on a farm near Ortonville, and my-y-y, those skies were big over the prairie. Have you ever been to Ortonville, young man?"

"No, ma'am, I haven't."

"It's farm country. Goose country, too. Why, in the fall those honkers would fly over in battalions, so many of them they'd fair block out the sun. And when they landed in a cornfield you could hear their voices bellering like blow horns clear over to Montevideo. Papa always shot one for Thanksgiving, and one for Christmas, too." They moved on toward the squad car, her hand on his arm, Christopher adjusting his stride to her baby steps while she told him about their Christmas dinners on the farm near Ortonville, her mother's sauerkraut stuffing and precisely what her mother had put into her beets to make them sweet and sour both, and how she herself had never mastered beets like her mother's.

At the squad car she needed help getting in, then swinging her legs to the front.

"Watch your purse," he said, pushing it up so he could slam the door.

Inside, he reported his whereabouts and destination to the dispatcher, and Mrs. Gurney asked, "Would you like to sample my cookies?"

"I certainly would. I'm a bachelor, so I don't get many homemade treats."

"I use only real butter, and cardamom. Some people think it's nutmeg, but it's not, it's cardamom. That's my secret." She had trouble opening the tin. Her fingers bent sharply from the end knuckle and her skin looked like mouse-spotted rice paper. "There we are," she said, when the lid finally gave.

He ate three cookies on the way to Mercy Hospital and told her he'd never tasted anything so delicious in his life, which put a smile on her wizened old face.

At Mercy, in the glaring white lights of the ER, he watched Mrs. Gurney being rolled away in a wheelchair with the tin on her lap, telling a young nurse about the cardamom and real butter she'd used in the cookies she'd brought for the doctors.

Back in his squad car, Christopher felt unutterably sad. The taste of the spice with the strange name—cardamom—lingered in his mouth. The faint smell of mothballs seemed to linger in the car, too, and he had the thought that maybe Mrs. Gurney kept them in her bed to preserve her very body. Poor old thing. Poor lonely old thing. Yet in spite of her loneliness, she had a need to give on Christmas Eve. What was more pitiful than a person with no one to give to?

It made him think of his own parents, who had been given two children and had squandered them both. What were they doing tonight in their dreary little apartment over there at Jackson Estates? Was there a tree? A special supper? Gifts? Anything? And where was Jeannie? Still shacked up in LA with her drug-pusher? Still fat and greasy-haired and living the reflection of their parents' lives? He imagined what it might be like if Jeannie had stayed around here, graduated from high school, gotten respectably married and had a couple of kids. What would it be like at her house tonight? Would he go there taking gifts to his nieces and nephews, and maybe help some brother-in-law put together toys for the kids' stockings? He tried to imagine his parents as grandparents, but the image wouldn't gel.

Lord, the city streets were so quiet on Christmas Eve. Cars at churches, but nowhere else. For once the bars were closed. Even the lighted Christmas decorations hanging from the lamp poles on Main Street looked forlorn.

He drove by Lee's house, but saw no activity. They, too, were probably at church.

He turned around in the circle at the end of Benton Street and cruised past her house once more, anxious for his shift to end so he could come back.

All the way back uptown his radio was still. At the west end of Main he kept going, right out onto the highway toward his apartment. Making sure his radio was on his belt, he went inside to his own refrigerator, opened the door and stood a long time contemplating the ham. It was wrapped in a mesh bag, must have weighed eighteen pounds, and one like it had been given in gratitude to every person on the staff who had responded to a call and saved the life of some rich people's son after he'd fallen into a swimming pool last summer.

There sat the ham.

Over at Jackson Estates sat his parents.

Reaching for the piece of meat he realized he wasn't so much different from Inez Gurney.

At Jackson Estates the hall smelled like stale cooked vegetables. Its walls were crosshatched with black marks. The corners of the woodwork were worn white. Some doors had been patched where boots had kicked through them. Three candy wrappers and a rusty tricycle sat halfway along the dingy corridor. He knocked at number six and waited. The Wise Men must have made it to Bethlehem faster than his mother made it to the door.

"Hi, Mavis," he said when she opened it.

"What do you want?"

"Just came to wish you Merry Christmas, that's all."

From inside, a gravelly voice yelled, "Who is it, Mavis? And hurry up and shut that goddamned door, will you? This place is built like a goddamn chicken coop!"

"Yeah, yeah!" she bellowed in a coarse whiskey-voice, "quit your bellyachin', you old sonofabitch." To Chris she said, "Well, come on in then, don't stand there in the hall while the old man chews my ass."

As he walked inside he heard his father coughing. The old man was sitting in a dilapidated chair with a metal TV tray beside him. A whiskey bottle and a shot glass shared the tray with a jar of Vicks, the *T.V. Guide,* a box of corn plasters and an empty metal plate from a TV dinner. Between the old man's throne and a similar arrangement four feet away, an artificial Christmas tree about a foot and a half high leaned like the Tower of Pisa, its permanently affixed lights looking hazy through the smoke from Mavis's cigarette, which still burned in an ashtray. She, too, was armed with a bottle and a shot glass. Her chosen libation, however, was peppermint schnapps. The room smelled of it, and the Vicks and the smoke, and the Salisbury steak gravy that congealed on the bottoms of their foil dishes.

"What do you say, Old Man?" Christopher said as he entered the sickening room and thumped the ham down on the adjacent kitchen table.

"Don't say nothin'. Got me a sonovabitch of a cold. What brings you around here all gussied up in your cop uniform? You wanna impress your ma and pa with how important you are?"

"Now, Ed, leave the boy alone," Mavis said, then burst into a fit of crackly coughing measuring about two packs a day on the nico-Richter scale.

"I brought you a ham," Chris told them.

"A ham . . . well, say, that's nice," said Mavis. "Here, have a drink."

"I'm on duty."

"Oh, that's right. Well, what the hell . . . just a little one. It's Christmas."

"I don't drink."

"Oh, that's right."

"He don't drink, Mavis," the old man sneered. "Our holier-than-thou, gun-totin' upstanding citizen cop don't touch the stuff to his lips, do you, Officer?"

Why had he come here again? Why had he set himself up for the hurt these occasional breakdowns in common sense always brought?

"You ought to think about drying out," he said to Ed. "I'll help you anytime you want."

"Come here to deliver your Christmas sermon, did you? I dry out when I *want* to dry out! I've told you that before! Think you can bring a goddamn ham in here and drop it on the table and start preaching, well, just get your ass out!"

"Now, Ed," Mavis said. "Chris, sit down."

"I can't stay. There are still emergency calls coming in even though it's Christmas Eve. I just thought . . ."

What had he thought? That they'd changed? Magically changed while marinating away here day after day in their self-made alcoholic stew?

Jesus, they were so foul and pathetic.

"Have you heard from Jeannie?" he asked.

"Not a word," replied Mavis. "You'd think she'd have the decency to send a card to her mother and dad at Christmastime, but no, not even that."

She didn't see it, didn't see any of it, not how unlovable they were, how undeserving of any consideration from their children. It took more than starting a child in a womb and spewing it forth to make a person deserving of the title "parent."

He felt himself growing physically sick, looking at them.

"Well, listen . . . enjoy the ham. I've got to go."

Mavis came to show him out; he wished she'd have remained in her chair where he need not smell the stale schnapps and smoke on her breath, or let her filthy garments brush his, or see her nicotine-stained fingers on the doorknob.

Thankfully, she didn't touch him or—worse—kiss his cheek as she sometimes remembered to do.

When the door closed behind him he bolted for fresh air, for the blameless, clear, star-studded night where somewhere people prayed in churches and gave each other gifts and sang carols around pianos.

And he thought, *Lee, please, be up when I get there at eleven.*

The Hillier Christmas tradition held that Orrin and Peg spend Christmas Eve at Lee's house and Christmas Day at Sylvia's. Lloyd came every year around noon of Christmas Eve day and stayed overnight so he'd be there in the morning for the opening of gifts. Janice, of course, was home from college, and to Lee's amazement, little Sandy Parker dropped in on Christmas Eve afternoon for about an hour, too. Though Lee was genuinely friendly to the girl, she found herself studying the fuzzy-haired, sloe-eyed brunette as the person with whom her son had recently begun practicing the rudiments of necking, and possibly—probably—petting.

The young people—dear, thoughtful hearts that they were—knew that this holiday would have a great, sad hole at its heart where Greg had once been, and they stopped over, too—Nolan, Sandy, Jane and Kim.

Candlelight church service was held at six, and afterward Lee fed everyone oyster stew and cranberry cake with hot brandied sauce, their traditional Christmas Eve fare.

They opened their gifts from Orrin and Peg but kept the rest for Christmas morning. They watched Pavarotti perform from some immense gothic temple with a 120-voice choir behind him. They missed Greg so terribly each of them went away to shed private tears at one time or another.

At ten o'clock, Orrin and Peg said they were going home.

Lee said, "Oh, can't you stay a little longer? Christopher gets off at eleven and he's coming over then."

"I'm sorry, honey, we can't. We'll be up fairly early to go over to Sylvia's and open gifts with them."

Janice said, "I didn't know Chris was coming over tonight. I thought he was coming in the morning."

"Poor guy had to work three to eleven on Christmas Eve, so I told him I'd save some oyster stew and cake for him and he could drop by for a midnight snack."

Peg said, "Wish him Merry Christmas from us. We might stop by tomorrow, or if you feel like it, come over to Sylvia's later on in the day."

"We might, but you know how it is. Everybody always likes to hang around here on Christmas Day. Play with their new toys."

When Orrin and Peg were gone, Lee said, "Time to stuff stockings." They had never given up the tradition. Each of them went to their rooms and found sacks of tiny gifts they'd squirreled away during the past few weeks, even Lloyd. The stocking that last year had said *Greg,* this year said *Chris.*

"I hope none of you mind my including Chris this year," Lee said.

Joey said, "Naw. Chris is neat."

Lloyd said, "Since when have any of us minded including Chris?"

Janice said, "I got something special for Chris's stocking."

"What?" her brother asked.

"None of your business. I got something special for you, too."

"What?"

She poked a tissue-wrapped ingot into his sock.

"Lemme see!"

"Get away, nosy!"

The two of them started tussling on the living room floor, and Lloyd smiled broadly at their antics.

They were all still up at 11:15 when Christopher got there. The tree was lit, the television was rerunning an old James Galway Christmas concert, and the stockings were hung from the arms of a dining room chair that had been set beside the tree and pressed into use as a substitute chimney for as long as it had been in the family.

When Christopher stepped in, still in uniform, he held a stack of gifts. The family surrounded him, exclaiming over the packages, taking his jacket, his hat, and wishing him Merry Christmas. Then Janice took his hand and led him into the living room.

"Come and see what's in here for you."

When he saw the stocking with his name on it, a powerful welling seemed to happen in his heart. He stared, battling the sting in his eyes, wondering how he'd managed to get so lucky as to have this family adopt him as they had. As one mesmerized, he reached . . .

And got his hand playfully slapped.

"No, not yet!" Janice scolded. "You have to wait for morning, the same as the rest of us."

"You don't ask much, do you?" he teased in reply.

Janice was now holding the hand she'd slapped, her fingers threaded possessively between Christopher's. "Come down here and look . . . there's more."

Indeed, there were gifts under the tree with his name on them. Several!

"Grampa and Joey and I talked it over, and we all decided you should stay here overnight, that way you'll be here when we all wake up in the morning. Mom, that's okay, isn't it? If Chris stays overnight?"

Christopher began to object. "Hey, wait a minute, Janice, I don't think—"

"Mom, that's okay, isn't it?" she repeated.

"Of course it's okay."

"Grampa sleeps in Greg's room," Janice explained, "and you can sleep on the sofa."

"Janice, really . . . I'm still in my uniform and . . ."

"Joey's got some baggy old sweats, haven't you, Joe?"

The decision seemed to be taken out of Christopher's hands. In short time, he had shucked off his tie, gun belt and bullet-proof vest, and was sitting on the living room floor with a bowl of oyster stew while the others lounged around with second pieces of cake. They turned the television off and kept only the tree lights on; he finished his stew and a piece of cake, and told them about Lola Gildress, Frank Tinker, Elda Minski and Inez Gurney.

He didn't tell them about taking the ham to his folks.

He told Lee later on, when everyone had gone to their rooms and he'd been given a toothbrush, blankets and a pillow, and Joey's sweats. She went down the hall, calling, "Goodnight, everyone," snapping out the lights and tapping on doors. "Everybody wake everybody else in the morning, okay?"

"Okay," they all replied, settling down in their rooms.

She made her way to the kitchen where one last light burned over the kitchen stove. "Joey-y-y-y," she called, "you forgot the kitchen stove light again." On her way past the living room, she called, " 'Night, Christopher. Don't fall asleep with those tree lights on."

He said, "Lee, come here a minute, will you?"

She entered the room where he was lying stretched out on his back with his hands stacked beneath his head, covered to the chest with an old quilt of her mother's.

She stood behind him and said quietly, "Yes?"

He reached a hand above his head. She put hers in it and he hauled her around to the side of the sofa where she knelt on the floor beside him.

He took her face in both his hands, studying what he could see of it with the tree lights behind her. He held it tenderly, his thumbs resting just beside her mouth, fanning softly over her skin.

"I love you, Lee," he said.

She hadn't expected it, not this soon, not this directly. She'd thought maybe, if they ever became intimate, he might say it someday. But this pure revelation, inspired not by some sexual tryst but by the spirit of Christmas, touched her as no passion-inspired words ever could. All within her strove toward a deeper relationship with him. She could no more withhold the words than she could keep from touching his face as she said them.

"I love you too, Christopher."

He didn't kiss her, merely sighed and pulled her down so her head lay on his chest, her forehead against his chin.

"I want to tell you something. I need to tell you, okay?"

With her ear against his chest, she could hear him swallow.

"Of course," she replied.

He waited several beats, as if gathering emotional equilibrium, before launching into it. "I went to see my parents tonight. I had taken Inez Gurney to the hospital and felt so damned sorry for her, all alone with nobody to be with on Christmas Eve. And after I got back in the squad car I started thinking about Mavis and Ed, and I suppose I identified a lot with old Inez. Hell, it was Christmas . . . and they were living right across town . . . and I hadn't seen them at all." He paused ruminatively then started again as if pulling himself from some unwanted wool gathering. "Anyway . . ." He cleared his throat. "I went to see them. I went over to my apartment and got a ham some grateful citizen had given each one of us in the department—and I took it over there." Again she heard him swallow thickly. "It was awful. The two of them, nothing but a pair of sick old drunks who really don't give a shit about me or about themselves. They just sit there drinking their lives away. It's just so damned pointless."

He stared at the tree lights: His tears had turned them into many-pointed stars.

She raised up so she could see his face. "Christopher, listen to me." She saw his glistening eyes, found a corner of the quilt and dried them. "They gave you birth, and for that you should be grateful. Somehow, out of all those misbegotten genes and chromosomes, a few of the right ones went to you and made you a good person who cares about your fellow man. But beyond that, they shirked every responsibility known to sociology. I will never again encourage you to go to them, because they don't deserve you. Alcoholism, they say, is an illness. But character is not. Their character, or lack of it, is inexcusable. Since I've known you, listened to you, learned what your childhood was like and how it's affected your adulthood, I've come to agree with you that parents *earn* love from their children, and they did nothing to earn yours. Now stop feeling guilty because you can't love them."

He kissed her forehead and said, "You're so damned good for me."

She was leaning on his chest with one arm, a hand in his hair while stroking his forehead repeatedly with her thumb. "Yes, I am," she whispered. "And you're good for me too."

He looked at her with some amazement. "Did you really say you love me?"

"Yes, I did. We both did . . . and not in the middle of a thrusting match on the floor either. There's some significance in that, isn't there?"

They both considered it awhile, then he said, "Thanks for the stocking."

"You don't know what's in it yet. Could be a stick and a lump of coal."

He'd been battling some wrenching inner emotions all evening, and they won at last. He gripped her hard, drawing her down against his chest, putting his face in her hair and squeezing his eyes shut against the sting within, the mixture of heavy-heartedness and lightheartedness this night had brought.

His parents—the failures.

This woman—the healer.

"Thanks for all of this," he said brokenly. "I don't know what the hell I did to deserve you."

She let him hold her, listening to him gulp down great knots of emotion until at last he freed her and she raised up to see his face.

"Feeling better now?"

He nodded and dried his eyes with his knuckles.

She kissed his mouth with extreme tenderness and whispered, "See you in the morning. No digging in the socks till everyone's up."

Janice awoke first, shortly after sunrise. She tiptoed to the kitchen and plugged in the electric coffeemaker, then stuck her head around the archway of the living room. Christopher lay on his side with both hands up near his face, one knee updrawn, protruding from the covers along with one bare foot.

She studied his foot—medium length, bony, with some pale hair on the toes.

She studied the palm of his right hand, fingers curled above it in repose. She studied his hair, so thick and manageable it scarcely looked mussed from his night's sleep. She studied his mouth, open a sliver as he slept, and imagined kissing it someday.

Down the hall a bedroom door opened and Christopher's eyelids flinched. The bathroom door closed and he woke up, saw Janice half-hidden around the doorway and went into a stretch with one elbow pointing at a corner of the ceiling.

"Oh . . . hi . . ." His words were distorted by the stretch. "Did I sleep too late?"

"No, everyone's just starting to wake up." She smiled. "Merry Christmas."

"Yeah, thanks, same to you. Is that coffee I smell?"

"Sure is. There'll be a jam-up in the bathroom, so go ahead and have a cup while you wait your turn."

"Thanks, I will."

"I heard you and Mom talking last night after I went to bed."

She waited while he wondered what she expected to hear him say.

"Yeah, I had something I needed to talk to her about."

"How long did you talk?"

"Not long. Ten minutes maybe."

"She's great, isn't she? You can talk to her about anything."

"Yeah, you sure can. But I knew that from Greg. He always told me that about her."

"It's been pretty awful around here without him since the holiday started, but we're all putting on a brave face."

"I know. I miss him, too."

She laid her cheek and one hand against the archway. "Thanks for filling in for him, Chris. Your being here means a lot to all of us. Especially to Mom."

How he and Lee managed to keep their feelings hidden throughout the rest of that day was an act of sheer determination. They sat on the living room floor and pulled the booty out of their stockings, still dressed in bathrobes and sweat suits, laughing at such findings as edible candy worms, bubble-gum "mosquito eggs," false eyelashes as long as spaghetti, socks with bear claws and footpads painted on them and red clown noses, which they all put on while they continued digging. Janice had bought Joey a sex manual for teenagers, which caused some laughter and some blushing, while Lloyd had gotten everyone coupons for McDonald's. In Christopher's stocking he also found tiny bottles of after-shave, a deck of playing cards, a key holder, a rubber stamp with his home address (from Joey, which surprised him because it meant they'd had long-term plans for his presence here this morning). And from Janice, two tickets to a Timberwolves game.

"If you need company, just let me know. I love the Wolves," she said.

"Gosh, thanks, Janice," he answered. "I just might."

When the stockings were emptied, they all got juice and coffee and settled down in the living room to open the gifts beneath the tree. Christopher had put plenty of thought into the gift he gave to each of them. For Joey, the object of every teenager's covetousness: a pair of Oakley sunglasses with dragonfly-blue lenses and Croakies to match. For Janice, a trip to Horst, which the gals at the police station assured him was the beauty shop of note in the Twin Cities. For Lloyd, a membership to a health club with a walking track. And for each of them, the last photograph he'd taken of Greg, blown up to a five-by-seven and framed.

The pictures brought tears, of course, but Lloyd put it best when he held the frame in one hand, wiped his eyes with the sleeve of his bathrobe and said, "We all needed this. We've been missing him a lot and haven't said anything. I don't know about the rest of you, but I've been sneaking off to wipe my eyes whenever he came to mind, which has been often. Now, thanks to Chris, he's here with us in this room again, in all our hearts at once. Thanks, Chris . . . thanks a lot."

When the emotional moment passed, they finished opening gifts. Joey gave him a paperback novel about a police detective, Lloyd a billfold, Janice a compact disc by Wynonna Judd, and Lee a coordinated sweater and shirt. It was only later, when he was taking the shirt out of the plastic sleeve and removing the pins, that he found, in the pocket, a fourteen-karat gold bracelet. Hanging from it by a golden thread was a small, flat red foil heart upon which the manufacturer's name was stamped in gold. Inside, on the space provided, she'd written *Love, Lee.*

He modeled his clothes—they fit—and kept on the wrinkled new shirt with his police trousers while they cleaned up the living room and ate a ham dinner, and tried Joey's new video game, and got a portion of the frame of a jigsaw puzzle put together. Finally, when he was getting ready to go home, he found a moment alone with Lee.

"I found the bracelet," he told her. "But it's too much."

"It's what I feel. Are you wearing it?"

He extended his wrist, proving that he'd had no intention of giving it up, too much or not. "Thank you, Lee. I really love it."

She touched the links with one finger. "So do I."

"And the heart."

She kissed his wrist where the warm gold chain crossed it.

"I wish you could stay."

"So do I. Are you going over to Sylvia's later on?"

"I'm not sure. It's awfully nice, just lolling around here."

"If I drive by, I'll give a honk. Well, I'd better say goodbye to the others."

Lloyd and Joey were in the living room playing the video game. They paused to say goodbye. Janice was in her bedroom trying on clothes. He knocked on her door and she came into the hall wearing a sweater with tags hanging from its wrist.

"Gotta go," he said. "Thanks for the best Christmas of my life."

"Thank you, too." She caught him around the neck with one arm and held him for only a moment. "And don't forget—call me if you want company at the Timberwolves."

He patted her back and they parted.

Lee saw him out. When he stood on the step and she held the door open behind him, he turned back and said, "I change shifts in three days, back to day shift, plus I have the whole New Year's weekend off. I want to take you out on New Year's Eve, so think up some excuse. Better yet, tell them the truth."

He left her with that challenge. She closed the door already beginning to scour her mind for explanations.

Chapter 14

⁓⁂⁓

Two days after Christmas, Lee received a beautiful greeting card from Christopher. In it he'd written:

Dear Lee,

Although I tried to tell you on Christmas Eve just how much it meant to me to be with you and your family for the holiday, I don't think I did a very good job. Your family is all that mine isn't, and being with you has been an education as well as a pleasure. If there were more families like yours, guys in my line of work would be put out of business. Being with you personally has come to be the best part of my life right now. You're a great lady, a special person, and a wonderful friend. Thanks a lot for everything you do for me, and especially for the Christmas gifts. The shirt and sweater are just what I like, but the bracelet—wow! I sure wasn't expecting that. I wear it every day and think of you when I put it on and when I see it there on my wrist. I'll never forget this Christmas as long as I live, and I have a feeling the same will be true about New Year's Eve. I just can't wait.

Love,
Christopher

It had been years since she'd received an affectionate greeting card from a man. Reading his words she felt romantic again, vibrant, eager—all the entirely feminine reactions of the wooed woman. It struck her as unusual that a man without a mother's positive influence would write a note such as this. He, too, was special to have done so. She reread the note time and again, sitting at home in the kitchen where they'd first kissed, thinking how unexpected was the advent of this young man into her personal life when she had not been looking for anyone to fill a gap. Indeed, she hadn't known the gap existed, now here he was, putting anticipation in her life, excitement in her days and a flurry in her widow's heart, which had been content to go unflurried for so many years.

How bizarre and unexpected to end up kneeling beside a man—especially one of Christopher's age—on a sofa on Christmas Eve and hearing that he loved her, telling him she loved him. Yet it was absolutely true. She loved him. What was to come of it, she had no idea, but the change it had wrought in her life felt so incredibly glorious she would go on gifting herself with his presence and enjoying each moment they spent together.

He called as she was sitting there reading his card for the fifth time. His voice had the power to turn her radiant within. He could say, simply, "Hi," as he did now, and in her breast happiness flowered, filled her with a wondrous sense of well-being, a benefaction that flowed on long after the conversation ended.

"I was reading your card," she told him, ". . . again."

"I meant every word in it."

"I loved every word in it. It's been years since I got a card like that from a man."

"You say that often—it's been years."

"Well, it has been. Do you mind?"

"No. Actually, it's sort of a thrill when I hear it. I like being the one bringing you back to life."

"You certainly are doing that."

"So how about dancing? Has it been years since you've done that, too?"

"Actually, it has been."

"Want to give it a whirl on New Year's Eve?"

"Yes!" she said, excited. "Oh, yes! I haven't bought a dancing dress in years!" He laughed. She laughed. "I said it again, didn't I?"

"A bunch of the guys from the department have reserved a block of tables at the Bel Ray ballroom. High Noon is playing."

"Who's High Noon?"

"The best country band around."

She gave a moment's thought to his invitation. "The department guys, huh?"

"You ready to face them as my date?"

"What do you think they'll say?"

"They'll tease me, but not when you're around."

"Well, if you can take it, I can take it. Are you a good dancer?"

"Passable. How about you?"

"I've got rhythm, but I'll probably be a little rusty."

"Want to go out to dinner first?"

"Dinner too? Christopher, you'll spoil me."

"I'd love to. How about if I pick you up at seven?"

"Fine." After a pause, she said, "Christopher, I'm so excited. I haven't been out on New Year's Eve since 1983."

"We'll make it a night you'll never forget."

She said to Janice and Joey, "Do either one of you object to Christopher taking me out on New Year's Eve?"

Joey said, "Not as long as you give me money to order a pizza."

Janice's expression drooped. "Oh, shoot! If I'd known, I wouldn't have made plans with Nolan and Jane."

Lee gazed at her daughter feeling somewhat miffed. Was she so old and decrepit that it was inconceivable Christopher might want to take her out *without* her children? Unbelievably, Janice failed to realize this was a real date. If it was a case of hiding in plain sight, so be it. Lee wasn't going to elucidate.

"The police department guys have reserved a bunch of tables at the Bel Ray ballroom and we're going out there."

"*Dancing?*" Janice exclaimed.

"Yes, dancing. Is there anything wrong with that?"

"Well, no, but . . . gosh, Mom, it's been a while, hasn't it?"

"Yes it has, and I'm pretty excited. What are you doing that night?"

"Going to a party at one of the girls' houses I worked with at The Gap last summer. She said I could bring anybody I want so I asked Nolan and Jane if they wanted to come along."

"What about you, Joey?"

"Could I have Denny stay overnight?"

"If it's okay with Denny's mom, and if she knows I won't be here till later. And no girls."

"No girls. Sandy is skiing in Colorado with her family, but will you pay for pizzas?"

"I'll pay for pizzas."

"All *right!*" He socked the air. "We can play video games all night!"

Lee bought a new dress. It was fun-loving, flouncy and had a two-tiered skirt in solid red. She bought red pumps to match, and real silk panty hose, then hung multicolored earrings on her ears and a glob of matching color above her sweetheart neckline.

Christopher came to pick her up dressed in jeans, sport coat, string tie and cowboy boots. He escorted her out after complimenting her looks, holding her coat, opening the door and in general acting as attentive as any normal young swain who comes a-courting.

When they'd left and Janice was still standing in the front hall with her saliva glands pumping, Joey said, "I think he likes Mom."

"Well, of course he likes Mom. *Everybody* likes Mom."

"But, I mean, I think they're going steady or something."

"Going steady! Oh, Joey, for heaven's sake, Mom is forty-five years old and Christopher's only thirty! He's just being nice to her because Greg is dead and he knows she'd be lonesome otherwise."

"Open your eyes, nipple-head! Look at how she was dressed! She didn't look like any old lady to me."

Janice rolled her eyes and headed back to the bathroom to finish combing her hair. Fourteen-year-old brothers could be so *dense!*

Janice was partially right. Christopher *was* being nice to Lee. Four blocks away, he had pulled his Explorer to the side of the street and was kissing her masterfully enough to suck off half the new lipstick she'd just applied. His left hand was inside her coat, caressing her breast, and his tongue was inside her mouth. When the kiss finally ended he said with his forehead against hers, "Are you sure you want to go dancing?"

"Yes," she answered, smiling. "First."

They ate at Finnegan's—lightly, because they talked and laughed and flirted so much that when the waiter came to claim their plates for the third time, they let him take them even though the food wasn't gone yet.

Christopher said, "Good God, you look pretty."

Lee said, "Good God, you look handsome."

"Is the dress new?"

"Everything's new. Me too, I think."

"You're going to be, before this night's over." He was holding her hands across the table, adoring her with his eyes. "I've got something for you." He released one hand, took a paper from his pocket and handed it to her. It was a green sheet, folded like a business letter. She opened it and read across the top "Lufkin Medical Laboratories." Lower down the page a single item jumped out at her: *HIV negative*.

Color leaped to her face. All within her seemed to surge to the sexual parts of her body. She gaped at him over the paper.

"Christopher . . . my God, you did it!"

"It seemed the wisest thing to do in today's world. But I don't want you to feel pressured because I did. The choice is still up to you."

She pressed a palm to her right cheek, then her left. "Mercy, am I blushing?"

"Yes, you are, and it's quite becoming."

"I can't believe you actually *did* it!"

"Why? I told you I would."

"But . . . but that was just . . . just speculation."

"Was it?"

She let her eyes be held by his. Her tone softened. "No, I guess it wasn't." And after a pause, "I didn't do anything like that though. Do you want me to?"

"Not if you and Bill were monogamous, and I think you were."

"Yes, we were."

"And there's been nobody else since, so I was the only one in question. Now that question is answered."

She took both his hands again. "That's quite an act of faith, Mr. Lallek."

He looked down at her knuckles while rubbing them with his thumbs. "That's what good relationships are built on, and I want ours to be the best."

She studied him with a loving expression in her eyes, then asked softly, "Would you mind very much if I got up, right here in the middle of this restaurant, and came over there and kissed you?"

He let a grin spread up one corner of his mouth . . . slowly. "You wouldn't sling your leg over my chair like you did that other time, would you?"

She grinned back, picturing herself in the red dress and high heels sitting astride him in this fancy restaurant with its candlelight and real linen. "I'll try to control myself."

He pulled on her hand and she got up to do as promised, surprising herself and him with her lack of compunction, even though they weren't sitting precisely in the *middle* of the restaurant, and even though the waiter wasn't anywhere in sight, and even though neither of them saw anyone they knew among the clientele.

She held his face in her two rough hands and put her mouth on his for only the briefest second. When their lips parted she kept her face close and whispered, "Do we really have to go dancing?"

And made him smile.

———

He could do the Texas two-step!

She watched the couples circling the floor counterclockwise, and balked as he tugged on her hand.

"But I can't do that!"

"How do you know?"

"Christopher, I'll embarrass you."

"Never. Come on, give it a try. We'll go out in the middle where we'll be out of traffic and I'll teach you a move or two."

She relented and let herself be taught, noting that there were others out there in the middle of the floor struggling through basic steps, too. Christopher told her, "They give lessons here a couple nights a week before the band starts playing, so there are always beginners."

As she'd told him, she *did* have rhythm, and it turned out to be less difficult than she'd imagined. Soon she was swinging under his arm, he was dipping under hers, and they were performing basic moves—the promenade and the wrap—quite smoothly as they circled the floor.

"I wouldn't have taken you for a dancer," she said while the *shh-shh-shh* of cowboy boots sandpapered the floor all around them.

"The last girl I dated—the one who moved to Texas—wanted me to learn. She and I took lessons together."

"I should thank her. This is fun."

"Ready to try something new?"

"Is it hard?"

"Naw, you can handle it. Now, get ready, I'm going to take you 'Around the World.' "

He lifted his hands and led her around his body in a full circle, spinning her round and round.

She laughed breathlessly as she faced him again and resumed the basic step.

"I did it!"

His smile was uncomplicated, pleased, and filled her with happiness.

At the tables reserved for police department personnel there were a lot of celebrating cops and wives, who were designated drivers. The mood was gay, at times raucous. Much to Lee's surprise, she was accepted as Christopher's date with none of the double-takes she'd expected. Pete Ostrinski asked her to dance and she followed him quite smoothly. Toni Mansetti inquired how her son was doing. The wife of Sergeant Anderson told her a ribald joke about panty hose that created a new round of laughter from all the other women who'd already heard it, and started them all casting dubious glances at their ankles, which played off the punch line and signaled more laughter. Christopher attempted to teach her an advanced move called the whip, but they got tangled up time after time and ended up laughing so much they gave up and decided they'd save it for next time.

The band struck up the Collin Raye song "Love Me," and Christopher took Lee's hand, sauntering onto the dance floor. "Come on," he said, "let's polish some belt buckles."

The mood had shifted. Couples were locked together in full-length embraces. The circling had stopped in favor of swaying in place and making gentle turns. The hall became dim with a bluish cast from the overhead canister lights trained on the band. A mirrored ball strewed reflected jewels of light across the faces and shoulders of the dancers. Christopher wrapped both arms around Lee, joining his hands on the shallows of her spine. She linked her fingers behind his neck, settled her hips against his and lifted her face to his happy one.

"Having fun?" he asked.

"Mmmm . . . you're the most fun this life has had for a long, long time."

He touched the end of his nose to hers, then tilted his head as if to kiss her.

"Your friends are watching," she murmured.

"I don't give a damn."

He kissed her and put pressure on her spine until his body changed the shape of her own and seemed to become an extension of it. Swaying, he dovetailed against her while the chorus of the song called repeatedly, "Love me . . . love me . . . love me . . ."

He put space between their faces and looked into her bedazzled rust-colored eyes. "What would you say if I said, 'Let's go, let's get out of here and get alone.' "

"Right now? Before the first set is even finished?"

He nodded, holding her hips flush to his, swiveling in rhythm with the music.

"I'd say, 'Let's.' "

"Do you mean it?"

"Let's just walk off this dance floor and get our coats at the coat check and not come back."

"They'll miss us and wonder where we went so early."

"I really don't care. Do you?"

"Not at all."

They sealed their pact with a smile, turned and threaded through the dancers, across the light-speckled floor toward the entrance, knowing full well they had made a silent covenant to consummate this relationship before the night was over.

Outside, it was bitter cold. They walked to Christopher's truck with their arms around each other. Inside, while he started the engine, he said, "Sit here by me." So she ignored her seat belt and rode to his apartment sitting on one foot with her arm around Christopher's shoulders and her cheek against the rough tweed of his shoulder. Once she kissed his jaw, once his ear. He found her free hand and pressed it upon his warm thigh beneath his own, where she could feel the muscles shift each time he moved his foot from the gas pedal to the brake and back again. He had the radio on, playing soft country songs that made conversation unnecessary. While they rode, he kept softly rubbing the backs of her fingers with the pads of his own.

At his apartment they parked in the garage and rode the elevator up. She watched with some residual amazement this young, virile man with his attractive close-cut hair as he bent to fit the key in the lock and open his door, knowing what would happen on the other side of it.

He switched on an overhead light, leaned his backside against the door, removed his cowboy boots and disposed of their coats. Then he took her hand and said,

"Come this way." She allowed herself to be towed down the hall to his bedroom while he hummed "Love Me" and loosened his string tie. In his bedroom, lit only by the negligent hall light that straggled around the doorway, he turned and kissed her, dipping his knees and circling her waist with both arms, then lifting her free of earthly ties and transporting her to the bed.

Their lives had been leading toward this for so long, and the decision to do it with full accord, thus they approached the next hour with both freedom and delight.

"Oh, Christopher," she whispered, as he came down upon her. "I want you so much."

"Then we're even . . . but say it again. I've waited so long to hear it."

"I want you so m—"

His mouth cut off her words and in the midst of the first wild and rolling kiss their hands dove straight as arrows to the objects of their desire. Through their clothing they petted the first time, telling each other with the curve and thrust of palms how it would be, how they wanted it to be, feeling warmth and arousal and the parting of limbs to give access. They were still for a moment, exploring, riveted by the combination of feelings beneath their own hands and the hands of the other. They lay apart, eyes open, faces tinted by the bisque light of the distant fixture that seemed to fall upward from their chins, highlighting their features as they went on accepting these gifts of feelings.

Her high-heeled pumps hit the floor . . . *thump* . . . *thump*. She closed her eyes and breathed "Ohh . . ." and rolled to her back, one foot flat on the bedspread, dress rucked up to her hips, giving herself over to the pure fleshly pleasure of feeling male hands upon her once again. He leaned over and kissed her breast, through layers of feminine apparel.

She said, "Please . . . could we get our clothes off, Christopher?"

He knelt in the middle of the bed and tugged her to her knees. "There's not much grace in taking clothes off. I didn't know how you felt about it."

"There's not much grace in having clothes on at a time like this. They do best on the floor."

He took off some of hers, she took off some of his, and each of them managed the most difficult pieces of their own. When they were naked, still kneeling in the middle of his bed, she abruptly straddled him, much as she had on that kitchen chair, their bodies close but unlinked.

"Hey, what's this?" he teased, surprised by how unceremoniously she took to his lap and flung both arms around his neck.

"I'm hiding."

"From what?"

"From your eyes. Sometimes, since that day we decorated your Christmas tree, I'd lie in bed and think about this moment and long for it and dread it at once."

"Why?" He leaned back and lifted a hand to touch her hairline with his fingertips.

"Because . . . I imagine the girls you've been with were young and perfect. Their skin was probably tight and tan and they didn't have stretch marks or wrinkles or veins that show, or terrible beat-up hands, or any of the unsightly things that forty-five-year-old women have."

"Lee," he said, tipping her off his lap and arranging his limbs half on top of her. "You're forgetting one thing." He kissed her once, his hand moving up her body, and whispered into her mouth, "I didn't love them."

With such simple words he stole her self-consciousness, which, like their clothing, seemed relegated to a puddle on the floor, leaving her free to enjoy her femininity. He lay on his side, braced up on an elbow, brushing a widespread hand up her leg, stomach and ribs, capturing first one breast, then the other, dipping his head to taste them, naked, for the first time. When he wet her skin, she wet her lips and reached a hand down for him, took him in hand and learned, with much pleasure, his intimate shape. It took little for him to bring her to climax—mere touches after all the years of dormancy. She lay in the wash of weak light from the hall and allowed him the greatest trust of all: to watch her at his mercy while her body quaked and spilled, while she uttered a coarse note in her arched throat and gripped his tangled bedspread in two fists.

Then he was above her on all fours, whispering into her mouth, "Do you want to put it on or should I?"

"What would you like?" she asked, realizing it had been a long time for him, too: There were parts of this ritual he'd undoubtedly spent time imagining.

"You do it," he answered, and laid the tiny packet in her hand.

He rolled to his back, hands thrown above his head, small sounds issuing from his throat as she touched him and ministered to him.

"Two years is too damn long," he said, his voice rumbly and deep while he lay with his eyes closed. "I can't imagine how you went without it for nine."

"Neither can I, now that I'm here."

"Please hurry . . . I'm dying."

"Oh, don't die," she begged, finishing, throwing herself across his chest, kissing his face. "Please don't die just yet. I've got some other things in mind I'd like to do with you." His arms scooped her in and he rolled at the same time, their limbs twining.

"Ah, sweet woman, you've just saved my life," he said.

They were avid and eager, stumbling through these initiate steps with the uncertainties of all first-time lovers, calling on playfulness to get them through the precarious moments of unset precedent.

The playfulness vanished, however, as their roll across the bed ended and two lovers found themselves captured in one another's eyes. A reverence stole their tongues. They could speak, at that moment, only with their eyes. Christopher centered himself above her, then in her, slowly and deeply.

"Lee . . . Lee . . ." he whispered against her lips. "At last."

Then together they became harmony and rhythm. The beat of their bodies became the culmination of the loving friendship they had formed in the past half-year. The sorrows of those months slid away. All those tears, all those talks, all those consolations had been leading to this. This! Christopher and Lee, making something extraordinary out of their ordinary selves.

"You . . . you," she said fiercely, gripping him with her heels and hands. ". . . All the time it was you and I didn't know it."

"I thought you'd say I was too young for you and you'd turn me away."

"I thought I was too old for you and I'd look foolish for even thinking this could happen."

"Never . . . I wanted this long before I first touched or kissed you."

"You feel so good. I've missed this so much."

"Tell me what you want . . . anything."

She wanted nothing, for she had the best life had to offer. Still he touched her, kissed her, caressed her in myriad ways, whispering, "Like this? Like this?"

And she whispered, "Yes . . . like that . . . oh yes."

She felt him stretch, and heard the snap of the bedside lamp. It brought her eyes flying open, staring up at him while his arm was still extended above his head.

"I want to see you. Do you mind?"

Shyness struck Lee. She wanted to say, Turn it off! In the light, their differences would be too boldly displayed, and all the faint cobwebbing of her age would leap out of hiding in the amber radiance from behind his shoulder. She wanted the room to remain dark, but while she was still caught by surprise, he settled astride her.

His crisp brown hair was disheveled by her finger tracks. His eyes loomed blue as oceans. By their insistent gaze he held her as he played with her breasts, reshaping them, stroking them, watching the backsides of his fingers circling round and round their florid tips, then beneath them, scribing half-moons before covering both mounds fully with his two broad hands.

"Say you don't mind," he beseeched in a husky lover's voice.

"I don't mind."

He could see that she did, that she was still self-conscious though he—her lover now—found her body beguiling. He bent forward, running his palm up over her brow as if feeling for fever, pushing the hair back from her face.

"Don't mind," he whispered, "don't mind, Lee. Let me love all of you the way I love the inner you."

She crooked an arm around his neck and drew his open mouth to hers, making a soft, acquiescent sound in her throat, wondering if the other man in her life had ever filled her with this much feeling, for at the moment, it hardly seemed possible. To kiss so, with tenderness tempering lust, yet lust an insistent accomplice, brought a luxuriance to their arousal. They had time and privacy and a healthy physical greed pressing them from within. "Oh, Christopher . . ." she murmured in a shaken voice. "You make me feel all the ways a woman wants to feel."

Again, he began moving within her.

She stroked his legs, spread her hands on his hips, watched the lamplight shift over his firm hide, his brow become beaded and his face sobered by passion. When his breathing grew forced, he fell forward, hands spread, elbows locked, blinking so slowly she thought he did not see her across the inches separating their faces, but watched instead his own inner feelings playing within some gilded screen in his mind.

He made some sounds, unmusical to all but her, the source of his pleasure.

When he came, he shuddered and collapsed like a craft running aground, falling upon her. She collected his thick bulk in both her arms and laced her fingers into his hair, finding his skull damp. The scent of him came from it—cosmetics and warm scalp and a touch of dance hall smoke.

She ran her nails over his head again and again, slowly, and he shivered once with his face out of sight above her shoulder.

When his pulse had slowed and his breathing evened, he caught her behind one knee with his heel and rolled them to their sides. He found a pillow and stuffed it beneath their heads, then for a long, serene time they studied each other's countenances, gauging their repletion in the tempo of their blinks and the laxness of their lips. She touched his lower one with a fingertip, then kissed him with a moth's touch.

He smiled.

"What are you thinking?" she asked.

"I'm not. I'm just being happy."

She rubbed his bottom lip. "It was very good for me."

"It was very good for me, too."

"What do you think are the chances of a woman coming the first time with a man?"

"I don't know."

"Pretty slim, I think."

"I was never sure if any girl did it with me before."

"Are you sure now?"

"Not a question in my mind, but it's probably because it's been so long for you. You were more than ready."

"You really think that?" She was still rubbing his lip.

"I told you once, I'm not really what you'd call a ladies' man."

"Well, you're this lady's man."

He clamped his teeth on her fingertip and sawed sideways, putting a faint white dot beneath her nail. He released it with a kiss and her fingertips settled against his chin. They closed their eyes for a while and rested, neither of them in a hurry to disjoin, enjoying the flaccid warmth of afterlove, the texture of his hirsute legs between her smooth ones, lazily moving a finger or a toe against one another. She thought about how liquid and relaxed her body felt. He thought about her reaching orgasm the first time with him.

In time he spoke quietly, his voice opening her eyes.

"Would it be tacky of me to ask about your sex life with your husband?"

"No, I don't think so. What we just did together removes a lot of barriers, don't you think?"

"So what was it like?"

She put some thought into her answer. "Guilt-ridden before marriage. Much better afterward, though it ran hot and cool. Sometimes we'd do it four times a week, sometimes only a couple of times a month. Just depended on what else was going on in our lives. We had to work a little harder at my orgasms than you and I did, though."

After a spell of silence, he lifted his head off the pillow and kissed her full on the mouth, then lay back as he'd been.

"You want to know something ironic?" he said. "I was scared to death that it wouldn't be as good for you with me as it had been with him. Everything you read says these things take time and patience to get right, so I figured . . ." He shrugged and his glance flickered away, then back at her, leaving the thought unfinished. "Once I said to you that I wasn't going to be scared of what might happen between us, but a lot of that was bravado. I was plenty scared, and most of it had to do with my being only thirty and you being so much older and experienced. That can be pretty intimidating for a man, you know. I thought, What if I make a play for her and she slaps my hand like I'm some naughty child?" After a pause he added, "But you didn't."

"Did you really think I'd do that?"

"I didn't know."

"Couldn't you tell I was falling for you?"

"Yes, but I thought you'd resist because of the unwritten social laws governing ages."

"Since we're making confessions, I have one of my own. When I first suspected that you were getting a crush on me, I thought, Gosh, he's so young. And I have to admit—I'm human—I had this other totally awful, unforgivable thought that did wonders for my ego: Wouldn't I look smart landing a boyfriend so young? It's been a real hang-up for me ever since, because it would make me a very shallow woman if that were my reason for going to bed with you, just to snag a younger man. Now we've done it, and I didn't do it for that reason at all; I did it because I love you and like you and respect you and have so much fun with you, but I have to admit—your age, your youth, your young, perfect body is a thrill I hadn't imagined."

He braced his head on one hand and used the other to push her slightly away so he could stroke her. He centered the butt of his hand between her breasts while fanning his fingers left and right, left and right, almost as if he were dusting her off.

"I'm glad we don't have to go through these firsts again. They're nerve-racking. Next time it'll be so much easier."

She smiled and teased, "Oh, so we're going to do this again?"

He went on watching his hand play across her soft skin. Goose bumps of pleasure had raised on her breasts, lifting the fine hair and puckering her nipples. "We're going to do this many, many times. As often as we can."

"A full-fledged affair, then—that's what we've started?"

He gave up dusting her breast and cupped her jaw instead while crooking an elbow beneath his ear.

"You can call it anything you want. Whatever it is, it's too damned good for a one-timer."

She studied him in the lamplight, which came from above and behind him, taking in the honey-hued nimbus outlining his brown hair, the russet lashes framing his blue eyes, his symmetrical features, which pleased her immeasurably. She studied his mouth, softened and polished by all the kissing they'd done . . . touched it as if unable to help herself. "Everything about you pleases me so much. I just can't believe this has happened, that we actually got beyond all those barriers. I'm liable to be insatiable for a while, making up for lost time."

"I won't mind." He caught her hand and began nipping its edge with his teeth. "Insatiable women are the best kind."

It was a toss-up who was more insatiable when she pushed him to his back and rolled atop him.

Later, she awakened him, lifting her head to read the alarm clock on the nightstand. They were beneath the covers by now, and her face held an irregularly shaped red blotch where it had been stuck to the hollow of his shoulder while she slept.

Coming awake, he looked down at her and smiled sleepily.

"Gotta go home," she whispered.

"Aw, no . . ." He rolled to face her, made a wishbone of his arms and captured her within them. "Noooo."

"I can't stay. Joey's at home with his friend Denny, and Janice will be coming home, too."

He lifted his head and left wrist, read his watch behind her back, then let himself go limp against the bedding again. "It's not even twelve yet."

"So, we jumped the gun a little bit."

He chuckled deep in his throat, eyes closed, arms lying loosely around her. "I wish you could stay here till morning."

"I know, so do I." She turned back the covers and got up. "But I can't."

He rolled to his back, joined his hands beneath his head and watched her begin to get dressed. Watched her step into her underwear, contort her arms to hook her rear-closing bra, then sit on the edge of the bed and skin her panty hose up her legs. Next came her dress, and when she had it on, he said, "Come around here. Let me zip it." She circled the foot of the bed and sat down with her back to him. He sat up and kissed her nape, threaded his arms inside her open dress, doubled them beneath her breasts and rested his mouth on the slope of her shoulder.

"I love watching you dress, watching you move around in my bedroom where I've imagined you doing just that."

She covered his arms with her own, felt them firm and warm inside the red crisp cloth of her bodice, tipped her head to one side and closed her eyes.

"I love this," she whispered, "just the feel of your arms around me. A man's arms are so different than a woman's. When you're without a man like I've been, you miss the sex, of course, but sometimes you miss this even more—just the touching, the rubbing together, letting your weight sag against somebody who's bigger, and smells different, and feels different than you. Promise me we'll do this sometime . . . just enjoy the feel of each other without having to make love."

"I promise. Now you have to promise me something."

"What?"

"To dress for me sometimes, the way you just did, slow and relaxed while I lie and watch you. It struck me a minute ago—anybody can watch a person undress, but watching them dress is even more intimate. You learn the order they do things—pants first, bra second, panty hose after that. Tonight, after I take you home, I'm going to picture that while I fall asleep."

She sighed, and let her head drop back, and they rocked gently with his arms still coiled about her and his lips on her neck. It would have been easy to fall back asleep, they were so contented with each other. But duty intruded, and she was forced to make her limbs move.

"I really do have to go. Zip me."

When he had, and she'd retrieved her jewelry from the nightstand, and slipped into her pumps, she took a page out of his notebook and watched while he rolled up to sit on the edge of the bed and find his discarded clothing, while he stood and pulled them on, buttoned his shirt before zipping his fly, then stuffed his tails in and tugged on the waist of his jeans, closed the waist button and—finally—zipped up.

"You're right," she said, sauntering over to stand before him, resting her elbows on his shoulders and toying with his hair. "There is something more intimate about it. I'd never thought about it before."

"Glad you enjoyed it," he said, smirking, buttoning his cuffs behind her back.

"And I thought of something else," she said.

"What's that?" He held her lightly by the ribs, his thumbs in the hollows just below her breasts.

"That if you'd just had sex with a stranger, you'd have trouble watching him dress. It would seem tawdry, wouldn't it? But watching you"—she kissed him lightly—"seemed like reading the P.S. on a love letter."

They rested their hips against each other and shared a single, splendid, soporific kiss.

When it ended, he said, very seriously, "I love you, Lee."

She imbibed the words, remaining silent while they seeped into her, filling all the empty troves that had been waiting years for this treasure.

Saying it became a reaffirmation, the ideal closing for this night of first intimacy.

"I love you too, Christopher."

And on that very fitting note, he took her home.

Chapter 15

⚘

On New Year's Day everyone in the Reston household slept late. It was 9:50 when Janice awoke. She opened her bedroom door and slogged down the hall toward the bathroom, noting with lazy indifference that her mother's door was still closed. The rarity of Lee Reston sleeping till late morning struck Janice as she returned to her room and opened her mother's door to peek inside.

Lee lay on her stomach with one arm crossed beneath her face and the other flopped up against the headboard. She was sprawled diagonally beneath the covers, breathing evenly. Her red dress lay neatly folded over the back of a chair. One standing red pump accompanied one fallen on the floor beneath her panty hose and bra.

Janice studied her mother and experienced a surge of embarrassment at the thought that Joey's deduction might be true. If it were, she, Janice, would look like a stupid fool. It must be true: Her mother had bought a new dress, a red dress with a tiered skirt and shoes to match! Lee, who seldom bought clothes, hadn't even showed it to Janice in advance, hadn't oohed and aahed over it the way one would expect her to. Had she been hiding it hoping Janice wouldn't be around when Christopher came to the house to pick her up?

She silently closed her mother's bedroom door and opened Joey's. It was stuffy inside, smelled like old sweat socks and some dried-up orange peels that were sitting on his windowsill. He, too, was sound asleep, on his back with his chin in the air at an odd angle and his hands, with their huge knuckles, relaxed on the bedclothes. Denny Whitman was dead to the world in a sleeping bag on the floor.

She went inside, closed the door behind her, picked her way carefully over Denny and tiptoed to her brother's bed.

"Hey, Joey," she whispered, sitting down beside him in her long flannel nightgown. "Hey, Joey, wake up."

Joey pushed her away with one leg and rolled to face the wall, mumbling some syllables that sounded like *gold* and *myrrh*.

She jostled him and whispered, "Joey, wake up. I've got to talk to you." She jostled him harder. "Darn it, Joey, will you turn over here!"

He did, with all the good nature of a pit bull.

"Jeez! Leave me alone, will ya? I'm still sleeping!"

"Joey, I have to ask you something. Be quiet so we don't wake up Denny."

"Ask me later."

"I just want to know what time Mom got home, that's all."

"I don't know."

"Well, were you up?"

"Yeah. It was early."

"Early?" Her heart lifted with hope.

"Yeah, before midnight, I know that much, 'cause Denny and me had the TV on." He was rubbing his eyes, then gave a huge yawn.

"Was Christopher with her?"

"No, he just dropped her off."

"He didn't come in?"

"No. Jeez, why don't you ask *her* all this stuff?"

"I can't ask her, not if what you said is true and she's dating him seriously. Do you really think she is?"

"Heck, I don't know. He's here all the time."

"But he wasn't here at midnight? You're sure?"

"No!" he whined, disgruntled. "I told you, he just dropped her off, and she came in and ate some popcorn with Denny and me, and she made us turn off our video games so she could see some stupid mob scene in Times Square."

"Well then, maybe she's not dating him. I mean, maybe they're just friends after all."

She stared hopefully at Joey. He only shrugged and said, "How should I know?"

"Wouldn't they have stayed together at least till midnight if they were going steady, as you put it? I mean . . . if you were with Sandy on New Year's Eve, what would you do at midnight?"

He blushed and said, "Jeez, why don't you leave a guy alone?"

"Joey, listen . . ." She put her hand over his and went on sincerely. "You're my brother. This is important. If she's dating Chris, and if it's serious, I think we should talk to Aunt Sylvia or somebody about it."

"Why?"

"So Aunt Sylvia can talk some sense into Mom."

"Why?"

"Well, she's fifteen years older than he is, for heaven's sake!"

"So what?"

"So what! How can you lie there and say 'So what'? Do you want her to make a fool of herself?"

Joey stared at her awhile and said, "I don't get it."

Exasperated, Janice doubled forward at the waist and scratched her head until her hair looked wiry. Joey was too young, after all. She was talking in a circle around the subject of sex, but he wasn't old enough to grasp it, and she realized it would be wrong of her to bring it up in the context of her mother and Chris. When Joey had used the term "going steady," Janice had translated it into "having an affair."

Yet she had no more proof than Joey did.

"Just listen," she advised. "You're around her more than I am now that I'm in school. But pay attention, will you, after I go back for third quarter?" She paused, but he kept looking at her blankly. "If she starts staying out late, or . . . or . . . well, you know . . . anything that keeps her away a lot, call me."

Before Joey could answer, Janice sensed herself being observed and looked down at the floor to find Denny Whitman awake and listening.

She jumped up off the bed. "Go back to sleep, you guys. Sorry I woke you."

When Lee got up, Janice studied her with sensors a-quiver, but her mother only came out of the bathroom smelling like toothpaste and put the coffeepot on, as usual. " 'Morning, dear," Lee said. "Did you have a good time last night?"

"It was okay. Did you?"

"I had a grand time, until I tried to do something called the whip. Nearly tore my arms off."

"The whip?"

"It's a country dance move. Christopher tried to teach it to me, but I messed it up so badly I'm afraid we gave up."

Janice studied her mother moving about the kitchen, opening drawers and finding bagels, slicing them and putting them under the broiler, getting out cream cheese and jam, finding a carton of orange juice and shaking it, doing all the ordinary things mothers do in the morning. What was she, Janice, staring at? Did she really think that if her mother was having an affair with Christopher it would show? That she'd look *different* this morning? A glimpse of a thought beamed across Janice's mind's eye, but she kept the beam narrow, so that it flashed too fast for her to picture her mother as the sexual partner of the man Janice herself had been trying to attract ever since she'd met him. But the thought had struck, and it left Janice grossly uncomfortable. Mothers simply were not to be considered sexual beings. Oh, maybe if fathers were still alive—but with anyone else the thought was unpalatable.

"Mom?"

Lee finished pouring a glass of juice and looked up at Janice, holding the carton stationary while its spout dripped. Janice was leaning back against the countertop, gripping her elbows tightly against her ribs, her bare toes curled into a scatter rug in front of the kitchen sink.

What's going on between you and Chris?

The unspoken question was foretold by the scowl on Janice's face, by her tight, self-imposed body hug, by the pinched look on her lips. Lee instinctively guessed what Janice was thinking, but if Janice wanted to know, let her ask. Lee herself was uneager to broach the subject, afraid of hurting Janice and reaping her censure. Furthermore, what was going on between herself and Christopher was too new, too fragile yet to broadcast and hold up to the family's dissatisfaction.

"Yes, honey?" Lee replied.

The question hovered between them, unspoken, while Lee poured a second glass of juice. As she was handing it to Janice the phone rang.

Janice answered, swinging to face the counter, presenting her back to her mother.

"Hello?" After a pause, Janice handed Lee the receiver, knuckles down over her shoulder. "It's for you."

Lee set down the juice glass, took the phone and said, "Happy New Year."

"Happy New Year to you too," Christopher said, sounding happy and smiley.

"Oh, hi, Christopher. How did you survive last night? Did I break any of your arms on that dance floor?"

"Not a one."

"I had a good time but my calves ache from dancing in high heels."

"I think maybe your calves ache from something else."

She laughed and he said, "I love you."

For Janice's sake she put a lilt of deceptive laughter in her voice. "Do you really? Heavens, I never would have guessed it."

"Could I bring over some lo mein later this afternoon and see you?"

"Do you think the Chinese restaurants will be open?"

"If they're not, we'll eat toast and watch football games."

"Fine. Let me get a nose count." She dropped the receiver from her ear and said, "Christopher wants to bring Chinese over later. Should we count you in?"

Without turning to face her mother, Janice said, "Sure," and walked from the room, leaving her orange juice untouched.

Janice watched them like a cat the entire time Christopher was there, but if they were intimate, they gave nothing away. Christopher sat most of the day with his nape caught on the davenport cushions, his ankles crossed, watching bowl games with Joey and Denny, rehashing plays with them. Lee, dressed in a gray sweat suit and terry-cloth footlets, read a book curled up in a living room chair. At five o'clock she got up to warm the car in preparation for taking Denny home. Christopher roused himself and offered, "I'll take him if you want."

"No, you're all comfortable there. I'll go. Back in ten minutes or so."

Janice thought, *If these two are messing around, I'm Mae West!* They both acted as if they needed a shot of testosterone.

Lee returned, warmed up the Chinese food in the microwave, brought everybody a plate in the living room and returned to her comfy chair to eat hers and continue reading.

At eight o'clock, Christopher stretched and said, "Well, I think I'll go."

Lee had difficulty pulling her eyes away from her book. "Just one min . . ." She raised a finger and kept on reading to the end of the paragraph.

"Don't stop reading. I can find my way out."

"Oh, no! No!" Lee returned to reality, leaving her chair with the book plopped facedown on the cushion. "It's just that I haven't read a book for so long. I kind of got lost in it."

"Well, keep on. You don't have to see me out."

She yawned, linked her fingers and inverted her hands straight out in front of herself, stretching everything from her waist up.

"Lazy day."

"Yeah, it was." He got his jacket and put it on in the front hall. "Thanks for letting me hang around underfoot." He kissed her cheek, making no secret of it while the two kids looked on from the front room. "Hey, Joey, Janice . . . see you, huh?"

When the door closed behind him, Janice decided with some relief, I was wrong, Joey was wrong, Christopher is no more to her than Greg's replacement.

It was 2 P.M.—Lee's lunch break—on the first business day following New Year's when she knocked on Christopher's apartment door. He flung it open and the two of them nearly ripped each other's skins off, lunging together. They kissed as if tomorrow it would be outlawed. He pinned her against the apartment door, then changed his mind and dragged her away from it to skin off her coat and drop it to the floor. The kiss was openmouthed, sexual, impatient—the lush, pervasive kind that ends imposed suppression and begins to mark territory. In the midst of it he captured her breasts, flattened them and her hard against the closed door. Their combined weight hit it with a bang that shuddered up their hipbones and echoed outside in the hall.

When it ended she held him none too gently by two fistfuls of hair above his ears. "Don't you ever do that to me again! I've never spent such a miserable day in my life! I wanted to come over to that sofa and flatten you underneath me, but all I could do was sit there across the room reading a silly book!"

He laughed and said, "Are you saying you wanted me?"

She put pressure on his hair and raved, "Wanted? Wanted!" then, growling, used his hair as a handle and wobbled his head around as if to tear it off his neck.

"How are your calf muscles?" he inquired with a crooked smile.

"Kiss me nice and I'll tell you."

He kissed her nice, gently this time, while she smoothed the hair she'd been clutching and left her hands gently cupping the back of his head.

When he once again looked down into her eyes, she said quietly, "My calf muscles could use some physical therapy."

"Ah," he replied, "I've got just the thing in mind."

He picked her up and carried her like a bride into the living room where the Christmas tree was gone and the furniture in its customary place. He dropped down on the sofa, tipping her off his lap and curling forward to hold and kiss her while her legs trailed over his thighs. Exploring her lips and tongue with his own, he freed the buttons up the front of her lavender smock. Beneath it she wore a sweater. His hand was already skimming up underneath it when she halted the kiss and told him, "Christopher, I have some really bad news."

His hand stopped and he sent a look of concern straight into her eyes.

"I got my period last night."

For three beats he only stared disbelievingly. Then he flung himself backward against the sofa as if he'd been shot, his head flopping back, eyes closed, hands dropping free of her while he groaned, "Ohhh . . . nooo . . . ."

"Sorry," she said with a shrug and a grimace.

"How many days?"

"Four or five."

He raised his head, opened his eyes and laid a finger across her mouth vertically. "Then you're no good to me, madam, because that's all I want you for, you know."

She kissed his finger and said, "Here I thought you loved me for my popcorn balls."

He squinted at one corner of the ceiling, thought for a moment, then turned a grin down her way. "Now that you've reminded me . . . I guess I *can* stick around for four or five days longer." He grabbed her elbows and hauled her up. "C'mere." When he'd righted her, amid some awkward adjusting of her weight and limbs, she ended up straddling his lap, his hands at her armpits between her sweater and smock. He tilted her forward and kissed her with the pressures of pre-intercourse set aside, replaced by a laxness perhaps even more enchanting. His lips were sublimely soft, moist and relaxed beneath hers as they exchanged four winsome, crisscross kisses—noses left . . . right . . . left . . . right. They took time, after the exchange, to study each other's eyes and faces appreciatively, their hands fluttering upon one another as idly as the fins of unswimming fish, his beside her breasts, hers at his back hairline. They were fine, rewarding minutes, those silent ones, while they recognized that sex could wait while their true allure for one another grew each moment they were together . . . and, too, each moment they were apart. Their eyes imparted the message, then they exchanged small possessive smiles at very close range.

"I'll tell you something," he said softly, "New Year's Day was hard on me, too. I knew I shouldn't come over, but I just had to."

"I'm glad you did. If you hadn't come to me, I'd have come to you, and I didn't have any idea how I'd explain myself."

He began to rebutton her smock. "It's hell having to explain yourself, isn't it?"

She combed his hair back with four fingers, enjoying the crisp coil of it, the combination of scents—shampoo, laundry, skin—that created the effusion peculiar to him.

"Janice knows," she said, scraping his skull lightly with her nails.

"I suspected as much. She was pretty aloof yesterday."

"I think she almost asked me in the morning."

Her smock was closed. He rested his hands on the crook of her waist. "What would you have said?"

She quit furrowing his hair. "I would have told her the truth."

"Would you really?"

She nodded so infinitesimally he believed her. "I just wanted some time for us first. We deserve that, I think, before I stir up the cauldron that's bound to boil over when everybody finds out."

"You really think so?"

She nodded, her eyes dropping to the V-neck of his sweater. "Everybody but Joey. He's crazy about you, and he's young enough that he doesn't have preconceptions. But Janice is going to be mortified. Sylvia is going to be shocked. And my mother . . ." Lee rolled her eyes, then settled them on something at her left. ". . . My mother will be the worst one of all."

"Does it matter so much, what they think?"

"Well, of course it matters." She needlessly adjusted his shirt collar over the neck of his sweater and left her hands flat on his collarbone. "They're my family."

"Are you saying they'll disown you or something?"

"No, they won't disown me."

"Then they'll disown me." He said it without rancor, looking up into her eyes, stating the likelihood as if it were something they must face and deal with.

She sighed and wound her arms around his head, drawing his face to her chest. "Oh, I hope not. I'd like to think they're less hypocritical than that."

They sat on, in the caramel light of afternoon that slanted through his windows, so happy to be together, accepting this unconventional pose in all its intimacy as their own. His face was turned aside while she plunged one hand into the hair at the crown of his head and worked her fingers as if shampooing, then stroked the hair to the limits of its short length before repeating the motion again and again. She couldn't get her fill of pleasure in touching the myriad textures of him after the many years' dearth of male textures. His hair, his jaw, his brow, the lobes of his ears, his ribs and chest; even the textures of his clothing seemed different from hers, draped over muscle so much firmer and a bone structure so much broader. His hand was up her back again, between the smock and sweater, absently marking time across her shoulder blades like an inverted pendulum.

He closed his eyes and drifted, enjoying, too, the distinct femaleness of her, the pressure of her legs wrapped around his hips, her nails on his skull, her palms on his clothing and her breath on his forehead. The sun warmed his left cheek while her breasts—soft and pliant—warmed his right. She was scented much like her flower

shop, herbal and lavender and floral all mixed together. His elbows, at her ribs, outlined a body circumference that seemed fragile compared to his own. Her shoulder
blades, when his fingertips brushed them, felt as insubstantial as bird wings.

Man . . . woman . . . different . . .

So incredibly, enjoyably different . . .

"You want something to eat?" he asked when they had both grown lazy and
indifferent to all but the sun and the motion of their hands.

"Mm . . ." she said against his hair, her eyes closed. "What have you got?"

"Some salami and cheese. Bagel chips. An apple."

"Mmm . . . do I have to?"

"You should eat something."

"I could live on this."

He smiled, nearly shivering beneath the gentle strokes of her hand on his
hair.

"What time do you have to get back?"

"I shouldn't stay long. Sylvia's got a dentist appointment this afternoon."

He sighed and regretfully withdrew from her arms, looking up at her with his
hair ruffled.

"Look at you, straddling me again. You're such a tart."

She clambered off, catching his hand, hauling him up behind her. "Come on,
let's find that salami."

Holding hands, they walked toward the kitchen, stone in love. But as they went
they wondered how much longer to keep their affair secret, and what it would lead
to and why whenever they discussed its outcome their tones became somber, as if
they were altering forever the future of their lives, though they did not know how.

Shortly after winter vacation ended, the school called Christopher. It was a silver-
bright winter day warm enough to raise steam off the melting sidewalks. Inside the
police department, where he was filling out an accident report, it smelled of late
morning coffee and gun-cleaning oil. He took the call and heard a woman's voice
inform him, "This is Cynthia Hubert, the principal at the junior high. We have a
seventh-grade student here, Judd Quincy, who's gotten into some trouble. He says
if we call you you'll come over here and bail him out."

Christopher sighed and let his shoulders sag, tilting back in his swivel chair.

"What's he done this time?"

"Stole some money out of a teacher's purse."

Christopher closed his eyes and pinched the bridge of his nose. Damn that kid.
He thought they'd been making progress.

"You sure he did it?"

"She caught him red-handed."

"Is the liaison officer there?"

"Yes, Judd is with him."

"Listen . . . don't do anything with him till I get there, okay?"

The principal's pause sounded strained with indecision. Finally she sighed and
said, "All right, we'll wait."

They had Judd in a counselor's office of Fred Moore Junior High when Christopher entered, in uniform. The room held an impacted, high-tension stillness often accompanying proven guilt. Judd sat in an aqua vinyl chair staring at his Air pump tennies. He looked skinny and unkempt. Christopher nodded to the liaison officer, Randy Woodward, from his own department. Behind Chris the principal entered, a stylish, thin, salt-and-pepper-haired woman wearing a straight gray dress and gold-rimmed glasses. He turned around and shook her hand. "Thanks for calling, Mrs. Hubert." He glanced down at Judd, still staring at his Air pumps, which by now looked as if they'd marched across Prussia on a foot soldier.

"Could I talk to him alone for a minute?" Chris asked.

The others went out and left the two of them alone.

Christopher shuffled over to stand before Judd, looking down on his bent head with its burry hair and birdlike neck, his rumpled, dirty T-shirt under a filthy denim jacket and jeans with tears across both knees. He stood a long time with his hands on his hips, the room quiet while from the outer office came the muted sounds of voices, and someone using a stapler, and a phone ringing persistently.

Finally Christopher asked, "Did you steal some money, Judd?"

The boy said nothing, only hung his head and studied the tongues of his tennies.

"Did you?" Chris repeated softly.

Judd nodded.

Words of rebuke somehow refused to form in Chris's mind. He'd lectured Judd so many times, had taken the tough-guy stance and made the kid realize the world wasn't fair but he'd just have to live with it, muddle his way through to adulthood, when he could finally make his own decisions. It struck Chris today, however: The kid was only twelve years old. To Judd, muddling his way through to seventeen, eighteen, whenever he might graduate from high school, must seem like asking him to become a Rhodes scholar. He was a scared, mixed-up, unloved little boy who probably hadn't been fed breakfast this morning, never mind kissed goodbye on his way out the door.

Suddenly Christopher found himself doing what he'd never done before: He went down on one knee and took Judd in his arms. Judd clung and started crying. Christopher held him firmly, swallowing hard to keep himself from doing the same, his nostrils narrowing at the stale smell coming from Judd's skin and clothing. He and Judd stayed that way, close and silent, while the secretary in the outer office seemingly used up an entire bar of staples, and every absentee in the school population called in sick. When Christopher tried to pull back, Judd clung harder.

"What went wrong?" Christopher asked. "Something at home?"

He felt Judd shrug.

"You want to get out of there? You want to live in a foster home?"

Judd said, "I want to live with you."

He pulled the boy's arms from around his neck and forced him to sit back on his chair. "I'm sorry, Judd, you can't. A person has to be licensed to give emergency foster care, and besides, what would I do with you when I work nights?"

"I'd be okay." Judd dried his eyes with the backs of his wrists. "I'd just watch TV and go to bed anytime you said I should."

It nearly killed Christopher to reply, "I'm sorry, Judd, it wouldn't work."

Judd looked up with more sincerity in his eyes than Christopher had ever seen there. "I could do stuff for you, maybe vacuum your place or warm up your can of soup for you."

That was Judd's idea of a meal, warming up your can of soup. Chris put his man-sized hand around Judd's boy-sized neck, wondering how much dirt was disguised by his dusky pigment. Then he got up and sat on the aqua-blue chair beside Judd's. He bent forward and rested his elbows on his knees.

"Tell me what happened at home."

"They took my free lunch tickets to buy coke with. Then they tried to give me some of it, said they was gonna turn me out—woo-hoo."

"Turn you out?"

"Yeah, you know—introduce me, sort of, to something new."

"The cocaine, you mean?"

Judd nodded while Christopher's adrenaline shot a stream of heat through his chest. It wasn't all that uncommon for parents like Judd's to fence their kids' subsidized lunch program tickets, but trying to get their own kid hooked on drugs was a new one on Chris. His innards seized up and he experienced the unholy desire to find Wendy and Ray Quincy and drive his fist into their faces until they needed plastic surgery.

"Now, let me get this straight." He lifted the kid's chin and forced his direct attention with a straight-line gaze. "Your mother and dad bought cocaine with your lunch money, then tried to get you to use it. You're sure that's how it was?"

Judd jerked his chin free. "I said that's how it was, and that's how it was."

"So you stole the money to eat lunch with?"

Judd had returned to shoe staring.

"Judd, I've got to have it straight this time, no lies, no half-truths. Is that why you stole the lunch money?"

The boy mumbled, "Yeah, I guess so."

"You guess so?"

"And 'cause I knew if I did, they'd call you."

Christopher left his chair and hunkered down facing Judd, sitting on one heel. "Hey, listen to me, okay? 'Cause this time it's really important. I can't put you in foster care without your parents' okay, and I don't think they'll give it. But we've got one other possibility. I've got the power to get you out of there and put you on a police hold for twenty-four hours. As soon as I do that a social worker will start proceedings with the county attorney, and there'll be a detention hearing before a judge. If we go that far, you'll have to tell the judge what you just told me, about your parents trying to get you to use coke. Will you do that?"

When it got that far, children often refused to testify against their parents, fearful at the last minute of losing their parents and home after all.

"Will you do that, Judd?"

Judd stared down at his dirty hands through plump tears that trembled on his lower eyelids.

"Can I live with you then?"

Don't break my heart like this, boy. "No, you can't, Judd. But there's a good chance I can be appointed your guardian during the proceedings."

"My guardian?" Judd looked up.

"It would be my sole purpose to look out for your welfare and make sure the correct decisions were made for you. But you have to understand—if I start this, if I put you on a twenty-four-hour police hold and talk to child protection, once they get in touch with the county attorney we're talking about taking you away from your parents permanently."

Judd thought that over for some time before coming up with one paltry defense of the mother who didn't deserve him. "My ma—sometimes she cooks supper."

Chris felt his throat thicken. When he spoke his voice sounded as if he were trying to swallow and talk simultaneously. "Yeah, I know. Sometimes they're okay. But most of the time they're not. They're sick, Judd, but they refuse to get help. Maybe if you don't live with them anymore they'll get it. We'd find you a good foster home where you'd get baths and meals and lunch money every day. But the choice is up to you—you've got to say."

"Could we still play basketball sometimes, you and me? And go to the workout room together?"

"Yes, Judd, we could. I'd make sure we did."

Judd found it impossible to make the final decision, so Christopher made it for him. He rose to his feet and put a hand on the boy's head. "Tell you what—we're going to get you out of school for today. You wait here, okay?"

In the principal's office he found Randy Woodward, Mrs. Hubert, and the teacher whose money had been stolen, Ms. Prothero. He closed the door and said without preamble, "I want to put him on police hold and get a court hearing."

"You think it'll do any good?" asked Woodward.

"I'm going after a CHIPS petition."

"A CHIPS petition?" said Woodward. "You're sure?" A CHIPS petition— Children in Need of Placement or Supervision—meant trying to remove a child permanently from his home. No responsible police officer or social worker began such a procedure without questioning himself to make sure it was the right thing to do.

"He stole the money because his parents fenced his subsidized lunch tickets and used the money to buy cocaine, then tried to get Judd to sniff some of it."

Ms. Prothero—a clean-cut all-American-girl type perhaps two years out of college—visibly blanched and put a hand to her mouth. Mrs. Hubert sat behind her desk looking sober but thoughtful. Randy Woodward said calmly, "I'd like to tie those sonsabitches on about a thirty-foot cable behind my snowmobile and go for a four-hour ride through the woods."

Christopher replied, "Trouble is, when they came to, they'd only ask for a snort. The boy needs a bath and some food. I don't think he's eaten in a while. He also needs clean clothes, which I don't think you'll find at his home. Will you contact Social Services?" he asked Woodward.

"Right away, if it's all right with Mrs. Hubert."

She nodded and said, "I think that's best."

"Ms. Prothero?"

The young woman came out of her daze, looking ill. "Yes, of course. Dear God, I had no idea it was that bad at his house."

Christopher said to Woodward, "I'll take him to the foster home myself after you make the call. He knows me. He's going to be scared."

"Sure. Glad to have you do it. These are the ones that break your heart."

Break your heart—sweet Jesus, this one damn near shredded Christopher's. He transported the scared little kid to a small, neat house on the southwest side of Anoka and walked him between the snowbanks up the driveway. Judd stared straight ahead, wearing a stoic expression and a denim jacket scarcely warm enough for mid-winter. All the while Chris remembered how hard Judd had hugged him in the counselor's office at school.

A buxom fiftyish woman in a moss-green sweater and slacks opened the door and let them inside.

"This is Mrs. Billings," Christopher told Judd.

She said, "Hello, Judd," with such false brightness it made Christopher feel guilty as hell for leaving the boy with her, though the house appeared clean and had holy pictures on the living room walls.

He said to the woman, "He needs food and a bath. He's on a twenty-four-hour hold pending a detention hearing."

Before leaving, he put a hand on Judd's shoulder. The boy was too tall to be knelt before, yet too short to be hugged chest to chest, so Christopher settled for a squeeze of the shoulder before he could no longer help himself and gathered Judd against him in a mismatched farewell hug. This time, before a stranger, Judd gave no hug in return.

"Hey, listen, you're going to be okay now."

"When will I see you again?"

"There'll be a hearing within twenty-four hours. The law won't allow me to be present at it, but I'll come to get you for it myself, in the squad car."

"You promise?"

"I promise."

"Will I go to school tomorrow?"

"No, probably not tomorrow. The hearing will probably be then."

"What's the hearing for?"

"Well, the legal language says it's a hearing for probable cause. That means the judge will decide if there's enough reason to keep you out of your home perma-nently. The county attorney will be coming to talk to you about it beforehand. Just tell the truth. Tell him what you told me at school."

Judd studied his friend the policeman with a downcast expression.

"Well, now, listen, I've got to go. I'm on duty, you know."

Judd nodded.

He ruffled the boy's hair, thanked Mrs. Billings and left. As he was opening his car door he glanced back at the house to find Judd standing motionlessly in the front window, watching him. Inside the squad, he had to blow his nose and clear his throat before he could pick up the radio and report to the dispatcher.

He realized something as he headed back toward Social Services to find out about when the hearing was scheduled: The kid hadn't lapsed into rap talk once today. Fear had robbed him of all vestiges of bravado.

He called Lee that night and said, "I've got to see you."

"Something's wrong," she said.

"Yeah, it's . . ." What was it? His job, his damned thankless job during the training for which he'd learned never to become emotionally involved with the people he served. "It's Judd."

She gave him permission straightaway, without asking a single further question. "Come anytime. I'll be here all night."

He got there at 8:30 feeling heavy-limbed, heavyhearted, and needing . . . needing something . . . something he couldn't quite put into words. Succor, maybe.

She let him into the shadowed front hall, took one look at his drawn face and said, "Darling, what is it?"

Without even removing his jacket, he took her in his arms and put his face against her hair. She folded her arms up his back and they stood in the dim entry behind a stub wall that left the back of her quite visible through the living room archway. The entry lights had been left off, as had those in the kitchen. One dim lamp cast light onto their ankles from the living room where, for once, no television chattered, no Joey sprawled.

"Just one of those days I could have done without."

"What happened to Judd?"

"I started legal proceedings to try to have him taken away from his parents permanently."

"What started it?"

He told her about the lunch tickets, the cocaine, the scene in the principal's office and taking Judd to the foster home. "The thing is, after all that kid's been through, I'm still not sure I'm doing the right thing."

"But, cocaine . . ."

"I know. I know." He held her loosely, needing the feel of her warmth and closeness, the faint pressure of her arms bolstering his back. "But I've been there, Lee, and I know how it feels. It's home, but it isn't like other kids' homes. Still it's the only one you've got, and if you lose your mom and dad, how do you know there'll be anybody there at all for you? I saw it in Judd's eyes today. I felt it when he latched onto me so damned hard I thought he'd break my neck. Then he said, 'I want to live with you, Chris,' and I had to say no. Jesus, Lee, you should have seen him. There he sat on that hard office chair, looking like some little refugee, dirty, bedraggled, smelling bad. He didn't even have on a decent winter jacket, and I knew damned well nobody'd fed him breakfast . . . and I've got an empty bedroom, and I make enough money that I could easily take good care of him, but what am I going to do with a boy of twelve when I work nights half the time and there's nobody to watch him?"

She had no answers. She only held him and let him go on whispering gruffly, working out his feelings.

"They warn you not to let this happen, never to get too close to kids like him, but what kind of a heartless human being would I be if I didn't?"

"Judd is warm and fed and being taken care of tonight. You did that much for him."

He sighed and rested his chin on her head, closing his eyes. He tried to draw strength from her, enough to blot out the difficult memories from that day, but they persisted. In time, he said, "The kids are the hardest part of this job. Not the felons, not the crooks, not even the accident victims. It's the kids that get to you."

"I know," she said, rubbing his back. "Greg always said the same thing."

"A couple years ago, the first year Greg joined the force, I got a call from the North Side saying someone had spotted a little girl walking down the street barefooted. It was a beautiful summer day, about two o'clock in the afternoon when I found her. I'd guess she was about three years old or so, and I swear to God, nobody had done one single thing for her that day. You could tell by her clothes that she'd dressed herself, poor little thing. She was wearing some dirty little dress and no panties underneath it at all, and then those bare feet, and her hair all scruffy and snarled. She was just toddling down the street dragging a hairless doll by one arm, blocks away from home. She'd just wandered out and nobody had even missed her. When I pulled the squad up beside her and got out, she was sucking on her fingers and crying, and even before I got to her, she reached up both arms, and once she'd put them around my neck, nobody could pry them loose. I had to call for a backup because she cried when I tried to let her go to drive my squad. I took her to the emergency foster home myself, and when I tried to give her to the woman there she sobbed and refused to let go of my neck." He was quiet awhile, then added, "I'll never forget that day as long as I live."

When he grew quiet, she said, "You mustn't feel guilty for not taking Judd."

"But I do. I started this big-brother relationship with him and I feel like I'm letting him down."

"You're too softhearted."

"How can a person be too softhearted?"

"Dear Christopher, this is one of the reasons why I love you."

"Oh, Lee . . ." He drew back and took her face in both hands, holding it like a chalice from which he would drink. He kissed her in gratitude, in beatitude, then continued holding her face.

"Tonight I wasn't sure if I needed a lover, a mother or a wife. So I came to you for all three."

"A wife?" she repeated.

"Cops have to lay a lot on their wives and I haven't got one." He grazed her cheeks with his thumbs. "Thanks for being here."

"If I was any help at all, I'm glad, but I have my own reasons for opening my door to you, and they're not totally altruistic." She went up on tiptoe and reached up one arm to draw his head down. "I thought about you all day long."

They were kissing when Joey came out of his bedroom and walked down the hall, stockingfooted. He entered the living room from the opposite end and came up short at the sight of his mother standing beyond the far archway of the room in the shadows of the entry hall, wrapped tightly in an embrace with somebody, kissing him.

He got a funny feeling in the pit of his stomach. A lift. A stir. An odd buoyant sensation that made his inner thighs feel liquidy and weak. It was Christopher, Joey was pretty sure, though all he could see was his jacket sleeves and his hands on his mother's back and head. He knew that jacket, though. Chris's left arm slipped down and caught his mother around the hips, pulling her deeper against himself. She whispered something Joey couldn't make out, and the murmur from a masculine voice confirmed that it was Christopher whose open hands came down and grasped his mother by both buttocks while she went up against him the way he'd seen in the movies.

He felt a blush cover his body and backed off into the hallway, standing motionless and undetected. He listened to their quiet murmurs and the long silences in between, then the more novel sound of slurpy kisses and humming sounds like he himself made when eating something he liked. He peeked around the corner again and saw Christopher's hand leave his mother's back and slide up under her sweater. The edge of the archway cut off his view, but he knew perfectly well Christopher was feeling up her breasts. Jeez! His *mother?* She still did stuff like that at her age? Wow, then they probably went all the way, too. Joey got all jacked-up feeling, all strange and tight and hard everyplace, and his breathing got windy. He took one last peek, then slipped silently into his mother's bedroom where the house's second telephone sat on her nightstand. He closed the door noiselessly, picked up the receiver and dialed by feel in the dark, then flopped on his back in the middle of her bed and said, "Hey, Denny, this is Joey. I gotta talk to you about the weirdest thing that just happened . . ."

Chapter 16

The judge ruled in favor of leaving Judd in foster care until a formal court hearing, which was scheduled for late February, though he denied Christopher the appointment as Judd's guardian, stating that the boy already had a county attorney and a social worker looking out for his welfare. Christopher returned Judd to Mrs. Billings's house and left him there with the promise that the two of them would work out together in the police weight room every Tuesday that Chris's schedule permitted.

Joey Reston decided he wouldn't tell anyone but Denny Whitman what he'd seen in the front hall at home. If he told Janice, she'd break up Christopher and their mother, and that would be the end of the rather sexually stimulating scenarios such as the one that had so fascinated him he'd decided to try a little of that stuff with Sandy Parker. Of course, he'd have to talk it all over with Denny first and make sure that when he finally put the move on his girlfriend, he did it right and didn't scare her off.

Janice had returned to college, and Lee made plans for an unabashed sexual reprise with Christopher on the first night it was possible.

She called him and said, "Joey has signed up for a class to get his driver's permit. He'll be gone for two hours tomorrow night, starting at seven o'clock. What are you doing?"

"I'm off. Can you come over?"

"Yes." She released a pent breath. "Just try to stop me."

"And I've got Friday off, too. What are you doing Friday night?"

"Nothing. And Joey's going to a basketball game."

"Two nights in a row. Shazam."

"Oh, Christopher, I haven't felt like this in years."

"Like what?"

"You know."

"Maybe I do, but tell me anyway."

"Sexy. Turned on. Thinking about it all the time. I suspect I should feel guilty, but I don't."

"Why should you feel guilty?"

"I'm lying to the kids."

"No, you're not. You're just reserving some of your private time for me and not telling them about it."

"A slanted view if I ever heard one."

"I've told you, anytime you want to tell them, straight to their faces, 'I'm dating Christopher,' just let me know. I'll come and tell them with you."

"Not yet," she said, a hoarder savoring her booty, "not just yet. I want you to myself for a while."

A silence fell while they pictured each other, and felt lucky and happy and yearny, as all new lovers feel when they must be apart.

"I wish I was with you now," he said.

"So do I."

"Are you in bed?" he asked.

"Yes." She called him every night at eleven, after lights out. "Are you?"

"Yes, in the dark. What are you wearing?"

"A really ugly old faded flannel nightgown. It must be ten years old."

"Are you lying on your back?"

"No, on my side, curled up with the phone on the pillow."

"Is the nightgown caught between your legs?"

His question did unbelievable things to her libido. "Is this one of those kinky telephone conversations I've heard about?"

"Yes, I suppose it is, but I've never had one like it before either, so don't go thinking I make a habit of this. Only with you. Is the nightgown caught between your legs?"

"Yes," she whispered, then closed her eyes, breathing as if his hands were upon her, picturing his face, his sturdy fingers, his unclothed body, while only silence connected their two telephones.

"Lee?" he whispered after a long while.

"Yes."

"Don't waste a minute getting over here after you drop Joey off."

She didn't. At 7:07 she was walking through his door, and by 7:09 neither of them had a stitch of clothing on. They didn't make it as far as his bedroom but tumbled to the living room floor where the radio was playing and two lamps were lit beside the sofa. This time, she hadn't a single inhibition about being seen in the light, but rolled with him, and spread her limbs at his bidding, and let him kiss her in the most intimate of places, which had been scented for that purpose.

Their coupling was greedy and untamed, a splendid natural compulsion carrying them from one pleasure to another after their forced celibacy. They explored poses balletic and profane, submitting completely to the unutterable joy of this act.

They had been kneeling, face-to-face, when she fell back, her arms upflung, her ribs forming a bridge where he spread one hand.

Her words came as an afterbeat. "I can feel you . . . clear up to . . . my heart . . . my God . . . my God . . . my God . . ."

"I never thought you'd be like this."

"I've never been . . . before . . ."

He hauled her up and she came with the same loose freedom as she'd fallen back, to kiss him and move upon him and mess his hair and wet his mouth with her own.

"Lee . . . Lee . . . I still can't believe I'm with you, and doing this."

She was forty-five, and flying free, and making up for so much lost time.

When she climaxed, he stifled her cry with a sofa pillow, afraid the tenants in the apartment below would hear. When he climaxed, she watched, smiling down their bodies, taking joy in the sight of them joined. In paroxysm he was beautiful, bowed back upon her with his jaw fallen open and his breath strident. She touched his damp brow and ran a finger into his open mouth, which settled closed as his eyes came open.

Afterward, they lay on their sides on the turfy texture of the carpet, holding each other with their legs and their gazes. Near their heads a branch of the ficus tree fluttered in the forced air rising up through the hot-air vent. The low bass beat of the radio reverberated along the floor and up into their ribs. Outside, snow pecked at the windows and wind prowled, but in the saffron light from the lamps Christopher and Lee felt warmed from within.

"You're something," he said, exhausted.

"I don't know where it came from."

"Too long without it."

"Something more, I think. This is a different me."

He touched her lower lip, misshaped it and let it spring back to its natural contour. "When I first started thinking about you in a sexual way, I imagined that you'd be very straight, very proper about it."

"I used to be. You've changed me."

"How did I manage that?"

"I don't know. You just . . ." She rolled to her back, one elbow jutting up, one breast flat and stretched, attracting his idle hand while their bodies remained in a liquid link below. "There you are, thirty and sturdy and making me into this sex-crazed woman where I used to be so . . . well, so functional, so oriented all day long at work. Now I lose track of what I'm doing, and I scheme to get away from the shop to meet you and do this, and a day without you seems like a month."

"It's the same for me. But it's more than sex. You're there for me in more ways than that."

"What ways?" she said, still lazing backward while he ran a fingertip over her ribs and around one nipple, down to her navel, inside it, then back up her center.

"The day after New Year's when you came here at noon and we couldn't make love, I felt contented just sitting with you on my lap in the sun. And when my job gets me down and I can come to you the way I did the other day when I put Judd in that foster home . . . that's all part of it for me. And that part is just as good as this part."

Smiling lazily, she rolled her shoulder toward him slightly, giving shape to her breast once more, so that it fit nicely into his hand.

"Just as good?" she teased.

"Well," he amended, grinning, "just about as good."

Her throat fluttered in a silent chuckle, then she rolled to lie face-to-face with him, lifting the hair at his nape with four fingers, studying his features while her laughter dissolved into something much more profound.

"For me too," she whispered.

She lifted her weight from the floor and bore it on one elbow, rolling slightly onto him to kiss him more affectionately than passionately.

"You've made me so happy," she said, strumming his hair back from his ears as if it were lute strings.

"I'm glad."

"And you know something?"

He waited, sated, for her to go on.

"I truly believe that the quality of a relationship can be measured by the quality of the time *after* making love. What do you think?"

He thought he wanted to spend the rest of his life with this woman, that's what he thought. Catching her neck in the crook of one elbow, he sighed her name, "Oh, Lee . . . ," and settled her in the bays and cays of his body, letting the unsaid speak louder than any words he could have replied.

She dreamed of Greg that night for only the third time since his death. The dream was simple, just a glimpse of him smiling and saying, "I took care of that hose, Mom," as he walked into the kitchen adjusting a red bill cap. She awakened disoriented, believing during those few fragile seconds before total wakefulness that he was still alive. Full awareness brought the hammer blows of her own heartbeat against the bedding, reminding her that he was truly dead and she'd never hear his voice or see his face again.

She touched things to make certain she was awake: the bedspread, her forehead, the nightstand, cool and solid at the tip of her outstretched arm.

What had the dream meant? And why had it come tonight right after she'd spent time with Christopher? Was it a signal that she truly was substituting Christopher for Greg, if not in the physical sense, then in the emotional?

That day, still melancholy from the dream, Lee received a second reminder of Greg—a telephone call from Nolan Steeg. "Hello," he said simply, "just wondering how you're doing." The sound of his voice clutched her with a deeper wistfulness, though she never failed to be touched by the sensitivity of the young people who continued calling this way instead of forgetting she'd ever known them and been part of their lives. Dear, thoughtful Nolan—how heartwarming to realize that he'd cared enough about Greg to continue caring about his family. He and Lee had a ten-minute visit about Nolan's job, Joey's driving, Janice's return to school, the winter weather. Finally, when they'd spoken of everything except the subject that was on both of their minds, Nolan said, "I don't know why, but I've been thinking of Greg so much today."

What a relief it was to speak directly of him at last.

"Oh, Nolan, me too . . . I dreamed of him last night."

"I never dream of him. I wish I would. It'd be nice to see him again."

"I can't believe you called today, just when I needed it. Not everybody realizes that I still need to talk about him sometimes."

"He was my friend my whole life long. It takes longer than a few months to get over losing him. I can't imagine how long it's going to take you. I'm just glad you're the kind I *can* talk to."

After Lee hung up she found her spirits fluctuating between happy recollections of the past and present self-pity. Nolan's call had sparked so many vivid memories of the two young boys through the years—in elementary school together, then in junior high like Joey was now, then in senior high, double-dating, going out for sports, polishing their first cars in the driveway, working barebacked in the sun while their car radios shook the leaves on the trees. At times during that day these images would bring a sting to Lee's eyes; at other times they would bring an unconscious smile, a healing acceptance.

But as if fate was out to undermine all the progress she'd made since last June, it had one more reminder in store. On her way home from work that night, she switched on the car radio, and what should be playing but Vince Gill's "When I Call Your Name." The chance of her hitting that particular song during the five-minute drive home was remote. Yet there it was, crooning out of the cold speakers, the third and most powerful reminder of Greg.

Music. Its nostalgia hit with an insidious impact. It was the most recent of his likes, this song that was still pouring forth from radios all over America, speaking to people's emotions on multiple levels. But not to Greg's. No longer to Greg's. What had he felt when he'd heard these words? Who had he thought of? Had there been a special girl he'd loved and lost and still longed for? A girl he might have eventually married? Had children with? Spent a happy life with?

That song began the thought that Lee had trained herself during the past seven months to shut out:

If only . . .

If only . . .

If only . . .

She didn't quite make it home before beginning to cry. Joey was there in the kitchen dropping some macaroni into boiling water when she walked in.

"Will you make some macaroni and cheese, Mom? But you gotta hurry. I've got to be at . . ." His expression grew fearful when he saw her tears. "Mom, what's wrong?"

He came to her straightaway and they hugged.

"Greg," she said through a stuffy nose. "I'm missing him something awful today."

He hugged her harder, standing very still.

"Me too. I wonder why."

"I don't know. Nolan called, too. He said the same thing."

"Why would we all be thinking of him at the same time?"

"Who knows? Earth rhythms, biorhythms, the pattern of the stars. We think we're healed, then we find out we're a long way from it."

"Yeah," he said in a croaky voice against her hair. "Bummer."

She rubbed his shoulder blades, smiled sadly and repeated, "Yeah . . . a real bummer." Over the last half year Joey had surpassed her in height. The realization only added to her gloominess: Soon he, too, would grow up and be gone from her. She drew back in spite of the thought, perhaps because of it, and forced life to take precedence over death.

"So. You've started some macaroni and cheese." She found several tissues and offered a couple to Joey. They blew their noses and wiped their eyes, and she turned down the stove burner before the macaroni boiled over. "And you've got to be at the high school at seven-thirty."

"Yeah," he said without much spirit. "Anoka's playing Coon Rapids." It was the biggest rivalry of the year.

She took his face in both hands and gave it a little love pat and smooch. "And pretty soon I won't have to give you a ride to these things anymore."

"Denny's mom is giving us a ride tonight."

"Well, good. Now, let's get this cheese sauce made."

When he was gone she cleaned up the kitchen and changed into blue jeans and a sweatshirt. The house was very quiet. The dishwasher made a rhythmic *thump-thump-thump* and sent out the lemony smell of steamy detergent. The houseplants needed watering but she suddenly despised the thought of watering one more plant, of touching one more leaf after a day, days, years of doing so. Suddenly she missed Janice so terribly much the center of her chest hurt—now where had that come from? She, who had adjusted to Janice's going off to college within months of her doing so. She dialed Janice's dorm number but nobody answered: Friday night, and what healthy, well-adjusted, pretty young coed wouldn't be out with friends? Lee hung up, braced both elbows on the kitchen counter and poked the tip of one finger into the leftover macaroni and cheese left cooling in a plastic storage dish.

Poke . . . poke . . . poke . . .

Holding her feelings at bay . . .

Holding . . . holding . . .

Until a sob burst forth with such ferociousness it laid her flat against the countertop, her hand lying limp beside the macaroni.

Christopher arrived when she was mopping up her face. He stepped inside with two rented videos and a red pie box from Bakers Square.

He asked the same question Joey had.

"Lee? What's wrong?"

She sniffled and said, "It's dumb."

He set down the videos and pie.

"What's dumb? Come here . . ." He went to her instead, and gathered her into his arms against the cold nylon of his jacket with the smell of winter captured in its filaments. Gently cupping the back of her neck, resting his lips on her forehead, he asked again, "What's dumb?"

"Greg," she got out before she began crying again.

He was the only one who didn't say anything, and it was precisely what she needed. Simply to be held, loved, rocked, petted, understood in silence by this man. The comfort of others mattered—it certainly had—but all day long she had yearned toward this minute when she could curl into a cocoon in Christopher's arms and feel at last the perfect consolation, for that's what he had become to her. No others, no matter how she loved or cared about them, could fulfill the need he had begun fulfilling in her day-to-day existence. Much as *he* had come to *her* when life got too complicated and sad, *she* now turned to *him*.

He let her cry for as long as she needed, then turned with one arm around her and walked slowly to the living room where they sat on the sofa in darkness softened only by the peachy light from the distant kitchen. She coiled up tightly against him like a snail beneath a leaf while he turned her legs to the side and draped them over his lap, laying his cheek on her hair.

In time she began telling him about her day, the trio of reminders that had rekindled her grief: the dream, Nolan's call and Greg's favorite song. She confessed her disappointment in discovering she wasn't healed of her grief after all.

"I guess I'm still what they call vulnerable, even after all these months."

" 'They'—who is 'they'?"

"The books, the magazines, the people who appear on talk shows. They all say you're vulnerable for a long time after a loss, and you should give yourself time before making changes in your life."

"Vulnerable to me, is that what you mean?"

"Oh, Christopher, I don't know what I mean. I thought I was over the worst of it, that's all; now here I am right back where I was seven months ago."

"Hardly. You've come a long way since then."

His coolheaded common sense reassured her. "I suppose you're right, and deep down inside I realize that I tend to get melodramatic. But this doesn't feel like melodrama. It feels like a great big empty ache that's never going to go away."

He could tell perfectly well what had happened today: She'd experienced a relapse of grief and had stepped back to assess her sexual relationship with him, which had begun to look suspiciously much like overreaction in the wake of loss. Were the two of them greedily grasping at life, proving they were not squandering it by engaging in this coital merry-go-round with each other? Were they fooling themselves about being in love in order to justify what they were doing on couches and floors and in his bed every chance they got? When the true period of mourning was over, would they find out they had merely used each other to get through it?

"You know, Lee, you're not the only one who's vulnerable here. What about me?"

She sat very still, with her legs still across his lap, one hand on his chest, feeling his heart beat along at a normal pace.

"Do you think we're both going to end up hurt when this is over?" she asked.

He gave no reply.

"Each of us will lose our best friend then, won't we?" she asked in a diminished voice.

He remained stone still. "You seem awfully sure this is going to be over someday."

Lee's mind ticked off the paramount reasons it would be: *His age. Her age. Mother. Janice.* What other outcome was possible? Surely someday there would be a painful breakup.

"Is this just a temporary fling for you, Lee?" he asked.

Now it was her turn to sit absolutely still.

"Is it?" he asked. When she made no reply, he pressed his point. "Are you waiting to get over your infatuation with me so you never have to tell your family?"

She pulled back sharply, looking up toward his shadowed face. "I don't know what you mean," she answered.

He rolled his head and looked at her. "You know something, Lee? That's the first lie I've ever heard you tell."

She bristled and lurched up from the couch, but he caught her arm and hauled her back against his side.

"Forget it," he said. "Tonight isn't the time to discuss it, right after you've had such a bad day anyway. I brought some pie. You want some pie? It's cream cheese and apple."

"I'm not in the mood right now." She rose with no resistance from him and walked out of the room. Left behind, he sighed and pulled himself to the edge of the sofa almost wearily, dropping his elbows to his knees and considering the situation for several minutes before pushing to his feet and following her to the kitchen.

She had put away the leftover macaroni and cheese and stood at the kitchen sink staring out the black window.

"Lee," he said with a note of apology, dropping a hand on her nape.

She stood stiffly beneath it. "What do you want me to do?" she asked.

"I don't know."

"Well, neither do I. Once people know about us everything will change, and I don't want that."

"All right." He dropped his hand from her. "All right. I just thought it might be easier if we were honest with them, and we could stop sneaking around."

They stood in the kitchen refusing to look at each other, wondering exactly what they wanted. Starting an affair was the simple part; continuing it was more difficult. If it were to be a temporary fling and nothing more, there was no reason for her children to know. If it was not, this was too soon to talk about it.

"Do you want me to go?" he asked.

"No."

"Then what do you want?"

"I want . . ." She turned and he saw uncertainty on her face. "I want to be bold and fearless, but I'm not. I'm afraid of what people will say."

He stood staring at her, part of him understanding, another part alienated by her reluctance to defy heaven and earth on his behalf. He was willing to defy it; why wasn't she? Yet he did understand. She had lost a husband and a son. She didn't want to lose a daughter, too, and who knew what reaction an outraged, infatuated twenty-three-year-old might have when she found out she'd been upstaged by her forty-five-year-old mother? And what about Lee's mother, father and sister?

He had no answers, so he escaped momentarily into serving up pie. He opened a cabinet door and got out two saucers, cut two pieces and found forks, then carried everything to the table. He sat down with his back to her and defiantly rammed one bite of pie into his mouth. It tasted like sadness.

"Aren't you going to eat your pie?" he asked.

She came, finally, and sat down, picked up her fork and took one bite, then stared at the wedge without eating more.

He studied her downcast face, her eyes that refused to meet his, her stubborn chin and the mouth that was trembling again after all the crying she'd done today. Hell, he hadn't intended to make her cry.

"Lee," he said in a tortured voice, "I'm sorry."

When she looked up he saw tears lining her eyelids, not quite plump enough to fall.

"I love you. You didn't need this tonight of all nights. I'm sorry."

They dropped their forks at the same moment and catapulted from their chairs into each other's arms, their hearts aching with love and fear and the realization that the hurt each of them had foreseen was already beginning.

"Sweet Jesus," he said, quite desperately, with his eyes closed, "I love you."

"Joey will be home in half an hour," she said. "We have to hurry."

He picked her up and carried her to the bedroom where they made love with an unmistakable tenderness, for here now was a new sexual mood: apology. It permeated their touches, murmurs, gazes.

For in Christopher lingered a profound regret for having added to her burden tonight rather than mitigating it, and in Lee the haunting suspicion that he was right, that she was hoping she'd get over him before her kids found out.

In the weeks that followed, however, life atoned. It gave them redemptive times together, rescuing them time and again from themselves, for in the presence of one another *self* tended to matter less. *Self* was somehow seen to, in all its wants, by their giving to each other.

Their primary frustration during that time was having so little time to themselves.

They stole hours.

They hoarded noons.

They grew expert at making love in ten minutes or less. Sometimes, though, friendship supplied the sustenance and sex waited. Friendship—by its thriving, simple force—drove their relationship to a new level of satisfaction.

Sex, they said to themselves, *well, yes, sex. But in all honesty anyone can achieve a certain level of expertise at sex, can't they?* Ah, but to be friends, now there was an accomplishment.

Perhaps they overplayed friendship because they'd been spooked by that exchange the night he'd suggested she might use him and lose him once this period of mourning had ended.

Christopher's deeper feelings caught up with him, however, one morning when everything had been so perfect his entire being was sated: all but that tiny corner of his wishes where a nagging hangnail of desire flapped each time it rubbed against his contentment.

Joey had spent the night before with the Whitman family at a motel with an indoor pool celebrating Denny's fifteenth birthday. For the first time ever, Christopher awakened at dawn with Lee in bed beside him.

He opened his eyes and saw her there, on her stomach with her left arm under the pillow, her right canted against his dark pine headboard. The daylight held too little candlepower to cast shadows, thus she reposed in the dusky prelight that gave her an allover hue of Spanish moss. Only her eyelashes stood out against the delicate gray colorlessness covering her exposed shoulder blades, arms and face. Her lips were open but she appeared unbreathing. Only her left eye showed. Beneath it a tiny furl of skin took on a first morning shadow along with another beside her nose, and yet another leading from it to the corner of her mouth. As he watched, her right thumb flinched, then her left leg, which was updrawn near his hip beneath the covers. That thumb—rough, slightly spatulate—bore the remnants of yesterday's work beneath its stubby nail. He loved, he'd discovered, her self-consciousness about her hands and the hands themselves, workworn, stained, crosshatched on the inner fingers by the abrasiveness of soil and colored by chlorophyll.

He rolled to his stomach, arranging his body in a mirror image of hers: pillow beneath his cheek, knee cocked and touching the tip of hers, his hand at the headboard seeking and finding hers, linking their fingers loosely while she continued slumbering, unaware of his touch. With his thumb he touched hers, rubbed its sandpapery pad and contemplated her face. He wanted the right to wake up beside her like this always. He wanted her coarse hands and her changeless hair and her relaxed mouth in his line of vision when he opened his eyes every morning for the rest of his life.

He waited to tell her so, watching in patience as the dawn gained strength and the light brought out pale hues upon her hair and skin. Her hair became bronze, her lips pink, her freckles rusty across her bare shoulders.

She opened her eye and found him watching her. Lifting her head, she scrubbed hard beneath her nose, squinting her eyes shut, then curled onto the pillow again. With their fingers still loosely linked, her left eye open, half her mouth visible, she smiled against her pillow.

"G'morning," she said, muffled.

"Good morning."

She closed her eye. "You've been watching me."

"Mm-hmm."

"For how long?"

"All night. Didn't want to waste a minute."

"Liar."

"Since dawn."

"Mmmm . . ." She acted as if she wanted to snooze some more, so he let her. His heart began racing, wondering how to pose the question, fearing she'd say no and force an end to their relationship. He thought about all the years he'd lived without really searching for the right one, then finding her in the most unlikely person of all. Thirty years of life funneling down into one crystallized moment that would affect all his days that followed. He'd never even thought of rehearsing this. He figured he'd know when the moment was right, and as for words—well, hell, a man just had to stumble through the best he could in spite of his hammering heart and his fears of rejection.

She might have dozed again, all the while he claimed her lax fingers and kept their thumbs matched, all the while the lump of anxiety rose from his chest to his throat and lay wedged against the pillow.

God in heaven, what if she said no? Where would he ever find another woman to equal her?

Her thumb began circling his slowly; she hadn't been dozing after all.

"Lee?" he said quietly.

Her left eye opened, its rusty iris dotted by deeper markings, like a tiger lily. "Hm?"

He lifted his head, carried her right hand down from the headboard and kissed the base of her thumb. Dread of her answer kept him mute so long that she said, "What, honey?"

He studied their joined hands while saying it. "I love you and I want to marry you."

Her head came up. Her face appeared in full, eyes wide while reactions volleyed across her face: stunned surprise, rejection of the moment for which she wasn't prepared, a weakness for him tempered by a realization of the strength she found with him.

"Oh, Christopher," she said, scuttling up, backing to the headboard, sitting with the blankets held above her bare breasts. "I was afraid you'd bring this up sometime."

"Afraid? I said I love you. You've said you love me. Why are you afraid?"

"There are fifteen years between us."

"We've known that since we first met, but we started this affair anyway." He sat up against the headboard, too, covered to the hip, the pillow at his back, his legs crossed and stretched straight out before him. "You'd have to do some pretty fancy talking to convince me that matters one single bit."

"You're blocking out what matters."

"For instance."

When she stubbornly refused to cite a reason, he did.

"Public opinion—shall we start with that?"

"All right, let's." Her voice had taken on an edge. "Or more to the point, family opinion, and I don't mean my mother's, or my sister's, or my father's, or Joey's. I mean Janice's. Let's start with her opinion."

"Let me reiterate something I've told you on several occasions. I never once—not by word, action or innuendo—made the slightest move on Janice. I hugged her a few times right after Greg died, but everybody was hugging everybody else then, so that doesn't count. Neither have I ever made any bones about the fact that I was taking you out or doing things with you. And if you recollect with any kind of honesty, you'll realize, neither did you."

She slid a thumbnail between her bottom teeth.

"Did you?" he insisted.

She locked both arms around her knees and replied meekly, "No."

"In fact, there were times when you asked your kids if they had any objections, weren't there?"

"Yes."

"As recently as New Year's Eve, right?"

"Yes."

He let that sink in before continuing. "Any feelings Janice supposed she had for me were strictly one-sided; and if you raised the kind of children I think you raised, she'll realize that you've got a right to happiness and she'll give us her blessings. If not . . ." He spread his hands and let them drop. "We'll face it when we have to. I don't have all the answers."

"But Janice would be mortified after the way she confided in me that she liked you, and after she bought you those tickets at Christmas and practically spelled it out that she'd like to go to that ball game with you."

"But is that our fault? Should we back away from each other just because Janice has a crush on me? I'll concede . . . she might be shocked when we first tell her, but she'll get used to the idea. So what other objections do you have?"

"They aren't objections, Christopher, they're common sense."

"What other common sense do you have, then?"

"I don't like your tone of voice."

"I don't like your answer!"

"I don't like any of this! We've never fought before."

"Well, damn it, Lee, that's what a man does when a woman turns down his proposal; he starts fighting for her!"

"All right," she said, spreading her hands as if pressing down the air at her hips. "All right." The blanket slipped down her breasts. She tugged it into place and pinned it beneath her arms. "You can disregard everything that's changeable but you can't disregard our ages. That part is never going to change."

"I don't want it to. I love you the way you are, you love me the way I am, and I don't see that changing as we grow older."

"But, Christopher—" She broke off her own objection, wagging her head as if this was all too exasperating.

" 'But, Christopher, what about kids.' That's what you were going to say, isn't it?" Their eyes met and he saw that some of her temper had dissolved. He felt his do the same and realized that this, above all, would be the most difficult to convince her of. When he spoke he put a wealth of earnest sincerity into his voice. "I don't want any, Lee. I've never wanted any. I told you that weeks ago. I've known since I was a kid myself that I didn't want to put any kid through what I've been through myself. And since I've grown up and become a police officer, I've seen so many poor, unloved, hungry little bastards that I just don't want to bring any into the world and risk putting them through that."

"But yours wouldn't *be* poor, unloved, hungry little bastards. You'd be such a good father," she said plaintively.

"I can be that to yours if I marry you. Maybe not to Janice, but to Joey. I love Joey already, and if I'm not mistaken he feels darn close to the same thing for me. I've been playing a father's role with him ever since Greg died, and if I marry you that'll just make it official."

She knew he was right about Joey, who worshiped the very breeze left by his passing.

He was hurrying on. "And you've forgotten about Judd. I've made a promise to myself that I'm going to stick by Judd till he's got a diploma in his hand and a reasonably firm foot into adulthood. He's going to need it. I'll have all the fathering I want, getting him over the hump . . . and you're right, I think I'll be good at it. Good enough to head that kid in the right direction, because whether he goes back to his parents or stays in foster care, he's got a hell of a lot to overcome, and I'm the one who can help him do it . . . me, who overcame it myself.

"As far as Janice is concerned, I don't think I'll ever be a father figure to her because she's too old, but I can round out the family and fill that space that's been vacant since Bill died. I know it'll take time with Janice, but once she falls in love— really falls in love with some nice young man she'll meet someday—she'll forget she ever looked at me twice. And when she sees that you're happy, she'll be happy, too."

Lee let her head fall back against the headboard and her eyes close. What peculiar and bittersweet luck they'd had to find each other and fall in love. How unfair that a chance thing like a number—fifteen—divided them and created a barrier to their happiness. She loved him—oh, her heart didn't question it for a moment— but with that love came a responsibility to look into a future that he was too young to heed, so she, with her greater life experience, must heed for him. She rolled her face toward him.

"You make everything sound so logical."

He took her hand and held it on the sheets between them. His voice was quiet when he replied, "There's nothing logical about love, not the way it happened to me. I just . . ." He shook his head in wonder. "Hell, I just fell. Hard. Sudden. Boom, there it was: *This is the woman I want to spend my life with.* It rattled me when I first realized it, but not for the reasons you think. I never cared that you were older or that people would talk. I got scared because I knew that when this day came and I asked you, you'd say exactly what you're saying."

He was staring at their joined hands, and she could see how devastated he'd be at her refusal. She loved him so incredibly much at that moment that she allowed herself the fantasy of picturing herself as his wife with everyone she knew ideally happy for her. But their situation offered too many obstacles for idealism. She tried to put all she felt into the quiet, loving tone of her voice.

"Please understand, Christopher . . . I have to say this. I'm a family woman, committed to family. To rob you of having children, who can bring so much joy into your life, seems like an act of selfishness, not of love."

"I told you, Lee . . ." He met her eyes and said with unflappable certainty, "I don't want any of my own."

"Everybody wants children of their own."

"You're wrong. You can't judge everybody by your own standards."

She sighed, deep and long, and let her shoulders droop as her gaze drifted beyond the foot of the bed. He rubbed his thumb over hers and said, "Fifty percent of American families aren't traditional anymore, did you know that? Fifty percent. We'd fit right in."

It might be true, but somehow she felt distanced from statistics, and unhumored by his pithy observation. Fifty percent . . . fifty. Lord, what had happened to this country?

They sat silently for a long time, involved in their private thoughts: he with disappointment creating a new knot in his throat, she with the worry that if she said yes he'd come to regret what he gave up years from now, when she aged before he, and when he wished he'd married someone younger and had children of his own, maybe even when her sexual drive died before his did. Within the next decade, possibly half a decade, she'd be facing menopause while he would hit the prime of his life saddled with her. There seemed, upon honest consideration, an actual edge of immorality to the idea of accepting his offer and doing that to him.

"Oh, Christopher," she sighed, "I don't know."

When he spoke, there was a note of appeal in his voice.

"Could we lie down, Lee? Please? Here it is, the first morning we ever wake up together, and you're over there against your pillow, and I'm over here against mine, and I'd rather be holding you while we talk about this."

She gave in to his gentle humoring and let him stack both their pillows. They settled down belly to belly, covered to the shoulder by blankets. They hugged, twining their legs and caressing one another's backs, though the embrace remained reassuring rather than sexual.

"Oh, Christopher," she sighed again, happy to be returned to his long, warm nakedness beneath the covers, but uncertain about their future just the same. "I'm sorry I got angry with you but this is such a hard decision."

"Do you realize," he said, "how fully I've already blended into your life? I do everything a husband would do. I help you buy your Christmas tree. I put it in the stand for you. I fix your hoses and level your washing machine and mow your lawn, and give your kids a talking to when they're sloughing off on their obligations to you. I comfort you when you're sad, and make love to you when you're happy, and sometimes I fill in that man's chair at the end of the table, and you love having me there, don't tell me you don't. I take your son out driving for the first time, and I go to his football games, and I'm the one who comes running when you're scared to death he's dead at midnight. Now, mind you, I didn't do this on purpose.

I didn't mean to inveigle myself into your home life, but the fact remains, it happened. For you to tell me a marriage wouldn't work between us is damned unbelievable, Lee."

"I never said it wouldn't work. I said there are obstacles."

"Life is full of obstacles. They're there to be surmounted."

She digested this piece of wisdom, the kind that usually came from her mouth. His warm palms worked at persuading her. Lord, how good it felt to lie like this with him, to feel him growing aroused against her. How easy it would be to say yes and enjoy this luxury every morning for the rest of her life. She had awakened alone for so many, many years. This was how men and women were meant to be, together. She imagined telling her mother she was going to marry him, then pushed the idea away because it interfered with the pleasure brought by his hands, his scent, his warmth and the sexuality he was stirring within them both.

"So, tell me something," he said, drawing back, finding her eyes. "If all the extraneous issues didn't exist—not the age difference, not Janice's crush, not all the public opinion we'll have to stand up to—if it were just you and me, knowing me the way you do now, loving me and knowing I love you . . . would you marry me?"

She looked into his beloved blue eyes and answered the way her heart dictated.

"Yes," she said without pause. "Yes, I would . . . but, Christopher, life isn't that ea—"

He laid a finger across her lips.

"There . . . you've said it. Yes, you'd marry me. You want to. Concentrate on that for a while—will you?—instead of examining the negative side of everything?"

They hugged full-length again, her smooth legs between his coarse-haired ones. "Oh, Christopher," she sighed—how many times had she sighed his name this morning? "I wish I could just say yes and it would be as simple as that."

"There was a spell a while back—we didn't talk about it, but I know what you were thinking. That maybe you had turned to me out of nothing more than desperation, just trying to get over losing Greg. I hope that's gone by now."

"It is . . . and I'm sorry I get those spells."

"Quit reading those books," he said. "They put ideas into your head. We're together because we love each other, not because we're leaning on each other out of desperation, right?"

She drew back to see his face. "Right," she whispered, "because we love each other."

He said it again, straight out, holding her face in both hands. "Marry me, Lee."

She closed her eyes and kissed him to give herself time to reason, but when she was under his naked influence, reason came with much more difficulty. He was fully aroused now, their legs were dovetailed tightly, and every sense within her responded to him.

"No fair," she whispered against his lips, "asking me when we're in a state like this."

"Marry me." They carried on this dialog between plucking kisses.

"May I have some time to think about it?"

"How much?"

"A day, a week, maybe just long enough to get rid of this enormous lump of morning insistence beneath the covers. I don't know how long, Christopher. I wish I did, but I don't."

"But do you love me?"

"Yes."

"Will you keep thinking about that while you're deciding?"

"Yes."

"Are you going to talk to anybody about it?"

"Probably not."

"Good, because I know a few of them who would try to talk you out of it."

"So do I."

Giving up the playfulness, rolling her full length beneath him, he declared with true passion, "Oh, God, I love you. Please say yes."

"I love you, too, and I'll try."

Chapter 17

⁓⁓

Near eight o'clock that morning they arose and showered. Lee used the bathroom first, got dressed and was looking into his refrigerator when he came out into the kitchen toweling his hair, wearing gray sweatpants that hung low on his belly.

"I want to cook you breakfast to celebrate our first night together, but there's nothing in here to cook."

He stood beside her searching the refrigerator, smelling like fresh shampoo and soap.

"Sorry, babe. I usually go out."

"Want to go to my house and eat? I've got lots of good things to put in an omelette. Joey won't be home yet, so it should be safe for you to take me home."

"Your house it is," he agreed, and went off to get dressed.

They drove separate cars and arrived at her house shortly before 9 A.M. When Lee pulled into the driveway her blood took a leap to her face: Janice's car was parked in front of the garage. Lee sat staring at it, gripping the steering wheel, holding her breath, then letting it gush out in resignation. Christopher parked behind her and walked past her window on his way to the garage. He raised the door and, when she'd driven inside, was waiting to open her car door. They stood in the cold garage gazing first at Janice's car, then at each other.

"Well, this is it, I guess," he said.

"I had no idea she was coming home."

"She didn't call and tell you?"

"No."

"So what are you going to tell her?"

"We could tell her we've been to church."

"In our blue jeans?"

"You're right. Besides, I always go to the ten o'clock service. I wonder when she got here."

"Judging from the frost on her windshield she's been here all night."

"I hope nothing's wrong. I'd better get inside and see."

When she turned away, he grabbed her arm. "Lee, I want to go in with you."

"She's going to be very angry."

"I can handle that."

"Embarrassed, too."

"I want us to face her together. Anything you're guilty of, I'm guilty of. Besides, if she's up she probably saw us both drive in, and I don't want it to look like I'm slinking off and leaving you to explain."

They went in together through the front door. Janice was standing by the kitchen table holding an ice pack on her jaw, glaring at them.

"Janice, what's wrong?" Lee moved straight toward her without stopping to remove her jacket.

"Nothing!" Janice snapped, her mouth cinching tight.

"What's wrong with your jaw?"

"A wisdom tooth. Where have you been, as if it isn't obvious!"

Lee removed her jacket and hung it on a chair. "At Chris's."

"All night? Mother, how could you?" Janice's face was flaming. She refused to look at Christopher.

"I'm sorry you found out this way."

"Where's Joey?"

"He spent the night at the Holiday Inn with the Whitmans."

"Does he know about what's been going on?"

"No."

"Oh my God, I can't believe this." Janice covered her face with one hand and turned away.

Christopher stood behind Lee's shoulder without touching her. "Your mom and I discussed whether or not to tell you but she decided she needed a little longer to sort out her feelings."

"Her feelings! Hers!" She spun on him. "What about mine? What about Joey's? This is disgusting!"

"Why?" he asked calmly.

"I'm not ignorant!" Janice snapped. "A woman doesn't stay out all night at a man's apartment without sex being involved. It is, isn't it?"

Lee snapped, "Janice, you're being rude."

Christopher remained calm. "Your mother and I have been seeing each other a lot since last June."

"Since my brother died! Say it the way it is! That's what started all this, isn't it? The classic mourning woman turns to the younger man for sympathy."

"I turned to her, too."

"Well, you could have told me! You could have . . . have said something be- fore I . . . before I . . ." Mortified, she escaped to the working part of the kitchen, turning her back on them once more. Christopher brushed around Lee's shoulder and took Janice's arm to gently turn her around.

"Things were complicated, Janice," he said quietly. She averted her burning face, refusing to look at him. "You know why." He released her arm.

She said to the floor, "I must have looked like a fool, giving you those tickets for Christmas, saying the stuff I did."

"No. I was the one in the wrong. I should have told you long before that, that I had feelings for your mom."

She glared up at him. "Then why didn't you?"

"Because we were no different than anyone else when we started dating. We didn't know what it would lead to."

Too embarrassed to stand so close to him, Janice shouldered around both him and Lee and stood defiantly at the opening where the hall led toward the bedrooms.

"Mother, he's thirty years old, for heaven's sake! What are people going to say?"

"Exactly what you are, I suppose. That he's too young for me. So should I give him up because I'll upset people?"

"You should give him up because you'll look like a fool!"

Lee felt herself begin to grow angry. "Do you think so, Janice? Why?"

Janice glared from her mother to Christopher and back again, her mouth clamped tightly shut.

"Why will I look like a fool, Janice? Because this *is* a sexual relationship?" Christopher opened his mouth to speak, but she held up a hand. "No, it's all right, Christopher. She's twenty-three years old; she's old enough to hear the truth. You're angry with me right now, Janice; well, I'm angry with you, too, because you're implying that because there's fifteen years difference between Christopher and me, he's using me. Do I have that correct?"

Janice blushed brighter and looked at the floor.

"Is that the kind of person you think Christopher is?"

Janice was too mortified to speak.

"You might as well know that it's been a big issue between us, one that we've talked about. Only it isn't only whether or not Christopher is using me, but whether I'm using him to get over Greg's death. I'm not. I love him. I'm sorry if that doesn't fit into your image of how a mother should act, but I do have feelings, I do have needs and I do get lonely. I even think about my future. I'm not old, Janice, I'm only older than Christopher, but who's to say how old is too old? Must I get permission from my family before I date a man?"

Janice looked up miserably. Tears shimmered on her eyelids. "But, Mother, he's Greg's friend. He's . . . he's more like your son."

"No. That's your viewpoint, not mine. Our relationship has totally changed in the last eight months. You might be interested to know that we became very, very good friends first before our relationship became intimate."

A hint of challenge came into Janice's voice when she asked, "What's Grandma going to say?"

Lee resisted the urge to look to Christopher for help. "Grandma will be very outspoken, and it won't be pleasant, but Grandma doesn't run my life. I do."

"Well, I can see that nothing I say is going to make you change your mind, so I'm going to bed. I've been up half the night waiting for you and my tooth hurts like the devil."

"Why didn't you call? I think you knew I'd be over at Christopher's. I would have come home."

"Because I wanted to know for sure. Now I do."

She spun on the ball of her foot and marched to her bedroom. When her door slammed, Lee and Christopher stood in the vacuum left by her anger, their emotions in chaos. The faucet was dripping. Lee went over and tried to turn it off, but the steady, monotonous sound continued. Finally Christopher moved up behind her and curved his hands over her shoulders. Wordlessly he turned her around and took her in his arms.

"I'm sorry," she said, feeling close to tears now that the first rush of rebuttal was over. "That must have been terrible for you."

"It was about what I expected. How about you?"

"What she said was. How I reacted was a surprise."

"A surprise?" he said.

"I thought I'd be brimming with guilt. Instead, when she started passing judgment I found myself getting angry. What right has she got to dictate my life? The trouble with my kids is, they've never seen me as a sexual person. All I've ever been is *Mom*. Ever since Bill died I've always been there for them and I guess they thought I always would be—exclusively. The idea that I could need a man for *that* stops them cold in their tracks."

"Still, I'm not sure you should have said that."

"Said what?" She drew back and cast him a bristly look.

"That our relationship is sexual."

"Why not? I have a right to that in my life, damn it, with you or any man I choose. I wanted her to know that."

"It was a jolt for her though, the way you said it."

"I wanted it out in the open."

"And now it is, that's for sure."

"Christopher, I don't want to fight with you, too!" She pulled away from him and put away a pot holder that was lying on the countertop, slamming the drawer with her hip. "And anyway, I don't know why we're fighting! First you say you want me to tell my kids, and we fight because I won't. Then I tell them and we fight because I did."

"Lee . . . Lee . . ." he said, taking her by the shoulders again, forcing her to face him. "Come on. I'm feeling my way here, too. I'm just trying to think of the best way to break this news to the rest of your family, because we're going to get more of what we just got from Janice, only I have a feeling it's going to be worse when it gets to your mother and your sister. They're really going to lay the guilt trip on you."

She lunged into his arms and held tight. "Oh, Christopher, I hate it when we argue. I love you. I want us to be together, but look what happens when we test the first person, and I haven't even mentioned marriage yet."

He drew back and gaped at her in surprise. "You mean you're thinking about it?"

"Well, of course I'm thinking about it. How could I not be? I love you. I don't want to spend the rest of my life alone."

"Oh, Lee . . ." The look in his eyes told her how she'd surprised him. Celebrating, however, took second place to the more serious message he had to impart. He held her by the slope of her neck and spoke earnestly into her eyes. "Then promise me you'll try to keep from getting angry when they tell you you're robbing the cradle, and when they accuse you of being a lonely, sad woman who doesn't know what she's doing, and when they say that you're being used and that I'm only after your house and your car and who knows what else, and that I'll grow tired of you as soon as the first young chick walks by in tight shorts and twitches her butt at me. Because unless I miss my guess, you're going to have to listen to that and a lot more. But the best way to fight that kind of attitude is by showing them that we're happy together, not by getting pissed off, okay?"

She rested her forehead against his chin and shut her eyes wearily. "Are they really going to say all that?"

"I think so."

They stood that way for a spell, taking strength from one another.

Finally Lee asked, "Will you?"

"Will I what?"

"Grow tired of me as soon as the first young chick twitches her butt at you?"

He put a finger beneath her chin and lifted it. "What do you think?"

"I've thought about it some—I won't lie to you and say I haven't."

"You wouldn't be normal if you hadn't, but that's one I can't combat with words. That's where trust comes in. If I say I love you and I want to commit myself to you for life, you just have to believe that I mean it, and we take it from there. Okay?"

Within a corner of her heart, peace settled. How convincing he was. How wise. Had he vowed never to look at another woman she would have been much less assured. His simple statement of ineluctable fact gave her pause to realize he had just put his finger on the basic element upon which all lasting marriages are built. Theirs—should it happen—would be strengthened by this belief, which she shared.

She reached up and kissed him in reply—not heavily, as if stamping her initial in sealing wax, but with a glancing touch of reassurance.

"I'd better go in and check on Janice's tooth. She'll be too stubborn to come back out here, and I think her jaw was swollen."

"Should I stay or go?"

"Stay. You came for breakfast and I'm going to fix it for you. I'll see to her first though."

Janice was lying on her side facing the wall when Lee sat down behind her.

"Is he gone?"

"No, he's still here. I'm going to make breakfast for him. What's happening with your wisdom tooth? Did it flare up suddenly?"

"It's all infected. I need to have it pulled."

"Which one? Upper or lower?"

"Lower."

"Turn over here."

"You *don't* have to worry about me. I can take care of myself," the girl declared.

"Janice, don't be so stubborn. I'm not going to stop worrying about *you* just because I'm dating *him*."

Janice flung herself onto her back and fixed her eyes on a piece of furniture behind Lee, who felt her brow.

"My heavens, girl, you have a fever. Have you taken any aspirin?"

"Yes."

"How long ago?"

"About three in the morning." The implication was clear: She'd been up waiting for her mother to return.

"I'll get you some more. Are you in bad pain?"

"It doesn't feel too pleasant but what can I do on a weekend? I'll just have to wait till morning to call Dr. Wing."

"Open your mouth. Let me see."

"Mother, it's infected and probably impacted, too. What's there to see?"

"Is there a bulge by the tooth?"

Janice rolled her eyes. "Yes, there's a bulge. But I won't die before morning, so just leave me alone."

Lee had no choice. When she returned with the aspirin and a glass of water, she said, "There *is* such a thing as emergency treatment for teeth, you know, so if it gets to that point I'll drive you to the hospital."

Janice popped the aspirins and chased them with water, handed the glass back to her mother and flung herself down facing the wall again. The message was clear: I'm not thanking you. I'm not forgiving you. I don't want to be mothered by you!

Lee stared at her daughter's back and left the room with a sigh.

On Monday afternoon at one o'clock an oral surgeon extracted both wisdom teeth from the right side of Janice's mouth. One was impacted and infected. The other, he said, would follow suit shortly, judging from its crowded condition and the angle at which it was pushing her other teeth.

She awakened from her sodium-pentathol slumber crying inexplicably—a natural reaction from the drug. One of the nurses on the office staff gave Lee instructions on how to care for her, how woozy Janice would be for a while and what to feed her to avoid a painful dry socket. Lee left the dentist's office carrying a prescription for pain pills and supporting a blubbering daughter, who continued to cry and babble, "I don't know why I'm crying so hard. I just don't know."

"It's from the drug," Lee explained. "It'll go away in an hour or so."

At home, Lee settled Janice into bed with a towel beneath her cheek and a mixing bowl to spit into. She gave her a pain pill and offered to heat up some chicken broth for her, then watched Janice's eyes fall shut as she was drawn down into the residual effects of the anesthetic.

Lee leaned over the bed and rubbed Janice's hair back from her forehead and kissed her.

In that moment, mothering became uncomplicated again as it had been when her children were babies. Smoothing a brow, administering a pill, cooking special foods when they were sick: These were the needs easy to fill. She found herself soothed—even healed—to be touching her daughter and seeing after her physical needs, especially after the rift created the previous day.

Janice, she thought, *please don't withdraw your love from me. Please don't make me choose between you and Christopher. There's no reason, darling, and it will break my heart if you keep turning away from me this way.*

Christopher called shortly before suppertime. "How's Janice?"

"She's asleep now, but she'll be hurting tonight. The dentist prescribed some pain pills though."

"Does she need anything? Can I do anything for you?"

"Just continue to be patient with my children," she replied. "It may take some time to win them over."

"That I can do, as long as I know there's a reason to. Have you thought any more about marrying me?"

"Yes, I've thought about it. It's *all* I've been thinking about."

"And?"

"And it sounds very appealing, but I still don't know."

"You know what?" he said.

"What?"

"I'm doing it again."

"Doing what again?"

"Playing the role of a husband and stepfather right this very minute. Think about it, Lee."

When his shift ended he stopped by on his way home.

"Hi," he said when Lee answered the door. "I can't stay. I've got a date with Judd, but I wanted to bring this for Janice. Tell her I hope she likes it."

He handed her a set of audio tapes of a current best-seller. "I thought it might be more relaxing for her to listen than to read it today."

She kissed his jaw and realized he was making it harder and harder for her to say no to his marriage proposal.

And too . . . he was doing it again.

What any good husband and dad would have done.

"Christopher brought you these."

Janice glanced back over her shoulder, studied the tapes her mother had dropped on the bed and said with asperity, "I already read it." She left them right where they'd fallen, turning her face to the wall.

Being shunned by her daughter hurt worse than Lee had ever imagined it could.

Being hurt by one child quite naturally drew her toward the other. In need of understanding, of an ally perhaps, maybe only a friendly smile, she went to Joey's room later that night. She found him sitting on the floor of his bedroom wrapping silver duct tape around his favorite pair of dilapidated Nikes.

"Hi," she said, leaning against his door frame.

"Oh, hi!" He looked back over his shoulder.

"May I come in?"

"Sure. How's Janice?"

"Sleeping. Grouchy."

"Man, I hope that never happens to me. Denny's dad says he's still got his wisdom teeth and they never gave him any trouble."

"It's more than Janice's wisdom teeth that's bothering her."

"What else?" He stopped taping and watched Lee cross to the bed and settle herself dead center on it, sitting Indian fashion. She was dressed in an oversized purple sweat suit with the sleeves pushed up to her elbows.

"She's upset with me."

"About what?"

"I'm going to be very honest with you, Joey, because this is really important to me."

"She must've figured it out about you and Chris, huh?"

Lee couldn't have hidden her surprise had she put a bag over her head. "Well, *you* don't seem too shocked. How long have you known?"

He shrugged and ran his hand repeatedly over the edge of the silver tape, smoothing it around the sole of the shoe. "I don't know. I saw you guys kissing one night, but I sort of figured, even before that."

"So what do you think about it?"

"Heck, I think it's cool."

Lee grinned. Who said girls were fun to raise? Give her a son anytime. Their temperaments were a lot less volatile.

"It's really serious, isn't it, Mom?"

"Yes, it is."

"That's what I figured. So, do ladies your age marry guys his age, or what?"

"I don't know of any who did, do you?"

He just shrugged and cut off another strip of tape.

"Would it bother you if I did?" she asked.

"Heck no. Why should it bother me?"

"People might tease you, say your mother's a baby snatcher, things like that."

"Jeez, people can be such dorks. If they said something like that, they don't know you. Or Chris either."

"He asked me last night," she admitted.

"To marry him?"

"Yes."

"Does Janice know that?"

"Not yet."

"Does Grandma know?"

"Grandma doesn't know any of this."

"Jeez, she'll shit a ring around herself when she finds out."

Lee laughed before she could stop herself. "You're not supposed to use language like that, young man."

"Yeah, well, I did, so ground me, Ma."

Lord, he was really growing up fast. She was going to enjoy the next three years with him. He was so refreshingly straightforward.

"So what'd you tell Chris?" Joey asked.

"I told him it was tempting."

"You wanna marry him?"

"Yes, I do."

"But you're scared of what Grandma will say, right?"

"Grandma, Janice, Sylvia, you. Well, not you anymore. You seem to be all right with the idea."

"Heck yes. You've been alone since Dad died. Sometimes I don't know how you stand it. I mean, me and Denny, we talk sometimes, you know? Like the night I saw you and Chris kissing the first time. I called him and I said to him that you were awful happy since you've been hangin' out with Chris, and it seems like you would have done stuff like that a long time ago."

"Kissing guys, you mean? I never wanted to until Chris came along."

"Really, Mom?" He studied her with a crooked grin on his mouth. "Then I think you should go for it."

No doubt about it, this son of hers was a gift. Lee sat on his bed with her elbows on her knees, smiling down at him while he slapped one more circuit of tape around his tennis shoe.

"I guess you know by now how much I love you. Are you going to wear those things that way?" she asked.

He held up his handiwork. "Heck yes. They're *hot!*"

"I seem to remember buying you some new ones for Christmas."

"Well, sure, and I love you, too, but not enough to throw these away just because they need a little tape job. These are my best ones."

She shook her head in wonderment, got off the bed, kissed the crown of his head and went into her bedroom to call Christopher and give him the latest *Children's Attitude Report.*

Janice stayed home one more day, then returned to school, still acting aloof toward her mother.

Lee worked that day, as usual, and returned home in the late afternoon to begin fixing supper. First she went down to the basement to throw the morning's load of laundry from the washer into the dryer. She was just coming up the basement stairs when the doorbell rang.

"Why, Mother!" she said, answering it. "What brings you over? And, Sylvia . . ." She had just left Sylvia at the store a half hour before.

Peg Hillier pushed past Lee with an officious air, removing her gloves.

"We've come to talk to you, Lee."

Lee watched her mother's back—stiff as a pikestaff—the swirl of her coat, the erectness of her neck, and knew she was in trouble.

"Oh. I bet I know what about."

"I'll just bet you do." Peg swung on her. "Janice called me."

Lee said, "Would you care to come in, Mother? Take off your coat? Sit down, maybe, and have a cup of coffee? You, too, Sylvia." She glanced outside. "Is this the whole army, or have you brought more? Where's Dad . . . and Lloyd? They should be here for this, too, shouldn't they?"

"Your attempt to be cute isn't fazing me in the least, Lee. Shut that door and tell me what in the ever-loving world has gotten into you! A woman of your age latching onto a boy your son's age!"

Lee shut the door resignedly and said, "Put your coats on the sofa. I'll make some coffee."

"I don't want any coffee! I want an explanation!"

"First of all, he's not my son's age. He's thirty years old and—"

"And you're forty-five. Good God, Lee, have you gone crazy?"

"Hardly, Mother. I fell in love."

"In love!" Peg's eyes seemed to protrude from her skull. "Is that what you call it? You've been sleeping with that boy! Janice said you admitted it!"

Sylvia added, "Lee, this is so shabby."

"So what did Mother do? Call you immediately and spread the news so you could come over here and bombard me together?"

"I agree with Mother. Your having an affair with Christopher is disgraceful, but we understand all the stresses you've been under since Greg died. It's natural that you'd want to turn to someone, but, Lee, a boy that age."

"He's not a boy! Will you quit saying that!"

"He might as well be, given your age difference."

Peg said, "I must admit, I never would have guessed he'd behave like this either. I thought he was such a fine young man. What in the world is he after?"

"After?"

"Yes, after! A man that age with a woman so old."

"So old. Gee, thanks, Mother."

"You may be willing to delude yourself, but I'm not. He was after exactly what he got! But to think he did it after you were so good to him, after you opened your doors to him, and took him into this family, and acted like a mother to him. To think that you'd let him seduce you!"

"Mother, I am telling you, we fell in love! It wasn't as if Greg died and I rolled into bed with Chris the next day! We began seeing each other and had so much fun together, and only then, after months, did our relationship become intimate."

"I don't want to hear it." Peg's face grew pinched and she looked aside.

Sylvia picked up the gauntlet. "You admitted to your own daughter that you've been sleeping with him. . . . Lee, what were you thinking of?"

"Am I not supposed to have any sex ever again? Is that it?" Lee's two attackers stared in stupefaction while she went on. "Am I supposed to be some dedicated little mama, waiting to darn my children's socks and cook their favorite foods when they come to visit me? Am I never supposed to want a life of my own?"

Sylvia replied, "Of course you can have a life of your own, but for heaven's sake, choose someone your own age to have it with."

"Why? Why is it so wrong that I chose Christopher?"

"Lee, be honest with yourself," Sylvia admonished. "This thing looks mighty quirky. You treated him like a son for how many years? Then when Greg dies the two of you grow thick as thieves, and pretty soon you're in bed together. How do you think it looks? And how long do you expect him to stick with you?"

"You might be interested to know, Sylvia, that Christopher has asked me to marry him."

"Oh, dear God," Peg breathed, putting a hand to her lips and dropping down hard on a kitchen chair.

"Marry him?" Sylvia, too, sat as if poleaxed.

"Yes. And I'm considering it."

"Oh, Lee, you don't know what you're doing. Greg hasn't been dead a year and, granted, you needed someone to get you through this terrible time, but to tie up with someone that young for life. How can it possibly last?"

"How can any marriage possibly last, given the divorce rates in this country today? If you love somebody, you have faith in them, you marry them assuming it will last because you've both said it will."

Peg took over. "You never joined any of those grief groups, but if you had you'd realize that you're doing exactly what they warn you not to do—jump into a relationship out of desperation. You're lonely, you've gone through a terrible ordeal losing Greg and you're facing the time when all your children will be gone. I understand that, dear, but look ahead. When you're sixty, he'll be forty-five. Do you really think he won't want a younger woman then?"

Lee refused to reply.

"And what about children?" Sylvia put in. "Doesn't he want any?"

"No."

"That's not natural."

"It's really none of your business though, is it, Sylvia? He and I have talked about all these things you two have thrown at me today, and if we've worked them out and I want to marry him, I expect you to honor my choice."

Peg and Sylvia exchanged glances that said Lee had truly lost good sense and just how were they going to convince her she was making the mistake of her life. Peg sighed dramatically and fixed an absent stare on the fruit basket in the middle of the table. She tried a new tactic.

"I just wonder what Bill would say."

"Oh, good God." Lee rolled her eyes. "Bill is dead, Mother. I'm alive. I have a lot of good healthy years ahead of me. It's unfair of you to suggest that I should remain faithful to a dead man."

"Oh, don't be so silly. I'm not suggesting that. But Bill was the children's father. What can this man ever be to them? Which brings up another nasty point. Janice told me that she confessed to you some time ago that she had feelings for Christopher herself."

"Yes, she did. But did she tell you if he ever returned the interest in any way whatsoever?" When Peg didn't answer, Lee hurried on. "No, he did not. Her attraction to Christopher complicated things for us, but we talked about it, too, and decided our own happiness counts for something. And we're the happiest when we're together."

"So you're not going to end it?"

"No, I'm not. He makes me happy. I make him happy. Why should I throw that away?"

"The day will come when you'll regret it."

"Maybe. But you could say that about half the choices you make in this life. On the other hand, the day may *never* come when I'll regret it, and how sad it would be if I'd thrown him away for nothing."

"So, are you really going to marry him?" Sylvia asked.

"I think so . . . yes, Sylvia."

Sylvia said, "Honestly, Lee, if it's just because of the . . . well, you know . . ." Sylvia stirred the air with her hand.

"I think the word you're looking for is 'sex,' Sylvia, and if it were just that, don't you think I'd have taken up with some man long before this? Sex is just one part of our relationship, and I'll freely admit that after so many years without it, it's sensational to have it available whenever I want it. But friendship and respect play equally important parts."

Sylvia had turned pink as a rare steak and didn't know where to rest her eyes.

"I'm sorry, Syl. I know it's a subject you never talk about, but you brought it up."

Sylvia's mouth was pinched as she went on superciliously. "I understand you stayed all night at his apartment Saturday night. What will your children think?"

"My son thinks I should marry him."

"He's fourteen years old. What does he know?"

"He knows Christopher. He loves him. He said, 'Hey, Ma, I think you should go for it.' "

Peg angled a disparaging look at her younger daughter. "And if you take Joey's advice, I'm still convinced you'll live to regret it."

"I think you'd better get used to the idea, Mother, because I'm going to say yes to Christopher."

Peg buried her face in both hands and propped her elbows on the table. "God in heaven, what will my friends say?"

"Ahh . . . There, you've hit upon your real problem, haven't you, Mother?"

"Well, it is a problem!" Peg spit, lifting her head suddenly. "People talk, you know!"

"Yes. Starting with my daughter—thank you, Janice."

"Don't you go blaming Janice!" Peg was getting angrier. "She did the right thing by calling me."

"Oh, yes, I can see that. This has been such an enlightening conversation. But it's true, Mother. You've saved your greatest worry for last: What will people think. You've always been so concerned about that. What will they think if I play Vince Gill at my son's funeral? What will they think if I bury him in his favorite cap? What will they think if I marry a handsome thirty-year-old man instead of some nice balding middle-aged bore who'll make me settle down and act my age?

"Well, the truth is, Mom, I don't care what they think. Because if they're looking down their noses at me, they aren't the kind of friends I'd value in the first place."

"You always were good at talking your way around things, Lee, but you won't be able to talk your way around this. People *will* whisper behind your back. Your children will undoubtedly be asked all kinds of pointed questions, and everyone at your father's and my country club will ask if it's true that he's only thirty."

"Then answer them honestly, Mother. Why can't you do that? Why can't you just say, 'Yes, he's thirty, and he's a fine man who's kind and considerate and cares about his fellow human beings, and who's made my daughter so happy, the happiest she's been since her first husband died.' Why can't you say that, Mother?"

"That's right!" Peg said self-righteously. "Turn the blame on me, as if I caused this disgraceful situation. Child, you exasperate me so!"

"Mother, I've always loved you, but you've never been able to admit when you're wrong, and this time you are."

"Lee, for heaven's sake!" Sylvia chided.

"You, too, Sylvia. You're wrong, too. I love this man. I'm going to marry him and make myself happy."

"Well, marry him then!" Peg shot up from her chair and marched toward the living room to get her coat. "But don't bring him to my house for Easter dinner!"

Chapter 18

"They said exactly what you said they'd say." Lee was on the telephone with Chris later that night.

"It was bad, I imagine."

"Horrible. But I held my temper like you asked me to."

"I take it that didn't help much."

"No. Except that I was proud of myself."

"You're really down though, I can tell." When she made no reply, he asked, "Aren't you?"

"Ohh . . ." She blew out a breath. "You know . . ." A moment of sadness came to complicate her irritation with this group of people she loved. "They're my only family."

"Yeah . . . I know the feeling. Ironic, isn't it? My family alienates me by caring too little, yours does it by caring too much."

"I suppose that's true, but it's hard to believe they care for me *at all* when they're trying to control my life."

"Honey, I'm really sorry you have to go through this." He sounded very sincere and sad on her behalf.

"Want to hear the funny part? My sister Sylvia, who's the world's biggest prude, couldn't even get herself to say the word when she wanted to chide me about my rampaging sex drive and how it was probably the only reason I wanted to marry you."

"You told them you were going to marry me?" His voice sounded as if he'd suddenly straightened his spine.

"Yes, I did, but, Christopher, I don't think that's the wisest thing to do right now. Everybody's all bent out of shape and giving me lectures, and I think it's best if I give them a chance to get used to the idea first."

"But you'll do it? You're saying yes?"

"I'm saying I want to."

"When, Lee?"

"I don't know when."

Some seconds passed while she sensed him visibly deflating. "All right." She could tell by his voice he was forcing himself not to push too hard. "I understand. But don't wait too long. Honey, I just love you so much. I don't want to waste any more time apart."

At the floral shop things became strained. From the very next day, Sylvia began cornering Lee when the others were beyond earshot, haranguing her with denunciations about her affair, scolding her for upsetting their mother so terribly and for setting a bad example for her children. Couldn't she see how improper it was? Hadn't their parents taught her such behavior was reprehensible? And with a man young enough to be her son! Didn't she realize he was only out to use her and would make a fool of her in the end? It just wasn't natural for a boy that age to fall for someone their age. Didn't she care at all that Mother and Dad's social circle would ask embarrassing questions? Why, even Sylvia's own children were already asking them.

"How did *they* find out?"

"They overheard me talking to Barry."

"Oh, great. Thanks a lot, Sylvia."

Sylvia threw down a stack of envelopes she'd been leafing through. "I'm not the guilty one here, Lee, so just watch it! Someone's got to make you come to your senses, and who else is it going to be? Mother? Janice? They're both so appalled they won't even speak to you!"

Unfortunately, it was true. Joey celebrated his fifteenth birthday, but Janice—who'd made a point of coming home on his birthday last year—remained at school and only sent him a card. Peg and Orrin sent a gift by mail and called with the excuse that they couldn't come over for birthday cake because Orrin had had some bridgework done on his teeth that day and his mouth was too sore.

Lloyd came, however, and brought Joey a big maroon sweatshirt with a big white *A* on the front, for next year when he'd be attending Anoka Senior High. The three of them went out for supper at Joey's favorite restaurant and Lloyd very discreetly mentioned, "The party's kind of small this year, isn't it?"

The whole story tumbled out, but Lloyd—kind, nonjudgmental Lloyd—merely said, "My, that is a problem, isn't it?"

———

Orrin came to Absolutely Floral one noon and said, "Lee, I'm taking you out to lunch," during which he told her seven times how upset her mother was, and how this foolishness of hers had to stop and she must tell that *boy* that he should go find someone his own age!

Lee's outrage boiled over. "You're all a bunch of backbiting hypocrites! Christopher was good enough for me when he was comforting me and acting as my support system after Greg died, and when he was picking up Janice at the airport, and sending you and Mom sympathy cards, and taking over a lot of the supportive duties that otherwise might have fallen to you! But now that he's been in my bed you treat him—both of us—like we're some sexual perverts! I don't think I like what that says about you!"

The meal ended on a bitter note with the two of them scarcely able to tolerate each other another minute.

Lee called Janice at college, as she usually did once a week, only to get perfunctory grunts for answers, delivered in a voice that said quite clearly, *I'm only tolerating this conversation, not taking part in it.* Lee asked when Janice would be coming home again and got the blunt reply, "I don't know."

Lee's attack on her father was immediately telegraphed throughout the family, and Lee received another sermon from Sylvia on right and wrong, this one more vitriolic than the last, as Sylvia defended her parents and chastised Lee for her treatment of them. The tension at Absolutely Floral got so pronounced that the other employees began to get grouchy, too. Then one day Pat Galsworthy said to Lee, "Are you *really* going out with a man who's only thirty years old?" Lee blew up at her and said it was none of her damned business, and if she wanted to keep her job she'd better stick to discussing floral trends with the *bookkeeper* when the two of them were holed up together.

Lee later apologized, but the truth was, the business was being affected by the rift between her and Sylvia. Finding it difficult to be civil to each other, the two of them became reluctant to sit down and discuss the ongoing daily matters—orders, billing, scheduling—which were so essential to having the enterprise run smoothly. This lack of communication was reflected in the botched routine, the scheduling snags and the general tension among all the store's employees.

Christopher called one Thursday and said, "Dress up in something classy. It's my night off and I'm taking you to dinner at the Carousel in downtown Saint Paul."

In the revolving restaurant, with the twinkling lights of the city dotting the night all around them, he produced a diamond ring with a rock so large it could not be worn beneath a leather glove.

"Oh, Christopher . . ." Lee said, gaping at the engagement ring in its blue velvet box. "Oh, look at this . . . what did you do?"

"I love you, Lee Reston. I want you to be my wife." He took her hand and put the ring on the proper finger. As usual, her nails were stubby and her skin rough.

"But it's so big. And what will I do with it when I'm handling dirt and flowers all day long?"

"Put it in a dresser drawer and put it on when you get home. Will you marry me?"

She looked up and felt tears beginning to gather.

"Oh, Christopher, I can't believe this is happening. I want to . . . you know I want to. But how can I?" The weight of the family's reaction bore down upon her, bringing a confusion of feelings. She loved this man and thought they could have a happy life together, but her decision was not as simplistic as that. "Everything else in my life is falling apart." She added in the gentlest voice she could muster, "I'm sorry . . . I can't wear this." She removed the ring and put it back in the box. "I just can't. It's much too beautiful for my ugly hands anyway."

He stared at the ring, forlorn, then at her, so disheartened she found it hard to meet his gaze. Finally he took her hands and held them on the tabletop.

"Lee, don't do this," he begged earnestly. "Please."

"You know what I'm going to say, don't you?"

"Don't. Don't say it, please . . ."

"But everybody's turned against me. Everybody."

"Except Joey."

"Yes, except Joey. But it's even affecting him. Janice didn't come for his birthday, and neither did his grandpa and grandma. Sylvia and I hardly speak to each other at work. Our business is becoming affected by all these bad feelings. What should I do?"

He dropped his eyes to their joined hands and rubbed the backs of hers with his thumbs. The expression on his face got even sadder, and his lengthening silence told her he recognized the problems he'd brought into her life, and that if she married him they would probably get worse. He hadn't the wherewithal, however, to cut her free by putting the ring back in his pocket.

The waiter came and presented their plates, steaming, fragrant, each a work of art. They mumbled "Thank you" and picked up their forks, pretending to eat, prodding the food instead.

Lee went on speaking in a hurt voice. "You know how important family has always been to me. I fought so hard to keep mine together after Bill died. My mom and dad have always been there for me, and Sylvia and I were best of friends. When we opened up the shop we got along so well even my mother couldn't believe it. And now . . ." She shrugged. "Now it's all falling apart."

"And so you're cutting me out."

"Don't put it that way."

"But it's true. I thought our relationship stood for something, but you're willing to write me off because your family doesn't approve. How do you think that makes me feel?"

"It hurts me too, Christopher."

He fixed his eyes on the night view outside the windows. As the restaurant revolved, it changed from the distant Minneapolis skyline to the dark strip of river. He had given up all pretense of eating and sat with his fingers on the stem of his water goblet. Finally, he turned back to her.

"Lee, I've never said one word against your family. I think that in spite of what they're doing to you, they're a good bunch of people. But they're condemning me not for myself but for my age. I honestly believe they know I'm a decent, law-abiding, fairly honorable guy who'll treat you the best he can for the rest of his life. But I'm only thirty, and you're forty-five, so they tell you you're crazy and it won't last, and they fill your head with all that garbage! But it's so damned unfair, and you're wrong to knuckle under to their pressure!"

"Maybe I am, but for the time being, that's the way it's got to be."

"For the time being—what does that mean?"

She took a deep breath and said the words that would break her heart. "It means I don't think I should see you anymore for a while."

He held himself still, as if to absorb the impact of her unwanted words. They both knew "for a while" could mean interminably. If her family disapproved now, would they be likely to change their stand in the future?

He set his teeth and studied the distant lights again, his face a mask of dejected stony lines.

"Please, Christopher, don't look that way. It's not what I want either."

He continued brooding while their suppers congealed into cold lumps on their plates. Finally he took his napkin from his lap, folded it, laid it beside his plate and, without looking at her, said, "Well, if it has to end let it end without harsh words. There's no sense in my being one more person to add to your woes. But if it's okay with you, Lee, I'd just as soon leave now. I'm not very hungry anymore."

It took them thirty minutes to drive from downtown St. Paul to Anoka. Through the entire trip he was painfully solicitous, holding her coat while she donned it, taking her elbow on their way to his truck, opening the door for her, seeing her safely inside. He adhered to the speed limit religiously all the way to her house, handling the vehicle perfectly, slowing for red lights with so much lead time her body scarcely swayed when they stopped. He kept the radio turned to a moderate level, adjusted the heat to hit her feet and signaled every turn.

All the while Lee felt as if a balloon were inflating inside her chest, shutting off more and more of her air, pressing against her lungs until there was less than enough left to sustain her.

Her heart ached.

Her eyes burned.

Her throat felt like a garden hose with a kink in it. If only he'd supplicate, rage, drive like a maniac. Instead, he maintained this perfect, stoic control.

At her house he left the engine idling and walked around to open her door, giving her a hand while she managed the long step down in her high heels, taking her elbow as they trod the icy sidewalk to the front step.

There she stopped, torn by what she was doing, aching already with the emptiness that was sure to slam her even harder when he drove away. The outside light had been left off, and the night wind swirled around their ankles. The late winter snow had grown dark with age and lay like a compressed gray blanket in the yard around them. The air held a chill dampness that permeated clothing, skin, going clear to the heart, it seemed.

He took her gloved hands in his and they stood with six inches of space between them, their chins lowered, staring at the dark concrete between their shoes.

She looked up.

He looked up.

And in that second when their eyes met, his life-saving control snapped. He clutched her against himself, hard, kissing her in an agony of forced farewell. It was a kiss that stamped love, possession, hurt and blame upon her, telling her in no uncertain terms how much he, too, would suffer when he walked away.

As suddenly as he'd grabbed her, he set her back by the arms and told her, "I won't be calling you. You know where I am if you want to see me."

Abruptly he spun, descended the two steps in one leap and stalked to his truck.

She had wept this hard before. Three times in her life she had wept this hard, so surely she would live through it. This was as fierce, consuming and debilitating as it had been when she'd cried for baby Grant . . . and for Bill . . . and for Greg. The difference was, she'd brought this on by choice.

Yet what other choice could she make?

She was a woman unused to hopelessness, so the question felt foreign going through her mind again and again that night. Another question glimmered: *How could people who love you put you through such hell?*

Over and over she relived Christopher's parting kiss, watched him turn and hurry away, heard the angry slam of his truck door and saw him squeal off down the road like a lunatic, accelerating with a roar that sent the rear end of the Explorer fishtailing up the street, hitting a snowbank on the opposite side and rebounding to the center. He had turned the radio up so loud she had heard it booming through his rolled-up windows. At the end of the block he'd blasted through a stop sign without slowing down.

This policeman.

This obeyer of laws.

This man whose heart she'd just broken.

She, with a broken heart of her own, lay on her bed as if she'd jumped from a tenth-story window, sobbing so loudly that her son woke up and opened her bedroom door a crack, whispering with fear in his voice, "Mom? . . . Mom? . . . What's wrong, Mom?"

She could not answer, did not want to answer, went on weeping and leaving Joey to worry and wonder—thoughtless wretch of a mother that she was.

She cried the tears of the lovelorn—the all-consuming spasmodic weeping that racked the entire body for hours on end, so bitterly sorry for herself that she didn't know how she'd survive the lonely days without him. Who would call to ask how her day had been? Who would show up at her door with a pie, or call to ask if she wanted to go walking or shopping for a Christmas tree? Who would hold her when she needed holding, and understand when she needed to cry sometimes, and be there to laugh with her during the happy times?

She lay sprawled on her side, inert, uninspired to act on her own behalf, to get up and find a new box of tissues, to get under the covers, to remove her clothing or her jewelry.

Her temples throbbed. Her eyes ached. Her nose felt raw. She couldn't sigh without shuddering.

I don't want to cry anymore. Please, don't let me cry anymore.

But even that thought brought fresh tears.

The last time she looked at the clock it was 4:34 and it hurt to pick up her head.

She awakened at 10:13 and jerked upright when she saw the time. She was over an hour late for work! She managed to get to her feet, then plopped back down, cradling her aching head. The bedspread was rucked into ridges like a topographic map. Her pillowcase needed washing. A pile of soggy tissues lay around her feet.

Oh God.

Oh God.

Oh God.

Let me get through this one day and then I'll be better.

When she forced herself to rise and began shuffling around, someone knocked on the door. Startled, she swung about just as Joey opened it and said doubtfully, "Mom, you all right?"

"Joey, what are you doing home? Isn't it a school day?"

"I didn't go today."

She was still dressed in the clothes from last night, wrinkled and misshapen—skirt, dress, nylons, sweater and all. It struck her suddenly how she must have scared him.

She closed her eyes and put a hand to her head, trying to stop it from bonging.

"Mom, what's wrong?"

It seemed as if he stood a quarter mile away. She trudged to him and draped her arms around him loosely. "Christopher and I broke up last night."

"Why?" he asked innocently.

His simple inquiry started the flow of tears again. The salt stung when it reached her raw, swollen eyelids.

"Everybody's having a shit-bird, that's why!" she said defiantly. "And it's so unfair, and I . . . I . . . ." The damned bawling started again. She hung on Joey's shoulders and showed him how girls act when they lose their boyfriends, wailing like wind in a knothole, abashed but unable to stop herself. Lord almighty, what was she doing blubbering on the poor kid's shoulder? He'd have enough of this when he was seventeen and broke up with some girl of his own.

Awkwardly he put his arms around her. "It's okay, Mom. Don't cry. I'm still here."

"Oh, Joey, I'm sorry . . . I'm sorry. I didn't mean to sc . . . scare you."

"Gosh, I thought it was going to be something awful, like you got cancer or something. If it's just Christopher, why don't you call him up and get back together? He really loves you, Mom, I can tell he does."

She got control of herself and withdrew from his arms. "If only it were that simple," she said, shuffling toward the bathroom. She switched on the light, made it to the mirror and mumbled, "Ye gods afrighty."

Joey had followed her to the doorway and stood looking in. "You do look like something on the floor of the meat-processing plant."

"Gee, thanks." She pushed the hair back from her forehead, what few strands weren't already standing up like dandelion stalks. She'd never known a face could have so much color without having been beaten up.

"Don't you think you'd better call the shop and tell Aunt Sylvia why you're late?"

"I'm not telling her one damn thing," she stated evenly, "except that I'm not coming in today. If she doesn't like it she can go suck a dead gladiola. What about you? I suppose I'd better call school and tell them I'll be bringing you in late."

"Could I not go today, Mom?"

That got her attention. She leaned back from the mirror and focused on him, still standing in the bathroom doorway. "Not go?"

"Let's both play hooky," he suggested. "We can think of something fun to do together."

Last night's engulfing cloud of depression began to show a sunny underbelly.

"You mean you want to spend the day out gallivanting with an old broad with purple sags all over her face and eyes that look like cow guts?"

"Yeah," he said, giving her a cheeky grin. "Sounds kind of fun."

She wandered over to him and leaned against the bathroom wall, propping one hand on her hip. "What are we going to do?"

He shrugged. "I d'know. We could . . ." He thought awhile, then finished brightly, ". . . go play a few games at the video parlor or go out shopping at the Mall of America, or how about having breakfast someplace, then going to a matinee? I could drive."

Out of the pit of her stomach started a gut-chuckle that grew as it rose, bringing an actual smile along with it.

"Oh, so that's your motive, is it?"

"Actually, I just thought of it now, but the whole program sounds better than going to school."

She surprised him by boosting off the wall and kissing his forehead. "Okay, it's a plan. Give me a half hour to repair the locker plant damage and I'll be ready to take off."

They decided they'd take turns choosing what to do next. They started at Circus, dropping thirteen dollars and fifty cents into various machines until Lee finally won a round of Afterburner over her son. Their next stop was the Dairy Queen Brazier, where they ate burgers, fries and banana splits. After that they drove clear over to St. Paul to Joe's Sporting Goods to check out the end-of-the-season ski sale, then to the Minneapolis Institute of Art, where they decided the Dutch artists were their favorites.

The day became one of those memorable pages out of the book of life that they would, in the future, turn to again and again. It was something they'd never done before, playing hooky. She had raised her children under the good old upper-midwest work ethic, but abandoning it for once bonded Lee and Joey as no parental guidance ever could.

Joey talked about his girlfriend, Sandy, and how nice she was, and admitted he was beginning to get "those feelings."

Lee talked about Christopher for much the same reason.

Joey said he really liked his math teacher, Mr. Ingram, and was thinking maybe he'd take geometry and trigonometry in senior high because Mr. Ingram said he was gifted in that area.

They talked about what Joey would like to do when he grew up.

"I don't want to be a cop," he said.

That brought up Greg, and how well they'd done in that regard, but what kinds of things still reminded them of him.

Joey asked if she'd ever done anything like this—playing hooky—with Janice or Greg. She said she hadn't; she'd been too busy after Daddy died, going to school, then starting the business, then worrying that an hour away from it might cause it to fail.

Joey said he liked her a lot better this way.

"Which way?" she asked.

He shrugged and said, "I don't know. You're just . . . happier, looser. I mean, you just said it yourself. A year ago you wouldn't have let me skip school. You'd have put me in the car and hauled me over there, then we wouldn't have gotten to do all this stuff together. You've changed a lot since Christopher's been around."

"Have I?" she asked sadly.

"Well, don't you think you have?"

Was it Christopher who had changed her? Greg's death? Or just getting older and wiser?

"Well, son," she said, dropping an arm around his shoulder, "it's been a heck of a year. Nobody goes through what we've been through without changing because of it. Anyway, I'm glad you like me better."

They were strolling along beside a marble carving called "Veiled Lady" when Joey stopped and looked his mother square in the face.

"Don't let them rip you off, Mom. Grandma and Aunt Sylvia and Janice, I mean. I know they've been telling you all kinds of stuff, but I think you should marry Chris."

She studied the statue, wondering how a veiled face could possibly be carved in stone. Yet there it was, face and veil both clearly visible in solid white rock.

She turned to Joey and took him in her arms. People nearby glanced curiously at the two of them, but Joey had matured enough to accept his mother's public displays of affection without cringing.

"I want to, Joey, so badly. But it's causing so much divisiveness in our family."

"Well, heck, what do they know?"

His unqualified support buoyed her heart. "Thank you, darling."

She released him and resumed moving down the deep corridor, her footsteps echoing, his squeaking as they ambled along.

"It means a lot to me that you told me," she said. "This whole day means a lot to me. Last night I didn't know how I was going to make it through another day. I thought I'd shrivel up and die without Christopher. But look. Here I am, enjoying this art gallery, proving how resilient the human spirit is. You helped me make it through the first day, and if I can make it through one, I can make it through the rest."

"So you're not going to see him again?"

"No, I'm not."

They kept walking.

He gazed up at a painting on his right.

She gazed at one on her left.

"You know what I think, Mom?"

The question repeated itself and came back to them in the lofty space through which they moved. Her wrist was hooked on his near shoulder. His hands were buried in the pockets of his unzipped winter jacket.

Click . . . squeak . . . click . . . squeak. Her flats and his taped-up tennies moved on together.

"I think you're making a big mistake."

That thought returned often during the slow progression of days while Lee and Christopher remained apart. How sluggishly time moved without the impetus of planned happiness to speed it along. How burdensome the duty of work without the leavening of play at its end. How lonely doing alone what one has done with another for so long.

They had eaten so many meals together, listened to so many songs on the radio, been in each other's houses, used each other's bathrooms, refrigerators, hairbrushes, silverware.

Reminders were everywhere.

He had left an Anoka police department ballpoint pen beside her telephone. On it was printed EMERGENCY? CALL 911. She felt as if every day were an emergency in which she was struggling to make sense out of the backwashes of life. Not an evening passed that didn't require immense resistance to keep from calling him the way the pen advised.

Foods she made reminded her of how he liked them. Popcorn. Chinese. Spaghetti and meatballs. Eating supper across the table from only Joey, Lee contemplated how in only three years he would be graduating from high school. Then what? Would she eat alone forever?

One day she turned over a flowered tablet and found a note he'd written when he'd stopped by on duty. It said *Anoka fairgrounds—alarm system.* He'd been called out to check one of the buildings and had left her with a peck on the mouth and an apology for not being able to stay longer.

She opened her glove compartment one night and found a small, powerful flashlight he'd bought and put there, scolding that she was too trusting and needed to safeguard herself more often than she did.

A magazine in her living room lay open to an article he'd been reading last time he'd been waiting for her to change clothes.

The washing machine spun itself off kilter again and she was nearly in tears before giving up and asking Jim Clements next door to come over and get it leveled for her.

She opened a cupboard door and found the vase in which he'd sent her the roses from another florist.

Countless times a day, the black-and-white Anoka police cars drove past the window of her shop. She never saw one without her heart giving a lurch that left her feeling empty and yearning for the rest of the day.

But nighttimes were the worst, lying alone in her bed, missing him with her body as well as with her mind, wondering how many more good years she had left and decrying the fact that she was squandering them to appease her family. Every night at eleven she would battle the urge to pick up the phone and say, "Hi, what are you doing? How was your day? When will I see you?" One night she actually lifted the receiver and dialed, then hung up on the first ring, rolled over and cried.

She tried to hide her despondency from Joey, but it lived inside her like a parasite, sucking away at her ability to enjoy life as she had before, to find fulfillment in her son's achievements and day-to-day activities, to feel satisfaction at the end of a well-worked day, to search out the good rather than the bad.

No, when she'd sent Christopher away she'd sent him with her optimism, humor, satisfaction, happiness—all the positive forces that had always driven her life. She tried to recover them, but her attempts at displaying her old spirit for Joey's sake looked, she knew, pitifully false.

It was much the same for Christopher.

Days without her took on a pointless mechanism. He worked. He ate. He lifted weights. He practiced at the shooting range. He took his Explorer in for an oil change. He took Judd to see a Bruce Lee movie. He didn't realize how he'd been avoiding his apartment, with all its memories of her, until the day he ran out of uniforms. How long since he'd done laundry? Eaten in the apartment? Opened the living room blinds?

He did what he had to do.

He washed and ironed his uniforms. Vacuumed the carpeting. Watered the plants. Changed his bedding.

The smell of her was still in it. Cosmetics, sex, woman—memories came billowing up out of the hot water when the sheets hit the washing machine.

She'd left a small bottle of hand lotion in his bathroom. She'd said he never had any when she wanted it, so she'd bought a bottle for her ever-rough, stained hands. After their breakup, he would sometimes uncap the lotion and smell it like a recovering alcoholic uncaps his liquor, sniffs it and makes wishes.

There were other reminders, too.

In his bathroom half a box of condoms.

In his refrigerator some strange-flavored pop she'd bought one time on impulse, saying it sounded so weird she had to try it. Chocolate-cherry soda. He kept it there in the hope that someday she'd come back and drink it as she'd planned.

In his Explorer a pack of tissues from the last time she'd had a cold.

In his living room the sofa where they'd first laid full-length together, the floor where they'd made love, the radio station they'd listened to while doing it, the plants she'd let him keep after Greg died and into whose soil she'd often stuck her finger to check for dryness.

The location of her flower shop, just around the corner from the police station, necessitated his passing it countless times a day. He never did so without glancing up hoping to see her watering plants in the window or coming out the door. But he never did. He saw only potted flowers behind the window glass and customers using the door.

Loneliness took on a new meaning during those late-winter days without her. Once he was in a drugstore buying deodorant and razor blades when he passed the racks of greeting cards. At a revolving one he paused, randomly plucked out several cards and read them.

I love you because . . .

I'm sorry . . .

When you're not here . . .

The sentimentality bludgeoned him as he read card after card and thought about sending one to her. One? Hell, he wanted to send her ten, a dozen, a card a day, their messages were so poignant. He loved her, he was sorry, when she wasn't here the green vitality of his life wilted.

They had been apart nearly six weeks when he went one Monday morning to Fred Moore Junior High to deliver some papers to the liaison officer. He was just approaching the glass-walled office when the door opened and Lee came out.

They saw each other and stopped dead in their tracks. Their hearts leaped. Their cheeks took fire.

"Lee," he said as the door drifted shut behind her.

"Hi, Christopher." She touched her chest as if her breath had grown sketchy. The halls were silent and empty with first hour in session.

"What are you doing here?"

"I washed Joey's gym shorts this weekend and naturally he forgot to take them this morning, so I had to drop them off. What are you doing here?"

"Dropping off some papers for the liaison officer."

They tried to think of more to say, but nothing mattered. All that mattered was looking into each other's eyes again, sending the silent messages that nothing had changed, the hurt lived on, the longing remained. They stood face-to-face, stealing these moments to look greedily at each other and feel their hearts come alive after feeling dead within for so long.

She was dressed in familiar clothes—her denim jacket with a lavender smock peeking out at the neck.

He was resplendent in his navy blue uniform with its silver badges and buttons, crisply knotted tie and visored cap.

The shiny floors of the school hall reflected the two of them standing motionless, loath to go their separate ways. But they could not stand there forever with their lips parted and their emotions turbulent.

He recovered first, shifting his weight to the opposite foot and rolling up the papers in one hand. "So, how's—" He cleared his throat and began again. "How's Joey?"

"He's just fine."

"Everybody else?"

"Oh, everybody's fine. How about Judd?"

"The papers are about him." He flourished the roll. "The court put him in permanent foster care and I think he's much happier already. He's in a house with four other children, and every one of them is from a different ethnic background."

"Oh, good. I'm so glad. I know how much you care about him."

A lull fell, then he asked, "So what have you been doing?"

A rapt expression had come over her face, a look filled with utter mesmerization. She acted as if she hadn't heard his question as a whispered admission fell from her lips.

"My God, I've missed you."

"I miss you too," he said, pained.

"Every night at eleven I think about picking up the phone."

"All you have to do is do it."

"I know. That's what's so hard."

"So nothing's changed with your family?"

"I don't talk to my family much."

"It's that bad?"

She couldn't begin to do justice to how bad it had been.

"I thought it was supposed to get better without me," he said.

"I know," she whispered while the force field of longing built and billowed around them.

"Then why are we going through this, Lee?"

"Because I . . . I . . . ." If she said any more she was going to cry, so she swallowed her excuse.

"It's still the age thing with you, isn't it? It's not just them, it's you too."

The office door opened and two students came out, chatting, carrying a tagboard sign and some masking tape. Both Lee and Christopher visibly started and stepped back, putting more space between them.

When the students' voices had trailed away, he said, "Well, listen . . . I have to go. Somebody's waiting for these." He indicated the tube of papers.

"Sure," she said. "Besides, this isn't the time or place."

He took another step backward and said, "It was good to see you. Every time I drive past your shop I hope you'll be in the window, but . . ." He shrugged and let the thought trail off.

"Christopher . . ." She reached out as if to detain him, but her touch fell short.

He reached out blindly behind himself for the handle of the glass door through which they could easily be seen by several office workers. "All you have to do is call, Lee."

With those words he retreated and left her standing in the empty hall.

Any progress she'd made was reversed by those few minutes of seeing his face, hearing his voice, learning that he remained in the same tortured state as she. Yearning . . . merciful Lord, she had never felt yearning as powerful as during those fleet, fraught seconds while she faced him in that hallway, while her heart reached and her blood coursed and she maintained a proper distance.

The following day and even the day after that she had only to recall their meeting to react the same way, with an upsurge of emotion spanning the cerebral to the sexual. How simply he elicited such response from her. He had only to step into her sphere to transform it and her into the realm of the extraordinary.

The letdown came with surefire pointedness, however, in the ordinary quiet of her own home.

She was back to crying again, failing to listen when Joey talked to her, sighing often and caring little about domestic duties. At the shop, the halting reconciliation that had begun between herself and Sylvia suffered a setback when her sister came to her one day as she was counting daffodils in a large white bucket.

"Lee, Barry met a man at his office who's about your age and—"

"No thank you."

"Well, aren't you going to let me finish?"

"Why should I? So you can fix me up with this guy and quit squirming over what you did to Christopher and me?"

"I'm not squirming."

Lee gave Sylvia a point-blank stare. "Well, you should be. If it wasn't for you I'd be married by now."

Sylvia had the grace to blush.

Lee put a rubber band around twelve daffodils, trimmed off their ends and stood them in the water. "I've been thinking, Sylvia. Would you be interested at all in letting me buy out your share of the business?"

Sylvia's mouth dropped open. "Lee, my God, is it that bad?"

"Or I suppose I could sell you my interest, but I still need a steady income, and with Joey only three years away from graduation I need to think about helping him out with college, and having something to keep myself busy after he's gone from home. That's why it would work better if I bought out your half rather than the other way around."

Sylvia rushed forward and touched Lee's hand. It was wet and held a Swiss army knife. This was the first time they'd touched since the breakup.

"Do you really want that, Lee?"

Lee removed her hand and concentrated on her work. "Yes, I think I do."

"Well, I don't."

The daffodils were all trimmed and clustered. Lee carried them away toward the front of the shop. "Think about it."

Her mother called her the next day at home, obviously alerted by Sylvia that Lee was beginning to show signs of disassociating herself from the family.

"Lee, Dad and I were wondering if you and Joey would like to come over for dinner one night this week."

"No, I'm sorry, Mother, we wouldn't."

She stunned Peg just as she had Sylvia.

"But . . ."

"Mother, I'm right in the middle of something here. I can't talk now."

"All right. Well . . . call me sometime."

Lee made no reply. It felt fantastic to pull a reversal of tactics on her mother.

Of course, Janice called too: By now it had become obvious the three of them were burning up the wires between their telephones.

Janice said, "Hi, Mom."

She replied coolly, "Hello, Janice."

"How are you?"

"Lonely," she replied.

Score three for Lee, she thought while Janice struggled for a response.

"Mom, Grandma called and said you're thinking about quitting business with Aunt Sylvia. You can't do that."

"Why?"

"Because . . . because it's so successful, and you love what you're doing."

"You know, Janice, I used to. But somehow it doesn't seem to matter much anymore."

"But you're so *good* at it."

"There's not much satisfaction in that fact either lately."

"If I came home this weekend, could we talk about it?"

"No. It's a decision I want to make on my own. And it's going to be a fairly busy weekend. I work on Saturday and there's a bake sale after church on Sunday. Then in the afternoon I planned to go to a matinee with Donna Clements."

Once again she'd flabbergasted her daughter by failing to issue the quick plea for Janice to come home so they could make peace at last.

Lee found she didn't want peace. Anger had taken over and it made her feel more alive than she had since this debacle began. When Janice hung up, Lee could almost picture her daughter standing motionless with her hand on the phone, staring at the wall, watching their way of life disintegrate.

Anger, manifested in that way, however, eroded Lee's spirit in the week following her emotional divorce from three of the people who mattered most in her life.

She grew churlish at work.

She cried at embarrassing moments.

She became snappish with Joey, who didn't deserve it.

He came into the bathroom one night after supper and found her on her hands and knees, scrubbing around the toilet bowl. With her butt facing the door, he couldn't tell she was crying.

"What you doin', Mom?" he asked innocently.

"What do you mean, what am I doing!" she retorted. "Can't you see what I'm doing? I'm scrubbing the toilet seat that you manage to piss on every time you go! Why boys can't hit a hole that big is beyond me! Then they leave it for the women to scrub up! Move! You're in my way!" She backed into his ankles and he leaped out of the way.

"I'll scrub it if you want me to," he said, hurt by her sudden attack.

"Oh sure, now you'll scrub it. Now that I've already done it! Just get out of my way!"

He slinked off and closed himself in his room. Later that night he heard his mother weeping the way she had the night she broke up with Christopher.

The phone rang at work the next day. Sylvia answered and laid the receiver on the counter. "It's Lloyd," she said.

Lee wiped her hands on her smock and felt hope infuse her spirits. Lloyd could always make her feel that way, and it had been so long since she'd talked to him or seen him. When she picked up the receiver her face held a note of gladness that matched her voice. "Lloyd?"

"Hello, dear."

"Oh, it's so good to hear from you."

"How are things over at that shop of yours today?"

"I'm surrounded by narcissus and pussy willows. Does that mean spring is here?"

"It must be, because I've caught a case of spring fever. I've been feeling a little cooped up here lately and I was wondering if you'd mind cheering up the life of a lonely old bachelor by going out to supper with him."

"Tonight?"

"That's what I was thinking. I've eaten a couple of those meals over at the Senior Citizens Center this week and they're enough to make you puke. What do you say to a nice fat juicy steak up at the Vineyard?"

"Oh, Lloyd, that sounds wonderful."

"I thought I'd come by for you at seven."

"I'll be ready."

When Lee hung up she caught Sylvia watching and wondering, but she divulged nothing.

At the Vineyard, Lloyd ordered a carafe of red wine. When the waitress had filled their glasses and left, he took a sip and said, "Well, I'll get right to the point, Lee." She felt her blood begin to plummet at his clipped, businessy tone. "The point being Christopher Lallek."

"Oh, Dad, not you too."

"No, no, not me too," he said, leaning forward as if with great enjoyment. "I'm not joining the ranks of those misguided fools who think they have a right to tell you how to run your life."

"You're not?" she said, amazed.

"Not at all. I came here to talk some sense into you, but not the kind of sense they'll agree with. Now, what's this I hear about you telling Christopher you aren't going to see him anymore?"

"Joey must have called you."

"He's been calling me quite regularly, as a matter of fact. And telling me how hard you are to live with lately, and how you cry yourself to sleep at night. A while back he told me all about a long talk the two of you had when you were walking through the art gallery. By the way, you made that boy feel like he had the greatest mom in the world by spending the day with him that way. But back to the issue at hand—you've broken up with Christopher."

"Yes, I have."

"Very noble . . . and very unwise, don't you think?"

She was too stunned to reply.

Lloyd covered her hand on the tabletop between them. "Lee, honey, I've known you for a long time. I've seen you sad and I've seen you happy, but I've never seen you any happier than during these past few months while you were seeing that young man. If I may be so crass, I'm not sure I ever saw you that happy when you were married to my son. I'm sure he'd forgive me for saying so because the two of you had a good marriage, and heaven knows I'm not taking anything away from that. But this . . . this young Lochinvar put a glow on you that hurt the eyes of those who don't wear it themselves. Could be some of them got a little jealous." He released her hand, took a drink of his wine, then studied the glass thoughtfully. "It's not easy to be stuck in a marriage that's twenty, thirty, forty years old and watch someone of your age fall in love and walk around looking like a ripe peach again. I'm not saying your mother and your sister don't have happy marriages. I'm just saying that the best of marriages get a little stale and shopworn after a while. And as for my granddaughter. That's pretty easy to understand. Naturally she'd get into a snit, being upstaged by her own mother.

"But don't you let any one of them talk you out of your happiness. You worked hard for it. You raised those kids and gave them nine good years after Bill died, and during that time you hardly ever thought of yourself. When you started dating Christopher you put yourself before them for once, and if you don't mind my saying so, it was high time. Children can get selfish, you know. You can give them so much of yourself that they expect it all."

"I haven't been giving them much of anything lately," she admitted.

"Well, that's a temporary thing. It's because when you're not happy you don't have as much to give. So what are you going to do about it?"

"I don't know."

"Don't you think the time has come for you to stand up to them—all of them, your mother, your sister and your daughter?"

"I thought that's what I'd been doing."

"No. What you've been doing is cutting off your nose to spite your face. What you need to do is go to that man you love and tell him you'll marry him, and let everybody else suck dead gladiolas—I believe that was the phrase, wasn't it?"

Lee laughed in spite of herself. The waitress brought their salads and Lloyd picked up his fork with scarcely a pause in his monologue.

"There's one other thought I've had, and I believe I've considered it quite thoroughly since the night when you told me about this whole ruckus those silly women have kicked up. I think Bill would give you his blessing if he could. He'd want you to be happy. After all, you're the mother of his children. If you're happy, they're going to be happy in the long run."

"Do you really think so, Dad?"

"Yes, I do."

"Mother suggested that I was being disloyal to Bill by taking up with Christopher."

Lloyd just shook his head. "Honestly, that woman. She means well, but sometimes I'd like to kick her butt. Mothers get . . . well, you know. They have this image in their heads of what's right for their daughters, and when it doesn't turn out that way they can get pretty forceful. They tell themselves they're doing it for their daughters' good, but they're really doing it to get their way."

"Oh, Lloyd, I can't tell you what a relief it is to hear you say these things."

"I'm only telling the truth. I'm not really one of your family, so I can look at the situation a lot more impartially than they can. Now eat your salad and stop looking as if you're going to leap off that chair and kiss me, because people will think I'm the one who's robbing the cradle."

"Lloyd Reston," she said, smiling at him very warmly, "you are the dearest, most sensible, lovable man in the world."

"Well, I'm close, but not quite the most. I expect that honor goes to this fellow you love. I've been around the two of you enough to see how you respect and admire each other and how doggone much fun you always manage to have when you're together."

"Yes, we do."

"And if I may be so bold . . . I understand that your affair was sexual, too. Well, I say, more power to you, Lee. That was probably the real burr under those women's saddles. You'll pardon me for saying it, but I've seen your sister touch her husband exactly once in all the years I've known them. As I remember he had a wood tick on his neck and she picked it off for him one time when we were picnicking somewhere. As for your mother and father—well, I'm not going to make any remarks about them, but I suspect, given their age, that lust has rather lost its stronghold over at their house.

"So I say, if you've found a virile young man who loves you to pieces and wants to sweep you off your feet, get swept. Now eat, I said."

Lee felt so light she was certain she'd float off her chair and bump the ceiling.

"May I say just one thing more?" she asked.

"Make it quick. My stomach is growling."

"I love you."

Lloyd lifted his gaze to his happy daughter-in-law and said, "Yes, I suppose you do. I've been around so long, what other choice do you have?"

He dug into his Caesar salad.

She dug into hers.

They wiped their mouths and exchanged messages over their linen napkins, smiling like conspirators.

Chapter 19

She had decided even before Lloyd dropped her at home. His blessing was all she'd needed to make her see how wrong she'd been to turn Christopher away. Lloyd's word carried more weight than all the others combined, for if he—the father of her first husband—could give her the right to second happiness, so surely should the others be able to do the same.

She kissed his cheek and he patted her arm before she stepped from his car and tripped to the house as if there were no earth beneath her feet.

With her impatient heart racing, she dialed Christopher's apartment.

"Be there, be there," she whispered, but got his answering machine instead.

This message was too momentous to leave on a tape recording: She dialed the police station and the dispatcher said, "He's working mid-shift, Mrs. Reston. He'll get off at eleven o'clock."

She checked her watch. It was after ten.

Suddenly she was racing. Into the bathroom, into the tub, out of the tub, into clean clothes, thinking, *Hang on, Christopher, I'm coming.*

At 10:45 she went into Joey's room and woke him up.

"Hey, Joey? . . . Honey?"

"Hm? Mom? What time is it? Feels like I just went to sleep."

"You did." She sat on the edge of his bed while the hall light slanted in a golden fan on the floor behind her. "It's only quarter to eleven. Sorry to wake you but I'm going over to Christopher's. I just wanted you to know in case you woke up and found me gone."

"To Christopher's?"

"I didn't think you'd mind."

"No. Hey, way to go, Mom."

"I may be gone late because he's just getting off work now."

"Grandpa must have done some fancy talking tonight."

"Yes, he did. And I'm going to do what he and you said I should do. I'm going to marry Chris."

"You are?" Even in the deep shadow she could see his crooked smile. "Gee, Mom, that's great."

"I'm going to tell him tonight."

"Well, in that case . . . maybe I shouldn't expect you till morning."

It struck Lee how society's perception of unmarried sex had changed in a single generation. Her own mother couldn't accept Lee's having an illicit affair, yet she could sit here on her son's bed and joke with him about it.

"I promise I'll be here to fix you breakfast."

"Waffles?" he asked.

"Is this extortion?" She hated making waffles . . . too much work.

"Well, heck, you can't blame a kid for trying."

"Okay, waffles."

"All *riiight.*"

"I owe you more than waffles though, don't I?"

"Aw, Mom . . ."

"Well, I do. I owe you an apology. I'm really sorry for how I acted the other day when you came into the bathroom. I had no right to bark at you and say the things I said. I know I hurt your feelings."

"Yeah, well, I figured out why."

"And you called Grandpa and told him to have a talk with me, right?"

"Well, you wouldn't listen to *me.*"

She arranged the covers across his chest and tipped forward, pinning him in place with the blankets. "You're a very perceptive young man, Joey Reston. You're going to make some woman an exceptional husband someday." She pecked him on the face.

"And it won't be long either. I just asked Sandy to marry me and she said yes. We're thinking maybe we'll go to school one more year and then do it."

Lee's mouth dropped open. Before the adrenaline reached her extremities, he laughed in falsetto and said, "Just kidding, Mom."

"Oh my God . . ." She put a hand to her heart. "You scared the living daylights out of me!"

"Just getting even for that tongue-lashing you gave me in the bathroom. I didn't think the waffles and the apology would quite cover it."

With the edge of a fist she thunked him on the chest. "You inconsiderate brat."

"Yeah, but you love me, right?"

"I do." She was laughing inside. "Yes, I surely do." She sat a moment on her son's bed, feeling happiness come and flood her, feeling things finally falling into place. "Well, I guess I'd better get going so I'm there when Christopher gets home."

"Tell him hi from me. And if he says yes, tell him he better be able to pee into the toilet bowl without getting any on the floor if he knows what's good for him."

"Joseph Reston!"

"G'night, Mom. Have a good time."

"Just you wait till April Fools' Day. I'm gonna get you so good."

"Hey, listen, woman. I gotta get some sleep. Tomorrow's a school day."

"All right, all right, I'm going."

She kissed him once more and headed for the door. As she reached it he said, "Seriously, Mom, I'm glad for you."

With a happy heart, she smiled and turned off the hall light.

It was 11:15 when she reached Christopher's place. Approaching his door she felt a quivering of anticipation within, the kind of anticipation a woman in her mid-forties believes gone with her salad days—that green, burgeoning optimism that she'd had when she'd married Bill, fresher perhaps because this love she felt was so unsought. It had chosen her; she had not chosen it. What a fool she'd been to let her family rob her of this happiness for even so short a time. This was *her* life, hers alone, and life was not a dress rehearsal. Fleet and final as it was, she owed herself the taking of all the happiness she could get from it, and Christopher was the key to so much of that happiness.

She knocked and waited, holding a vision of him inside her head and an eagerness within her heart. In seconds his voice came from the other side of the door.

"Who is it?" Ever the policeman, ever cautious.

"It's Lee."

The dead bolt clacked and the door opened, bumping aside his black work shoes, which sat on the rug. He stood before her in stocking feet, still dressed in his uniform, his hair pressed flat from the rim of his hat, holding a yellow plastic container of microwave Beefaroni from which a spoon protruded. The room smelled like the freshly heated food.

"Well, this is a surprise."

"Not at all. We both knew the other day at school that we couldn't stay apart."

"You might have known but I didn't. I thought it was really over for good."

She offered a fey smile, letting her eyes wander up to his hair, down to his dear blue eyes and full lips. "Would you mind, Officer Lallek, if I came in there and kissed you?"

She stepped over his shoes, unceremoniously took him in her arms and kissed him. He kissed her too, holding her with one arm while the other hand was occupied by his snack. It was a kiss of sentimental sweetness, unrushed rather than unruly. She fit so nicely beneath his downturned head with its neatly trimmed hair and closed eyes. The shape and texture of his lips and tongue were as familiar to Lee as the interior of her own mouth. She took her time enjoying the kiss, washing him with an almost lazy swoop of her tongue that said she had been a very silly woman, indeed. When the kiss ended they stood peacefully, smiling at each other.

"Mmm . . . what are you eating?"

"Beefaroni."

"Tastes good."

"You want one? I can heat one for you."

"Hm-mm . . . wouldn't taste nearly as good firsthand. Would you like to finish yours though?"

"Not particularly, now that you're here."

"Do anyway. I'll watch."

He grinned wryly. "You'll watch?"

She rested her forearms against his bullet-proof vest and traced the outline of his lips with an index finger. "I'll watch these," she murmured, "closing around the spoon and moving while you chew. I've missed watching these."

He chuckled and said, "We police officers meet all kinds."

"Eat your cheap noodles," she said in a rich caviar voice.

He freed his hands and stood before her plying the spoon, keeping his eyes on her over the plastic cup. When his mouth was full she kissed his cheek, which was puffed slightly, its muscles shifting as he chewed. He smiled, swallowed and said, "You miss me or what?"

"Huh-uh. That's not why I'm going to marry you. I'm going to marry you so you can level my washing machine and mow my grass, shovel my snow, stuff like that."

The spoon stopped halfway to his mouth. He leaned back to give himself ample space to see her face. "You're going to marry me?"

"Yes, I am, Officer Lallek. I'm going to elope with you."

"Elope!"

"Quicker than you can say Chef Boyardee Beefaroni."

"You don't say."

"I'm tired of people telling me what I should and shouldn't do. I'm tired of sleeping alone and eating alone and watching you cruise by my house at night when you think I'm sleeping and I won't see you."

"Since when did—"

"I *saw* you. You went past on Sunday night at ten, and the next night just before you got off duty, and plenty of other nights, too."

"How about tonight?"

"I wasn't home. I was out with Lloyd getting preached to. Then when I got home I took a bath and put perfume behind my knees and put on clean underwear and told Joey I was coming over here to propose to you."

"Is that so? Clean underwear? And perfume where?"

"In all the places where two can enjoy it more than one."

"Here, hold this." He handed her the container, then swung her up like a hammock in his arms and ordered, "Flip that dead bolt."

When she had, he carried her to the kitchen where the bright lights were lit over the table and the silverware drawer hung open.

"Set that down on the cabinet," he ordered.

She got rid of the container, then doubled her arms around his neck while he carried her to the bedroom. Above the bed he released her knees, letting her slide down his body until she knelt on the mattress. Holding her face in both hands, he kissed her, a long flowing river of a kiss upon which they drifted together, with the promise of a much longer ride ahead. When it ended they remained close, breathing on each other in the dark, setting their hearts on a straight, mutual course toward permanence. The levity they'd shared at her arrival had been dispelled by the import of this solemn moment.

"Christopher, I'm sorry," she whispered. "I loved you and I listened to them. I'm sorry."

"It's been hell without you."

"For me too."

"I didn't want to come between you and your family though. I still don't."

"Lloyd made me see that it's their problem, not ours. If they love me they'll accept you, and they love me. I know they do, so I'm willing to give them a second chance. Will you marry me, Christopher?"

"I'd marry you here and now if I could."

"I meant it when I said I want to elope. Do you think we could?"

"You're serious!" he said, surprised anew.

"Yes, I am. I'm not giving anyone a chance to influence me again. I just want us to get on a plane and go someplace. The only one I'll tell is Lloyd, because I'll have to ask him if he can stay at the house with Joey while we're gone. I always thought it would be so romantic to be married in a garden. Do you think we could use the tickets to Longwood Garden, or is it still winter in Pennsylvania?"

"I'm afraid it's still winter there. But it's spring down South. Maybe we could find someplace down there."

"Oh, do you mean it, Christopher? You'll really do it?"

"I have vacation time coming. I can talk to my sergeant and see what they'll give me off. For a reason as good as this they might be willing to rearrange the schedule."

"Oh good. Now could we quit making plans and take this metal vest off you? It's such a nuisance."

While he began loosening his tie and unbuttoning his shirt, she walked on her knees to the far side of the bed and fell to all fours to switch on a bedside lamp. By its light she returned to him, taking over her share of the duties she so relished, ridding him of the vesture that symbolized his profession, which had brought the two of them together. While they undressed she wondered as she had so often—did Greg know? Could he smile down from some celestial plane and see how happy the two of them were? Did he grin and say, "Nice work, Grandpa?" Had he found his little brother somewhere up there, and were the two of them pleased at this mortal bliss their mother and Greg's best friend had found?

As the last pieces of clothing dropped, her wondering ceased and she fell with Christopher, already embraced. And in their reach and flow to one another they became splendid beings celebrating not only their bodies but also their love.

It took them two days to find the proper garden and make arrangements. On the third, a Thursday, they flew to Mobile, Alabama, where they rented a car and drove straight to the Mobile Infirmary. There they had the required blood tests and walked out four hours later with the results. These they took to the Mobile County Courthouse at the intersection of Government and Royal streets, where they bought their wedding license and made arrangements with one Richard Tarvern Johnson, the administrative assistant to the judge of probate, to meet them the following morning at eleven o'clock at the near end of the bridge spanning Mirror Lake in Bellingrath Gardens.

Lee Reston had never before seen azaleas blooming in their natural habitat. She saw them on her wedding day, more than 250,000 plants, some of them nearly 100 years old, in every conceivable shade of pink, cascading from bushes higher than her head, lining pathways, surrounding the boles of moss-draped water oaks, reflected in the pools, lakes and in the current of the Isle-aux-Oies River, beside which the Bellingrath estate had been built.

The gardens sprawled over an 800-acre setting, boasting latticed bowers, sparkling fountains, bubbling cascades, verdant lawns and flowers . . . everywhere flowers. Christopher had trouble keeping Lee moving while they walked toward their rendezvous with Johnson. She kept gazing overhead at the immense oaks and sighing, "Ohh, look." And at rainbows of tulips and daffodils lining the walkways. "Oh, look at *those*. I've never seen anything like it in my life." And at the flood of purple hyacinths that turned the air to ambrosia. "Oh, smell them, Christopher! I think I'm getting dizzy, they smell so grand!"

He tugged on her hand. "Come along, sweetheart, we'll tour the gardens later on. We don't want to be late for our own wedding."

The bridge at Mirror Lake was arched, with wooden latticework supporting its railings. It spanned the lake across which could be seen the rockery and the summer house, each surrounded by colorful blooms. At the near end of the bridge, Johnson, the marriage official of Mobile County, was waiting. He was a dyed-in-the-wool southerner with the accent to prove it, a man in his mid-forties, with thinning blond hair, glasses and a smile that said he much preferred the jewelled setting of Bellingrath to the libraryish rooms of the courthouse where he usually performed his nuptial duties.

He had sold them their wedding license the previous day and recognized them as they approached.

"Good mornin', Mister Lallek, Mizz Reston. And a fine one it is for a weddin'."

"Good morning, Mister Johnson," they returned in unison.

"Aren't these azaleas something? I swear."

Christopher said, "Mrs. Reston owns a florist shop. I've had trouble getting her here without dawdling."

Johnson chuckled and said, "A place like this would make anyone dawdle. Well . . . shall we get started?"

There were only the three of them: Johnson in his business suit; Lee in a taupe organdy dress and high heels, holding a single calla lily; Christopher in a navy blue suit with a fragrant gardenia in his lapel. Only the three of them and a pair of swans on the lake behind them, and off to one side a wading flock of sunset-colored flamingos going about their business of eating their lunch and standing on one leg while digesting it. Some finches chittered to one another in the low flowers beside the lake, and an occasional sparrow or warbler tattled from the water oak above their head.

No guests to seat.

No caterers bustling in the wings.

No pomp or circumstance.

Only two people in love, relaxed on their wedding day.

"We can do this however you prefer," Johnson said. "I'm here to make it official. I can read some words from a book or you can say whatever you like."

Christopher and Lee looked at each other. He was holding her Instamatic camera. She was holding her lily. Neither of them had given a thought to ceremony. Truly, it had been celebrated on the night they'd agreed to do this, with only the two of them present.

Christopher decided. "I'd like to say something myself."

"So would I."

"Very well," Johnson agreed. "Whenever you're ready."

Christopher set the camera on the grass at their feet and held both of Lee's hands.

"Well . . ." he said, then halted to do some thinking. He looked into her eyes, then blew out a breath containing a trace of a laugh, because he had no idea what to say. At last he made a good start.

"I love you, Lee. I've loved you for long enough to know that you make a better person of me, and I think that's important. I want to be with you for the rest of my life. I promise to be faithful, and to help you raise Joey, and to take care of both of you the best I can. I promise to be good to you and to take you to as many gardens as we can possibly see in the rest of our life, and to respect you and love you till my dying day, which won't be hard at all." He smiled and she did, too. "Oh, and one more thing. I promise to respect your family, too, and to show them in every way I know how that this marriage was the right thing for both of us." He paused for thought. "Oh, the ring . . ." He fished it from his pocket, not the immense rock he'd tried to give her earlier, but a plain gold band they'd chosen together, one with no jewels that would have to be left in the dresser drawer, just a sturdy circle that could stand up to the daily beating to which it would be subjected.

"I love you," he said, slipping it on her finger. "And you were right. This ring is much better because you'll never have to take it off." He smiled directly into her eyes, then said to Johnson, "I guess that's all."

Johnson nodded and said, "Mizz Reston?"

She looked down at Christopher's hands within her own, then up at his face, wholly happy and at peace.

"You've been such a gift to me, Christopher. You came into my life when I least expected it, at a time when I needed someone so badly. Little did I know that I'd fall in love with you. How lucky I am that I did. And I'll keep loving you till the end of our days. I'll be there for you when your job gets you down. I know it's not always easy to be a policeman's wife, but who knows better than I what I'm getting into? I promise that I'll support you in all the causes you espouse, especially with kids, because I'm sure that Judd won't be the last one you'll be a stand-in father to. I'll do whatever I can for them, and I'll give you the freedom to do what you must for them. I'll make a home for us, and it will always be open to your friends . . . and your family, if you choose. I'll go to every garden on the face of this earth that you're willing to take me to." She smiled broadly, winning a smile from him. Soon her expression softened. "Somehow the old words are best . . . in sickness and in health, for richer, for poorer, till death do us part. That's how I'll love you." Gently, she said, "Give me the other ring."

He took it from his pocket and she put it on his finger, then kissed it. Raising her eyes again to his, she whispered, "I love you, Christopher."

"I love you, Lee."

They kissed. Behind them on the water a pair of swans floated toward each other, and for an instant as they passed, their heads and necks formed a heart, as if a blessing were being extended upon the vows just spoken.

Mr. Johnson said, "Let it be known that the state of Alabama recognizes this marriage as true and legal and that a record of it will be kept on file in the Mobile County Courthouse."

The ceremony was over but had been so brief it left a lull of uncertainty, as if the bride and groom were thinking, *Shouldn't it have taken longer?* Johnson made it official. "Congratulations, Mr. and Mrs. Lallek." He shook both their hands and said, "Now if you'll sign the wedding certificate, that'll about do it."

When they'd both signed, he snapped a picture of them with Lee's camera. Then a passing tourist snapped one of all three of them.

"Well, good luck to you both," Johnson bid.

He left them there beside the lake, chuckling into each other's eyes because in some respects the few official words spoken by him seemed like a farce. Vows were, after all, a thing of the heart, not of recorded signatures and dates.

When he'd departed, Christopher captured Lee's hand and swung her against his chest. "Come here, Mrs. Lallek. Let's try that again."

This kiss was overseen only by the swans and the buttermilk clouds that washed the blue sky with an overlay of white. It went on as long as Lee could permit without getting impatient for their tour of the gardens to begin. She pulled away first. Being a creature devoid of coyness, she put it to him honestly, "Kiss me later, Christopher. I'm just too anxious to see all those flowers."

They spent their first three hours as Mr. and Mrs. Lallek strolling the gardens and snapping pictures of each other.

They spent their wedding night at a place called Kerry Cottage, a restored carriage house on the grounds of an antebellum mansion named Sharrow. The owner, one Mrs. Ramsay, a thin, horsey-faced matron with gray hair that waved naturally, tightly against her skull, said she would do some telephoning and put off some relatives who were driving down for the night from Monroeville. "They never pay me a red cent and expect breakfast on the table at the stroke of eight. Cousin Grace can just come another time. Tonight you two newlyweds will have the best room I've got."

She fed them glazed cornish game hens filled with pine-nut stuffing at a table in the garden beneath a hawthorn tree, which she said was planted by her great-great-granddaddy before the Civil War. When dusk fell she lit a hurricane candle and brought them amaretto cream cake poised upon a lake of vanilla cream. On the cream she'd scribed two interlocked hearts of chocolate syrup. She touched each of her guests on the shoulder and said wistfully, "May your lives together be as happy as mine was with the Colonel." Choosing not to elaborate on who the Colonel was, she filled their glasses with something she called iced mint malmsey and disappeared into the shadows.

They toasted.

They drank.

They gazed.

They took time to adore each other while the night beckoned them toward the privacy of their garden cottage. Still, they sat on, savoring the anticipation and the resonance of the feelings stirring between them. The iced mint malmsey was slightly bitter but refreshing. Above their heads the leaves of the hawthorn tree rustled like dry paper in a faint night breeze. Beneath their elbows the pierced metal of the garden tabletop grew cool upon their skin. The light from the candle illuminated their faces to a Rubenesque glow.

Christopher emptied his glass, set it on the tabletop with a soft *tink* and said, "Mrs. Lallek . . . ," testing it on his tongue before going on. "Would you care to retire now?"

"Mr. Lallek," she replied, smiling into his eyes, "I would like very much to retire now."

He pushed back his chair. It resounded like a muffled bell as it bumped over the cobbles. He pulled hers out and she rose, taking his arm.

"Shall we find Mrs. Ramsay and thank her?"

"By all means."

They ambled toward the house on the uneven bricks with the smell of wisteria in their nostrils.

"I find myself speaking differently here," he said. "Listen to me, at home I'd say *talking,* here I say speaking. There I say *should,* here I say *shall.* What is it?"

"The South definitely casts a spell."

It continued casting its spell as they thanked and bid goodnight to their hostess, sauntered arm in arm 'neath a spreading live oak, past their own hawthorn, and made their way to the carriage house with its testered, draped bed. There, the coverlet was already turned down and a pair of good-night candies waited on their pillows.

She was naked when he laid her down and stretched out beside her.

"Lee . . . oh Lee," he murmured. "My wife at last."

She spoke his name and drew him in, close to her body, closer still to her soul. "Christopher . . . my husband."

Wife.

Husband.

Lovers.

In the rich, rife southern night, they wanted no more.

Lloyd got the idea all on his own. He took only Joey into his confidence before sending out the invitations.

To his granddaughter, Janice.

To Sylvia and Barry Eid.

To Orrin and Peg Hillier.

And to Judson Quincy.

You're invited to a wedding supper honoring the marriage of Lee Reston and Christopher Lallek, who were married at Bellingrath Gardens last Friday. Supper will be served at the bridal couple's future home at 1225 Benton Street, on Wednesday evening at 5:00 p.m. Please don't disappoint them or me.

Sincerely,
Lloyd Reston

They all called immediately upon receipt of their letters, everyone outspoken and miffed, haranguing Lloyd as if he were to blame for Lee's lack of good sense. To each one he'd say, "Just a minute, Joey wants to talk to you."

And Joey would spill out his honest enthusiasm. "Hey, Grandma, isn't it great? You're coming, aren't you? Mom called and she's so dang happy! So am I! So is Grandpa Lloyd! He and I are making the wedding supper and neither one of us knows what we're doing exactly, but we're looking through recipe books for something that sounds good and easy. Are you coming?"

Each one hung up, frowning, hoist by her own petard. Lee's own son was ecstatic. Lee's former father-in-law had given his blessing to the union. The two of them, inept stumblebums in the kitchen, were going to prepare a meal of celebration and asked only that the rest of the family be in attendance.

How in heaven's name could they say no without looking like total jerks?

————

Lloyd solicited Judd's help. He picked up both him and Joey immediately after school and the three of them set Lee's kitchen table with her best china. They hung three paper wedding bells on the light fixture. They cut up about five pounds of beef sirloin, seared it in a big soup pot, whacked up some onions and mushrooms, poured in some burgundy and bouillon, put in the proper spices and hoped a woman would show up to thicken it into beef burgundy when the time was right.

They cut up a salad, opened up three cans of whole-kernel corn, prepared instant rice in the microwave, got a bread basket lined with a napkin like Lee always did, tore apart the dinner buns, put two sticks of butter on a plate and hid the bakery-decorated cake on the top shelf of Joey's closet.

Shortly before 4 P.M., Lloyd put on his jacket and said to the boys, "Now, don't forget. If nobody's here by five, take all the extra plates off the table, okay? I should have your mother and Chris back here by five-thirty at the latest. That's if their plane gets in on time."

Christopher drove on the way home from the airport. Lee delivered a monologue on Bellingrath Gardens. Her spiel never slowed until they reached her house only to find there was no room for the Explorer in the driveway.

". . . could go back again to . . ." Lee interrupted herself in the middle of the thought. She gaped at the collection of vehicles. "That looks like Mother's car. And Janice's . . . and Sylvia and Barry's." Her head snapped around and her eyes lit on the man in the backseat. "Lloyd, what have you done?"

"Let's go inside and see."

She looked terrified as she got out of the truck and stood beside it, staring at the house. Christopher took her arm. Above her head, he exchanged glances with Lloyd.

"What *did* you do, Lloyd?"

"Invited them, that's all."

"But, Dad . . ." she said. "None of them knows."

"They do now."

"Oh hell," she groaned, and looked for help to Christopher, who had none to offer.

"We might as well go face them," he said.

The boys had loud music playing. Lee's mother was stirring something on the stove. Her father was opening a bottle of wine. Sylvia was fussing over a bouquet of white roses on the center of the table. They all appeared intentionally busy except the boys, who came to the door babbling excitedly.

Lee got a hug from Joey. Christopher said, "Well, for heaven's sake, Judd is here, too!" and got a high five and congratulations from him. The others gave up their preoccupation and hovered on the perimeter while Joey and Judd went on bragging loudly about the preparations they'd made with Lloyd, and the music kept playing, and Lee stood barely inside her own front door afraid to take the seven or eight steps that would carry her to the others. She felt as awkward as a singer who's begun on the wrong key. At her shoulder she felt Christopher waiting for her to move, while behind them Lloyd hung up coats in the closet.

Finally she said, "Well . . . this is a nice surprise," and made her feet move.

She reached Sylvia first, and felt her heart clubbing as they remained that one step apart, their emotions strained and wavering. Who moved first? Lee, perhaps, taking that initial difficult step toward amity.

Their hug was stilted, their elbows in the air above each other's shoulders, their backsides jutting while Sylvia whispered in Lee's ear, "I think you're crazy. It'll never work."

Lee whispered back, "Just watch and see."

Her mother came next. This hug was harder, but bore much the same message. "Have you lost your mind, eloping? When Lloyd told me I nearly died."

"Thanks for coming, Mother."

Orrin's hug was the first genuine one. "Your mother says you're crazy, but I've never seen you look happier, honey."

"Thanks, Daddy. I am." She turned to the last person. "Janice . . . honey, it's so good to see you." Janice was blushing and hanging back. Lee's embrace broke the ice. The two hugged longer and harder than they had in many months, feeling relief sluice in and mend the rift that had held them aloof for weeks. "Oh, Mom . . ." Janice's whisper was unsteady. Lee heard her gulp in a futile effort to control her emotions. She rubbed the center of Janice's back, hard, a connection that said, *Don't cry, dear, everything's going to be just fine now.*

In the hubbub of greetings, those between Lee's family and Christopher were perfunctory at best, but Janice—bless her heart—exhibited grace under pressure and gave her mother the kindest wedding gift she could give by approaching Christopher straightaway and, blushing though she was, offering a genuine hug.

"It's easy to see how happy you both are. Congratulations."

"Thank you, Janice, from both your mother and me."

"I just want you to know, I've met a guy I really like a lot. We're going out on our second date tomorrow night."

Christopher smiled and said, "Good for you. Bring him home soon so we can meet him."

Looking on, Lee felt a welling of emotion that pushed at her throat and seemed to billow within her heart. She turned away and went around the corner of the kitchen to dry her eyes in private. Christopher saw and followed. Coming up behind her he locked an arm across her chest. She gripped it with both hands and tipped her head back against him, closing her eyes, swallowing hard.

"Oh, Christopher . . ." she whispered.

"I know," he replied, and kissed her hair.

Judd came barging around the corner and came up short. "Could I change the CD? Oh! Something wrong?"

Joey came right behind him and said, "No you can't. Come on, dummy, leave 'em alone."

And somehow, eyes got dried, the kitchen got invaded, the beef burgundy got thickened, food got dished up and everyone got seated. Vince Gill was singing from the living room. Some glasses were filled with wine. Some were filled with Sprite. Food and chatter were being passed around the table. The noise and confusion of family mealtime worked its magic at replacing the faltering relationships that would still need some work in the future.

Lloyd arose with his glass in his hand. "If I may—"

"No, Grandpa," Joey interrupted. "This time I think it's my job."

After a hesitation of surprise, Lloyd resumed his chair with a pleased smile and turned the floor over to his grandson.

Joey stood and lifted his glass of Sprite to each person in turn as he toasted.

"To Grandpa Lloyd, for getting us together. To Aunt Sylvia for bringing the flowers. To Uncle Barry for bringing Aunt Sylvia . . ." Everyone laughed. "To Judd, who's just going to have to learn to like country music instead of rap. To my sister, Janice, who I'm glad to have back home. To Grandma and Grandpa Hillier for giving us the best mom in the world. But most of all to Mom and Christopher, the new bride and groom. I hope you guys always stay as happy as you are today, and I hope you go away often and leave me with Grandpa Lloyd, because I get by with all kinds of stuff when he's here. Man, I ate pizza every night and stayed up till eleven-thirty and he let me drive the car over to Sandy's house!"

When the laughter died down, Joey continued. "Seriously . . . I learned some things this year about what really matters. We all did. So I'll just end by saying, Mom, Christopher, we all wish you a long and happy life together. That goes from all of us here"—his eyes circled the table, then lifted toward heaven—"and from those up there. Dad? Greg? Grant? Nice to know you're all together. Put in a good word for these two, will you?"

While around the wedding table glasses touched, hearts softened, and a bride had difficulty keeping her eyes dry, three souls looked down from their ethereal dwelling above, exchanged smiles of satisfaction and, with their arms around each other, ambled off to wait.